Waiting for the Biblioburro

Esperando el Biblioburro

by Monica Brown
por Monica Brown

illustrations by John Parra
ilustraciones por John Parra

translation by
Adriana Domínguez

traducción por
Adriana Domínguez

TRICYCLE PRESS

Acknowledgments

The author would like to acknowledge Simon Romero of the *New York Times* and Valentina Canavesio of Ayoka Productions, who shed light on Luis Soriano Bohórquez's work for literacy. Most special thanks, however, go to Luis himself, for his participation and support of this book.

Agradecimientos

La escritora agradece a Simon Romero de *The New York Times* y a Valentina Canavesio de Ayoka Productions, quienes compartieron información sobre el trabajo de Luis Soriano Bohórquez para incrementar el alfabetismo. Agradece especialmente, a Luis mismo, por su participación y apoyo de este libro.

The Library of Congress has cataloged the English hardcover edition of this work as follows:

Waiting for the Biblioburro / by Monica Brown ; illustrations by John Parra — 1st ed.

p. cm.

Summary: When a man brings to a remote village two burros, Alfa and Beto, loaded with books the children can borrow, Ana's excitement leads her to write a book of her own as she waits for the Biblioburro to return. Includes glossary of Spanish terms and a note on the true story of Colombia's Biblioburro and mobile libraries in other countries.

[1. Biblioburro—Fiction. 2. Books and reading—Fiction. 3. Libraries—Fiction. 4. Soriano, Luis—Fiction. 5. Colombia—Fiction.]

I. Parra, John, ill. II. Title.

PZ7.B81644 Wai 2011 [E]—dc22 2010024183

ISBN 978-0-553-53879-3 (bilingual trade) — ISBN 978-0-553-53894-6 (bilingual lib. bdg.)

MANUFACTURED IN CHINA

Design by Chloe Rawlins

Typeset in Celestia Antiqua and Putain

The illustrations in this book were created with acrylics on board.

November 2016

10 9 8

Random House Children's Books supports the First Amendment and celebrates the right to read.

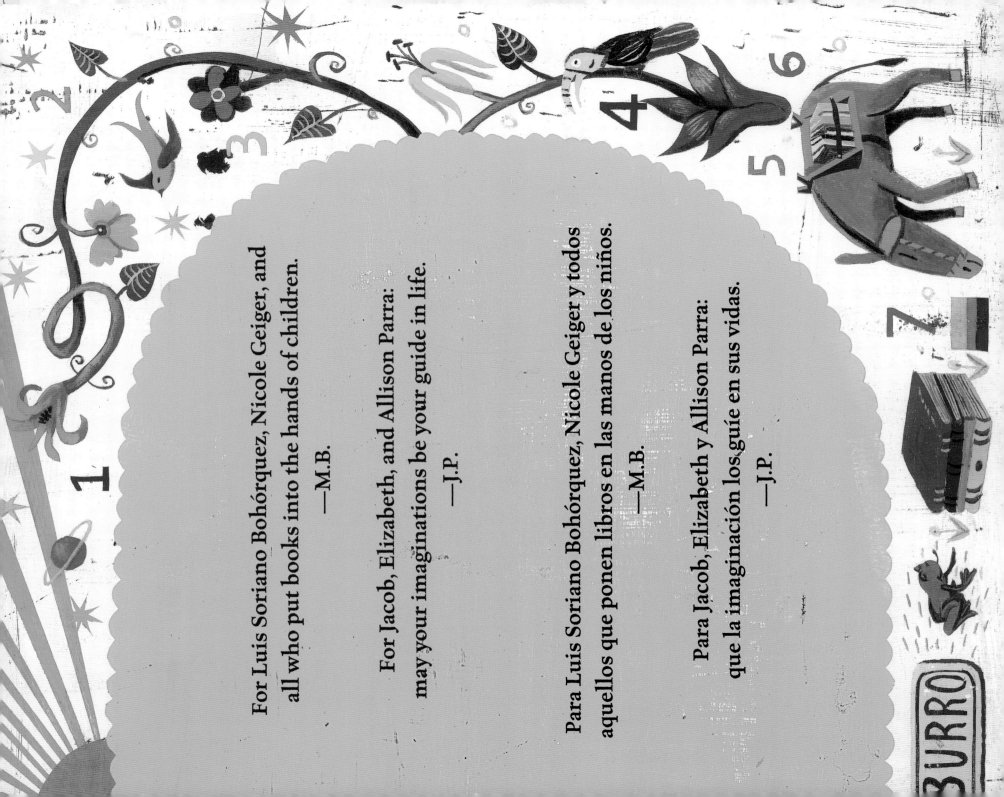

For Luis Soriano Bohórquez, Nicole Geiger, and all who put books into the hands of children.

—M.B.

For Jacob, Elizabeth, and Allison Parra: may your imaginations be your guide in life.

—J.P.

Para Luis Soriano Bohórquez, Nicole Geiger y todos aquellos que ponen libros en las manos de los niños.

—M.B.

Para Jacob, Elizabeth y Allison Parra: que la imaginación los guíe en sus vidas.

—J.P.

On a hill behind a tree, there is a house.
In the house, there is a bed and on the bed
there is a little girl named Ana, fast asleep,
dreaming about the world outside and
beyond the hill.

En una colina detrás de una árbol, hay una casa.
En la casa, hay una cama y en la cama hay una
niña llamada Ana, durmiendo profundamente
y soñando sobre el mundo fuera de su casa,
más allá de la colina.

When Ana wakes up to the rooster's *quiquiriquí*, Papi is already at work on the farm and Mami is busy in the garden. Ana bathes her little brother and feeds the goats and collects the eggs to sell at the market.

Cuando Ana se despierta con el quiquiriquí del gallo, papi ya está trabajando en la granja y mami está ocupada en el jardín. Ana baña a su hermanito, le da de comer a las cabras y recoge los huevos para vender en el mercado.

After breakfast, Ana and her mother walk down the hill. Ana closes her eyes against the sun and wishes she was back in the cool of the house with her *libro*, her book.

Después del desayuno, Ana y su madre bajan de la colina. Ana cierra los ojos frente al sol y desea estar en el fresco de su casa con su libro.

Ana has read her book, her only book, so many times she knows it by heart. The book was a gift from her teacher for working so hard on her reading and writing. But last fall, her teacher moved far away, and now there is no one to teach Ana and the other children in her village.

Ana ha leído su libro —su único libro— tantas veces, que lo sabe de memoria. El libro fue un regalo de su maestra por haberse esforzado tanto en sus tareas de lectura y escritura. Pero el otoño pasado, su maestra se mudó lejos y ahora no hay quien pueda enseñar a Ana y el resto de los niños de su pueblo.

So, at night, on her bed in the house on the hill, Ana makes up her own *cuentos* and tells the stories to her little brother to help him fall asleep. She tells him stories about make-believe creatures that live in the forest and the mountains and the sea. She wishes for new stories to read, but her teacher with the books has gone.

Por eso, de noche, en su cama en la casa de la colina, Ana inventa sus propios cuentos y se los narra a su hermanito para ayudarlo a dormir. Le cuenta historias sobre criaturas que viven en el bosque, en las montañas y en el mar. Desea nuevas historias para leer, pero la maestra con los libros se ha marchado.

One morning, Ana wakes up to the sounds of *tacatac!* Clip-clop!
and a loud *iii-aah, iii-aah!* When Ana looks down the hill below
her house, she sees a man with a sign that reads *Biblioburro*.
With the man, there are two *burros*. What are they carrying?

Una mañana, Ana se despierta con el sonido de *¡tacatac, clip-clop!*
Y un ruidoso *¡iii-aah! ¡iii-aah!* Cuando Ana mira hacia abajo de la
colina, ve un hombre con un letrero que dice *Biblioburro*.
El hombre tiene dos burros. ¿Qué traen?

Libros! Books!

Ana runs down the hill to the man with the sign and the *burros* and the books. Other children run to him too, skipping down hills and stomping through the fields.

¡Libros!

Ana baja la colina corriendo hacia el hombre con el letrero y los burros y los libros. Otros niños también corren hacia él, bajando las colinas brincando y pisando fuerte por el campo.

"Who are you? Who are they?" the children ask.

The man says, "I am a librarian, a *bibliotecario*, and these are my *burros*, Alfa and Beto. Welcome to the Biblioburro, my *biblioteca*."

"But, *señor*," Ana says, "I thought libraries were only in big cities and buildings."

"Not this one," says the librarian. "This is a *moving library*."

Then he spreads out his books and invites the children to join him under a tree.

—¿Quién es usted? ¿Quiénes son ellos? —preguntan los niños.

El hombre contesta: —Soy un bibliotecario y estos son mis burros, Alfa y Beto. Bienvenidos al Biblioburro, mi biblioteca.

—Pero, señor —dice Ana— yo pensaba que las bibliotecas existían solo en las grandes ciudades y en edificios.

—Ésta no —dice el bibliotecario—. Ésta es una biblioteca móvil.

Luego saca sus libros e invita a los niños a acompañarlo bajo el árbol.

"Once upon a time," the librarian begins, sharing the story of an elephant who swings from a spider's web. He reads from books with beautiful pictures, then helps the little ones learn their abecedario.

He sings, "A, B, C, D, E, F, G . . ."

"Especially you," says the librarian with a smile.

"Me too?" asks Ana.

Finally, he says, "Now it's your turn. Pick out books and in a few weeks I will be back to collect them and bring you new ones."

—Había una vez —comienza el bibliotecario, contando la historia de un elefante que se balancea de una telaraña. Lee libros con ilustraciones hermosas y después ayuda a los pequeños a aprender el abecedario.

Canta: "A, B, C, D, E, F, G . . ."

—Especialmente tú —dice el bibliotecario con una sonrisa.

—¿Yo también? —pregunta Ana.

Al fin, dice: —Ahora les toca a ustedes. Elijan libros y en unas semanas regresaré a recogerlos y a traerles otros.

So many *cuentos!*

While Alfa and Beto chomp the sweet grass under the tree, Ana picks up book after book and finds pink dolphins and blue butterflies, castles and fairies, talking lions and magic carpets.

¡Tantos cuentos!

Mientras Alfa y Beto mastican la dulce hierba debajo del árbol, Ana toma libro tras libro y encuentra delfines rosados, mariposas azules, castillos y hadas, leones que hablan y alfombras mágicas.

"Someone should write a story about your *burros*," Ana tells the librarian, rubbing Alfa's nose and feeding more grass to Beto.

"Why don't you?" he asks. Then he packs up the books and is off.

"Enjoy!" he calls to the children. "I will be back."

Ana runs up the hill to her house, hugging the books to her chest. She can't wait to share her books with her brother, and that night she reads until she can't keep her eyes open any longer.

—Alguien debería escribir una historia sobre tus burros —le dice Ana al bibliotecario mientras frota la nariz de Alfa y le da más hierba a Beto.

—¿Por qué no lo haces tú? —pregunta él. Luego guarda los libros y comienza su camino.

—¡Que los disfruten! —le dice en voz alta a los niños—. Volveré.

Ana sube la colina corriendo hacia su casa y abrazando los libros contra el pecho. Tiene muchas ganas de compartirlos con su hermano y esa noche los lee hasta que no puede mantener los ojos abiertos.

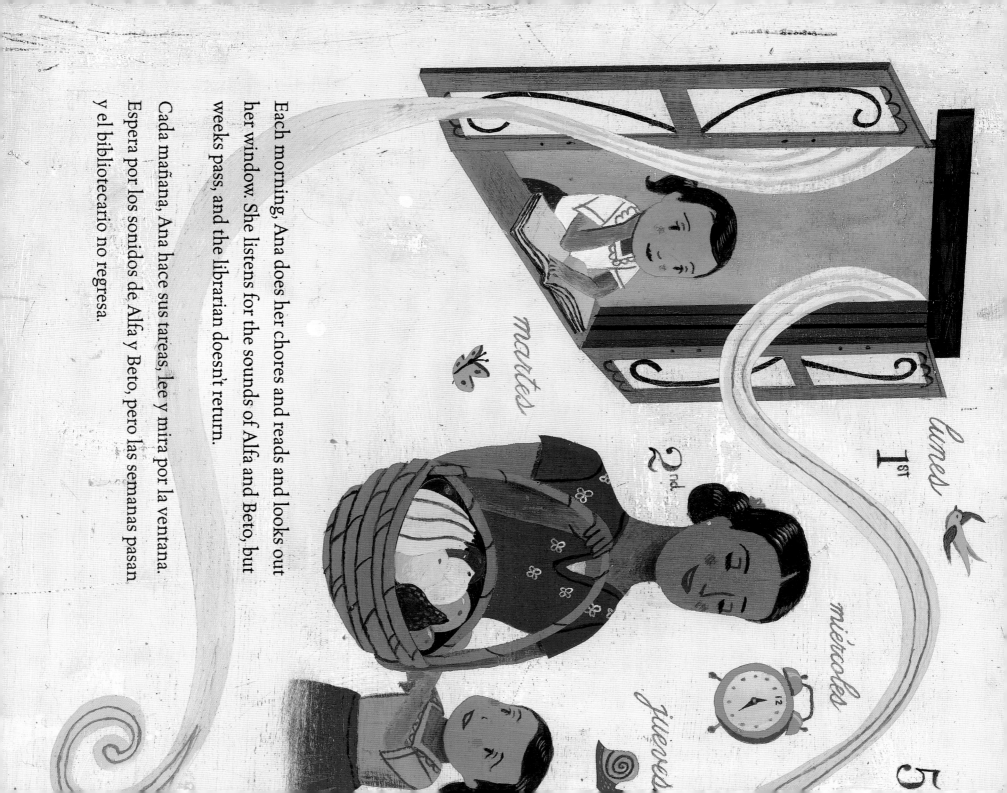

Each morning, Ana does her chores and reads and looks out her window. She listens for the sounds of Alfa and Beto, but weeks pass, and the librarian doesn't return.

Cada mañana, Ana hace sus tareas, lee y mira por la ventana. Espera por los sonidos de Alfa y Beto, pero las semanas pasan y el bibliotecario no regresa.

lunes 1ˢᵀ

martes 2ⁿᵈ

miércoles

jueves 5

"When will he come back?" she asks her mother, who smiles and says, "Go read, Ana."
"When will he come back?" she asks her mother, who smiles and says, "Go draw, Ana."
"When will he come back?" she asks her mother, who smiles and says, "Go write, Ana."
"When will he come back?" she asks her mother, who finally says, "Go to bed, Ana!"

—¿Cuándo regresará? —le pregunta a su madre, quien sonríe y le contesta: —Ve a leer, Ana.
—¿Cuándo regresará? —le pregunta a su madre, quien sonríe y le contesta: —Ve a dibujar, Ana.
—¿Cuándo regresará? —le pregunta a su madre, quien sonríe y le contesta: —Ve a escribir, Ana.
—¿Cuándo regresará? —le pregunta a su madre, quien finalmente dice: —¡Ve a dormir, Ana!

One night, Ana dreams she is flying over her country on a butterfly's back. In her dream, she crosses mountains and oceans and rivers and jungles, bringing stories everywhere she goes. Stories fly from her mouth and fingers like magic, falling into the hands of the children waiting below.

When Ana wakes up, she misses Alfa and Beto and the Biblioburro's books. She remembers that the librarian told her that she could write a book, and so, with paper and string and colored pencils, she does.

Una noche, Ana sueña que está volando sobre su país en la espalda de una mariposa. En su sueño, cruza montañas, océanos, ríos y junglas, trayendo historias a doquiera que va. Las historias salen de su boca y de sus dedos como magia, cayendo en las manos de los niños que las esperan debajo.

Cuando Ana se despierta, extraña a Alfa y Beto y a los libros del Biblioburro. Recuerda que el bibliotecario le dijo que podía escribir un libro, entonces, toma papel, hilo y lápices de colores y lo hace.

Finally, just when Ana thinks she'll never see the Biblioburro again, she wakes up to *iii-aah, iii-aah!* and children yelling.

She runs down the hill with her library books and a special surprise of her very own.

"I wrote this *cuento* for you," she says.

"*¡Qué bueno!*" the librarian says, and then he reads *her* story to the children under the tree.

Finalmente, cuando Ana piensa que nunca va a volver a ver al Biblioburro, se despierta con un *¡iii-aah! ¡iii-aah!* Y el grito de los niños.

Baja la colina corriendo con los libros prestados y su propia sorpresa.

—Escribí este cuento para usted —dice.

—¡Qué bueno! —contesta el bibliotecario y lee la historia de Ana a los niños debajo del árbol.

When it's time to go, Ana's book is packed carefully on the *burro's* back, ready to be carried away, over the hills and through the fields to another child who is . . .

A la hora de partir, guarda cuidadosamente el libro de Ana sobre el lomo del burro, que está pronto para llevarlo, sobre las colinas y a través de los campos a otro niño que está . . .

asleep on a bed, in a house, on a hill behind a tree, dreaming of Alfa and Beto and all the new stories the Biblioburro will bring.

durmiendo en una cama, en una casa, en una colina detrás de un árbol, soñando con Alfa y Beto y todas las historias nuevas que traerá el Biblioburro.

AUTHOR'S NOTE

How far would you go for a book? How far would a librarian travel to bring a book to you?

Around the world, there are many librarians, and libraries, that travel long distances, just like the Biblioburro. In Kenya, camel caravans deliver books to nomads in the desert. In Sweden, Stockholm's "floating library" delivers books to islanders via book boats. In Zimbabwe, there is a donkey-drawn mobile cart library. In the United States, bookmobiles started out as book wagons.

This book was inspired by a particular librarian I was honored to get to know—Luis Soriano Bohórquez. Near La Gloria, Colombia, this teacher and librarian delivers books to children in remote villages with the help of his two donkeys, Alfa and Beto. Luis's Biblioburro program is an inspiration to us all. To learn more about Luis, check out cnn.com/2010/LIVING/02/25/cnnheroes .soriano/.

This book is a celebration of Luis and all the teachers and librarians who bring books to children everywhere—across deserts, fields, mountains, and water.

NOTA DE LA AUTORA

¿Qué tan lejos irías por un libro? ¿Qué tan lejos viajaría un bibliotecario para traerte un libro?

Alrededor del mundo hay muchos bibliotecarios y bibliotecas que viajan grandes distancias, como Biblioburro. En Kenya, caravanas de camellos llevan libros a nómadas en el desierto. En Suecia, la "biblioteca flotante" de Estocolmo lleva libros a isleños sobre botes-bibliotecas. En Zimbabue, hay una biblioteca móvil en un carro tirado por un burro. En Estados Unidos, las bibliotecas móviles comenzaron con carretas de libros.

Este libro fue inspirado por un bibliotecario en particular que tuve el honor de conocer: Luis Soriano Bohórquez. Por la zona de La Gloria, Colombia, este maestro y bibliotecario lleva libros a niños en pueblos remotos con la ayuda de sus burros, Alfa y Beto. El programa Biblioburro de Luis sirve para inspirarnos a todos. Para saber más acerca de Luis, visite: cnn.com/2010/LIVING/02/25 /cnnheroes.soriano/.

Este libro rinde homenaje a Luis y a todos los maestros y bibliotecarios que llevan libros a niños en todas partes del mundo—a través de desiertos, campos, montañas y mares.

GLOSSARY OF SPANISH TERMS

abecedario: alphabet

biblioteca: library

bibliotecario: librarian

burro: donkey

cuento: story

domingo: Sunday

había una vez: once upon a time

iii-aah: hee-haw

jueves: Thursday

libro: book

lunes: Monday

martes: Tuesday

miércoles: Wednesday

quiquiriquí: cock-a-doodle-doo

sábado: Saturday

señor: sir

tacatac: clip-clop

viernes: Friday

qué bueno: that's good

2. **Identification and analysis of the financial reporting issues**

a. Issue identification

Read the case and look for potential financial reporting issues. To do this, you need to know the accounting principles and rules and have an understanding of the business and the business transactions. Issues are usually about deciding whether or not to **recognize** something (revenues, liabilities etc.), deciding how to **measure** financial statement elements (leave them as they are or write them down or off), or how to **present/disclose** these items in the financial statements (treat them as current or long–term, debt or equity, discontinued or continuing operations, etc.).

b. Ranking issues

Focus on the more important issues. In other words, focus first on the issues that are material to the users of the information (those that are more complex and/or those that affect any of the key numbers or ratios identified above). You should identify right away what you consider to be material.

c. Analysis

The analysis should consider both qualitative and quantitative aspects. It should also look at the issue from different perspectives. For example, in a revenue recognition issue, should the revenue be recognized now or later? Consider only the relevant alternatives.

Qualitative:

- Each perspective must be supported by making reference to GAAP and accounting theory (including the conceptual framework). For example, recognize the revenue now because... or recognize it later because...

- Make sure the analysis is case specific—i.e., that it refers to the facts of the specific case.

- Make strong arguments for both sides of the discussion. If the issue is a real issue, there is often more than one way to account for the transaction or event.

- Make sure that the analysis considers the substance of the transaction from a business and economic perspective.

Quantitative:

- Calculate the impact of the different perspectives on key financial statement numbers/ratios. Would this decision be relevant to users?

- Calculate what the numbers might look like under different accounting methods, if they are relevant.

3. **Recommendations**

After each issue is analyzed, conclude on how the items should be accounted for. Your conclusion should be based on your role and the financial reporting objective that you identified earlier.

TENTH CANADIAN EDITION

INTERMEDIATE
ACCOUNTING

Donald E. Kieso, PhD, CPA
KPMG Peat Marwick Emeritus Professor of Accounting
Northern Illinois University
DeKalb, Illinois

Jerry J. Weygandt, PhD, CPA
Arthur Andersen Alumni Professor of Accounting
University of Wisconsin
Madison, Wisconsin

Terry D. Warfield, PhD
Associate Professor
University of Wisconsin
Madison, Wisconsin

Nicola M. Young, MBA, FCA
Saint Mary's University
Halifax, Nova Scotia

Irene M. Wiecek, FCPA, FCA
University of Toronto
Toronto, Ontario

Bruce J. McConomy, PhD, CPA, CA
Wilfrid Laurier University
Waterloo, Ontario

WILEY

Dedicated to accounting educators in Canada and to the students in their intermediate financial accounting courses. Embracing continuing change as standards evolve in a multiple-GAAP world.

I would like to say a special thank you to Nickie who transitions off this book as Bruce transitions on. You are an amazing analytical thinker, Nickie, and this text exists today largely through your significant contributions. I will miss our lengthy technical and theoretical conversations that always seemed to start innocently enough with "one quick question..." I have learned so much from you and it has been a privilege and pleasure working with you.

—Irene

Library and Archives Canada Cataloguing in Publication

Intermediate accounting / Donald E. Kieso ... [et al.]. — 10th Canadian ed.

Includes index.

ISBN 978-1-118-30084-8 (v. 1).—ISBN 978-1-118-30085-5 (v. 2)

1. Accounting—Textbooks. I. Kieso, Donald E.

HF5636.I56 2013   657'.044   C2012-906693-1

Production Credits

Acquisitions Editor: Zoë Craig
Vice President and Publisher: Veronica Visentin
Vice President, Marketing: Carolyn Wells
Marketing Manager: Anita Osborne
Editorial Manager: Karen Staudinger
Production Manager: Tegan Wallace
Developmental Editor: Daleara Jamasji Hirjikaka
Media Editor: Channade Fenandoe

Editorial Assistant: Luisa Begani
Design & Typesetting: Lakeside Group Inc.
(Gail Ferreira Ng-A-Kien)
Cover Design: Lakeside Group Inc.
(John Lightfoot)
Cover Photo: ©istockphoto.com/bagi998
Printing and Binding: Courier

References to the *CICA Handbook—Accounting* are reprinted (or adapted) with permission from the Canadian Institute of Chartered Accountants (CICA), Toronto, Canada. Any changes to the original material are the sole responsibility of the author (and/or publisher) and have not been reviewed or endorsed by the CICA.

The IASB, the IFRS Foundation, the authors and the publishers do not accept responsibility for any loss caused by acting or refraining from acting in reliance on the material in this publication, whether such loss is caused by negligence or otherwise.

Questions adapted from (Financial Accounting: Assets (FA) Exams or Financial Accounting: Liabilities & Equities (FA3) Exams) published by the Certified General Accountants Association of Canada, © CGA-Canada, (2012), reproduced with permission. All rights reserved. Because of regular Tax Act updates, changes to IFRS and the *CICA Handbook*, the contents of these examinations may be out of date; therefore the accuracy of the contents is the sole responsibility of the user.

Printed and bound in the United States of America

1 2 3 4 5 CC 17 16 15 14 13

Brief Contents

Contents

Cash Is King

The Canadian Press Images-Marco Beauregard

CHANCES ARE, most Canadians have at least some Canadian Tire "money" in a wallet or drawer that they have received as a reward for paying with cash or debit card at the iconic retailer. Canadian Tire has been handing out paper coupons that can be used to buy merchandise since 1958, making it Canada's oldest customer loyalty program. More than 1 billion Canadian Tire notes, ranging in denominations of 5 cents to $2 are in circulation. The notes are made from authentic bank note paper and today use the latest anti-counterfeiting technology. But unlike real money, the notes feature not an image of a prime minister or monarch, but the fictional character Sandy McTire, designed by a Canadian Tire employee in 1961.

Keeping up with the electronic times, in 2000, Canadian Tire launched a co-branded MasterCard credit card, giving customers Canadian Tire "money" electronically no matter where they use the card. In 2012, in Nova Scotia the retailer piloted the Canadian Tire "Money" Advantage, an electronic customer rewards program that allows customers to collect points by making purchases at its stores and gas bars that can also be redeemed for Canadian Tire merchandise. The company awards more than $100 million to customers every year through its loyalty programs. Eight in 10 Canadians visit a Canadian Tire store each year.

All of these customer rewards create liabilities for Canadian Tire, since there is a good chance that customers will redeem the rewards and the company will have to honour its obligation to provide free merchandise. Canadian Tire's franchised dealers pay the company to acquire the paper "money," which the dealers then hand out to customers. An obligation arises when that happens, because the dealers retain the right to return the money to the company for a cash refund. An obligation also arises when the company issues points to customers using the Canadian Tire MasterCard credit card. "These obligations are measured at fair value by reference to the fair value of the awards for which they could be redeemed based on the estimated probability of their redemption and are expensed to sales and marketing in the Consolidated Statements of Income," the company says in its 2011 annual report.

Because paper Canadian Tire "money" has no expiry date, the company has an indefinite obligation to honour the coupons whenever customers find them in their coat pockets or the bottoms of their hockey bags.

Sources: Canadian Tire Corporation, Limited, 2011 annual report; "Canadian Tire Money: A History of Loyalty Program Innovation," corporate website, http://corp.canadiantire.ca; "Canadian Tire's Loyalty Offering Becomes More Valuable with Canadian Tire 'Money' Advantage Rewards," company news release, February 12, 2012.

Non-Financial and Current Liabilities

LEARNING OBJECTIVES

After studying this chapter, you should be able to:

1. Understand the importance of non-financial and current liabilities from a business perspective.

2. Define liabilities, distinguish financial liabilities from other liabilities, and identify how they are measured.

3. Define current liabilities and identify and account for common types of current liabilities.

4. Identify and account for the major types of employee-related liabilities.

5. Explain the recognition, measurement, and disclosure requirements for decommissioning and restoration obligations.

6. Explain the issues and account for unearned revenues.

7. Explain the issues and account for product guarantees and other customer program obligations.

8. Explain and account for contingencies and uncertain commitments, and identify the accounting and reporting requirements for guarantees and commitments.

9. Indicate how non-financial and current liabilities are presented and analyzed.

10. Identify differences in accounting between IFRS and ASPE and what changes are expected in the near future.

This chapter explains the basic principles underlying the accounting and reporting for many common current liabilities and for a variety of non-financial liabilities, such as unearned revenues, product warranty and other customer obligations, and asset retirement obligations. Contingencies, commitments, and guarantees are also addressed. Issues related to long-term financial liabilities are explained in Chapter 14.

The chapter is organized as follows:

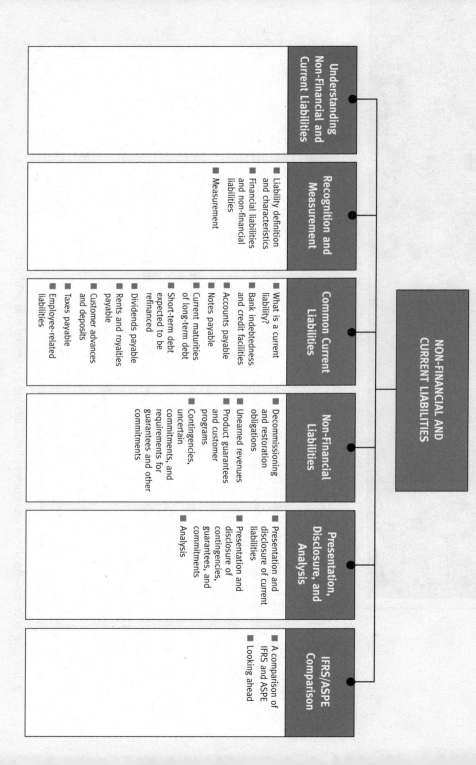

NON-FINANCIAL AND CURRENT LIABILITIES

Understanding Non-Financial and Current Liabilities

Recognition and Measurement
- Liability definition and characteristics
- Financial liabilities and non-financial liabilities
- Measurement

Common Current Liabilities
- What is a current liability?
- Bank indebtedness and credit facilities
- Accounts payable
- Notes payable
- Current maturities of long-term debt
- Short-term debt expected to be refinanced
- Dividends payable
- Rents and royalties payable
- Customer advances and deposits
- Taxes payable
- Employee-related liabilities

Non-Financial Liabilities
- Decommissioning and restoration obligations
- Unearned revenues
- Product guarantees and customer programs
- Contingencies, uncertain commitments, and requirements for guarantees and other commitments

Presentation, Disclosure, and Analysis
- Presentation and disclosure of current liabilities
- Presentation and disclosure of contingencies, guarantees, and commitments
- Analysis

IFRS/ASPE Comparison
- A comparison of IFRS and ASPE
- Looking ahead

UNDERSTANDING NON-FINANCIAL AND CURRENT LIABILITIES

Objective 1

Understand the importance of non-financial and current liabilities from a business perspective.

The asset and liability approach to accounting, as evidenced in the conceptual framework, requires that asset and liability definitions govern the recognition of all other accounting elements. Volume 1 of this text concentrated on the recognition and measurement of a variety of assets, and Volume 2 continues by beginning with a closer look at liabilities in general and then several specific types of common liabilities.

The explanations in this chapter about non-financial liabilities under international standards are based on current IAS 37 *Provisions, Contingent Liabilities and Contingent Assets*, and we provide an overview of materials underlying expected revisions to this standard.[1] While the expected revisions indicate the IASB's thinking as this text went to print, they are not effective until they are incorporated into a final standard. Therefore, we limit our discussion of expected revisions to the "Looking Ahead" section of the chapter. The final standard, when issued, will be a new IFRS entitled *Non-Financial Liabilities* covering liabilities not within the scope of other standards.

There are many kinds of liabilities. As a consumer, a common one you're familiar with is a warranty. When you purchase a new automobile or computer, one major consideration is the length of the warranty provided by the manufacturer or retailer, and whether you should pay an additional amount to extend the warranty. From the seller's perspective, the warranty provided to customers represents a liability to be reported on the statement of financial position. It's considered a liability because the manufacturer or retailer has an obligation to repair or replace any defects that are covered in the warranty, usually for no additional charge. A typical warranty on a new automobile is three years or 60,000 kilometres. As a consumer, you might choose to extend the warranty to five or six years. As a manufacturer or retailer, the warranty you offer will affect your competitive advantage over other vendors, and will complicate your accounting over the life of the warranty. There are several alternatives for accounting for warranty transactions that we will explore in this chapter.

It is important for businesses to properly account for their liabilities so they can keep an eye on their cash flow. Cash flow management is a key control factor for most businesses. Taking advantage of supplier discounts for prompt payment is one step companies can take to control their cash flows. Control of expenses and related accounts payable can improve the efficiency of a business, and can be particularly important during economic downturns.

In this chapter, we focus on current liabilities and non-financial liabilities. As we will see, companies need to account for typical items such as trade accounts payable and less obvious liabilities including constructive obligations that arise based on past practice. We will look at the related definitions under IFRS and ASPE next before examining the detailed accounting requirements.

Underlying Concept

To be able to properly classify specific financial instruments, proper definitions are needed for assets, liabilities, and equities. The conceptual framework definitions are used as the basis for settling difficult classification issues.

RECOGNITION AND MEASUREMENT

Liability Definition and Characteristics

Objective 2

Define liabilities, distinguish financial liabilities from other liabilities, and identify how they are measured.

Chapter 2 of this text presented the elements of financial statements and their definitions. It explained that the FASB and IASB are considering developing revised definitions of terms such as "assets" and **liabilities** as part of their conceptual framework project. In this text, we apply the current definitions as they are now being used, but briefly discuss the items under consideration by the IASB as it moves toward developing new standards in the "Looking Ahead" section of the chapter. Illustration 13-1 provides the definition of liabilities in the existing IFRS and in the *CICA Handbook*, Part II.[2]

Illustration 13-1

Definition of Liabilities

Definition in Existing IFRS and *CICA Handbook*, Part II (a summary)

A **liability** is an obligation that arises from past transactions or events, which may result in a transfer of assets or provision of services.

Liabilities have three essential characteristics:

1. They embody a **duty or responsibility**.
2. The entity has **little or no discretion to avoid the duty**.
3. The **transaction** or event that obliges the entity **has occurred**.

The three characteristics of a liability are essential to the current definition. First, a liability must represent a duty or responsibility; for example, to pay a supplier for goods that it has purchased. The entity has little (or no) discretion to avoid the obligation, otherwise there would be negative consequences such as the supplier suing for breach of contract. And the liability relates to a transaction that has occurred (the goods were purchased, they have been delivered and title has passed). So an economic obligation exists **at the date of the statement of financial position.** The existence of a present obligation is not always clear, as we will see later in this chapter. For example, there may be uncertainty about whether an event that has occurred results in a present obligation, or how a law or regulation applies to that event. Judgement is needed in many circumstances, with management drawing on evidence such as the entity's past experience, other entities' experience with similar items, and opinions of experts and others.[3]

The idea that an entity must have a duty or responsibility to perform in a particular way suggests it is required to bear the economic obligation, and this requirement can be **enforced by legal or equivalent means.** This means that a law, or contract enforceable by law, or a constructive obligation exists. **A constructive obligation** arises when past or present company practice shows that the entity has indicated to others that it will accept a specific responsibility and other parties can reasonably expect the entity to meet its responsibility. For example, a company may be required by provincial legislation to provide 4% vacation pay to its employees, but it may have paid 6% over the past number of years. Therefore, even though the company may not be required by law or contract to pay the extra 2%, the expectation is that it will continue to provide it. This is a constructive obligation, and amounts owing at the date of the statement of financial position are recognized as a liability, based on the 6%.

All entities must comply with the statutes, laws, and regulations in the legal jurisdiction in which they operate; however, these result in liabilities only if the entity violates their provisions. A liability does not result if the transaction or event obliging the company has not yet taken place.

Under current **recognition** requirements, non-financial liabilities are recognized only if it is probable (that is, more likely than not) that the obligation would result in an outflow of cash or other economic resources from the entity. That is, the uncertainty of the amount is an issue as to whether the obligation is recognized as a liability.

Financial Liabilities and Non-Financial Liabilities

Because a number of accounting standards refer to the recognition, measurement, and reporting of **financial instruments** specifically, it is important to be able to identify those that are financial **liabilities.** Under both accounting standards for private enterprises (ASPE) and IFRS, a **financial liability** is any liability that is a **contractual obligation:**

1. to deliver cash or other financial assets to another entity or

2. to exchange financial assets or financial liabilities with another entity under conditions that are potentially unfavourable to the entity.[4]

Note that this definition requires the liability to be based on an obligation that is created by a contract. Liabilities that are created by legislation, such as income taxes payable, do not qualify as financial liabilities and therefore are not covered by the same accounting standards as financial liabilities. In this chapter, most current liabilities are financial in nature, but if the obligation will be met by the delivery of goods or services, such as in the case of unearned revenue and warranty obligations, it is not considered a financial liability.

The classification of liabilities into financial and non-financial liabilities is important because the accounting standard that applies depends on how the liability is classified.

Measurement

Financial Liabilities

Financial liabilities are recognized initially at their fair value. After acquisition, though, most of the financial liabilities that are discussed in this and later chapters are accounted for **at their amortized cost**.[5] Consistent with cost-based measurement, transaction costs that are a direct result of the issue of the liability are debited to (deducted from) its original fair value. Alternatively, transaction costs associated with the issue of financial liabilities that are accounted for after acquisition **at fair value** are recognized in net income as they are incurred.

When liabilities are short-term in nature, such as regular trade payables with 30- or 60-day payment terms, they are usually accounted for on practical grounds at their maturity value. This is appropriate because the difference between the liability's fair value and its maturity value is not significant. The slight overstatement of liabilities that results from carrying many current liabilities at their maturity value is accepted if it is immaterial.

Non-Financial Liabilities

Non-financial liabilities, on the other hand, are usually not payable in cash. Therefore, they are measured in a different way. **ASPE** does not separately address the issue of non-financial liabilities, so these are measured in a variety of ways, depending on the specific liability. For example, unearned revenue is usually measured at the fair value of the goods or services to be delivered in the future, and, where matching is an issue, the obligations are measured based on management's best estimate of the cost of the goods or services to be provided in the future.

Under IFRS, non-financial liabilities are measured initially and at each subsequent reporting date at the best estimate of the amount the entity would rationally pay at the date of the statement of financial position to settle the present obligation. This is usually the present value of the resources needed to fulfill the obligation, measured at the expected value or probability-weighted average of the range of possible outcomes.[6]

With this introduction to liabilities, we now take a closer look at specific current liabilities found on most companies' statements of financial position.

COMMON CURRENT LIABILITIES

What Is a Current Liability?

Because liabilities result in a future disbursement (payment) of assets or services, one of their most important features is the timing of when they are due. Obligations that mature in the short term place a demand on the entity's current assets. They are demands that must be satisfied on time and in the ordinary course of business if operations are to continue. Liabilities with a distant due date generally do not result in a claim on the company's current assets and are therefore classified differently. This difference in timing and the effect on current assets is a major reason for the division of liabilities into (1) current liabilities and (2) non-current liabilities.

Another reason for classifying current assets and liabilities separately from long-term assets and liabilities is to provide information about the working capital used by the entity in its normal operating cycle. The normal **operating cycle** is the period of time between acquiring the goods and services for processing in operations and receiving cash from the eventual sale of the processed goods and services. Industries that manufacture products that go through an aging process and certain capital-intensive industries may have an operating cycle of much longer than one year. On the other hand, most retail and service establishments have several operating cycles in a single year. The operating cycle is sometimes referred to as the cash-to-cash cycle. If the length of the cycle is not obvious, accounting standards often assume it is 12 months.

The definition of a **current liability** and of the length of the operating cycle is directly related to that of a current asset. A liability is classified as current under IFRS when one of the following conditions is met:

1. It is expected to be settled in the entity's normal operating cycle.

2. It is held primarily for trading.

3. It is due within 12 months from the end of the reporting period.

4. The entity does not have an unconditional right to defer its settlement for at least 12 months after the date of the statement of financial position.[7]

ASPE provides a similar definition, suggesting that current liabilities include amounts payable within one year from the date of the balance sheet or within the normal operating cycle, when that is longer than a year.[8] There may be minor differences in application.

A variety of current liabilities commonly found in the financial statements of companies are illustrated next.

Bank Indebtedness and Credit Facilities

A major element of a company's cash position is its bank indebtedness for current operating purposes and its **line of credit** or **revolving debt** arrangements related to this debt. Instead of having to negotiate a new loan every time it needs funds, a company generally enters into an agreement with its bank that allows it to make multiple borrowings up to a negotiated limit. As previous borrowings are partly repaid, the company is permitted to borrow again under the same contract. Because the financial institution commits itself to making money available to the entity, the bank often charges an additional fee for this service over and above the interest that it charges on the funds that are actually advanced. Under such agreements, the financial institution usually requires collateral and often sets restrictions on the company's activities or financial statement ratios that must be maintained.

The amount of actual bank indebtedness is reported on the statement of financial position, while the total funds that the credit arrangement allows the company to borrow and any restrictions that are imposed by the financial institution are disclosed in the notes.

Borrowings and growth must be carefully managed! Maintaining close working relationships with customers, banks, suppliers, and other creditors is central to getting through the crunch. Based in British Columbia, **Pacific Safety Products Inc. (PSP)** enjoyed a 69% increase in sales in one year several years ago and suffered the liquidity problems that often come with such success. The company's annual report indicated that one of PSP's major challenges during the year had been to manage its cash flow so that it could pay suppliers. This was necessary to ensure a continuous flow of raw materials that were needed in the manufacturing process in order to meet customer orders on a timely basis.

PSP thus reported bank indebtedness of almost $3 million in its current liabilities at the company's year end. Providing details on the indebtedness, a note to the financial statements indicated a maximum operating line of credit of $3 million with the Bank of Nova Scotia, which was secured by accounts receivable, inventory, and an assignment of insurance. The note also reported that the company was not in compliance with the covenants imposed by the bank for its current ratio and tangible net worth, but that the bank was allowing PSP to operate outside its covenants.

One year later, PSP reported sales that were only 75% of those reported for the preceding fiscal year, but its cash flow from operating activities was almost twice as high as in the earlier period! The uncollected receivables from one year earlier had been collected and this allowed the company to get over the cash crunch. Bank indebtedness was reduced to only $102,417, the operating line was reduced to $2 million, and the company was once again in compliance with the covenants imposed by the bank.

Accounts Payable

Accounts payable, or trade **accounts payable,** are balances owed to others for goods, supplies, or services related to the entity's ordinary business activities that are purchased on open account. This means that evidence of the obligations' existence comes from regular invoices rather than from separate contracts for each transaction. Accounts payable arise because of the time lag between the receipt of goods and services and the payment for them. This period of extended credit is usually stated in the terms of sale and purchase—for example, 2/10, n/30 or 1/10, E.O.M., net 30—and is commonly 30 to 60 days long.[9]

Most accounting systems are designed to record liabilities for purchases of goods when the goods are received. Sometimes there is a delay in recording the goods and the related liability on the books, such as when waiting for an invoice. If title has passed to the purchaser before the goods are received, the transaction should be recorded when the title passes. Attention must be paid to transactions that occur near the end of one accounting period and the beginning of the next so that the goods and services received (the inventory or expense) are recorded in the same accounting period as the liability (accounts payable) and both are recorded in the proper period. Chapter 8 discussed this cut-off issue in greater detail and illustrated the entries for accounts payable and purchase discounts.

Notes Payable

Law

Notes payable are written promises to pay a certain sum of money on a specified future date and may arise from purchases, financing, or other transactions. In some industries, instead of the normal procedure of extending credit on an open account, notes (often referred to as **trade notes payable**) are required as part of the sale or purchase transaction. Notes payable to banks or loan companies are generally created by cash loans. Notes may be classified as current (short-term) or long-term (non-current), depending on the payment due date. Notes may also be interest-bearing or non–interest-bearing (that is, zero-interest-bearing) and accounting for them is the mirror image of accounting for notes receivable illustrated in Chapter 7.

Interest-Bearing Note Issued

Assume that Provincial Bank agrees to lend $100,000 on March 1, 2014, to Landscape Corp. and the company signs a $100,000, four-month, 12% note. The entry to record the cash received by Landscape Corp. on March 1 is:

March 1	Cash	100,000	
	Notes Payable		100,000

A	=	L	+ SE
+100,000		+100,000	

Cash flows: ↑ 100,000 inflow

If Landscape Corp. has a December 31 year end but prepares financial statements semi-annually, an adjusting entry is required to recognize the four months of interest expense and interest payable of $4,000 ($100,000 × 12% × $^{4}/_{12}$) on June 30. The adjusting entry is:

June 30	Interest Expense	4,000	
	Interest Payable		4,000

A =	L	+ SE
	+4,000	−4,000

Cash flows: No effect

At maturity on July 1, Landscape Corp. pays the note's face value of $100,000 plus the $4,000 of interest. The entry to record payment of the note and accrued interest is as follows:

A = L + SE
−104,000 −104,000
Cash flows: ↓ 104,000 outflow

July 1	Notes Payable	100,000	
	Interest Payable	4,000	
	Cash		104,000

Zero-Interest-Bearing Note Issued

A zero-interest-bearing note may be issued instead of an interest-bearing note. Despite its name, a **zero-interest-bearing note does have an interest component**. The interest is just not added on top of the note's face or maturity value; instead, it is included in the face amount. The interest is the difference between the amount of cash received when the note is signed and the higher face amount that is payable at maturity. The borrower receives the note's present value in cash and pays back the larger maturity value.

To illustrate, assume that Landscape Corp. issues a $100,000, four-month, zero-interest-bearing note payable to the Provincial Bank on March 1. The note's present value is $96,154, based on the bank's discount rate of 12%. Landscape's entry to record this transaction is as follows:

A = L + SE
+96,154 +96,154
Cash flows: ↑ 96,154 inflow

| March 1 | Cash | 96,154 | |
| | Notes Payable[10] | | 96,154 |

Notes Payable is credited for the note's fair value, which is less than the cash due at maturity. In effect, this is the amount borrowed. If Landscape Corp. prepares financial statements at June 30, the interest expense for the four-month period to June 30 must be recognized along with the increase in the Note Payable, $96,154 × 12% × 4/12 = $3,846, as follows:

A = L + SE
+3,846 −3,846
Cash flows: No effect

| June 30 | Interest Expense | 3,846 | |
| | Notes Payable | | 3,846 |

The Notes Payable account now has a balance of $96,154 + $3,846 = $100,000. This is the amount borrowed plus interest to June 30 at 12%. On July 1 the note is repaid:

A = L + SE
−100,000 −100,000
Cash flows: ↓ 100,000 outflow

| July 1 | Notes Payable | 100,000 | |
| | Cash | | 100,000 |

The accounting issues related to long-term notes payable are discussed in Chapter 14.

Current Maturities of Long-Term Debt

Bonds, mortgage notes, and other long-term indebtedness that mature within 12 months from the date of the statement of financial position—**current maturities of long-term debt**—are reported as current liabilities. When only part of a long-term obligation is to be paid within the next 12 months, as in the case of a mortgage or of serial bonds that are to be retired through a series of annual instalments, **only the maturing portion of the principal of the long-term debt is reported as a current liability**. The balance is reported as a long-term liability.

Portions of long-term obligations that will mature in the next 12 months should not be included as current liabilities if, by contract, they are to be retired by assets accumulated for this purpose that properly have not been reported as current assets. In this situation, no current assets are used and no other current liabilities are created in order to repay the maturing liability. Therefore, it is correct to classify the liability as long-term.

A liability that is **due on demand** (that is, callable by the creditor), or that will be due on demand within a year, is also classified as a current liability. Often companies have debt agreements that, while due on demand, have payment schedules set up to pay the obligation over a number of years. The management of these entities may argue that only the portion due to be paid within 12 months should be classified as current. Managers further argue that financial statement readers will be misled if the whole of the debt is reported as a current liability, because the company's liquidity position is misrepresented. The standard setters, on the other hand, indicate that all of such **callable debt** meets the definition of a current liability, and that additional information about the callable debt can be explained in the notes to the financial statements.

Law

Liabilities often become callable by the creditor if there is a violation of a debt agreement. For example, most debt agreements require the borrower to maintain a minimum ratio of equity to debt or, as illustrated in the Pacific Safety Products situation above, specify minimum current ratio requirements.

If a long-term debt agreement is violated and the liability becomes payable on demand, the debt is reclassified as current. Under IFRS, this position holds, even if the lender agrees between the date of the statement of financial position and the date the financial statements are released that it will not demand repayment because of the violation. This position is consistent with the fact that, at the date of the statement of financial position, the entity did not have an unconditional right to defer the payment beyond 12 months from the reporting date. That right could only be exercised by the lender.

Under ASPE, the liability is reclassified to the current category unless:

1. the creditor waives in writing the covenant (agreement) requirements, **or**

2. the violation has been cured or rectified within the grace period that is usually given in these agreements, **and**

3. it is likely that the company will not violate the covenant requirements within a year from the date of the statement of financial position.[11]

Short-Term Debt Expected to Be Refinanced

Short-term debt obligations are amounts scheduled to mature within one year from the date of the statement of financial position. However, a classification issue arises when such a liability is expected to be refinanced on a long-term basis, and therefore current assets are not expected to be needed for them. Where should these **short-term obligations expected to be refinanced** on a long-term basis be reported?[12]

At one time, the accounting profession generally agreed with not including short-term obligations in current liabilities if they were "expected to be refinanced" on a long-term basis. Because the profession gave no specific guidelines, however, determining whether a short-term obligation was "expected to be refinanced" was usually based solely on management's **intent**. Classification was not clear-cut and the proper accounting was therefore uncertain. For example, a company might want a five-year bank loan but handles the actual financing with 90-day notes that it keeps renewing. In this case, is the loan long-term debt or a current liability?

Consistent with the international standard for callable debt, under IFRS, if the debt is due within 12 months from the reporting date, it is classified as a current liability. This classification holds even if a long-term refinancing has been completed before the financial statements are released. The only exception accepted for continuing long-term classification is if, at the date of the statement of financial position, the entity expects to refinance it or roll it over **under an existing agreement** for at least 12 months and the decision is **solely at its discretion.**

Also consistent with the ASPE standard for callable debt, the short-term liability expected to be refinanced is classified as a current liability unless either the liability has been refinanced on a long-term basis or there is a non-cancellable agreement to do so before the financial statements are completed and nothing stands in the way of completing the refinancing. That is, if there is irrefutable evidence by the time the financial statements are completed that the debt has been or will be converted into a long-term obligation, ASPE allows currently maturing debt to be classified as long-term on the balance sheet.

If an actual refinancing occurs, the amount of the short-term obligation that is excluded from current liabilities cannot be higher than the proceeds from the new obligation or equity securities that are used to retire it. For example, assume that Montavon Winery has $3 million of short-term debt at the reporting date. The company then issues $2 million of long-term debt after the date of the statement of financial position but before the financial statements are issued. It uses the proceeds from the issue to partially liquidate the short-term liability. If the net proceeds from the issue of the new long-term debt total $2 million, only $2 million of the short-term debt can be excluded from current liabilities.

Under IFRS, the whole $3 million of maturing debt would still be classified as a current obligation. That is, the international standard has a more stringent requirement: the agreement must be firm **at the date of the statement of financial position.**

Another issue is whether a short-term obligation can be excluded from current liabilities if it is paid off after the date of the statement of financial position and then replaced by long-term debt before the financial statements are issued. To illustrate, assume that Marquardt Limited pays off short-term debt of $40,000 on January 17, 2015, and issues long-term debt of $100,000 on February 3, 2015. Marquardt's financial statements dated December 31, 2014, are issued on March 1, 2015. Because the refinancing does not appear to be linked to the short-term debt, ASPE requires the debt to be classified as current. In addition, because its repayment occurred **before** funds were obtained through long-term financing, the repayment **used existing** current assets. Illustration 13-2 shows this situation.

Illustration 13-2

Short-Term Debt Paid Off after Date of the Statement of Financial Position (SFP) and Later Replaced by Long-Term Debt under Both Standards

December 31, 2014 SFP date	January 17, 2015	February 3, 2015	March 1, 2015 SFP issued
Liability $40,000 How to classify?	Liability of $40,000 paid off	Issues long-term debt of $100,000	Liability of $40,000 classified as current

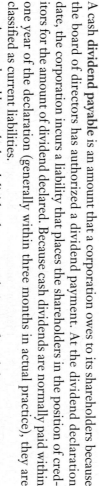

Underlying Concept

Preferred dividends in arrears are economic obligations for which the entity is the obligor, but they are not present obligations until declared. Using a note to disclose the preferred dividends in arrears improves the predictive value of the financial statements.

Dividends Payable

A cash **dividend payable** is an amount that a corporation owes to its shareholders because the board of directors has authorized a dividend payment. At the dividend declaration date, the corporation incurs a liability that places the shareholders in the position of creditors for the amount of dividend declared. Because cash dividends are normally paid within one year of the declaration (generally within three months in actual practice), they are classified as current liabilities.

Accumulated but undeclared dividends on cumulative preferred shares **are not recognized as a liability,** because **preferred dividends in arrears** are not an obligation until formal action is taken by the board of directors to authorize the distribution. Nevertheless, the company is required to disclose the existence of cumulative dividends that are undeclared in a note to the financial statements.

Dividends that are payable in the form of additional shares **are not recognized as a liability.** Such share or stock dividends (discussed in Chapter 15) do not meet the definition of a liability because they do not require future outlays of economic resources. In addition, they are not enforceable in that the board of directors can revoke them at any time before they are issued. On declaration, an entry is prepared that reduces (debits) Retained Earnings and credits a contributed capital account such as Stock Dividends Distributable. This latter account is reported in the shareholders' equity section because it represents a transfer of equity from retained earnings to contributed capital.

Rents and Royalties Payable

Law

Rents and royalties payable are another common type of current liability. This obligation may be created by a **contractual agreement in which payments are conditional on the amount of revenue that is earned or the quantity of product that is produced or extracted.** For example, franchisees are usually required to pay franchise fees to the franchisor that are calculated as a percentage of sales. Tenants in shopping centres may be obligated to pay additional rents on sales that are above a predetermined amount. Manufacturers may have licensing agreements that require them to pay the holder of a patent a royalty for each unit that the manufacturer produces.

Liabilities for expenses that are based on revenues earned or units produced are usually easy to measure. For example, if a lease calls for a fixed rent payment of $500 per month and 1% of all sales over $300,000 per year, the annual rent obligation amounts to $6,000 plus $0.01 of each dollar of revenue over $300,000. Or a royalty agreement may require the accrual of $1 per unit that is produced under the patented process, or the accrual of $0.50 on every barrel of oil that is extracted, with the accrued amount then paid to the owner of the mineral rights. As each additional unit of product is produced or extracted, an additional obligation, usually a current liability, is created.

Customer Advances and Deposits

A company's current liabilities may include returnable cash deposits or customer advances that are received from customers and employees. Deposits may be received from customers to guarantee the performance of a contract or service or to guarantee the payment of expected future obligations. For example, telephone companies often require deposits from customers when they install a phone. Some companies require their employees to make deposits for the return of keys or other company property. Deposits may also be received from tenants to cover possible future damage to property.

Are the deposits current or long-term obligations? Their initial classification depends on the conditions attached to the specific deposit. For example, if the entity does not have the right to defer the settlement of the deposit for a period of at least 12 months from the date of the statement of financial position, the deposit is reported as a current liability.

Taxes Payable

Sales Tax

Provincial sales taxes on transfers of tangible property and on certain services must be collected from customers and remitted to the tax authority, usually a provincial or territorial government.[13] The balance in the Sales Tax Payable account is the liability for sales taxes that have been collected from customers but not yet remitted to the appropriate government. The following entry shows the accounting for a sale on account of $3,000 when a 4% sales tax is in effect:

Accounts Receivable	3,120
Sales Revenue	3,000
Sales Tax Payable	120

A	=	L	+	SE
+3,120		+120		+3,000

Cash flows: No effect

Goods and Services Tax

Most businesses in Canada are subject to the Goods and Services Tax (GST). The GST, a **value-added tax** of 5% (since July 1, 2008), is a tax on the value added to the goods and services provided by each taxable entity. The net amount that an entity pays to the Canada Revenue Agency (CRA), which administers this tax, is determined as follows. The entity deducts its **input tax credit** (the GST the company paid on goods and services it purchased from suppliers) from the amount of GST the company collected, on behalf of the government, on sales to its customers. The Harmonized Sales Tax (HST) is accounted for **in the same way** as the GST in those provinces that have agreed on the combined provincial tax and GST.[14]

Accounting for the GST involves setting up a liability account—GST Payable—that is credited with GST charged on sales, and an asset account—GST Receivable—that is debited for GST paid to suppliers. Normally, the amount that is collected on sales is higher than the amount paid on purchases, and a net remittance is therefore made to the Canada Revenue Agency. Since GST is also paid on purchases of capital assets, it is possible for the GST Receivable account to have a larger balance. In these instances, a claim for reimbursement is made to the CRA.

Let's look at the accounting for the GST. Purchases of taxable goods and services are recorded by debiting the GST Receivable account for the amount of GST to be paid and debiting the appropriate asset or expense account(s) for the purchase price. Since the GST paid is recoverable from the federal government, the GST is not included in the cost of the item(s) acquired. As an example, assume that Bateman Limited purchases merchandise for $150,000 plus GST of 5% ($7,500). The entry to record this transaction is as follows, assuming a perpetual inventory system is used:

Inventory	150,000	
GST Receivable	7,500	
Accounts Payable		157,500

A	=	L	+	SE
+157,500		+157,500		

Cash flows: No effect

If these goods are sold for $210,000 plus GST of 5% ($10,500), the sale entry is:

Accounts Receivable	220,500	
Sales Revenue		210,000
GST Payable		10,500

A	=	L	+	SE
+220,500		+10,500		+210,000

Cash flows: No effect

In many cases, GST and sales taxes are levied on the same sale and purchase. Assume, for example, that Smith Ltd. sells supplies to Jones Corp. for $1,000 and both a 7% provincial sales tax and 5% GST are charged on this amount. The entry made by each company follows:

Smith Ltd. (vendor company)		
Accounts Receivable	1,120	
Sales Revenue		1,000
Sales Tax Payable		70
GST Payable		50
(To record sale to Jones Corp.)		

Jones Corp. (purchaser company)		
Supplies Expense	1,070	
GST Receivable	50	
Accounts Payable		1,120
(To record purchase from Smith Ltd.)		

Notice that the purchaser includes the provincial sales tax **in the cost** of the goods or services purchased. The provincial sales tax, unlike the GST, is not recoverable by the purchaser.[15] In the provinces with a Harmonized Sales Tax, the full HST amount is treated as shown for the GST.

Because companies are permitted under the legislation to offset the receivable and payable amounts, only the net balance of the two accounts is reported on the statement of financial position. Until a net credit balance is remitted to the Receiver General for Canada, it is reported as a current liability. A net debit balance, on the other hand, is reported as a current asset.

Income Tax

In Canada, federal and provincial income taxes are levied on a company's taxable income. Most businesses consider the amount of income tax payable as an estimate because corporate tax returns are often finalized after the financial statements have been issued. In addition, the meaning and application of numerous tax rules, especially new ones, are debatable and often depend on a court's interpretation. Using the best information and advice available, a business prepares its income tax return at the end of its fiscal year and calculates its best estimate of the income tax payable for the period.

Assume that Forest Ltd. determines, based on its taxable income for the year, that an income tax liability of $21,000 is payable, and further assume that no accruals or instalments have been made during the year. Forest makes the following entry at year end:

Current Tax Expense	21,000	
Income Tax Payable		21,000

A = L + SE
+21,000 −21,000
Cash flows: No effect

Most corporations are required to make periodic tax instalments (payments) throughout the year based on the previous year's income tax or estimates of the current year's income tax. If Forest Ltd. had made a $20,000 tax instalment at the end of the year, the following entry would also have been made.

Income Tax Payable	20,000	
Cash		20,000

A = L + SE
−20,000 −20,000
Cash flows: ↓ 20,000 outflow

Assuming the $21,000 tax liability from above, Forest Ltd. would then report an Income Tax Payable balance of $1,000 in the current liabilities section of its year-end statement of financial position ($21,000 − $20,000). Alternatively, if the company had made instalments of $23,000, there would be a $2,000 debit balance in the Income Tax Payable account ($23,000 − $21,000). This is reported as Income Tax Receivable, a current asset.

An alternative approach that is often used charges (debits) the instalment payments to expense. When the tax return is completed at year end and the actual amount of tax for the year is calculated, the expense is then adjusted. This series of entries is as follows:

Instalment payments of $20,000

Current Tax Expense	20,000	
Cash		20,000

Income taxes per tax return: $21,000

Current Tax Expense	1,000	
Income Tax Payable		1,000

Instalment payments of $23,000

Current Tax Expense	23,000	
Cash		23,000

Income taxes per tax return: $21,000

Income Tax Receivable	2,000	
Current Tax Expense		2,000

Regardless of the approach used, the resulting financial statements are identical.

Law

If, in a later year, the CRA assesses an additional tax on an earlier year's income, Income Tax Payable is credited and the income tax expense is usually charged to current operations. However, if the additional tax was caused by an obvious arithmetic error that occurred when the amount of tax was originally calculated, the error is corrected through retained earnings.

It is common for there to be differences between taxable income **under the tax laws** and accounting income **under generally accepted accounting principles.** Because of these differences, the total income tax payable to the government in any specific year may differ substantially from the total income tax expense reported on the financial statements. Chapter 18 focuses on the problems of accounting for income tax and presents an extensive discussion of related issues that are both complex and interesting.

Unlike corporations, proprietorships and partnerships are not taxable entities. It is the individual proprietor and the members of a partnership, not the business itself, that are subject to personal income taxes on their share of the business's taxable income; therefore, income tax liabilities do not appear on the financial statements of proprietorships and partnerships.

Employee-Related Liabilities

Amounts that are owed to employees for salaries or wages at the end of an accounting period are reported as a current liability called Salaries and Wages Payable. The following additional items related to employee compensation are also usually reported as current liabilities:

1. Payroll deductions
2. Short-term compensated absences
3. Profit-sharing and bonuses

Objective 4

Identify and account for the major types of employee-related liabilities.

Law

Payroll Deductions

The most common types of **payroll deductions** are employee income taxes, Canada (or Quebec) Pension Plan contributions, Employment Insurance premiums, and miscellaneous items such as other insurance premiums, employee savings, and union dues. Any amounts that have been deducted but not yet remitted to the proper authority by the end of the accounting period are recognized as current liabilities. This is also true for any matching amounts that the employer is required to pay.

Canada (Quebec) Pension Plan (CPP/QPP). The Canada and Quebec pension plans are financed by the governments through a tax on both the employer and the employee. All employers are required to collect the employee's share of this tax. They deduct it from the employee's gross pay and remit it on a regular basis to the government along with the employer's share. Both the employer and the employee are taxed at the same rate (which was 4.95% each in 2012) based on the employee's gross pay up to maximum contributory earnings of $46,600. This maximum amount is determined by subtracting the basic yearly exemption of $3,500 from the maximum amount of pensionable earnings of $50,100. The maximum annual contribution for each of the employee and employer was therefore 4.95% of $46,600, or $2,306.70 in 2012.

Employment Insurance. Another payroll tax that the federal government levies on both employees and employers is used for the system of Employment Insurance (EI). Employees must pay a premium of 1.83% (2012) of insurable earnings to an annual maximum contribution of $839.97 while the employer is required to contribute 2.562% or 1.4 times the amount of employee premiums.[16] Insurable earnings are gross wages above a preset minimum and below a maximum amount of $45,900. Both the premium rates and insurable earnings are adjusted periodically.

Income Tax Withholding. Income tax laws require employers to withhold from each employee's pay the approximate amount of income tax that will be due on those wages. The amount of income tax that is withheld is calculated by the employer according to a government-prescribed formula or a government-provided income tax deduction table, and depends on the length of the pay period and each employee's wages, marital status, claimed dependants, and other permitted deductions.

Illustration of Payroll Deductions. Assume a weekly payroll of $10,000 that is entirely subject to CPP (4.95%), Employment Insurance (1.83%), income tax withholdings of $1,320, and union dues of $88. The entry to record the salaries and wages paid and the employee payroll deductions is:

Salaries and Wages Expense	10,000	
Employee Income Tax Deductions Payable		1,320
CPP Contributions Payable		495
EI Premiums Payable		183
Union Dues Payable		88
Cash		7,914

A = L + SE
−7,914 +2,086 −10,000

Cash flows: ↓ 7,914 outflow

The required employer payroll taxes are recognized as compensation-related expenses in the same accounting period as the payroll is recorded. The entry for the required employer contributions is as follows:

Payroll Tax Expense	751	
CPP Contributions Payable ($495 × 1.0)		495
EI Premiums Payable ($183 × 1.4)		256

A = L + SE
+751 −751

Cash flows: No effect

The employer then sends to the Receiver General for Canada the amount of income tax, CPP, and EI deductions withheld from the employees, along with the employer's required contributions for CPP and EI. The entry to record the payment to the CRA for the payroll described above is:

Employee Income Tax Deductions Payable	1,320	
CPP Contributions Payable ($495 + $495)	990	
EI Premiums Payable ($183 + $256)	439	
Cash		2,749

A = L + SE
−2,749 −2,749

Cash flows: ↓ 2,749 outflow

Until they are remitted to the government and the union, these amounts are all reported as current liabilities. In a manufacturing enterprise, all payroll costs (wages, payroll taxes, and fringe benefits) are allocated to appropriate cost accounts such as Direct Labour, Indirect Labour, Sales Salaries, or Administrative Salaries.

This abbreviated and somewhat simplified discussion of payroll costs and deductions does not give a clear sense of the large volume of records and clerical work that is involved in maintaining a sound and accurate payroll system.

Short-Term Compensated Absences

Compensated absences are periods of time taken off from active employment for which employees are paid, such as statutory holidays and vacation. The entitlement to such benefits is one of two types:

1. accumulating or
2. non-accumulating.

Underlying Concept

Accounting for obligations for compensated absences is based on liability definition, recognition, and measurement concepts.

Accumulating Rights to Benefits.   Employers are required under provincial law to give each employee vacation equal to a specified number of days, or to pay them in lieu of the vacation. As a result, employers have an **unconditional obligation** for vacation pay that accrues (or accumulates) as the employees work. This obligation—or liability—is usually satisfied by paying employees their regular salaries when they are absent from work while taking vacation.

Employees may have **vested rights** to some of their benefits that accumulate with service. This means that the employer is legally required to pay the benefits even if the employee no longer works for the organization; thus, vested rights do not depend on an employee's continued service. For example, assume that you have earned four days of vacation as at December 31, the end of your employer's fiscal year. Because vacation pay is prescribed by law, your employer will have to pay you for these four days even if you resign from your job. In this case, your four days of vacation pay is a vested right and the costs are accrued by the company as expense **in the period in which the benefit is earned by the employee.**

Now assume that a company offers its employees an entitlement to vacation days above the legal requirement. Further assume that this entitlement **is not vested**, but that the right to any unused additional vacation can be carried forward to future periods. If you continue to work for the company, you are entitled to the additional unused vacation days, but if you leave the company, you lose the right to them. Although the rights are not vested, they are accumulated rights and the company will have to honour the majority of those benefits that have been earned. **Accumulated rights**, therefore, are rights that accrue with employee service. They are not necessarily vested but can still be carried forward to future periods if they are not used in the period in which they are earned. In accounting for accumulated rights, the employer recognizes an expense and a liability for the cost of these compensated absences as they are earned by employees, but the estimated cost and obligation take into account the fact that, because of employee turnover, some of these benefits will never be paid.

Entitlement to **sick pay** varies greatly among employers. In some companies, sick pay vests and employees are allowed to accumulate unused sick time. They can take time off from work with pay even though they are not ill, or they will be paid for the unused sick days when they leave the company. In this case, an obligation exists to pay future amounts; therefore, **the liability and expense are accrued** as the employees earn the benefit. This type of longer term liability is discussed in Chapter 19.

When sick days accumulate with time, but do not vest (that is, they are paid only when an employee is absent due to illness), it may be very difficult to estimate the expense that is associated with the benefits earned by the employees. In estimating the obligation, management takes into account the likelihood that many of the accumulated benefits will never be paid. Usually if the estimate is an immaterial amount, no accrual is made and the entity accounts for such non-vesting sick pay on a pay-as-you-go basis. This means that the expense is recognized in the accounts as the sick days are taken.

What rate should be used to accrue the compensated absence expense and liability: the current rate or an estimated future rate? The **best measure is the additional amount the entity expects to pay in the future** as a result of the benefits accumulated to the reporting date.[17] Many companies use the current rate of pay as the best estimate of the future amount, but other companies use future amounts that are likely to be paid, or that have already been agreed on under collective agreements, for example.

To illustrate, assume the following information for Amutron Limited that began operations on January 1, 2014.

- The company employs 10 individuals who are paid $480 per week, and this is the best estimate of the following year's wages as well.

- A total of 20 weeks of vacation is earned by all employees in 2014, but none is taken during the year.

- In 2015, the vacation weeks earned in 2014 are used when the current rate of pay has increased to $500 per week.

The entry at December 31, 2014, to accrue the vacation pay entitlement earned by the employees is as follows:

Salaries and Wages Expense	9,600	
Vacation Wages Payable ($480 × 20)		9,600

A	=	L	+	SE
+9,600				−9,600

Cash flows: No effect

At December 31, 2014, the company reports a current liability of 20 weeks × $480 or $9,600 on its statement of financial position, and an expense of $9,600 for the benefits earned by employees in 2014. In 2015, the vacation time that is paid for (and that was earned in 2014) is recorded as follows:

Vacation Wages Payable	9,600	
Salaries and Wages Expense	400	
Cash ($500 × 20)		10,000

A	=	L	+	SE
−10,000		−9,600		−400

Cash flows: ↓ 10,000 outflow

In 2015, the vacation weeks are used and the liability is eliminated. Note that the difference between the cash paid and the reduction in the liability account is recorded as an adjustment to Wages Expense in the period when it is paid. This difference occurs because the liability account was accrued at the lower rate of $480 per week. The cash paid, however, is based on the rate of pay in effect when the benefit is taken. If the future pay rates had been estimated accurately and used to calculate the accrual in 2014, then the cash paid in 2015 would have been the same as the liability.

Non-Accumulating Rights to Benefits. **Non-accumulating compensated absences**, on the other hand, are benefits that employees are entitled to by virtue of their employment and the occurrence of an obligating event. The rights to these benefits do not vest and are accounted for differently than those that accumulate with service. A good example is the additional compensation and time off for parental (maternity, paternity, and adoption) leave beyond what the government provides, and some short-term disability benefits. Employees' rights to such benefits do not accrue as they work, but only when the requirements of the parental leave or short-term disability plan have been met.[18]

Because the employer has no basis on which to accrue the costs of these benefits and the associated liability, no entry is made until the obligating event occurs. When the parental leave is taken or the employee becomes disabled, the **total** estimated liability and expense associated with the event is recognized at that time. This **event accrual method** of accounting is applied as follows. Assume that Resource Corp. provides a parental leave benefit plan that promises to pay a qualifying employee, for a period of up to one year, an amount equal to the difference between the employee's current salary and the amount paid by Employment Insurance during the leave. Sue Kim, an employee, applies for and is granted a one-year parental leave to begin on April 18. Resource Corp. calculates that the benefit payable to Sue Kim will be $200 per week. The company makes the following entry when she begins her leave on April 18:

Employee Benefit Expense	10,400	
Parental Leave Benefits Payable		10,400
($200 × 52 weeks = $10,400)		

A	=	L	+	SE
		+10,400		−10,400

Cash flows: No effect

As the compensated absence (the parental leave) is taken and Sue Kim is paid, the liability is reduced. Assuming Resource Corp. has a biweekly payroll, the following entry is made each pay period (disregarding payroll deductions):

The compensated absences discussed in this section of the chapter are all relatively short-term in nature. When the associated obligations will be met within 12 months from the date of the statement of financial position, there is no need to discount the future cash outflows when measuring the outstanding liability.[19]

Parental Leave Benefits Payable		400	
Cash			400

A	=	L	+	SE
−400		−400		

Cash flows: ↓ 400 outflow

Profit-Sharing and Bonus Agreements

Many companies have a **bonus** or a **profit-sharing** plan for their employees. These plans may be open to all employees or be restricted to those in managerial positions or perhaps only to key officers of the company. Payments under such plans are in addition to the regular salary or wage and may be a percentage of the employees' regular rates of pay, or they may depend on productivity increases or the amount of the company's annual profit. From the entity's viewpoint, **bonus and profit-sharing payments to employees** are considered additional compensation and are therefore a type of wage or salary expense in determining the net income for the year. Obligations for amounts outstanding are usually reported as current liabilities at the reporting date because they relate to and are based on the results of the period just ended, and are usually payable in the near term.

To illustrate, assume that a company has income before bonuses of $100,000 for 2014. The company has an annual bonus plan and determines in January 2015 that it will pay out bonuses of $10,700 related to the prior year. An adjusting entry dated December 31, 2014, is made to record the bonus as follows:

Bonus Expense		10,700	
Bonus Payable			10,700

A	=	L	+	SE
		+10,700		−10,700

Cash flows: No effect

In January 2015, when the bonus is paid, the entry is:

Bonus Payable		10,700	
Cash			10,700

A	=	L	+	SE
−10,700		−10,700		

Cash flows: ↓ 10,700 outflow

Underlying Concept

Accounting for bonuses or profit-sharing plans follows underlying concepts. For example, in Japan, traditionally bonuses to members of boards of directors were considered distributions of profits and therefore were charged against retained earnings.

It is important to be careful when calculating bonus and profit-sharing amounts, especially if the formula specifies that the bonus is based on **after-tax** income. Because the additional amount to be paid is itself a tax-deductible expense, simultaneous equations may have to be set up and solved to determine both the expense and tax amounts. Keep in mind that under IFRS, bonus and profit-sharing payments are accrued for constructive obligations where a reasonable estimate of the obligation can be made; that is, where the entity has no realistic alternative but to make the payments as a result of past practice (IAS 19.19).

NON-FINANCIAL LIABILITIES

Most liabilities that companies incur can be measured fairly accurately by the amount of cash (or the cash equivalent value of other financial assets) that the company must give up to discharge the obligation. In addition, the timing of the payment is usually clear. However, some liabilities are more difficult to measure because the obligations will be met with goods and services (that is, non-financial resources), and the timing of meeting the obligation and its amount are not fixed. Examples include unearned revenues, product guarantees and warranties, and obligations under customer loyalty programs. Other examples include obligations related to the dismantling and retirement of assets. These are referred to under IFRS as **provisions**: liabilities of uncertain timing or amount.

Even though the amount and timing of these obligations may not be known, whenever they involve unconditional obligations that are enforceable and that exist at the date of the statement of financial position, they are liabilities. We start by reviewing two such obligations where there is little or no uncertainty about the existence of the liability, although there may be uncertainty about its measurement.

Decommissioning and Restoration Obligations

Objective 5

Explain the recognition, measurement, and disclosure requirements for decommissioning and restoration obligations.

In many industries, the construction and operation of long-lived assets means taking on obligations associated with the eventual retirement of those assets. For example, when a mining company opens up a strip mine, it likely also makes a commitment to restore the land on which the mine is located once the mining activity is completed. Similarly, when an oil company erects an offshore drilling platform, it may be obligated to dismantle and remove the platform at the end of its useful life. Such obligations occur in a variety of ways. For example, they may arise from purchasing an asset before it is used (such as the erection of an oil rig), or they may increase over time through normal operations (such as a mine site that expands over time). Further examples of restorative activities include the following:

1. Decommissioning nuclear facilities

2. Dismantling, restoring, and reclaiming oil and gas properties

3. Certain closure, reclamation, and removal costs of mining facilities

4. Closure and post-closure costs of landfills

In general, the obligation associated with the retirement of a long-lived asset that results from acquiring, constructing, developing, or operating it must be recognized by the company **in the period when the obligation is incurred**.[20] This liability is known as an **asset retirement obligation (ARO)** or **site restoration obligation**.

While this general principle underlies both the IFRS and ASPE standards, there is a difference in the type of obligation that is recognized and which activities' costs are capitalized as part of the capital asset's cost. A table indicating the differences was presented in Chapter 10, and it is reproduced here as Illustration 13-3.

Law

Illustration 13-3

IFRS/ASPE Application Differences

	IFRS	ASPE
Category of obligations	Recognizes costs of **both legal** and **constructive obligations**, such as when an entity creates an expectation in others through its own actions that it will meet this obligation.	Recognizes costs associated with **legal obligations** only.
Category of activities	Costs included as capital assets are only those related to the acquisition of the asset, not those related to the subsequent production of goods or services (product costs).	Costs included as capital assets are retirement obligations resulting from both the acquisition of the asset and its subsequent use in producing inventory, such as the mining of coal.

The first difference relates to the fact that IFRS recognizes a broader group of non-financial obligations as liabilities: both legal and constructive obligations. The position on the second difference is consistent with the concept that costs incurred in the production of goods and services are inventory or product costs. ASPE recognizes all such costs as part of the capital asset. Because the costs capitalized to property, plant, and equipment under ASPE are often amortized subsequently as product costs, this GAAP difference may not have a significant effect on financial results.

Measurement

The liability is initially measured at "the best estimate of the expenditure required to settle the present obligation" at the reporting date.[21] Under the proposed revisions to the international standard, a similar measurement objective is identified as the amount the entity "would rationally pay at the end of the reporting period to be relieved of the present obligation." Because the obligation will often be met many years in the future, discounting the future costs is one requirement in determining the present amount required. Significant application guidance is provided on how this measurement should be approached.

Recognition and Allocation

As explained in Chapter 10, the estimated ARO costs associated with the asset's acquisition are added to the carrying amount of the related asset and a liability is recognized for the same amount. An asset retirement cost is recorded as part of the cost of the related asset because it is considered necessary in order to acquire and operate the asset, and to receive its economic benefits. Because no future economic benefit is associated with capitalized asset retirement costs as a stand-alone asset, these costs are not recorded separately from the asset account.

Later, the ARO cost is amortized to expense over the related asset's useful life. While the straight-line method is acceptable, other systematic and rational allocations are also allowed. As the expected retirement obligation and costs increase due to further damage to the site from production activities, ASPE adds these to both the recognized liability and to the capital asset account, adjusting the future depreciation rate. Under IFRS, the obligation amount is increased; however, the incremental costs caused by production are added to inventory as production overhead costs.

Note that environmental cleanup costs that are required after such events as a major oil spill or accidental runoff of chemicals into a water table **do not result in an asset retirement obligation and addition to the cost base** of the underlying asset. These catastrophes do not result in future benefits, and therefore do not justify an increase in any asset's cost.

Illustration of Accounting for Initial Recognition

To illustrate the accounting for the obligation, assume that on January 1, 2014, Wildcat Oil Corp. erects an oil platform off the Newfoundland coast. Wildcat is legally required to dismantle and remove the platform at the end of its five-year useful life. The total cost of dismantling and removal is estimated to be $1 million. Based on a 10% discount rate, the present value of the asset retirement obligation is $620,920 ($1 million × 0.62092). To keep our example relatively simple, Wildcat makes the following entry to recognize this liability under both ASPE and IFRS:

Jan. 1, 2014	Drilling Platform	620,920
	Asset Retirement Obligation	620,920

A = L + SE
+620,920 +620,920
Cash flows: No effect

If only 80% of the $1-million estimate is caused by the asset acquisition itself, with the other 20% caused by the use of the platform in production, only 80% of the $620,920 is recognized at January 1, 2014. This is the only part that is a present obligation at that date. As the platform is used and the retirement costs increase due to production, the present value of the estimated increase in the obligation is added to the production overhead costs (IFRS) or to the Drilling Platform asset (ASPE). To keep our example relatively simple, let's assume that 80% of the $1-million estimate is caused by acquisition of the asset and the remaining 20% relates to production in the first year that the asset is used. Wildcat would initially recognize 80% of this liability under both ASPE and IFRS:

Jan. 1, 2014	Drilling Platform	496,736	
	Asset Retirement Obligation		496,736

A	=	L	+ SE
+496,736		+496,736	

Cash flows: No effect

Over the asset's life, the retirement cost is depreciated. Using the straight-line method, Wildcat makes the following entry in 2014 and similar entries in 2015, 2016, 2017, and 2018 to record this expense:

Dec. 31, 2014	Depreciation Expense ($496,736 ÷ 5)	99,347	
	Accumulated Depreciation – Drilling Platform		99,347

A	=	L	SE
–99,347			–99,347

Cash flows: No effect

In addition, because the liability is measured on a discounted basis, interest on the liability is accrued each period. An entry is made at December 31, 2014, to record the expense and the related increase or **accretion** in the carrying amount of the liability. Under IFRS, the interest adjustment to the liability account **due to the passage of time** is recognized as a borrowing cost. Under ASPE, it is recognized as an operating expense on the income statement—accretion expense—but not as interest or a borrowing cost. Illustration 13-4A shows the difference in treatment between ASPE and IFRS.

Illustration 13-4A

Accretion/Interest Expense on ARO

A	=	L	+	SE
		+49,674		–49,674

Cash flows: No effect

IFRS

Dec. 31, 2014			
Interest Expense		49,674	
Asset Retirement			
Obligation			49,674
($496,736 × 10%)			

ASPE

Dec. 31, 2014			
Accretion Expense		49,674	
Asset Retirement			
Obligation			49,674
($496,736 × 10%)			

On December 31, 2014, Wildcat estimates that the increase in the ARO in 2014 incurred related to the production of oil in 2014 was $136,602. Under ASPE, the increase in cost would be added to the cost of the drilling platform. Under IFRS, the added cost would be charged to production (that is, inventory, assuming the oil was not yet sold). The related journal entries are shown in Illustration 13-4B.

Illustration 13-4B

Accounting for Increases in ARO Relating to Production

A	=	L	+	SE
+136,602		+136,602		

Cash flows: No effect

IFRS

Dec. 31, 2014			
Inventory		136,602	
Asset Retirement			
Obligation			136,602

ASPE

Dec. 31, 2014			
Drilling Platform		136,602	
Asset Retirement			
Obligation			136,602

In 2015 and subsequent years, under ASPE, the depreciation expense for the drilling platform would be increased to reflect the additional amount capitalized on December 31, 2014. Under IFRS, cost of goods sold would be increased as the inventory is sold. As mentioned above, because the drilling costs capitalized to property, plant, and equipment under ASPE are often amortized subsequently as product costs, this ASPE/IFRS difference may not have a significant effect on financial results.

On January 10, 2019, Wildcat pays Rig Reclaimers, Inc. for dismantling the platform at the contract price of $995,000. Wildcat then makes the following entry to record the settlement of the liability:

Jan. 10, 2019	Asset Retirement Obligation	1,000,000*	
	Gain on Settlement of ARO		5,000
	Cash		995,000

*ARO on Dec. 31, 2014 = (496,736 × 1.10) + 136,602 = 683,012. Taking into account the time value of money, this would increase as follows (to December 31, 2018): 683,012 × 1.1 × 1.1 × 1.1 × 1.1 = 683,012 × (1.1)⁴ = 1,000,000 (rounded).

A = L + SE
−995,000 = −1,000,000 +5,000

Cash flows: ↓ 995,000 outflow

Subsequent Recognition and Measurement of AROs: Summary

To summarize, under ASPE, the expense for the interest element (accretion) is calculated first. This is followed by an adjustment to the carrying amount of the Asset Retirement Obligation account for any increase or decrease in the cost estimates. This adjustment is also made to the carrying amount of the long-lived asset to which it relates and, of course, to the amount of annual depreciation.[22] IFRIC 1 indicates that IFRS is applied in a similar way, except that the change in obligation due to production would be inventoried instead of added to the capital asset's cost.

Real World Emphasis

Objective 6
Explain the issues and account for unearned revenues.

Unearned Revenues

When a company receives cash or other assets in advance for specific goods or services to be delivered or performed in the future, the entity recognizes the obligation as a liability. For example, a magazine publisher such as Rogers Publishing Limited receives payments from customers when subscriptions to magazines such as *Maclean's* are ordered, and an airline such as Air Canada usually sells tickets in advance for flights. For their part, retail stores increasingly issue gift certificates that can be redeemed for merchandise. In all these situations, the assets received in advance require the entity to perform in the future. This obligation is a liability that is generally referred to as **unearned revenue**. The company's liability is measured at the fair value of the outstanding obligation and this revenue is then recognized as the goods are delivered or the services are provided.

To illustrate, assume that the Rambeau Football Club sells 5,000 season tickets at $50 each for its five-game home schedule. The entry for the sale of the season tickets is:

| Cash | 250,000 | |
| Unearned Revenue | | 250,000 |

A = L + SE
+250,000 = +250,000

Cash flows: ↑ 250,000 inflow

As each game is completed, the following entry is made to recognize the revenue earned:

| Unearned Revenue | 50,000 | |
| Revenue | | 50,000 |

A = L + SE
−50,000 = +50,000

Cash flows: No effect

The balance in the Unearned Revenue account is reported as a current liability in the statement of financial position. As the Rambeau Football Club plays each game, part of the obligation is met, revenue is earned, and a transfer is made from unearned revenue to a revenue account on the income statement. The costs associated with that revenue are deducted as expenses in the same period to determine the period's net income.

Unearned revenue is material for some companies. In the airline industry, for example, tickets sold for future flights represent a significant portion of total current liabilities. WestJet's advance ticket sales represented 45.9% of its current liabilities at December 31,

2011, up from 40.1% at December 31, 2010. At the same dates, **Air Canada** reported advance ticket sales equal to 49.3% and 44.0% of current liabilities, respectively. The following table shows specific unearned revenue (statement of financial position) accounts and earned revenue (income statement) accounts that might be used in different industries.

Industry Type	Account Title	
	Unearned Revenue	**Earned Revenue**
Airline	Advance Ticket Sales	Passenger Revenue
Magazine publisher	Deferred Subscription Revenue	Subscription Revenue
Hotel	Advance Room Deposits	Room Revenue
Equipment maintenance	Unearned Maintenance Contract Fees	Maintenance Contract Revenue

Real World Emphasis

Alternative Terminology

Unearned Revenue and Earned Revenue account names often vary by industry.

Objective 7

Explain the issues and account for product guarantees and other customer program obligations.

Product Guarantees and Customer Programs

Businesses often offer continuing care or other customer programs that require the entity to provide goods and services after the initial product or service has been delivered. This is an area where the accounting for the entity's continuing obligations has been evolving. Historically, an expense approach has been used to account for the outstanding liability, but some recent standards have moved to an approach we call the revenue approach. Let us start with an overview of these two approaches and then see how they are applied in specific situations.

Expense approach. Under some circumstances, the outstanding liability is measured at the cost of the economic resources needed to meet the obligation. The **expense approach** makes the assumption that along with the liability that is required to be recognized at the reporting date, the associated expense needs to be measured and matched with the revenues of the period. In fact, the need to match expenses has driven this approach over the years. As the actual costs are incurred in subsequent periods, the liability is reduced. This is similar to the proposed contract-based approach for quality assurance warranties, discussed in Chapter 6.

Significant Change

Revenue approach. Under other circumstances, the outstanding liability is measured at the value of the obligation—an output price rather than an input price or cost measure. This is the situation when assets are received in advance for a variety of performance obligations to be delivered in the future. Under the **revenue approach**, the proceeds received for any goods or services yet to be delivered or performed are unearned at the point of sale. Until the revenue is earned, the obligation—the liability—is reported at its sales or fair value. The liability is then reduced as the revenue is earned. Revenue recognition concerns are at the base of this approach. This is similar in many respects to the proposed contract-based approach to revenue recognition explained in Chapter 6 where the liability represents a performance obligation for insurance type warranties that are sold separately. Revenue is recognized when the service is provided and the performance obligation is satisfied.

There are two major differences between these approaches:

1. Under the expense approach, the liability is **measured at the estimated cost** of meeting the obligation. Under the revenue approach, the liability recognized is **measured at the value of the service** to be provided, not at its cost.

2. Under the expense approach, and assuming the estimate of the cost of the obligation to be met in the future is close to the actual future cost, there is **no effect on future income**.[23] Under the revenue approach, **future income is affected**. Some amount of unearned revenue is recognized as a liability, and this is recognized as revenue in future periods when it is earned or the performance obligation is met. Any expenses

associated with that revenue are also recognized in the future. Therefore, **future income amounts are affected** by the profit or loss earned on the delivery of the goods or services provided in subsequent periods.

Product Guarantees and Warranty Obligations

A **warranty (product guarantee)** is a promise made by a seller to a buyer to correct problems experienced with a product's quantity, quality, or performance. Warranties are commonly used by manufacturers to promote sales. Automakers, for example, attract additional business by extending the length of their new-car warranty. For a specified period of time following the date of sale to the consumer, a manufacturer may promise to be responsible for all or part of the cost of replacing defective parts, to perform any necessary repairs or servicing without charge, to refund the purchase price, or even to double your money back. Warranties and product guarantees are **stand-ready obligations** at the reporting date that result in future costs that are often significant.

Accounting for warranties is in a state of transition. In the past and still applied in some cases, as a holdover from times when the matching principle predominated, the expense approach was widely used. Increasingly today, the asset and liability view and faithful representation drive the accounting model, resulting in the **bifurcation** or separation of the proceeds received into two or more revenue amounts for the various deliverables promised. Two examples are provided that illustrate how these approaches are applied to warranties.

Expense Approach Illustrated. In this situation, the warranty is **provided with** an associated product or service, with no additional fee being charged for it. All of the revenue from the sale of the product or service is considered earned on delivery of the product or service, but matching requires that all costs associated with that revenue be recognized as an expense in the same accounting period as the sale. Therefore, the future costs to be incurred to make good on the outstanding warranty are estimated and recognized in the same period as the sale, along with the associated obligation (liability) to provide the warranty service in the future. As the actual costs are incurred in subsequent periods, the warranty liability is reduced.

Assume that Denson Corporation begins production of a new machine in July 2014, and sells 100 units for $5,000 each by its year end, December 31, 2014. Denson provides a one-year warranty promising to fix any inherent manufacturing problems. The company has estimated, from experience with a similar machine, that the warranty cost will average $200 per unit. Under IFRS, the estimate is measured using a probability-weighted expected value, while ASPE will probably use the value of the most likely estimate.[24] Denson incurs $4,000 in actual warranty costs in 2014 to replace parts on machines that were sold before December 31, 2014, and costs of $16,000 in 2015. Illustration 13-5 shows how the expense approach recognizes these events.

(continued)

Illustration 13-5

Expense Approach and Warranty Liability Entries

Sale of 100 machines at $5,000 each, July to December, 2014:		
Accounts Receivable	500,000	
Sales Revenue		500,000
Actual warranty costs incurred, July to December, 2014:		
Warranty Expense	4,000	
Materials, Cash, Payables, etc.		4,000
Year-end adjusting entry to accrue outstanding warranty obligations at December 31, 2014:		
Warranty Expense	16,000	
Warranty Liability		16,000

Illustration 13-5

Expense Approach and Warranty Liability Entries (continued)

December 31, 2014 financial statement amounts reported:		
Income Statement		
Sales Revenue	$500,000	
Warranty Expense	$20,000	
Statement of Financial Position		
Warranty Liability	$16,000	

Actual warranty costs incurred, 2015:

Warranty Expense	16,000	
Materials, Cash, Payables, etc.		16,000

Adjusting entry, December 31, 2015, to adjust liability account to correct balance of $0:

Warranty Liability	16,000	
Warranty Expense		16,000

December 31, 2015 financial statement amounts reported:		
Income Statement		
Sales Revenue	$0	
Warranty Expense	$0	
Statement of Financial Position		
Warranty Liability	$0	

Underlying Concept

Using the cash method when the costs are immaterial or the warranty period is short is a proper application of the materiality concept.

The entries illustrate the fact that the actual warranty costs are initially charged to expense as they are incurred. At the end of the accounting period, the remaining estimated expense associated with the 2014 sales is recognized and the liability account is adjusted for the same amount. At December 31, 2014, the liability was increased to $16,000 as this additional expense was recognized, and at December 31, 2015, it was adjusted to the correct balance at that time of $0, as was the 2015 expense.

In situations where the warranty costs are very immaterial or when the warranty period is relatively short, the product guarantee may be accounted for on a cash basis. Under the **cash basis**, warranty costs are charged to expense as they are incurred; that is, they are recognized in expense **in the period when the seller or manufacturer honours the warranty**. No liability is recognized for future costs arising from warranties, and the expense is not necessarily recognized in the period of the related sale. If the cash basis is applied to the facts in the Denson Corporation example, $4,000 is recorded as warranty expense in 2014 and $16,000 as warranty expense in 2015, with the total sales being recorded as revenue in 2014. This method is used for income tax purposes, but not generally for financial reporting purposes.

Revenue Approach Illustrated. Under the revenue approach, the warranty service is considered to be a separate deliverable from the underlying product or service sold. It is either sold as a **separate** service or its price is considered to be **bundled** with the selling price of the associated goods. In the latter case, the amount of revenue attributable to the warranty has to be broken out and recognized separately. Under this method, the proceeds received for (or allocated to) the separate service to maintain the product in good order are unearned at the point of sale. The revenue is earned as the warranty service is provided.

To illustrate, assume that Hamlin Corp. sells equipment for $20,000 on January 2, 2014. Included with the equipment is a warranty agreement for two years, during which time Hamlin agrees to repair and maintain the equipment. Warranty agreements similar to this are available separately and are estimated to have a stand-alone value of $1,200. Therefore, Hamlin allocates $1,200 of the proceeds of the bundled sale to the warranty contract. The entry to record the sale on January 2, 2014, is:

Cash	20,000	
Sales Revenue		18,800
Unearned Warranty Revenue		1,200

A = L + SE
+20,000 +1,200 +18,800

Cash flows: ↑ 20,000 inflow

This approach recognizes revenue as Hamlin performs under the warranty contract. Assuming the revenue is earned evenly over the two-year contract term, the entry to remeasure the unearned revenue account to its correct balance at December 31, 2014, is as follows:

Unearned Warranty Revenue	600
Warranty Revenue	600

A = L + SE
    −600 +600
Cash flows: No effect

If costs of $423 were incurred in 2014 as a result of servicing this contract, Hamlin's entry is:

Warranty Expense	423
Materials, Cash, Payables, etc.	423

A = L + SE
  +423 −423
Cash flows: No effect

In 2015, the remainder of the unearned warranty revenue is recognized and any costs incurred under the contract are recognized in 2015 expense. If the costs of performing services under the extended warranty contract are not expected to be incurred in a straight-line pattern (as historical evidence might indicate), revenue is recognized over the contract period in the same pattern as the costs are expected to be incurred. In addition, if the costs of providing services under the contract are expected to be more than the remaining unearned revenue (in other words, it is an **onerous contract**), a loss and related liability are recognized for any expected shortfall.

Which approach is considered GAAP? Under both ASPE and IFRS, the principle is clear that revenue that covers a variety of deliverables (bundled sales) should be unbundled and the revenue allocated to the various goods or services that are required to be performed. This method has been used increasingly over the past few years. Even more support for the revenue approach is found in the IFRS draft standards covering these liabilities. These refer to the fact that it is an extremely rare circumstance when a liability cannot be measured reliably, and they require that the liability be measured at the value of the obligation, not its cost. The revenue approach is also consistent with the contract-based view being developed for proposed revenue recognition standards. In the future, this approach will likely be the only one permitted when guarantees are involved.

Customer Loyalty Programs

As indicated in our opening story, customer **loyalty programs**, such as those offered by Sears, the Bay, and Shoppers Drug Mart, are very popular, with all of them promising future benefits to the customer in exchange for current sales. Canadians' participation in such loyalty programs is high, with over 90% of Canadians belonging to at least one consumer rewards program in a recent year, up nine percentage points over two years earlier.[25] Other programs that have been adopted widely include the frequent flyer programs that are used by all major airlines. On the basis of mileage or the number of trips accumulated, frequent flyer members are awarded discounted or free airline tickets. Airline customers can earn miles toward free travel by making long-distance phone calls, staying in hotels, and charging items such as groceries and gasoline on a credit card.

How should companies account for such programs? Standard setters now interpret programs where customer loyalty credits are awarded to be revenue arrangements with multiple deliverables. Under IFRS, IFRIC Interpretation 13 *Customer Loyalty Programmes* requires the revenue from the original transaction to be allocated between the award credits and the other components of the sale. The fair value of the award credits is recognized as unearned revenue, a liability. This is later recognized in revenue when the credits are exchanged for the promised awards. The issue of accounting for loyalty programs is not explicitly addressed in ASPE; however, the general principle that the revenue recognition criteria should be applied "to the separately identifiable components of a single transaction in order to reflect the substance of the transaction" is reflected in ASPE.[26]

Premiums and Rebates

Many companies offer premiums or other benefits to customers in return for box tops, coupons, labels, wrappers, or other evidence of having purchased a particular product. The **premiums** may be such items as silverware, dishes, small appliances, toys, or cash values against future purchases.

Printed coupons that can be redeemed for a cash discount on items purchased are extremely popular marketing tools, as is the cash rebate, which the buyer can obtain by returning the store receipt, a rebate coupon, and Universal Product Code (UPC label or bar code) to the manufacturer. **Contests** have also been widely used to get consumers' attention and their sales dollars, with the **Tim Hortons** "Roll up the Rim to Win" promotion being one of the most successful contests in Canadian history. A wide variety of prizes are offered, including automobiles, vacations, major sporting events tickets, and free coffee!

With the life of many contests running a few months and the average coupon being valid for an average of approximately six months, many companies have the practical problem of accounting for these marketing costs, as they affect more than one fiscal period. Historically, such programs have been accounted for under the expense approach. The accounting issue relates to the fact that while these promotions **increase current sales revenue**, the associated costs are often incurred **in future periods**. The matching concept requires companies to deduct the total estimated costs against the current period's revenue and the cost is charged to an expense account such as Premium or Promotion Expense. In addition, the obligations existing at the date of the statement of financial position must also be recognized and reported in a liability account such as Estimated Liability for Premiums or Estimated Liability for Coupons Outstanding.

The following hypothetical example illustrates the accounting treatment commonly used for premium offers. In 2014, Fluffy Cakemix Corporation offers its customers a large non-breakable mixing bowl in exchange for $1.00 and 10 box tops. The mixing bowl costs Fluffy Cakemix Corporation $2.30, and the company estimates that 60% of the box tops will be redeemed. Illustration 13-6 shows the journal entries to account for the premium offer.

Illustration 13-6

Premium Offers – ASPE vs. IFRS

1. Purchase of 20,000 mixing bowls at $2.30 each:

Inventory of Premiums	46,000	
Cash		46,000

A = L + SE
0 = 0   0

Cash flows: ↓ 46,000 outflow

2. Sales of 300,000 boxes of cake mix at $2.10. We consider two alternative scenarios below: (a) Fluffy Cakemix is a small Canadian company following ASPE and prefers to use the expense approach and (b) Fluffy Cakemix is a public company following IFRS and prefers the revenue approach. Assume that 5% of the amount received from customers relates to the premiums to be awarded.

ASPE—Expense Approach

Cash	630,000	
Sales Revenue		630,000

ASPE
A   =   L   +   SE
+630,000   0   +630,000

IFRS—Revenue Approach

Cash	630,000	
Sales Revenue		598,500
Unearned Revenue		31,500

IFRS
A   =   L   +   SE
+630,000   +31,500   +598,500

Cash flows: ↑ 630,000 inflow

3. Redemption of 60,000 box tops, receiving $1.00 with every 10 box tops, and the delivery of 6,000 mixing bowls (60,000 ÷ 10). (Note: this represents one third of the total of the premiums expected to be awarded. See part 4 below for the calculation.)

(continued)

Illustration 13-6

Premium Offers – ASPE vs. IFRS (continued)

ASPE				
A	=	L	+	SE
–7,800				–7,800

IFRS				
A	=	L	+	SE
–7,800		–10,500		+2,700

Cash flows: ↑ 6,000 inflow

Under the expense approach, the December 31, 2014 statement of financial position of Fluffy Cakemix Corporation reports an inventory of premium mixing bowls of $32,200 as a current asset and an estimated liability for premiums of $15,600 as a current liability. The 2014 income statement reports a $23,400 premium expense among the selling expenses. Under the revenue approach, the December 31, 2014 statement of financial position of Fluffy Cakemix Corporation reports an inventory of premium mixing bowls of $32,200 as a current asset and an estimated liability for unearned sales revenue of $21,000 as a current liability. The 2014 income statement reports a $7,800 premium revenue and an estimated liability for unearned sales revenue of $10,500.

If the costs associated with premiums and rebates are really **marketing expenses**, the expense approach applied in the illustration is a reasonable way to account for them. On the other hand, IAS 18.13 and IFRIC 13 suggest that it may be more appropriate to use the revenue approach, and allocate some of the consideration received from the sales transaction to unearned revenue.

ASPE—Expense Approach

Cash	6,000	
[(60,000 ÷ 10) × $1.00]		
Premium Expense	7,800	
Inventory of		
Premiums		13,800
(60,000/10) ×		
2.30 = $13,800		

IFRS—Revenue Approach

Cash	6,000	
[(60,000 ÷ 10) × $1.00]		
Premium Expense	7,800	
Inventory of		
Premiums		13,800
(60,000/10) ×		
$2.30 = $13,800		
Unearned Revenue	10,500	
Sales Revenue		10,500
($31,500 ×		
1/3) = $10,500		

4. Under ASPE, assuming Fluffy Cakemix uses the expense approach, it would also require the following adjusting entry to recognize the remaining expense and estimated liability for outstanding premiums at the end of the period. This journal entry would not be required under the IFRS under the revenue approach.

Premium Expense 15,600
Estimated Liability for Premiums 15,600

	ASPE—Expense Approach	IFRS—Revenue Approach
	15,600	N/A

Calculation:

Total boxes sold in 2014		300,000
Total estimated redemptions (60%)		180,000
Box tops redeemed in 2014		60,000
Estimated future redemptions		120,000
Cost per premium: $2.30 – $1.00 =		$1.30
Cost of estimated claims outstanding:		
(120,000 ÷ 10) × $1.30 =		$15,600

ASPE

A	=	L	+	SE
		+15,600		–15,600

Cash flows: No effect

Objective 8

Explain and account for contingencies and uncertain commitments, and identify the accounting and reporting requirements for guarantees and commitments.

Contingencies, Uncertain Commitments, and Requirements for Guarantees and Other Commitments

Contingencies and Uncertain Commitments

Companies are often involved in situations where it is uncertain whether an obligation to transfer cash or other assets actually exists at the statement of financial position date or

Real World Emphasis

what amount will be required to settle the obligation. For example, **Research In Motion Limited** provided four pages of information about litigation and legal proceedings in the Management Discussion & Analysis (MD&A) section of its annual report and further discussion in the notes to its financial statements for its year ended February 26, 2011. The litigation mostly involved alleged patent infringements. **Thomson Reuters Corporation** also discussed lawsuits and legal claims in notes to its December 31, 2011 financial statements. In addition, the company stated that the outcome of the proceedings was subject to future resolution and the uncertainties of litigation. The company stated that when the claims are resolved, they are not expected to have a material adverse effect.

Broadly speaking, these situations are referred to as contingencies. A **contingency** is "an existing condition or situation involving uncertainty as to possible gain or loss to an enterprise that will ultimately be resolved when one or more future events occur or fail to occur. Resolution of the uncertainty may confirm the acquisition of an asset or the reduction of a liability."[27] As indicated in Chapter 5, **gain contingencies** and **contingent assets** are not recorded in the accounts and our discussion is limited to uncertainty and the recognition of liabilities. How the uncertainty is dealt with currently in accounting is explained below for both ASPE and IFRS. Another approach that reflects the on-going thinking about contingencies and provisions under IFRS, based on IAS 37 *Provisions, Contingent Liabilities and Contingent Assets*, is described briefly in the Looking Ahead section of the chapter.

Current Approach to the Recognition and Measurement of Contingencies.
Under current ASPE, the term **contingent liability** includes the **whole population** of existing or possible obligations that depend on the occurrence of one or more future events to confirm either their existence or the amount payable, or both. As we'll see below, some of these contingent liabilities are recognized in the accounts, some require only note disclosure, and others are not referred to at all in the financial statements. Under existing international standards, the term "contingent liability" is used **only** for those existing or possible obligations that are **not** recognized.

The approach taken by current standards to deal with whether a liability should be recognized when there is a contingency is to determine the probability of a future event occurring (or not occurring) that would establish whether the outcome is a loss. How likely it is that a future event will confirm the incurrence of a loss and a liability can range from highly probable to remote or unknown.

Under ASPE, the following range is used:

Term	Interpretation
Likely	High
Unlikely	Slight
Not determinable	Cannot be determined

ASPE

A contingent loss is recognized in income and as a liability **only if both the following conditions** are met:[28]

1. It is **likely** that a future event will confirm that an asset has been impaired or a liability has been incurred at the date of the financial statements.

2. The loss amount can be **reasonably estimated**.

Aside from the "likely" probability, the first condition requires that the liability relate to events that occurred on or before the date of the statement of financial position. The second criterion indicates that it has to be possible to make a reasonable and reliable estimate of the liability; otherwise, it cannot be accrued as a liability. The evidence that is used to estimate the liability may be the company's own experience, the experience of other companies in the industry, engineering or research studies, legal advice, or educated guesses by personnel who are in the best position to know. Often, **a range of possible amounts** may be determined. If a specific amount within the range is a better estimate than others, this is the amount that is accrued. If no particular amount is better than another, the bottom of the range is recognized, and the amount of the remaining exposure to possible loss is disclosed in the notes.

When the liability recognition criteria are not met because of the inability to determine a reasonable estimate of the loss amount, or the likelihood of a confirming future event cannot be determined, or when the entity is exposed to loss above the amount accrued, additional information is disclosed in the notes to the statements. Information is disclosed about: (1) the nature of the contingency, (2) the estimated amount of the contingent loss or a statement that an estimate cannot be made, and (3) the extent of exposure to losses in excess of the amount that has been recognized.

Under current IFRS requirements, provisions are required for situations such as lawsuits where it is more likely than not that a present obligation exists. Because it is more likely than not the company will lose, these are considered liabilities (not "contingent liabilities") under IFRS. Provisions are not required for contingent liabilities under IFRS as these are defined as "possible obligations" whose existence will only be confirmed by uncertain future events that may or may not occur. So, for example, for a lawsuit where it is not probable that an outflow of resources will be required to settle an obligation, the obligation would be considered a contingent liability. To summarize, the recognition criterion used to determine if a provision should be recognized is based on whether it is **"probable"** that there will be an outflow of resources. Probable is interpreted to mean "more likely than not." This is a somewhat lower hurdle than the "likely" required under ASPE. If the amount cannot be measured reliably, the item would be considered a contingent liability and no liability is recognized under IFRS either; however, the standard indicates that it is only in very rare circumstances that this would be the case.

If recognized, IAS 37 requires the best estimate and an "expected value" method to be used to measure the liability. This approach assigns weights to the possible outcomes according to their associated probabilities if a range of possible amounts is available. Unless the likelihood of needing future resources to settle a contingent liability is **remote**, disclosures are required about the nature of these uncertain amounts and, if practicable: (1) an estimate of its financial effect, (2) information about the uncertainties related to the amount or timing of any outflows, and (3) whether any reimbursements are possible.

As you might expect, using the terms "likely" or "probable" as a basis for determining the accounting for contingencies and provisions involves considerable judgement and subjectivity, as does the requirement that the amounts be "reliably measurable." Practising accountants often express concern over the wide variety of interpretations of these terms. Current accounting practice for these situations relies heavily on the exact language that is used in responses from lawyers. However, the language of lawyers may be necessarily biased and protective rather than predictive of the outcome. As a result, the recognition of losses and liabilities varies considerably in practice. There is agreement, however, that general risks that are inherent in business operations, such as the possibility of war, strike, uninsurable catastrophes, or an economic recession, are not accounting "contingencies" and are neither recognized nor reported in the financial statements.

The table below identifies some common examples of potential losses and how they are generally accounted for now.

Loss Related to	Not Accrued	May Be Accrued[a]
1. Risk of damage of enterprise property by fire, explosion, or other hazards		X
2. General or unspecified business risks	X	
3. Risk of damage from catastrophes assumed by property and casualty insurance companies including reinsurance companies	X	

(continued)

	Not Accrued	May Be Accrued[a]
4. Threat of expropriation of assets		X
5. Pending or threatened litigation		X
6. Actual or possible claims and assessments		X
7. Guarantees of indebtedness of others[b]		X
8. Agreements to repurchase receivables (or the related property) that have been sold		X

[a] Will be accrued when all recognition criteria are met regarding likelihood and measurability.
[b] See chapter section on Financial Guarantees

The most common types of loss contingencies and provisions have to do with litigation, claims by others, and assessments.[29] To recognize a loss and a liability in the accounts, **the cause for litigation must have occurred on or before the date of the financial statements**. It does not matter if the company did not become aware of the existence or possibility of the lawsuit or claims until after the date of the financial statements.

To evaluate the **likelihood of an unfavourable outcome**, management considers the nature of the litigation, the progress of the case, the opinion of legal counsel, the experience of the company and others in similar cases, and any company response to the lawsuit.[30] **Estimating the amount of loss** from pending litigation, however, can rarely be done with any certainty. And, even if the evidence that is available at the date of the statement of financial position does not favour the defendant, it is not reasonable to expect the company to publish in its financial statements a dollar estimate of the likely negative outcome. Such specific disclosures could weaken the company's position in the dispute and encourage the plaintiff to step up its efforts for more compensation. There is a fine line between a shareholder's right to know about potential losses and information that could hurt the company's interests.

Note 37 of the December 31, 2011 year-end financial statements of **adidas AG**, shown in Illustration 13-7, provides an example of disclosures related to contingencies.

Real World Emphasis

Illustration 13-7

Note Disclosure of Contingencies and Commitments—adidas AG

Note 37. Commitments and contingencies (extracts):
Other financial commitments
The Group has other financial commitments for promotion and advertising contracts, which mature as follows:

Financial commitments for promotion and advertising (€ in millions)

	Dec. 31, 2011	Dec. 31, 2010
Within 1 year	681	613
Between 1 and 5 years	1,918	1,474
After 5 years	1,244	695
Total	3,843	2,782

Commitments with respect to advertising and promotion maturing after five years have remaining terms of up to 19 years from December 31, 2011.

Litigation
The Group is currently engaged in various lawsuits resulting from the normal course of business, mainly in connection with distribution agreements as well as intellectual property rights. The risks regarding these lawsuits are covered by provisions when a reliable estimate of the amount of the obligation can be made. In the opinion of Management, the ultimate liabilities resulting from such claims will not materially affect the consolidated financial position of the Group.

Financial Guarantees

Closely related to the topic of contingencies are the requirements for companies to account for and provide information about a variety of types of financial guarantees that they have provided. One of the most common types is a financial guarantee contract. In this situation, one party (the guarantor) contracts to reimburse a second party for a loss incurred if a third party (the debtor) does not make required payments when due.[31] Such a guarantee qualifies as a financial liability because the guarantor has an unconditional obligation to transfer cash in the future if the debtor fails to meet its obligations. How is such a guarantee reported in the financial statements?

Under ASPE, such guarantees fall under the loss contingency standards discussed earlier in this section of the chapter, as well as the disclosure provisions for guarantees set out in an accounting guideline.[32] Specific disclosures are required even if the probability of having to make payments under the guarantee is remote. Users are interested in knowing what types of guarantees the company has made, the maximum potential obligation the company is exposed to, how much has been recognized in the accounts as a liability, and the prospects for recovery from third parties.

Under IFRS, the guarantee is recognized initially at fair value, usually equal to the premium charged by the guarantor. After this, it is measured at the higher of:

1. the best estimate of the payment that would be needed to settle the obligation at the reporting date, and

2. any unamortized premium received as a fee for the guarantee (unearned revenue).[33]

Similar to warranties, if this is a single obligation, the best estimate would be the "most likely" amount. However, if there are many similar obligations, the expected value of the possible outcomes is determined. The time value of money is taken into consideration if the effects are significant. In addition to reconciling the opening to the closing balance for this type of obligation, the additional disclosures are similar to those under ASPE. The objective under both sets of standards is to give readers better information about the entity's obligations and **particularly about the risks that are assumed as a result of issuing guarantees.**

Illustration 13-8 presents **RONA inc.**'s disclosure on guarantees from Note 21 of the company's financial statements for its year ended December 25, 2011 (in thousands).

Real World
Emphasis

Illustration 13-8

Disclosure of Guarantees—
RONA inc.

Guarantees

In the normal course of business, the Company reaches agreements that could meet the definition of "guarantees".

The Company guarantees mortgages for an amount of $1,257. The terms of these loans extend until 2012 and the net carrying amount of the assets held as security, which mainly include land and buildings, is $5,389.

Pursuant to the terms of inventory repurchase agreements, the Company is committed towards financial institutions to buy back the inventory of certain customers at an average of 64% of the cost of the inventories to a maximum of $44,961. In the event of recourse, this inventory would be sold in the normal course of the Company's operations. These agreements have undetermined periods but may be cancelled by the Company with a 30-day advance notice. In the opinion of management, the likelihood that significant payments would be incurred as a result of these commitments is low.

Commitments

Companies conduct business by entering into agreements with customers, suppliers, employees, and other parties. These **executory contracts**—contracts where neither party has yet performed—are not recognized as liabilities in the accounts. Although they are not recognized as liabilities at the date of the statement of financial position, unrecognized **contractual commitments** or **contractual obligations** commit the company and its assets into the future. While it would not be reasonable or desirable to require companies to disclose all of their outstanding contractual obligations, it is useful to have them highlight commitments that have certain characteristics. As discussed in Chapter 8, if there are unavoidable costs associated with completing a contract that exceed the benefits to be received, it would be considered an onerous contract. This concept also applies to commitments. For example, onerous contracts include instances where a company is commited to executing a contract at a loss or paying the other party a penalty for failing to fulfill the contract.

Disclosures are therefore required of commitments to make expenditures that are abnormal relative to the company's financial position and usual operations and for commitments that involve significant risk. Examples include major property, plant, and equipment and intangible asset expenditure commitments, and commitments to make lease payments.[34]

PRESENTATION, DISCLOSURE, AND ANALYSIS

Presentation and Disclosure of Current Liabilities

Objective 9

Indicate how non-financial and current liabilities are presented and analyzed.

The current liability accounts are commonly presented in Canada as the first classification in the statement of financial position's liabilities and shareholders' equity section. IFRS illustrates an "upside-down" presentation in IAS 1 *Presentation of Financial Statements*, with the long-term assets and liabilities at the top and the current assets and liabilities at the bottom of the statement of financial position. However, this form of presentation is not required by the standard. In some instances, current liabilities are presented as a group immediately below current assets, with the total of the current liabilities deducted from the current assets total. Although this presentation is not seen often, it is an informative one that focuses on the company's investment in **working capital.**

Within the current liabilities section, the accounts may be listed in the order of either their maturity or liquidation preference, whichever provides more useful information to readers of the financial statements. Many companies list bank indebtedness first (sometimes called "commercial paper," "bank loans," or "short-term debt"), regardless of their relative amounts, then follow with accounts payable, notes payable, and then end the section with the current portion of long-term debt. An excerpt from the May 7, 2011 balance sheet of **Empire Company Limited** is presented in Illustration 13-9. Empire Company has considerable real estate holdings in addition to its activities in the food and grocery industry, and is best known for its Sobeys chain of stores. The company did not move to fully adopt IFRS until its May 2012 financial statements. Compare this with the current liabilities section of IFRS-reporting **Marks & Spencer Group plc** at its April 2, 2011 year end, as shown in Illustration 13-10. This company reports in millions of British pound sterling (£). Marks & Spencer is a well-known international retail giant based in the United Kingdom. Both these excerpts are representative of the types of current liabilities that are found in the reports of many corporations.

Real World Emphasis

Illustration 13-9

Balance Sheet Presentation of Current Liabilities—Empire Company Limited

(in millions)	May 7, 2011	May 1, 2010
LIABILITIES		
Current		
Bank indebtedness (Note 10)	$ 8.1	$ 17.8
Accounts payable and accrued liabilities	1,689.0	1,621.6
Income taxes payable	—	19.5
Long-term debt due within one year (Note 11)	49.7	379.4
Liabilities relating to assets held for sale	12.7	—
Future taxes liabilities (Note 18)	46.6	50.9
	1,806.1	2,089.2

Consolidated statement of financial position

Liabilities	Notes	As at 2 April 2011 £m	As at 3 April 2010 £m
Current liabilities			
Trade and other payables	21	1,347.6	1,153.8
Borrowings and other financial liabilities	22	602.3	482.9
Partnership liability to the Marks & Spencer			
UK Pension Scheme	12	71.9	71.9
Derivative financial instruments	23	50.7	27.1
Provisions	24	22.7	25.6
Current tax liabilities		115.0	129.2
		2,210.2	1,890.5

Illustration 13-10

Statement of Financial Position Presentation of Current Liabilities—Marks & Spencer Group plc

Real World Emphasis

As indicated earlier in the chapter, IAS 37 uses the term "provisions" to refer to liabilities where there is uncertainty about their timing or the amount of the future expenditure. It requires that companies report provisions separately and provide a reconciliation of the opening and closing balances of each class of provisions. It is likely that anticipated amendments to IAS 37 will replace the term "provision" and use the general term "liability" instead.

Entities should disclose enough supplementary information about their current liabilities so that readers can understand and identify the entity's current needs for cash. Such information usually includes identifying the major classes of current liabilities, such as bank loans, trade credit and accrued liabilities, income taxes, dividends, and unearned revenue. Also, amounts owing to officers, directors, shareholders, and associated companies are reported separately from amounts that are owed to enterprises that the reporting entity deals with at arm's length. Secured liabilities and any assets that have been pledged as collateral are identified clearly.

Presentation and Disclosure of Contingencies, Guarantees, and Commitments

Under ASPE, companies are required to disclose their contingent liabilities when any of the following is true:

1. It is likely that a future event will confirm the existence of a loss but the loss cannot be reasonably estimated.

2. A loss has been recognized, but there is an exposure to loss that is higher than the amount that was recorded.

3. It is not possible to determine the likelihood of the future confirming event.

Companies reporting under ASPE are also required to report any contractual obligations that are significant relative to their current financial position of future operations. In addition, guarantors must report information about any guarantees they have made, even if the likelihood of having to make any payments is slight. This includes information about the nature of the guarantees, maximum potential payments, potential recoveries, and the existence of any collateral. Under IFRS, companies are required to disclose a brief description for each class of contingent liability, unless the probability of outflow is remote. They are also encouraged to disclose an estimate of the financial effect of the liability.

Empire Company Limited, referred to above in Illustration 13-9, provides information in Note 23 to its financial statements for the year ended May 7, 2011, as follows:

Guarantees and commitments relative to:

- Letters of credit and credit enhancements through standby letters of credit
- Franchisee bank loan guarantees, franchise lease obligation guarantees including equipment leases
- Minimum rent payable under operating lease commitments

Contingencies relative to:

- Canada Revenue Agency reassessments for GST (fiscal years 1999 and 2000) where Sobeys has filed a Notice of Objection
- Director, officer, and particular employee indemnification in excess of insurance policy provisions
- Ordinary course of business claims and litigation to which management considers the company's exposure to be immaterial, although it is unable to predict with certainty

Marks & Spencer Group plc's Note 27, from its 2011 financial statements, reports on the following contingencies and commitments:

- Capital expenditure commitment related to its interest in a joint venture
- Commitment to purchase property, plant, and equipment if there is a change in trading arrangements with certain warehouse operators
- Commitments for payments under non-cancellable operating leases

Analysis

Because the ability to pay current obligations as they come due is critical to a company's short-term financial health and continued existence, analysts pay particular attention to the current liabilities section of the statement of financial position. As with most financial statement items, it is not the absolute dollar amount of the current liabilities that is important, but rather its relationship to other aspects of the company's position and results.

Current liabilities result from **both operating and financing activities.** Trade liabilities, provisions, and other liabilities that **arise from operations**—such as payroll, rent, insurance, and taxes payable—are the most common. In addition, advances from customers are a source of operating credit, and it is important to distinguish them from other operating sources. Why? This liability requires the company to provide a service or product in the future rather than make cash payments, and will therefore result in the recognition of revenue in the future. An increase in this category of liability predicts future revenues, not cash outflows.

Short-term notes and the current portion of long-term debt result **from financing activities.** The company must either generate operating cash flows to repay these liabilities or arrange for their refinancing. Refinancing, however, may not always be possible or may come at a higher cost to the borrower than the original note or debt.

Identifying current liabilities separately from long-term obligations is important because it provides information about the company's liquidity. **Liquidity** refers to a company's ability to convert assets into cash to pay off its current liabilities in the ordinary course of business. The higher the proportion of assets expected to be converted to cash to liabilities currently due, the more liquid the company. A company with higher liquidity is better able to survive financial downturns and has a better chance of taking advantage of investment opportunities that arise.

As indicated in earlier chapters of the text, basic ratios such as net cash flow provided by operating activities to current liabilities and the turnover ratios for receivables and inventory **are useful in assessing liquidity.** Three other key ratios are the current ratio, the acid-test ratio, and the days payables outstanding.

The **current ratio** is the ratio of total current assets to total current liabilities. The formula is shown in Illustration 13-11.

$$\text{Current ratio} = \frac{\text{Current assets}}{\text{Current liabilities}}$$

The current ratio shows how many dollars of current assets are available for each dollar of current liabilities. Sometimes it is called the **working capital ratio** because working capital is the excess of current assets over current liabilities. The higher the ratio, the more likely it is that the company can generate cash to pay its currently maturing liabilities.

A company with a large amount of current assets that is made up almost entirely of inventory may have a satisfactory current ratio, but it may not be very liquid. The current ratio does not show whether or not a portion of the current assets is tied up in slow-moving inventories. With inventories—especially raw materials and work in process—there is a question of how long it will take to transform them into finished goods, to convert the finished product into accounts receivable by selling it, and then to collect the amounts that customers owe. Better information may be provided to assess liquidity by eliminating inventories and other non-liquid current assets such as prepaid expenses from the current asset ratio numerator. Many analysts prefer to use the resulting **acid-test** or **quick ratio**, shown in Illustration 13-12. This ratio relates quick assets—such as cash, investments held for trading purposes, and receivables, which are all easily convertible to cash—to total current liabilities.

$$\text{Acid-test ratio} = \frac{\text{Cash} + \text{Marketable securities} + \text{Net receivables}}{\text{Current liabilities}}$$

The current ratio and quick ratio are especially useful when analyzing a company over time and when comparing it with other companies in the same industry.

The third ratio, the **days payables outstanding**, zeroes in on how long it takes a company to pay its trade payables. In other words, it determines the average age of the payables. **Trade payables** are amounts that the entity owes to suppliers for providing goods and services related to normal business operations; that is, they are amounts that result from operating transactions. When cash is managed well, the payment of payables is delayed as long as possible, but done in time to meet the due date. If there is a trend where the age of the payables outstanding is increasing, particularly if it is above the normal credit period for the industry, it may indicate liquidity problems for the company. Illustration 13-13 shows the formula for this ratio.

$$\text{Days payables outstanding} = \frac{\text{Average trade accounts payable}}{\text{Average daily cost of goods sold}}$$
or average daily cost of total operating expenses

The formula provides a better result if all the suppliers that are represented in the payables amount (the numerator) provide the goods and services that are captured in the cost of goods sold amount (the denominator). If the trade accounts payable include the suppliers for most of the company's operating goods and services in addition to the inventory purchases, analysts prefer to use the "average daily cost of total operating expenses" as the denominator.

To illustrate the calculation of these ratios, partial balance sheet and income statement information is provided in Illustration 13-14 for the year ended January 28, 2012, for **Reitmans (Canada) Limited**, a women's clothing retailer. The amounts are reported in thousands of Canadian dollars.

Real World Emphasis

Illustration 13-14

Selected Financial Statement Information—Reitmans (Canada) Limited

Balance Sheet (extracts)
As at January 28, 2012, and January 29, 2011
(in thousands)

	2012	2011
ASSETS		
CURRENT ASSETS		
Cash and cash equivalents (note 5)	$ 196,835	$ 230,034
Marketable securities	71,442	70,413
Trade and other receivables	3,033	2,866
Derivative financial asset (note 6)	751	—
Income taxes recoverable	4,735	—
Inventories (note 7)	78,285	73,201
Prepaid expenses	11,902	12,491
Total Current Assets	366,983	389,005
CURRENT LIABILITIES		
Trade and other payables (note 12)	$ 63,875	$ 64,093
Derivative financial liability (note 6)	1,505	—
Deferred revenue (note 13)	22,278	19,834
Income taxes payable	—	5,998
Current portion of long-term debt (note 14)	1,474	1,384
Total Current Liabilities	89,132	91,309
Statements of Earnings		
Sales	$1,019,397	$1,059,000
Cost of goods sold (note 7)	363,333	350,671
Gross profit	656,064	708,329
Selling and distribution expenses	547,367	528,676
Administrative expenses	46,878	55,511
Results from operating activities	61,819	124,142

The calculation of the current, acid-test, and days payables outstanding ratios for Reitmans is as follows:

$$\text{Current ratio} = \frac{\text{Current assets}}{\text{Current liabilities}} = \frac{\$366,983}{\$89,132} = 4.1$$

$$\text{Acid-test ratio} = \frac{\text{Quick assets}}{\text{Current liabilities}} = \frac{\$196,835 + \$71,442 + \$3,033 + \$751 + \$4,735}{\$89,132} = 3.1$$

$$\text{Days payables outstanding} = \frac{\text{Average trade accounts payable}}{\text{Average daily cost of goods sold}}$$

or

$$\frac{\text{Average trade accounts payable}}{\text{Average daily total operating expenses}}$$

$$= \frac{\dfrac{\$63,875 + \$64,093}{2}}{\dfrac{\$363,333 + \$547,367 + \$46,878}{365}} = \frac{\$63,984}{\$2,624} = 24.4 \text{ days}$$

While a 4.1-to-1 current ratio and a 3.1-to-1 quick ratio appear in the higher-than-necessary range, it is often difficult to make a definite statement about a company's liquidity from these ratios alone. What amounts to an acceptable ratio depends on the industry and how it operates. In some industries, companies need significant amounts of current and quick assets compared with their current liabilities. In other industries, such as those that generate cash from cash sales or whose receivables and inventory turn over quickly, companies may be very liquid with low current and quick ratios. Too high a ratio may indicate poor deployment of assets in cash, near-cash, receivables, and inventory, as there are carrying costs associated with maintaining these balances. Reitmans probably converts a significant portion of its inventory to cash on a daily basis as customers pay cash or use debit or credit cards such as Visa and MasterCard. (Credit card slips from these two companies are deposited daily as if they were cash.) The length of its cash cycle is reduced because it does not have to carry large receivable balances. For these reasons, Reitmans' working capital ratios could be lower and still indicate ample liquidity. An analyst might question why this company's ratios are so high.

Reitmans' accounts payable are, on average, 24.4 days old. It appears that the company is not experiencing problems keeping up with payments, especially since cash and cash equivalents exceed current liabilities! It may be that supplier credit terms are in the 30-day range. It is difficult to draw any definite conclusions about these numbers by themselves. They need to be compared with results from previous years, with credit policies, and with the ratios of other companies in the same industry.

IFRS/ASPE COMPARISON

A Comparison of IFRS and ASPE

Illustration 13-15 indicates the differences between ASPE and IFRS as this text went to print, and an indication of what was expected in the revised standard on liabilities, a replacement of IAS 37 *Provisions, Contingent Liabilities and Contingent Assets*.

Looking Ahead

As indicated earlier in the chapter, accounting for a variety of liabilities, including contingencies, is in a state of transition. What underlies the proposed changes is the work being carried out by the IASB and the FASB on the conceptual framework—particularly the revised definition of a "liability" and how the recognition criteria are applied. In the existing standards, a liability is recognized if it is **probable** that it will require an outflow of resources in the future. The proposed changes reflect the shift of the "probability" criterion from being part of the recognition criteria for the element, to how an existing obligation is measured.

Under the proposed recognition and measurement requirements, a liability would be **recognized** whenever an unconditional obligation exists at the reporting date. Any uncertainty about the amount to be sacrificed in the future is then taken into account in the **measurement** of the liability. So, the probability of having to give up entity resources would become part of the measurement aspect. A significant amount of application guidance is expected as part of any revisions, particularly to help in determining if a present obligation exists at the reporting date. The measurement basis would change to an "exit" (or "relief") value—the amount the entity would pay a third party to relieve it of its obligation.

The *Exposure Draft of Proposed Amendments to IAS 37 Provisions, Contingent Liabilities and Contingent Assets* has suggested that the term "contingent liabilities" be eliminated. As mentioned above, under the proposed changes to IFRS, liabilities would only arise from **unconditional** (or **non-contingent**) obligations. This is a more conceptually defensible approach to determining what is recognized as a non-financial liability. As discussed above, uncertainty about the amounts that might be payable would be taken into account in the **measurement** of the liability, not its **existence**.

It is also likely that accounting for guarantees will be covered by the same recognition and measurement standards as other liabilities, and contingencies. If there is an unconditional (stand-ready) obligation to make good under the guarantee at the date of the statement of financial position, the liability would be recognized and measured for inclusion in the liability section of the statement of financial position.

As this text went to print, the completion date for the elements and recognition phase of the conceptual framework project was uncertain, with the project being put on hold until the IASB finished discussions about its future work plan. A finalized IFRS on liabilities to replace IAS 37 *Provisions, Contingent Liabilities and Contingent Assets* was still planned but the timing was uncertain. The Accounting Standards Board is expected to propose changes to the accounting standards in Part II of the *CICA Handbook* every few years, particularly as they affect the conceptual framework.

Illustration 13-15

IFRS and ASPE Comparison Chart

	ASPE—*CICA Handbook*, Part II, Sections 1510, 1540, 3110, 3280, 3290, 3856, and Accounting Guideline 14	IFRS—IAS 1, 7, 19, 37, and 39; IFRIC 13	IAS 19, IASB Exposure Draft of Proposed Amendments to IAS 37, June 2005; and Exposure Draft ED/2010/1 Measurement of Liabilities in IAS 37, Proposed Amendments to IAS 37, January 2010	References to Related Illustrations and Select Brief Exercises
Scope and definitions – Terminology	A liability is an obligation arising from past transactions and events, the settlement of which may result in the transfer or use of assets, provision of services, or other yielding of economic benefits in the future.	A liability is a present obligation arising from past events in which the settlement is expected to result in an outflow of resources that embody economic benefits.	A liability is defined in the same way as in IAS 37. A clarification is made explaining that an obligation only needs to be capable of resulting in an asset outflow; no specific degree of certainty has to exist about that outflow.	Illustration 13-1
	Contingent liability refers to uncertain situations, some of which may be recognized as a liability and others not.	A contingent liability refers only to those that do not meet the recognition criteria.	The contingent liability term is eliminated.	BE 13-25
	The term "provision" is not defined.	A provision is defined as a liability of uncertain timing or amount.	The term "liability" replaces the term "provision."	BE 13-26
Scope	No specific accounting standard addresses non-financial liabilities.	IAS 37 basically addresses non-financial liability issues, including guarantees and onerous contracts.	The revised standard will apply to all liabilities unless covered by another standard.	
	Accounting for financial guarantees is addressed by the loss contingency standards.	Financial guarantees may be covered by insurance standards.	No change.	Illustration 13-8
	Customer loyalty programs are not explicitly addressed in the standards.	Customer loyalty programs are addressed by IFRIC 13, which requires the current proceeds to be split between the original transaction and the award credits (as unearned revenue).	When the IASB completes its revenue recognition project, warranties and refunds will be transferred to a new revenue project.	Illustration 13-6

(continued)

	ASPE—CICA Handbook, Part II, Sections 1510, 1540, 3110, 3280, 3290, 3856, and Accounting Guideline 14	IFRS—IAS 1, 7, 19, 37, and 39; IFRIC 13	IAS 19, IASB Exposure Draft of Proposed Amendments to IAS 37, June 2005; and Exposure Draft ED/2010/1 Measurement of Liabilities in IAS 37, Proposed Amendments to IAS 37, January 2010	References to Related Illustrations and Select Brief Exercises
Recognition — Restoration and de-commissioning obligations	Recognizes costs associated with legal obligations only.	Recognizes costs of both legal and constructive obligations.	Recognize a liability if it meets the definition of a liability and can be reliably measured; management considers all available evidence to determine the existence of an obligation.	Illustration 13-3
	Costs recognized are capitalized to property, plant, and equipment.	Costs capitalized associated with the asset are recognized as property, plant, and equipment; those that accrue as a result of production are considered product costs and are charged to inventory.	No changes are expected for decommissioning obligations.	Illustration 13-3
— Contingencies and uncertain commitments	Recognize if occurrence of a future confirming event is "likely," meaning a high probability, and measurable.	Recognize if occurrence of a future confirming event is "probable," meaning more likely than not, and measurable—a lower threshold than under ASPE.	Recognize a liability if it meets the definition of a liability and can be reliably measured; management considers all available evidence to determine the existence of an obligation. The probability thresholds are removed.	BE 13-25
		A potential reimbursement is recognized only when virtually certain of recovery.	The right to reimbursement is recognized when it can be reliably measured.	Illustration 13-4B
— Contingent gains	Contingent gains are not recognized.	A provision is measured at the best estimate of the expenditure required to settle the present obligation at the balance date or to transfer it to a third party.	A liability is measured at the amount an entity would rationally pay to be relieved of the present obligation: the lowest of the present value of the resources needed to fulfill the obligation; the amount needed to cancel the obligation; and the amount needed to transfer it to a third party.	N/A
Measurement — Non-Financial liabilities	The most likely value is used.	A probability-weighted expected value is required where a large population of items is being measured.	Probability-weighted measures continue to be used.	
	An asset retirement obligation is measured at the best estimate of the expenditure required to settle the present obligation at the date of the statement of financial position or transfer it to a third party.			
	The interest adjustment recognized to the Asset Retirement Obligation account due to the passage of time is recognized as Accretion Expense.	The interest adjustment to the Asset Retirement Obligation account due to the passage of time is recognized as a borrowing cost (interest expense).	There is no change from existing IFRS.	BE13-18 and BE 13-19 Illustration 13-4A

(continued)

	ASPE—CICA Handbook, Part II, Sections 1510, 1540, 3110, 3280, 3290, 3856, and Accounting Guideline 14	IFRS—IAS 1, 7, 19, 37, and 39; IFRIC 13	IAS 19, IASB Exposure Draft of Proposed Amendments to IAS 37, June 2005; and Exposure Draft ED/2010/1 Measurement of Liabilities in IAS 37, Proposed Amendments to IAS 37, January 2010	References to Related Illustrations and Select Brief Exercises
– Contingencies and uncertain commitments	Measure the amount of the liability at the best estimate in the range of possible outcomes; if none, use lowest point in the range and disclose the remaining exposure to loss.	Measure the amount at the probability-weighted expected value of the loss.	The same measurement as described above applies to all obligations within the scope of IAS 37.	BE 13-26
Presentation – Current/non-current classification	If long-term debt becomes callable due to a violation of a debt agreement, it can be reported as long-term under certain conditions.	If long-term debt becomes callable due to a violation of a debt agreement, it cannot be reported as long-term even if the creditor agrees not to call the debt before the date the statements are released.	There is no change from existing IFRS.	BE 13-11
	Short-term debt expected to be refinanced is reported as long-term if refinanced on a long-term basis before the statements are completed.	Short-term debt expected to be refinanced is reported as a current liability even if refinanced on a long-term basis before the statements are released, unless refinanced under an existing agreement at the reporting date and solely at the entity's discretion.	There is no change from existing IFRS.	BE 13-12
	No guidance is provided for onerous contractual obligations such as may occur with purchase commitments.	A liability and loss are required to be recognized for onerous contracts if the unavoidable costs exceed the benefits from receiving the contracted goods or services.	There is no change from existing IFRS.	Illustration 8-3 and subsequent discussion.
Disclosure	There are no general disclosure requirements for liabilities similar to the provisions. All disclosures are less extensive than required under international standards.	IAS 37 identifies specific disclosures for "provisions" including descriptions and a reconciliation of balances between beginning and ending balances.	Disclosures are similar to those in IAS 37 with increased requirements in situations where liabilities are not recognized due to lack of reliability of measurement and situations of uncertainty of existence.	

(continued)

Illustration **13-15**

IFRS and ASPE Comparison Chart
(continued)

SUMMARY OF LEARNING OBJECTIVES

1 Understand the importance of non-financial and current liabilities from a business perspective.

Cash flow management is a key control factor for most businesses. Taking advantage of supplier discounts for prompt payment is one step companies can take. Control of expenses and related accounts payable can improve the efficiency of a business, and can be particularly important during economic downturns.

2 Define liabilities, distinguish financial liabilities from other liabilities, and identify how they are measured.

Liabilities are defined as present obligations of an entity arising from past transactions or events that are settled through a transfer of economic resources in the future. They must be enforceable on the entity. Financial liabilities are a subset of liabilities. They are contractual obligations to deliver cash or other financial assets to another party, or to exchange financial instruments with another party under conditions that are potentially unfavourable. Financial liabilities are initially recognized at fair value, and subsequently either at amortized cost or fair value. ASPE does not specify how non-financial liabilities are measured. However, unearned revenues are generally measured at the fair value of the goods or services to be delivered in the future, while others are measured at the best estimate of the amount the entity would rationally pay at the date of the statement of financial position to settle the present obligation.

3 Define current liabilities and identify and account for common types of current liabilities.

Current liabilities are obligations that are payable within one year from the date of the statement of financial position or within the operating cycle if the cycle is longer than a year. IFRS also includes liabilities held for trading and any obligation where the entity does not have an unconditional right to defer settlement beyond 12 months after the date of the statement of financial position. There are several types of current liabilities. The most common are accounts and notes payable, and payroll-related obligations.

4 Identify and account for the major types of employee-related liabilities.

Employee-related liabilities include (1) payroll deductions, (2) compensated absences, and (3) profit-sharing and bonus agreements. Payroll deductions are amounts that are withheld from employees and result in an obligation to the government or other party. The employer's matching contributions are also included in this obligation. Compensated absences earned by employees are company obligations that are recognized as employees earn an entitlement to them, as long as they can be reasonably measured. Bonuses based on income are accrued as an expense and liability as the income is earned.

5 Explain the recognition, measurement, and disclosure requirements for decommissioning and restoration obligations.

A decommissioning, restoration, or asset retirement obligation (ARO) is an estimate of the costs a company is obliged to incur when it retires certain assets. It is recorded as a liability and is usually long-term in nature. Under ASPE, only legal obligations are recognized. They are measured at the best estimate of the cost to settle them at the date of the statement of financial position, and the associated cost is included as part of the cost of property, plant, and equipment. Under IFRS, both legal and constructive obligations are recognized. They are measured at the amount the entity would rationally pay to be relieved of the obligation, and are capitalized as part of PP&E or to inventory, if due to production activities. Over time, the liability is increased for the time value of money and the asset costs are amortized to expense. Entities disclose information about the nature of the obligation and how it is measured, with more disclosures required under IFRS than ASPE.

6 Explain the issues and account for unearned revenues.

When an entity receives proceeds in advance or for multiple deliverables, unearned revenue is recognized to the extent the entity has not yet performed. This is measured at the fair value of the remaining goods or services that will be delivered. When costs remain to be incurred in revenue transactions where the revenue is considered earned and has been recognized, estimated liabilities and expenses are recognized at the best estimate of the expenditures that will be incurred. This is an application of the matching concept.

7 Explain the issues and account for product guarantees and other customer program obligations.

Historically, an expense approach has been used to account for the outstanding liability, but some recent standards have moved toward the revenue approach. Under the expense approach, the outstanding liability is measured at the cost of the economic resources needed to meet the obligation. The assumption is that along with the liability that is required to be recognized at the reporting date, the associated expense needs to be measured and matched with the revenues of the period. Under the revenue approach, the outstanding liability is measured at the value of the obligation. The proceeds received for any goods or services yet to be delivered or performed are considered to be unearned at the point of sale. Until the revenue is earned, the obligation—the liability—is reported at its sales or fair value. The liability is then reduced as the revenue is earned.

8 Explain and account for contingencies and uncertain commitments, and identify the accounting and reporting requirements for guarantees and commitments.

Under existing standards, a loss is accrued and a liability recognized if (1) information that is available before the issuance of the financial statements shows that it is likely (or more likely than not under IFRS) that a liability has been incurred at the date of the financial statements, and (2) the loss amount can be reasonably estimated (under IFRS, it would be a rare situation where this could not be done). An alternative approach likely to be required in new standards being developed by the IASB is described in the Looking Ahead section of the chapter.

Guarantees in general are accounted for similarly to contingencies. Commitments, or contractual obligations, do not usually result in a liability at the date of the statement of financial position. Information about specific types of outstanding commitments is reported at the date of the statement of financial position.

9 Indicate how non-financial and current liabilities are presented and analyzed.

Current liability accounts are commonly presented as the first classification in the liability section of the statement of financial position, although under IFRS, a common presentation is to present current assets and liabilities at the bottom of the statement. Within the current liability section, the accounts may be listed in order of their maturity or in order of their liquidation preference. IFRS requires information about and reconciliations of any provisions. Additional information is provided so that there is enough to meet the requirement of full disclosure. Information about unrecognized loss contingencies is reported in notes to the financial statements, including their nature and estimates of possible losses. Commitments at year end that are significant in size, risk, or time are disclosed in the notes to the financial statements, with significantly more information required under IFRS. Three common ratios used to analyze liquidity are the current, acid-test, and days payables outstanding ratios.

10 Identify differences in accounting between IFRS and ASPE and what changes are expected in the near future.

Private enterprise and international standards are substantially the same. However, there are some classification differences. ASPE does not address "provisions," and there are differences related to which decommissioning and restoration liabilities are recognized and how the costs are capitalized, and how the probability and measurement criteria are applied to contingencies. In addition, requires considerably more disclosure. Looking ahead, revisions to the existing standards are being proposed by the IASB and FASB that will likely be applied, at least in part, under *CICA Handbook*, Part II in the future. The major changes relate to the recognition and measurement standards for non-financial liabilities.

Quiz

KEY TERMS

Brief Exercises

(LO 1)   BE13-1   Wellson Corporation has current assets, including cash, accounts receivable, and inventory, and current liabilities, including accounts payable and short-term notes payable. The company has effective systems in place for granting credit to customers, collecting overdue accounts, and managing inventory. (a) Discuss why management of working capital is important for effective business operations. (b) Discuss how Wellson can improve its management of working capital.

(LO 3)   BE13-2   Roley Corporation uses a periodic inventory system and the gross method of accounting for purchase discounts. On July 1, Roley purchased $60,000 of inventory, terms 2/10, n/30, f.o.b. shipping point. Roley paid freight costs of $1,200. On July 3, Roley returned damaged goods and received a credit of $6,000. On July 10, Roley paid for the goods. Prepare all necessary journal entries for Roley.

(LO 3)   BE13-3   Refer to the information for Roley Corporation in BE13-2. Assume instead that Roley uses the net method of accounting for purchase discounts. Prepare all necessary journal entries for Roley.

(LO 3)   BE13-4   Upland Limited borrowed $40,000 on November 1, 2014, by signing a $40,000, three-month, 9% note. Prepare Upland's November 1, 2014 entry; the December 31, 2014 annual adjusting entry; and the February 1, 2015 entry.

(LO 3)   BE13-5   Refer to the information for Upland Limited in BE13-4. Assume that Upland uses reversing entries. Prepare the 2015 journal entry(ies) for Upland.

(LO 3)   BE13-6   Takemoto Corporation borrowed $60,000 on November 1, 2014, by signing a $61,350, three-month, zero-interest-bearing note. Prepare Takemoto's November 1, 2014 entry; the December 31, 2014 annual adjusting entry; and the February 1, 2015 entry.

(LO 3)   BE13-7   DeGroot Limited conducts all of its business in a province with HST of 13%. Prepare the summary journal entry to record the company's sales for the month of July, during which customers purchased $37,000 of goods on account.

(LO 3)   BE13-8   Louise Incorporated operates in Alberta, where it is subject to GST of 5%. In August, Louise purchased $29,400 of merchandise inventory, and had sales of $45,000 on account. Louise uses a periodic inventory system. Prepare the summary entry to record the purchases for August, the summary entry to record sales for August, and the subsequent entry to record the payment of any GST owing to the government.

(LO 3) **BE13-9** Clausius Ltd. made four quarterly payments of $3,200 each to the CRA during 2014 as instalment payments on its estimated 2014 tax liability. At year end, Clausius's controller completed the company's 2014 tax return, which showed income tax of $20,000 on its 2014 income. Prepare the summary entry for the quarterly tax instalments and the year-end entry to recognize the 2014 income tax. Identify any year-end statement of financial position amount that is related to income tax and indicate where it should be reported.

(LO 3) **BE13-10** Refer to the information about Clausius Ltd. in BE13-9. Assume instead that the tax return indicated 2014 income tax of $10,200. Prepare the year-end entry to recognize the 2014 income tax. Identify any year-end statement of financial position amount that is related to income tax and indicate where it should be reported.

(LO3, 10) **BE13-11** At December 31, 2014, Parew Corporation has a long-term debt of $600,000 owing to its bank. The existing debt agreement imposes several covenants related to Parew's liquidity and solvency. At December 31, 2014, Parew was not in compliance with the covenants related to its current ratio and debt to total assets ratio; however, the bank was allowing Parew to operate outside of its covenants. Parew prepares financial statements in accordance with IFRS. (a) Should the debt be reported as a current liability at December 31, 2014? (b) How would your answer to part (a) be different if Parew prepared financial statements in accordance with ASPE?

(LO3, 10) **BE13-12** At December 31, 2014, Burr Corporation owes $500,000 on a note payable due February 15, 2015. Assume that Burr follows IFRS and that the financial statements are completed and released on February 20, 2015. (a) If Burr refinances the obligation by issuing a long-term note on February 14 and by using the proceeds to pay off the note due February 15, how much of the $500,000 should be reported as a current liability at December 31, 2014? (b) If Burr pays off the note on February 15, 2015, and then borrows $1 million on a long-term basis on March 1, how much of the $500,000 should be reported as a current liability at December 31, 2014? (c) How would the answers to parts (a) and (b) be different if Burr prepared financial statements in accordance with ASPE?

(LO 4) **BE13-13** Whirled Corporation's weekly payroll of $23,000 included employee income taxes withheld of $3,426, CPP withheld of $990, EI withheld of $920, and health insurance premiums withheld of $250. Prepare the journal entry to record Whirled's weekly payroll.

(LO 4) **BE13-14** Refer to the information for Whirled Corporation in BE13-13. Assume now that the employer is required to match every dollar of the CPP contributions of its employees and to contribute 1.4 times the EI withholdings. (a) Prepare the journal entry to record Whirled's payroll-related expenses. (b) Prepare Whirled's entry to record its payroll-related payment to the CRA.

(LO 4) **BE13-15** At December 31, 2014, 30 employees of Kasten Inc. have each earned two weeks of vacation time. The employees' average salary is $500 per week. Prepare Kasten's December 31, 2014 adjusting entry.

(LO 4) **BE13-16** Laurin Corporation offers parental benefits to its staff as a top-up on Employment Insurance benefits so that employees end up receiving 100% of their salary for 12 months of parental leave. Ruzbeh Awad, who earns $74,000 per year, announced that he will be taking parental leave for a period of 17 weeks starting on December 1, 2014. Assume that the Employment Insurance program pays him a maximum of $720 per week for the 17 weeks. Prepare all entries that Laurin Corporation must make during its 2014 fiscal year related to the parental benefits plan as it applies to Ruzbeh Awad.

(LO 4) **BE13-17** Mayaguez Corporation pays its officers bonuses based on income. For 2014, the bonuses total $350,000 and are paid on February 15, 2015. Prepare Mayaguez's December 31, 2014 adjusting entry and the February 15, 2015 entry.

(LO 5, 10) **BE13-18** Lu Corp. erected and placed into service an offshore oil platform on January 1, 2014, at a cost of $10 million. Lu is legally required to dismantle and remove the platform at the end of its nine-year useful life. Lu estimates that it will cost $1 million to dismantle and remove the platform at the end of its useful life and that the discount rate to use should be 8%. Prepare the entry to record the asset retirement obligation.

(LO5, 10) **BE13-19** Refer to the information for Lu Corp. in BE13-18. Prepare any necessary adjusting entries that are associated with the asset retirement obligation and the asset retirement costs at December 31, 2014, assuming that Lu follows (a) IFRS, and (b) ASPE.

(LO5, 10) **BE13-20** Refer to the information for Lu Corp. in BE13-18 and BE13-19. Assume that the increase in the asset retirement obligation in 2014 related to the production of oil in 2014 was $54,027. Prepare any necessary entries to record the increase in the asset retirement obligation at December 31, 2014, assuming that Lu follows (a) IFRS, and (b) ASPE.

(LO 7) **BE13-21** Jupiter Corp. provides at no extra charge a two-year warranty with one of its products, which was first sold in 2014. In that year, Jupiter sold products for $2.5 million and spent $63,000 servicing warranty claims. At year end, Jupiter estimates that an additional $420,000 will be spent in the future to service warranty claims related to the 2014 sales. Prepare Jupiter's journal entry(ies) to record the sale of the products, the $63,000 expenditure, and the December 31 adjusting entry under the expense approach.

(LO 7) **BE13-22** Refer to the information for Jupiter Corp. in BE13-21. Prepare entries for the warranty that recognize the sale as a multiple deliverable with the warranty as a separate service that Jupiter bundled with the selling price of the product. Sales in 2014 occurred evenly throughout the year. Warranty agreements similar to this are available separately, are estimated to have a stand-alone value of $600,000, and are earned over the warranty period as follows: 2014 – 25%, 2015 – 50%, and 2016 – 25%. Also prepare the entry(ies) to record the $63,000 expenditure for servicing the warranty during 2014, and the adjusting entry required at year end, if any, under the revenue approach.

(LO 7) **BE13-23** Henry Corporation sells home entertainment systems. The corporation also offers to sell its customers a two-year warranty contract as a separate service. During 2014, Henry sold 20,000 warranty contracts at $99 each. The corporation spent $180,000 servicing warranties during 2014, and it estimates that an additional $900,000 will be spent in the future to service the warranties. Henry recognizes warranty revenue based on the proportion of costs incurred out of total estimated costs. Prepare Henry's journal entries for (a) the sale of warranty contracts, (b) the cost of servicing the warranties, and (c) the recognition of warranty revenue.

(LO 7) **BE13-24** Wynn Corp. offers a set of building blocks to customers who send in three codes from Wynn cereal, along with $1. Wynn purchased 100,000 building block sets in 2014 for $2.50 each, and paid for them by cash. During 2014, Wynn sold one million boxes of cereal for $4 per box. Wynn estimates that 10% of the sales amount received from customers relates to the building block sets to be awarded. The company expects 30% of the codes to be sent in, and in 2014, 240,000 codes were redeemed. Prepare all necessary journal entries for 2014 if (a) Wynn follows IFRS and prefers to use the revenue approach, and (b) Wynn follows ASPE and prefers to use the expense approach.

(LO 8,10) **BE13-25** At December 31, 2014, Lawton & Border Inc. is involved in a lawsuit. Under existing standards in IAS 37, (a) prepare the December 31 entry assuming it is probable (and very likely) that Lawton & Border will be liable for $700,000 as a result of this suit. (b) Prepare the December 31 entry, if any, assuming it is probable (although not likely) that Lawton & Border will be liable for a payment as a result of this suit. (c) Would your answer change if it was not probable that Lawton & Border would be liable? (d) Repeat parts (a) and (b) assuming that Lawton & Border follows ASPE.

(LO 8) **BE13-26** Siddle Corp. was recently sued by a competitor for patent infringement. Lawyers have determined that it is probable (and very likely) that Siddle will lose the case, and that Siddle will have to pay between $100,000 and $250,000 in damages. In light of this case, Siddle is considering establishing a $100,000 self-insurance allowance. Siddle follows IFRS. (a) What entry(ies), if any, should Siddle record in respect of this lawsuit? (b) Repeat part (a) assuming that Siddle follows ASPE.

(LO 9) **BE13-27** Yuen Corporation shows the following financial position and results for the three years ended December 31, 2014, 2015, and 2016 (in thousands):

	2016	2015	2014
Cash	$ 650	$ 700	$ 600
Fair value–net income investments	500	500	500
Accounts receivable	900	1,000	1,300
Inventory	4,900	4,600	4,000
Prepaid expenses	1,300	1,000	900
Total current assets	$ 8,250	$ 7,800	$ 7,300
Accounts payable	$ 1,550	$ 1,700	$ 1,750
Accrued liabilities	2,250	2,000	1,900
Total current liabilities	$ 3,800	$ 3,700	$ 3,650
Cost of goods sold	$15,000	$18,000	$17,000

For each year, calculate the current ratio, quick ratio, and days payables outstanding ratio, and comment on your results.

Exercises

(LO 2, 4) E13-1 (Balance Sheet Classification of Various Liabilities) The following items are to be reported on a balance sheet.

1. Accrued vacation pay
2. Income tax instalments paid in excess of the income tax liability on the year's income
3. Service warranties on appliance sales
4. A bank overdraft
5. Employee payroll deductions unremitted
6. Unpaid bonus to officer
7. A deposit received from a customer to guarantee performance of a contract
8. Sales tax payable
9. Gift certificates sold to customers but not yet redeemed
10. Premium offers outstanding
11. A royalty fee owing on units produced
12. A personal injury claim pending
13. Current maturities of long-term debts to be paid from current assets
14. Cash dividends declared but unpaid
15. Dividends in arrears on preferred shares
16. Loans from officers
17. GST collected on sales in excess of GST paid on purchases
18. An asset retirement obligation
19. The portion of a credit facility that has been used

Instructions

(a) How would each of the above items be reported on the balance sheet according to ASPE? If you identify an item as a liability, indicate whether or not it is a financial liability.

(b) Would your classification of any of the above items change if they were reported on a statement of financial position prepared according to IFRS?

(LO 3) E13-2 (Accounts and Notes Payable) The following are selected 2014 transactions of Darby Corporation.

Sept. 1 Purchased inventory from Orion Company on account for $50,000. Darby uses a periodic inventory system and records purchases using the gross method of accounting for purchase discounts.

Oct. 1 Issued a $50,000, 12-month, 8% note to Orion in payment of Darby's account.

1 Borrowed $75,000 from the bank by signing a 12-month, non–interest-bearing $81,000 note.

Instructions

(a) Prepare journal entries for each transaction.

(b) Prepare adjusting entries at December 31, 2014.

(c) Calculate the net liability, in total, to be reported on the December 31, 2014 statement of financial position for (1) the interest-bearing note, and (2) the non–interest-bearing note.

(d) Prepare the journal entries for the payment of the notes at maturity.

(e) Repeat part (d) assuming the company uses reversing entries. (Show the reversing entries at January 1, 2015.) Would the use of reversing entries be efficient for both types of notes?

(LO 3) E13-3 (Liability for Returnable Containers) Diagnostics Corp. sells its products in expensive, reusable containers. The customer is charged a deposit for each container that is delivered and receives a refund for each container that is returned within two years after the year of delivery. When a container is not returned within the time limit, Diagnostics accounts for the container as being sold at the deposit amount. Information for 2014 is as follows:

Containers held by customers at December 31, 2013, from deliveries in:

| | 2012 | $170,000 | |
| | 2013 | 480,000 | $650,000 |

Containers delivered in 2014

| 2012 | $115,000 | $894,000 |
| 2013 | 280,000 | |

Containers returned in 2014 from deliveries in:

| 2013 | 310,400 | |
| 2014 | 705,400 | |

Instructions

(a) Prepare all journal entries required for Diagnostics Corp. for the reusable containers during 2014.

(b) Calculate the total amount that Diagnostics should report as a liability for reusable containers at December 31, 2014.

(c) Should the liability calculated in part (b) be reported as current or long-term? Explain.

(AICPA adapted)

(LO 3)   E13-4   (Entries for Sales Taxes) Sararas Corporation is a merchant and operates in the province of Ontario, where the HST rate is 13%. Sararas uses a perpetual inventory system. Transactions for the business for the month of March are as follows:

Mar. 1   Paid March rent to the landlord for the rental of a warehouse. The lease calls for monthly payments of $5,500 plus 13% HST.

3   Sold merchandise on account and shipped merchandise to Marcus Ltd. for $20,000, terms n/30, f.o.b. shipping point. This merchandise cost Sararas $11,000.

5   Granted Marcus a sales allowance of $500 (exclusive of taxes) for defective merchandise purchased on March 3. No merchandise was returned.

7   Purchased merchandise for resale on account from Tinney Ltd. at a list price of $14,000, plus applicable tax.

12   Purchased a desk for the shipping clerk, and paid by cash. The price of the desk was $600 before applicable tax.

31   Paid the monthly remittance of HST to the Receiver General.

Instructions

(a) Prepare the journal entries to record these transactions on the books of Sararas Company.

(b) Assume instead that Sararas operates in the province of Alberta, where PST is not applicable. Prepare the journal entries to record these transactions on the books of Sararas.

(c) Assume instead that Sararas operates in a province where 10% PST is also charged on the 5% GST. Prepare the journal entries to record these transactions on the books of Sararas.

(LO 3)   E13-5   (Income Tax) Shaddick Corp. began its 2014 fiscal year with a debit balance of $11,250 in its Income Tax Receivable account. During the year, the company made quarterly income tax instalment payments of $8,100 each. In early June, a cheque was received from the for Shaddick's overpayment of 2013 taxes. The refunded amount was exactly as Shaddick had calculated it would be on its 2013 income tax return. On completion of the 2014 income tax return, it was determined that Shaddick's income tax based on 2014 income was $37,800.

Instructions

(a) Prepare all journal entries that are necessary to record the 2014 transactions and events.

(b) Indicate how the income tax will be reported on Shaddick's December 31, 2014 statement of financial position.

(c) Assume that the cheque from the CRA in early June is for $2,750. The difference arose because of calculation errors on Shaddick's tax return. How would the difference be accounted for and where would it be shown on Shaddick's financial statements?

Digging
Deeper

(LO 3, 4,   E13-6   (Financial Statement Impact of Liability Transactions) The following is a list of possible transactions.
7, 8)**
1. Purchased inventory for $80,000 on account (assume perpetual system is used).

2. Issued an $80,000 note payable in payment of an account (see item 1 above).

3. Recorded accrued interest on the note from item 2 above.

4. Borrowed $100,000 from the bank by signing a $112,000, six-month, non-interest-bearing note.

5. Recognized four months of interest expense on the note from item 4 above.

6. Recorded cash sales of $75,260, which includes 6% sales tax.

7. Recorded salaries and wages expense of $35,000. The cash paid was $25,000; the difference was due to various amounts withheld.

8. Recorded employer's payroll taxes.

9. Accrued accumulated vacation pay.

10. Signed a $2-million contract with Construction Corp. to build a new plant.

11. Recorded bonuses due to employees.

12. Recorded a provision on a lawsuit that the company will probably lose.

13. Accrued warranty expense (assume expense approach).

14. Paid warranty costs that were accrued in item 13 above.

15. Recorded sales of product and separately sold warranties.

16. Paid warranty costs under contracts from item 15 above.

17. Recognized warranty revenue (see item 15 above).

18. Recorded estimated liability for premium claims outstanding.

19. Recorded the receipt of a cash down payment on services to be performed in the next accounting period.

20. Received the remainder of the contracted amount and performed the services related to item 19 above.

Instructions

Set up a table using the format that follows and, using ASPE, analyze the effects of the 20 transactions on the financial statement categories in the table. Use the following codes: increase (I), decrease (D), or no net effect (NE).

Transaction	Assets	Liabilities	Owners' Equity	Net Income
1				

(LO 3, 10) E13-7 (Refinancing of Short-Term Debt) On December 31, 2014, Hornsby Corporation had $1.2 million of short-term debt in the form of notes payable due on February 2, 2015. On January 21, 2015, in order to ensure that they had sufficient funds to pay for their short-term debt when it matured, the company issued 25,000 common shares for $38 per share, receiving $950,000 in proceeds after brokerage fees and other costs of issuance. On February 2, 2015, the proceeds from the sale of the shares, along with an additional $250,000 cash, were used to liquidate the $1.2-million debt. The December 31, 2014 balance sheet is issued on February 23, 2015.

Instructions

(a) Assuming that Hornsby follows ASPE, show how the $1.2 million of short-term debt should be presented on the December 31, 2014 balance sheet, including the note disclosure.

(b) Assuming that Hornsby follows IFRS, explain how the $1.2 million of short-term debt should be presented on the December 31, 2014 statement of financial position.

(c) Considering only the effect of the $1.2-million short-term notes payable, would Hornsby's current ratio appear higher if Hornsby followed ASPE, or if Hornsby followed IFRS? Discuss your answer from the perspective of a creditor.

Digging
Deeper

(LO 3, 10) E13-8 (Refinancing of Short-Term Debt) On December 31, 2014, Zimmer Corporation has $7.9 million of short-term debt in the form of notes payable that will be due periodically in 2015 to Provincial Bank. On January 28, 2015, Zimmer enters into a refinancing agreement with the bank that will permit it to borrow up to 60% of the gross amount of its accounts receivable. Receivables are expected to range between a low of $5.7 million in May and a high of $7 million in October during the year 2015. The interest cost of the maturing short-term debt is 15%, and the new agreement calls for a fluctuating interest rate at 1% above the prime rate on notes due in 2016. Zimmer's December 31, 2014 balance sheet is issued on February 15, 2015.

Instructions

(a) Assuming that Zimmer follows ASPE, prepare a partial balance sheet for Zimmer Corporation at December 31, 2014, that shows how its $7.9 million of short-term debt should be presented, including any necessary note disclosures.

(b) Assuming that Zimmer follows IFRS, explain how the $7.9 million of short-term debt should be presented on the December 31, 2014 statement of financial position.

(LO 4) E13-9 (Payroll Tax Entries) The payroll of Sumerlus Corp. for September 2014 is as follows. Total payroll was $485,000. Pensionable (CPP) and insurable (EI) earnings were $365,000. Income taxes in the amount of $85,000 were withheld, as were $8,000 in union dues. The Employment Insurance tax rate was 1.83% for employees and 2.562% for employers, and the CPP rate was 4.95% for employees and 4.95% for employers.

(LO 4)   E13-10   (Compensated Absences—Vacation and Sick Pay) Mustafa Limited began operations on January 2, 2013. The company employs nine individuals who work eight-hour days and are paid hourly. Each employee earns 10 paid vacation days and six paid sick days annually. Vacation days may be taken after January 15 of the year following the year in which they are earned. Sick days may be taken as soon as they are earned; unused sick days accumulate. Additional information is as follows:

	Actual Hourly Wage Rate		Vacation Days Used by Each Employee		Sick Days Used by Each Employee	
	2013	2014	2013	2014	2013	2014
	$10	$11	0	9	4	5

Mustafa Limited has chosen to accrue the cost of compensated absences at rates of pay in effect during the period when they are earned and to accrue sick pay when it is earned.

Instructions

(a) Prepare the journal entry(ies) to record the transactions related to vacation entitlement during 2013 and 2014.

(b) Prepare the journal entry(ies) to record the transactions related to sick days during 2013 and 2014.

(c) Calculate the amounts of any liability for vacation pay and sick days that should be reported on the statement of financial position at December 31, 2013, and 2014.

(d) How would your answers to parts (b) and (c) change if the entitlement to sick days did not accumulate?

Digging Deeper

(LO 4)   E13-11   (Compensated Absences—Vacation and Sick Pay) Refer to the data in E13-10 and assume instead that Mustafa Limited has chosen not to recognize paid sick leave until it is used, and has chosen to accrue vacation time at expected future rates of pay without discounting. The company uses the following projected rates to accrue vacation time:

Year in Which Vacation Time Was Earned	Projected Future Pay Rates Used to Accrue Vacation Pay
2013	$10.75 per hour
2014	$11.60 per hour

Instructions

(a) Prepare the journal entry(ies) to record the transactions related to vacation entitlement during 2013 and 2014.

(b) Prepare the journal entry(ies) to record the transactions related to sick days during 2013 and 2014.

(c) Calculate the amounts of any liability for vacation pay and sick days that should be reported on the statement of financial position at December 31, 2013, and 2014.

Instructions

(a) Prepare the necessary journal entries to record the payroll if the salaries and wages paid and the employer payroll taxes are recorded separately.

(b) Prepare the entries to record the payment of all required amounts to the CRA and to the employees' union.

(c) For every dollar of salaries and wages that Sumerlus commits to pay, what is the actual payroll cost to the company?

(d) Discuss any other costs, direct or indirect, that you think would add to the company's costs of having employees.

Digging Deeper

(LO 4)   E13-12   (Compensated Absences—Parental Benefits) Goldwing Corporation offers enriched parental benefits to its staff. While the government provides compensation based on Employment Insurance legislation for a period of 12 months, Goldwing increases the amounts received and extends the period of compensation. The benefit program tops up the amount received to 100% of the employee's salary for the first 12 months, and pays the employee 75% of his or her full salary for another six months after the Employment Insurance payments have ceased.

Zeinab Jolan, who earns $54,000 per year, announced to her manager in early June 2014 that she was expecting a baby in mid-November. On October 29, 2014, nine weeks before the end of the calendar year and Goldwing's fiscal year, Zeinab began her 18-month maternity leave. Assume that the Employment Insurance program pays her a maximum of $720 per week for 52 weeks.

Instructions

Round all answers to the nearest dollar.

(a) Prepare all entries that Goldwing Corporation must make during its 2014 fiscal year related to the maternity benefits plan in regard to Zeinab Jolan. Be sure to include the date of each entry.

(b) Prepare one entry to summarize all entries that the company will make in 2015 relative to Zeinab Jolan's leave.

(c) Calculate the amount of maternity benefits payable at December 31, 2014, and 2015. Explain how these amounts will be shown on the company's statement of financial position.

(LO 4) E13-13 (Bonus Calculation and Income Statement Preparation) The incomplete income statement of Justin Corp. follows.

Sales revenue	$10,000,000
Cost of goods sold	7,000,000
Gross profit	3,000,000
Administrative and selling expenses	$1,000,000
Profit-sharing bonus to employees	?
Income before income taxes	?
Income taxes	?
Net income	$?

The employee profit-sharing plan requires that 20% of all profits remaining after the deduction of the bonus and income tax be distributed to the employees by the first day of the fourth month following each year end. The income tax rate is 30%, and the bonus is tax-deductible.

Instructions

(a) Complete the condensed income statement of Justin Corp. for the year 2014. You will need to develop two simultaneous equations to solve for the bonus amount: one for the bonus and one for the tax.

(b) Prepare the journal entry to record the bonus at December 31, 2014.

(LO 5) E13-14 (Asset Retirement Obligation) On January 1, 2014, Offshore Corporation erected a drilling platform at a cost of $5,460,000. Offshore is legally required to dismantle and remove the platform at the end of its six-year useful life, at an estimated cost of $950,000. Offshore estimates that 70% of the cost of dismantling and removing the platform is caused by acquiring the asset itself, and that the remaining 30% of the cost is caused by using the platform in production. The present value of the increase in asset retirement obligation related to the production of oil in 2014 and 2015 was $32,328 and $34,914, respectively. The estimated residual value of the drilling platform is zero, and Offshore uses straight-line depreciation. Offshore prepares financial statements in accordance with IFRS.

Instructions

(a) Prepare the journal entries to record the acquisition of the drilling platform, and the asset retirement obligation for the platform, on January 1, 2014. An appropriate interest or discount rate is 8%.

(b) Prepare any journal entries required for the platform and the asset retirement obligation at December 31, 2014.

(c) Prepare any journal entries required for the platform and the asset retirement obligation at December 31, 2015.

(d) Assume that on December 31, 2019, Offshore dismantles and removes the platform for a cost of $922,000. Prepare the journal entry to record the settlement of the asset retirement obligation. Also assume its carrying amount at that time is $950,000.

(e) Repeat parts (a) through (d) assuming that Offshore prepares financial statements in accordance with ASPE.

(LO 5) E13-15 (Asset Retirement Obligation) Crude Oil Limited purchased an oil tanker depot on July 2, 2014, at a cost of $600,000 and expects to operate the depot for 10 years. After the 10 years, the company is legally required to dismantle the depot and remove the underground storage tanks. It is estimated that it will cost $75,000 to do this at the end of the depot's useful life. Crude Oil follows ASPE.

Instructions

(a) Calculate the present value of the asset retirement obligation (that is, its fair value) on the date of acquisition, based on an effective interest rate of 6%. Prepare the journal entries to record the acquisition of the depot and the asset retirement obligation for the depot on July 2, 2014.

(b) Prepare any journal entries required for the depot and the asset retirement obligation at December 31, 2014. Crude Oil uses straight-line depreciation. The estimated residual value of the depot is zero.

(c) On June 30, 2024, Crude Oil pays a demolition firm to dismantle the depot and remove the tanks at a cost of $80,000. Prepare the journal entry for the settlement of the asset retirement obligation.

(d) Prepare the schedule to calculate the balance in the asset retirement obligation account for all years from 2014 to 2024, assuming there is no change in the estimated cost of dismantling the depot.

Digging Deeper

(e) Show how all relevant amounts will be reported on Crude Oil Limited's financial statements at December 31, 2014.

(f) How would the accretion expense be reported on the statement of cash flows?

(g) Discuss how Crude Oil would account for the asset retirement costs and obligation if the company reported under IFRS. Be specific.

(LO 7) **E13-16 (Warranties—Expense Approach and Cash Basis)** Cléroux Corporation sold 150 colour laser copiers in 2014 for $4,000 each, including a one-year warranty. Maintenance on each machine during the warranty period averages $300.

Instructions

(a) Prepare entries to record the machine sales and the related warranty costs under the expense approach. Actual warranty costs incurred in 2014 were $17,000.

(b) Based on the information above and assuming that the cash basis is used, prepare the appropriate entries.

(c) Is the method in (b) ever acceptable under GAAP? Explain.

(LO 7) **E13-17 (Warranties—Expense Approach)** Cool Sound Corporation manufactures a line of amplifiers that carry a three-year warranty against defects. Based on experience, the estimated warranty costs related to dollar sales are as follows: first year after sale—2% of sales; second year after sale—3% of sales; and third year after sale—4% of sales. Sales and actual warranty expenditures for the first three years of business were:

	Sales	Warranty Expenditures
2012	$ 810,000	$ 6,500
2013	1,070,000	17,200
2014	1,036,000	62,000

Instructions

(a) Calculate the amount that Cool Sound Corporation should report as warranty expense on its 2014 income statement and as a warranty liability on its December 31, 2014 statement of financial position. Assume that all sales are made evenly throughout each year and that warranty expenditures are also evenly spaced according to the rates above.

(b) Assume that Cool Sound's warranty expenditures in the first year after sale end up being 4% of sales, which is twice as much as was forecast. How would management account for this change?

(LO 7) **E13-18 (Warranties—Expense Approach and Revenue Approach)** Selzer Equipment Limited sold 500 Rollomatics on account during 2014 for $6,000 each. During 2014, Selzer spent $30,000 servicing the two-year warranties that are included in each sale of the Rollomatic. All servicing transactions were paid in cash.

Instructions

(a) Prepare the 2014 entries for Selzer using the expense approach for warranties. Assume that Selzer estimates that the total cost of servicing the warranties will be $120,000 for two years.

(b) Prepare the 2014 entries for Selzer assuming that the warranties are not an integral part of the sale, but rather a separate service that is considered to be bundled with the selling price. Assume that of the sales total, $160,000 is identified as relating specifically to sales of warranty contracts. Selzer estimates the total cost of servicing the warranties will be $120,000 for two years. Because the repair costs are not incurred evenly, warranty revenues are recognized based on the proportion of costs incurred out of the total estimated costs.

(c) What amounts would be shown on Selzer's income statement under parts (a) and (b)? Explain the resulting difference in the company's net income.

(d) Assume that the equipment sold by Selzer undergoes technological improvements and management now has no past experience on which to estimate the extent of the warranty costs. The chief engineer believes that product warranty costs are likely to be incurred, but they cannot be reasonably estimated. What advice would you give on how to account for and report the warranties?

(LO 7) **E13-19 (Warranties—Expense Approach and Revenue Approach)** Novack Machinery Corporation manufactures equipment to a very high standard of quality; however, it must still provide a warranty for each unit sold, and there are instances where the machines do require repair after they have been put into use. The company started in business in 2014, and as the controller, you are trying to determine whether to use the expense or the revenue approach to measure the warranty obligation. You would like to show the company president how this choice would affect the financial statements for 2014, and advise him of the better choice, keeping in mind that the revenue approach is consistent with IFRS, and there are plans to take the company public in a few years.

You have determined that sales for the year were 1,000 units, with a selling price of $3,000 each. The warranty is for two years, and the estimated warranty cost averages $200 per machine. Actual costs of servicing warranties for the year were $105,000. You have done some research and determined that if the revenue approach were to be used, the portion of revenue allocated to the warranty portion of the sale would be $350. Because the costs of servicing warranties are not incurred evenly, warranty revenues are recognized based on the proportion of costs incurred out of the total estimated costs.

Instructions

(a) For both the expense and the revenue approach, prepare the necessary journal entries to record all of the transactions described, and determine the warranty liability and expense amounts for 2014.

(b) What are the advantages and disadvantages of the two choices? What do you think is the best choice in this situation? Why?

(LO 7) **E13-20** **(Premium Entries)** Moleski Corporation includes one coupon in each box of soap powder that it produces, and 10 coupons are redeemable for a premium (a kitchen utensil). In 2014, Moleski Corporation purchased 8,800 premiums at $0.90 each and sold 120,000 boxes of soap powder at $3.30 per box. In total, 44,000 coupons were presented for redemption in 2014. It is estimated that 60% of the coupons will eventually be presented for redemption. Moleski uses the expense approach to account for premiums.

Instructions

(a) Prepare all the entries that would be made for sales of soap powder and for the premium plan in 2014.

(b) What amounts relative to soap powder sales and premiums would be shown on Moleski's financial statements for 2014?

(LO 7) **E13-21** **(Premiums)** Three independent situations follow.

Situation 1: Marquart Stamp Corporation records stamp service revenue and provides for the cost of redemptions in the year stamps are sold to licensees. The stamps can be collected and then redeemed for discounts on future purchases from Marquart as an incentive for repeat business. Marquart's past experience indicates that only 80% of the stamps sold to licensees will be redeemed. Marquart's liability for stamp redemptions was $13 million at December 31, 2013. Additional information for 2014 is as follows:

Stamp service revenue from stamps sold to licensees	$9,500,000
Cost of redemptions (stamps sold prior to 1/1/14)	6,000,000

If all the stamps sold in 2014 were presented for redemption in 2015, the redemption cost would be $5.2 million.

Instructions

What amount should Marquart report as a liability for stamp redemptions at December 31, 2014?

Situation 2: In packages of its products, ITSS Inc. includes coupons that may be presented at retail stores to obtain discounts on other ITSS products. Retailers are reimbursed for the face amount of coupons redeemed plus 10% of that amount for handling costs. ITSS honours requests for coupon redemption by retailers up to three months after the consumer expiration date. ITSS estimates that 60% of all coupons issued will eventually be redeemed. Information relating to coupons issued by ITSS during 2014 is as follows:

Consumer expiration date	12/31/14
Total face amount of coupons issued	$800,000
Total payments to retailers as at 12/31/14	$330,000

Instructions

(a) What amount should ITSS report as a liability for unredeemed coupons at December 31, 2014?

(b) What amount of premium expense should ITSS report on its 2014 income statement?

Situation 3: Baylor Corp. sold 700,000 boxes of pie mix under a new sales promotion program. Each box contains one coupon that entitles the customer to a baking pan when the coupon is submitted with an additional $4.75 from the customer. Baylor pays $5.00 per pan and $1.25 for shipping and handling. Baylor estimates that 60% of the coupons will be redeemed even though only 105,000 coupons had been processed during 2014. Each box of pie mix is sold for $4.50, and Baylor estimates that $1.00 of the sale price relates to the baking pan to be awarded. Baylor follows IFRS and accounts for its promotional programs in accordance with the revenue approach and IFRIC 13.

Instructions

(a) What amount should ITSS report as a liability for unredeemed coupons at December 31, 2014?

(b) What amount of premium expense should ITSS report on its 2014 income statement?

Digging Deeper

Digging Deeper

Instructions

(a) What amount related to the promotional program should Baylor report as a liability at December 31, 2014?

(b) What amount of premium expense will Baylor report on its 2014 income statement as a result of the promotional program?

(c) Prepare any necessary 2014 journal entries to record revenue, the liability, and coupon redemptions.

(d) Discuss the conceptual merit of recording the sales revenue related to unredeemed coupons as unearned premium revenue.

(AICPA adapted)

(LO 7) E13-22 (Premiums) Timo van Leeuwen operates a very busy roadside fruit and vegetable stand from May to October every year as part of his farming operation, which has a December 31 year end. Each time a customer purchases over $10 of produce, Timo gives the customer a special fruit-shaped sticker that can't be copied. If a customer collects 10 of these stickers, they can have $10 worth of produce for no charge. The stickers must be redeemed by June 30 of the following year. During the current year, 25,000 stickers were given out to customers. Timo knows from experience that some stickers will never be cashed in, as the customer may not shop at his stand frequently enough to collect 10 stickers, or they get lost or forgotten. In previous years, 10% of stickers have been redeemed. During the current year, 6% of the stickers given out were redeemed. Timo uses the expense approach to account for premiums and estimates that product costs are 60% of their selling prices.

Instructions

(a) Determine the amount that should be reported as premium expense on the December 31 income statement and the amount of any liability at December 31.

(b) Prepare all the necessary journal entries to record the premium expense associated with the stickers and the related liability at year end.

(LO 7) E13-23 (Coupons and Rebates) St. Thomas Auto Repairs is preparing the financial statements for the year ended November 30, 2014. As the accountant, you are looking over the information regarding short-term liabilities, and determining the amounts that should be reported on the balance sheet. St. Thomas Auto Repairs reports under ASPE. The following information regarding new corporate initiatives has been brought to your attention.

1. The company printed a coupon in the local newspaper in November 2014. The coupon permits customers to take 10% off the cost of any service between November 1, 2014, and January 30, 2015. The newspaper has a circulation of 10,000 customers. In November, 30 coupons were used, resulting in sales reductions of $250. It is expected that 50 more coupons will be used before January 30, and the average sales transaction for the company is $75.

2. In order to reduce the costs associated with production downtime due to sick days taken, the company developed a new plan in 2014. Employees are permitted up to six sick days per year with pay. If these days are not all used, then 50% of the unused time will be accumulated and can be used as paid vacation within the next year; otherwise, the rights will expire at the end of the next fiscal year. During 2014, two employees were eligible for the plan and each used two of their six days. The daily rate of pay for each employee is $100. These two individuals are long-term employees of the company who are unlikely to resign in the near future and who have been relatively healthy in the past.

3. The company is considering starting a customer loyalty program. The program would involve tracking the purchases of each customer on a small card that is retained by the customer. Each time a customer reaches $250 in total purchases, a $10 discount would be offered on the next purchase.

Instructions

(a) For items that affect the 2014 financial statements, determine the amount of any liability that should be reported and the related expense.

(b) Discuss the issues that the proposed customer loyalty program raises from an accounting standpoint. Explain how the program should be accounted for.

(LO 8, 10) E13-24 (Contingencies and Commitments) Four independent situations follow.

Situation 1: During 2014, Sugarpost Inc. became involved in a tax dispute with the CRA. Sugarpost's lawyers have informed management that Sugarpost will likely lose this dispute. They also believe that Sugarpost will have to pay the CRA between $900,000 and $1.4 million. After the 2014 financial statements were issued, the case was settled with the CRA for $1.2 million.

Instructions

What amount, if any, should be reported as a liability for this contingency as at December 31, 2014, assuming that Sugarpost follows ASPE?

Situation 2: Toward the end of Su Li Corp.'s 2014 fiscal year, employer–union talks broke off, with the wage rates for the upcoming two years still unresolved. Just before the new year, however, a contract was signed that gave employees a 5% increase in their hourly wage. Su Li had spent $1.2 million in wages on this group of workers in 2014.

Instructions

Prepare the entry, if any, that Su Li Corp. should make at December 31, 2014. Briefly explain your answer.

Situation 3: On October 1, 2014, the provincial environment ministry identified Jackhammer Chemical Inc. as a potentially responsible party in a chemical spill. Jackhammer's management, along with its legal counsel, have concluded that it is likely that Jackhammer will be found responsible for damages, and a reasonable estimate of these damages is $5 million. Jackhammer's insurance policy of $9 million has a clause requiring a deductible of $500,000.

Instructions

(a) Assuming ASPE is followed, how should Jackhammer Chemical report this information in its financial statements at December 31, 2014?

(b) Briefly identify any differences if Jackhammer were to follow IFRS.

Situation 4: Etheridge Inc. had a manufacturing plant in a foreign country that was destroyed in a civil war. It is not certain who will compensate Etheridge for this destruction, but Etheridge has been assured by that country's government officials that it will receive a definite amount for this plant. The compensation amount will be less than the plant's fair value, but more than its carrying amount.

Instructions

How should the contingency be reported in the financial statements of Etheridge Inc. under ASPE?

(LO 9) **E13-25 (Ratio Calculations and Discussion)** Kawani Corporation has been operating for several years, and on December 31, 2014, presented the following statement of financial position.

KAWANI CORPORATION
Statement of Financial Position
December 31, 2014

Cash	$ 40,000	Accounts payable	$ 70,000
Accounts receivables	75,000	Mortgage payable	140,000
Inventory	95,000	Common shares (no par)	160,000
Equipment (net)	220,000	Retained earnings	60,000
	$430,000		$430,000

Cost of goods sold in 2014 was $420,000, operating expenses were $51,000, and net income was $27,000. Accounts payable suppliers provided operating goods and services. Assume that total assets are the same in 2013 and 2014.

Instructions

Calculate each of the following ratios:

(a) Current ratio (b) Acid-test ratio (c) Debt-to-total-assets ratio (d) Rate of return on assets (e) Days payables outstanding

For each ratio, also indicate how it is calculated and what its significance is as a tool for analyzing the company's financial soundness.

(LO 9) **E13-26 (Ratio Calculations and Analysis)** Harold Limited's condensed financial statements provide the following information:

HAROLD LIMITED
Statement of Financial Position

	Dec. 31, 2014	Dec. 31, 2013
Cash	$ 52,000	$ 60,000
Accounts receivable (net)	198,000	80,000
Fair value-net income investments (short-term)	80,000	40,000
Inventory	440,000	360,000
Prepaid expenses	3,000	7,000
Total current assets	773,000	547,000
Property, plant, and equipment (net)	857,000	853,000
Total assets	$1,630,000	$1,400,000
Accounts payable	$ 220,000	$ 145,000
Other current liabilities	20,000	15,000
Bonds payable	400,000	400,000
Common shareholders' equity	990,000	840,000
Total liabilities and shareholders' equity	$1,630,000	$1,400,000

Income Statement
For the Year Ended December 31, 2014

Sales	$1,640,000
Cost of goods sold	(800,000)
Gross profit	840,000
Selling and administrative expense	(440,000)
Interest expense	(40,000)
Net income	$ 360,000

Instructions

(a) Determine the following:

1. Current ratio at December 31, 2014
2. Acid-test ratio at December 31, 2014
3. Accounts receivable turnover for 2014
4. Inventory turnover for 2014
5. Days payables outstanding for 2014
6. Rate of return on assets for 2014
7. Profit margin on sales

(b) Prepare a brief evaluation of the financial condition of Harold Limited and of the adequacy of its profits.

(c) In examining the other current liabilities on Harold Limited's statement of financial position, you notice that unearned revenues have declined in the current year compared with the previous year. Is this a positive indicator about the client's liquidity? Explain.

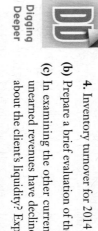

Digging
Deeper

(LO 9) E13-27 (Ratio Calculations and Effect of Transactions) Financial information for Cao Inc. follows.

CAO INC.
Statement of Financial Position
December 31, 2014

Cash		$ 45,000	Notes payable (short-term)	$ 50,000
Receivables	$110,000		Accounts payable	32,000
Less: Allowance	15,000	95,000	Accrued liabilities	5,000
Inventories		170,000	Share capital (52,000 shares)	260,000
Prepaid insurance		8,000	Retained earnings	141,000
Land		20,000		
Equipment (net)		150,000		
		$488,000		$488,000

Income Statement
For the Year Ended December 31, 2014

Sales		$1,400,000
Cost of goods sold		
Inventory, Jan. 1, 2014	$200,000	
Purchases	790,000	
Cost of goods available for sale	990,000	
Inventory, Dec. 31, 2014	170,000	
Cost of goods sold		820,000
Gross profit on sales		580,000
Operating expenses		170,000
Net income		$ 410,000

Instructions

(a) Calculate the following ratios or relationships of Cao Inc. Assume that the ending account balances are representative unless the information provided indicates differently.

1. Current ratio
2. Inventory turnover
3. Receivables turnover
4. Average age of receivables (days sales outstanding)
5. Average age of payables (days payables outstanding)
6. Earnings per share
7. Profit margin on sales
8. Rate of return on assets

(b) For each of the following transactions, indicate whether the transaction would improve, weaken, or have no effect on the current ratio of Cao Inc. at December 31, 2014.

1. Writing off an uncollectible account receivable for $2,200
2. Receiving a $20,000 down payment on services to be performed in 2015
3. Paying $40,000 on notes payable (short-term)
4. Collecting $23,000 on accounts receivable
5. Purchasing equipment on account
6. Giving an existing creditor a short-term note in settlement of an open account owed

Problems

P13-1 The following are selected transactions of Pendlebury Department Store Ltd. for the current year ending December 31.

1. On February 2, the company purchased goods having cash discount terms of 2/10, n/30 from Hashmani Limited for $46,000. Purchases and accounts payable are recorded using the periodic system at net amounts after cash discounts. The invoice was paid on February 26.

2. On April 1, Pendlebury purchased a truck for $50,000 from Schuler Motors Limited, paying $5,000 cash and signing a one-year, 8% note for the balance of the purchase price.

3. On May 1, the company borrowed $83,000 from First Provincial Bank by signing a $92,000 non–interest-bearing note due one year from May 1.

4. On June 30 and December 31, Pendlebury remitted cheques for $19,000 each as instalments on its current year tax liability.

5. On August 14, the board of directors declared a $13,000 cash dividend that was payable on September 10 to shareholders of record on August 31.

6. On December 5, the store received $750 from Jefferson Players as a deposit on furniture that Jefferson Players is using in its stage production. The deposit is to be returned to the theatre company after it returns the furniture on January 15.

7. On December 10, the store purchased new furniture and fixtures for $8,000 on account. Sales tax of 8% and GST of 5% were charged by the supplier on the purchase price.

8. During December, cash sales of $79,000 were recorded, plus 8% sales tax and 5% GST that must be remitted by the 15th day of the following month. Both taxes are levied on the sale amount to the customer.

9. Pendlebury's lease for its store premises calls for a $2,500 monthly rental payment plus 3% of all sales. The payment is due one week after month end.

10. Pendlebury is legally required to restore the area surrounding one of its new store parking lots, when the store is closed in 12 years. Pendlebury estimates that the fair value of this obligation at December 31 is $46,000.

11. The corporate tax return indicated taxable income of $205,000. Pendlebury's income tax rate is 20%.

Instructions

(a) Prepare all the journal entries that are necessary to record the above transactions when they occurred and any adjusting journal entries relative to the transactions that would be required to present fair financial statements at December 31. Date each entry.

(b) Identify the current liabilities that will be reported on the December 31 statement of financial position, and indicate the amount of each one.

(c) Prepare the journal entries for transactions 7 and 8 above if the 8% sales tax was applied on the purchase or sale amount plus the GST.

(d) Why is the liabilities section of the statement of financial position of primary significance to bankers?

(e) How are current liabilities related to current assets?

Digging Deeper

P13-2 Bian Inc. financed the purchase of equipment costing $85,000 on January 1, 2014, using a note payable. The note requires Bian to make annual $32,389 payments of blended interest and principal on January 1 of the following three years, beginning January 1, 2015. The note bears interest at the rate of 7%.

Instructions

(a) Prepare the debt amortization schedule for the note over its term.

(b) Prepare the journal entry(ies) that are required for the year ended December 31, 2014, and the first instalment payment on January 1, 2015.

(c) Prepare the statement of financial position presentation of the note at December 31, 2014. (Include both the current and long-term portions.)

(d) Prepare the statement of financial position presentation of the note at December 31, 2015.

(e) Redo part (c) assuming that the equipment was purchased on July 1, 2014, and the payments are due beginning July 1, 2015.

P13-3 Hrudka Corp. has manufactured a broad range of quality products since 1988. The following information is available for the company's fiscal year ended February 28, 2014. Hrudka follows ASPE.

1. The company has $4 million of bonds payable outstanding at February 28, 2014, that were issued at par in 2003. The bonds carry an interest rate of 7%, payable semi-annually each June 1 and December 1.

2. Hrudka has several notes payable outstanding with its primary banking institution at February 28, 2014. In each case, the annual interest is due on the anniversary date of the note each year (same as the due dates listed). The notes are as follows:

Due Date	Amount Due	Interest Rate
Apr. 1, 2014	$150,000	8%
Jan. 31, 2015	200,000	9%
Mar. 15, 2015	500,000	7%
Oct. 30, 2016	250,000	8%

3. Hrudka uses the expense approach to account for warranties. The company has a two-year warranty on selected products, with an estimated cost of 1% of sales being returned in the 12 months following the sale, and a cost of 1.5% of sales being returned in months 13 to 24 following sale. The warranty liability outstanding at February 28, 2013, was $5,700. Sales of warrantied products in the year ended February 28, 2014, were $154,000. Actual warranty costs incurred during the current fiscal year are as follows:

Warranty claims honoured on 2012–2013 sales	$4,900
Warranty claims honoured on 2013–2014 sales	1,100
	$6,000

4. Regular trade payables for supplies and purchases of goods and services on open account are $414,000 at February 28, 2014. Included in this amount is a loan of $23,000 owing to an affiliated company.

5. The following information relates to Hrudka's payroll for the month of February 2014. The company's required contribution for EI is 1.4 times that of the employee contribution; for CPP it is 1.0 times that of the employee contribution.

Salaries and wages outstanding at February 28, 2014	$220,000
EI withheld from employees	9,500
CPP withheld from employees	16,900
Income taxes withheld from employees	48,700
Union dues withheld from employees	21,500

6. Hrudka regularly pays GST owing to the government on the 15th of the month. Hrudka's GST transactions include the GST that it charges to customers and the GST that it is charged by suppliers. During February 2014, purchases attracted $28,000 of GST, while the GST charged on invoices to customers totalled $39,900. At January 31, 2014, the balances in the GST Receivable and GST Payable accounts were $34,000 and $60,000, respectively.

7. Other miscellaneous liabilities included $50,000 of dividends payable on March 15, 2014; $25,000 of bonuses payable to company executives (75% payable in September 2014, and 25% payable the following March); and $75,000 in accrued audit fees covering the year ended February 28, 2014.

8. Hrudka sells gift cards to its customers. The company does not set a redemption date and customers can use their cards at any time. At March 1, 2013, Hrudka had a balance outstanding of $950,000 in its Unearned Revenues—Gift Cards account. The company received $225,000 in cash for gift cards purchased during the current year and $375,000 in redemptions took place during the year. Based on past experience, 15% of customer gift card balances never get redeemed. At the end of each year, Hrudka recognizes 15% of the opening balance of Unearned Revenues as earned during the year.

Instructions

(a) Prepare the current liability section of the February 28, 2014 balance sheet of Hrudka Corp. Identify any amounts that require separate presentation or disclosure under ASPE.

(b) For each item included as a current liability, identify whether the item is a financial liability. Explain.

(c) If you have excluded any items from the category of current liabilities, explain why you left them out.

(d) Assume that Hrudka Corp. is not in compliance with the debt covenants in the note payable due October 30, 2016, in item 2 above. How would this affect the classification of the note on the balance sheet?

(e) For a manufacturer such as Hrudka, how should the revenue from unredeemed gift cards be shown on the income statement, as opposed to revenue from redeemed gift cards?

Digging Deeper

P13-4 Healy Corp., a leader in the commercial cleaning industry, acquired and installed, at a total cost of $110,000 plus 15% HST, three underground tanks for the storage of hazardous liquid solutions needed in the cleaning process. The tanks were ready for use on February 28, 2014.

The provincial ministry of the environment regulates the use of such tanks and requires them to be disposed of after 10 years of use. Healy estimates that the cost of digging up and removing the tanks in 2024 will be $28,000. An appropriate interest or discount rate is 6%.

Healy also manufactures commercial cleaning machines that it sells to dry cleaning establishments throughout Nova Scotia. During 2014, Healy sold 20 machines at a price of $12,000 each plus 15% HST. The machines were sold with a two-year warranty for parts and labour. Similar warranty agreements are available separately and are estimated to have a stand-alone value of $970. Sales in 2014 occurred evenly throughout the year. Any revenue related to the warranty agreements is assumed to be earned evenly over the two-year contract term as follows: 2014 – 25%, 2015 – 50%, and 2016 – 25%. Healy estimates the total cost of servicing the warranties will be $10,800 over the two-year contract term. Healy incurred actual warranty expenditures of $2,700 in 2014.

Instructions

Answer the following, assuming Healy follows IFRS and has a December 31 fiscal year end.

(a) Assuming straight-line depreciation and no residual value for the tanks at the end of their 10-year useful life, what is the balance in the asset Storage Tanks account, net of accumulated depreciation, at December 31, 2014?

(b) What is the balance of the asset retirement obligation liability at December 31, 2016, assuming there has been no change to the estimate of the final cost of disposal?

(c) Determine the balance of the warranty-related liability that would be reported on the December 31, 2014 statement of financial position. Ignore HST and assume that Healy uses the revenue approach to account for warranties.

(d) Determine the Warranty Expense that would be reported on Healy's 2014 income statement.

(e) Healy follows a policy of filing its HST return on December 31 each year and either sending a cheque or request-ing a refund on this date. Assuming there are no other HST transactions during the year, will Healy be sending a cheque or requesting a refund on December 31, 2014? What will be the amount of the cheque paid or refund claimed?

(f) From the perspective of a financial statement user, comment on Healy's assumption that revenue related to the warranty agreements is earned evenly over the three-year contract term.

P13-5 Sultanaly Company Limited pays its office employees each week. A partial list follows of employees and their payroll data for August. Because August is the vacation period, vacation pay is also listed.

Employee	Weekly Pay	Vacation Pay to Be Received in August
Mark Olly	$ 450	$ 900
Bill Ganton	110	220
Laurie Evans	250	
Louise Bérubé	1,250	
Jeff Huziak	480	2,500

Assume that the income tax withheld is 10% of wages and that union dues withheld are 1% of wages. Vacations are taken the second and third weeks of August by Olly, Ganton, and Bérubé. The Employment Insurance rate is 1.83% for employees and 1.4 times that for employers. The CPP rate is 4.95% each for employee and employer.

Instructions

(a) Make the journal entries that are necessary for each of the four August payrolls. The entries for the payroll and for the company's payroll tax are made separately.

(b) Make the entry to record the monthly payment of accrued payroll liabilities.

(c) Prepare the entry to accrue the 4% vacation entitlement that was earned by employees in August. (No entitlement is earned on vacation pay.)

P13-6 The following is a payroll sheet for Bayview Golf Corporation for the month of September 2014. The Employment Insurance rate is 1.83% and the maximum annual deduction per employee is $839.97. The employer's obligation for Employment Insurance is 1.4 times the amount of the employee deduction. Assume a 10% income tax rate for all employees, and a 4.95% CPP premium charged to both the employee and employer, up to an annual maxi-mum of $2,306.70 per employee. Union dues are 1% of earnings.

Name	Earnings to Aug. 31	September Earnings	Income Tax Withholding	CPP	EI	Union Dues
L. Meloche	$ 6,800	$ 800				
P. Groot	6,300	700				
D. Beauchamp	7,600	1,100				
C. Regier	13,600	1,900				

Instructions

(a) Complete the payroll sheet and make the necessary entry to record the payment of the payroll.

(b) Make the entry to record the employer's payroll tax expense.

(c) Make the entry to record the payment of the payroll liabilities. Assume that the company pays all payroll liabilities at the end of each month.

(d) What is the total expense that the company will report in September 2014 relative to employee compensation?

P13-7 Huang Inc. has a contract with its president, Ms. Shen, to pay her a bonus during each of the years 2014, 2015, and 2016. Assume a corporate income tax rate of 30% during the three years. The profit before deductions for bonus and income tax was $250,000 in 2014, $308,000 in 2015, and $350,000 in 2016. The president's bonus of 12% is deductible for tax purposes in each year and is to be calculated as follows:

1. In 2014, the bonus is to be based on profit before deductions for bonus and income tax.

2. In 2015, the bonus is to be based on profit after deduction of bonus but before deduction of income tax.

3. In 2016, the bonus is to be based on profit before deduction of bonus but after deduction of income tax.

Instructions

Calculate the amounts of the bonus and the income tax for each of the three years.

P13-8 In preparing Sahoto Corporation's December 31, 2014 financial statements under ASPE, the vice-president, finance, is trying to determine the proper accounting treatment for each of the following situations.

1. As a result of uninsured accidents during the year, personal injury suits for $350,000 and $60,000 have been filed against the company. It is the judgement of Sahoto's lawyers that an unfavourable outcome is unlikely in the $60,000 case but that an unfavourable verdict for approximately $225,000 is likely in the $350,000 case.

2. In early 2014, Sahoto received notice from the provincial environment ministry that a site the company had been using to dispose of waste was considered toxic, and that Sahoto would be held responsible for its cleanup under provincial legislation. The vice-president, finance, discussed the situation over coffee with the vice-president, engineering. The engineer stated that it would take up to three years to determine the best way to remediate the site and that the cost would be considerable, perhaps as much as $500,000 to $2 million or more. The engineering vice-president advocates recognizing at least the minimum estimate of $500,000 in the current year's financial statements. The financial vice-president advocates just disclosing the situation and the inability to estimate the cost in a note to the financial statements.

3. Sahoto Corporation has a foreign division that has a net carrying amount of $5,725,000 and an estimated fair value of $8.7 million. The foreign government has told Sahoto that it intends to expropriate the assets and business of all foreign investors. Based on settlements that other firms have received from this same country, Sahoto expects to receive 40% of the fair value of its properties as compensation.

4. Sahoto's chemical products division consists of five plants and is uninsurable because of the special risk of injury to employees and losses due to fire and explosion. The year 2014 is considered one of the safest in the division's history because there were no losses due to injury or casualty. Having suffered an average of three casualties a year during the rest of the past decade (ranging from $60,000 to $700,000), management is certain that next year the company will not be so fortunate.

Instructions

(a) Prepare the journal entries that should be recorded as at December 31, 2014, to recognize each of the situations above.

(b) Indicate what should be reported relative to each situation in the financial statements and accompanying notes. Explain why.

(c) Are there any ethical issues involved in accounting for contingencies?

P13-9 Ramirez Inc., a publishing company, is preparing its December 31, 2014 financial statements and must determine the proper accounting treatment for the following situations. The company has retained your firm to help with this task.

1. Ramirez sells subscriptions to several magazines for a one-year, two-year, or three-year period. Cash receipts from subscribers are credited to Unearned Subscriptions Revenue, and this account had a balance of $2.3 million at December 31, 2014. Outstanding subscriptions at December 31, 2014, expire as follows:

During 2015	$600,000
During 2016	500,000
During 2017	800,000

2. On January 2, 2014, Ramirez discontinued collision, fire, and theft coverage on its delivery vehicles and became self-insured for these risks. Actual losses of $50,000 during 2014 were charged to delivery expense. The 2013 premium for the discontinued coverage amounted to $80,000 and the controller wants to set up a reserve for self-insurance by a debit to delivery expense of $30,000 and a credit to the reserve for self-insurance of $30,000.

3. A suit for breach of contract seeking damages of $1 million was filed by an author against Ramirez on July 1, 2014. The company's legal counsel believes that an unfavourable outcome is likely. A reasonable estimate of the court's award to the plaintiff is between $300,000 and $700,000. No amount within this range is a better estimate of potential damages than any other amount.

4. Ramirez's main supplier, Bartlett Ltd., has been experiencing liquidity problems over the last three quarters. In order for Bartlett's bank to continue to extend credit, Bartlett has asked Ramirez to guarantee its indebtedness. The bank loan stands at $500,000 at December 31, 2014, but the guarantee extends to the full credit facility of $900,000.

5. Ramirez's landlord has informed the company that its warehouse lease will not be renewed when it expires in six months' time. Ramirez entered into a $2-million contract on December 15, 2014, with Complete Construction Company Ltd., committing the company to building an office and warehouse facility.

6. During December 2014, a competitor company filed suit against Ramirez for industrial espionage, claiming $1.5 million in damages. In the opinion of management and company counsel, it is reasonably possible that damages

Ethics

will be awarded to the plaintiff. However, the amount of potential damages awarded to the plaintiff cannot be reasonably estimated.

Instructions

(a) For each of the above situations, provide the journal entry that should be recorded as at December 31, 2014, under ASPE, or explain why an entry should not be recorded. For each situation, identify what disclosures are required, if any.

(b) Would your answer to any of the above situations change if Ramirez followed current IFRS standards?

P13-10 Brooks Corporation sells portable computer equipment with a two-year warranty contract that requires the corporation to replace defective parts and provide the necessary repair labour. During 2014, the corporation sells for cash 400 computers at a unit price of $2,500. Based on experience, the two-year warranty costs are estimated to be $155 for parts and $185 for labour per unit. (For simplicity, assume that all sales occurred on December 31, 2014.) The warranty is not sold separately from the equipment, and no portion of the sales price is allocated to warranty sales. Brooks follows ASPE.

Instructions

Answer parts (a) to (d) based on the information above.

(a) Record the 2014 journal entries, assuming the cash basis is used to account for the warranties.

(b) Record the 2014 journal entries, assuming the accrual basis expense approach is used to account for the warranties.

(c) What liability relative to these transactions would appear on the December 31, 2014 balance sheet and how would it be classified if the cash basis is used?

(d) What liability relative to these transactions would appear on the December 31, 2014 balance sheet and how would it be classified if the accrual basis expense approach is used?

Answer parts (e) to (h) assuming that in 2015 the actual warranty costs incurred by Brooks Corporation were $21,400 for parts and $39,900 for labour.

(e) Record the necessary entries in 2015, applying the cash basis.

(f) Record the necessary entries in 2015, applying the accrual basis expense approach.

(g) Which method of accounting for warranties would you recommend to the company? Why?

(h) Assume that the warranty costs incurred by Brooks Corporation in 2016 were substantially higher than estimated. How would the company deal with the discrepancy between the estimated warranty liability and the actual warranty expense?

Digging
Deeper

P13-11 Smythe Corporation sells televisions at an average price of $850 and they come with a standard one-year warranty. The company also offers each customer a separate three-year extended warranty contract for $90 that requires the company to perform periodic services and replace defective parts. The extended warranty begins one year after the purchase date. During 2014, the company sold 300 televisions and 270 extended warranty contracts for cash. Company records indicate that warranty costs in the first year after purchase average $25 per set: $15 for parts and $10 for labour. Smythe estimates the average three-year extended warranty costs as $20 for parts and $40 for labour. Assume that all sales occurred on December 31, 2014, and that all warranty costs are expected to be incurred evenly over the warranty period. Smythe uses the expense approach for the one-year warranty and the revenue approach for the extended warranty contracts.

Instructions

Answer parts (a) and (b) based on the information above.

(a) Record any necessary journal entries in 2014.

(b) What liabilities relative to these transactions would appear on the December 31, 2014 statement of financial position and how would they be classified?

Answer parts (c) and (d) assuming that in 2015 Smythe Corporation incurred actual costs relative to 2014 television warranty sales of $4,410 for parts and $2,940 for labour.

(c) Record any necessary journal entries in 2015 relative to the 2014 television warranties.

(d) What amounts relative to the 2014 television warranties would appear on the December 31, 2015 statement of financial position and how would they be classified?

Answer parts (e) and (f) assuming that in 2016 Smythe Corporation incurred the following costs relative to the extended warranties sold in 2014: $2,000 for parts and $3,000 for labour.

(e) Record any necessary journal entries in 2016 relative to the 2014 television warranties.

(f) What amounts relative to the 2014 television warranties would appear on the December 31, 2016 statement of financial position and how would they be classified?

P13-12 Renew Energy Ltd. (REL) manufactures and sells directly to customers a special long-lasting rechargeable battery for use in digital electronic equipment. Each battery sold comes with a guarantee that will replace free of charge any battery that is found to be defective within six months from the end of the month in which the battery was sold. On June 30, 2014, the Estimated Liability Under Battery Warranty account had a balance of $45,000, but by December 31, 2014, this amount had been reduced to $5,000 by charges for batteries returned.

REL has been in business for many years and has consistently experienced an 8% return rate. However, effective October 1, 2014, because of a change in the manufacturing process, the rate increased to 10%. Each battery is stamped with a date at the time of sale so that Bartlett has developed information on the likely pattern of returns during the six-month period, starting with the month following the sale. (Assume no batteries are returned in the month of sale.)

Month Following Sale	% of Total Returns Expected in the Month
1st	20%
2nd	30%
3rd	20%
4th	10%
5th	10%
6th	10%
	100%

For example, for January sales, 20% of the returns are expected in February, 30% in March, and so on. Sales of these batteries for the second half of 2014 were:

Month	Sales Amount
July	$1,800,000
August	1,650,000
September	2,050,000
October	1,425,000
November	1,000,000
December	900,000

REL's warranty also covers the payment of the freight cost on defective batteries returned and on new batteries sent as replacements. This freight cost is 10% of the sales price of the batteries returned. The manufacturing cost of a battery is roughly 60% of its sales price, and the salvage value of the returned batteries averages 14% of the sales price. Assume that REL follows IFRS and that it uses the expense approach to account for warranties.

Instructions

(a) Calculate the warranty expense that will be reported for the July 1 to December 31, 2014 period.

(b) Calculate the amount of the provision that you would expect in the Estimated Liability Under Battery Warranty account as at December 31, 2014, based on the above likely pattern of returns.

P13-13 To increase the sales of its Sugar Kids breakfast cereal, Kwiecien Corporation places one coupon in each cereal box. Five coupons are redeemable for a premium consisting of a child's hand puppet. In 2014, the company purchases 40,000 puppets at $1.50 each and sells 480,000 boxes of Sugar Kids at $3.75 a box. Kwiecien estimates that $0.20 of the sale price relates to the hand puppet to be awarded. From its experience with other similar premium offers, the company estimates that 40% of the coupons issued will be mailed back for redemption. During 2014, 115,000 coupons are presented for redemption.

Instructions

(a) Prepare the journal entries that should be recorded in 2014 relative to the premium plan, assuming that the company follows a policy of charging the cost of coupons to expense as they are redeemed and adjusting the liability account at year end.

(b) Prepare the journal entries that should be recorded in 2014 relative to the premium plan, assuming that the company follows a policy of charging the full estimated cost of the premium plan to expense when the sales are recognized.

(c) How would the accounts resulting from the entries in parts (a) and (b) above be presented on the 2014 financial statements?

(d) Prepare the journal entries that should be recorded in 2014 relative to the premium plan, assuming that the company follows IFRS and accounts for its promotional programs in accordance with the revenue approach and IFRIC 13.

(e) How would the accounts resulting from the entries in part (d) above be presented on the 2014 financial statements?

(f) Compare your answer to part (c) with your answer to part (e). Which approach to accounting for premiums would you recommend to the company? Why?

Digging Deeper

P13-14 The Hwang Candy Corporation offers a CD as a premium for every five chocolate bar wrappers that customers send in along with $2.00. The chocolate bars are sold by the company to distributors for $0.30 each. The purchase price of each CD to the company is $1.80; in addition, it costs $0.50 to mail each CD. The results of the premium plan for the years 2014 and 2015 are as follows (all purchases and sales are for cash):

	2014	2015
CDs purchased	250,000	330,000
Chocolate bars sold	2,895,400	2,743,600
Wrappers redeemed	1,200,000	1,500,000
2014 wrappers expected to be redeemed in 2015	290,000	
2015 wrappers expected to be redeemed in 2016		350,000

Instructions

(a) Prepare the journal entries that should be made in 2014 and 2015 to record the transactions related to the Hwang Candy Corporation's premium plan using the expense approach.

(b) Indicate the account names, amounts, and classifications of the items related to the premium plan that would appear on the statement of financial position and the income statement at the end of 2014 and 2015.

(c) For each liability that you identified in part (b), indicate whether it is a financial liability. Explain.

P13-15 Mullen Music Limited (MML) carries a wide variety of musical instruments, sound reproduction equipment, recorded music, and sheet music. MML uses two sales promotion techniques—warranties and premiums—to attract customers.

Musical instruments and sound equipment are sold with a one-year warranty for replacement of parts and labour. The estimated warranty cost, based on experience, is 2% of sales.

A premium is offered on the recorded and sheet music. Customers receive a coupon for each dollar spent on recorded music or sheet music. Customers may exchange 200 coupons plus $20 for a CD player. MML pays $34 for each CD player and estimates that 60% of the coupons given to customers will be redeemed.

MML's total sales for 2014 were $7.2 million: $5.4 million from musical instruments and sound reproduction equipment, and $1.8 million from recorded music and sheet music. Replacement parts and labour for warranty work totalled $164,000 during 2014. A total of 6,500 CD players used in the premium program were purchased during the year and there were 1.2 million coupons redeemed in 2014.

The expense approach is used by MML to account for the warranty and premium costs for financial reporting purposes. The balances in the accounts related to warranties and premiums on January 1, 2014, were:

Inventory of premiums	$ 39,950
Estimated liability for premiums	44,800
Warranty Liability	136,000

Instructions

(a) MML is preparing its financial statements for the year ended December 31, 2014. Determine the amounts that will be shown on the 2014 financial statements for the following:

1. Warranty expense
2. Warranty Liability
3. Premium expense
4. Inventory of premiums
5. Estimated liability for premiums

(b) Assume that MML's auditor determined that both the one-year warranty and the coupons for the CD players were, in fact, revenue arrangements with multiple deliverables that should be accounted for under the revenue approach. Explain how this would change the way in which these two programs were accounted for in part (a).

(CMA adapted. Used with permission.)

P13-16 Dungannon Enterprises Ltd. sells a specialty part that is used in widescreen televisions and provides the ultimate in screen clarity. To promote sales of its product, Dungannon launched a program with some of its smaller customers. In exchange for making Dungannon their exclusive supplier, Dungannon guarantees these customers to their creditors so that Dungannon will assume the customers' long-term debt in the event of non-payment to the creditors. In addition to charging for parts, Dungannon also charges a fee to customers who take the guarantee program, and bases the fee on the time frame that the guarantee covers, which is typically three years. In the current fiscal year, these fees amounted to $30,000 for the three-year coverage period.

Six months before Dungannon's fiscal year end, one of its customers, Hutter Corp., began to experience financial difficulties and missed two months of mortgage payments. Hutter's lender then called on Dungannon to make the mortgage payments. At its fiscal year end on December 31, 2014, Dungannon had recorded a receivable of $15,000 related to the payments made by Dungannon on Hutter's behalf. Hutter owes the lender an additional $30,000 at this point. The lender is contemplating putting a lien on Hutter's assets that were pledged as collateral for the loans but the collateral involves rights on development of new state-of-the-art three-dimensional television technology that is still unproven. Dungannon follows ASPE.

Instructions

(a) Prepare all required journal entries and adjusting entries on Dungannon's books to recognize the transactions and events described above.

(b) Identify any disclosures that must be made as a result of this information and prepare the note disclosure for Dungannon for the period ended December 31, 2014.

P13-17 Hamilton Airlines is faced with two situations that need to be resolved before the financial statements for the company's year ended December 31, 2014, can be issued.

1. The airline is being sued for $4 million for an injury caused to a child as a result of alleged negligence while the child was visiting the airline maintenance hangar in March 2014. The suit was filed in July 2014. Hamilton's lawyer states that it is likely that the airline will lose the suit and be found liable for a judgement costing anywhere from $400,000 to $2 million. However, the lawyer states that the most probable judgement is $800,000.

2. On November 24, 2014, 26 passengers on Flight No. 901 were injured upon landing when the plane skidded off the runway. On January 11, 2015, personal injury suits for damages totalling $5 million were filed against the airline by 18 injured passengers. The airline carries no insurance. Legal counsel has studied each suit and advised that it can reasonably expect to pay 60% of the damages claimed.

Instructions

(a) Prepare any disclosures and journal entries for the airline required by (1) ASPE, and (2) IFRS in the preparation of the December 31, 2014 financial statements.

(b) Ignoring the 2014 accidents, what liability due to the risk of loss from lack of insurance coverage should Hamilton Airlines record or disclose? During the past decade, the company has experienced at least one accident per year and incurred average damages of $3.2 million. Discuss fully.

Case

Refer to the Case Primer on the Student Website and in *WileyPLUS* to help you answer this case.

CA13-1 ABC Airlines (ABC) carried more than 11.9 million passengers to over 160 destinations in 17 countries in 2014. ABC is the descendant of several predecessor companies, including AB Air and BC Airlines. The amalgamated company was created in 1999. In the years that followed, the world air travel industry slumped and caused many airlines to go bankrupt or suffer severe financial hardship. ABC weathered the storm by going through a significant restructuring. One of the changes as a result of the restructuring was to have ABC employees take share options as part of their remuneration. This resulted in employees investing $200 million in the company. The company is privately owned.

In 2014, ABC was still suffering losses, now partly due to increased competition and falling seat prices. Losses were $187 million in 2012 and $194 million in 2013. The CEO announced a new restructuring plan that would hopefully put an end to the continuing losses. The plan focused on three areas: improved network profitability, decreased overhead costs, and decreased labour costs. For the latter, employees were asked to accept reduced wages over a four-year period. Just like most companies, ABC is now concerned with increasing market share and maintaining customer loyalty.

On the company's website, the following advertisement appears:

"Fly 5, Fly Free—Fly five times with ABC Airlines and its worldwide partners and earn a free trip. The more you fly, the more the world is within reach."

Free flights have been offered by ABC in the past through its well-publicized frequent flyer program. Under the program, customers earn points for flying with ABC and, once they accumulate enough points, they can then use them to take free flights. In the notes to its financial statements, ABC notes that the incremental costs of frequent flyer points are accrued as the entitlements to free flights are earned. The accrual is included as part of accrued liabilities.

Excerpts from the 2014 financial statements follow (in millions):

Total assets (including current assets of $456.5)	$1,866
Current liabilities	765
Long-term debt	841
Preferred shares	289
Common shares	407
Deficit	(436)
Total liabilities and equity	$1,866

Instructions

Adopt the role of company management and discuss the treatment of the "Fly 5, Fly Free" program for financial reporting purposes. The company is interested in understanding how the program would be accounted for under both IFRS and ASPE.

Integrated Cases

IC13-1 Envirocompany Limited (EL) is a pulp and paper company that has been in operation for 50 years. Its shares trade on a major stock exchange. It is located in a small town in Northern Ontario and employs thousands of people. In fact, the town exists mainly because of the jobs created by EL. Its equipment is fairly outdated and pollutes the surrounding water and air with chemicals that have been shown to be carcinogens. The old equipment is part of the reason for the company's "success" since it is all paid for and requires little maintenance. The employees tolerate the pollution because EL gives them good jobs and keeps the local economy going.

Last year, a new chairman of the board of directors was appointed to EL, Charles Champion. He first became aware of the size of the pollution problem before being appointed to the board and he felt that he would like to do something about it. He took this mission as a personal challenge. In the first year of his appointment, he commissioned several in-depth studies on how EL might reduce or eliminate the pollution. He wanted to be careful to protect himself and the other members of the board because directors were increasingly being held personally liable for the actions of companies. The company has begun cultivating an image implying that it would like to become more environmentally conscious while at the same time preserving jobs.

Most studies pointed to the old machinery and recommended that it be replaced by new state-of-the-art equipment. Cost estimates ran into the millions of dollars and the board of directors felt that the company would not be able to survive that type of expenditure. One study proved that the company would not even be in business any more, given the cost of new environmentally friendly equipment, declining demand for unrecycled newsprint, and increasing competition from abroad. That study was quickly put away on a shelf.

Recent environmental studies have shown that the pollutants were seeping into the water table and finding their way into neighbouring communities. The studies showed that there were increasing incidences of birth defects in animals and humans in the affected areas, including increases in sterility for certain aquatic and marine life. This caused several politicians to start grandstanding and calling for tighter pollution controls and steeper fines.

In the past year, there have been reports of people living downstream getting sick, apparently from the chemical pollutants from EL. One individual threatened to sue, and EL's lawyers were privately acknowledging the potential for a class action suit. EL has insurance that would cover up to $1 million in damages.

Meanwhile, the accountants were struggling with how to account for the problem in the year-end statements.

Instructions

Adopt the role of the company controller and discuss the financial reporting issues.

IC13-2 Landfill Limited (LL) is a private company that collects and disposes of household garbage. Waste is collected and trucked to local disposal sites where it is dumped and then covered with topsoil. The disposal sites are owned by LL and were financed by debt from Bank Inc. at an average interest rate of 5%.

LL has several disposal sites that will be filled with garbage and later sold as industrial land. LL estimates that the sites will take 20 years on average to fill up. Varying amounts of garbage will be dumped each year. Salvage values are not known at the time although land normally holds its value unless toxic chemicals are found.

Government regulations require that the company perform capping, closure, and post-closure activities. Capping involves covering the land with topsoil and planting vegetation. Closure activities include drainage, engineering, and demolition. Post-closure activities include maintaining the landfill once the government has given final certification.

Instructions

Adopt the role of the company controller and discuss the financial reporting issues.

They also include monitoring the ground and surface water, gas emissions, and air quality. If the land is sold, the purchaser reduces the acquisition cost by an estimate of this cost. LL must also guarantee that the land is toxin free and if it is later found to contain toxins, LL will pay for cleanup.

In the past year, one of these landfill sites was sold. However, the company recently received notification from the purchaser's lawyers that high levels of toxins had been found leaking into the water table.

Obtaining new contracts, as well as keeping old ones, depends on many factors. These include competitive bidding, the company's profile in the community, its past work performance, its financial stability, and having a history of adhering strictly to environmental standards. Financial statements are therefore relevant in the process of obtaining new contracts as they are examined by those who award them.

Instructions

Adopt the role of the company auditor and discuss the financial reporting issues. Landfill Limited is one of your new audit clients this year. The client is interested in how these issues would be accounted for under both ASPE and IFRS.

IC13-3   Candelabra Limited (CL) is a manufacturing company that is privately owned. The company's production facilities produce a significant amount of carbon dioxide, and currently the town is suing CL for polluting the surrounding area. The company is enjoying a period of significant prosperity and earnings have been steadily increasing. CL plans to double in size within the next 10 years. The production facility was financed by a 100-year bond that pays 5% interest annually. The bond includes a covenant that stipulates that the debt to equity ratio must not exceed 2:1. The debt to equity ratio is currently just below this threshold.

The government has recently introduced a system to control pollution whereby each company is allocated a certain number of "carbon credits." The carbon credits allow the company to produce a certain amount of carbon dioxide as a by-product from its production facilities. CL has been allocated a fixed number of these credits by the government at no cost. If CL produces more carbon dioxide than allowed, it will have to pay a fine. CL is pretty sure that it will exceed the amount allowed under the government-allotted carbon credits. Many companies in the surrounding area have extra carbon credits and as a result, the government has established an informal marketplace whereby companies can trade their extra credits. The value of the contracts changes depending on supply and demand.

CL has purchased several carbon credit contracts in the marketplace just in case. At the time it acquired the contracts, there was an oversupply and so CL was able to acquire them at very little cost. Currently, demand for the credits has increased significantly.

As another backup plan, CL is investigating diverting excess carbon dioxide to an underground cave that is situated on company-owned property. Currently, CL has spent a significant amount of funds to investigate the feasibility of diverting and storing the extra carbon dioxide it produces. The engineers working on the project are still not convinced of the feasibility of this type of storage on a larger scale. At present, they have started to store some excess carbon dioxide there on a test basis.

In order to fund the work on the cave, the company has issued shares. The shares are redeemable in cash at the company's option if its carbon dioxide levels (excluding any amounts that will be stored in the cave) reach a certain point. The shares are currently held by a large pension company.

Instructions

Assume the role of CL's auditors and analyze the financial reporting issues. Please note where there are differences between IFRS and ASPE.

Writing Assignments

WA13-1   You, the ethical accountant, are the new controller at ProVision Corporation. It is January 2015 and you are currently preparing the December 31, 2014 financial statements. ProVision manufactures household appliances. It is a private company and has the choice for 2014 to follow ASPE or IFRS. During your review of the accounts and discussion with the lawyer, you discover the following possible liabilities.

1. ProVision began production of a new dishwasher in June 2014, and by December 31, 2014, had sold 100,000 units to various retailers for $500 each. Each dishwasher is sold with a one-year warranty included. The company estimates that its warranty expense per dishwasher will amount to $25. By year end, the company had already paid out $1 million in warranty expenditures on 35,000 units. ProVision's records currently show a warranty expense of $1 million for 2014. Warranties similar to these are available for sale for $75. (Show both the expense approach and the revenue approach as alternatives. Assume that the revenue approach could be used by both ASPE and IFRS.)

2. ProVision's retail division rents space from Meadow Malls. ProVision pays a rental fee of $6,000 per month plus 5% on the amount of yearly retail profits that is over $500,000. ProVision's CEO, Burt Wilson, tells you that he had instructed the previous accountant to increase the estimate of bad debt expense and warranty costs in order to keep the retail division's profits at $475,000.

Ethics

3. ProVision's lawyer, Robert Dowski, informed you that ProVision has a legal obligation to dismantle and remove the equipment used to produce the dishwashers and clean up the rental premises as part of the lease agreement. The equipment, costing $10 million, was put into production on June 1, 2014, and has a useful life of 120 months. The dismantling and removal costs are estimated to be $3 million. In addition, as a result of the production process, there are clean-up costs incurred, estimated to be $5,000 per month during production, which will be totally paid (estimated in total to be $600,000) when the equipment is removed. (The appropriate discount rate to be used for determining the present value of the cash flows is 0.5% per month.)

4. ProVision is the defendant in a patent infringement lawsuit filed by Heidi Golder over ProVision's use of a hydraulic compressor in several of its products. Dowski claims that, if the suit goes against ProVision, the loss may be as much as $5 million. It is more likely than not that ProVision will have to pay some amount on settlement. Although the exact amount is not known, the lawyer has been able to assign probabilities and expected payment amounts as follows: 20% probability that the settlement will be $5 million, 35% probability that the settlement required will be $3 million, and 45% that no settlement will be required.

Instructions

(a) In the form of a memorandum to the CFO, address each of the above issues. Explain what the problem is and what choices the company has to report these liabilities under ASPE or IFRS. Prepare the journal entries that would be required under adoption of either standard. Explain any differences in the reported income under the various approaches.

(b) Identify any issues that you consider unethical and suggest what should be done.

WA13-2   Antigonish Corporation includes the following items in its liabilities at its year end, December 31, 2014:

1. Accounts payable, $420,000, due to suppliers in January 2015

2. Notes payable, $1.5 million, maturing on various dates in 2017

3. Deposits from customers on equipment ordered from Antigonish, $250,000

4. Salaries payable, $37,500, due on January 14, 2015

5. Bonds payable, $2.5 million, maturing on July 1, 2015. The company has been able to renegotiate an agreement from the bondholders to roll over this maturity date to July 1, 2018. This agreement was settled on January 21, 2015.

Instructions

In answering each of the following, note any differences between IFRS and ASPE.

(a) What are the essential characteristics that make an item a liability?

(b) What distinguishes a current liability from a long-term liability?

(c) What distinguishes a financial liability from a non-financial liability?

(d) Indicate for each of the above liabilities if it should be reported as current or non-current at the December 31, 2014 report date.

WA13-3   City Goods Limited is a sports clothing and equipment retailer, which has a chain of 10 stores across Canada. You have just been hired as the new controller for the company. You are currently meeting with the CFO to discuss some accounting-related topics that have arisen in the preparation of the company's January 31, 2015 financial statements. City Goods is a private company. The following is a summary of your notes from this meeting.

1. Customer loyalty program: In this fiscal year, the company implemented a new customer loyalty program that grants "CG points" to members based on the amount they spend in the store. The points have no expiry date and can be redeemed against future purchases in the store. The company has already determined that the fair value of each point is $0.50. During the year, 700,000 points were awarded to members, of which 80,000 were subsequently redeemed for purchases in the stores. The company anticipates that 90% of the points will be redeemed at some point in time.

2. The company entered into an agreement on April 1, 2011, to lease a retail location for five years. In December 2014, City Goods decided to close that retail location due to very poor sales. The company has not been able to sublet the premises and is not able to terminate the lease agreement. The monthly lease payment, which includes all operating costs, is $2,300 per month.

3. The company has a policy of refunding purchases by dissatisfied customers, as long as it is within two years from the date of purchase. This refund policy is not documented, but the company has made a practice of doing so in the past. During the year, the company's sales totalled $35 million. From experience, the company has determined the following probabilities for returns: there is a 25% probability that returns will represent 6% of total sales, 55% probability that they will represent 4% of total sales, and 20% probability that they will represent 2% of total sales.

During the year, there were returns on current year's sales of $1.1 million, on which refunds were made.

Instructions

For each of the issues above, explain the situation and the appropriate accounting treatment under ASPE and IFRS. Show any required journal entries. Where necessary, you can use a discount rate of 0.5% per month.

WA13-4 Conduit Corporation has 45 current employees: 5 managers and 40 non-managers. The average wage paid is $250 per day for non-managers. The company has just finished negotiating a new employee contract with the non-managers that would see this increase by 3% effective January 1, 2015. The company's fiscal year end is December 31, 2014. You are the controller for Conduit and are completing the year-end adjusting journal entries. The company has the following employee benefit plans.

1. Non-manager employees are entitled to two sick leave days per month. If any days are not taken, they may accumulate and be taken as vacation or paid in cash. The sick days may be carried forward to the end of the next year. At the end of the year, there were 60 accumulated sick leave days that had not yet been taken.

2. Parental leave: Any employee is entitled to one year's parental leave. The company will pay the amount to top up the employee's annual salary at the time the leave is taken. The company will pay the amount to top up the unemployment benefits received to make up the employee's annual salary at the time the leave is taken. Currently, there is one employee on parental leave, who started her maternity leave on December 15, 2014. It is expected that the top-up required will be $1,000 per month for 12 months and the employee was paid $500 on December 31, 2014. There is another employee who is trying to adopt a child and has also said that he will want paternity leave at the time the adoption occurs. The top-up is also estimated to be $1,000 per month for this employee.

3. A profit-sharing plan provides for employees to receive a bonus of 3% of net profit before taxes for all employees who worked for the company during the year. The net profit before taxes is estimated to be $2 million. The bonus is allocated 30% to the five managers and 70% to the remaining employees. However, the bonus is not paid until October 31 of the following year, and only to employees who remain with the company. The company expects a 5% turnover by October 31, 2015, for the non-manager group.

4. The company pays on average three weeks' vacation pay, even though Conduit's legal obligation is only for two weeks. This vacation pay accumulates and can be carried over for up to one year. However, if the employee leaves before the vacation is taken, then they are only legally entitled to the two-week rate. At the end of the year, there were 10 non-manager employees who had only taken one week of their annual entitlement during 2014. There is a probability of 15% that one of these employees will leave before the full vacation accrual is taken.

5. The company is being sued by a former employee. The non-manager employee contends that not enough severance was paid when he was let go in June 2014. The ex-employee's lawyers are asking for a severance payment of two weeks' pay for each year worked, which in this case was 25 years. The company agreed to pay the employee severance of $30,000 when he was asked to leave the company. This $30,000 has already been accrued in the accounting records. The case is still being disputed and will go to arbitration early in March 2015. Conduit's lawyers believe that the probabilities of settlements for additional amounts (over and above the $30,000) are as follows: 25% probability of settling at $20,000, 60% probability of settling at $28,000, and 15% probability of settling at $30,000.

Instructions

You are the controller for Conduit and are completing the year-end adjusting journal entries. Discuss each of the above issues and determine the journal entries that would be required under IFRS and ASPE. Also determine whether the benefits are accumulating or non-accumulating and vesting or not vesting.

WA13-5

Instructions

Write a brief essay highlighting the differences between IFRS and ASPE noted in this chapter, discussing the conceptual justification for each.

RESEARCH AND FINANCIAL ANALYSIS

RA13-1 Shoppers Drug Mart Limited

Real World Emphasis

Shoppers Drug Mart Limited's 2011 annual financial statements can be found at the end of this volume. The company is Canada's largest drug store chain.

Instructions

Review the consolidated statements of financial position and notes to the financial statements of Shoppers Drug Mart Limited and answer the following questions.

(a) What makes up the current liabilities reported at December 31, 2011? Be as specific as possible.

(b) What is the nature of the current liability Provisions?

(c) Calculate Shoppers' current ratio and quick ratio for December 31, 2011, and the two preceding fiscal periods. Comment on the company's liquidity.

RA13-2 Canadian Tire Corporation, Limited

Real World Emphasis

The 2011 financial statements and 10-year financial review of Canadian Tire Corporation, Limited can be found at www.sedar.com.

Instructions

(a) What makes up Canadian Tire's current liabilities? Suggest at least five different types of liabilities that are likely included in Trade and Other Payables. What is included in Deposits?

(b) What were Canadian Tire's working capital, acid-test ratio, and current ratio for the two most recent years of data that are provided? How do these results compare with the measures for five years ago? Comment on the company's current liquidity in general, and compared with its liquidity five years ago. What role does the inventory turnover have in assessing liquidity in general, and for Canadian Tire specifically? What is in the accounts receivable and what role does it play in assessing liquidity for Canadian Tire? Can a turnover ratio be calculated for these accounts receivable?

(c) What is the current portion of long-term debt? Explain clearly what makes up this amount. If the company does not borrow any additional long-term funds during 2012, how much would you expect to see on the 2012 balance sheet as the current portion of long-term debt? Explain clearly what would make up this amount. Are there any concerns arising from this amount?

(d) What types of commitments and contingencies has Canadian Tire reported in its financial statements? Identify which items are commitments and which are contingencies. What is management's reaction to the contingencies?

(e) What covenants does the company have to maintain under its existing debt agreements? Was it in compliance at the year end? (Hint: See the Capital Management Disclosures note.)

RA13-3 Deutsche Lufthansa AG

Real World Emphasis

The financial statements of **Deutsche Lufthansa AG** for the year ended December 31, 2011, are available on the www.lufthansa.com website.

Instructions

(a) What is included in the current liabilities for Lufthansa and how have the percentages of each item to total current liabilities changed from 2010 to 2011?

(b) What specific items are included in Other Provisions, Trade Payables and Other Financial Liabilities, and Advanced Payments Received, Deferred Income, and Other Non-Financial Liabilities? What is included in Liabilities from Unused Flight Documents?

(c) What types of employee benefit liabilities are included in "Other Provisions"? How does the company estimate environmental obligations?

(d) What changes have occurred in Other Provisions between December 31, 2010, and December 31, 2011? Prepare a reconciliation of the opening and closing balance for 2011.

(e) How does the company currently account for the bonus miles program, Lufthansa's customer loyalty program? What is the amount in liabilities that represents this obligation? How many miles have been accumulated? (See Note 2 of the 2011 financial statements.)

(f) What contingencies does the company have? Have any of these been recognized?

(g) What makes up the current portion of borrowings for Lufthansa's most recently reported fiscal year end? Be specific.

RA13-4 Research Topics

There are many interesting company programs and circumstances that relate to the definition, recognition, and measurement of liabilities. Examples include customer loyalty programs, retail gift cards, corporate restructuring obligations, air miles programs, product liability lawsuits, liability accruals on interim financial statements, environmental liabilities, onerous contracts, and many employee benefit programs.

Instructions

Choose one of the programs or circumstances listed above. Research your choice using international and Canadian sources, and prepare a one-page summary of the liability recognition and measurement issues that are involved. If possible, identify any accounting standards that may help resolve the issues.

ENDNOTES

1 The underlying materials are the 2005 Exposure Draft of Proposed Amendments to IAS 37 *Provisions, Contingent Liabilities and Contingent Assets*, the related January 2010 Exposure Draft *Measurement of Liabilities in IAS 37* and the later decision of the IASB to pause the project until it completes its ongoing deliberations about its work plan.

2 *CICA Handbook—Accounting*, Part II, Section 1000.29 and IFRS Conceptual Framework 4.15–4.19.

3 This continues to be an issue. See IASB Staff Paper, *Summary of Decisions Reached Since Publishing Exposure Draft: Liabilities—Amendments to IAS 37*, September 30, 2009, p. 5.

4 IAS 32 *Financial Instruments: Presentation*, para. 11. Copyright © 2012 IFRS Foundation. All rights reserved. Reproduced by Wiley Canada with the permission of the IFRS Foundation ®. No permission granted to third parties to reproduce or distribute.

5 At the intermediate-level study of accounting, the only financial liabilities discussed that are held for trading purposes and later accounted for at fair value are derivatives. These financial liabilities are discussed in Chapter 16.

6 The standard also addresses the issue of possible reimbursements that apply when an entity settles a provision. In this case, a reimbursement must be virtually certain of being received, so there may be timing differences between when a non-financial liability is recognized and when the corresponding recovery is recognized.

7 IAS 1 *Presentation of Financial Statements*, para. 69. The FASB and IASB have made a tentative decision in their joint Financial Statement Presentation project (December 2009) that the current (short-term) and non-current (long-term) classifications should be based only on a fixed period of one year. In June 2010, the IASB decided to do more outreach before finalizing and publishing a revised exposure draft on financial statement presentation. In July 2010, a "Staff Draft" of an exposure draft was published suggesting that the terminology "current" would be replaced by "short-term" and would be based on a fixed period of one year from the reporting date.

8 *CICA Handbook—Accounting*, Part II, Section 1510.08 to 1510.11.

9 As explained in Chapter 7, 2/10, n/30 means there is a 2% discount if the invoice is paid within 10 days with the full amount due in 30 days; and 1/10, E.O.M. net 30 means that there is a 1% discount if the invoice is paid before the 10th of the following month with full payment due by the 30th of the following month.

10 Alternatively, the note payable could have been recorded at its face value of $100,000, with the $3,846 difference between the cash received and the face value debited to Discount on Notes Payable. Discount on Notes Payable is a contra account to Notes Payable and therefore is subtracted from Notes Payable on the balance sheet.

11 *CICA Handbook—Accounting*, Part II, Section 1510.14.

12 Refinancing a short-term obligation on a long-term basis means either replacing it with a long-term obligation or with equity securities or renewing, extending, or replacing it with short-term obligations for an uninterrupted period that is more than one year from the date of the company's balance sheet.

13 The rate of provincial sales tax (PST) varies from province to province. When this text went to print, Alberta and the territories had no sales tax, while Ontario's rate was 8%, Manitoba's and British Columbia's was 7%, and Saskatchewan charged 5%. The tax is usually applied to the sale amount, although in Quebec (7.5%) and Prince Edward Island (10%), it is applied to the selling price plus the GST, increasing the effective provincial rate. As discussed below, in some provinces, such as Ontario and Nova Scotia, the PST and GST have been combined into a harmonized sales tax (HST) and PEI's will be combined in 2013.

14 In Ontario, New Brunswick, Newfoundland and Labrador, and Nova Scotia, the provincial retail sales tax has been combined with the federal Goods and Services Tax (5%) to form the HST. The 13% HST (15% in Nova Scotia) is administered for the most part by the Canada Revenue Agency and is accounted for on the same basis as the GST for the other provinces and territories. British Columbia moved to apply a single HST (12%) to replace its existing PST and the federal GST in 2010, but the decision was reversed in a sales tax referendum in 2011. Reinstatement of PST and GST in British Columbia was scheduled for 2013. In Quebec, both the Quebec Sales Tax and the GST are administered by the province and both taxes are applied as value-added taxes, similar to the GST.

15 One exception is in the province of Quebec. The Quebec Sales Tax and the GST are both administered by the province, where all amounts paid are recoverable by the entity through a system of input tax refunds, similar to the input tax credits for the GST.

16 The Quebec rates are somewhat lower than in the rest of Canada because Quebec separately provides parental benefits under a different plan.

17 IAS 19.16 *Employee Benefits* specifies that the "expected cost of accumulating paid absences" should be measured as "the additional amount that the entity expects to pay as a result of the unused entitlement that has accumulated at the end of the reporting period." ASPE does not specifically address this issue.

18 In Canada, statutory parental leave comes under the Employment Insurance program. Many companies, however, offer additional paid parental leave benefits to their employees above the regulated absence from the workplace, usually once they are considered permanent employees.

19 Longer-term employee benefit obligations associated with compensated absences, including post-retirement benefits, are the subject of Chapter 19.

20 ASPE recognizes this type of liability only when a reasonable estimate can be made of the amount.

21 *CICA Handbook–Accounting*, Part II, Section 3110.09 (*Asset Retirement Obligations*) and IAS 37.36 (*Provisions, Contingent Liabilities and Contingent Assets*). Copyright © 2012 IFRS Foundation. All rights reserved. Reproduced by Wiley Canada with the permission of the IFRS Foundation ®. No permission granted to third parties to reproduce or distribute.

22 *CICA Handbook–Accounting*, Part II, Section 3110 *Asset Retirement Obligations*, paras. 19–21.

23 To the extent that the estimates are not exact, future income will be affected by the difference between the estimated expense/liability and the actual costs incurred. These differences are usually minor.

24 For this example, the authors are assuming the result is the same under both methods. These measurements are explained in Chapter 2. In summary, IFRS requires that all possible outcomes be weighted by the probability of their occurrence, and that the sum of these weighted amounts is the expected value to be used as the cost estimate. ASPE does not dictate any particular method, so the outcome that is most probable could be chosen as the cost estimate.

25 Based on research by Colloquy, a service provider for the global loyalty-marketing industry, as reported in *CAmagazine*, November 2009, p. 9.

26 IFRIC 13, paragraphs 5 to 8 and *CICA Handbook–Accounting*, Part II, Section 3400.11.

27 *CICA Handbook–Accounting*, Part II, Section 3290.05.

28 Loss contingencies that result in the incurrence of a liability (under ASPE) are the most relevant ones for the discussion in this chapter. IFRS defines a "provision" as "a liability of uncertain timing or amount." Provisions under IFRS capture items, such as lawsuits, that are considered loss contingencies under ASPE. In short, the terminology is different between ASPE and current IFRS, but the underlying accounting decisions of whether to accrue or disclose items such as lawsuits are quite similar.

29 The CICA's *Financial Reporting in Canada, 2008 Edition* reports that the four most common types of contingent losses disclosed by its sample of 200 Canadian companies were lawsuits, environmental matters, contingent consideration, and possible tax reassessments.

30 For some companies, litigation presents significant costs in employee time and legal fees, even if the outcomes are positive. For example, in 2003, giant **Walmart Stores Inc.** reported that it was the target of 6,649 active lawsuits of all sorts.

31 IASB, IAS 39.9. This chapter does not discuss the revenue recognition issues for insurance contracts.

32 *CICA Handbook–Accounting*, Part II, Disclosure of Guarantees, AcG-14.

33 For further details, see IAS 37 and IAS 39.47.

34 *CICA Handbook–Accounting*, Part II, Contractual Obligations, Section 3280.

When Long-Term Debt Is Good Business

IN THE RAILWAY INDUSTRY, long-term debt financing is crucial as companies typically do not have enough free cash flow for huge infrastructure projects, which can cost billions of dollars and take years to build and pay off. Railroads generally use whatever combination of borrowing and issuing equity that would result in the debt to equity ratio that they and the markets are most comfortable with. The industry's ideal rate of debt to equity is about 1:1, says Walter Spracklin, an analyst covering Canadian transportation companies for investment firm RBC Capital Markets. Put another way, the railway industry's target is a 50% debt to total capitalization ratio. (Capitalization is debt plus equity.)

For any company, the first source of funding for large-scale projects is internally generated free cash flow, Mr. Spracklin explains. If it doesn't have enough free cash flow to pay off the project in one to two years, a company needs outside funding.

It's preferable to borrow rather than issue equity in the form of more shares, Mr. Spracklin says. Equity costs more than debt for two reasons. First, debt payments are tax-deductible, whereas issuing equity is not. Second, debt payments are a fixed level of cost, unlike equity.

Railways in North America, once fiercely competitive and barely profitable, "transformed themselves" in the 1980s due to deregulation, Mr. Spracklin says. Before deregulation, companies were unable to charge higher rates, and a slew of mergers resulted. In 1980, there were 39 major railroads on the continent. Today, there are half a dozen, including two in Canada: Canadian National Railway Company and Canadian Pacific.

Given the current stability in the industry, why would railways want to go into long-term debt to acquire smaller companies, build new lines, or buy new rolling stock (trains)? It's because these companies owe it to themselves and their shareholders to maximize opportunities to earn a good return on investment. "If you're in an industry that generates high levels of return on invested capital because of the nature of that industry, being less competitive and able to charge higher rates, you will want to invest as much as you possibly can. If you can earn a rate of return on existing projects that is well in excess of your cost of capital, you'd want to do as many projects out there that you can possibly take on," Mr. Spracklin says.

14 | Long-Term Financial Liabilities

LEARNING OBJECTIVES

After studying this chapter, you should be able to:

1. Understand the nature of long-term debt financing arrangements.

2. Understand how long-term debt is measured and accounted for.

3. Understand when long-term debt is recognized and derecognized, including how to account for troubled debt restructurings.

4. Explain how long-term debt is presented on the statement of financial position.

5. Identify disclosure requirements.

6. Calculate and interpret key ratios related to solvency and liquidity.

7. Identify major differences in accounting standards between IFRS and ASPE, and what changes are expected in the near future.

PREVIEW OF CHAPTER 14

Long-term debt and financial liabilities continue to play an important role in our capital markets because companies and governments need large amounts of capital to finance their growth. In many cases, the most effective way to obtain capital is by issuing long-term debt. This chapter explains the accounting issues that are related to long-term debt and financial liabilities. The more basic issues regarding bonds and notes will be covered in this chapter, while the more complex instruments will be discussed in Chapter 16. As you might expect, the accounting for long-term notes payable mirrors the accounting for long-term notes receivable, which was presented in Chapter 7. Special topics such as pensions and leases will be discussed in Chapters 19 and 20.

The chapter is organized as follows:

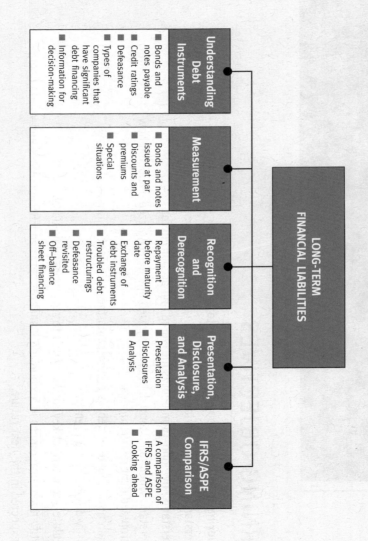

LONG-TERM FINANCIAL LIABILITIES

Understanding Debt Instruments
- Bonds and notes payable
- Credit ratings
- Defeasance
- Types of companies that have significant debt financing
- Information for decision-making

Measurement
- Bonds and notes issued at par
- Discounts and premiums
- Special situations

Recognition and Derecognition
- Repayment before maturity date
- Exchange of debt instruments
- Troubled debt restructurings
- Defeasance revisited
- Off-balance sheet financing

Presentation, Disclosure, and Analysis
- Presentation
- Disclosures
- Analysis

IFRS/ASPE Comparison
- A comparison of IFRS and ASPE
- Looking ahead

UNDERSTANDING DEBT INSTRUMENTS

Objective 1
Understand the nature of long-term debt financing arrangements.

Long-term debt consists of obligations that are not payable within a year or the operating cycle of the business, whichever is longer, and will therefore require probable sacrifices of economic benefits in the future. Bonds payable, long-term notes payable, mortgages payable, pension liabilities, and lease liabilities are examples of long-term debt or liabilities.[1]

The process that leads to incurring long-term debt is often very formal. For example, the bylaws of corporations usually require that the board of directors and the shareholders give their approval before bonds can be issued or other long-term debt arrangements can be contracted. When companies arrange for financing, the details of the arrangements are generally documented in legal contracts. The contracts determine the rights and obligations of the lender and borrower and state the terms of the arrangement including the interest rate, the due date or dates, call provisions, property pledged as security, and sinking fund requirements.

The contracts may also include **restrictive covenants** (terms or conditions) that are meant to limit activities and protect both lenders and borrowers. Examples of these types of covenants include working capital and dividend restrictions, and limitations on incurring additional debt. Covenants to restrict the amount of additional debt are common. Additional debt increases the risk of insolvency and there is a limit to the amount of risk that creditors are willing to accept even though some lenders can tolerate more risk than others.

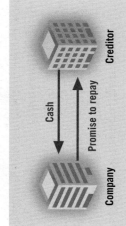

Creditor

Promise to repay

Cash

Company

Law

Bonds and Notes Payable

Bonds are the most common type of long-term debt that companies report on their statements of financial position.

Characteristics

The main purpose of bonds is to borrow for the long term when the amount of capital that is needed is too large for one lender to supply. When bonds are issued in $100, $1,000, or $10,000 denominations, a large amount of long-term indebtedness can be divided into many small investing units, which makes it possible for more than one lender to participate in the loan.

Law

A bond is created by a contract known as a **bond indenture** and represents a promise to pay both of the following: (1) a sum of money at a designated maturity date, and (2) periodic interest at a specified rate on the maturity amount (face value). Individual bonds are evidenced or supported by a paper certificate and they typically have a $1,000 face value. Bond interest payments are usually made semi-annually, but the interest rate is generally expressed as an annual rate.

An entire bond issue may be sold to an investment banker who acts as a selling agent and markets the bonds. In such arrangements, investment bankers may do one of two things. They may underwrite the entire issue by guaranteeing a certain sum to the corporation, thus taking the risk of selling the bonds for whatever price the agent can get (which is known as **firm underwriting**). They may instead sell the bond issue for a commission that will be deducted from the proceeds of the sale (which is known as **best efforts underwriting**). Alternatively, the issuing company may choose to place a bond issue privately by selling the bonds directly to a large institution—which may or may not be a financial institution—without the aid of an underwriter. This situation is known as **private placement**.

Finance

The difference between current notes payable and long-term notes payable is the maturity date. As discussed in Chapter 13, short-term notes payable are expected to be paid within a year or the operating cycle, whichever is longer. Long-term notes are similar in substance to bonds as both have fixed maturity dates and carry either a stated or implicit interest rate. However, notes do not trade as easily as bonds in the organized public securities markets, and sometimes do not trade at all.

Underlying Concept

Even though the legal form of a note is different from a bond, the economic substance is the same as they both represent liabilities. They therefore receive substantially the same treatment from an accounting perspective, depending on the features that the specific note or bond carries.

Types

The following are some of the more common types of long-term debt that are found in practice. Each type of instrument has specific contractual features that manage risk for the company and/or the holder. For instance, a secured bond is less risky and therefore often has a lower rate of interest. Any feature that gives the holder more choice or options is generally more desirable to the investor, who may be willing to pay a premium for the flexibility. Where the company has choices and options, such as an option to convert the bond into shares, this may be seen as less desirable by the investors since the choices and options are beyond their control. Each feature noted below changes the riskiness and desirability of the instruments and therefore affects the pricing of the instrument.

Registered and Bearer (Coupon) Bonds. Bonds that are issued in the owner's name are called **registered bonds.** To sell a registered bond, the current certificate has to be surrendered and a new certificate is then issued. A **bearer** or **coupon bond,** however, is not recorded in the owner's name and may therefore be transferred from one owner to another by simply delivering it to the new owner.

Secured and Unsecured Debt. **Secured debt** is backed by a pledge of some sort of collateral. **Mortgage bonds or notes** are secured by a claim on real estate. **Collateral trust bonds or notes** are secured by shares and bonds of other corporations. Debt instruments that are not backed by collateral are **unsecured;** for example, **debenture bonds.** **Junk bonds** are unsecured and also very risky, and therefore pay a high interest rate. These bonds are often used to finance leveraged buyouts.

Term, Serial, and Perpetual Bonds or Notes. Debt issues that mature on a single date are called **term bonds or notes,** and issues that mature in instalments are called **serial bonds or notes.** Serial bonds are frequently used by schools, municipalities, and provincial or federal governments. **Perpetual bonds or notes** have unusually long terms; that is, 100 years or more, or no maturity date. These are often referred to as century or millennium bonds, depending on the length of the term.

Income, Revenue, and Deep Discount Bonds. **Income bonds** pay no interest unless the issuing company is profitable. **Revenue bonds** have this name because the interest on them is paid from a specified revenue source. **Deep discount bonds or notes**—which are also referred to as **zero-interest debentures, bonds, or notes**—have very little or no interest each year and therefore are sold at a large discount that basically provides the buyer with a total interest payoff (at market rates) at maturity.

Commodity-Backed Bonds. Commodity-backed debt, also called **asset-linked debt,** is redeemable in amounts of a commodity, such as barrels of oil, tonnes of coal, or ounces of rare metal.

Callable, Convertible Bonds and Notes and Debt with Various Settlement and Other Options. **Callable bonds and notes** give the issuer the right to call and retire the debt before maturity. (These are sometimes referred to as demand loans.) **Convertible debt** allows the holder or the issuer to convert the debt into other securities such as common shares. Certain bonds or other financial instruments give the issuer the option to repay or settle the principal in either cash or common shares, or give the right to decide to the holder.

One of the more interesting innovations in the bond market is bonds whose interest or principal payments are tied to changes in the weather. The incidence of unusual and extreme weather events has been increasing, along with potential losses from these often unexpected events. Many insurers are feeling the impact of this in terms of profits. The Office of the Superintendent of Financial Institutions, the regulatory body in Canada for financial institutions including insurance companies, has signalled that it is open to allowing insurance companies to issue these weather bonds to help manage risk.

Holders of the bonds would lose their rights to some or all of the interest and/or principal payments if a "triggering event" occurred. A triggering event could be anything from an excess amount of rainfall to a hailstorm or drought. Why would an investor buy this type of security? The instrument would have to be priced to compensate for the riskiness of the instrument by offering a higher interest return or being sold at a discount.

These instruments are part of a larger group of instruments sometimes referred to as catastrophe bonds ("cat" bonds), which are used globally. The bonds are often sold in private placement offerings, meaning that they are sold to large institutional investors. Because many bonds do not repay the principal if the triggering event occurs, they are referred to as "principal-at-risk variable-rate notes."

Credit Ratings

A credit rating is assigned to each new public bond issue by independent credit rating agencies. This rating reflects a current assessment of the company's ability to pay the amounts that will be due on that specific borrowing. The rating may be changed up or down during the issue's outstanding life because the quality is constantly monitored. Note that institutional investors, such as insurance companies and pension funds, invest heavily in **investment grade securities**. Investment grade securities are high-quality securities (not speculative) and therefore only certain securities qualify. There is pressure on a company to ensure that its debt instruments are rated investment grade so that it can have greater access to capital. Credit rating analysts review many business models and industry factors when they make their determinations. Trends in costs and revenues are especially important.

Two major companies, Moody's Investors Service and Standard & Poor's Corporation, issue quality ratings on every public debt issue. The following graph shows the categories of ratings issued by Standard & Poor's, along with historical default rates on bonds receiving these ratings.[2] As expected, bonds receiving the highest quality rating of AAA have the lowest historical default rates. Bonds rated below BBB, which are considered below investment grade ("junk bonds"), experience very high default rates.

What Do the Numbers Mean?

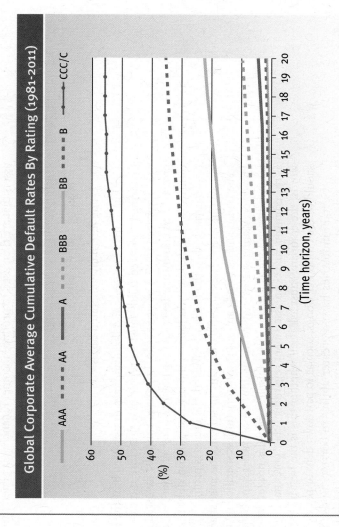

Global Corporate Average Cumulative Default Rates By Rating (1981–2011)

AAA · · · AA —— A · · · BBB —— BB · · · B ——•—— CCC/C

(%) 60 50 40 30 20 10 0

0 1 2 3 4 5 6 7 8 9 10 11 12 13 14 15 16 17 18 19 20
(Time horizon, years)

Debt ratings reflect credit quality. The market closely monitors these ratings when determining the required yield and pricing of bonds at issuance and in periods after issuance, especially if a bond's rating is upgraded or downgraded. It is not surprising, then, that bond investors and companies that issue bonds keep a close watch on debt ratings, both when bonds are issued and while the bonds are outstanding.

Defeasance

Law

Occasionally, a company may want to extinguish or pay off debt before its due date, but economic factors, such as early repayment penalties, may stop it from doing so. One option is to set aside the money in a trust or other arrangement and allow the trust to repay the original debt (principal and interest) as it becomes due according to the original

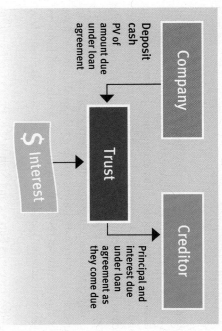

Finance %

agreement. To do this, the company must set aside sufficient funds so that the investment and any return will be enough to pay the principal and interest directly to the creditor. This is known as **defeasance**. If the creditor of the original debt agrees to look to the trust for repayment and give up its claim on the company, this is known as **legal defeasance**.

In this case, the trust becomes the debtor and the creditor looks to the trust for payment since the company no longer has a contractual obligation under the original loan agreement. A new legal agreement would be agreed to by all parties that notes that the principal and interest payments would be made by the trust.

Types of Companies that Have Significant Debt Financing

As noted in earlier chapters, the business model involves obtaining financing to invest in assets that are then used to produce income. Financing is generally obtained through three sources:

1. Borrowing

2. Issuing equity (shares)

3. Using internally generated funds

There are advantages and disadvantages to using each of the above-noted sources of financing. Borrowed funds must be repaid and therefore increase liquidity and solvency risk. However, on the positive side, borrowed funds (if invested properly) can increase profits. This is known as **leverage**: the practice of using other people's money to maximize returns to shareholders. As long as the interest paid on debt financing is less than the return earned when the funds are invested, the excess is profit.

Issuing shares does not affect liquidity or solvency because share capital does not need to be repaid and dividends are not mandatory (unless specified by the terms of the share). However, issuing shares may result in dilution of ownership. Using internally generated funds is fine as long as the company's business model is producing excess funds and as long as the company makes an assessment regarding other potential uses for the funds. In other words, the company must ask itself whether this is the best use of funds or whether they should be used for other things, such as to pay down debt or pay dividends to shareholders.

Certain industries have a greater ability to borrow funds. These include capital-intensive industries (those with significant tangible assets), such as transportation and hotel companies. Lenders are able to structure the lending agreements in such a way as to secure the loans with the underlying tangible assets. For instance, **Canadian Pacific Railway Limited**, a hotel and railway transportation company, has a long-term debt to equity ratio of 1.77:1 based on its 2011 financial statements. **Trimac Transportation Ltd**, a trucking company, has a long-term debt to equity ratio of 1.93:1 based on its 2011 financial statements.

Information for Decision-Making

Companies must manage their cash flows and borrowings to ensure that there are enough funds to continue to operate and to maximize profits and benefit from opportunities. Continued access to low-cost funds is important. For this reason, the amount of long-term debt financing is an important ratio. Too little long-term debt financing means the company is not taking advantage of leverage. Too much means the company may be overextended. This could result in higher costs of capital, and possibly the inability to access additional debt financing should the need arise.

For all these reasons, financial ratios that focus on liquidity and debt are monitored. These include ratios such as current ratio, debt to equity, debt to total assets, and times interest earned.

MEASUREMENT

Objective 2

Understand how long-term debt is measured and accounted for.

When issued, bonds and notes are valued at the present value of their future interest and principal cash flows (generally representing fair value). The initial carrying value is adjusted by any directly attributable issue costs.[3]

Bonds and Notes Issued at Par

When bonds are issued on an interest payment date at par (that is, at face value), no interest has accrued and there is no premium or discount. The accounting entry is made simply for the cash proceeds and the bonds' face value. To illustrate, assume that a company plans to issue 10-year term bonds with a par value of $800,000, dated January 1, 2014, and bearing interest at an annual rate of 10% payable semi-annually on January 1 and July 1. If it decides to issue them on January 1 at par, the entry on its books would be as follows:

Cash	800,000	
Bonds Payable		800,000

$$
\begin{array}{ccccc}
A & = & L & + & SE \\
+800{,}000 & & +800{,}000 & &
\end{array}
$$

Cash flows: ↑ 800,000 inflow

The entry to record the first semi-annual interest payment of $40,000 ($800,000 × 0.10 × ½) on July 1, 2014, would be:

Interest Expense	40,000	
Cash		40,000

$$
\begin{array}{ccccc}
A & = & L & + & SE \\
-40{,}000 & & & & -40{,}000
\end{array}
$$

Cash flows: ↓ 40,000 outflow

The entry to record accrued interest expense at December 31, 2014 (the year end), would be:

Interest Expense	40,000	
Interest Payable		40,000

$$
\begin{array}{ccccc}
A & = & L & + & SE \\
& & +40{,}000 & & -40{,}000
\end{array}
$$

Cash flows: No effect

In Chapter 7, we discussed the recognition of a $10,000, three-year note issued at face value by Scandinavian Imports to Bigelow Corp. In this transaction, the stated rate and the effective rate were both 10%. The time diagram and present value calculation in Chapter 7 for Bigelow Corp. would be the same for the issuer of the note, Scandinavian Imports, in recognizing the note payable. Because the note's present value and its face value are the same ($10,000), no premium or discount is recognized. The issuance of the note is recorded by Scandinavian Imports as follows:

Cash	10,000	
Notes Payable		10,000

$$
\begin{array}{ccccc}
A & = & L & + & SE \\
+10{,}000 & & +10{,}000 & &
\end{array}
$$

Cash flows: ↑ 10,000 inflow

Discounts and Premiums

The issuance and marketing of bonds to the public does not happen overnight. It usually takes weeks or even months. Underwriters must be arranged, the approval of the relevant securities commission must be obtained, audits and the issuance of a prospectus may be required, and certificates must be printed. Frequently, the terms in a bond indenture are decided well in advance of the bond sale. Between the time the terms are set and the time the bonds are issued, the market conditions and the issuing corporation's financial position may change significantly. Such changes affect the bonds' marketability and, thus, their selling price.

A bond's selling price is set by the supply and demand of buyers and sellers, relative risk, market conditions, and the state of the economy. The investment community values a bond at the present value of its future cash flows, which consist of (1) interest and (2) principal. The rate that is used to calculate the present value of these cash flows is the interest rate that would give an acceptable return on an investment that matches the issuer's risk characteristics.

The interest rate that is written in the terms of the bond indenture (and is ordinarily printed on the bond certificate) is known as the **stated, coupon,** or **nominal rate.** This rate, which is set by the bond issuer, is expressed as a percentage of the bond's **face value,** also called the **par value, principal amount,** or **maturity value.** If the rate that is required by the investment community (the buyers) is different from the stated rate, when buyers calculate the bond's present value, the result will be different from the bond's face value, and its purchase price will therefore also differ. The difference between the bond's face value and its present value is either a **discount** or **premium.**[4] If the bonds sell for less than their face value, they are being sold at a discount. If the bonds sell for more than their face value, they are being sold at a premium.

The interest rate that is actually earned by the bondholders is called the **effective yield** or **market rate.** If bonds sell at a **discount,** the effective yield is **higher** than the stated rate. Conversely, if bonds sell at a **premium,** the effective yield is **lower** than the stated rate. While the bond is outstanding, its price is affected by several variables, but especially by the market rate of interest. There is an inverse relationship between the market interest rate and the bond price. That is, when interest rates increase, the bond's price decreases, and vice versa.

To illustrate the calculation of the present value of a bond issue, assume that Discount Limited issues $100,000 in bonds that are due in five years and pay 9% interest annually at year end. At the time of issue, the market rate for such bonds is 11%. Illustration 14-1 shows both the interest and the principal cash flows.

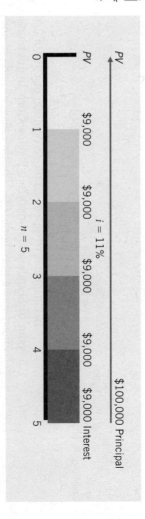

Illustration 14-1

Present Value Calculation of Bond Selling at a Discount

PV

0	1	2	3	4	5
	$9,000	$9,000	$9,000	$9,000	$9,000 Interest

$i = 11\%$

$n = 5$

$100,000 Principal

PV

The actual principal and interest cash flows are discounted at an 11% rate for five periods as follows:

Present value of the principal: $100,000 × 0.59345		$59,345
Present value of the interest payments: $9,000 × 3.69590		33,263
Present value (selling price) of the bonds		$92,608

By paying $92,608 at the date of issue, the investors will realize an effective rate or yield of 11% over the five-year term of the bonds. These bonds would therefore sell at a discount of $7,392 ($100,000 − $92,608). Note that the price at which the bonds sell is typically stated as a percentage of their face or par value. For example, we would say that the Discount Limited bonds sold for 92.6 (92.6% of par). If Discount Limited had received $102,000, we would say the bonds sold for 102 (102% of par).

When bonds sell below their face value, it means that investors are demanding a rate of interest that is higher than the stated rate. The investors are not satisfied with the stated rate because they can earn a greater rate on alternative investments of equal risk. Because they cannot change the stated rate, they therefore refuse to pay face value for the bonds and instead achieve the effective rate of interest that they require by lowering the amount invested in the bonds. The result is that the investors receive interest at the stated rate calculated on the face value, but they are essentially earning an effective rate that is higher than the stated rate because they paid less than face value for the bonds. Although notes do not trade as readily as bonds in stock markets, the same issues arise where the stated rate on the notes is different from the market rate at the date of issuance.

Most long-term debt is subsequently measured at amortized cost. Under this method, the interest is adjusted for any premium or discount over the life of the bond.

Straight-Line Method

The **straight-line method** is valued for its simplicity. It might be used by companies whose financial statements are not constrained by GAAP or by companies following ASPE that choose the straight-line method as part of their accounting policy.[5]

If the $800,000 of bonds illustrated earlier were issued on January 1, 2014, at 97 (meaning 97% of par), the issuance would be recorded as follows:

Cash ($800,000 × 0.97)	776,000	
Bonds Payable		776,000

A	=	L	+	SE
+776,000		+776,000		

Cash flows: ↑ 776,000 inflow

Because of its relationship to interest, discussed above, the discount is amortized and charged to interest expense over the period of time that the bonds are outstanding.

Under the straight-line method, the amount that is amortized each year is constant. For example, using the bond discount above of $24,000, the amount amortized to interest expense each year for 10 years is $2,400 ($24,000 ÷ 10 years) and, if amortization is recorded annually, it is recorded as follows:

Interest Expense	2,400	
Bonds Payable		2,400

A	=	L	+	SE
		+2,400		−2,400

Cash flows: No effect

At the end of the first year, 2014, as a result of the amortization entry above, the unamortized balance of the discount is $21,600 ($24,000 − $2,400).

If the bonds were dated and sold on October 1, 2014, and if the corporation's fiscal year ended on December 31, the discount amortized during 2014 would be only 3/12 of 1/10 of $24,000, or $600. Three months of accrued interest must also be recorded on December 31.

A premium on bonds payable is accounted for in much the same way as a discount on bonds payable. If the $800,000 of par value, 10-year bonds are dated and sold on January 1, 2014, at 103, the following entry is made to record the issuance:

Cash ($800,000 × 1.03)	824,000	
Bonds Payable		824,000

A	=	L	+	SE
+824,000		+824,000		

Cash flows: ↑ 824,000 inflow

At the end of 2014 and for each year that the bonds are outstanding, the entry to amortize the premium on a straight-line basis is:

Bonds Payable	2,400	
Interest Expense		2,400

A   =   L   +   SE
         −2,400   +2,400
Cash flows: No effect

Bond interest expense is increased by amortizing a discount and decreased by amortizing a premium. Amortization of a discount or premium under the effective interest method is discussed later in this chapter.

Some bonds are **callable** by the issuer after a certain date and at a stated price so that the issuing corporation may have the opportunity to reduce its debt or take advantage of lower interest rates. Whether or not the bond is callable, any premium or discount must be amortized over the bond's life up to the maturity date because it is not certain that the issuer will call the bond and redeem it early.

Bond interest payments are usually made semi-annually on dates that are specified in the bond indenture. When bonds are issued between interest payment dates, bond buyers will pay the seller the interest that has accrued from the last interest payment date to the date of issue. By paying the accrued interest, the purchasers of the bonds are, in effect, paying the bond issuer in advance for the portion of the full six-month interest payment that the purchasers are not entitled to (but will receive) since they have not held the bonds during the entire six-month period. The purchasers will receive the full six-month interest payment on the next semi-annual interest payment date.

To illustrate, assume that $800,000 of par value, 10-year bonds, dated January 1, 2014, and bearing interest at an annual rate of 10% payable semi-annually on January 1 and July 1, are issued on March 1, 2014, at par plus accrued interest. The entry on the books of the issuing corporation is:

Cash	813,333	
Bonds Payable		800,000
Interest Expense ($800,000 × 0.10 × ²/₁₂)		13,333*

*Interest Payable might be credited instead

A   =   L   +   SE
+813,333   +800,000   +13,333
Cash flows: ↑ 813,333 inflow

The purchaser is thus advancing two months of interest because on July 1, 2014, four months after the date of purchase, six months of interest will be received by the purchaser from the issuing company. The issuing company makes the following entry on July 1, 2014:

Interest Expense	40,000	
Cash		40,000

A   =   L   +   SE
−40,000   −40,000
Cash flows: ↓ 40,000 outflow

The expense account now contains a debit balance of $26,667, which represents the proper amount of interest expense: four months at 10% on $800,000.

The above illustration was simplified by having the January 1, 2014 bonds issued on March 1, 2014, at par. If, however, the 10% bonds were issued at 102, the entry on March 1 on the issuing corporation's books would be:

Cash [($800,000 × 1.02) + ($800,000 × 0.10 × 2/12)] 829,333
   Bonds Payable 816,000
   Interest Expense 13,333

A = L + SE
+829,333 +816,000 +13,333
Cash flows: ↑ 829,333 inflow

The premium would be amortized from the date of sale, March 1, 2014, not from the date of the bonds, January 1, 2014.

Effective Interest Method

A common method for amortizing a discount or premium is the **effective interest method**. This method is required under IFRS and allowed as an accounting policy choice under ASPE. Under the effective interest method, the steps are as follows:

1. Interest expense is calculated first by multiplying the **carrying value**[6] of the bonds or notes at the beginning of the period by the effective interest rate.

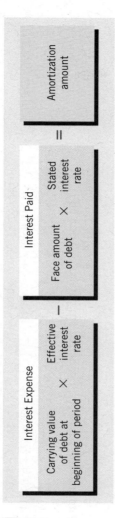

Bond Discount and Premium Amortization Calculation

Interest Expense			Interest Paid			Amortization amount
Carrying value of debt at beginning of period	×	Effective interest rate	−	Face amount of debt	×	Stated interest rate	=	

2. The discount or premium amortization is then determined by comparing the interest expense with the interest to be paid.

Illustration 14-2 shows the formula for calculating the amortization under this method. The effective interest method produces a periodic interest expense that is equal to a constant percentage of the bonds' or notes' carrying value.

Both the effective interest and straight-line methods result in the same total amount of interest expense over the term of the bonds.

Example: Bonds Issued at a Discount. To illustrate the amortization of a discount using the effective interest method, assume that Master Corporation issued $100,000 of 8% term bonds on January 1, 2014, that are due on January 1, 2019, with interest payable each July 1 and January 1. Because the investors required an effective interest rate of 10%, they paid $92,278 for the $100,000 of bonds, creating a $7,722 discount. The $7,722 discount is calculated as in Illustration 14-3.[7]

Calculation of Discount on Bonds Payable

Maturity of bonds payable		$100,000
Present value of $100,000 due in 5 years at 10%,		
interest payable semi-annually ($100,000 × 0.61391)	$61,391	
Present value of $4,000 interest payable semi-annually		
for 5 years at 10% annually ($4,000 × 7.72173)	30,887	
Proceeds from sale of bonds		92,278
Discount on bonds payable		$ 7,722

The five-year amortization schedule appears in Illustration 14-4.

Illustration 14-4

Bond Discount Amortization Schedule

SCHEDULE OF BOND DISCOUNT AMORTIZATION
Effective Interest Method–Semi-Annual Interest Payments
5-Year, 8% Bonds Sold to Yield 10%

Date	Cash Paid	Interest Expense	Discount Amortized	Carrying Amount of Bonds
1/1/14				$ 92,278
7/1/14	$ 4,000ᵃ	$ 4,614ᵇ	$ 614ᶜ	92,892ᵈ
1/1/15	4,000	4,645	645	93,537
7/1/15	4,000	4,677	677	94,214
1/1/16	4,000	4,711	711	94,925
7/1/16	4,000	4,746	746	95,671
1/1/17	4,000	4,783	783	96,454
7/1/17	4,000	4,823	823	97,277
1/1/18	4,000	4,864	864	98,141
7/1/18	4,000	4,907	907	99,048
1/1/19	4,000	4,952	952	100,000
	$40,000	$47,722	$7,722	

ᵃ $4,000 = $100,000 × 0.08 × 6/12   ᶜ $614 = $4,614 − $4,000
ᵇ $4,614 = $92,278 × 0.10 × 6/12   ᵈ $92,892 = $92,278 + $614

The entry to record the issuance of Master Corporation's bonds at a discount on January 1, 2014, is:

Cash   92,278
   Bonds Payable   92,278

Cash flows: ↑ 92,278 inflow

A   =   L   +   SE
+92,278   +92,278

The journal entry to record the first interest payment on July 1, 2014, and amortization of the discount is:

Interest Expense   4,614
   Bonds Payable   614
   Cash   4,000

Cash flows: ↓ 4,000 outflow

A   =   L   +   SE
−4,000   +614   −4,614

The journal entry to record the interest expense accrued at December 31, 2014 (the year end), and amortization of the discount is:

Interest Expense   4,645
   Interest Payable   4,000
   Bonds Payable   645

Cash flows: No effect

A   =   L   +   SE
    +4,645   −4,645

Example: Bonds Issued at Premium. If instead it had been a market where the investors were willing to accept an effective interest rate of 6% on the bond issue described above, they would have paid $108,530 or a premium of $8,530, calculated as in Illustration 14-5.

Illustration 14-5

Calculation of Premium on Bonds Payable

Maturity value of bonds payable
Present value of $100,000 due in 5 years at 6%, interest
payable semi-annually ($100,000 × 0.74409) $74,409

                                      $100,000

Illustration 14-5

Calculation of Premium on Bonds Payable (continued)

Present value of $4,000 interest payable semi-annually for 5 years at 6% annually ($4,000 × 8.53020)	34,121
Proceeds from sale of bonds	108,530
Premium on bonds payable	$ 8,530

The five-year amortization schedule appears in Illustration 14-6.

Illustration 14-6

Bond Premium Amortization Schedule

SCHEDULE OF BOND PREMIUM AMORTIZATION
Effective Interest Method–Semi-Annual Interest Payments
5-Year, 8% Bonds Sold to Yield 6%

Date	Cash Paid	Interest Expense	Premium Amortized	Carrying Amount of Bonds
1/1/14				$108,530
7/1/14	$ 4,000a	$ 3,256b	$ 744c	107,786d
1/1/15	4,000	3,234	766	107,020
7/1/15	4,000	3,211	789	106,231
1/1/16	4,000	3,187	813	105,418
7/1/16	4,000	3,162	838	104,580
1/1/17	4,000	3,137	863	103,717
7/1/17	4,000	3,112	888	102,829
1/1/18	4,000	3,085	915	101,914
7/1/18	4,000	3,057	943	100,971
1/1/19	4,000	3,029	971	100,000
	$40,000	$31,470	$8,530	

a $4,000 = $100,000 × 0.08 × 6/12
b $3,256 = $108,530 × 0.06 × 6/12
c $744 = $4,000 − $3,256
d $107,786 = $108,530 − $744

The entry to record the issuance of the Master Corporation bonds at a premium on January 1, 2014, is:

Cash	108,530	
Bonds Payable		108,530

A = L + SE
+108,530 +108,530
Cash flows: ↑ 108,530 inflow

The journal entry to record the first interest payment on July 1, 2014, and amortization of the premium is:

Interest Expense	3,256	
Bonds Payable	744	
Cash		4,000

A = L + SE
-4,000 -744 -3,256
Cash flows: ↓ 4,000 outflow

As the discount or premium should be amortized as an adjustment to interest expense over the life of the bond, it results in a **constant interest rate** when it is applied to the carrying amount of debt that is outstanding at the beginning of any specific period.

Accruing Interest. In our examples up to now, the interest payment dates and the date the financial statements were issued were the same. For example, when Master Corporation sold bonds at a premium, the two interest payment dates coincided with the financial reporting dates. However, what happens if Master wishes to report financial statements at the end of February 2014? In this case, as Illustration 14-7 shows, the premium is prorated by the appropriate number of months to arrive at the proper interest expense.

Illustration 14-7

Calculation of Interest Expense

The journal entry to record this accrual is:

Interest accrual ($4,000 × 2/6)		$1,333.33
Premium amortized ($744 × 2/6)		(248.00)
Interest expense (Jan. to Feb.)		$1,085.33

A	=	L	+	SE
		+1,085		−1,085

Cash flows: No effect

If the company prepares financial statements six months later, the same procedure is followed to amortize the premium, as Illustration 14-8 shows.

Bonds Payable		
Interest Expense	1,085	
Interest Payable		1,333

Illustration 14-8

Calculation of Premium Amortization

Premium amortized (Mar.–June) ($744 × 4/6)		$496.00
Premium amortized (July–Aug.) ($766 × 2/6)		255.33
Premium amortized (Mar.–Aug. 2014)		$751.33

The calculation is much simpler if the straight-line method is used. In the Master situation, for example, the total premium is $8,530 and this amount needs to be allocated evenly over the five-year period. The premium amortization per month is therefore $142 ($8,530 ÷ 60 months).

Special Situations

Non-Market Rates of Interest—Marketable Securities

Financial liabilities should initially be recognized at fair value, which is generally the exchange value that exists when two arm's-length parties are involved in a transaction. If a zero-interest-bearing (non-interest-bearing) **marketable** security is issued for cash only, its fair value is the cash received by the security's issuer. The implicit or **imputed interest rate** is the rate that makes the cash that is received now equal to the present value of the amounts that will be received in the future. This rate should also equal the market rate of interest. The difference between the security's face amount and the present value is a discount and is amortized to interest expense over the life of the note.

To illustrate the entries and the amortization schedule, assume that your company is the one that issued the $10,000, three-year, zero-interest-bearing note to Jeremiah Company that was illustrated in Chapter 7. Let's assume further that the note is marketable. The implicit rate that equated the total cash to be paid ($10,000 at maturity) to the present value of the future cash flows ($7,721.80 cash proceeds at the date of issuance) was 9%. Assume that the market rate of interest for a similar note would also be 9%. (The present value of $1 for three periods at 9% is $0.77218.) The time diagram that shows the one cash flow is as follows:

Finance

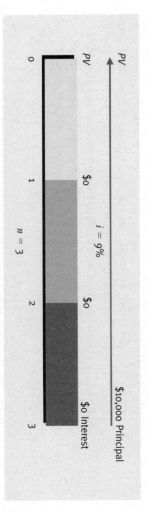

The entry to record issuance of the note would be:

| Cash | 7,722 | |
| Notes Payable | | 7,722 |

A	=	L	+	SE
+7,722		+7,722		

Cash flows: ↑ 7,722 inflow

The discount is amortized and interest expense is recognized annually. The three-year discount amortization and interest expense schedule is shown in Illustration 14-9 using the effective interest method.

Illustration 14-9

Schedule of Note Discount Amortization

SCHEDULE OF NOTE DISCOUNT AMORTIZATION
Effective Interest Method
0% Note Discounted at 9%

	Cash Paid	Interest Expense	Discount Amortized	Carrying Amount of Note
Date of issue				$ 7,721.80
End of year 1	$-0-	$ 694.96[a]	$ 694.96[b]	8,416.76[c]
End of year 2	-0-	757.51	757.51	9,174.27
End of year 3	-0-	825.73[d]	825.73	10,000.00
	$-0-	$2,278.20	$2,278.20	

[a] $7,721.80 × 0.09 = $694.96
[b] $694.96 − 0 = $694.96
[c] $7,721.80 + $694.96 = $8,416.76
[d] Adjustment to compensate for rounding

Interest expense at the end of the first year using the effective interest method is recorded as follows:

| Interest Expense ($7,722 × 9%) | 695 | |
| Notes Payable | | 695 |

A	=	L	+	SE
		+695		−695

Cash flows: No effect

The total amount of the discount, $2,278 in this case, represents the interest expense to be incurred and recognized on the note over the three years.

Non-Market Rates of Interest—Non-marketable Instruments

If the loans or notes do not trade on a market (that is, they are not securities) and the interest rate is a non-market interest rate, the situation must be analyzed carefully. The cash consideration that is given may not be equal to the fair value of the loan or note. Normally, in an arm's-length reciprocal transaction, the loan would be issued with an interest rate approximating the market rate and therefore the consideration would approximate fair value. If the loan is issued with an interest rate that is less than the market rate, this concession should be accounted for separately.

In these cases, the entity must measure the value of the loan by discounting the cash flows using the market rate of interest, which is done by considering similar loans with similar terms. Any difference between the cash consideration and the discounted amount (the fair value of the loan) would be booked to net income unless it qualified for some other asset or liability.[8]

For example, assume that a government entity issues at face value a zero-interest-bearing loan that is to be repaid over five years with no stated interest. In doing this, the government is giving an additional

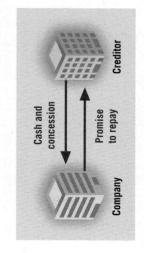

Cash and concession
Promise to repay
Creditor
Company

benefit to the company beyond the debt financing. It is forgiving the interest that the company would normally be charged. Thus, the company is getting a double benefit—the loan and a grant for the interest that would otherwise be paid. The extra benefit would be accounted for separately as a government grant.

To illustrate, assume that to help a company finance the construction of a building, the government issues a $100,000, five-year, zero-interest-bearing note at face value when the market rate of interest is 10%. To record the loan, the company records a discount of $37,908, which is the difference between the loan's $100,000 face amount and its fair value of $62,092 ($100,000 × the present value factor for five years at 10% = $100,000 × 0.62092). The rest may be booked to the related building account under government grant accounting since it relates to the construction of an asset. The issuer's journal entry is:

Cash	100,000	
Notes Payable		62,092
Buildings		37,908

A	=	L	+	SE
+62,092		+62,092		

Cash flows: ↑ 100,000 inflow

The discount is subsequently amortized to interest expense. The net value of the building (that is, net of the government grant) is depreciated, thus spreading the grant over the life of the asset.[9] In this situation, the writeoff of the discount and the amortization of the government grant are at different rates.

Notes Issued for Property, Goods, and Services

When a non-marketable debt instrument is exchanged for property, goods, or services in a bargained, arm's-length transaction, there are additional measurement issues. As with other transactions, it should be booked at fair value. But what is the fair value? If the issued debt is a marketable security, the value of the transaction would be easy to determine. If it is not, we must try to estimate the fair value. Normally, for monetary transactions, when measuring the transaction's price, we first try to measure the value of the monetary asset or liability and, if this is not possible, we then attempt to value the non-monetary assets in the transaction. In this case, the note is a monetary liability and so we would try to value this first. The note could be valued using a valuation technique such as discounting. Similar to the previous example, the cash flows from the debt instrument could be discounted using a market rate of interest for similar debt with similar terms. If this is not possible, and if the fair value of the property, goods, or services is readily determinable, this fair value of the property, goods, or services could then be used to measure the transaction.

For example, assume that Scenic Development sold land having a cash sale price of $200,000 to Health Spa, Inc. in exchange for Health Spa's five-year, $293,860, zero-interest-bearing note. The $200,000 cash sale price represents the present value of the $293,860 note discounted at 8% for five years. The 8% interest rate is the market rate for a similar loan with similar terms. If both parties were to record the transaction on the sale date at the $293,860 face amount of the note, Health Spa's Land account and Scenic's sales would be overstated by $93,860 because the $93,860 is the interest for five years at an effective rate of 8%. Interest revenue to Scenic and interest expense to Health Spa for the five-year period would also then be correspondingly understated by $93,860.

The transaction could be measured by using a valuation technique to measure the value of the debt or alternatively by using the fair value of the land ($200,000) if it is not possible to measure the debt. In this case, we know the fair value of the land and we also know that the market rate is 8%. Since the present value of the note is equal to the land value, we use $200,000. The difference between the cash sale price of $200,000 and the face amount of the note, $293,860, represents interest at an effective rate of 8% and the transaction is recorded at the exchange date as follows:

Health Spa, Inc.			Scenic Development Company		
Land	200,000		Notes Receivable	200,000	
Notes Payable		200,000	Sales Revenue		200,000

A = L + SE
+200,000 +200,000

Cash flows: No effect

A = L + SE
+200,000 +200,000

Cash flows: No effect

During the five-year life of the note, Health Spa annually amortizes a portion of the discount of $93,860 as a charge to interest expense. Scenic Development records interest revenue totalling $93,860 over the five-year period by also amortizing the discount.

If a higher interest rate were determined to be the market rate of interest, the land and selling price would be measured at a lower amount since there is an inverse relationship between the discount rate and the present value of the cash flows. This might cause us to question whether the so-called cash sales price of the land has been overstated since the vendor would want to receive consideration equal to the fair value of the land. At some point, a judgement call is required to determine which is more reliable: the imputed interest rate or the stated fair value of the asset.

Fair Value Option

Generally, long-term debt is measured at amortized cost; however, as discussed earlier in the text, there is an option to value financial instruments at fair value (referred to as the **fair value option**). Although ASPE allows the fair value option for all financial instruments, IFRS explicitly requires that the option be used only where fair value results in more relevant information. This would be the case where the use of fair value eliminates or reduces measurement and/or recognition inconsistencies or where the financial instruments are managed or performance is evaluated on a fair value basis.

One significant issue arises when the fair value option is used for measuring the entity's own debt instruments. As a general rule, fair value should always incorporate information about the riskiness of the cash flows associated with a particular instrument (including information about the entity's own liquidity and solvency). However, this gives some peculiar and counterintuitive results; that is, if the debt increases in risk, it would have a lower fair value, thus resulting in recognition of a gain for the company that issued it. Therefore, even though the company is worse off, it recognizes a gain.

IFRS 13, which deals with fair value measurement, requires that non-performance risk (which includes credit risk) be included in the fair value measurement.[10] IFRS 9 requires that subsequent changes in fair value that arise on remeasurement of the fair value of financial liabilities under the fair value option be presented in Other Comprehensive Income.[11] Under ASPE, all changes in fair value are recognized in net income where the fair value option is selected.

As an example, assume that Friction Limited has bonds outstanding in the amount of $100,000. The company has chosen to apply the fair value option in accounting for this liability. At the end of the current year, the company's credit risk has increased and therefore the fair value of its debt is $95,000. Assume that the change in fair value is due solely to the change in credit risk. Illustration 14-10 shows how the gain would be accounted for.

Significant Change

Illustration 14-10

Use of the Fair Value Option in Valuing a Long-Term Liability (IFRS versus ASPE)

	IFRS: IFRS 9 (mandatorily adoptable 2015)		ASPE and IFRS pre-2015: IAS 39	
To record the change in fair value of debt that is accounted for under the fair value option				
Bonds Payable	5,000		5,000	
Unrealized Gain or Loss				5,000
Unrealized Gain or Loss - OCI		5,000		

A = L + SE
-5,000 +5,000

Cash flows: No effect

RECOGNITION AND DERECOGNITION

Like all financial instruments, long-term debt is recognized in the financial statements when the company becomes party to the contractual provisions (when the financing deal is finalized or bonds are issued). The debt remains on the books until it is extinguished. When debt is extinguished, it is **derecognized** from the financial statements. If the instrument is held to maturity, no gain or loss is calculated. This is because any premium or discount and any issue costs will be fully amortized at the date the instrument matures. As a result, the carrying amount will be equal to the instrument's maturity (face) value. And as the maturity or face value is also equal to the instrument's market value at that time, there is no gain or loss.

From a financial reporting perspective, the **extinguishment of debt** is recorded when either of the following occurs:

1. The debtor discharges the liability by paying the creditor.

2. The debtor is legally released from primary responsibility for the liability by law or by the creditor (for example, due to cancellation or expiry).[12]

Repayment before Maturity Date

In some cases, debt is extinguished before its maturity date. The amount paid on extinguishment before maturity, including any call premium and expenses of reacquisition or early repayment, is called the **reacquisition price.** On any specified date, the bond's net carrying amount is the amount that is payable at maturity, adjusted for any unamortized premium or discount and cost of issuance. If the net carrying amount is more than the reacquisition price, the excess amount is a gain from extinguishment; conversely, if the reacquisition price exceeds the net carrying amount, the excess is a loss from extinguishment. At the time of reacquisition, the unamortized premium or discount and any costs of issue that apply to the bonds must be amortized up to the reacquisition date.

To illustrate, assume that on January 1, 2011, General Bell Corp. issued bonds with a par value of $800,000 at 97 (which is net of issue costs), due in 20 years. Eight years after the issue date, the entire issue is called at 101 and cancelled. The loss on redemption (extinguishment) is calculated as in Illustration 14-11, which uses straight-line amortization for simplicity.

Objective 3

Understand when long-term debt is recognized and derecognized including how to account for troubled debt restructurings.

Illustration 14-11

Calculation of Loss on Redemption of Bonds

Reacquisition price ($800,000 × 1.01)		$808,000
Net carrying amount of bonds redeemed:		
Face value	$800,000	
Unamortized discount ($24,000[a] × 12/20)	(14,400)	
(amortized using straight-line basis)		785,600
Loss on redemption		$ 22,400

[a]$800,000 × (1 – 0.97)]

The entry to record the reacquisition and cancellation of the bonds is:

Bonds Payable	785,600	
Loss on Redemption of Bonds	22,400	
Cash		808,000

A = L + SE
−808,000 −785,600 −22,400
Cash flows: ↓ 808,000 outflow

Exchange of Debt Instruments

The replacement of an existing issuance with a new one is sometimes called **refunding**. Generally, an exchange of debt instruments that have **substantially different terms** between a borrower and lender is viewed as an extinguishment of the old debt and the issuance of a new one.[13]

Companies may refund or replace debt to get more favourable terms. These early extinguishments would generally be bound by the initial debt agreement. (For example, there are provisions that allow early repayment.) The debtor may experience a loss and sometimes a gain depending on the prepayment options in the original agreement. If the bonds are marketable securities, the company can simply buy them back in the marketplace.

Sometimes, however, companies are forced to repay or restructure their debt due to inability to make interest and principal payments. This is sometimes referred to as troubled debt restructuring. An example of the accounting for a settlement through an exchange of debt instruments is noted in the next section.

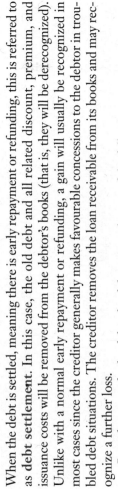

Underlying Concept

If the new debt is substantially the same as the old debt, the economic substance is that it is a continuation of the old debt, even though, legally, the old debt may have been settled.

Troubled Debt Restructurings

Law

A troubled debt restructuring occurs when, for economic or legal reasons that are related to the debtor's financial difficulties, a creditor grants a concession to the debtor that it would not offer in ordinary circumstances. This is what separates a troubled debt restructuring from an ordinary early repayment or exchange.

A troubled debt restructuring can be either one of these two basic types of transactions:

1. **Settlement** of the debt at less than its carrying amount

2. **Continuation** of the debt, but with a **modification** of its terms

Settlement of Debt

Finance

When the debt is settled, meaning there is early repayment or refunding, this is referred to as **debt settlement**. In this case, the old debt and all related discount, premium, and issuance costs will be removed from the debtor's books (that is, they will be derecognized). Unlike with a normal early repayment or refunding, a gain will usually be recognized in most cases since the creditor generally makes favourable concessions to the debtor in troubled debt situations. The creditor removes the loan receivable from its books and may recognize a further loss.

In order to settle the debt, the debtor may do one of the following:

1. Transfer non-cash assets (real estate, receivables, or other assets).

2. Issue shares.

3. Issue new debt to another creditor and use the cash to repay the existing debt.

If non-cash assets are used to settle the debt, the debtor will recognize a gain or loss on the disposal of the asset for the amount of the difference between the fair value of those assets and their carrying amount (book value). The creditor may force the debtor to transfer the asset if there is a legal charge on the asset (such as in the case of collateral or a mortgage). This is referred to as a **loan foreclosure**. The creditor takes the underlying security (the asset) as a replacement for payment of the loan.

To illustrate a transfer of assets, assume that Halifax City Bank has loaned $20 million to Union Trust. Union Trust in turn has invested these monies in residential apartment buildings, but because of low occupancy rates it cannot meet its loan obligations. Halifax City Bank agrees to accept from Union Trust a building with a fair value of $16 million in full settlement of the $20-million loan obligation. The building has a recorded value of $21 million on the books of Union Trust, net of accumulated depreciation of $5 million.

Assume that no prior allowance for doubtful accounts has been set up on the note and no impairment has been recognized on the building.[14] The entry to record this transaction on the books of Halifax City Bank (the creditor) is as follows:

Buildings	16,000,000	
Loss on Impairment	4,000,000	
Notes Receivable		20,000,000

A	=	L	+	SE
−4,000,000				−4,000,000

Cash flows: No effect

The building is recorded at its fair value, and a charge is made to the income statement to reflect the loss.[15]

The entry to record this transaction on the books of Union Trust (the debtor) is as follows:

Accumulated Depreciation—Buildings	5,000,000	
Notes Payable	20,000,000	
Loss on Sale of Buildings	5,000,000	
Buildings		26,000,000
Gain on Restructuring of Debt		4,000,000

A	=	L	+	SE
−21,000,000		−20,000,000		−1,000,000

Cash flows: No effect

Union Trust has a loss on the disposal of building in the amount of $5 million, which is the difference between the $21-million book value and the $16-million fair value. In addition, it has a gain on restructuring of debt of $4 million, which is the difference between the $20-million carrying amount of the note payable and the $16-million fair market value of the real estate.

To illustrate the granting of an equity interest (that is, shares), assume that Halifax City Bank had agreed to accept from Union Trust 320,000 of Union's common shares, with a market value of $16 million, in full settlement of the $20-million loan obligation. Assume also that the bank had previously recognized a loss on impairment of $4 million. Halifax decides to treat the investments as FV-NI. The entry to record this transaction on the books of Halifax City Bank (the creditor) is as follows:

FV-NI Investments	16,000,000	
Allowance for Doubtful Accounts	4,000,000	
Notes Receivable		20,000,000

A	=	L	+	SE
0				

Cash flows: No effect

The shares that are received by Halifax City Bank are recorded as an investment and at their fair value (equal to market value) on the date of the restructuring.

The entry to record this transaction on the books of Union Trust (the debtor) is as follows:[16]

Notes Payable	20,000,000	
Common Shares		16,000,000
Gain on Restructuring of Debt		4,000,000

A	=	L	+	SE
		−20,000,000		+20,000,000

Cash flows: No effect

In some cases, a debtor will have serious short-term cash flow problems that lead it to request one or a combination of the following modifications:

1. Reduction of the stated interest rate
2. Extension of the maturity date of the debt's face amount
3. Reduction of the debt's face amount

4. Reduction or deferral of any accrued interest

5. Change in currency

If there are substantial modifications, however, the transaction is treated like a settlement. The modifications would be considered substantial in either of these two situations:

1. The discounted present value under the new terms (discounted using the original effective interest rate) is at least 10% different from the discounted present value of the remaining cash flows under the old debt.

2. There is a change in creditor and the original debt is legally discharged.[17]

If one of these conditions is met, the transaction is considered a settlement. Otherwise, it is treated as a modification.

When the economic substance is a **settlement**, the old liability is eliminated and a new liability is assumed. The new liability is measured at the present value of the revised future cash flows discounted at the current prevailing market interest rate, as is done for the initial recording of a bond. The gain is measured as the difference between the current present value of the revised cash flows and the carrying value of the old debt.

Assume that on December 31, 2014, Manitoba National Bank enters into a debt restructuring agreement with Resorts Development Corp., which is experiencing financial difficulties. The bank restructures a $10.5-million loan receivable issued at par (interest paid up to date) by doing all of the following:

1. It reduces the principal obligation from $10.5 million to $9 million.

2. It extends the maturity date from December 31, 2014, to December 31, 2018.

3. It reduces the interest rate from 12% to 8%. (The market rate is currently 9%.)

Is this a settlement or a modification? Has a substantial modification in the debt occurred? The test to establish whether this is a settlement or not involves the cash flows. The present value of both cash flow streams is calculated as follows, using the historic rate as the discount rate for consistency and comparability:

Old debt: PV = $10,500,000 (since the debt is currently due)

New debt: PV = $9,000,000 (PVF$_{4,12\%}$) + $720,000 (PVFOA$_{4,12\%}$) (see Tables A-2 and A-4)

New debt: PV = $9,000,000 (0.63552) + $720,000 (3.03735) = $7,906,572

The new debt's value differs by more than 10% of the old debt's value, so the renegotiated debt would therefore be considered a settlement, and a gain would be recorded through the following journal entry:

Notes Payable	10,500,000	
Notes Payable		8,708,468
Gain on Restructuring of Debt		1,791,532

A	=	L	+	SE
		−1,791,532		+1,791,532

Cash flows: No effect

Because it is new debt, it would be recorded at the present value of the new cash flows at the market interest rate as follows: PVF$_{4,9\%}$ + PVFOA$_{4,9\%}$ = $9,000,000 (0.70843) + $720,000 (3.23972) = $8,708,468.

Manitoba National Bank would record any loss on the same basis as an impaired loan, as discussed earlier. That is, the recorded amount of the loan receivable would be reduced to the amount of the net cash flows receivable (but under the modified terms) discounted at the historical effective interest rate that is inherent in the loan. Because it is a restructuring, the uncollectible amount would be written off (as opposed to setting up an allowance).

Non-Substantial Modification of Terms

Where debt is exchanged but the terms of the new debt are not substantially different (modified) from the old debt, the accounting is different. The old debt is seen to continue to exist but with new terms. A new effective interest rate is imputed by equating the carrying amount of the original debt with the present value of the revised cash flows.

Looking back to our example above for Manitoba National Bank and Resorts Development Corp., if the substantial modification test was not met, the debt would remain on the books at $10.5 million and no gain or loss would be recognized. As a result, no entry would be made by Resorts Development Corp. (debtor) at the date of restructuring. The debtor would calculate a new effective interest rate, however, in order to record interest expense in future periods. In this case, the new rate is calculated by relating the pre-restructure carrying amount ($10.5 million) to the total future cash flows ($9 million + [4 × $720,000]). Using a financial calculator or spreadsheet formula, we can determine that the rate to discount the total future cash flows ($11,880,000) to the present value that is equal to the remaining balance ($10.5 million) is 3.46613%.

Based on the effective rate of 3.46613%, the schedule in Illustration 14-12 is prepared.

Illustration 14-12

Schedule Showing Reduction of Carrying Amount of Note

RESORTS DEVELOPMENT CORP. (DEBTOR)

Date	Interest Paid (8%)	Interest Expense (3.46613%)	Reduction of Carrying Amount	Carrying Amount of Note
12/31/14				$10,500,000
12/31/15	$ 720,000ᵃ	$ 363,944ᵇ	$ 356,056ᶜ	10,143,944
12/31/16	720,000	351,602	368,398	9,775,546
12/31/17	720,000	338,833	381,167	9,394,379
12/31/18	720,000	325,621	394,379	9,000,000
	$2,880,000	$1,380,000	$1,500,000	

ᵃ$720,000 = $9,000,000 × 0.08
ᵇ$363,944 = $10,500,000 × 3.46613%
ᶜ$356,056 = $720,000 − $363,944

Thus, on December 31, 2015 (the date of the first interest payment after the restructuring), the debtor makes the following entry:

December 31, 2015		
Notes Payable	356,056	
Interest Expense	363,944	
Cash		720,000

A	=	L	+	SE
−720,000		−356,056		−363,944

Cash flows: ↓ 720,000 outflow

A similar entry (except for different amounts for debits to Notes Payable and Interest Expense) is made each year until maturity. At maturity, the following entry is made:

December 31, 2018		
Notes Payable	9,000,000	
Cash		9,000,000

A	=	L	+	SE
−9,000,000		−9,000,000		

Cash flows: ↓ 9,000,000 outflow

In this case also, Manitoba National Bank would account for the restructuring as an impaired loan.

There is one last point regarding troubled debt situations. Most debt is generally measured at amortized cost. In certain situations, however, the debt may be measured at fair value under the fair value option or in certain hedging situations. If a company is having financial difficulties, its solvency risk increases and the capital markets generally penalize the company with higher cost of capital and interest rates. Where liabilities are carried at fair value, the debt must be continually remeasured. Discounting at a higher interest rate and/or incorporating lower cash flows in the estimation of fair value would mean a lower fair value, resulting in a gain on revaluation. Should gains be recognized on remeasurement of a company's own debt due to a decline in ability to pay? This question was discussed earlier under the fair value option heading. Under present GAAP, the gain would be recognized in net income. Although, if IFRS 9 is followed, the gain would be recognized in OCI.

The decision tree in Illustration 14-13 summarizes the process for deciding how to account for early retirements and modifications of debt.

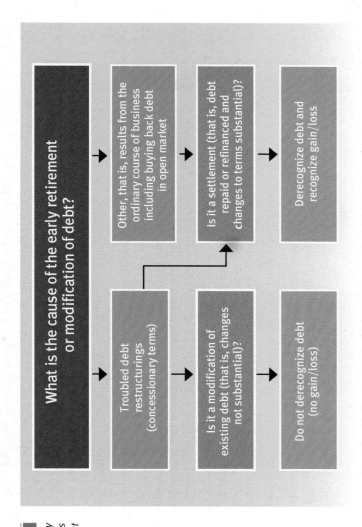

Illustration 14-13

Accounting for Early Retirements and Modifications of Debt

Note that in other than troubled debt situations, companies would generally not exchange debt because there is little economic incentive to do so. They would either buy back the debt in the open market or exercise an early prepayment option, if one existed in the original debt agreement. The creditor no longer has any claim on the company and therefore the company treats the transaction as an extinguishment and thus derecognized accounting and the debt would be derecognized.

Defeasance Revisited

Earlier in the chapter, we discussed defeasance. Let's revisit defeasance and look at the accounting. Where **legal defeasance** occurs, the debt is extinguished and the creditor looks to the trust for repayment. The creditor no longer has any claim on the company and therefore the company treats the transaction as an extinguishment and thus derecognizes the liability.

In some cases, however, the company does not inform the creditor of the arrangement or the creditor does not release the company from the primary obligation to settle the debt. Thus the original loan agreement is still in force. This version of the arrangement is often called **in-substance defeasance**. Does in-substance defeasance result in extinguishment of the debt on the company's books? In essence, if the trust is properly set up—for example, the money is invested in low-risk or risk-free investments in an irrevocable trust—it can be argued that the debt has been pre-paid and there is little risk to the company. On the other hand, the company still has the primary obligation according to the original loan agreement. IFRS and ASPE do not allow derecognition of debt under in-substance defeasance arrangements since the company still owes the money.

Off-Balance Sheet Financing

Theory

Finance

Off-balance sheet financing occurs when a company structures a financing deal that results in the obligations not being recorded as debt on the statement of financial position. It is an issue of extreme importance to accountants as well as to general management. Because increased debt signals increased solvency risk, there is a reporting bias to keep low debt levels on the SFP. From a user perspective, however, the amount of debt is very relevant and, in the interest of transparency, all debt should be recognized on the SFP. This is an area where the level of information asymmetry may be significant.

Off-balance sheet financing can take many different forms. The accounting issues can be complex and IFRS and ASPE differ as to how to account for these items. Since these items are dealt with in more detail in other chapters and courses, the specific GAAP differences will not be covered here.

Some examples of off-balance sheet financing follow.

1. **Non-consolidated entities:** Under GAAP, a parent company does not have to consolidate an entity that is less than 50% owned where there is no control. IFRS 10 is a newly issued standard that defines control. ASPE has differing standards regarding what constitutes control as was discussed in Chapter 2. In addition, ASPE allows an accounting policy choice between the equity method and cost, even where control does exist. In such cases, the parent therefore does not report the assets and the liabilities of the entity. Instead, the parent reports only the investment on its statement of financial position. As a result, users of the financial statements might not understand that the entity has considerable debt that the parent may ultimately be liable for if the entity runs into financial difficulty. Investments were discussed in Chapter 9.

2. **Special purpose entities or variable interest entities:** A special purpose entity (SPE) or variable interest entity (VIE) is an entity that a company creates to perform a special project or function. For example, SPEs or VIEs might be formed to do the following:

   (a) Access financing. For example, companies sometimes set up SPEs and VIEs to buy assets, such as accounts receivable or investments, from the company. The company then sells the assets to the SPE/VIE in return for cash, thus obtaining financing. Investors invest in the SPE/VIE to benefit from the return on the assets and certain tax advantages. This process is known as a **securitization of** assets. In this way, the company essentially takes a pool of assets and turns it into securities. Whether the company treats this as a sale or financing was discussed in Chapter 7.

   (b) Take on risk from the company. As in the example above, the sale of the receivables or investments eliminates price and cash flow risks for the company as it now holds cash instead of the riskier receivables or investments. The SPEs/VIEs provide a ready market for buying the assets.

   (c) Isolate certain assets from other company assets. For example, the pension assets of company employees are often segregated in a trust fund or SPE. This arrangement allows greater security for the employees and the company gets certain tax advantages when it contributes money to the plan. Recognition of unfunded pension obligations is discussed in Chapter 19.

   SPEs and VIEs thus serve valid business functions. They only become a problem when they are used primarily to make a company's statement of financial position look better by disguising risk. As a general rule, these entities should be consolidated when the company is the main beneficiary of the SPE/VIE. Except for the overview that has just been presented, the accounting for SPEs and VIEs is beyond the scope of this book.

3. **Operating leases:** Another way that companies keep debt off the SFP is by leasing. Instead of owning the assets, companies lease them. By meeting certain conditions, the company has to report only rent expense each period and provide note disclosure of the transaction. Accounting for leases is discussed in Chapter 20.

The accounting profession's response to these off–balance sheet financing arrangements has been to tighten up the accounting guidance for guarantees, SPEs, leases, and pensions and also to mandate increased note disclosure requirements. This response follows an efficient markets philosophy. The important question has not been whether the presentation is off–balance sheet, but whether the items are disclosed at all.[18]

The IASB is currently working on this issue of what constitutes the economic entity. A new definition for the reporting entity was being established as part of the conceptual framework project.

PRESENTATION, DISCLOSURE, AND ANALYSIS

Objective 4
Explain how long-term debt is presented on the statement of financial position.

The reporting of long-term debt is one of the most controversial areas in financial reporting. Because long-term debt has a significant impact on a company's cash flow, reporting requirements must be substantive and informative. One problem is that the definition of a liability and the recognition criteria in the conceptual framework are not precise enough to prevent the argument from being made that certain obligations do not need to be reported as debt.

Presentation

Current versus Long-Term

Companies that have large amounts and many issues of long-term debt often report only one amount in the statement of financial position and give details about the amount through comments and schedules in the accompanying notes. Long-term debt that **matures within one year** should generally be reported as a **current liability**, unless it will be retired using something other than current assets. If the debt is to be refinanced, the company must treat it as current unless the refinancing has occurred before the release of the financial statements or a refinancing agreement is in place.[19] IFRS requires that the financing be in place by the date of the statement of financial position.[20]

Where it is more relevant to present information according to liquidity, the entity should present assets and liabilities in order of liquidity. If this is the case, the amounts to be recovered or paid within the next 12 months should be disclosed.[21]

Debt versus Equity

As financial instruments become more complex, the line between what is debt and what is equity is becoming more blurred. As noted above, there is significant pressure on companies to watch their debt levels. The debt-versus-equity issue will be discussed in Chapter 16, which examines more complex financial instruments.

Disclosures

Objective 5
Identify disclosure requirements.

Note disclosures generally indicate the following:

- the nature of the liabilities,
- maturity dates,

- interest rates,
- call provisions,
- conversion privileges,
- restrictions imposed by the creditors, and
- assets designated or pledged as security.

Any assets that have been pledged as security for the debt should be shown as such in the assets section of the statement of financial position. The fair value of the long-term debt should also be disclosed. Disclosure is required of future payments for sinking fund requirements and maturity amounts of long-term debt during each of the next five years. Disclosures are also required regarding risks related to the debt (such as solvency and liquidity). The purpose of these disclosures is to help financial statement users evaluate the amounts and timing of future cash flows.

Disclosure requirements are significant. The paragraph above is just a very high-level summary. IFRS 7 details the disclosure requirements for IFRS whereas Section 3856 covers this off under ASPE. Disclosure requirements under ASPE are less than under IFRS.

Analysis

A company's level of debt is a very high-profile number. Many investors and creditors focus on this number for resource allocation decisions. How much debt is the right amount? It depends. The higher the debt, the greater the risk that the company may not be able to repay it. Capital markets respond to this additional solvency risk by increasing the cost of capital and making it more difficult for companies with high debt levels to access additional capital.

As mentioned earlier in the chapter, lenders put covenants in lending agreements stating the amount of debt that a company is allowed to have. Covenants normally state certain financial tests and ratios that the borrower must meet or the debt will become payable. Because of this, restrictive covenants can encourage reporting bias. The company may feel forced to meet the test even if it means using aggressive accounting to do so. Although debt holders assume that the covenants will protect them, covenants are often written in a way that can be interpreted (or misinterpreted) in different ways. Therefore, covenants may provide little or no protection.

Long-term creditors and shareholders are interested in a company's long-term **solvency**, particularly its ability to pay interest as it comes due and to repay the face value of debt at maturity. **Debt to total assets** and **times interest earned** are two of several ratios that provide information about debt-paying ability and long-term solvency. Companies have a vested interest in making sure that they manage their debt levels in a way that does not weaken their solvency position. The **debt to total assets ratio** measures the percentage of the total assets that is provided by creditors. It is calculated by dividing total debt (both current and long-term liabilities) by total assets, as shown in the following formula:

$$\text{Debt-to-total assets} = \frac{\text{Total debt}}{\text{Total assets}}$$

The **higher the percentage** of debt to total assets, the **greater the risk** that the company may be unable to meet its maturing obligations.

The **times interest earned ratio** indicates the company's ability to meet interest payments as they come due. The higher the ratio, the better the company's ability to ensure that its interest payments are made. It is calculated by dividing income before interest expense and income taxes by interest expense:

Objective 6
Calculate and interpret key ratios related to solvency and liquidity.

Ethics

Underlying Concept

Users of financial statements must be aware when covenants exist so that they understand the potential for misstating the financial statements. Whenever these conditions are important for users to have a complete understanding of the company's financial position and results of operations, they should be described in the body of the financial statements or the accompanying notes.

$$\text{Times interest earned} = \frac{\text{Income before income taxes and interest expense}}{\text{Interest expense}}$$

To illustrate these ratios, we will use data from the **Shoppers Drug Mart (SDM)** 2011 annual report, which disclosed total liabilities of $3,032 million, total assets of $7,300 million, interest expense of $67 million ($3 million of which are capitalized), income tax expense of $233 million, and net income of $614 million. SDM's debt to total assets ratio is calculated as follows:

$$\begin{aligned} \text{Debt-to-total assets} &= \text{Total debt/total assets} \\ &= \$3,032/\$7,300 \\ &= 41.5\% \end{aligned}$$

SDM has a moderate debt to total assets percentage of 41.5%. The company is largely capitalized by equity.

The interest coverage ratio is calculated as follows:

$$\begin{aligned} \text{Interest coverage ratio} &= \text{Income before income taxes and interest expense/interest expense} \\ &= \$914/67 \\ &= 13.6 \text{ times (a healthy coverage ratio)} \end{aligned}$$

This is due to the fact that debt levels are reasonable and the company is profitable.

Objective 7

Identify major differences in accounting standards between IFRS and ASPE, and what changes are expected in the near future.

IFRS/ASPE COMPARISON

A Comparison of IFRS and ASPE

Illustration 14-14 summarizes the differences in accounting for long-term financial liabilities between IFRS and ASPE.

	ASPE—*CICA Handbook*, Part II, Sections 1510, 1521, and 3856	IFRS—IAS 1, 29 and 32 IFRS 7 and 9	References to Related Illustrations and Select Brief Exercises
Measurement	There is specific guidance on measuring related party transactions (which will be covered in Chapter 23).	There is no specific guidance on related-party transactions.	See Chapter 23—BE 23-11, 12, 13 and 14.
	Subsequently, liabilities are generally measured at amortized cost using the effective interest or other method (unless measured at fair value under the fair value option or because it is a derivative, with a few exceptions).	Subsequently, liabilities are generally measured at amortized cost using the effective interest method (unless measured at fair value under the fair value option or because it is a derivative).	See Chapter 9—Illustrations 9-4 and 9-6 and subsequent journal entries (note that Chapter 9 deals with the amortization issue from the asset side but the calculations are similar on the liability side).

(*continued*)

Illustration 14-14

IFRS and ASPE Comparison Chart

ASPE—CICA Handbook, Part II, Sections 1510, 1521, and 3856	IFRS—IAS 1, 29 and 32 IFRS 7 and 9	References to Related Illustrations and Select Brief Exercises
Where the fair value option is used, credit risk is incorporated into the measurement and resulting gains/losses are booked through net income.	Where the fair value option is used, credit risk is incorporated into the measurement and resulting gains/losses are booked through net income. However, if IFRS 9 is adopted early, gains/losses related to changes in credit risk are booked though Other Comprehensive Income.	Illustration 14-10 and BE 14-18
Presentation Normally the balance sheet is segregated into current/non-current; however, this may not be appropriate for certain industries.	Normally the SFP is segregated into current/non-current except where presentation on the basis of liquidity is more relevant (then debt is presented in order of liquidity).	BE 14-24
Refinanced long-term debt may be classified as long-term where refinanced by date of issue of financial statements.	Refinanced long-term debt may be classified as long-term where refinanced by SFP date.	BE 14-20

Illustration 14-14

IFRS and ASPE Comparison Chart (continued)

Looking Ahead

The IASB and FASB are currently working on several projects related to long-term debt as follows:

1. **Financial instruments project:** The IASB and FASB continue to work on IFRS 9. They are currently looking at making the FV-OCI option available to debt instruments. This standard is meant to eventually replace the current standard (IAS 39). The mandatory adoption date has been deferred to 2015 for IFRS 9 so that the FASB and IASB can continue to study the issues in hopes of bringing about greater convergence.

2. **Financial instruments with the characteristics of equity:** The IASB paused this project because it had a number of other projects on the go. This will affect how debt and equity instruments are classified and presented on the statement of financial position.

3. **Conceptual framework project:** As part of this project, the standard setters are trying to identify the economic entity for financial reporting purposes and are looking at the definition of control. This was discussed briefly in Chapter 2.

SUMMARY OF LEARNING OBJECTIVES

1 Understand the nature of long-term debt financing arrangements.

Incurring long-term debt is often a formal procedure. Corporation bylaws usually require the approval of the board of directors and the shareholders before bonds can be issued or other long-term debt arrangements can be contracted. Generally, long-term debt has various covenants or restrictions. The covenants and other terms of the agreement between the borrower and the lender are stated in the bond indenture or note agreement. Notes are similar in substance to bonds but do not trade as readily in capital markets, if at all.

The variety of types of bonds and notes is a result of attempts to attract capital from different investors and risk takers and to satisfy the issuers' cash flow needs.

External credit rating agencies rate bonds and assign a credit rating based on the riskiness. The credit rating helps investors decide whether to invest in a particular bond. Companies sometimes extinguish debt early using a defeasance arrangement. In a defeasance arrangement, funds are deposited into a trust and the trust continues to make the regularly scheduled payments until maturity.

By using debt financing, companies can maximize income through the use of leverage. Capital-intensive industries often have higher levels of debt. Continued access to low-cost debt is important for maximizing shareholder value.

2 Understand how long-term debt is measured and accounted for.

The investment community values a bond at the present value of its future cash flows, which consist of interest and principal. The rate that is used to calculate the present value of these cash flows is the interest rate that provides an acceptable return on an investment that matches the issuer's risk characteristics. The interest rate written in the terms of the bond indenture and ordinarily appearing on the bond certificate is the stated, coupon, or nominal rate. This rate, which is set by the issuer of the bonds, is expressed as a percentage of the bond's face value, which is also called the par value, principal amount, or maturity value. If the rate used by the buyers differs from the stated rate, the bond's present value calculated by the buyers will differ from the bond's face value. The difference between the bond's face value and the present value is either a discount or a premium. Long-term debt is measured at fair value on initial recognition, including

transaction costs where the instruments will subsequently be valued at amortized cost. Subsequently, the instruments are measured at amortized cost or, in certain limited situations, fair value, under the fair value option.

The discount (premium) is amortized and charged (credited) to interest expense over the period of time that the bonds are outstanding. IFRS requires the effective interest method; however, ASPE allows a choice and often smaller private entities use the straight-line method.

Bonds and notes may be issued with zero interest or for a non-monetary consideration. Measurement of the bonds and the consideration must reflect the underlying substance of the transaction. In particular, reasonable interest rates must be imputed. The fair value of the debt and of the non-monetary consideration should be used to value the transaction.

3 Understand when long-term debt is recognized and derecognized, including how to account for troubled debt restructurings.

At the time of reacquisition, the unamortized premium or discount and any costs of issue that apply to the debt must be amortized up to the reacquisition date. The amount that is paid on extinguishment or redemption before maturity, including any call premium and expense of reacquisition, is the reacquisition price. On any specified date, the debt's net carrying amount is the amount that is payable at maturity, adjusted for unamortized premium or discount and the cost of issuance. Any excess of the net carrying amount over the reacquisition price is a gain from extinguishment, whereas the excess of the reacquisition price over the net carrying amount is a loss from extinguishment. Legal defeasance results in derecognition of the liability. In-substance defeasance does not.

Where debt is settled by exchanging the old debt with new debt (generally in troubled debt situations), it is treated as a settlement where the terms of the agreements are substantially different, including a size test, and where the new debt is with a new lender. If not treated as a settlement, it is treated as a modification of the old debt and a new interest rate is imputed.

Off-balance sheet financing is an attempt to borrow funds in such a way that the obligations are not recorded. One type of off-balance sheet financing involves the use of certain variable interest entities. Accounting standard setters are studying this area with the objective of coming up with a new definition of what constitutes the reporting entity.

4 Explain how long-term debt is presented on the statement of financial position.

Companies that have large amounts and many issues of long-term debt often report only one amount in the SFP and support this with comments and schedules in the accompanying notes. Long-term debt that matures within one year should be reported as a current liability, unless it will be retired without using current assets. If the debt is to be refinanced, converted into shares, or retired from a bond retirement fund, it should continue to be reported as non-current and accompanied by a note explaining the method to be used in its liquidation unless certain conditions are met.

5 Identify disclosure requirements.

Note disclosures are significant and generally indicate the nature of the liabilities, maturity dates, interest rates, call provisions, conversion privileges,

restrictions imposed by the creditors, and assets designated or pledged as security as well as other details.

6 Calculate and interpret key ratios related to solvency and liquidity.

Debt to total assets and times interest earned are two ratios that provide information about debt-paying ability and long-term solvency.

7 Identify major differences in accounting standards between IFRS and ASPE, and what changes are expected in the near future.

IFRS and ASPE are largely converged as they relate to long-term debt. Small differences relate to whether the debt is presented as current or non-current and in measurement. For example, ASPE has measurement standards for related-party transactions. The standard setters are working on several large projects, including the conceptual framework and financial instruments with the characteristics of equity.

Quiz

Brief Exercises

(LO 1) BE14-1 Richter Corporation is a retailer in the technology industry with a 10-year bond issue outstanding. At the time of issuance on January 1, 2014, the bonds were assigned a BBB– credit rating by Standard & Poor's, and the market rate for the bonds was 9%. Due to new competition in the industry, Richter experienced four consecutive quarters of increasing losses and deteriorating financial position in 2014. (a) Discuss the potential impact on the bonds' credit rating, if any. (b) Discuss the potential impact on investors' required yield on the bonds, if any.

(LO 1) BE14-2 Dowty Incorporated, a telecommunications equipment manufacturer, has a debt to total assets ratio of 55%, while competing companies of similar size operating in the same industry have an average debt to total assets ratio of 62%. Dowty is planning to expand its operations by adding two new plants next year. (a) Discuss three sources for financing the expansion. (b) Recommend the most suitable source of financing for Dowty, based on the information provided.

(LO 2) BE14-3 Buchanan Corporation issues $500,000 of 11% bonds that are due in 10 years and pay interest semi-annually. At the time of issue, the market rate for such bonds is 10%. Calculate the bonds' issue price.

(LO 2) BE14-4 Chieh, Inc. issued a $300,000, four-year, 8% note at face value to Cedar Bank on January 1, 2014, and received $300,000 cash. The note requires annual interest payments each December 31. Prepare Chieh's journal entries to record (a) the note issuance and (b) the December 31 interest payment.

(LO 2) BE14-5 On May 1, 2014, Jadeja Corporation, a publicly listed corporation, issued $200,000 of five-year, 8% bonds, with interest payable semi-annually on November 1 and May 1. The bonds were issued to yield a market interest rate of 6%. Jadeja uses the effective interest method. (a) Calculate the present value (issue price) of the bonds on May 1. (b) Record the issue of the bonds on May 1. (c) Prepare the journal entry to record the first and second interest payments on November 1, 2014, and May 1, 2015.

(LO 2) BE14-6 Marta Corporation issued a $75,000, four-year, zero-interest-bearing note to Samson Corp. on January 1, 2014, and received $47,664 cash. The implicit interest rate is 12%. Marta uses the effective interest method. (a) Prepare Marta's journal entry for the January 1 issuance. (b) Prepare Marta's journal entry for the December 31 recognition of interest. (c) Assume that the effective interest of 12% had not been provided in the data. Prove the effective interest rate of 12% using a financial calculator or computer spreadsheet functions. (d) Prepare an effective-interest amortization table for the note.

(LO 2) BE14-7 Brestovacki Corporation issued a $50,000, five-year, 5% note to Jernigan Corp. on January 1, 2014, and received a piece of equipment that normally sells for $38,912. The note requires annual interest payments each December 31. The market interest rate for a note of similar risk is 11%. Prepare Brestovacki's journal entry for (a) the January 1, 2014 issuance and (b) the December 31, 2014 interest payment using the effective interest method.

(LO 2) BE14-8 Khajepour Corporation issued a $140,000, four-year, zero-interest-bearing note to Saccomanno Corp. on January 1, 2014, and received $140,000 cash. In addition, the company agreed to sell merchandise to Saccomanno for an amount less than the regular selling price over the four-year period. The market interest rate for similar notes is 8%. Khajepour uses the effective interest method. Prepare Khajepour's January 1 journal entry.

(LO 2) BE14-9 Pflug Ltd. signed an instalment note on January 1, 2014, in settlement of an account payable of $40,000 owed to Mott Ltd. Pflug is able to borrow funds from its bank at 11%, whereas Mott can borrow at the rate of 10%. The note calls for two equal payments of blended principal and interest to be made at December 31, 2014, and 2015. Calculate the amount of the equal instalment payments that will be made to Mott Ltd.

(LO 2) BE14-10 Watson Corporation issued $500,000 of 8%, 10-year bonds on January 1, 2014, at face value. The note requires annual interest payments each December 31. Costs associated with the bond issuance were $25,000. Watson follows ASPE and uses the straight-line method to amortize bond issue costs. Prepare the journal entry for (a) the January 1, 2014 issuance and (b) the December 31, 2014 interest payment and bond issuance cost amortization. (c) What are the general principles surrounding accounting for transaction costs associated with the issue of notes or bonds?

(LO 2) BE14-11 Grenier Limited issued $300,000 of 10% bonds on January 1, 2014. The bonds are due on January 1, 2019, with interest payable each July 1 and January 1. The bonds are issued at face value. Grenier uses the effective interest method. Prepare the company's journal entries for (a) the January issuance, (b) the July 1, 2014 interest payment, and (c) the December 31, 2014 adjusting entry.

(LO 2) BE14-12 Assume that the bonds in BE14-11 were issued at 98. Assume also that Grenier Limited records the amortization using the straight-line method. Prepare the journal entries related to the bonds for (a) January 1, (b) July 1, and (c) December 31.

(LO 2)   **BE14-13**   Assume that the bonds in BE14-11 were issued at 103. Assume also that Grenier Limited records the amortization using the straight-line method. Prepare the journal entries related to the bonds for (a) January 1, (b) July 1, and (c) December 31.

(LO 2)   **BE14-14**   Stevens Corporation issued $700,000 of 9% bonds on May 1, 2014. The bonds were dated January 1, 2014, and mature on January 1, 2019, with interest payable each July 1 and January 1. The bonds were issued at face value plus accrued interest. Stevens uses the effective interest method. Prepare the company's journal entries for (a) the May 1 issuance, (b) the July 1 interest payment, and (c) December 31.

(LO 2)   **BE14-15**   On January 1, 2014, Quinton Corporation issued $600,000 of 7% bonds that are due in 10 years. The bonds were issued for $559,229 and pay interest each July 1 and January 1. The company uses the effective interest method. Assume an effective rate of 8%. (a) Prepare the company's journal entry for the January 1 issuance. (b) Prepare the company's journal entry for the July 1 interest payment. (c) Prepare the company's December 31 adjusting entry. (d) Assume that the effective interest of 8% was not given in the data. Prove the effective interest rate of 8% using a financial calculator or computer spreadsheet functions. (e) Prepare the first three payments of an effective-interest amortization table for the bonds.

(LO 2)   **BE14-16**   Assume that the bonds in BE14-15 were issued for $644,635 and the effective interest rate was 6%. (a) Prepare the company's journal entry for the January 1 issuance. (b) Prepare the company's journal entry for the July 1 interest payment. (c) Prepare the company's December 31 adjusting entry. (d) Assume that the effective interest of 6% was not given in the data. Prove the effective interest rate of 6% using a financial calculator or computer spreadsheet functions. (e) Prepare the first three payments of an effective-interest amortization table for the bonds.

(LO 2)   **BE14-17**   Teton Corporation issued $600,000 of 8% bonds on November 1, 2014, for $644,636. The bonds were dated November 1, 2014, and mature in 10 years, with interest payable each May 1 and November 1. The company uses the effective interest method with an effective rate of 6%. Prepare the company's December 31, 2014 adjusting entry.

(LO 2)   **BE14-18**   Hanson Incorporated issued $1 million of 7%, 10-year bonds on July 1, 2013, at face value. Interest is payable each December 31. The company has chosen to apply the fair value option in accounting for the bonds. A risk assessment at December 31, 2014, shows that Hanson's credit risk has increased, and as a result, the fair value of the bonds is $900,000 on that date. Prepare the company's journal entries on December 31, 2014, if Hanson follows (a) ASPE, (b) IAS 39, and (c) IFRS 9 (mandatorily adoptable in 2015)

(LO 3)   **BE14-19**   On January 1, 2014, Henderson Corporation retired $500,000 (face value) of bonds at 99. At the time of retirement, the unamortized premium was $9,750. Prepare the corporation's journal entry to record the reacquisition of the bonds.

(LO 3)   **BE14-20**   Assume that Theo Limited has a loan that is currently due at year end. The debt is being refinanced with a 5-year loan and the deal to refinance the debt is signed two days after year end. How would the original loan be classified in the year end statements under IFRS and ASPE? Theo presents a classified statement of financial position.

(LO 3)   **BE14-21**   Lawrence Incorporated owes $100,000 to Ontario Bank Inc. on a two-year, 10% note due on December 31, 2014. The note was issued at par. Because Lawrence is in financial trouble, Ontario Bank agrees to extend the maturity date of the note to December 31, 2016, reduce the principal to $75,000, and reduce the interest rate to 8%, payable annually on December 31. Present value of the new debt is calculated as $72,397. Lawrence prepares financial statements in accordance with IFRS. Prepare the journal entry on Lawrence's books on December 31, 2014, 2015, and 2016.

(LO 3)   **BE14-22**   On January 1, 2014, Steinem Corporation established a special purpose entity to buy $1 million of accounts receivable from Steinem. Investors have invested in the special purpose entity to benefit from the return on assets and certain tax advantages. The special purpose entity has used the cash invested by the investors to purchase the $1 million of accounts receivable from Steinem. (a) Has Steinem's liquidity improved as a result of this transaction? (b) Will Steinem's statement of financial position show increased debt or equity as a result of this transaction? (c) What type of transaction is this, and from the perspective of an investor, what is the related risk?

(LO 4)   **BE14-23**   At December 31, 2014, Hyasaki Corporation has the following account balances:

Bonds Payable—Due January 1, 2022 (face value, $2,000,000) $1,912,000
Bond Interest Payable   80,000

Show how the above accounts should be presented on the December 31, 2014 statement of financial position, and with the proper classifications.

(LO 4)   **BE14-24**   Ling Corporation has the following liabilities at December 31, 2014: accounts payable $20,000; long-term debt $100,000 (due in two years, current portion $20,000); and bonds payable $200,000 (due in five years). Prepare the liabilities section of the statement of financial position if Ling presents liabilities (a) in order of liquidity, and (b) segregated into current and non-current.

(LO 6) **BE14-25** Beekers Incorporated had total debt of $1 million and $1.2 million at December 31, 2014 and 2015, respectively, and total assets of $2 million and $2.2 million at December 31, 2014 and 2015, respectively. Evaluate the company's debt-paying ability in 2014 and 2015.

Exercises

(LO 1) **E14-1** **(Features of Long-Term Debt)** The following examples describe possible features or characteristics of long-term debt:

1. The debt agreement includes a covenant that requires the debtor to maintain a minimum amount of working capital.

2. The stated rate of a bond issue is less than the market rate.

3. The debt is backed by a claim on the debtor's real estate.

4. The debt agreement includes a covenant that limits the amount of additional debt that the debtor can incur.

5. The debt matures on a single date in 20 years.

6. The bond gives the holder the right to call the debt before maturity.

7. The debtor arranges for defeasance of the debt.

8. The debt is a debenture bond.

Instructions

(a) Match each example in the preceding list to the number below that best describes it:

   i. Increases the riskiness of the long-term debt

   ii. Decreases the riskiness of the long-term debt

   iii. Does not affect the riskiness of the long-term debt

(b) For a feature or characteristic that increases the riskiness of the long-term debt, discuss the effect of the feature or characteristic on investors' required yield on the long-term debt.

(LO 1, 2) **E14-2** **(Information Related to Various Bond Issues)** Anaconda Inc. has issued three types of debt on January 1, 2014, the start of the company's fiscal year:

1. $10 million, 10-year, 13% unsecured bonds, with interest payable quarterly (the bonds were priced to yield 12%)

2. $2.5 million par of 10-year, zero-coupon bonds at a price to yield 12% per year

3. $15 million, 10-year, 10% mortgage bonds, with interest payable annually to yield 12%

Instructions

Prepare a schedule that identifies the following items for each bond:

(a) The maturity value

(b) The number of interest periods over the life of the bond

(c) The stated rate for each interest period

(d) The effective interest rate for each interest period

(e) The payment amount per period

(f) The present value of the bonds at the date of issue

(g) Each instrument has different features. Comment on how the instruments are different, discussing the underlying nature of the debt. Which bonds are riskiest and why?

(LO 2) **E14-3** **(Entries for Bond Transactions)** Two independent situations follow:

1. On January 1, 2014, Divac Limited issued $300,000 of 10-year, 9% bonds at par. Interest is payable quarterly on April 1, July 1, October 1, and January 1.

2. On June 1, 2014, Verbitsky Inc. issued at par, plus accrued interest, $200,000 of 10-year, 12% bonds dated January 1. Interest is payable semi-annually on July 1 and January 1.

Instructions

For each of these two independent situations, prepare journal entries to record:

(a) The issuance of the bonds   **(c)** The accrual of interest on December 31

(b) The payment of interest on July 1

(LO 2)   E14-4   (Entries for Bond Transactions—Effective Interest) Foreman Inc. issued $800,000 of 10%, 20-year bonds on January 1, 2014, at 102. Interest is payable semi-annually on July 1 and January 1. Foreman Inc. uses the effective interest method of amortization for any bond premium or discount. Assume an effective yield of 9.75%. (With a market rate of 9.75%, the issue price would be slightly higher. For simplicity, ignore this.)

Instructions

Prepare the journal entries to record the following (round to the nearest dollar):

(a) The issuance of the bonds

(b) The payment of interest and the related amortization on July 1, 2014

(c) The accrual of interest and the related amortization on December 31, 2014

(LO 2)   E14-5   (Entries for Bond Transactions—Straight-Line) Foreman Inc. issued $800,000 of 20-year, 10% bonds on January 1, 2014, at 102. Interest is payable semi-annually on July 1 and January 1. The company uses the straight-line method of amortization for any bond premium or discount.

Instructions

(a) Prepare the journal entries to record the following:

1. The issuance of the bonds

2. The payment of interest and the related amortization on July 1, 2014

3. The accrual of interest and the related amortization on December 31, 2014

(b) Briefly explain how the entries would change depending on whether Foreman follows IFRS or ASPE.

(LO 2)   E14-6   (Entries for Non-Interest-Bearing Debt) On January 1, 2014, Guillemette Inc. makes the following acquisitions:

1. Purchases land having a fair market value of $300,000 by issuing a five-year, non-interest-bearing promissory note in the face amount of $505,518.

2. Purchases equipment by issuing an eight-year, 6% promissory note having a maturity value of $275,000 (interest payable annually).

The company has to pay 11% interest on funds from its bank.

Instructions

(a) Record Guillemette's journal entries on January 1, 2014, for each of the purchases.

(b) Record the interest at the end of the first year on both notes using the effective interest method.

(LO 2)   E14-7   (Imputation of Interest) Two independent situations follow.

1. On January 1, 2014, Spartan Inc. purchased land that had an assessed value of $390,000 at the time of purchase. A $600,000, non-interest-bearing note due on January 1, 2017, was given in exchange. There was no established exchange price for the land, and no ready market value for the note. The interest rate that is normally charged on a note of this type is 12%.

2. On January 1, 2014, Geimer Furniture Ltd. borrowed $4 million (face value) from Aurora Inc., a major customer, through a non-interest-bearing note due in four years. Because the note was non-interest-bearing, Geimer Furniture agreed to sell furniture to this customer at lower than market price. A 10% rate of interest is normally charged on this type of loan.

Instructions

(a) For situation 1, determine at what amount the land should be recorded at January 1, 2014, and the interest expense to be reported in 2014 related to this transaction. Discuss how the assessed value of the land could be used in this situation.

(b) For situation 2, prepare the journal entry to record this transaction and determine the amount of interest expense to report for 2014.

(LO 2)   E14-8   (Purchase of Land with Instalment Note) Desrocher Ltd. issued an instalment note on January 1, 2014 (with a required yield of 9%), in exchange for land that it purchased from Safayeni Ltd. Safayeni's real estate agent had listed the land on the market for $120,000. The note calls for three equal blended payments of $43,456 that are to be made at December 31, 2014, 2015, and 2016.

Instructions

(a) Discuss how the purchase price of the land will be established.

(b) Using time value of money tables, a financial calculator, or computer spreadsheet functions, prove that the note will cost Desrocher Ltd. 9% interest over the note's full term.

(c) Prepare an effective-interest amortization table for the instalment note for the three-year period.

(d) Prepare Desrocher's journal entry for the purchase of the land.

(e) Prepare Desrocher's journal entry for the first instalment payment on the note on December 31, 2014.

(f) From Safayeni Ltd.'s perspective, what are the advantages of an instalment note compared with a regular interest-bearing note?

Digging Deeper

(LO 2) E14-9 (Purchase of Equipment with Non-Interest-Bearing Debt) To meet customer demand for its product, Armada Inc. decided to purchase equipment from Southern Ontario Industries on January 2, 2014, and expand its production capacity. Armada issued an $800,000, five-year, non–interest-bearing note to Southern Ontario Industries for the new equipment when the prevailing market interest rate for obligations of this nature was 12%. The company will pay off the note in five $160,000 instalments that are due at the end of each year over the life of the note. Armada uses the effective interest method for amortization of any premium or discount.

Instructions

(Round to the nearest dollar in all calculations.)

(a) Prepare the journal entry(ies) at the date of purchase.

(b) Prepare the journal entry(ies) at the end of the first year to record the payment and interest.

(c) Prepare the journal entry(ies) at the end of the second year to record the payment and interest.

(LO 2) E14-10 (Purchase of Computer with Non-Interest-Bearing Debt) Collins Corporation purchased a computer on December 31, 2014, paying $30,000 down and a further $75,000 payment due on December 31, 2017. An interest rate of 10% is implicit in the purchase price. Collins uses the effective interest method and has a December 31 year end. Collins prepares financial statements in accordance with ASPE.

Instructions

(a) Prepare the journal entry(ies) at the purchase date. (Round to two decimal places.)

(b) Prepare any journal entry(ies) required at December 31, 2015, 2016, and 2017.

(c) Can Collins choose a different method of amortizing any premium or discount on its notes payable? Explain your answer.

(LO 2) E14-11 (Entries for Bond Transactions) On January 1, 2014, Osborn Inc. sold 12% bonds having a maturity value of $800,000 for $860,651.79, which provides the bondholders with a 10% yield. The bonds are dated January 1, 2014, and mature on January 1, 2019, with interest payable on January 1 of each year. The company follows IFRS and uses the effective interest method.

Instructions

(a) Prepare the journal entry at the date of issue.

(b) Prepare a schedule of interest expense and bond amortization for 2014 through 2017.

(c) Prepare the journal entry to record the interest payment and the amortization for 2014.

(d) Prepare the journal entry to record the interest payment and the amortization for 2016.

(e) If Osborn prepares financial statements in accordance with ASPE, can Osborn choose a different method of amortizing any premium or discount on its bonds payable? Explain your answer.

(LO 2) E14-12 (Amortization Schedules—Straight-Line) Minor Inc. sells 10% bonds having a maturity value of $3 million for $2,783,724. The bonds are dated January 1, 2014, and mature on January 1, 2019. Interest is payable annually on January 1.

Instructions

Set up a schedule of interest expense and discount amortization under the straight-line method.

(LO 2) E14-13   (Amortization Schedule—Effective Interest) Assume the same information as in E14-12.

Instructions

(a) Set up a schedule of interest expense and discount amortization under the effective interest method. (*Hint:* The effective interest rate must be calculated.)

(b) Which method of discount amortization results in higher interest expense for the year ended December 31, 2014? Which method of discount amortization results in higher interest expense for the year ended December 31, 2018? Explain the results. From the perspective of a user of Minor's financial statements, which method would you prefer the company to use, if you would like the company's income statement to reflect the most faithfully representative measure of net income?

Digging Deeper

(LO 2) E14-14   (Determine Proper Amounts in Account Balances) Four independent situations follow.

1. Wen Corporation incurred the following costs when it issued bonds: printing and engraving costs, $25,000; legal fees, $69,000; and commissions paid to underwriter, $70,000.

2. Griffith Inc. sold $3 million of 10-year, 10% bonds at 104 on January 1, 2014. The bonds were dated January 1, 2014, and pay interest on July 1 and January 1.

3. Kennedy Inc. issued $600,000 of 10-year, 9% bonds on June 30, 2014, for $562,500. This price provided a yield of 10% on the bonds. Interest is payable semi-annually on December 31 and June 30.

4. Bergevin Corporation issued $800,000 of bonds on January 1, 2014, with interest payable each January 1. The carrying amount of the bonds on December 31, 2014, is $850,716.97. Bergevin has chosen to apply the fair value option in accounting for the bonds. An assessment of the company's credit risk at December 31, 2014, shows that it has increased, and as a result, the fair value of the bonds is $838,000 on that date. Bergevin prepares financial statements in accordance with IFRS.

Instructions

(a) In situation 1, what accounting treatment could be given to these costs?

(b) In situation 2, if Griffith follows ASPE and uses the straight-line method to amortize bond premium or discount, determine the amount of interest expense to be reported on July 1, 2014, and December 31, 2014.

(c) In situation 3, if Kennedy uses the effective interest method, determine the amount of interest expense to record if financial statements are issued on October 31, 2014.

(d) In situation 4, what accounting treatment should be given to the bonds at December 31, 2014?

(LO 2) E14-15   (Interest-Free Government Loans) Russell Forest Products Limited needed to upgrade a burner at its sawmill in Cochrane, Ontario, to comply with new air pollution standards. The new burner, which is used to burn the scrap wood from its sawing operations, will not only reduce the amount of pollution, but will supply heat for the plant facility, including the wood dryer. In order to encourage Russell Forest Products Limited in its compliance with the standards, the Province of Ontario extended an interest-free loan of $400,000 on December 31, 2014. The only conditions in obtaining the interest-free loan are that the loan proceeds be applied directly to the construction costs and that the loan be repaid in full on December 31, 2022. Russell Forest Products Limited borrowed the remaining funds from the bank for the construction of the burner and will be paying interest at the rate of 7% per year.

Instructions

(a) Discuss the issues related to obtaining the interest-free loan from the Province of Ontario.

(b) Prepare an amortization table for the loan using the effective interest method. Present the first three years of the loan.

(c) Prepare the entry on December 31, 2014, to record the interest-free loan.

(d) Prepare any adjusting journal entry that is necessary at December 31, 2015, the company's fiscal year end, concerning any interest on the note.

(LO 2, 4) E14-16   (Entries and Questions for Bond Transactions) On June 30, 2014, Mosca Limited issued $4 million of 20-year, 13% bonds for $4,300,920, which provides a yield of 12%. The company uses the effective interest method to amortize any bond premium or discount. The bonds pay semi-annual interest on June 30 and December 31.

Instructions

(a) Prepare the journal entries to record the following transactions:

1. The issuance of the bonds on June 30, 2014

2. The payment of interest and the amortization of the premium on December 31, 2014

3. The payment of interest and the amortization of the premium on June 30, 2015

4. The payment of interest and the amortization of the premium on December 31, 2015

(b) Show the proper statement of financial position presentation for the liability for bonds payable on the December 31, 2014 statement of financial position.

(c) Answer the following questions.

1. What amount of interest expense is reported for 2014?

2. Will the bond interest expense that is reported in 2014 be the same as, greater than, or less than the amount that would be reported if the straight-line method of amortization were used?

3. What is the total cost of borrowing over the life of the bond?

4. Will the total bond interest expense for the life of the bond be greater than, the same as, or less than the total interest expense if the straight-line method of amortization were used?

(LO 3) E14-17 (Entries for Retirement and Issuance of Bonds) Friedman Corporation had bonds outstanding with a maturity value of $500,000. On April 30, 2014, when these bonds had an unamortized discount of $10,000, they were called in at 104. To pay for these bonds, Friedman had issued other bonds a month earlier bearing a lower interest rate. The newly issued bonds had a life of 10 years. The new bonds were issued at 103 (face value $500,000). Issue costs related to the new bonds were $3,000. All issue costs were capitalized. Friedman prepares financial statements in accordance with IFRS.

Instructions

Ignoring interest, calculate the gain or loss and record this refunding transaction.

(LO 2, 4) E14-18 (Entries for Retirement and Issuance of Bonds—Straight-Line) On June 30, 2007, Auburn Limited issued 12% bonds with a par value of $800,000 due in 20 years. They were issued at 98 and were callable at 104 at any date after June 30, 2014.

Because of lower interest rates and a significant change in the company's credit rating, it was decided to call the entire issue on June 30, 2014, and to issue new bonds. New 10% bonds were sold in the amount of $1 million at 102; they mature in 20 years. The company follows ASPE and uses straight-line amortization. The interest payment dates are December 31 and June 30 of each year.

Instructions

(a) Prepare journal entries to record the retirement of the old issue and the sale of the new issue on June 30, 2014.

(b) Prepare the entry required on December 31, 2014, to record the payment of the first six months of interest and the amortization of the bond premium.

(LO 3) E14-19 (Entries for Retirement and Issuance of Bonds—Effective Interest) Refer to E14-18 and Auburn Limited.

Instructions

Repeat the instructions of E14-18 assuming that Auburn Limited follows IFRS and uses the effective interest method. Provide an effective-interest table for the bonds from the inception of the bond to the date of the redemption. (*Hint:* You need to first calculate the effective interest rate on the 2007 and 2014 bonds. Round the semi-annual interest percentage to three decimal places.)

(LO 3) E14-20 (Entry for Retirement of Bond; Costs for Bond Issuance) On January 2, 2009, Kowalchuk Corporation, a small company that follows ASPE, issued $1.5 million of 10% bonds at 97 due on December 31, 2018. Legal and other costs of $110,000 were incurred in connection with the issue. Kowalchuk Corporation has adopted the policy of capitalizing and amortizing the legal and other costs incurred by including them with the bond recorded at the date of issuance. Interest on the bonds is payable annually each December 31. The $110,000 in issuance costs are being deferred and amortized on a straight-line basis over the 10-year term of the bonds. The discount on the bonds is also being amortized on a straight-line basis over the 10 years. (The straight-line method is not materially different in its effect compared with the effective interest method.)

The bonds are callable at 102 (that is, at 102% of their face amount), and on January 2, 2014, the company called a face amount of $850,000 of the bonds and retired them.

Instructions

(a) Ignoring income taxes, calculate the amount of loss, if any, that the company needs to recognize as a result of retiring the $850,000 of bonds in 2014. Prepare the journal entry to record the retirement.

(b) How would the amount of the loss calculated in part (a) differ if the policy for Kowalchuk Corporation had been to carry the bonds at fair value and thus expense the costs of issuing the bonds at January 2, 2009? Assuming that Kowalchuk Corporation had followed this policy, prepare the journal entry to record the retirement. Assume the redemption price approximates fair value.

(c) How would your answers to (a) and (b) change if Kowalchuk were to follow IAS 39?

Digging Deeper

(LO 3) **E14-21 (Entries for Retirement and Issuance of Bonds)** Robinson, Inc. had outstanding $5 million of 11% bonds (interest payable July 31 and January 31) due in 10-years. On July 1, it issued $7 million of 15-year, 10% bonds (interest payable July 1 and January 1) at 98. A portion of the proceeds was used to call the 11% bonds at 102 on August 1. The unamortized bond discount for the 11% bonds was $120,000 on August 1. Robinson prepares financial statements in accordance with IFRS.

Instructions

Prepare the necessary journal entries to record the issue of the new bonds and the retirement of the old bonds.

(LO 3) **E14-22 (Impairments)** On December 31, 2013, Mohr Inc. borrowed $81,241 from Par Bank, signing a $125,000, five-year, non-interest-bearing note. The note was issued to yield 9% interest. Unfortunately, during 2014 Mohr began to experience financial difficulty. As a result, at December 31, 2014, Par Bank determined that it was probable that it would receive only $93,750 at maturity. The market rate of interest on loans of this nature is now 11%. Both companies prepare financial statements in accordance with IFRS.

Instructions

(a) Prepare the entry to record the issuance of the loan by Par Bank on December 31, 2013.

(b) Prepare the entry (if any) to record the impairment of the loan on December 31, 2014, by Par Bank.

(c) Prepare the entry (if any) to record the impairment of the loan on December 31, 2014, by Mohr.

(LO 3) **E14-23 (Settlement of Debt)** Strickland Inc. owes Heartland Bank $200,000 plus $18,000 of accrued interest. The debt is a 10-year, 10% note. During 2014, Strickland's business declined due to a slowing regional economy. On December 31, 2014, the bank agrees to accept an old machine and cancel the entire debt. The machine has a cost of $390,000, accumulated depreciation of $221,000, and a fair value of $180,000. The bank plans to dispose of the machine at a cost of $6,500. Both Strickland and Heartland Bank prepare financial statements in accordance with IFRS.

Instructions

(a) Prepare the journal entries for Strickland Inc. and Heartland Bank to record this debt settlement. Assume Heartland had previously recognized an allowance for doubtful accounts for the impairment prior to the settlement.

(b) How should Strickland report the gain or loss on disposal of the machinery and on the restructuring of debt in its 2014 income statement?

(c) Assume that instead of transferring the machine, Strickland decides to grant the bank 15,000 of its common shares, which have a fair value of $190,000. This is in full settlement of the loan obligation. Assuming that Heartland Bank treats Strickland's shares as fair value-net income investments, prepare the entries to record the transaction for both parties. Assume Heartland had previously recognized an allowance for doubtful accounts for the impairment prior to the settlement.

(LO 3) **E14-24 (Term Modification—Debtor's Entries)** On December 31, 2014, Green Bank enters into a debt restructuring agreement with Troubled Inc., which is now experiencing financial trouble. The bank agrees to restructure a $2-million, 12% note receivable issued at par by the following modifications:

1. Reducing the principal obligation from $2 million to $1.9 million

2. Extending the maturity date from December 31, 2014, to December 31, 2017

3. Reducing the interest rate from 12% to 10%

Troubled pays interest at the end of each year. On January 1, 2018, Troubled Inc. pays $1.9 million in cash to Green Bank. Troubled prepares financial statements in accordance with IFRS.

Instructions

(a) Discuss whether or not Troubled should record a gain.

(b) Calculate the rate of interest that Troubled should use to calculate its interest expense in future periods.

(c) Prepare the interest payment entry for Troubled on December 31, 2016.

(d) What entry should Troubled make on January 1, 2018?

(LO 3) **E14-25 (Term Modification—Creditor's Entries)** Assume the same information as in E14-24 and answer the following questions related to Green Bank (the creditor). Green Bank prepares financial statements in accordance with IFRS.

Instructions

(a) What interest rate should Green Bank use to calculate the loss on the debt restructuring?

(b) Calculate the loss that Green Bank will suffer from the debt restructuring. Prepare the journal entry to record the loss.

(c) Prepare the amortization schedule for Green Bank after the debt restructuring.

(d) Prepare the interest receipt entry for Green Bank on December 31, 2016.

(e) What entry should Green Bank make on January 1, 2018?

(LO 3) E14-26 (Settlement—Debtor's Entries) Use the same information as in E14-24 but assume now that Green Bank reduced the principal to $1.6 million rather than $1.9 million. On January 1, 2018, Troubled Inc. pays $1.6 million in cash to Green Bank for the principal. The market rate is currently 10%.

Instructions

(a) Can Troubled record a gain under this term modification? If yes, calculate the gain.

(b) Prepare the journal entries to record the gain on Troubled's books.

(c) What interest rate should Troubled use to calculate its interest expense in future periods? Will your answer be the same as in E14-24? Why or why not?

(d) Prepare the amortization schedule of the note for Troubled after the debt restructuring.

(e) Prepare the interest payment entries for Troubled on December 31, 2015, 2016, and 2017.

(f) What entry should Troubled make on January 1, 2018?

(LO 3) E14-27 (Settlement—Creditor's Entries) Use the information in E14-24 and the assumptions in E14-26 and answer the following questions related to Green Bank (the creditor).

Instructions

(a) What interest rate should Green Bank use to calculate the loss on the debt restructuring?

(b) Calculate the loss that Green Bank will suffer under this new term modification. Prepare the journal entry to record the loss on Green Bank's books.

(c) Prepare the amortization schedule for Green Bank after the debt restructuring.

(d) Prepare the interest receipt entry for Green Bank on December 31, 2015, 2016, and 2017.

(e) What entry should Green Bank make on January 1, 2018?

(LO 3) E14-28 (Debtor/Creditor Entries for Settlement of Troubled Debt) Vargo Limited owes $270,000 to First Trust Inc. on a 10-year, 12% note due on December 31, 2014. The note was issued at par. Because Vargo is in financial trouble, First Trust Inc. agrees to extend the maturity date to December 31, 2016, reduce the principal to $220,000, and reduce the interest rate to 5%, payable annually on December 31. The market rate is currently 5%. Both Vargo and First Trust prepare financial statements in accordance with IFRS.

Instructions

(a) Prepare the journal entry on Vargo's books on December 31, 2014, 2015, and 2016.

(b) Prepare the journal entry on First Trust's books on December 31, 2014, 2015, and 2016.

(LO 3) E14-29 (Debtor/Creditor Entries for Settlement of Troubled Debt) Grumpy Limited owes $137,300 to Bank One Inc. on a 10-year, 11% note due on December 31, 2014. The note was issued at par. Because Grumpy is in financial trouble, Bank One Inc. agrees to accept a piece of equipment (with original cost of $100,000 and carrying value of $55,000 on Grumpy's books at December 31, 2014) and cancel the entire debt. The equipment has a fair value of $82,500. Both Grumpy and Bank One prepare financial statements in accordance with IFRS.

Instructions

(a) Prepare the journal entry on Grumpy's books for the debt settlement.

(b) Prepare the journal entry on Bank One's books for the debt settlement. Assume that the impairment has already been accrued through the Allowance for Doubtful Accounts.

(LO 4) E14-30 (Classification of Liabilities) The following are various accounts:

1. Bank loans payable of a winery, due March 10, 2018 (the product requires aging for five years before it can be sold)

2. $10 million of serial bonds payable, of which $2 million is due each July 31

3. Amounts withheld from employees' wages for income tax

4. Notes payable that are due January 15, 2017

5. Interest payable on a note payable (the note is due January 15, 2017, and the interest is due June 30, 2015)

6. Credit balance in a customer's account arising from returns and allowances after collection in full of the account

7. Bonds payable of $2 million maturing June 30, 2018

8. An overdraft of $1,000 in a bank account (no other balances are carried at this bank)

9. An overdraft of $1,000 in a bank account (other accounts are carried at this bank and have positive account balances)

10. Deposits made by customers who have ordered goods

Instructions

(a) Indicate whether each of the items above should be classified under IFRS on December 31, 2014, as a current or long-term liability or under some other classification. Consider each item independently from all others; that is, do not assume that all of them relate to one particular business. If the classification of some of the items is doubtful, explain why in each case.

(b) Assume instead that the company follows ASPE. Repeat part (a) for the items that would be classified differently.

(LO 4) **E14-31 (Classification)** The following items are found in a company's financial statements:

1. Interest expense (credit balance)

2. Gain on restructuring of debt

3. Mortgage payable (payable in equal amounts over the next three years)

4. Debenture bonds payable (maturing in five years)

5. Notes payable (due in four years)

6. Income bonds payable (due in three years)

Instructions

(a) Indicate how each of these items should be classified in the financial statements under IFRS.

(b) Assume instead that the company follows ASPE. Repeat part (a) for the items that would be classified differently.

(LO 5) **E14-32 (Long-Term Debt Disclosure)** At December 31, 2014, Reddy Inc. has three long-term debt issues outstanding. The first is a $2.2-million note payable that matures on June 30, 2017. The second is a $4-million bond issue that matures on September 30, 2018. The third is a $17.5-million sinking fund debenture with annual sinking fund payments of $3.5 million in each of the years 2016 through 2020.

Instructions

Prepare the note disclosure that is required for the long-term debt at December 31, 2014.

Problems

Digging Deeper

P14-1 Sabonis Cosmetics Inc. purchased machinery on December 31, 2014, paying $50,000 down and agreeing to pay the balance in four equal instalments of $40,000 that are payable each December 31. An assumed interest rate of 8% is implicit in the purchase price. Sabonis prepares financial statements in accordance with IFRS.

Instructions

(a) Prepare the journal entries that would be recorded for the purchase and for the payments and interest on December 31, 2014, 2015, 2016, 2017, and 2018.

(b) From the lender's perspective, what are the advantages of an instalment note compared with an interest-bearing note?

Digging Deeper

P14-2 On June 1, 2014, MacDougall Corporation approached Silverman Corporation about purchasing a parcel of undeveloped land. Silverman was asking $240,000 for the land and MacDougall saw that there was some flexibility in the asking price. MacDougall did not have the necessary funds to make a cash offer to Silverman and proposed to give, in return for the land, a $300,000, five-year promissory note that bears interest at the rate of 4%. The interest is to be paid annually to Silverman Corporation on June 1 of each of the next five years. Silverman insisted that the note taken in return become a mortgage note. The amended offer was accepted by Silverman, and MacDougall signed a mortgage note for $300,000 due June 1, 2019. MacDougall would have had to pay 10% at its local bank if it were to secure the necessary cash for the land purchase. Silverman, on the other hand, could borrow the funds at 9%. Both MacDougall and Silverman have calendar year ends.

Instructions

(a) Discuss how MacDougall Corporation would determine a value for the land in recording the purchase from Silverman Corporation.

(b) What is the difference between a promissory note payable and a mortgage note payable? Why would Silverman Corporation insist on obtaining a mortgage note payable from MacDougall Corporation?

(c) Calculate the purchase price of the land and prepare an effective-interest amortization table for the term of the mortgage note payable that is given in the exchange.

(d) Prepare the journal entry for the purchase of the land.

(e) Prepare any adjusting journal entry that is required at the end of the fiscal year and the first payment made on June 1, 2015, assuming no reversing entries are used.

(f) Assume that Silverman had insisted on obtaining an instalment note from MacDougall instead of a mortgage note. Then do the following:

1. Calculate the amount of the instalment payments that would be required for a five-year instalment note. Use the same cost of the land to MacDougall Corporation that you determined for the mortgage note in part (a).

2. Prepare an effective-interest amortization table for the five-year term of the instalment note.

3. Prepare the journal entry for the purchase of the land and the issuance of the instalment note.

4. Prepare any adjusting journal entry that is required at the end of the fiscal year and the first payment made on June 1, 2015, assuming no reversing entries are used.

5. Compare the balances of the two different notes payable and related accounts at December 31, 2014. Be specific about the classifications on the statement of financial position.

6. Consider why Silverman would insist on an instalment note in this case?

P14-3 The following amortization and interest schedule is for the issuance of 10-year bonds by Capulet Corporation on January 1, 2014, and the subsequent interest payments and charges. The company's year end is December 31 and it prepares its financial statements yearly.

Amortization Schedule

Year	Cash	Interest	Amount Unamortized	Carrying Amount
Jan. 1, 2014			$5,651	$ 94,349
2014	$11,000	$11,322	5,329	94,671
2015	11,000	11,361	4,968	95,032
2016	11,000	11,404	4,564	95,436
2017	11,000	11,452	4,112	95,888
2018	11,000	11,507	3,605	96,395
2019	11,000	11,567	3,038	96,962
2020	11,000	11,635	2,403	97,597
2021	11,000	11,712	1,691	98,309
2022	11,000	11,797	894	99,106
2023	11,000	11,894	–0–	$100,000

Instructions

(a) Indicate whether the bonds were issued at a premium or a discount and explain how you can determine this fact from the schedule.

(b) Indicate whether the amortization schedule is based on the straight-line method or the effective interest method and explain how you can determine which method is used. Are both amortization methods accepted for financial reporting purposes?

(c) Determine the stated interest rate and the effective interest rate.

(d) Based on the schedule above, prepare the journal entry to record the issuance of the bonds on January 1, 2014.

(e) Based on the schedule above, prepare the journal entry or entries to reflect the bond transactions and accruals for 2014. (Interest is paid January 1.)

(f) Based on the schedule above, prepare the journal entry or entries to reflect the bond transactions and accruals for 2022. Capulet Corporation does not use reversing entries.

P14-4 Venzuela Inc. is building a new hockey arena at a cost of $2.5 million. It received a down payment of $500,000 from local businesses to support the project, and now needs to borrow $2 million to complete the project. It therefore decides to issue $2 million of 10-year, 10.5% bonds. These bonds were issued on January 1, 2014, and pay interest annually on each January 1. The bonds yield 10% to the investor and have an effective interest rate to the issuer of 10.4053% (increased effective interest rate due to the capitalization of the bond issue costs). Any additional funds that are needed to complete the project will be obtained from local businesses. Venzuela Inc. paid and capitalized $50,000 in bond issuance costs related to the bond issue. Venzuela prepares financial statements in accordance with IFRS.

Instructions

(a) Prepare the journal entry to record the issuance of the bonds on January 1, 2014.

(b) Prepare a bond amortization schedule up to and including January 1, 2019, using the effective interest method.

(c) Assume that on July 1, 2017, the company retires half of the bonds at a cost of $1,065,000 plus accrued interest. Prepare the journal entry to record this retirement.

(d) Assume that the costs incurred by Venzuela Inc. to issue the bonds totalled $50,000 as above. If Venzuela Inc. chose to apply the fair value option and thus expense these costs, how would this affect the amount of interest expense that is recognized by Venzuela Inc. each year and over the 10-year term of the bonds in total, compared with its current accounting practice of capitalizing the bond issue costs? Assume that Venzuela would apply the fair value option under IAS 39.

P14-5 In the following two independent cases, the company closes its books on December 31:

1. Armstrong Inc. sells $2 million of 10% bonds on March 1, 2014. The bonds pay interest on September 1 and March 1. The bonds' due date is September 1, 2017. The bonds yield 12%.

2. Ouelette Ltd. sells $6 million of 11% bonds on June 1, 2014. The bonds pay interest on December 1 and June 1. The bonds' due date is June 1, 2018. The bonds yield 10%. On October 1, 2015, Ouelette buys back $1.2 million worth of bonds for $1.4 million (includes accrued interest).

Instructions

For the two cases above, prepare all of the relevant journal entries from the time of sale until the date indicated. (For situation 1, prepare the journal entries through December 31, 2015; for situation 2, prepare the journal entries through December 1, 2016.) Use the effective interest method for discount and premium amortization (prepare any necessary amortization tables). Amortize any premium or discount on the interest dates and at year end. (Assume that no reversing entries were made.)

P14-6 Selected transactions on the books of Pfaff Corporation follow:

May 1, 2014	Bonds payable with a par value of $700,000, which are dated January 1, 2014, are sold at 105 plus accrued interest. They are coupon bonds, bear interest at 12% (payable annually at January 1), and mature on January 1, 2024. (Use an interest expense account for accrued interest.)
Dec. 31	Adjusting entries are made to record the accrued interest on the bonds and the amortization of the proper amount of premium. (Use straight-line amortization.)
Jan. 1, 2015	Interest on the bonds is paid.
April 1	Par value bonds of $420,000 are repurchased at 103 plus accrued interest and are retired. (Bond premium is to be amortized only at the end of each year.)
Dec. 31	Adjusting entries are made to record the accrued interest on the bonds, and the proper amount of premium amortized.

Instructions

(a) Assume that Pfaff follows ASPE. Prepare the journal entries for the transactions above.

(b) How would your answers to the above change if Pfaff were to follow IFRS?

P14-7 On December 31, 2014, Faital Limited acquired a machine from Plato Corporation by issuing a $600,000, non-interest-bearing note that is payable in full on December 31, 2018. The company's credit rating permits it to borrow funds from its several lines of credit at 10%. The machine is expected to have a five-year life and a $70,000 residual value.

Instructions

(a) Prepare the journal entry for the purchase on December 31, 2014.

(b) Prepare any necessary adjusting entries related to depreciation of the asset (use straight-line) and amortization of the note (use the effective interest method) on December 31, 2015.

(c) Prepare any necessary adjusting entries related to depreciation of the asset and amortization of the note on December 31, 2016.

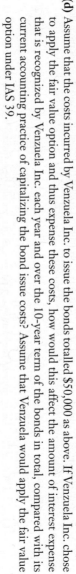

(d) Assume that on December 31, 2014, prior to purchasing the machine, Faital had total debt of $432,000 and total assets of $896,000. From the perspective of a creditor, discuss the effect of the purchase on Faital's debt-paying ability.

P14-8   Benoit Inc. issued 25-year, 9% mortgage bonds in the principal amount of $3 million on January 2, 2000, at a discount of $150,000. It then amortized the discount through charges to expense over the life of the issue on a straight-line basis. The indenture securing the issue provided that the bonds could be called for redemption in total but not in part at any time before maturity at 104% of the principal amount, but it did not provide for any sinking fund.

On December 18, 2014, the company issued 20-year, 11% debenture bonds in the principal amount of $4 million at 102 and the proceeds were used to redeem the 25-year, 9% mortgage bonds on January 2, 2015. The indenture securing the new issue did not provide for any sinking fund or for retirement before maturity. Benoit prepares financial statements in accordance with ASPE.

Instructions

(a) Prepare journal entries to record the issuance of the 11% bonds and the retirement of the 9% bonds.

(b) Indicate the income statement treatment of the gain or loss on redemption of bonds and prepare the note disclosure that is required. Assume that 2015 income from operations is $3.2 million and that the weighted number of shares outstanding is 1.5 million and the income tax rate is 25%.

P14-9   Four independent situations follow:

1. On March 1, 2014, Wilkie Inc. issued $4 million of 9% bonds at 103 plus accrued interest. The bonds are dated January 1, 2014, and pay interest semi-annually on July 1 and January 1. In addition, Wilkie incurred $27,000 of bond issuance costs.

2. On January 1, 2014, Langley Ltd. issued 9% bonds with a face value of $500,000 for $469,280 to yield 10%. The bonds are dated January 1, 2014, and pay interest annually. Langley prepares financial statements in accordance with ASPE.

3. Chico Building Inc., a private company that prepares financial statements in accordance with ASPE, has several long-term bonds outstanding at December 31, 2014. These long-term bonds have the following sinking fund requirements and maturities for the next six years:

	Sinking Fund	Maturities
2015	$300,000	$100,000
2016	$100,000	$250,000
2017	$100,000	$100,000
2018	$200,000	–0–
2019	$200,000	$150,000
2020	$200,000	$100,000

4. In the long-term debt structure of Czeslaw Inc., the following three bonds were reported: mortgage bonds payable, $10 million; collateral trust bonds, $5 million; bonds maturing in instalments, secured by plant equipment, $4 million.

Instructions

(a) For situation 1, calculate the net amount of cash received by Wilkie as a result of the issuance of these bonds.

(b) For situation 2, what amount should Langley report for interest expense in 2014 related to these bonds, assuming that it uses the effective interest method for amortizing any bond premium or discount? Could Langley choose to use the straight-line method for amortizing any bond premium or discount?

(c) For situation 3, indicate how this information should be reported in Chico's financial statements at December 31, 2014.

(d) For situation 4, determine the total amount of debenture bonds that is outstanding, if any.

P14-10   On April 1, 2014, Taylor Corp. sold 12,000 of its $1,000 face value, 15-year, 11% bonds at 97. Interest payment dates are April 1 and October 1, and the company uses the straight-line method of bond discount amortization. On March 1, 2015, Taylor extinguished 3,000 of the bonds by issuing 100,000 shares. At this time, the accrued interest was paid in cash to the bondholders whose bonds were being extinguished. In a separate transaction on March 1, 2015, 120,000 of the company's shares sold for $31 per share.

Instructions

Prepare Taylor Corp.'s journal entries to record the following:

(a) April 1, 2014: issuance of the bonds

(b) October 1, 2014: payment of the semi-annual interest

(c) December 31, 2014: accrual of the interest expense

(d) March 1, 2015: extinguishment of 3,000 bonds by the issuance of common shares (no reversing entries are made)

P14-11 Refer to P14-10 and Taylor Corp.

Instructions

Repeat the instructions of P14-10 assuming that Taylor Corp. uses the effective interest method. Provide an effective interest table for the bonds for two interest payment periods. (*Hint:* You need to first calculate the effective interest rate on the bonds. Round the semi-annual interest percentage to four decimal places.)

P14-12 On January 1, 2014, Batonica Limited issued a $1.2-million, five-year, zero-interest-bearing note to Northern Savings Bank. The note was issued to yield 8% annual interest. Unfortunately, during 2014 Batonica fell into financial trouble due to increased competition. After reviewing all available evidence on December 31, 2014, Northern Savings Bank decided that the loan was impaired. Batonica will probably pay back only $800,000 of the principal at maturity. Both Batonica and Northern Savings Bank prepare financial statements in accordance with IFRS.

Instructions

(a) Prepare journal entries for both Batonica and Northern Savings Bank to record the issuance of the note on January 1, 2014. (Round to the nearest $10.)

(b) Assuming that both Batonica and Northern Savings Bank use the effective interest method to amortize the discount, prepare the amortization schedule for the note.

(c) Under what circumstances can Northern Savings Bank consider Batonica's note to be impaired?

(d) Estimate the loss that Northern Savings Bank will suffer from Batonica's financial distress on December 31, 2014. What journal entries should be made to record this loss?

P14-13 Daniel Perkins is the sole shareholder of Perkins Inc., which is currently under bankruptcy court protection. As a debtor in possession, he has negotiated a revised loan agreement with United Bank. Perkins Inc.'s $600,000, 10-year, 12% note was refinanced with a $600,000, 10-year, 5% note. Assume the market rate of interest is 12% at the refinancing date. Both Perkins and United Bank prepare financial statements in accordance with IFRS.

Instructions

(a) What is the accounting nature of this transaction?

(b) Prepare the journal entry to record this refinancing (1) on the books of Perkins Inc. and (2) on the books of United Bank.

(c) Discuss whether the financial statements provide the information that would be useful to managers and potential investors in this situation.

P14-14 Shahani Corporation is having financial difficulty and has therefore asked Bajwa National Bank to restructure its $3-million, 10%, 10% note outstanding. The note was issued at par and has three years remaining. The current market rate for a loan of this nature is 12%. Both Shahani and Bajwa National Bank prepare financial statements in accordance with IFRS.

Instructions

For each of the following independent situations related to the above scenario, prepare the journal entry that Shahani and Bajwa National Bank would make for the restructuring that is described.

(a) Bajwa National Bank agrees to take an equity interest in Shahani by accepting common shares valued at $2.2 million in exchange for relinquishing its claim on this note.

(b) Bajwa National Bank agrees to accept land in exchange for relinquishing its claim on this note. The land has a carrying amount of $1,050,000 and a fair value of $2.5 million.

(c) Bajwa National Bank agrees to modify the terms of the note so that Shahani does not have to pay any interest on the note over the three-year period.

(d) Bajwa National Bank agrees to reduce the principal balance down to $2.3 million and to require interest only in the second and third year at a rate of 9%.

P14-15 Dilemma Inc. owes Stauskas Bank a $250,000, 10-year, 15% note issued at par. The note is due today, December 31, 2014. Because Dilemma Inc. is in financial trouble, Stauskas agrees to accept 60,000 shares of Dilemma's common shares, which are currently selling for $1.40; to reduce the note's face amount to $150,000; to extend the maturity date to December 31, 2018; and to reduce the interest rate to 6%. Interest will continue to be due on December 31 of each year, and one year of interest is outstanding as at December 31, 2014. The current market rate is 15%. Both Dilemma and Stauskas Bank prepare financial statements in accordance with IFRS.

Instructions

(a) Prepare all the necessary journal entries on the books of Dilemma Inc. from the time of the restructuring through maturity.

(b) Prepare all the necessary journal entries on the books of Stauskas Bank from the time of the restructuring through maturity.

P14-16 At December 31, 2013, Shutdown Manufacturing Limited had outstanding a $300,000, 12% note payable to Thornton National Bank. Dated January 1, 2011, the note was issued at par and due on December 31, 2014, with interest payable each December 31. During 2014, Shutdown notified Thornton that it might be unable to meet the scheduled December 31, 2014 payment of principal and interest because of financial difficulties. On September 30, 2014, Thornton sold the note, including interest accrued since December 31, 2013, for $280,000 to Orsini Foundry, one of Shutdown's oldest and largest customers. On December 31, 2014, Orsini agreed to accept inventory that cost $240,000 but was worth $315,000 from Shutdown in full settlement of the note. Thornton, Shutdown, and Orsini prepare financial statements in accordance with IFRS.

Instructions

(a) Prepare the journal entry to record the September 30, 2014 transaction on the books of Thornton, Shutdown, and Orsini. For each company, indicate whether the transaction is a restructuring of troubled debt.

(b) Prepare the journal entries to record the December 31, 2014 transaction on the books of Shutdown and Orsini. For each company, indicate whether this transaction is a restructuring of troubled debt.

P14-17 Mazza Corp. owes Tsang Corp. a $110,000, 10-year, 10% note issued at par plus $11,000 of accrued interest. The note is due today, December 31, 2014. Because Mazza Corp. is in financial trouble, Tsang Corp. agrees to forgive the accrued interest and $10,000 of the principal, and to extend the maturity date to December 31, 2017. Interest at 10% of the revised principal will continue to be due on December 31 of each year. Assume the market rate of interest is 10% at the date of refinancing. Mazza and Tsang prepare financial statements in accordance with IFRS.

Instructions

(a) Is this a settlement or a modification?

(b) Prepare a schedule of the debt reduction and interest expense for the years 2014 through 2017.

(c) Calculate the gain or loss for Tsang Corp. and prepare a schedule of the receivable reduction and interest income for the years 2014 through 2017.

(d) Prepare all the necessary journal entries on the books of Mazza Corp. for the years 2014, 2015, and 2016.

(e) Prepare all the necessary journal entries on the books of Tsang Corp. for the years 2014, 2015, and 2016.

Case

Refer to the Case Primer on the Student Website and in *WileyPLUS* to help you answer this case.

CA14-1 Pitt Corporation is interested in building a pop can manufacturing plant next to its existing plant in Montreal. The objective would be to ensure a steady supply of cans at a stable price and to minimize transportation costs. However, the company has been experiencing some financial problems and has been reluctant to borrow any additional cash to fund the project. The company is not concerned about the cash flow problems of making payments; instead, its real concern is the impact of adding long-term debt to its balance sheet.

The president of Pitt, Aidan O'Reilly, approached the president of Aluminum Can Corp. (ACC), its major supplier, to see if some agreement could be reached. ACC was anxious to work out an arrangement, since it seemed inevitable that Pitt would begin its own can production. ACC could not afford to lose the account.

After some discussion, a two-part plan was worked out. First ACC will construct a plant on Pitt's land next to the existing plant, and the plant will initially belong to ACC. Second, Pitt will sign a 20-year purchase agreement. Under the purchase agreement, Pitt will express its intention to buy all of its cans from ACC and pay a unit price that at normal capacity would cover labour and material, an operating management fee, and the debt service requirements on the new plant. The expected unit price, if transportation costs are taken into consideration, is lower than the current market price. If Pitt ends up not taking enough production in any specific year and if the excess cans cannot be sold at a high enough price on the open market, Pitt agrees to make up any cash shortage so that ACC can make the payments on its debt. The bank is willing to make a 20-year loan for the plant, taking the plant and the purchase agreement as collateral. At the end of 20 years, the plant will become Pitt's.

Integrated Cases

IC14-1 Finishing International Enterprises (FIE), a private company based in Vancouver, is Canada's largest dealer of heavy equipment, such as tractors, grapple skidders, and backhoes. The company sells, rents, finances, and provides customer support for all of the heavy equipment it finances.

FIE is owned by Tony Finishing, who provides the strategic vision, while all of the accounting functions are the responsibility of Chen Yi, the controller. Tony has determined that FIE will be expanding into the United States next year. FIE has been able to reduce its debt load over the years but still relies heavily on its creditors for continued support and growth. The bank has never asked for an audit before, but recently, Tony met with the bank to make some routine changes to the banking agreement. He was told the company would have to provide audited statements for the year ended December 31, 2014, given its expansion into the United States. The bank has also stipulated that FIE must maintain a total debt to equity ratio of no more than 1 to 1 (that is, for every $1 in equity, there should be no more than $1 in debt), where debt is defined as all liabilities, including payables and accruals.

Lento & Partners LLP (L&P) has been FIE's accountants for many years. It is now January 2015, and you are the senior accountant at L&P who has been responsible for FIE's year end in the past. Tony has asked you to come in before year end to help Chen establish accounting policies to ensure that FIE is in compliance with GAAP. You meet with Tony and Chen and note the following.

1. During the year, FIE sold 2,000 small tractors for $2,600 each, including a one-year warranty. Maintenance on each machine during the warranty period averages $380. During the year, actual warranty costs incurred were $180,000. FIE is currently using the cash basis to record the warranty expense.

2. On October 1, 2014, the provincial environment ministry identified FIE as a potentially responsible party in a chemical spill in its Hamilton warehouse. Management, along with legal counsel, has concluded that it is likely that they will be responsible for damages, and a reasonable range of these damages is $500,000 to $750,000. FIE's insurance policy of $1 million has a deductible clause of $250,000. Management has yet to record this transaction in the books.

3. The company purchased a new piece of machinery on January 1, 2014. The purchase was financed though an interest-free five-year loan, whereby it is required to pay back $500,000 in each year. Management recorded the asset and liability at $2.5 million in the books. Management was excited about this promotion as the interest rate normally charged on a similar loan would have been 9%. FIE uses the straight-line method to amortize the asset, which has a seven-year useful life.

4. On January 1, 2013, FIE constructed a warehouse on property it leased for a five-year period. FIE will be required to remove the warehouse and restore the property to its original condition at the end of the lease term. Inflation-adjusted costs of removing the warehouse and restoring the property are estimated to be $200,000. In 2013, management recorded a liability for $200,000 in the books. No additional entries have been made.

5. On January 1, 2014, FIE issued 30,000 redeemable and retractable preferred shares at a value of $10 per share. The shares are redeemable by FIE at any time after January 2018. The shares are retractable for $10 per share at any time up to January 2018, after which the retractable feature expires. The preferred shares require the payment of a mandatory dividend of $2 per share during the retraction period, after which the dividends become non-cumulative and non-mandatory (that is, paid at the discretion of the board).

FIE's balance sheet reveals that the corporation has $1.6 million in debt and $2,850,000 in equity. Tony stated that since equity is greater than debt by $1,250,000, he is planning on paying a large $800,000 dividend on his common shares, which "will still allow the debt to equity ratio covenant (1:1) to be maintained." FIE's credit-adjusted risk-free rate is 8%.

Instructions

Adopt the role of the controller and discuss the financial reporting issues. The company is a private company. (*Hint:* Use first principles.) Where IFRS and ASPE are different, the controller would like to know.

IC14-2 RTL is a family owned and operated business that prints flyers and banners. It has been in operation for over 20 years and is being passed on to the next generation. Profits from the last two years have been significantly declining. This is a direct result of the changing landscape of the industry, which has been moving toward digital printing. RTL management has an aggressive plan to change the revenue mix from traditional to digital printing.

To finance this transition, RTL borrowed money from the bank at the end of 2012 for the purchase of digital printing equipment. Some changes were made to the original equipment to accommodate for the printing of banners.

Instructions

Provide a report to Tony and Chen outlining your recommendation on accounting policies and other important issues. Note where there are differences between ASPE and IFRS.

Despite an increase in digital sales, RTL did not achieve its revenue target for 2013 or 2014. In addition to the slow digital revenue growth, RTL has recently lost its top two traditional print clients, who accounted for 50% of overall revenues. Management is concerned with RTL's ability to continue making payments on the outstanding loan under the current conditions.

Management is actively communicating with the bank regarding potential alternatives. Given RTL's history with the bank, concessions will be made by the bank including a reduction of the interest rate from 10% to 8%, a three-year extension of the current maturity, and a reduction of principal from $2 million to $1.5 million. The restructuring agreement was signed just before year end. Management is confident that the old debt should be eliminated from the balance sheet. The current market discount rate is 9%.

RTL also has a new sales plan that it is offering to digital customers. Revenue contracts include an upfront non-refundable fee and a term of two to three years. Customers are charged a per-unit fee for each digital print and a flat fee for any change in concept or design. Each contract has a minimum value so RTL earns a flat rate even if digital printing jobs are never performed. The catch to the lucrative contracts are that RTL must be available to print on-demand 24 hours a day, 7 days a week. All of RTL's current digital print customers are small businesses, two of which have recently filed for bankruptcy.

RTL plans to use the digital printing equipment only for five years. At the end of this period, RTL is expecting to pay $100,000 for any modifications necessary to update and prepare the equipment for sale to another vendor. A liability of $100,000 has already been recorded in the books in 2012. The accountant who prepared the journal entry has asked the controller to review this past transaction for accuracy.

Instructions

It is the end of 2014. The financial controller is preparing notes for the upcoming meeting with the auditors. Adopt the role of the controller and discuss any financial reporting issues that should be addressed before the meeting. Identify the necessary journal entries. RTL would like to use more simplified GAAP if possible.

Writing Assignments

WA14-1 Lindall Limited (LL) has a 10-year loan issued by the bank that is due in five years. The VP Finance feels that the company is carrying too much debt on its statement of financial position and would like to repay the loan early. Unfortunately the early repayment penalty is significant and therefore LL is looking for other options to reduce the amount of debt on the statement of financial position. Currently, the company is looking at the following transaction:

- Set up a trust that will be used to repay the principal and interest on the original loan as these payments come due.
- Transfer funds to the trust in the amount equal to the present value of the principal and interest payments.
- Invest the funds in low-risk investments such that the investments will be able to generate sufficient return to make the principal and interest payments.

The VP Finance is not sure whether they need the bank to discharge the original loan and agree to look to the trust for repayment (legal defeasance). She would like to derecognize the debt on the LL statement of financial position once the deal is in place. LL follows IFRS.

Instructions

Adopt the role of the ethical accountant and discuss the financial reporting issues. What is the difference between legal defeasance and in-substance defeasance? How does this affect the accounting? Are there arguments for removing the debt under both legal and in-substance defeasance? How should the company account for the defeasance arrangement?

Ethics

WA14-2 On January 1, 2014, Branagh Limited issued for $1,075,230 its 20-year, 13% bonds that have a maturity value of $1 million and pay interest semi-annually on January 1 and July 1. The bond issue costs were not material in amount. Three presentations follow of the statement of financial position long-term liability section that might be used for these bonds at the issue date:

1. Bonds payable (maturing January 1, 2034)	$1,075,230
2. Bonds payable principal (face value $1,000,000, maturing January 1, 2034)	97,220[a]
Bonds payable interest (semi-annual payment of $65,000)	978,010[b]
Total bond liability	$1,075,230
3. Bonds payable principal (maturing January 1, 2034)	$1,000,000
Bonds payable interest ($65,000 per period for 40 periods)	2,600,000
Total bond liability	$3,600,000

[a] The present value of $1 million due at the end of 40 (six-month) periods at the yield rate of 6% per period
[b] The present value of $65,000 per period for 40 (six-month) periods at the yield rate of 6% per period

Instructions

(a) Discuss the conceptual merit(s) of each of the three date-of-issue statement of financial position presentations shown above.

(b) Explain why investors would pay $1,075,230 for bonds that have a maturity value of only $1 million.

(c) Assuming that, at any date during the life of the bonds, a discount rate is needed to calculate the carrying value of the obligations that arise from a bond issue, discuss the conceptual merit(s) of using the following for this purpose:

1. The coupon or nominal rate
2. The effective or yield rate at date of issue

(d) If the obligations arising from these bonds are to be carried at their present value and this is calculated according to the current market rate of interest, how would the bond valuation at dates after the date of issue be affected by an increase or a decrease in the market rate of interest?

WA14-3   Thompson Limited (a private company with no published credit rating) completed several transactions during 2014. In January, the company purchased under contract a machine at a total price of $1.2 million. It is payable over five years with instalments of $240,000 per year, with the first payment due January 1, 2014. The seller considered the transaction to be an instalment sale with the title transferring to Thompson at the time of the final payment. If the company had paid cash for the machine, all at the time of the sale, the machine would have cost $1,050,000. The company could have borrowed funds from the bank to buy the machine at an interest rate of 7%. It is expected that the machine will last 10 years.

On July 1, 2014, Thompson issued $10 million of general revenue bonds priced at 99 with a coupon of 10% payable July 1 and January 1 of each of the next 10 years to a small group of large institutional investors. As a result, the bonds are closely held. The July 1 interest was paid and on December 30 the company transferred $500,000 to the trustee, Holly Trust Limited, for payment of the January 1, 2015 interest.

Thompson purchased $500,000 (face value) of its 6% convertible bonds for $455,000. It expects to resell the bonds at a later date to a small group of private investors.

Finally, due to the economic conditions, Thompson was able to obtain some government financing to assist with the purchase of some updated technology to be used in the plant. The government provided a $500,000 loan with an interest rate of 1% on December 31, 2014. The company must repay $500,000 in five years: December 31, 2019. Interest payments of $5,000 are due for the next five years, starting on December 31, 2015. The company could have borrowed a similar amount of funds for an interest rate of 6% on December 31, 2014.

Instructions

(a) As Thompson's accountant, prepare journal entries for the machine purchase and the government loan transactions described above. As Thompson is a private company, indicate any differences in treatment that might arise under ASPE and IFRS. For any fair value discussions, outline the level of fair value hierarchy that has been used.

(b) Having prepared the statement of financial position as at December 31, 2014, you have presented it to the company president. She asks you the following questions about it. Answer these questions by writing a brief paragraph that justifies your treatment of the items in the statement of financial position.

1. Why is the new machine being valued at $1,050,000 on the books, when we are paying $1.2 million in total? Why has depreciation been charged on equipment being purchased under contract? Title has not yet passed to the company and, therefore, the equipment is not yet our asset. Would it not be more correct for the company to show on the left side of the statement of financial position only the amount that has been paid to date instead of showing the full contract price on the left side and the unpaid portion on the right side? After all, the seller considers the transaction an instalment sale.

2. Bond interest is shown as a current liability. Did we not pay our trustee, Holly Trust Limited, the full amount of interest that is due this period?

3. The repurchased bonds (sometimes referred to as treasury bonds) are shown as a deduction from bonds payable issued. Why are they not shown as an asset, since they can be sold again? Are they the same as bonds of other companies that we hold as investments?

4. What is this government grant showing on the statement of financial position? We received a loan, not a grant, since we have to pay it back. Why is the government loan showing substantially less than the $500,000 that we will have to repay?

WA14-4   Part I The appropriate method of amortizing a premium or discount on issuance of bonds is the effective interest method under IFRS. ASPE allows either the effective interest rate or the straight-line method.

Part II Gains or losses from the early extinguishment of debt that is refunded can theoretically be accounted for in three ways:

1. They can be amortized over the remaining life of old debt.

2. They can be amortized over the life of the new debt issue.

3. They can be recognized in the period of extinguishment.

Instructions—Part I

(a) What is the effective interest method of amortization and what are the differences and similarities between it and the straight-line method of amortization?

(b) How is interest calculated using the effective interest method? Why and how do amounts that are obtained using the effective interest method differ from amounts that are calculated under the straight-line method?

Instructions—Part II

(a) Provide supporting arguments for each of the three theoretical methods of accounting for gains and losses from the early extinguishment of debt.

(b) Which of the above methods is generally accepted as the appropriate amount of gain or loss that should be shown in a company's financial statements?

WA14-5

Instructions

Write a brief essay highlighting the differences between IFRS and ASPE noted in this chapter, discussing the conceptual justification for each. As part of this essay, include a discussion of the differences in capital disclosure requirements.

WA14-6 The IASB has been working on determining whether or not an entity's credit risk should be incorporated into the measurement of the liability. The Staff Paper that accompanies the Discussion Paper on Credit Risk in Liability Measurement, dated June 2009, outlines three reasons to support this treatment and three arguments cited against this treatment. (This paper is available at www.iasb.org.) The examples below clarify the issues being addressed.

The example given in the paper discusses a regular bond payable that will be settled in cash and will be valued using an effective rate of interest based on the market's assessment of credit risk and the entity's ability to pay. For example, this might be 7%; in other words, the company would have to pay 7% interest on these bonds and this is used as the effective interest rate to value these bonds at the time the bonds are issued. In addition, suppose that the company also has an asset retirement obligation that will be settled in the provision of services in the future. This will also require some outlay of cash in future and the value of the liability is determined by discounting these future cash flows using a discount rate that incorporates the time value of money and the risks specific to the liability. In many cases, this could be different from the 7% used for the bonds. Should the same discount rate, which incorporates credit risk, be used to determine this liability? Or should the asset retirement obligation be discounted using a default risk-free rate of interest?

Furthermore, as market rates change, should the value of the liabilities also be changing to reflect this? Let's say that the current market rate one year later required for the bond is 8% and this increase is due to a lower credit rating for the entity. Under current accounting standards, the bonds payable does not get revalued since it is reported at amortized cost. Should the bonds payable now be revalued and the effective interest rate changed? The asset retirement obligation would get revalued using the most current discount rates at each reporting period.

Note that the IASB has revised IFRS 9 requiring that the changes in fair value due to credit risk be presented as other comprehensive income. IFRS 9 will be mandatory in 2015 and the IASB has reopened discussions on IFRS 9 in hopes of harmonizing with U.S. GAAP, so IFRS 9 will likely change.

Instructions

(a) Explain the meaning of "non-performance risk."

(b) Using the example of a bond payable and an asset retirement obligation, discuss the arguments for and against incorporating credit risk into the measurement of liabilities.

(c) What are the alternatives for measuring liabilities?

RA14-1 Shoppers Drug Mart

Refer to the year-end financial statements and accompanying notes of **Shoppers Drug Mart** (SDM).

Instructions

Using ratio and other analyses, prepare an assessment of SDM's solvency and financial flexibility for the periods ended December 31, 2011, and January 1, 2011.

RA14-2 Loblaw Companies Limited and Empire Company Limited

Instructions

Access the financial statements for **Loblaw Companies Limited** for the year ended December 31, 2011, and **Empire Company Limited** for the year ended May 7, 2011, through SEDAR (www.sedar.com) and then answer the following questions.

(a) Calculate the debt-to-total-asset ratio and the times interest earned ratio for these two companies. Comment on the quality of these two ratios for both companies.

(b) What financial ratios do both companies use in the annual reports to monitor and present their debt financial condition? Do both companies use the same ratios? Are the ratios calculated in the same way?

(c) Review the type of debt that each company has issued and provide a brief description of the nature of debt issued. What credit rating does each company have? (This can be found in the Management Discussion and Analysis section.) If the credit rating has changed, comment on why this has happened. Compare the debt ratings of the two companies and comment on whether this is what would be expected given the analysis done in part (a).

(d) Review each company's Capital Management Disclosure note. For each company, explain its objectives in managing the capital, what is included in capital and the total of managed capital, the key ratios that are monitored, and any covenants that are imposed on the company.

(e) Do the companies have any variable interest entities? If so, explain the nature of these entities and how they have been reported by the companies. How did the accounting change (if at all) when the companies switched to IFRS?

RA14-3 DBRS

DBRS is a large bond-rating agency in Canada.

Instructions

Access the agency's website at www.dbrs.com and answer the following.

(a) How does DBRS rate the debt of food retailer companies? In other words, what is its methodology? List the factors considered in assessing the general business risk profile, the general financial risk profile (specific ratios considered), and industry-specific factors.

(b) What ratings has DBRS given to Loblaw Companies Limited and Empire Company Limited?

(c) Comment on why the ratings in (b) might have been given.

(d) Is it possible to have different ratings on different debt instruments in the same company? Explain.

RA14-4 Air Canada

Real World
Emphasis

Instructions

Access the financial statements for Air Canada for the year ended December 31, 2011, through SEDAR (www.sedar.com) and then answer the following questions.

(a) Calculate the debt to equity ratio. In your opinion, is this a high or low ratio? Discuss.

(b) Go to the DBRS website at www.dbrs.com. What ratings has DBRS given to Air Canada?

(c) Go to note 25 of the financial statements. This note deals with the transition to IFRS and explains the impact of the transition. What is the impact on accounting for long-term debt instruments and variable interest entities? (*Hint:* look at note 25(i) and (vii)).

ENDNOTES

[1] "Long-term debt" and "long-term liabilities" meet the definition of a financial liability in *CICA Handbook—Accounting*, Part II, Section 3856 and IAS 32 because they represent contractual obligations to deliver cash. These terms have the same meaning and are used interchangeably throughout the text.

[2] Data source: Standard & Poor's Corp. Standard & Poor's Financial Services LLC (S&P) does not guarantee the accuracy, completeness, timeliness or availability of any information, including ratings, and is not responsible for any errors or omissions (negligent or otherwise), regardless of the cause, or for the results obtained from the use of ratings. S&P gives no express or implied warranties, including, but not limited to, any warranties of merchantability or fitness for a particular purpose or use. S&P shall not be liable for any direct, indirect, incidental, exemplary, compensatory, punitive, special or consequential damages, costs, expenses, legal fees, or losses (including lost income or profits and opportunity costs) in connection with any use of ratings. S&P's ratings are statements of opinions and are not statements of fact or recommendations to purchase, hold or sell securities. They do not address the market value of securities or the suitability of securities for investment purposes, and should not be relied on as investment advice.

[3] *CICA Handbook—Accounting*, Part II, Section 3856.07 and IAS 39.43. Note that where the liabilities will subsequently be measured at fair value (for example, under the fair value option), the transaction costs should not be included in the initial measurement. Instead, the costs would be expensed.

[4] Until the 1950s, it was common for corporations to issue bonds with low, even-percent coupons (such as 4%) to demonstrate their financial soundness. Frequently, the result was larger discounts. More recently, it has become acceptable to set the stated rate of interest on bonds in more precise terms (such as 6⅞%). Companies usually try to match the stated rate as closely as possible to the market or effective rate at the time of issue. While discounts and premiums continue to occur, their absolute size tends to be much smaller, and often it is immaterial. A study conducted in the mid-1980s documented that, out of 685 new debt offerings, none were issued at a premium. Approximately 95% were issued either with no discount or at a price above 98. Now, however, zero-interest (deep discount) bonds are more popular, which causes substantial discounts.

[5] Although the effective interest method is required under IFRS per IAS 39.47, ASPE does not specify that this method must be used and therefore the straight-line method is also an option.

[6] The book value, also called the carrying value, equals the face amount minus any unamortized discount, or plus any unamortized premium. As previously noted, issue costs are deducted as long as the instrument is not subsequently measured using fair value. For simplicity's sake, these costs are assumed to be zero in most of the examples.

[7] Because interest is paid semi-annually, the interest rate that is used is 5% (10% × 6/12) and the number of periods is 10 (5 years × 2).

[8] *CICA Handbook—Accounting*, Part II, Section 3856.A8 and IAS 39.AG64.

[9] Note that a deferred credit/revenue account could be used to record the government grant or alternatively a contra asset account. Government grants were discussed in Chapter 10.

[10] IFRS 13.42.

[11] IFRS 9.5.7.7. Note that IFRS 9 is not mandatorily adoptable until 2015 (although it may be adopted early). Until that time, IAS 39 would be followed. IAS 39 does not prescribe any special treatment for gains and losses arising from remeasurement of financial liabilities under the fair value option and so, if a financial liability were accounted for under the fair value option, all gains and losses would be recognized in net income similar to ASPE.

[12] *CICA Handbook—Accounting*, Part II, Section 3856.26 and IAS 39.39.

[13] *CICA Handbook—Accounting*, Part II, Section 3856.27, IAS 39.40, and IAS 39.AG57.

[14] In reality, a loss should likely have been recognized when the bank first determined that the loan was impaired. This would usually be done before a loan is restructured or settled.

[15] The creditor must decide whether the asset meets the criteria to be classified as held for sale. If it does, the asset will subsequently be valued at its fair value less the costs to sell it.

[16] This type of transaction is sometimes referred to as a debt for equity swap. IFRIC Interpretation 19 deals with the accounting by the debtor (only) and supports the measurement of the common shares issued at fair value. For the debtor, general accounting principles would require the investment in the shares to be initially recognized at fair value. This is supported by *CICA Handbook—Accounting*, Part II, Section 3856.28.

[17] *CICA Handbook—Accounting*, Part II, Section 3856.A52 and IAS 39.40/AG62.

[18] It is unlikely that the accounting profession will be able to stop all types of off-balance sheet transactions. Developing new financial instruments and arrangements to sell to customers is profitable for investment banking firms, especially where there is a demand for them. Many banks are discontinuing these types of products, however, due to the highly publicized negative connotations surrounding SPEs, the abuse of which was one reason for the downfall of **Enron Corporation.**

[19] *CICA Handbook—Accounting*, Part II, Section 1510.10.

[20] IAS 1.72.

[21] *CICA Handbook—Accounting*, Part II, Section 1510.02 and IAS 1.61.

Cumulative Coverage: Chapters 13 and 14

The following information is obtained from the 2014 records of Chef's Spoon Incorporated, a company that produces high-quality kitchenware. The company has a June 30 year end and follows ASPE.

1. The total payroll of Chef's Spoon was $460,000 for the month of June 2014. Income taxes withheld were $110,000. The employment insurance is 1.98% for the employee and 1.4 times the employee premium for the employer. The CPP/QPP contributions are 4.95% for each. No employee earned more than the maximum insurable or pensionable earnings. Payroll is entered at the end of the month, and paid at the first of the next month. The remittance of taxes, CPP, and EI takes place the following month.

2. At the end of May, the vacation pay accrual account had a balance of $50,000. No vacations were taken in June and 70 employees who earned an average salary of $40,000 per year earned 4% vacation pay, and another 20 employees, who earned an average salary of $125,000, earned 8% vacation pay.

3. In January 2014, a worker was injured in the factory in an accident partially the result of his own negligence. The worker has sued Chef's Spoon for $800,000. Legal counsel believes it is somewhat possible that the outcome of the suit will be unfavourable and that the settlement would cost the company from $250,000 to $500,000.

4. The company sued one of its suppliers for providing raw materials used in Chef's Spoon products that contained a highly toxic plastic, and it is involved in a pending court case. Chef's Spoon's lawyers believe it is likely that the company will be awarded damages of $1.5 million.

5. On February 1, the company purchased equipment for $90,000 from Culinary Universe Company, paying $30,000 in cash and giving a one-year, 8% note for the balance. This transaction has not been recorded by Chef's Spoon yet because the $30,000 cash payment was made by a personal cheque from a key shareholder. The shareholder is asking to be repaid for this amount by July 15.

6. In order to keep up with the competition, the company needed to modernize its operations by building a new warehouse and production facility. The company had been able to save $1 million in cash but would need to come up with $4.2 million to finance the balance of the construction costs. After much analysis, the CEO made the decision to issue $4.2-million, five-year, 6% bonds since it would be cheaper than getting a loan from the bank. The bonds were finally issued February 1, 2014, and would pay interest on February 1 and August 1. The bonds yield 5% and are callable at 103. The bonds yield 5% and are callable at 103. The company uses the effective interest method to amortize bond discount and premium amounts.

7. During the 2014 fiscal year, the company opened its first retail store. This store sold products manufactured by Chef's Spoon, but also purchased from other suppliers of kitchen products. The retail store is located in a high-traffic shopping mall, and the company took control of the space on July 1, 2013. After two months of renovation work, the store opened and has been very successful. Sales in the first 10 months of operations totalled $1,523,000. The lease agreement required monthly rental payments of $15,000 due at the beginning of each month, and, if the total store sales exceeded $1,250,000 during the lease year, the company was required to pay additional rent of 1% of sales over $1,250,000.

8. The retail store sells several premium kitchenware items and gives its customers a coupon with each premium kitchenware item sold. In return for three coupons, customers receive a complimentary spice container that the company purchases for $1.20 each. Chef's Spoon's experience indicates that 60% of the coupons will be redeemed. During the 10 months ended June 30, 2014, 100,000 premium kitchenware items were sold, and 45,000 coupons were redeemed. As of June 30, no entries have been recorded with respect to the coupons.

Instructions

(a) For each transaction above, prepare the necessary journal entries to record the liability at year end, and any transactions that have not been properly recorded for the June 30, 2014 year end. If any transaction does not require an entry, explain in detail why no entry is needed, and what disclosure is required, if any.

(b) On August 31, 2015, Chef's Spoon Inc. called 40% of the bonds payable. Prepare the required journal entry for the retirement on this date.

Shareholders' Equity Is Not Always Equitable

Bloomberg via Getty Images

OWNING SHARES in a publicly traded company essentially means being a part owner, which exposes shareholders to the rewards but also the risks of ownership. When a company goes bankrupt, shareholders may lose all of their investment. A recent Canadian example is the former telecommunications giant Nortel Networks.

Nortel, once the ninth-most valuable corporation globally, saw its share price peak in August 2000 at $124.50, giving it a market value of nearly $440 billion. Shortly after, the worldwide dot-com bust dragged down its share price. In the next decade, the company struggled with falling customer orders, tougher competition, management missteps, and an accounting scandal. As Nortel focused on reorganizing and getting its accounting house in order, it filed for bankruptcy protection in January 2009, the day before a debt payment of $107 million was due. Its shares stopped trading in June 2009 at $0.18.

The company did not emerge from bankruptcy. Its remaining assets were sold. More than 6,000 of its patents were auctioned off, sold in 2011 to a consortium of tech firms, including

Apple, Microsoft, and Research In Motion, for U.S. $4.5 billion in cash.

The proceeds of the sale went to pay off some of the money owed to some creditors. When a company goes bankrupt, there is a hierarchy of who gets paid. At the top of the list are secured debt holders, followed by trade and other creditors. The last on the list are shareholders. Many companies have two types or classes of shares: common and preferred. Preferred shareholders, as the name sounds, get preference over common shareholders as creditors. Common shareholders' rights are residual, meaning they get whatever is left over when everyone else has been paid.

In the case of Nortel, neither class of shareholders was expected to get a penny back from their investment in the bankruptcy proceedings, which raised nearly $9 billion to pay creditors at the top of the hierarchy. "Nortel does not expect that the Company's common shareholders or the NNL (Nortel Networks Limited) preferred shareholders will receive any value from Nortel's creditor protection proceedings and expects that the proceedings will result in the cancellation of these equity interests," the company said in a news release.

Sources: The Canadian Press, "Nortel Bankruptcy Mediation Begins with $9 Billion on the Table," *Toronto Star*, April 24, 2012; Theresa Tedesco, "Nortel Trial to Open Old Wounds," *Financial Post*, January 14, 2012; "Nortel Completes Sale of Patents and Patent Applications," company news release, July 29, 2011.

15 | Shareholders' Equity

LEARNING OBJECTIVES

After studying this chapter, you should be able to:

1. Discuss the characteristics of the corporate form of organization, rights of shareholders, and different types of shares.

2. Explain how to account for the issuance, reacquisition, and retirement of shares, stock splits, and dividend distribution.

3. Understand the components of shareholders' equity and how they are presented.

4. Understand capital disclosure requirements.

5. Calculate and interpret key ratios relating to equity.

6. Identify the major differences in accounting between ASPE and IFRS, and what changes are expected in the near future.

After studying the appendices to this chapter, you should be able to:

7. Explain how to account for par value and treasury shares.

8. Explain how to account for a financial reorganization.

Capital markets are highly important in any economy that functions based on private ownership rather than government ownership. The markets provide a forum where prices are established, and these prices then become signals and incentives that guide the allocation of the economy's financial resources. More and more individuals and entities are investing in the capital marketplace (which includes stock markets and exchanges, as well as other arenas). This chapter explains the various accounting issues for different types of shares or equity instruments' that corporations issue to raise funds in capital markets. The chapter also examines the accounting issues for retained earnings and other components of shareholders' equity.

The chapter is organized as follows:

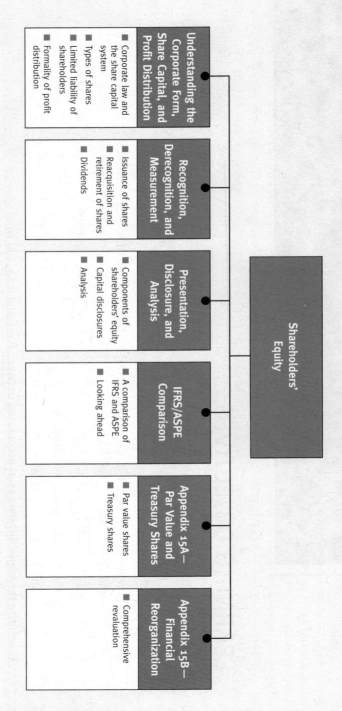

Shareholders' Equity

Understanding the Corporate Form, Share Capital, and Profit Distribution
- Corporate law and the share capital system
- Types of shares
- Limited liability of shareholders
- Formality of profit distribution

Recognition, Derecognition, and Measurement
- Issuance of shares
- Reacquisition and retirement of shares
- Dividends

Presentation, Disclosure, and Analysis
- Components of shareholders' equity
- Capital disclosures
- Analysis

IFRS/ASPE Comparison
- A comparison of IFRS and ASPE
- Looking ahead

Appendix 15A— Par Value and Treasury Shares
- Par value shares
- Treasury shares

Appendix 15B— Financial Reorganization
- Comprehensive revaluation

Law

Finance

Objective 1

Discuss the characteristics of the corporate form of organization, rights of shareholders, and different types of shares.

UNDERSTANDING THE CORPORATE FORM, SHARE CAPITAL, AND PROFIT DISTRIBUTION

Of the three primary forms of business organization—the proprietorship, the partnership, and the corporation—the most common form of business is the corporate

Many different meanings are attached to the word **capital** because the word is often used differently by various user groups. In corporate **finance**, for example, capital commonly refers to **sources of financing**. In **law**, capital is considered that portion of shareholders' equity that is required by statute to **be retained in the business for the protection of creditors**. Accountants use the word "capital" when referring not only to shareholders' equity but also to long-term assets (capital assets) or to whether an expenditure should be treated as an asset (capitalized) or expensed. It is therefore important to pay careful attention to **the context** in which the term is being used.

form. Although the corporate form has several advantages (as well as disadvantages) over the other two forms, its main advantage is that a corporation is a **separate legal entity** and, therefore, the entity's owners have **greater legal protection** against lawsuits. An additional important advantage is that incorporation involves the issue of shares, which gives **access to capital markets** for companies that choose to raise funds in this way.

Corporations may be classified by the nature of their ownership as follows:

1. Public sector corporations

(a) Government units such as municipalities, cities, and so on. No shares issued.

(b) Government business enterprises such as Canada Post and provincial liquor control boards (that is, companies owned by the government and sometimes referred to as Crown corporations). Shares issued.

2. Private sector corporations

(a) Not-for-profit: entities whose main objective is something other than profit (such as churches, charities, and colleges). No shares issued.

(b) For-profit: companies whose main objective is to increase shareholder value and maximize profit. Shares issued.

Private companies: companies whose shares are held by a few shareholders and are not available for public purchase. These entities are governed by shareholder agreements, which dictate who may hold the shares and how shareholder interests may or may not be transferred or disposed of. There are many private companies in Canada, from small businesses to large corporate entities such as McCain Foods and Maple Lodge Farms.

Public companies: companies whose shares are available for purchase by the general public, normally through a stock exchange, such as the Toronto Stock Exchange (TSX), or stock market, such as the TSX Venture Exchange.[2] Public companies must follow securities laws that have been established by provincial securities commissions, corporations law, and finally rules established by the exchanges and markets that the companies trade on.

This text focuses on the for-profit type of corporation operating in the private sector. Public sector entities and not-for-profit entities are generally covered in advanced accounting courses.

What Do the Numbers Mean?

Real estate income or investment trusts (REITs) have created a lot of interest in the last couple of decades. Legally, these funds are often set up as limited purpose **trust funds.** Their activities are restricted and they may be fairly passive. Under the Income Tax Act, as long as the trust pays out its income to investors, the trust itself pays no income tax. The investors then pay tax on the cash that they receive from the trust. Investors are referred to as "unitholders" and their liability is normally limited, but not as limited as the liability of a shareholder. It is important for the trustees of the trust (essentially the fund management) to ensure that the trust's insurance and other legal actions protect the unitholders adequately.

Real World Emphasis

REITs are special purpose entities, otherwise known as variable interest entities. Their special purpose is to invest in real estate. **Canadian Real Estate Investment Trust** is the oldest REIT in the Canadian marketplace, having listed on the TSX in 1993. The trust was started in 1984. In Canada, many other industries followed the REIT model in order to take advantage of the tax structure, including trusts for Yellow Pages, Swiss Water Decaffeinated, Enbridge, Gateway Casino, Boston Pizza, and A&W. In 2007, the Canadian government passed a law to revoke the tax-free status of these non-real estate trusts. The change in law was phased in gradually by 2011 and these non-real estate trusts are no longer exempt from taxes.

Corporate Law and the Share Capital System

Anyone who wants to establish a corporation must submit articles of incorporation to the provincial or federal government, depending on whether the person wants to do business

Law

in a specific province or across Canada. Once the requirements are properly fulfilled, the corporation charter is issued, and the corporation is recognized as a legal entity under the relevant business corporations act. While the provisions of most provincial business corporations acts are reasonably similar, there are some differences. Consequently, when legal aspects are discussed in this chapter, the discussion will only consider the Canada Business Corporations Act (CBCA).

The articles of incorporation specify such things as the company name,[3] place of registered office, classes and maximum numbers of shares authorized, restrictions of rights to transfer shares, number of directors, and any restrictions on the corporation's business. Once it has been incorporated, the corporation prepares share certificates and issues them to shareholders.

A corporation's share capital is generally made up of a large number of units or shares. These shares may be organized into groups or **classes**, such as Class A shares versus Class B shares. Within a class, each share is exactly equal to every other share. The number of shares that are possessed determines each owner's interest. If a company has only one class of shares and it is divided into 1,000 shares, a person owning 500 shares has one half of the corporation's ownership interest, and a person holding 10 shares would have a one-hundredth interest.

Each share has certain rights and privileges that can only be restricted by provisions in the articles of incorporation. If there are no restrictive provisions, each share gives the following **basic or inherent rights:**

1. To share proportionately in profits and losses

2. To share proportionately in management (that is, the share gives the right to vote for directors)

3. To share proportionately in the corporate assets upon liquidation of the corporation

The CBCA allows a corporation to assign a fourth right: the right to share proportionately in any new issues of shares of the same class. This right is known as a **preemptive right.**

The first three rights are expected in the ownership of any business; the last right may be used in a corporation to protect each shareholder's proportional interest in the enterprise. The preemptive right protects an existing shareholder from the involuntary dilution of the shareholder's ownership interest. Without this right, the corporation would be able to issue additional shares without notifying the shareholders and at prices that are not favourable to the shareholders. This could result in the shareholders' specific percentage interest (the proportional ownership of the corporation) being reduced. Because the preemptive right that attaches to existing shares makes it inconvenient for corporations to make large issuances of additional shares, as they frequently do in acquiring other companies, many corporations have eliminated it.

The great advantage of the share system is that it makes it very easy to transfer an interest in a business from one individual to another. Individuals who own shares in a corporation may sell them to others at any time and at any price without obtaining the consent of the company or other shareholders. Each share is the personal property of the owner and may be disposed of at will.[4] For its part, the corporation is only required to maintain a list or subsidiary ledger of shareholders, which it needs as a guide to dividend payments, issuance of share rights, voting proxies, and similar elements. Because shares of public companies are so easily and frequently transferred, the corporation must update the subsidiary ledger of shareholders periodically, generally before every dividend payment or shareholders' meeting. Major stock exchanges require controls over record keeping that are costly for the typical corporation. As a result, public companies generally outsource this task to registrars and transfer agents that specialize in providing services for recording and transferring shares.

Types of Shares

Common Shares

In every corporation, there is one class of shares that represents the basic ownership interest. That class is called common shares. **Common shares** represent the residual ownership interest in the company, suffer the ultimate risks of loss, and receive the benefits of success. A common shareholder is not guaranteed annual dividends and is not guaranteed assets upon dissolution of the corporation. However, common shareholders generally control the corporation management through the voting rights attached to these shares.[5] They also tend to profit the most if the company is successful. If a corporation has only one authorized issue of capital shares, that issue is, by definition, common shares, and this is true even if the corporation's charter does not designate the shares as common.

Shares may be **in-substance common shares**. These are shares that, even though they have the same characteristics as common shares, cannot be or are not called common shares for legal purposes. The following should be considered when deciding whether to treat financial instruments as common shares for financial statement purposes.

- Subordination: The shares do not have a preferred rank over other shares for dividend distributions or for the distribution of company assets upon windup of the company.

- Risks and rewards of ownership: The shares participate in the earnings/losses of the company and the appreciation/depreciation in value of the company.

- Obligation to transfer value: These shares have no obligation to transfer value. Given that they represent a residual interest in the company, they have value only if the company's net assets have value.

- No other common shares: All shares in the class in question have the same features.

- Redemption: The shares are retractable/redeemable only upon windup of the company.[6]

Preferred Shares

Nature of Preferred Shares. In an effort to attract all types of investors, corporations may offer two or more classes of shares, with each class having different rights or privileges. The preceding section pointed out that each share of a particular issue has the same rights as other shares of the same issue and that there are three inherent rights in every share. By special contracts between the corporation and its shareholders, some of these rights may be sacrificed by the shareholder in return for other special rights or privileges. This creates special classes of shares, and because they have certain preferential rights, such shares are usually called **preferred shares**. In return for any special preference, the preferred shareholder is always required to sacrifice some of the basic rights of common share interests.

A typical type of preference is to give the preferred shareholders a priority claim on earnings and on assets (upon dissolution or windup of the company), compared with the claims of the common shareholders. This means that preferred shareholders are assured a dividend, usually at a stated rate, before any amount may be distributed to the common shareholders. They are also assured that if the company goes bankrupt, they rank before the common shareholders in terms of getting their money back. In return for this preference, the preferred shareholders may sacrifice the right to a voice in management or the right to share in profits beyond the stated rate.

Instead of issuing both common and preferred shares, a company may accomplish much the same thing by issuing two classes of shares, Class A shares and Class B shares. In this case, one of the issues is the common share and the other issue has some preference or restriction of basic shareholder rights. Preferred shares may be issued with a dividend

Law

Underlying Concept

Common shares carry the residual risks and rewards of ownership.

preference that is expressed as a **percentage of the issue price**. Thus, holders of 8% preferred shares issued at $100 are entitled to an annual dividend of $8 per share. This share is commonly referred to as an 8% preferred share. The dividend may also be expressed as a **specific dollar amount** per share; for example, $8 per share. A preference as to dividends does not assure shareholders that dividends will be paid; it only means that the stated dividend rate or amount that applies to the preferred share must be paid before any dividends can be paid on the common shares.

Features of Preferred Shares.   A corporation may attach whatever preferences or restrictions it desires to a preferred share issue, and in whatever combination (as long as it does not specifically violate its incorporation law), and it may issue more than one class of preferred share. Some preferred share features include the following:

1. **Cumulative.** Dividends on cumulative shares that are not paid in any given year are known as dividends in arrears and must be made up in a later year before any profits can be distributed to common shareholders. There is no liability, however, until the board of directors **declares** a dividend. According to common law, if the corporate charter is silent about the cumulative feature, the preferred share is considered cumulative.

2. **Convertible.** This feature allows the company or holder to exchange the shares for common shares at a predetermined ratio. Thus, the shareholder has the relative security of the preferred share yet may gain from the appreciation of the company by converting preferred shares to common shares.

3. **Callable/redeemable.** The issuing corporation can call or redeem at its option (through its own choice) the outstanding preferred shares at specified future dates and at stipulated prices. The callable feature permits the corporation to use the capital that it has obtained through the issuance of such shares until the need has passed or having the issued shares is no longer an advantage. The existence of a call price or prices tends to set a ceiling on the market value of the preferred shares unless they are convertible into common shares. When a preferred share is called for redemption, any dividends in arrears must be paid.

4. **Retractable.** The holders of the shares can put or sell their shares to the company, normally after having given adequate notice, and the company must then pay the holders for the shares. The retraction option makes this instrument more attractive to the holders as it gives them more choice.

5. **Participating.** Participating preferred shareholders share (at the same rate as common shareholders) in any profit distributions that are higher than the prescribed rate of the preferred share. That is, a 5% preferred share, if it is fully participating, will receive not only its 5% return, but also dividends at the same rate that is paid to common shareholders if the latter are paid amounts higher than 5% of stated value. Note that participating preferred shares are not always fully participating. That is, they can also be partially participating. For example, provision may be made that a 5% preferred share will be participating up to a maximum total rate of 10%, after which it ceases to participate in additional profit distributions, or a 5% preferred share may participate only in additional profit distributions that exceed a 9% dividend rate on the common share.

Ethics

Finance

Preferred shares are often issued instead of debt because a company's debt to equity ratio has become too high. The issuing company may structure the instrument such that its legal form represents shares in hopes of avoiding treating the instruments as debt on the financial statements. Accounting for preferred shares can be complex because of their many and varied features and because accountants must account for the instruments in accordance with their economic substance as opposed to their legal form. Chapter 16 discusses the more complex aspects of these financial instruments.

Finally, issuances of common, preferred, or other shares may be made through **private placements**[7] as opposed to through the stock markets and exchanges. The difference between the two is that the company remains private if it has no shares that trade on a stock market or exchange and it is therefore not subject to the same regulations as a public company.

Limited Liability of Shareholders

Law

Those who own a corporation—the shareholders—contribute cash, property, or services to the enterprise in return for ownership shares. The property or service that has been invested in the enterprise is the limit on a shareholder's possible loss. That is, if the corporation has losses that are so large that the remaining assets are not enough to pay creditors, the creditors have no recourse against the personal assets of the individual shareholders. This is unlike in a partnership or proprietorship, where the owners' personal assets can be accessed to satisfy unpaid claims against the enterprise. Ownership interests in a corporation are legally protected against such a contingency. The shareholders are thus said to have **limited liability**: they may lose their investment but they cannot lose more than their investment.

While the corporate form of organization gives the protective feature of limited liability to the shareholders, it also stipulates that the amount of the shareholders' investment that is represented in share capital accounts cannot be withdrawn unless all prior claims on corporate assets have been paid. This means that the corporation must maintain this capital until dissolution of the corporation. Upon dissolution, it must then satisfy all prior claims before distributing any amounts to the shareholders. In a proprietorship or partnership, the owners or partners may withdraw amounts whenever and in whatever amount they choose because all their personal assets can be accessed to protect creditors from loss.

Shares issued by corporations must be without a nominal or par value (according to the CBCA). This simply means that all proceeds from the issuance of the shares must be credited to the appropriate share capital account and become part of the shareholders' investment referred to above. In some provinces and in the United States, shares that have a fixed per-share amount printed on each share certificate are called **par value shares.**

Par value has only one real significance: in jurisdictions where the concept of par value is legally allowed, it establishes the maximum responsibility of a shareholder in the event of insolvency or other involuntary dissolution. Par value is thus not value in the ordinary sense of the word. It is merely an amount per share that has been determined by the incorporators of the company and stated in the corporation charter or certificate of incorporation. Appendix 15A discusses par value shares in greater detail.

Formality of Profit Distribution

Legality of Dividend Distribution

Law

An enterprise's owners decide what to do with profits that are realized through operations. Profits may be left in the business for a future expansion or simply to have a margin of safety, or they may be withdrawn and divided among the owners. In a proprietorship or partnership, this decision is made by the owner or owners informally and requires no specific action. In a partnership, the partnership agreement would usually specify how profits or losses are to be shared. In a corporation, however, profit distribution (referred to as **dividends**) is controlled by certain legal restrictions. Not all shares carry the right to receive dividends.

First, no amounts may be distributed among the owners unless the corporate capital is kept intact. This restriction is based on the presumption that there have to be sufficient net assets or security left in the corporation to satisfy the liability holders after any assets have been distributed to shareholders as dividends. Various tests of corporate solvency have been used over the years. Under the CBCA, dividends may not be declared or paid if there are reasonable grounds for believing that (1) the corporation is, or would be after the dividend, unable to pay its liabilities as they become due; or (2) the realizable value of the corporation's assets would, as a result of the dividend, be less than the total of its liabilities and stated or **legal capital** for all classes of shares.

Second, distributions to shareholders must be formally approved by the board of directors and recorded in the minutes of the board's meetings. As the top executive body in the corporation, the board of directors must make certain that no distributions are made to shareholders that are not justified by profits, and directors are generally held personally liable to creditors if liabilities cannot be paid because company assets have been illegally paid out to shareholders.

Third, dividends must be in full agreement with preferences created by the share capital contracts. Once the corporation has entered into contracts with various classes of shareholders, the stipulations of such contracts must be followed.

Finance

Financial Condition and Dividend Distribution

Determining the proper amount of dividends to pay is a difficult financial management decision. Companies that are paying dividends are extremely reluctant to reduce or eliminate their dividends, because they believe that this action could be viewed negatively by the securities market. As a consequence, companies that have been paying cash dividends will make every effort to continue to do so.

Very few companies pay dividends in amounts equal to their legally available retained earnings. The major reasons that companies have for limiting the dividend amount are as follows:

1. There are agreements (bond covenants) with specific creditors that require all or a portion of the earnings to be retained in the form of assets in order to build up additional protection against possible loss.

2. The company wants to retain assets that would otherwise be paid out as dividends, in order to finance growth or expansion. This is sometimes called internal financing, reinvesting earnings, or plowing the profits back into the business.

3. The company wants to smooth out dividend payments from year to year by accumulating earnings in good years and using such accumulated earnings as a basis for dividends in bad years.

4. The company wants to build up a cushion or buffer against possible losses or errors in the calculation of profits.

Dividend policies vary among corporations. Some older, well-established firms take pride in a long, unbroken string of quarterly dividend payments.[8] They would lower or not declare the dividend only if they were forced to do so by a sustained decline in earnings or a critical shortage of cash. Growth companies, on the other hand, pay few or no cash dividends because their policy is to expand as rapidly as internal and external financing permit. Investors in these companies hope that their share price will appreciate in value and that they will realize a profit when they sell their shares. In other words, they hope to benefit from capital appreciation.

Good business management means paying attention to more than just the legality of dividend distribution. **Economic conditions** also need to be considered and, most importantly, liquidity. Assume the following extreme situation:

Statement of Financial Position

Plant assets	$500,000	Share capital	$400,000
		Retained earnings	100,000
	$500,000		$500,000

The company has a retained earnings credit balance, and generally, unless the balance is restricted, the company can therefore declare a dividend of $100,000. But because all its assets are plant assets and used in operations, paying a cash dividend of $100,000 would require selling plant assets or borrowing.

Even if we assume a statement of financial position that shows current assets, the question remains whether those assets are needed for other purposes.

Statement of Financial Position

Cash	$100,000	Current liabilities	$ 60,000
Plant assets	460,000	Share capital	$400,000
		Retained earnings	100,000
			500,000
	$560,000		$560,000

The existence of current liabilities implies very strongly that some of the cash is needed to meet current debts as they mature. In addition, day-to-day cash requirements for payrolls and other expenditures that are not included in current liabilities also require cash.

Thus, before a dividend is declared, management must consider the availability of funds to pay the dividend. Other demands for cash should also perhaps be investigated by preparing a cash forecast. A dividend should not be paid unless both the present and future financial position appear to justify the distribution. Directors must also consider the effect of inflation and replacement costs before making a dividend commitment. During a period of significant inflation, some costs that are charged to expense under historical cost accounting are understated in terms of comparative purchasing power. This is because the amounts represent older dollars since the asset was purchased earlier when the dollars were likely worth more. Because these costs are not adjusted for inflation, income is therefore overstated.

The non-payment of dividends can also significantly impact a company. For instance, **Torstar Corporation** has Class B shares that are normally non-voting, but if the company does not pay dividends for eight consecutive quarters, the shares then have voting rights.

What Do the Numbers Mean?

RECOGNITION, DERECOGNITION, AND MEASUREMENT

Issuance of Shares

Objective 2

Explain how to account for issuance, reacquisition, and retirement of shares, stock splits, and dividend distribution.

In issuing shares, the following procedures are followed: First, the shares must be **authorized**. Next, shares are **offered for sale** and contracts to sell shares are entered into. Finally, amounts to be received for the shares are **collected** and the **shares are issued**.

Share Issue—Basic

Shares are sold for the price that they will bring in the marketplace. Normally the company will hire specialists (such as investment banking firms and underwriters) to value the shares[9] and help **promote and sell them**. As payment for their services, the underwriters take as commission a percentage of the total share consideration that is received from investors. The **net** amount that is received by the company becomes the credit to common or preferred shares. For example, assume that Video Electronics Corporation is organized with 10,000 authorized common shares. The only entry that is made for this authorization is a memorandum entry. There is no journal entry since there is no monetary amount involved in the authorization. If 500 shares are then issued for cash at $10 per share, the entry should be:

Finance

A = L + SE
+5,000   +5,000

Cash flows: ↑ 5,000 inflow

| Cash | 5,000 | |
| Common Shares | | 5,000 |

Entries for preferred shares are the same as for common shares as long as the preferred shares are classified as equity.[10] As par value shares are relatively uncommon in Canada, the issues that are unique to them are covered in Appendix 15A.

Shares Sold on a Subscription Basis

Shares may also be sold on a subscription basis. Sales of **subscribed shares** generally occur when new, small companies go public or when corporations offer shares to employees so they can participate in the business ownership. When a share is sold on a subscription basis, its full price is not received immediately. Normally, only a **partial payment** is made, and the share is not issued until the full subscription price is received.

The journal entries for handling shares that are sold on a subscription basis are illustrated by the following example. Assume that Lubradite Corp. offers shares on a subscription basis to selected individuals, giving them the right to purchase 10 common shares at a price of $20 per share. Fifty individuals accept the company's offer and agree to pay 50% down and the remaining 50% at the end of six months. Lubradite's entries would be as follows:

At date of receipt of subscriptions

Share Subscriptions Receivable (10 × $20 × 50)	10,000	
Common Shares Subscribed		10,000
(To record receipt of subscriptions for 500 shares.)		

A = L + SE
+5,000   +5,000

Cash flows: No effect

Cash	5,000	
Share Subscriptions Receivable		5,000
(To record receipt of first instalment representing 50% of total due on subscribed shares.)		

A = L + SE
+5,000   +5,000

Cash flows: ↑ 5,000 inflow

Underlying Concept

Subscriptions receivable appear to meet the definition of an asset since they represent a future benefit to the company in terms of incoming cash. However, treating them as an asset results in the share capital increasing even though the shares are not yet issued. This does not provide transparent financial reporting.

Whether the Subscriptions Receivable account should be presented as an asset or a contra equity account is a matter of professional judgement, although conceptually, it makes sense to record it as a reduction of equity. In the United States, the Securities and Exchange Commission (SEC) requires the latter treatment. ASPE provides guidance for share purchase loan receivables, which will be discussed later in the chapter.

When the final payment is received and the shares are issued, the entries are:

Ethics

Six months later

Cash	5,000	
Share Subscriptions Receivable		5,000
(To record receipt of final instalment on subscribed shares.)		

A = L + SE
+5,000   +5,000

Cash flows: ↑ 5,000 inflow

Common Shares Subscribed	10,000	
Common Shares		10,000
(To record issuance of 500 shares upon receipt of final instalment from subscribers.)		

A = L + SE
            0

Cash flows: No effect

Defaulted Subscription Accounts

Sometimes a subscriber is unable to pay all instalments and therefore defaults on the agreement. The question is what to do with the balance of the subscription account and the amount that has already been paid in. The answer is determined by the subscription contract, corporate policy, and any applicable law of the jurisdiction of incorporation. The possibilities include returning the amount already paid by the subscriber (possibly after deducting some expenses), treating the amount paid as forfeited and therefore transferring it to the Contributed Surplus account, or issuing fewer shares to the subscriber so that the number of shares issued is equivalent to what the subscription payments already received would have paid for fully.

For example, assume that a subscriber to 50 Lubradite common shares defaults on the final payment. If the subscription contract stated that amounts paid by the defaulting subscriber would be refunded, Lubradite would make the following entry when the default occurs, assuming that the refund was to be paid at a later date:

Common Shares Subscribed	1,000	
Share Subscriptions Receivable		500
Accounts Payable		500

(To record default on 50 shares subscribed for $20 each and on which 50% had been paid.)

A	=	L	+	SE
		+500		−500.
		+500		

Cash flows: No effect

If the amount paid by the subscriber were forfeited, there would be a $500 credit to Contributed Surplus as this is a **capital transaction**.

Shares Issued with Other Securities (Lump-Sum Sales)

Generally, corporations sell each class of shares separately so that they can determine the proceeds for each class and, ordinarily, even for each lot of shares in the class. Occasionally, however, two or more classes of securities are issued for a single payment or lump sum. It is not uncommon, for example, for more than one type or class of security to be issued in the acquisition of another company. The accounting problem in such **lump-sum sales** is the allocation of the proceeds among the several classes of securities, or determining how to measure the separate classes of shares.

Two possible measurement techniques are used: (1) the **relative fair value method** and (2) the **residual value method**.[11] These measurement techniques are often used in accounting, even for issues that are not lump-sum share issues. The first method values each instrument according to its fair value and then proportionally allocates the lump-sum value to each instrument. The second method values one instrument (often the one that is easier to measure) and then allocates the rest of the amount to the other instrument. Examples of these methods are presented in other chapters. These same techniques are used to bifurcate bundled sales for revenue recognition purposes (Chapter 6), allocate the costs of inventory and/or PP&E in basket or lump-sum purchases (Chapters 8 and 10), and measure the respective parts of compound financial instruments (Chapter 16).

Costs of Issuing Shares

Direct incremental costs that are incurred to sell shares, such as underwriting costs, accounting and legal fees, printing costs, and taxes, should be reported as a reduction of the amounts paid in. Issue costs are therefore debited to Share Capital because they are capital transactions rather than operating transactions.

Management salaries and other indirect costs related to the share issue should be expensed as they are incurred because it is difficult to establish a relationship between these costs and the proceeds that are received from the sale. In addition, corporations annually incur costs for maintaining the shareholders' records and handling ownership transfers. These recurring costs, which are mainly registrar and transfer agents' fees, are normally charged to expense in the period in which they are incurred.

Aside from the case of shares sold on a subscription basis, sometimes companies issue shares but do not require the purchaser to pay right away. This may be the case for instances where the company lends its employees money to buy new shares. There is controversy in such cases about how this receivable should be presented on the SFP. Some argue that the receivable should be recorded as an asset like other receivables. Others argue that the receivable should be reported as a reduction of shareholders' equity.

The SEC requires companies to use the latter approach (similar to the accounting for shares sold on a subscription basis) because the risk of collection on these types of transactions is often very high. IFRS is not definitive on this issue but the conceptual framework would support presenting the receivables as a reduction of shareholders' equity unless there is substantial evidence that the company is not at risk for declines in the value of the shares and there is reasonable assurance that the company will collect the amount in cash. ASPE specifically supports this approach.[12]

Ethics

Unfortunately, this issue surfaced with **Enron Corporation.** Starting in early 2000, Enron issued shares of its common stock to four "special purpose entities" and in exchange it received notes receivable. Enron then increased its assets and shareholders' equity, a move the company subsequently called an accounting error. As a result, Enron's 2000 audited financial statements overstated assets and shareholders' equity by $172 million. Enron's 2001 unaudited statements overstated them by $828 million. The $1-billion overstatement was 8.5% of Enron's previously reported equity as at June 30—a material amount.

Sources: Jonathan Weil, "Basic Accounting Tripped Up Enron," "Financial Statements Didn't Add Up," and "Auditors Overlook Simple Rule," *Wall Street Journal,* November 11, 2001, p. C1; George J. Benston and Al L. Hargraves, "Enron: What Happened and What We Can Learn from It," *Journal of Accounting and Public Policy,* 21 (2002), pp. 105–127; Daniel Fisher, "Enron's Real Financials," Forbes.com, February 3, 2003.

Reacquisition and Retirement of Shares

It is not unusual for companies to buy back their own shares. In fact, share buybacks now exceed dividends as a form of distribution to shareholders.[13] While corporations have varied reasons for purchasing their outstanding shares, some of the major ones are as follows:

1. **To increase earnings per share and return on equity.** By reducing shares outstanding and reducing shareholders' equity, certain performance ratios are often improved, such as earnings per share and return on equity. In 2011, **CGI Group** (Canada's largest information technology outsourcing firm) spent $287 million to buy back its own shares. This pushed the share price up 11.6%.

2. **To provide shares for employee share compensation contracts or to meet potential merger needs. Honeywell Inc.** reported that part of its purchase of 1 million common shares was to be used for employee share option contracts. Other companies acquire shares to have them available for business acquisitions.

3. **To stop takeover attempts or to reduce the number of shareholders.** By reducing the number of shares that are held by the public, the current owners and management may find it easier to keep outsiders from gaining control or significant influence. When Ted Turner tried to acquire **CBS,** CBS started a substantial buyback of its shares.

4. **To make a market in the share.** By purchasing shares in the marketplace, management creates a demand that may stabilize the share price or, in fact, increase it. Over a period of four years, **Nexfor Inc.,** a large North American producer of building materials, repurchased and cancelled 15.5 million shares for $122 million (representing 10% of the company's shares). The company commented that the shares were undervalued and represented a good deal.

5. **To return cash to shareholders.** In 2012, **AbitibiBowater Inc.**'s board of directors authorized the repurchase of up to 10% of the company's common stock using excess cash. The company noted that it was taking advantage of the strong position of the company to return cash to shareholders.

Some publicly held corporations have chosen to go private; that is, they decided to eliminate public (outside) ownership by purchasing their entire float of outstanding shares. This is often done through a **leveraged buyout**, which is when management or another employee group purchases the company shares and finances the purchase by using the company assets as collateral.

Once shares are reacquired, they may either be retired or held in the treasury for re-issue. If they are not retired, such shares are referred to as **treasury shares.** Technically, a treasury share is a corporation's own share that has been reacquired after having been issued and fully paid. In Canada, the CBCA, with minor exceptions, requires that repur-chased shares be cancelled and, if a company's articles of incorporation limit the number of authorized shares, that the shares be restored to the status of authorized but unissued shares. While some provincial jurisdictions do allow treasury shares to exist, such shares remain relatively uncommon in Canada.[14] This is unlike the United States, where many companies hold treasury shares.[15] Appendix 15A briefly reviews the accounting for these shares.

When shares are purchased or redeemed by the issuing corporation, it is likely that the price paid will differ from the amount that was received for the shares when they were issued. As this is a capital transaction, any gains or losses are booked through equity[16] (rather than through the income statement).

If the acquisition cost is greater than the original cost, then the acquisition cost should be allocated as follows:

1. First, to Share Capital, in an amount equal to the par, stated, or assigned value of the shares

2. Second, for any excess after the first allocation, to Contributed Surplus, to the extent that the contributed surplus was created by a net excess of proceeds over cost on a can-cellation or resale of shares of the same class

3. Third, for any excess after the second allocation, to Contributed Surplus in an amount equal to the pro rata share of the portion of contributed surplus that arose from trans-actions, other than those above, in the same class of shares

4. Last, for any excess after the third allocation, to Retained Earnings

If the acquisition cost is less than the original cost, then the acquisition cost should be allocated as follows:

1. First, to Share Capital, in an amount equal to the par, stated, or assigned value of the shares

2. Second, for the difference after the first allocation, to Contributed Surplus

For shares with no par value (which means most shares in Canada), the assigned value is equal to the average per share amount in the account for that class of shares at the trans-action date. The difference between the stated or assigned value and the lower cost of acquisition is credited to Contributed Surplus and is seen as a contribution by the original shareholders that now accrues to the remaining shareholders.

Applying the formulas noted above, in cases where the acquisition cost is greater than the assigned cost, this would normally result in debiting Share Capital (step 1) and Retained Earnings (step 4). Contributed Surplus would only be adjusted if there were a prior balance in the Contributed Surplus account that related to the shares that are being acquired.

To illustrate, assume that Cooke Corporation has the following in its shareholders' equity accounts:

On January 30, 2014, Cooke purchased and cancelled 500 Class A shares at a cost of $4 per share. The required entry is:

Share capital:		
Class A, 10,500 shares issued and outstanding		$ 63,000
Class B, 50,000 shares issued and outstanding		100,000
Total share capital		163,000
Retained earnings		300,000
Total shareholders' equity		$463,000

Class A Shares [500 × ($63,000 ÷ 10,500)] | | 3,000
Cash | | 2,000
Contributed Surplus* | | 1,000

*Average per share amount (assigned value) = $63,000 ÷ 10,500 = $6. Excess of assigned value over reacquisition cost = $6 − 4 = $2 per share for 500 shares.

A = L + SE
−2,000 −2,000

Cash flows: ↓ 2,000 outflow

On September 10, 2014, the company purchased and cancelled an additional 1,000 Class A shares. The purchase cost was $8 per share. The transaction is recorded as follows:

Class A shares [1,000 × ($60,000 ÷ 10,000)] | | 6,000
Contributed Surplus* | | 1,000
Retained Earnings | | 1,000
Cash | | 8,000

*Equals the whole amount of the excess from the above

A = L + SE
−8,000 −8,000

Cash flows: ↓ 8,000 outflow

IFRS gives no specific guidance for the reacquisition and retirement of shares. However, the accounting may end up being similar to ASPE if basic principles are followed.

Dividends

There are basically two classes of dividends:

1. Those that are a return on capital (a share of the earnings)

2. Those that are a return of capital, referred to as **liquidating dividends**

The natural expectation of any shareholder who receives a dividend is that the corporation has operated successfully and that he or she is receiving a share of its earnings. A liquidating dividend should therefore be adequately described in the financial statements. This type of dividend will be discussed in greater depth later in the chapter.

Dividends are commonly paid in cash but occasionally they are paid in shares or other assets. **Dividends generally reduce the total shareholders' equity in the corporation,** because the equity is reduced, through an immediate or promised future distribution of assets. Stock dividends are different, however. When a stock dividend is declared, the corporation does not pay out assets or incur a liability. It issues additional shares to each shareholder and nothing more. Both types of dividends are discussed below.

Cash Dividends

The board of directors votes on the declaration of dividends and if the resolution is properly approved, the dividend is declared. Before the dividend is paid, a current list of shareholders must be prepared. For this reason, there is usually a time lag between the declaration and payment. A resolution approved at the January 10 (**date of declaration**) meeting of the board of directors might be declared payable on February 5 (**date of payment**) to all shareholders of record on January 25 (**date of record**).[17]

The period from January 10 to January 25 gives time for any transfers in process to be completed and registered with the transfer agent. The time from January 25 to February 5 provides an opportunity for the transfer agent or accounting department, depending on who does this work, to prepare a list of shareholders as at January 25 and to prepare and mail dividend cheques.

To illustrate the declaration and payment of an ordinary dividend that is payable in cash, assume that on June 10 Rajah Corp. declared a cash dividend of 50 cents a share on 1.8 million shares and payable on July 16 to all shareholders of record on June 24. The following entries are required:

At date of declaration (June 10)		
Dividends	900,000	
Dividends Payable		900,000

$$A = L + SE$$
$$+900,000 \quad -900,000$$
Cash flows: No effect

At date of record (June 24)		
No entry		

At date of payment (July 16)		
Dividends Payable	900,000	
Cash		900,000

$$A = L + SE$$
$$-900,000 \quad -900,000$$
Cash flows: ↓ 900,000 outflow

To have a ledger account that shows the amount of dividends declared during the year, the company can debit Dividends instead of debiting Retained Earnings at the time of declaration. This account is then closed to Retained Earnings at year end. Dividends may be declared either as a certain percentage of par or stated value, such as a 6% dividend, or as an amount per share, such as 60 cents per share. In the first case, the rate is multiplied by the par or stated value of outstanding shares to get the total dividend; in the second, the amount per share is multiplied by the number of shares outstanding. **Cash dividends are not declared and paid on treasury shares since the shares are owned by the company itself.**

Dividends in Kind

Dividends that are payable in corporation assets other than cash are called property dividends or dividends in kind. Property dividends may be merchandise, real estate, or investments, or whatever form the board of directors designates. Because of the obvious difficulties of dividing units and delivering them to shareholders, the usual property dividend is in the form of securities of other companies that the distributing corporation holds as an investment.

A property dividend is a non-reciprocal transfer of nonmonetary assets between an enterprise and its owners. These dividends should generally be measured at the fair value of the asset that is given up unless they are considered to represent a spinoff or other form of restructuring or liquidation, in which case they should be recorded at the carrying value of the nonmonetary assets or liabilities transferred.[18] No gain or loss would be recorded in the second instance.

When the U.S. Supreme Court decided that **DuPont's** 23% investment in **General Motors** violated antitrust laws, DuPont was ordered to divest itself of the GM shares within 10 years. The shares represented 63 million of GM's 281 million shares then outstanding. DuPont could not sell the shares in one block of 63 million, nor could it sell 6 million shares annually for the next 10 years without severely depressing the value of the GM shares. At that time, the entire yearly trading volume in GM shares was not even 6 million shares. DuPont solved its problem by declaring a property dividend and distributing the GM shares as a dividend to its own shareholders.

What Do the Numbers Mean?

Stock Dividends

Management may want to "capitalize" part of the earnings (that is, reclassify amounts from earned to contributed capital) so that earnings are retained in the business on a permanent basis. In this case, it may issue a **stock dividend**. No assets are distributed and each shareholder has exactly the same proportionate interest in the corporation, and the same total book value, after the issue of the stock dividend as before the declaration. The book value per share is lower, however, after the issue of the stock dividend as before the declaration. The

There is no clear guidance on how to account for stock dividends. The major issue is whether or not they should be treated in the same way as other dividends.[19] If they are treated like other dividends, they should be recorded by debiting Retained Earnings and crediting Share Capital. In terms of measuring the transaction, fair value would be used (measured by looking at the market value of the shares issued, at the declaration date).

Where the stock dividends give the option to the holder to receive them in cash or shares, the stock dividend is considered a nonmonetary transaction under GAAP and must be treated as a regular dividend, valued at fair value.[20] Where there is no option to receive the dividend in cash, GAAP is silent; however, the CBCA states that for stock dividends, the declared amount of the dividend must be added to the stated capital account. The CBCA does not allow shares to be issued until they are fully paid for, at an amount not less than the fair equivalent of money that the corporation would have received had the shares been issued for cash. Therefore, if the company is incorporated under the CBCA, all stock dividends should be recorded as dividends and measured at fair value.

To illustrate a stock dividend, assume that a corporation has 1,000 common shares outstanding and retained earnings of $50,000. If the corporation declares a 10% stock dividend, it issues 100 additional shares to current shareholders. If it is assumed that the shares' fair value at the time of the stock dividend is $130 per share and that the shareholders had the option to take the dividend in cash but chose not to, the entry is:

	At date of declaration and distribution	
Dividends	13,000	
Common Shares		13,000

A = L + SE
0

Cash flows: No effect

If the dividend is declared before it is distributed, then the journal entry would be a debit to Dividends or Retained Earnings and a credit to Stock Dividends Distributable. Upon share issue, the journal entry would be a debit to Stock Dividends Distributable and a credit to Common Shares. Note that no asset or liability has been affected. The entry merely reflects a reclassification of shareholders' equity. No matter what the fair value is at the time of the stock dividend, each shareholder retains the same proportionate interest in the corporation. Illustration 15-1 proves this point.

(continued)

Illustration 15-1

Effects of a Stock Dividend

Before dividend:

Common shares, 1,000 shares		$100,000
Retained earnings		50,000
Total shareholders' equity		$150,000

Shareholders' interests:

A—400 shares, 40% interest, book value	$ 60,000
B—500 shares, 50% interest, book value	75,000
C—100 shares, 10% interest, book value	15,000
	$150,000

Illustration 15-1

Effects of a Stock Dividend (continued)

After declaration and distribution of 10% stock dividend:

If fair value ($130) is used as basis for entry

Shareholders' common shares, 1,100 shares	$113,000
Retained earnings ($50,000 – $13,000)	37,000
Total shareholders' equity	$150,000

Shareholders' interests:

A—440 shares, 40% interest, book value	$ 60,000
B—550 shares, 50% interest, book value	75,000
C—110 shares, 10% interest, book value	15,000
	$150,000

Note, in Illustration 15-1, that the total shareholders' equity has not changed as a result of the stock dividend. Also note that the proportion of the total shares outstanding that is held by each shareholder is unchanged.

Liquidating Dividends

Some corporations use contributed surplus as a basis for dividends. Without proper disclosure of this fact, shareholders may wrongly believe that the corporation has been paying dividends out of profits. We mentioned in Chapter 11 that companies in the extractive industries may pay dividends equal to the total of accumulated income and depletion. The portion of these dividends that is in excess of accumulated income represents a return of part of the shareholders' investment.

For example, assume that McChesney Mines Inc. issued a dividend to its common shareholders of $1.2 million. The cash dividend announcement noted that $900,000 should be considered income and the remainder a return of capital. The entry is:

At date of declaration

Retained Earnings (or Dividends)	900,000	
Contributed Surplus	300,000	
Dividends Payable		1,200,000

$$A = L + SE$$
$$+1,200,000 \quad -1,200,000$$

Cash flows: No effect

In some cases, management may simply decide to cease business and declare a liquidating dividend. In these cases, liquidation may take place over several years to ensure an orderly and fair sale of all assets.

Dividend Preferences

The examples that now follow illustrate the effects of various dividend preferences on dividend distribution to common and preferred shareholders. Assume that in a given year, $50,000 is to be distributed as cash dividends, outstanding common shares have a book value of $400,000, and 1,000 $6-preferred shares are outstanding (issued for $100,000). Dividends would be distributed to each class as follows, under the particular assumptions:

1. If the preferred shares are non-cumulative and non-participating, the effects are shown in Illustration 15-2:

Illustration 15-2

Dividend Distribution, Non-Cumulative and Non-Participating Preferred Shares

	Preferred	Common	Total
$6 × 1,000	$6,000	$ -0-	$ 6,000
The remainder to common	-0-	44,000	44,000
Totals	$6,000	$44,000	$50,000

2. If the preferred shares are cumulative and non-participating, and dividends were not paid on the preferred shares in the preceding two years, the effects are shown in Illustration 15-3:

Illustration 15-3

Dividend Distribution, Cumulative and Non-Participating Preferred, Shares with Dividends in Arrears

	Preferred	Common	Total
Dividends in arrears, $6 × 1,000 for 2 years	$12,000	$ -0-	$12,000
Current year's dividend, $6 × 1,000	6,000	-0-	6,000
The remainder to common	-0-	32,000	32,000
Totals	$18,000	$32,000	$50,000

3. If the preferred shares are non-cumulative and fully participating, the effects are shown in Illustration 15-4.[21]

Illustration 15-4

Dividend Distribution, Non-Cumulative and Fully Participating Preferred Shares

	Preferred	Common	Total
Current year's dividend, $6	$ 6,000	$24,000	$30,000
Participating dividend—pro rata	4,000	16,000	20,000
Totals	$10,000	$40,000	$50,000

The participating dividend was determined as follows:

Current year's dividend:

Preferred, $6 × 1,000 = $6,000
Common, 6% of $400,000 = $24,000 (= a like amount)

The 6% represents $6,000 on preferred shares/$100,000

Amount available for participation ($50,000 − $30,000)

Carrying value of shares that are to participate ($50,000 − $30,000)

Rate of participation ($20,000/$500,000)

Participating dividend:

Preferred (4% of $100,000)
Common (4% of $400,000)

	Preferred	Common
	$ 30,000	
	$ 20,000	
	$500,000	
	4%	
	$ 4,000	
	16,000	
	$ 20,000	

4. If the preferred shares are cumulative and fully participating, and if dividends were not paid on the preferred shares in the preceding two years (the same procedure that was used in example 3 is used again here to carry out the participation feature), the effects are shown in Illustration 15-5:

Illustration 15-5

Dividend Distribution, Cumulative and Fully Participating Preferred Shares, with Dividends in Arrears

	Preferred	Common	Total
Dividends in arrears, $6 × 1,000 for 2 years	$12,000	$ -0-	$12,000
Current year's dividend, $6	6,000	24,000	30,000
Participating dividend, 1.6% ($8,000/$500,000)	1,600	6,400	8,000
Totals	$19,600	$30,400	$50,000

Stock Splits

If a company has undistributed earnings over several successive years and has thus accumulated a sizable balance in retained earnings, the market value of its outstanding shares is likely to increase. Shares that were issued at prices of less than $50 a share can easily reach a market value of more than $200 a share. The higher the share's market price, the harder it is for some investors to purchase it. The managements of many corporations believe that, for better public relations, the corporation's shares should be widely owned. They wish, therefore, to have a market price that is low enough to be affordable to the majority of potential investors.

To reduce the market value of shares, the common device that is used is the stock split.[22] From an accounting standpoint, no entry is recorded for a stock split; a memorandum note, however, is made to indicate that the number of shares has increased.

Differences between a Stock Split and Stock Dividend

Law

From a legal standpoint, a **stock split** is distinguished from a stock dividend, because a stock split results in an increase in the number of shares outstanding with no change in the share capital or the retained earnings amounts. As noted earlier, legally, the stock dividend may result in an increase in both the number of shares outstanding and the share capital while reducing the retained earnings (depending on the legal jurisdiction).

A stock dividend, like a stock split, may also be used to increase the share's marketability. If the stock dividend is large, it has the same effect on market price as a stock split. In the United States, the profession has taken the position that, whenever additional shares are issued to reduce the unit market price, then the distribution more closely resembles a stock split than a stock dividend. **This effect usually results only if the number of shares issued is more than 20% to 25% of the number of shares that were previously outstanding.**[23] A stock dividend of more than 20% to 25% of the number of shares previously outstanding is called a **large stock dividend**.

In principle, it must be determined whether the large stock dividend is more like a stock split or a dividend (from an economic perspective). Professional judgement must be used in determining this as there is no specific guidance under ASPE or IFRS.

Legal requirements must be considered as a constraint. As noted earlier, for instance, companies that are incorporated under the CBCA must measure any newly issued shares at market (including those issued as stock dividends). This means, therefore, that all stock dividends for such companies are to be treated as dividends and measured at market. On the other hand, in jurisdictions where legal requirements for stated share capital values are not a constraint, the following options would be available for stock dividends:

1. Treat as a dividend (debit retained earnings and credit common shares) and measure at either the market value of the shares or their par or stated value.

2. Treat as a stock split (memo entry only).

The SEC supports the second approach for large stock dividends of more than 25%. Illustration 15-6 summarizes and compares the effects of dividends and stock splits.

Declaration and Distribution of Dividends and Stock Splits

Effect on:	Declaration of Cash Dividend	Payment of Cash Dividend	(Small) Stock Dividend	(Large) Stock Dividend	Stock Split
Retained earnings	Decrease	—	Decrease[a]	Decrease[b]	—
Common shares	—	—	Increase	Increase	—
Contributed surplus	—	—	—	—	—
Total shareholders' equity	Decrease	—	—	—	—
Working capital	Decrease	—	—	—	—
Total assets	—	Decrease	—	—	—
Number of shares outstanding	—	—	Increase	Increase	Increase

[a] Generally equal to market value of shares.

[b] May be equal to par, stated value of shares or market value. Note that some companies may choose to interpret GAAP such that the dividend is treated as a stock split. In Canada, this is a matter of judgement and is governed by legal requirements regarding the value of stated capital and economic substance.

PRESENTATION, DISCLOSURE, AND ANALYSIS

Objective 3

Understand the components of shareholders' equity and how they are presented.

Components of Shareholders' Equity

Owners' equity in a corporation is defined as **shareholders' equity** or corporate capital. The following four categories normally appear as part of shareholders' equity:

1. Common and/or preferred shares
2. Contributed surplus
3. Retained earnings (deficit)
4. Accumulated other comprehensive income[24]

The first two categories, shares and contributed surplus, form the contributed capital. The third and fourth categories, retained earnings and accumulated other comprehensive income, represent the enterprise's earned capital.

Illustration 15-7 shows a partial statement of financial position for **Loblaw Companies Limited**.

Illustration 15-7

Excerpt from the 2011 Financial Statements for Loblaw Companies Limited

(millions of Canadian dollars)	As at Dec. 31, 2011	As at Jan. 1, 2011	As at Jan. 3, 2010
Shareholders' Equity			
Common Share Capital (note 19)	1,540	1,475	1,308
Retained Earnings	4,414	4,122	3,771
Contributed Surplus (note 21)	48	1	1
Accumulated Other Comprehensive Income	5	5	1
Total Shareholders' Equity	**6,007**	**5,603**	**5,080**
Total Liabilities and Shareholders' Equity	**$17,428**	**$16,841**	**$16,090**

Contributed (paid-in) capital is the total amount that shareholders provide to the corporation for it to use in the business. **Earned capital** is the capital that is created by the business operating profitably. It consists of all undistributed income that remains invested in the enterprise. The distinction between paid-in capital and earned capital is important from both legal and economic points of view. Legally, there are restrictions on dividend payouts. These were discussed earlier in the chapter. Economically, management, shareholders, and others want to see earnings for the **corporation's** continued existence and growth. Maintaining the level of contributed capital is also a goal.[25]

Illustration 15-8 shows an example of a consolidated statement of changes in shareholders' equity for Loblaw. Note that under ASPE, given that other comprehensive income and accumulated other comprehensive income do not exist, companies provide a statement of changes in retained earnings only. Changes in share capital and contributed surplus are generally shown in the notes.

Consolidated Statement of Changes in Shareholders' Equity

(millions of Canadian dollars except where otherwise indicated)	Common Share Capital	Retained Earnings	Contributed Surplus	Accumulated Other Comprehensive Income	Total Shareholders' Equity
Balance at January 1, 2011	**$1,475**	**$4,122**	**$ 1**	**$5**	**$5,603**
Net earnings	—	769	—	—	769
Other comprehensive loss (note 22)	—	(208)	—	—	(208)

(continued)

(millions of Canadian dollars except where otherwise indicated)	Common Share Capital	Retained Earnings	Contributed Surplus	Accumulated Other Comprehensive Income	Total Shareholders' Equity
Total Comprehensive Income	—	**561**	—	—	**561**
Dividend reinvestment plan (note 19)	43	—	—	—	43
Net effect of share-based compensation (notes 19 and 21)	28	—	47	—	75
Common shares purchased for cancellation (note 19)	(6)	(33)	—	—	(39)
Dividends declared per common share – $0.84	—	(236)	—	—	(236)
	65	292	47	—	404
Balance at December 31, 2011	**$1,540**	**$4,414**	**$48**	**$5**	**$6,007**

See accompanying notes to the consolidated financial statements.

Illustration 15-8

Example of Disclosures of Changes in Shareholders' Equity—Loblaw Companies Limited

Contributed Surplus

The term "surplus" is used in an accounting sense to designate the excess of net assets over the total paid-in, par or stated value of a corporation's shares. As previously mentioned, this surplus is further divided between earned surplus (retained earnings) and contributed surplus. Contributed surplus may be affected by a variety of transactions or events, as Illustration 15-9 shows.

- Par value share issue and/or retirement (see Appendix 15A)
- Treasury share transactions (see Appendix 15A)
- Liquidating dividends
- Financial reorganizations (see Appendix 15B)
- Stock options and warrants (see Chapter 16)
- Issue of convertible debt (see Chapter 16)
- Forfeited share subscriptions
- Donated assets by a shareholder
- Redemption or conversion of shares

Illustration 15-9

Transactions that May Affect Contributed Surplus

Retained Earnings (Deficit)

The basic source of retained earnings—earnings retained for use in the business—is income from operations. Shareholders assume the greatest risk in enterprise operations as shareholders' equity declines with any losses. In return, they also reap the rewards, sharing in any profits resulting from enterprise activities. Any income that is not distributed among the shareholders becomes additional shareholders' equity. Net income includes a considerable variety of income sources. These include the enterprise's main operation (such as manufacturing and selling a product), plus any secondary activities (such as disposing of scrap or renting out unused space), plus the results of unusual items. All lead to net income that increases retained earnings. The more common items that either increase or decrease retained earnings are summarized in Illustration 15-10.

RETAINED EARNINGS

Debits	Credits
1. Net loss	1. Net income
2. Prior period adjustments (error corrections) and certain changes in accounting principle	2. Prior period adjustments (error corrections) and certain changes in accounting principle
3. Cash, property, and most stock dividends	3. Adjustments due to financial reorganization
4. Some treasury share transactions	

Illustration 15-10

Transactions that Affect Retained Earnings

Accumulated Other Comprehensive Income

Accumulated other comprehensive income is the cumulative change in equity that is due to the revenues and expenses, and gains and losses that stem from non-shareholder transactions that are excluded from the calculation of net income. It is considered to represent earned income as well. Comprehensive income was previously discussed in Chapters 4, 5, 9, and 10 and will be referred to in Chapter 16. Recall that the concept of comprehensive income is not applicable under ASPE.

Capital Disclosures

Objective 4
Understand capital disclosure requirements.

Numerous disclosures are required under GAAP regarding capital.[26] For example, basic disclosures include the amounts of authorized share capital, issued share capital, and changes in capital since the last SFP date.[27] Under IFRS, the company is required to disclose the changes in all equity accounts—including retained earnings, accumulated other comprehensive income, and share capital—since the last SFP date in the statement of changes in equity (instead of the statement of retained earnings). In many corporations, there are restrictions on retained earnings or dividends and these should be disclosed. The note disclosure should reveal the source of the restriction, pertinent provisions, and the amount of retained earnings that is restricted, or the amount that is unrestricted. Restrictions may be based on maintaining a certain retained earnings balance, the corporation's ability to observe certain working capital requirements, additional borrowing, and other considerations.

The following details would normally be disclosed on the face of the statement of financial position, in the statement of changes in shareholders' equity (under IFRS), or in the notes:

1. The authorized number of shares or a statement noting that this is unlimited

2. The existence of unique rights (such as dividend preferences and the amounts of such dividends, redemption and/or retraction privileges, conversion rights, and whether or not the dividends are cumulative)

3. The number of shares issued and amount received

4. Whether the shares are par value or no par value

5. The amount of any dividends in arrears for cumulative preferred shares

6. Details of changes during the year (presented in the statement of changes in equity under IFRS)

7. Restrictions on retained earnings

Under IFRS, companies must also disclose information about their objectives, policies, and processes for managing capital. They must include summary quantitative data about what the company manages as capital and about any changes in capital.[28] The reason for requiring this disclosure is to give users of financial statements better insight into the way the company's capital is managed. Additional detailed disclosures are required under IFRS. Illustration 15-11 shows a sample of these types of disclosures for Bombardier Inc.[29]

30. CAPITAL MANGEMENT

The Corporation's capital management strategy is designed to maintain strong liquidity and to optimize its capital structure in order to reduce costs and improve its ability to seize strategic opportunities. The Corporation analyzes its capital structure using global metrics, which are based on a broad economic view of the Corporation. The Corporation manages and monitors its global metrics such that it can achieve an investment-grade profile.

(continued)

The Corporation adjusted its global metrics to align them to those that the Corporation believes should be used to assess its creditworthiness and to reflect the new accounting rules under IFRS:

- Adjusted debt now includes the sale and leaseback obligation, as this obligation is recognized on the consolidated statements of financial position under IFRS. In addition, adjusted debt now excludes:
  - the fair value of derivatives designated in fair value hedge relationships, as such derivatives are related to our interest rate hedging program (i.e. they do not represent a principal repayment obligation); and
  - the net retirement benefit liability which is now monitored separately from our global metrics (see below).
- Adjusted interest was redefined to include interest paid (as per the supplemental information provided in the consolidated statements of cash flows), an interest adjustment for operating leases and accretion expense on sale and leaseback obligations.

Furthermore, the Corporation no longer monitors the capitalization metric as such metrics have become less relevant, in particular in the context of the volatile equity measurement that arises under IFRS.

The Corporation's objectives with regard to its global metrics are as follows:

- adjusted EBIT to adjusted interest ratio greater than 5.0; and
- adjusted debt to adjusted EBITDA ratio lower than 2.5.

Global metrics – The following global metrics do not represent the ratios required for bank covenants. A reconciliation of the global metrics to the most comparable IFRS financial measures are provided in the Non-GAAP financial measures section of the MD&A for the fiscal year ended December 31, 2011.

GLOBAL METRICS

	December 31, 2011	January 31, 2011
Adjusted EBIT[1]	$1,271	$1,262
Adjusted interest[2]	$ 271	$ 251
Adjusted EBIT to adjusted interest ratio	**4.7**	**5.0**
Adjusted debt[3]	$5,311	$5,296
Adjusted EBITDA[4]	$1,657	$1,683
Adjusted debt to adjusted EBITDA ratio[5]	**3.2**	**3.1**

[1] Represents EBIT plus interest adjustment for operating leases, and interest received (as per the supplemental information provided in the consolidated statements of cash flows, adjusted, if needed, for the settlement of fair value hedge derivatives before their contractual maturity dates).

[2] Represents interest paid (as per the supplemental information provided in the consolidated statements of cash flows), plus accretion expense on sale and leaseback obligations and interest adjustments for operating leases.

[3] Represents long-term debt adjusted for the fair value of derivatives designated in fair value hedge relationships plus sale and leaseback obligations and the net present value of operating lease obligations.

[4] Represents EBITDA plus amortization and interest, adjusted for operating leases, and interest received (as per the supplemental information provided in the consolidated statements of cash flows, adjusted, if needed, for the settlement of derivatives before their contractual maturity dates).

[5] The fiscal year ended December 31, 2011 comprises 11 months of BA's results and 12 months of BT's results.*

In addition to the above global level metrics, the Corporation separately monitors its net retirement benefit liability which amounted to $3,213 million as at December 31, 2011 ($1,946 million as at January 31, 2011). The measurement of this liability is dependent on numerous key long-term assumptions such as those regarding future compensation increases, inflation rates, mortality rates and current discount rates. In recent years, this liability has been particularly volatile due to changes in discount rates. Such volatility is exacerbated by the long-term nature of the obligation. For example, discount rates have reached an historical low during the fiscal year ended December 31, 2011 resulting in a net retirement benefit liability increase of $1.5 billion. The Corporation closely monitors the impact of the net retirement benefit liability on its future cash flows and has introduced significant risk mitigation initiatives in recent years in this respect. For details on the increase in the net benefit retirement liability due to changes in discount rate assumptions and risk mitigation initiatives, see the Retirement benefits section of the MD&A.

In order to adjust its capital structure, the Corporation may issue or reduce long-term debt, make discretionary contributions to pension funds, repurchase or issue share capital, or vary the amount of dividends paid to shareholders.

See note 29 – Credit facilities for a description of bank covenants.

*Please note that BA refers to Bombardier Aerospace and BT to Bombardier Transportation.

Analysis

Several ratios use amounts related to shareholders' equity to evaluate a company's **profitability** and **long-term solvency**. The following four ratios are discussed and illustrated next: (1) rate of return on common shareholders' equity, (2) payout ratio, (3) price earnings ratio, and (4) book value per share.

Rate of Return on Common Shareholders' Equity

A widely used ratio that measures profitability from the common shareholders' viewpoint is **rate of return on common shareholders' equity**. This ratio shows how many dollars of net income were earned for each dollar invested by the owners. It is calculated by dividing net income less preferred dividends by average common shareholders' equity. For example, assume that Garber Inc. had net income of $360,000, declared and paid preferred dividends of $54,000, and had average common shareholders' equity of $2,550,000. Garber's ratio is calculated as follows:

$$\text{Rate of return on common shareholders' equity} = \frac{\text{Net income} - \text{Preferred dividends}}{\text{Average common shareholders' equity}}$$

$$= \frac{\$360,000 - \$54,000}{\$2,550,000}$$

$$= 12\%$$

As the calculation shows, because preferred shares are present, preferred dividends are deducted from net income to calculate the income available to common shareholders. Similarly, the carrying value of preferred shares is deducted from total shareholders' equity to arrive at the amount of common shareholders' equity used in this ratio.

When the rate of return on total assets is lower than the rate of return on the common shareholders' investment, the company is said to be trading on the equity at a gain. **Trading on the equity** describes the practice of using borrowed money at fixed interest rates or issuing preferred shares with constant dividend rates in hopes of obtaining a higher rate of return on the money used (this is sometimes also referred to as **leverage**). As these debt issues must be given a prior claim on some or all of the corporate assets, the advantage to common shareholders of trading on the equity must come from borrowing at a lower rate of interest than the rate of return that is obtained on the assets that have been borrowed. If this can be done, the capital obtained from bondholders or preferred shareholders earns enough to pay the interest or preferred dividends and to leave a margin for the common shareholders. When this occurs, trading on the equity is profitable.

Payout Ratio

Another measure of profitability is the **payout ratio**, which is the ratio of cash dividends to net income. If preferred shares are outstanding, this ratio is calculated for common shareholders by dividing cash dividends paid to common shareholders by net income available to common shareholders. Assuming that Troy Corp. has cash dividends of $100,000, net income of $500,000, and no preferred shares outstanding, the payout ratio is calculated as follows:

$$\text{Payout ratio} = \frac{\text{Cash dividends to common}}{\text{Net income} - \text{Preferred dividends}}$$

$$= \frac{\$100,000}{\$500,000}$$

$$= 20\%$$

For some investors, it is important that the payout be high enough to provide a good yield on the shares.[30] However, payout ratios have declined for many companies because many investors now view appreciation in the share value as more important than the dividend amount.

Price Earnings Ratio

The **price earnings (P/E) ratio** is an oft-quoted statistic that analysts use in discussing the investment potential of an enterprise. It is calculated by dividing the share's market price by the earnings per share. For example, assuming that Soreson Corp. has a market price of $50 and earnings per share of $4, its price earnings ratio would be calculated as follows:

$$\text{Price earnings ratio} = \frac{\text{Market price of share}}{\text{Earnings per share}}$$

$$= \$50/\$4$$

$$= 12.5$$

Book Value per Share

A much-used basis for evaluating net worth is the book or equity value per share. Book value per share is the amount that each share would receive if the company were liquidated, based on the amounts reported on the SFP. However, the figure loses much of its relevance if the valuations on the statement of financial position do not approximate the fair market value of the assets. **Book value per share** is calculated by dividing common shareholders' equity by the number of common shares outstanding. Assuming that Chen Corporation's common shareholders' equity is $1 million and it has 100,000 shares outstanding, its book value per share is calculated as follows:

$$\text{Book value per share} = \frac{\text{Common shareholders' equity}}{\text{Number of shares outstanding}}$$

$$= \frac{\$1,000,000}{100,000}$$

$$= \$10 \text{ per share}$$

When preferred shares are present, an analysis of the covenants involving the preferred shares should be studied. If preferred dividends are in arrears, the preferred shares are participating, or the preferred shares have a redemption or liquidating value higher than their carrying amount, then retained earnings must be allocated between the preferred and common shareholders in calculating book value.

To illustrate, assume that the following situation exists.

Shareholders' equity	Preferred	Common
Preferred shares, 5%	$300,000	
Common shares		$400,000
Contributed surplus		37,500
Retained earnings	-0-	162,582
Totals	$300,000	$600,082
Shares outstanding		4,000
Book value per share		$150.02

In the preceding calculation, it is assumed that no preferred dividends are in arrears and that the preferred shares are not participating. Now assume that the same facts exist except that the 5% preferred shares are cumulative and participating up to 8%, and that dividends for three years before the current year are in arrears. The common shares' book value is then calculated as follows, assuming that no action has yet been taken concerning dividends for the current year.

Shareholders' equity	Preferred	Common
Preferred shares, 5%	$300,000	
Common shares		$400,000
Contributed surplus		37,500
Retained earnings:		
Dividends in arrears (3 years at 5% a year)	45,000	
Current year requirement at 5%	15,000	20,000
Participating additional 3%	9,000	12,000
Remainder to common	-0-	61,582
Totals	$369,000	$531,082
Shares outstanding		4,000
Book value per share		$132.77

In connection with the book value calculation, the analyst should also consider the following items: the number of authorized and unissued shares, the number of treasury shares on hand, any commitments with respect to the issuance of unissued shares or the reissuance of treasury shares, and the relative rights and privileges of the various types of shares authorized.

Objective 6

Identify the major differences in accounting between ASPE and IFRS, and what changes are expected in the near future.

IFRS/ASPE COMPARISON
A Comparison of IFRS and ASPE

Illustration 15-12 summarizes the major differences in accounting for equity between ASPE and IFRS.

	ASPE—CICA Handbook, Part II, Sections 3240, 3251, and 3856	IFRS—IAS 1 and 7	References to Related Illustrations and Select Brief Exercises
Recognition/ derecognition	Specific guidance is given for reacquisition of shares. The cost should be allocated first to share capital, then to contributed surplus, and then to retained earnings.	No explicit guidance is given, although the accounting may end up the same using basic principles.	N/A
	Receivables for loans issued to buy shares are recognized as assets if the shareholder is at risk for changes in value of the shares and there is reasonable assurance that the company will be able to collect in cash. Otherwise, they are not recognized or if recognized, are presented as contra equity.	No explicit guidance is given, although the accounting may end up the same due to basic principles.	N/A

(continued)

	ASPE—*CICA Handbook*, Part II, Sections 3240, 3251, and 3856	IFRS—IAS 1 and 7	References to Related Illustrations and Select Brief Exercises
Measurement	Specific guidance is given for comprehensive revaluation of assets where a financial reorganization of the company occurs. Assets are revalued, the debt and equity accounts are adjusted to reflect the new capital structure, and any deficit or retained earnings are reclassified to other equity accounts.	No explicit guidance is given for accounting for financial reorganizations. Note that IFRS allows revaluation of property, plant, and equipment and intangibles (using the revaluation method), financial instruments (under the fair value option), and investment properties (under the fair value method). These are covered in other chapters, including 10, 14, and 16.	Comprehensive revaluation accounting is covered in Appendix 15B.
	Dividends in kind that represent a spinoff of assets to shareholders are measured at carrying value unless it is a transaction with controlling shareholders, in which case the transaction is treated as a related party transaction and may be remeasured.	No explicit guidance is given; however, related party transactions are not remeasured.	Related party transactions are covered in Chapter 23.
Presentation	Changes in retained earnings are presented in a retained earnings statement. Changes in capital accounts are presented in the notes. The concept of comprehensive income is not discussed.	Changes in all equity accounts are presented in a separate statement of changes in equity.	Illustration 15-8 gives an example of the statement of changes in shareholders' equity. Examples of this statement as well as statements of changes in retained earnings are given throughout the text.
Disclosures	Specific disclosures about how a company manages its capital are not explicitly mandated.	Specific disclosures are required regarding how a company manages its capital.	Illustration 15-11

Illustration 15-12

IFRS and ASPE Comparison Chart

Looking Ahead

The IASB and FASB are working on several projects, including the financial statement presentation project and the project on liabilities and equity. The financial statement project was discussed in Chapter 4.

At the time of writing, the liabilities/equity project had been put on hold. The IASB is looking to do some research on identifying financial instruments, which are difficult to classify as debt or equity under the current standards. Any changes to the standards will need to be done in conjunction with the work on the conceptual framework on defining elements.

SUMMARY OF LEARNING OBJECTIVES

1 Discuss the characteristics of the corporate form of organization, rights of shareholders, and different types of shares.

The three main forms of organization are the proprietorship, partnership, and corporation. Incorporation gives shareholders protection against claims on their personal assets and allows greater access to capital markets.

If there are no restrictive provisions, each share carries the following rights: (1) to share proportionately in profits and losses, (2) to share proportionately in management (the right to vote for directors), and (3) to share proportionately in corporate assets upon liquidation. An additional right to share proportionately in any new issues of shares of the same class (called the preemptive right) may also be attached to the share.

Preferred shares are a special class of share that possess certain preferences or features that common shares do not have. Most often, these features are a preference over dividends and a preference over assets in the event of liquidation. Many other preferences may be attached to specific shares. Preferred shareholders give up some or all of the rights normally attached to common shares.

2 Explain how to account for the issuance, reacquisition, and retirement of shares, stock splits, and dividend distribution.

Shares are recognized and measured at net cost when issued. Shares may be issued on a subscription basis, in which case they are not considered legally issued until they are paid up. Shares may also be issued as a bundle with other securities, in which case the cost must be allocated between the securities. The residual or relative fair value methods (sometimes referred to as the incremental or proportional methods) may be used to allocate the cost.

If the reacquisition cost of the shares is greater than the original cost, the acquisition cost is allocated to share capital, then contributed surplus, and then retained earnings. If the cost is less, the cost is allocated to share capital (to stated or assigned cost) and to contributed surplus.

Dividends paid to shareholders are affected by the dividend preferences of the preferred shares. Preferred shares can be cumulative or non-cumulative, and fully participating, partially participating, or non-participating.

A stock dividend is a capitalization of retained earnings that generally results in a reduction in retained earnings and a corresponding increase in certain contributed capital accounts. The total shareholders' equity remains unchanged with a stock dividend. A stock split results in an increase or decrease in the number of shares outstanding. However, no accounting entry is required.

3 Understand the components of shareholders' equity and how they are presented.

Contributed surplus is additional surplus coming from shareholder transactions. Accumulated other comprehensive income is accumulated non-shareholder income that has not been booked through net income. ASPE does not discuss this concept. The shareholders' equity section of a balance sheet includes Share Capital, Contributed Surplus, Retained Earnings, and Accumulated Other Comprehensive Income. A statement of changes in shareholders' equity is required under IFRS.

4 Understand capital disclosure requirements.

Basic disclosure requirements include authorized and issued share capital and changes during the period. Rights attached to shares should be presented, and where dividends are in arrears, this should also be disclosed. Where there are restrictions on retained earnings or dividends, this should be disclosed. Under IFRS, companies must also disclose information about their objectives, policies, and processes for managing capital and show summary quantitative information regarding what the company considers its capital.

5 Calculate and interpret key ratios relating to equity.

Common ratios used in this area are the rate of return on common shareholders' equity, payout ratio, price earnings ratio, and book value per share.

6 Identify the major differences in accounting between ASPE and IFRS, and what changes are expected in the near future.

In several cases, ASPE provides more guidance, as noted in the comparison chart. IFRS requires a statement of changes in shareholders' equity, whereas ASPE requires a statement of changes in retained earnings (with additional note disclosure regarding the changes in equity). The IASB and FASB are continuing to work on a financial statements project as well as a liability and equity project.

KEY TERMS

APPENDIX 15A

PAR VALUE AND TREASURY SHARES

Objective 7
Explain how to account for par value and treasury shares.

Neither par value shares nor treasury shares are allowed under the Canada Business Corporations Act. As mentioned in the chapter, however, these types of shares are allowed under certain provincial business corporations acts and are common in the United States. For this reason, they will now be discussed in greater detail in this appendix.

Par Value Shares

The par value of a share has no relationship to its fair market value. At present, the par value that is associated with most capital share issuances is very low ($1, $5, or $10). To show the required information for the issuance of par value shares, accounts must be kept for each class of share as follows:

1. **Preferred or common shares.** These accounts reflect the par value of the corporation's issued shares. They are credited when the shares are originally issued. No additional entries are made in these accounts unless additional shares are issued or shares are retired.

2. **Contributed surplus (paid-in capital in excess of par or additional paid-in capital in the United States).** This account indicates any excess over par value that was paid in by shareholders in return for the shares issued to them. Once it has been paid in, the excess over par becomes a part of the corporation's paid-in capital, and the individual shareholder has no greater claim on the excess paid in than all other holders of the same class of shares.

To illustrate how these accounts are used, assume that Colonial Corporation sold, for $1,100, 100 shares with a par value of $5 per share. The entry to record the issuance is:

Cash	1,100	
Common Shares		500
Contributed Surplus		600

A = L + SE
+1,100   +1,100
Cash flows: ↑ 1,100 inflow

When the shares are repurchased and cancelled, the same procedure is followed as was described in the chapter.

Treasury Shares

Treasury shares are created when a company repurchases its own shares but does not cancel them. Generally, the repurchase and resale are treated as a single transaction. The repurchase of treasury shares is the first part of a transaction that is completed when the shares are later resold. Consequently, the holding of treasury shares is viewed as a transitional phase between the beginning and end of a single activity.

When shares are purchased, the total cost is debited to Treasury Shares on the statement of financial position. This account is shown as a deduction from the total of the components of shareholders' equity in the SFP. An example of such disclosure follows:

Shareholders' equity:		
Common shares, no par value; authorized 24,000,000 shares;		
issued 19,045,870 shares, of which 209,750 are in treasury	$ 27,686,000	
Retained earnings	253,265,000	
		280,951,000
Less: Cost of treasury shares		(7,527,000)
Total shareholders' equity		$273,424,000

When the shares are sold, the Treasury Shares account is credited for their cost. If they are sold at more than their cost, the excess is credited to Contributed Surplus. If they are sold at less, the difference is debited to Contributed Surplus (if it is related to the same class of shares) and then to Retained Earnings. If the shares are subsequently retired, the journal entries shown in the chapter would be followed.

Note also that dividends on treasury shares should be reversed since a company cannot receive dividend income on its own shares (dr. Dividends Payable, cr. Retained Earnings).

SUMMARY OF LEARNING OBJECTIVE FOR APPENDIX 15A

7 Explain how to account for par value and treasury shares.

These shares may only be valued at par value in the common or preferred share accounts. The excess goes to contributed surplus. On a repurchase or cancellation, the par value is removed from the common or preferred share accounts and any excess or deficit is booked to contributed surplus or retained earnings, as was discussed for no par shares.

Treasury shares are created when a company repurchases its own shares and does not cancel or retire them at the same time; that is, they remain outstanding. The single-transaction method is used when treasury shares are purchased. This method treats the purchase and subsequent resale or cancellation as part of the same transaction.

APPENDIX 15B

FINANCIAL REORGANIZATION

Objective 8

Explain how to account for a financial reorganization.

A corporation that consistently suffers net losses accumulates negative retained earnings, or a deficit. Shareholders generally presume that dividends are paid out of profits and retained earnings and, therefore, a deficit sends a very negative signal about the company's ability to pay dividends. In addition, certain laws in some jurisdictions specify that no dividends may be declared and paid as long as a corporation's paid-in capital has been reduced by a deficit. In these cases, a corporation with a debit balance of retained earnings must accumulate enough profits to offset the deficit before it can pay any dividends.

This situation may be a real hardship on a corporation and its shareholders. A company that has operated unsuccessfully for several years and accumulated a deficit may have finally turned the corner. The development of new products and new markets, the arrival of a new management group, or improved economic conditions may point to much improved operating results in the future. However, if the law prohibits dividends until the deficit has been replaced by earnings, the shareholders must wait until such profits have been earned, which can take quite a long time. Furthermore, future success may depend on obtaining additional funds through the sale of shares, but if no dividends can be paid for some time, the market price of any new share issue is likely to be low, assuming the shares can be marketed at all.

Thus, a company with excellent prospects may not be able to carry out its plans because of a deficit, although present management may have had nothing at all to do with the years during which the deficit was built up. To allow the corporation to go ahead with its plans might well be in everyone's best interest; to require it to eliminate the deficit through profits might actually force it to liquidate.

One way that a company that has gone through financial difficulty can proceed with its plans without having to recover from a deficit is a **financial reorganization**. A financial reorganization is defined as:

a substantial realignment of an enterprise's equity and non-equity interests such that the holders of one or more of the significant classes of non-equity interests and the holders of all of the significant classes of equity interests give up some (or all) of their rights and claims on the enterprise.[31]

In other words, in a financial reorganization, creditors often give up their claim on the company and take back ownership rights (shares).

A financial reorganization is the outcome of negotiation and results in an eventual agreement between non-equity and equity holders in the corporation. These negotiations may take place under a legal act (such as the Companies' Creditors Arrangement Act) or a less formal process.[32] The result gives the company a fresh start and the accounting is often referred to as **fresh start accounting**.

Comprehensive Revaluation

When a financial reorganization occurs, where the same party does not control the company both before and after the reorganization, and where new costs are reasonably determinable, the company's assets and liabilities should undergo a **comprehensive revaluation**.[33]

Under ASPE, this requires three steps:[34]

1. The deficit balance (retained earnings) is brought to zero. Any asset writedowns or impairments that existed before the reorganization should be recorded first. The deficit is reclassified to Share Capital, Contributed Surplus, or a separately identified account within Shareholders' Equity.

2. The changes in debt and equity that have been negotiated are recorded. Often, debt is exchanged for equity, reflecting a change in control.

3. The assets and liabilities are comprehensively revalued. This step assigns appropriate going concern values to all assets and liabilities based on the negotiations. The difference between the carrying values before the reorganization and the new values after is known as a **revaluation adjustment**. The revaluation adjustment and any costs incurred to carry out the financial reorganization are accounted for as capital transactions and are closed to Share Capital, Contributed Surplus, or a separately identified account within Shareholders' Equity. Note that the new costs of the identifiable assets and liabilities must not be greater than the entity's fair value if this is known.[35]

Entries Illustrated

The series of entries that follows illustrates the accounting procedures that are applied in a financial reorganization. Assume that New Horizons Inc. shows a deficit of $1 million before the reorganization comes into effect on June 30, 2014. Under the terms of the negotiation, the creditors are giving up rights to payment of the $150,000 debt in return for 100% of the common shares. The original shareholders agree to give up their shares.

1. **Restate impairments of assets that existed before the reorganization:**

Deficit	750,000	
Inventory (loss on writedown)		225,000
Intangible Assets – Patents (loss on writedown)		525,000

A	=	L	+	SE
−750,000				−750,000

Cash flows: No effect

Elimination of deficit against contributed capital:

Common Shares	1,750,000	
Deficit		1,750,000

A	=	L	+	SE
				0

Cash flows: No effect

2. **and 3. Restate assets and liabilities to recognize unrecorded gains and losses and to record the negotiated change in control:**

Buildings (gain on write-up)	400,000	
Notes Payable (gain on writedown)	150,000	
Common Shares		550,000

A	=	L	+	SE
+400,000		−150,000		+550,000

Cash flows: No effect

Note that, if there is no change in control, ASPE does not allow a comprehensive revaluation.

When a financial reorganization occurs and is accounted for as such, the following requirements must be fulfilled:

1. The proposed reorganization should receive the **approval** of the corporation's shareholders before it is put into effect.

2. The new asset and liability valuations should be **fair** and not deliberately understate or overstate assets, liabilities, and earnings.

3. After the reorganization, the corporation must have a zero balance of retained earnings, although it may have contributed surplus arising from the reorganization.

Disclosure

In the period of the reorganization, the following must be disclosed:

1. The date of the reorganization

2. A description of the reorganization

3. The amount of the change in each major class of assets, liabilities, and shareholders' equity resulting from the reorganization

In the following fiscal period, in subsequent reports, the following must be disclosed:

1. The date of the reorganization

2. The revaluation adjustment amount and the shareholders' equity account in which it was recorded

3. The amount of the deficit that was reclassified and the account to which it was reclassified

SUMMARY OF LEARNING OBJECTIVE FOR APPENDIX 15B

8 Explain how to account for a financial reorganization.

A corporation that has accumulated a large debit balance (deficit) in retained earnings may enter into a process known as a financial reorganization. During a reorganization, creditors and shareholders negotiate a deal to put the company on a new footing. This generally involves a **change in control** and a **comprehensive revaluation** of assets and liabilities. The procedure consists of the following steps: (1) The deficit is reclassified so that the ending balance in Retained Earnings is zero. (2) The change in control is recorded. (3) All assets and liabilities are comprehensively revalued at current values so that the company will not be burdened with having to complete inventory or fixed asset valuations in following years.

KEY TERMS

comprehensive revaluation, p. 967
financial reorganization, p. 967

fresh start accounting, p. 967

revaluation adjustment, p. 968

Quiz

Brief Exercises

Note: All assignment material with an asterisk (*) relates to the appendices to the chapter.

(LO 1) **BE15-1** Explain the pros and cons of incorporating.

(LO 1) **BE15-2** List the types of dividends. Why do companies or investors have a preference for one or the other?

(LO 1) **BE15-3** Walter Corporation has three classes of shares: Series A, Series B, and Class A. How should Walter classify and present the different classes if the characteristics of each class are as follows?

Series A shares	The shares are mandatorily redeemable and carry a dividend rate of 4%.
Series B shares	The shares are cumulative and carry a dividend rate of $2 per share. They are subordinated to the Series A shares for dividend distribution.
Class A shares	The shares are subordinated to both Series A and Series B shares for dividend distribution and participate in the earnings and losses of the company above a non-cumulative dividend of $0.50 per share. The shares have a voting right of one vote per share.

(LO 2) **BE15-4** Bonata Inc. sells 1,400 common shares on a subscription basis at $65 per share on June 1 and accepts a 45% down payment. On December 1, Bonata collects the remaining 55% and issues the shares. Prepare the company's journal entries.

(LO 2) **BE15-5** On March 1, Kramers Inc. sells 1,000 common shares to its employees at $25 per share and lends the money to the employees to buy the new shares. The employees pay 50% of the price on the transaction date and pay the balance in one year. (a) Prepare the company's necessary journal entries. (b) Assuming a December 31 fiscal year end, how should the receivable for the uncollected amount on the share issue be presented on the statement of financial position (1) under ASPE and (2) under IFRS?

(LO 2) **BE15-6** Platinum Corporation issued 4,000 of its common shares for $66,000. The company also incurred $1,700 of costs associated with issuing the shares. Prepare the journal entry to record the issuance of the company's shares.

(LO 2) **BE15-7** Higgins Inc. has 52,000 common shares outstanding. The shares have an average cost of $21 per share. On July 1, 2014, Higgins reacquired 800 shares at $56 per share and retired them. (a) Prepare the journal entry to record this transaction if Higgins prepares financial statements in accordance with ASPE. (b) Discuss how the answer to part (a) may be different if Higgins prepared financial statements in accordance with IFRS.

(LO 2) **BE15-8** Spencer Corporation has 50,000 common shares outstanding, with an average issue price per share of $8. On August 1, 2014, the company reacquired and cancelled 600 shares at $40 per share. There was Contributed Surplus of $0.25 per share at the time of the reacquisition (total $12,500), which arose from net excess of proceeds over cost on a previous cancellation of common shares. (a) Prepare the journal entry to record this transaction if Spencer prepares financial statements in accordance with ASPE. (b) Discuss how the answer to part (a) may be different if Spencer prepared financial statements in accordance with IFRS.

(LO 2) **BE15-9** Hamza Inc. declared a cash dividend of $0.60 per share on its 1.5 million outstanding shares. The dividend was declared on August 1 and is payable on September 9 to all shareholders of record on August 15. Prepare all necessary journal entries for those three dates.

(LO 2) **BE15-10** Mallard Inc. owns shares of Oakwood Corporation that are classified as part of Mallard's trading portfolio and accounted for using the fair value through net income model. At December 31, 2013, the securities were carried in Mallard's accounting records at their cost of $850,000, which equalled their fair value. On September 21, 2014, when the securities' fair value was $1.3 million, Mallard declared a property dividend that will result in the Oakwood securities being distributed on October 23, 2014, to shareholders of record on October 8, 2014. Prepare all necessary journal entries for the three dates.

(LO 2) **BE15-11** On April 20, Raule Mining Corp. declared a dividend of $400,000 that is payable on June 1. Of this amount, $150,000 is a return of capital. Prepare the April 20 and June 1 journal entries for Raule.

(LO 2) **BE15-12** Chadwick Corporation has 450,000 common shares outstanding. The corporation declares a 6% stock dividend when the shares' fair value is $30 per share (their carrying value is $18 per share). Prepare the journal entries for the company for both the date of declaration and the date of distribution.

(LO 2) **BE15-13** Kindey Corporation has 185,000 common shares outstanding with a carrying value of $20 per share. Kindey declares a 4-for-1 stock split. (a) How many shares are outstanding after the split? (b) What is the carrying value per share after the split? (c) What is the total carrying value after the split? (d) What journal entry is necessary to record the split?

(LO 3) BE15-14 Lu Corporation has the following account balances at December 31, 2014:

Common Shares Subscribed	$ 250,000
Common Shares—No Par Value	310,000
Subscriptions Receivable	80,000
Retained Earnings	1,340,000
Contributed Surplus	320,000
Accumulated Other Comprehensive Income	560,000

Prepare the December 31, 2014 shareholders' equity section of the statement of financial position.

(LO 3) BE15-15 The Sawgrass Corporation, a public company, reported the following balances at January 1, 2014:

Common Shares—No Par Value (32,000 shares issued, unlimited authorized)	$ 800,000
Retained Earnings	1,500,000
Contributed Surplus	145,000
Accumulated Other Comprehensive Income	40,000

During the year ended December 31, 2014, the following summary transactions occurred:

Net income earned during the year	$400,000
Holding gain on fair value-other comprehensive income investments	25,000
Reduction of contributed surplus during the year due to repurchase of common shares	17,500
Reduction of common shares account balance during the year due to repurchase of 1,000 common shares	25,000
Dividends paid during the year on common shares	70,000
Issued 2,000 common shares during the year	100,000

(a) Prepare a statement of changes in shareholders' equity for the year as required under IFRS.

(b) Prepare the shareholders' equity section of the statement of financial position at December 31.

(c) How would the answer to parts (a) and (b) be different if Sawgrass prepared financial statements in accordance with ASPE?

(LO 5) BE15-16 Arthur Corporation has the following selected financial data:

	2014	2013
Net income	$ 720,000	$ 680,000
Total assets	5,136,000	4,525,000
Preferred shares, 4%, cumulative	600,000	600,000
Common shares	350,000	350,000
Retained earnings	2,786,000	2,190,000
Accumulated other comprehensive income	145,000	130,000
Total shareholders' equity	3,881,000	3,270,000
Cash dividends paid in the year	124,000	170,000
Market price of common shares	$97.46	$64.33
Weighted average number of common shares	80,000	80,000

There were no preferred dividends in arrears. (a) Calculate the following ratios for 2014: (1) rate of return on common shareholders' equity, (2) payout ratio, (3) price earnings ratio, (4) book value, and (5) rate of return on total assets. (b) Is Arthur Corporation trading on the equity?

(LO 7) *BE15-17 Sullivan Limited issued 2,000 shares of no par value common shares for $79,000. Prepare Sullivan's journal entry if (a) the shares have no par value, and (b) the shares have a par value of $11 per share.

(LO 7) *BE15-18 Hanover Corporation has 750,000 shares outstanding. The shares have an average cost of $45 per share. On September 5, 2014, the company repurchases 1,500 of its own shares at $75 per share and does not cancel them. The shares are classified as treasury shares. On November 20, 2014, the company resells 1,000 of the treasury shares at $80 per share. Prepare the journal entries for the repurchase and subsequent sale of the treasury shares.

(LO 7) *BE15-19 Use the information for Hanover Corporation in BE15-18. Assume now that the company resells the 1,000 treasury shares at $55 per share. Prepare the journal entries for the repurchase and subsequent sale of the treasury shares.

(LO 8) *BE15-20 Tsui Corporation went through a financial reorganization by writing down its buildings by $107,000 and eliminating its deficit, which was $182,000 before the reorganization. As part of the reorganization, the creditors agreed to take back 55% of the common shares in lieu of payment of the debt of $1.8 million (Notes Payable). Prepare the entries to record the financial reorganization assuming that Tsui follows ASPE.

Exercises

(LO 2)   E15-1   (Recording Issuance of Common and Preferred Shares) Victoria Corporation was organized on January 1, 2014. It is authorized to issue 400,000 common shares and 100,000 preferred shares with a $7 dividend. The following share transactions were completed during the first year:

Jan. 10	Issued 200,000 common shares for cash at $23 per share.	
Mar. 1	Issued 17,000 preferred shares for cash at $119 per share.	
Apr. 1	Issued 3,000 common shares for land. The asking price for the land was $67,000; its fair value was $60,000.	
May 1	Issued 20,000 common shares for cash at $18 per share.	
Aug. 1	Issued 1,000 common shares to lawyers in payment of their bill of $19,000 for services rendered in helping the company organize.	
Sept. 1	Issued 32,500 common shares for cash at $16 per share.	
Nov. 1	Issued 1,500 preferred shares for cash at $125 per share.	

Instructions

Prepare the journal entries to record the above transactions.

(LO 2)   E15-2   (Subscribed Shares) Callaghan Inc. decided to sell shares to raise additional capital so that it could expand into the rapidly growing service industry. The corporation chose to sell these shares through a subscription basis and publicly notified the investment world. The offering was 40,000 shares at $22 a share. The terms of the subscription were 35% down and the balance at the end of six months. All shares were subscribed for during the offering period.

Instructions

(a) Prepare the journal entries for the original subscription, the collection of the down payments, the collection of the balance of the subscription price, and the issuance of the shares.

(b) Discuss how the Share Subscriptions Receivable account should be presented on the statement of financial position if it is still outstanding at the end of the reporting period.

(c) Discuss how Callaghan should account for the balance in the subscription account and the amounts already collected if the subscriber defaults before making the final payment.

(LO 2)   E15-3   (Share Issuances and Repurchase) As of December 31, 2013, Cayenne Corporation has 40,000 common shares outstanding. During 2014, the company took part in the following selected transactions.

1. Issued 6,000 common shares at $25 per share, less $2,000 in costs related to the issuance of the shares.

2. Issued 3,750 common shares for land appraised at $130,000. The shares were actively traded on a national stock exchange at approximately $32 per share on the date of issuance.

3. Purchased and retired 500 of the company's shares at $29 per share. The repurchased shares have an average issue price per share of $34.

Instructions

(a) Prepare the journal entries to record the three transactions listed.

(b) When shares are repurchased, is the original issue price of those individual shares relevant? Explain.

(LO 2)   E15-4   (Correcting Entries for Equity Transactions) Stankovic Inc. recently hired a new accountant with extensive experience in accounting for partnerships. Because of the pressure of the new job, the accountant was unable to review what he had learned earlier about corporation accounting. During the first month, he made the following entries for the corporation's no par value capital shares:

May 12	Cash	221,000	
	Common Shares		221,000
	(Issued 13,000 common shares at $17 per share.)		
10	Cash	400,000	
	Common Shares		400,000
	(Issued 8,000 preferred shares at $50 per share.)		
15	Common Shares	15,000	
	Cash		15,000
	(Purchased and retired 1,000 common shares at $15 per share.)		

31	Cash	9,000
	Common Shares		5,000
	Gain on Sale of Shares		4,000
	(Issued 500 shares at $18 per share.)		

Instructions

Based on the explanation for each entry, prepare the entries that should have been made for the capital share transactions. Explain your reasoning.

(LO 2) E15-5 (Preferred Dividends) The outstanding share capital of Meadowcrest Corporation consists of 3,000 shares of preferred and 7,000 common shares for which $280,000 was received. The preferred shares carry a dividend of $7 per share and have a $100 stated value.

Instructions

Assuming that the company has retained earnings of $95,000 that is to be entirely paid out in dividends and that preferred dividends were not paid during the two years preceding the current year, state how much each class of shares should receive under each of the following conditions.

(a) The preferred shares are non-cumulative and non-participating.

(b) The preferred shares are cumulative and non-participating.

(c) The preferred shares are cumulative and participating.

(d) Assume that Meadowcrest's current year net income was $90,000. Calculate the current year payout ratio under each of the conditions above. Comment on the results of your analysis from the perspective of a potential investor.

Digging Deeper

(LO 2) E15-6 (Preferred Dividends) McNamara Limited's ledger shows the following balances on December 31, 2014:

Preferred shares outstanding: 25,000 shares	$ 625,000
Common shares outstanding: 40,000 shares	3,000,000
Retained earnings	890,000

Instructions

Assuming that the directors decide to declare total dividends in the amount of $445,000, determine how much each class of shares should receive under each of the conditions that follow. Note that one year's dividends are in arrears on the preferred shares, which pay a dividend of $1.50 per share.

(a) The preferred shares are cumulative and fully participating.

(b) The preferred shares are non-cumulative and non-participating.

(c) The preferred shares are non-cumulative and are participating in distributions in excess of a 10% dividend rate on the common shares.

(LO 2) E15-7 (Participating Preferred and Stock Dividend) The following is the shareholders' equity section of Suozzi Corp. at December 31, 2014:

Preferred shares,[a] authorized 100,000 shares; issued 25,000 shares	$ 750,000
Common shares (200,000 authorized, 60,000 issued)	1,800,000
Contributed surplus	1,150,000
Total paid-in capital	3,700,000
Retained earnings	2,470,500
Total shareholders' equity	$6,170,500

[a] The preferred shares have a $5 dividend rate, are cumulative, and participate in distributions in excess of a $3 dividend on the common shares.

Instructions

(a) No dividends were paid in 2012 or 2013. On December 31, 2014, Suozzi wants to pay a cash dividend of $4 a share to common shareholders. How much cash would be needed for the total amount to be paid to preferred and common shareholders?

(b) The company decides instead that it will declare a 15% stock dividend on the outstanding common shares. The shares' fair value is $105 per share. Prepare the entry on the date of declaration.

(c) The company decides instead to acquire and cancel 10,500 common shares. The current fair value is $105 per share. Prepare the entry to record the retirement, assuming contributed surplus arose from previous cancellations of common shares.

(LO 2) E15-8   (Dividend Entries) The following data were taken from the statement of financial position accounts of Bedard Corporation on December 31, 2014:

Current assets	$1,040,000
FV-NI investments	824,000
Common shares (no par value, no authorized limit, 600,000 shares issued and outstanding)	6,000,000
Contributed surplus	350,000
Retained earnings	1,840,000

Instructions

Prepare the required journal entries for the following unrelated events in January 2015.

(a) A 6% stock dividend is declared and distributed at a time when the shares' fair value is $48 per share.

(b) A 4-for-1 stock split is effected.

(c) A dividend in kind is declared on January 8, 2015, and paid on January 28, 2015, in fair value–net income investments. The investments have a carrying amount of $160,000 (fair value at December 31, 2014) and a January 8 fair value of $165,000.

(LO 2) E15-9   (Stock Split and Stock Dividend) The common shares of Hoover Inc. are currently selling at $143 per share. The directors want to reduce the share price and increase the share volume before making a new issue. The per share carrying value is $34. There are currently 1 million shares issued and outstanding.

Instructions

(a) Prepare the necessary journal entries assuming that:

1. The board votes a 2-for-1 stock split.
2. The board votes a 100% stock dividend.

(b) Briefly discuss the accounting and securities market differences between these two methods of increasing the number of shares outstanding.

(LO 2) E15-10   (Entries for Stock Dividends and Stock Splits) The shareholders' equity accounts of Chatsworth Inc. have the following balances on December 31, 2014:

Common shares, 400,000 shares issued and outstanding	$10,000,000
Contributed surplus	2,300,000
Retained earnings	42,400,000

Common shares are currently selling on the Prairie Stock Exchange at $59.

Instructions

Prepare the appropriate journal entries for each of the following cases.

(a) A stock dividend of 10% is declared and issued.

(b) A stock dividend of 100% is declared and issued.

(c) A 2-for-1 stock split is declared and issued.

(LO 2, 3) E15-11   (Dividends and Shareholders' Equity Section) Falkon Corp. reported the following amounts in the shareholders' equity section of its December 31, 2013 statement of financial position:

Preferred shares, $8 dividend (10,000 shares authorized, 2,000 shares issued)	$200,000
Common shares (100,000 authorized, 25,000 issued)	100,000
Contributed surplus	155,000
Retained earnings	250,000
Accumulated other comprehensive income	75,000
Total	$780,000

During 2014, the company had the following transactions that affect shareholders' equity.

1. Paid the annual 2013 $8 per share dividend on preferred shares and a $3 per share dividend on common shares. These dividends had been declared on December 31, 2013.
2. Purchased 3,700 shares of its own outstanding common shares for $35 per share and cancelled them.
3. Issued 1,000 shares of preferred shares at $105 per share (at the beginning of the year).
4. Declared a 10% stock dividend on the outstanding common shares when the shares were selling for $45 per share.
5. Issued the stock dividend.

6. Declared the annual 2014 $8 per share dividend on preferred shares and a $2 per share dividend on common shares. These dividends are payable in 2015.

The contributed surplus arose from net excess of proceeds over cost on a previous cancellation of common shares. Total assets at December 31, 2013, were $940,000, and total assets at December 31, 2014, were $916,000. The company follows IFRS.

Instructions

(a) Prepare journal entries to record the transactions above.

(b) Prepare the December 31, 2014 shareholders' equity section. Assume 2014 net income was $450,000 and comprehensive income was $455,000.

(c) Prepare the statement of changes in shareholders' equity for the year ended December 31, 2014.

(d) Calculate the rate of return on common shareholders' equity and the rate of return on total assets for 2014. Is Falkon trading on the equity? Evaluate the results from the perspective of a common shareholder.

Digging Deeper

(LO 2, 3) E15-12 (Statement of Changes in Shareholders' Equity) Miss M's Dance Studios Ltd. is a public company, and accordingly uses IFRS for financial reporting. The corporate charter authorizes the issue of up to 1 million common shares and 50,000 preferred shares with a $2 dividend. At the beginning of the December 31, 2014 year, the opening account balances indicated that 25,000 common shares had been issued for $4 per share, and no preferred shares had been issued. Opening retained earnings were $365,000. The transactions during the year were as follows:

Jan.	15	Issued 10,000 common shares at $6 per share.
Feb.	12	Issued 2,000 preferred shares at $60 per share.
June	30	Declared and paid dividend on common shares of $1.50 per share.
Sept.	2	Issued 5,000 common shares in exchange for land valued at $25,000.
Oct.	31	Declared and paid dividend on preferred shares of $2 per share.
Nov.	15	Purchased and retired 500 preferred shares at $62 per share.
Dec.	31	Reported net income of $532,000.

Instructions

(a) Prepare journal entries to record the transactions above.

(b) Prepare the statement of changes in shareholders' equity.

(LO 2, 3) E15-13 (Equity Transactions and Statement of Changes in Shareholders' Equity) On January 1, 2014, Copeland Ltd. (a public company) had the following shareholders' equity accounts:

Preferred shares, $5-non-cumulative, no par value, unlimited number authorized, none issued	–0–
Common shares, no par value, unlimited number authorized, 800,000 issued	$5,600,000
Retained earnings	1,323,000
Accumulated other comprehensive income	142,000

The following selected transactions occurred during 2014:

Jan.	2	Issued 100,000 preferred shares at $25 per share.
Mar.	5	Declared the quarterly cash dividend to preferred shareholders of record on March 20, payable April 1.
Apr.	18	Issued 130,000 common shares at $11 per share.
June	5	Declared the quarterly cash dividend to preferred shareholders of record on June 20, payable July 1.
Sept.	5	Declared the quarterly cash dividend to preferred shareholders of record on September 20, payable October 1.
Dec.	5	Declared the quarterly cash dividend to preferred shareholders of record on December 20, payable January 1.
Dec.	31	Net income for the year was $374,000.

Instructions

(a) Prepare journal entries to record the transactions above.

(b) Post the entries to the shareholders' equity T accounts.

(c) Prepare the statement of changes in shareholders' equity for the year.

(d) Prepare the shareholders' equity section of the statement of financial position at December 31.

(e) Prepare the financing activities section of the statement of cash flows for the year ended December 31.

(LO 2, 3, 5) ***E15-14** **(Shareholders' Equity Section)** Radford Corporation's charter authorized 1 million shares of $11 par value common shares, and 300,000 shares of 6% cumulative and non-participating preferred shares, with a par value of $100 per share. The corporation made the following share transactions through December 31, 2014: 300,000 common shares were issued for $3.6 million and 10,000 preferred shares were issued for machinery valued at $1,475,000. Subscriptions for 10,500 common shares have been taken, and 30% of the subscription price of $16 per share has been collected. The shares will be issued upon collection of the subscription price in full. In addition, 10,000 common shares have been purchased for $15 and retired. The Retained Earnings balance is $180,000 before considering the transactions above.

Instructions

(a) Prepare the shareholders' equity section of the statement of financial position in good form.

(b) Repeat part (a) assuming the common shares and preferred shares are no par.

(c) Discuss the alternative presentations of the share subscriptions receivable account. Would the presentation of the receivable affect the book value or the rate of return on shareholders' equity?

Digging Deeper

(LO 2, 6) **E15-15** **(Equity Items on Statement of Financial Position)** The following are selected transactions that may affect shareholders' equity.

1. Recorded accrued interest earned on a note receivable.

2. Declared a cash dividend.

3. Effected a stock split.

4. Recorded the expiration of insurance coverage that was previously recorded as prepaid insurance.

5. Paid the cash dividend declared in item 2 above.

6. Recorded accrued interest expense on a note payable.

7. Recorded an increase in the fair value of a fair value–other comprehensive income (FV-OCI) investment that will be distributed as a property dividend. The carrying amount of the FV-OCI investment was greater than its cost. The shares are traded in an active market.

8. Declared a property dividend (see item 7 above).

9. Distributed the investment to shareholders (see items 7 and 8 above).

10. Declared a stock dividend.

11. Distributed the stock dividend declared in item 10.

12. Repurchased common shares for less than their initial issue price.

Instructions

(a) In the table below, assuming the company follows IFRS (including IAS 39), indicate the effect that each of the 12 transactions has on the financial statement elements that are listed. Use the following codes: increase (I), decrease (D), and no effect (NE).

Item	Assets	Liabilities	Shareholders' Equity	Share Capital	Cont. Surplus	Retained Earnings	Acc. Other Compr. Income	Net Income

(b) Would the effect of any of the above items change if the company were to follow ASPE?

(LO 3) **E15-16** **(Shareholders' Equity Section)** Brubacher Corporation's post-closing trial balance at December 31, 2014, was as follows:

BRUBACHER CORPORATION
Post-Closing Trial Balance
December 31, 2014

	Dr.	Cr.
Accounts payable		$ 310,000
Accounts receivable	$ 480,000	
Accumulated depreciation—buildings		185,000
Accumulated other comprehensive income		100,000

	Dr.	Cr.
Contributed surplus—common		1,460,000
Allowance for doubtful accounts		30,000
Bonds payable		300,000
Buildings	1,450,000	
Cash	190,000	
Common shares		200,000
Dividends payable on preferred shares (cash)		4,000
Inventories	360,000	
FV-NI investments	200,000	
Land	400,000	
Preferred shares		500,000
Prepaid expenses	40,000	
Retained earnings		201,000
Treasury shares (10,000 common shares)	170,000	
Totals	$3,290,000	$3,290,000

At December 31, 2014, Brubacher had the following numbers for its common and preferred shares:

	Common	Preferred
Authorized	600,000	60,000
Issued	200,000	10,000
Outstanding	190,000	10,000

The dividends on preferred shares are $5 cumulative. In addition, the preferred shares have a preference in liquidation of $50 per share.

Instructions

Prepare the shareholders' equity section of Brubacher's statement of financial position at December 31, 2014. The company follows IFRS.

(AICPA adapted)

(LO 5) E15-17 (Comparison of Alternative Forms of Financing) What follows are the liabilities and shareholders' equity sections of the statements of financial position for Kao Corp. and Bennington Corp. Each has assets totalling $4.2 million.

Kao Corp.		
Current liabilities		$ 300,000
Long-term debt, 10%		1,200,000
Common shares		2,000,000
(100,000 shares issued)		
Retained earnings		700,000
(Cash dividends, $220,000)		
		$4,200,000

Bennington Corp.		
Current liabilities		$ 600,000
Common shares		2,900,000
(145,000 shares issued)		
Retained earnings		700,000
(Cash dividends, $328,000)		
		$4,200,000

For the year, each company has earned the same income before interest and tax.

	Kao Corp.	Bennington Corp.
Income before interest and taxes	$1,200,000	$1,200,000
Interest expense	120,000	–0–
	1,080,000	1,200,000
Income taxes (30%)	324,000	360,000
Net income	$ 756,000	$ 840,000

At year end, the market price of Kao's shares was $101 per share; it was $63.50 for Bennington's.

Instructions

(a) Which company is more profitable in terms of return on total assets?

(b) Which company is more profitable in terms of return on shareholders' equity?

(c) Which company has the greater net income per share? Neither company issued or reacquired shares during the year.

(d) From the point of view of income, is it advantageous to Kao's shareholders to have the long-term debt outstanding? Why or why not?

(e) What is each company's price earnings ratio?

(f) What is the book value per share for each company?

(LO 8) *E15-18 (Financial Reorganization) The following account balances are available from the ledger of Yutao Shui Corporation on December 31, 2013:

Common Shares (20,000 shares authorized and outstanding)	$1,000,000
Retained Earnings (deficit)	(190,000)

On January 2, 2014, the corporation put into effect a shareholder-approved reorganization by agreeing to pass the common shares over to the creditors in full payment of the $260,000 Notes Payable, writing up Buildings by $135,600, and eliminating the deficit. Assume that Yutao Shui follows ASPE.

Instructions

Prepare the required journal entries for the financial reorganization of Yutao Shui Corporation.

(LO 8) *E15-19 (Financial Reorganization) The condensed balance sheets of Rockford Limited, a small private company that follows ASPE, follow for the periods immediately before, and one year after, it had completed a financial reorganization:

	Before Reorganization	One Year After		Before Reorganization	One Year After
Current assets	$ 300,000	$ 420,000	Common shares	$2,400,000	$1,550,000
Buildings (net)	1,700,000	1,290,000	Contributed surplus	220,000	160,000
	–0–	–0–	Retained earnings	(620,000)	
	$2,000,000	$1,710,000		$2,000,000	$1,710,000

For the year following the financial reorganization, the company reported net income of $190,000 and depreciation expense of $80,000, and paid a cash dividend of $30,000. As part of the reorganization, the company wrote down inventories by $120,000 in order to reflect circumstances that existed before the reorganization. Also, the deficit, and any revaluation adjustment, was accounted for by charging amounts against contributed surplus until it was eliminated, with any remaining amount being charged against common shares. The common shares are widely held and there is no controlling interest. No purchases or sales of plant assets and no share transactions occurred in the year following the reorganization.

Instructions

Prepare all the journal entries made at the time of the reorganization.

Problems

P15-1   Transactions of Kent Corporation are as follows.

1. The company is granted a charter that authorizes the issuance of 150,000 preferred shares and 150,000 common shares without par value.

2. The founders of the corporation are issued 10,000 common shares for land valued by the board of directors at $210,000 (based on an independent valuation).

3. Sold 15,200 preferred shares for cash at $110 per share.

4. Repurchased and cancelled 3,000 shares of outstanding preferred shares for cash at $100 per share.

5. Paid $85,000 in dividends that were declared in the previous period.

6. Repurchased for cash and cancelled 500 shares of the outstanding common shares issued in item 2 above at $49 per share.

7. Issued 2,000 preferred shares at $99 per share.

Instructions

(a) Prepare entries in journal form to record the transactions listed above. No other transactions affecting the capital share accounts have occurred.

(b) Assuming that the company has retained earnings from operations of $1,032,000, prepare the shareholders' equity section of its statement of financial position after considering all the transactions above.

(c) Why is the distinction between paid-in capital and retained earnings important?

(d) How would the repurchase of the preferred shares differ if the preferred shares were retractable or callable/redeemable?

P15-2 Oregano Inc. was formed on July 1, 2011. It was authorized to issue 300,000 shares of no par value common shares and 100,000 shares of cumulative and non-participating preferred shares carrying a $2 dividend. The company has a July 1 to June 30 fiscal year. The following information relates to the company's shareholders' equity account.

Common Shares

Before the 2013–14 fiscal year, the company had 110,000 outstanding common shares issued as follows:

1. 95,000 shares issued for cash on July 1, 2011, at $31 per share

2. 5,000 shares exchanged on July 24, 2011, for a plot of land that cost the seller $70,000 in 2001 and had an estimated fair value of $220,000 on July 24, 2011

3. 10,000 shares issued on March 1, 2012; the shares had been subscribed for $42 per share on October 31, 2011

Oct. 1, 2013	Subscriptions were received for 10,000 shares at $46 per share. Cash of $92,000 was received in full payment for 2,000 shares and share certificates were issued. The remaining subscription for 8,000 shares was to be paid in full by September 30, 2014, and the certificates would then be issued on that date.
Nov. 30, 2013	The company purchased 2,000 of its own common shares on the open market at $39 per share. These shares were restored to the status of authorized but unissued shares.
Dec. 15, 2013	The company declared a 5% stock dividend for shareholders of record on January 15, 2014, to be issued on January 31, 2014. The company was having a liquidity problem and could not afford a cash dividend at the time. The company's common shares were selling at $52 per share on December 15, 2013.
June 20, 2014	The company sold 500 of its own common shares for $21,000.

Preferred Shares

The company issued 50,000 preferred shares at $44 per share on July 1, 2011.

Cash Dividends

The company has followed a schedule of declaring cash dividends each year in December and June and making the payment to shareholders of record in the following month. The cash dividend declarations have been as follows since the company's first year and up until June 30, 2014:

Declaration Date	Common Shares	Preferred Shares
Dec. 15, 2012	$0.30 per share	$3.00 per share
June 6, 2013	$0.30 per share	$1.00 per share
Dec. 15, 2014	—	$1.00 per share

No cash dividends were declared during June 2014 due to the company's liquidity problems.

Retained Earnings

As at June 30, 2013, the company's Retained Earnings account had a balance of $690,000. For the fiscal year ending June 30, 2014, the company reported net income of $40,000.

In March 2013, the company received a term loan from Alberta Bank. The bank requires the company to establish a sinking fund and restrict retained earnings for an amount equal to the sinking fund deposit. The annual sinking fund payment of $50,000 is due on April 30 each year; the first payment was made on schedule on April 30, 2014.

Instructions

(a) Prepare the shareholders' equity section of the company's statement of financial position, including appropriate notes, as at June 30, 2014, as it should appear in its annual report to the shareholders.

(b) Prepare the journal entries for the 2013–14 fiscal year.

(c) Discuss why the common shareholders might be willing to accept a stock dividend during the year rather than a cash dividend.

(CMA adapted. Used with permission.)

Digging Deeper

Digging Deeper

P15-3 Parker Corporation's charter authorizes the issuance of 1 million common shares and 500,000 preferred shares. The following transactions involving share issues were completed. Assume that Parker follows IFRS and that each transaction is independent of the others.

1. Issued 4,200 common shares for machinery. The machinery had been appraised at $74,500, and the seller's carrying amount was $58,600. The common shares' most recent market price is $18 a share.

2. Voted a $6 dividend on both the 17,000 shares of outstanding common and the 40,000 shares of outstanding preferred.

3. Issued 2,500 common shares and 1,200 preferred shares for a lump sum of $125,000. The common shares had been selling at $13 and the preferred at $80.

4. Issued 2,200 common shares and 135 preferred shares for furniture. The common shares had a fair value of $14 per share and the furniture was appraised at $36,000.

Instructions
Prepare the journal entries to record the transactions.

P15-4 Manitoba Deck System Corporation (MDSC) is a public company whose shares are actively traded on the Toronto Stock Exchange. The following information relates to MDSC:

Jan. 1, 2014	The company is granted a charter that authorizes the issuance of 500,000 no par value common shares, and 250,000 no par value preferred shares that entitle the holder to a $4 per share annual dividend.
Jan. 10, 2014	Issues 15,000 common shares to the founders of the corporation for land that has a fair value of $450,000.
Mar. 10, 2014	Issues 4,000 preferred shares for cash for $100 per share.
Apr. 15, 2014	The company issues 110 common shares to a car dealer in exchange for a used vehicle. The asking price for the car is $6,400. At the time of the exchange, the common shares are selling at $55 per share.
Aug. 20, 2014	MDSC decides to issue shares on a subscription basis to select individuals, giving each person the right to purchase 250 common shares at a price of $60 per share. Forty individuals accept the company's offer and agree to pay 10% down and the remainder in three equal instalments.
Oct. 11, 2014	MDSC issues 3,000 common shares and 600 preferred shares for a lump sum of $230,000 cash. At the time of sale, both the common and preferred shares are actively traded. The common shares are trading at $58 each; the preferred shares at $105 each.
Dec. 31, 2014	MDSC declares cash dividends totalling $26,000, payable on January 31, 2015, to holders of record on January 15, 2015.

Instructions
(a) Prepare the general journal entries to record the transactions.

(b) Provide support for the exchange value of the April 15, 2014 transaction, referring to the conceptual framework.

(Adapted from CGA – Canada Examination)

Digging Deeper

P15-5 Kanish Corporation's general ledger includes the following account balances:

Contributed Surplus	Common Shares	Retained Earnings
Balance $8,000	Balance $270,000	Balance $85,000

The Contributed Surplus account arose from net excess of proceeds over cost on a previous cancellation of common shares. The average cost of the common shares bought and cancelled in the first two transactions is $30 per share.

Instructions
Assuming that the above balances existed before any of the transactions that follow, record the journal entries for each transaction.

(a) Bought and cancelled 430 shares at $38 per share.

(b) Bought and cancelled 200 shares at $44 per share.

(c) Sold 3,200 shares at $41 per share.

(d) Sold 1,500 shares at $47 per share.

(e) Bought and cancelled 1,000 shares at $50 per share.

P15-6 Stellar Corp. had the following shareholders' equity on January 1, 2014:

Common shares, 300,000 shares authorized, 100,000 shares issued and outstanding	$ 270,000
Contributed surplus	310,000
Retained earnings	2,300,000
Total shareholders' equity	$2,880,000

The contributed surplus arose from net excess of proceeds over cost on a previous cancellation of common shares. Stellar prepares financial statements in accordance with ASPE.

The following transactions occurred, in the order given, during 2014.

1. Subscriptions were sold for 12,000 common shares at $26 per share. The first payment was for $10 per share.

2. The second payment for the sale in item 1 above was for $16 per share. All payments were received on the second payment except for 2,000 shares.

3. In accordance with the subscription contract, which requires that defaulting subscribers have all their payments refunded, a refund cheque was sent to the defaulting subscribers. At this point, common shares were issued to subscribers who had fully paid on the contract.

4. Repurchased 22,000 common shares at $29 per share. They were then retired.

5. Sold 5,000 preferred shares and 3,000 common shares together for $300,000. The common shares had a fair value of $31 per share.

Instructions

(a) Prepare the journal entries to record the transactions for the company for 2014.

(b) Assume that the subscription contract states that defaulting subscribers forfeit their first payment. Prepare the journal entries for items 2 to 4 above.

(c) Discuss how Stellar may have determined the fair value of its common shares, given that the company prepares financial statements in accordance with ASPE and is a private company.

P15-7 Original Octave Inc. (OOI) is a widely held, publicly traded company that designs equipment for tuning musical instruments. Information about its shareholders' equity is as follows.

ORIGINAL OCTAVE INC.
Shareholders' Equity
December 31, 2013

Share capital	
Preferred shares, no par value, $8, cumulative, and participating	
(20,000 authorized; 1,000 issued and outstanding)	$100,000
Common shares, no par value	
(1,000,000 authorized; 40,000 issued and outstanding)	500,000
Contributed capital, preferred share retirement	20,000
Retained earnings	620,000
	280,000
Shareholders' equity	$900,000

The preferred share dividend was not paid in 2013.

Several transactions affecting shareholders' equity took place during the fiscal year ended December 31, 2014, and are summarized in chronological order as follows.

1. Exchanged 10,000 common shares for a prototype piano tuning machine. The machine was valued at $100,000 by an independent appraiser. On the transaction date, OOI's shares were actively trading at $10 per share.

2. Purchased and retired 10,000 common shares at $15 per share.

3. Paid the annual dividend on the preferred shares. The common shares were then paid a $2 per share dividend.

Original Octave's net income for 2014 was $65,000.

Instructions

(a) Prepare journal entries for each of the three transactions.

(b) Calculate the company's payout ratio for 2014. Would the payout ratio for 2014 be different if the preferred share dividend was paid in 2013? Comment on the results of your analysis from the perspective of a potential investor.

Digging
Deeper

*P15-8   Laurentian Corporation had the following shareholders' equity at January 1, 2014.

Preferred shares, 8%, $100 par value, 10,000 shares authorized, 4,000 shares issued	$ 400,000
Common shares, $2 par value, 200,000 shares authorized, 80,000 shares issued	160,000
Common shares subscribed, 10,000 shares	20,000
Contributed surplus—preferred	20,000
Contributed surplus—common	940,000
Retained earnings	780,000
	2,320,000
Less: Common share subscriptions receivable	40,000
Total shareholders' equity	$2,280,000

The contributed surplus accounts arose from amounts received in excess of the par value of the shares when issued. During 2014, the following transactions occurred:

1. Equipment was purchased in exchange for 100 common shares. The shares' fair value on the exchange date was $12 per share.

2. Sold 1,000 common shares and 100 preferred shares for the lump-sum price of $24,500. The common shares had a market price of $14 at the time of the sale.

3. Sold 2,000 preferred shares for cash at $102 per share.

4. All of the subscribers paid their subscription prices into the firm.

5. The common shares subscribed were issued.

6. Repurchased and retired 1,000 common shares at $15 per share.

7. Net income for 2014 was $246,000.

Instructions

Prepare the shareholders' equity section for the company as at December 31, 2014. (The use of T accounts may help you organize the material.)

P15-9   The books of Binkerton Corporation carried the following account balances as at December 31, 2014:

Cash	$ 1,300,000
Preferred shares, $2 cumulative dividend, non-participating, 25,000 shares issued	750,000
Common shares, no par value, 300,000 shares issued	15,000,000
Contributed surplus (preferred)	150,000
Retained earnings	327,000

The preferred shares have dividends in arrears for the past year (2013). At its annual meeting on December 21, 2014, the board of directors declared the following: The current year dividends shall be $2 per share on the preferred and $0.70 per share on the common; the dividends in arrears shall be paid by issuing one share of common shares for each 10 shares of preferred held.

The preferred shares are currently selling at $80 per share and the common shares at $20 per share. Net income for 2014 is estimated at $56,000.

Instructions

(a) Prepare the journal entries that are required for the dividend declaration and payment, assuming that they occur at the same time.

Digging Deeper

(b) Could the company give the preferred shareholders two years of dividends and common shareholders a $0.70 per share dividend, all in cash? Explain your reasoning.

P15-10   Lasson Corp. has 5,000 preferred shares outstanding (no par value, $2 dividend), which were issued for $150,000, and 30,000 no par value common shares, which were issued for $550,000.

Instructions

The following schedule shows the amount of dividends paid out over the last four years. Allocate the dividends to each type of share under assumptions (a) and (b). Express your answers in per share amounts and using the format that is shown.

Assumptions

	(a) Preferred, non-cumulative, and non-participating		Preferred, cumulative, participating		(b) Preferred, cumulative, and fully participating	
	Preferred	Common	Preferred	Common	Preferred	Common

Year	Paid-out
2011	$ 8,000
2012	$ 24,000
2013	$ 60,000
2014	$126,000

P15-11 Guoping Limited provides you with the following condensed statement of financial position information:

Assets		Liabilities and Shareholders' Equity		
Current assets	$ 40,000	Current and long-term liabilities		$100,000
Investments in Geneva Company— fair value through net income (10,000 shares)	60,000	Shareholders' equity		
		Common shares^a	$ 20,000	
Equipment (net)	250,000	Contributed surplus	110,000	
Intangibles	60,000	Retained earnings	180,000	310,000
Total assets	$410,000	Total liabilities and shareholders' equity		$410,000

^a 10,000 shares issued and outstanding.

Instructions

(a) For each transaction below, indicate the dollar impact (if any) on the following five items: (1) total assets, (2) common shares, (3) contributed surplus, (4) retained earnings, and (5) shareholders' equity. (Each situation is independent.)

1. The company declares and pays a $0.50 per share dividend.
2. The company declares and issues a 10% stock dividend when the shares' market price is $12 per share.
3. The company declares and issues a 40% stock dividend when the shares' market price is $17 per share.
4. The company declares and distributes a property dividend. The company gives one Geneva share for every two company shares held. Geneva is selling for $12 per share on the date when the property dividend is declared.
5. The company declares a 3-for-1 stock split and issues new shares.

(b) What are the differences between a stock dividend and a cash or property dividend?

P15-12 Some of the account balances of Vos Limited at December 31, 2013, are as follows:

$6 Preferred shares (no par, 2,000 shares authorized, 2,000 shares issued and outstanding)	$520,000
Common shares (no par, 100,000 shares authorized, 50,000 shares issued and outstanding)	500,000
Contributed surplus	103,000
Retained earnings	774,000
Accumulated other comprehensive income	22,350

The price of the company's common shares has been increasing steadily on the market; it was $21 on January 1, 2014, and advanced to $24 by July 1 and to $27 at the end of the year 2014. The preferred shares are not openly traded but were appraised at $120 per share during 2014. Vos follows IFRS and had net income of $154,000 during 2014.

Instructions

(a) Prepare the journal entries for each of the following.

1. The company declared a property dividend on April 1. Each common shareholder was to receive one share of Waterloo Corp. for every 10 shares outstanding. Vos had 8,000 shares of Waterloo (2% of the outstanding shares), and had purchased them in 2009 for $68,400. The shares are accounted for using the fair value through other comprehensive income (FV-OCI) model. The accumulated other comprehensive income relates only to these shares. The fair value of the Waterloo shares was $16 per share on April 1. The property dividend was distributed on April 21 when the fair value of the Waterloo shares was $18.50. The Waterloo shares remained at a fair value of $18.50 until year end.
2. On July 1, the company declared a 5% stock dividend to the remaining common shareholders. The stock dividend was distributed July 22.
3. A shareholder, in an effort to persuade Vos to expand into her city, donated to the company a plot of land with an appraised value of $42,000.

Digging Deeper

(b) Prepare the shareholders' equity section of Vos's statement of financial position at December 31, 2014.

(c) How should Vos account for the difference in fair value of the Waterloo shares between the date of declaration and date of distribution? Does the declaration of a property dividend create a financial liability?

Digging Deeper

P15-13 Perfect Ponds Incorporated is a backyard pond design and installation company. The company was incorporated during 2014, with 1 million common shares, and 50,000 preferred shares with a $3 dividend rate. Perfect Ponds follows ASPE. The following transactions took place during the first year of operations with respect to these shares:

Jan. 1   The articles of incorporation were filed and state that 1 million common shares and 50,000 preferred shares are authorized.

Jan. 15   30,000 common shares were sold by subscription to three individuals, who each purchased 10,000 shares for $50 per share. The terms require 10% of the balance to be paid in cash immediately. The balance was to be paid by December 31, 2015, at which time the shares will be issued.

Feb. 20   70,000 common shares were sold by subscription to seven individuals, who each purchased 10,000 shares for $50 per share. The terms require that 10% of the balance be paid in cash immediately, with the balance to be paid by December 31, 2014. Shares are to be issued once the full payment had been received.

Mar. 3   50,000 common shares were sold by an underwriter for $52 per share. The underwriter charged a 5% commission on the sale.

May 10   The company paid $2,000 to a printing company for costs involved in printing common share certificates. As well, an invoice for legal fees related to the issue of common shares was received for $15,000.

Sept. 23   The company issued a combination of 2,000 common and 1,000 preferred shares to a new shareholder for a total price of $200,000. The company was unable to estimate a fair value of the preferred shares, and the most recent sale of common shares was used to estimate the value of the common share portion of the transaction.

Nov. 28   The company wanted to recognize the efforts of a key employee and offered him the opportunity to purchase 500 common shares for $52, to be paid by December 31, 2015. No interest was to be charged on the outstanding balance; however, the shares were issued immediately.

Dec. 31   Of the seven subscriptions issued on February 20, five subscriptions were paid in full and two subscribers defaulted. According to the subscription contract, the defaulting subscribers would not be issued shares for any amount that had been paid and no money would be refunded.

Dec. 31   The company declared a dividend of $200,000 for 2014. Net income for the year was $800,000.

Instructions

(a) Prepare the journal entries to record the transactions for the year.

(b) Prepare the shareholders' equity section of the balance sheet as of December 31, 2014.

(c) Provide support for the statement of financial position presentation of the November 28 transaction, referring to the conceptual framework.

Digging Deeper

P15-14 Secord Limited has two classes of shares outstanding: preferred ($6 dividend) and common. At December 31, 2013, the following accounts and balances were included in shareholders' equity:

Preferred shares, 300,000 shares issued (authorized, 1,000,000 shares)	$ 3,000,000
Common shares, 1,000,000 shares (authorized, unlimited)	10,000,000
Contributed surplus—preferred	200,000
Contributed surplus—common	17,000,000
Retained earnings	5,500,000
Accumulated other comprehensive income	250,000

The contributed surplus accounts arose from net excess of proceeds over cost on previous cancellations of shares of each respective class. The following transactions affected shareholders' equity during 2014:

Jan. 1   Issued 25,000 preferred shares at $25 per share.
Feb. 1   Issued 50,000 common shares at $20 per share.
June 1   Declared a 2-for-1 stock split (common shares).
July 1   Purchased and retired 30,000 common shares at $15 per share.
Dec. 31   Net income is $2.1 million; comprehensive income is $2,050,000.
Dec. 31   The preferred dividend is declared, and a common dividend of $0.50 per share is declared.

Assume that Secord follows IFRS.

Instructions

(a) Prepare the statement of changes in shareholders' equity and the shareholders' equity section of the statement of financial position for the company at December 31, 2014. Show all supporting calculations.

(b) How would the answer to part (a) be different if Secord followed ASPE?

P15-15 Gateway Corporation has outstanding 200,000 no par value common shares that were issued at $10 per share. The balances at January 1, 2014, were $21 million in its retained earnings account; $4.3 million in its contributed surplus account; and $1.1 million in its accumulated other comprehensive income account. During 2014, the company's net income was $3.2 million and comprehensive income was $3,350,000. A cash dividend of $0.70 per share was declared and paid on June 30, 2014, and a 5% stock dividend was declared and distributed to shareholders of record at the close of business on December 31, 2014. You have been asked to give advice on how to properly account for the stock dividend. The existing company shares are quoted on a national stock exchange. The shares' market price per share has been as follows:

Oct. 31, 2014	$31
Nov. 30, 2014	33
Dec. 31, 2014	38
Average price over the two-month period	35

Instructions

(a) Prepare a journal entry to record the cash dividend.

(b) Prepare a journal entry to record the stock dividend.

(c) Prepare the shareholders' equity section (including a schedule of retained earnings) of the company statement of financial position for the year 2014 based on the information given. Write a note to the financial statements that states the accounting basis for the stock dividend.

(d) Prepare a statement of changes in shareholders' equity for the year 2014.

Case

Refer to the Case Primer on the Student Website and in *WileyPLUS* to help you answer this case.

*CA15-1 "You can't write up assets," said Nick Toby, internal audit director of Nadir International Inc., to his boss, Jim Majewski, vice-president and chief financial officer. "Nonsense," said Jim, "I can do this as part of a quasi-reorganization of our company." For the last three years, Nadir International, a farm equipment manufacturing firm, has experienced a downturn in its profits as a result of stiff competition with overseas firms and a general downturn in the North American economy. The company is hoping to turn a profit by modernizing its property, plant, and equipment. This will require Nadir International to raise a lot of money. Management is very optimistic as to the future of the company, as the economy is entering a significant growth period.

Over the past few months, Jim has tried to raise funds from various financial institutions, but they are unwilling to lend capital. The reason they give is that the company's net book value of fixed assets on the balance sheet, based on historic cost, is not large enough to sustain major funding. Jim attempted to explain to bankers and investors that these assets are more valuable than their recorded amounts, especially since the company used accelerated amortization methods and tended to underestimate the useful lives of assets. Jim also believes that the company's land and buildings are substantially undervalued because of rising real estate prices over the past several years.

Jim's proposed solution to raise funds is a simple one: First, declare a large dividend to company shareholders that results in Retained Earnings having a large debit balance. Then, write up the fixed assets of Nadir International to an amount that is equal to the deficit in the Retained Earnings account.

Instructions

Adopt the role of the internal auditor and discuss the financial reporting issues. Nadir is thinking of going public.

Integrated Cases

IC15-1 Sandolin Incorporated (SI) is a global, diversified firm whose shares trade on the major Canadian and U.S. stock markets. It owns numerous toll highways, several companies in the energy business, and an engineering consulting firm. Currently, its shares are trading at a 52-week high and its credit rating on all debt issues is AA. This is partly due to its revenues, which have doubled, and is also due to a recent restructuring. The restructuring is in the energy business and allows the company to position itself as a low-cost competitor in the industry. The restructuring involved laying off 5,000 employees and mothballing several oil and gas wells. The cost to extract oil and gas from the wells is currently too high. The company plans to retain the wells and work on new technology to reduce the extraction costs. SI is in the process of putting together its annual financial statements and the VP Finance, Santos Suarez, is planning to meet with the company's auditors next week for a preliminary audit planning meeting. Santos is concerned about a phone call that he recently received from the government, as it was threatening legal action relating to the transportation part of the business. Among other things, SI owns a highway that stretches approximately 100 km across a major urban centre. The road is very profitable since non-toll roads in the area are congested and people use the toll road to commute. SI recently raised toll rates on the road and the government is claiming it is prohibited from doing this without government consent, which the government does not plan to give. Santos is concerned that if this news gets out, the credit rating and share price will suffer. SI believes that its contract allows it to change toll rates whenever it wants. SI's lawyers have reviewed the contracts and feel that SI's position is justifiable. The value of the toll road as a business is substantially less if the company loses the right to change the tolls.

While reviewing the company's dramatic increase in revenues, Santos became aware of a new type of transaction that the company has been entering into with increasing frequency in the past two months. As part of the energy business, SI employs a group of traders who make deals that reduce the company's exposure to fluctuating commodity prices. According to several e-mails between the traders, the deals are known as "round trip" trades. Several large trades involved purchases and sales with the same party for the same volume at substantially the same price. They have been treated as sales and account for 40% of the increase in revenues. The trader's position is that the company does make a commission on these deals, which adds up depending on the volume. The company never takes possession of the commodity that is being bought and sold.

Just before year end, the company acquired a mid-sized engineering firm. As part of the deal, the company issued shares to the vendor. The value of the issued shares was higher than the fair value of the engineering firm and the vendor gave SI a one-year note receivable for the difference. If profits from the engineering firm exceed a certain threshold—in other words, if the firm outperforms expectations—the note will not be paid. Currently, SI has recorded the note receivable as an asset.

Instructions

Adopt the role of Santos Suarez and analyze the financial reporting issues.

IC15-2   Wind and Solar Inc. (WSI) is in the business of providing electricity. The company is a new company just starting up this year (2013). Currently, it is owned by Winifred Wind and Winston Chang. Both Winston and Winifred own 50% of the common shares of the company. Under the terms of the shareholder agreement, either party may buy the other out at a price of 10 times the current net income. This buyout clause becomes effective immediately; WSI plans to go public within five years if all goes well.

During the year, the company obtained financing from the local bank and purchased land on which it has built large wind turbines (windmills) and solar panels. The company will be generating electrical energy through wind power and solar power. The loan was used to finance the construction of the windmills and solar panels. Under the terms of the loan, the company must maintain a debt to equity ratio of 1:1.

The cost of building windmills and wind turbines is very expensive and as a result, half way through the year, the company had used up all of the bank financing. The bank declined to advance more funds. Winston and Winifred entered into an agreement with Windy Developments (WD) to help them build more windmills. Under the terms of the agreement, WD will advance the funds needed to build the windmills up front. In return, WSI has agreed to pay WD a percentage of the revenues generated from the windmills once they become operational. The new windmills are 50% complete.

WSI has several engineers working on the projects who are currently not being paid a salary for their services. Instead, they have been given shares in the company. WSI has set aside 10% of the total shares outstanding in order to remunerate the engineers. Under the terms of this agreement, the engineers may convert their shares to cash at the end of 2014. WSI plans to have a valuation done of the company at the end of 2014 and 10% of the value will be attributable to the engineers' shares. The valuation will be based on the average income from 2013 and 2014.

During 2013, some of the windmills and solar panels were up and running and had started to generate revenues. The company's largest customer was the local government, which had signed a contract with WSI to purchase half of the output of electricity for 2013 and 2014. At a minimum, the government was locked in to pay $1 million. The price per KW hour was fixed upfront and the government had already paid half of the money in advance. The contract was non-cancellable and even if WSI was unable to deliver the minimum amount of electricity, the government would still be committed to pay the full $1 million. The government noted that it considered the $1 million as a type of grant in support of the development of clean energy and was happy to pay the funds in order to support the clean energy movement.

By the end of 2013, Winston had decided that he wanted Winifred to buy out his shares according to the shareholder agreement. The first year of operations had been so stressful for him that he had developed several health problems.

Instructions

Adopt the role of the company's auditors and discuss the financial reporting issues.

Writing Assignments

WA15-1 Algonquin Corporation sold 50,000 common shares on a subscription basis for $40 per share. By December 31, 2014, collections on these subscriptions totalled $1.3 million. None of the subscriptions has been paid in full so far. Algonquin is a private company.

Instructions

(a) Discuss the meaning of the account Common Shares Subscribed and indicate how it is reported in the financial statements.

(b) Discuss the arguments in favour of reporting Subscriptions Receivable as a current asset.

(c) Discuss the arguments in favour of reporting Subscriptions Receivable as a contra equity account.

(d) Indicate how these 50,000 shares would be presented on Algonquin's December 31, 2014 balance sheet under the method discussed in (c) above.

(e) Suppose that Algonquin also has a benefit plan that allows employees to purchase shares of the company, and take two years to pay for the shares. When an employee agrees to purchase the shares, the shares are shown as issued and an Employee Share Loan Receivable Account is set up. As payments are made by the employee, this loan receivable account is reduced. Discuss the reporting issues related to this receivable account under IFRS and ASPE.

WA15-2 Under IFRS, "equity" is defined under the Framework for Preparation and Presentation of Financial Statements. Under ASPE, a definition of equity is provided in the *CICA Handbook*, Part II, Section 1000.

Instructions

Answer the following questions that relate to these sections and what is reported as equity.

(a) Define and discuss the term "equity."

(b) In reporting equity, various subcategories are required. Outline these equity components under ASPE and IFRS and explain why there are differences.

(c) How does ASPE report changes in these components? How does IFRS report these changes? Why are these presentations different?

(d) What transactions or events change owners' equity under IFRS? Under ASPE?

(e) What are some examples of changes within owners' equity that do not change the total amount of owners' equity under IFRS? Under ASPE?

WA15-3 The directors of Amman Corporation are considering issuing a stock dividend. They have asked you to discuss this option by answering the following questions.

Instructions

(a) What is a stock dividend? How is a stock dividend distinguished from a stock split, both from a legal standpoint and from an accounting standpoint?

(b) For what reasons does a corporation usually declare a stock dividend? A stock split?

(c) Discuss the amount of retained earnings, if any, that should be capitalized in connection with a stock dividend.

(AICPA adapted)

WA15-4 Henning Inc. is a medium-sized manufacturer that has been experiencing losses for the five years that it has been in business. Henning is a private company. Although the operations for the year just ended resulted in a loss, several important changes resulted in a profitable fourth quarter, and the company's future operations are expected to be profitable. The treasurer, Peter Henning, suggests that there be a financial reorganization to eliminate the accumulated deficit of $650,000.

Ethics

Instructions

(a) What are the characteristics of a financial reorganization? In other words, what does it consist of?

(b) List the conditions that generally justify a financial reorganization.

(c) Adopt the role of the ethical accountant and discuss the propriety of the treasurer's proposals to eliminate the deficit of $650,000.

(AICPA adapted)

WA15-5 The definition of equity relies on the definition of a liability. The current definition of equity is that it is the residual amount of the assets after deducting liabilities. Consequently, the definition of a liability is critical to determining what equity is. In addition, financial instruments are classified as equity only if they do not meet the definition of a liability. FASB, however, has described three approaches for defining an equity instrument from a non-equity instrument: basic ownership, ownership-settlement, and reassessed expected outcomes. FASB decided on the use of "basic ownership" to define an equity instrument.

From the perspective of the conceptual framework, discuss the validity of both this account and the Accumulated Other Comprehensive Income account.

Instructions

Using information available from the IASB website (www.ifrs.org), answer the following questions. You may find the following document helpful with this analysis: "Discussion Paper—Financial Instruments with Characteristics of Equity—September 2008."

(a) Explain the three approaches for identifying an equity instrument: basic ownership, ownership settlement, and reassessed expected outcomes.

(b) Explain the IASB's preliminary decision on the characteristics of an equity instrument.

(c) Under each of the above three approaches, assess how a convertible bond that is convertible into a fixed number of shares (regardless of the current share price at the time of conversion) would be classified. How would a convertible bond that was convertible into a variable number of shares, depending on the current share price, be reported under each of the above approaches?

WA15-6

Instructions

Write a brief essay highlighting the differences between IFRS and accounting standards for private enterprises noted in this chapter, discussing the conceptual justification for each. As part of this essay, include a discussion of the differences in capital disclosure requirements as well as provide insight as to the additional information provided by capital disclosures to market participants.

WA15-7 The board of directors of Titus Inc. is considering issuing new preferred shares of the company in order to raise capital. They have asked you to discuss some of the available features that could be attached to the shares.

Instructions

(a) Briefly describe why a company may attach various attributes to shares.

(b) Explain some of the various share options available.

(c) Describe how the various attributes associated with each type of share will affect the share from a financing perspective.

RESEARCH AND FINANCIAL ANALYSIS

Real World Emphasis

RA15-1 Magna International Inc.

The **Magna International Inc.** financial statements for the year ended December 31, 2011, can be found on SEDAR (www.sedar.com).

Instructions

(a) The company has many different types of shares authorized, issued, and/or outstanding at the end of 2011. Prepare a chart that shows the following: name of share class, number of authorized shares, number of issued and outstanding shares, number of votes per share, and rights in terms of dividends.

(b) Why would a company structure its capital in this way? Is there a need for the various classes of shares? How does this structure compare with prior years?

(c) Calculate the average book value per share for the 2010 and 2011 year ends. Compare these values with the closing share price at each year end. (*Hint:* Look at the Annual Information Form.)

(d) Describe the various types of share transactions that occurred from 2009 to 2011.

(e) How much was paid in dividends during 2011, and what kinds of dividends were paid?

(f) For 2010 and 2011, calculate the rate of return on shareholders' equity, the payout ratio, and the price earnings ratio based on the closing share price for the year end. Comment on the amounts calculated.

(g) Examine the Capital Disclosure note. What are the company's objectives in managing its capital? How does it measure its capital and what is included in capital?

RA15-2 Bank of Montreal and Royal Bank of Canada

The Bank of Montreal and Royal Bank of Canada financial statements for the year ended October 31, 2012, can be found on SEDAR (www.sedar.com).

Instructions

(a) What is the average carrying value of each company's common shares? Compare these values with market prices. What stock exchanges do these banks trade on?

(b) What is the authorized share capital of each company?

(c) Comment on how each company presents its common shares and shareholders' equity.

(d) Describe the changes (number of shares and price) in each company's common share accounts over the past three years. What types of activities are contributing to the changes?

(e) What amounts of cash dividends per share were declared by each company during 2012? What were the dollar amount effects of the cash dividends on each company's shareholders' equity?

(f) What is each company's rate of return on common shareholders' equity for the year ended 2012? Which company gets the higher return on the equity of its shareholders?

RA15-3 Canadian Tire Corporation Limited

Refer to the financial statements and accompanying notes and discussion of Canadian Tire Corporation Limited for the year ended December 31, 2011, and answer the following questions. The financial statements are available on SEDAR at www.sedar.com.

Instructions

(a) What are the issued and authorized shares for both classes of shares that the company has? What percentage of the authorized shares is issued?

(b) Compare the rights that are attached to each share. Are the class A shares more like preferred shares or common shares?

(c) Why does the company repurchase shares every year? How successful was it in achieving its objective in 2011?

(d) How did the company account for the excess of the amount paid on reacquisition over the carrying value of the shares for 2011? Recreate the journal entry.

(e) What was the average carrying value of the shares at the beginning of the year? What average price were the shares repurchased at? Compare this with the market prices of the shares.

(f) Review the capital disclosure note. What are the company's objectives in managing its capital? How does it monitor its capital? What is included in capital for the company?

Real World Emphasis

Real World Emphasis

RA15-4 Suncor Energy Inc.

On May 14, 2008, Suncor Energy Inc. completed a 2-for-1 stock split of its common shares. Access the 2008 and 2007 annual reports from the company's website (www.suncor.ca).

Instructions

(a) Why might Suncor have declared a stock split?

(b) What impact did the stock split have on (1) total shareholders' equity, (2) total book value, (3) number of outstanding shares, and (4) book value per share? Examine the 2007 numbers as originally filed and the restated 2007 comparison numbers in the 2008 annual reports to reflect this change for number of shares outstanding, the total dollar value of common shares outstanding, and earnings per share data.

(c) What impact did the split have on the shares' market value? What has since happened to their market price?

RA15-5 Statements of Changes in Equity

IFRS requires statements of changes in shareholders' equity. ASPE only requires a statement of retained earnings.

Instructions

(a) Discuss why these differences occur.

(b) Review the statement of changes of Lufthansa AG (available at www.lufthansa.com) for the year ended December 31, 2011.

1. Explain the various components that are reconciled in the statement of changes.

2. Comment on why users might find the statement of changes in equity more useful than a statement of retained earnings.

3. Which of these components found on Lufthansa's statement for changes in equity would be similar to a private enterprise?

RA15-6 Impact of Different Legal Systems on IFRS

Companies from many countries have moved to, or are in the process of moving to, IFRS. Evidence has shown that it is preferable to adopt IFRS in its entirety, with no differences from the standards. This chapter shows how much the legal environment affects the accounting for shares. Different countries will have differing legal systems and environments, which may affect the accounting on a country-by-country basis.

Instructions

How should this situation be dealt with, in your opinion?

RA15-7 Tembec Inc.

Access the 2008 annual report of Tembec Inc. for the period ended September 27, 2008, from SEDAR (www.sedar.com). Note that this accounting would follow the current ASPE requirements.

Instructions

(a) Read Note 1 to Tembec's financial statements for the year ended September 27, 2008. Describe the Plan of Arrangement that was implemented on February 29, 2008. What was the value of the new equity that was issued?

(b) Explain what is required to implement "fresh start" accounting. When is it allowed to be done?

(c) How was the restructuring completed? Prepare the appropriate journal entries from the information provided in Note 1. Use the account names that the company used.

(d) How was the "fresh start" accounting applied? Explain the nature of the fair value adjustments and how much was required to adjust each asset and liability account.

RA15-8 Rogers Sugar Inc.

Real World Emphasis

Access the 2012 annual report of **Rogers Sugar Inc.** for the period ended September 29, 2012, from SEDAR (www.sedar.com).

Instructions

(a) Describe the makeup of the company's current capital share structure, including details of any current year changes to the structure. Does this structure fall in line with the authorized capital of the company described in the capital disclosures?

(b) Review the company's capital management objectives. Briefly describe the company's objectives of capital management and how the company is maintaining the objective.

ENDNOTES

[1] An equity instrument is "any contract that evidences a residual interest in the assets of an entity after deducting its liabilities," according to the *CICA Handbook–Accounting*, Part II, Section 3856.05(e) and IAS 32.11. Most shares (including common and preferred shares) may be considered equity instruments; however, some preferred shares with debt-like features are classified as financial liabilities. These will be discussed in Chapter 16.

[2] An exchange is a more formal marketplace that is more heavily regulated and uses a specific mechanism for pricing shares. Companies must meet certain requirements to be initially listed on the exchange, and then must continue to meet these ongoing requirements to remain listed. These requirements include numerous financial tests, such as asset and revenue levels. Stock markets use a different share pricing mechanism and are generally less heavily regulated. There is a wide range of types of stock markets. At the more formal end of the range is NASDAQ and at the less formal end are alternate trading systems, which are unstructured, Internet-based marketplaces where interested buyers and sellers may meet and trade shares. The TSX is the senior exchange in Canada, whereas the TSX Venture Exchange deals with smaller, start-up companies.

[3] Under the CBCA, the name must include the words "Incorporated," "Limited," or "Corporation," or their respective short forms, in either English or French.

[4] The company issuing the shares records a journal entry only when it first issues and sells the shares and when it buys them back. When shareholders buy and sell shares from each other, this is not recorded by the company.

[5] Shareholders who have voting rights elect the board of directors to make major decisions for them.

[6] *CICA Handbook–Accounting*, Part II, Section 3856.A27 and A28 and IAS 32.16A to D.

[7] The term "private placement" refers to a situation where the shares are only offered privately to a select group of interested investors. In other words, they are not floated for sale on the stock exchange or market. Private placements are often directed at large institutional or individual investors.

[8] **Bank of Montreal** and **Bank of Nova Scotia** have been paying dividends consistently since 1829 and 1833, respectively. The Bank of Montreal notes on its website that it is the "longest-running dividend-paying" company in Canada. It seeks to pay out 40% to 50% of its earnings over time.

[9] The shares are valued using valuation models that include expected future cash flow or operating income from the company. This often results in pressure on the income numbers since a higher income results in a higher share price.

[10] Some of the more complex features of preferred shares that were noted earlier can result in their being accounted for as debt.

[11] These methods are sometimes referred to as the proportional method (relative fair value method) and the incremental method (residual value method). Conceptually, the relative fair value method is preferable where fair values are available. However, sometimes the method is mandated by GAAP. For example, for convertible debt under IFRS, the debt is valued first and the remaining balance is allocated to the equity portion.

[12] *CICA Handbook–Accounting*, Part II, Section 3251.10.

[13] At the beginning of the 1990s, the situation was just the opposite; that is, share buybacks were less than half the level of dividends. As previously discussed, companies are extremely reluctant to reduce or

14 According to the CICA's *Financial Reporting in Canada, 2005*, only 13 out of 200 companies reported treasury shares.

15 *Accounting Trends and Techniques 2010* (American Institute of Certified Public Accountants) indicates that, of its selected list of 500 companies, 340 carried common stock in treasury.

16 IAS 32.33 requires any consideration paid or received to be recognized directly in equity but does not specify how to allocate between the various equity accounts. ASPE 3240 specifies the treatment. Legal and tax requirements of the specific jurisdiction must be taken into account.

17 Determining the date of record is not always straightforward. It is generally the day prior to what is known as the ex-dividend date. Theoretically, the ex-dividend date is the day after the date of record. However, to allow time for the transfer of shares, stock exchanges generally advance the ex-dividend date by two to four days. Therefore, a party who owns the shares on the day prior to the expressed ex-dividend date receives the dividend, and a party who buys the stock on or after the ex-dividend date does not receive the dividend. Between the declaration date and the ex-dividend date, the market price of the shares includes the dividend.

18 *CICA Handbook–Accounting*, Part II, Section 3831.14. Note that if the transaction is with a controlling shareholder, then *CICA Handbook–Accounting*, Part II, Section 3840 dealing with related parties applies. IFRS does not allow related party transactions to be remeasured.

19 From a tax perspective, the Canada Revenue Agency treats stock dividends received in the same way as other dividends.

20 *CICA Handbook–Accounting*, Part II, Section 3831, paras. .05 (f)(ii) and .06.

21 When preferred shares are participating, there may be different agreements on how the participation feature is executed. However, if there is no specific agreement, the following procedure is recommended:

(a) After the preferred shares are assigned their current year's dividend, the common shares will receive a "like" percentage. In example 3, this amounts to 6% of $400,000.

(b) If there is a remainder of declared dividends for participation by the preferred and common shares, this remainder will be shared in proportion to the carrying value in each share class. In example 3, the proportion is:

Preferred $100,000/500,000 × $20,000 + $4,000
Common $400,000/500,000 × $20,000 + $16,000

22 Some companies use reverse stock splits. A reverse stock split reduces the number of shares outstanding and increases the price per share. This technique is used when the share price is unusually low. Note that a company's debt covenants or listing requirements might require that the company's shares trade at a certain level. A reverse stock split might help get the price up to where the company needs it to be.

23 *Accounting Research and Terminology Bulletin No. 43*, par. 13.

24 Accumulated other comprehensive income is used under IFRS to represent the cumulative balance of other comprehensive income. ASPE does not mention either other comprehensive income or accumulated other comprehensive income.

25 In Chapter 4, the concept of **capital maintenance** was discussed. The idea of creating shareholder value is based on at least retaining contributed capital and, ideally, causing it to grow through earnings. Note that the AcSB is moving away from the earned versus contributed distinction, since it is felt that income that is included as other comprehensive income is not really earned by the company nor is it contributed. It might be argued, however, that the income is indeed earned since management made decisions that resulted in these gains/losses.

26 *CICA Handbook–Accounting*, Part II, Sections 3240, 3251, and 3856 and IFRS 7.

27 *CICA Handbook–Accounting*, Part II, Section 3240.20–.22 and IAS 1.79.

28 IAS 1.134–.138.

29 ASPE does not explicitly require these disclosures. This is because many private companies have shares that are closely held and therefore this type of information is not necessarily required in the statements.

30 Another closely watched ratio is the dividend yield: the cash dividend per share divided by the market price. This ratio gives investors some idea of the rate of return that will be received in the form of cash dividends.

31 *CICA Handbook–Accounting*, Part II, Section 1625.03.

32 *CICA Handbook–Accounting*, Part II, Section 1625.15.

[33] *CICA Handbook–Accounting*, Part II, Section 1625.04.

[34] IFRS does not explicitly cover accounting for financial reorganizations, although the same accounting principles and procedures may be applied as noted under ASPE where legally permissible. IFRS already allows revaluation of investment properties; property, plant, and equipment; as well as intangibles. In addition, financial instruments are allowed to be valued at fair value if certain conditions are met.

[35] *CICA Handbook–Accounting*, Part II, Section 1625.35 – 42.

Investing in Catastrophes

© istockphoto.com/jonathansloane

WHAT IF YOU COULD make money by betting that a certain natural disaster would not happen in a certain place at a certain time, causing a certain amount of damage? That is essentially what happens when investors buy catastrophe bonds, one of many different kinds of complex financial instruments that companies may hold and have to account for.

Catastrophe bonds were created in the 1990s after insurance companies suffered heavy claims from property damage caused by natural events, mainly hurricanes in the United States. To help spread the risk of such catastrophes, insurers started issuing catastrophe bonds as a new source of reinsurance—essentially insurance on insurance. Insurance companies are prepared to pay investors to provide money for a rainy day, to be called when large catastrophes occur that cause billions of dollars in damage that the companies will have to pay out claims for among their policyholders.

At a very high level, catastrophe bonds work very similarly to corporate and government bonds. They pay a series of premiums or coupons to the investor—quarterly, semi-annually, or annually—for a certain length of time, usually three years. When the bond matures, the principal is paid back. However, the investor may not get their principal back if a catastrophe of a magnitude specified in the bond occurs before the bond matures. This is similar to when a corporation goes bankrupt before a corporate bond matures and the investor loses the principal.

Historically, the small universe of catastrophe bonds has generated returns at about the same rate of return as corporate bonds, so why would investors want to take a chance on them? It's because catastrophe bonds, unlike more traditional bonds, are linked to nature—not the economy. "You are able to lower overall portfolio risk by investing into assets which are not correlated with each other," says Ryan Bisch, a principal with Mercer, a global investment consulting firm. "The expectation is that a loss in your catastrophe bonds shouldn't be linked to any loss in your equity portfolio and that's what you're trying to do, to take advantage of diversification," says Mr. Bisch, the Canadian leader for Mercer's alternative investment service.

Catastrophe bond issuers use sophisticated modelling to calculate the likelihood of huge disasters, and independent bond rating agencies will assess the risk of such bonds defaulting to communicate this to investors before the bonds are issued. The higher the probability of a certain-sized disaster, the higher the coupon payment and overall potential return to investors, Mr. Bisch explains.

A few catastrophe bonds have been triggered and defaulted, such as the one that applied to the earthquake and tsunami off Japan in 2011. "It can be full loss on an individual bond," Mr. Bisch says. "It's not an investment that every investor is comfortable with."

16 Complex Financial Instruments

LEARNING OBJECTIVES

After studying this chapter, you should be able to:

1. Understand what derivatives are and how they are used to manage risks.

2. Understand how to account for derivatives.

3. Analyze whether a hybrid/compound instrument issued for financing purposes represents a liability, equity, or both.

4. Explain the accounting for hybrid/compound instruments.

5. Describe the various types of stock compensation plans.

6. Describe the accounting for share-based compensation.

7. Identify the major differences in accounting between ASPE and IFRS, and what changes are expected in the near future.

After studying the Chapter 16 appendices, you should be able to:

8. Understand how derivatives are used in hedging and explain the need for hedge accounting standards.

9. Understand how to apply hedge accounting standards.

10. Account for share appreciation rights plans.

11. Understand how options pricing models are used to measure financial instruments.

PREVIEW OF CHAPTER 16

Uncommon in the past, complex financial instruments are now used by companies in many different industries. Companies use these instruments in an effort to manage risk, gain access to pools of financing, and minimize the cost of capital and taxes. In response to this trend, the accounting profession has developed a framework for dealing with these instruments in the financial statements. Earlier in the text, the accounting was discussed for basic financial instruments, including accounts and notes receivable/payable, investments, loans, and shares. This chapter focuses on complex financial instruments, such as hybrid and compound debt and equity instruments and derivatives.[1] Since employee compensation plans often include derivatives such as stock options, these plans will also be discussed in this chapter.

The chapter is organized as follows:

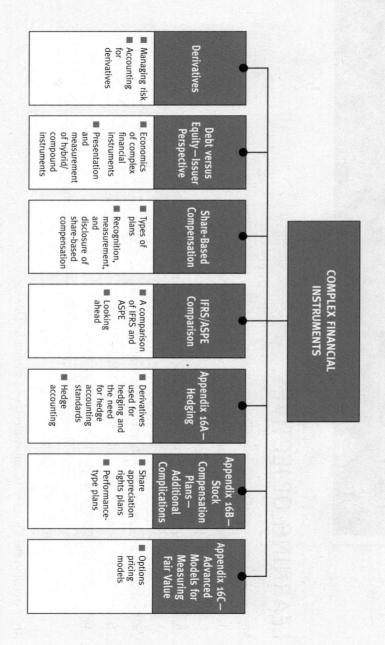

COMPLEX FINANCIAL INSTRUMENTS

Derivatives
- Managing risk
- Accounting for derivatives

Debt versus Equity—Issuer Perspective
- Economics of complex financial instruments
- Presentation and measurement of hybrid/compound instruments

Share-Based Compensation
- Types of plans
- Recognition, measurement, and disclosure of share-based compensation

IFRS/ASPE Comparison
- A comparison of IFRS and ASPE
- Looking ahead

Appendix 16A— Hedging
- Derivatives used for hedging and the need for hedge accounting standards
- Hedge accounting

Appendix 16B— Stock Compensation Plans— Additional Complications
- Share appreciation rights plans
- Performance-type plans

Appendix 16C— Advanced Models for Measuring Fair Value
- Options pricing models

DERIVATIVES

If you recall from previous chapters, **financial instruments** are contracts that create both a financial asset for one party and a financial liability or equity instrument for the other party.[2] Financial instruments can be primary or derivative. **Primary financial instruments** include most basic financial assets and **financial liabilities**, such as receivables and payables, as well as **equity instruments**, such as shares. The accounting issues for primary financial instruments were covered in earlier chapters. **Derivative instruments**, on the other hand, are more complex. They are called derivatives because they derive (get) their value from an **underlying** primary instrument, index, or non-financial item, such as a commodity (called the "underlying"). Derivatives may trade on exchanges such as the Canadian Derivatives Exchange and "over-the-counter" markets. Where there is a market for the derivative, it is easier to value. Certain derivatives do not trade on any exchange or market (for instance, certain executive stock options are tailor-made, as opposed to standardized, foreign exchange forward contracts).

Accounting standards define derivatives as financial instruments that create rights and obligations that have the effect of transferring, between parties to the instrument, one or more of the financial risks that are inherent in an underlying primary instrument. They transfer risks that are inherent in the underlying primary instrument without either party having to hold any investment in the underlying.[3]

Derivatives have three characteristics:

1. Their value changes in response to the **underlying instrument (the "underlying")**.

2. They require **little or no initial investment.**

3. They are settled at a **future** date.

Options, forwards, and futures are common types of derivative instruments. As a basic rule, derivatives are measured at fair value with gains and losses booked through net income. Derivatives may be embedded in contracts. This means that the contract has more than one part: a host (non-derivative) part and one or more derivatives.

The accounting for the common types of derivative instruments will be discussed further in this chapter. Special accounting exists for derivatives that are part of a hedging relationship and this is discussed in Appendix 16A. The notion of an **underlying** will be illustrated with examples throughout the chapter. The accounting for **embedded derivatives** is complex and in flux and is generally beyond the scope of this text. Having said that, the chapter will discuss this area briefly in the context of compound instruments issued by companies.

Finance

Objective 1
Understand what derivatives are and how they are used to manage risks.

Managing Risks

Why do derivatives exist? In short, they exist to help companies manage risks. Companies operate in an environment of constant change caused by volatile markets, new technology, and deregulation, among other things. This increases overall business risk as well as financial risk. The response from the financial community has been to develop products to manage some of these risks, with one result being the rise of derivatives. Recall from Appendix 5A the differing types of risks that a company faces. Managers of successful companies have always and will continue to manage risks to minimize unfavourable financial consequences and to maximize shareholder value. While managing risk helps keep uncertainty at an acceptable level (which may differ depending on the stakeholders), it also has its costs.

There are many layers of costs relating to the use of derivatives. Three categories of costs are as follows:

1. Direct costs

2. Indirect costs

3. Other costs, such as opportunity costs

Underlying Concept

As always, the benefits of entering into certain transactions, especially complex ones, should exceed the costs; otherwise, the company will be reducing shareholder value rather than creating it.

In order to enter into contracts that manage risk, such as insurance and derivative contracts, transaction costs are normally incurred, including bank service charges, brokerage fees, and insurance premiums. These are the **direct**, visible costs that are charged by an intermediary or the other party to the transaction. Then there are **indirect**, less visible costs. For example, the activity of researching, analyzing, and executing these transactions uses a significant amount of employee time. Finally, there are **other costs** which may not be so visible. For example, the use of too many complicated financial instruments increases the complexity of financial statements and therefore reduces their transparency and understandability. Given the current climate, capital markets may penalize such companies by increasing costs of capital and/or limiting or denying access to capital. Another type of hidden cost is the **opportunity cost,** because managing risk sometimes results in limiting the potential or opportunity for gain. Companies must consider all of the costs that are associated with derivatives and weigh them against the benefits.

The growth in the use of derivatives has been aided by the development of powerful calculation and communication technology, which provides new ways to analyze information about markets as well as the power to process high volumes of payments. Thanks to these developments, many corporations are now using derivatives extensively and successfully.

The International Swaps and Derivatives Association (ISDA) was founded in 1985 and has 810 member organizations from 57 countries. The ISDA describes itself as being among the world's largest global financial trade associations as measured by number of member firms. In 2009, the ISDA completed a survey of the world's major companies as identified in the Fortune Global 500. The research shows that 471 of the 500 companies use derivatives and that this percentage has been growing since the prior survey was done in 2003. The following chart[4] is taken from the survey and shows the types of derivatives contracts that these companies are entering into. Note the extensive use of foreign currency ("forex") and interest rate derivatives. The numbers reflect the percentage of total companies in the survey that use each type of derivative.

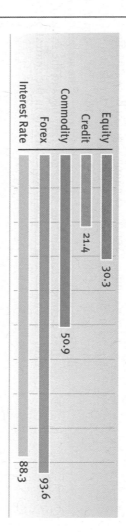

The research shows that there is widespread use of derivatives in many industries. The chart[5] below illustrates this, showing the percentage of surveyed companies in each industry that use derivatives.

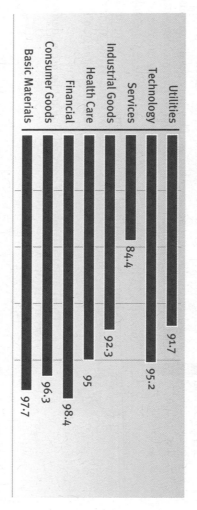

Given the widespread use of these instruments, accounting standard setters are striving to ensure that they are properly reflected in the financial statements. Because of the complexity of the derivative contracts and how they are used by companies to manage risk, the financial reporting issues are significant.

As mentioned above, companies use derivatives to manage risks, and especially financial risks. There are various kinds of financial risks, and they are defined in IFRS as follows.[6]

1. **"Credit risk:** The risk that one party to a financial instrument will cause a financial loss for the other party by failing to discharge (respect) an obligation."

2. **"Liquidity risk:** The risk that an entity will have difficulty meeting obligations that are associated with financial liabilities...."

3. **Market risk**: The risk that the fair value or future cash flows of a financial instrument will fluctuate because of changes in market prices." There are three types of market risk: currency risk, interest rate risk, and other price risk.

(a) "**Currency risk**: The risk that the fair value or future cash flows of a financial instrument will fluctuate because of changes in foreign exchange rates."

(b) "**Interest rate risk**: The risk that the fair value or future cash flows of a financial instrument will fluctuate because of changes in market interest rates."

(c) "**Other price risk**: The risk that the fair value or future cash flows of a financial instrument will fluctuate because of changes in market prices (other than price changes arising from **interest rate risk** or **currency risk**), whether those changes are caused by factors that are specific to the individual financial instrument or its issuer, or factors that affect all similar financial instruments being traded in the market."

It is important for companies and users of financial statements to identify and understand which risks a company currently has and how it plans to manage these risks. Keep in mind that derivatives often expose the company to additional risks. As long as the company identifies and manages these risks, this is not a problem. There is a problem, however, when stakeholders do not understand the risk profile of derivative instruments. The use of derivatives can be dangerous, and it is critical that all the parties involved understand the risks and rewards involved with these contracts.[7]

An entity might use derivatives to reduce or offset various risks (normally referred to as **hedging**). It is also possible to enter into derivative contracts to create positions that are expected to be profitable.[8] Both are acceptable strategies and depend on the company's risk tolerance profile; that is, the nature of the risks that the company can comfortably undertake and the amount of exposure to each risk that it is willing to accept. There are special optional accounting rules that a company can use when a derivative is used to hedge certain risk. Although hedging will be discussed in the body of the chapter, **hedge accounting** will be discussed in Appendix 16A due to its added complexity.

What types of business models and processes generate financial risk? Virtually all business models generate financial (and indeed other) risks. The following are some examples:

- Any business that purchases commodities such as fuel, agricultural products, or renewable resources as inputs has a **market risk** associated with these inputs. These companies know that commodity prices vary significantly depending on supply and demand. This affects the company's profitability and may lead to volatile net income. Often, the commodities are priced in different currencies, which creates a **currency risk.**

- Likewise, any company that sells commodities has a **market risk.** Depending on the commodity pricing when the commodity is sold, the company might make more or less profit, which again can lead to volatile or unpredictable net income.[9]

- Companies that sell on credit have **credit risks**: the risk that the customer or other party (counterparty) may fail to make a payment.

- Companies that borrow money or incur liabilities increase **liquidity risk**: the risk that they will not be able to pay their obligations. Debt also creates **interest rate risk.**

- Companies that buy goods, finance purchases, create inventory, sell goods, and collect receivables have **market risks**: the risk that the value of the assets will change while the company is holding them.

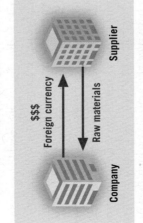

Foreign currency $$$
Raw materials
Company → Supplier

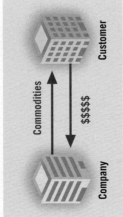

Commodities
$$$$$
Company → Customer

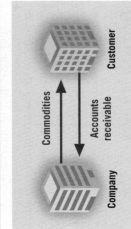

Commodities
Accounts receivable
Company → Customer

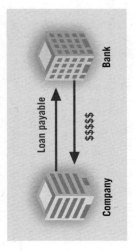

Loan payable
$$$$$
Company → Bank

Remember that derivative transactions may be the most efficient way of managing these risks. Alternatively, or in addition, the company may rely on other tools to manage the risks, including internal controls (such as credit checks on customers to reduce or eliminate credit risk).

A company may try to structure its business model such that it is not exposed to certain financial risks and thus does not need to manage them. For instance, by having a policy of selling only for cash, the company is not exposed to credit risk. By using "just-in-time" inventory ordering, a company gets rid of the market risk associated with stockpiling or holding inventory.

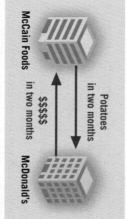

Producers and Consumers as Derivative Users

McCain Foods Limited is a large producer of potatoes for the consumer market. Assume that McCain believes that the present price for potatoes is excellent, but that McCain will need two months to harvest its potatoes and deliver them to market. The company has **market risk** related to its inventory. Because the company is concerned that the price of potatoes will drop, it signs a contract in which it agrees to sell its potatoes today at the current market price, but for delivery in two months. This locks in the market price. Known as a **forward contract**, this type of contract reduces the **market risk** related to the potatoes (both in terms of price and cash flows).

Who would buy this contract? Suppose **McDonald's Corporation** is on the other side of the contract and it wants to have potatoes (for french fries) in two months and is worried that prices will increase.[10] McDonald's also has **market risk**. It therefore agrees to delivery in two months at the current fixed price because it knows that it will need potatoes in two months and that it can make an acceptable profit at the current price level. McDonald's is also managing its **market risk**.

In this situation, if the price of potatoes increases before delivery, you might conclude that McCain loses and McDonald's wins. Conversely, if prices decrease, McCain wins and McDonald's loses. However, the objective is not to gamble on the outcome. In other words, regardless of which way the price moves, both companies should be pleased because both have received a price at which they can make an acceptable profit. In summary:

- Both companies have existing risks because of the way they do business (their business model).

- Both seek to manage these risks.

- Both are using derivatives to reduce these risks.

- Both are seen to be hedging their risks because they are reducing uncertainty.

Commodity prices are volatile and depend on factors such as weather, crop disasters, and general economic conditions. For the producer of a product and its consumer to plan effectively, it makes good sense to lock in specific future revenues or input costs in order to run their businesses successfully. This is a key way to manage cash flows to limit the risk of going bankrupt.

Speculators and Arbitrageurs as Derivative Users

In some cases, instead of a company like McDonald's buying the contract, a **speculator** may purchase the contract from McCain. The speculator is not trying to reduce risk, however. Instead the objective is to maximize potential returns by being exposed to greater risks. The speculator is betting that the price of potatoes will increase and that the value of the forward contract will therefore also increase. The speculator, who may be in the market for only a few hours, will then sell the forward contract to another speculator or to a company like McDonald's. The speculator will never take delivery of the potatoes as this was never the intention. The goal was to generate a cash profit from trading in the derivative instrument itself. The difference between this transaction and the earlier hedging transaction is that in the earlier transaction the company was entering into a derivative to reduce a pre-existing risk. In the case of the speculator, there is no pre-existing risk, just a desire to take on additional risk in the hope of increasing profits.

Another user of derivatives is an **arbitrageur**. These market players try to take advantage of inefficiencies in different markets. They try to lock in profits by simultaneously entering into transactions in two or more markets. For example, an arbitrageur might trade in a futures contract and at the same time in the commodity that underlies the futures contract, hoping to achieve small price gains on the difference between the two. Arbitrageurs exist because there is information asymmetry in different markets. This occurs when the same information is not available to all market participants in the different markets. Some markets are more efficient than others. The arbitrageurs force the prices in the different markets to move toward each other since they create demand and supply where previously there might not have been any, thus driving the prices either up or down.

Speculators and arbitrageurs are very important to markets because they keep the market liquid on a daily basis.

Theory

Accounting for Derivatives

Objective 2
Understand how to account for derivatives.

The basic principles regarding accounting for derivatives are as follows:

1. Financial instruments (including financial derivatives) and certain non-financial derivatives represent rights or obligations that meet the definitions of assets or liabilities and should be recognized in financial statements when the entity becomes party to the contract.

2. Fair value is the most relevant measure.

3. Gains and losses should be booked through net income.

Special optional hedge accounting exists for derivatives and other items that have been designated as being part of a hedging relationship for accounting purposes. These are described in Appendix 16A.

Recall the discussion regarding fair value measurement from Chapter 2 and Appendix 2A. Appendix 16C discusses more advanced measurement techniques and models.

Non-Financial Derivatives and Executory Contracts

Derivatives may be financial or non-financial. An example of a financial derivative is a forward contract to buy U.S. dollars. An example of a non-financial derivative is a contract to buy pork bellies or potatoes as in the earlier example. GAAP provides accounting guidance for financial instruments (including financial derivatives), as well as certain non-financial derivatives. Thus many commodities futures are accounted for in the same manner as financial derivatives.

What about purchase commitments? Are they derivatives? For instance, many companies enter into contracts intending to take delivery of raw material in the future in order to lock in a supply of raw materials. These contracts may be structured as commodities futures or forward contracts in legal form and therefore are derivatives from a finance perspective. However, they may also be structured as regular purchase commitments. Under both types of contracts, the company is agreeing to take delivery of the raw materials at an agreed-upon price in the future. What separates the two types of contracts from an accounting perspective? What makes the forwards and futures derivatives from a finance perspective but not the purchase commitments? Should they both be accounted for as derivatives?[11]

Purchase commitments are generally labelled as **executory contracts**: contracts to do something in the future (where no cash or product changes hands up front). Note that derivatives are similarly contracts to do something in the future and could arguably also be referred to as executory contracts. In this regard, the two are similar. Purchase commitments are not structured as derivatives contracts from a legal perspective, however, and

Law

they do not trade on commodities exchanges (as do futures and options, for instance).[12] Historically, these contracts have not been recognized in the financial statements. An issue exists, however, because technically, purchase commitments meet the accounting definition of derivatives. This is because their value changes with the value of the underlying (in this case the raw material); there is no investment up front and the contract will be settled in the future.

Under ASPE, purchase commitments are not accounted for as derivatives because they are not exchange traded and therefore are difficult to measure. They are therefore not recognized until the goods are received. IFRS considers whether contracts have net settlement features, meaning that they can be settled on a net basis by paying cash or other assets as opposed to taking delivery of the underlying product.[13] For contracts with net settlement features, as long as the company intends to take delivery of the raw materials, the contracts are designated as "expected use," and are not accounted for as derivatives. Purchase contracts that must be settled by taking delivery or delivering the underlying products are not accounted for as derivatives. As such, they are not recognized until delivery of the underlying non-financial asset takes place (for example, the inventory is delivered or received).

Illustration 16-1 analyzes the nature of purchase commitments and forward/futures/options contracts that relate to non-financial assets such as commodities.

	Purchase commitments for non-financial assets (such as inventory)	Forward/futures/options to buy/sell non-financial assets (such as inventory)
Legal form	Purchase contract/commitment. Generally does not include net settlement clause.	Forward/futures/option contract
Does it trade on a market (thus establishing liquidity and fair value)?	No	Yes and generally net settleable
Does it meet the definition of an executory contract (that is, does it promise to do something in the future where neither party has yet performed)?	Yes. A contract is signed up front but no money or goods change hands until later.	Yes. A contract is signed up front but no money or goods change hands until later.
Does it meet the definition of a derivative (that is, does its value depend on underlying, there is little or no upfront investment, and it will be settled in future)?	Yes. The value of the contract depends upon the value of the underlying (for example, inventory), there is no upfront investment, and it will be settled in the future.	Yes. The value of the contract depends upon the value of the underlying (for, example, inventory), there is no upfront investment, and it will be settled in the future.
Perspective for accounting purposes	Generally accounted for as an unexecuted contract and not recognized until the underlying non-financial item is delivered. (Derivative accounting does not apply to these contracts either because they are not exchange traded [ASPE] or because they are not settleable on a net basis [IFRS]).	Generally accounted for as a derivative (recognized and measured at FV-NI). Under ASPE these contracts are accounted for as derivatives only if exchange traded. Accounted for as an executory contract under IFRS, where there is no net settlement feature or where one exists but the company expects to take delivery or deliver the underlying asset.

Illustration 16-1

Accounting for Contracts Involving Non-Financial Assets

Law

We will now discuss three basic types of derivatives: options and warrants, forwards, and futures.

Options and Warrants

Options and warrants are derivative instruments. An option or warrant gives the holder the contractual right to acquire or sell an underlying instrument at a fixed price (the **exercise** or **strike price**—the agreed-upon price at which the option may be settled) within a defined term (the **exercise period**). A good example is an option to purchase shares of a company for a fixed price, on a specified date. The **underlying** is the shares; that is, this option derives its value from the share price of the underlying shares. If the share price goes up, the option is worth more. If it goes down, the option may become worth less.

The option allows the holder to protect himself or herself against declines in the market value of the underlying shares but also allows the holder to participate in increases in the share value without having to hold the actual shares. Derivative instruments do not result in the transfer of the underlying (the shares in our example) at the contract's inception and perhaps not even when it matures. They also require a relatively low upfront investment (which is the cost of the option premium). The cost of the option is a fraction of the cost of the actual share itself. Before the end of the option period, the holder may sell the option to capture the value. The holder has the right to exercise the option but is not obliged to buy the shares at the exercise price.

A Framework for Options.   Options may be purchased (**purchased options**) or written by a company (**written options**). If a company **purchases** an option, it will pay a fee or premium and gain a right to do something. If a company **writes** an option, it charges a fee or premium and gives the holder/purchaser the right to do something. The "right" in question may be either of the following:

1. A right to **buy** the underlying (**a call option**)
2. A right to **sell** the underlying (**a put option**)

The framework is shown in Illustration 16-2.

Illustration 16-2
A Framework for Options

	Call—right to buy	**Put**—right to sell
Written	Sell option for $ Transfer rights to buy shares/underlying	Sell option for $ Transfer rights to sell shares/underlying
Purchased	Pay $ for option Obtain right to buy shares/underlying	Pay $ for option Obtain right to sell shares/underlying

A written option is riskier for the company because the writer has no control over whether it will be required to deliver something. The company is obligated to perform under the option. This is different from a purchased option, which gives the company the right but not the obligation to do something. Assume that a company writes or sells an option for $5 cash. Because this creates an obligation for the company that has written the option, the option is generally accounted for as a liability.

An example of a purchased call option follows.

Illustration of a Purchased Call Option.   Assume that Abalone Inc. purchases a **call option** contract on January 2, 2014, from Baird Investment Corp.[14] The option gives Abalone the right to purchase 1,000 Laredo Corp. shares (the underlying) at $100 per share (the exercise/strike price), and it expires April 30, 2014. For the right to buy the shares at this fixed price, Abalone pays a premium of $400. This is a financial derivative because the underlying is a financial asset (the Laredo shares).

At the time of the transaction, Laredo shares are trading at $100. If

the price of Laredo shares increases above $100, Abalone can exercise the option and purchase the shares for $100 per share. Alternatively, Abalone may sell the option to someone else. Here, Baird has the market risk associated with the shares. Abalone has market risk associated with the option itself, or the $400. At worst, the option becomes worthless and

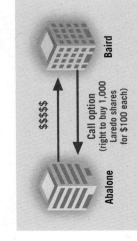

Abalone loses the $400. If Baird has written the option without holding an investment in Laredo (a "naked" position), it will suffer a loss if the price of Laredo increases. If Baird holds shares in Laredo offsetting the option sold (a "covered call"), its profit on the investment will be limited to the difference between $100 and the price it paid for the shares plus the $400 premium received from Abalone. If Laredo's share price never increases above $100 per share, the call option is worthless and Abalone recognizes a loss equal to the initial price of the call option.

The following journal entry would be made by Abalone at the acquisition date of January 2, 2014:

Derivatives—Financial Assets/Liabilities	400	
Cash		400

A	=	L	+	SE
0				

Cash flows: ↓ 400 outflow

The option premium is composed of two amounts: (1) the intrinsic value and (2) the time value. Illustration 16-3 shows the formula to calculate the option premium.

Option Premium Formula

Option Premium	=	Intrinsic Value	+	Time Value

Intrinsic value is the difference between the market price of the underlying and the strike or exercise price at any point in time. It represents the amount that would be realized by the option holder if the option were exercised immediately. On January 2, 2014, the intrinsic value of the option related to the Laredo shares is zero because the market price is equal to the strike price of $100. **Time value** refers to the option's value over and above its intrinsic value. Time value reflects the option's value over and above its intrinsic value. Time value reflects the possibility that the option will have a **fair value greater than zero because there is some expectation that the price of Laredo shares will increase above the strike price during the option term.** As indicated, the option's time value is $400.[15]

On March 31, 2014, the price of Laredo shares has increased to $120 per share and the intrinsic value of the call option contract is now $20,000. That is, Abalone could exercise the call option and purchase 1,000 shares from Baird for $100 per share and then sell the shares in the market for $120 per share. This gives Abalone a potential gain of $20,000 ($120,000 − $100,000) on the option contract.

The options may be worth more than this due to the time value component; that is, the shares may increase in value over the remaining month. Assume the options are trading at $20,100. In addition, we must consider the original cost of the option. The entry to record this change in value of the option at March 31, 2014, is as follows:[16]

Derivatives—Financial Assets/Liabilities	19,700	
Gain		19,700[a]

[a] $20,100 − $400

A	=	L	+	SE
+19,700				+19,700

Cash flows: No effect

At March 31, 2014, the call option is reported on the statement of financial position (SFP) at its fair value of $20,100 and the net gain increases net income for the period. The options are "in-the-money"; that is, they have value.

On April 1, 2014, assuming the shares are still worth $120 and Abalone settles the option in cash rather than by taking delivery of the shares of Laredo, the entry to record the settlement of the call option contract with Baird is as follows:

Cash	20,000	
Loss	100[17.]	
Derivatives—Financial Assets/Liabilities		20,100

A = L + SE
-100   -100

Cash flows: ↑ 20,000 inflow

Illustration 16-4 summarizes the effects of the call option contract on net income.

Illustration 16-4
Effect on Income—Option

Transaction	Income (Loss) Effect
Net increase in value of call option	$19,700
($20,100 − $400)	
Settle call option	(100)
Total net income	$19,600[a]

[a] This amount is net of $400 cost for the right to participate in the increase in the value of the shares.

On April 1, 2014, Abalone could have taken delivery of the shares under the option contract. Assuming that the company decides to present the investment in the shares as FV-NI, the entry to record this is as follows:

Date			
March 31, 2014			
April 1, 2014	FV-NI Investment	120,000	
	Loss	100	
	Cash		100,000
	Derivatives—Financial Assets/Liabilities		20,100

A = L + SE
-100   -100

Cash flows: ↓ 100,000 outflow

Abalone could have purchased the Laredo shares directly on January 2 instead of buying an option. To make the initial investment in Laredo shares, Abalone would have had to pay the full cost of the shares up front and would therefore have had to pay more cash than it did for the option. If the price of the Laredo shares then increased, Abalone would realize a gain; however, Abalone would also be at risk for a loss if the Laredo shares declined in value.

We will return to the discussion of options in Appendix 16A. Chapter 17 will also revisit the option framework when looking at the potentially dilutive impact of options in calculating earnings per share.

Forwards

A **forward contract** is another type of derivative. Under a forward contract, the parties to the contract each commit up front to do something in the future. For example, one party commits to buy an item (referred to as the underlying) and the other to sell the item at a specified price on a specified date. The price and time period are locked in under the contract. The contracts are specific to the transacting parties based on their needs. These instruments generally do not trade on exchanges because the terms are unique to the parties involved (that is, the terms are not standardized as most exchange-traded contracts are).

Usually banks buy and sell these contracts or act as intermediaries between the parties to the contract. Forwards are measured at the present value of any future cash flows under the contract—discounted at a rate that reflects risk.

Illustration of a Forward Contract. To illustrate, assume that on January 2, 2014, Abalone Inc. agrees to buy $1,000 in U.S. currency for

Finance

Law

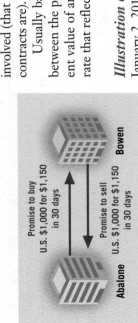

Promise to buy
U.S. $1,000 for $1,150
in 30 days

Promise to sell
U.S. $1,000 for $1,150
in 30 days

Abalone   Bowen

Finance

$1,150 in Canadian currency in 30 days from Bowen Bank. The forward contract not only transfers to the holder the right to increases in value of the underlying (in this case, U.S. dollars), it also creates an obligation to pay a fixed amount at a specified date (in this case, $1,150). This is different than the purchased option, which creates a right but not an obligation: with a purchased option, the holder may choose to exercise the option but does not have to. The forward contract transfers the **currency risk** inherent in the Canada–U.S. exchange rate. In addition, the contract creates credit risk and liquidity risk. The credit risk is the risk that at the end of the contract, the counterparty (Bowen in this case) will not deliver the underlying (U.S. $1,000). The liquidity risk is the risk that Abalone will not be able to honour its commitment to deliver Canadian $1,150 at the end of the contract. This is a financial derivative because the underlying is a financial asset: foreign currency.

Upon inception, the contract is priced such that the value of the forward contract is zero. Assume in the example above that the date on which the transaction is entered into, U.S. $1 = Canadian $1.10. No journal entry would be recorded at this point because we must consider the fair value of the contract—not just the difference between the spot rate[18] and the forward rate. Like the option, the value of the forward considers both the intrinsic value and the time value component. It is generally valued at the present value of the future net cash flows under the contract.

Under derivatives accounting, subsequently, the forward is remeasured at fair value. The value will vary depending on interest rates as well as on what is happening with the spot prices (the current value) and forward prices (future value as quoted today) for the U.S. dollar. If the U.S. dollar appreciates in value, in general, the contract will have value since Abalone has locked in to pay only $1,150 for the U.S. $1,000. Assuming that the fair value of the contract is $50, on January 5, 2014, Abalone would record the following:

Derivatives—Financial Assets/Liabilities	50	
Gain		50

A	=	L	+	SE
+50	=			+50

Cash flows: No effect

The derivative would be presented as an asset on the statement of financial position and measured at fair value with gains and losses, both unrealized and realized, being booked through net income.

Suppose on January 31, the contract moves into a loss position; that is, if the contract were settled today, the company would suffer an overall loss of $30. This might occur for instance if the value of the U.S. currency declines. In this case, Abalone is locked in to pay $1,150 for something that is worth less than that amount. The following journal entry would be booked:

Loss	80	
Derivatives—Financial Assets/Liabilities		80

A	=	L	+	SE
−80	=			−80

Cash flows: No effect

The original gain is reversed and the additional loss must be booked.

The forward contract meets the definition of a financial liability because it is a contractual obligation to exchange financial instruments with another party under conditions that are potentially unfavourable. The Derivatives—Financial Assets/Liabilities account would therefore be presented as a liability on the SFP. Since the derivative contract can sometimes be an asset while at other times it can be a liability, it can be presented as either an asset or a liability on the SFP.

Assume that on February 1, the settlement date, the U.S. dollar is worth $1.04 Canadian. The following entry would be booked to settle the contract if it was settled on a net basis:

Loss	80	
Derivatives—Financial Assets/Liabilities	30	(to eliminate carrying value)
Cash		110[a]

[a] U.S. $1,000 × (1.15 − 1.04)

A   =   L   +   SE
-110   -30   -80
Cash flows: ↓ 110 outflow

If instead Abalone actually took delivery of the U.S. dollars, the following journal entry would be booked:

Cash	1,040	(U.S. $ at the spot/current exchange rate)
Derivatives—Financial Assets/Liabilities	30	(to eliminate carrying value)
Loss	80	
Cash		1,150

A   =   L   +   SE
-110   -30   -80
Cash flows: ↓ 110 outflow

Futures

Futures contracts, another popular type of derivative, are the same as forwards except for the following:

1. They are standardized as to amounts and dates.

2. They are exchange traded and therefore have ready market values.

3. They are settled through clearing houses, which generally removes the credit risk.

4. There is a requirement to put up collateral in the form of a "margin" account. The margin account represents a percentage of the contract's value. Daily changes in the value of the contract are settled daily against the margin account by the clearing house (known as marking to market) and resulting deficiencies in the margin account must be made up daily.

The initial margin is treated as a deposit account similar to a bank account, and is increased or decreased as the margin amount changes. The gain or loss on the contract, reflected in the daily change in the account, is recognized in income.

Illustration of a Futures Contract.

For example, assume Forward Inc. entered into a futures contract to sell grain for $1,000 on an exchange. The broker requires a $100 initial margin (normally a percentage of the market value of the contract or a fixed amount multiplied by the number of contracts). This amount is deposited in cash with the broker. Like the forward, the futures contract would have a zero value up front. This is a non-financial derivative because the underlying is a non-financial commodity (grain).

At the date when the contract is entered into, the following journal entry would be booked to show the margin that has been deposited with the broker. The contract is otherwise valued at $0 on inception.

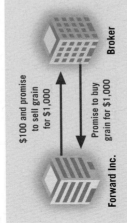

$100 and promise to sell grain for $1,000

Promise to buy grain for $1,000

Forward Inc.   Broker

| Deposits | 100 | |
| Cash | | 100 |

A   =   L   +   SE
0
Cash flows: ↓ 100 outflow

Finance

Assume that the value of the grain increases after the contract has been entered into. The contract is marked to market by the broker. Assume that the market value of the contract decreases by $50. This is because Forward has agreed to sell the grain for a fixed amount that is lower than the current market value. The clearing house then requires

Forward to deposit an additional $50. The entries to record the loss and the additional deposit would be:

Loss	50	
Derivatives—Financial Assets/Liabilities		50
Deposits	50	
Cash		50

A = L + SE
−50   −50
Cash flows: ↓ 50 outflow

If the contract is closed out (settled net without delivering the grain) with no further changes in value, the following entry would be booked.

Cash	100	
Derivatives—Financial Assets/Liabilities	50	
Deposits		150

A = L + SE
0
Cash flows: ↑ 100 inflow

Forward suffered a loss of $50, which was booked to net income already through the journal entries above. This is because it had agreed to sell the grain for $1,000 when it was worth more. Instead of delivering the grain, Forward paid the difference in cash—thus locking in the loss. Note that the net impact is a loss of $50 on the contract. On the income statement, a decision would be made about how to present the loss since it is now realized.

Derivatives Involving the Entity's Own Shares

Sometimes companies enter into derivative contracts that deal with their own shares. For instance, a company might buy or write options dealing with its own shares or enter into forward contracts to buy or sell its own shares at a future date. Examples of "own equity" derivative instruments include:

1. Options
   (a) Purchased call or put options to buy/sell the entity's own shares
   (b) Written call or put options to buy/sell the entity's own shares

2. Forwards
   (a) To buy the entity's own shares
   (b) To sell the entity's own shares

Assume Abalone Inc. paid $400 to Baker Corp. for the right to buy 1,000 of Abalone's own common shares for $30 each. Assume further that the contract may only be settled by exercising the option and buying the shares. Why would Abalone do this? Perhaps Abalone is looking to buy back its own shares to boost share values.

Should the cost of the option be treated as an investment as in the earlier example where the underlying is a share from another company as opposed to the entity's own shares? This is a presentation issue. IFRS states that this transaction would be presented as a reduction from shareholders' equity and not as an investment.[19] Contracts where the entity agrees to issue a fixed number of its own shares for a fixed amount of consideration are also generally presented as equity (for example, written call options and forwards to sell shares). This is sometimes referred to as the "fixed for fixed" principle when discussing how to account for derivatives that are settleable with own equity instruments. ASPE is silent on this matter but general principles would support presenting the financial instrument as contra equity since it does not meet the definition of an asset.

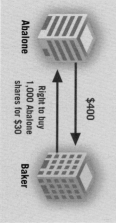

Abalone → Baker
$400
Right to buy 1,000 Abalone shares for $30

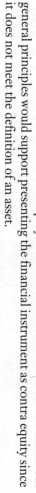

Not all contracts involving own equity instruments are treated as equity, however. Some end up being treated as financial liabilities or financial assets. This area of accounting is very complex and is beyond the scope of this text. This is also an area of transition. As a general rule, any analysis should go back to basic principles and definitions. The following exceptions exist.

1. *Fixed for fixed override:* When a derivative contract is entered into that creates an obligation to pay cash or other assets even if it is for a fixed number of the entity's shares (for example, a written put option or forward contract to buy shares), it overrides the "fixed for fixed" principle noted earlier and the contract should generally be treated as a financial liability. Therefore, any time there is an obligation to pay cash, a financial liability is recognized.

2. *Settlement options:* Where the derivative contract allows choice in how the instruments will be settled (for example, one party can choose to settle net in cash or by exchanging shares), the instrument is a financial asset/liability by default under IFRS unless all possible settlement options result in it being an equity instrument.[20] Under ASPE, the instrument would likely be treated as equity if the entity can avoid settling with cash or other assets (that is, where the entity has the option to choose the way the contract is settled and can avoid paying cash or other assets).

Illustration 16-5 summarizes IFRS requirements for own equity instruments. As mentioned above, ASPE is not as explicit in this area and generally the analysis defaults to whether the definition of a liability is met or not.

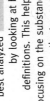

Underlying Concept

Often, complex transactions are best analyzed by looking at basic definitions. This helps by focusing on the substance of the transaction.

Illustration 16-5

Summary of Accounting for Own Equity Instruments under IFRS

	Presentation under IFRS	Analysis
Written call options	Equity	Holder has the right to buy a **fixed** number of its own shares for a **fixed** amount of cash and no contractual obligation to pay cash.
Written put options	Financial liabilities	Holder has the right to sell a **fixed** number of its own shares to the company for a **fixed** amount of cash. Even though this is a fixed for fixed contract, the obligation to pay cash creates a liability.
Purchased call/put options	Contra equity	The company has the right to buy or sell a **fixed** amount of its own shares for a **fixed** amount of cash. There is no contractual obligation to pay cash. This is therefore equity.
Forward contract to buy shares	Financial liabilities	The company has committed to buy a **fixed** number of its own shares for a **fixed** amount of cash. Even though this is a fixed for fixed contract, the obligation to pay cash creates a liability.
Forward contract to sell shares	Equity	The company has committed to sell a **fixed** number of its own shares for a **fixed** amount of cash. There is no contractual obligation to pay cash. This is therefore equity.
Contracts that may or will be settled net (settlement option)	Financial assets/liabilities	These are not fixed for fixed contracts because they will be settled either in cash (net) or a variable number of shares that equal the net cash settlement value.

DEBT VERSUS EQUITY—ISSUER PERSPECTIVE

Objective 3

Analyze whether a hybrid/compound instrument issued for financing purposes represents a liability, equity, or both.

Finance

Economics of Complex Financial Instruments

In companies with very simple capital structures, financing is obtained through debt instruments (loans, bonds, and debentures) and common shares. Both these simple financing vehicles have very different legal and economic characteristics. Debt instruments are generally repaid, pay interest, and rank in preference to common shares upon windup or liquidation. Common shares, on the other hand, are seen as permanent capital, pay dividends, and are residual in nature, meaning that upon windup or liquidation, the shareholders get whatever is left after paying off all debts. These characteristics are summarized in the chart in Illustration 16-6.

	Loan or Bonds Payable	Common Shares
Term	Maturity date/repayment schedule.	Permanent capital.
Return to investor/lender	Interest, which is a function of the principal amount, time, and risk.	Dividends, which are a function of profits, cash flows, value of shares, and company policy.
Seniority in terms of liquidation, windup, or bankruptcy	Often secured by assets of the company. Generally ranks in preference upon liquidation, windup, or bankruptcy.	Unsecured residual interest. Shareholders get whatever is left after other capital providers such as creditors are paid out.[21]
Advantages to entity	Interest is tax deductible.	Does not increase solvency or liquidity risk.
	Company does not have to give up ownership.	Company does not have to pay out dividends.
	Leverage (maximize profits to shareholders by using the money of creditors).	Unsecured and so assets not at risk except in bankruptcy.
Disadvantages to entity	Too much debt increases liquidity and solvency risk and may result in higher cost of capital and/or lack of access to capital.	Issuance of more shares dilutes existing shareholder base.
		Missed leverage opportunity.

Over the years, the capital markets have sought to profit from the best attributes of both these types of instruments and have created many hybrid-type instruments that are neither straight debt (sometimes referred to as "plain vanilla" debt) nor straight common shares. **Hybrid/compound instruments** have more than one component, including debt and equity (such as debt with detachable warrants), or may have the dual attributes of both debt and equity. Preferred shares were probably the first hybrid or compound instrument. They are not quite common shares because they rank in preference to common shares regarding dividend payout and payout upon liquidation, windup, or bankruptcy. They often pay dividends annually, similar to debt. Other examples of hybrids or compound instruments are certain convertible debt instruments, term preferred shares, and mandatorily redeemable shares.

From an economic perspective, every time a new instrument is issued, it is priced or benchmarked against the standard instruments of debt and common shares, keeping in mind tax treatments that may be more or less favourable depending on whether the instrument is seen as debt or equity. So companies may, for instance, be able to pay less interest if the instrument also gives the holder some equity-like features (for instance, a conversion option). These designer-type financial instruments allow companies to create a specific type of instrument, keeping in mind the amount of capital required, desired risk profile, and acceptable cost of capital. Unfortunately, sometimes one of the design criteria includes a desire to show less debt on the statement of financial position.

Ethics

Presentation and Measurement of Hybrid/ Compound Instruments

Objective 4

Explain the accounting for hybrid/compound instruments.

Why is there so much fuss about hybrid/compound instruments? The capital marketplace focuses on liquidity and solvency and these are calculated using financial statement numbers. Excessive debt on an SFP signals increased riskiness and will affect the cost of capital and ultimately access to capital. Given that demand exists by both companies and investors for these types of instruments, and given the current accounting model that requires separate presentation of debt and equity, accountants must figure out a way to systematically and consistently classify these instruments such that the financial statements provide useful information to users including investors and creditors.

For this reason, these hybrid/compound instruments must be analyzed carefully for accounting purposes. They may be classified as debt, equity, or as part debt and part equity. The economic substance must be reviewed as well as contractual terms. Does the contract obligate the entity to pay out cash or other assets? If so, some or all of the instrument is a liability.

Presentation of Hybrid/Compound Instruments

When analyzing whether the contract is debt, equity, or both, consider the following:

1. Contractual terms

   (a) Does the instrument explicitly obligate the entity to pay out cash or other assets?

   (b) Does the instrument give the holder the choice to force the company to pay out cash (in which case it may create an obligation for the entity)?

   (c) Are there settlement options (in which case, it may create an obligation for the entity)?

2. Economic substance

   Does the instrument contain any equity-like features that may need to be separated out? Keep in mind that generally when the instrument gives the holder increased flexibility or choice, the instrument is worth more. For instance, a convertible bond (explained below) is worth more because it allows the holder to have the security of debt but also exposes the investors to the risks and rewards of share ownership. Thus, part of the instrument is equity-like.

3. Definitions of financial statement elements

   A **financial liability** is defined under both ASPE and IFRS as a contractual obligation to do either of the following:

   (a) deliver cash or another financial asset to another party, or

   (b) exchange financial instruments with another party under conditions that are potentially unfavourable.

   In addition, under IFRS, the definition of a financial liability includes guidance where the instrument is settleable using the entity's shares instead of cash. Essentially, where the company settles the instrument using a variable number of shares (instead of cash), it is still a financial liability. This is supported by ASPE as well, although it is not part of the definition.

   An **equity instrument** under both ASPE and IFRS is any contract that represents a residual interest in the assets of an entity after deducting all of its liabilities.

   In addition, under IFRS, the guidance includes the following with respect to instruments settleable in the entity's own equity instruments. The instrument is equity only if it

Finance

will be settled by exchanging a **fixed number** of the issuer's own equity instruments for a **fixed amount** of cash or other assets (and it is not a liability).[22]

These definitions are critical in determining how to present the instruments.

Illustration 16-7 shows some examples of hybrid/compound instruments indicating SFP presentation.

Illustration 16-7

Examples of Hybrid/Compound Instruments

Contract	Presentation
Convertible debt (convertible at the option of the holder into a fixed number of common shares of the company).	Part liability and part equity. The conversion option is essentially an embedded written call option and this part is equity since a fixed number of shares will be issued. The debt carries with it a contractual obligation to pay interest and principal.*
Puttable shares (holder has the option to require the company to take the instruments back and pay cash).	Liability. This instrument contains a written put option that requires the entity to pay cash or other assets if the option is exercised. The holder has the right to exercise the option and therefore this is beyond the entity's control. The exception to this is noted in the next example below.
Shares that give the holder the option to require the company to surrender a pro rata share of net assets upon windup.	Equity. Although these are technically liabilities because of the put option, they may be presented as equity as long as they are "in-substance common shares." (Recall these criteria from Chapter 15.)
Mandatorily redeemable preferred share.	Liability. The mandatory redemption imposes a contractual obligation to deliver cash or other assets. As an exception, high/low preferred shares are presented as equity under ASPE (see the chapter text below this illustration).
Debt with detachable warrants. The warrants are for a fixed number of shares.	Liability and equity. Since the warrants are detachable, they are separate financial instruments and are treated as written call options. The instruments allow for a fixed number of shares to be exchanged for a fixed amount of cash. The debt carries with it a contractual obligation to pay interest and principal.*
Preferred shares that must be repaid if certain conditions are met (for example, if the market price of the common shares exceed a certain threshold).	Liability. Under IFRS, a liability exists since the contingent settlement provision is based on an event outside the company's control. Under ASPE, the instrument would be accounted for as a liability only where the contingency is highly likely to occur.[23]
Debt that will be settled by issuing a variable number of common shares equal to the face value of the debt (or where the holder has the option to require settlement in cash or a variable number of shares).	Liability. The common shares are used as currency to settle the obligation, which is equal to the face value of the debt regardless of who has the option to choose.
Perpetual debt.	Liability. The economic value of this instrument is determined by discounting the interest payments (which represent a contractual obligation to pay cash).

*Note that ASPE allows the entity to measure the equity portion at $0 as an accounting policy choice. This will be discussed later in the chapter.

Redeemable shares are often used in tax and succession planning. Many small businesses are created and run by individuals who at some point decide that they would like to hand the company over to their children. One orderly way of doing this that minimizes taxes is through the use of redeemable preferred shares, sometimes referred to as **high/low preferred shares**. The business assets can be transferred to a new company, which makes it possible to take advantage of special tax provisions that minimize taxes, and the owner takes redeemable preferred shares as part of the consideration. The children then buy the common shares in the new company for a nominal amount, which allows them to benefit from subsequent increases in the company's value. This also gives them some or all of the voting control since the common shares would normally be voting shares.

The redemption amount of the preferred shares is set at the company's fair value at the time of the transaction. This means that the fair value is frozen for the individual at a point in time (which is why the label "estate freeze" is sometimes given to this type of transaction). All subsequent increases in value will go to the children through ownership of the common shares. The owner of the former company will eventually get his or her money (which represents the fair value of the assets that he or she put in) out of the new company at a future point by redeeming the preferred shares.

This is a good example of yet another business reason to use complex financial instruments. Note that the redemption feature causes this instrument to be recorded as a (huge) liability since the company has an obligation to deliver cash upon redemption. Many small business owners are not happy with this accounting since it makes the company look highly leveraged when, in fact, the shares will normally not be redeemed in the short- or medium-term. Treating the shares as liabilities on the balance sheet may also cause the company to violate pre-existing debt covenants. As a result of this, ASPE requires these particular instruments to be treated as equity.[24]

One last presentation issue is whether the financial instruments should be offset against other financial instruments when presented on the SFP. When a company offsets one or more financial instruments, such as financial assets and liabilities, the instruments are generally shown as a net number. For instance, if the company has a receivable of $100 and a payable of $75, and they are presented on a net basis, only net assets of $25 would be presented. The potential problem with this is that it tends to obscure the fact that the $25 asset is really made up of the two components. Therefore there are some restrictions on offsetting.

When can a company show these amounts on a net basis? Only when certain criteria are met, as follows:

1. The company has a legally enforceable right[25] to net the amounts (in other words, if the instruments were to be settled, then they could legally be settled on a net basis).

2. The company intends to settle the instruments on a net basis or simultaneously (that is, collect the receivable and immediately pay out the payable).[26]

Measurement of Hybrid/Compound Instruments

Upon initial recognition, financial instruments are measured at fair value, which is generally the exchange value. If they have components of both debt and equity, they may require bifurcation (splitting into debt and equity). This is therefore a measurement issue. Whatever the classification that is chosen upon inception, this classification continues to be used until the instrument is removed from the SFP.

The **measurement** of hybrid/compound instruments is complicated by the fact that the economic value of these instruments can be attributed to **both** the debt and equity components. That is, the instrument is neither 100% debt nor 100% equity, and instead is part debt and part equity. How should these two components be measured?

As noted in previous chapters, there are two approaches to allocating the value of a transaction to its respective parts: the **residual value method** (sometimes referred to as the **incremental method**) and the **relative fair value method** (sometimes referred to as the **proportional method**). These tools have been referred to in earlier chapters and used for instance to help bifurcate bundled sales and purchases. The mechanics are the same. The methods are recapped briefly below.

1. Relative fair value method: Determine the market values of similar individual instruments. For instance, for convertible debt, determine the value of straight debt without the conversion feature and the value of the option to convert. This is easier to do if

Underlying Concept

Well-defined measurement tools help cope with measurement uncertainty. These tools ultimately help in preparing financial information that is more reliable.

there are existing markets for both these instruments as separate items. However, measurement of the debt portion can also be done by a PV calculation, discounting at the market rate for similar debt. Measurement of the option portion can be done using an options pricing model.[27] The components are then assigned these values. If the total is greater than or less than the instrument's issue price, the difference is pro-rated based on the respective market or fair values and is then allocated to each of the components.

2. Residual value method: Value only one component (the one that is easier to value, which is often the debt component). The other component is valued at whatever is left.

IFRS requires the use of the residual value method, with any debt components being valued first and the residual being allocated to the equity components. ASPE allows the equity component to be valued at zero or the residual value method to be used, with the more easily measurable component being valued first.[28] Subsequently, debt is measured at amortized costs unless the fair value option is selected (or it is a derivative).

Let's look at a very common financial instrument—convertible debt—and how it is accounted for.

Convertible Debt

A **convertible bond** is a bond that may be converted into common shares of the company. It combines the benefits of a bond with the privilege of exchanging it for common shares **at the holder's option.** It is purchased by investors who want the security of a bond hold-ing—guaranteed interest—plus the added option of conversion if the value of the common shares increases significantly.

Corporations issue convertible debt for two main reasons. One is the desire to raise equity capital without giving up more ownership control than necessary. To illustrate, assume that a company wants to raise $1 million at a time when its common shares are selling at $45 per share. Such an issue would require selling 22,222 shares (ignoring issue costs). By selling 1,000 bonds at $1,000 par, and with each bond being convertible into 20 common shares, the enterprise may raise $1 million by committing only 20,000 common shares.[29] Investors may be willing to take the bonds since they give the investors greater security (especially if the bonds are secured by company assets) yet allow them to participate in the company growth through the option to convert the bonds to common shares.

A second, more common reason that companies have for issuing convertible securities is to obtain debt financing at cheaper rates. Many enterprises would have to issue debt at higher interest rates unless a convertible feature was attached. The conversion privilege entices the investor to accept a lower interest rate than would normally be the case on a straight debt issue. For example, **Amazon.com** at one time issued convertible bonds that paid interest at an effective yield of 4.75%, which was much lower than Amazon.com would have had to pay if it had issued straight debt. For this lower interest rate, the investor received the right to buy Amazon.com's common shares at a fixed price until the bonds' maturity.

Finance
%

Real World Emphasis

There are reporting issues in the accounting for convertible debt at all of the follow-ing times:

1. Issuance

2. Conversion

3. Retirement

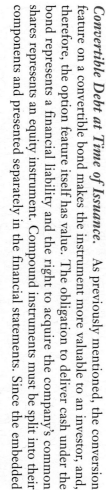
ASPE

Convertible Debt at Time of Issuance. As previously mentioned, the conversion feature on a convertible bond makes the instrument more valuable to an investor, and, therefore, the option feature itself has value. The obligation to deliver cash under the bond represents a financial liability and the right to acquire the company's common shares represents an equity instrument. Compound instruments must be split into their components and presented separately in the financial statements. Since the embedded option to convert to common shares is an equity instrument, that part of the instrument is presented as equity. The remaining component is presented as a liability. Recall that ASPE allows an accounting policy choice to measure the equity portion at $0.

For example, assume that Bond Corp. offers three-year, 6% convertible bonds (par $1,000). Each $1,000 bond may be converted into 250 common shares, which are currently trading at $3 per share. Similar straight bonds carry an interest rate of 9%. One thousand bonds are issued at par.

Allocating the proceeds to the liability and equity components under the residual value or incremental method involves valuing one component first and then allocating the rest of the value to the other component. Assume that the company decides to use the residual method and measure the debt first. The bond may be measured at the PV of the stream of interest payments ($1 million × 6% for three years) plus the PV of the bond itself ($1 million) all discounted at 9%, which is the market rate of interest. The remainder of the proceeds is then allocated to the option. This allocation is shown in Illustration 16-8.

Total proceeds (at par in this case)	$1,000,000
Less:	
Value of bonds (PV annuity 3 years, 9%, $60,000 + PV $1,000,000, in 3 years, 9%)	(924,061)
Incremental value of option	$ 75,939

The journal entry to record the issuance would be as follows:

	IFRS		ASPE, valuing the equity component at zero as an accounting policy choice*	
Cash	1,000,000		1,000,000	
Bonds Payable		924,061		1,000,000
Contributed Surplus—Conversion Rights		75,939		0

*ASPE also allows the residual method to be used with the more easily measurable component being measured first. Normally the debt component is more easily measurable so this option is consistent with IFRS.

Convertible Debt at Time of Conversion. If bonds are converted into other securities, the main accounting problem is to determine the amount at which to record the securities that have been exchanged for the bond. Assume that holders of the convertible debt of Bond Corp. decide to convert their convertible bonds before the bonds mature. The bond discount will be partially amortized at this point. Assume that the unamortized portion is $14,058. The entry to record the conversion would be as follows:

Bonds Payable ($1,000,000 − $14,058)	985,942	
Contributed Surplus—Conversion Rights	75,939	
Common Shares		1,061,881

This method, referred to as the **book value method** of recording the bond conversion, is the method that is required under IFRS and ASPE.[30] Support for the book value approach is based on the argument that an agreement was established at the date that the bond was issued either to pay a stated amount of cash at maturity or to issue a stated number of shares of equity securities. Therefore, when the debt is converted to equity in accordance with the pre-existing contract terms, no gain or loss would be recognized upon conversion.[31] Any accrued interest that was forfeited would be treated as part of the new book value of the shares (and credited to Common Shares).

Illustration 16-8

Incremental Allocation of Proceeds between Liability and Equity Components

IFRS

A	=	L	+	SE
+1,000,000		+924,061		+75,939

ASPE

A	=	L	+	SE
+1,000,000		+1,000,000		

Cash flows: ↑ 1,000,000 inflow

A	=	L	+	SE
		−985,942		+985,942

Cash flows: No effect

Underlying Concept

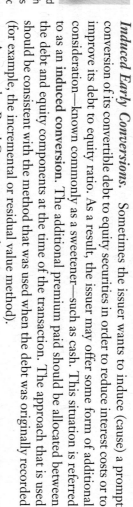

Note that the convertible debt in the example above is treated to as an **induced conversion**. The additional premium paid should be allocated between the same as the debt with detachable warrants. This is because the economic substance of the instruments is the same: they both have debt and give the holder the option to hold shares.

Induced Early Conversions. Sometimes the issuer wants to induce (cause) a prompt conversion of its convertible debt to equity securities in order to reduce interest costs or to improve its debt to equity ratio. As a result, the issuer may offer some form of additional consideration—known commonly as a sweetener—such as cash. This situation is referred to as an **induced conversion**. The additional premium paid should be allocated between the debt and equity components at the time of the transaction. The approach that is used should be consistent with the method that was used when the debt was originally recorded (for example, the incremental or residual value method).

Assume that Bond Corp. wants to reduce interest costs at some point during the life of the debt. It therefore offers an additional cash premium of $15,000 to the bondholders to convert, and at a time when the carrying amount of the debt was $972,476. Assume further that the **residual value method** was used to allocate the issue price originally between debt and equity components, with the debt being measured at its discounted cash flows and the equity being valued as the residual amount. The bond's fair value at the conversion time is $981,462 (ignoring the conversion feature) due to lower market interest rates. The first step in the allocation of the inducement premium is to determine the difference between the bonds' fair value and carrying value:

$$\$981,462 - \$972,476 = \$8,986$$

Then the residual method would be used to allocate the inducement premium between the debt and equity components (since this method was originally used):

$$\$15,000 - \$8,986 = \$6,014$$

Thus, $8,986 would be treated as a debt retirement cost and $6,014 as a capital transaction similar to a share redemption cost. The journal entry would be as follows:

Bonds Payable	972,476	
Loss on Redemption of Bonds	8,986 (above)	
Contributed Surplus—Stock Options	75,939 (previously calculated)	
Retained Earnings	6,014 (above)	
Common Shares		1,048,415
Cash		15,000

The shares are now valued at the total carrying amount of the bonds, plus the option, as follows:

$$\$972,476 + \$75,939 = \$1,048,415$$

Retirement of Convertible Debt. The normal retirement of the liability component of convertible debt at maturity (its repayment) is treated the same way as non-convertible bonds, as explained in Chapter 14. The equity component remains in Contributed Surplus. What happens, however, if the instrument is retired early and the company pays off the debt with cash? Assume that Bond Corp. decides to retire the convertible debt early and offers the bondholders $1,070,000 cash, which is the fair value of the instrument at the time of early retirement. The following journal entry would be booked:

$$
\begin{aligned}
A &= L + SE \\
-15,000 &= -972,476 + 957,476
\end{aligned}
$$

Cash flows: ↓ 15,000 outflow

Bonds Payable	972,476	
Loss on Redemption of Bond	8,986	
Contributed Surplus—Conversion Rights	75,939	
Retained Earnings	12,599	
Cash		1,070,000

$$A = L + SE$$
$$-1,070,000 \quad -972,476 \quad -97,524$$

Cash flows: ↓ 1,070,000 outflow

The amounts related to the instrument (including the bonds payable, any remaining discount, and the contributed surplus) are zeroed out and the loss is allocated between the debt portion and the equity portion. The portion allocated to the debt is the same as the amount in the previous example (that is, the difference between the debt's carrying value and its fair value). If the residual method is used, the rest is allocated to the equity portion. Note that the fair value of $1,070,000 includes the fair value of the bond and the embedded option. The option is also removed from the books as it is seen as settled.

Interest, Dividends, Gains, and Losses

Once the determination is made to classify something on the SFP as debt, equity, or part debt and part equity, the related interest, dividends, gains, and losses must be consistently treated. For instance, a term preferred share would be presented as a liability and, therefore, related dividends would be booked as interest or dividend expense and charged to the income statement (not to Retained Earnings).

Underlying Concept

Dividends would normally be debited to Retained Earnings; however, because the economic substance of a term preferred share is debt, dividends on term preferred shares are treated as interest or dividend expense.

SHARE-BASED COMPENSATION

Thus far, we have covered off several instances in previous chapters where shares and other equity instruments are used as compensation (instead of cash); for instance, when purchasing inventory and fixed assets. This section focuses on stock compensation plans that remunerate or compensate employees for services provided.

It is generally agreed that effective compensation programs:

1. Motivate employees to high levels of performance
2. Help retain executives and recruit new talent
3. Base compensation on employee and company performance
4. Maximize the employee's after-tax benefit and minimize the employer's after-tax cost
5. Use performance criteria that the employee can control

Although straightforward cash compensation plans (salary and, perhaps, a bonus) are an important part of any compensation program, they are oriented to the short term. Many companies recognize that a more long-run compensation plan is often needed in addition to cash.

Finance

Long-term compensation plans aim to develop a strong loyalty toward the company. An effective way to do this is to give the employees an equity interest based on changes in their company's long-term measures, such as increases in earnings per share, revenues, share price, or market share. These plans come in many different forms. Essentially, they provide the executive or employee with the opportunity to receive shares or cash in the future if the company's performance is satisfactory. Stock-based compensation plans also help companies conserve cash. When they are used, the company does not expend any cash. In fact, if options are used to compensate employees, the employees actually pay cash into the company when they exercise the option. Start-up companies find this very useful since they are often cash-poor in that early phase.

Types of Plans

Many different types of plans are used to compensate employees and especially management. In all these plans, the reward amount depends on future events. Consequently, continued employment is a necessary element in almost all types of plans. The popularity of a particular plan usually depends on prospects in the stock market and tax considerations. For example, if it appears that appreciation will occur in a company's shares, a plan that offers the option to purchase shares is attractive to an executive.

Conversely, if it appears that price appreciation is unlikely, then compensation might be tied to some performance measure such as an increase in book value or earnings per share.

Four common compensation plans that illustrate different objectives are:

1. Compensatory stock option plans (CSOPs)

2. Direct awards of stock

3. Stock appreciation rights plans (SARs)

4. Performance-type plans

The main accounting issues relate to recognition of the plan (determining when the cost of the plan should be recognized) and measurement (determining how the cost should be measured). SARs and performance-type plans will be discussed in Appendix 16B.

Stock Options Revisited

Before looking at the accounting for employee stock option plans, it is useful to revisit the earlier discussion about options in this chapter. So far, options have been discussed in the following contexts:

1. as derivatives, used to manage risk (hedge or speculation) and

2. as debt with detachable warrants (options), used as sweeteners with bonds to access pools of capital and reduce the cost of capital.

The above instruments are sometimes **exchange-traded options**; that is, they trade on an options or stock exchange. Companies also use stock options for the following reasons:

1. To **give employees an opportunity to own part of the company**, with the issue being made to a wide group of people (such as all employees). Another benefit of these plans if they are widely subscribed to is that the company raises cash. These are generally called **employee stock option or purchase plans (ESOPs)**.

2. To **remunerate management or employees.** These are called **compensatory stock option plans (CSOPs).**

3. As **compensation in a particular purchase or acquisition transaction,** with the stock options being provided instead of paying cash or another asset, or incurring a liability. For instance, a company might buy another company and pay for the investment with stock options. These are valued at fair value. The accounting is similar to the accounting covered in Chapter 10 under acquisition of assets upon issuance of shares.

Illustration 16-9 reviews the different types of options and option plans. Note that ESOPs and CSOPs are generally not traded on an exchange. As a result, the fair value cannot be measured as readily.

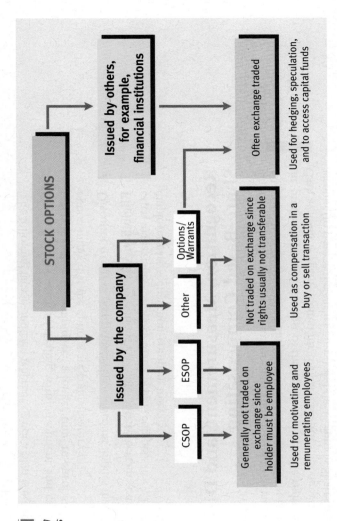

Illustration 16-9

Different Ways of Using Options

What is the difference between ESOPs and CSOPs in terms of accounting? The answer has to do with the underlying nature of the transaction. The main difference between the two plans is that with ESOPs, the employee usually pays for the options (either fully or partially). Thus these transactions are seen as **capital** transactions (charged to equity accounts). The employee is investing in the company. CSOPs, on the other hand, are primarily seen as an **alternative way to compensate** the employees for their services, like a barter transaction. The services are rendered by the employee in the act of producing revenues. This information must be recognized on the income statement as an operating transaction (expensed).

Illustration 16-10 summarizes the difference between CSOPs and non-compensatory plans, or ESOPs.

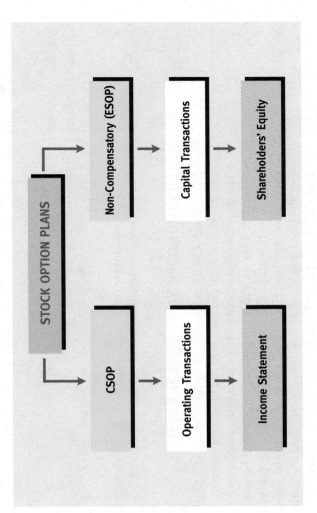

Illustration 16-10

Compensatory versus Non-Compensatory Plans

The following factors indicate whether or not a plan is compensatory:

1. **Option terms** (such as dealing with enrolment and cancellation): Non-standard terms that give the employees a longer time to enrol and the ability to cancel the option imply that the options are compensatory.

2. **Discount from market price:** A large discount implies that the plan is compensatory.[32]

3. **Eligibility:** Making options available only to certain restricted groups of employees, often management, implies that a plan is compensatory. Plans that are available to all employees are seen as non-compensatory.[33]

Recognition, Measurement, and Disclosure of Share-Based Compensation

Objective **6**

Describe the accounting for share-based compensation.

Under an ESOP, when an option or share right is sold to an employee, the Cash account is debited and the Contributed Surplus or other equity account is credited for the amount of the premium (that is, the cost of the option). When the right or option is exercised, the Cash account is again debited for the exercise price, along with the Contributed Surplus account (to reverse the earlier entry) and the Common Shares account is credited to show the issuance of the shares.

To illustrate, assume that Fanco Limited set up an ESOP that gives employees the option to purchase company shares for $10 per share. The option premium cost is $1 per share and Fanco has set aside 10,000 shares. On January 1, 2014, employees purchase 6,000 options for $6,000. The journal entry is as follows:

Cash	6,000	
Contributed Surplus—Stock Options		6,000

A = L + SE
+6,000 +6,000
Cash flows: ↑ 6,000 inflow

Subsequently, all 6,000 options are exercised, resulting in 6,000 shares being issued. The journal entry is as follows:

Cash	60,000	
Contributed Surplus—Stock Options	6,000	
Common Shares		66,000

A = L + SE
+60,000 +60,000
Cash flows: ↑ 60,000 inflow

If the options are never exercised, any funds that were received by the company on the sale of the options would remain in Contributed Surplus.

Compensatory Stock Option Plans

Even though CSOPs do not usually involve a transfer of cash when the options are first granted, they are still recognized in the financial statements and measured at fair value.[34] The transaction has economic value since many employees accept the stock options in lieu of salary or a bonus. When the options are granted, the employees presumably are motivated to work harder. The economic value lies in the potential for future gain when the options are exercised. How should the fair value of the transaction be measured? Recall that an option gets its value from two components: the intrinsic value component and a time value component. While the intrinsic value may be easy to measure (the shares' fair value less the exercise price), the time value component is more difficult to measure. Even though it is difficult to value the stock options themselves, it is even more difficult to value the services rendered by the employees.

The compensation cost that arises from employee stock options should be recognized as the services are being provided.[35]

Determining Expense. The total compensation expense is calculated on the date when the options are granted to the employee (**the grant date**) and is based on the fair value of the options that are expected to vest.[36] The grant date is the date when the employee and company agree on the value of what is to be exchanged. **The grant date is therefore the measurement date.** Fair value for public companies is estimated using market prices, and if not available, using a valuation technique (for example, an options pricing model). No adjustments are made after the grant date for any subsequent changes in the share price, either up or down. The options pricing model incorporates several input measures:

1. The exercise price

2. The expected life of the option

3. The current market price of the underlying stock

4. The volatility of the underlying stock

5. The expected dividend during the option life

6. The risk-free rate of interest for the option life

The **measurement date** may be later for plans that have variable terms (that is, if the number of shares and/or option price are not known) that depend on events after the date of grant. For such variable plans, the compensation expense may have to be estimated based on assumptions about the final number of shares and the option price (usually at the exercise date).

Allocating Compensation Expense. In general, compensation expense is recognized in the periods in which the employee performs the service (the **service period**). Unless something different is specified, the service period is the **vesting period**: the time between the grant date and the vesting date. Thus, the total compensation cost is determined at the grant date and allocated to the periods that benefit from the employee services. Illustration 16-11 presents the relevant dates and time frames.

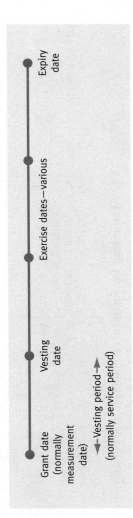

Key Dates in Accounting for Stock Option Plans

To illustrate the accounting for a stock option plan, assume that on November 1, 2014, the shareholders of Chen Corp. approve a plan that grants options to the company's five executives to purchase 2,000 shares each of the company's common shares. The options are granted on January 1, 2015, and may be exercised at any time after December 31, 2016. The exercise price per share is $60.

To keep this illustration simple, we will assume that the fair value, as determined using an options pricing model, results in a total compensation expense of $220,000. The following section discusses the recognition of compensation expense at various dates.

1. **Grant date:** Recall that the option's value is recognized as an expense in the periods in which the employee performs services. In the case of Chen Corp., assume that the documents that are associated with the issuance of the options indicate that the

expected period of benefit/service is two years, starting on the grant date. The journal entries to record the transactions related to this option are as follows:

January 1, 2015

No entry

A = L + SE
0

Cash flows: No effect

December 31, 2015

| Compensation Expense | 110,000 | |
| Contributed Surplus—Stock Options ($220,000 ÷ 2) | | 110,000 |

A = L + SE
0

Cash flows: No effect

December 31, 2016

| Compensation Expense | 110,000 | |
| Contributed Surplus—Stock Options | | 110,000 |

The compensation expense is allocated evenly over the two-year service period, assuming that equal service is provided during the entire period.

2. **Exercise date:** If 20% or 2,000 of the 10,000 options were exercised on June 1, 2018 (three years and five months after date of grant), the following journal entry would be recorded:

June 1, 2018

Cash (2,000 × $60)	120,000	
Contributed Surplus—Stock Options (20% × $220,000)	44,000	
Common Shares		164,000

A = L + SE
+120,000　+120,000

Cash flows: ↑ 120,000 inflow

3. **Expiration:** If the remaining stock options are not exercised before their expiration date, the balance in the Contributed Surplus account would remain. If the company kept several Contributed Surplus accounts, the balance would be shifted to a specific Contributed Surplus account that is used for options that have expired. The entry to record this transaction at the date of expiration is:

Contributed Surplus—Stock Options	176,000	
Contributed Surplus—Expired Stock Options		176,000
(80% × $220,000)		

A = L + SE
0

Cash flows: No effect

4. **Accounting for forfeitures:** The fact that a stock option is not exercised does not make it incorrect to record the costs of the services received from executives that have been attributed to the stock option plan. However, if a stock option is forfeited because an employee fails to satisfy a service requirement (for instance, if the employee leaves the company), the estimate of the compensation expense that has been recorded should be adjusted as a change in estimate (credit Compensation Expense and debit Contributed Surplus). ASPE allows a choice: either estimate forfeitures up front or account for them as they occur. IFRS requires the former treatment. If estimated up front, the entity will likely have to adjust subsequently to reflect the actual number of options forfeited.[37]

Direct Awards of Stock

Stock may be awarded directly as compensation for services provided by an employee. This type of transaction is more broadly known as a **nonmonetary reciprocal transaction**. The transaction is nonmonetary because it involves little or no cash, and it is reciprocal because it is a two-way transaction. The company gives something up (shares) and gets something in return (the employee's services).

Almost all **business** transactions are reciprocal. As a **nonmonetary** transaction, direct awards of stock are recorded at the fair value of the item that is given up (the stock).[38] For instance, instead of paying a cash salary, the company may offer company shares as remuneration. This would be recorded as salary expense at the shares' fair value. The value of the shares is used because it is difficult to value the services provided.

Companies whose shares are traded on stock exchanges are able to measure the value of the options more readily since they can measure volatility. Private companies, however, do not have volatility measures yet must nonetheless attempt to measure it.

Private companies have another issue. If they issue CSOPs to their employees, how do the employees realize the value? If an employee exercises the option and buys the shares, there is no ready market in which to sell the shares and the value is therefore locked in. Often private companies will offer to buy back the shares from the employee. If the company has a policy and past practice of repurchasing the shares, does this create a liability? This requires professional judgement but a good argument may be made for recognizing a liability instead of equity. In other words, the past practice of repurchasing the shares and the probability that this will be done again (since the employees cannot sell the shares elsewhere) support the recognition of a liability. The company in substance has an obligation to the employee.[39] The liability would have to be remeasured on an ongoing basis with the difference being charged to income as compensation expense.

Most CSOPs are equity settled; that is, they will be settled by issuing shares to the employee. Sometimes, the CSOPs are cash settled or there is a choice between cash and equity. This will be addressed in Appendix 16B.

Disclosure of Compensation Plans

Full disclosure should be made of the following:

- The accounting policy that is being used
- A description of the plans and modifications
- Details of the numbers and values of the options issued, exercised, forfeited, and expired
- A description of the assumptions and methods being used to determine fair values
- The total compensation cost included in net income and contributed surplus
- Other[40]

IFRS/ASPE COMPARISON

Objective 7

Identify the major differences in accounting between ASPE and IFRS, and what changes are expected in the near future.

Many complex financial instruments exist and must be accounted for in the company's financial statements. It is important to understand the nature of the instruments from an economic perspective: why would the company issue this type of instrument and why would an investor invest in it? It is also important to understand what creates the instrument's value. This will help in understanding the economic substance of the instrument. The accounting issues relate to presentation (determining if it is debt or equity, or both) and measurement.

Derivatives have been the focus of some very negative publicity in the past few years with companies suffering significant losses and perhaps even going bankrupt due to derivative instruments. This is partially due to the complexity of these contracts and the fact that they are not well understood by many who use them.

Do complex accounting standards add any value in the capital marketplace? They certainly add to the costs of preparing financial statements. Accountants in industry must stay up to date on these standards, as must the auditors. There is a very real risk that investors and creditors do not understand the standards and perhaps may not even have the educational background that is required to be able to work through the complexities.

A Comparison of IFRS and ASPE

Illustration 16-12 compares IFRS with ASPE for complex financial instruments, providing additional information relative to the information included in the comparison illustrations in Chapters 14 and 15.

	Accounting Standards for Private Enterprises (ASPE)—CICA Handbook, Part II, Sections 3856 and 3870	IFRS—IAS 32, 39, and IFRS 2	References to Related Illustrations and Select Brief Exercises
Presentation – Purchase commitments	Accounted for as executory contracts since not exchange traded.	Accounted for as executory contracts unless the contracts allow for net settlement and the entity does not expect to take delivery of the inventory (in which case they are treated as derivatives).	BE 16-2
– Own equity instruments	Less detailed guidance is provided under ASPE. Consider the basic definitions of financial liability and equity. If the definition of a liability is not met, then the instrument is presented as equity.	The definitions of financial liabilities and equity instruments include references to instruments settled in the entity's own instruments. As a general rule, the instrument is equity only if it **will be** settled by issuing a fixed number of shares **and** there is no contractual obligation.	For most instruments this will be the same treatment. More complex scenarios are beyond the scope of the text.
– Certain puttable shares	Treated as equity if certain criteria are met including under certain tax planning arrangements. The criteria establish whether the instruments are "in-substance" equity instruments. This was also discussed in Chapter 15.	Treated as equity if certain criteria are met. No special treatment for certain tax planning arrangements. The criteria establish whether the instruments are "in-substance" equity instruments. This was also discussed in Chapter 15.	BE 16-15
Recognition – Hybrid/compound instruments with contingent settlement provisions	Instruments with contingent settlement provisions are financial liabilities if the contingency is highly likely to occur.	Instruments with contingent settlement provisions represent liabilities where the contingency is outside the control of the issuer.	BE 16-16
Measurement – Components of compound instruments	May measure the equity component at $0. Alternatively, measure the component that is most easily measurable and apply the residual to the other component. Where a financial liability is indexed to the entity's financial performance or changes in equity, it is measured at the higher of the amortized cost and the amount owing at the balance sheet date given the index feature.	Always measure the debt component first (generally at the present value of the cash flows). The rest of the value is assigned to equity since it is a residual item. A financial liability that is indexed to the entity's financial performance or changes in equity would be analyzed to determine if an embedded derivative exists. Embedded derivatives are beyond the scope of the text.	Illustration 16-8 BE 16-10 and BE 16-11

(continued)

	Accounting Standards for Private Enterprises (ASPE)—*CICA Handbook*, Part II, Sections 3856 and 3870	IFRS—IAS 32, 39, and IFRS 2	References to Related Illustrations and Select Brief Exercises
– CSOP when using an options pricing model	Allowed to value the entire financial instruments at fair value under the fair value option.	Allowed to value the entire financial instruments at fair value under the fair value option as long as certain conditions are met.	Illustration 14-10
	Volatility is not readily available for private entities but an attempt must be made to measure. May choose whether to recognize forfeitures up front or later.	Volatility generally measurable. Must estimate forfeitures up front.	No difference as long as recognize forfeitures upfront under ASPE.
Presentation – Equity settled CSOP for private entities	Generally presented as equity although history of repurchasing the shares after the employee has exercised the CSOP may indicate that the CSOP is a liability.	N/A	N/A
Recognition and measurement – Hedge accounting (Appendix 16A)	Does not specify accounting for fair value hedges or cash flow hedges. Instead, the standard lists certain types of specific hedging transactions that may qualify for hedge accounting including hedges of anticipated transactions and hedges of interest-bearing assets and liabilities. Hedge accounting generally stipulates that the hedging item is not recognized until it is settled (using accrual accounting).	Specifies fair value hedges and cash flow hedges. Under fair value hedge accounting, the hedged item is valued at fair value with gains and losses booked through income. Under cash flow hedge accounting, the gains and losses on the hedging item are booked through OCI and may be recycled to income when the hedged item is booked to net income.	Illustrations 16A-1, 2, 3, 7, 8, 9, and 11
– Accounting for cash-settled and other stock compensation plans (Appendix 16B)	Cash-settled plans such as SARs are measured at intrinsic value. Entities have a choice as to how to measure equity-settled SARs.	Cash-settled plans are measured at fair value (using valuation methods such as options pricing models, which incorporate both intrinsic value and time value). All equity-settled instruments are measured at fair value.	BE 16-20 and BE 16-21

Illustration 16-12

IFRS and ASPE Comparison Chart

Looking Ahead

As previously mentioned in Chapters 14 and 15, the IASB has been working on numerous projects relating to financial instruments. The project on hedging will attempt to ensure that hedge accounting acknowledges how hedges are used to mange risks and the project dealing with the definitions of liabilities versus equity will attempt to encourage more consistent application of the standards. The hedge accounting project has been split into two phases: a general hedge accounting phase and a macro hedging phase. The IASB is in the process of field testing the draft new standards for general hedge accounting and plans to issue a discussion paper on macro hedging in 2013. Many of the proposed changes relating to general hedge accounting are beyond the scope of this text. Fair value and cash flow hedge accounting as presented in this chapter would still apply.

As of the time of writing, the project on liabilities versus equity had been put on hold.

SUMMARY OF LEARNING OBJECTIVES

1 Understand what derivatives are and how they are used to manage risk.

Derivatives are financial instruments that derive (get) their value from an underlying instrument. They are attractive since they transfer risks and rewards without having to necessarily invest directly in the underlying instrument. They are used for both speculative purposes (to expose a company to increased risks in the hope of increased returns) and for hedging purposes (to reduce existing risk).

Financial risks include credit, currency, interest rate, liquidity, market, and other price risks. Credit risk is the risk that the other party to a financial instrument contract will fail to deliver. Currency and interest rate risk are the risk of a change in value and cash flows due to currency or interest rate changes. Liquidity risk is the risk that the company itself will not be able to honour the contract due to cash problems. Finally, market risk is the risk of a change in value and/or cash flows related to market forces.

2 Understand how to account for derivatives.

Derivatives are recognized on the SFP on the date that the contract is initiated. They are remeasured, on each SFP date, to their fair value. The related gains and losses are recorded through net income. Written options create liabilities. Futures contracts require the company to deposit a portion of the contracts' value with the broker/exchange. The contracts are marked to market by the broker/exchange daily and the company may have to deposit additional funds to cover deficiencies in the margin account. Purchase commitments that are net settleable and are not "expected use" contracts are accounted for as derivatives under IFRS. Under ASPE, purchase commitments are never accounted for as derivatives because they are not exchange-traded futures contracts. Exchange-traded derivatives relating to commodities are generally accounted for as derivatives under ASPE. Special hedge accounting may affect how derivatives are accounted for.

Under IFRS, derivatives that are settleable in the entity's own equity instruments are accounted for as equity (or contra-equity) if they will be settled by exchanging a fixed amount of equity instruments for a fixed amount of cash or other assets and they do not create an obligation to deliver cash or other assets. Otherwise, they are financial assets/liabilities. In general, if the instruments are net settleable or have settlement options, they most often do not

meet the criteria for equity presentation and are therefore financial assets/liabilities. IFRS provides significantly more guidance with respect to the accounting for these instruments.

3 Analyze whether a hybrid/compound instrument issued for financing purposes represents a liability, equity, or both.

Complex instruments include compound and hybrid instruments where the legal form may differ from the economic substance. The economic substance dictates the accounting. The main issue is that of presentation: should the instrument be presented as debt or equity? The definitions of debt and equity are useful in analyzing this. It is also important to understand what gives the instruments their value from a finance or economic perspective. If an instrument has both debt and equity components, use of the proportional and incremental methods will help in allocating the carrying value between the two components. There are differences in measuring compound financial instruments under IFRS versus ASPE. Related interest, dividends, gains, and losses are treated in a way that is consistent with the SFP presentation.

4 Explain the accounting for hybrid/compound instruments.

The method for recording convertible bonds at the date of issuance is different from the method that is used to record straight debt issues. As the instrument is a compound instrument and contains both debt and equity components, these must be measured separately and presented as debt and equity, respectively. Any discount or premium that results from the issuance of convertible bonds is amortized, assuming the bonds will be held to maturity. If bonds are converted into other securities, the principal accounting problem is to determine the amount at which to record the securities that have been exchanged for the bond. The book value method is often used in practice. ASPE allows an entity to value the equity portion of compound instruments at $0.

5 Describe the various types of stock compensation plans.

Stock compensation includes direct awards of stock (when a company gives the shares to an employee as compensation), compensatory stock option plans whereby an employee is given stock options in lieu of salary, share appreciation rights (SARs), and performance-type plans. SARs and performance-type plans are discussed in Appendix 16B.

Employee stock option plans are meant to motivate employees and raise capital for the company. They are therefore capital transactions. Compensatory stock option plans are operating transactions since they are meant to compensate the employee for service provided.

6 Describe the accounting for share-based compensation.

CSOPs and direct awards of stock are measured at fair value (using an options pricing model) at the grant date. The cost is then allocated to expense over the period that the employee provides service.

As noted above, SARs and performance-type plans are discussed in Appendix 16B.

7 Identify the major differences in accounting between ASPE and IFRS, and what changes are expected in the near future.

The differences are noted in the comparison chart. The stock-based compensation standards are largely converged and stable; however, the IASB is currently working on several projects relating to financial instruments including defining equity versus liabilities and hedging.

KEY TERMS

APPENDIX 16A

HEDGING

Derivatives Used for Hedging and the Need for Hedge Accounting Standards

Objective 8
Understand how derivatives are used in hedging and explain the need for hedge accounting standards.

In the body of the chapter, we discussed basic issues related to derivatives. This appendix will focus on the **accounting for hedging**. How does hedging actually reduce risk from an economic perspective and what are the accounting implications?

Companies that are already exposed to financial risks because of existing business transactions that arise from their business models may choose to protect themselves by managing and reducing those risks. For example, most public companies borrow and lend substantial amounts in credit markets and are therefore exposed to significant financial risks. They face substantial risk that the fair values or cash flows of interest-sensitive assets or liabilities will change if interest rates increase or decrease (known as **interest rate risk**).

These same companies often also have cross-border transactions or international operations that expose them to **exchange rate risk**. The borrowing activity creates **liquidity risk** for the company and the lending activity creates credit risk.

Because the value and/or cash flows of derivative financial instruments can vary according to changes in interest rates, foreign currency exchange rates, or other external factors, derivatives may be used to offset the associated risks. Using derivatives or other instruments to offset risks is called **hedging**. In a hedging relationship, there is a **hedged item** (the risk or exposure) and a hedging item (often a derivative contract entered into to reduce risk). A properly hedged position should result in no economic loss to the company. It may result in no gain, and there may be costs involved to effect the transactions, but it should limit or eliminate any potential losses. It reduces uncertainty and risk, and therefore volatility, and that is what gives hedging its value.

It is important to separate the **act of hedging** to reduce economic and financial risks from the **accounting** for these hedges. Hedge accounting is optional and in some cases not even necessary. A company may choose to apply it or not. It is an accounting policy choice.

Why do we need special accounting rules for hedges? They exist in part due to our **mixed measurement model** (fair value, amortized cost, and cost) and the **treatment of the related gains and losses where fair value is used**. They also exist because sometimes we **need to hedge future transactions that are not yet recognized on the SFP.**

Symmetry in Accounting—No Need for Special Hedge Accounting

Consider the situation where a company has a U.S. $100 receivable that is due in 30 days. The company is exposed to a **foreign currency risk.** Each time the currency rate changes, the economic value of the asset changes. Under existing IFRS and ASPE at each SFP date, we revalue the asset to reflect the current spot rate for the U.S. dollar. If the U.S. dollar depreciates against the Canadian dollar, the receivable is worth less and the resulting loss gets booked to the income statement. Now let's assume that the company does not want this foreign currency exposure (the hedged item) and it enters into a forward contract (the hedging item) to sell U.S. dollars for $102 Canadian in 30 days. This provides an **effective (economic) hedge** against changes in the value of the asset. If the U.S. dollar subsequently depreciates in value, then the forward contract increases in value because, under the contract, we can still sell the U.S. $100 for $102 Canadian no matter what happens to the exchange rate. From an **economic perspective,** the gains on the forward offset the losses on the receivable. From an **accounting perspective,** this gain gets booked to the income statement and thus offsets the loss on the receivable. In this case, because the losses on the receivable offset the gains on the forward, **no special hedge accounting is needed.**

No Symmetry in Accounting—Potential Need for Special Hedge Accounting

If instead, the company had an investment in a security classified as fair value through other comprehensive income, losses due to decreases in the value of the security would be booked to Other Comprehensive Income. Suppose the company decided to purchase an option (the hedging item) to sell the security at a fixed price. This would protect it against future declines in value of the shares (the hedged item) and would therefore be an effective (economic) hedge against future losses. If the value of the shares declined, the value of the option to sell at a set price would increase, resulting in a gain. This gain would normally be booked to net income since the option is a derivative. In this case, even though the gains and losses offset from an economic perspective, there is asymmetry in the accounting because the loss is booked to Other Comprehensive Income and the gain to net income. The company needs to decide whether it wants to use hedge accounting to ensure that the gains and losses will offset in net income. The journal entries for this example will be looked at later in this appendix.

Finance

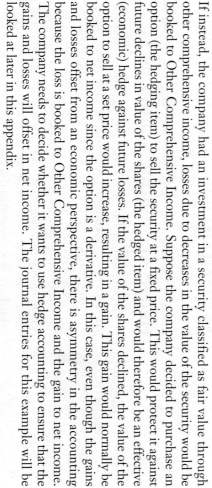

Underlying Concept

Using hedge accounting increases transparency—reflecting the decrease in income volatility where the company has hedged its positions.

Hedge Accounting

Objective 9
Understand how to apply hedge accounting standards.

Hedge accounting is optional and modifies the normal accounting. It is designed to ensure that the timing of the recognition of gains/losses in net income is the same for both the hedged item and the hedging item, it will result in recognition and measurement that is different than under pre-hedge accounting GAAP. Thus, it is important to ensure that the hedge is effective and properly identified and documented in order to allow it to qualify for special treatment. Hedges may qualify for optional hedge accounting when the following criteria are met.[41]

1. At the inception of the hedge, the entity must do the following:

   (a) **Identify** the exposure (such as exposure to foreign exchange fluctuations).

   (b) **Designate** that hedge accounting will be applied.

   (c) **Document** the risk management objectives and strategies, the hedging relationship, the items being hedged and used to hedge, the methods of assessing the effectiveness of the hedge, and the method of accounting for the hedge.

2. At the inception and throughout the term, the entity should have reasonable assurance that the relationship is **effective and consistent with the risk management policy.** As a result, all of the following must be respected:

   (a) The effectiveness of the hedge should be reliably measurable.[42]

   (b) The hedging relationship should be reassessed regularly.

   (c) Where the hedge involves forecasted transactions, it should be probable that these transactions will occur.

Under ASPE, hedge accounting is greatly simplified, with only certain pre-specified transactions qualifying for optional hedge accounting treatment. These include anticipated purchase/sale of a commodity hedged with a forward contract, anticipated foreign exchange denominated transactions hedged with a forward contract, interest-bearing assets/liabilities hedged with interest rate or cross currency swaps, and net investments in a foreign subsidiary.

Under IFRS, hedge accounting divides hedges into two basic groups: fair value hedges and cash flow hedges. **Fair value hedge** accounting is used to account for hedges of exposures relating to recognized assets/liabilities and unrecognized purchase commitments. **Cash flow hedge** accounting is used to account for hedges of exposures relating to future cash flows such as future interest payments on variable rate debt. Each will be discussed below.

Fair Value Hedges

A derivative may be used to hedge or offset the exposure to changes in the fair value of a recognized asset or liability (or of a previously unrecognized firm commitment),[43] and thus reduce market (price) risk.[44] In a perfectly hedged position, the economic gain/loss on the fair value of the derivative (the hedging item) and that of the hedged asset or liability (the hedged item) should be equal and offsetting. Hedge accounting modifies the current accounting. Under fair value hedge accounting, the hedged item must be recognized on the SFP and measured (or remeasured) at fair value and the related gains/losses must be booked through net income. So for instance, if the asset was normally measured at cost, it would have to be remeasured to fair value under hedge accounting. In addition, if the gains/losses were normally booked through OCI, a journal entry would be booked to reclassify them to net income under hedge accounting.

A typical fair value hedge is the use of **put options** (options to sell an investment at a pre-set price) or a forward contract (to sell the investment at a pre-set price) to hedge the risk that an investment will decline in value. Let's look at an example.

Using Hedge Accounting—Recognized Assets as Hedged Items.

To illustrate, assume that Pathay Inc. purchases an investment for $1,000. This exposes the company to a market risk—the risk that the shares will decline in value. The shares trade on a local stock exchange. Assume further that the investment is designated as fair value through other comprehensive Income (FV-OCI) under IFRS and therefore it will be carried at its fair value, with gains and losses normally being booked through Other Comprehensive Income. Under ASPE, the shares are accounted for as FV-NI investments since there is an active market. Illustration 16A-1 shows the journal entries to record the initial investment at January 1, 2015:

Illustration 16A-1

Acquisition of Investment

	IFRS		ASPE	
FV-OCI Investments	1,000			
FV-NI Investments			1000	
Cash		1,000		1,000

A = L + SE
0   0

Cash flows: ↓ 1,000 outflow

Assume that on the same date, the company also enters into a derivative contract in which it purchases an option to sell the shares at $1,000 to protect itself against losses in value of the security. The cost of the option is $10. If the value of the shares declines, the company can sell the shares under the option for $1,000—thus limiting any loss. As a derivative, the option will be measured at fair value, with subsequent gains and losses booked to net income. Illustration 16A-2 shows the journal entry.

Illustration 16A-2

Acquisition of Derivative Contract to Hedge Market Risk

	IFRS		ASPE	
Derivatives—Financial Assets/Liabilities	10		10	
Cash		10		10

A = L + SE
0   0

Cash flows: ↓ 10 outflow

If at December 31, 2015, the investment's fair value increased by $50, the derivative would decrease in value by $50. (In actual fact, the loss on the option would not exactly offset the gains on the investment as the value of the option incorporates other variables.) The journal entries to record this are as follows in Illustration 16A-3.

Illustration 16A-3

Recognition of Change in Value of Derivative and Hedge Accounting

	IFRS: optional hedge accounting		ASPE: not eligible for hedge accounting	
FV-OCI Investments	50			
FV-NI Investments			50	
Unrealized Gain or Loss		50		50
Derivatives—Financial Assets/Liabilities	50		50	

A = L + SE
0   0

Cash flows: No effect

As previously mentioned, the derivative is always valued at fair value, with the gains/losses being booked to net income. However, normally the gain on the FV-OCI investment would be booked to Other Comprehensive Income under IFRS. There is therefore a mismatch. Hedge accounting under IFRS allows the gain on the hedged item to be booked through net income so it may be offset by the loss on the derivative as noted in the journal entry above. Hedge accounting allows us to modify the way we would normally account for the FV-OCI investment. This is a fair value hedge under IFRS, since the hedged item is the risk that the value of the investment, which is a recognized asset, will decline. As noted in the illustration, this transaction is not eligible for hedge accounting under ASPE (since it is not on the list of allowable transactions noted earlier). In the end, the impact on net income is the same when we compare the accounting for this transaction under ASPE (without using hedge accounting) and IFRS (using hedge accounting). This is because under ASPE, where OCI does not exist, the accounting is symmetrical and the gains and losses offset without having to apply hedge accounting.

Using Hedge Accounting—Purchase Commitments as Hedged Items.   Assume the company has committed to purchase a certain amount of raw materials at a fixed price denominated in U.S. dollars in order to secure a stable supply of the raw materials. This would create a foreign currency risk as the price is fixed in U.S. dollars, the value of which will vary over time. Normally, a company would not recognize purchase commitments for which it intends to take delivery of the raw materials unless there was a contingent loss that was measurable and probable.[45]

Assume further that the company chooses to hedge the risk by entering into a forward contract to purchase U.S. dollars at a future date at a fixed exchange rate. This would lock in the rate and therefore remove the foreign currency risk. The forward would be recognized on the SFP and measured at fair value, with gains and losses being recorded in net income. If the purchase commitment were not recognized on the SFP, there would be a mismatch. Therefore, per IFRS under hedge accounting, the purchase commitment would also need to be recognized on the SFP and measured at fair value (with gains/losses booked through net income). Since this might be difficult to measure, the entity may choose to account for this under IFRS as a cash flow hedge. As we will see later, this would result in leaving the purchase commitment off-balance sheet and booking any unrealized gains or losses on the forward contract through OCI.

Under ASPE hedge accounting, neither the purchase commitment nor the derivative would be recognized until the goods were delivered and the contracts settled. The raw materials would be measured using the locked in forward exchange rate for the U.S. dollars.

Cash Flow Hedges

A cash flow hedge deals with transactions that offset the effects of future variable cash flows, such as future interest payments on variable rate debt. Because the debt is a variable rate, the interest to be paid out will fluctuate, and this therefore makes future cash flows uncertain. Since the hedged position (that is, the potential change in future interest payments) is not yet recognized on the SFP, the gains/losses related to changes in value (and hence the cash flows) are not captured. Thus, under hedge accounting per IFRS, any gains/losses on the hedging item should not be included in net income either. They are therefore recognized in Other Comprehensive Income.

Recall that under ASPE, the term Other Comprehensive Income is not used. Therefore, hedge accounting under ASPE for these types of transactions essentially requires that the hedging item not be recognized until the transaction is settled. (In other words, it remains off-balance sheet.) The purchase commitment example above illustrates this.

In a cash flow hedge, the company is trying to protect itself against variations in future cash flows. Different derivative instruments may be used to effect this. Let's look at an example.

Using Hedge Accounting—Interest Rate Swaps as Hedging Items.   When a company has a series of similar transactions that it wants to hedge, a **swap contract** may be used. A swap is a transaction between two parties in which the first party promises to make a series of payments to the second party. Similarly, the second party promises to make simultaneous payments to the first party. The parties swap payments. A swap is a series of forward contracts. The most common type of swap is the **interest rate swap**, in which one party makes payments based on a fixed or floating rate and the second party does just the opposite. In most cases, financial institutions and other intermediaries find the two parties, bring them together, and handle the flow of payments between the two parties, as shown in Illustration 16A-4.

To illustrate the accounting for a cash flow hedge, assume that Jones Corporation issues $1 million of five-year, floating-rate bonds on January 2, 2015. The entry to record this transaction is as follows:

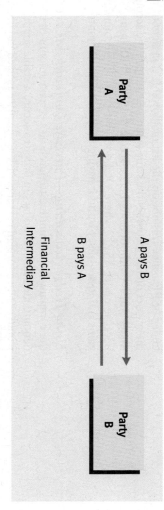

Party A → A pays B → Party B

Party B → B pays A → Party A

Financial Intermediary

	January 2, 2015	
Cash	1,000,000	
Bonds Payable		1,000,000

A floating interest rate was offered to appeal to investors, but Jones is concerned about the cash flow uncertainty associated with the variable rate interest. To protect against the **cash flow uncertainty**, Jones decides to hedge the risk by entering into a five-year interest rate swap. Under the terms of the swap contract, the following will occur:

1. Jones will pay fixed payments at 8% (based on the $1-million amount) to a counterparty.

2. Jones will receive, from the counterparty, variable or floating rates that are based on the market rate in effect throughout the life of the swap contract.

As Illustration 16A-5 shows, by using this swap, Jones can change the interest on the bonds payable from a floating rate to a fixed rate. Jones thus swaps the floating rate, assumed to be 9% in the example, for a fixed rate.

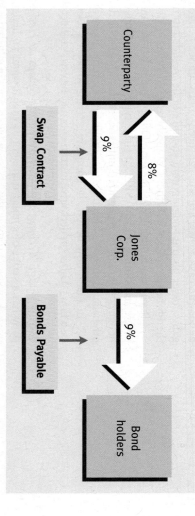

Counterparty

Swap Contract 9% 8%

Jones Corp.

Bonds Payable 9%

Bond holders

The settlement dates for the swap correspond to the interest payment dates on the debt (December 31). On each interest payment (**settlement date**), Jones and the counterparty will calculate the difference between current market interest rates (9% in the example) and the fixed rate of 8%, and settle the difference.[46] Both parties will also need to value the swap contract on each SFP date using a discounted cash flow model. If interest rates rise, the value of the swap contract to Jones increases (Jones has a gain), while at the same time Jones's floating-rate debt obligation becomes larger (Jones has an economic loss). The swap is an effective risk management tool in this setting because its

Finance

%

value is related to the same underlying (interest rates) that will affect the value of the floating-rate bond payable. Thus, if the swap's value goes up, it offsets the loss related to the debt obligation.

Assuming that the swap was entered into on January 2, 2015 (the same date as the issuance of the debt), the swap at this time has no value and there is therefore no need for a journal entry.

January 2, 2015

No entry required. Memorandum to indicate that the swap contract is signed.

At the end of 2015, the interest payment on the bonds is made to the bondholders. Assume the floating rate is 9%. The journal entry to record this transaction is as follows:

December 31, 2015

Interest Expense	90,000	
Cash (9% × $1,000,000)		90,000

A = L + SE
−90,000   −90,000
Cash flows: ↓ 90,000 outflow

At the end of 2015, market interest rates have increased to 9%, and the value of the swap contract has therefore increased. Recall (see Illustration 16A-5) that in the swap Jones is to receive a floating rate of 9%, or $90,000 ($1,000,000 × 9%), and pay a fixed rate of 8%, or $80,000. Jones therefore receives $10,000 ($90,000 − $80,000) as a settlement payment on the swap contract on the first interest payment date. The entry to record this transaction is booked as an interest rate adjustment as follows:

December 31, 2015

Cash	10,000	
Interest Expense		10,000

A = L + SE
+10,000   +10,000
Cash flows: ↑ 10,000 inflow

In addition, assume that the fair value of the interest rate swap has increased by $40,000. This increase in value is recorded as follows:[47]

December 31, 2015

Derivatives—Financial Assets/Liabilities	40,000	
Unrealized Gain or Loss—OCI		40,000

A = L + SE
+40,000   +40,000
Cash flows: No effect

As a derivative, as previously noted, this swap contract is recognized on the SFP, and the gain in fair value is normally reported in net income. Under IFRS hedge accounting, this is a cash flow hedge and the gain on the hedging item (the swap) is reported in Other Comprehensive Income (as opposed to net income). This is because there is asymmetry in the accounting under pre-hedge accounting GAAP. The losses on the bond payable (due to the fact that it is a variable rate loan and interest rates keep rising) do not get recognized because they are opportunity costs. This is a cash flow hedge because it relates to the anticipated changes in interest rates related to the variable rate loan.

The unrealized gain will gradually be reflected in net income when the benefit of the locked-in (lower) interest rate is realized as reduced interest expense, as the earlier entries showed. By the end of the swap contract, the value of the contract will be nil and the company will have recorded net interest expense that reflects the fixed rate. Illustration 16A-6 shows the presentation of a cash flow hedge on the SFP.

Illustration 16A-6

Statement of Financial Position Presentation of Cash Flow Hedge

JONES CORPORATION
Statement of Financial Position (partial)
December 31, 2015

Non-current assets:	
Swap contract	$ 40,000
Long-term liabilities	
Bonds payable	$1,000,000
Equity	
Other comprehensive income	$ 40,000

The effect on the Jones Corporation SFP is the addition of the swap asset. On the income statement, interest expense of $80,000 is reported. Jones has effectively changed the debt's interest rate from variable to fixed. That is, by receiving a floating rate and paying a fixed rate on the swap, the floating rate on the bond payable is converted to variable, which results in an effective interest rate of 8% in 2015. The economic gain on the swap offsets the economic loss related to the debt obligation (since interest rates are higher), and therefore the net gain or loss on the hedging activity is zero. Hedge accounting under IFRS allows us to record the gain or loss on the hedging activity is zero. Hedge accounting under IFRS allows us to record the gain outside of net income since the economic substance is that the risk has been neutralized.

Under ASPE hedge accounting, the swap contract is not recognized on the balance sheet. Instead only the payments/receipts of interest are accrued as interest expense/income adjustments as shown in the journal entries under IFRS.

One last point on interest rate swaps. As noted above, they may be used as cash flow hedges. They may also be used as fair value hedges and be eligible for hedge accounting under both IFRS and ASPE. Interest rate swaps would protect against changes in fair value of a recorded asset or liability that would occur when market interest rates change and where the asset or liability has a fixed interest rate. They can be used to offset fixed interest rate payments on a debt obligation to take advantage of lower interest rates or to offset a decline in the value of a bond investment when market interest rates are increasing. In the previous example, assume instead that the $1,000,000 debt had a fixed interest rate of 8% and that the company was concerned that interest rates were declining. The company decides to enter into a swap contract to protect itself against the risk of further declines in interest rates (and potential increases in the fair value of the liability). Under the swap agreement, the company will receive 8% and pay variable rates. As a derivative (before any hedge accounting), the swap would be recognized on the SFP, re-measured at reporting dates, and gains/losses would be recognized in income. If IFRS hedge accounting were used this would be a fair value hedge because it relates to the risk that the fair value of the fixed-rate liability is increasing due to declining interest rates. Under IFRS fair value hedge accounting, the liability would be revalued to fair value with gains/losses being booked through income so that they offset the gains/losses on the swap. Therefore, if the fair value of the debt decreased by $40,000 (due to increases in interest rates) and the fair value of the swap decreased by a corresponding $40,000, the following entries would be booked:

	December 31, 2015	
Unrealized Gain or Loss	40,000	
Derivative – Financial Assets/Liabilities		40,000
Bonds Payable	40,000	
Unrealized Gain or Loss		40,000

A	=	L	+	SE
−40,000		−40,000		

Cash flows: No effect

Under ASPE hedge accounting, these journal entries would not be booked and as noted earlier, only the payments/receipts of interest would be booked. Interestingly, while the swap contract eliminates **risk** created by fixed interest rates, it exposes the company to

cash flow risk. Financial instruments are bundles of different types of risks. A company must choose which risks, if any, it wants to eliminate, and always keep in mind that the hedging instrument may carry new risks.

Using Hedge Accounting—Anticipated Purchases as Hedged Items. Another example of a cash flow hedge is a hedge of an anticipated future transaction, such as a raw material purchase.

To illustrate the accounting for cash flow hedges under IFRS, assume that in September 2015, Allied Can Co. anticipates purchasing 1,000 metric tonnes of aluminum in January 2016. Allied is concerned that prices for aluminum will increase in the next few months, and it wants to protect against possible price increases for aluminum inventory. To hedge the risk that it might have to pay for higher prices for inventory in January 2016, Allied enters into a cash-settled aluminum forward contract.

The contract requires Allied to pay any difference between $1,550 per tonne and the spot price for aluminum, if lower, to the counterparty. If the price of aluminum increases, the counterparty will make a payment for the difference to Allied.[48] The contract matures on the expected purchase date in January 2016. The underlying for this derivative is the price of aluminum. If the price of aluminum rises above $1,550, the value of the contract to Allied increases because Allied will be able to purchase the aluminum at the lower price of $1,550 per tonne.

Assume that the contract was entered into on September 1, 2015, and that the price to be paid today for inventory to be delivered in January, the forward price, was equal to the current spot price adjusted for the time between September and January. On a net present value basis, the fair value of this contract will be zero. Therefore no entry is necessary.

September 1, 2015

No entry required. Memorandum to indicate that the contract is signed.

Assume that at December 31, 2015, the price for January delivery of aluminum has increased. The fair value of the contract has therefore also increased, with its value now assumed to be $25,000. Allied would make the following entry as shown in Illustration 16A-7 to record this increase in the value of the forward contract.

	IFRS: optional hedge accounting	ASPE: optional hedge accounting
Derivatives—Financial Assets/Liabilities	25,000	N/A
Unrealized Gain or Loss—OCI	25,000	N/A

The derivative contract is reported on the SFP as an asset. The gain on the contract would normally be recorded through net income. However, under IFRS hedge accounting, it is reported as part of Other Comprehensive Income. Since Allied has not yet purchased and sold the inventory, this is an anticipated transaction. In this type of transaction, gains or losses on the futures contract are accumulated in equity as part of Other Comprehensive Income until the period in which the inventory is sold and earnings is affected.

Under ASPE hedge accounting, the derivative contract would not be recognized until it is settled (when the inventory is recognized). The gain/loss would be recorded as an adjustment to inventory.

Assume now that in January 2016, Allied purchases (separately) 1,000 metric tonnes of aluminum for $1,575. It would make the following entry as shown in Illustration 16A-8.

Illustration 16A-7

Change in Value of Derivative Contract

$$A = L + SE$$
$$+25,000 \quad\quad +25,000$$

Cash flows: No effect

Illustration 16A-8
Acquisition of Inventory

	IFRS: optional hedge accounting	ASPE: optional hedge accounting
Inventory ($1,575 × 1,000 tonnes)	1,575,000	1,575,000
Cash	1,575,000	1,575,000

A = L + SE
0

Cash flows: ↓ 1,575,000 outflow

At the same time, Allied makes final settlement on the derivative contract and makes the following entry as shown in Illustration 16A-9.

Illustration 16A-9
Settlement of Derivative Contract

	IFRS: optional hedge accounting	ASPE: optional hedge accounting
Cash	25,000	25,000
Derivatives—Financial Assets/Liabilities ($1,575,000 − $1,550,000)	25,000	25,000
Inventory		

A = L + SE
0

Cash flows: ↑ 25,000 inflow

Through use of the derivative contract, Allied has been able to fix the cost of its inventory. The $25,000 contract settlement payment offsets the amount paid to purchase the inventory at the prevailing market price of $1,575,000. The result is that the net cash outflow is at $1,550 per metric tonne, as desired. In this way, Allied has hedged the cash flow for the purchase of inventory, as shown in Illustration 16A-10.

Illustration 16A-10
Effect of Hedge on Cash Flows

Anticipated Cash Flows
Wish to fix cash paid
for inventory at $1,550,000

=

Actual Cash Flows
Actual cash paid	$1,575,000
Less: Cash received on future contract	(25,000)
Final cash paid	$1,550,000

There are no income effects at this point. The gain on the futures contract is accumulated in equity as part of Accumulated Other Comprehensive Income under IFRS until the period when the inventory is sold and earnings is affected through cost of goods sold.

For example, assume that the aluminum is processed into cans, the finished goods. The total cost of the cans (including the aluminum purchases in January 2016) is $1.7 million. Allied sells the cans in July 2016 for $2 million. The entry to record the sale is as follows in Illustration 16A-11.

Illustration 16A-11
Recognition of Sale of Finished Goods

	IFRS: optional hedge accounting		ASPE: optional hedge accounting	
Cash	2,000,000		2,000,000	
Sales Revenue		2,000,000		2,000,000
Cost of Goods Sold	1,700,000		1,675,000	
Inventory		1,700,000		1,675,000
Unrealized Gain or Loss—OCI	25,000		N/A	
Cost of Goods Sold		25,000		N/A

IFRS
A = L + SE
+300,000 +300,000

Cash flows: ↑ 2,000,000 inflow

ASPE
A = L + SE
+325,000 +325,000

Cash flows: ↑ 2,000,000 inflow

The gain on the futures contract, which was reported as part of Other Comprehensive Income, now reduces the cost of goods sold. As a result, the cost of aluminum included in the overall cost of goods sold is $1,550,000. The derivative contract has worked as planned to manage the cash paid for aluminum inventory and the amount of cost of goods sold. Note that under IFRS, this entry could also be made at the date when the inventory was acquired, except that the credit would be booked to Inventory. Thus, the cost of goods sold in July 2016 would be $1,675,000 (versus $1,700,000).

SUMMARY OF LEARNING OBJECTIVES FOR APPENDIX 16A

8 Understand how derivatives are used in hedging and explain the need for hedge accounting standards.

Any company or individual that wants to protect itself against different types of business risk often uses derivative contracts to achieve this objective. In general, where the intent is to manage and reduce risk, these transactions involve some type of hedge. Derivatives are useful tools for this since they have the effect of transferring risks and rewards between the parties to the contract. Derivatives can be used to hedge a company's exposure to fluctuations in interest rates, foreign currency exchange rates, equity, or commodity prices.

Hedge accounting is optional accounting that ensures that properly hedged positions will reduce volatility in net income created by hedging with derivatives. It seeks to match gains and losses from hedged positions with those of the hedging items so that they may be offset.

9 Understand how to apply hedge accounting standards.

Since this is special accounting, companies must ensure that there is in fact a real hedge (that the contract insulates the company from economic loss or undesirable consequences) and that the hedge remains effective. Proper documentation of the risks and risk management strategy is important. Under

IFRS, there are fair value hedges and cash flow hedges. A fair value hedge reduces risks relating to fair value changes of recorded assets and liabilities as well as purchase commitments. Cash flow hedges protect against future losses due to future cash flow changes relating to exposures that are not captured on the SFP. ASPE does not discuss fair value or cash flow hedges but rather stipulates the accounting for certain types of specific hedge transactions.

Properly hedged positions reduce income fluctuations because gains and losses are offset. Under IFRS, for cash flow hedges, the gains and losses on the hedging items are booked through Other Comprehensive Income and are brought into net income in the same (future) period that the hedged items are booked to net income. For fair value hedges, hedge accounting adjusts the hedged asset to ensure that it is recognized and measured at fair value and that related gains/losses are booked through net income. Both types of hedges ensure that the gains/losses of the hedged and hedging positions offset. Under ASPE hedge accounting, the hedging item (which is generally a derivative) is not recognized on the balance sheet until the hedging item is settled. Thus both the hedged item (usually a future transaction) and the hedging item (the derivative) are off-balance sheet and there is no mismatch.

KEY TERMS

APPENDIX 16B

STOCK COMPENSATION PLANS— ADDITIONAL COMPLICATIONS

Two common stock compensation plans (beyond the stock option plans discussed in the chapter) that illustrate different accounting issues are:

1. Share appreciation rights plans
2. Performance-type plans

These will be discussed below. In addition, this appendix will discuss briefly account-ing where settlement options exist.

Objective 10

Account for share appreciation rights plans.

Share Appreciation Rights Plans

One of the main drawbacks of compensatory stock option plans is that in order to realize the stock options benefit, the employees must exercise the options and then sell the shares. This is a somewhat complex process and usually involves incurring transaction costs. One solution to this problem was the creation of **share appreciation rights (SARs)**. In this type of plan, the executive or employee is given the right to receive compensation equal to the share appreciation, which is defined as the excess of the shares' fair value at the date of exercise over a pre-established price. This share appreciation may be paid in cash, shares, or a combination of both.

The major advantage of SARs is that the employee often does not have to make a cash outlay at the date of exercise, and instead receives a payment for the share appreciation. Unlike shares that are acquired under a stock option plan, the shares that constitute the basis for calculating the appreciation in a SARs plan are not issued. The executive is awarded only cash or shares having a fair value equivalent to the appreciation.

As indicated earlier, the usual date for measuring compensation related to stock com-pensation plans is the date of grant. However, with SARs, the final amount of the cash (or shares, or combination of the two) to be distributed is not known until the date of exer-cise—the measurement date. Therefore, total compensation expense cannot be measured until this date.

How then should compensation expense be recorded during the interim periods from the date of grant to the date of exercise? This determination is not easy because it is impossible to know what the total compensation cost will be until the date of exercise, and the service period will probably not coincide with the exercise date.

For cash settled SARs, ASPE and IFRS differ in how to measure the value of the SAR and hence the compensation between the date of grant and date of exercise. Under ASPE, the value of the SAR is estimated using what is known as the **intrinsic value method**. The intrinsic value method measures the value of the SAR by starting with the market or fair value of the share, deducting the pre-established price noted in the SAR, and multiplying by the number of SARs outstanding. IFRS requires use of an options pricing model to esti-mate fair value of the SAR.[49] Both are attempts to measure the value of the SAR and the options pricing model is a more complex and sophisticated valuation technique.

Regardless of how fair value is estimated for the compensation and liability, this total estimated compensation expense is then allocated over the service period, to record an expense (or decrease expense if the market price falls) in each period. At the end of each interim period, the total compensation expense reported to date should equal the percentage of the total service period that has elapsed, multiplied by the estimated compensation cost.

For example, assume that at the end of an interim period, the service period is 40% complete and the total estimated compensation is $100,000. At this time, the cumulative compensation expense reported to date should equal $40,000 ($100,000 × 0.40). As a second example, assume the following: In the first year of a four-year plan, the company charges one fourth of the appreciation to date. In the second year, it charges off two fourths or 50% of the appreciation to date, less the amount that was already recognized in the first year. In the third year, it charges off three fourths of the appreciation to date, less the amount recognized previously, and in the fourth year it charges off the remaining compensation expense.

A special problem arises when the exercise date is later than the service period. In the previous example, if the SARs were not exercised at the end of four years, it would be necessary to account for the subsequent change in value of the SAR and compensation in the fifth year. In this case, the compensation expense is adjusted whenever a change in value of the SAR occurs in subsequent reporting periods until the rights expire or are exercised, whichever comes first.

Increases or decreases in the fair value of the SARs between the date of grant and the exercise date, therefore, result in a change in the measure of compensation. Some periods will have credits to compensation expense if the fair value falls from one period to the next; the credit to Compensation Expense, however, cannot exceed previously recognized compensation expense. In other words, cumulative compensation expense cannot be negative.

To illustrate, assume that Hotels, Inc. establishes a SARs program on January 1, 2015, which entitles executives to receive cash at the date of exercise (anytime after the service period) for the difference between the shares' fair value and the pre-established or stated price of $10 on 10,000 SARs. The SAR's fair value on December 31, 2015, is $30,000 and the service period runs for two years (2015 to 2016). Illustration 16B-1 shows the amount of compensation expense to be recorded each period, assuming that the executives exercise their rights after holding the SARs for three years.

SHARE APPRECIATION RIGHTS
Schedule of Compensation Expense

(1)	(2)	(3)	(4)			
Date	Fair Value of SAR[a]	Percentage Accrued[b]	Cumulative Compensation Accrued to Date	Expense 2015	Expense 2016	Expense 2017
12/31/15	$30,000	50%	$15,000	$15,000		
			$55,000			
12/31/16	$70,000	100%	$70,000		$55,000	
			(20,000)			
12/31/17	$50,000	100%	$50,000			$(20,000)

[a]Cumulative compensation for unexercised SARs to be allocated to periods of service.
[b]The percentage accrued is based on a two-year service period (2015 to 2016).

Illustration 16B-1
Compensation Expense, Share Appreciation Rights

In 2015, Hotels would record compensation expense of $15,000 because 50% of the $30,000 total compensation cost estimated at December 31, 2015, is allocable to 2015.

In 2016, the fair value increased to $70,000; therefore, the additional compensation expense of $55,000 ($70,000 − $15,000) was recorded. The SARs were held through 2017, during which time the fair value decreased to $50,000. The decrease is recognized by recording a $20,000 credit to Compensation Expense and a debit to Liability Under Share Appreciation Rights Plans. Note that after the service period ends, since the rights are still outstanding, the rights are adjusted to fair value at December 31, 2017. Any such credit to Compensation Expense cannot exceed previous charges to expense that can be attributed to that plan.

As the compensation expense is recorded each period, the corresponding credit should be to a liability account if the stock appreciation is to be paid in cash. According to GAAP, SARs that call for settlement in cash are indexed liabilities and the measurement date is therefore the settlement date.[50]

The entry to record compensation expense in the first year, assuming that the SARs ultimately will be paid in cash, is as follows:

Compensation Expense	15,000	
Liability Under Share Appreciation Rights Plan		15,000

A = L + SE
+15,000 −15,000

Cash flows: No effect

The liability account would be credited again in 2016 for $55,000 and debited for $20,000 in 2017, when the negative compensation expense is recorded. The entry to record the negative compensation expense is as follows:

Liability Under Share Appreciation Rights Plan	20,000	
Compensation Expense		20,000

A = L + SE
−20,000 +20,000

Cash flows: No effect

At December 31, 2017, the executives receive $50,000. The entry removing the liability is as follows:

Liability Under Share Appreciation Rights Plan	50,000	
Cash		50,000

A = L + SE
−50,000 −50,000

Cash flows: ↓ 50,000 outflow

There are some complexities involved with SARs. Sometimes there are choices as to how the instrument will be settled (in cash or shares). Judgement should be used to determine whether the instrument should be accounted for as an equity-settled instrument (like the CSOP) or a cash-settled instrument (like the SAR above). Under ASPE, SARs that require equity settlement are presented as equity. The issuer can choose to estimate the SAR's fair value using the intrinsic value method or other valuation technique, such as the options pricing model.[51] Under IFRS, equity-settled SARs are presented as contributed surplus and measured at fair value using an options pricing model.[52]

SARs are often issued in combination with compensatory stock options (referred to as **tandem** or **combination plans**). The executive must then select which of the two sets of terms to exercise and which one to cancel. The existence of alternative plans running concurrently poses additional problems. Based on the facts available each period, it must be determined which of the two plans is more likely to be exercised and that plan is then accounted for and the other is ignored.

Performance-Type Plans

Some executives have become disenchanted with stock compensation plans in which payment depends ultimately on an increase in the common shares' market price. They do not like having their compensation and judgement of performance at the mercy of the stock market's erratic behaviour. As a result, there has been a large increase in the use of **performance-type plans** that award the executives common shares (or cash) if specified performance criteria are attained during the performance period (generally three to five years). Many large companies now have some type of plan that does not rely on share price appreciation. The performance criteria usually include increases in return on assets or equity, growth in sales, growth in earnings per share (EPS), or a combination of these factors.

A performance-type plan's measurement date is the date of exercise because the number of shares that will be issued or the cash that will be paid out when performance is achieved is not known at the date of grant. The company must use its best estimates to measure the compensation cost before the date of exercise. The compensation cost is allocated to the periods involved in the same way as is done with stock appreciation rights; that is, the percentage approach is used.

Tandem or combination awards are popular with these plans. The executive has the choice of selecting between a performance or stock option award. Companies such as **General Electric** and **Xerox** have adopted plans of this nature. In these cases, the executive has the best of both worlds: if either the share price increases or the performance goal is achieved, the executive gains. Sometimes, the executive receives both types of plans, so that the monies received from the performance plan can finance the exercise price on the stock option plan.

SUMMARY OF LEARNING OBJECTIVE FOR APPENDIX 16B

10 **Account for share appreciation rights plans.**

SARs are popular because the employee can share in increases in value of the company's shares without having to purchase them. The increases in value over a certain amount are paid to the employee as cash or shares. Obligations to pay cash represent a liability that must be remeasured. The cost is therefore continually adjusted, with the measurement date being the exercise date. The related expense is spread over the service period. If the SARs are not exercised at the end of the service period, the liabil-

ity must continue to be remeasured. Cash-settled SARs are measured using intrinsic values under ASPE and fair value (using options pricing models) under IFRS. Some SARs are settled using equity instruments. These are treated as equity and measured at fair value. ASPE allows an accounting policy choice as to how to measure equity-settled SARs.

Performance type plans are tied to performance (of the entity, the individual, or a group of individuals). There is therefore more measurement uncertainty.

KEY TERMS

combination plans, p. 1040

intrinsic value method, p. 1038

share appreciation rights (SARs), p. 1038

tandem plans, p. 1040

APPENDIX 16C

ADVANCED MODELS FOR MEASURING FAIR VALUE

Options Pricing Models

Finance

Chapter 2 introduced the use of a framework for determining fair values. Basic models for calculating fair value include discounted cash flow models, which were reviewed in that chapter. This appendix goes one step further and looks briefly at more advanced models for measuring fair value.

There are numerous **options pricing models** and they are usually covered in more advanced finance texts and courses. The Black-Scholes and binomial tree options pricing models are two of these models.

Options pricing models incorporate the following information (at a minimum) as inputs to the model:

1. The exercise price. This is the price at which the option may be settled. It is agreed upon by both parties to the contract.

2. The expected life of the option. This is the term of the option. It is agreed upon by both parties to the contract. Some options may only be settled at the end of the term (known as European options) while others may be settled at points during the term (known as American options).

3. The current market price of the underlying stock. This is readily available from the stock market.

4. The volatility of the underlying stock. This is the magnitude of future changes in the market price. Volatility looks at how the specific stock price moves relative to the market.

5. The expected dividend during the option life.

6. The risk-free rate of interest for the option life. In general, government bonds carry a return that is felt to be the risk-free return.

Where possible, the fair value is more robust if the inputs make use of external and objective market information. For items such as volatility and dividends, judgement is required in arriving at the input value. Entities look to historical data to help determine these amounts, but care should be taken because historical data are not necessarily indicative of the future. In addition, for some entities, such as newly listed companies, there will be no history. In this case, the entity may look to similar entities in the same industry. The same problem exists for private entities. For these entities, the company also benchmarks against other similar companies and industries in an attempt to calculate the volatility measure.

Any other inputs that a knowledgeable market participant would consider in valuing the option would also be taken into account. These include the employees' ability to exercise the option (whether it is restricted or not and whether the option may be exercised early or not).

Recall further that financial instrument values have two components: an **intrinsic value** component and a **time value** component. These two components are used in the

- Black-Scholes model, which requires the following two amounts to be calculated. Note that this model can be used with published tables.

1. *The standard deviation of proportionate changes in the fair value of the asset underlying the options, multiplied by the square root of the time to expiry of the option.* This amount relates to the time value portion and the potential for the value of the asset underlying the option to change over time. The volatility of the shares as compared with the volatility of the market in general is an important factor here. The more volatile the shares, the greater the fair value of the options. This is because the volatility introduces more risk and the higher the risk, the higher the return.

2. *The ratio of the fair value of the asset underlying the option to the present value of the option exercise price.* This relates to the intrinsic value.

The calculations of the fair value using options pricing models are beyond the scope of this text.

models such as the Black-Scholes and binomial tree models. Where possible, valuation techniques should use available external inputs to ensure that they are more objective. Having said this, significant judgement goes into determining fair values using options pricing models.

Quiz

SUMMARY OF LEARNING OBJECTIVE FOR APPENDIX 16C

11 Understand how options pricing models are used to measure financial instruments.

Fair value is most readily determined where there is an active market with published prices. Where this is not the case, a valuation technique is used. More basic techniques include discounted cash flows. More complex techniques include options pricing

Brief Exercises

Note: All assignment material with an asterisk (*) relates to an appendix to the chapter.

(LO 1, 2) BE16-1 Saver Rio Ltd. purchased options to acquire 1,000 common shares of Spender Limited for $20 per share within the next six months. The premium (cost) related to the options was $500. How should this be accounted for in the financial statements of Saver Rio? Explain which financial risks the transaction exposes the entity to.

(LO 1, 2) BE16-2 On February 1, 2014, Daily Produce Ltd. entered into a purchase commitment contract to buy apples from Farmers Corporation. According to the contract, Daily Produce could settle the contact on a net basis; however, Daily Produce intends to take delivery of the apples so that they can be sold in its grocery stores. On April 1, 2014, Daily Produce takes delivery of the apples for cost of $1,000, and charges the amount on account. (a) How should this be accounted for in Daily Produce's financial statements if it applies IFRS? (b) How should this be accounted for in Daily Produce's financial statements if it applies ASPE? (c) Explain which financial risks the transaction exposes the entity to.

(LO 1, 2) BE16-3 On January 1, 2014, Ginseng Inc. entered into a forward contract to purchase U.S. $5,000 for $5,280 Canadian in 30 days. On January 15, the fair value of the contract was $35 (reflecting the present value of the future cash flows under the contract). Assume that the company would like to update its records on January 15. (a) Prepare only the necessary journal entries on January 1 and 15, 2014. (b) Explain which financial risks the transaction exposes the entity to.

(LO 2) BE16-4 Refer to BE16-3. Assume the same facts except that the forward contract is a futures contract that trades on the Futures Exchange. Ginseng Inc. was required to deposit $25 with the stockbroker as a margin. Prepare the journal entries to update the books on January 1 and 15.

(LO 2) **BE16-5** On January 1, 2014, Pacer Ltd. paid $1,000 for the option to buy 5,000 of its common shares for $25 each. The contract stipulates that it may only be settled by exercising the option and buying the shares. How should this be accounted for in the financial statements of Pacer Ltd.? Assume that Pacer Ltd. complies with IFRS.

(LO 3, 4) **BE16-6** Jamieson Limited, a publicly accountable enterprise, issued century bonds that will not be due until 2114. The bonds carry interest at 5%. Explain how this instrument should be presented on the statement of financial position.

(LO 3, 4) **BE16-7** Silky Limited, a private company that complies with accounting standards for private enterprises (ASPE), has redeemable preferred shares outstanding that carry a dividend of 5%. If the shares are not redeemed within five years, the dividend will double every five years from then on. How should Silky account for this instrument? How should Silky treat the dividends associated with the redeemable preferred shares?

(LO 3, 4) **BE16-8** Milano Ltd. issued 1,000 preferred shares for $10 per share. The preferred shares pay an annual, cumulative dividend of $0.50 per share, and become mandatorily redeemable if net income drops below $500,000 in any fiscal year. Discuss how Milano Ltd. should account for the preferred shares under IFRS. Would the accounting for the preferred shares differ if Milano Ltd. adopted ASPE?

(LO 3, 4) **BE16-9** During 2014, Genoa Limited issued retractable preferred shares. The shares may be presented to the company by the holder for redemption after 2017. Explain how these should be presented in the financial statements under IFRS and ASPE.

(LO 3, 4) **BE16-10** On January 1, 2014, MacGregor Ltd. issued 1,000 3-year, 5% convertible bonds at par of $1,000, with interest payable each December 31. Each bond is convertible into 100 common shares, and the current fair value of each common share is $8 per share. Similar straight bonds carry an interest rate of 9%. (a) Calculate the PV of the debt component by itself. (b) How should MacGregor record the issuance if it follows IFRS? (c) How should MacGregor record the issuance if it follows ASPE?

(LO 4) **BE16-11** Bantry Capital Ltd. issued 500 $1,000 bonds at 103. Each bond was issued with 10 detachable stock warrants. After issuance, similar bonds were sold at 97, and the warrants had a fair value of $2.50. (a) Record the issuance of the bonds and warrants assuming that Bantry Capital follows IFRS. (b) Assuming that Bantry Capital follows ASPE, discuss the two options available to record the issuance of the bonds and warrants, and prepare the journal entry for each option.

(LO 4) **BE16-12** Refer to BE16-11 except assume that the instruments are convertible bonds and that they have now been converted. Assume that Bantry Capital Ltd. follows ASPE, and that all of the proceeds were allocated to the debt component upon initial recognition. At time of conversion, the unamortized bond premium was $10,000, and the common shares had a fair value of $50 per share. Record the conversion using the book value method.

(LO 4) **BE16-13** Century Ltd. issued 15,000 common shares upon conversion of 10,000 preferred shares. The preferred shares were originally issued at $8 per share and the Contributed Surplus—Conversion Rights account for the preferred shares had a balance of $8,000. The common shares were trading at $13 per share at the time of conversion. Record the conversion of the preferred shares.

(LO 4) **BE16-14** Davison Corporation has puttable common shares outstanding. These shares give the holder the option to require Davison to repurchase the shares for cash. In the event of liquidation, the holders of these shares are also entitled to a pro rata share of Davison's net assets (where net assets are those assets that remain after all other claims on the company's assets are satisfied). The shares do not have a preferred rank over other shares for dividend distributions, and there are no other common shares. (a) How should the shares be classified on the statement of financial position if Davison applies IFRS? (b) Would the answer to part (a) be different if Davison applies ASPE?

(LO 4) **BE16-15** Next Generation Corporation (a private company) has preferred shares outstanding, which require Next Generation to redeem the shares for cash at an amount equal to fair value of the company's business assets at the time of issuance of the preferred shares. The preferred shares are held by Richard Parent (the founder and former president of Parent Corporation), who intends to redeem the preferred shares at some point in the future. At the time of issuance of the preferred shares, Parent had transferred the business assets of Parent Corp. to Next Generation (a newly established corporation at the time) as part of an estate freeze transaction, and received these preferred shares as consideration. (a) How should the preferred shares be classified on the statement of financial position if Next Generation follows IFRS? (b) Would the answer to part (a) be different if Next Generation follows ASPE? (c) Discuss why this type of transaction involving preferred shares is called an "estate freeze."

(LO 4) **BE16-16** In January 2014, Parker Inc. issued preferred shares that must be redeemed by Parker if the fair value of the company's common shares exceeds $100 per share. At time of issuance of the preferred shares, Parker's common shares had a fair value of $60 per share. At December 31, 2014, Parker's common shares have a fair value of $50 per share, and it is considered unlikely that Parker's common shares will exceed a fair value of $100 per share. (a) How should the preferred shares be classified on the statement of financial position as at December 31, 2014, if Parker follows IFRS? (b) Would the answer to part (a) be different if Parker follows ASPE?

(LO 5) **BE16-17** List the various types of stock compensation plans.

(LO 5) **BE16-18** Explain the differences between employee and compensatory option plans and other options.

(LO 6) **BE16-19** On January 1, 2014, Blaine Corporation granted 4,000 options to executives. Each option entitles the holder to purchase one share of Blaine's common shares at $40 per share at any time after January 1, 2016. The shares' market price is $55 per share on the date of grant, and the required service period is two years. Prepare Blaine's journal entries for January 1, 2014, and December 31, 2014, and 2015. Assume that the options' fair value as calculated using an options pricing model is $106,000. Ignore forfeitures for simplification purposes.

(LO 10) ***BE16-20** Alison Inc. established a stock appreciation rights (SARs) program on January 1, 2014, which entitles executives to receive cash at the date of exercise for the difference between the shares' fair value and the pre-established price of $20 on 5,400 SARs. The required service period is two years. The shares' fair value is $22 per share on December 31, 2014, and $34 per share on December 31, 2015. The SARs are exercised on January 1, 2016. (a) Calculate Alison's compensation expense for 2014 and 2015 assuming it follows ASPE. (b) Would the accounting for the SARs program differ if Alison adopted IFRS?

(LO 10) ***BE16-21** Spencer Ltd. established a stock appreciation rights (SARs) program on January 1, 2014, which entitles executives to receive cash at the date of exercise (anytime in the next three years) for the difference between the shares' fair value and the pre-established price of $20 on 10,000 SARs. As of December 31, 2014, the shares' fair value is $30 per share, the SARs' fair value is $150,000, and the executives have not exercised their rights yet. The service period runs for two years (2014 to 2015), and at December 31, 2014, the service period is considered 50% complete. (a) Record compensation expense for 2014 assuming that Spencer follows IFRS. (b) Record compensation expense for 2014 assuming that Spencer follows ASPE.

(LO 10) ***BE16-22** Explain what performance-type plans are and how they differ from other types of compensatory plans.

(LO 10) ***BE16-23** Explain how options pricing models are useful in determining fair value. What are the inputs to such models?

Exercises

(LO 11) **E16-1** **(Derivative Transaction)** On January 2, 2014, Jackson Corporation purchased a call option for $350 on Walter's common shares. The call option gives Jackson the option to buy 1,000 shares of Walter at a strike price of $25 per share any time during the next six months. The market price of a Walter share was $25 on January 2, 2014 (the intrinsic value was therefore $0). On March 31, 2014, the market price for Walter stock was $38 per share, and the fair value of the option was $15,500.

Instructions

(a) Prepare the journal entry to record the purchase of the call option on January 2, 2014.

(b) Prepare the journal entry(ies) to recognize the change in the call option's fair value as of March 31, 2014.

(c) What was the effect on net income of entering into the derivative transaction for the period January 2 to March 31, 2014?

(d) Based on the available facts, explain whether the company is using the option as a hedge or for speculative purposes.

(e) Explain which financial risks the transaction exposes the entity to.

(LO 1, 2) **E16-2** **(Derivative Transaction)** On April 1, 2014, Petey Ltd. paid $150 for a call to buy 500 shares of NorthernTel at a strike price of $25 per share any time during the next six months. The market price of NorthernTel's shares was $25 per share on April 1, 2014. On June 30, 2014, the market price for NorthernTel's stock was $34.50 per share, and the fair value of the option was $5,000.

Instructions

(a) Prepare the journal entry to record the purchase of the call option on April 1, 2014.

(b) Prepare the journal entry(ies) to recognize the change in the call option's fair value as of June 30, 2014.

(c) Prepare the journal entry that would be required if Petey Ltd. exercised the call option and took delivery of the shares as soon as the market opened on July 1, 2014.

(d) Why is there a gain or loss when the option is exercised?

Digging
Deeper

(LO 2) **E16-3 (Purchase Commitment)** On January 1, 2014, Fresh Juice Ltd. entered into a purchase commitment contract to buy 10,000 oranges from a local company at a price of $0.50 per orange anytime during the next year. The contract provides Fresh Juice with the option either to take delivery of the oranges at any time over the next year, or to settle the contract on a net basis for the difference between the agreed-upon price of $0.50 per orange and the market price per orange for any oranges that have not been delivered. As at January 31, 2014, Fresh Juice Ltd. did not take delivery of any oranges, and the market price for an orange was $0.49.

Instructions

(a) Assuming that Fresh Juice Ltd. follows IFRS, how should Fresh Juice Ltd. account for this purchase agreement if it fully intends to take delivery of all 10,000 oranges over the next year? Provide any required journal entries at January 1 and January 31.

(b) How would your answer to part (a) change if Fresh Juice Ltd. did not intend to take delivery of the oranges? Provide any required journal entries at January 1 and January 31.

(c) Assuming that Fresh Juice Ltd. follows ASPE, how would Fresh Juice Ltd. account for this purchase agreement if it fully intends to take delivery of all 10,000 oranges over the next year?

(LO 2) **E16-4 (Derivatives Involving the Entity's Own Shares)** Merry Ltd., paid $250 for the option to buy 1,000 of its common shares for $15 each. The contract stipulates that it may only be settled by exercising the option and buying the shares. Merry Ltd. follows IFRS.

Instructions

(a) Provide the journal entry required to account for the purchase of the call option.

(b) Assume that the contract allows both parties a choice to settle the option by either exchanging the shares or settling on a net basis. Would this change your conclusion in part (a)?

(LO 2, 3, 4, 8) **E16-5 (Various Complex Financial Instruments)** The following situations occur independently.

1. A company knows that it will require a large quantity of euros to pay for some imports in three months. The current exchange rate is satisfactory, and as a result, the company purchases a forward contract committing it to acquire 10 million euros at the current exchange rate in three months' time.

2. A shipping company uses large quantities of fuel to power its ships. Shipping rates are set well in advance of when the actual transportation of goods will take place. The company purchases forward contracts for fuel to ensure that it knows the price it will have to pay for fuel in the future. The contracts are exchange-traded futures.

3. An exporting company exports a significant amount of wheat to China. In order to protect itself against the risk that prices will drop significantly, it uses a just-in-time inventory management system to keep stock at the lowest possible levels.

4. A manufacturing company uses a large quantity of steel in its products. In order to ensure the cost of this steel is known, the company enters into executory contracts where it agrees to take delivery of predetermined quantities of steel at predetermined prices in the future.

5. A company pays a shareholder $5,000 for the right to buy 500 of its own common shares for $25 per share at a future date. The contract is not net settleable.

6. A company enters into a futures contract with a margin account to sell its grain for $2,500.

7. A company issues preferred shares on January 1, 2014, with the following terms and conditions: the shares are redeemable by the company for $50/share on January 1, 2017, and the redemption price doubles every 12 months after January 1, 2017.

8. A company issues debt with detachable warrants. The warrants can be sold separately, and entitle the holder to purchase one share at a future date for a predetermined price.

9. A company issues debt that, at the option of the holder, can be converted into 100,000 common shares of the company.

10. A company issues shares that can be redeemed for a fixed amount at the request of the shareholder at any time.

Instructions

For each of the above situations, describe the type of financial instrument involved, when it should be recognized in the financial statements, the measurement that should be used for accounting purposes, and how gains or losses should be recorded. Assume the company is not using hedge accounting. Be sure to note if there are differences between ASPE and IFRS for any items.

(LO 4) E16-6 (Issuance and Conversion of Bonds) The following are unrelated transactions.

1. On March 1, 2014, Loma Corporation issued $300,000 of 8% non-convertible bonds at 104, which are due on February 28, 2034. In addition, each $1,000 bond was issued with 25 detachable stock warrants, each of which entitled the bondholder to purchase one of Loma's no par value common shares for $50. The bonds without the warrants would normally sell at 95. On March 1, 2014, the fair value of Loma's common shares was $40 per share and the fair value of each warrant was $2. Loma prepares its financial statements in accordance with IFRS.

2. Grand Corp. issued $10 million of par value, 9%, convertible bonds at 97. If the bonds had not been convertible, the company's investment banker estimates they would have been sold at 93. Grand Corp. has adopted ASPE, and would like to explore all options available to report the convertible bond.

3. Hussein Limited issued $20 million of par value, 7% bonds at 98. One detachable stock purchase warrant was issued with each $100 par value bond. At the time of issuance, the warrants were selling for $6. Hussein Limited has adopted ASPE.

4. On July 1, 2014, Tien Limited called its 9% convertible bonds for conversion. The $10 million of par value bonds were converted into 1 million common shares. On July 1, there was $75,000 of unamortized discount applicable to the bonds, and the company paid an additional $65,000 to the bondholders to induce conversion of all the bonds. At the time of conversion, the balance in the account Contributed Surplus—Conversion Rights was $270,000, and the bond's fair value (ignoring the conversion feature) was $9,955,000. The company records conversion using the book value method. The company prepares its financial statements using IFRS.

5. On December 1, 2014, Horton Company issued 500 of its $1,000, 9% bonds at 103. Attached to each bond was one detachable stock purchase warrant entitling the holder to purchase 10 of Horton's common shares. On December 1, 2014, the fair value of the bonds, without the stock warrants, was 95, and the fair value of each stock warrant was $50. Horton Company prepares its financial statements in accordance with IFRS.

Instructions

Present the required entry(ies) to record each of the above transactions.

(LO 4) E16-7 (Conversion of Bonds) Daisy Inc. issued $6 million of 10-year, 9%, convertible bonds on June 1, 2014, at 98 plus accrued interest. The bonds were dated April 1, 2014, with interest payable April 1 and October 1. Bond discount is amortized semi-annually on a straight-line basis. Bonds without conversion privileges would have sold at 97 plus accrued interest.

On April 1, 2015, $1.5 million of these bonds were converted into 30,000 common shares. Accrued interest was paid in cash at the time of conversion but only to the bondholders whose bonds were being converted. Assume that the company follows IFRS.

Instructions

(a) Prepare the entry to record the issuance of the convertible bonds on June 1, 2014.

(b) Prepare the entry to record the interest expense at October 1, 2014. Assume that interest payable was credited when the bonds were issued. (Round to nearest dollar.)

(c) Prepare the entry(ies) to record the conversion on April 1, 2015. (The book value method is used.) Assume that the entry to record amortization of the bond discount using the straight-line method and interest payment has been made.

(d) Assume that Daisy follows ASPE. Discuss how the issuance of convertible bonds is recorded, and prepare the entry(ies) to record the issuance of the convertible bonds on June 1, 2014.

(e) What do you believe was the likely fair value of the common shares as of April 1, 2015 (the date of conversion)?

Digging Deeper

(LO 4) E16-8 (Conversion of Bonds) Vargo Limited had $2.4 million of bonds payable outstanding and the unamortized premium for these bonds amounted to $44,500. Each $1,000 bond was convertible into 20 preferred shares. All bonds were then converted into preferred shares. The Contributed Surplus—Conversion Rights account had a balance of $22,200. Assume that the company follows IFRS.

Instructions

(a) Assuming that the book value method was used, what entry would be made?

(b) From the perspective of the bondholders, what is the likely motive for the conversion of bonds into preferred shares? What are the advantages of each investment that are given up or obtained by the bondholders who chose to convert their investment?

Digging Deeper

(LO 4)   **E16-9   (Conversion of Bonds and Expired Rights)** Dadayeva Inc. has $3 million of 8% convertible bonds outstanding. Each $1,000 bond is convertible into 30 no par value common shares. The bonds pay interest on January 31 and July 31. On July 31, 2014, the holders of $900,000 of these bonds exercised the conversion privilege. On that date, the market price of the bonds was 105, the market price of the common shares was $36, the carrying value of the common shares was $18, and the Contributed Surplus—Conversion Rights account balance was $450,000. The total unamortized bond premium at the date of conversion was $210,000. The remaining bonds were never converted and were retired when they reached the maturity date. Assume that the company follows IFRS.

Instructions

(a) Assuming that the book value method was used, record the conversion of the $900,000 of bonds on July 31, 2014.

(b) Prepare the journal entry that would be required for the remaining amount in Contributed Surplus—Conversion Rights when the maturity of the remaining bonds is recorded.

(LO 4)   **E16-10   (Conversion of Bonds)** On January 1, 2014, when the fair value of its common shares was $80 per share, Hammond Corp. issued $10 million of 8% convertible debentures due in 20 years. The conversion option allowed the holder of each $1,000 bond to convert the bond into five common shares. The debentures were issued for $10.8 million. The bond payment's present value at the time of issuance was $8.5 million and the corporation believes the difference between the present value and the amount paid is attributable to the conversion feature. On January 1, 2015, the corporation's common shares were split 2 for 1, and the conversion rate for the bonds was adjusted accordingly. On January 1, 2016, when fair value of the corporation's common shares was $135 per share, holders of 30% of the convertible debentures exercised their conversion option. Hammond Corp. applies ASPE, and uses the straight-line method for amortizing any bond discounts or premiums.

Instructions

(a) Prepare the entry to record the original issuance of the convertible debentures.

(b) Using the book value method, prepare the entry to record the exercise of the conversion option. Show supporting calculations in good form.

(c) How many shares were issued as a result of the conversion?

(d) From the perspective of Hammond Corp., what are the advantages and disadvantages of the conversion of the bonds into common shares?

(LO 4)   **E16-11   (Conversion of Bonds)** Shankman Corporation had two issues of securities outstanding: common shares and an 8% convertible bond issue in the face amount of $8 million. Interest payment dates of the bond issue are June 30 and December 31. The conversion clause in the bond indenture entitles the bondholders to receive 40 no par value common shares in exchange for each $1,000 bond. The value of the equity portion of the bond issue is $60,000. On June 30, 2014, the holders of $1.2 million of the face value bonds exercised the conversion privilege. The market price of the bonds on that date was $1,100 per bond and the market price of the common shares was $35. The total unamortized bond discount at the date of conversion was $500,000.

Instructions

Prepare the entry to record the exercise of the conversion option, using the book value method. Assume the company follows IFRS.

(LO 4)   **E16-12   (Conversion of Bonds)** On January 1, 2014, Olson Corporation issued $6 million of 10-year, 7%, convertible debentures at 104. Investment bankers believe that the debenture would have sold at 102 without the conversion privilege. Interest is to be paid semi-annually on June 30 and December 31. Each $1,000 debenture can be converted into five common shares of Olson after December 31, 2015. On January 1, 2016, $400,000 of debentures is converted into common shares, and on March 31, 2016, an additional $400,000 of debentures is converted into common shares. Fair value of Olson's common shares is $110 and $115 per share on January 1, 2016, and March 31, 2016, respectively. Accrued interest at March 31 will be paid on the next interest date. Bond premium is amortized on a straight-line basis. Olson follows ASPE.

Instructions

(a) Make the necessary journal entries for

1. December 31, 2015
2. January 1, 2016
3. March 31, 2016
4. June 30, 2016

Record the conversions using the book value method.

(b) From the perspective of the debenture holders, why would they be motivated to wait for the conversion of the bonds into common shares? What are the risks involved in waiting and what could the bondholders ultimately give up by waiting too long?

(LO 4) **E16-13 (Issuance of Bonds with Detachable Warrants)** On September 1, 2014, Oxford Corp. sold at 102 (plus accrued interest) 5,200 of its $1,000 face value, 10-year, 9%, non-convertible bonds with detachable stock warrants. Each bond carried two detachable warrants; each warrant was for one common share at a specified option price of $10 per share. Shortly after issuance, the warrants were selling for $5 each. Assume that no fair value is available for the bonds. Interest is payable on December 1 and June 1. Oxford Corp. prepares its financial statements in accordance with ASPE.

Instructions

(a) Prepare in general journal format the entry to record the issuance of the bonds under both options available under ASPE.

(b) From the perspective of a creditor, discuss the effect of each option on Oxford Corp.'s debt to total assets ratio.

(AICPA adapted)

(LO 4) **E16-14 (Issuance of Bonds with Redemption Feature)** On January 1, 2014, Tiamund Corp. sold at 103, 100 of its $1,000 face value, 5-year, 9%, non-convertible, retractable bonds. The retraction feature allows the holder to redeem the bonds at an amount equal to three times net income, to a maximum of $1,200 per bond. Tiamund has net income of $250, $350, and $450 for the fiscal years of December 31, 2014, 2015, and 2016, respectively. Tiamund Corp. prepares its financial statements in accordance with ASPE.

Instructions

(a) Prepare the entry to record the issuance of the bonds.

(b) Using straight-line amortization, how much would the bond be carried at on the statement of financial position for the 2014, 2015, and 2016 year ends?

(LO 6) **E16-15 (Issuance and Exercise of Stock Options)** On November 1, 2013, Aymar Corp. adopted a stock option plan that granted options to key executives to purchase 45,000 common shares. The options were granted on January 2, 2014, and were exercisable two years after the date of grant if the grantee was still a company employee; the options expire six years from the date of grant. The option price was set at $42, and total compensation expense was estimated to be $550,000. Note that the calculation did not take into account forfeitures.

On April 1, 2015, 3,500 options were terminated when some employees resigned from the company. The fair value of the shares at that date was $28. All of the remaining options were exercised during the year 2016: 31,500 on January 3 when the fair value was $52, and 10,000 on May 1 when the fair value was $58 a share. Assume that the entity follows ASPE and has chosen not to reflect forfeitures in its upfront estimate of compensation expense.

Instructions

(a) Prepare journal entries relating to the stock option plan for the years 2014, 2015, and 2016. Assume that the employees perform services equally in 2014 and 2015, and that the year end is December 31.

(b) What is the significance of the fact that the pricing model did not take into account forfeitures? Would taking expected forfeitures into account make the estimate of the total compensation expense higher or lower?

(c) List the types of stock compensation plans and discuss the objectives of effective stock compensation plans.

(d) What are the main differences between an employee stock option plan and a compensatory stock option plan?

(LO 6) **E16-16 (Issuance, Exercise, and Termination of Stock Options)** On January 1, 2014, Harwood Corporation granted 20,000 options to key executives. Each option allows the executive to purchase one share of Harwood's common shares at a price of $25 per share. The options were exercisable within a two-year period beginning January 1, 2016, if the grantee was still employed by the company at the time of the exercise. On the grant date, Harwood's shares were trading at $20 per share, and a fair value options pricing model determined total compensation to be $750,000. Management has assumed that there will be no forfeitures as they do not expect any of the key executives to leave.

On May 1, 2016, 8,000 options were exercised when the market price of Harwood's shares was $31 per share. The remaining options lapsed in 2017 because executives decided not to exercise their options. Management was indeed correct in their assumption regarding forfeitures in that all executives remained with the company. Assume that Harwood follows IFRS.

Instructions

(a) Prepare the necessary journal entries related to the stock option plan for the years ended December 31, 2014, through 2017.

Digging Deeper

Digging Deeper

(b) What is the significance of the $20 market price of the Harwood shares at the date of grant? Would the exercise price normally be higher or lower than the market price of the shares on the date of grant?

(c) What is the significance of the $31 market price of the Harwood shares at May 1, 2016, the date of the exercise of the stock options?

(d) What likely happened to the market price of the shares in 2017?

(e) What motive might an employee have for delaying the exercise of the stock option? What are the risks involved?

(LO 6) **E16-17 (Issuance, Exercise, and Termination of Stock Options)** On January 1, 2014, Kasan Corp. granted stock options to its chief executive officer. This is the only stock option that Kasan offers and the details are as follows:

Option to purchase:	5,000 common shares
Option price per share:	$62.00
Fair value per common share on date of grant:	$57.00
Stock option expiration:	The earlier of eight years after issuance or the employee's cessation of employment with Kasan for any reason other than retirement
Date when options are first exercisable:	The earlier of four years after issuance or the date on which an employee reaches the retirement age of 65
Fair value of options on date of grant:	$10.00

On January 1, 2019, 4,000 of the options were exercised when the fair value of the common shares was $78. The remaining stock options were allowed to expire. The CEO remained with the company throughout the period.

Instructions

Record the journal entries at the following dates. Assume that the entity follows ASPE and has decided not to include an estimate of forfeitures upon initial recognition of the compensation expense.

(a) January 1, 2014

(b) December 31, 2014, the fiscal year end of Kasan Inc.

(c) January 1, 2019, the exercise date

(d) December 31, 2021, the expiry date of the options

(LO 9) ***E16-18 (Cash Flow Hedge)** On January 2, 2014, Thompson Corp. issued a $100,000, four-year note at prime plus 1% variable interest, with interest payable semi-annually. On the same date, Thompson entered into an interest rate swap where it agreed to pay 6% fixed and receive prime plus 1% for the first six months on $100,000. At each six-month period, the variable rate will be reset. The prime interest rate is 5.7% on January 2, 2014, and is reset to 6.7% on June 30, 2014. Thompson follows ASPE and uses hedge accounting. Assume that the swap qualifies for hedge accounting under ASPE.

Instructions

(a) Calculate the net interest expense to be reported for this note and the related swap transaction as of June 30 and December 31, 2014.

(b) Prepare the journal entries relating to the interest for the year ended December 31, 2014.

(c) Explain why this is a cash flow hedge.

(LO 9) ***E16-19 (Cash Flow Hedge)** On January 2, 2014, Yellowknife Corp. issues a $10-million, five-year note at LIBOR, with interest paid annually. To protect against the cash flow uncertainty related to interest payments that are based on LIBOR, Yellowknife entered into an interest rate swap to pay 6% fixed and receive LIBOR based on $10 million for the term of the note. The LIBOR rate for the first year is 5.8%. The LIBOR rate is reset to 6.6% on January 2, 2015. Yellowknife follows ASPE and uses hedge accounting. Assume that the criteria for hedge accounting under ASPE are met.

Instructions

(a) Calculate the net interest expense to be reported for this note and related swap transactions as of December 31, 2014, and 2015.

(b) Prepare the journal entries relating to the interest for the years ended December 31, 2014, and 2015.

(c) Explain why this is a cash flow hedge.

(d) Explain how the accounting would change if the company were to use hedge accounting under IFRS.

(LO 9) *E16-20 (Fair Value Hedge) Timothy Corp. issued a $1-million, four-year, 7.5% fixed-rate interest only, nonprepayable bond on December 31, 2013. Timothy later decided to hedge the interest rate and change from a fixed rate to variable rate, so it entered into a swap agreement with M&S Corp. The swap agreement specified that Timothy will receive a fixed rate of 7.5% and pay variable rate interest with settlement dates that match the interest payments on the instrument. Assume that interest rates declined during 2014 and that Timothy received $13,000 as a net settlement on the swap for the settlement at December 31, 2014. The loss related to the debt (due to interest rate changes) was $48,000. The value of the swap contract increased by $48,000. The company follows IFRS. Assume criteria for hedge accounting are met and that the company has chosen to use hedge accounting.

Instructions

(a) Prepare the journal entry to record the payment of interest on December 31, 2014.

(b) Prepare the journal entry to record the receipt of the swap settlement on December 31, 2014.

(c) Prepare the journal entry to record the change in the fair value of the swap contract on December 31, 2014.

(d) Prepare the journal entry to record the change in the fair value of the bond on December 31, 2014 (under hedge accounting).

(e) Explain why fair value hedge accounting can be applied to this hedge.

(f) Assume that the company applies hedge accounting under ASPE. How would the journal entries change?

(LO 10) *E16-21 (Stock Appreciation Rights) Barrett Limited established a stock appreciation rights program that entitled its new president, Angela Murfitt, to receive cash for the difference between the Barrett Limited common shares' fair value and a pre-established price of $32 (also fair value on December 31, 2013), on 40,000 SARs. The date of grant is December 31, 2013, and the required employment (service) period is four years. The common shares' fair value fluctuated as follows: December 31, 2014, $36; December 31, 2015, $40; December 31, 2016, $45; December 31, 2017, $36; December 31, 2018, $48. Barrett Limited recognizes the SARs in its financial statements. Angela Murfitt exercised half of the SARs on June 1, 2019 when the share price was $46. Assume that Barrett follows ASPE.

Instructions

(a) Prepare a five-year (2014 to 2018) schedule of compensation expense pertaining to the 40,000 SARs granted to Murfitt.

(b) Prepare the journal entry for compensation expense in 2014, 2017, and 2018 pertaining to the 40,000 SARs.

(c) Prepare the entry at June 1, 2019, for the exercise of the SARs.

(d) If Barrett Limited was a publicly accountable entity, would your answer to part (a) differ? Explain.

(e) From the perspective of an investor, comment on the effect of Barrett's SARs program on the company's reported profit, for the years 2014 to 2018.

(LO 10) *E16-22 (Stock Appreciation Rights) At the end of its fiscal year, December 31, 2014, Javan Limited issued 200,000 stock appreciation rights to its officers that entitled them to receive cash for the difference between the fair value of its shares and a pre-established price of $12. The fair value fluctuated as follows: December 31, 2015, $15; December 31, 2016, $11; December 31, 2017, $21; December 31, 2018, $19. The required service period is four years, and the exercise period is three years from the end of the service period. The company recognizes the SARs in its financial statements. Assume that Javan follows ASPE.

Instructions

(a) Prepare a schedule that shows the amount of compensation expense that is allocable to each year that is affected by the stock appreciation rights plan.

(b) Prepare the entry at December 31, 2018, to record compensation expense, if any, in 2018.

(c) Prepare the entry at January 1, 2019, assuming that all 200,000 SARs are exercised on that date, and that fair value of the shares on that date was $19.

(d) Does the calculation of compensation expense for 2016 reflect the drop in fair value of the shares to below the pre-established price of $12 per share? Why or why not?

(LO 10) *E16-23 (Stock Appreciation Rights) Parsons Limited established a stock appreciation rights program that entitled its new president, Brandon Sutton, to receive cash for the difference between the shares' fair value and a pre-established price of $32 (also fair value on December 31, 2013), on 50,000 SARs. The date of grant is December 31, 2013, and the required employment (service) period is four years. The president exercised all of the SARs on December 31, 2018. The shares' fair value fluctuated as follows: December 31, 2014, $36; December 31, 2015, $39; December 31, 2016, $45; December 31, 2017, $36; December 31, 2018, $48. The company recognizes the SARs in its financial statements. Assume that Parsons follows ASPE.

Instructions

(a) Prepare a five-year (2014 to 2018) schedule of compensation expense pertaining to the 50,000 SARs granted to Brandon Sutton.

(b) Prepare the journal entry for compensation expense in 2014, 2017, and 2018 relative to the 50,000 SARs.

(c) From the perspective of the employee, contrast the features of a stock appreciation right to the features of a compensatory stock option.

(d) Discuss what a performance-type compensation plan is, giving examples.

Digging
Deeper

Problems

P16-1 The treasurer of Hing Wa Corp. has read on the Internet that the stock price of Ewing Inc. is about to take off. In order to profit from this potential development, Hing Wa purchased a call option on Ewing common shares on July 7, 2014, for $240. The call option is for 200 shares (notional value), and the strike price is $70. The option expires on January 31, 2015. The following data are available with respect to the call option:

Date	Fair Value of Option	Market Price of Ewing Shares
Sept. 30, 2014	$1,340	$76 per share
Dec. 31, 2014	$ 825	$73 per share
Jan. 4, 2015	$1,200	$75 per share

Instructions

Prepare the journal entries for Hing Wa for the following dates:

(a) July 7, 2014: Invests in call option on Ewing shares.

(b) September 30, 2014: Hing Wa prepares financial statements.

(c) December 31, 2014: Hing Wa prepares financial statements.

(d) January 4, 2015: Hing Wa settles the call option net on the Ewing shares (that is, without buying the shares).

P16-2 Refer to P16–1, but assume that Hing Wa wrote (sold) the call option for a premium of $240 (instead of buying it). Assume that the market price of the shares and the fair value of the option is otherwise the same.

Instructions

Prepare the journal entries for Hing Wa for the following dates:

(a) July 7, 2014: Sale of the call option on Ewing shares.

(b) September 30, 2014: Hing Wa prepares financial statements.

(c) December 31, 2014: Hing Wa prepares financial statements.

(d) January 4, 2015: Hing Wa settles the call option net on the Ewing shares (that is, without selling the shares).

P16-3 Brondon Corp. purchased a put option on Mykia common shares on July 7, 2014, for $480. The put option is for 350 shares, and the strike price is $50. The option expires on January 31, 2015. The following data are available with respect to the put option:

Date	Fair Value of Option	Market Price of Mykia Shares
Sept. 30, 2014	$250	$56 per share
Dec. 31, 2014	$100	$58 per share
Jan. 31, 2015	$ 0	$62 per share

Instructions

Prepare the journal entries for Brondon Corp. for the following dates:

(a) July 7, 2014: Invests in put option on Mykia shares.

(b) September 30, 2014: Brondon prepares financial statements.

(c) December 31, 2014: Brondon prepares financial statements.

(d) January 31, 2015: Put option expires.

P16-4 Biotech Inc. purchased an option to buy 10,000 of its common shares for $35 each. The option cost $750, and explicitly stipulates that it may only be settled by exercising the option and buying the shares.

Instructions

(a) Provide the journal entry required to account for the purchase of the call option assuming Biotech Inc. complies with IFRS.

(b) Assume that the contract allows both parties a choice to settle the option by either exchanging the shares or settling on a net basis. Would this change your conclusion in part (a)?

(c) Assume that Biotech Inc. complies with ASPE. Would this change your conclusion in part (a)?

P16-5 The shareholders' equity section of Finley Inc. at the beginning of the current year is as follows:

Common shares, 1,000,000 shares authorized, 300,000 shares issued and outstanding	$3,600,000
Retained earnings	570,000

During the current year, the following transactions occurred.

1. The company issued 100,000 rights to the shareholders. Ten rights are needed to buy one share at $32 and the rights are void after 30 days. The shares' market price at this time was $34 per share.

2. The company sold to the public a $200,000, 10% bond issue at par. The company also issued with each $100 bond one detachable stock purchase warrant, which provided for the purchase of common shares at $30 per share. Shortly after issuance, similar bonds without warrants were selling at 96 and the warrants at $8.

3. All but 10,000 of the rights issued in item 1 were exercised in 30 days.

4. At the end of the year, 80% of the warrants in item 2 had been exercised, and the remaining were outstanding and in good standing.

5. During the current year, the company granted stock options for 5,000 common shares to company executives. The company, using an options pricing model, determined that each option is worth $10. The exercise or strike price is $30. The options were to expire at year end and were considered compensation for the current year.

6. All but 1,000 shares related to the stock option plan were exercised by year end. The expiration resulted because one of the executives failed to fulfill an obligation related to the employment contract.

Instructions

(a) Prepare general journal entries for the current year to record each of the transactions. Assume the company follows IFRS.

(b) Prepare the shareholders' equity section of the statement of financial position at the end of the current year. Assume that retained earnings at the end of the current year is $750,000.

(c) Assume instead that the executive in items 5 and 6 had fulfilled the employment contract, and that the stock options expired because the share price was lower than the exercise or strike price. Would it be incorrect to have recorded compensation expense related to the expired stock options, during the service period? Why or why not? Would the journal entry to record the expiration be any different than the journal entry for item 6 recorded in part (a)? If so, prepare the journal entry.

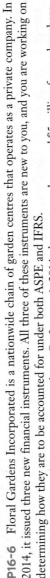

Digging Deeper

P16-6 Floral Gardens Incorporated is a nationwide chain of garden centres that operates as a private company. In 2014, it issued three new financial instruments. All three of these instruments are new to you, and you are working on determining how they are to be accounted for under both ASPE and IFRS.

The first financial instrument was a loan. On January 1, 2014, the company borrowed $5 million from a key shareholder at a rate of 3%, at a time when the market rate of interest was 5%. In order to convince the shareholder to loan the money to the company at a rate lower than the market rate of interest, the company agreed that in five years, the shareholder would have the option of either accepting full repayment of the debt, or receiving 500,000 shares in the company.

The second financial instrument was one that you benefited from. The company gave its 10 key management employees a compensatory stock option plan for the first time. The purpose was to provide additional remuneration for key employees at a time when financial constraints were making it difficult for the company to pay additional salaries. The plan allowed the key employees to purchase 5,000 options to purchase shares for $50 each when they were generally considered to be worth $100. The options were granted on January 1, 2014, and could be exercised at the end of the year or anytime in the next two years. Total compensation expense was estimated to be $550,000, and the expected period of benefit was one year beginning on the grant date. No other management employee exercised their options during the year, but you exercised all of your options on December 31, 2014.

The final new transaction that you have to determine how to account for is a forward contract. The company had not used these before, but as the Canada/U.S. exchange rate had been very good toward the end of the year, the company decided to purchase its U.S. currency needs for 2015 in advance. The company agreed to buy $7 million in U.S. currency for $7,070,000 (U.S. $1 = Canadian $1.01) on December 15, 2014, from Foreign Currency Inc. Any changes in value of the Canadian dollar would be transferred to Floral Gardens. On December 31, 2014, the U.S. dollar strengthened in relation to the Canadian dollar, and the new value was U.S. $1 = Canadian $1.02.

Instructions

(a) Prepare all the 2014 journal entries to account for the three financial instruments under both ASPE (assuming that the company chooses to value the equity component of compound instruments at $0) and IFRS.

(b) Determine the carrying amount of each statement of financial position item at year end, December 31, 2014, under both ASPE and IFRS.

P16-7 Nutmeg Inc., a publicly accountable enterprise that reports in accordance with IFRS, issued convertible bonds for the first time on January 1, 2014. The $1 million of five-year, 10% (payable annually on December 31, starting December 31, 2014), convertible bonds were issued at 108, yielding 8%. The bonds would have been issued at 98 without a conversion feature, and yielding a higher rate of return. The bonds are convertible at the investor's option.

The company's bookkeeper recorded the bonds at 108 and, based on the $1,080,000 bond carrying value, recorded interest expense using the effective interest method for 2014. He prepared the following amortization table:

Date	Cash Interest (10%)	Effective Interest (8%)	Premium Amortization	Carrying Amount of Bonds
Jan. 1, 2014				$1,080,000
Dec. 31, 2014	$100,000	$86,400	$13,600	1,066,400

You were hired as an accountant to replace the bookkeeper in November 2015. It is now December 31, 2015, the company's year end, and the CEO is concerned that the company's debt covenant may be breached. The debt covenant requires Nutmeg to maintain a maximum debt to equity ratio of 2.3. Based on the current financial statements, the debt-to-equity ratio would be 2.6. The CEO recalls hearing that convertible bonds should be reported by separating out the liability and equity components, yet he does not see any equity amounts related to the bonds on the current financial statements. He has asked you to look into the bond transactions recorded and make any necessary adjustments. He would also like you to explain how any adjustments that you make affect the debt to equity ratio.

Instructions

(a) Determine the amount that should have been reported in the equity section of the statement of financial position at January 1, 2014, for the conversion right, considering that the company must comply with IFRS. Prepare the journal entry that should have been recorded on January 1, 2014.

(b) Explain whether ASPE offers any alternatives that are not available under IFRS.

(c) Using a financial calculator or computer spreadsheet functions, calculate the effective rate (yield rate) for the bonds. Leave at least four decimal places in your calculation.

(d) Prepare a bond amortization schedule from January 1, 2014, to December 31, 2018, using the effective interest method and the corrected value for the bonds.

(e) Prepare the journal entry(ies) dated January 1, 2015, to correct the bookkeeper's recording errors in 2014. Ignore income tax effects.

(f) Prepare the journal entry at December 31, 2015, for the interest payment on the bonds.

(g) Explain the effect that the error correction prepared in part (e) has on the debt to equity ratio.

Digging Deeper

P16-8 On January 1, 2014, Biron Corp. issued $1.2 million of five-year, zero-interest-bearing notes along with warrants to buy 1 million common shares at $20 per share. On January 1, 2014, Biron had 9.6 million common shares outstanding and the market price was $19 per share. Biron Corp. received $1 million for the notes and warrants. If offered alone, on January 1, 2014, the notes would have been issued to yield 12% to the creditor. Assume that the company follows IFRS.

Instructions

(a) Prepare the journal entry(ies) to record the issuance of the zero-interest-bearing notes and warrants for the cash consideration that was received.

(b) Prepare an amortization table for the note using the effective interest method.

(c) Prepare adjusting journal entries for Biron Corp. at the end of its fiscal year of December 31, 2014.

(d) Prepare the journal entry required for Biron Corp. if half of the warrants are exercised on January 1, 2017.

P16-9 On September 30, 2014, Gargiola Inc. issued $4 million of 10-year, 8%, convertible bonds for $4.6 million. The bonds pay interest on March 31 and September 30 and mature on September 30, 2024. Each $1,000 bond can be converted into 80 no par value common shares. In addition, each bond included 20 detachable warrants. Each warrant can be used to purchase one common share at an exercise price of $15. Immediately after the bond issuance, the warrants traded at $3 each. Without the warrants and the conversion rights, the bonds would have been expected to sell for $4.2 million.

On March 23, 2017, half of the warrants were exercised. The common shares of Gargiola Inc. were trading at $20 each on this day.

Immediately after the payment of interest on the bonds, on September 30, 2019, all bonds outstanding were converted into common shares. Assume the entity follows IFRS.

Instructions

(a) Prepare the journal entry to record the issuance of the bonds on September 30, 2014.

(b) Using a financial calculator or computer spreadsheet functions, calculate the effective rate (yield rate) for the bonds. Leave at least four decimal places in your calculation.

(c) Prepare a bond amortization schedule from September 30, 2014, to September 30, 2019, using the effective interest rate.

(d) Prepare the December 31, 2014 year-end adjusting journal entries and the payment of interest on March 31, 2015. Assume that Gargiola Inc. does not use reversing entries.

(e) Prepare the journal entry to account for the exercise of the warrants on March 23, 2017. How many common shares were issued in this transaction?

(f) Prepare the journal entry to account for the bond redemption on September 30, 2019.

(g) How many shares were issued on September 30, 2019? What do you believe was the likely market value of the common shares as of the date of the conversion, September 30, 2019?

P16-10 Vanstone Corp., a public company, adopted a stock option plan on November 30, 2014, that designated 70,000 common shares as available for the granting of options to officers of the corporation at an exercise price of $8 a share. The market value was $12 a share on November 30, 2014.

On January 2, 2015, options to purchase 28,000 shares were granted to President Don Pedro: 15,000 for services to be rendered in 2015, and 13,000 for services to be rendered in 2016. Also on that date, options to purchase 14,000 shares were granted to Vice-President Beatrice Leonato: 7,000 for services to be rendered in 2015, and 7,000 for services to be rendered in 2016. The shares' market value was $14 a share on January 2, 2015. The options were exercisable for a period of one year following the year in which the services were rendered. On January 2, 2015, the value of the options was estimated at $400,000.

In 2016, neither the president nor the vice-president exercised their options because the shares' market price was below the exercise price. The shares' market value was $7 a share on December 31, 2016, when the options for 2015 services lapsed.

On December 31, 2017, both the president and vice-president exercised their options for 13,000 and 7,000 shares, respectively, when the market price was $16 a share. The company's year end is December 31.

Instructions

Prepare the necessary journal entries in 2014 when the stock option plan was adopted, in 2015 when the options were granted, in 2016 when the options lapsed, and in 2017 when the options were exercised.

P16-11 On December 31, 2014, Master Corp. had a $10-million, 8% fixed-rate note outstanding that was payable in two years. It decided to enter into a two-year swap with First Bank to convert the fixed-rate debt to floating-rate debt. The terms of the swap specified that Master will receive interest at a fixed rate of 8% and will pay a variable rate equal to the six-month LIBOR rate, based on the $10-million amount. The LIBOR rate on December 31, 2014, was 7%. The LIBOR rate will be reset every six months and will be used to determine the variable rate to be paid for the following six-month period. Master Corp. designated the swap as a fair value hedge. Assume that the hedging relationship meets all the conditions necessary for hedge accounting and that IFRS is a constraint. The six-month LIBOR rate and the swap and debt fair values were as follows:

Date	6-Month LIBOR Rate	Swap Fair Value	Debt Fair Value
Dec. 31, 2014	7.0%		$10,000,000
June 30, 2015	7.5%	$(200,000)	9,800,000
Dec. 31, 2016	6.0%	60,000	10,060,000

Instructions

(a) Present the journal entries to record the following transactions:

1. The entry, if any, to record the swap on December 31, 2014

2. The entry to record the semi-annual debt interest payment on June 30, 2015

3. The entry to record the settlement of the semi-annual swap amount receivable at 8%, less the amount payable at LIBOR, 7%

4. The entry, if any, to record the change in the debt's fair value at June 30, 2015

5. The entry, if any, to record the change in the swap's fair value at June 30, 2015

(b) Indicate the amount(s) reported on the statement of financial position and income statement related to the debt and swap for the year ended December 31, 2014.

(c) Indicate the amount(s) reported on the statement of financial position and income statement related to the debt and swap for the six months ended June 30, 2015.

(d) Indicate the amount(s) reported on the statement of financial position and income statement related to the debt and swap for the year ended December 31, 2015.

*P16-12   LEW Jewellery Corp. uses gold in the manufacture of its products. LEW anticipates that it will need to purchase 500 ounces of gold in October 2014 for jewellery that will be shipped for the holiday shopping season. However, if the price of gold increases, LEW's cost to produce its jewellery will increase, which could reduce its profit margins.

To hedge the risk of increased gold prices, on April 1, 2014, LEW enters into a gold futures contract and designates this contract as a cash flow hedge of the anticipated gold purchase (under IFRS). The notional amount of the contract is 500 ounces, and the terms of the contract require LEW to purchase gold at a price of $300 per ounce on October 31, 2014 or to settle the contract net on the basis of the difference between the $300 and the gold price at October 31. LEW expects to settle the contract net on a net basis. Assume the following data with respect to the price of the futures contract. Assume no margin deposits were paid.

Date	Fair Value of Futures Contract
Apr. 1, 2014	$ –0–
June 30, 2014	$5,000
Sept. 30, 2014	$7,500
Oct. 31, 2014	$7,500

Instructions

Prepare the journal entries for the following transactions:

(a) April 1, 2014: Inception of the forward contract.

(b) June 30, 2014: LEW prepares financial statements.

(c) September 30, 2014: LEW prepares financial statements.

(d) October 31, 2014: LEW purchases 500 ounces of gold at the market price of $315 per ounce, and settles the futures contract on a net basis.

(e) December 20, 2014: LEW sells for $350,000 jewellery containing the gold purchased in October 2014. The cost of the finished goods inventory is $200,000.

(f) Indicate the amount(s) reported on the statement of financial position and statement of comprehensive income related to the futures contract for the six months ended June 30, 2014.

(g) Indicate the amount(s) reported on the statement of comprehensive income related to the futures contract and the inventory transactions for the year ended December 31, 2014.

(h) Explain how the accounting would be different using hedge accounting under ASPE.

Cases

Real World Emphasis

Refer to the *Case Primer* on the Student Website and in *WileyPLUS* to help you answer these cases.

*CA16-1   Air Canada is Canada's largest domestic and international airline, providing scheduled and charter air transportation for passengers and cargo. The airline industry has suffered many difficulties and financial setbacks in the past decade. The high costs associated with operating an airline have claimed many "victims," including Canadian Airlines, which was purchased by Air Canada in 2000 in a highly publicized takeover battle. One of the largest cost components on Air Canada's income statement is aircraft fuel.

Since aircraft fuel is a commodity good, its price is subject to significant fluctuations. The cost of a barrel of aircraft fuel is determined by supply and demand relationships and other global economic conditions that affect production. As a result, Air Canada, like all other airlines, faces a high amount of uncertainty about the cost that it will be required to pay for aircraft fuel. In order to reduce the uncertainty and attempt to limit exposure, Air Canada uses a fuel hedging strategy to manage the risk. The notes to the company's 2011 financial statements describe the airline's strategy for its fuel hedging and provide additional disclosure as follows:

Fuel Price Risk

Fuel price risk is the risk that future cash flows arising from jet fuel purchases will fluctuate because of changes in jet fuel prices. In order to manage its exposure to jet fuel prices and to help mitigate volatility in operating cash flows, the Corporation enters into derivative contracts with financial intermediaries. The Corporation uses derivative contracts based on jet fuel, heating oil and crude-oil based contracts. Heating oil and crude-oil derivatives are used due to the relative limited liquidity of jet fuel derivative instruments on a medium to long-term horizon since jet fuel is not traded on an organized futures exchange. The Corporation's policy permits hedging of up to 75% of the projected jet fuel purchases for the next 12 months, 50% for the next 13 to 24 months and 25% for the next 25 to 36 months. These are maximum (but not mandated) limits. There is no minimum monthly hedging requirement. There are regular reviews to adjust the strategy in light of market conditions. The Corporation does not purchase or hold any derivative financial instrument for speculative purposes.

During 2011:

- The Corporation recorded a loss of $26 in Loss on financial instruments recorded at fair value related to fuel derivatives ($11 loss in 2010).

- The Corporation purchased crude-oil call options and collars covering a portion of 2011 and 2012 fuel exposure. The cash premium related to these contracts was $35.

- Fuel derivative contracts cash settled with a net fair value of $31 in favour of the Corporation ($27 in favour of the counterparties in 2010).

As of December 31, 2011, approximately 23% of the Corporation's anticipated purchases of jet fuel for 2012 are hedged at an average West Texas Intermediate ("WTI") equivalent capped price of US$114 per barrel. The Corporation's contracts to hedge anticipated jet fuel purchases over the 2012 period are comprised of call options and call spreads. The fair value of the fuel derivatives portfolio at December 31, 2011 is $11 in favour of the Corporation ($33 in favour of the Corporation in 2010) and is recorded within Prepaid expenses and other current assets.

The following table outlines the notional volumes per barrel along with the WTI equivalent weighted average floor and capped price for each year currently hedged by type of derivative instruments as at December 31, 2011.

Derivative Instruments	Term	Volume (bbls)	WTI Weighted Average Floor Price (US$/bbl)	WTI Weighted Average Capped Price (US$/bbl)
Call options	2012	5,279,106	not applicable	$115
Call spreads	2012	360,000	not applicable	$107

The Corporation is expected to generate fuel hedging gains if oil prices increase above the average capped price.

Instructions

Discuss the various accounting issues that arise as a result of Air Canada's aircraft fuel hedging strategy. Specifically, discuss whether or not it makes sense for the company to use hedge accounting (which is optional) and from an accounting perspective, what type of hedge this is.

CA16-2 The executive officers of Coach Corporation have a performance-based compensation plan that links performance criteria to growth in earnings per share. When annual EPS growth is 12%, the Coach executives earn 100% of a predetermined bonus amount; if growth is 16%, they earn 125%. If EPS growth is lower than 8%, the executives receive no additional compensation.

In 2014, Joanna Tse, the controller of Coach, reviews year-end estimates of bad debt expense and warranty expense. She calculates the EPS growth at 15%. Peter Reiser, a member of the executive group, remarks over lunch one day that the estimate of bad debt expense might be decreased, increasing EPS growth to 16.1%. Tse is not sure she should do this, because she believes that the current estimate of bad debts is sound. On the other hand, she recognizes that a great deal of subjectivity is involved in the calculation.

Instructions

Discuss the financial reporting issues. Assume this is a public company.

Integrated Cases

Ethics

IC16-1 On-line Deals Inc. (ODI) is in the business of selling things on-line. The company is currently owned by two founding partners, Jay and Wen. Due to the rise in Internet commerce, Jay and Wen are thinking about taking the company public. Revenues have increased steadily over the past few years and demand for this type of service appears to be growing.

ODI sells airline tickets as well as hotel rooms. Sometimes it will buy a block of rooms or airline flights from a company and sell them on-line to interested individuals. Other times airline and hotel companies advise ODI when they have excess capacity and ODI passes this information on to its customers, hoping that they will buy. All transactions are booked as revenues when the customer pays for them. The amount of revenues is generally equal to the fair value of the flight or hotel room (which is equal to what the customer pays).

During the year, in response to increased competition from other on-line businesses, ODI has spent a significant amount of money on revamping its website. It unveiled the "new look" just before year end and customers appear to really like the new features built into the website. In this business, it is very important to have a fresh and current look to the website to keep customers coming back. ODI has a large staff of dedicated information technology and service staff who deal with this. Like Jay and Wen, the senior management team do not yet draw salaries from the company but are paid with stock options. It is very difficult to determine the value of these options as the company is not yet public.

In the past year, the company's website and customer database were attacked by computer hackers. This was very embarrassing for ODI and many customers were very angry. Jay and Wen made a public announcement that they would spend whatever it took to increase security so it would never happen again. Several customers are suing the company in a class action lawsuit. The case goes to trial early next year. ODI's lawyers are a bit worried since similar lawsuits for other companies have ended up with the company paying out a fairly large settlement. Part of the problem in this case was that ODI relies on an outside company (Store All Inc., or SAI) that stores all of its data. The breach occurred at SAI although Jay and Wen also know that part of the problem was their own computer system, on which they had spent significant funds to develop. ODI has since terminated its dealings with SAI and is in the process of building a new company-owned technology facility that will be up and running by next year. The new facility is state of the art and is very expensive. Jay and Wen have been heavily involved in the design of the new facility. They have been discussing with their lawyers their intention to sue SAI for the problems caused.

In order to finance the new facility, ODI issued financial instruments to a large institutional investor. The terms of the financial instruments are below:

- The face value is $100 million.
- They are repayable when revenues exceed two times the historic revenue levels.
- Each year, the financial instruments pay out a dividend of 3%.
- An annual audit must be performed.

Instructions

Adopt the role of the auditors and discuss the financial reporting issues.

IC16-2 Saltworks Inc. (SI) produces salt. Its main assets are two pieces of property that have two salt mines in them (mine 1 and mine 2). Both mines are currently in production. The salt exists in a crystalline layer of rock that rests about 50 metres below ground level. In order to mine the salt, tunnels are created by drilling through the rock. When the salt layer is reached, several holes are drilled into the salt layer to the bottom of the layer. Spring water is then fed through the holes. The water dissolves the salt and a cave is gradually created over time that is filled with salty water. The salt water is siphoned out of the hole, concentrated, and dried. It is then ground up and packaged. The life of a salt mine is about 30 years. Mine 1 is almost fully mined, so there is very little salt left. Mine 2 is a new mine and the tunnels are currently being dug. So far, $500,000 of costs have been incurred this year to drill and build tunnels for mine 2.

Mine 1 is completely depreciated and has a zero carrying value (net book value). Recently, SI discovered a new vein of salt in the mountain where mine 1 previously existed. The company's engineers feel that this new mine (mine 3) will produce at least as much salt as mine 1. Costs of $300,000 have been incurred to date to locate and test the salt. The salt from mine 3 is of a different quality and SI is not sure that a market currently exists for this salt nor that the costs of mining will be recoverable from future revenues. Nonetheless, the company plans to continue developing the mine in the meantime to confirm this.

The mountain that houses mine 2 is covered with pine trees. An unrelated company (Logging Co. or LC) has approached SI for the rights to cut the trees down. SI has agreed to sell these rights for $400,000, which has been paid upfront. The contract gives LC the right to cut down a certain number of trees over the next three years. In order to gain access to the trees, logging roads must be built. LC has approached SI about sharing the costs (equally) of building the roads. SI has agreed as it feels it can use the roads later to transport salt. Already, costs of $1 million have been incurred to build the roads. Unfortunately, the work done to date on the roads has to be redone due to excessive rainfall, which led to a huge flood. The flood washed out parts of the new road.

During the year (before the flood), SI had purchased a weather derivative contract. SI paid a premium of $100,000 for the contract. Under the terms of the contract, the counterparty will pay to SI $500,000 if more than 250 mm of rain falls within a certain period (causing flooding). Since this has happened, SI has approached the counterparty for payout.

A local environmental group has discovered that LC will be cutting down trees and is currently in discussions with SI. The group's members are demanding that SI replant the mountain with small seedlings that will grow into trees and eventually replace the trees that will be cut down. Although no contracts have been signed and SI has not specifically agreed to any course of action, SI has assured the group that it is company policy to be environmentally conscientious.

SI's president recently had a meeting with the CEO of a public company that is looking to purchase SI in the next year. The CEO is anxious to have a look at SI's financial statements and has asked that they be prepared in accordance with IFRS.

Instructions

Assume the role of the accountant for SI and discuss the financial reporting issues relating to the above. SI is a private company. (*Hint:* Use the conceptual framework to analyze any issues that are more complex.)

IC16-3   Great Canadian Gaming Corporation operates casinos, racetracks, slot machines, and other entertainment venues. Its shares trade on the TSX. The following is an excerpt from the 2011 financial statement note 31, which itemizes and quantifies the impact of switching to IFRS.

Real World Emphasis

TRANSITION TO IFRS
b) Reconciliation of Canadian GAAP to IFRS

IFRS 1 requires an entity to reconcile equity and comprehensive income from historical Canadian GAAP to IFRS at the Transition Date and as at, and for the period ending on, the last Canadian GAAP reporting date. The following represents the reconciliations from historical Canadian GAAP to IFRS for the respective periods noted for equity, net loss and comprehensive loss:

RECONCILIATION OF EQUITY

As at	Note	December 31, 2010	January 1, 2010
Shareholders' equity under Canadian GAAP		$419.1	$434.4
Differences increasing (decreasing) reported shareholders' equity:			
Impairments of long-lived assets	i	(10.6)	(26.8)
Fair value as deemed cost	ii	(10.9)	(10.9)
Contingent consideration	iii	(1.1)	—
Amortization	iv	2.2	—
Income taxes	vii	2.4	6.7
Shareholders' equity under IFRS		$401.1	$403.4

RECONCILIATION OF NET LOSS

For the year ended	Note	December 31, 2010
Net loss under Canadian GAAP		$ (21.9)
Differences in GAAP decreasing (increasing) reported net loss:		
Impairments	i	16.2
Contingent consideration	iii	(1.1)
Amortization	iv	2.2
Foreign currency translation adjustment	v	0.4
Stock-based compensation	vi	0.6
Income taxes	vii	(4.3)
Net loss under IFRS		$ (7.9)

RECONCILIATION OF COMPREHENSIVE LOSS

For the year ended	December 31, 2010
Comprehensive loss under Canadian GAAP	$ (21.8)
Differences in GAAP decreasing (increasing) reported comprehensive loss:	
Differences in net loss, net of tax	14.0
Foreign currency translation adjustments	(0.4)
Comprehensive loss under IFRS	$ (8.2)

Writing Assignments

WA16-1 For various reasons, a corporation may issue options and warrants that give their holder the right to purchase the corporation's common shares at specified prices that, depending on the circumstances, may be less than, equal to, or greater than the current market price. For example, warrants may be issued to:

1. Existing shareholders on a pro rata basis
2. Certain key employees under an incentive stock option plan
3. Purchasers of the corporation's bonds

Instructions

For each of the three examples of who may receive issues of options and warrants:

(a) Explain why the warrants/options are used.

(b) Discuss the significance of the price (or prices) at which the warrants/options are issued (or granted) in relation to (1) the current market price of the company's shares, and (2) the length of time over which they can be exercised.

(c) Describe the information that should be disclosed in the financial statements or notes that are prepared when stock warrants/options are outstanding in the hands of the three groups of holders listed above.

(AICPA adapted)

WA16-2 Some complex financial instruments require that the Black-Scholes formula be used to measure their fair value. Examples of these complex instruments include derivatives that are options, bonds issued by the entity that are convertible into shares of the entity, and compensatory stock option plans.

Instructions

(a) For each example provided, explain why it requires the use of the Black-Scholes model in measuring fair value. Discuss how these instruments are initially recorded and subsequently measured under IFRS and ASPE.

(b) Discuss the inputs required in using the Black-Scholes formula for compensatory stock option plans and where this information comes from. Discuss the implications in determining the inputs under IFRS and ASPE.

(c) State the impact on the year-over-year compensation expense for newly granted compensatory stock option plans of making the following changes to the inputs used for the Black-Scholes formula, assuming all other inputs remain unchanged:

1. The risk-free rate has increased from 3% to 5%.
2. The volatility has decreased from 45% to 30%.
3. The expected life has increased from four years to six years.

(d) The Black-Scholes formula was originally designed to determine the fair value of options that are exchange traded. As a result, there has been some disagreement as to whether or not the Black-Scholes formula is the appropriate method to be used for measuring compensatory stock options. What are some of the arguments put forth to support this view? (Consider differences between exchange-traded options on shares and compensatory stock options provided to employees.)

WA16-3 Many companies expose themselves to various financial risks, primarily due to their business models (the way they conduct business).

Instructions

(a) Discuss the preceding statement by identifying the various financial risks and giving real life examples. In creating shareholder value, why is it important for a company to manage risk?

(b) Explain what a derivative is. What are the three key characteristics? Give some examples of derivatives.

(c) Explain what is meant by the act of hedging from an economic perspective. What is meant by the use of hedge accounting? When might a company opt for hedge accounting to report an economic hedge? When might a company decide not to use hedge accounting for an economic hedge?

Instructions

As an independent analyst, provide a critical analysis of the reconciling items. (*Hint:* Access the financial statements on www.sedar.com and review the rest of note 31, which explains the differences.) Compare and contrast the prechangeover GAAP with IFRS.

*WA16-4 CopMin Inc. is a private enterprise that is involved in copper mining operations. The company currently owns two operating mines. It is January 1, 2014, and CopMin has recently entered into two types of contracts. For its Papula Mine, it has entered into a sales contract with one of its major customers. As part of this contract, it has agreed to sell 75% of its annual production at a fixed price that increases 1% each year for inflation. The contract is for five years (until December 31, 2018) and cash will be received on delivery of the copper, which will be made on a monthly basis. For its second mine, Minera Mine, the company has purchased a variety of option contracts to sell copper that are exchange traded. The company has options on 60% of the mine's production for 2014 and 40% of production for 2015. The company has the option to sell copper at a fixed price and all of the contracts can be settled on a net cash basis any time before expiry. The company paid a fee to buy these option contracts at the time they were purchased.

Instructions

(a) Explain how CopMin would record these two different contracts under IFRS and ASPE. Assume no hedge accounting.

(b) How would your answer in part (a) change if the contract for the Papula Mine could be settled net in cash?

*WA16-5 Soron Limited is a private company that uses derivatives to mitigate a variety of risks. The ethical accountant, Leon Price, has just been hired as the new controller and has recently met with the CEO. The CEO has just explained to him the following derivatives that the company is currently party to. The CEO has further explained that he would like to avoid showing the losses on the financial statements. Assume any requirements for hedge accounting are met.

1. The company recently purchased 10,000 shares in a company. These shares are publicly traded. At the same time, the company purchased exchange-traded options to sell these shares at a future date.

2. The company recently sold goods to a customer in the United States and the invoice was priced in U.S. dollars, which should be collected in six months. At the same time, to mitigate the loss on the exchange value of this receivable, Soron entered into a forward contract to sell the same amount of U.S. dollars in six months.

3. Soron has a division that operates in Australia. All of the transactions in this division are translated into Canadian dollars for reporting purposes. In order to mitigate the risk of the exchange rate fluctuation between the Australian dollar and the Canadian dollar, the company has entered into forward contracts to buy Australian dollars in the future at varying amounts over the next year. These forward contracts have experienced a foreign exchange loss in the current year as the Canadian dollar appreciated relative to the Australian dollar.

Instructions

Assume the role of Leon Price, the ethical accountant, and explain to the CEO how the three transactions should be reported under IFRS and ASPE.

WA16-6 Sometimes an entity issues financial instruments that require settlement using its own shares. Examples of these include purchased or written options to buy or sell its own shares, or forward contracts to buy or sell its own shares.

Instructions

Explain the accounting issues that result from the existence of these instruments. How does IFRS tend to treat these types of instruments? Give examples to support the different treatments that are available under IFRS. Note any differences under ASPE.

WA16-7

Write a brief essay highlighting the differences between IFRS and ASPE noted in this chapter, discussing the conceptual justification for each.

WA16-8 RIT Co. has an investment of 5,000 shares in a public company, SIT Ltd. In October 2014, RIT Co. purchased put options for SIT Ltd. shares at a price of $2 per put option. The strike price associated with the put options is $100 per share, which is equal to the current trading price of the shares.

Instructions

(a) What is the purpose of the put options purchased by RIT Co.?

(b) How would RIT account for the purchase of the put options? Assume that the value of the shares of SIT subsequently decline. How would this be accounted for?

(c) Is this accounting treatment transparent?

WA16-9

Write a brief essay to explain both the similarities and the differences that exist between hedging and speculation.

Ethics

RESEARCH AND FINANCIAL ANALYSIS

RA16-1 Potash Corporation of Saskatchewan Inc.

Access the financial statements of Saskatoon-based PotashCorp., a global fertilizer producer, from the company's website or SEDAR (www.sedar.com) for the year ended December 31, 2011.

Instructions

(a) The company has several stock-based compensation plans. Compare and contrast these plans, noting such things as who is eligible, whether they have to buy shares to access any benefit, what the benefit or compensation is based on (profits or stock price), vesting periods, expiry periods, how the compensation cost is determined, where the offsetting amounts are reported (equity or liabilities), and when the compensation expense is recorded and whether it is adjusted or not. Prepare a chart to present your findings. (*Note:* Summarize the same type of plans together.)

(b) Review the financial statements and discuss how the stock plans are accounted for. How much was reported to compensation expense, contributed surplus, and liabilities during the year?

(c) Comment on any professional judgement that is used in accounting for the stock option plans. How have these estimates changed from 2008 to 2011? Comment on what the impact on the compensation expense would be as a result of changes in each of these inputs, if all other inputs remained unchanged.

RA16-2 Canadian Tire Corporation

Access the annual report of Canadian Tire Corporation for the year ended December 31, 2011, from the company's website or SEDAR (www.sedar.com). According to the annual report, the company operates more than 488 retail stores across Canada, selling automotive parts, accessories, and services; sports and leisure products; and home products.

Instructions

(a) Read the Management Discussion and Analysis portion of the annual report.

(b) Identify and summarize the various business and financial risks that the company is exposed to. Explain how these risks stem from the underlying nature of the business (that is, the business model).

(c) How is the company dealing with its foreign currency and interest rate risks?

(d) What derivatives are used by the company? What does the company use hedge accounting for? (See Note 3.)

(e) From Note 39, determine the fair values of the derivatives at the year end. In determining the fair value of these derivatives, what fair value hierarchy has been used? Prepare a schedule outlining the fair value of the cash flow hedges, the fair value hedges, and those derivatives not designated as hedges for accounting purposes.

RA16-3 Loblaw Companies Limited

Access the financial statements of Loblaw Companies Limited for the year ended December 31, 2011. The statements are available on the company's website or SEDAR (www.sedar.com).

Instructions

(a) During 2008, the company issued second preferred shares—Series A. Describe the terms of these shares and how the company measures and reports these shares. Explain why this presentation is required.

(b) How much were the shares originally issued for? What amount is showing on the statements with respect to these shares at the 2011 year end? Why is the amount different?

(c) How much was paid in dividends on these shares during 2011? How was the cost of these dividends reported?

(d) Review the company's capital management note. How are these preferred shares treated?

RA16-4 Deutsche Lufthansa AG

Access the financial statements of Deutsche Lufthansa AG for the year ended December 31, 2011. These can be found at the company's website (http://investor-relations.lufthansa.com).

Instructions

(a) Discuss the company's business model (that is, how it earns income).

(b) Identify and summarize the various financial risks that the company is exposed to. (See the discussion on Financial Opportunities and Risks in the annual report.) How is the company dealing with its financial risks and what are its objectives in managing these risks? What types of derivatives are used for hedging purposes?

(c) Read the Risks and Opportunities Report to the financial statements. How many of the various risks noted in part (b) are hedged?

(d) Also from the Risks and Opportunities Report, what derivative instruments, if any, are being used by the company to hedge its risks related to commodities? Identify which derivatives are designated as cash flow hedges and which are designated as fair value hedges for 2011. Explain why the hedges have been designated as cash flow or fair value.

(e) How have the fair values of the derivatives been determined?

(f) Related to the derivatives, how much was moved from other comprehensive income to earnings during the year?

Real World Emphasis

ENDNOTES

[1] Many derivatives are self-standing but some are embedded in other contracts. Compound and hybrid instruments often contain embedded derivatives.

[2] *CICA Handbook–Accounting*, Part II, Section 3856.05 and IAS 32.11.

[3] *CICA Handbook–Accounting*, Part II, Section 3856.05 and IAS 39.9.

[4] *ISDA Research Notes*, Spring 2009, International Swaps and Derivatives Association, Inc.

[5] Ibid.

[6] IFRS 7 Appendix A and *CICA Handbook–Accounting*, Part II, Section 3856.A66. Copyright © 2012 IFRS Foundation. All rights reserved. Reproduced by Wiley Canada with the permission of the IFRS Foundation ®. No permission granted to third parties to reproduce or distribute.

[7] There are some well-publicized examples of companies that have suffered sizable losses as a result of using derivatives. For example, companies such as **Showa Shell Sekiyu** (Japan), **Metallgesellschaft** (Germany), **Proctor & Gamble** (United States), and **Air Products & Chemicals** (United States) have incurred significant losses from investments in derivative instruments. Companies sometimes suffer losses because they take too much risk, they do not understand the markets or positions taken, or they suffer from the timing of closing out the contracts and positions.

[8] When companies create positions that are expected to be profitable, there is often a risk of loss as well. Some refer to this as speculating.

[9] All business inputs have price risks associated with them. There is always a risk that prices to acquire the inputs will vary over time.

[10] Why would one party think that prices will rise and the other that they will fall? The same information is rarely available to all parties. In most contract negotiations, there is information asymmetry, which leads to the parties sometimes expecting different outcomes.

[11] Recall that derivatives are contracts themselves just like the purchase commitment and it is the terms of the contract that give rise to contractual rights and obligations that accountants must then account for. Sometimes, accounting is complicated by the fact that accountants like to put labels like "derivatives"

on things. This labelling complicates the accounting since standard setters must determine whether it is appropriate to apply the label (and the designated accounting) or not.

[12] Commodities contracts generally trade in liquid markets and by virtue of the fact that they trade on an exchange, they have a net cash settlement feature. This means that the option exists to close out the position and take cash instead of delivery of the underlying product itself.

[13] Per IAS 39.6, there are various ways in which contracts can be settled net in cash or other financial instruments, including:
– where explicitly allowed by contract,
– where there is a history of settling net in cash or taking delivery and immediately selling the item for profit, or
– where the item is readily convertible to cash. (Items are readily convertible to cash where there is a ready market to buy/sell the items.)

The ability to settle net is an important differentiating feature since where it does not exist, the contract will have to settle by delivering or taking delivery of the underlying. There is no choice. Where net settlement is an option, then an additional hurdle must be cleared to prove that the contract was entered into for expected use.

[14] Baird Investment Corp. is referred to as the **counterparty**. Recall that derivatives are financial instruments. Recall also that financial instruments are a contract between two parties. Counterparties frequently are investment bankers or other entities that hold inventories of financial instruments.

[15] The value is estimated using options pricing models, such as the Black-Scholes model. The fair value estimate is affected by the volatility of the underlying stock, the expected life of the option, the risk-free rate of interest, and expected dividends on the underlying shares during the option term. This model is further explained in Appendix 16C.

[16] The decline in value of the time value portion of the options from $400 to $100 reflects both the decreased likelihood that the Laredo shares will continue to increase in value over the option period and the shorter time to maturity of the option contract.

[17] A loss exists due to the decrease in the time value component of the option. As time passes, the time value component declines and is zero, at the end of the contract.

[18] Spot rate is the current market rate.

[19] IAS 32 *Financial Instruments: Presentation*, Illustrative Examples. There is quite a comprehensive group of examples presented in IAS 32. This area is currently being studied by the IASB.

[20] IAS 32.26. The IASB made this decision to prevent entities from designing financial instruments so as to achieve a certain accounting outcome per the basis for the Conclusions document for IAS 32. Note that ASPE looks to the basic definitions of financial liabilities and equity to resolve the presentation issue. Whether a contract can or may be settled net is an interesting question. If the contract is a non-traded contract between two parties (as opposed to involving instruments that trade in the marketplace) then this would be presumably determined by the terms of the contract. However, when the derivatives are purchased in the capital marketplace (such as a stock market/exchange), the entity may trade out of the position (settle net) by selling the contract in the open market. Thus, derivatives that trade in the marketplace involving settlement in own equity instruments are most likely accounted for as financial assets/liabilities and not equity instruments because they effectively allow for net settlement.

[21] This actually depends upon the laws in the respective legal jurisdiction.

[22] This was mentioned earlier in this chapter when discussing derivatives. Recall also that Chapter 15 provided a discussion about "in-substance shares," which are treated as equity as long as certain conditions are met even though the holder has the option to require the entity to pay cash.

[23] *CICA Handbook—Accounting*, Part II, Section 3856.A26.

[24] *CICA Handbook—Accounting*, Part II, Section 3856.23. These types of transactions generally relate more to private entities and not public entities and therefore are not mentioned in IFRS.

[25] The legally enforceable right could exist, for instance, due to the contracts governing the instruments, laws in certain jurisdictions, or rules governing the operation of stock exchanges (if the instruments are traded on a particular exchange).

[26] *CICA Handbook—Accounting*, Part II, Section 3856.24 and IAS 32.42.

[27] Calculation of this amount using an options pricing model is beyond the scope of this course and would generally be covered in a finance course. Appendix 16C provides a brief recap of options pricing models.

[28] *CICA Handbook—Accounting*, Part II, Section 3856.22 and IAS.32.31.

[29] In fact, the bonds would sell at a premium due to the embedded stock option.

[30] *CICA Handbook—Accounting*, Part II, Section 3856.A34 and IAS 32.AG32.

[31] An alternative approach that has some conceptual merit uses the market value to record the conversion. Under this method, the common shares would be recorded at market value (their market value or the market value of the bonds); the contributed surplus, bonds payable, and discount amounts would be zeroed out; and a gain/credit or loss/debit would result. Since the Canada Business

Corporations Act requires shares to be recorded at their cash equivalent value, legal requirements would tend to partially support this approach.

32 Note that a company might offer an option under an ESOP at less than the fair value of the option. As long as this discount is small and effectively represents the issue costs that a company might otherwise have incurred had it done a public offering, this is not seen as compensatory.

33 IFRS 2.4 and *CICA Handbook–Accounting*, Part II, Section 3870.28. Note that the wording of the respective standards is different although the substance of the content is the same. IFRS approaches the analysis differently, looking at whether the employee is acting in the role of shareholder or employee.

34 *CICA Handbook–Accounting*, Part II, Section 3870.24. IFRS 2.10 and .11.

35 Stock options that are issued to non-employees in exchange for other goods or services must be measured according to their fair value as nonmonetary transactions.

36 To "vest" means to earn the rights to something. An employee's award becomes vested at the date that the employee's right to receive or retain shares of stock or cash under the award no longer depends on the employee remaining in the employer's service or fulfilling some other prescribed condition.

37 *CICA Handbook–Accounting*, Part II, Section 3870.43-.46 and IFRS 2.19 and .20.

38 *CICA Handbook–Accounting*, Part II, Section 3870.24. and IFRS 2.11.

39 *CICA Handbook–Accounting*, Part II, Section 3870.03.

40 *CICA Handbook–Accounting*, Part II, Section 3870.65-.68 and IFRS 2.44-.52.

41 *CICA Handbook–Accounting*, Part II, Section 3856.31 and IAS 39.88.

42 Under IFRS, effectiveness is proven by showing that the changes in the hedged item are highly correlated with the changes in the hedging item. Although no method is specified in the standard, regression analysis is often used. Under ASPE, the entity must prove that the critical terms of the contracts for the hedged and hedging items are essentially the same (thus indirectly proving that the hedge will be effective). This is known as the "critical terms match" test.

43 If a firm commitment such as a purchase commitment is hedged, then the commitment itself must be recognized on the SFP so that resulting gains and losses offset the gains and losses generated by the hedging item.

44 Note that the trade-off to reducing market risk with a derivative is an increase in credit, liquidity, and operational risks (the risk related to designing and monitoring the hedge position).

45 If the terms of the contract allowed the contract to be settled net in cash (instead of taking delivery of the raw material), it may meet the definition of a derivative and have to be recognized as being such, as noted earlier in the chapter (under IFRS). If the purchase commitment was recognized as a derivative and it was hedged with a derivative, there would be no need for special hedge accounting as both would be recognized and measured at fair value with gains/losses booked through net income such that they offset.

46 The decision to make an interest rate swap is based on a recognized index of market interest rates. The most commonly used index is the London Interbank Offer Rate, or LIBOR. The prime lending rate is another rate that is commonly referenced in loan agreements and other financial instruments. This rate is set periodically by the Bank of Canada. The interest rates that are attached to various instruments are normally above prime (such as P + 1% or P + 2%).

47 Theoretically, this fair value change reflects the present value of expected future differences in variable and fixed interest rates and any changes in the counterparty's credit risk.

48 Under the net settlement feature, the actual aluminum does not have to be exchanged. Rather, the parties to the contract may settle by paying the cash difference between the forward price and the price of aluminum on the settlement date.

49 IFRS 2.30-.33. Note that IFRS 2 is scoped out of IFRS 13 *Fair Value Measurements*. ASPE refers to the shares' market price/value. Since the shares of private entities do not trade on exchanges by definition, the standard assumes internal markets for the shares.

50 *CICA Handbook–Accounting*, Part II, Section 3870.39.

51 *CICA Handbook–Accounting*, Part II, Section 3870.64.

52 IFRS 2.33.

© istockphoto.com/H-Agall

Catching the Market by Surprise

WHEN A PUBLIC COMPANY announces its quarterly or annual financial results, the amount of earnings is usually not a surprise. Often, the company will signal ahead of time to the market what it thinks its earnings will be, such as by holding a conference call with investors and analysts to provide earnings guidance. Analysts who closely monitor the company's financial statements will issue predictions about upcoming results based on earnings guidance, past numbers, the company's announcements about sales and revenues during the period, and economic conditions in general and for the industry.

But sometimes, announced earnings will be above or below what the market expected, which is called an earnings surprise. One reason this occurs is the information asymmetry in the market; that is, the companies know more about their performance than the analysts do, until the results are announced. Earnings surprises are published daily by the NASDAQ stock exchange for the benefit of investors, though the Toronto Stock Exchange does not do this. Investors want to know a company's earnings per share: how much each share contributes to income.

What are the implications for a company after an earnings surprise? It has no legal or financial obligation to meet anyone's expectations, but the market will react. A negative earnings surprise—when a company's earnings are lower than expected—usually results in its share price falling, while a positive earnings surprise—when a company's earnings are higher than expected—usually results in its share price rising. These share price increases or decreases, known as post-earnings announcement drift, can last for days or even months after earnings are announced. One theory for this phenomenon is that not all investors have sophisticated knowledge to correctly interpret relevant earnings information.

Research has found that most companies tend to share good news with investors right away. But some companies may understate their expected earnings in advance of releasing results in order to get a positive earnings surprise and therefore an increase in share price. If positive earnings surprises happen too often, the market eventually catches on and revises a company's earnings expectations upwards, closer to its actual recent earnings.

Sources: David Milstead, "Investors Eye Guidance as Earnings Season Begins," *Globe and Mail*, January 6, 2013; Jonathan Ratner, "Positive Earnings Surprises Not That Surprising," *Financial Post*, July 25, 2012; Dennis Y. Chung and Karel Hrazdil, "Market Efficiency and the Post-Earnings Announcement Drift," *Contemporary Accounting Research*, Vol. 28, No. 3 (Fall 2011), pp. 926–956; Allison Koester, Russell Lundholm, and Mark Soliman, "Attracting Attention in a Limited Attention World: An Exploration of the Forces Behind Positive Extreme Earnings Surprises," unpublished paper, September 2010.

Earnings per Share

LEARNING OBJECTIVES

After studying this chapter, you should be able to:

1. Understand why earnings per share (EPS) is an important number.

2. Understand when and how earnings per share must be presented, including related disclosures.

3. Calculate earnings per share for companies with a simple capital structure.

4. Calculate earnings per share for companies with a complex capital structure.

5. Identify the major differences in accounting between ASPE and IFRS, and what changes are expected in the near future.

PREVIEW OF CHAPTER 17

Earnings per share data are frequently reported in the financial press and are widely used by shareholders and potential investors in evaluating a company's profitability and value. This chapter examines how basic and diluted earnings per share figures are calculated and what information they contain.

The chapter is organized as follows:

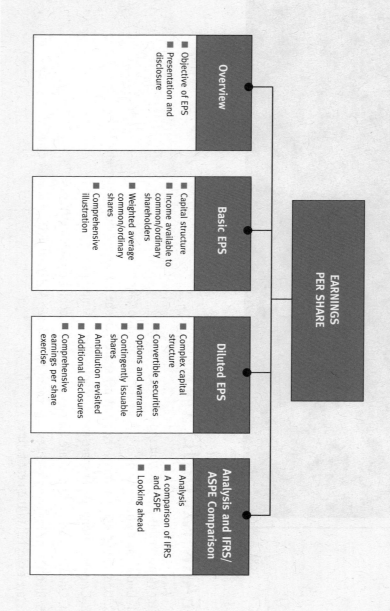

EARNINGS PER SHARE

Overview
- Objective of EPS
- Presentation and disclosure

Basic EPS
- Capital structure
- Income available to common/ordinary shareholders
- Weighted average common/ordinary shares
- Comprehensive illustration

Diluted EPS
- Complex capital structure
- Convertible securities
- Options and warrants
- Contingently issuable shares
- Antidilution revisited
- Additional disclosures
- Comprehensive earnings per share exercise

Analysis and IFRS/ASPE Comparison
- Analysis
- A comparison of IFRS and ASPE
- Looking ahead

OVERVIEW

Objective of EPS

Common[1] shareholders need to know how much of a company's available income can be attributed to the shares that they own. This helps them assess future dividend payouts and the value of each share. As noted in Chapters 15 and 16, common shares are different from other forms of financing, such as debt and preferred shares. Common shareholders have a residual interest in the company. The return on investment is not based on a predetermined interest rate, the passage of time or a face value (as it is for debt). If the company does well, common shareholders are the ones who gain the most. Similarly, if a company does not do well, common shareholders stand to lose the most. (There may not be anything left after a company covers its costs and obligations.) How big is the common shareholders' part of the profit pie? How is it affected by financial instruments such as convertible debt and options? Earnings per share disclosures help investors (both existing shareholders and potential investors) by indicating the amount of income that is earned by each common share: in other words, the common shareholders' piece of the earnings pie. Common shares are sometimes referred to as ordinary shares. The basic calculation is shown in Illustration 17-1.

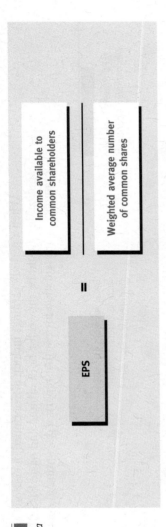

Illustration 17-1

The EPS Formula

EPS $=$ $\dfrac{\text{Income available to common shareholders}}{\text{Weighted average number of common shares}}$

Note that EPS is normally calculated only for common shares. The calculation is done for both basic EPS and diluted EPS. **Basic EPS** looks at actual earnings and the actual number of common shares outstanding (with this number prorated for the amount of time that the shares have been outstanding). **Diluted EPS** is a **"what if"** calculation that takes into account the possibility that financial instruments such as convertible debt and options (and others) might have a negative impact on existing shareholder returns and, therefore, the shares' value. This chapter will deal first with the calculations for basic EPS and then the calculations for diluted EPS.

Presentation and Disclosure

Because of the importance of earnings per share information, companies whose shares trade on a stock exchange or market or companies that are in the process of listing on a stock exchange or market are required to report this information on the face of the income statement.[2] ASPE does not require EPS calculations or disclosures in the financial statements. This is because of cost-benefit considerations as well as the fact that these entities may be closely held. Generally, earnings per share information is reported below income in the income statement.

When the income statement presents discontinued operations, earnings per share should be disclosed for income from continuing operations, discontinued operations, and net income.[3] The EPS numbers related to discontinued operations may be disclosed on the face of the statement or in the notes. The EPS data in Illustration 17-2 are representative of this disclosure, and assume that the EPS numbers for discontinued operations are presented on the face of the income statement.

Illustration 17-2

Income Statement Presentation of EPS Components

Earnings per share:

Income from continuing operations	$4.00
Loss from discontinued operations, net of tax	(0.60)
Net income	$3.40

These disclosures make it possible for users of the financial statements to know the specific impact of income from continuing operations on EPS, as opposed to a single EPS number, which also includes the impact of gains and losses on operations that will not continue in the future. If a corporation's capital structure is complex, the earnings per share presentation would include both basic and diluted EPS, as shown in Illustration 17-3.

Illustration 17-3

EPS Presentation—Complex Capital Structure

Earnings per common share:

Basic earnings per share	$3.80
Diluted earnings per share	$3.35

When a period's earnings include discontinued operations, per share amounts (where applicable) should be shown for both diluted and basic EPS. Illustration 17-4 gives an example of a presentation format that reports a discontinued operation.

Illustration 17-4

EPS Presentation, with Discontinued Operations

Basic earnings per share:	
Income before discontinued operations	$3.80
Discontinued operations	(0.80)
Net income	$3.00
Diluted earnings per share:	
Income before discontinued operations	$3.35
Discontinued operations	(0.65)
Net income	$2.70

IFRS requires the following:

1. Earnings per share amounts must be shown for all periods that are presented.

2. If there has been a stock dividend or stock split, all per share amounts of prior period earnings should be restated using the new number of outstanding shares.

3. If diluted EPS data are reported for at least one period, they should be reported for all periods that are presented, even if they are the same as basic EPS.

4. When the results of operations of a prior period have been restated for instance, as a result of an error correction, the corresponding earnings per share data should also be restated. The restatement's effect should then be disclosed in the year of the restatement.

BASIC EPS

Capital Structure

Objective 3

Calculate earnings per share for companies with a simple capital structure.

When a corporation's capital structure consists only of common shares and preferred shares and/or debt without conversion rights, the company is said to have a **simple capital structure**. In contrast, a company is said to have a **complex capital structure** if the structure includes securities that could have a dilutive or negative effect (that is, a lowering effect) on earnings per common share. In the EPS formula given in Illustration 17-1, any increase in the denominator will result in a decrease in EPS. These other, potentially dilutive securities are called potential common shares. A **potential common/ordinary share** is a security or other contract that may give its holder the right to obtain a common/ordinary share during or after the end of the reporting period. Examples are debt and equity instruments (such as preferred shares) that are convertible into common shares, warrants, options, and contingently issuable shares.[4] **Contingently issuable shares** are shares that are issuable for little or no consideration once a condition involving uncertainty has been resolved.[5] For instance, in an acquisition of another company, the acquirer may promise to issue some additional shares (at a later date) as part of the purchase consideration if the acquired company performs well.

Companies with simple capital structures only need to calculate and present basic EPS. Those with complex capital structures must calculate and present both basic and diluted EPS. The table in Illustration 17-5 summarizes the reporting requirements.

Illustration **17-5**

EPS Reporting Requirements
for Different Capital Structures

Capital Structure	Major Types of Equity Instruments	Impact on EPS Calculations
Simple	— Common (residual, voting) shares — Preferred shares	— Need only calculate basic EPS
Complex	— Common shares — Potential common shares • Convertible preferred shares • Convertible debt • Options/warrants • Contingently issuable shares • Other	— Must calculate basic and diluted EPS

The calculation of earnings per share for a simple capital structure involves two items: income available to common/ordinary shareholders and the weighted average number of common shares outstanding. These are examined separately in the next sections.

Finance

Income Available to Common/Ordinary Shareholders

As noted earlier, basic EPS looks at **actual** earnings that are left or available after paying operating costs (including interest) and after paying or setting aside funds for dividends on shares that rank in preference (most often preferred shares) over the common shares.

Illustration 17-6 shows the concept of income available to common shareholders as a residual component of income.

Illustration **17-6**

Income Available to Common
Shareholders (CSH)

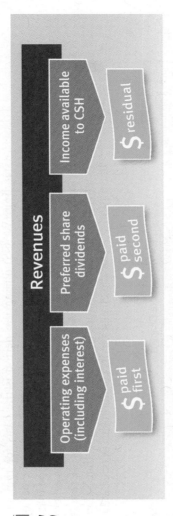

Income available to common shareholders is equal to net income less amounts that have been set aside to cover obligations of other instruments, such as preferred shares that rank in preference over common shares. Since these instruments are senior, they rank in preference in terms of return on investment and these funds must be set aside before looking at how much is available for the common or residual shareholders.

When a company has both common and preferred shares outstanding, the dividends for the current year on these preferred shares are subtracted from net income to arrive at income available to common shareholders.

In reporting earnings per share information, dividends declared on preferred shares should be subtracted from income from continuing operations **and** from net income to arrive at income available to common shareholders. If dividends on preferred shares are declared and a net loss occurs, the preferred dividend increases the loss in calculating the loss per share. If the preferred shares are cumulative and the dividend is not declared in the current year, an amount equal to the dividend that should have been declared for the current year only should be subtracted from net income or added to the net loss. Dividends in arrears for previous years would have been included in the previous years' calculations.

Assume, for example, that Michael Limited has net income of $3 million and two classes of preferred shares, in addition to common shares. Class A preferred shares are cumulative and carry a dividend of $4 per share. There are 100,000 shares outstanding throughout the year. No dividend declaration has been made and no dividends have been paid during the year. Class B preferred shares are non-cumulative and carry a dividend of $3 per share. There are 100,000 shares outstanding throughout the year and the dividends have not been declared or paid in the current year. The income available for common shareholders would be calculated as follows:

Net income	$3,000,000
Less:	
Preferred dividends—Class A	(400,000)
Income available to common shareholders	$2,600,000

Note that the Class A share dividends are deducted even though they have not been declared or paid. This is because they are cumulative and will eventually have to be paid. No dividends are set aside for the Class B shares since they are non-cumulative and have not been declared. Because they are non-cumulative, the company never has to make up a lost dividend to the Class B shareholders.

Weighted Average Common/Ordinary Shares

In all calculations of earnings per share, the **weighted average number of shares outstanding (WACS)** during the period is the basis for the per share amounts that are reported. Shares that are issued or purchased during the period affect the amount outstanding and must be weighted by the fraction of the period that they have been outstanding. The rationale for this approach is that the income was generated on the issue proceeds for only part of the year. Accordingly, the number of shares outstanding should be weighted by the same factor. To illustrate, assume that Salomski Inc. has the data in Illustration 17-7 for the changes in its common shares outstanding for the period.

Illustration 17-7

**Common Shares Outstanding,
Ending Balance—
Salomski Inc.**

Date	Share Changes	Shares Outstanding
Jan. 1	Beginning balance	90,000
Apr. 1	Issued 30,000 shares for cash	30,000
		120,000
July 1	Repurchased 39,000 shares	(39,000)
		81,000
Nov. 1	Issued 60,000 shares for cash	60,000
Dec. 31	Ending balance	141,000

To calculate the weighted average number of shares outstanding, the calculation is done as in Illustration 17-8.

Illustration 17-8

Weighted Average Number of
Shares Outstanding

Dates Outstanding	(A) Shares Outstanding	(B) Fraction of Year	(C) Weighted Shares (A × B)
Jan. 1–Mar 31	90,000	3/12	22,500
Apr. 1–June 30	120,000	3/12	30,000
July 1–Oct. 31	81,000	4/12	27,000
Nov. 1–Dec. 31	141,000	2/12	23,500
Weighted average number of shares outstanding			103,000

As illustrated, 90,000 shares were outstanding for three months, which translates to 22,500 whole shares for the entire year. Because additional shares were issued on April 1, the number of shares outstanding changes and these shares must be weighted for the time that they have been outstanding. When 39,000 shares were repurchased on July 1, this reduced the number of shares outstanding and a new calculation again has to be made to determine the proper weighted number of shares outstanding.

Stock Dividends, Splits, and Reverse Splits

When stock dividends or stock splits occur, calculation of the weighted average number of shares requires a restatement of the shares outstanding before the stock dividend or split.[6] For example, assume that a corporation had 100,000 shares outstanding on January 1 and issued a 25% stock dividend on June 30. For purposes of calculating a weighted average for the current year, the additional 25,000 shares outstanding as a result of the stock dividend are assumed to have been outstanding since the beginning of the year. Thus, the weighted average for the year would be 125,000 shares.

The issuance of a stock dividend or stock split requires a restatement (which is applied retroactively), but the issuance or repurchase of shares for cash does not. Why? Stock splits and stock dividends do not increase or decrease the net enterprise's assets; only additional shares are issued. Therefore, the weighted average number of shares must be restated. By restating the number, valid comparisons of earnings per share can be made between periods before and after the stock split or stock dividend. Conversely, the issuance or purchase of shares for cash changes the amount of net assets. The company earns either more or less in the future as a result of this change in net assets. Stated another way, a stock dividend or split does not change the shareholders' total investment; it only increases (or decreases if it is a reverse stock split) the **number** of common shares.

To illustrate how a stock dividend affects the calculation of the weighted average number of shares outstanding, assume that Baiye Limited has the data in Illustration 17-9 for the changes in its common shares during the year.

Illustration 17-9

Shares Outstanding, Ending
Balance—Baiye Limited

Date	Share Changes	Shares Outstanding
Jan. 1	Beginning balance	100,000
Mar. 1	Issued 20,000 shares for cash	20,000
		120,000
June 1	60,000 additional shares (50% stock dividend)	60,000
		180,000
Nov. 1	Issued 30,000 shares for cash	30,000
Dec. 31	Ending balance	210,000

Illustration 17-10 shows the calculation of the weighted average number of shares outstanding.

Dates Outstanding	(A) Shares Outstanding	(B) Restatement	(C) Fraction of Year	(D) Shares Weighted (A × B × C)
Jan. 1–Feb. 28	100,000	1.50	2/12	25,000
Mar. 1–May 31	120,000	1.50	3/12	45,000
June 1–Oct. 31	180,000		5/12	75,000
Nov. 1–Dec. 31	210,000		2/12	35,000
Weighted average number of shares outstanding				180,000

The shares outstanding before the stock dividend must be restated. The shares outstanding from January 1 to June 1 are adjusted for the stock dividend so that these shares are stated on the same basis as shares issued after the stock dividend. Shares issued after the stock dividend do not have to be restated because they are already on the new basis. The stock dividend simply restates existing shares. A stock split is treated in the same way.

If a stock dividend or stock split occurs after the end of the year, but before the financial statements are issued, the weighted average number of shares outstanding for the year (and any other years presented in comparative form) must be restated. For example, assume that Hendricks Corp. calculates its weighted average number of shares to be 100,000 for the year ended December 31, 2014. On January 15, 2015, before the financial statements are issued, the company splits its shares 3 for 1. In this case, the weighted average number of shares used in calculating earnings per share for 2014 would be 300,000 shares. If earnings per share information for 2013 is provided as comparative information, it also must be adjusted for the stock split.

Mandatorily Convertible Instruments

Where common shares will be issued in future due to mandatory conversion of a financial instrument that is already outstanding, it is assumed that the conversion has already taken place for EPS calculation purposes. For these instruments, the denominator of the basic EPS calculation would be adjusted as though the instruments had already been converted to common shares and that the common shares were outstanding. An adjustment may be needed for the numerator depending on how the instruments were presented in the financial statements (that is, as debt, common shares, or preferred shares). Note that if the instruments were presented as common share equity already, there would be no need to adjust the numerator and the concern would only be to ensure the number of common shares was adjusted for these shares that were not yet outstanding.

Contingently Issuable Shares

Contingently issuable shares are potential common shares, as mentioned earlier. If these shares are issuable simply with the passage of time (as with the mandatorily convertible instruments noted above), they are not considered contingently issuable since it is certain that time will pass. Where they are issuable based on something else (for example, profit levels or performance targets), they are included in the calculation of basic EPS when the conditions are satisfied.

Comprehensive Illustration

Leung Corporation has income of $580,000 before discontinued operations (net of tax) of $240,000. In addition, it has declared preferred dividends of $1 per share on 100,000 preferred shares outstanding. Leung Corporation also has the data shown in Illustration 17-11 for changes in its common shares outstanding during 2014.

Illustration 17-11

Shares Outstanding, Ending Balance—Leung Corp.

Dates	Share Changes	Shares Outstanding
Jan. 1	Beginning balance	180,000
May 1	Purchased 30,000 shares	30,000
		150,000
July 1	300,000 additional shares issued (3-for-1 stock split)	300,000
		450,000
Dec. 31	Issued 50,000 shares for cash	50,000
Dec. 31	Ending balance	500,000

To calculate the earnings per share information, the weighted average number of shares outstanding is first determined as in Illustration 17-12.

Illustration 17-12

Weighted Average Number of Shares Outstanding

Dates Outstanding	(A) Shares Outstanding	(B) Restatement	(C) Fraction of Year	(D) Shares Weighted (A × B × C)
Jan. 1–Apr. 30	180,000	3	4/12	180,000
May 1–Dec. 31	150,000	3	8/12	300,000
Weighted average number of shares outstanding				480,000

In calculating the weighted average number of shares, the shares sold on December 31, 2014, are ignored because they have not been outstanding during the year. Income before discontinued operations and net income are then divided by the weighted average number of shares to determine the earnings per share. Leung Corporation's preferred dividends of $100,000 are subtracted from income before discontinued operations ($580,000) to arrive at income from continuing operations available to common shareholders of $480,000 ($580,000 − $100,000). Deducting the preferred dividends from the income from continuing operations has the effect of also reducing net income without affecting the amount of the discontinued operations. The final amount is referred to as income available to common shareholders. Illustration 17-13 shows the calculation of income available to common shareholders.

Illustration 17-13

Calculation of Income Available to Common Shareholders

	(A) Income Information	(B) Weighted Shares	(C) Earnings per Share (A ÷ B)
Income from continuing operations available to common shareholders	$480,000	480,000	$1.00
Income from discontinued operations (net of tax)	240,000	480,000	0.50
Income available to common shareholders	$720,000	480,000	$1.50

Disclosure of the per share amount for the discontinued operations (net of tax) must be reported either on the face of the income statement or in the notes to the financial statements. Income and per share information would be reported as in Illustration 17-14.

Illustration 17-14

Earnings per Share, with Discontinued Operations

Income from continuing operations	$580,000
Income from discontinued operations, net of tax	240,000
Net income	$820,000

(continued)

Illustration 17-14

Earnings per Share, with
Discontinued Operations
(continued)

Earnings per share:
Income from continuing operations	$1.00
Income from discontinued operations, net of tax	0.50
Net income	$1.50

DILUTED EPS

Complex Capital Structure

Finance

Objective 4

Calculate earnings per
share for companies
with a complex capital
structure.

One problem with a basic EPS calculation is that it fails to recognize the potentially dilutive impact on outstanding shares when a corporation has dilutive securities in its capital structure. **Dilutive securities must be considered because their conversion or exercise often decreases earnings per share.** This adverse effect can be significant and, more important, unexpected, unless financial statements call attention to the potentially dilutive effect.

A complex capital structure exists when a corporation has potential common shares such as convertible securities, options, warrants, or other rights that could dilute earnings per share if they are converted or exercised. **Therefore, as noted earlier, when a company has a complex capital structure, both basic and diluted earnings per share are generally reported.** The calculation of diluted EPS is similar to the calculation of basic EPS. The difference is that diluted EPS includes the effect of all dilutive potential common shares that were outstanding during the period, on both income and shares. The formula in Illustration 17-15 shows the relationship between basic EPS and diluted EPS.

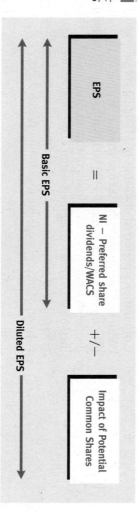

Illustration 17-15

Relationship between Basic
and Diluted EPS

$$\text{EPS} = \frac{\text{NI} - \text{Preferred share dividends/WACS}}{} +/- \text{Impact of Potential Common Shares}$$

Basic EPS

Diluted EPS

Note that companies with complex capital structures will not report diluted EPS if the securities in their capital structure are antidilutive. **Antidilutive securities** are securities that, upon conversion or exercise, increase earnings per share (or reduce the loss per share). The purpose of presenting both EPS numbers is to inform financial statement users of situations that may occur and to provide worst-case dilutive situations. If the securities are antidilutive, the likelihood of conversion or exercise is considered remote. **Thus, companies that have only antidilutive securities report only the basic EPS number.**[7]

The calculation of basic EPS was shown in the previous section. The discussion in the following sections addresses the effects of convertible and other dilutive securities on EPS calculations.

Convertible Securities

At conversion, convertible securities are exchanged for common shares. Convertible securities are therefore potential common shares and may be dilutive. The method that is used to measure the dilutive effects of a potential conversion on EPS is sometimes called the **if-converted method.**[8]

If-Converted Method

The if-converted method for convertible debt or preferred shares assumes both of the following:

1. It assumes that the convertible securities are converted at the **beginning of the period** (or at the time of the security issuance, if they are issued during the period).[9]

2. It assumes **the elimination of related interest, net of tax** or a preferred share dividend. If the debt/equity had been converted at the beginning of the period, there would be no bond interest expense/preferred dividend. No tax effect is calculated for preferred share dividends, because preferred dividends generally are not tax-deductible.

Thus the denominator—the weighted average number of shares outstanding—is increased by the additional shares that are assumed to be issued. The numerator—net income—is increased by the amount of interest expense, net of tax or preferred share dividends, that is associated with those convertible securities.

As an example, assume that Field Corporation has net income for the year of $410,000 and a weighted average number of common shares outstanding during the period of 100,000 shares. The basic earnings per share is therefore $4.10 ($410,000 ÷ 100,000).

The company has two convertible debenture bond issues outstanding.[10] One is a 6% issue sold at 100 (total $1 million) in a prior year and convertible into 20,000 common shares. The other is a 10% issue sold at 100 (total $500,000) on April 1 of the current year and convertible into 32,000 common shares. The tax rate is 30%.

As shown in Illustration 17-16, to determine the numerator, we add back the interest on the if-converted securities less the related tax effect. Because the if-converted method assumes that conversion occurs at the beginning of the year, no interest on the convertible securities is assumed to be paid during the year. The interest on the 6% convertible bonds is $60,000 for the year ($1,000,000 × 6%). The increased tax expense is $18,000 ($60,000 × 0.30), and the interest added back net of taxes is $42,000 [$60,000 − $18,000, or simply $60,000 × (1 − 0.30)].

Because the 10% convertible bonds are issued after the beginning of the year, the shares that are assumed to have been issued on that date, April 1, are weighted as outstanding from April 1 to the end of the year. In addition, the interest adjustment to the numerator for these bonds would only reflect the interest for nine months. Thus, the interest added back on the 10% convertible security would be $26,250 [$500,000 × 10% × 9/12 year × (1 − 0.30)]. The calculation of earnings (the numerator) for diluted earnings per share is shown in Illustration 17-16. Note that both debentures are individually dilutive.

Net income for the year	$410,000
Add: Adjustment for interest (net of tax)	
6% debentures ($60,000 × [1 − 0.30])	42,000
10% debentures ($100,000 × 9/12 × [1 − 0.30])	26,250
Adjusted net income	$478,250

The calculation of the weighted average number of shares adjusted for dilutive securities—the denominator in a diluted earnings per share calculation—is shown in Illustration 17-17.

Weighted average number of shares outstanding	100,000
Add: Shares assumed to be issued:	
6% debentures (as of beginning of year)	20,000
10% debentures (as of date of issue, April 1; 9/12 × 32,000)	24,000
Weighted average number of shares adjusted for dilutive securities	144,000

Field Corporation would then report earnings per share based on a dual presentation on the face of the income statement; that is, it would present both basic and diluted earnings per share.[11] The presentation is shown in Illustration 17-18.

Illustration 17-18

Earnings per Share Disclosure

Net income for the year	$410,000
Earnings per share:	
Basic earnings per share ($410,000 ÷ 100,000)	$4.10
Diluted earnings per share ($478,250 ÷ 144,000)	$3.32

Other Factors

The example above assumed that Field Corporation's debentures were sold at their face amount. If the bonds were instead sold at a premium or discount, interest expense would have to be adjusted each period to account for this occurrence. Therefore, the amount of interest expense added back, net of tax, to net income is the interest expense reported on the income statement, not the interest paid in cash during the period. Likewise, because the convertible debentures are compound instruments, a portion of the proceeds would actually be allocated to the equity component, and the discount rate on the debt would be the market interest rate on straight debt. Finally, if the company had the option to settle the debentures using shares or cash, we would assume shares were used. (Further discussion of these factors is beyond the scope of this text.)

The conversion rate on a dilutive security may change over the period that the dilutive security is outstanding. In this situation, for the diluted EPS calculation, the most advantageous conversion rate available to the holder is used.[12] For example, assume that a convertible bond was issued January 1, 2012, with a conversion rate of 10 common shares for each bond starting January 1, 2014, beginning January 1, 2017, the conversion rate is 12 common shares for each bond; and beginning January 1, 2022, it is 15 common shares for each bond. In calculating diluted EPS in 2012, the conversion rate of 15 shares to one bond would be used.

Options and Warrants

Recall from Chapter 16 that stock options allow the holder to buy or sell shares at a preset price (the **exercise price**). The company may either **write** the options or **purchase** them. The options may also allow the holder to buy the shares (**call options**) or sell the shares (**put options**).[13]

Written Options

When the company writes or sells the options, it gives the holder or purchaser the right to either buy (call) or sell (put) the shares. **Thus, if the holder or purchaser decides to exercise the options, the company will have to deliver (either buy or sell the shares).** Generally speaking, the holder of the options will exercise the right if the options are in the money. They are in the money if the holder of the options will benefit from exercising them. If the option is a call option—giving the holder the right to buy the shares at a pre-set price—the holder will exercise it if the pre-set or exercise price is lower than the current market price. **Written options and their equivalents must be included in the diluted EPS calculations if they are dilutive. Generally speaking, they are dilutive when they are written options that are in the money.**

Assume, for example, that Gaddy Limited sold (or wrote) **call options** for $2 that allow the purchaser to buy shares of Gaddy at $10 (the exercise price). At the time, Gaddy shares were trading at $9. Assume further that the market price of Gaddy shares subsequently increases to $15. The options are now in the money since they have value to the holder. If the holder exercises the options, Gaddy will have to issue its own shares for the exercise price ($10). This will result in dilution for Gaddy and so must be considered in the diluted EPS calculation. Note that if the shares of Gaddy never go above $10, the holder will not exercise them and the options will expire. Expired options as well as options that are not in the money are excluded from the diluted EPS calculation.

If Gaddy had instead sold **put options** that allow the purchaser to sell shares of Gaddy to Gaddy at an exercise price of $8, these might also be dilutive. Assume that when the put options were issued, Gaddy shares were $9, and that the shares subsequently went down to $6. If the put option is exercised, Gaddy will have to buy the shares from the option holder and will have to pay $8—the exercise price. Again, this must be incorporated in the diluted EPS calculation as it is in the money for the holder. The holder can sell the shares for more than their market value. Once again, if the options expire or are not in the money, they are not included in the diluted EPS calculation (since it is assumed that they will not be exercised).

Written put options, where the company may be forced to buy the shares at an unfavourable price, are the same as **forward purchase contracts.** Forward purchase contracts are included in the calculations if they represent a liability; that is, if the forward purchase price is higher than the average market price. Similarly, written call options are the same as **forward sales contracts.** Forward sales contracts are also included in the calculations if they represent a liability; that is, if the forward selling price is lower than the market price. In both cases, the instruments are in the money to the other party.

Purchased Options

Purchased options, on the other hand, do not result in the company having an obligation (as opposed to written options, which do result in an obligation). When the company buys options, it obtains the right but not the obligation to buy (call) or sell (put) its own shares. When will it exercise these options? Like any option holder, it is assumed that the company will exercise the options when they are in the money. Thus, when the underlying shares in a purchased call option have a market value that is greater than the exercise price, they are in the money. Alternatively, when the underlying shares in a purchased put option have a market value that is less than the exercise price, the options are in the money and it is assumed that they will be exercised.

Illustration 17-19 summarizes this.

Finance

Illustration 17-19
In-the-Money Options

	Call	Put
Written	In the money when market price is greater than exercise price	In the money when market price is less than exercise price
Purchased	In the money when market price is greater than exercise price	In the money when market price is less than exercise price

Purchased options will always be antidilutive since they will only be exercised when they are in the money and this will always be favourable to the company. They are therefore not considered in the calculation.[14]

Treasury Stock Method

Written options and warrants, and their equivalents, are included in earnings per share calculations through what is sometimes referred to as the treasury stock and/or reverse treasury stock method.

The treasury stock method applies to **written call options and equivalents** and assumes that:

1. the options and warrants or equivalents are exercised **at the beginning of the year** (or on the date of issue if it is later), and

2. the proceeds are used to purchase common shares for the treasury at the **average market price during the year.**

If the exercise price is lower than the average market price, then the proceeds from exercise are not sufficient to buy back all the shares. This would result in more shares being issued than purchased and the effect will therefore be dilutive. **The excess number of the shares to be issued over the number of shares that would be purchased is added to the weighted average number of shares outstanding in calculating the diluted earnings per share. Note that no adjustment is made to the numerator.**

Assume, for example, that 1,500 (written) call options are outstanding at an exercise price of $30 for a common share. The average common share market price per share is $50. Because the market price is greater than the exercise price, the options are considered in the money and the holder is assumed to exercise them. The holder can buy the shares for a price that is less than market price—a bargain. By applying the treasury stock method, there would be 600 incremental shares outstanding, calculated as in Illustration 17-20.[15]

Illustration 17-20

Calculation of Incremental Shares

Proceeds from exercise of 1,500 options (1,500 × $30)	$45,000
Shares issued upon exercise of options	1,500
Treasury shares purchasable with proceeds ($45,000 ÷ $50)	900
Incremental shares outstanding (additional potential common shares)	600

Thus, if the exercise price of the call option or warrant is lower than the shares' market price, dilution occurs because, on a net basis, more common shares are assumed to be outstanding after the exercise. If the exercise price of the call option or warrant is higher than the shares' market price, the options would not be exercised and would therefore be irrelevant to the EPS calculation.[16] As a practical matter, a simple average of the weekly or monthly prices is adequate, as long as the prices do not fluctuate significantly.

To illustrate the application of the treasury stock method, assume that Kubitz Industries, Inc. has net income for the period of $220,000. The average number of shares outstanding for the period was 100,000 shares. Hence, basic EPS, ignoring all dilutive securities, is $2.20. The average number of shares that are issuable under written call options at an option price of $20 per share is 5,000 shares (although the options are not exercisable at this time). The average market price of the common shares during the year was $28. Illustration 17-21 shows the calculation.

Illustration 17-21

Calculation of Earnings per Share—Treasury Stock Method

	Basic Earnings per Share	Diluted Earnings per Share
Average number of shares issuable under options:		
Option price per share		5,000
		× $20
Proceeds upon exercise of options		$100,000
Average market price of common shares		$28
Treasury shares that could be repurchased with proceeds ($100,000 ÷ $28)		3,571
Excess of shares under option over the treasury shares that could be repurchased		
(5,000 − 3,571)—potential incremental common shares		1,429
Average number of common shares outstanding		100,000
Total average number of common shares outstanding and potential common shares	100,000 (A)	101,429 (C)
Net income for the year	$220,000 (B)	$220,000 (D)
Earnings per share	$2.20 (B ÷ A)	$2.17 (D ÷ C)

Reverse Treasury Stock Method

The **reverse treasury stock method** is used for (written) put options and forward purchase contracts. It assumes both of the following:

1. The company would issue enough common shares **at the beginning of the year** in the marketplace (at the average market price) to generate sufficient funds to buy the shares under the option/forward.

2. The proceeds from the above would be used to buy back the shares under the option/forward at the beginning of the year.

If the options are in the money, the company would have to buy the shares back under the options/forward at a higher price than the market price. Thus, it would have to issue more shares at the beginning of the year to generate sufficient funds to meet the obligation under the option/forward.

Assume, for example, that 1,500 (written) put options are outstanding at an exercise price of $30 for a common share. The average market price per common share is $20. Because the market price is less than the exercise price, the options are considered in the money and the holder is assumed to exercise them. The holder can sell the shares for a price that is higher than market price—again, a bargain. By applying the reverse treasury stock method, there would be 750 additional (incremental) shares outstanding, calculated as in Illustration 17-22.

Illustration 17-22
Calculation of Incremental Shares

Amount needed to buy 1,500 shares under put option (1,500 × $30)	$45,000
Shares issued in market to obtain $45,000 ($45,000 ÷ $20)	2,250
Number of shares purchased under the put options	1,500
Incremental shares outstanding (potential common shares)	750

This is dilutive because there would be 750 more shares outstanding. If the market price were higher than the exercise price, the options would never be exercised. (This is because the holder could sell the shares in the marketplace for a higher amount.) Thus, options that are not in the money are ignored in the diluted EPS calculation. Likewise, when the forward purchase price of a forward purchase contract is lower than the market price, the forward contract is antidilutive because the company would theoretically have to issue fewer shares in the marketplace in order to generate sufficient money to honour the forward contract. In other words, it would issue fewer shares than it would buy back, resulting in fewer common shares outstanding (not more).

Contingently Issuable Shares

Contingently issuable shares are potential common shares, as mentioned earlier. If the shares are issuable upon attaining a certain earnings or market price level, for instance, and this level is met at the end of the year, they should be considered as outstanding from the beginning of the year for the calculation of diluted earnings per share. If the conditions have not been met, however, the diluted EPS may still be affected. The number of contingently issuable shares included in the diluted EPS calculation would be based on the number of shares (if any) that would be issuable if the end of the reporting period were the end of the contingency period and if the impact were dilutive.

For example, assume that Walz Corporation purchased Cardella Limited in 2014 and agreed to give the shareholders of Cardella 20,000 additional shares in 2016 if Cardella's net income in 2015 is $90,000. Assume also that in 2014 Cardella's net income is $100,000, which is higher than the $90,000 target for 2015. Because the contingency of stipulated earnings of $90,000 is already being attained in 2014, and because 2014 is treated as though it were the end of the contingency period, Walz's diluted earnings per share for

2014 would include the 20,000 contingent shares in the calculation of the number of shares outstanding.

Antidilution Revisited

In calculating diluted EPS, the combined impact of all dilutive securities must be considered. However, it is necessary to first determine which potentially dilutive securities are in fact individually dilutive and which are antidilutive. As was stated earlier, securities that are antidilutive have to be excluded from EPS calculations; they therefore cannot be used to offset dilutive securities.

Recall that antidilutive securities are securities whose inclusion in earnings per share calculations **would increase earnings per share (or reduce net loss per share).** Convertible debt is antidilutive if the addition to income of the interest (net of tax) would cause a greater percentage increase in income (the numerator) than a conversion of the bonds would cause a percentage increase in common and potentially dilutive shares (the denominator). In other words, convertible debt is antidilutive if conversion of the security would cause common share earnings to increase by a greater amount per additional common share than the earnings per share amount before the conversion.

To illustrate, assume that Kohl Corporation has a $1-million, 6% debt issue that is convertible into 10,000 common shares. Net income for the year is $210,000, the weighted average number of common shares outstanding is 100,000 shares, and the tax rate is 30%. In this case, assume also that conversion of the debt into common shares at the beginning of the year requires the adjustments to net income and the weighted average number of shares outstanding that are shown in Illustration 17-23.

Net income for year	$210,000	Average number of shares outstanding	100,000
Add: Adjustment for interest (net of tax) on 6% debentures $60,000 × (1 − 0.30)	42,000	Add: Shares issued upon assumed conversion of debt	10,000
Adjusted net income	$252,000	Average number of common and potential common shares	110,000

Basic EPS = $210,000 ÷ 100,000 = $2.10
Diluted EPS = $252,000 ÷ 110,000 = $2.29 (Antidilutive)

As a shortcut, the convertible debt can also be identified as antidilutive by comparing the incremental EPS resulting from conversion, $4.20 ($42,000 additional earnings ÷ 10,000 additional shares), with EPS before inclusion of the convertible debt, $2.10. With options or warrants, whenever the option or warrant is not in the money, it is irrelevant to the calculations because the holder would not exercise it.

Additional Disclosures

Complex capital structures and a dual presentation of earnings require the following additional disclosures in note form:

1. The amounts used in the numerator and denominator in calculating basic and diluted EPS

2. A reconciliation of the numerators and denominators of basic and diluted per share calculations for income before discontinued operations (including the individual income and share amounts of each class of securities that affects EPS)

3. Securities that could dilute basic EPS in the future but were not included in the calculations because they have antidilutive features

4. A description of common share transactions that occur after the reporting period that would have significantly changed the EPS numbers

Illustration 17-24 presents an example of the reconciliation and related disclosure that is needed to meet the standard's disclosure requirements. Assume that stock options to purchase 1 million common shares at $85 per share were outstanding during the second half of 2014 but that the options are antidilutive.

Illustration 17-24

Reconciliation for Basic and Diluted EPS

For the Year Ended December 31, 2014

	Income (Numerator)	Shares (Denominator)	Per Share Amount
Net Income	$7,500,000		
Less: Preferred stock dividends	(45,000)		
Basic EPS			
Income available to common shareholders	7,455,000	3,991,666	$1.87
Warrants		30,768	
Convertible preferred shares	45,000	308,333	
4% convertible bonds (net of tax)	60,000	50,000	
Diluted EPS			
Income available to common shareholders after assumed conversions	$7,560,000	4,380,767	$1.73

Related disclosure: Stock options to purchase 1 million common shares at $85 per share were outstanding during the second half of 2014 but were not included in the calculation of diluted EPS because the options' exercise price was greater than the average market price of the common shares. The options were still outstanding at the end of 2014 and expire on June 30, 2021.

One final note on additional disclosures: an entity may choose to report additional per share calculations based on other reported components of comprehensive income. If this is done, the weighted average number of shares would be the same and the basic and diluted EPS numbers must be presented with equal prominence.

Maple Leaf Foods recognized a charge of $80 million in its 2011 financial statements relating to restructuring (including severance, site closings, asset impairment, and other costs). In 2011, the overall net income was about $87 million, resulting in a basic earnings per share of 59 cents per share. In the MD&A, management disclosed an "adjusted EPS" figure that was calculated on net income before the restructuring, and other fair value adjustments. This resulted in a positive EPS number of 1.01 cents per share—almost double.

The company wanted to show the results of operations before the one-time costs so users could see how the rest of the business operations were performing. It felt that this additional information would be the most useful. As previously discussed in the text, care should be taken when presenting and using non-GAAP measures as they are non-standardized. In addition, it is important to remember that EPS is based on net income as opposed to comprehensive income.

What Do the Numbers Mean?

Real World Emphasis

Comprehensive Earnings per Share Exercise

The purpose of the following exercise is to show the method of calculating dilution when many securities are involved. Illustration 17-25 presents a section of the statement of financial position of Andrews Corporation, our assumed company; assumptions about the company's capital structure follow the illustration.

Long-term debt:

Notes payable, 14%	$ 1,000,000
7% convertible bonds payable	2,000,000
9% convertible bonds payable	3,000,000
Total long-term debt	$ 6,000,000

Shareholders' equity:

$10 cumulative dividend, convertible preferred shares, no par value; 100,000 shares authorized, 20,000 shares issued and outstanding		$ 2,000,000
Common shares, no par value; 5,000,000 shares authorized, 400,000 shares issued and outstanding		400,000
Contributed surplus		2,100,000
Retained earnings		9,000,000
Total shareholders' equity		$13,500,000

Notes and Assumptions

December 31, 2014

1. Options were granted or written in July 2012 to purchase 30,000 common shares at $15 per share. The average market price of Andrews' common shares during 2014 was $25 per common share. The options expire in 2022 and no options were exercised during 2014.

2. The 7% bonds were issued in 2013 at face value. The 9% convertible bonds were issued on July 1, 2014, at face value. Each convertible bond is convertible into 50 common shares (each bond has a face value of $1,000).

3. The $10 cumulative, convertible preferred shares were issued at the beginning of 2011. Each preferred share is convertible into four common shares.

4. The average income tax rate is 30%.

5. The 400,000 common shares were issued at $1 per share and were outstanding during the entire year.

6. Preferred dividends were not declared in 2014.

7. Net income was $1.2 million in 2014.

8. No bonds or preferred shares were converted during 2014.

Instructions

(a) Calculate basic earnings per share for Andrews for 2014.

(b) Calculate diluted earnings per share for Andrews for 2014, following these steps:

1. Determine, for each dilutive security, the incremental per share effect if the security is exercised or converted. Where there are multiple dilutive securities, rank the results from the lowest earnings effect per share to the largest; that is, rank the results from the most dilutive to least dilutive. The instruments with the lowest incremental EPS calculation will drag the EPS number down the most and are therefore most dilutive.

2. Beginning with the basic earnings per share based upon the weighted average number of common shares outstanding, recalculate the earnings per share by adding the most dilutive per share effects from the first step. If the results from this recalculation are less than EPS in the prior step, go to the next most dilutive per

share effect and recalculate the earnings per share. This process is continued as long as each recalculated earnings per share amount is smaller than the previous amount. The process will end either because there are no more securities to test or because a particular security maintains or increases the earnings per share (that is, it is antidilutive).

(c) Show the presentation of earnings per share for Andrews for 2014.

Solution to Comprehensive EPS Exercise

(a) Basic earnings per share

The calculation of basic earnings per share for 2014 starts with the amount based upon the weighted average number of common shares outstanding, as shown below.

Net income	$1,200,000
Less: $10 cumulative, convertible preferred share dividend requirements	200,000
Income applicable to common shareholders	$1,000,000
Weighted average number of common shares outstanding	400,000
Earnings per common share	$2.50

Note the following points about the above calculation:

1. When preferred shares are cumulative, the preferred dividend is subtracted to arrive at the income that is applicable to common shares, whether or not the dividend is declared.

2. The earnings per share of $2.50 is calculated as a starting point because the per share amount is not reduced by the existence of convertible securities and options.

(b) Diluted earnings per share

The steps in calculating diluted EPS are now applied to Andrews Corporation. (Note that net income and income available to common shareholders are not the same since the preferred dividends are cumulative.) Andrews Corporation has four items that could reduce EPS: options, 7% and 9% convertible bonds, and the convertible preferred shares.

The first step in calculating diluted earnings per share is to determine an incremental per share effect for each potentially dilutive security. Illustrations 17-26 through 17-29 show these calculations. Anything that is less than basic EPS is potentially dilutive.

Number of shares under option	30,000
Option price per share	× $15
Proceeds upon assumed exercise of options	$450,000
Average 2014 market price of common shares	$ 25
Treasury shares that could be acquired with proceeds ($450,000 ÷ $25)	18,000
Excess shares under option over treasury shares that could be repurchased (30,000 − 18,000)	12,000
Per share effect:	
Incremental numerator effect: None	
Incremental denominator effect: 12,000 shares	
Therefore potentially dilutive	$ 0

Illustration 17-26
Incremental Impact of Options

Illustration 17-27

Incremental Impact of 7% Bonds

Interest expense for year ($2,000,000 × 7%)		$140,000
Income tax reduction due to interest (30% × $140,000)		42,000
Interest expense avoided (net of tax)		$ 98,000
Number of common shares issued, assuming conversion of bonds (2,000 bonds × 50 shares)		100,000
Per share effect:		
Incremental numerator effect: $98,000		
Incremental denominator effect: 100,000 shares		$ 0.98

Therefore potentially dilutive

Illustration 17-28

Incremental Impact of 9% Bonds

Interest expense for year ($3,000,000 × 9%)		$270,000
Income tax reduction due to interest (30% × $270,000)		81,000
Interest expense avoided (net of tax)		$189,000
Number of common shares issued, assuming conversion of bonds (3,000 bonds × 50 shares)		150,000
Per share effect (outstanding 1/2 year):		
Incremental numerator effect: $189,000 x 0.5 = $94,500		
Incremental denominator effect: 150,000 shares × 0.5 = 75,000		$ 1.26

Therefore potentially dilutive

Illustration 17-29

Incremental Impact of Preferred Shares

Dividend requirement on cumulative preferred (20,000 shares × $10)		$200,000
Income tax effect (dividends not a tax deduction): None		-0-
Dividend requirement avoided		$200,000
Number of common shares issued, assuming conversion of preferred (4 × 20,000 shares)		80,000
Per share effect:		
Incremental numerator effect: $200,000		
Incremental denominator effect: 80,000 shares		$ 2.50

Therefore neutral

Illustration 17-30

Ranking of Potential Common Shares (Most Dilutive First)

Illustration 17-30 shows the ranking of all four potentially dilutive securities.

	$ Effect Per Share
Options	-0-
7% convertible bonds	0.98
9% convertible bonds	1.26
$10 convertible preferred	2.50

The next step is to determine earnings per share and, through this determination, to give effect to the ranking in Illustration 17-30. Starting with the basic earnings per share of $2.50 calculated previously, add the incremental effects of the options to the original calculation, as shown in Illustrations 17-31 to 17-34.

Illustration 17-31

Step-by-Step Calculation of Diluted EPS, Adding Options First (Most Dilutive)

Options

Income applicable to common shareholders		$1,000,000
Add: Incremental numerator effect of options: None		-0-
Total		$1,000,000

(continued)

Illustration 17-31

Step-by-Step Calculation of Diluted EPS, Adding Options First (Most Dilutive) (continued)

Weighted average number of common shares outstanding	400,000
Add: Incremental denominator effect of options—Illustration 17-26	12,000
Total	412,000
Recalculated earnings per share ($1,000,000 ÷ 412,000 shares)	$ 2.43

Since the recalculated earnings per share is reduced (from $2.50 to $2.43), the effect of the options is dilutive. Again, this effect could have been anticipated because the average market price exceeded the option price ($15).

Illustration 17-32 shows the recalculated earnings per share assuming the 7% bonds are converted.

Illustration 17-32

Step-by-Step Calculation of Diluted EPS, Adding 7% Bonds Next (Next Most Dilutive)

7% Bonds

Numerator from previous calculation	$1,000,000
Add: Interest expense avoided (net of tax)—Illustration 17-27	98,000
Total	$1,098,000
Denominator from previous calculation (shares)	412,000
Add: Number of common shares assumed issued upon conversion of bonds—Illustration 17-27	100,000
Total	512,000
Recalculated earnings per share ($1,098,000 ÷ 512,000 shares)	$ 2.14

Since the recalculated earnings per share is reduced (from $2.43 to $2.14), the effect of the 7% bonds is dilutive.

Next, in Illustration 17-33, earnings per share is recalculated assuming the conversion of the 9% bonds.

Illustration 17-33

Step-by-Step Calculation of Diluted EPS, Adding 9% Bonds Next (Next Most Dilutive)

9% Bonds

Numerator from previous calculation	$1,098,000
Add: Interest expense avoided (net of tax)—Illustration 17-28	94,500
Total	$1,192,500
Denominator from previous calculation (shares)	512,000
Add: Number of common shares assumed issued upon conversion of bonds—Illustration 17-28	75,000
Total	587,000
Recalculated earnings per share ($1,192,500 ÷ 587,000 shares)	$ 2.03

Since the recalculated earnings per share is reduced (from $2.14 to $2.03), the effect of the 9% convertible bonds is dilutive.

The final step (Illustration 17-34) is the recalculation that includes the 10% preferred shares.

Illustration 17-34

Step-by-Step Calculation of Diluted EPS, Adding Preferred Shares Next (Least Dilutive)

Preferred Shares

Numerator from previous calculation	$1,192,500
Add: Dividend requirements avoided—Illustration 17-29	200,000
Total	$1,392,500
Denominator from previous calculation (shares)	587,000

(continued)

Illustration 17-34

Step-by-Step Calculation of Diluted EPS, Adding Preferred Shares Next (Least Dilutive) (continued)

Add: Number of common shares assumed issued upon conversion of preferred—Illustration 17-29	80,000
Total	667,000
Recalculated earnings per share ($1,392,500 ÷ 667,000 shares)	$ 2.09

The effect of the $10 convertible preferred shares is anti-dilutive, because the per share effects result in a higher EPS of $2.09. Since the recalculated earnings per share is not reduced, the effects of the convertible preferred shares are not used in the calculation. Diluted earnings per share to be reported is therefore $2.03.

(c) **Presentation of EPS**

The disclosure of earnings per share on the income statement for Andrews Corporation is shown in Illustration 17-35.

Illustration 17-35

Presentation of EPS

Net Income	$1,200,000
Basic earnings per common share	$ 2.50
Diluted earnings per common share	$ 2.03

Illustration 17-36 summarizes the calculations for the comprehensive EPS exercise. In summary, when calculating EPS, follow the steps noted below:

Illustration 17-36

Summary of Calculations for the Comprehensive EPS Exercise

	Income	Shares	Per share amounts
Net Income	$1,200,000		
Less: Preferred stock dividends (20,000 × $10)	(200,000)		
Basic EPS	$1,000,000	400,000	$2.50
Options		12,000	
	1,000,000	412,000	2.43
7 % Bonds	98,000	100,000	
	1,098,000	512,000	2.14
9 % Bonds	94,500	75,000	
	1,192,500	587,000	2.03
Preferred shares	200,000	80,000	
Diluted Earnings Per Share	$1,392,500	667,000	$2.09

1. For basic EPS: calculate income available to common shareholders and weighted average number of common shares. Divide.

2. For diluted EPS:

(a) Obtain income available to common shareholders and weighted average number of common shares from the basic EPS calculation. This is your starting point.

(b) Identify potential dilutive securities (potential common shares).

(c) Calculate the incremental impact on EPS for each potential dilutive security. In other words, if the security was converted, what would be the impact on the numerator and denominator of the EPS calculation?

(d) Rank the potentially dilutive security from most dilutive to least.

(e) Recalculate EPS by starting with the most dilutive security first. If the recalculated EPS number is lower, add in the next most dilutive security. Stop when the recalculated EPS is lowest. This is the diluted EPS.

ANALYSIS AND IFRS/ASPE COMPARISON

Analysis

Objective 5

Identify the major differences in accounting between ASPE and IFRS, and what changes are expected in the near future.

Underlying Concept

The problem with setting standards for calculating EPS is that many of these dilutive financial instruments are very complex and it is not always easy to break them down into their economic components.

Finance

EPS is one of the most highly visible standards of measurement for assessing management stewardship and predicting a company's future value. It is therefore a very important number and, because of this importance, IFRS is very specific regarding its calculation.

Recall Illustration 17-6, which showed the common shareholders' claim on only residual income. Earnings per share provides shareholders with information that helps them predict the value of their shareholdings. The diluted EPS calculation is especially useful since there are many potential common shares outstanding through convertible securities, options and warrants, and other financial instruments, and shareholders need to understand how these instruments can affect their holdings. From an economic perspective, it is therefore important to carefully analyze the potential dilutive impact of the various securities instruments, and the IASB is helping make it possible to do such analyses by continually striving to ensure greater transparency in EPS calculations. Sometimes this is not so easy due to the complexity of the financial statements.

Earnings per share is also useful in valuing companies. When companies or their shares are valued, "earnings" are often discounted to arrive at an estimated value. While there are many different ways of doing this, discounted cash flow calculations (with earnings often used as a substitute for the calculation) or NPV (net present value) calculations are commonly used to estimate company or share value. Ideally, a **normalized or sustainable cash flow or earnings** number should be used in the valuation calculation since earnings or net income may be of higher or lower quality (as noted in Chapter 4). However, since calculating normalized or sustainable cash flows and earnings requires significant judgement, when valuing common shares, the EPS number is sometimes used instead since it is felt to be more reliable and all-inclusive.

The price earnings ratio provides useful information by relating earnings to the price that the shares are trading at. It is sometimes used to generate a quick estimate of the value of the shares, and therefore the company. It allows an easy comparison with other companies and the information is often readily available. The price earnings ratio divides the price of the share by the earnings per share number. The result is often called the **multiplier**. The multiplier shows the per share value that each dollar of earnings generates. For example, if the share value is $10 and EPS is $1, the multiplier is 10 (10 ÷ 1). **Therefore, each additional dollar of earnings is felt to generate an additional $10 in share price.** This is a very rough calculation only, especially when you think of the judgement that went into calculating that EPS number in the first place. Consider the hundreds of financial reporting choices, such as accounting methods, measurement uncertainty, bias, and other judgements. This is one of the major reasons why preparers of financial statements must be aware of the impact of all financial reporting decisions on the bottom line.

A Comparison of IFRS and ASPE

The main difference between the standards is that ASPE does not prescribe standards for calculating EPS at all. The EPS standards therefore only apply to publicly accountable entities in Canada and private enterprises that choose to apply IFRS.

Looking Ahead

Where do we go from here? As the accounting for derivatives and financial instruments continues to evolve, standard setters are gradually revisiting other areas to determine the

SUMMARY OF LEARNING OBJECTIVES

1 Understand why earnings per share (EPS) is an important number.

Earnings per share numbers give common shareholders an idea of the amount of earnings that can be attributed to each common share. This information is often used to predict future cash flows from the shares and to value companies.

2 Understand when and how earnings per share must be presented, including related disclosures.

Under IFRS, EPS must be presented for all public companies or companies that are intending to go public. The calculations must be presented on the face of the income statement for net income from continuing operations and net income (for both basic EPS and diluted EPS in the case of complex capital structures). When there are discontinued operations, the per share impact of these items must also be shown, but it can be shown either on the face of the income statement or in the notes. Comparative calculations must also be shown.

3 Calculate earnings per share for companies with a simple capital structure.

Basic earnings per share is an actual calculation that takes income available to common shareholders and divides it by the weighted average number of common shares outstanding during the period.

4 Calculate earnings per share for companies with a complex capital structure.

Diluted earnings per share is a "what if" calculation that considers the impact of potential common shares. Potential common shares include convertible debt and preferred shares, options and warrants, contingently issuable shares, and other instruments that may result in additional common shares being issued by the company. They are relevant because they may cause the present interests of the common shareholders to become diluted.

The if-converted method considers the impact of convertible securities such as convertible debt and preferred shares. It assumes that the instruments are converted at the beginning of the year (or issue date, if later) and that any related interest or dividend is thus avoided.

The treasury stock method looks at the impact of written call options on EPS numbers. It assumes that the options are exercised at the beginning of the year and that the money from the exercise is used to buy back shares in the open market at the average common share price.

The reverse treasury stock method looks at the impact of written put options. It assumes that the options are exercised at the beginning of the year and that the company first issues shares in the market (at the average share price) to obtain sufficient funds to buy the shares under the option.

Antidilutive potential common shares are irrelevant since they would result in diluted EPS calculations that are higher than the basic EPS. Diluted EPS must show the worst possible EPS number. Note that purchased options and written options that are not in the money are ignored for purposes of calculating diluted EPS because they are either antidilutive or will not be exercised.

impact of the standards for financial instruments on these other areas. Earnings per share is one such area.

Conversion features included in instruments, such as convertible debt and convertible preferred shares, are in substance embedded options. For instance, in many convertible debt instruments, the conversion feature represents a written call option. Why, then, would we not treat these embedded options as we treat stand-alone options? Why not use the treasury stock or reverse treasury stock method instead of the if-converted method?

Some derivative instruments, such as written put options and forwards to purchase the entity's own shares, are in fact liabilities. How should they be treated for EPS purposes?

With respect to financial instruments that are carried at fair value with gains/losses being booked through net income, many feel that the potentially dilutive impact is already captured when the instruments are revalued to their fair value. This includes some derivatives that are settleable in the entity's own equity instruments, which are treated as financial assets/liabilities.

At the time of writing, the IASB and FASB had paused work on the EPS project.

5 Identify the major differences in accounting between ASPE and IFRS, and what changes are expected in the near future.

ASPE does not prescribe accounting standards for EPS. The IASB and FASB were working on a revised plan of action to study the issues. At the time of writing, work on the project was paused.

KEY TERMS

antidilutive securities, p. 1076
basic EPS, p. 1069
call options, p. 1078
complex capital structure, p. 1070
contingently issuable shares, p. 1070
diluted EPS, p. 1069
exercise price, p. 1078
if-converted method, p. 1076

income available to common shareholders, p. 1071
in the money, p. 1078
potential common/ordinary share, p. 1070
put options, p. 1078
reverse treasury stock method, p. 1081
simple capital structure, p. 1070

treasury stock method, p. 1080
weighted average number of shares, p. 1072

Quiz

Brief Exercises

(LO 1, 2) BE17-1 The 2014 income statement of Schmidt Corporation showed net income of $1,230,000 and a loss from discontinued operations of $105,000. Schmidt had 40,000 common shares outstanding all year. (a) Calculate earnings per share for 2014 as it should be reported to shareholders. (b) Discuss why Schmidt Corporation's reporting of earnings per share is useful to financial statement users.

(LO 3) BE17-2 Hedley Corporation had 2014 net income of $1.4 million. During 2014, Hedley paid a dividend of $5 per share on 100,000 preferred shares. Hedley also had 220,000 common shares outstanding during the year. Calculate Hedley's 2014 earnings per share.

(LO 3) BE17-3 Assume the same information for Hedley Corporation as in BE17-2 except that the preferred shares are non-cumulative and the dividend has not been declared or paid.

(LO 3) BE17-4 Assume the same information for Hedley Corporation as in BE17-2 except that the preferred shares are cumulative and the dividends have not yet been declared or paid.

(LO 3) BE17-5 Bentley Corporation had 120,000 common shares outstanding on January 1, 2014. On May 1, 2014, Bentley issued 65,000 shares. On July 1, Bentley repurchased and cancelled 22,000 shares. Calculate Bentley's weighted average number of shares outstanding for the year ended December 31, 2014.

(LO 3) BE17-6 Laurin Limited had 42,000 common shares outstanding on January 1, 2014. On March 1, 2014, Laurin issued 20,000 shares in exchange for equipment. On July 1, Laurin repurchased and cancelled 10,000 shares. On October 1, 2014, Laurin declared and issued a 10% stock dividend. Calculate the weighted average number of shares outstanding for Laurin for the year ended December 31, 2014.

(LO 3) BE17-7 Assume the same information as in BE17-6 except that on October 1, 2014, Laurin declared a 3-for-1 stock split instead of a 10% stock dividend.

(LO 3) BE17-8 Assume the same information as in BE17-6 except that on October 1, 2014, Laurin declared a 1-for-2 reverse stock split instead of a 10% stock dividend.

(LO 3) BE17-9 Tomba Corporation had 300,000 common shares outstanding on January 1, 2014. On May 1, Tomba issued 30,000 shares. (a) Calculate the weighted average number of shares outstanding for the year ended December 31, 2014, if the 30,000 shares were issued for cash. (b) Calculate the weighted average number of shares outstanding for the year ended December 31, 2014, if the 30,000 shares were issued in a stock dividend.

(LO 3) BE17-10 Ethan Corporation had 100,000 common shares outstanding on December 31, 2013. During 2014, the company issued 12,000 shares on March 1, retired 5,000 shares on July 1, issued a 20% stock dividend on October 1, and issued 18,000 shares on December 1. For 2014, the company reported net income of $400,000 after a loss from discontinued operations of $50,000 (net of tax). The company issued a 2-for-1 stock split on February 1, 2015, and the

(LO 4) **BE17-11** Francine Limited was incorporated with share capital consisting of 100,000 common shares. In January 2014, it issued 20,000 mandatorily convertible preferred shares. The terms of the prospectus for the issuance of the preferred shares require the convertible preferred shares to be converted into common shares, at the rate of one preferred share for one common share, during the fourth quarter of 2015. The preferred shares pay an annual dividend of $4 per share. Assume that for the fiscal year ended December 31, 2014, the company made an after-tax profit of $140,000. Calculate the 2014 earnings per share.

(LO 4) **BE17-12** Milliken Corporation reported net income of $700,000 in 2014 and had 115,000 common shares outstanding throughout the year. Also outstanding all year were 9,500 of cumulative preferred shares, with each being convertible into two common shares. The preferred shares pay an annual dividend of $5 per share. Milliken's tax rate is 30%. Calculate Milliken's 2014 diluted earnings per share.

(LO 4) **BE17-13** Thiessen Corporation earned net income of $300,000 in 2014 and had 100,000 common shares outstanding throughout the year. Also outstanding all year was $800,000 of 10% bonds that are convertible into 26,000 common shares. Thiessen's tax rate is 25%. Calculate Thiessen's 2014 diluted earnings per share. For simplicity, ignore the IFRS requirement to record the debt and equity components of the bonds separately.

(LO 4) **BE17-14** Assume the same information as in BE17–13 except that the 10% bonds are convertible into 10,000 common shares. Calculate Thiessen's 2014 diluted earnings per share.

(LO 4) **BE17-15** Melanie Corporation reported net income of $550,000 in 2014 and had 900,000 common shares outstanding throughout the year. On May 1, 2014, Melanie issued 5% convertible bonds. Each $1,000 bond is convertible into 120 common shares. Total proceeds at par amounted to $1 million, and was allocated to the liability and equity components under the residual value method. The liability component was measured first, at present value of the stream of interest payments plus present value of the bond maturity value, all discounted at 8% (the interest rate that applies to similar straight bonds). At the time of issuance, the liability component was recorded at $922,685. Melanie's tax rate is 30%. Calculate Melanie's 2014 diluted earnings per share.

(LO 4) **BE17-16** Assume the same information as in BE17–15 except that Melanie reported net income of $350,000 in 2014. Calculate Melanie's 2014 diluted earnings per share.

(LO 4) **BE17-17** Lawrence Limited has 150,000 common shares outstanding throughout the year. On June 30, Lawrence issued 28,000 convertible preferred shares that are convertible into one common share each. Calculate the weighted average common shares for purposes of the diluted EPS calculations. Assume that the preferred shares are dilutive.

(LO 4) **BE17-18** Bedard Corporation reported net income of $300,000 in 2014 and had 200,000 common shares outstanding throughout the year. Also outstanding all year were 45,000 (written) options to purchase common shares at $10 per share. The average market price for the common shares during the year was $15 per share. Calculate the diluted earnings per share.

(LO 4) **BE17-19** Glavin Limited purchased 40,000 call options during the year. The options give the company the right to buy its own common shares for $9 each. The average market price during the year was $12 per share. Calculate the incremental shares outstanding for Glavin Limited.

(LO 4) **BE17-20** Use the same information as in BE17–19 and assume that Glavin also wrote put options that allow the holder to sell Glavin's shares to Glavin at $13 per share. Calculate the incremental shares outstanding for Glavin Limited.

(LO 4) **BE17-21** Assume the same information as in BE17–19 except that Glavin purchased put options to give it the option of selling its own common shares for $10 each. How should the options be treated for purposes of the diluted EPS calculation?

(LO 4) **BE17-22** Assume the same information as in BE17–20 except that the put options allow the holder to sell Glavin's shares to Glavin at $11 each. How should these options be treated for purposes of the diluted EPS calculation?

Exercises

(LO 3) **E17-1** **(Weighted Average Number of Shares)** On January 1, 2014, Saigon Distillers Inc. had 475,000 common shares outstanding. On April 1, the corporation issued 47,500 new common shares to raise additional capital. On July 1, the corporation declared and distributed a 20% stock dividend on its common shares. On November 1, the corporation repurchased on the market 45,000 of its own outstanding common shares to make them available for issuances relating to its key executives' outstanding stock options.

Instructions

(a) Calculate the weighted average number of shares outstanding as at December 31, 2014.

(b) Assume that Saigon Distillers Inc. had a 1-for-5 reverse stock split instead of a 20% stock dividend on July 1, 2014. Calculate the weighted average number of shares outstanding as at December 31, 2014.

(LO 1, 3) **E17-2 (Weighted Average Number of Shares)** Gogeon Inc. uses a calendar year for financial reporting. The company is authorized to issue 50 million common shares. At no time has Gogeon issued any potentially dilutive securities. The following list is a summary of Gogeon's common share activities:

Number of common shares issued and outstanding at December 31, 2012	6,500,000
Shares issued as a result of a 10% stock dividend on September 30, 2013	650,000
Shares issued for cash on March 31, 2014	2,500,000
Number of common shares issued and outstanding at December 31, 2014	9,650,000

Gogeon issued its 2014 financial statements on February 28, 2015. A 3-for-1 stock split of Gogeon's common shares occurred on March 31, 2015.

Instructions

(a) Calculate the weighted average number of common shares to use in calculating earnings per common share for 2013 on the 2013 comparative income statement.

(b) Calculate the weighted average number of common shares to use in calculating earnings per common share for 2013 on the 2014 comparative income statement.

(c) Calculate the weighted average number of common shares to use in calculating earnings per common share for 2014 on the 2014 comparative income statement.

(d) Calculate the weighted average number of common shares to use in calculating earnings per common share for 2014 on the 2015 comparative income statement.

(e) Calculate the weighted average number of common shares to use in calculating earnings per common share for 2015 on the 2015 comparative income statement.

(f) Referring to how EPS is used and applied, discuss why the weighted average number of common shares must be adjusted for stock dividends and stock splits.

(CMA adapted. Used with permission.)

(LO 2, 3) **E17-3 (EPS—Simple Capital Structure)** Koala Inc. had 210,000 common shares outstanding on December 31, 2013. During 2014, the company issued 8,000 shares on May 1 and retired 14,000 shares on October 31. For 2014, the company reported net income of $229,690 after a loss from discontinued operations of $40,600 (net of tax).

Instructions

(a) Calculate earnings per share for 2014 as it should be reported to shareholders.

(b) Assume that Koala Inc. issued a 3-for-1 stock split on January 31, 2015, and that the company's financial statements for the year ended December 31, 2014, were issued on February 15, 2015. Calculate earnings per share for 2014 as it should be reported to shareholders.

(c) Discuss why Koala Inc.'s reporting of earnings per share is useful to financial statement users.

(d) Is it possible for a corporation to have a simple capital structure one fiscal year and a complex capital structure in another fiscal year? If yes, how could this happen?

(LO 2, 3) **E17-4 (EPS—Simple Capital Structure)** On January 1, 2014, Logan Limited had shares outstanding as follows:

6% cumulative preferred shares, $100 par value, 10,000 shares issued and outstanding	$1,000,000
Common shares, 200,000 shares issued and outstanding	2,000,000

To acquire the net assets of three smaller companies, the company authorized the issuance of an additional 330,000 common shares. The acquisitions were as follows:

Date of Acquisition	Shares Issued
Company A: April 1, 2014	190,000
Company B: July 1, 2014	100,000
Company C: October 1, 2014	40,000

On May 14, 2014, Logan realized a $97,000 gain (before tax) on a discontinued operation from a business segment that had originally been purchased in 1997.

On December 31, 2014, the company recorded income of $680,000 before tax, not including the discontinued operation gain. Logan has a 30% tax rate.

Instructions

(a) Calculate earnings per share for 2014 as it should be reported to shareholders.

(b) Assume that Logan declared a 1-for-2 reverse stock split on February 10, 2015, and that the company's financial statements for the year ended December 31, 2014, were issued on February 28, 2015. Calculate earnings per share for 2014 as it should be reported to shareholders.

(c) What determines that Logan has a simple capital structure?

(LO 3) E17-5 (EPS—Simple Capital Structure) On January 1, 2014, Poelman Corp. had 580,000 common shares outstanding. During 2014, it had the following transactions that affected the common share account:

Feb. 1	Issued 180,000 shares.	
Mar. 1	Issued a 10% stock dividend.	
May 1	Acquired 200,000 common shares and retired them.	
June 1	Issued a 3-for-1 stock split.	
Oct. 1	Issued 60,000 shares.	

The company's year end is December 31.

Instructions

(a) Determine the weighted average number of shares outstanding as at December 31, 2014.

(b) Assume that Poelman earned net income of $3,456,000 during 2014. In addition, it had 100,000 of 9%, $100 par, non-convertible, non-cumulative preferred shares outstanding for the entire year. Because of liquidity limitations, however, the company did not declare and pay a preferred dividend in 2014. Calculate earnings per share for 2014, using the weighted average number of shares determined in part (a).

(c) Assume the same facts as in part (b), except that the preferred shares were cumulative. Calculate earnings per share for 2014.

(d) Assume the same facts as in part (b), except that net income included a loss from discontinued operations of $432,000, net of applicable income tax. Calculate earnings per share for 2014.

(e) What is the reasoning behind using a weighted average calculation for the number of shares outstanding in the EPS ratio?

Digging Deeper

(LO 3) E17-6 (EPS—Simple Capital Structure) Esau Inc. presented the following data:

Net income	$5,500,000
Preferred shares: 50,000 shares outstanding,	
8% cumulative, not convertible	
8% cumulative, not convertible	$5,000,000
Common shares: Shares outstanding, Jan. 1, 2014	650,000
Issued for cash, May 1, 2014	100,000
Acquired treasury shares for cash, Sept. 1, 2014 (shares cancelled)	150,000
2-for-1 stock split, Oct. 1, 2014	

As of January 1, 2014, there were no dividends in arrears. On December 31, 2014, Esau declared and paid the preferred dividend for 2014.

Instructions

(a) Calculate earnings per share for the year ended December 31, 2014.

(b) Discuss what the effect would be on your calculation in (a) if the stock split had been declared on January 30, 2015, instead of on October 1, 2014, assuming the financial statements of Esau Inc. for the year ending December 31, 2014, were issued after January 30, 2015.

(c) Assume that Esau did not declare or pay a preferred dividend in 2014. Calculate earnings per share for the year ended December 31, 2014.

(d) Assume that as of January 1, 2014, Esau had two years of dividends in arrears, and that on December 31, 2014, Esau declared and paid the dividends in arrears and the preferred dividend for 2014. Calculate earnings per share for the year ended December 31, 2014.

(e) Assume that the preferred shares are non-cumulative, and that the preferred dividend was paid in 2014. Calculate earnings per share for the year ended December 31, 2014.

(f) Assume that the preferred shares are non-cumulative, and that Esau did not declare or pay a preferred dividend in 2014. Calculate earnings per share for the year ended December 31, 2014.

(g) Discuss the effect of a stock split on Esau Inc.'s market price per share. Would a current shareholder favour Esau Inc.'s declaration of a stock split?

Digging Deeper

(LO 3) E17-7 (EPS—Simple Capital Structure) A portion of the combined statement of income and retained earnings of Nestor Inc. for the current year ended December 31, 2014 follows:

Income before discontinued operations	$ 30,000,000
Loss from discontinued operations, net of applicable income tax (Note 1)	2,205,000
Net income	27,795,000
Retained earnings at beginning of year	93,250,000
	121,045,000
Dividends declared:	
On preferred shares, $6.00 per share	$ 540,000
On common shares, $1.75 per share	14,875,000
	15,415,000
Retained earnings at end of year	$105,630,000

Note 1. During the year, Nestor Inc. suffered a loss from discontinued operations of $2,205,000 after the applicable income tax reduction of $735,000.

At the end of 2014, Nestor Inc. has outstanding 12.5 million common shares and 90,000 shares of 6% preferred. On April 1, 2014, Nestor Inc. issued 1 million common shares for $32 per share to help finance the loss.

Instructions

(a) Calculate the earnings per share on common shares for 2014 as it should be reported to shareholders.

(b) Assume that Nestor Inc. issued a 20% stock dividend on September 1, 2014. Calculate the earnings per share on common shares for 2014 as it should be reported to shareholders.

(LO 3) E17-8 (EPS—Simple Capital Structure) At January 1, 2014, Ming Limited's outstanding shares included the following:

280,000 $50 par value, 7%, cumulative preferred shares
900,000 common shares

Net income for 2014 was $2,130,000. No cash dividends were declared or paid during 2014. On February 15, 2015, however, all preferred dividends in arrears were paid, together with a 5% stock dividend on common shares. There were no dividends in arrears before 2014.

On April 1, 2014, 550,000 common shares were sold for $10 per share and on October 1, 2014, 310,000 common shares were purchased for $20 per share.

The financial statements for 2014 were issued in March 2015.

Instructions

(a) Calculate earnings per share for the year ended December 31, 2014.

(b) What is the significance of the declaration and payment date of February 15, 2015, for the dividend on preferred shares? What effect, if any, will this transaction have on the December 31, 2014 financial statements?

(c) Would your answer in part (b) change if the dividend arrears on preferred shares were for two years as at December 31, 2014?

Digging Deeper

(LO 4) E17-9 (EPS with Convertible Bonds, Various Situations) In 2013, Digital Inc. issued $75,000 of 8% bonds at par, with each $1,000 bond being convertible into 100 common shares. The company had revenues of $17,500 and expenses of $8,400 for 2014, not including interest and tax (assume a tax rate of 30%). Throughout 2014, 2,000 common shares were outstanding, and none of the bonds were converted or redeemed. (For simplicity, assume that the convertible bonds' equity element is not recorded.)

Instructions

(a) Calculate diluted earnings per share for the year ended December 31, 2014.

(b) Repeat the calculation in (a), but assume that the 75 bonds were issued on September 1, 2014 (rather than in 2013), and that none have been converted or redeemed.

(LO 4)   **(c)** Repeat the calculation in (a), but assume that 25 of the 75 bonds were converted on July 1, 2014.

E17-10   (EPS with Convertible Bonds) On June 1, 2012, Gustav Corp. and Gabby Limited merged to form Fallon Inc. A total of 800,000 shares were issued to complete the merger. The new corporation uses the calendar year as its fiscal year.

On April 1, 2014, the company issued an additional 400,000 shares for cash. All 1.2 million shares were outstanding on December 31, 2014. Fallon Inc. also issued $600,000 of 20-year, 8% convertible bonds at par on July 1, 2014. Each $1,000 bond converts to 40 common shares at any interest date. None of the bonds have been converted to date. If the bonds had been issued without the conversion feature, the annual interest rate would have been 10%.

Fallon Inc. is preparing its annual report for the fiscal year ending December 31, 2014. The annual report will show earnings per share figures based on a reported after-tax net income of $1,540,000 (the tax rate is 30%).

Instructions

(a) Determine for 2014 the number of shares to be used in calculating:

1. Basic earnings per share   **2.** Diluted earnings per share

(b) Determine for 2014 the earnings figures to be used in calculating:

1. Basic earnings per share   **2.** Diluted earnings per share

(LO 4)   **E17-11   (EPS with Convertible Bonds and Preferred Shares)** Ottey Corporation issued $4 million of 10-year, 7% callable convertible subordinated debentures on January 2, 2014. The debentures have a face value of $1,000, with interest payable annually. The current conversion ratio is 14:1, and in two years it will increase to 18:1. At the date of issue, the bonds were sold at 98 to yield a 7.2886% effective interest rate. Bond discount is amortized using the effective interest method. Ottey's effective tax was 25%. Net income in 2014 was $7.5 million, and the company had 2 million shares outstanding during the entire year. For simplicity, ignore the requirement to record the debentures' debt and equity components separately.

Instructions

(a) Prepare a schedule to calculate both basic and diluted earnings per share for the year ended December 31, 2014.

(b) Discuss how the schedule would differ if the security were convertible preferred shares.

(c) Assume that Ottey Corporation experienced a substantial loss of income for the fiscal year ending December 31, 2014. How would you respond to the argument made by a friend who states: "The interest expense from the conversion of the debentures is not actually saved, and there is no income tax to be paid on the additional income that is assumed to have been created from the conversion of the debentures."

Digging Deeper

(LO 4)   **E17-12   (EPS with Convertible Bonds and Preferred Shares)** On January 1, 2014, Shaylyn Limited issued $2.5 million of face value, 10-year, 7% bonds at par. Each $1,000 bond is convertible into 15 common shares. Shaylyn's net income in 2014 was $250,000, and its tax rate was 30%. The company had 100,000 common shares outstanding throughout 2014. None of the bonds were exercised in 2014. For simplicity, ignore the requirement to record the bonds' debt and equity components separately.

Instructions

(a) Calculate diluted earnings per share for the year ended December 31, 2014.

(b) Calculate diluted earnings per share for 2014, assuming the same facts as above, except that $1.5 million of 7% cumulative convertible preferred shares was issued instead of the bonds. Each $100 preferred share is convertible into four common shares.

(LO 4)   **E17-13   (EPS with Convertible Bonds and Preferred Shares)** Mininova Corporation is preparing earnings per share data for 2014. The net income for the year ended December 31, 2014, was $400,000 and there were 60,000 common shares outstanding during the entire year. Mininova has the following two convertible securities outstanding:

10% convertible bonds (each $1,000 bond is convertible into 25 common shares)	$100,000
5% convertible $100 par value preferred shares (each share is convertible into two common shares)	$50,000

Both convertible securities were issued at face value in 2011. There were no conversions during 2014, and Mininova's income tax rate is 24%. The preferred shares are cumulative. For simplicity, ignore the requirement to record the debt and equity components of the bonds separately.

Instructions

(a) Calculate Mininova's basic earnings per share for 2014.

(b) Calculate Mininova's diluted earnings per share for 2014.

(c) Recalculate Mininova's basic and diluted earnings per share for 2014, assuming instead that the preferred shares pay a 14% dividend.

(LO 4) **E17-14 (EPS with Convertible Bonds with Conversion and Preferred Shares)** Use the same information as in E17–13, except for the changes in part (c). Assume instead that 40% of the convertible bonds were converted to common shares on April 1, 2014.

Instructions

(a) Calculate Mininova's weighted average common shares outstanding.

(b) Calculate Mininova's basic earnings per share for 2014.

(c) Calculate Mininova's diluted earnings per share for 2014.

(d) What do you notice about the results of the diluted earnings per share calculation when conversions occur during the year and when they do not occur?

Digging Deeper

(LO 4) **E17-15 (EPS with Convertible Bonds and Preferred Shares)** Hayward Corporation had net income of $50,000 for the year ended December 31, 2014, and weighted average number of common shares outstanding of 10,000. The following information is provided regarding the capital structure:

1. 7% convertible debt, 200 bonds each convertible into 40 common shares. The bonds were outstanding for the entire year. The income tax rate is 25%. The bonds were issued at par ($1,000 per bond). No bonds were converted during the year.

2. 4% convertible, cumulative $100 preferred shares, 1,000 shares issued and outstanding. Each preferred share is convertible into two common shares. The preferred shares were issued at par and were outstanding the entire year. No shares were converted during the year.

Instructions

(a) Calculate the basic earnings per share for 2014.

(b) Briefly explain the if-converted method.

(c) Calculate the diluted earnings per share for 2014, using the if-converted method. For simplicity, ignore the requirement to record the debt and equity components of the bond separately.

(d) When Hayward Corporation issued the 7% convertible debt, would the company's interest rate on straight debt have been higher or lower than 7%? Explain your answer.

Digging Deeper

(LO 4) **E17-16 (EPS with Options, Various Situations)** Vimeo Corp.'s net income for 2014 is $90,000. The only potentially dilutive securities outstanding were 1,000 call options issued during 2013, with each option being exercisable for one share at $14. None have been exercised, and 50,000 common shares were outstanding during 2014. The average market price of the company's shares during 2014 was $20.

Instructions

(a) Calculate diluted earnings per share for the year ended December 31, 2014 (round to nearest cent).

(b) Assuming that the 1,000 call options were instead issued on October 1, 2014 (rather than in 2013), calculate diluted earnings per share for the year ended December 31, 2014 (round to nearest cent). The average market price during the last three months of 2014 was $20.

(c) How would your answers for parts (a) and (b) change if, in addition to the information for parts (a) and (b), the company issued (wrote) 1,000 put options with an exercise price of $10?

(LO 4) **E17-17 (EPS with Warrants)** Howard Corporation earned $480,000 during a period when it had an average of 100,000 common shares outstanding. The common shares sold at an average market price of $23 per share during the period. Also outstanding were 18,000 warrants that could each be exercised to purchase one common share for $10.

Instructions

(a) Are the warrants dilutive?

(b) Calculate basic earnings per share.

(c) Calculate diluted earnings per share.

(LO 4) E17-18 (EPS with Contingent Issuance Agreement) Purchaser Inc. recently purchased Target Corp., a large home-painting corporation. One of the terms of the merger was that if Target's net income for 2015 was $110,000 or more, 10,000 additional shares would be issued to Target's shareholders in 2016. Target's net income for 2014 was $120,000.

Instructions

(a) Would the contingent shares have to be considered in Purchaser's 2014 earnings per share calculations?

(b) Assume the same facts, except that the 10,000 shares are contingent on Target achieving a net income of $130,000 in 2015. Would the contingent shares have to be considered in Purchaser's earnings per share calculations for 2014?

(c) Provide support for the accounting treatment of the contingent shares discussed in part (a), referring to the conceptual framework.

Digging
Deeper

Problems

P17-1 Mavis Corporation is a new audit client of yours and has not reported earnings per share data in its annual reports to shareholders in the past. The treasurer, Andrew Benninger, has asked you to provide information about the reporting of earnings per share data in the corporation's financial statements.

Instructions

(a) Define the term "earnings per share" as it applies to a corporation with a capitalization structure that is composed of only one class of common shares. Explain how earnings per share should be calculated and how the information should be disclosed in the corporation's financial statements.

(b) Discuss the treatment, if any, that should be given to each of the following items in calculating the earnings per common share for financial statement reporting:

1. Outstanding preferred shares issued at a premium with a par value liquidation right

2. The exercise at a price below market value but above carrying amount of a call option on common shares that was issued during the current fiscal year to officers of the corporation.

3. The replacement of a machine immediately before the close of the current fiscal year at a cost that is 20% above the original cost of the replaced machine. The new machine will perform the same function as the old machine, which was sold for its carrying amount.

4. The declaration of current dividends on cumulative preferred shares.

5. The existence of purchased call options that allow the company to purchase shares of its own common shares at a price that is lower than the average market price

6. The acquisition of some of the corporation's outstanding common shares during the current fiscal year. The shares were classified as treasury shares.

7. A 2-for-1 stock split of common shares during the current fiscal year

P17-2 Loretta Corporation is preparing the comparative financial statements to be included in the annual report to shareholders. Loretta's fiscal year ends May 31. The following information is available.

1. Income from operations before income tax for Loretta was $1.4 million and $660,000, respectively, for the fiscal years ended May 31, 2015, and 2014.

2. Loretta experienced a loss from discontinued operations of $500,000 from a business segment disposed of on March 3, 2015.

3. A 25% combined income tax rate applies to all of Loretta Corporation's profits, gains, and losses.

4. Loretta's capital structure consists of preferred shares and common shares. The company has not issued any convertible securities or warrants and there are no outstanding stock options.

5. Loretta issued 150,000 of $100 par value, 6% cumulative preferred shares in 2007. All of these shares are outstanding, and no preferred dividends are in arrears.

6. There were 1.5 million common shares outstanding on June 1, 2013. On September 1, 2013, Loretta sold an additional 300,000 common shares at $17 per share. Loretta distributed a 15% stock dividend on the common shares outstanding on December 1, 2014.

7. These were the only common share transactions during the past two fiscal years.

Instructions

(a) Determine the weighted average number of common shares that would be used in calculating earnings per share on the current comparative income statement for:

1. The year ended May 31, 2015
2. The year ended May 31, 2014

(b) Starting with income from operations before income tax, prepare a comparative income statement for the years ended May 31, 2015, and 2014. Assume that Loretta discloses all applicable earnings per share data on the face of the income statement.

(c) A corporation's capital structure is the result of its past financing decisions. Furthermore, the earnings per share data that are presented on a corporation's financial statements depend on the corporation's capital structure.

1. Explain why Loretta Corporation is considered to have a simple capital structure.
2. Describe how earnings per share data would be presented for a corporation that had a complex capital structure.

(CMA adapted. Used with permission.)

P17-3 Audrey Inc. has 1 million common shares outstanding as at January 1, 2014. On June 30, 2014, 4% convertible bonds were converted into 100,000 additional shares. Up to that point, the bonds had paid interest of $250,000 after tax. Net income for the year was $1,298,678. During the year, the company issued the following:

1. June 30: 10,000 call options giving holders the right to purchase shares of the company for $30
2. Sept. 30: 15,000 put options allowing holders to sell shares of the company for $25

On February 1, Audrey also purchased in the open market 10,000 call options on its own shares, allowing it to purchase its own shares for $27. Assume the average market price for the shares during the year was $35.

Instructions

(a) Calculate the required EPS numbers under IFRS. For simplicity, ignore the impact that would result from the convertible debt being a hybrid security.

(b) Show the required presentations on the face of the income statement.

P17-4 Use the same information for Audrey Inc. as in P17-3, but also assume the following.

1. On September 30, 200,000 convertible preferred shares were redeemed. If they had been converted, these shares would have resulted in an additional 100,000 common shares being issued. The shares carried a dividend rate of $3 per share to be paid on September 30. No conversions have ever occurred.

2. There are 10,000 of $1,000, 5% convertible bonds outstanding with a conversion rate of three common shares for each bond starting January 1, 2015. Beginning January 1, 2018, the conversion rate is six common shares for each bond; and beginning January 1, 2022, it is nine common shares for each bond. The tax rate is 30%.

Instructions

(a) Calculate the required EPS numbers under IFRS. For simplicity, ignore the impact that would result from the convertible debt being a hybrid security.

(b) Show the required presentations on the face of the income statement.

P17-5 Tseng Corporation Ltd. has the following capital structure at the following fiscal years ended December 31:

	2014	2013
Number of common shares	375,000	330,000
Number of non-convertible, non-cumulative preferred A shares	10,000	10,000
Amount of 7% convertible bonds	$2,000,000	$2,000,000

The following additional information is available.

1. On July 31, 2014, Tseng Corporation exchanged common shares for a large piece of equipment. This was the only transaction that resulted in issuance of common shares in 2014.

2. Income before discontinued operations for 2014 was $950,000, and a loss from discontinued operations of $150,000 was recorded, net of applicable tax recovery.

3. During 2014, dividends in the amount of $4.00 per share were paid on the preferred A shares.

4. Each $1,000 bond can be converted into 20 common shares.

5. There were unexercised stock options, outstanding since 2011, that allow holders to purchase 20,000 common shares at $40.00 per share.

6. Written warrants to purchase 20,000 common shares at $60.00 per share were outstanding at the end of 2013, and no warrants were exercised in 2014.

7. The average market value of the common shares in 2014 was $50.00.

8. Tseng's tax rate is 30%.

9. Tseng declared and paid a $100,000 dividend to common shareholders on June 1, 2014.

Instructions

(a) Determine the weighted average number of common shares that would be used in calculating earnings per share for the year ended December 31, 2014.

(b) Starting with the heading "Income before discontinued operations," prepare the bottom portion of the income statement for the year ended December 31, 2014. Assume that Tseng Corporation discloses all applicable earnings per share data on the face of the income statement.

(AICPA adapted)

P17-6   Bryce Corporation is preparing the comparative financial statements for the annual report to its shareholders for the fiscal years ended May 31, 2014, and May 31, 2015. The income from operations was $1.8 million and $2.5 million, respectively, for each year. In both years, the company incurred a 10% interest expense on $2.4 million of debt for an obligation that requires interest-only payments for five years. The company experienced a loss of $600,000 from the discontinued operation of its Scotland facility in February 2015. The company uses a 30% effective tax rate for income tax.

The capital structure of Bryce Corporation on June 1, 2013, consisted of 1 million common shares outstanding and 20,000 of $50, par value, 6% cumulative preferred shares. There were no preferred dividends in arrears, and the company had not issued any convertible securities, options, or warrants.

On October 1, 2013, Bryce sold an additional 500,000 common shares at $20 per share. Bryce distributed a 20% stock dividend on the common shares outstanding on January 1, 2014. On December 1, 2014, Bryce was able to sell an additional 800,000 common shares at $22 per share. These were the only common share transactions that occurred during the two fiscal years.

Instructions

(a) Identify whether the capital structure at Bryce Corporation is a simple or complex capital structure, and explain why.

(b) Determine the weighted average number of shares that Bryce Corporation would use in calculating earnings per share for the fiscal year ended:
   1. May 31, 2014
   2. May 31, 2015

(c) Prepare, in good form, a comparative income statement that begins with income from operations for Bryce Corporation for the fiscal years ended May 31, 2014, and May 31, 2015. Assume that Bryce Corporation discloses all applicable earnings per share data on the face of the income statement.

(CMA adapted. Used with permission.)

P17-7   Shari Patel of the controller's office of Diamond Corporation was given the assignment of determining the basic and diluted earnings per share values for the year ending December 31, 2014. Patel has gathered the following information.

1. The company is authorized to issue 8 million common shares. As at December 31, 2013, 2 million shares had been issued and were outstanding.

2. The per share market prices of the common shares on selected dates were as follows:

	Price per Share
July 1, 2013	$20.00
Jan. 1, 2014	21.00
Apr. 1, 2014	25.00
July 1, 2014	11.00
Aug. 1, 2014	10.50
Nov. 1, 2014	9.00
Dec. 31, 2014	10.00

3. A total of 700,000 shares of an authorized 1.2 million convertible preferred shares had been issued on July 1, 2013. The shares were issued at $25, and have a cumulative dividend of $3 per share. The shares are convertible into common shares at the rate of one convertible preferred share for one common share. The rate of conversion is to be automatically adjusted for stock splits and stock dividends. Dividends are paid quarterly on September 30, December 31, March 31, and June 30.

4. Diamond Corporation is subject to a 30% income tax rate.

5. The after-tax net income for the year ended December 31, 2014, was $11,550,000.

The following specific activities took place during 2014:

1. January 1: A 5% common stock dividend was issued. The dividend had been declared on December 1, 2013, to all shareholders of record on December 29, 2013.

2. April 1: A total of 400,000 shares of the $3 convertible preferred shares were converted into common shares. The company issued new common shares and retired the preferred shares. This was the only conversion of the preferred shares during 2014.

3. July 1: A 2-for-1 split of the common shares became effective on this date. The board of directors had authorized the split on June 1.

4. August 1: A total of 300,000 common shares were issued to acquire a factory building.

5. November 1: A total of 24,000 common shares were purchased on the open market at $9 per share and cancelled.

6. Cash dividends to common shareholders were declared and paid as follows:

April 15: $0.30 per share
October 15: $0.20 per share

7. Cash dividends to preferred shareholders were declared and paid as scheduled.

Instructions

(a) Determine the number of shares to use in calculating basic earnings per share for the year ended December 31, 2014.

(b) Determine the number of shares to use in calculating diluted earnings per share for the year ended December 31, 2014.

(c) Calculate the adjusted net income amount to use as the numerator in the basic earnings per share calculation for the year ended December 31, 2014.

P17-8   Isabelle Leclerc is the controller at Camden Pharmaceutical Industries, a public company. She is currently preparing the calculation for basic and diluted earnings per share and the related disclosure for Camden's external financial statements. The following is selected financial information for the fiscal year ended June 30, 2014:

CAMDEN PHARMACEUTICAL INDUSTRIES
Selected Statement of Financial Position Information
June 30, 2014

Long-term debt

Notes payable, 10%	$ 1,000,000
7% convertible bonds payable	5,000,000
10% bonds payable	6,000,000
Total long-term debt	$12,000,000

Shareholders' equity

Preferred shares, $4.25 cumulative, 100,000 shares	
authorized, 25,000 shares issued and outstanding	$ 1,250,000
Common shares, unlimited number of shares	
authorized, 1,000,000 shares issued and outstanding	4,500,000
Contributed surplus—conversion rights	500,000
Retained earnings	6,000,000
Total shareholders' equity	$12,250,000

The following transactions have also occurred at Camden:

1. Options were granted by the company in 2012 to purchase 100,000 shares at $15 per share. Although no options were exercised during 2014, the average price per common share during fiscal year 2014 was $20.

2. Each bond was issued at face value. The 7% convertible debenture will convert into common shares at 50 shares per $1,000 bond. It is exercisable after five years and was issued in 2013. Ignore any requirement to record the bonds' debt and equity components separately.

3. The $4.25 preferred shares were issued in 2012.

4. There are no preferred dividends in arrears, and preferred dividends were not declared in fiscal year 2014.

5. The 1 million common shares were outstanding for the entire 2014 fiscal year.

6. Net income for fiscal year 2014 was $1.5 million, and the average income tax rate was 30%.

Instructions

(a) For the fiscal year ended June 30, 2014, calculate the following for Camden Pharmaceutical Industries:

1. Basic earnings per share

2. Diluted earnings per share

(b) Explain how premiums and discounts on outstanding convertible bonds affect the calculation of diluted earnings per share.

(c) From the perspective of a common shareholder, provide support for the treatment of the preferred dividends in calculating Camden Pharmaceutical Industries' basic and diluted earnings per share.

P17-9 An excerpt from the statement of financial position of Earl Limited follows:

EARL LIMITED
Selected Statement of Financial Position Information
At December 31, 2014

Long-term debt

Notes payable, 10%	$ 2,000,000
4% convertible bonds payable	3,000,000
6% convertible bonds payable	4,000,000
Total long-term debt	$ 9,000,000

Shareholders' equity

$0.80 cumulative, no par value, convertible preferred shares (unlimited number of shares authorized, 280,000 shares issued and outstanding)	$ 4,000,000
Common shares, no par value (5,000,000 shares authorized, 1,800,000 shares issued and outstanding)	18,000,000
Contributed surplus	100,000
Retained earnings	5,000,000
Total shareholders' equity	$27,100,000

Notes and Assumptions
December 31, 2014

1. Options were granted/written in 2013 that give the holder the right to purchase 50,000 common shares at $12 per share. The average market price of the company's common shares during 2014 was $18 per share. The options expire in 2022 and no options were exercised in 2014.

2. The 4% bonds were issued in 2013 at face value. The 6% convertible bonds were issued on July 1, 2014, at face value. Each convertible bond is convertible into 80 common shares (each bond has a face value of $1,000).

3. The convertible preferred shares were issued at the beginning of 2014. Each share of preferred is convertible into one common share.

4. The average income tax rate is 31%.

5. The common shares were outstanding during the entire year.

6. Preferred dividends were not declared in 2014.

7. Net income was $1,750,000 in 2014.

8. No bonds or preferred shares were converted during 2014.

Instructions

(a) Calculate basic earnings per share for 2014.

(b) Calculate diluted earnings per share for 2014. For simplicity, ignore the requirement to record the debt and equity components of the bonds separately.

(c) From the perspective of a common shareholder, provide support for the treatment of the preferred dividends in calculating Earl Limited's basic and diluted earnings per share.

(d) Discuss how a potential shareholder's investment decision may be affected if diluted earnings per share was not reported.

P17-10 Benoit Limited had net income for the fiscal year ending June 30, 2014, of $16.4 million. There were 2 million common shares outstanding throughout 2014. The average market price of the common shares for the entire fiscal year was $75. Benoit's tax rate was 30% for 2014.
Benoit had the following potential common shares outstanding during 2014:

1. Options to buy 100,000 common shares at $60 per share

2. 800,000 convertible preferred shares entitled to a cumulative dividend of $8 per share. Each preferred share is convertible into two common shares.

3. 5% convertible debentures with a principal amount of $100 million, issued at par. Each $1,000 debenture is convertible into 20 common shares.

Instructions

For the fiscal year ended June 30, 2014, calculate the following for Benoit Limited. For simplicity, ignore the requirement to record the debt and equity components separately.

(a) Basic earnings per share

(b) Diluted earnings per share

P17-11 As auditor for Checkem & Associates, you have been assigned to review Tao Corporation's calculation of earnings per share for the current year. The controller, Mac Taylor, has supplied you with the following calculations:

Net income	$3,374,960

Common shares issued and outstanding:

Beginning of year	1,285,000
End of year	1,200,000
Average	1,242,500

Earnings per share:

$$\frac{\$3,374,960}{1,242,500} = \$2.72 \text{ per share}$$

You have gathered the following additional information:

1. The only equity securities are the common shares.

2. There are no options or warrants outstanding to purchase common shares.

3. There are no convertible debt securities.

4. Activity in common shares during the year was as follows:

Outstanding, Jan. 1	1,285,000
Shares acquired, Oct. 1	(250,000)
	1,035,000
Shares issued, Dec. 1	165,000
Outstanding, Dec. 31	1,200,000

Instructions

(a) Based on the information, do you agree with the controller's calculation of earnings per share for the year? If you disagree, prepare a revised calculation.

Digging Deeper

(b) Assume the same facts except that call options had also been issued for 140,000 common shares at $10 per share. These options were outstanding at the beginning of the year and none had been exercised or cancelled during the year. The average market price of the common shares during the year was $20 and the ending market price was $25. Prepare a calculation of earnings per share.

P17-12 The following information is for Polo Limited for 2014:

Net income for the year	$2,300,000
8% convertible bonds issued at par ($1,000 per bond), with each bond convertible into 30 common shares	2,000,000
6% convertible, cumulative preferred shares, $100 par value, with each share convertible into 3 common shares	4,000,000
Common shares (600,000 shares outstanding)	6,000,000
Stock options (granted in a prior year) to purchase 75,000 common shares at $20 per share	750,000
Tax rate for 2014	30%
Average market price of common shares	$25 per share

There were no changes during 2014 in the number of common shares, preferred shares, or convertible bonds outstanding. For simplicity, ignore the requirement to book the convertible bonds' equity portion separately.

Instructions

(a) Calculate basic earnings per share for 2014.

(b) Calculate diluted earnings per share for 2014.

(c) Discuss how a potential shareholder's investment decision may be affected if diluted earnings per share was not reported.

P17-13 Jackie Enterprises Ltd. has a tax rate of 30% and reported net income of $8.5 million in 2014. The following details are from Jackie's statement of financial position as at December 31, 2014, the end of its fiscal year:

Long-Term Debt:

Bonds payable due Dec. 31, 2020, 10% (issued at par)	$ 5,000,000
Bonds payable, face value $9,000,000, due Dec. 31, 2024, 7.25%, convertible into common shares at the investor's option at the rate of two shares per $100 of bonds	8,600,000

Shareholders' Equity:

Preferred shares, $4.50 cumulative, convertible, convertible into common shares at the rate of two common shares for each preferred share, 120,000 shares outstanding	$ 5,500,000
Preferred shares, $3.00 cumulative, convertible, convertible into common shares at the rate of one common share for each preferred share, 400,000 shares outstanding	10,000,000
Common shares, 1,700,000 shares outstanding	750,000
Contributed surplus—conversion rights for bonds	
Retained earnings	9,500,000

Other information:

1. Quarterly dividends were declared on March 1, June 1, September 1, and December 1 for the preferred shares and paid 10 days after the date of declaration.

2. Dividends paid on common shares amounted to $980,000 during the year and were paid on December 20, 2014.

3. Interest expense on bonds payable totalled $1,178,200, including bond discount amortization, which is recorded using the effective interest amortization method.

4. There were no issuances of common shares during the 2014 fiscal year, and no conversions.

Instructions

(a) Determine the amount of interest expense incurred in 2014 for each of the bonds outstanding at December 31, 2014.

(b) Calculate basic earnings per share for 2014.

(c) Determine the potential for dilution for each security that is convertible into common shares.

(d) Calculate diluted earnings per share for 2014.

(e) What is the significance of the preferred share dividends being paid quarterly? What impact, if any, does this frequency in payment have on the calculation of diluted earnings per share?

Digging
Deeper

P17-14 The following information is available for Dylan Inc., a company whose shares are traded on the Toronto Stock Exchange:

Net income	$150,000
Average market price of common shares during 2014 (adjusted for stock dividend)	$20
December 31, 2014 (fiscal year end) market price of common shares	$20
Income tax rate for fiscal year 2014	30%

Transactions in common shares during 2014:

	Change	Cumulative shares
Jan. 1, 2014, common shares outstanding		90,000
Mar. 1, 2014, issuance of common shares	30,000	120,000
June 1, 2014, 10% stock dividend	12,000	132,000
Nov. 1, 2014, repurchase of common shares	(30,000)	102,000

Other information:

1. For all of the fiscal year 2014, $100,000 of 6% cumulative convertible bonds have been outstanding. The bonds were issued at par and are convertible into a total of 10,000 common shares (adjusted for the stock dividend) at the option of the holder, and at any time after issuance.

2. Stock options for 20,000 common shares have been outstanding for the entire 2014 fiscal year, and are exercisable at the option price of $25 per share (adjusted for the stock dividend).

3. For all of the fiscal year 2014, $100,000 of 4% cumulative convertible preferred shares have been outstanding. The preferred shares are convertible into a total of 15,000 common shares (adjusted for the stock dividend) at the option of the holder, and at any time after January 2019.

Instructions

(a) Determine the weighted average number of common shares that would be used in calculating earnings per share for the year ending December 31, 2014.

(b) Calculate basic earnings per share for 2014.

(c) Determine the potential for dilution for each security that is convertible into common shares.

(d) Calculate diluted earnings per share for 2014. For simplicity, ignore the requirement to record the debt and equity components of the bonds separately.

Case

Refer to the Case Primer on the Student Website and in *WileyPLUS* to help you answer this case.

Ethics

CA17-1 Canton Products Inc. has been in business for quite a while. Its shares trade on a public exchange and it is thinking of expanding onto the New York and London Stock Exchanges. Recently, however, the company has run into cash flow difficulties. The CEO is confident that the company can overcome this problem in the longer term as it has a solid business model; however, in the shorter term, Canton needs to be very careful in managing its cash flows. Of particular concern is the fact that it has multiple potential common shares outstanding that cause the diluted earnings per share numbers to be significantly lower than the company's basic EPS. This in turn has recently caused Canton's stock price to decline and is affecting the company's ability to get the best interest rates on its bank loans.

At a recent meeting with the CFO, the CEO decided to exchange the company's convertible senior subordinated notes (the old notes) for new senior subordinated notes (the new notes). The notes were held by a large institutional investor that agreed to the exchange. The old notes were convertible into 25 shares for each $1,000 note. The new notes have a net share settlement provision that requires that, upon conversion, the company will pay the holders up to $1,000 in cash for each note, plus an excess amount that would be settled in shares at a fixed conversion price (30 shares for each $1,000 note in the total consideration). The notes may only be turned in if the share price exceeds 20% of the fixed conversion price.

It is now year end and the share price is trading above the fixed conversion price but well below the 20% premium level. The note therefore cannot be turned in (converted). The CEO feels that the share price will not exceed the 20% premium for a couple of years.

Instructions

Adopt the role of the auditors and discuss the issues related to the new notes.

Integrated Case

IC17-1 Tiziana's Foods Limited (TFL) is in the supermarket business. It is a public company and is thinking of going private (that is, buying up all of its shares that are available). The funds will come from a private consortium. The consortium has offered to buy all the shares if the share price hits a certain level. Although the company has come through some tough times, things have been looking up recently. This is partially due to a new strategy to upgrade the stores and increase square footage.

TFL obtains revenues from two sources: in-store sales to customers and fees from sales of new franchises and continuing franchise fees. This year was a banner year for sales of new franchises. The company sold and booked revenues for 10 new franchised stores. Most of these new stores have not yet opened but locations have been found and deposits have been taken from each of the franchisees.

Under the terms of the franchise contracts, TFL has agreed to absorb any losses that the stores suffer for the first five years. Based on market research, however, and the location of the new stores, it is highly unlikely that losses will occur. Just in case, TFL has requested that franchisees deposit a certain amount of money in a trust fund. In addition, TFL has agreed to issue shares of TFL to the franchisees if the stores are profitable in the first two years.

During the year, TFL issued long-term debt that is convertible into common shares of the company. The number of common shares varies depending on the share price. Because of the potential for taking the company private, TFL agreed to certain concessions. If the company goes private, TFL must pay back 120% of the face value of the debt.

Instructions

Assume the role of the controller and discuss the financial reporting issues.

Writing Assignments

WA17-1 "Earnings per share" (EPS) is the most commonly featured financial statistic for corporations. For many securities, the daily published quotations of share prices include a "times earnings" figure that is based on EPS. Stock analysts often focus their discussions on the EPS of the corporations that they study.

Instructions

(a) Explain how the calculation of EPS is affected by dividends or dividend requirements on classes of preferred shares that may be outstanding.

(b) One of the technical procedures that applies to EPS calculations is the treasury stock method. Briefly describe the circumstances that can make it appropriate to use the treasury stock method.

(c) Convertible debentures are considered potentially dilutive common shares. Explain how convertible debentures are handled in regard to EPS calculations. Does the treatment change if the convertible bond can be settled in cash or shares at the issuer's option?

(d) An article in *Report on Business* magazine titled "The magic number: The price-to-earnings ratio deserves its favoured status—as long as you use it right," written by Fabrice Taylor (February 2010), noted that the long-term average of all shares for the "times earnings" figure was about 19 times. Taylor went on to state that **Maple Leaf Foods Inc.** was (currently) trading at a P/E (price-to-earnings) ratio of 100 times EPS for 2008, and **Finning International Inc.** was trading at a P/E ratio of 442 times the past year's EPS. Maple Leaf Foods in the past year had suffered large losses due to product recalls. Finning is a seller of Caterpillar equipment whose sales and earnings fluctuate with commodity prices.

Are these companies' share prices too high? What might be causing these times earnings multiples to be so high? What other information would be needed before this determination could be made?

(AICPA adapted)

WA17-2 Matt Kacskos is a shareholder of Howat Corporation and has asked you, the firm's accountant, to explain why his employee stock options were not included in diluted EPS. In order to explain this situation, you must briefly explain what dilutive securities are, why they are and are not included in the EPS calculation, and why some securities are antidilutive and therefore are not included in this calculation.

Instructions

(a) Write Kacskos a one-and-a-half page letter explaining why the warrants are not included in the calculation. Use the following data to help you explain this situation.

1. Howat Corporation earned $228,000 during the period, when it had an average of 100,000 common shares outstanding.

2. The common shares sold at an average market price of $25 per share during the period.

3. Also outstanding were 15,000 employee stock options that could be exercised by the holder to purchase one common share at $30 per option.

(b) The IASB proposed in its Exposure Draft issued in 2008 that the year-end price of the shares be used, rather than the average price for the year. Assuming that the year-end market price was $33 per share, would this change your answer in part (a)? Why or why not?

(c) Now assume that the company in the past has made a practice of settling the stock options in cash. Consequently, the stock options have been reported as a liability at fair value, with changes in fair value reflected in net earnings. The 2008 Exposure Draft proposed that, if the options are reported at fair value through profit or loss, then these should not be adjusted for in the diluted EPS. Make arguments to support this new proposed treatment.

(d) Stock options (not just employee stock options) are used for various purposes by companies. Briefly explain the business reasons for companies issuing stock options.

WA17-3 On July 1, 2013, Seaway Tools Limited acquired Marine Machinery from John Tweel. The consideration was paid in 100,000 shares issued to Tweel, in addition to contingent consideration. The agreement also allowed for the following:

1. If Marine's profits for the next three years averaged $5 million or more, 50,000 more shares would be issued to Tweel at December 31, 2015 Marine's profits for 2013, 2014, and 2015 were $7 million, $9 million, and $6 million, respectively.

2. Seaway would grant 3,000 new shares for each new customer that Marine attracts with an initial contract value of more than $500,000 during 2013 and 2014. During 2013, Marine had two customers that met this criterion, with contracts signed on August 1 and November 1. During 2014, Marine had five new customers meeting that criterion, with two contracts signed March 1, one contract signed May 1, and two contracts signed September 1.

The consolidated earnings for Seaway were $22 million, $19 million, and $24 million for the years ending December 31, 2013, 2014, and 2015, respectively. The number of shares outstanding for Seaway at January 1, 2013, before the acquisition, was 1 million.

Instructions

Determine the basic and diluted earnings per share for Seaway for 2013 and 2014. (Refer to IAS 33, paragraph 52 to assist you with these calculations.)

WA17-4 IFRS allows per share amounts to be reported on items other than earnings.

Instructions

(a) Adopt the role of the ethical accountant and write a short essay on the pros and cons of allowing companies to include alternate per share amounts in their annual reports. What other types of per share data might be helpful for investors?

(b) Currently, per share data is only required on the profit or loss for the year. What would be the arguments to support the disclosure of comprehensive income per share also? What would be some arguments to discourage this disclosure?

(c) Find an example of a company's disclosure of per share data for other than earnings per share.

Ethics

RESEARCH AND FINANCIAL ANALYSIS

RA17-1 British Sky Broadcasting Group plc

British Sky Broadcasting Group plc (BSkyB) operates the leading pay television broadcast service in the United Kingdom and Ireland. Shares of the company trade on the London Stock Exchange and the NYSE. The company produces financial statements in accordance with IFRS. Access the company's annual report for the year ended June 30, 2012, from its website (http://corporate.sky.com). We know from the annual report (page 63) that the company's shares traded between £6.97 and $8.49 per share.

Instructions

(a) Determine how the company has calculated the basic and diluted earnings per share and verify the calculations, where possible. That is, verify (by examining the relevant notes) the number of shares outstanding, adjustments made to the ordinary shares, and the dilutive shares added. Note any information that is missing in order for you to make this determination. What amounts were determined to be antidilutive? Using the share prices disclosed in the question, determine why the company has concluded that there are some items that are antidilutive.

(b) Assume that all conditions have been met for share option awards. Determine the amount of shares that would be added for the dilution using the treasury stock method for 2012. (Make note of any assumptions you have made.)

(c) BSkyB has also disclosed other information on a per share basis. Explain this other per share data. Why has the company provided this information? If you were an investor, would you find it useful?

RA17-2 Molson Coors Brewing Company

Molson Coors Brewing Company has a year end of December 31. Access the company's 2011 annual report from the company website (www.molsoncoors.com).

Instructions

(a) What types of per share information does the company provide?

(b) Does the company have a complex or simple capital structure? List the types of shares that the company has outstanding. How has the number of shares been determined for the basic EPS?

(c) Describe the types of share-based compensation the company has. Identify any potential common shares that would be included in the diluted earnings per share calculation.

(d) Discuss how the company calculated its diluted earnings per share and explain any choices that it made. Explain the items that were found to be antidilutive by the company and the reasons provided.

RA17-3 BCE Inc.

One way of improving a company's EPS is to reduce the number of shares outstanding. Access the financial statements for BCE Inc. for the year ended December 31, 2011, from the company's website (www.bce.ca) or SEDAR. Excerpts from the 2009 financial statements have also been provided below:

Note 8: Earnings Per Share

The following table is a reconciliation of components used in the calculation of basic and diluted earnings per common share from continuing operations.

	2009	2008	2007
Earnings from continuing operations	1,749	1,033	3,959
Earnings from continuing operations	(107)	(124)	(131)
Dividends on preferred shares			
Earnings from continuing operations – basic	1,642	909	3,828
Weighted average number of common shares outstanding (in millions)			
Weighted average number of common shares outstanding – basic	772.9	805.8	804.8
Assumed exercise of stock options(1)	—	1.4	2.1
Weighted average number of common shares outstanding – diluted	772.9	807.2	806.9

(1) The calculation of the assumed exercise of stock options includes the effect of the average unrecognized future compensation cost of dilutive options. It does not include anti-dilutive options, which are options that would not be exercised because their exercise price is higher than the average market value of a BCE Inc. common share. The number of excluded options was 10,508,239 in 2009, 4,646,531 in 2008 and 5,278,529 in 2007.

Instructions

(a) What per share information has the company provided each year?

(b) What types of shares does the company have outstanding? What are the dividend payments required on these shares?

(c) How have the earnings from continuing operations been determined for each year from 2007 to 2011? Why has this adjustment been made? Why were the earnings for 2007 and 2008 significantly different from the other years presented? You may need to refer to the relevant years' financial statements for details.

(d) What has the weighted average number of shares been each year for the period 2007 to 2011 for the basic EPS? Why does this change from year to year? Recalculate the basic earnings per share from continuing operations as if the weighted average number of shares outstanding had remained the same since 2007. Assuming that the company's share price trades at around 12 times earnings, what has been the impact each year of the reduction in the number of shares on the share price?

(e) Review the calculation of the diluted earnings per share. What has caused the dilution impact? What has been excluded from the calculation and why?

RA17-4 EPS Harmonization

The FASB and the IASB have been working together to resolve the remaining differences between FASB Statement 128, *Earnings per Share*, and IAS 33 *Earnings per Share*. In August 2008, the IASB issued an Exposure Draft outlining proposed changes to the earnings per share standard. The project has currently been deferred.

Instructions

From the IASB website (www.iasb.org), review the Exposure Draft. Discuss the issues raised and comment on whether the changes will result in better financial reporting.

ENDNOTES

[1] IFRS refers to common shares as "ordinary shares." The terms will be used interchangeably here.

[2] IAS 33 *Earnings per Share* stipulates this in IAS 33.66 and 33.67/A.

[3] IAS 33.68.

[4] IAS 33.5 and .7.

[5] IAS 33.5.

[6] IAS 33.28.

[7] IAS 33.41.

[8] This terminology is used in the United States and was used in pre-2011 Canadian GAAP. IAS 33 does not label the calculations although the calculations themselves are essentially the same.

[9] IAS 33.36.

[10] To simplify, the consequences of measuring and presenting the debt and equity components of the convertible debentures separately have been ignored for this example. When initially recognized, convertible debentures would have been recognized as part debt and part equity under IFRS. The interest expense would be calculated using the market interest rate for straight debt; that is, without the conversion feature. This assumption has been made throughout the chapter and the end of chapter material.

[11] The conversion of bonds is dilutive because EPS with conversion ($3.32) is less than basic EPS ($4.10).

[12] IAS 33.39.

[13] Note that IAS 33 was not updated when IAS 32 was revised to provide guidance on accounting for instruments that are settled using the entity's own equity instruments (including options and forwards). IAS 33 therefore is not conceptually consistent with IAS 32 as it relates to these types of instruments, and the IASB and FASB had plans to revise the standard. This is discussed further in the Looking Ahead section at the end of this chapter.

[14] IAS 33.62.

[15] The incremental number of shares can be calculated in a simpler way: (Market price − Option price) ÷ Market price × Number of options = Number of shares ($50 − $30) ÷ $50 × 1,500 options = 600 shares

[16] Note that options and warrants have basically the same assumptions and problems regarding calculation, although the warrants may allow or require the tendering of some other security, such as debt, in lieu of cash upon exercise. In such situations, the accounting becomes quite complex and is beyond the scope of this book.

Cumulative Coverage: Chapters 15 to 17

Homeland Corporation is a public company listed on the TSX with a December 31 year end. At the beginning of the current year, there were unlimited common shares authorized with 100,000 issued and outstanding. These shares had a carrying amount of $4 million, and there was $150,000 in retained earnings and $100,000 in contributed surplus (of which $75,000 was created by a net excess of proceeds over cost on a previous cancellation of common shares; the remainder resulted from the issue of compensatory stock options in 2013).

The following transactions took place during the 2014 fiscal year:

January 1 Homeland Corp. issued $5 million of 12%, five-year, convertible bonds, with interest payable annually on December 31. Each $1,000 bond can be converted into 20 common shares. In addition, each $1,000 bond included 10 detachable warrants, where each warrant can be used to purchase one share of common stock at an exercise price of $55. The company intends to use the effective interest amortization method for any bond discount or premium.

Common shares were trading at the time for $45 and a valuator indicated that the warrants had a fair market value of $3. The bond issue with attached warrants sold out at 103. Without the warrants and the conversion rights, the bond issue would have traded at 98.

June 1 By this date, the market price for shares had increased to $55. As a result, 30% of the bonds outstanding were converted into common shares when the market price was $55 per share. The company uses the book value method to record bond conversions.

July 31 50% of the outstanding warrants were exercised when the common shares were trading at $56 per share.

October 1 Homeland Corp. granted 2,000 options to executives in 2013. Each option entitled the holder to purchase one common share for $55 during 2014. These options were valued using an option pricing model at $25,000. On October 1, 2014, 1,200 of the options were exercised when the market price was $58.

December 1 Homeland Corp. purchased and retired 10,000 shares in the open market for $57 per common share.

December 31 The remaining compensatory stock options expired as the executive to whom they had been issued failed to complete his employment contract. The possibility that someone might not complete their employment contract was not taken into account in the option pricing model that was used to determine the value of these stock options.

The net income from operations after tax was $4 million and the tax rate was 25%. The average common share price during 2014 was $52. Income tax expense was $1 million and dividends were paid on December 31 at $2.50 per share.

Instructions

(a) Prepare the appropriate journal entries to record the above transactions.

(b) Prepare any necessary year-end journal entries.

(c) Determine basic and diluted earnings per share, and prepare the presentation of EPS for the income statement.

(d) Complete the statement of shareholders' equity.

A Win-Win Move for the Double Double™

Courtesy Tim Hortons

FEW THINGS ARE as quintessentially Canadian as a trip to Tim Hortons® for a Double Double and maybe some Timbits® to go. In fact, loyal customers may be surprised to discover that the Canadian icon had actually been a U.S.-registered company for years. However, this is no longer the case now that "Tims" has come home.

Tim Hortons Inc. completed its reorganization as a Canadian public company in September 2009. In addition to operational and administrative benefits, a key reason for the move back across the border was the income tax savings, explains Mike Myskiw, Tim Hortons' Vice President, Tax and Treasurer. The federal government has been lowering its general corporate income tax rate, which stood at 15% in 2012. That year, provincial corporate income tax rates ranged from 10 to 16%. In comparison, the U.S. federal rate is 35%. Add state taxes and the U.S. rate could be up to 40%.

"We still feel that that was the best move," Mr. Myskiw says of returning to Canada. "The fiscal incentives that Canada provides are better than the U.S. right now as far as taxes go." In 2012, the effective tax rate that Tim Hortons paid, averaged across every jurisdiction it does business in, was approximately 28%.

The reorganization did not change the way Tim Hortons accounts for income taxes. Although

it is a foreign private issuer listed on the New York Stock Exchange, as well as the Toronto Stock Exchange, in 2012, it prepared its financial statements in accordance with U.S. GAAP, and filed annual and quarterly reports with the Securities and Exchange Commission in the U.S. instead of filing as a foreign private issuer.

Even though Tim Hortons has effectively moved back to Canada, it has no plans to adopt IFRS in the foreseeable future, Mr. Myskiw says. "Our shareholder base is on both sides of the border so we want to be comparable to the other quick service restaurant chains in the U.S."

There are a number of other benefits of repatriating. Head office has always been in Canada, as are most executives, so it makes sense from an operational perspective. It will also make it easier to expand within Canada and internationally. Under Canada's exemption system, companies doing business abroad pay the corporate taxes of that foreign country and, when they repatriate the foreign income, they are exempt from paying Canadian corporate taxes. With the U.S. system, when the company repatriates foreign income, it has to pay the U.S. corporate taxes and then claim a corporate tax credit for the international taxes paid.

All in all, it's a win-win situation for Tim Hortons and its shareholders.

18 | Income Taxes

LEARNING OBJECTIVES

After studying this chapter, you should be able to:

1. Understand the importance of income taxes from a business perspective.

2. Explain the difference between accounting income and taxable income, and calculate taxable income and current income taxes.

3. Explain what a taxable temporary difference is, determine its amount, and calculate deferred tax liabilities.

4. Explain what a deductible temporary difference is, determine its amount, and calculate deferred tax assets.

5. Prepare analyses of deferred tax balances and record deferred tax expense.

6. Explain the effect of multiple tax rates and tax rate changes on income tax accounts, and calculate current and deferred tax amounts when there is a change in substantively enacted tax rates.

7. Account for a tax loss carryback.

8. Account for a tax loss carryforward, including any note disclosures.

9. Explain why the Deferred Tax Asset account is reassessed at the statement of financial position date, and account for the deferred tax asset with and without a valuation allowance account.

10. Identify and apply the presentation and disclosure requirements for income tax assets and liabilities, and apply intraperiod tax allocation.

11. Identify the major differences between ASPE and IFRS for income taxes.

After studying Appendix 18A, you should be able to:

12. Apply the temporary difference approach (future income taxes method) of accounting for income taxes in a comprehensive situation.

As our opening story indicates, companies spend a considerable amount of time and effort trying to minimize their income tax payments. This is important because income taxes are a major cost of doing business for most corporations. At the same time, companies must present financial information to the investment community that provides a clear picture of present and potential tax obligations and tax benefits. In this chapter, we discuss the basic standards that both publicly accountable and private enterprises must follow in reporting income taxes. The content and organization of the chapter are as follows.

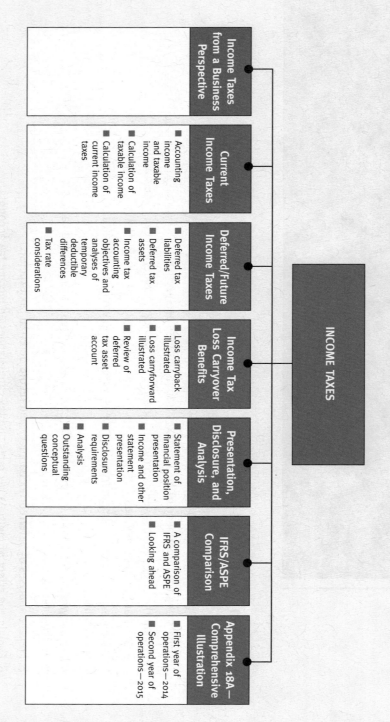

Objective 1

Understand the importance of income taxes from a business perspective.

INCOME TAXES FROM A BUSINESS PERSPECTIVE

When a company decides where to set up its operations, a major consideration is the tax rate that it will face on its profits. The link between taxes and economic growth has been recognized in studies by organizations such as the Organisation for Economic Co-operation and Development (OECD). A recent OECD study looked at the impact on economic growth of a variety of taxes, including property taxes, consumption taxes (such as the GST), personal income taxes, and corporate income taxes. The results suggest that, of the various tax options available to OECD countries, corporate income taxes had the most negative effect on gross domestic product per capita.[1]

The fact that corporate taxes can slow growth may help to explain why governments in Canada have steadily reduced corporate tax rates for more than 20 years. For example, the combined federal and provincial tax rate for general corporations in Canada declined from an average of approximately 43% in 2000 to approximately 28% in 2012. The combined federal and provincial tax rates ranged from 25% to 31% for most provinces and territories in 2012.[2]

Accounting for income taxes is important for businesses, individuals, and governments. In this chapter we focus on accounting for taxes by businesses in Canada. We leave the details of how to prepare corporate tax returns for courses that specialize in that subject. Our focus is on financial reporting by companies once they have determined the amount of taxes that they owe.

Up to this point, you have learned the basic principles that corporations use to report information to investors and creditors. Corporations file income tax returns following the Income Tax Act (and related provincial legislation), which is administered by the Canada Revenue Agency (CRA).[3] Because IFRS and ASPE standards and methods differ in several ways from tax regulations, adjustments usually need to be made to the income reported on the financial statements when determining the income that is taxable under tax legislation. That is, the current year's pre-tax income on the **income statement** (the income amount as determined by applying IFRS or ASPE) and the company's taxable income usually differ. This is highlighted in Illustration 18-1.

Law

Illustration 18-1

Income Statement Differences between IFRS and Tax Reporting

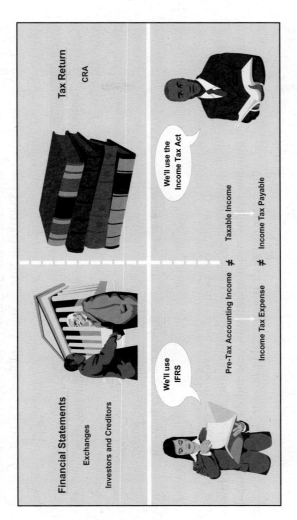

Let's take a closer look at these differences between accounting income and taxable income.

CURRENT INCOME TAXES

Accounting Income and Taxable Income

Objective 2

Explain the difference between accounting income and taxable income, and calculate taxable income and current income taxes.

Accounting income is a financial reporting term that is also known as "income before taxes," "income for financial reporting purposes," or **accounting profit**, as it is referred to in IAS 12 *Income Taxes*. In this chapter, it is a pre-tax concept, and we will use the terms "income" and "profit" interchangeably. Accounting income is determined according to IFRS or ASPE and is measured with the objective of providing useful information to investors and creditors. **Taxable income**, on the other hand, is a tax accounting term and indicates the amount on which income tax payable is calculated. Taxable income is determined according to the Income Tax Act and Regulations, which are designed to raise money to support government operations. It is also referred to as "income for tax purposes," or, under IAS 12, as **taxable profit**.

Illustration 18-2
Accounting Income

To illustrate how differences in IFRS and tax rules affect financial reporting and taxable income, assume that Chelsea Inc. reported revenues of $130,000 and expenses of $60,000 on its income statement in each of its first three years of operations. Illustration 18-2 shows the (partial) income statements over these three years.

CHELSEA INC.
IFRS Reporting

	2014	2015	2016	Total
Revenues	$130,000	$130,000	$130,000	
Expenses	60,000	60,000	60,000	
Accounting income	$ 70,000	$ 70,000	$ 70,000	$210,000

Following tax regulations, Chelsea reports the same expenses to the CRA in each of the years. However, the $130,000 of revenue that was reported each year was taxable in different accounting periods: taxable revenues were $100,000 in 2014, $150,000 in 2015, and $140,000 in 2016, as shown in Illustration 18-3.

Illustration 18-3
Taxable Income

CHELSEA INC.
Tax Reporting

	2014	2015	2016	Total
Revenues	$100,000	$150,000	$140,000	
Expenses	60,000	60,000	60,000	
Taxable income	$ 40,000	$ 90,000	$ 80,000	$210,000

In reality, companies do not submit revised income statements for the tax return that list only taxable revenues and deductible expenses. Instead, they prepare a schedule that begins with accounting income and they then adjust this amount for each area of difference between it and taxable income. Chelsea's schedules would appear as in Illustration 18-4.

Illustration 18-4
Schedule to Reconcile
Accounting Income to
Taxable Income

CHELSEA INC.

	2014	2015	2016
Accounting income	$70,000	$70,000	$70,000
Less revenue taxable in a future period	(30,000)		
Add revenue recognized in previous period, taxable in current period		20,000	10,000
Taxable income	$40,000	$90,000	$80,000
Taxes payable (25% assumed rate)	$10,000	$22,500	$20,000

Calculation of Taxable Income

Reversing and Permanent Differences

Let's take a more detailed look at the differences between accounting income and taxable income. The Chelsea Inc. example above illustrates how to calculate taxable income when there is only one such difference. In reality, many adjustments may be needed. The major reasons for differences between accounting and taxable income follow, and examples of each type are provided.[4]

1. ***Revenues or gains are taxable after they are recognized in accounting income.*** A sale may be recorded in the current accounting period with a debit to a receivable and a credit to revenue, but the revenue may not be included in taxable income until a future year when the receivable is actually collected in cash. There is a timing difference that will reverse in the future. A similar difference may also apply to a gain on sale or to holding gains recognized on assets being held, as these amounts may not be taxable until they have been **realized**; that is, received in cash. Examples include:

- Instalment sales that are recognized when the sale takes place for financial reporting purposes and on the cash basis for tax purposes

- Contracts that are accounted for under the percentage-of-completion method for financial reporting purposes and the completed contract or zero-profit basis for tax purposes, resulting in some or all of the related gross profit being deferred for tax purposes

- Unrealized holding gains that are recognized in income or in OCI on investments or other assets carried at fair value, but which are not taxable until the assets are sold and the gains realized

Note that for discussions later in the chapter, in all of these examples, the IFRS or ASPE statement of financial position reports an asset (an account receivable, or construction in process, or an investment account) with a carrying amount that is higher than its tax value would be on a tax statement of financial position, if one were prepared.[5] This is the basis for understanding deferred (or future) income taxes later in the chapter.

2. ***Expenses or losses are deductible for tax purposes after they are recognized in accounting income.*** Some expenses or losses that are recognized for accounting purposes are not allowed to be deducted for tax purposes until a future period. For example, for financial statement purposes, an expense may have to be accrued, but for tax purposes it may not be deductible as an expense until it is paid. That is, it is only when the liability is eventually settled that the expense or loss is deductible in calculating taxable income. Examples include the following:

- Product warranty liabilities

- Estimated losses and liabilities related to restructuring

- Litigation accruals

- Accrued pension costs

- Holding or impairment losses on investments or other assets

In all these examples, notice that a liability (or contra asset or direct asset reduction) is recognized on the statement of financial position when the expense or loss is recognized for financial reporting purposes. For tax purposes, however, the expense is not recognized in the current period and, therefore, neither is a tax liability or reduction in the asset's tax value.

3. ***Revenues or gains are taxable before they are recognized in accounting income.*** A company may recognize cash that it received during the year as unearned revenue if it is an advance payment for goods or services to be provided in future years. For tax purposes, the advance payment may have to be included in taxable income when the cash is received. When the entity recognizes this revenue on the income statement in later years when the goods or services are provided to customers, these amounts can be deducted in calculating taxable income. This is because they were included in taxable income in the year the cash was received. They cannot be taxed twice. Examples include the following:

- Subscriptions, royalties, and rentals received in advance

- Sale and leaseback gains, including a deferral of profit on a sale for financial reporting purposes that would be reported as realized for tax purposes

  Once again, the statement of financial position is also affected. There is a difference between the carrying amount of the liability account such as Unearned Revenue and its tax base.

4. **Expenses or losses are deductible before they are recognized in accounting income.** The cost of assets such as equipment, for example, is deducted for financial statement purposes according to whichever depreciation method the company uses for financial statement purposes. For tax purposes, the capital cost allowance (CCA) method must be used. Therefore, depending on which accounting method was chosen, the asset's cost may be deducted faster for tax purposes than it is expensed for financial reporting purposes. When this happens, taxable income in the early years of the asset's life is lower than the accounting income. Because the asset's capital cost is the total amount that can be depreciated both on the books and for tax purposes, this means that future taxable incomes will be higher than the accounting incomes in those future years. Other examples include the following:

- Property and resources that are depreciated/depleted faster for tax purposes than for financial reporting purposes

- Deductible pension funding that exceeds the pension expense that is recognized

- Prepaid expenses that are deducted in calculating taxable income in the period when they are paid

  These, too, will result in the carrying amount of a statement of financial position account (equipment, at cost less accumulated depreciation, for example) that is different from its tax base (the equipment's undepreciated capital cost or UCC).

5. **Permanent differences.** Some differences between taxable income and accounting income are permanent. **Permanent differences** are caused by items that (1) are included in accounting income but never in taxable income, or (2) are included in taxable income but never in accounting income. Examples of items that are included in accounting income but never in taxable income are:

- **Non-tax-deductible expenses** such as fines and penalties, golf and social club dues, and expenses related to the earning of non-taxable revenue;

- **Non-taxable revenue**, such as dividends from taxable Canadian corporations, and proceeds on life insurance policies carried by the company on key officers or employees

  Examples of items that are included in taxable income but never in accounting income are depletion allowances of natural resources that exceed the resources' cost.

  Since **permanent** differences affect only the period in which they occur, there are no deferred or future tax consequences associated with the related statement of financial position accounts.

  The situations identified in numbers 1 to 4 above are known as **reversible differences or timing differences.** Their accounting treatment and tax treatment are **the same,** but the **timing** of when they are included in accounting income and when they are included in taxable income **differs.** These reversible or timing differences result in a temporary difference between the carrying amount of the asset or liability and its tax base, which we discuss further below.

Multiple Differences Illustrated

To illustrate a situation when there are multiple differences between accounting income and taxable income, assume that BT Corporation reports accounting income of $200,000 in each of the years 2014, 2015, and 2016. Assume also that the company is subject to a 30% tax rate in each year, and has the following differences between income reported on the financial statements and taxable income:

1. Revenue of $18,000 on a sale to a customer in 2014 is recognized for financial reporting purposes in 2014. The revenue is considered taxable when the customer pays the account—in equal monthly payments over 18 months beginning January 1, 2015.

2. A premium of $5,000 is paid in each of 2015 and 2016 for life insurance that the company carries on key officers. This is not deductible for tax purposes, but is expensed for accounting purposes.

3. A warranty with an estimated cost of $30,000 was provided on sales in 2014. This amount was recognized as expense in the same year. It was expected that $20,000 of the warranty work would be performed in 2015 and $10,000 in 2016, and this is what actually happened. For tax purposes, warranty expenses are not deductible until the expenditures are actually incurred.[6]

The first and third items above are **reversible** differences. The second item is a **permanent** difference with no future tax consequences. The reconciliation of BT's accounting income to its taxable income for each year is shown in Illustration 18-5.

Illustration 18-5

Calculation of Taxable Income

	2014	2015	2016
Accounting income	$200,000	$200,000	$200,000
Adjustments:			
Revenue from 2014 sale	(18,000)	12,000	6,000
Warranty expense	30,000	(20,000)	(10,000)
Non-deductible insurance expense		5,000	5,000
Taxable income	$212,000	$197,000	$201,000

The analysis always starts with pre-tax income reported on the income statement. This is adjusted to the taxable amount as follows: revenue items that are not taxable until a future period are deducted, and expenses that are not deductible in the year are added back. This explains the $18,000 deduction of the 2014 sale amount as this was included in 2014's accounting income but is not taxable in 2014. It will be taxable in 2015 and 2016 as the difference reverses; that is, as the receivable is collected. In 2015 and 2016, the amounts collected will be added to the accounting incomes reported to calculate the taxable income for each year.

Starting with pre-tax accounting income and adjusting it to taxable income also explains why the $30,000 of warranty expense is added back to accounting income in 2014. Because BT Corporation did not make any payments under the warranty in 2014, the company cannot deduct any warranty expense for tax purposes. The full amount of $30,000 was deducted in calculating accounting income in 2014, so it is all added back in determining taxable income. The warranty costs are deducted in calculating taxable income in the years they are actually paid by the company (that is, in 2015 and 2016) even though no warranty expense was deducted in the accounting incomes of those two years.

The original difference and its reversal affect taxable income. The **original** or **originating difference** is the cause of the initial difference between accounting and taxable income amounts. An example is the $30,000 original difference related to warranty expense in 2014. The **reversal**, on the other hand, causes the opposite effect in subsequent years, such as the $20,000 and $10,000 warranty expense differences in 2015 and 2016.

The $5,000 life insurance premium is added back to 2015 and 2016's accounting income because it was deducted as an expense in calculating accounting income in each of those years. It is not a deductible expense for tax purposes in any year and the $5,000 will not affect any future year's taxable income. Its effect is **permanent**.

Calculation of Current Income Taxes

While the calculation of taxable income may sometimes be challenging, the calculation of current tax expense and income taxes payable in this chapter is straightforward. To determine this amount, the current rate of tax is simply applied to the company's taxable income. Continuing with the BT Corporation example above and the taxable incomes determined in Illustration 18-5, the calculation of the company's current tax expense and income taxes payable for each of the three years is shown in Illustration 18-6.

	2014	2015	2016
Taxable income	$212,000	$197,000	$201,000
Tax rate	30%	30%	30%
Income tax payable and current tax expense	$ 63,600	$ 59,100	$ 60,300

The year-end adjusting entries to record current income tax each year are as follows:

Dec. 31, 2014	Current Tax Expense	63,600	
	Income Tax Payable		63,600
Dec. 31, 2015	Current Tax Expense	59,100	
	Income Tax Payable		59,100
Dec. 31, 2016	Current Tax Expense	60,300	
	Income Tax Payable		60,300

This method of calculating income tax expense is straightforward and is known as the **taxes payable method**. It is one of the methods that is permitted under ASPE.

Notice that although BT Corporation reported identical accounting income in each year and the tax rate stayed the same, the current **tax expense differs each year**. This fluctuation is caused mainly by the reversible differences created by the 2014 sale and warranty expense. Conceptually, the income tax expense reported on the income statement **should be directly related to the accounting income that is reported**, not to the amount that is taxable in the period. Therefore, another method, based on an asset and liability approach to income taxes, is required under IFRS and is permitted as the other accounting policy choice under ASPE. This method—the **future income taxes method**—starts with the calculation of current income taxes as described above. It then adjusts for the effects of any changes in **future income tax assets and future income tax liabilities** and recognizes these effects as **future income tax expense**. Note that the terminology used in the international standards for this same method is the **temporary difference approach**; the related tax assets and liabilities are called **deferred tax assets** and **deferred tax liabilities**, and the associated expense is referred to as **deferred tax expense**. The terms "future" and "deferred" are used interchangeably. This method is explained next.

DEFERRED/FUTURE INCOME TAXES

As indicated above, reversible differences that affect taxable income each year result in an effect on the amount of income taxes payable in the future as the differences reverse. The accumulated tax effects of these differences are recognized on the balance sheet as future tax assets and future tax liabilities. The adjustment of these differences at the reporting date dictates the amount of deferred tax expense (or future income tax expense) to be recognized. The **deferred tax expense** and the **current tax expense** are then both reported on the income statement as components of income tax expense for the period.

The basic principle that underlies deferred taxes is as follows: If the recovery of an asset or settlement of a liability that is reported on the statement of financial position will result in the company's having to pay income taxes in the future, a future or deferred tax liability is recognized on the current period's statement of financial position. Alternatively,

Alternative Terminology

IFRS uses the terms current tax expense (income) and deferred tax expense (income), whereas ASPE suggests current income tax expense (benefit) and future income tax expense (benefit). We use the ASPE term "benefit" rather than "income" when describing tax-related income statement accounts, and we use the other terms interchangeably in this text.

if the recovery or settlement results in deferred tax reductions (benefits), a future or deferred tax asset is recognized on the current statement of financial position. This is explained further in the next sections.

The **tax base** or **tax basis** of an asset or liability is similar to a measurement attribute, such as historical cost and fair value (IFRS uses the term "base" and ASPE uses "basis"). The **tax base of an asset** is the amount that will be deductible for tax purposes against any taxable economic benefits that will flow to the company when it recovers the carrying amount of the asset. If the economic benefit will not be taxable, the tax base is equal to the carrying amount.[7] A good example is the UCC of a depreciable asset. This amount is usually different from the asset's carrying amount in the accounting records. In other words, it is the amount that is attributed for tax purposes to the statement of financial position item. Examples from *CICA Handbook*, Part II, Section 3465 on Income Taxes and IAS 12 *Income Taxes* will help explain how this is applied.

Example 1. A capital asset was acquired at an original cost (and tax base) of $1,000. By the end of Year 3, capital cost allowance totalling $424 has been deducted when calculating taxable income for Years 1 to 3. Therefore, the tax base of this asset at the end of Year 3 is $1,000 − $424 = $576. This is its UCC. Going back to the definition of tax base provided above, this is the amount that will be deductible for tax purposes in the future as the asset is used to generate cash flows and its carrying amount on the statement of financial position is recovered.

Example 2. An investment in another company's shares was purchased at a cost of $1,000. Regardless of whether this investment is accounted for on the statement of financial position at fair value or at cost, when it is sold the company has to deduct the cost of the investment from the proceeds received to determine taxable income. The tax base of the investment is therefore $1,000.

Example 3. A company has trade accounts receivable with a carrying amount of $10,000. The related revenue is taxable as it is earned and is included in taxable income as it is recognized in the accounts. When this asset's carrying amount of $10,000 is recovered (that is, as the customer pays the account), the amount received will not be taxable, so the tax base is equal to its carrying amount. Therefore, its tax base is $10,000.

Example 4. A company holds a life insurance policy on the company president. The policy has a cash surrender value and carrying amount on the statement of financial position of $100,000. If the company receives the $100,000 on the president's death, the proceeds are not taxable under the Income Tax Act. Based on the definition above, the tax base of this asset is the same as its carrying amount. There are no tax consequences.

The **tax base of a liability** is its carrying amount on the statement of financial position reduced by any amount that will be deductible for tax purposes in future periods. The tax base of revenue received in advance is its carrying amount, less any amount that will not be taxable in the future. When a liability can be settled for its carrying amount without any tax consequences, its tax base is the same as its carrying amount. Again, let us look at some examples.

Example 1. A company has an accrued liability with a carrying amount of $1,000. The related expense that was included in accounting income when the expense was accrued is deductible for tax purposes only when it is paid. According to the definition above, the tax base of the accrued liability is its carrying amount ($1,000) less the amount deductible for tax purposes in future periods ($1,000). Therefore, its tax base is $0.

Example 2. A company receives $1,000 of interest in advance and recognizes this as unearned revenue, a liability. The interest was taxed on a cash base, when it was received. The tax base of the unearned revenue is its carrying amount ($1,000) less the amount that will not be taxable in the future ($1,000), thus, $0.

Example 3. A company reports an accrued liability of $200 and the related expenses were deducted for tax purposes in the same period the expense and liability were recognized.

The company also reports a loan payable of $500. In both cases, there is no income tax consequence when the liability is paid in the future. The tax base of the accrued liability and of the loan payable is the same as the carrying amount of each liability on the books (that is, $200 and $500, respectively).

There may be situations where an item has a tax base but it is not recognized as an asset or liability on the statement of financial position. Consider the example of research and development phase costs that have been expensed in the accounts as incurred, but that are deductible for tax purposes in a future year. Although the carrying amount on the statement of financial position is $0, the tax authorities allow the company to reduce future taxable income. The tax base of these research costs would be the amount that would be permitted as a deduction in future periods.

The difference between the tax base of an asset or liability and its reported amount in the statement of financial position is called a **temporary difference**. There are two types. A **taxable temporary difference** will result in taxable amounts in future years when the carrying amount of the asset is received or the liability is settled. That is, the effect is an increase in taxable income and income taxes in the future. A **deductible temporary difference** will decrease taxable income and taxes in the future. We will first look at the effects of **taxable** temporary differences and then discuss **deductible** temporary differences.

Deferred Tax Liabilities

Taxable Temporary Differences

In the Chelsea Inc. example in Illustrations 18-2 to 18-4 above, the company reported revenue of $130,000 on its 2014 income statement. For tax purposes, Chelsea reported only $100,000 of taxable revenue, the amount that was collected in cash in the year. At the end of 2014, the carrying amount of accounts receivable on the statement of financial position is $30,000 (that is, $130,000 − $100,000 collected). What is the tax base of the accounts receivable? Going back to the definition of the tax base of an asset, it is the amount that can be deducted for tax purposes from the $30,000 received. In this case, the full $30,000 will be taxable as it is collected—no amount can be deducted from this. Therefore, the tax value of the accounts receivable is $0.

In the future period when Chelsea collects the $30,000 in accounts receivable, the $30,000 will be taxable and the company will have to pay income tax on it. Therefore, the difference between the carrying amount and tax value of the accounts receivable is a taxable amount—a taxable temporary difference.

What will happen to this $30,000 temporary difference that originated in 2014 for Chelsea Inc.? Assuming that Chelsea expects to collect $20,000 of the receivables in 2015 and $10,000 in 2016, this will result in taxable amounts of $20,000 in 2015 and $10,000 in 2016. These future taxable amounts will cause future taxable income to be increased, along with the amount of income taxes to be paid. Illustration 18-7 presents the original difference, the reversal or turnaround of this temporary difference, and the resulting taxable amounts in future periods.

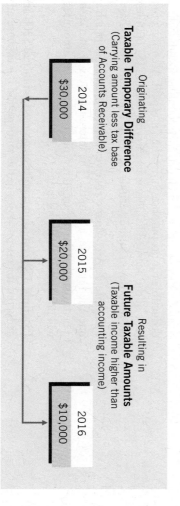

Illustration 18-7

Reversal of Temporary Difference, Chelsea Inc.

Originating
Taxable Temporary Difference
(Carrying amount less tax base of Accounts Receivable)

2014	2015	2016
$30,000	$20,000	$10,000

Resulting in
Future Taxable Amounts
(Taxable income higher than accounting income)

An assumption that underlies a company's IFRS or ASPE statement of financial position is that the assets and liabilities will be recovered and settled, respectively, at least at their reported amounts (carrying amounts). This assumption means that under accrual accounting we need to recognize the future tax consequences of temporary differences in the current year. In other words, it is necessary to recognize in the current period the amount of income taxes that will be payable, reduced, or refunded when the assets' currently reported amounts are recovered or the liabilities are settled.

In our example, we assumed that Chelsea will collect the accounts receivable and report the $30,000 collection as taxable revenue in 2015 and 2016. Based on this, additional income tax will have to be paid in those years. We therefore record the future tax related to the collection of the receivable in Chelsea's books **in 2014.**

Calculation of Deferred Tax Liability

A **deferred tax liability** or **future income tax liability** is the future tax consequence of a taxable temporary difference. It represents the increase in taxes payable in future years as a result of a taxable temporary difference existing at the end of the current year. Recall from the Chelsea example that income tax payable is $10,000 ($40,000 × 25%) in 2014 (Illustration 18-4). In addition, there is a deferred tax liability at the end of 2014 of $7,500, calculated as shown in Illustration 18-8.

Illustration **18-8**

Calculation of Deferred Tax Liability, End of 2014

Carrying amount of accounts receivable	$30,000
Tax base of accounts receivable	–0–
Taxable temporary difference at the end of 2014	30,000
Future tax rate	25%
Deferred tax liability at the end of 2014	$ 7,500

Another way to calculate the deferred tax liability is to **prepare a schedule that shows the taxable amounts by year** as a result of existing temporary differences, as is shown in Illustration 18-9. A detailed schedule like this is needed when the tax rates in future years are different and the calculations are more complex.

Illustration **18-9**

Schedule of Future Taxable Amounts

	Future Years		
	2015	2016	Total
Future taxable amounts	$20,000	$10,000	$30,000
Future tax rate	25%	25%	
Deferred tax liability at the end of 2014	$ 5,000	$ 2,500	$ 7,500

Because it is the first year of operation for Chelsea, there is no deferred tax liability at the beginning of the year. The calculation of the current, deferred, and total income tax expense for 2014 is shown in Illustration 18-10.

Illustration **18-10**

Calculation of Income Tax Expense, 2014

Current tax expense, 2014 (from Illustration 18-4)		
Taxable income × tax rate ($40,000 × 25%)		$10,000
Deferred tax expense, 2014		
Deferred tax liability, end of 2014	$7,500	
Less: Deferred tax liability, beginning of 2014	–0–	
Income tax expense (total) for 2014		7,500
		$17,500

This calculation indicates that income tax expense has two components: current tax expense (the amount of income tax payable or refundable for the current period) and deferred tax expense. **Deferred or future income tax expense is the change** in the statement of financial position deferred tax asset or liability account from the beginning to the end of the accounting period.

Journal entries are needed to record both the current and deferred taxes. Taxes due and payable are credited to Income Tax Payable, while the increase in deferred taxes is credited to Deferred Tax Liability. These tax entries could be combined into one entry. However, because disclosure is required of both components, using two entries makes it easier to keep track of the current tax expense and the deferred tax expense. For Chelsea Inc., the following entries are made at the end of 2014:

Current Tax Expense	10,000	
Income Tax Payable		10,000

A = L + SE
   +10,000 −10,000

Cash flows: No effect

Deferred Tax Expense	7,500	
Deferred Tax Liability		7,500

A = L + SE
   +7,500 −7,500

Cash flows: No effect

At the end of 2015 (the second year), the taxable temporary difference—the difference between the carrying amount ($10,000) and tax base ($0) of the accounts receivable—that relates to the 2014 sales is $10,000. (Remember that $20,000 of the 2014 receivable was collected in 2015.) The $10,000 difference is multiplied by the applicable future tax rate to determine the deferred tax liability of $2,500 ($10,000 × 25%) to be reported at the end of 2015. Both the current and deferred tax expense for 2015 are calculated in Illustration 18-11.

Illustration 18-11

Calculation of Income Tax Expense, 2015

Current tax expense, 2015 (from Illustration 18-4)		
Taxable income × tax rate ($90,000 × 25%)		$22,500
Deferred tax expense, 2015		
Deferred tax liability, end of 2015 ($10,000 × 25%)	$2,500	
Less: Deferred tax liability, beginning of 2015	7,500	(5,000)
Income tax expense (total) for 2015		$17,500

The journal entries to record income taxes for 2015 are:

Current Tax Expense	22,500	
Income Tax Payable		22,500

A = L + SE
   +22,500 −22,500

Cash flows: No effect

Deferred Tax Liability	5,000	
Deferred Tax Benefit		5,000

A = L + SE
   −5,000 +5,000

Cash flows: No effect

Notice in the second entry that an **income tax expense with a credit balance** is often referred to as an **income tax benefit**, or as indicated in IAS 12, it is a **tax income** account. To avoid confusion between the terms "taxable income" and "tax income," we use the term "income tax benefit" in our examples.

In the entry to record deferred taxes at the end of 2016, the Deferred Tax Liability balance is reduced by another $2,500. Illustration 18-12 shows this ledger account as it appears at the end of 2016.

Illustration 18-12

Deferred Tax Liability Account
after Reversals

Deferred Tax Liability

		2014
2015	5,000	7,500
2016	2,500	
		–0–

Balance

As you can see, the Deferred Tax Liability account has a zero balance at the end of 2016.

Deferred Tax Assets

Deductible Temporary Differences

Objective **4**
Explain what a deductible temporary difference is, determine its amount, and calculate deferred tax assets.

To help explain deductible temporary differences and deferred tax assets, assume that Cunningham Inc. sells microwave ovens on which it offers a two-year warranty accounted for using an expense approach. In 2015, the company estimated its warranty expense related to its 2015 sales of microwave ovens to be $500,000. Cunningham expects that $300,000 of these warranty costs will actually be incurred in 2016, and $200,000 in 2017.

Cunningham reports the $500,000 of warranty expense on its 2015 income statement and a related estimated liability for warranties of $500,000 on its December 31, 2015 statement of financial position. For tax purposes, warranty costs are deductible only when the costs are actually incurred. Therefore, no warranty expense can be deducted in determining 2015's taxable income. Because $500,000 **will be deductible in future periods** when the warranty obligation is settled, the tax base of the warranty liability at December 31, 2015, is $0. There is a temporary difference of $500,000 related to the warranty liability.

Because of this temporary difference, Cunningham Inc. recognizes **in 2015** the tax benefits (positive tax consequences) associated with the tax deductions in the future. These future deductible amounts will cause taxable income to be less than accounting income in 2016 and 2017. The deferred tax benefit is reported on the December 31, 2015 statement of financial position as a **deferred tax asset.**

Cunningham's temporary difference originates in one period (2015) and reverses over two periods (2016 and 2017). This situation is diagrammed in Illustration 18-13.

Illustration 18-13

Reversal of Temporary
Difference, Cunningham Inc.

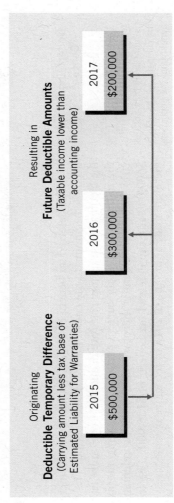

Originating
Deductible Temporary Difference
(Carrying amount less tax base of
Estimated Liability for Warranties)

2015
$500,000

Resulting in
Future Deductible Amounts
(Taxable income lower than
accounting income)

2016	2017
$300,000	$200,000

Calculation of Deferred Tax Assets

A **deferred tax asset** or **future income tax asset** is the future tax consequence of a **deductible temporary difference.** In other words, it represents the reduction in taxes payable or the increase in taxes refundable in future years as a result of a deductible temporary difference that exists at the end of the current year.[8]

To illustrate the deferred tax asset and income tax benefit, we continue with the Cunningham example. The warranty expense recognized on the income statement in 2015 is not deductible for tax purposes until the period when the actual warranty costs are incurred. Therefore, a deduction will be allowed for tax purposes in 2016 and again in 2017 as the liability for warranties is settled, causing taxable income in those years to be lower than accounting income. The deferred tax asset at the end of 2015 (assuming a 25% tax rate for 2016 and 2017) is calculated in Illustration 18-14.

Illustration 18-14

Calculation of Deferred Tax Asset, End of 2015

Carrying amount of warranty liability	$500,000
Tax base of warranty liability	-0-
Deductible temporary difference at the end of 2015	500,000
Future tax rate	25%
Deferred tax asset at the end of 2015	$125,000

Another way to calculate the deferred tax asset is to prepare a schedule like the one in Illustration 18-15. It shows the deductible amounts that are scheduled for the future as a result of the deductible temporary difference.

Illustration 18-15

Schedule of Future Deductible Amounts

	Future Years		
	2016	2017	Total
Future deductible amounts	$300,000	$200,000	$500,000
Future tax rate	25%	25%	
Deferred tax asset at the end of 2015	$ 75,000	$ 50,000	$125,000

Assuming that 2015 is Cunningham's first year of operations and that income tax payable for this year is $600,000, income tax expense is calculated as shown in Illustration 18-16.

Illustration 18-16

Calculation of Income Tax Expense, 2015

Current tax expense, 2015 (given)
Taxable income × tax rate	$600,000

Deferred tax expense/benefit, 2015
Deferred tax asset, end of 2015	$125,000
Less: Deferred tax asset, beginning of 2015	-0-
	(125,000)
Income tax expense (total) for 2015	$475,000

The deferred tax benefit of $125,000 results from the increase in the deferred tax asset from the beginning to the end of the accounting period. The deferred tax benefit captures the fact that the warranty costs are deductible from future taxable income and recognizes this in the accounts in the current period. The total income tax expense of $475,000 on the 2015 income statement is therefore made up of two elements: a current tax expense of $600,000 and the deferred tax benefit of $125,000. The following journal entries are therefore made at the end of 2015 to recognize income taxes:

Current Tax Expense	600,000	
Income Tax Payable		600,000

$$A = L + SE$$
$$+600,000 \quad -600,000$$
Cash flows: No effect

Deferred Tax Asset	125,000	
Deferred Tax Benefit		125,000

$$A = L + SE$$
$$+125,000 \quad +125,000$$
Cash flows: No effect

Assuming warranty costs are incurred in the same amounts that were expected, the liability for warranties at the end of 2016 has a carrying amount of $500,000 − $300,000 = $200,000. The tax base of this liability is still $0 and the future deductible amount is now $200,000. Therefore, the deferred tax asset at the end of 2016 is 25% of $200,000, or $50,000. Assuming the income tax payable for 2016 is $440,000, income tax expense for the year is calculated as shown in Illustration 18-17.

Calculation of Income Tax Expense, 2016

Current tax expense, 2016 (given)		$440,000
Taxable income × tax rate		
Deferred tax expense/benefit, 2016		
Deferred tax asset, end of 2016	$ 50,000	
Less: Deferred tax asset, beginning of 2016	(125,000)	75,000
Income tax expense (total) for 2016		$515,000

As expected, a reduction in the deferred tax asset account, as with assets in general, results in an increase in the expense to be recognized. The journal entries to record income taxes in 2016 are:

Current Tax Expense	440,000	
Income Tax Payable		440,000

$$A = L + SE$$
$$+440,000 \quad -440,000$$

Cash flows: No effect

Deferred Tax Expense	75,000	
Deferred Tax Asset		75,000

$$A = L + SE$$
$$-75,000 \quad -75,000$$

Cash flows: No effect

The total income tax expense of $515,000 on the income statement for 2016 is made up of two parts: a current tax expense of $440,000 and a deferred tax expense of $75,000. You may have noticed that the deferred tax expense of $75,000 that is recognized in 2016 **is not related to future events at all.** In this case, it represents the reversal of a deferred tax benefit that originated in a prior year. The deferred tax expense or benefit measures the change in the deferred tax liability or asset account over the period. It is a combination of originating and reversing temporary differences, changing tax rates, and other events discussed later in this chapter.

At the end of 2017, the Deferred Tax Asset balance is further reduced by $50,000, as shown in the T account in Illustration 18-18. Deferred tax expense in 2017 is $50,000.

Deferred Tax Asset Account after Reversals

Deferred Tax Asset		
2015	125,000	75,000 2016
		50,000 2017
Balance	−0−	

Some analysts dismiss deferred tax assets and deferred tax liabilities when they assess a company's financial position. However, these accounts meet the conditions set out in the conceptual framework to be recognized as assets and liabilities.

Deferred Tax Asset

1. It contributes to future net cash flows.
2. Access to the benefit is controlled by the entity.
3. It results from a past transaction or event.

Deferred Tax Liability

1. It is an obligation.
2. It represents a future sacrifice of economic resources.
3. It results from a past transaction or event.

A study by B. Ayers found that the market views deferred tax assets and liabilities in much the same way as it views other assets and liabilities, and that FASB's SFAS No. 109 increased the usefulness of future tax amounts in financial statements.

In addition, the reaction of market analysts to the writeoff of deferred taxes in the past supports treating them as assets, as does management's treatment of them. When Air Canada ran into financial problems, it reduced its $400-million balance in its future income tax asset account at the end of one year to zero at the end of the next year. The reason? Because the airline was not sure that it would be able to generate enough taxable income in the future, its ability to realize any benefits from future deductible amounts was questionable. Like other assets with uncertain benefits, this asset was written down.

Sources: B. Ayers, "Deferred Tax Accounting Under SFAS No. 109: An Empirical Investigation of Its Incremental Value-Relevance Relative to APB No. 11," *The Accounting Review* (April 1998); "Air Canada Reports Final Year 2002 and Fourth Quarter Financial Results," company news release, May 13, 2003; John R. Graham, Jana S. Raedy, and Douglas A. Shackelford, "Research in Accounting for Income Taxes," *Journal of Accounting and Economics* (2011).

Income Tax Accounting Objectives and Analyses of Temporary Deductible Differences

Income Tax Accounting Objectives

One objective of accounting for income taxes is to recognize the amount of tax that is payable or refundable for the current year. In Chelsea Inc.'s case, income tax payable is $10,000 for 2014.

A second objective is **interperiod tax allocation**: to recognize the tax effects in the accounting period when the transactions and events are recognized for financial reporting purposes. We saw how this was achieved in the Cunningham example. Accounting for the effect of future taxes on the statement of financial position in this way is what underlies the **future income taxes method**, also known as the **temporary difference approach**. The following table illustrates how the statement of financial position amount reported for the warranty liability mirrors the net future cash outflows of Cunningham.

	End of 2015	End of 2016
Deferred Tax Asset		
Economic resources needed to settle the obligation:		
Future resources needed to settle the warranty liability	$500,000	$200,000
Future tax savings as liability is settled	125,000	50,000
Net future economic resources needed	$375,000	$150,000
Net liabilities reported on the statement of financial position:		
Warranty liability (in liabilities)	$500,000	$200,000
Deferred tax asset (in assets)	125,000	50,000
Net liabilities reported	$375,000	$150,000

A similar table could be constructed for Chelsea's receivables and deferred tax liability to show that the net amount of these two accounts corresponds to the net cash inflow expected as the receivables are collected.

In addition to ensuring that the statement of financial position amounts faithfully represent economic reality, deferred taxes also affect the amount of income tax expense reported in each year. With interperiod tax allocation, the expense amount is related primarily to the revenues and expenses that are reported on each year's income statement. This is shown in Illustration 18-19 for Chelsea Inc. In some years, total income tax expense is greater than taxes payable, and in others it is less. The net result is to report income tax expense that is based on the income statement amounts—in this case 25% of

Objective 5
Prepare analyses of deferred tax balances and record deferred tax expense.

the accounting income, or $22,500. Deferred taxes affect the tax expense reported in all years where there are originating and reversing differences.

Illustration **18-19**

Accounting Income and Total Income Tax Expense

CHELSEA INC.
Financial Reporting of Income Tax Expense

	2014	2015	2016
Revenues	$130,000	$130,000	$130,000
Expenses	60,000	60,000	60,000
Income before income tax	70,000	70,000	70,000
Less income tax expense:			
Current tax expense	10,000	22,500	20,000
Deferred tax expense	7,500	(5,000)	(2,500)
	17,500	17,500	17,500
Net income	$ 52,500	$ 52,500	$ 52,500

Analysis of Multiple Differences Illustrated

As can be seen in the recent financial statements of Canadian public companies, there are a variety of causes of temporary differences that result in deferred tax assets and liabilities. These include differences between the tax base and carrying amounts of plant and equipment, tax loss carryforwards, pension assets and liabilities, share issue costs, intangible assets, site restoration and asset retirement obligations, and goodwill, among others.

We will now illustrate the analysis that underlies the accounting for deferred tax accounts on the statement of financial position and deferred tax expense or benefit on the income statement when there are multiple temporary differences. We return to the BT Corporation example used earlier in the chapter to explain current income taxes. You were asked to assume that BT Corporation reports accounting income of $200,000 in each of the years 2014, 2015, and 2016; that the company is subject to a 30% tax rate in each year; and that it has the following differences between income reported on the financial statements and taxable income.

1. For tax purposes, royalty revenue of $18,000 recorded in 2014 is reported over an 18-month period at an equal amount each month as it is collected, beginning January 1, 2015. The entire revenue is recognized for financial reporting purposes in 2014.

2. A premium of $5,000 is paid in each of 2015 and 2016 for life insurance that the company carries on key officers. This is a non-deductible expense for tax purposes, but is considered a business expense for accounting purposes.

3. A warranty with an associated expense of $30,000, provided on sales in 2014, was recognized in the same year. It was expected that $20,000 of the warranty work would be performed in 2015 and $10,000 in 2016, and this is what actually happened.

The calculations of taxable income and current tax expense are shown in Illustrations 18-5 and 18-6. We now continue with the example to see how this information affects the statement of financial position and deferred tax assets and liabilities.

All differences between the accounting income and taxable income are considered in reconciling the income reported on the financial statements to taxable income. However, **only those that result in temporary differences are considered when determining deferred tax amounts for the statement of financial position.** When there are multiple differences, a schedule is prepared of the statement of financial position accounts whose carrying amounts and tax bases are different.

For BT Corporation, the royalty revenue from 2014 resulted in an $18,000 difference between the carrying amount and the tax base of its accounts receivable at the end of 2014. The sale and receivable were recognized in 2014, but no payments were received until 2015; no amounts were included in taxable income in 2014. The receivable's tax value is therefore $0. Another way to look at this is that, for tax purposes, neither the account receivable nor the royalty revenue has been recognized.

The life insurance premium expense is a permanent difference. It is not reversible and has no deferred tax consequences. Therefore, it is not considered in calculating deferred taxes.

BT Corporation ended 2014 with a warranty liability on its books of $30,000 because none of the actual warranty work had been carried out as at the end of the year. For tax purposes, however, no warranty expense or associated warranty liability has been recognized at December 31, 2014. The liability's tax value is therefore $0.

The company's analysis and calculation of the temporary differences, the net deferred tax asset or liability, and the deferred tax expense or benefit for 2014 are shown in Illustration 18-20. Because the same tax rate is assumed for all periods, calculating the deferred tax asset and liability is simplified. If the tax rate for future years has been legislated at differing rates, it would be better to use a separate schedule to calculate the deferred tax amounts as set out in Illustrations 18-9 and 18-15.

Illustration 18-20

Calculation of Deferred Tax
Asset/Liability and Deferred
Tax Expense—2014

Statement of Financial Position Account	Tax Base	—	Carrying Amount	=	Deductible (Taxable) Temporary Difference	×	Tax Rate	=	Deferred Tax Asset (Liability)
Accounts receivable	$-0-		$18,000		$(18,000)		.30		$(5,400)
Warranty liability	-0-		(30,000)		30,000		.30		9,000
Net deferred tax asset, December 31, 2014									3,600
Net deferred tax asset (liability) before adjustment									-0-
Increase in deferred tax asset, and deferred tax benefit, 2014									$ 3,600

In 2014, BT has two originating differences that result in temporary differences. One results in a deferred tax asset and the other in a deferred tax liability. While separate entries could be made to each of these accounts, the analyses and entries in this chapter work with one net account. Statement of financial position presentation is covered later in the chapter. If you find the concept of tax base confusing, it may help to focus on the related temporary difference column in Illustration 18-20. For the accounts receivable, while the $18,000 has already been included in net income, it will only be taxable when the related cash is received. Therefore, in the future BT will be required to pay tax on the $18,000 (taxable temporary difference). For the warranty, the $30,000 was expensed for accounting purposes but will only be deductible for tax purposes when the repairs are made in the future. Therefore, the $30,000 future tax deduction results in a deductible temporary difference.

The journal entries to record income taxes for 2014, based on the above analysis and the analysis for current tax expense in Illustration 18-6, are:

Current Tax Expense	63,600	
Income Tax Payable (see Illustration 18-6)		63,600

A = L + SE
+63,600 −63,600
Cash flows: No effect

Deferred Tax Asset	3,600	
Deferred Tax Benefit		3,600

A = L + SE
+3,600   +3,600
Cash flows: No effect

Illustration 18-21 sets out the analysis of the temporary differences at the end of 2015. The two differences that originated in 2014 have begun to reverse. The account receivable has been reduced to $6,000 at the end of 2015, and the warranty liability outstanding is now only $10,000. Again, as Illustration 18-21 shows, the deferred tax expense or benefit is determined **by the change** in the deferred tax asset or liability account on the statement of financial position.

Illustration 18-21

Calculation of Deferred Tax Asset/Liability and Deferred Tax Expense—2015

Statement of Financial Position Account	Tax Base	−	Carrying Amount	=	(Taxable) Deductible Temporary Difference	×	Tax Rate	=	Deferred Tax Asset (Liability)
Accounts receivable	$-0-		$ 6,000		$ (6,000)		.30		$(1,800)
Warranty liability	-0-		$(10,000)		10,000		.30		3,000
Net deferred tax asset, December 31, 2015									1,200
Less: Net deferred tax asset before adjustment									3,600
Decrease in deferred tax asset, and deferred tax expense, 2015									$ 2,400

The journal entries to record income taxes at December 31, 2015, are:

Current Tax Expense   59,100
   Income Tax Payable (see Illustration 18-6)   59,100

A	=	L	+	SE
		+59,100		−59,100

Cash flows: No effect

Deferred Tax Expense   2,400
   Deferred Tax Asset   2,400

A	=	L	+	SE
−2,400				−2,400

Cash flows: No effect

As indicated in Illustration 18-22, by the end of 2016 all differences have reversed, leaving no temporary differences between statement of financial position amounts and tax values.

Illustration 18-22

Calculation of Deferred Tax Asset/Liability and Deferred Tax Expense—2016

Statement of Financial Position Account	Tax Base	−	Carrying Amount	=	(Taxable) Deductible Temporary Difference	×	Tax Rate	=	Deferred Tax Asset (Liability)
Accounts receivable	$-0-		$-0-		$-0-		N/A		$ -0-
Warranty liability	-0-		-0-		-0-		N/A		-0-
Net deferred tax asset, December 31, 2016									-0-
Less: Net deferred tax asset before adjustment									1,200
Decrease in deferred tax asset, and deferred tax expense, 2016									$1,200

The journal entries at December 31, 2016, reduce the Deferred Tax Asset account to zero and recognize $1,200 in deferred tax expense for 2016.

Current Tax Expense   60,300
   Income Tax Payable (see Illustration 18-6)   60,300

A	=	L	+	SE
		+60,300		−60,300

Cash flows: No effect

Deferred Tax Expense   1,200
   Deferred Tax Asset   1,200

A	=	L	+	SE
−1,200				−1,200

Cash flows: No effect

Illustration 18-23 provides a summary of the bottom portion of the income statements for BT Corporation for each of the three years.

Illustration 18-23

BT Corporation Income Statements—2014, 2015, and 2016

BT CORPORATION
Income Statements (partial) for the Years

	2014	2015	2016
Income before income tax expense	$200,000	$200,000	$200,000
Less income tax expense:			
Current expense	63,600	59,100	60,300
Deferred expense (benefit)	(3,600)	2,400	1,200
	60,000	61,500	61,500
Net income	$140,000	$138,500	$138,500

Total income tax expense reported in 2014, 2015, and 2016 is $60,000, $61,500, and $61,500, respectively. Although the statutory or enacted rate (the rate set by government legislation) of 30% applies for all three years, the effective rate is 30% for 2014 ($60,000 ÷ $200,000 = 30%) and 30.75% for 2015 and 2016 ($61,500 ÷ $200,000 = 30.75%). The **effective tax rate** is calculated by dividing total income tax expense for the period by the pre-tax income reported on the financial statements. The difference between the enacted and effective rates in 2015 and 2016 of 0.75% in this case is caused by the $5,000 non-deductible life insurance expense ([$5,000 × 0.30] ÷ $200,000).

Tax Rate Considerations

Objective 6

Explain the effect of multiple tax rates and tax rate changes on income tax accounts, and calculate current and deferred tax amounts when there is a change in substantively enacted tax rates.

In the previous illustrations, the enacted tax rate did not change from one year to the next. To calculate the deferred tax account reported on the statement of financial position, the temporary difference was simply multiplied by the current tax rate because it was expected to apply to future years as well. Tax rates do change, however.

Future Tax Rates

What happens if tax rates (or tax laws) are different for future years? Accounting standards take the position that the income tax rates to use should be the ones that are expected to apply when the tax liabilities are settled or tax assets are realized. These would normally be the future tax rates that have been enacted at the statement of financial position date. The accounting standard does recognize, however, that situations may exist where a **substantively enacted rate** or tax law may be more appropriate.[9] To illustrate the use of different tax rates, we use the example of Warlen Corp. At the end of 2014, this company has a temporary difference of $300,000, as determined in Illustration 18-24.

Illustration 18-24

Calculation of Temporary Difference

Net carrying amount of depreciable assets	$1,000,000
Tax base of depreciable assets (UCC)	700,000
Taxable temporary difference	$ 300,000

This is a **taxable** temporary difference because, to date, Warlen has deducted $300,000 more CCA on its tax returns than it has deducted depreciation expense on its income statements. We know this because the UCC is $300,000 lower than the assets' net carrying amount in the accounts. When Warlen Corp. calculates taxable income in the future, it will have to add back its depreciation expense and deduct a lower amount of CCA. The result will be a taxable income that is higher than the accounting income.

Continuing with this example, assume that the $300,000 will reverse and that the tax rates that are expected to apply in the following years on the resulting taxable amounts are as shown in Illustration 18-25.

Illustration 18-25

Deferred Tax Liability Based on Future Rates

	Total	2015	2016	2017	2018	2019
Future taxable amounts	$300,000	$80,000	$70,000	$60,000	$50,000	$40,000
Tax rate		30%	30%	25%	20%	20%
Deferred tax liability	$ 78,000	$24,000	$21,000	$15,000	$10,000	$ 8,000

As indicated, the deferred tax liability is $78,000—the total deferred tax effect of the temporary difference at the end of 2014.

Because the Canadian tax system provides incentives by reducing the income tax rates that may be applied to taxable income, the rate used to calculate deferred tax amounts includes the tax rate reductions, provided it is expected that the company will qualify for the rate reductions in the periods of reversal.[10] The general principle is to use the rates that are expected to apply to the taxable income in the periods when the temporary differences are expected to reverse, provided that the rates are enacted or substantively enacted at the statement of financial position date. The AcSB, IASB, and FASB standards all agree that discounting deferred tax assets and liabilities **is not permitted.**

Revision of Future Tax Rates

When a change in the tax rate is enacted (or substantively enacted) into law, **its effect on the existing deferred tax asset and liability accounts is recorded immediately as an adjustment to income tax expense in the period of the change.**

Assume that on September 10, 2014, a new income tax rate is enacted that lowers the corporate rate from 30% to 25%, effective January 1, 2016. To illustrate this change, we use the example of Hostel Corp. If Hostel Corp. has one temporary difference at the beginning of 2014 related to $3 million of excess capital cost allowance, then it has a Deferred Tax Liability account at January 1, 2014, with a balance of $900,000 ($3,000,000 × 30%). If taxable amounts related to this difference are scheduled to increase the taxable income equally in 2015, 2016, and 2017, the deferred tax liability at September 10, 2014, is now $800,000, calculated as shown in Illustration 18-26.

Illustration 18-26

Schedule of Future Taxable Amounts and Related Tax Rates

	Total	2015	2016	2017
Future taxable amounts	$3,000,000	$1,000,000	$1,000,000	$1,000,000
Tax rate		30%	25%	25%
Revised deferred tax liability	$ 800,000	$ 300,000	$ 250,000	$ 250,000

An entry is made on September 10, 2014, to recognize the $100,000 decrease ($900,000 − $800,000) in the deferred tax liability:

Deferred Tax Liability	100,000	
Deferred Tax Benefit		100,000

A	=	L	+	SE
		−100,000		+100,000

Cash flows: No effect

While ASPE does not require separate disclosure of the future tax expense or benefit due to a change in tax rates, IFRS does.

Law

When governments change their income tax rates, the effect on corporate Canada can be a substantial hit or a tax windfall! As an example, the last time the federal, Alberta, and Saskatchewan governments significantly reduced future tax rates, it resulted in tax windfalls for many companies in the oil industry. The federal rate fell from 21% in 2007, to 16.5% in 2011 and 15% in 2012. Companies reporting large deferred tax liabilities saw immediate reductions as they remeasured these liabilities. A concurrent increase in earnings of these companies was reported as the reduction in the deferred income tax liability was taken into income through a deferred tax benefit. **Husky Energy Inc.**, an integrated energy and energy-related company, for example, indicated that the reduction in tax rates increased its profits for 2007 by $395 million, helping its net earnings increase by 16.8% for the year (significantly higher than the 4.5% that it would have increased without the adjustment). **Canadian Natural Resources Ltd.**, Canada's second-largest independent petroleum producer at the time, recognized a similar gain from the tax rate change, some $864 million, which helped to bring its reported net earnings in 2007 to more than $2.6 billion!

Sources: "Corporation Tax Rates," Canada Revenue Agency, available at http://www.cra-arc.gc.ca/tx/bsnss/tpcs/crprtns/rts-eng.html; Husky Energy Inc. Annual Report 2007; Canadian Natural Resources Ltd. Annual Report 2007.

Basic corporate tax rates do not change often, and the current rate is therefore normally used.[11] However, changes in provincial rates, the small business deduction, foreign tax rates, and surcharges on all levels of income affect the effective rate and may require adjustments to the deferred tax accounts.

To this point in the chapter, the following topics have been covered:

- Recognition and measurement of current tax expense (benefit) and the associated income taxes that are currently payable (receivable). This describes the taxes payable approach to accounting for income taxes.

- Explanation of temporary differences and why deferred tax assets and deferred tax liabilities are required to be recognized and measured under the temporary difference approach, in addition to the current income taxes.

- Recognition and measurement of deferred tax assets and deferred tax liabilities and the associated deferred tax expense or benefit.

- Explanation of the tax rates to use and how changes in the rates are accounted for.

Appendix 18A provides a comprehensive example to help you cement your understanding of the analyses needed to support the income tax entries for the year. The example illustrates interperiod tax allocation with multiple temporary differences and a tax rate change over a two-year period.

INCOME TAX LOSS CARRYOVER BENEFITS

A loss for income tax purposes or tax loss occurs when the year's tax-deductible expenses and losses exceed the company's taxable revenues and gains. The tax system would be unfair if companies were taxed during profitable periods and received no tax relief during periods of losses. Therefore, a company pays no income tax in a year in which it incurs a tax loss. In addition, the tax laws permit taxpayers to use a tax loss of one year to offset taxable income of other years. This is accomplished through the tax loss carryback and carryforward provisions of income tax legislation, which allow taxpayers to benefit from tax losses—either by recovering taxes that were previously paid or by reducing taxes that will otherwise be payable in the future.

A corporation can choose to carry a tax loss back against taxable income of the immediately preceding three years. This is a **loss carryback**. Alternatively, it can choose to carry losses forward to the 20 years that immediately follow the loss. This is a **loss carryforward**.[12] Or, it may choose to do both. Illustration 18-27 presents a diagram of the carryover periods, assuming a tax loss is incurred in 2014.

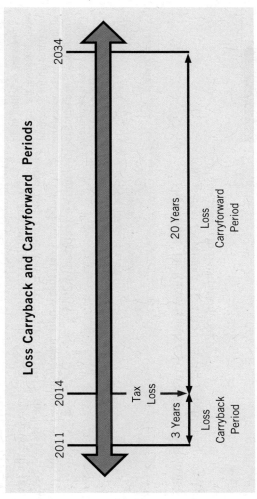

Loss Carryback and Carryforward Periods

If a loss is carried back, it is usually applied against the earliest available income—2011 in the example above. The **benefit from a loss carryback** is the **recovery of some or all of the taxes** that were paid in those years. The tax returns for the preceding years are refiled, the current-year tax loss is deducted from the previously reported taxable income, and a revised amount of income tax payable is determined for each year. This figure is then compared with the taxes that were actually paid for each of the preceding years, and the government is asked to refund the difference.

If a corporation decides to carry the loss forward, or if the full amount of the loss could not be absorbed in the carryback period, **the tax loss can be used to offset taxable income in the future so that taxes for those future years are reduced or eliminated.** The decision on how to use a tax loss depends on factors such as its size, the results of the previous years' operations, past and anticipated future tax rates, and other factors in which management sees the greatest tax advantage.[13]

Tax losses are relatively common and can be large. Companies that have suffered substantial losses are often attractive merger candidates because, in certain cases, the acquirer may use these losses to reduce its taxable income and, therefore, its income taxes. In a sense, a company that has suffered substantial losses may find itself worth more "dead than alive" because of the economic value related to the tax benefit that another company may be able to use.[14] The following sections discuss the accounting treatment of loss carrybacks and carryforwards.

Loss Carryback Illustrated

To illustrate the accounting procedures for a tax loss carryback, assume that Groh Inc. has the taxable incomes and losses shown in Illustration 18-28. Assume also that there are no temporary or permanent differences in any year.

Year	Taxable Income or Loss	Tax Rate	Tax Paid
2011	$ 75,000	30%	$22,500
2012	50,000	25%	12,500
2013	100,000	30%	30,000
2014	200,000	20%	40,000
2015	(500,000)	—	–0–

In 2015, Groh Inc. incurs a tax loss that it decides to carry back. The carryback is applied first to 2012, the third year preceding the loss year. Any unused loss is then carried back to 2013, and then to 2014. Groh files amended tax returns for each of the years 2012, 2013, and 2014, receiving refunds for the $82,500 ($12,500 + $30,000 + $40,000) of taxes paid in those years.

For accounting purposes, the $82,500 represents the **tax benefit of the loss carryback**. The tax benefit is recognized in 2015, the loss year, because the tax loss gives rise to a tax refund (an asset) that is both measurable and currently realizable. The following journal entry is prepared in 2015:

Income Tax Receivable	82,500	
Current Tax Benefit		82,500

The Income Tax Receivable is reported on the statement of financial position as a current asset at December 31, 2015. The tax benefit is reported on the income statement for 2015 as shown in Illustration 18-29.

GROH INC.
Income Statement (partial) for 2015

Income (loss) before income taxes	$(500,000)
Income tax benefit	
Current benefit due to loss carryback	82,500
Net income (loss)	$(417,500)

If the tax loss carried back to the three preceding years is less than the taxable incomes of those three years, the only entry needed is similar to the one above. For Groh Inc., however, the $500,000 tax loss for 2015 is more than the $350,000 in total taxable income from the three preceding years; **the remaining $150,000 loss can therefore be carried forward**. The accounting for a tax loss carryforward is explained next.

Loss Carryforward Illustrated

If a net operating loss is not fully absorbed through a carryback or if the company decides not to carry the loss back, **the loss can be carried forward for up to 20 years**. Because carryforwards are used to offset expected future taxable income, the tax benefit associated with a loss carryforward is represented by future tax savings: reductions in taxes in the future that would otherwise be payable. In order to actually benefit from this loss, the company must generate future taxable income. In some cases, the ability to do this may be highly uncertain.

The accounting issue, then, is whether the tax benefit of a loss carryforward should be recognized **in the loss year when the potential benefits arise, or in future years when the benefits are actually realized**. IFRS indicates that the potential benefit must be **probable**. While this term is not defined in the income tax standard, **probable** is defined as **more likely than not** in another standard of IFRS, and the IASB agreed that this was its meaning in its joint project on harmonizing tax standards with U.S. GAAP. ASPE (the future income taxes method) takes the position that the potential benefit of unused tax losses meets the definition of an asset **to the extent that it is more likely than not that the benefit will be realized**; that is, more likely than not that there will be future taxable income against which the losses can be applied.

When it is probable that a tax loss carryforward will result in future economic benefits, it is accounted for in the same way as a deductible temporary difference: a deferred tax asset is recognized in an amount equal to the expected benefit.

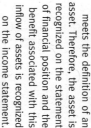

Future Taxable Income Probable

To illustrate the accounting for an income tax loss carryforward, we continue with the Groh Inc. example. In 2015, after carrying back as much of the loss as possible to the three preceding years, the company has a $150,000 tax loss available to carry forward. Assuming that it is probable that the company will **generate sufficient taxable income in the future** so that the benefit of the remaining $150,000 loss will be realized, Groh records a deferred tax asset. If a tax rate of 20% applies to future years, the asset recognized is $30,000 ($150,000 $\times$ 20%). The journal entries to record the benefits of the carryback and the carryforward in 2015 are as follows:

To recognize benefit of loss carryback

Income Tax Receivable	82,500	
Current Tax Benefit		82,500

A	=	L	+	SE
+82,500				+82,500

Cash flows: No effect

To recognize benefit of loss carryforward

Deferred Tax Asset	30,000	
Deferred Tax Benefit		30,000

A	=	L	+	SE
+30,000				+30,000

Cash flows: No effect

The Deferred Tax Asset account on the statement of financial position is a measure of the expected future tax savings from the loss, and because this asset is recognized, a $30,000 deferred tax benefit is reported on the income statement. The 2015 income statement appears as shown in Illustration 18-30.

GROH INC.

Income Statement (partial) for 2015

Income (loss) before income taxes		$(500,000)
Income tax benefit		
Current benefit due to loss carryback	$82,500	
Deferred tax benefit due to loss carryforward	30,000	112,500
Net income (loss)		$(387,500)

Illustration 18-30

Recognition of the Benefit of the Loss Carryback and Carryforward in the Loss Year

For 2016, assume that Groh returns to profitability and has taxable income of $200,000 from the year's operations, subject to a 20% tax rate. In this year, then, Groh can deduct the carryforward loss from the 2016 taxable income, and reduce the tax that would otherwise be payable in the year. In other words, in 2016 Groh **realizes** the benefit of the tax loss carryforward that was **recognized** for accounting purposes in 2015. The income tax payable for 2016 is determined in Illustration 18-31.

Taxable income before loss carryforward, 2016	$ 200,000
Tax loss carryforward deduction	(150,000)
Revised taxable income for 2016	50,000
Tax rate	20%
Income tax payable for 2016 and current tax expense	$ 10,000
Deferred tax asset, opening balance ($150,000 $\times$ 0.2)	$ 30,000
Deferred tax asset, December 31, 2016 ($0 $\times$ 0.2)	–0–
Deferred tax expense, 2016	$ 30,000

Illustration 18-31

Calculation of Income Tax Payable in the Year the Loss Carryforward Is Realized

The journal entries to record income taxes for 2016 are:

Current Tax Expense	10,000	
Income Tax Payable		10,000

A = L + SE
+10,000 −10,000

Cash flows: No effect

Deferred Tax Expense	30,000	
Deferred Tax Asset		30,000

A = L + SE
−30,000 −30,000

Cash flows: No effect

The first entry records income taxes payable for 2016 and, therefore, current tax expense. The second entry records the using up of the tax benefit that was captured as a deferred tax asset the previous year.

The 2016 income statement in Illustration 18-32 shows that the 2016 total income tax expense is based on 2016's reported income. The **benefit of the tax loss** is not reported in 2016. It was already reported in 2015.

GROH INC.
Income Statement (partial) for 2016

Income before income taxes		$200,000
Income tax expense		
Current	$10,000	
Deferred	30,000	40,000
Net income		$160,000

Future Taxable Income Not Probable

Let's return to the Groh Inc. example and 2015. A tax asset (Income Tax Receivable) was recognized in 2015 because Groh knew that the company would receive $82,500 of benefits from $350,000 of the tax loss. This left $150,000 of tax losses to carry forward. We assume now that the company's future profitability is uncertain and that at December 31, 2015, there is not enough evidence that there will be future taxable income to deduct these losses against. Therefore, we cannot recognize the potential tax benefit of the loss carryforward as an asset. In this case, the only 2015 income tax entry is:

Income Tax Receivable	82,500	
Current Tax Benefit		82,500

A = L + SE
+82,500 +82,500

Cash flows: No effect

The presentation in the 2015 income statement in Illustration 18-33 reflects the entry made—**only the benefit related to the loss carryback is recognized.** However, the unrecognized potential tax benefit associated with the remaining $150,000 of tax losses is relevant information for financial statement readers. Therefore, the amounts and expiry dates of unrecognized (unbooked) tax losses are disclosed. This makes readers aware of the possibility of future benefits (reduced future tax outflows) from the loss, even though the likelihood of realizing these benefits at the reporting date is too uncertain for them to be recognized in the body of the statements.

Illustration 18-33

Recognition of Benefit of Loss Carryback Only

GROH INC.
Income Statement (partial) for 2015

Income (loss) before income taxes	$(500,000)
Income tax benefit	
Current benefit due to loss carryback (see note)	82,500
Net income (loss)	$(417,500)

Note: The company has not recognized any benefits associated with $150,000 of tax losses that are available for carryforward. These will expire by 2035.

Assume now that in 2016 the company performs better than expected, generating taxable income of $200,000 from its annual operations. After applying the $150,000 loss carryforward, tax is payable on only $50,000 of income. With a tax rate of 20%, the following entry is made:

Current Tax Expense	10,000	
Income Tax Payable ($50,000 × 20%)		10,000

A = L + SE
+10,000 −10,000

Cash flows: No effect

This entry recognizes the taxes currently payable in the year. Because the potential tax benefit associated with the loss carryforward **was not recognized in 2015, it is recognized in 2016**, the year it is realized. The $10,000 of current tax expense is actually made up of two components: income taxes of $40,000 accrued on the 2016 income of $200,000, and a $30,000 tax reduction from the realization of the unrecorded loss carryforward. Separate disclosure of the benefit from the loss carried forward is not required under ASPE, but is required under IFRS if it makes up a major component of tax expense. Illustration 18-34 shows the 2016 income statement.

Illustration 18-34

Recognition of Benefit of Loss Carryforward when Realized

GROH INC.
Income Statement (partial) for 2016

Income before income taxes	$200,000
Current tax expense (note)	10,000
Net income	$190,000

The note to the financial statements (if required) would state that current tax expense includes a $30,000 benefit from deducting a previously unrecognized tax loss carryforward.

If 2016's taxable income had been less than $150,000, only a portion of the unrecorded tax loss could have been applied. The entry to record 2016 income taxes would have been similar to the entry above. In addition, a note to the financial statements is provided to disclose the amount and expiry date of the remaining unused loss.

Carryforward with Valuation Allowance

In the Groh Inc. example above, we assumed that the company's future was uncertain, and that there was insufficient evidence that the company would be able to benefit from the remaining $150,000 of 2015 tax losses available to be carried forward. As a result, no deferred tax asset was recognized in 2015.

There is an alternative recognition approach to this situation. Under it, a deferred tax asset is recognized for the full amount of the tax effect on the $150,000 loss carryforward, **along with an offsetting valuation allowance**, a contra account to the deferred tax asset account. Because the net effect on the financial statements is the same, this valuation allowance approach is also permitted under ASPE. The valuation allowance approach is not consistent with existing IAS 12 *Income Taxes*. The international standard allows recognition of a deferred tax asset only to the extent that future tax benefits are probable.

How does a valuation allowance work? Assuming that the entry for the loss carryback has already been made, the following entries recognize the tax effect of the full $150,000 loss carryforward and the valuation allowance to bring the deferred tax asset account to its realizable value of zero at December 31, 2015:

Deferred Tax Asset ($150,000 × 20%)	30,000	
Deferred Tax Benefit		30,000

A	=	L	+	SE
+30,000				+30,000

Cash flows: No effect

Deferred Tax Expense	30,000	
Allowance to Reduce Deferred Tax Asset		30,000
to Expected Realizable Value		

A	=	L	+	SE
–30,000				–30,000

Cash flows: No effect

The latter entry, which sets up the allowance account, indicates that there is not enough evidence that the company will benefit from the tax loss in the future. The effect on the financial statements is the same whether these two entries are made or the deferred tax asset is not recognized in the accounts at all. The income statement under the allowance approach is identical to the statement provided in Illustration 18-33.

Now assume that the company performs better than expected in 2016, generating taxable income of $200,000. After applying the $150,000 loss carryforward, tax is payable on only $50,000 of income. With a tax rate of 20%, the entry for current taxes is:

Current Tax Expense	10,000	
Income Tax Payable ($50,000 × 20%)		10,000

A	=	L	+	SE
		+10,000		–10,000

Cash flows: No effect

Because the amount of tax losses available to carry forward to future years has changed, the Deferred Tax Asset account and its valuation allowance are adjusted. In this case, no tax losses remain.

Deferred Tax Expense	30,000	
Deferred Tax Asset		30,000

A	=	L	+	SE
–30,000				–30,000

Cash flows: No effect

Allowance to Reduce Deferred Tax Asset to	30,000	
Expected Realizable Value		
Deferred Tax Benefit		30,000

A	=	L	+	SE
+30,000				+30,000

Cash flows: No effect

The deferred tax expense of $30,000 (from adjusting the tax asset account) cancels out the $30,000 deferred tax benefit (from adjusting the allowance account). In this case, the income statement reports only the current tax expense of $10,000, as set out in Illustration 18-34, when neither the tax asset nor the allowance was recognized.

To summarize, IFRS currently requires an "affirmative judgement" approach by recognizing deferred tax assets only to the extent that it is probable that deductible temporary differences, unused tax losses, and income tax reductions will result in a deferred tax benefit. This approach differs from the "impairment approach" recommended by the FASB in

SFAS 109. The U.S. method recognizes a deferred tax asset for all deductible temporary differences, unused tax losses, and income tax reductions and **offsets them with an impairment allowance** for the portion of the asset that does not meet the "more likely than not" threshold. ASPE permits either approach. As part of the short-term convergence project between the IASB and the FASB, the IASB had planned to move to the SFAS 109 valuation allowance approach, but this proposed change was not implemented when the IASB decided to narrow the scope of its income tax project in 2010.

Review of Deferred Tax Asset Account

Objective 9

Explain why the Deferred Tax Asset account is reassessed at the statement of financial position date, and account for the deferred tax asset with and without a valuation allowance account.

Both IFRS and ASPE recommend recognizing a deferred tax asset for most deductible temporary differences and for the carryforward of unused tax losses and other income tax reductions, **to the extent that it is probable that the deferred tax asset will be realized;** in other words, as long as taxable income is more likely than not to be available to apply the deductions against. Consistent with the reporting for all assets, the Deferred Tax Asset account must be reviewed at each reporting date to ensure that its carrying amount is appropriate.

Assume that Jensen Corp. has a deductible temporary difference or loss carryforward of $1 million at the end of its first year of operations. Its tax rate is 20% and a deferred tax asset of $200,000 ($1,000,000 × 20%) is recognized on the basis that it is more likely than not that enough taxable income will be generated in the future. The journal entry to record the deferred tax benefit and the change in the deferred tax asset is:

| Deferred Tax Asset | 200,000 | |
| Deferred Tax Benefit | | 200,000 |

A	=	L	+	SE	
+200,000				+200,000	

Cash flows: No effect

If, at the end of the next period, the deductible temporary difference or loss carryforward remains at $1 million but now only $750,000 meets the criterion for recognition, the deferred tax asset is recalculated as 20% of $750,000, or $150,000. The entry to be made depends on whether the allowance approach is used or not. Both methods of adjusting the asset account are shown in Illustration 18-35.

Revaluation of Deferred Tax Asset Account

A	=	L	+	SE	
−50,000				−50,000	

Cash flows: No effect

Direct Adjustment

| Deferred Tax Expense | 50,000 | |
| Deferred Tax Asset | | 50,000 |

Allowance Method

| Deferred Tax Expense | 50,000 | |
| Allowance to Reduce Deferred Tax Asset to Expected Realizable Value | | 50,000 |

If a valuation account is used, it is reported on the statement of financial position as a deduction from the Deferred Tax Asset account (or is explained in the notes). Regardless of approach, the net amount reported is identical. The accounts are reported within the asset section of the statement of financial position as shown in Illustration 18-36.

Statement of Financial Position Presentation of Remaining Deferred Tax Asset

Direct Adjustment

| Deferred tax asset | $150,000 |

Allowance Method

Deferred tax asset	$200,000
Less: Allowance to reduce deferred tax asset to expected realizable value	(50,000)
Deferred tax asset (net)	$150,000

At the end of the next period when the deferred tax asset and its realizable value are evaluated, assume it is now more likely than not that $850,000 of the original $1 million will be deductible in the future. This means the tax asset should be reported at $170,000 ($850,000 × 20%). The entry in Illustration 18-37 adjusts the accounts. Notice that a net value of $170,000 means that the allowance needs to be adjusted to $30,000. Once again, the net effect of the two approaches is identical. However, the valuation allowance method has the advantage of retaining the relationship between the Deferred Tax Asset account and the future deductible amounts.

Illustration 18-37

Revaluation of Deferred Tax Asset Account

A	=	L	+	SE
+20,000				+20,000

Cash flows: No effect

Direct Adjustment

Deferred Tax Asset	20,000	
Deferred Tax Benefit		20,000

Allowance Method

Allowance to Reduce Deferred Tax Asset to Expected Realizable Value	20,000	
Deferred Tax Benefit		20,000

Law

The accounting standards offer guidance on how to determine whether it is probable that future taxable income of an appropriate nature, and relating to the same taxable entity and the same tax authority, will be available. The following possible sources of taxable income may be available **under the tax law** to realize a tax benefit for deductible temporary differences, tax loss carryovers, and other tax reductions:

1. Future reversals of existing taxable temporary differences

2. Future taxable income before taking into account reversing temporary differences, tax loss, and other tax reductions

3. Taxable income available in prior carryback years

4. Tax-planning strategies that would, if necessary, be implemented to realize a deferred tax asset. Tax strategies are actions that are prudent and feasible, and that would be applied.

When an entity has a history of recent tax losses, or circumstances are unsettled, or if the carryforward period allowed by tax law is about to expire, it must look for substantive reasons to justify recognition of a tax asset. Both favourable and unfavourable evidence is considered, with more weight attached to objectively verifiable evidence.[15] If the entity concludes that it is not probable that appropriate future taxable income will be available, a deferred tax asset is not recognized or a previously recognized tax asset is removed.

The deferred or future tax asset account is also reviewed to determine whether conditions have changed, because it may now be reasonable to recognize a deferred tax asset that was previously unrecognized. If conditions have changed, the associated tax benefit is recognized in the income statement of the same period. If the entity uses a valuation allowance account, the full deferred tax asset is already included in the account, and it is the allowance that needs to be adjusted (in this case, reduced).

Real World Emphasis

Agrium Inc., headquartered in Calgary, Alberta, produces and markets agricultural nutrients and industrial products and is a retail supplier of agricultural products and services in both North and South America. As seen in the excerpt from Note 6 to the company's 2010 financial statements in Illustration 18-38, Agrium reports information about its future income tax assets, including those related to its losses available to be carried forward. Agrium reported under Canadian GAAP in 2010, which is similar to ASPE requirements. Therefore Agrium is permitted to use a valuation allowance, and chose to do so in 2010 and prior years.

Illustration 18-38

Future Income Tax Assets and Valuation Allowance — Agrium Inc.

As at December 31
(millions of U.S. dollars)

6. Income Taxes

	2010	2009
Future income tax assets		
Loss carryforwards expiring through 2030	92	25
Asset retirement obligations and environmental remediation	75	80
Employee future benefits and incentives	73	64
Receivables, inventories and accrued liabilities	105	92
Other	19	9
Future income tax assets before valuation allowance	364	270
Valuation allowance	(71)	(21)
Total future income tax assets, net of valuation allowance	293	249

In this excerpt, Agrium provides information about the sources of the temporary differences that result in future deductible amounts and future income tax assets. For the U.S. $364 million of future income tax assets at December 31, 2010, a valuation allowance of U.S. $71 million was needed.

PRESENTATION, DISCLOSURE, AND ANALYSIS

Statement of Financial Position Presentation

Because income taxes have a unique nature, income tax assets and liabilities have to be reported separately from other assets and liabilities on the statement of financial position.

Income Taxes Receivable or Payable Currently

Income tax amounts **currently** receivable or payable are reported separately from **deferred** or **future** tax assets and liabilities. They are reported as current assets or current liabilities, and cannot be netted against one another unless there is a legal right of offset. This means that the receivable and payable usually have to belong to the same taxable entity, they have to relate to the same tax authority, and the authority has to allow a single net payment. This presentation is the same whether ASPE or IFRS is being applied.

Because corporations are required to make several instalment payments to the Canada Revenue Agency during the year, there could be a debit balance in the Income Tax Payable account. When this occurs, it is reported as a current asset called Prepaid Income Taxes or Income Taxes Receivable. An income tax refund that is the result of carrying a current year's tax loss back against previous years' taxable income is also reported as an income tax receivable and current asset.

Deferred Tax Assets and Liabilities

The presentation of deferred or future tax asset and liability accounts differs under ASPE and IFRS. The **IFRS requirements** are the easier to apply—all deferred tax assets and liabilities are reported as **non-current** items on a classified statement of financial position.

Under ASPE requirements, however, future income tax assets and future income tax liabilities are segregated into current and non-current categories. The classification of an individual future income tax liability or asset **as current or non-current** is determined by

---

Objective 10

Identify and apply the presentation and disclosure requirements for income tax assets and liabilities, and apply intraperiod tax allocation.

Law

Underlying Concept

The principle about netting similar assets and liabilities only when there is a legal right of offset and the intention is to settle them on a net base is applied consistently through the accounting standards.

the classification of the asset or liability underlying the specific temporary difference. Let's see what this means.

Step 1.
What is the classification of the asset or liability that resulted in the tax asset or liability? A tax asset or tax liability caused by a temporary difference in an asset or liability classified as non-current is identified as non-current. A tax asset or tax liability caused by a temporary difference in a current asset or liability on the balance sheet, such as with tax losses, the future tax account is classified according to the expected reversal date of the temporary difference: if within 12 months from the reporting date, it is current; otherwise, it is non-current.

Step 2.
Determine the net current amount by netting the various future income tax asset and liability amounts that are classified as current. If the net result is an asset, report it on the balance sheet as a current asset; if it is a liability, report it as a current liability.

Step 3.
Determine the net non-current amount by netting the various future income tax assets and liabilities that are classified as non-current. If the net result is an asset, report it on the balance sheet as a non-current asset; if it is a liability, report it as a long-term liability.

To illustrate, assume that K. Scoffi Limited has four future income tax items at December 31, 2015. K. Scoffi reports under ASPE, has chosen to apply the future income taxes payable method of accounting for its income taxes, and operates under a single tax jurisdiction. The analysis in Illustration 18-39 shows how each temporary difference and related future income tax asset or liability is classified.

Illustration 18-39

Classification of Temporary Differences as Current or Non-Current under ASPE

Temporary Difference Related To:	Resulting Future Tax		Related Balance Sheet Account	Related Balance Sheet Account Classification
	Asset	Liability		
1. **Rent collected in advance:** recognized when earned for accounting purposes and when received for tax purposes	$42,000		Unearned Rent	Current
2. Use of **straight-line depreciation** for accounting purposes and accelerated depreciation for tax purposes		$214,000	Equipment	Non-current
3. Recognition of **revenue** in the period of sale for accounting purposes and during the period of collection for tax purposes		45,000	Accounts Receivable	Current
4. **Warranty liabilities:** recognized for accounting purposes at time of sale; for tax purposes at time paid	12,000		Estimated Liability under Warranties	Current
Totals	$54,000	$259,000		

If K. Scoffi has a single future tax liability account with a balance of $259,000 − $54,000 = $205,000 in it, an analysis similar to this is needed to identify each component.

The future taxes to be classified as "current" net to a $9,000 asset ($42,000 + $12,000 − $45,000), and the future taxes to be classified as "non-current" net to a $214,000 liability. Consequently, K. Scoffi's future taxes will appear on the December 31, 2015 balance sheet as shown in Illustration 18-40.

Current assets	
Future income tax asset	$9,000
Long-term liabilities	
Future income tax liability	$214,000

As indicated earlier, a future income tax asset or liability **may not be related to a specific asset or liability**. One example is research costs that are recognized as expenses in the accounts when they are incurred but deferred and deducted in later years for tax purposes. Another example is a tax loss carryforward. In both cases, a future income tax asset is recognized, but there is no related, identifiable asset or liability for financial reporting purposes. In these situations, future income taxes are classified according to the date the temporary difference is expected to reverse or the tax benefit is expected to be realized.

If K. Scoffi reports as a publicly accountable enterprise under IFRS, one net deferred tax liability of $205,000 is presented as a non-current liability.

Similar to taxes currently receivable or payable, **deferred** or **future** income tax assets and liabilities also cannot be netted against one another unless they relate to the same taxable entity and the same tax authority and there is a legal right to settle or realize them at the same time. This is required whether ASPE or international standards are being applied.

Income and Other Statement Presentation

Intraperiod tax allocation refers to how and where the income tax expense or benefit for the period—for both current and deferred taxes—is reported on the income and other statements that reflect transactions that attract income tax. A good place to start is to understand that the objective is to report the tax cost or benefit in the same place as **the underlying transaction or event that gave rise to the tax.** This means that the current and deferred tax expense (or benefit) of the current period related to **income before discontinued operations, discontinued operations, other comprehensive income, adjustments reported in retained earnings, and capital transactions is reported with the related item.**

To illustrate intraperiod tax allocation, assume that Copy Doctor Inc. has a tax rate of 25% and reports the following pre-tax amounts in 2015:

- A loss from continuing operations of $500,000
- Income from discontinued operations of $900,000, of which $210,000 is not taxable
- An unrealized holding gain of $25,000 on investments accounted for at fair value through other comprehensive income (FV-OCI). Assume that this will be taxable as ordinary income when it is realized

Illustration 18-41 presents an analysis that is useful in determining how and where the current tax expense or benefit will be reported.

	Continuing Operations	Discontinued Operations	OCI	Total
Accounting income (loss)	($500,000)	$900,000	$25,000	$425,000
Deduct non-taxable permanent difference		(210,000)		(210,000)
Deduct originating difference: gain taxable when realized			(25,000)	(25,000)
Taxable income	($500,000)	$690,000	$ –0–	$190,000
Current tax expense/tax payable at 25%	($125,000)	$172,500	$ –0–	$47,500

Whenever income tax is reported separately so that it appears with a particular component of comprehensive income or in another statement, prepare your analysis by setting up a separate column for each component that attracts tax, as shown in the illustration. Note that the Canada Revenue Agency is not interested in where the company reports various amounts on the IFRS or ASPE financial statements. It is interested only in the last column of the illustration; that is, in what is taxable in the year and what is not. Based on the analysis, the entry to record current income tax is:

Current Tax Expense—Discontinued Operations	172,500	
Current Tax Benefit		125,000
Income Tax Payable		47,500

A	=	L	+	SE	
		+47,500		−47,500	

Cash flows: No effect

Deferred taxes are also allocated to the financial statement items that attract tax. In this case, we assume that the $25,000 temporary difference between the carrying amount of the FV-OCI investments and their tax base is the only temporary difference in this and previous years. Illustration 18-42 shows the calculations to determine deferred taxes.

Illustration 18-42

Analysis, Intraperiod Tax Allocation—Deferred Taxes, 2015

	Continuing Operations	Discontinued Operations	OCI	Total
Taxable temporary difference, Dec. 31, 2015	$-0-	$-0-	$25,000	$25,000
Deferred tax liability at 25% future rate, Dec. 31, 2015	$-0-	$-0-	$ 6,250	$ 6,250
Less deferred tax liability before adjustment	-0-	-0-	-0-	-0-
Deferred tax expense, 2015	$-0-	$-0-	$ 6,250	$ 6,250

The calculations are the same as those earlier in the chapter, with added columns for the different parts of the statements that attract tax. In this example, the only temporary difference is related to an item of other comprehensive income. The tax effect therefore is reported there as well. The entry to record deferred taxes is:

Deferred Tax Expense—OCI	6,250	
Deferred Tax Liability		6,250

A	=	L	+	SE	
		+6,250		−6,250	

Cash flows: No effect

Illustration 18-43 shows how the income taxes calculated above are reported in the financial statements along with the items that attract the tax. The tax amounts are taken directly from the entries or the analysis.

Illustration 18-43

Statement Presentation—
Intraperiod Tax Allocation

COPY DOCTOR INC.
Income Statement
Year Ended December 31, 2015

Income (loss) from continuing operations before tax	$(500,000)
Less: Current tax benefit	125,000
Income from discontinued operations	$ 900,000
Less: Current tax expense	(172,500)
	$ 727,500
Net income	$ 352,500
	$(375,000)

(continued)

Illustration 18-43

*Statement Presentation —
Intraperiod Tax Allocation*
(continued)

Statement of Comprehensive Income
Year Ended December 31, 2015

Net income		$ 352,500
Other comprehensive income:		
Unrealized gains, FV-OCI investments	$ 25,000	
Less: Deferred tax expense	(6,250)	18,750
Comprehensive income		$ 371,250

As far as the Copy Doctor example above goes, accounting under IFRS and ASPE is the same. However, there is a difference in how intraperiod allocation is applied when current and deferred taxes relate to transactions recognized in equity or other comprehensive income of a prior period. IFRS requires that, where practical, the tax effect in the current year be traced back to where the transaction was originally reported and be presented in the same statement as in the prior period. Under ASPE, income taxes are charged or credited to various equity accounts only for items recognized in the current period. Notice that this difference applies only when there is no current period event or transaction associated with the change in current or deferred taxes.[16]

In terms of real-world examples, we can look to **CGI Group Inc.**, a Canadian-based company that manages information technology and offers business process services. For its year ended September 30, 2011, CGI Group Inc. reported income tax expense separately for earnings from continuing operations, earnings from discontinued operations, and four individual unrealized gain amounts reported in other comprehensive income.

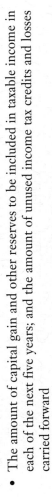

Real World Emphasis

Disclosure Requirements

Taxes Payable Method

If a company reporting under ASPE chooses the taxes payable accounting policy to report income taxes, a limited amount of information is required to be disclosed:

- The income tax expense or benefit included in determining income (loss) before discontinued operations; and the amount related to transactions recognized in equity

- A reconciliation of the actual tax rate or expense or benefit to the statutory amount for income (loss) before discontinued operations, with information about major reconciling items

- The amount of capital gain and other reserves to be included in taxable income in each of the next five years; and the amount of unused income tax credits and losses carried forward

This limited information provides a financial statement reader with significant information about areas where there are temporary differences and potential increases in taxable income in the medium term.

Future Income Taxes Method

If a company reporting under ASPE chooses the future income taxes accounting policy, again, only limited disclosures are required:

- The amounts of current and of future income tax expense or benefit included in income before discontinued operations; and the amount related to capital transactions or transactions recognized in equity

- The amount of unused income tax losses, income tax reductions, and deductible temporary differences for which no future income tax asset is recognized

In addition, any enterprise reporting under ASPE whose income is not taxed because it is taxable directly to its owners is required to disclose this fact.

The disclosure situation changes for publicly accountable entities reporting under IFRS. The IFRS requirements are extensive, with the following types of information identified:

- Separate disclosure of the major components of income tax expense or benefit, and the source of both current and deferred taxes

- The amount of current and deferred tax recognized in equity in the period; and tax expense for each component of OCI

- A reconciliation of the effective tax rate to the statutory rates for the period and an explanation of changes in the statutory rates relative to the prior period

- Information about unrecognized deferred income tax assets and the underlying deductible temporary differences and unused tax losses, as well as supporting evidence for recognized deferred tax assets

- Information about each type of temporary difference and the deferred tax asset or liability recognized on the statement of financial position

Real World Emphasis

The actual standard, IAS 12 *Income Taxes*, is the best source to refer to for the specific disclosures mandated for publicly accountable enterprises. Excerpts from the 2011 financial statements of Switzerland-based **Nestlé Group** are provided in Illustration 18-44 to indicate what the disclosures involve. The deferred tax asset and liability accounts on the balance sheet are provided, followed by the company's complete income tax note, Note 14. Nestlé reports amounts in millions of Swiss francs (CHF). Using the bulleted list of required disclosures above, see if you can find the specific information in these excerpts.

Illustration 18-44

Disclosure of Deferred Income Taxes—Nestlé Group

Consolidated balance sheet as at 31 December 2011

In millions of CHF	Notes	2011	2010
Assets			
Non-current assets			
Deferred tax assets	14	2,476	1,911
Liabilities and equity			
Non-current liabilities			
Deferred tax liabilities (a)	14	2,060	1,371

14. Taxes

14.1 Taxes recognised in the income statement

In millions of CHF	2011	2010
Components of taxes		
Current taxes (a)	2,554	2,917
Deferred taxes	(301)	181
Taxes reclassified to other comprehensive income	859	248
Taxes reclassified to equity	—	(3)
Taxes from continuing operations	**3,112**	**3,343**
Taxes from discontinued operations	350	
Total taxes	**3,112**	**3,693**
Reconciliation of taxes		
Expected tax expense at weighted average applicable tax rate	3,054	2,882
Tax effect of non-deductible or non-taxable items	(202)	(10)
Prior years' taxes	(215)	(129)
Transfers to unrecognised deferred tax assets	83	53
Transfers from unrecognised deferred tax assets	(123)	(20)
Changes in tax rates	23	9
Withholding taxes levied on transfers of income	313	353

(continued)

Other, incl. taxes on capital	179	205
Taxes from continuing operations	**3,112**	**3,343**

(a) Current taxes related to prior years represent a tax expense of CHF 35 million (2010: tax expense of CHF 25 million).

The expected tax expense at weighted average applicable tax rate is the result from applying the domestic statutory tax rates to profits before taxes of each entity in the country it operates. For the Group, the weighted average applicable tax rate varies from one year to the other depending on the relative weight of the profit of each individual entity in the Group's profit as well as the changes in the statutory tax rates.

14.2 Taxes recognised in other comprehensive income

In millions of CHF	2011	2010
Tax effects relating to		
Currency retranslations	64	195
Fair value adjustments on available-for-sale financial instruments	(29)	(11)
Fair value adjustments on cash flow hedges	159	21
Actuarial gains/(losses) on defined benefit schemes	665	63
	859	268

14.3 Reconciliation of deferred taxes by type of temporary differences recognised in the balance sheet

In millions of CHF

	Property, plant and equipment	Goodwill and intangible assets	Employee benefits	Inventories, receivables, payables and provisions	Unused tax losses and unused tax credits	Other	Total
At 1 January 2010	(1,068)	(1,089)	1,965	822	307	(139)	798
Currency retranslations	116	87	(149)	(88)	(28)	(18)	(80)
Deferred tax (expense)/income	(134)	(157)	(98)	101	39	68	(181)
Modification of the scope of consolidation	(7)	(7)	8	2	—	7	3
At 31 December 2010	**(1,093)**	**(1,166)**	**1,726**	**837**	**318**	**(82)**	**540**
Currency retranslations	5	(12)	(24)	(24)	(15)	4	(66)
Deferred tax (expense)/income	(223)	(46)	408	10	62	90	301
Modification of the scope of consolidation	(36)	(360)	10	14	1	12	(359)
At 31 December 2011	**(1,347)**	**(1,584)**	**2,120**	**837**	**366**	**24**	**416**

In millions of CHF	2011	2010
Reflected in the balance sheet as follows:		
Deferred tax assets	2,476	1,911
Deferred tax liabilities	(2,060)	(1,371)
Net assets	**416**	**540**

14.4 Unrecognised deferred taxes

The deductible temporary differences as well as the unused tax losses and tax credits for which no deferred tax assets are recognised expire as follows:

In millions of CHF	2011	2010
Within one year	20	56
Between one and five years	314	276
More than five years	1,479	1,648
	1,813	1,980

(continued)

Illustration 18-44

Disclosure of Deferred Income
Taxes—Nestlé Group
(continued)

At 31 December 2011, the unrecognised deferred tax assets amount to CHF 464 million (2010: CHF 544 million).

In addition, the Group has not recognised deferred tax liabilities in respect of unremitted earnings that are considered indefinitely reinvested in foreign subsidiaries. At 31 December 2011, these earnings amount to CHF 12.9 billion (2010: CHF 13.3 billion). They could be subject to withholding and other taxes on remittance.

Analysis

The extensive disclosures related to current and deferred taxes are required for several reasons, some of which we now discuss.

Assessment of Quality of Earnings

Ethics

In trying to assess the quality of a company's earnings, many investors are interested in the reconciliations between accounting and tax numbers. Profits that are improved by a favourable tax effect should be examined carefully, particularly if the tax effect is non-recurring. Accounting for deferred tax assets is an area that requires considerable judgement and may, therefore, be open to abuse. To justify the recognition of deferred tax assets on the balance sheet and tax benefits on the income statement, it takes only a small amount of optimism for management to expect flows of future taxable income against which to apply tax losses and other future deductible amounts. Valuation of deferred tax assets, either directly or through an adjustment of the valuation allowance account, usually affects bottom-line income on a dollar-for-dollar basis.

A good example of this is the case of **Stelco Inc.**, once a strong Canadian steel producer. In one year, the company's loss of $217 million was reduced by $81 million of future income tax benefits, while $139 million of future income tax assets were reported on its balance sheet. In the next year, the company's $9 million of income was increased by an $11-million future income tax benefit, and $161 million of net future income tax assets were reported on the balance sheet. $74 million of which was classified as a current asset. The future deductible amounts underlying the tax asset accounts were related to the recognition of employee retirement benefit expenses in excess of amounts paid, and income tax losses carried forward.

To have classified $74 million of the future income tax asset as a current asset, management must have expected the upcoming year to be an excellent one for the company! As it turned out, sales volume and prices were down, costs increased, and the cash position deteriorated, resulting in Stelco obtaining an order to launch a court-supervised restructuring under the Companies' Creditors Arrangement Act.

Regardless of management's motivations in assessing the value of future income tax assets, financial statement readers should be aware of how big a part judgement plays in these measurements.

Better Predictions of Future Cash Flows

Real World Emphasis

Examining the future portion of income tax expense provides information about whether taxes payable are likely to be higher or lower in the future. A close examination may provide insight into the company's policies on capitalization of costs and revenue recognition, and on other policies that give rise to differences between the accounting income reported and taxable income. As a result, it may be possible to predict upcoming reductions in future income tax liabilities and additional cash required for income tax payments. Such a situation may lead to a loss of liquidity.[17]

From disclosures of the amounts and expiration dates of losses being carried forward, analysts can estimate income that a company may recognize in the future and on which it

Real World Emphasis

will pay no income tax. For example, **Versatile Systems Inc.**, a British Columbia company, focuses on software development and sales of computer software, hardware, and system integration services. Versatile reported in its 2011 consolidated financial statements that the company had U.S. $28,631,801 of tax losses and deductions that it could use to offset future taxable income. Versatile also provides information about when the operating losses expire, the jurisdiction in which the losses are available for carryforward, and the extent to which a valuation allowance has been provided.

Outstanding Conceptual Questions

The FASB and IASB believe that the future income tax or temporary difference approach, also known as the asset-liability method, is the most conceptually sound method of accounting for income taxes. Its objectives are to recognize the amount of taxes payable or refundable for the current year, and tax liabilities and tax assets for the future tax consequences of events that have been recognized in the financial statements or tax returns.

Although this method is considered to be the most appropriate approach for publicly accountable enterprises, some conceptual questions remain.

Finance

No Discounting

Without discounting the asset or liability (that is, by not considering its present value), financial statements do not indicate the appropriate benefit of a tax deferral or the burden of a tax prepayment. This makes it more difficult to compare the financial statements, because a dollar in a short-term deferral is presented as being of the same value as a dollar in a longer-term deferral.

Recognition of Deferred Tax Assets

Some professionals believe that future deductible amounts arising from operating loss carryforwards are different than future deductible amounts arising from other causes. One rationale for this view is that a deferred tax asset arising from normal transactions results in a tax prepayment: a prepaid tax asset. In the case of losses available to carry forward, no tax prepayment has been made. Others argue that realization of a loss carryforward is less likely and thus should require a more severe test than for a net deductible amount arising from normal operations.

These controversies exist within the temporary difference approach. Others argue that a completely different type of approach should be used to report deferred taxes. In addition, advances in the conceptual framework project are removing the criterion of "probability" from the definition of both an asset and a liability and incorporating it in the measurement of the elements instead. Questions arise about whether deferred tax liabilities are, in fact, "present obligations." And, are deferred tax assets really "present economic resources"? When these new concepts are applied to the asset-liability approach to income taxes, it is likely that different recognition and measurement decisions may result.

IFRS/ASPE COMPARISON

A Comparison of IFRS and ASPE

Objective 11
Identify the major differences between ASPE and IFRS for income taxes.

While other differences exist between ASPE and IFRS than those indicated in Illustration 18-45, many relate to complexities in income tax accounting that are beyond the scope of this text.

Illustration **18-45**
IFRS and ASPE
Comparison Chart

	Accounting Standards for Private Enterprises (ASPE)—*CICA Handbook*, Part II, Section 3465	IFRS—IAS 12	References to Related Illustrations and Select Brief Exercises
Scope, definitions, and terminology	Terminology used: • Accounting income • Taxable income (taxable loss) • Future income tax	• Tax expense (tax benefit) • Tax basis • More than likely	Terminology used: • Accounting profit • Taxable profit (tax income) • Deferred tax	• Tax expense (tax income) • Tax base • Probable	Illustration 18-6 BE18-3 and BE18-22
Recognition	A company chooses either the taxes payable method or the future income taxes method as its accounting policy. The future income taxes method is also known as the asset and liability approach and the temporary difference approach.		No choice is permitted. All companies apply the temporary difference approach, almost identical to the ASPE future income taxes approach.		Illustrations 18-35, 18-36, and 18-37 BE18-15, BE18-16, and BE18-17
	A future income tax asset is permitted to be recognized for all deductible temporary differences, unused tax losses, and income tax reductions. For presentation purposes, a valuation allowance is permitted to be used to bring the future income tax asset to the amount that is more likely than not to be realized in the future.		A deferred tax asset is permitted to be recognized only to the extent that it is probable that it will be realized in the future. A valuation account is not used.		
Presentation	Future income tax assets and liabilities are classified as current or non-current based on the classification of the underlying asset or liability that resulted in the future income tax amount. When there is no related balance sheet account, the classification is based on when the temporary difference is expected to reverse.		All deferred tax asset and liability accounts are classified as non-current.		Illustrations 18-39 and 18-40 Illustrations 18A-5 and 18A-6 BE18-21
	There is no reporting of income taxes in equity accounts unless it is for a current period transaction that affects equity.		IFRS requires "backward tracing" of current period tax changes that relate to items charged or credited to equity or OCI in prior periods. In the current period, the tax effect is reported on the statement the item was originally reported on.		N/A
Disclosure	Less information is required to be disclosed under both the taxes payable and future income taxes methods of accounting for income taxes than is required under IFRS.		Considerably more information is required to be reported under IFRS, including details that explain changes in most tax-related accounts, the reasons for temporary differences, and a breakdown of major components of deferred tax expense for the period.		Illustration 18-44
	An enterprise whose income is not taxed because it is taxed directly to its owners is required to identify this situation.		There is no similar disclosure requirement.		N/A

Looking Ahead

In March 2009, the IASB issued an Exposure Draft (ED) of a standard to replace IAS 12 *Income Taxes*. The intent is to eliminate many of the differences between the IFRS and FASB standards. The ED did not propose to change the fundamental approach to accounting for taxes (the balance sheet liability approach). However, it did seek to eliminate differences in the application of and exceptions to this method as used under IFRS, U.S., and Canadian standards.

Among the harmonization moves the ED recommended are the following:

- moving to the Canadian and U.S. approach to classification of deferred tax assets and liabilities on the balance sheet,

- requiring the use of a valuation allowance approach for the recognition and measurement of deferred tax assets, and

- removing the "backward tracing" of current tax changes that relate to a prior-year item in equity or OCI.

The 2009 ED also dealt with accounting for **uncertain tax positions**; that is, how to handle uncertainty in tax measurements.

In December 2010, the IASB decided to narrow the scope of the income tax project. It clarified how to measure deferred taxes when the recovery of an asset would be through use versus sale, when the asset is carried at fair value. In short, the presumption is that recovery would be through sale. The IASB has left open the possibility that a fundamental review of the accounting for income taxes could be part of a future consultation process.

SUMMARY OF LEARNING OBJECTIVES

1 Understand the importance of income taxes from a business perspective.

When a company decides where to set up its operations, a major consideration is the tax rate that it will face on its profits. The fact that corporate taxes can slow growth may help to explain why governments in Canada have steadily reduced corporate tax rates over time. For example, the combined federal and provincial tax rate declined from an average of approximately 43% to approximately 28% between 2000 and 2012.

2 Explain the difference between accounting income and taxable income, and calculate taxable income and current income taxes.

Accounting income is calculated in accordance with generally accepted accounting principles. Taxable income is calculated in accordance with prescribed tax legislation and regulations. Because tax legislation and GAAP have different objectives, accounting income and taxable income often differ. To calculate taxable income, companies start with their accounting income and then add and deduct items to adjust the GAAP measure of income to what is actually taxable and tax deductible in the period.

Current tax expense and income taxes payable are determined by applying the current tax rate to taxable income.

3 Explain what a taxable temporary difference is, determine its amount, and calculate deferred tax liabilities.

A taxable temporary difference is the difference between the carrying amount of an asset or liability and its tax base with the consequence that, when the asset is recovered or the liability is settled in the future for an amount equal to its carrying value, the taxable income of that future period will be increased. Because taxes increase in the future as a result of temporary differences that exist at the balance sheet date, the future tax consequences of these taxable amounts are recognized in the current period as a deferred tax liability.

4 Explain what a deductible temporary difference is, determine its amount, and calculate deferred tax assets.

A deductible temporary difference is the difference between the carrying amount of an asset or liability and its tax base with the consequence that, when the asset is recovered or the liability is settled in the future for an amount equal to its book value, the taxable income of that future period will be reduced. Because taxes are reduced in the future as a result of temporary differences that exist at the balance sheet date, the future tax consequences of these deductible amounts are recognized in the current period as a deferred tax asset.

5 Prepare analyses of deferred tax balances and record deferred tax expense.

The following steps are taken: (1) identify all temporary differences between the carrying amounts and tax bases of assets and liabilities at the balance sheet date; (2) calculate the correct net deferred tax asset or liability balance at the end of the period; (3) compare the balance in the deferred tax asset or liability before the adjustment with the correct balance at the balance sheet date—the difference is the deferred tax expense/benefit; and (4) make the journal entry, which is based on the change in the amount of the net deferred tax asset or liability.

6 Explain the effect of multiple tax rates and tax rate changes on income tax accounts, and calculate current and deferred tax amounts when there is a change in substantively enacted tax rates.

Tax rates other than the existing rates can be used only when the future tax rates have been enacted into legislation or substantively enacted. Deferred tax assets and liabilities are measured at the tax rate that applies to the specific future years in which the temporary difference is expected to reverse. When there is a change in the future tax rate, its effect on the future tax accounts is recognized immediately. The effects are reported as an adjustment to deferred tax expense in the period of the change.

7 Account for a tax loss carryback.

A company may carry a taxable loss back three years and receive refunds to a maximum of the income taxes paid in those years. Because the economic benefits related to the losses carried back are certain, they are recognized in the period of the loss as a tax benefit on the income statement and as an asset (income tax receivable) on the balance sheet.

8 Account for a tax loss carryforward, including any note disclosures.

A post-2009 tax loss can be carried forward and applied against the taxable incomes of the next 20 years. If the economic benefits related to the tax loss are more likely than not to be realized during the carryforward period, they are recognized in the period of the loss as a deferred tax benefit in the income statement and as a deferred tax asset on the balance sheet. Otherwise, they are not recognized

in the period of the loss as a deferred tax benefit in the income statement and as a deferred tax asset on the balance sheet.

9 Explain why the Deferred Tax Asset account is reassessed at the statement of financial position date, and account for the deferred tax asset with and without a valuation allowance account.

Every asset must be assessed to ensure that it is not reported at an amount higher than the economic benefits that are expected to be received from the use or sale of the asset. The economic benefit to be received from the deferred tax asset is a reduction in deferred taxes payable. If it is unlikely that sufficient taxable income will be generated in the future to allow the future deductions, the income tax asset may have to be written down. If previously unrecognized amounts are now expected to be realizable, a deferred tax asset is recognized. These entries may be made directly to the deferred tax asset account or through a valuation allowance contra account.

10 Identify and apply the presentation and disclosure requirements for income tax assets and liabilities, and apply intraperiod tax allocation.

Under all methods, current income taxes payable or receivable are reported separately as a current liability or current asset. Under ASPE and assuming a single tax authority, future income tax assets and deferred tax accounts are all classified as non-current. Current and deferred tax expense is reported separately with income before discontinued operations, discontinued operations, items in OCI, retained earnings, and other capital. Separate disclosure is required of the amounts and expiry dates of unused tax losses, and the amount of deductible temporary differences for which no deferred tax asset has been recognized. ASPE calls for limited disclosures, but under IFRS, additional disclosures are required about temporary differences and unused tax losses, the major components of income tax expense, and the reasons for the difference between the statutory tax rate and the effective rate indicated on the income statement.

in the financial statements. Alternatively, ASPE also allows the use of a contra valuation allowance account, but this approach is not envisaged under current IFRS. Disclosure is required of the amounts of tax loss carryforwards and their expiry dates. If previously unrecorded tax losses are subsequently used to benefit a future period, the benefit is recognized in that future period.

11 Identify the major differences between ASPE and IFRS for income taxes.

ASPE allows an accounting policy choice—either the taxes payable method or the future income taxes method—while IFRS requires use of a method consistent with the future income taxes method, the temporary difference approach. The current differences relate to terminology, the balance sheet classification of deferred/future tax assets and liabilities, use of a valuation allowance, and the extent of disclosure.

KEY TERMS

accounting income, p. 1115
accounting profit, p. 1115
deductible temporary difference, p. 1122
deferred tax expense, p. 1120
deferred tax assets, p. 1120
deferred tax liabilities, p. 1120
effective tax rate, p. 1132
future income tax assets, p. 1120
future income tax expense, p. 1120
future income tax liabilities, p. 1120
future income taxes method, p. 1120
income tax benefit, p. 1124

interperiod tax allocation, p. 1128
intraperiod tax allocation, p. 1145
loss carryback, p. 1134
loss carryforward, p. 1135
loss for income tax purposes, p. 1134
more likely than not, p. 1136
originating difference, p. 1119
permanent differences, p. 1118
probable, p. 1136
reversible differences, p. 1118
substantively enacted rate, p. 1132
taxable income, p. 1115
taxable profit, p. 1115

taxable temporary difference, p. 1122
tax base/basis, p. 1121
tax base of an asset, p. 1121
tax base of a liability, p. 1121
tax income, p. 1124
tax loss, p. 1134
taxes payable method, p. 1120
temporary difference, p. 1122
temporary difference approach, p. 1120
timing differences, p. 1118
valuation allowance, p. 1139

APPENDIX 18A

COMPREHENSIVE ILLUSTRATION

Objective 12
Apply the temporary difference approach (future income taxes method) of accounting for income taxes in a comprehensive situation.

The example below walks you through a comprehensive illustration of an income tax problem with several temporary and permanent differences. It assumes the reporting company either reports under IFRS or applies the future income taxes method under ASPE. The illustration follows one company through two complete years, 2014 and 2015. Study it carefully. It should help cement your understanding of the concepts and procedures presented in the chapter.

First Year of Operations—2014

Allman Corporation, which began operations early in 2014, produces various products on a contract basis. The company's year end is December 31. Each contract generates a gross profit of $80,000 and some of Allman's contracts provide for the customer to pay on an instalment basis. In such cases, the customer pays one fifth of the contract revenue in the year of the sale and one fifth in each of the following four years. Gross profit is recognized in the year when the contract is completed for financial reporting purposes (accrual basis) and in the year when cash is collected for tax purposes (cash basis). Information on Allman's operations for 2014 is as follows:

1. In 2014, the company completed seven contracts that allow the customer to pay on an instalment basis. The related gross profit of $560,000 on sales of $1.5 million (to be

collected at a rate of $300,000 per year beginning in 2014) is recognized for financial reporting purposes, but only $112,000 of gross profit on these sales is reported on the 2014 tax return. Future collections on the related instalment receivables are expected to result in taxable amounts of $112,000 in each of the next four years.

2. At the beginning of 2014, Allman Corporation purchased depreciable assets with a cost of $540,000. For financial reporting purposes, Allman depreciates these assets using the straight-line method over a six-year service life with no residual value expected. For tax purposes, the assets fall into CCA Class 8, permitting a 20% rate, and for the first year the half-year rule is applied. Any UCC remaining at the end of 2019 is expected to be tax deductible in that year as a terminal loss. Illustration 18A-1 shows the depreciation and net asset value schedules for both financial reporting and tax purposes:

	Accounting		Tax	
Year	Depreciation	Carrying Amount, End of Year	CCA	UCC, End of Year
2014	$ 90,000	$450,000	$ 54,000	$486,000
2015	90,000	360,000	97,200	388,800
2016	90,000	270,000	77,760	311,040
2017	90,000	180,000	62,208	248,832
2018	90,000	90,000	49,766	199,066
2019	90,000	—	199,066	—
	$540,000		$540,000	

Illustration 18A-1

Depreciation and net asset value schedules for financial reporting and tax purposes

3. The company guarantees its product for two years from the contract completion date. During 2014, the total product warranty liability accrued for financial reporting purposes was $200,000, and the 2014 expenditures for repairs under the warranty liability were $44,000. The remaining liability of $156,000 is expected to be settled by expenditures of $56,000 in 2015 and $100,000 in 2016.

4. At December 31, 2014, the company accrued non-taxable dividends receivable of $28,000, the only dividend revenue reported for the year.

5. During 2014, non-deductible fines and penalties of $26,000 were paid.

6. The 2014 accounting income before taxes is $412,000.

7. The enacted tax rate for 2014 is 30%, and for 2015 and future years it is 20%.

8. The company is expected to have taxable income in all future years.

Taxable Income, Income Tax Payable, and Current Tax Expense—2014

The first step in determining the company's income tax payable for 2014 is to calculate its taxable income. Each step in this calculation has to be thought through carefully. Remember that you are starting with what is included in the current year's revenues and expenses (the accounting income) and are adjusting this to what the net taxable amount is. The income taxes levied on the taxable amount are the taxes payable and also the current tax expense for the year. Illustration 18A-2 shows the results.

Accounting income for 2014	$ 412,000
Permanent differences:	
Non-taxable revenue—dividends	(28,000)
Non-deductible expenses—fines and penalties	26,000
Reversible differences:	
Deferred gross profit for tax purposes ($560,000 – $112,000)	(448,000)
Depreciation per books in excess of CCA ($90,000 – $54,000)	36,000
Warranty expense per books in excess of amount deductible for	
tax purposes ($200,000 – $44,000)	156,000
Taxable income for 2014	$ 154,000
Income tax payable and current tax expense for 2014:	
$154,000 × 30%	$ 46,200

Deferred Tax Assets and Liabilities at December 31, 2014, and 2014 Deferred Tax Expense

Because deferred tax expense is the difference between the opening and closing balance of the deferred income tax asset or liability account, the next step is to determine the net deferred tax asset or liability at the end of 2014. (The opening balance in this case is $0 because this is the first year of operations.) This represents the net tax effect of all the temporary differences between the carrying amounts and tax bases of related assets and liabilities on December 31, 2014. Illustration 18A-3 summarizes the temporary differences, the deferred tax asset and liability amounts, the correct balance of the net deferred tax liability account at December 31, 2014, and the amount required for the deferred tax expense entry.

Balance Sheet Account	Tax Base	–	Carrying Amount	=	(Taxable) Deductible Temporary Difference	×	Tax Rate	=	Deferred Tax Asset (Liability)
Instalments receivable	$752,000		$1,200,000		$(448,000)		.20		$(89,600)
Plant and equipment	486,000		450,000		36,000		.20		7,200
Warranty liability	–0–		(156,000)		156,000		.20		31,200
Net deferred tax liability, December 31, 2014									(51,200)
Net deferred tax asset (liability) before adjustment									–0–
Increase in deferred tax liability account, and deferred tax expense for 2014									$(51,200)

Let's review each step in this illustration. Allman Corporation recognized all the profit on the 2014 instalment sales in its 2014 income statement. None of the $560,000 of gross profit is deferred for financial reporting purposes. However, only $112,000 of the gross profit is recognized in taxable income. Therefore, the remaining $448,000 ($560,000 – $112,000) of gross profit is deferred for tax purposes and the taxable temporary difference will be included in taxable income in the future as the outstanding receivables on the sales are collected. The tax base of the instalments receivable account is $752,000. The temporary difference will result in taxable amounts in the future. At the enacted rate of 20%, this will cause an additional $89,600 of income tax to be payable in the future.

The carrying amount of the depreciable assets is $450,000 at the end of 2014, but their undepreciated capital cost, or tax value, is $486,000. Because the company has taken $36,000 **less CCA** than depreciation to the end of 2014, in the future there will be

$36,000 **more CCA** deductible for tax purposes than depreciation taken on the books. Therefore, the $36,000 is a deductible temporary difference that will cause future taxes to be reduced by $7,200. Comparing the CCA and depreciation schedules over the next few years reveals that in some years (2015, 2019, and onwards) excess CCA will be claimed, while in others (2016, 2017, and 2018) less CCA than depreciation will be claimed. These net out at December 31, 2014, to $36,000 more CCA than depreciation in the future.

Allman reports a warranty liability of $156,000 on its December 31, 2014 statement of financial position. This whole amount will be deductible when calculating taxable income in the future when the actual warranty expenditures are made and the liability settled. Because Allman has not yet recognized the $156,000 of expenses for tax purposes, the tax base of the liability is $0. This third temporary difference, therefore, is a deductible temporary difference and, at a 20% rate, will result in future tax savings of $31,200.

The key to the analysis is to determine whether taxable income **in a future period will be increased or decreased**. If increased, it is a **taxable** temporary difference; if decreased, it is a **deductible** temporary difference.

The tax effect of each temporary difference is calculated by using the tax rate that applies for each specific future year in which the difference reverses. In this case, because the tax rates for all future years are identical, the deferred tax amounts can be calculated by simply applying the 20% rate to the temporary differences at the end of 2014 as shown in Illustration 18A-3. If the tax rates for each future year are not the same, a separate schedule setting out when each temporary difference is expected to reverse is needed, such as the one shown in Illustration 18A-4.

Illustration 18A-4

Schedule of Reversals of Temporary Differences at December 31, 2014

(Taxable) deductible temporary differences	Total		Future Years			
		2015	2016	2017	2018	2019
Instalments receivable	$(448,000)	$(112,000)	$(112,000)	$(112,000)	$(112,000)	
Plant and equipment	36,000	7,200	(12,240)	(27,792)	(40,234)	$109,066
Warranty liability	156,000	56,000	100,000			
Net (taxable) deductible amount	$(256,000)	$ (48,800)	$ (24,240)	$(139,792)	$(152,234)	$109,066
Tax rate enacted for year		20%	20%	20%	20%	20%
Net deferred tax asset (liability)	$ (51,200)	$ (9,760)	$ (4,848)	$ (27,958)	$ (30,447)	$ 21,813

Income Tax Accounting Entries—2014

The entries to record current (Illustration 18A-2) and deferred taxes (Illustration 18A-3) for 2014 are:

Current Tax Expense	46,200	
Income Tax Payable		46,200

A = L + SE
+46,200 −46,200
Cash flows: No effect

Deferred Tax Expense	51,200	
Deferred Tax Liability		51,200

A = L + SE
+51,200 −51,200
Cash flows: No effect

Financial Statement Presentation—2014

If Allman Corporation reports under IFRS (and is a single taxable entity dealing with a single taxation authority), the company is permitted to net its deferred tax asset of $38,400

($7,200 + $31,200) and deferred tax liability of $89,600 to report one net deferred tax liability of $51,200 as a non-current liability. Otherwise, the deferred tax asset and the deferred tax liability are reported separately. IFRS does not permit any deferred tax accounts to be reported in current assets or current liabilities.

Under ASPE, however, the future income tax assets and liabilities are classified as current and non-current on the statement of financial position based on the classifications of the related assets and liabilities that underlie the temporary differences. They are then summarized into one net current and one net non-current amount (again, assuming a single taxable entity and the same taxation authority). The classification of Allman Corporation's future tax account at the end of 2014 under ASPE is shown in Illustration 18A-5.

Illustration 18A-5

ASPE Classification of Future Income Tax Asset/Liability Accounts

Statement of Financial Position Account	Classification of Statement of Financial Position Account	Future Income Tax Asset (Liability)*	Classification of Future Income Tax Asset (Liability) Current	Classification of Future Income Tax Asset (Liability) Non-current
Instalments receivable (deferred gross profit)	Mixed: current and non-current	$(89,600)	$(22,400)	$(67,200)
Plant and equipment	Non-current	7,200		7,200
Warranty liability	Mixed: current and non-current	31,200	11,200	20,000
		$(51,200)	$(11,200)	$(40,000)

*From Illustration 18A-3

For the first temporary difference, the related account on the statement of financial position is the instalments receivable. The instalments receivable are classified partially as a current asset and partially as long-term. Because one fourth of the gross profit relates to the receivable due in 2015, this portion of the receivable is a current asset and the current portion of the future income tax liability is $22,400 ($89,600 × 1/4). The $67,200 remainder ($89,600 − $22,400) of the future income tax liability is non-current.

The plant and equipment are classified as long-term, so the resulting future income tax asset is classified as non-current. The warranty liability account, like the instalment receivables, is split between the current and long-term categories. Our assumption is that $56,000 of the liability is reported as current and the remaining $100,000 as non-current. The current portion of the future income tax asset, therefore, is $11,200 ($56,000 ÷ $156,000 × $31,200). The remainder ($31,200 − $11,200 = $20,000) is non-current.

Under ASPE, using the future income taxes method of accounting for income taxes, the $51,200 net future income tax liability is reported on the statement of financial position in two parts. A future income tax liability of $11,200 is reported as a **current liability**, and a future income tax liability of $40,000 is reported as a **long-term liability**. The statement of financial position presentation is shown in Illustration 18A-6 under IFRS and under ASPE. The income statement presentation is the same under both standards.

Illustration 18A-6

Financial Statement Presentation—2014

Statement of Financial Position, December 31, 2014–IFRS Presentation

Current liabilities	
Income tax payable	$ 46,200
Long-term liabilities	
Deferred tax liability	$ 51,200

(continued)

Illustration 18A-6
Financial Statement Presentation—2014 (continued)

IFRS → ← ASPE

Balance Sheet, December 31, 2014—ASPE Presentation

Current liabilities	
Income tax payable	$ 46,200
Future income tax liability	$ 11,200
Long-term liabilities	
Future income tax liability	$ 40,000

Income Statement, Year Ended December 31, 2014—IFRS and ASPE

Income before income tax		$412,000
Income tax expense		
Current	$46,200	
Deferred/Future	51,200	97,400
Net income		$314,600

Second Year of Operations—2015

1. During 2015, the company collected one fifth of the original sales price (or one quarter of the outstanding receivable at December 31, 2014) from customers for the receivables arising from contracts completed in 2014. Recovery of the remaining receivables is still expected to result in taxable amounts of $112,000 in each of the following three years.

2. In 2015, the company completed four new contracts with a total selling price of $1 million (to be paid in five equal instalments beginning in 2015), earning a gross profit of $320,000. For financial reporting purposes, the full $320,000 is recognized in 2015. For tax purposes, however, the gross profit is deferred and taken into taxable income as the cash is received; that is, one fifth, or $64,000, in 2015 and one fifth in each of 2016 to 2019.

3. During 2015, Allman continued to depreciate the assets acquired in 2014 according to the depreciation and CCA schedules in Illustration 18A-1. Therefore, depreciation expense of $90,000 is reported on the 2015 income statement and CCA of $97,200 is claimed for tax purposes.

4. Information about the product warranty liability and timing of warranty expenditures at the end of 2015 is shown in Illustration 18A-7.

Illustration 18A-7
Warranty Liability and Expenditure Information

Balance of liability at beginning of 2015	$156,000
Accrual of expense reported on the 2015 income statement	180,000
Expenditures related to contracts completed in 2014	(62,000)
Expenditures related to contracts completed in 2015	(50,000)
Balance of liability at end of 2015	$224,000

Estimated timing of warranty expenditures:

$ 94,000 in 2016 on 2014 contracts	
50,000 in 2016 on 2015 contracts	
80,000 in 2017 on 2015 contracts	
$224,000	

5. During 2015, non-taxable dividend revenue recognized is $24,000.

6. A loss of $172,000 is accrued for financial reporting purposes because of pending litigation. This amount is not tax deductible until the period when the loss is realized, which is estimated to be 2020.

7. Accounting income for 2015 is $504,800.

8. The tax rate in effect for 2015 is 20%; in late December, revised tax rates of 25% were enacted for 2016 and subsequent years.

Remeasurement of Deferred Tax Liability Account because of Tax Rate Change

Whenever new tax rates are substantively enacted that affect the measurement of deferred tax assets and liabilities already on the books, the balances in the deferred tax accounts are restated. This is recognized at the date the rates are changed. In the case of Allman Corporation, the rates were increased in late December 2015; therefore, this is when the adjusting entry is made. The remeasurement is carried out on the temporary differences existing before the rate is changed, in this case those at the beginning of 2015. Illustration 18A-8 indicates how this is done.

				Future Years			
(Taxable) deductible temporary differences	**Total**	**2015**	**2016**	**2017**	**2018**	**2019**
Net (taxable) deductible amount (from Illustration 18A-4)	$(256,000)	$(48,800)	$(24,240)	$(139,792)	$(152,234)	$109,066
Revised tax rate		20%	25%	25%	25%	25%
Revised net deferred tax asset (liability)	$ (61,560)	$ (9,760)	$ (6,060)	$ (34,948)	$ (38,059)	$ 27,267
Net deferred tax liability before change in rates	(51,200)					
Adjustment: increase in deferred tax liability	$ (10,360)					

Illustration 18A-8
Adjustment for Change in Income Tax Rates

The entry to recognize the effect of the change in rates is:

Deferred Tax Expense   10,360
    Deferred Tax Liability   10,360

A = L + SE
    +10,360   −10,360

Cash flows: No effect

Illustration 18A-8
Adjustment for Change in Income Tax Rates

Taxable Income, Income Tax Payable, and Current Tax Expense—2015

Taxable income, income tax payable, and current tax expense for 2015 are calculated in Illustration 18A-9.

Accounting income for 2015	$ 504,800
Permanent difference: Non-taxable revenue—dividends	(24,000)
Reversible differences:	
Gross profit on 2014 instalment sales, taxable in 2015	112,000
Deferred gross profit for tax—2015 contracts ($320,000 − $64,000)	(256,000)
CCA in excess of depreciation per books ($97,200 − $90,000)	(7,200)
Deductible warranty expenditures from 2014 contracts	(62,000)

(continued)

Illustration 18A-9
Calculation of Taxable Income and Taxes Payable—2015

Illustration 18A-9

Calculation of Taxable Income and Taxes Payable—2015 (continued)

Warranty expense per books—2015 contracts in excess of amount deductible for tax purposes ($180,000 − $50,000)		130,000
Loss accrual per books not deductible in 2015		172,000
Taxable income for 2015		$ 569,600
Income tax payable and current tax expense for 2015: $569,600 × 20%		$ 113,920

Deferred Tax Assets and Liabilities at December 31, 2015, and 2015 Deferred Tax Expense

The next step is to determine the correct balance of the net deferred tax asset or liability account at December 31, 2015. The amount required to adjust this account to its correct balance is deferred tax expense/benefit for 2015.

Illustration 18A-10 summarizes the temporary differences at December 31, 2015, the deferred tax effects of these differences, the correct ending balance of the statement of financial position deferred tax account, and the amount required for the deferred tax benefit entry.

Illustration 18A-10

Determination of Deferred Tax Assets, Liabilities, and Deferred Tax Expense/Benefit—2015

Balance Sheet Account	Tax Base	−	Carrying Amount	=	(Taxable) Deductible Temporary Difference	×	Tax Rate	=	Deferred Tax Asset (Liability)
Instalments receivable									
–2014 sales	$564,000		$900,000		$(336,000)		.25		$(84,000)
–2015 sales	544,000		800,000		(256,000)		.25		(64,000)
Plant and equipment	388,800		360,000		28,800		.25		7,200
Warranty liability									
–2014 sales	–0–		(94,000)		94,000		.25		23,500
–2015 sales	–0–		(130,000)		130,000		.25		32,500
Litigation liability	–0–		(172,000)		172,000		.25		43,000
Net deferred tax liability, December 31, 2015									(41,800)
Net deferred tax asset (liability) before adjustment (51,200) + (10,360)									(61,560)
Decrease in deferred tax liability, and deferred tax benefit for 2015									$ 19,760

The temporary difference caused by deferring the profit on the instalment sales for tax purposes again results in a taxable temporary difference and a deferred tax liability. The company has no deferred profits in the accounts—it has all been recognized in income. For tax purposes, three fifths of the 2014 profit of $560,000 (that is, $336,000) is still deferred at December 31, 2015, while four fifths of the 2015 profit of $320,000 (that is, $256,000) is deferred. These amounts will be taxable and increase taxable income in the future.

To the end of 2015, $28,800 less CCA has been claimed than depreciation. This can be seen by comparing the book value of the plant and equipment of $360,000 with its UCC or tax base of $388,800 at the same date. In the future, there will be $28,800 more CCA deductible for tax purposes than depreciation taken on the books. This will reduce future taxable income. The temporary difference due to warranty costs will result in deductible amounts in each of 2016 and 2017 as this difference reverses, and the $172,000 loss that is not deductible for tax this year will be deductible in the future.

Again, because the future tax rates are identical for each future year, the deferred tax liability can be calculated by applying the 25% rate to the total of the temporary differences. If instead the rates had been changed to 25% for 2016, 26% for 2017, and 27% thereafter, for example, a schedule similar to the one in Illustration 18A-4 would be prepared.

Income Tax Accounting Entries—2015

The entries to record current and deferred taxes for 2015 are:

Current Tax Expense	113,920	
Income Tax Payable (Illustration 18A-9)		113,920

A =	L	+	SE
	+113,920		−113,920

Cash flows: No effect

Deferred Tax Liability (Illustration 18A-10)	19,760	
Deferred Tax Benefit		19,760

A =	L	+	SE
	−19,760		+19,760

Cash flows: No effect

Financial Statement Presentation—2015

Continuing the assumptions about Allman set out above Illustration 18A-5, a net deferred tax liability of $41,800 is reported as a non-current liability under IFRS.[18] The ASPE classification of Allman Corporation's deferred tax account at the end of 2015 is shown in Illustration 18A-11.

Illustration 18A-11

ASPE Classification of Future Income Tax Asset/Liability Accounts

Statement of Financial Position Account	Classification of Statement of Financial Position Account	Future Income Tax Asset (Liability)*	Classification of Future Tax Asset (Liability)	
			Current	Non-current
Instalments receivable (deferred gross profit)				
−2014 sales	Mixed: current and non-current	$(84,000)	$(28,000)	$(56,000)
−2015 sales	Mixed: current and non-current	(64,000)	(16,000)	(48,000)
Plant and equipment	Non-current	7,200		7,200
Warranty liability	Current			
−2014 sales	Mixed: current and non-current	23,500	23,500	
−2015 sales		32,500	12,500	20,000
Litigation liability	Non-current	43,000		43,000
		$(41,800)	$ (8,000)	$(33,800)

*From Illustration 18A-10

The future income tax accounts related to the deferred gross profit follow the statement of financial position classification of the receivables. Of the amounts owed on the 2014 sales, one third will be collected in 2016 so one third of the receivable is reported in current assets. One third of the future income tax liability ($1/3 \times \$84,000 = \$28,000$) is also classified as a current item, with the remaining two thirds reported as non-current. The deferred gross profit on the 2015 sales is analyzed the same way—in this case, one quarter is current and three quarters non-current. The warranty liability related to 2014 sales is all expected to be paid within the next year; therefore, it is a current liability on the statement of financial position. The related future income tax asset is also designated as current. Of the $130,000 warranty liability related to the 2015 sales, $50,000 is expected to be met in 2016 and is included in current liabilities. The current portion of the future income tax asset is therefore $12,500 ($50,000 ÷ $130,000 × $32,500), and the remainder is long-term.[19] The litigation liability is reported outside current liabilities and so is its related future income tax account.

Under ASPE, using the future income taxes method of accounting for income taxes, the $41,800 net future income tax liability is reported on the statement of financial position in two parts. A future income tax liability of $8,000 is reported as a **current liability**, and a future income tax liability of $33,800 is reported as a **long-term liability**. The statement of financial position presentation is shown in Illustration 18A-12 under IFRS and under ASPE. The income statement presentation is the same under both sets of standards, although there is no ASPE requirement to separately disclose the major components of tax expense other than the current income tax and future income tax expense amounts.

Illustration 18A-12

Financial Statement Presentation—2015

Statement of Financial Position, December 31, 2015–IFRS Presentation

Current liabilities	
Income tax payable	$113,920
Long-term liabilities	
Deferred tax liability	$ 41,800

Balance Sheet, December 31, 2015–ASPE Presentation

Current liabilities	
Income tax payable	$113,920
Future income tax liability	$ 8,000
Long-term liabilities	
Future income tax liability	$ 33,800

Income Statement, Year Ended December 31, 2015–IFRS and ASPE

Income before income tax		$504,800
Income tax expense (benefit)		
Current	$113,920	
Deferred/Future (see Note 1)	(9,400)	104,520
Net income		$400,280

Note 1. The deferred/future income tax benefit is the net result of a tax benefit of $19,760 from originating and reversing temporary differences, and a tax expense of $10,360 resulting from a change in tax rates in the year.

SUMMARY OF LEARNING OBJECTIVE FOR APPENDIX 18A

12 **Apply the temporary difference approach (future income taxes method) of accounting for income taxes in a comprehensive situation.** In a comprehensive situation, take the following steps. (1) Calculate the current tax expense and payable; (2) determine the taxable and deductible temporary differences as the difference between the carrying amounts and tax bases of the assets and liabilities; calculate the correct balance of the deferred tax asset or liability account; (3) determine the deferred tax expense as the adjustment needed to the existing balance; (4) Make an adjusting entry to restate the deferred tax asset or liability amounts if a change in the future tax rates has been substantively enacted; and (5) Classify the net deferred/future tax asset or liability according to the accounting standards being applied.

Note: In the end-of-chapter material that follows, the simplifying assumption is made that all companies use the term "deferred" (used by IFRS) rather than the term "future" (used by ASPE) for the income tax accounts related to temporary differences. It is also assumed that where warranties are used as an example of a temporary/timing difference, the company is following the expense warranty approach, and not accounting for the warranty as a separate performance obligation.

Brief Exercises

(LO 1) **BE18-1** Faber Corporation is a young start-up technology company with steadily increasing sales in its first six months of operations. Faber's head office is located in a country in Eastern Europe, where the company would be subject to a corporate income tax rate of 28%. Next year, Faber plans to launch international sales of its products in a country in Asia (where the corporate income tax rate is 35%) and one in South America (where the corporate income tax rate is 38%). (a) What is the effect of income taxes on a company's profits? (b) What is the effect of income taxes on a company's cash flows? (c) Considering only the effect of income taxes, in which country should Faber register its company?

(LO 2) **BE18-2** In 2014, Shafali Corporation had accounting income of $248,000 and taxable income of $198,000. The difference is due to the use of different depreciation methods for tax and accounting purposes. The tax rate is 25%. Calculate the amount to be reported as income tax payable at December 31, 2014.

(LO 2) **BE18-3** Nilson Inc. had accounting income of $156,000 in 2014. Included in the calculation of that amount is insurance expense of $5,000, which is not deductible for tax purposes. In addition, the undepreciated capital cost (UCC) for tax purposes is $14,000 lower than the net carrying amount of the property, plant, and equipment, although the amounts were equal at the beginning of the year. Prepare Nilson's journal entry to record 2014 taxes, assuming IFRS and a tax rate of 25%.

(LO 2, 3, 5) **BE18-4** Anugraham Corp. follows IFRS and began operations in 2014 and reported accounting income of $275,000 for the year. Anugraham's CCA exceeded its book depreciation by $40,000. Anugraham's tax rate for 2014 and years thereafter is 35%. In its December 31, 2014 statement of financial position, what amount of deferred tax liability should be reported?

(LO 2, 5) **BE18-5** Using the information from BE18-3, calculate the effective rate of income tax for Nilson Inc. for 2014. Also make a reconciliation from the statutory rate to the effective rate, using percentages.

(LO 3, 5) **BE18-6** At December 31, 2014, Naifa Inc. owned equipment that had a book value of $145,000 and a tax base of $114,000 due to the use of different depreciation methods for accounting and tax purposes. The enacted tax rate is 30%. Calculate the amount that Naifa should report as a deferred tax liability at December 31, 2014.

(LO 3, 5) **BE18-7** Using the information from BE18-4, and assuming that the $40,000 difference is the only difference between Anugraham's accounting income and taxable income, prepare the journal entry(ies) to record the current tax expense, deferred tax expense, income tax payable, and the deferred tax liability.

(LO 4) **BE18-8** At December 31, 2014, Camille Corporation had an estimated warranty liability of $170,000 for accounting purposes and $0 for tax purposes. (The warranty costs are not deductible until they are paid.) The tax rate is 25%. Calculate the amount that Camille should report as a deferred tax asset at December 31, 2014.

(LO 4, 5) **BE18-9** At December 31, 2013, Chai Inc. had a deferred tax asset of $40,000. At December 31, 2014, the deferred tax asset is $62,000. The corporation's 2014 current tax expense is $70,000. What amount should Chai report as total 2014 income tax expense?

(LO 5) **BE18-10** At December 31, 2013, Ambuir Corporation had a deferred tax liability of $35,000. At December 31, 2014, the deferred tax liability is $52,000. The corporation's 2014 current tax expense is $53,000. What amount should Ambuir report as total 2014 income tax expense?

(LO 5) **BE18-11** Chua Corporation has a taxable temporary difference related to depreciation of $715,000 at December 31, 2014. This difference will reverse as follows: 2015, $53,000; 2016, $310,000; and 2017, $352,000. Enacted tax rates are 25% for 2015 and 2016, and 31% for 2017. Calculate the amount that Chua should report as a deferred tax asset or liability at December 31, 2014.

(LO 6) **BE18-12** At December 31, 2013, Palden Corporation had a deferred tax asset of $675,000, resulting from future deductible amounts of $2.7 million and an enacted tax rate of 25%. In May 2014, new income tax legislation is signed into law that raises the tax rate to 27% for 2014 and future years. Prepare the journal entry for Palden to adjust the deferred tax account.

(LO 7) **BE18-13** Ayesha Corporation had the following tax information:

In 2014, Ayesha suffered a net operating loss of $550,000, which it decided to carry back. The 2014 enacted tax rate is 29%. Prepare Ayesha's entry to record the effect of the loss carryback.

Year	Taxable Income	Tax Rate	Taxes Paid
2011	$390,000	35%	$136,500
2012	325,000	30%	97,500
2013	400,000	30%	120,000

(LO 7, 8) BE18-14 Kyle Inc. incurred a net operating loss of $580,000 in 2014. Combined income for 2011, 2012, and 2013 was $460,000. The tax rate for all years is 35%. Prepare the journal entries to record the benefits of the carryback and the carryforward, assuming it is more likely than not that the benefits of the loss carryforward will be realized.

(LO 7, 8) BE18-15 Use the information for Kyle Inc. given in BE18-14, but assume instead that it is more likely than not that the entire tax loss carryforward will not be realized in future years. Prepare all the journal entries that are necessary at the end of 2014 assuming (a) that Kyle does not use a valuation allowance account, and (b) that Kyle does use a valuation allowance account.

(LO 7, 8) BE18-16 Use the information for Kyle Inc. given in BE18-15. Assume now that Kyle earns taxable income of $25,000 in 2015 and that at the end of 2015 there is still too much uncertainty to recognize a deferred tax asset. Prepare all the journal entries that are necessary at the end of 2015 assuming (a) that Kyle does not use a valuation allowance account, and (b) that Kyle does use a valuation allowance account.

(LO 7, 8) BE18-17 At December 31, 2014, Aminder Corporation has a deferred tax asset of $340,000. After a careful review of all available evidence, it is determined that it is more likely than not that $70,000 of this deferred tax asset will not be realized. Prepare the necessary journal entry assuming (a) that Aminder does not use a valuation allowance account, and (b) that Aminder does use a valuation allowance account.

(LO 10) BE18-18 In 2014, Borovya Limited purchased shares of Gurvir Corp. at a cost of $45,000. This was the first time the company had ever acquired an investment to be accounted for at fair value through other comprehensive income (FV-OCI). At December 31, 2014, the Gurvir Corp. shares had a fair value of $41,000. Borovya Limited's income tax rate is 30%. Assume that any gains that are ultimately realized on the sale of the Gurvir Corp. shares will be taxable as ordinary income when the gains are realized. Prepare the necessary journal entries to record the unrealized loss and the related income taxes in 2014. Prepare the statement of comprehensive income for Borovya Limited, beginning with the line for net income of $55,000. Assume Borovya Limited reports under IFRS.

(LO 10) BE18-19 Sandeep Corporation had income before income tax of $230,000 in 2014. Sandeep's current tax expense is $43,000, and deferred tax expense is $27,000. (a) Prepare Sandeep's 2014 income statement, beginning with income before income tax. (b) Calculate Sandeep's effective tax rate.

(LO 10) BE18-20 Kolby Inc. reported income from continuing operations of $71,000 and a loss from discontinued operations of $10,000 in 2014, all before income taxes. All items are fully taxable and deductible for tax purposes. Prepare the bottom of the income statement for Kolby Inc., beginning with income from continuing operations before income tax. Assume a tax rate of 25%.

(LO 10, 11) BE18-21 Sonia Corporation has historically followed ASPE, but is considering a change to IFRS. It has temporary differences at December 31, 2014, that result in the following statement of financial position future income tax accounts:

Deferred tax liability, current	$38,000
Deferred tax asset, current	$52,000
Deferred tax liability, non-current	$96,000
Deferred tax asset, non-current	$27,000

Indicate how these balances will be presented in Sonia's December 31, 2014 statement of financial position, assuming (a) Sonia reports under the ASPE future/deferred taxes method, and (b) Sonia follows IFRS for reporting purposes.

(LO 11) BE18-22 Using the information from BE18-3, prepare Nilson's journal entry to record 2014 income tax. Assume a tax rate of 25% and that Nilson uses the taxes payable method of accounting for income taxes under ASPE.

Exercises

(LO 2) E18-1 (Terminology, Relationships, Calculations, Entries)

Instructions

Complete the following statements by filling in the blanks or choosing the correct answer in the parentheses.

(a) In a period in which a taxable temporary difference reverses, the reversal will cause taxable income to be (less than/greater than) accounting income.

(b) In a period in which a deductible temporary difference reverses, the reversal will cause taxable income to be (less than/greater than) accounting income.

(c) If a $76,000 balance in the Deferred Tax Asset account were calculated using a 25% rate, the underlying temporary difference would amount to $ _____.

(d) Deferred taxes (are/are not) recorded to account for permanent differences.

(e) If a taxable temporary difference originates in 2014, it causes taxable income of 2014 to be (less than/greater than) accounting income for 2014.

(f) If total income tax expense is $50,000 and deferred tax expense is $65,000, then the current portion of the total income tax expense is referred to as a current tax (expense/benefit) of $ _____.

(g) If a corporation's tax return shows taxable income of $100,000 for Year 2 and a tax rate of 25%, how much will appear on the December 31, Year 2 statement of financial position for "Income tax payable" if the company has made estimated tax payments of $16,500 for Year 2? $ _____.

(h) An increase in the Deferred Tax Liability account on the statement of financial position is recorded by a (debit/credit) to the Deferred Tax Expense account.

(i) An income statement that reports current tax expense of $82,000 and a deferred tax benefit of $23,000 will report total income tax expense of $ _____.

(j) Under ASPE, a valuation account may be used whenever it is judged to be more likely than not that a portion of a deferred tax asset (will be/will not be) realized.

(k) If the tax return shows total income taxes due for the period of $75,000 but the income statement shows total income tax expense of $55,000, the difference of $20,000 is referred to as a deferred tax (expense/benefit).

(l) If a company's income tax rate increases, the effect will be to (increase/decrease) the amount of a deferred tax liability and _____ (increase/decrease) the amount of a deferred tax asset.

(m) The difference between the tax base of an asset or liability and its carrying amount is called a _____ difference. Differences between accounting income and taxable income that will reverse in the future are called _____ differences.

(LO 2) E18-2 (One Reversing Difference through Three Years, One Rate) Aabid Corporation reports the following amounts in its first three years of operations.

	2014	2015	2016
Taxable income	$245,000	$121,000	$125,000
Accounting income	160,000	139,000	131,000

The difference between taxable income and accounting income is due to one reversing difference. The tax rate is 30% for all years and the company expects to continue with profitable operations in the future.

Instructions

(a) For each year, (1) identify the amount of the reversing difference originating or reversing during that year, and (2) indicate the amount of the temporary difference at the end of the year.

(b) Indicate the balance in the related deferred tax account at the end of each year and identify it as a deferred tax asset or liability.

(LO 2) E18-3 (Intraperiod Tax Allocation—Other Comprehensive Income) Hang Technologies Inc. held a portfolio of shares and bonds that it accounted for using the fair value through other comprehensive income model at December 31, 2014. This was the first year that Hang had purchased investments. In part due to Hang's inexperience, by December 31, 2014, the market value of the portfolio had dropped below its original cost by $28,000. Hang recorded the necessary adjustments at December 31, 2014, and was determined to hold the securities until the unrealized loss of 2014 could be recovered. By December 31, 2015, Hang's goals of recovery had been realized and the original portfolio of shares and bonds had a fair market value $5,500 higher than the original purchase costs. Hang's income tax rate is 30% for all years. Assume that any gains that will ultimately be realized on the sale of the shares and bonds are taxable as ordinary income when they are realized. Hang applies IFRS.

Instructions

(a) Prepare the journal entries at December 31, 2014, to accrue the unrealized loss on Hang's securities and the related income tax.

(b) Prepare the journal entries at December 31, 2015, to accrue the unrealized gain on the securities and the related income tax.

(c) Prepare a comparative statement of comprehensive income for the fiscal years ending December 31, 2014, and 2015. Assume net income of $100,000 in each fiscal year.

(LO 2, 3, 4) **E18-4 (Identifying Reversing or Permanent Differences and Showing Effects)** The accounting for the items in the numbered list that follows is commonly different for financial reporting purposes than it is for tax purposes.

1. For financial reporting purposes, the straight-line depreciation method is used for plant assets that have a useful life of 10 years; for tax purposes, the CCA declining-balance method is used with a rate of 20% (ignore the half-year rule).

2. A landlord collects rents in advance. Rents are taxable in the period when they are received.

3. Non-deductible expenses are incurred in obtaining income that is exempt from taxes.

4. Costs of guarantees and warranties are estimated and accrued for financial reporting purposes.

5. Instalment sales are accounted for by the accrual method for financial reporting purposes and the cash basis for tax purposes.

6. For some assets, straight-line depreciation is used for both financial reporting and tax purposes but the assets' lives are shorter for tax purposes.

7. Pension expense is reported on the income statement before it is funded. Pension costs are deductible only when they are funded.

8. Proceeds are received from a life insurance company because of the death of a key officer (the company carries a policy on key officers).

9. The company reports dividends received from taxable Canadian corporations as investment income on its income statement, even though the dividends are non-taxable.

10. Estimated losses on pending lawsuits and claims are accrued for financial reporting purposes. These losses are tax deductible in the period(s) when the related liabilities are settled.

11. Security investments accounted for using the fair value through net income (FV-NI) model are adjusted at the end of the year to their fair value. This is the first year that the company has such investments and the fair value is lower than the cost.

12. An impairment loss is recorded for goodwill in the current accounting period.

Instructions

(a) Match each item in the preceding list to the number below that best describes it:

   i. A reversing difference that will result in future deductible amounts and, therefore, will usually give rise to a deferred tax asset

   ii. A reversing difference that will result in future taxable amounts and, therefore, will usually give rise to a deferred tax liability

   iii. A permanent difference

(b) For each item in the preceding list, indicate if the amounts that are involved in the current year will be added to or deducted from accounting income to arrive at taxable income.

(LO 2, 3, 4, 5) **E18-5 (Two Reversing Differences, Future Taxable and Deductible Amounts, No Beginning Deferred Taxes, One Tax Rate)** Sayaka Tar and Gravel Ltd. operates a road construction business. In its first year of operations, the company obtained a contract to construct a road for the municipality of Cochrane West, and it is estimated that the project will be completed over a three-year period starting in June 2014. Sayaka uses the percentage-of-completion method of recognizing revenue on its long-term construction contracts. For tax purposes, and in order to postpone the tax on such revenue for as long as possible, Sayaka uses the completed-contract method allowed by the CRA. By its first fiscal year end, the accounts related to the contract had the following balances:

Accounts Receivable	$320,000
Construction in Process	500,000
Revenue from Long-Term Contracts	500,000
Construction Expenses	350,000
Billings on Construction in Process	400,000

The accounts related to the equipment that Sayaka purchased to construct the road had the following balances at the end of the first fiscal year ending December 31, 2014, for accounting and tax purposes:

Equipment	$1,100,000
Accumulated Depreciation—Equipment	170,000
Undepreciated Capital Cost	980,000

Sayaka's tax rate is 25% for 2014 and subsequent years. Income before income tax for the year ended December 31, 2014, was $195,000. Sayaka reports under the ASPE future/deferred income taxes method.

Instructions

(a) Calculate the deferred tax asset or liability balances at December 31, 2014.

(b) Calculate taxable income and income tax payable for 2014.

(c) Prepare the journal entries to record income taxes for 2014.

(d) Prepare the income statement for 2014, beginning with the line "Income before income tax."

(e) Provide the balance sheet presentation for any resulting deferred tax balance sheet accounts at December 31, 2014. Be specific about the classification.

(f) Repeat the balance sheet presentation in part (e) assuming Sayaka follows IFRS.

(LO 2, 3, 4, 5) **E18-6 (Two Reversing Differences, Future Taxable and Deductible Amounts, Beginning Deferred Taxes, One Tax Rate)** Refer to E18-5 for Sayaka Tar and Gravel Ltd., and assume the same facts for the fiscal year ending December 31, 2014. For the second year of operations, Sayaka made progress on the construction of the road for the municipality. The account balances at December 31, 2015, for the construction project and the accounting and tax balances of accounts related to the equipment used for construction follow (the balances at December 31, 2014, are also listed):

	2015	2014
Accounts Receivable	$ 105,000	$ 320,000
Construction in Process	940,000	500,000
Revenue from Long-Term Contracts	440,000	500,000
Construction Expenses	410,000	350,000
Billings on Construction in Process	390,000	400,000
Equipment	1,100,000	1,100,000
Accumulated Depreciation—Equipment	460,000	170,000
Undepreciated Capital Cost	620,000	980,000

Sayaka's tax rate continues to be 25% for 2015 and subsequent years. Income before income tax for the year ended December 31, 2015, was $120,000.

Instructions

(a) Calculate the deferred tax asset or liability balances at December 31, 2015.

(b) Calculate taxable income and income tax payable for 2015.

(c) Prepare the journal entries to record income taxes for 2015.

(d) Prepare a comparative income statement for 2014 and 2015, beginning with the line "Income before income tax."

(e) Provide the comparative balance sheet presentation for any resulting deferred tax balance sheet accounts at December 31, 2014, and 2015. Be specific about the classification.

(f) Repeat the balance sheet presentation in part (e) assuming Sayaka follows IFRS.

(LO 2, 3, 4, 5) **E18-7 (Two Reversing Differences, Future Taxable and Deductible Amounts, Beginning Deferred Taxes, Change in Tax Rate)** Refer to E18-6 for Sayaka Tar and Gravel Ltd., and assume the same facts as in E18-6 for the fiscal year ending December 31, 2015, except that the enacted tax rate for 2016 and subsequent years was reduced to 20% on September 15, 2015.

Instructions

(a) Prepare the journal entry to record the effect of the change in the enacted tax rate.

(b) Calculate any deferred tax balances at December 31, 2015.

(c) Calculate taxable income and income tax payable for 2015.

(d) Prepare the journal entries to record income taxes for 2015.

(e) Prepare a comparative income statement for 2014 and 2015, beginning with the line "Income before income tax" and provide details about the components of income tax expense.

(f) Provide the comparative statement of balance sheet presentation for any resulting deferred tax balance sheet accounts at December 31, 2014, and 2015. Be specific about the classification.

(g) Repeat the statement of financial position presentation in part (e) assuming Sayaka follows IFRS.

(LO 2, 3, 4, 5) **E18-8** **(Reversing and Permanent Differences, Future Taxable Amount, No Beginning Deferred Taxes)** Christina Inc. follows IFRS and accounts for financial instruments based on IFRS 9. Christina holds a variety of investments, some of which are accounted for at fair value through net income and some of which are accounted for at fair value through other comprehensive income. On January 1, 2014, the beginning of the fiscal year, Christina's accounts and records include the following information:

	Cost	Market Value
Fair value through net income investments	$60,000	$60,000
Fair value through other comprehensive income investments	71,000	71,000

Market values for the FV-NI investments and FV-OCI investments at December 31, 2014, were $58,000 and $75,000, respectively. Computers that are used to track investment performance were purchased during 2014 for $10,000. For tax purposes, assume the computers are in Class 10 with a CCA rate of 30%. Depreciation expense for the year was $2,000. Christina recorded meals and entertainment expenses of $24,000 related to "wining and dining" clients. The CRA allows 50% of these costs as a deductible business expense.

Christina's income before income tax for 2014 is $110,000. This amount does not include any entries to adjust investments to market values at December 31, 2014. Christina's tax rate for 2014 is 25%, although changes enacted in tax legislation before December 31, 2014, will result in an increase in this rate to 30% for 2015 and subsequent taxation years. Assume that these rates apply to all income that is reported. There were no deferred tax accounts at January 1, 2014.

Instructions

(a) Prepare journal entries to reflect the difference between the carrying amount and market value for the above investments at Christina's year end of December 31, 2014.

(b) Explain the tax treatment that should be given to the unrealized gains or losses reported on Christina's statement of income and statement of comprehensive income.

(c) Calculate the deferred tax asset or liability balances at December 31, 2014, and indicate their classification.

(d) Calculate taxable income and income tax payable for 2014.

(e) Prepare the journal entries to record income taxes for 2014.

(LO 2, 3, 5) **E18-9** **(One Reversing Difference, Future Taxable Amounts, One Rate, No Beginning Deferred Taxes)** Raman Limited had investments in securities on its statement of financial position for the first time at the end of its fiscal year ending December 31, 2014. Raman reports under IFRS and its investments in securities are to be accounted for at fair value through net income. During 2014, Raman reports realized losses and gains on the trading of shares and bonds resulted in investment income, which is fully taxable in the year. Raman also accrued unrealized gains at December 31, 2014, which are not taxable until the investment securities are sold. The portfolio of trading securities had an original cost of $314,450 and a fair value on December 31, 2014, of $318,200. The entry recorded by Raman on December 31, 2014, was as follows:

FV-NI Investments	3,750	
Investment Income or Loss		3,750

Income before income tax for Raman was $302,000 for the year ended December 31, 2014. There are no other permanent or reversing differences in arriving at the taxable income for Raman Limited for the fiscal year ending December 31, 2014. The enacted tax rate for 2014 and future years is 30%.

Instructions

(a) Explain the tax treatment that should be given to the unrealized gain that Raman Limited reported on its income statement.

(b) Calculate the deferred tax balance at December 31, 2014.

(c) Calculate the current income tax for the year ending December 31, 2014.

(d) Prepare the journal entries to record income taxes for 2014.

(e) Prepare the income statement for 2014, beginning with the line "Income before income tax."

(f) Provide the statement of financial position presentation for any resulting income tax statement of financial position accounts at December 31, 2014. Be clear on the classification you have chosen and explain your choice.

(g) Repeat part (f) assuming Raman follows the ASPE future/deferred income taxes method and has chosen the fair value through net income model to account for its securities investments.

(LO 2, 3, 5) **E18-10   (One Reversing Difference, Future Taxable Amounts, One Rate, No Beginning Deferred Taxes)** Sorpon Corporation purchased equipment very late in 2014. Based on generous capital cost allowance rates provided in the Income Tax Act, Sorpon Corporation claimed CCA on its 2014 tax return but did not record any depreciation as the equipment had not yet been put into use. This temporary difference will reverse and cause taxable amounts of $25,000 in 2015, $30,000 in 2016, and $40,000 in 2017. Sorpon's accounting income for 2014 is $200,000 and the tax rate is 30% for all years. There are no deferred tax accounts at the beginning of 2014.

Instructions

(a) Calculate the deferred tax balance at December 31, 2014.

(b) Calculate taxable income and income tax payable for 2014.

(c) Prepare the journal entries to record income taxes for 2014.

(d) Prepare the income tax expense section of the income statement for 2014, beginning with the line "Income before income tax."

(LO 2, 3, 5) **E18-11   (One Reversing Difference, Future Taxable Amounts, One Rate, Beginning Deferred Taxes)** Use the information for Sorpon Corporation in E18-10, and assume that the company reports accounting income of $180,000 in each of 2015 and 2016, and no temporary differences other than the one identified in E18-10.

Instructions

(a) Calculate the deferred tax balances at December 31, 2015, and 2016.

(b) Calculate taxable income and income tax payable for 2015 and 2016.

(c) Prepare the journal entries to record income taxes for 2015 and 2016.

(d) Prepare the income tax expense section of the income statements for 2015 and 2016, beginning with the line "Income before income tax."

(e) What trend do you notice in the amount of net income reported for 2015 and 2016 in part (d)? Is this a coincidence? Explain.

Digging Deeper

(LO 2, 3, 5, 6) **E18-12   (One Temporary Difference, Future Taxable Amounts, No Beginning Deferred Taxes, Change in Rate)** Use the information for Sorpon Corporation in E18-10, and assume that the company reports accounting income of $180,000 in each of 2015 and 2016, and no reversing differences other than the one identified in E18-10. In addition, assume now that Sorpon Corporation was informed on December 31, 2015, that the enacted rate for 2016 and subsequent years is 25%.

Instructions

(a) Calculate the deferred tax balances at December 31, 2015, and 2016.

(b) Calculate taxable income and income tax payable for 2015 and 2016.

(c) Prepare the journal entries to record income taxes for 2015 and 2016.

(d) Prepare the income tax expense section of the income statements for 2015 and 2016, beginning with the line "Income before income tax."

(LO 2, 4, 5) **E18-13   (Permanent and Reversing Differences, Calculating Taxable Income, Entry for Taxes)** Melissa Inc. reports accounting income of $105,000 for 2014, its first year of operations. The following items cause taxable income to be different than income reported on the financial statements.

1. Capital cost allowance (on the tax return) is greater than depreciation on the income statement by $16,000.

2. Rent revenue reported on the tax return is $24,000 higher than rent revenue reported on the income statement.

3. Non-deductible fines appear as an expense of $15,000 on the income statement.

4. Melissa's tax rate is 30% for all years and the company expects to report taxable income in all future years. Melissa reports under the ASPE future/deferred income taxes method.

Instructions

(a) Calculate taxable income and income tax payable for 2014.

(b) Calculate any deferred tax balances at December 31, 2014.

(c) Prepare the journal entries to record income taxes for 2014.

(d) Prepare the income tax expense section of the income statement for 2014, beginning with the line "Income before income tax."

(e) Reconcile the statutory and effective rates of income tax for 2014.

(f) Provide the balance sheet presentation for any resulting deferred tax balance sheet accounts at December 31, 2014. Be specific about the classification.

(g) Repeat part (f) assuming Melissa follows IFRS.

(LO 2, 4, 5) E18-14 (One Reversing Difference, Future Deductible Amounts, One Rate, No Beginning Deferred Taxes) Jenny Corporation recorded warranty accruals as at December 31, 2014, in the amount of $150,000. This reversing difference will cause deductible amounts of $50,000 in 2015, $35,000 in 2016, and $65,000 in 2017. Jenny's accounting income for 2014 is $135,000 and the tax rate is 25% for all years. There are no deferred tax accounts at the beginning of 2014.

Instructions

(a) Calculate the deferred tax balance at December 31, 2014.

(b) Calculate taxable income and current income tax payable for 2014.

(c) Prepare the journal entries to record income taxes for 2014.

(d) Prepare the income tax expense section of the income statement for 2014, beginning with the line "Income before income tax."

(LO 2, 4, 5) E18-15 (One Reversing Difference, Future Deductible Amounts, One Rate, Beginning Deferred Taxes) Use the information for Jenny Corporation in E18-14, and assume that the company reports accounting income of $155,000 in each of 2015 and 2016 and the warranty expenditures occurred as expected. No reversing difference exists other than the one identified in E18-14.

Instructions

(a) Calculate the deferred tax balances at December 31, 2015, and 2016.

(b) Calculate taxable income and income tax payable for 2015 and 2016.

(c) Prepare the journal entries to record income taxes for 2015 and 2016.

(d) Prepare the income tax expense section of the income statements for 2015 and 2016, beginning with the line "Income before income tax."

(e) What trend do you notice in the amount of net income reported for 2015 and 2016 in part (d)? Is this a coincidence? Explain.

Digging Deeper

(LO 2, 4, 5, 6) E18-16 (One Temporary Difference, Future Taxable Amount Becomes Future Deductible Amount, One Rate, Change in Rate) Refer to the information for Raman Limited in E18-9. Following the year ended December 31, 2014, Raman continued to actively trade its securities investments until the end of its 2015 fiscal year, when it was forced to sell several of them at a loss, because of the need for cash for operations. By December 31, 2015, the portfolio of investments contained a single investment in shares, which was purchased in November 2015. Raman Limited had paid $42,000 for these remaining shares. At December 31, 2015, the shares' market value was $40,000. Income before income tax for Raman was $120,000 for the year ended December 31, 2015. There are no other permanent or timing differences in arriving at the taxable income for Raman Limited for the fiscal year ending December 31, 2015. The enacted tax rate for 2015 and future years is 30%.

Instructions

(a) Prepare the necessary journal entry for Raman Limited to accrue the unrealized loss on its securities investments.

(b) Explain the tax treatment that should be given to the unrealized accrued loss that Raman Limited reported on its income statement.

(c) Calculate the deferred tax balance at December 31, 2015.

(d) Calculate the current income taxes for 2015.

(e) Prepare the journal entries to record income taxes for 2015. Assume that there have been no entries to the ending balances of deferred taxes reported at December 31, 2014.

(f) Prepare the income statement for 2015, beginning with the line "Income before income tax."

(g) Provide the presentation for the statement of financial position for any resulting deferred tax accounts at December 31, 2015. Be clear on the classification you have chosen and explain your choice.

(h) Prepare the journal entries in part (e) under the assumption that, late in 2015, the income tax rate changed to 28% for 2016 and subsequent years.

(i) Repeat the balance sheet presentation in part (g) assuming Raman reports under the ASPE future/deferred income taxes method and has chosen the fair value through net income model to account for its securities investments.

(LO 2, 4, 5, 6) **E18-17 (One Reversing Difference, Future Deductible Amounts, No Beginning Deferred Taxes, Change in Rate)** Use the information for Jenny Corporation in E18-14, and assume that the company reports accounting income of $155,000 in each of 2015 and 2016, and that there is no reversing difference other than the one identified in E18-14. In addition, assume now that Jenny Corporation was informed on December 31, 2015, that the enacted rate for 2016 and subsequent years is 28%.

Instructions

(a) Calculate the deferred tax balances at December 31, 2015, and 2016.

(b) Calculate taxable income and income tax payable for 2015 and 2016.

(c) Prepare the journal entries to record income taxes for 2015 and 2016.

(d) Prepare the income tax expense section of the income statements for 2015 and 2016, beginning with the line "Income before income tax."

(LO 2, 5, 11) **E18-18 (Depreciation, Reversing Difference over Five Years, Determining Taxable Income, Taxes Payable Method)** Zak Corp. purchased depreciable assets costing $600,000 on January 2, 2014. For tax purposes, the company uses CCA in a class that has a 40% rate. For financial reporting purposes, the company uses straight-line depreciation over five years. The enacted tax rate is 34% for all years. This depreciation difference is the only reversing difference the company has. Assume that Zak has income before income tax of $340,000 in each of the years 2014 to 2018.

Instructions

(a) Calculate the amount of capital cost allowance and depreciation expense from 2014 to 2018, as well as the corresponding balances for carrying amount and undepreciated capital cost of the depreciable assets at the end of each of the years 2014 to 2018.

(b) Determine the amount of taxable income in each year from 2014 to 2018.

(c) Determine the amount of deferred taxes that should be reported in the statement of financial position for each year from 2014 to 2018.

(d) Prepare the journal entries to record income taxes for each year from 2014 to 2018.

(e) Prepare the income tax entry(ies) to record income taxes for each year, assuming the management and owners have decided on the taxes payable method.

(LO 2, 6) **E18-19 (Deferred Tax Liability, Change in Tax Rate)** Yen Inc.'s only temporary difference at the beginning and end of 2014 is caused by a $3.3-million deferred gain for tax purposes on an installment sale of a plant asset. The related receivable (only one half of which is classified as a current asset) is due in equal instalments in 2015 and 2016. The related deferred tax liability at the beginning of the year is $990,000. In the third quarter of 2014, a new tax rate of 29% is enacted into law and is scheduled to become effective for 2016. Taxable income is expected in all future years.

Instructions

(a) Determine the amount to be reported as a deferred tax liability at the end of 2014. Indicate its proper classification(s) if Yen Inc. applies ASPE.

(b) Indicate the classification of the deferred tax asset or liability account if Yen Inc. applies IFRS.

(c) Prepare the journal entry (if any) that is necessary to adjust the deferred tax liability when the new tax rate is enacted into law.

(LO 6) **E18-20 (One Difference, Multiple Rates, Beginning Deferred Taxes, Change in Rates)** At the end of 2013, Valerie Corporation reported a deferred tax liability of $31,000. At the end of 2014, the company had $201,000 of temporary differences related to property, plant, and equipment. Depreciation expense on this property, plant, and equipment has been lower than the CCA claimed on Valerie's income tax returns. The resulting future taxable amounts are as follows:

2015	$ 67,000
2016	50,000
2017	45,000
2018	39,000
	$201,000

The tax rates enacted as of the beginning of 2013 are as follows: 31% for 2013 and 2014; 30% for 2015 and 2016; and 25% for 2017 and later. Taxable income is expected in all future years.

Instructions

(a) Calculate the deferred tax account balance at December 31, 2014.

(b) Prepare the journal entry for Valerie to record deferred taxes for 2014.

(c) Early in 2015, after the 2014 financial statements were released, new tax rates were enacted as follows: 29% for 2015 and 27% for 2016 and later. Prepare the journal entry for Valerie to recognize the change in tax rates.

(LO 7) **E18-21 (Loss Carryback and Carryforward)** Alliance Inc. reports the following incomes (losses) for both book and tax purposes (assume the carryback provision is used where possible):

Year	Accounting Income (Loss)	Tax Rate
2011	$ 120,000	25%
2012	90,000	25%
2013	(280,000)	30%
2014	40,000	30%

The tax rates listed were all enacted by the beginning of 2011.

Instructions

(a) Prepare the journal entries for each of the years 2011 to 2014 to record income taxes, assuming at December 31, 2013, that it was more likely than not that the company would not be able to benefit from the remaining losses available to carry forward.

(b) Prepare the income tax section of the income statements for each of the years 2011 to 2014, beginning with the line "Income (loss) before income tax."

(LO 7, 8) **E18-22 (Carryback and Carryforward of Tax Loss)** The accounting income (loss) figures for Farah Corporation are as follows:

2009	$ 160,000
2010	250,000
2011	80,000
2012	(160,000)
2013	(380,000)
2014	130,000
2015	145,000

Accounting income (loss) and taxable income (loss) were the same for all years involved. Assume a 32% tax rate for 2009 and 2010, and a 28% tax rate for the remaining years.

Instructions

Prepare the journal entries for each of the years 2011 to 2015 to record income tax expense and the effects of the tax loss carrybacks and carryforwards, assuming Farah Corporation uses the carryback provision first. All income and losses relate to normal operations and it is more likely than not that the company will generate substantial taxable income in the future.

(LO 7, 8) **E18-23 (Loss Carryback and Carryforward)** Riley Inc. reports the following pre-tax incomes (losses) for both financial reporting purposes and tax purposes:

Year	Accounting Income (Loss)	Tax Rate
2012	$ 120,000	34%
2013	90,000	34%
2014	(280,000)	38%
2015	220,000	38%

The tax rates listed were all enacted by the beginning of 2012. Riley reports under the ASPE future/deferred income taxes method.

Instructions

(a) Prepare the journal entries for each of the years 2012 to 2015 to record income tax, assuming the tax loss is first carried back, and that at the end of 2014, the loss carryforward benefits are judged more likely than not to be realized in the future.

(b) Using the assumption as in part (a), prepare the income tax section of the 2014 and 2015 income statements, beginning with the line "Income (loss) before income tax."

(c) Prepare the journal entries for 2014 and 2015, assuming that it is more likely than not that 25% of the carryforward benefits will not be realized. This company does not use a valuation allowance.

(d) Using the assumption in part (c), prepare the income tax section of the 2014 and 2015 income statements, beginning with the line "Income (loss) before income tax."

(LO 7, 8, 10) E18-24 (Loss Carryback and Carryforward Using a Valuation Allowance) Refer to the information for Riley Inc. in E18-23.

Instructions

(a) Assume that Riley Inc. uses a valuation allowance to account for deferred tax assets, and also that it is more likely than not that 25% of the carryforward benefits will not be realized. Prepare the journal entries for 2014 and 2015.

(b) Based on your entries in part (a), prepare the income tax section of the 2014 and 2015 income statements, beginning with the line "Income (loss) before income tax."

(c) Indicate how the deferred tax asset account will be reported on the December 31, 2014 and 2015 statements of financial position.

(d) Assume that on June 30, 2015, the enacted tax rates changed for 2015. Should management record any adjustment to the accounts? If yes, which accounts will be involved and when should the adjustment be recorded?

(e) Repeat part (c) assuming Riley Inc. follows IFRS.

(LO 9) E18-25 (Deferred Tax Asset—Different Amounts to Be Realized) Brandon Corp. had a deferred tax asset account with a balance of $101,500 at the end of 2013 due to a single temporary difference of $290,000 related to warranty liability accruals. At the end of 2014, this same temporary difference has increased to $315,000. Taxable income for 2014 is $887,000. The tax rate is 35% for all years.

Instructions

(a) Calculate and record income taxes for 2014, assuming that it is more likely than not that the deferred tax asset will be realized.

(b) 1. Assuming it is more likely than not that $25,000 of the deferred tax asset will not be realized, prepare the journal entries to record income taxes for 2014. Brandon does not use a valuation allowance account.
2. In 2015, prospects for the company improved. While there was no change in the temporary deductible differences underlying the deferred tax asset account, it was now considered more likely than not that the company would be able to make full use of the temporary differences. Prepare the entry, if applicable, to adjust the deferred tax asset account.

(LO 9) E18-26 (Deferred Tax Asset—Different Amounts to Be Realized; Valuation Allowance) Refer to the information provided about Brandon Corp. in E18-25.

Instructions

(a) Assuming that it is more likely than not that $25,000 of the deferred tax asset will not be realized, prepare the journal entries to record income taxes for 2014. Brandon uses a valuation allowance account.

(b) In 2015, prospects for the company improved. While there was no change in the temporary deductible differences underlying the deferred tax asset account, it was now considered more likely than not that the company would be able to make full use of the temporary differences. Prepare the entry, if applicable, to adjust the deferred tax asset and related account(s).

(LO 10) E18-27 (Three Differences, Classification of Deferred Taxes) Darrell Corporation reports under IFRS and at December 31, 2014, the company had a net deferred tax liability of $375,000. An explanation of the items that make up this balance follows:

Temporary Differences	Resulting Balances in Deferred Tax Account
1. Excess of accumulated tax depreciation over book depreciation	$230,000
2. Accrual, for book purposes, of estimated loss contingency from pending lawsuit that is expected to be settled in 2014. The loss will be deducted on the tax return when it is paid.	(80,000)
3. Accrual method (account receivable) used for book purposes and instalment method used for tax purposes for an isolated instalment sale of an investment, due in 2015.	225,000
	$375,000

Digging Deeper

Instructions

(a) Indicate how deferred tax should be presented on Darrell Corporation's December 31, 2014 statement of financial position.

(b) How would your response to part (a) change if Darrell Corporation followed the ASPE future/deferred income taxes method?

(LO 10) **E18-28 (Interperiod Tax Allocation—Discontinued Operations)** Geoff Corp.'s operations in 2014 had mixed results. One division, Vincent Group, again failed to earn income at a rate that was high enough to justify its continued operation, and management therefore decided to close the division. Vincent Group earned revenue of $118,000 during 2014 and recognized total expenses of $110,500. The remaining two divisions reported revenues of $273,000 and total expenses of $216,000 in 2014.

In preparing the annual income tax return, Geoff Corp.'s controller took into account the following information:

1. The CCA exceeded depreciation expense by $3,700. There were no depreciable assets in the Vincent Group division.

2. Included in Vincent's expenses is an accrued litigation loss of $5,100 that is not deductible for tax purposes until 2015.

3. Included in the continuing divisions' expenses are the president's golf club dues of $4,500, and included in their revenues are $1,700 of dividends from taxable Canadian corporations.

4. There were no deferred tax account balances for any of the divisions on January 1, 2014.

5. The tax rate for 2014 and future years is 35%.

6. Geoff Corp. reports under IFRS.

Instructions

(a) Calculate the taxable income and income tax payable by Geoff Corp. in 2014 and the deferred tax asset or liability balances at December 31, 2014.

(b) Prepare the journal entry(ies) to record income tax for 2014.

(c) Indicate how income taxes will be reported on the income statement for 2014 by preparing the bottom portion of the statement, beginning with "Income before income tax and discontinued operations." Assume that 10,000 common shares were outstanding throughout 2014.

(d) Provide the statement of financial position presentation for any resulting deferred tax accounts at December 31, 2014. Be specific about the classification.

(e) How would your response to (d) change if Geoff Corp. followed the ASPE future/deferred income taxes method?

(LO 10, 11) **E18-29 (Taxes Payable Method)** Refer to the information in E18-9 for Raman Limited. Assume that the company reports under ASPE and that the taxes payable method of accounting is used for income tax.

Instructions

(a) Prepare the journal entry(ies) to record income tax at December 31, 2014.

(b) Prepare the income statement for 2014, beginning with the line "Income before income tax."

(c) Provide the statement of financial position presentation for any resulting income tax accounts at December 31, 2014.

(d) Prepare the disclosures that are necessary because the taxes payable method is being used.

(e) Now that Raman Limited has adopted the taxes payable method, how do you think the creditors to this accounting policy would react when they read Raman's financial statements? Explain.

(LO 10, 11) **E18-30 (Taxes Payable Method)** Refer to the information in E18-13 for Melissa Inc. Assume that the company follows the taxes payable method of accounting for income taxes under ASPE. During the year, Melissa Inc. made tax instalment payments of $42,000.

Instructions

(a) Calculate taxable income and income tax expense for the year ended December 31, 2014.

(b) Prepare the journal entry(ies) to record income taxes at December 31, 2014.

(c) Prepare the income statement for 2014, beginning with the line "Income before income tax."

(d) Provide the balance sheet presentation for any resulting income tax accounts at December 31, 2014.

Digging Deeper

(LO 10, 11)   **E18-31   (Taxes Payable Method)** As the new accountant for Carly's Pet Express Inc., a line of pet boutiques, you are developing the financial statement disclosures for the 2014 financial statement note on income taxes. The company uses ASPE, and has selected the taxes payable method. The statutory tax rate is currently 28%. During 2014, net income before tax was $185,000. CCA exceeded depreciation expense by $25,000. The only permanent difference was the non-deductible portion of meals and entertainment costs, which was 50% of $20,000.

Instructions

(a) Determine the income tax expense to be recorded using the taxes payable method and record the necessary journal entry.

(b) Prepare the reconciliation of actual tax rate to the statutory rate as required for inclusion in the financial statement note on income taxes.

Problems

P18-1 Anthony Ltd. began business on January 1, 2013. At December 31, 2013, it had a $6,000 balance in the deferred tax liability account that pertains to property, plant, and equipment previously acquired at a cost of $1.2 million. The property, plant, and equipment is being depreciated on a straight-line basis over six years for financial reporting purposes, and is a Class 8—20% asset for tax purposes. Depreciation expense for financial reporting purposes was $100,000 for 2013. Anthony's income before income tax for 2014 was $80,000. Anthony Ltd. follows the ASPE future/deferred income taxes method.

The following items caused the only differences between accounting income before income tax and taxable income in 2014.

1. In 2014, the company paid $75,000 for rent; of this amount, $25,000 was expensed in 2014. The other $50,000 will be expensed equally over the 2015 and 2016 accounting periods. The full $75,000 was deducted for tax purposes in 2014.

2. Anthony Ltd. pays $12,000 a year for a membership in a local golf club for the company's president.

3. Anthony Ltd. now offers a one-year warranty on all its merchandise sold. Warranty expenses for 2014 were $12,000. Cash payments in 2014 for warranty repairs were $6,000.

4. Meals and entertainment expenses (only 50% of which are ever tax deductible) were $16,000 for 2014.

5. Depreciation expense was $200,000 and CCA was $216,000 for 2014. No new assets were acquired in the year, and there were no asset disposals.

Income tax rates have not changed over the past five years.

Instructions

(a) Calculate the balance in the Deferred Tax Asset or Liability account at December 31, 2014.

(b) Calculate income tax payable for 2014.

(c) Prepare the journal entries to record income taxes for 2014.

(d) Prepare the income tax expense section of the income statement for 2014, beginning with the line "Income before income tax."

(e) Indicate how deferred taxes should be presented on the December 31, 2014 balance sheet.

(f) How would your response to parts (a) to (e) change if Anthony reported under IFRS?

P18-2 At December 31, 2013, Chloe Corporation had a temporary difference (related to pensions) and reported a related deferred tax asset of $30,000 on its balance sheet. At December 31, 2014, Chloe has five temporary differences. An analysis reveals the following:

Temporary Difference	Future (Taxable) Deductible Amounts		
	2015	2016	2017
1. Pension liability: expensed as incurred on the books; deductible when funded for tax purposes	$30,000	$ 20,000	$ 10,000
2. Royalties collected in advance: recognized when earned for accounting purposes and when received for tax purposes	76,000	—	—
3. Accrued liabilities: various expenses accrued for accounting purposes and recognized for tax purposes when paid	24,000	—	—

Temporary Difference	Future (Taxable) Deductible Amounts		
	2015	2016	2017
4. Deferred gross profit: profits recognized on instalment sales when sold for book purposes, and as collected for tax purposes	(36,000)	(36,000)	(36,000)
5. Equipment: straight-line depreciation for accounting purposes, and CCA for tax purposes	(90,000)	(50,000)	(40,000)
	$ 4,000	$ (66,000)	$ (66,000)

The enacted tax rate has been 30% for many years. In November 2014, the rate was changed to 28% for all periods after January 1, 2016. Assume that the company has income tax due of $180,000 on the 2014 tax return and that Chloe follows the ASPE future/deferred income taxes method.

Instructions

(a) Indicate how deferred taxes should be presented on Chloe Corporation's December 31, 2014 balance sheet.

(b) How would your response to part (a) change if Chloe reported under IFRS?

(c) Calculate taxable income for 2014.

(d) Calculate accounting income for 2014.

(e) Draft the income tax section of the 2014 income statement, beginning with the line "Income before income tax." Provide as much information as possible about the components of income tax expense.

P18-3 Eloisa Corporation applies IFRS. Information about Eloisa Corporation's income before income tax of $63,000 for its year ended December 31, 2014, includes the following:

1. CCA reported on the 2014 tax return exceeded depreciation reported on the income statement by $100,000. This difference, plus the $150,000 accumulated taxable temporary difference at January 1, 2014, is expected to reverse in equal amounts over the four-year period from 2015 to 2018.

2. Dividends received from taxable Canadian corporations were $15,000.

3. Rent collected in advance and included in taxable income as at December 31, 2013, totalled $60,000 for a three-year period. Of this amount, $40,000 was reported as unearned for book purposes at December 31, 2014. Eloisa reports unearned revenue as a current liability if it will be recognized in income within 12 months from the balance sheet date. Eloisa paid a $2,880 interest penalty for late income tax instalments. The interest penalty is not deductible for income tax purposes at any time.

4. Equipment was disposed of during the year for $90,000. The equipment had a cost of $105,000 and accumulated depreciation to the date of disposal of $37,000. The total proceeds on the sale of these assets reduced the CCA class; in other words, no gain or loss is reported for tax purposes.

5. Eloisa recognized a $75,000 loss on impairment of a long-term investment whose value was considered impaired. The Income Tax Act only permits the loss to be deducted when the investment is sold and the loss is actually realized. The investment was accounted for at amortized cost.

6. The tax rates are 30% for 2014, and 25% for 2015 and subsequent years. These rates have been enacted and known for the past two years.

Instructions

(a) Calculate the balance in the Deferred Tax Asset or Liability account at December 31, 2013.

(b) Calculate the balance in the Deferred Tax Asset or Liability account at December 31, 2014.

(c) Prepare the journal entries to record income taxes for 2014.

(d) Indicate how the Deferred Tax Asset or Liability account(s) will be reported on the comparative statements of financial position for 2013 and 2014.

(e) Prepare the income tax expense section of the income statement for 2014, beginning with "Income before income tax."

(f) Calculate the effective rate of tax. Provide a reconciliation and explanation of why this differs from the statutory rate of 30%. Begin the reconciliation with the statutory rate.

(g) How would your response to parts (a) to (f) change if Eloisa reported under ASPE?

P18-4 The accounting income of Stephani Corporation and its taxable income for the years 2014 to 2017 are as follows:

Year	Accounting Income	Taxable Income	Tax Rate
2014	$460,000	$299,000	25%
2015	420,000	294,000	30%
2016	390,000	304,200	30%
2017	460,000	644,000	30%

The change in the tax rate from 25% to 30% was not enacted until early in 2015.

Accounting income for each year includes an expense of $40,000 that will never be deductible for tax purposes. The remainder of the difference between accounting income and taxable income in each period is due to one reversing difference for the depreciation of property, plant, and equipment. No deferred taxes existed at the beginning of 2014.

Instructions

(a) Calculate the current and deferred tax expense or benefit for each of the four years. Also calculate the balance of the deferred tax balance sheet account at the end of each fiscal year from 2014 to 2017.

(b) Prepare journal entries to record income taxes in all four years.

(c) Prepare the bottom of the income statement for 2015, beginning with the line "Income before income tax."

P18-5 Jordan Corporation reports under IFRS. The following information applies to Jordan Corporation.

1. Prior to 2013, taxable income and accounting income were identical.

2. Accounting income was $1.7 million in 2013 and $1.4 million in 2014.

3. On January 1, 2013, equipment costing $1 million was purchased. It is being depreciated on a straight-line basis over eight years for financial reporting purposes, and is a Class 8—20% asset for tax purposes.

4. Tax-exempt interest income of $60,000 was received in 2014.

5. The tax rate is 35% for all periods.

6. Taxable income is expected in all future years.

7. Jordan Corporation had 100,000 common shares outstanding throughout 2014.

Instructions

(a) Calculate the amount of capital cost allowance and depreciation expense for 2013 and 2014, and the corresponding carrying amount and undepreciated capital cost of the depreciable assets at the end of 2013 and 2014.

(b) Determine the amount of current and deferred tax expense for 2014.

(c) Prepare the journal entry(ies) to record 2014 income taxes.

(d) Prepare the bottom portion of Jordan's 2014 income statement, beginning with the line "Income before income tax."

(e) Indicate how deferred taxes should be presented on the December 31, 2014 statement of financial position.

(f) How would your responses to parts (a) to (e) change if Jordan Corporation followed the ASPE future/deferred income taxes method?

P18-6 The accounting records of Steven Corp., a real estate developer, indicated income before income tax of $850,000 for its year ended December 31, 2014, and of $525,000 for the year ended December 31, 2015. The following data are also available.

1. Steven Corp. pays an annual life insurance premium of $11,000 covering the top management team. The company is the named beneficiary.

2. The carrying amount of the company's property, plant, and equipment at January 1, 2014, was $1,256,000, and the UCC at that date was $998,000. Steven recorded depreciation expense of $175,000 and $180,000 in 2014 and 2015, respectively. CCA for tax purposes was $192,000 and $163,500 for 2014 and 2015, respectively. There were no asset additions or disposals over the two-year period.

3. Steven deducted $211,000 as a restructuring charge in determining income for 2013. At December 31, 2013, an accrued liability of $199,500 remained outstanding relative to the restructuring, which was expected to be completed in the next fiscal year. This expense is deductible for tax purposes, but only as the actual costs are incurred and paid for. The actual restructuring of operations took place in 2014 and 2015, with the liability reduced to $68,000 at the end of 2014 and $0 at the end of 2015.

4. In 2014, property held for development was sold and a profit of $52,000 was recognized in income. Because the sale was made with delayed payment terms, the profit is taxable only as Steven receives payments from the purchaser. A 10% down payment was received in 2014, with the remaining 90% expected in equal amounts over the following three years.

5. Non-taxable dividends of $3,250 in 2014 and of $3,500 in 2015 were received from taxable Canadian corporations.

6. In addition to the income before income tax identified above, Steven reported a before-tax gain on discontinued operations of $18,800 in 2014.

7. A 30% rate of tax has been in effect since 2012.

Steven Corp. follows the ASPE future/deferred income taxes method.

Instructions

(a) Determine the balance of any deferred tax asset or liability accounts at December 31, 2013, 2014, and 2015.

(b) Determine 2014 and 2015 taxable income and current tax expense.

(c) Prepare the journal entries to record current and deferred tax expense for 2014 and 2015.

(d) Identify how the deferred tax asset or liability account(s) will be reported on the December 31, 2014 and 2015 balance sheets.

(e) Prepare partial income statements for the years ended December 31, 2014 and 2015, beginning with the line "Income from continuing operations before income tax."

(f) How would your response to parts (a) to (e) change if Steven Corp. reported under IFRS?

P18-7 Andrew Weiman and Mei Lee are discussing accounting for income taxes. They are currently studying a schedule of taxable and deductible amounts that will arise in the future as a result of existing temporary differences. The schedule applies to a company that reports under the ASPE future/deferred income taxes method. The schedule is as follows:

	Current Year		Future Years			
	2014	2015	2016	2017	2018	
Taxable income	$50,000					
Taxable amounts		$75,000	$75,000	$ 75,000	$75,000	
Deductible amounts				(2,400,000)		
Enacted tax rate	30%	28%	26%	24%	24%	

Instructions

(a) Explain the concept of future taxable amounts and future deductible amounts as shown in the schedule.

(b) Determine the balance of the deferred tax asset and deferred tax liability accounts on the December 31, 2014 balance sheet. Assuming all temporary differences originated in 2014, prepare the journal entry to recognize income tax expense for 2014.

(c) Assume that this company is not expected to perform well in the future due to a sluggish economy and in-house management problems. Identify any concerns you may have about reporting the deferred tax asset/liability account as calculated.

(d) Company management determines that it is unlikely that the company will be able to benefit from all of the future deductible amounts. Early in 2015, after the entries in part (b) have been made, but before the financial statements have been finalized and released, management estimates that $2.0 million of the $2.4 million in future deductible amounts will not be used, and that the remaining amount will be deductible in 2017. Prepare the entry that is required to recognize this, assuming the company uses a valuation allowance to adjust the deferred tax asset account.

(e) When finalizing the 2015 financial statements, management estimates that, due to the prospects for an economic recovery, it is now more likely than not that the company will benefit from a total of $2.1 million of the future deductible amounts: $600,000 in 2017 and $1.5 million in 2018. Prepare the journal entry that is required, if any, to adjust the allowance account at December 31, 2015.

(f) Indicate how the deferred tax accounts will be reported on the December 31, 2014 and 2015 balance sheets after taking into account the information in parts (d) and (e) above. Explain how these would differ, if at all, if the company did not use a valuation allowance account.

(g) How would your responses to part (f) change if the company followed IFRS?

P18-8 Sarah Corp. reported the following differences between statement of financial position carrying amounts and tax bases at December 31, 2013:

	Carrying Amount	Tax Base
Depreciable assets	$125,000	$93,000
Warranty liability (current liability)	18,500	-0-
Pension liability (long-term liability)	34,600	-0-

The differences between the carrying amounts and tax bases were expected to reverse as follows:

	2014	2015	After 2015
Depreciable assets	$17,500	$12,500	$ 2,000
Warranty liability	18,500	-0-	-0-
Accrued pension liability	11,000	11,000	12,600

Tax rates enacted at December 31, 2013, were 31% for 2013, 30% for 2014, 29% for 2015, and 28% for 2016 and later years.

During 2014, Sarah Corp. made four quarterly tax instalment payments of $8,000 each and reported income before income tax on its income statement of $109,400. Included in this amount were dividends from taxable Canadian corporations of $4,300 (non–taxable income) and $20,000 of expenses related to the executive team's golf dues (non–tax-deductible expenses). There were no changes to the enacted tax rates during the year.

As expected, book depreciation in 2014 exceeded the capital cost allowance claimed for tax purposes by $17,500, and there were no additions or disposals of property, plant, and equipment during the year. A review of the 2014 activity in the warranty liability account in the ledger indicated the following:

Balance, Dec. 31, 2013	$18,500
Payments on 2013 product warranties	(18,900)
Payments on 2014 product warranties	(5,600)
2014 warranty accrual	28,300
Balance, Dec. 31, 2014	$22,300

All warranties are valid for one year only. The Pension Liability account reported the following activity:

Balance, Dec. 31, 2013	$34,600
Payment to pension trustee	(70,000)
2014 pension expense	59,000
Balance, Dec. 31, 2014	$23,600

Pension expenses are deductible for tax purposes, but only as they are paid to the trustee, not as they are accrued for financial reporting purposes.

Sarah Corp. reports under IFRS.

Instructions

(a) Calculate the deferred tax asset or liability account at December 31, 2013, and explain how it should be reported on the December 31, 2013 statement of financial position.

(b) Calculate the deferred tax asset or liability account at December 31, 2014.

(c) Prepare all income tax entries for Sarah Corp. for 2014.

(d) Identify the balances of all income tax accounts at December 31, 2014, and show how they will be reported on the comparative statements of financial position at December 31, 2014, and 2013, and on the income statement for the year ended December 31, 2014.

(e) How would your responses to parts (a) and (d) change if Sarah Corp. followed the ASPE future/deferred income taxes method?

P18-9 The following are two independent situations related to future taxable and deductible amounts that resulted from temporary differences at December 31, 2014. In both situations, the future taxable amounts relate to property, plant, and equipment depreciation, and the future deductible amounts relate to settlements of litigation that were previously accrued in the accounts.

1. Alia Corp. has developed the following schedule of future taxable and deductible amounts:

	2015	2016	2017	2018	2019
Deductible amounts	$300	$300	$300	$ 200	$100
Taxable amounts	0	0	0	(1,800)	0

Alia reported a net deferred tax liability of $500 at January 1, 2014.

2. Khoi Corp. has the following schedule of future taxable and deductible amounts:

	2015	2016	2017	2018
Taxable amounts	$400	$400	$ 400	$400
Deductible amounts	0	0	(3,000)	0

Khoi Corp. reported a net deferred tax asset of $600 at January 1, 2014.

Both Alia Corp. and Khoi Corp. have taxable income of $4,000 in 2014 and expect to have taxable income in all future years. The tax rates enacted as of the beginning of 2014 are 30% for 2014 to 2017, and 35% for 2018 and subsequent years. All of the underlying temporary differences relate to non-current assets and liabilities. Both Khoi and Alia report under IFRS.

Instructions

(a) Determine the deferred tax assets or liabilities that will be reported on each company's December 31, 2014 statement of financial position.

(b) For each of these two situations, prepare journal entries to record income taxes for 2014. Show all calculations.

(c) Provide the presentation of deferred tax accounts on each company's December 31, 2014 statement of financial position, including their correct classification.

(d) How would your response to part (c) change if Khoi and Alia followed the ASPE future/deferred income taxes method?

P18-10 The following information was disclosed during the audit of Shawna Inc.:

Year	Amount Due per Tax Return
2014	$105,000
2015	84,000

1. On January 1, 2014, equipment was purchased for $400,000. For financial reporting purposes, the company uses straight-line depreciation over a five-year life, with no residual value. For tax purposes, the CCA rate is 25%.

2. In January 2015, $225,000 was collected in advance for the rental of a building for the next three years. The entire $225,000 is reported as taxable income in 2015, but $150,000 of the $225,000 is reported as unearned revenue on the December 31, 2015 statement of financial position. The $150,000 of unearned revenue will be earned equally in 2016 and 2017.

3. The tax rate is 30% in 2014 and all subsequent periods.

4. No temporary differences existed at the end of 2013. Shawna expects to report taxable income in each of the next five years. Its fiscal year ends December 31.

Shawna Inc. follows IFRS.

Instructions

(a) Calculate the amount of capital cost allowance and depreciation expense for 2014 and 2015, and the corresponding carrying amount and undepreciated capital cost of the depreciable assets at December 31, 2014, and 2015.

(b) Determine the balance of the deferred tax asset or liability account at December 31, 2014, and indicate the account's classification on the statement of financial position.

(c) Prepare the journal entry(ies) to record income taxes for 2014.

(d) Draft the bottom of the income statement for 2014, beginning with "Income before income tax."

(e) Determine the balance of the deferred tax asset or liability account at December 31, 2015, and indicate the account's classification on the December 31, 2015 statement of financial position.

(f) Prepare the journal entry(ies) to record income taxes for 2015.

(g) Prepare the bottom of the income statement for 2015, beginning with "Income before income tax."

(h) Provide the comparative statement of financial position presentation for the deferred tax accounts at December 31, 2014, and 2015. Be specific about the classification.

(i) Is it possible to have more than two accounts for deferred taxes reported on a statement of financial position? Explain.

(j) How would your response to part (h) change if Shawna Inc. reported under the ASPE future/deferred income taxes method?

P18-11 The following information relates to Pearline Corporation's transactions during 2014, its first year of operations.

1. Income before income tax on the income statement for 2014 was $110,000.

2. In addition, Pearline reported a loss due to the writedown of land of $46,000 for financial reporting purposes.

3. Pearline reported a tax-deductible financing charge of $5,700 on its 2014 statement of retained earnings. The charge is for interest on a financial instrument that is legally debt, but in substance is equity for financial reporting purposes.

4. The tax rate enacted for 2014 and future years is 30%. Since this was Pearline Corporation's first taxation year, no instalments on account of income taxes were required or paid by Pearline.

5. Differences between the 2014 GAAP amounts and their treatment for tax purposes were as follows:

   (a) Warranty expense accrued for financial reporting purposes amounted to $15,000. Warranty payments deducted for taxes amounted to $12,000. Warranty liabilities were classified as current on the balance sheet.

   (b) Of the loss on writedown of land of $46,000, 25% will never be tax deductible. The remaining 75% will be deductible for tax purposes evenly over the years from 2015 to 2017. The loss relates to the loss in value of company land due to contamination.

   (c) Gross profit on construction contracts using the percentage-of-completion method for book purposes amounted to $30,000. For tax purposes, gross profit on construction contracts amounted to $0 as the completed-contract method is used and no contracts were completed during the year. Construction costs amounted to $270,000 during the year.

   (d) Depreciation of property, plant, and equipment for financial reporting purposes amounted to $60,000. CCA charged on the tax return amounted to $80,000. The related property, plant, and equipment cost $300,000 when it was acquired early in 2014.

   (e) A $3,500 fine paid for a violation of pollution laws was deducted in calculating accounting income.

   (f) Dividend revenue earned on an investment was tax exempt and amounted to $1,400.

6. Taxable income is expected for the next few years.

Pearline Corporation follows the ASPE future/deferred income taxes method.

Instructions

(a) Calculate Pearline Corporation's deferred tax asset or liability at December 31, 2014.

(b) Calculate the taxable income for 2014. Show all details of the adjustments to accounting income to arrive at taxable income.

(c) Prepare the journal entry(ies) to record income taxes for 2014.

(d) Prepare a partial 2014 income statement, beginning with "Income before income tax."

(e) Prepare a statement of retained earnings for the year ended December 31, 2014, assuming no dividends were declared in the year.

(f) Show how the balance of all the tax asset or liability accounts will be reported on the December 31, 2014 balance sheet.

(g) Calculate the effective rate of tax. Provide a reconciliation and explanation of why this differs from the statutory rate of 30%. Begin the reconciliation with the statutory rate.

(h) How would your response to part (f) change if Pearline Corporation followed IFRS?

P18-12 Carly Inc. reported the following accounting income (loss) and related tax rates during the years 2009 to 2015:

Year	Accounting Income (Loss)	Tax Rate
2009	$ 70,000	20%
2010	25,000	20%
2011	60,000	20%
2012	80,000	30%
2013	(210,000)	35%
2014	70,000	30%
2015	90,000	25%

Accounting income (loss) and taxable income (loss) were the same for all years since Carly began business. The tax rates from 2012 to 2015 were enacted in 2012.

Instructions

(a) Prepare the journal entries to record income taxes for the years 2013 to 2015. Assume that Carly uses the carryback provision where possible and expects to realize the benefits of any loss carryforward in the year that immediately follows the loss year.

(b) Indicate the effect of the 2013 entry(ies) on the December 31, 2013 statement of financial position if Carly follows the ASPE future/deferred income taxes method. Indicate as well the effect on the statement of financial position if Carly reports under IFRS.

(c) Show how the bottom portion of the income statement would be reported in 2013, beginning with "Loss before income tax."

(d) Show how the bottom portion of the income statement would be reported in 2014, starting with "Income before income tax."

(e) Prepare the journal entries for the years 2013 to 2015 to record income taxes, assuming that Carly uses the carryback provision where possible but is uncertain if it will realize the benefits of any loss carryforward in the future. Carly does not use a valuation allowance.

(f) Assume now that Carly uses a valuation allowance account along with its deferred tax asset account. Identify which entries in part (e) would differ and prepare them.

(g) Based on your entries in part (e), indicate how the bottom portion of the income statements for 2013 and 2014 would be reported, beginning with "Income (loss) before income tax."

Digging
Deeper

(h) From a cash flow perspective, can you think of any advantage in using the valuation allowance for financial reporting purposes? Can you think of any advantages in not using it?

P18-13 Chen Corporation reported income before income tax for the year ended December 31, 2014, of $1,645,000. In preparing the 2014 financial statements, the accountant discovered an error that was made in 2013. The error was that a piece of land with a cost of $40,000 had been recognized as an operating expense in error. The balance reported as retained earnings at December 31, 2013, was $5,678,000, and the net book value of property, plant, and equipment (excluding land) was $1,352,000 at the same date. During 2014, Chen Corporation acquired additional equipment with a cost of $16,000.

In completing the corporate tax return for the 2014 year, the company controller noted that the 2014 depreciation expense was $365,000, CCA claimed was $300,000, and non-deductible income tax penalties and interest of $2,500 and golf club dues of $4,500 were incurred in the year. In addition, the accounting allowance for doubtful accounts exceeded the tax reserve for uncollectible amounts by $20,000, although they were equal at the beginning of the year. At the end of 2013, the company had temporary differences of $135,000, due to lower depreciation expense than CCA claimed on the corporate tax return. The resulting future taxable amounts and the dates they were expected to reverse at December 31, 2013, were:

2014	$ 65,000
2015	40,000
2016	30,000
	$135,000

The tax rate is 35% for all years. Chen Corporation applies ASPE and uses the future/deferred income taxes method of accounting.

Instructions

(a) Calculate the balance sheet deferred tax account balance at December 31, 2013.

(b) Determine the effect of the prior period error on the December 31, 2013 balance sheet and prepare the journal entry to correct the error. Assume that the 2013 income tax return is refiled.

(c) Prepare the journal entries to record income taxes for the 2014 year.

(d) Indicate how the income taxes will be reported on the financial statements for 2014 by preparing the bottom portion of the income statement beginning with "Income before income tax." Also prepare the Statement of Retained Earnings for the year ended December 31, 2014, assuming no dividends were declared during the year.

P18-14 Aaron Engines Ltd. operates small engine repair outlets and is a tenant in several of Tran Holdings Inc.'s strip shopping malls. Aaron signed several lease renewals with Tran that each called for a three-month rent-free period. The leases start at various dates and are for three to five years each. As with all of Tran's tenants, Aaron pays rent quarterly, three months in advance, and records the payments initially to Prepaid Rent.

The rent-free period obtained in the lease agreement with Tran Holdings Inc. reduces the overall rental costs of the outlets over the term of each lease. Aaron's accounting policy requires the leasing costs of each outlet to be allocated evenly over the term of the lease to fairly match expenses with revenues. Aaron accrues rent expense during the rent-free period to an account called Rent Payable. Following the rent-free period, the Rent Payable account is amortized to Rent Expense over the remaining term of the lease. For tax purposes, Aaron must use the cash basis and is unable to deduct the rent expense accrued during the rent-free periods. On its tax return, Aaron can only deduct the actual rent payments when they are made.

The balances for the accounts related to prepaid rent and rent payable under leases as well as payments for interest to earn tax-exempt income and payments for golf club dues for the years ending December 31, 2015 and 2014, follow:

	2015	2014
Prepaid Rent (assume current classification and no balance at Dec. 31, 2013)	$ 92,000	$ 89,000
Rent Payable (assume non-current classification and no balance at Dec. 31, 2013)	133,000	146,000
Golf Dues Expense	11,000	13,000
Interest Expense (incurred to earn tax-exempt income)	6,000	4,000

In 2014, Aaron's tax rate is 28%, and for subsequent years it is 27%. Income before income tax for the year ended December 31, 2014, was $884,000. During 2015, Aaron's tax rate changed to 29% for 2015 and subsequent years. Income before income tax for the year ended December 31, 2015, was $997,000. Assume that Aaron Engines Ltd. applies ASPE.

Instructions

(a) Calculate the deferred tax asset or liability balances at December 31, 2014, and 2015.

(b) Calculate taxable income and income tax payable for 2014 and 2015.

(c) Prepare the journal entries to record income taxes for 2014 and 2015.

(d) Prepare a comparative income statement for 2014 and 2015, beginning with the line "Income before income tax."

(e) Provide the comparative balance sheet presentation for any resulting deferred tax accounts at December 31, 2014, and 2015. Be specific about the classification.

(f) Calculate the effective rate of tax for 2015. Provide a reconciliation and explanation of why this differs from the statutory rate of 29%. Begin the reconciliation with the statutory rate.

(g) How would your responses to parts (a) to (f) change if Aaron applied IFRS instead of ASPE?

P18-15 On December 31, 2013, Quirk Inc. has taxable temporary differences of $2.2 million and a deferred tax liability of $616,000. These temporary differences are due to Quirk having claimed CCA in excess of book depreciation in prior years. Quirk's year end is December 31. At the end of December 2014, Quirk's substantially enacted tax rate for 2014 and future years was changed to 30%.

For the year ended December 31, 2014, Quirk's accounting loss before tax was ($494,000). The following data are also available.

1. Pension expense was $87,000 while pension plan contributions were $111,000 for the year (only actual pension contributions are deductible for tax).

2. Business meals and entertainment were $38,000 (one-half deductible for tax purposes).

3. For the three years ending December 31, 2013, Quirk had cumulative, total taxable income of $123,000 and total income tax expense/income tax payable of $51,660.

4. During 2014, the company booked estimated warranty costs of $31,000 and these costs are not likely to be incurred until 2018.

5. In 2014, the company incurred $150,000 of development costs (only 50% of which are deductible for tax purposes).

6. Company management has determined that it is probable that only one half of any loss carryforward at the end of 2014 will be realized.

7. In 2014, the amount claimed for depreciation was equal to the amount claimed for CCA.

Instructions

Prepare the journal entries to record income taxes for the year ended December 31, 2014, and the income tax reconciliation note.

Case

Refer to the Case Primer on the Student Website and in *WileyPLUS* to help you answer this case.

CA18-1 Baker Company Limited (BCL) was founded in 2012 and its first year of operations turned out to be a good one, as start-up years go, since the company not only broke even but actually showed a very small profit. Just as the company was getting established in the market, however, a full-fledged recession hit in 2013 and had devastating effects. Demand for BCL's products in retail markets declined as consumers tightened their purse strings. Through tight cost controls, however, BCL managed to hold its own and still recorded a small profit in 2013.

While the recession finally petered out by the end of 2014, BCL did end up feeling its effects, as the company was unable to remain profitable and suffered large operating losses that year. In fact, the losses were significantly greater than the profits that were reported in the previous two years. Despite this change, BCL management was not overly alarmed by the losses and had the following comments to make.

The losses were expected given the widespread recession. Since the bulk of our sales are in retail markets, and with unemployment levels being at record highs, it is not surprising that consumer demand has fallen off. If BCL is compared with the industry, you will see that we did much better than our competitors, some of whom went bankrupt.

Keep in mind that we are a relatively new company and managed to record a profit in two out of our first three years. We attribute this to our strong management team and our ability as a streamlined company to react to the recession with cost control measures and an aggressive, yet flexible sales staff.

We see ourselves positioned for a new growth spurt given that the economy seems to have recovered and a lot of "dead wood" (competition) has been cleared out. As a matter of fact, in that regard, the recession will have a positive impact on our short- to mid-term growth potential.

BCL is on the verge of introducing two new products that will revolutionize the industry and assure us a solid earnings base for the future. These products will be introduced in 2015 and we have already lined up sufficient buyers such that we predict we will at least break even in terms of net income in 2015. This is a very conservative forecast.

Although the effects of the recession were lessening, unemployment was still high in early 2015 and consumer spending had not increased significantly. Some economists were predicting that it would take two or three years for consumer confidence and spending to pick up to pre-recession levels.

Instructions

Adopt the role of the company's auditor and determine whether BCL should recognize the benefits of the losses suffered in the 2014 financial statements. Assume BCL is a private company. Note any differences between IFRS and ASPE.

Integrated Case

IC18-1 Cauchy Inc. (CI) has just had a planning meeting with its auditors. There were several concerns that had been raised during the meeting regarding the draft financial statements for the December 31, 2014 year end. CI is a public company whose shares list on the TSX. It has recently gone through a major expansion and, as a result, there are several financial reporting decisions that need to be made for the upcoming year-end financial statements. The expansion has been financed in the short term with a line of credit from the bank; however, the company plans to raise capital in the equity markets in the new year. It is hoped that the expansion will increase profitability, although it is too early to tell. Just before year end, the company purchased a number of investments as follows:

- 20% of the common shares of KL Corp. CI was able to appoint one member to KL's board of directors (which has four members in total). CI is unsure as to whether it will hold on to this investment for the longer term or sell it if the share price increases. The company has currently set a benchmark that if the share price increases by more than 25%, it will liquidate the investment. KL has been profitable over the past few years and the share price is on an upward trend. The original reason for entering into this transaction was to create a strategic alliance with KL that will help ensure a steady supply of high-quality raw materials from KL to CI.

- Corporate bonds. These bonds are five-year bonds that bear interest at 5% (which is in excess of market interest rates). As a result, the company paid a premium for the bonds. The bonds are convertible to common shares of the company. It is CI's intent to hold on to these bonds to maturity, although if there were an unforeseen cash crunch, it might have to cash them in earlier.

The company completed a significant sale to a new U.S. customer on credit on December 31, 2014. Under the terms of the agreement, CI will provide services to the customer over a one-year period. The sales agreement includes a non-refundable upfront fee for a significant amount, which the company has recognized as revenue. As part of the deal, CI will provide access to significant proprietary information (which it has already done) and then provide ongoing analysis and monitoring functions as a service to the customer. It is not specified in the contract whether the rights to the proprietary information are transferable but CI is taking the position that they are. The proprietary information is of no value as a separate item if not transferable. During the year, CI renewed service contracts for some of its other major customers under similar deals.

The receivable for this large sale is in U.S. dollars. Half of this has been hedged using a forward contract to sell U.S. dollars at a fixed rate. The other half is hedged through a natural hedge since the company has some U.S. dollar payables. The auditor has asked that the company prepare some notes analyzing the need for hedge accounting for this transaction and explaining the risks associated with the sales transaction and hedge transactions.

This has been a bad year for the company due to one-time charges on a lawsuit settlement, and currently the draft statements are showing a loss. The company's tax accountants have determined that the company will also have a loss for tax purposes.

Instructions

Assume the role of the controller and analyze the financial reporting issues.

Writing Assignments

WA18-1 The amount of income taxes that is due to the government for a period of time is rarely the same as the amount of income tax expense that is reported on the income statement for that same period under IFRS and one of the alternatives under ASPE.

Instructions

(a) Explain the objectives of accounting for income taxes in general purpose financial statements.

(b) Explain the basic principles that are applied in accounting for income taxes at the date of the financial statements to meet the objectives discussed in part (a).

(c) Explain how the recognition of deferred tax accounts on the balance sheet is consistent with the conceptual framework, noting the differences between IFRS and ASPE.

(d) Using the definition of an asset and a liability (from Chapter 2), discuss why deferred tax assets and deferred tax liabilities as currently measured and reported might not meet this definition.

WA18-2 The temporary difference approach for recording deferred taxes is an integral part of generally accepted accounting principles.

Instructions

(a) Indicate whether each of the following independent situations results in a timing (reversing) difference or a permanent difference in the year. Explain your answer. Be sure to note any differences between ASPE and IFRS.

1. Estimated warranty costs (covering a three-year warranty) are expensed for financial reporting purposes at the time of sale but deducted for income tax purposes when they are paid.

2. Equity investments have a quoted market value that is recorded at fair value through net income and is adjusted to their fair value at the balance sheet date.

3. The depreciation on equipment is different for book and income tax purposes because of different bases of carrying the asset, which was acquired in a trade-in. The different bases are a result of different rules that are used for book and tax purposes to calculate the cost of assets acquired in a trade-in.

4. A company properly uses the equity method to account for its 30% investment in another taxable Canadian corporation. The investee pays non-taxable dividends that are about 10% of its annual earnings.

5. Management determines that the net realizable value of the inventory is below cost, causing a writedown in the current year.

6. A company reports a contingent loss (ASPE) or provision (IFRS) that it expects will result from an ongoing lawsuit. The loss is not reported on the current year's tax return. Half the loss is a penalty it expects to be charged by the courts. This portion of the loss is not a tax-deductible expenditure, even when it is paid.

7. The company uses the revaluation model for reporting its land and buildings. Due to current economic conditions, the fair value of the properties declined and the writedown was recorded against the revaluation surplus reported in equity.

8. The company settles its retirement obligation on a drilling platform that is put out of service. The actual settlement was less than the amount accrued, and the company recognizes a gain on settlement in its accounting net income.

(b) Discuss the nature of any deferred tax accounts that result from the situations in part (a) above, including their possible classifications in the company's balance sheet. Indicate how these accounts should be reported. Note any differences between IFRS and the asset-liability method under ASPE.

WA18-3 The following are common items that are treated differently for financial reporting purposes than they are for tax purposes:

1. The excess amount of a charge to the accounting records (allowance method) over a charge to the tax return (direct writeoff method) for uncollectible receivables

2. The excess amount of accrued pension expense over the amount paid

3. The receipt of dividends from a taxable Canadian corporation that are treated as income for accounting purposes but are not subject to tax

4. Expenses incurred in obtaining tax-exempt income

5. A trademark that is acquired directly from the government and is capitalized and amortized over subsequent periods for accounting purposes and expensed for tax purposes

6. A prepaid advertising expense that is deferred for accounting purposes and deducted as an expense for tax purposes

7. Premiums paid on life insurance of officers (where the corporation is the beneficiary)

8. A penalty paid for filing a late tax return

9. Proceeds of life insurance policies on lives of officers

10. Restructuring costs that are recognized as an unusual item on the income statement and are not deductible until actual costs are incurred

11. Unrealized gains and losses that are recognized on investments recorded as FV-NI or FV-OCI and are not taxable or deductible until realized for tax purposes

12. Excess depletion for accounting purposes over the amount taken for tax purposes

13. The estimated gross profit on a long-term construction contract that is reported in the income statement, with some of the gross profit being deferred for tax purposes

Instructions

(a) Indicate for each item above if the situation is a permanent difference or a reversing difference resulting in a temporary difference.

(b) Indicate for each item above if the situation will usually create future taxable amounts resulting in a deferred tax liability or future deductible amounts resulting in a deferred tax asset, or whether it will have no future tax implications.

Ethics

WA18-4 Henrietta Aguirre, the ethical accountant, is the newly hired Director of Corporate Taxation for Mesa Incorporated, which is a publicly traded corporation. Aguirre's first job with Mesa was to review the company's accounting practices for deferred taxes. In doing her review, she noted differences between tax and book depreciation methods that permitted Mesa to recognize a sizable deferred tax liability on its balance sheet. As a result, Mesa did not have to report current tax expenses.

Aguirre also discovered that Mesa had an explicit policy of selling off plant and equipment assets before they reversed in the deferred tax liability account. This policy, together with the rapid expansion of Mesa's capital asset base, allowed Mesa to defer all income taxes payable for several years, at the same time as it reported positive earnings and an increasing EPS. Aguirre checked with the legal department and found the policy to be legal, but she is uncomfortable with the ethics of it.

Instructions

(a) Why would Mesa have an explicit policy of selling assets before they reversed in the deferred tax liability account?

(b) What are the ethical implications of Mesa's deferral of income taxes?

(c) Who could be harmed by Mesa's ability to defer income taxes payable for several years, despite positive earnings?

(d) In a situation such as this, what might be Aguirre's professional responsibilities as an ethical accountant in today's business world?

WA18-5   Under the temporary difference approach, the tax rates used for deferred tax calculations are those enacted at the balance sheet date, based on how the reversal will be treated for tax purposes.

Instructions

For each of the following situations, discuss the impact on deferred tax balances.

(a) At December 31, 2014, Golden Corporation has one temporary difference that will reverse and cause taxable amounts in 2015. In 2014, new tax legislation sets tax rates equal to 35% for 2014, 30% for 2015, and 24% for 2016 and the years thereafter.

Explain what circumstances would require Golden to calculate its deferred tax liability at the end of 2014 by multiplying the temporary difference by:

1. 35%

2. 30%

3. 24%

(b) Record Inc. uses the fair value method for reporting its investment properties. The company has an investment property with an original cost of $5 million and a tax carrying amount of $3.5 million due to cumulative capital cost allowance claimed to date of $1.5 million. This asset is increased to its fair value of $8 million for accounting purposes. No equivalent adjustment is made for tax purposes. The tax rate is 30% for normal business purposes. If the asset is sold for more than cost, the cumulative capital cost allowance of $1.5 million will be included in taxable income as recaptured depreciation, but sale proceeds in excess of cost will be taxable at 15%. Calculate the related deferred balance assuming:

1. The value of the asset will be recovered through its use.

2. The value of the asset will be recovered by selling the asset.

(c) Assume the same above for parts (a) and (b), but the company is now revaluing a tract of land and a building that are included in property, plant, and equipment. The change in revaluation has been reported in other comprehensive income. All numbers remain the same as discussed in parts (a) and (b) above. What differences in the tax impact, if any, would be required?

WA18-6   LGS Inc. is a private company. You have recently been hired as the CFO for the company and are currently finalizing the company year-end report for December 31, 2015. The company has an option to follow either IFRS or ASPE, and has not yet made the choice. Three situations have arisen affecting the company's reporting of income taxes. These situations are described below (assume that tax rates are 28%).

1. Shortly after you were hired, you found that a prior period adjustment had been made in 2014, and the deferred tax liability account was adjusted through retained earnings as part of this error correction. The difference between the accounting value and the tax value of the related asset is $1 million. Originally, the rate used to record the deferred tax liability was 25%. In 2015, the enacted tax rate on this difference is now 28% and therefore an adjustment must be made to the financial tax liability account.

2. The company has a building that has been recently appraised at a fair value of $10 million. Currently, the building's carrying value is $6.5 million and its original cost was $8 million. Accumulated capital cost allowance booked to date on the building is $2.3 million. (Ignore the one-time adjustments allowed to property, plant, and equipment for first-time adopters for IFRS or ASPE.)

3. LGS bought some equity investments during the year that are not publicly traded for a total cost of $340,000. The company purchased these as an investment to be sold in the near future. Currently, the shares have been valued at December 31, 2014, for $510,000. There were no dividends received on this investment during the year.

Instructions

For each of the situations described above, discuss the options for reporting the income tax implications under IFRS and ASPE.

WA18-7

Instructions

Write a brief essay highlighting the differences between IFRS and ASPE noted in this chapter, discussing the conceptual justification for each.

RESEARCH AND FINANCIAL ANALYSIS

RA18-1 Stora Enso Oyj

The complete financial statements of **Stora Enso Oyj** for the company's year ended December 31, 2011, are available at the company's website (www.storaenso.com). Refer to Stora Enso's financial statements and accompanying notes and answer the following questions.

Instructions

(a) Identify all income tax accounts reported on the December 31, 2011 statement of financial position. Explain clearly what each account represents.

(b) What are the temporary differences that existed at December 31, 2011, and resulted in the deferred taxes? Which of these differences might relate to the deferred tax assets and which ones to the deferred tax liabilities? Explain the reasons for your answers.

(c) Reconcile the opening balance to the closing balance for the deferred tax accounts for the year ended December 31, 2011. What are the major transactions causing the balance to change from January 1 to December 31?

(d) Does Stora Enso's management think it is probable that the benefits related to future deductible amounts will be realized? Explain. What are the gross amounts of the loss carryforwards that the company has available and what are the expiry dates for these losses?

(e) Has Stora Enso applied intraperiod tax allocation in 2011? Explain.

(f) How much income tax did Stora Enso pay in 2011? Where did you find this information?

(g) What was the effective tax rate for Stora Enso in 2011? In 2010? What were the major causes of the differences between the statutory and effective tax rates for 2011 and 2010? For each reason you give, indicate whether the effective rate was made higher or lower than the statutory rate.

RA18-2 Gildan Activewear Inc.

Gildan Activewear Inc. is a Canadian company that manufactures and sells activewear, socks, and underwear. Manufacturing is primarily done in Honduras and the Dominican Republic and sales are made worldwide.

Instructions

Through SEDAR (www.sedar.com) or Gildan's website (www.gildan.com), obtain a copy of the company's financial statements for its year ended September 30, 2012, and answer the following questions.

(a) Review the consolidated statements of earnings and comprehensive income for 2012 and 2011. What was the income tax expense for each year? Did the company apply intraperiod tax allocation in 2012 or 2011? Why or why not? How much does the company show as income taxes payable on the consolidated statements of financial position for the fiscal year ends 2012 and 2011? What was reported regarding cash flows of current income taxes in 2012 and 2011, and where did you find this information?

(b) What was the company's effective tax rate for 2012? For 2011? What was the statutory rate in each of these years? What caused the differences? Be specific about whether the effective rate was increased or decreased as a result of each cause that you identify. Note 20 will aid you.

(c) For each deferred tax account reported on the September 30, 2012 consolidated statement of financial position, explain what underlies the balance that is reported. For each temporary difference, identify the SFP asset or liability where the tax basis and book value differ.

(d) What are the losses that the company has available to carry forward? When do these losses expire? How has the company accounted for these losses? Note 20 will aid you.

RA18-3 Comparative Analysis

Real World Emphasis

Alimentation Couche-Tard Inc., Loblaw Companies Limited, and **Empire Company Limited** are three companies in the same industry. Because of this, the expectation is that their operations and financial positions are also similar.

Instructions

Go to SEDAR (www.sedar.com) or the companies' websites and, using Alimentation Couche-Tard's financial statements for the year ended April 29, 2012, Loblaw's financial statements for the year ended December 31, 2011, and Empire's financial statements for the year ended May 5, 2012, answer the following questions.

(a) Identify what industry all three companies are in.

(b) Identify all the areas where the three companies used intraperiod tax allocation. This requires a careful reading of some of the notes to the financial statements as well as the main statements themselves. Prepare a schedule of the total income tax provision (expense) or recovery (benefit) for each company, and identify where the provision or recovery was reported.

(c) Compare the three companies' deferred tax assets and/or deferred tax liabilities, and identify, as much as possible, what temporary differences are responsible for these accounts. Would you expect companies in the same industry to have similar types of temporary differences? Do they?

(d) Would you expect the three companies to be subject to similar income tax legislation and tax rates? Are their statutory rates the same? Explain. Compare the companies' statutory and effective rates and explain why there are differences, if any.

RA18-4 International Comparison

Real World Emphasis

Different countries have different statutory tax rates. Choose an industry and select five companies that operate in different countries. Access these companies' most recent financial statements and make note of their statutory and effective income tax rates.

Alternatively, use the railway industry and the following companies:

Canadian National Railway: Canada

Deutsche Bahn: Germany

East Japan Railway: Japan

NSB Group: Norway

National Railroad Passenger Corporation (Amtrak): United States

Instructions

Access the most recent reports for the five companies you chose. For each company, identify its year end, country of operation, statutory income tax rates, and effective tax rates. Discuss any similarities or differences found.

ENDNOTES

1 See J. Arnold, "Do Tax Structures Affect Aggregate Economic Growth?: Empirical Evidence from a Panel of OECD Countries," OECD Economics Department Working Papers, No. 643, OECD Publishing, 2008.

2 Canada Revenue Agency, www.cra-arc.gc.ca/tx/bsnss/tpcs/crprtns/rts-eng.html.

3 Proprietorships and partnerships do not pay income taxes as separate legal entities. Instead, their income is taxed as part of the proprietor's or partners' income as individuals. Prior to 2011, organizations that organized as income trusts also generally did not have their income taxed, because they distribute the income to their unitholders. Taxes that are owed on such distributions were obligations of the unitholders. The favourable tax treatment for most income trusts was phased out by 2011.

4 At the risk of oversimplification, it can be said that the Income Tax Act follows a principle of having the tax follow the cash flow. Although taxable income is based mainly on income reported under IFRS or ASPE, in cases where the timing of cash flows is significantly different from the timing of revenue recognition, revenues tend to be taxable as they are received in cash and expenses are allowed as deductions when they are paid.

5 Note that no one prepares a "tax" statement of financial position—it is just a concept. However, if there were one, the tax values that are referred to here are what would be on that statement of financial position, and they would be based on how the transaction is accounted for, for tax purposes. If the revenue is not yet recognized for tax purposes, there would be no receivable either. That is, the tax basis of the receivable is $0. Similarly, the tax value of the investments would be their original cost.

6 Where warranties are used as an example of a temporary/timing difference in this chapter, it is assumed that the company is following the expense warranty approach, and not accounting for the warranty as a separate performance obligation. This treatment is consistent with the the example provided in IAS 12.25. As discussed in Chapter 6, the accounting treatment for warranties is expected to be clarified as part of the IASB's new contract-based revenue recognition model.

7 See IAS 12.7.

8 CICA Handbook—Accounting, Part II, Section 3465.02(d) indicates that future income tax assets also include the income tax benefits that arise through the carryforward of unused tax losses and unused income tax reductions, excluding investment tax credits. IAS 12 Income Taxes, para 5, also states that deferred tax assets arise from the carryforward of unused tax losses and tax credits. These are discussed later in the chapter.

9 CICA Handbook—Accounting, Part II, Section 3465.51 to .54 and IAS 12 Income Taxes paras. 46 to 49. Copyright © IFRS Foundation. All rights reserved. Reproduced by Wiley Canada with the permission of the IFRS Foundation ®. No permission granted to third parties to reproduce or distribute.

Under ASPE, there must be persuasive evidence that the government is able and committed to enacting the proposed change in the foreseeable future in order to use a substantively enacted rate or tax law. This usually means that the legislation or regulation has to have been drafted in an appropriate form and tabled in Parliament, and the government will be able to pass the legislation. IFRS indicates that the announced tax rate or law can be used only when the government announcements of tax changes have the substantive effect of actual enactment.

10 ASPE indicates that it must be more likely than not that the company will be eligible for the reduced tax rate. Examples of tax incentives include the small business deduction, the manufacturing and processing profits deduction, and the scientific research and development credits.

11 The federal general corporate income tax rate has gradually dropped from 28% to 15% between 2001 and 2012. Federal budgets tabled after the time of writing could change these rates further, one way or the other.

12 The carryforward period has been increasing. The 2004 federal budget increased it from 7 years to 10, and the 2006 budget increased it again to 20 years. Note also that the references in this chapter to tax losses are limited to non-capital losses. Special rules apply to capital losses.

13 At one time, it was common practice when refiling prior years' returns to reduce the amount of CCA claimed, thus increasing the amount of taxable income in those prior years. The company could then absorb more of a current year tax loss. With the recent extensions of the carryforward period, now at 20 years, this option is now not commonly allowed.

14 When Sears Canada Inc. bought 19 Eaton's stores for $80 million, $20 million of the price was for approximately $175 million of tax losses accumulated by Eaton's. The $20 million could not be distributed until five years after Sears had benefited from it. This was because the Canada Revenue Agency could legally appeal the company's use of the losses. The $20 million was finally paid out in 2006.

[15] Examples of positive evidence that might support the recognition of a tax asset include a firm sales backlog that will produce more than enough taxable income to realize the deferred tax asset, or a history of strong earnings and evidence that the loss is due to a specific identifiable and non-recurring cause.

[16] Let's look at an example. Assume an entity reports a correction of a prior period error in retained earnings in Year 5. As a result, a deferred tax liability is recognized on the Year 5 statement of financial position and a deferred tax expense is netted against the retained earnings adjustment in the same year. In Year 6, the tax rate increases, also increasing the balance of the deferred tax liability recognized in Year 5. Under ASPE, the related deferred tax expense is reported on the Year 6 income statement. There is no backward tracing to the retained earnings statement. Under IFRS, the increased tax expense in Year 6 is reported in retained earnings. The IASB may change this requirement in the future to harmonize with the FASB approach, which is also similar to ASPE.

[17] R.P. Weber and J.E. Wheeler, in "Using Income Disclosures to Explore Significant Economic Transactions," *Accounting Horizons* (September 1992), discuss how deferred (future) tax disclosures can be used to assess the quality of earnings and to predict future cash flows.

[18] Alternatively, if more than one tax jurisdiction was involved or these were the consolidated financial statements of a number of taxable entities, IFRS requires that the deferred tax assets be reported separately from the deferred tax liabilities. In this case, the deferred tax liability of $148,000 relating to the deferred gross profit would be reported separately from the total of all the deferred tax assets of $106,200.

[19] If Allman Corporation classifies all warranty liabilities as current because the company defines the operating cycle as including the two-year warranty period, then the entire future tax asset related to the warranties would be reported as a current amount.

The information regarding Tim Hortons set forth herein are part of and/or may include: (i) excerpts from financial statements included in reports filed by Tim Hortons Inc. with the U.S. Securities and Exchange Commission (SEC) and the Canadian securities administrators that have been reproduced with permission but not endorsed or confirmed by Tim Hortons, and (ii) other data and information generated by third parties unaffiliated with Tim Hortons Inc. in connection with its financial results and/or other information. Accordingly, Tim Hortons Inc. makes no representation of warranty as to, and expressly disclaims responsibility regarding, the accuracy or completeness of any of the information related to Tim Hortons, or the inquiries, analysis or interpretation regarding any such information, that is described above and/or otherwise included herein. This information should not be relied upon for purposes of trading in the securities of Tim Hortons or otherwise. You may find current financial and other information prepared by Tim Hortons Inc. at its investor relations website at www.timehortons-invest.com, or as filed with the SEC and the Canadian securities administrators at www. sec.gov and www.sedar.com, respectively. Tim Hortons, Double Double and Timbits are trademarks of the TDL Marks Corporation. Used with permission.

Controlling Pension Costs

© istockphoto.com/Athony Seebaran

THE ROYAL BANK OF CANADA (RBC) recently joined the growing number of Canadian companies ending its defined benefit pension plan in an effort to control pension costs. As of January 1, 2012, all new full-time RBC employees are covered by a defined contribution pension plan after six months of service. Employees hired before that date will continue to be covered under the defined benefit pension plan.

Defined benefit pension plans, which guarantee a certain pension amount to employees upon retirement, are expensive to employers because they must cover any shortfalls in the value of investments held in the plans. Defined contribution pension plans, on the other hand, guarantee the employer will contribute a certain amount to employees' pensions, but there's no certainty how much money employees will receive in retirement.

To help compensate for the lack of certainty regarding benefits and remain a competitive employer, RBC increased its contributions to its defined contribution pension plan, including how much it will match employees' own contributions to the plan.

Retirees covered by RBC's defined benefit pension plan receive pension and other benefits—including health, dental, and life insurance—based on their years of service, contributions, and their final salary when they retire. Even though the company switched to a defined contribution plan for new employees, it is still responsible for paying benefits to retirees enrolled in the defined benefit plan.

The cost of defined benefit pension plans can vary widely over time. It depends on economic factors, such as interest rates, the value of the investments in the pension fund, and employees' salary upon retirement, and on demographic factors, such as retirees' life expectancy. RBC periodically calculates its benefit expenses and obligations using several factors, including the expected rate of return on assets in the pension funds, trends in health care costs, and projected salary increases. Its pension funds hold investments that are largely equity and fixed income securities, whose value can change quickly.

With more than 50,000 employees in Canada, RBC's pension costs are no small matter. The company contributed $283 million to its pension plans and $45 million to other post-employment benefit plans in 2011, while it expected to pay $457 million and $65 million into those plans, respectively, in 2012. A company spokesperson says the move to a defined contribution plan should stabilize pension costs in the long term.

Sources: Barbara Shecter, "RBC Ends Defined-Benefit Pensions for New Hires," *Financial Post,* September 23, 2011; Marowits Ross, The Canadian Press, "Royal Bank Moving to DC Pension Plan for New Hires," *Investment Executive,* September 25, 2011; RBC Annual Report, 2011.

Pensions and Other Employee Future Benefits

LEARNING OBJECTIVES

After studying this chapter, you should be able to:

1. Understand the importance of pensions from a business perspective.

2. Identify and account for a defined contribution benefit plan.

3. Identify and explain what a defined benefit plan is and the related accounting issues.

4. Explain what the employer's benefit obligation is, identify alternative measures for this obligation, and prepare a continuity schedule of transactions and events that change its balance.

5. Identify transactions and events that change benefit plan assets, and calculate the balance of the assets.

6. Explain what a benefit plan's funded status is, calculate it, and identify what transactions and events change its amount.

7. Identify the components of pension expense, and account for a defined benefit pension plan under the immediate recognition approach.

8. Account for defined benefit plans with benefits that vest or accumulate other than pension plans.

9. Identify the types of information required to be presented and disclosed for defined benefit plans, prepare basic schedules, and be able to read and understand such disclosures.

10. Identify differences between the IFRS and ASPE accounting for employee future benefits and what changes are expected in the near future.

After studying Appendix 19A, you should be able to:

11. Explain and apply basic calculations to determine current service cost, the defined benefit obligation, and past service cost for a one-person defined benefit pension plan.

After studying Appendix 19B, you should be able to:

12. Identify the components of pension benefit cost, and account for a defined benefit pension plan when using the deferral and amortization approach under ASPE; determine the pension plan accounts reported in the financial statements and explain their relationship to the funded status of the plan.

PREVIEW OF CHAPTER 19

Since employers are concerned about the well-being of their employees, organizations have established a variety of employee future benefit programs. For example, private pension and other post-retirement benefit plans are common in companies of all sizes. In early 2012, more than 6 million Canadian workers belonged to employer pension plans. Most of them, about 5 million, were members of plans whose assets were held in trusteed pension funds (which are governed by the provisions of a trust agreement). The remainder were in plans managed principally by insurance company contracts. The market value of the assets held in trusteed pension funds in Canada totalled $1.1 trillion at the end of the first quarter of 2012.[1]

A pension is part of an employee's overall compensation package. Post-retirement health care and other benefits are also often part of this package. The substantial growth of these plans, in terms of both how many employees are covered and the dollar amount of benefits, has made their costs very large in relation to many companies' financial position, results of operations, and cash flows. This is made clear in the opening story about the Royal Bank of Canada, but it is not alone in taking steps to reduce such costs. This chapter discusses the accounting issues related to these future benefits.

The chapter is organized as follows:

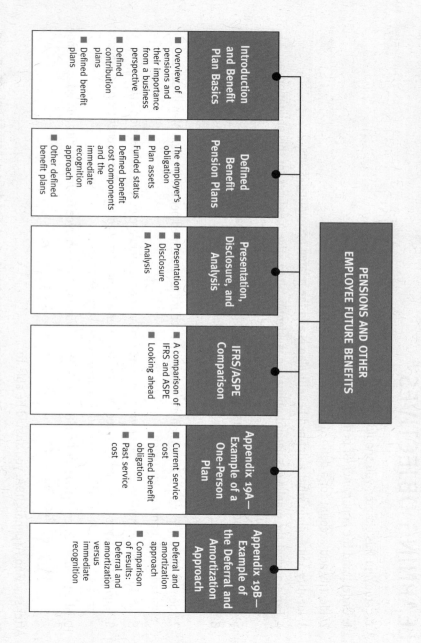

PENSIONS AND OTHER EMPLOYEE FUTURE BENEFITS

Introduction and Benefit Plan Basics
- Overview of pensions and their importance from a business perspective
- Defined contribution plans
- Defined benefit plans

Defined Benefit Pension Plans
- The employer's obligation
- Plan assets
- Funded status
- Defined benefit cost components and the immediate recognition approach
- Other defined benefit plans

Presentation, Disclosure, and Analysis
- Presentation
- Disclosure
- Analysis

IFRS/ASPE Comparison
- A comparison of IFRS and ASPE
- Looking ahead

Appendix 19A— Example of a One-Person Plan
- Current service cost
- Defined benefit obligation
- Past service cost

Appendix 19B— Example of the Deferral and Amortization Approach
- Deferral and amortization approach
- Comparison of results: Deferral and amortization versus immediate recognition

INTRODUCTION AND BENEFIT PLAN BASICS

Objective 1

Understand the importance of pensions from a business perspective.

Overview of Pensions and Their Importance from a Business Perspective

Pension plans of Canadian companies continue to be in the news. For example, one recent report indicates that "ninety percent of the roughly 400 defined-benefit pension plans overseen by Canada's federal regulator are underfunded, meaning they cannot meet their liabilities should their plans be wound up today, as is required by law."[2] One of the most extreme examples of how complicated accounting for pensions can be, and how important pension deficits have become, is Air Canada. In its 2011 annual report, the company notes that it has 10 separate plans registered under the Canadian Pension Benefits Standards Act, in addition to international plans in the United States, United Kingdom, and Japan. The company also has a variety of plans that are not registered. Its defined benefit pension plans provide pensions to retired employees as well as termination and death benefits. To complicate matters further, other employee benefits must be accounted for by Air Canada. These include health and disability benefits for employees who are still active, and for those who have already retired.

Aside from the cost of administering all of these plans, and negotiating changes to the plans with a variety of unions, how much do the plans cost the company? For 2011, Air Canada indicates a pension benefits expense of $152 million, other employee future benefits expense of $112 million, and additional costs recognized in other comprehensive income of $2.4 billion! At the end of 2011, Air Canada reported pension and other benefit liabilities on its consolidated statement of financial position of $5.6 billion (an increase of over $2.2 billion from the prior year). At the end of 2011, the company reported overall shareholders' equity of negative $4.1 billion. If you consider this information in relation to the basic equation of Assets = Liabilities + Equity you readily see the significant impact of underfunded pensions on Air Canada's financial position.

The company attributes much of the increase in its pension and other benefit liabilities to a decrease in the interest rate it uses to determine its pension liabilities. We will see later in the chapter why the changes in interest rates, and interest rate assumptions, are so important for companies.

Chapter Overview

This chapter introduces basic terminology, categories of benefits, and how to account for benefit plans that are relatively straightforward. We then explain the key underlying components of defined benefit plans—such as the company's defined benefit obligation and assets of pension plans—and what causes them to change. These components and changes in them are the basic building blocks for employee future-benefits accounting. By understanding them, you will better visualize and understand some of the new concepts that are introduced in the chapter. Appendix 19A provides a simplified example of a one-person pension plan to help you better visualize and understand pension accounting, even if the individual standards differ or change later.

After this, we describe approaches to the recognition and measurement of the statement of financial position benefit liability (or asset) and the period's benefit cost associated with a defined benefit plan. We then set out what constitutes current GAAP under IFRS and ASPE for such plans. Appendix 19A provides a simplified example of a one-person pension plan to help you better visualize and understand some of the new concepts that are introduced in the chapter. Appendix 19B provides an example of the deferral and amortization approach, which, at the time of writing this book, was allowed under ASPE.

Short-term benefits that are provided while employees are actively employed, such as regular vacations and occasional sick days, were discussed in Chapter 13, as were short-term absences to which employees may be entitled, such as parental leave and short-term disability leave.

As mentioned, this chapter discusses the accounting and reporting for a variety of employee future benefits that are earned by employees and that are expected to be provided to them on a long-term basis. Examples of these benefit plans include:

- Post-retirement plans such as pensions and plans that provide health care or life insurance benefits after an employee's retirement.

- Post-employment plans with benefits that are provided after employment but before retirement. These include long-term disability income benefits, long-term severance benefits, and continuation of benefits such as health care and life insurance.

- Plans covering accumulating and vested compensated absences. This type of benefit includes payments made while an employee is absent from work. It also includes unrestricted sabbatical leaves and accumulated sick days that vest or are taken as paid vacation.

Nature of Pension Plans

A pension plan is an arrangement in which an employer provides benefits (payments) to employees after they retire, for services that the employees provided while they were working. Pension accounting may refer **either to accounting for the employer or accounting for the pension plan.** This chapter focuses on the employer's accounting. The company or employer is the organization that sponsors the pension plan. It incurs the cost and contributes to the pension fund. The fund is the entity that receives the employer contributions (and employee contributions, if any), administers the pension assets, and makes the benefit payments to the pension recipients (the retired employees). Illustration 19-1 sets out the three participants in a pension plan and the flow of cash among them.

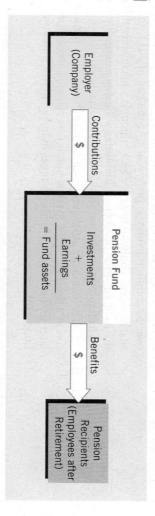

Illustration 19-1

*Flow of Cash among Pension
Plan Participants*

The pension plan in the illustration is **funded.**[3] This means that the employer (company) sets money aside for future pension benefits by making payments to a funding agency that is responsible for accumulating the pension plan assets and for making payments to the recipients as the benefits come due. The assets that are transferred become the assets of the pension plan, which is a separate legal entity. They are not company assets.

In **contributory plans,** the employees pay part of the cost of the stated benefits or voluntarily make payments to increase their benefits. In **non-contributory plans,** the employer bears the entire cost. Companies generally design pension plans in accordance with federal income tax laws that permit deduction of the employer's and employees' contributions to the pension fund and offer tax-free status for earnings on the pension fund assets. The pension benefits are taxable when they are received by the pensioner.

The plan is a separate legal and reporting entity for which a set of books is maintained and financial statements are prepared. General purpose financial statements for pension plans are not covered in this chapter but they are set out in Part IV of the *CICA Handbook* and in IAS 26. This chapter is devoted to issues that relate to **the employer** as the sponsor of pension and other employee future benefit plans.

The need for proper administration of pension funds, as well as sound accounting, becomes apparent when you appreciate the size of these funds. The following list shows the pension benefit plan expense, fund assets, and shareholders' equity of a sample of large Canadian companies for 2011.

Company	Pension Cost/ Expense in millions	Pension Fund Assets in millions	Shareholders' Equity in millions
ManuLife Financial Corporation	$183	$ 2,931	$24,879
Canadian Pacific Railway Limited	46	9,215	4,649
Suncor Energy Inc.	160	2,499	38,600
Bombardier Inc. (U.S. $)	175	6,395	671
BCE Inc.	150	16,384	14,759

As the list shows, pension expense can be a substantial amount, and the fund assets are sometimes larger than the shareholders' equity of the company that sponsors the plan. Employee future benefit plans can also be described as indicated in Illustration 19-2.

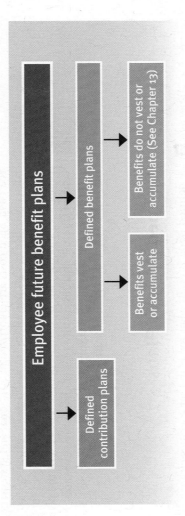

Employee future benefit plans

Defined contribution plans

Defined benefit plans

Benefits vest or accumulate

Benefits do not vest or accumulate (See Chapter 13)

Illustration 19-2

Categories of Employee Future Benefit Plans

The two most common types of pension plans are defined contribution plans and defined benefit plans. Defined contribution plans are fairly straightforward, so we begin with this type of plan. Most of the chapter explains the accounting for defined benefit plans in which the benefits vest or accumulate.[4] We discuss the concept of vesting further below.

Defined Contribution Plans

Objective 2

Identify and account for a defined contribution benefit plan.

Law

A **defined contribution (DC) plan** is a post-employment benefit plan that specifies how the entity's contributions or payments into the plan are determined, rather than identifying what benefits will be received by the employee or the method of determining those benefits.[5] In other words, the employer's contributions are defined; the employee's benefits are not. The IFRS definition in IAS 19 *Employee Benefits* extends the explanation of a DC plan to include the fact that, once the entity pays those contributions into the fund, it has no further obligation to make additional payments, even if the fund ends up not having enough assets to pay the employee benefits. Under a defined contribution plan, the amounts paid in are usually attributed to specific individuals. The contributions may be a fixed sum—for example, $5,000 per year—or they may be related to salary, such as 6% of regular plus overtime earnings. No promise is made about the ultimate benefit that will be paid out to the employees.

For a DC pension plan, the amounts that are contributed are usually turned over to an independent third party or trustee who acts on behalf of the beneficiaries (the participating employees). The trustee assumes ownership of the pension assets and is responsible for their investment and distribution. The trust is separate and distinct from the employer. The size of the pension benefit that the employee finally collects under the plan depends on the amounts that have been contributed to the pension trust, the income that has accumulated in the trust, the treatment of forfeitures of funds created by the termination of employees before retirement, and the investment alternatives available on retirement.

Because **the contribution is defined**, the accounting for a defined contribution plan is straightforward. The employer's obligation is dictated by the amounts to be contributed. Therefore, a liability is reported on the employer's statement of financial position only if the required contributions have not been made in full, and an asset is reported if more than the required amount has been contributed. Discounting is not generally an issue as long as the amounts due are expected to be paid in the 12-month period following the reporting date. The annual **benefit cost** (that is, the **pension expense**) is simply the amount that the company is obligated to contribute to the plan.[6] The employer generally has no other obligation and assumes no other risk relative to this plan.

ASPE discusses other possible components of the associated cost and liability. When a defined contribution plan is first established, or when it is later amended, the employer may be required to make contributions for employee services that were provided before the start of the plan or its amendment. This obligation is referred to as **prior or past service cost**. Such costs are amortized in a rational and systematic way and are added to the current service cost as part of the annual pension expense, over the period that the organization is expected to realize the economic benefits from the plan change. This period could be as short as just the current period. The cost of the plan for the period might also contain interest charges on any related discounted amounts and a reduction for interest earned on any unallocated plan surplus. Under IFRS, these past service costs are generally recognized immediately in expense.

Defined Benefit Plans

Objective 3
Identify and explain what a defined benefit plan is and the related accounting issues.

A **defined benefit (DB) plan** is a plan that specifies either the benefits to be received by an employee or the method of determining those benefits. In other words, the employee's benefits are defined; the employer's contributions are not fixed. One example is a plan that provides an entitlement to a lump-sum payment of $5,000 on the employee's 10th and 25th anniversaries of employment with the employer company. Another is a plan that provides an annual pension benefit on retirement equal to 2% of the average of the employee's best three years of salary multiplied by the number of years of employment.

The most complex type of benefit plan provides defined benefits that vest in the employee based on the employee's length of service. Employees' rights to post-employment medical benefits, for example, generally vest after the employee has worked a specified number of years, and the amount of benefit usually increases with the length of service. **Vesting** means that an employee keeps the rights to the benefit even if the employee no longer works for the entity. That is, if an employee whose benefits have vested leaves the company, the individual will still receive those benefits. If they are not vested when the employee leaves, the rights to the benefits are lost.

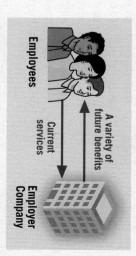

EXAMPLE

Employers promise a number of future benefits in exchange for current service. Employees may be entitled to some of these benefits even if they leave the company. The major accounting issue is "How do we measure the employer's obligation, and in which accounting periods should the cost of the benefits be recognized?"

A variety of future benefits

Current services

Employees

Employer Company

Law

Other long-term employee benefits, including unrestricted time off for long service or sabbatical leave, deferred compensation, and other compensated absences, may also fit the description of defined benefit plans with benefits that vest or accumulate. All of these benefit plans have something in common: **the entitlement to the benefits increases with the length of the employee's service.** **The objective** in accounting for these plans, therefore, is for the expense and liability related to these plans to be recognized over the accounting periods in which the related services are provided by the employees.

As discussed, a defined benefit pension plan identifies the pension benefits that an employee will receive after retiring. These benefits typically are a function of an employee's years of service and compensation level in the years approaching retirement. To ensure that appropriate resources are available to pay the benefits at retirement, there is usually a requirement that funds be set aside during the service life of the employees.

The **employees** are the beneficiaries of a defined **contribution** trust, but the **employer** is the beneficiary of a defined **benefit** trust. The trust's main purpose under a defined benefit plan is to safeguard assets and to invest them so that there will be enough to pay the employer's obligation to the employees. **In form**, the trust is a separate entity; **in substance**, the trust assets and liabilities belong to the employer. That is, **as long as the plan continues, the employer is responsible for paying the defined benefits, no matter what happens in the trust.** The employer must make up any shortfall in the accumulated assets held by the trust. If excess assets have accumulated in the trust, it may be possible for the employer to recapture them either through reduced future funding or through a reversion of funds, depending on the trust agreement, plan documents, and governing legislation.[7]

With a defined benefit plan, the employer assumes the economic risks: the employee is secure because the benefits to be paid on retirement are predefined, but the employer is at risk because the cost is uncertain.[8] The cost depends on factors such as employee turnover, mortality, length of service, and compensation levels, as well as investment returns that are earned on pension assets, inflation, and other economic conditions over long periods of time.

Because the cost to the company is affected by a wide range of uncertain future variables, it is not easy to measure the pension cost and liability that have to be recognized each period as employees provide services to earn their pension entitlement. In addition, an appropriate funding pattern must be established to assure that enough funds will be available at retirement to provide the benefits that have been promised. Whatever funding method is decided on, it should provide enough money at retirement to meet the benefits defined by the plan. Note that **the expense to be recognized each period is not the same as the employer's cash funding contribution,** just as depreciation expense recognized on the use of plant and equipment is not measured in terms of how the asset is financed. The accounting issues related to defined benefit plans are complex, but interesting.

At one time, most employer-sponsored pension plans in Canada were of the defined benefit or DB type. The majority of plans now are DC plans, and the percentage is growing. However, in terms of pension assets, the amount that is in defined benefit plans continues to be disproportionately high.

The issues that are associated with pension plans involve complicated mathematical considerations. Companies therefore use the services of actuaries to ensure that the plan is appropriate for the employee group covered. **Actuaries** are individuals who are trained through a long and rigorous certification program to assign probabilities to future events and their financial effects.[9] The insurance industry also employs actuaries to assess risks and to advise the industry on the setting of premiums and other aspects of insurance policies. Employers rely heavily on actuaries for help in developing, implementing, and determining the funding of pension plans.

An actuary's chief purpose in pension accounting is to ensure that the company has established an appropriate funding pattern to meet its pension obligations. This calculation requires a set of assumptions to be established and the continued monitoring of these assumptions to ensure that they are realistic. Actuaries make predictions, called **actuarial assumptions,** about mortality rates, employee turnover, interest and earnings rates, early

Law

Finance

retirement frequency, future salaries, and any other factors that need to be considered for pension plans. They also calculate the various pension measures that affect the financial statements, such as the pension obligation, the annual cost of servicing the plan, and the cost of amendments to the plan. Defined benefit pension plans rely heavily on information and measurements provided by these specialists.

Because DB pension plans will be used extensively in this chapter to explain how to account for DB plans, basic information about the nature of pension plans is provided next.

DEFINED BENEFIT PENSION PLANS

Significant Change

Accounting for employee future benefits such as pensions has undergone significant change in recent years, with the IASB introducing new requirements effective January 1, 2013, and with changes being considered under ASPE and by FASB. However, the foundations on which employee future benefit accounting is based have not changed significantly. The first is the employer's obligation to pay out benefits in the future for the employees' services up to the date of the statement of financial position. This is estimated by the actuary. The second foundation is setting aside plan assets to fund this obligation. Understanding the nature of the **defined benefit obligation** (referred to in **ASPE** as the **accrued benefit obligation**) and **plan assets (fund assets)**, and the transactions and events that affect their measurement, helps clarify the study of accounting for benefit plans, even as the standards change.

The Employer's Obligation

Alternative Measures of the Pension Obligation

Most companies agree that an employer's **pension obligation** is the deferred compensation obligation that it has to its employees for their service under the terms of the pension plan. Determining that obligation is not simple, though, because there are different ways of measuring it.

One measure of the pension obligation is based only on the benefits that vest. **Vested benefits** are those that an employee is entitled to receive even if he or she provides no additional services to the company. Most pension plans require a specific minimum number of years of service to the employer before an employee achieves the status of having vested benefits. Actuaries calculate the **vested benefit obligation** using vested benefits only, at current salary levels, under the **vested benefit method.**

Another way to measure the obligation is using both vested and non-vested benefits. On this basis, the deferred compensation amount is calculated on all years of employees' service—**both vested and non-vested**—using current salary levels. This basis of measurement is called the **accumulated benefit method.**

A third method calculates the deferred compensation amount using both vested and non-vested service, and incorporates future salaries projected to be earned over the period to retirement. This way of measuring the pension obligation is called the **projected benefit method.** Because future salaries are expected to be higher than current salaries, this approach results in the largest measure of the pension obligation.

Deciding which measure to use is a critical choice because it affects the amount of the pension liability and the annual pension expense reported. The diagram in Illustration 19-3 presents the differences in these three methods. Regardless of the approach used, the estimated future benefits to be paid are discounted to their present value.

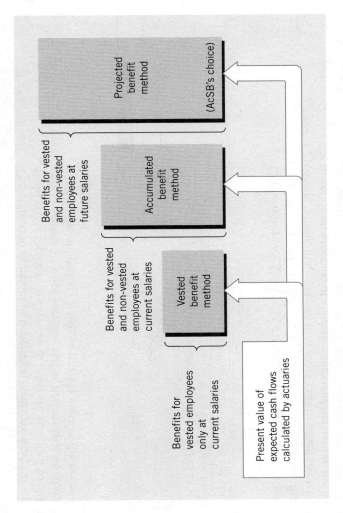

Illustration **19-3**

Different Methods of Measuring the Pension Obligation

Underlying Concept

The FASB and the IASB have both studied whether the liability should include estimates of future salaries. This debate centres on whether a company can have a liability today that is based in part on future salaries that have not yet been earned.

Which of these methods is generally accepted as providing the best measure of the obligation? The FASB, IASB, and Canadian Accounting Standards Board (AcSB) have all adopted the **projected benefit method** to calculate the defined benefit obligation (known as the **accrued benefit obligation [ABO]** under ASPE) as the best measure specifically for accounting purposes. The **defined benefit obligation (DBO) for accounting purposes** is the present value of vested and non-vested benefits earned to the date of the statement of financial position, with the benefits measured using employees' future salary levels.[10]

Critics of using projected salaries argue that it results in future obligations being added to existing ones. Those in favour of the defined benefit obligation counter that a promise by an employer to pay benefits based on a percentage of the employees' future salary is far different from a promise to pay a percentage of their current salary, and that this difference should be reflected in the pension liability and pension expense.

The **accrued benefit obligation (ABO) for funding purposes** represents another measure. It is used under ASPE for the immediate recognition approach, and it is discussed later in this chapter. The ABO for funding purposes tends to focus more on current salary levels and often uses a different discount rate. Regardless of the measure of the obligation chosen for accounting purposes, regulators use a variety of different measures for determining the level of contributions that plan sponsors are required by law to remit to the pension fund.

Changes in the Defined Benefit Obligation

The measurement of the defined benefit obligation is central to accounting for pension costs. At any point in time, the DBO represents the actuarial present value of the cost of the benefits attributed to employee services that have been provided to date. A simplified example of the measurement of the DBO for accounting purposes in a one-person pension plan is provided in Appendix 19A, and you may find it useful to read this material before proceeding.

Illustration 19-4 summarizes the DBO from the perspective of the transactions and events that change its amount. The DBO increases as employees provide further services and earn additional benefits, and as interest is added to this outstanding discounted liability.

The obligation decreases as benefit payments are made to retirees. In addition, the DBO might either increase or decrease as plans are amended to change the future benefits that were promised for prior services, and as the actuarial assumptions change that are used to calculate the obligation. Actuaries provide most of the necessary measurements related to the DBO.

	Defined benefit obligation (DBO), at beginning of period
+	Current service cost
+	Interest cost
−	Benefits paid to retirees
±	Past service costs of plan amendments during period
±	Actuarial gains (−) or losses (+) during period
=	Defined benefit obligation (DBO), at end of period

Current Service Cost.   The **current service cost** is the cost of the benefits that are to be provided in the future in exchange for the services that the employees provided in the current period. In measuring the service cost to assign to each period, standard setters had to decide on a method of allocating the estimated cost to the individual years during which the entitlement to the benefits builds. Should the total cost be allocated based on the percentage of salary earned by the employee during the year relative to the total estimated career compensation (that is, **prorated on salaries**)? Or should it be allocated based on an equal amount per year of service (that is, **prorated on service**)? The standard setters decided on the latter method that accrues a relatively equal charge each period—the projected unit credit method.[11]

To calculate current service cost, the actuary predicts the additional benefits that must be paid under the plan's benefit formula as a result of the employees' current year of service and then discounts the cost of these benefits to their present value. For example, consider the following pension benefit formula:

By working an additional year, the employee earns an entitlement to a larger pension, and the company's pension obligation for accounting purposes increases by the present value of 2% of the employee's estimated final salary for each year of expected retirement.[12] Appendix 19A provides a simplified example of this calculation.

For defined benefit plans where future benefits depend on or are increased by the length of service, the actuary bases the accounting calculations on future salary levels and then attributes the cost of the future benefits to the accounting periods, usually between the date of hire and the date when the employee becomes eligible for full benefits. This is known as the **attribution period**. The obligation to provide benefits is attributed to the periods in which the employee provides the service that gives rise to the benefits. While the date of hire is the most common date for employees to begin earning benefits, it may be a later date, and eligibility for full benefits may occur before the date of retirement.

Interest Cost.   Because future benefit plans are deferred compensation arrangements—the benefits are essentially elements of wages that are deferred—the time value of money has to be considered. As the obligation is not paid until each employee retires, it is measured on a discounted basis. As time to retirement passes, **interest accrues on the defined benefit obligation just as it does on any discounted debt.** The interest is based on the DBO that is outstanding during the period, taking into account any material changes in its balance during that period. So, for example, if the plan was modified and past service costs had been awarded at the first of the year, the interest cost would have increased as well because the opening benefit liability would have been higher. Similarly the timing of benefit payments would impact the DBO outstanding at various times in the year and would affect the interest cost.

What interest rate should be used? Both IFRS and ASPE require the use of a current market rate, determined by reference to the current yield on high-quality debt instruments such as high-quality corporate bonds. The objective is to have the discount rate reflect the estimated timing and amount of the expected benefit payments. Changes to IFRS in 2013 require that the discount rate used in relation to the DBO and the plan assets be the same rate. (ASPE, however, allows for different rates to be used for the obligation and the plan assets under the deferral and amortization approach summarized in Appendix 19B.) ASPE also allows a current **settlement rate** to be used, instead of the current yield on high-quality corporate bonds. This is the rate implied in an insurance contract that could be purchased to effectively settle the pension obligation. The rate to be used is the rate at the end of the reporting period and it is reassessed at each such date. Note that minor changes in the interest rate used to discount pension benefits can dramatically affect the measurement of the employer's obligation. For example, a 1% decrease in the discount rate might increase pension liabilities by 15%!

Benefits Paid to Retirees. The pension fund trustee is responsible for making payments of the pension benefits to the former employees. Similar to all liabilities, as obligations are met, the balance of the remaining obligation is reduced.

Past Service Costs. When a defined benefit plan is either initiated (begun) or amended, credit is often given to employees for years of service that they provided before the date of initiation or amendment. As a result of these credits for prior services, the actuary remeasures the DBO, and it usually ends up being larger than it was before the change. The increase in the DBO on the date that the plan is initiated or amended is known as **past service cost**, the cost of the retroactive benefits. This increase is often substantial, and under the 2013 changes to IFRS it now is included in pension benefit cost in the income statement (rather than being deferred and amortized). See Appendix 19A for a simplified illustration.

In recent years, because they want to reduce the very significant costs that are associated with post-retirement plans, many companies have been negotiating reductions in some of their plan benefits. When this happens, there is a **decrease** in the DBO that relates to past services, and a **past service benefit** is recognized.

Actuarial Gains and Losses. **Actuarial gains and losses** related to the DBO (the liability) can result from either: (1) a change in actuarial assumptions, which means a change in the assumptions about the occurrence of future events that affect the measurement of the future benefit costs and obligations; or (2) an **experience gain or loss**, which is the difference between what has actually occurred and the previous actuarial assumptions about what would occur. When later events show that assumptions were inaccurate, adjustments are needed.

In estimating the DBO, actuaries make assumptions about such variables as mortality rates, retirement rates, turnover rates, disability rates, and rates of salary escalation (increase). Any difference between these assumed rates and the ones that are actually experienced changes the amount of the DBO. Actual experience is rarely exactly the same as actuarial predictions. An unexpected gain or loss that changes the amount of the DBO due to short-term experience varying from what had been assumed is sometimes referred to as an **experience gain or loss**.[13] Actuarial gains and losses also occur when the assumptions that are used by the actuary in calculating the DBO are revised, because this too causes a change in the amount of the obligation. An example is the effect of a change in the interest rate used to discount the pension cash flows on the measurement of the obligation. Because experience gains and losses are similar to and affect the DBO in the same way as changes in actuarial assumptions, both types are generally referred to as **actuarial gains and losses**.

To illustrate, assume that a company's calculated defined benefit obligation—based on its opening balance and the year's service cost, interest cost, benefits paid, and plan amendments—was $962,000 at December 31, 2014. If the company's actuaries, using December 31, 2014 estimates in their actuarial calculations, determine that the defined benefit obligation is actually $975,000, then the company has suffered an actuarial loss of $13,000 ($975,000 − $962,000). If the actuary calculates a reduced obligation, the result is an actuarial gain. Whatever the result, the DBO is adjusted to its most recent actuarial valuation. The adjustment flows through OCI under IFRS, or net income under ASPE's immediate recognition approach. However, it may be deferred and amortized if using the corridor approach under ASPE. (The corridor approach, used to amortize the net accumulated gain or loss when its balance is considered too large, is explained in Appendix 19B.)

Plan settlements and curtailments also affect the amount of the defined benefit obligation. For example, settlements substantially settle or discharge all (or part) of the benefit obligation, while curtailments generally reduce the expected years of future service for active employees. A detailed examination of settlements and curtailments is outside the scope of this chapter.

Plan Assets

Plan Asset Composition

The benefit plan assets are the other major foundation on which pension accounting is based. **Plan assets** are assets that have been set aside in a trust or other legal entity that is separate from the employer company. The assets are restricted and can be used only to settle the related defined benefit obligation: they cannot be used for meeting the claims of other company creditors. The plan assets are made up mainly of cash and investments in debt and equity securities that are held to earn a reasonable return, generally at a minimum of risk. Other investments, such as real estate investment property, are also common plan holdings for larger plans. As will be explained later, the plan assets increase by the return on plan assets, with the difference between the (actual) return on plan assets and the (expected) interest income on plan assets being treated as a remeasurement gain or loss under the new IFRS rules.[14] The remeasurement gain or loss on the plan assets is combined with the actuarial gain or loss on the DBO and is charged to OCI under IFRS. (ASPE works differently depending on whether the immediate recognition or deferral and amortization approach is chosen, as we will see later in the chapter and in Appendix 19B.)

Objective 5

Identify transactions and events that change benefit plan assets, and calculate the balance of the assets.

Changes in Plan Assets

As can be seen in Illustration 19-5, the fund assets change as a result of contributions from the employer (and employee, if the plan is contributory) and from the return on plan assets generated on the assets that have been invested. The pool of assets is reduced by payments to retirees.

Illustration 19-5

Plan Assets—Continuity Schedule

	Plan assets, fair value at beginning of period
+	Contributions from employer company, and employees if applicable
±	Actual return
−	Benefits paid to retirees
=	Plan assets, fair value at end of period

Contributions. The amount of an employer company's contributions to the plan has a direct effect on the plan's ability to pay the DBO. Who and what determine how much a company contributes to the plan? In Canada, pension plans come under either federal or provincial pension legislation as well as regulations of the Canada Revenue Agency (CRA). The CRA stipulates the amount of the contributions that are tax deductible to the company and the conditions on the payment of benefits out of the plan. Federal and provincial laws dictate the funding requirements.[15]

Return on Plan Assets. The **return on plan assets** can be thought of as the income generated on the assets being held by the trustee, less the cost of administering the fund. The return that is earned on these assets usually increases the fund balance. The return on plan assets is made up of dividends, interest, and gains and losses from the sale of investments, as well as profits that are generated on any real estate investments. In addition, because the assets are measured at fair value, both realized and unrealized gains and losses on the assets are included as part of the return on plan assets. Including the realized and unrealized gains and losses explains why the return could increase the plan assets in one year and decrease them in another. In years when stock and/or bond markets decline significantly, the reduction in fair value may be greater than the other forms of income that are reported and the actual return on plan assets will be a loss.

Because the return on plan assets can be highly variable from one year to the next, actuaries ignore short-term fluctuations when they develop a funding pattern to accumulate assets to pay benefits in the future. Instead, they calculate an expected long-term rate of return and apply it to the fair value of the fund assets to arrive at an **expected return** on plan assets.[16] Under IFRS, the same discount rate is applied to the DBO and the plan assets (that is, the rate for high-quality corporate bonds). The interest cost on the DBO combined with the interest income on the plan assets together comprise the net interest on the net defined benefit liability or asset, which is charged to net income.

Benefits Paid. The plan trustee pays out benefits to the retirees according to the plan formula and pension agreement.

Funded Status

The measures of the DBO and plan assets are fundamental to pension accounting. Because of this, accounting standards specify that they should be measured as at the date of the annual financial statements.[17] Under IFRS, both the plan assets and DBO are required to represent reporting date values. (More specifically, the net defined benefit liability/asset is to be measured with "sufficient regularity that the amounts recognised in the financial statements do not differ materially from the amounts that would be determined at the end of the reporting period" [IAS 19.58].)

Calculation of Funded Status

As indicated in Illustration 19-6, the difference between the DBO and the pension assets' fair value at a point in time is known as the plan's **funded status.** A plan with more liabilities than assets is **underfunded** and has a funded status liability. A plan with accumulated assets that are greater than the related obligation is **overfunded** and is said to have a funded status asset.[18]

Defined benefit obligation (DBO), end of period
− Fair value of plan assets, end of period
‾‾‾‾‾‾‾‾‾‾‾‾‾‾‾‾‾‾‾‾‾‾‾‾‾‾‾‾‾‾‾‾‾‾‾‾‾
= Plan's funded status, end of period

DBO > Plan assets = **underfunded** = a funded status liability
Plan assets > DBO = **overfunded** = a funded status asset

Illustration 19-6

Funded Status

Accounting for Changes in Funded Status

Now that you have been introduced to most of the components that are needed to account for a DB pension plan, it is time to look at how companies actually account for such plans.

Pension accounting would be relatively straightforward if all the changes in the DBO, as defined for accounting purposes, and in the fund assets (except for the cash contributions made by the employer company to the fund assets) were recognized as part of the pension expense and as a change in the net defined benefit liability/asset on the statement of financial position (SFP). The SFP account would have the same balance as the funded status, and the income statement account along with the company contributions into the plan would explain the change in the funded status. But this is only one approach to calculating the benefit cost and the net defined benefit liability/asset on the SFP. For a variety of reasons, pension accounting has introduced several variations in how and when these amounts are recognized. The methods now in use by IFRS and ASPE are explained next.

Defined Benefit Cost Components and the Immediate Recognition Approach

You have already been introduced to the components that make up the pension benefit cost. As we have discussed, under IFRS some of this cost is reflected in net income and some in other comprehensive income. They are the events that change the balances of the DBO and the fund assets and, therefore, the funded status. These are:

- Service cost (current and past service)
- Net interest (the net of interest on the DBO and plan assets)
- Remeasurements (actuarial gains and losses including the return on plan assets to the extent not included in net interest)

While there is general agreement that pension costs should be accounted for on the accrual basis and recognized in the accounting periods that benefit from the employees' service, not everyone agrees on when certain cost components should be included in current year expense. Two approaches to accounting for pension expense and the related SFP account are:

1. the immediate recognition approach, and
2. the deferral and amortization approach.

At the time of writing this book, ASPE permitted companies to make an accounting policy choice between the immediate recognition and the deferral and amortization approaches, while IFRS applied a form of the immediate recognition approach. Within these approaches, there are areas where choices are permitted.

The main changes introduced under IFRS that became effective in 2013 are as follows:

1. The elimination of the ability to defer and amortize past service costs or benefits and actuarial gains or losses. The corridor approach disappears. (The deferral and amortization approach was still allowed under ASPE at the time this book went to press, and it is discussed in detail in Appendix 19B, along with the corridor approach.)
2. Requiring the net employee benefit liability or asset to be reported on the SFP, and for it to be based on the funded status of the plan. Instead of being calculated as the net of the plan assets and the defined benefit obligation, however, it can be characterized as the net amount owing to the plan or net receivable from the plan. The net benefit asset may not equal the net of the plan assets and the DBO. It would be adjusted for the effect, if any, of the plan asset ceiling test. See IAS 19.57 for details.

3. Requiring changes in the net employee benefit liability or asset on the SFP during the period to be included as components of the defined benefit cost. The changes are reported either in net income or in other comprehensive income (OCI) as follows:

(a) Current and past service cost—in **net income**

(b) Interest on the net employee benefit liability or asset—in **net income**

(c) Gains and losses from remeasurements included in the net employee benefit liability or asset—in **OCI.**

The differences between ASPE and IFRS also affect the resulting pension asset or liability reported on the statement of financial position. We use the example of Zarle Corporation and its defined benefit pension plan as set out in Illustration 19-8 to explain the immediate recognition approach. The deferral and amortization approach is explained later (in Appendix 19B) using details related to the pension plan of Trans Corp.

Under an **immediate recognition approach,** the pension expense is made up of all items affecting the funded status during the period except the company contributions into the plan assets:

Significant
Change

1. **Current service cost and interest cost.** Both the service cost for benefits earned by employees and the interest cost accrued on the DBO during the current period are recognized and included in pension expense in the same period.

2. **Actual return on plan assets.** Under IFRS, the same discount rate is used for interest cost on the DBO and for the interest assumed to be earned on the plan assets. The **actual return** earned on the plan assets, which is typically a positive amount, reduces the cost to the employer of sponsoring an employee pension plan. If a negative return is generated, the pension cost is increased.

Under the immediate recognition approach for ASPE, the actual return on plan assets is used in the calculations of pension expense charged to net income. Under IFRS, the actual return on plan assets is allocated between pension expense on the statement of comprehensive income, and other comprehensive income. Specifically the interest on the net defined benefit liability/asset is recognized in net income (IAS 19.57). The return on plan assets other than interest on the net defined benefit liability/asset is recognized in OCI.[19]

3. **Past service cost.** Plan amendments instantly change the amount of the employer's obligation, and the total cost (or benefit) of the amendment is recognized immediately in pension expense.

4. **Actuarial gains and losses.** When actuarial gains and losses are recognized as a component of pension expense in the same period they are incurred, the reported expense tends to fluctuate significantly from year to year. As you might expect, the immediate recognition approach under ASPE makes no adjustment for this. Instead, ASPE recognizes the full amount of the actuarial gain or loss in pension expense each period. IFRS is similar in that the gains and losses are not deferred, but under IFRS the actuarial gains or losses are included in OCI rather than in net income.

Other components of expense are identified in the accounting standard, including changes to the DBO from plan settlements and curtailments. These are beyond the scope of this text. In addition, a part of the change in the valuation allowance related to the funded status asset (if any) is also included. The limit on the carrying amount of a net defined benefit asset on the statement of financial position due to the asset ceiling test is explained briefly later in this chapter.

Illustration of Immediate Recognition Approach

A work sheet is used to illustrate how the transactions affecting the DBO and fund assets are accumulated in the accounts. **It is important to note two things.**

1. **Neither the DBO nor the fund assets are recognized directly in the sponsoring company's accounts;** they are both **off-balance sheet or memo accounts.** The fund assets belong to the benefit trust, and the DBO is a liability of the sponsoring company only to the extent there are not enough assets in the fund to cover the total obligation.

2. When applying the immediate recognition approach under ASPE, **the accrued benefit obligation** is based on an actuarial valuation used for **funding purposes,** not the accrued benefit obligation used for accounting purposes. It represents the obligation at the date of the statement of financial position. (To simplify matters, in the following example we assume that the ABO based on the actuarial valuation used for **funding purposes under ASPE** is equal to the DBO that would be calculated under **IFRS.**)

A unique pension work sheet is used to keep track of pension expense and the Net Defined Benefit Liability/Asset account on the statement of financial position, as well as the off-balance sheet amounts. As its name suggests, the work sheet is a working tool; it is not a journal or part of the general ledger. It merely accumulates the information needed to make the pension journal entries. The format of the work sheet that illustrates the relationship among all the components is shown in Illustration 19-7.[20]

Illustration 19-7

Basic Format of Pension Work Sheet

	A	B	C	D	F	G
		General Journal Entries			Memo Record	
1	Items	Annual Pension Expense	Cash	Net Defined Benefit Liability/ Asset	Defined Benefit Obligation	Plan Assets
2						
3						
4						
5						
6						

The left-hand columns of the work sheet under "General Journal Entries" determine the entries to be recorded in the formal general ledger accounts. The right-hand "Memo Record" columns maintain balances on the defined benefit obligation and the plan assets, based on amounts provided by the actuary and pension plan trustee. On the first line of the work sheet, the beginning balances are recorded. Subsequently, transactions and events that relate to the pension plan are entered, using debits and credits and using both sets of records as if there were just one set for recording the entries. For each transaction or event, the debits must equal the credits, and the balance in the Net Defined Benefit Liability/Asset column must equal the net balance in the Memo Record columns. If the DBO is greater than the plan assets, a pension liability is reported on the statement of financial position. If the DBO is less than the plan assets, a pension asset results.

Let's walk through the immediate recognition model by using the facts and circumstances set out in Illustration 19-8 that apply to Zarle's pension plan for the three-year period from 2013 to 2015.

Illustration 19-8

Zarle Corporation Pension Plan, 2013–2015

	2013	2014	2015
Fair value of plan assets, first of year			
Defined benefit obligation (DBO) (assumed to equal the ABO for funding purposes under ASPE)	$100,000	$111,000	$134,100
Current service cost for year	100,000	112,000	212,700
Interest or discount rate on the DBO/plan assets	9,000	9,500	13,000
	10%	10%	10%
Cost of past service benefits granted January 1, 2014	–0–	80,000	–0–

(continued)

Illustration 19-8

Zarle Corporation Pension Plan, 2013–2015 (continued)

	2013	2014	2015
Actual earnings on plan assets for year	10,000	11,100	12,000
Employer contributions for year (funding)	8,000	20,000	24,000
Benefits paid to retirees by trustee for year	7,000	8,000	10,500
Actuarial loss due to change in actuarial assumptions	–0–	–0–	28,530
Plan assets, end of year	111,000	134,100	159,600
DBO, end of year	112,000	212,700	265,000
Funded status, end of year—over- or (under)-funded	(1,000)	(78,600)	(105,400)

The Basics—2013 Work Sheet and Entries. Assume that Zarle Corporation begins its 2013 fiscal year with a DBO of $100,000, plan assets of $100,000, and a $0 balance in its Net Defined Benefit Liability/Asset account on the statement of financial position.

Using the information found in Illustration 19-8, Illustration 19-9 presents the work sheet, including the beginning balances and all the pension transactions that Zarle Corporation needs to account for in 2013. The beginning balances of the defined benefit obligation and the pension plan assets are recorded on the work sheet's first line in the memo record. They are not recorded in the accounts and, therefore, are not reported as a liability and an asset in Zarle Corporation's financial statements. Notice that, although they are "off-balance sheet," the January 1, 2013 funded status of $0 is the same as the balance of $0 in the net defined benefit liability/asset line on the statement of financial position on that date. Under the immediate recognition approach, the funded status and the amount of the statement of financial position account are the same.[21]

Illustration 19-9

Pension Work Sheet—2013

	General Journal Entries			Memo Record	
Items	Annual Pension Expense	Cash	Net Defined Benefit Liability/Asset	Defined Benefit Obligation	Plan Assets
Balance, Jan. 1, 2013			–0–	100,000 Cr.	100,000 Dr.
(a) Service cost	9,000 Dr.			9,000 Cr.	
(b) Interest cost	10,000 Dr.			10,000 Cr.	
(c) Actual/expected return	10,000 Cr.				10,000 Dr.
(d) Contribution		8,000 Cr.			8,000 Dr.
(e) Benefits paid				7,000 Dr.	7,000 Cr.
Expense entry, 2013	9,000 Dr.		9,000 Cr.		
Contribution entry, 2013		8,000 Cr.	8,000 Dr.		
Balance, Dec. 31, 2013			1,000 Cr.	112,000 Cr.	111,000 Dr.

Entry (a) in Illustration 19-9 records the service cost component, which increases the defined benefit obligation by $9,000 and increases pension expense by $9,000. Entry (b) accrues the interest cost, increasing both the DBO and pension expense by $10,000. (This is the $100,000 weighted average balance of the defined benefit obligation multiplied by the discount rate of 10%.) Note that in all chapter examples and end-of-chapter problem material, unless specified otherwise, **it is assumed that current service cost is credited at year end and that contributions to the fund and benefits paid to retirees are year-end cash flows.** Such an assumption is needed in order to determine the average balances outstanding for calculating any interest and expected return amounts. (We relax this assumption in the third year of our example.)

Entry (c) records the actual return on plan assets (for ASPE) or expected return based on the discount rate (under IFRS), which increases the plan assets and decreases pension expense. Entry (d) reflects Zarle Corporation's contribution (funding) of assets to the pension fund; cash is decreased by $8,000 and plan assets are increased by $8,000. Entry (e) records the benefit payments made to retirees, which result in equal $7,000 decreases in the plan assets and the defined benefit obligation.

Zarle makes the following journal entry on December 31, 2013, to formally record the pension expense under both IFRS and ASPE for the year. (The journal entries are the same under IFRS and ASPE because there are no actuarial gains or losses, and there is no difference between expected and actual return in 2013.)

Pension Expense	9,000	
Net Defined Benefit Liability/Asset		9,000

A = L + SE
    +9,000 −9,000
Cash flows: No effect

When Zarle Corporation issued its $8,000 cheque to the pension fund trustee late in the year, it made the following entry:

Net Defined Benefit Liability/Asset	8,000	
Cash		8,000

A = L + SE
−8,000 −8,000
Cash flows: ↓ 8,000 outflow

The credit balance in the Net Defined Benefit Liability/Asset account of $1,000 represents the funded status—the difference between the DBO of $112,000 and the fund assets of $111,000. This should not be surprising because all the transactions that affected the DBO and plan assets, except for the benefits paid, also affected the statement of financial position. The benefits paid decrease the fund assets and the DBO in equal amounts with no effect on the funded status.

In addition, the statement of financial position liability account also represents the excess of the accumulated pension expense recognized to date over the accumulated contributions made to date—a $1,000 liability. Although we are not told what expense was reported and contributions were made in prior years, we can tell that these amounts were equal at January 1, 2013. This is because the Net Defined Benefit Liability/Asset account balance was $0 at that date.

2014 Work Sheet and Entries with Past Service Costs. One question that standard setters have wrestled with is whether the past service costs or credits that are associated with the adoption or amendment of pension plans should be fully recognized in net income when the plan is initiated or amended. Under the immediate recognition approach, the conclusion is that the costs, although significant, all relate to past services and that there is no justification for deferring their recognition to future periods' income statements. We will see this assumption challenged in the deferral and amortization approach explained in Appendix 19B.

To illustrate how past service costs affect the pension accounts, we continue with Zarle Corporation in 2014. The work sheet's first line shows the beginning balances of the Net Defined Benefit Liability/Asset account and the components of the plan's funded status. Zarle amends its defined benefit pension plan on January 1, 2014, to grant prior service benefits to certain employees. The company's actuaries determine that this causes an increase in the defined benefit obligation of $80,000.

Illustration 19-10 presents all the pension "entries" and information used by Zarle Corporation in 2014. The work sheet's first line shows the beginning balances of the Net Defined Benefit Liability/Asset account and the components of the plan's funded status. Entry (f) records Zarle Corporation's granting of prior service benefits by adding $80,000 to the defined benefit obligation and its immediate recognition in Pension Expense. Entries (g), (h), (i), (j), and (k) are similar to the corresponding entries in 2013. Notice that the interest cost on the DBO is the year's interest at 10% on the average balance outstanding for the year. Because the past service costs were granted effective January 1, the balance outstanding for the year was $112,000 + $80,000 = $192,000.

Illustration 19-10

Pension Work Sheet—2014

	A	B	C	D	F	G
1		**General Journal Entries**			**Memo Record**	
2	**Items**	**Annual Pension Expense**	**Cash**	**Net Defined Benefit Liability/ Asset**	**Deferred Benefit Obligation**	**Plan Assets**
3	Balance, Dec. 31, 2013			1,000 Cr.	112,000 Cr.	111,000 Dr.
4	(f) Past service cost	80,000 Dr.			80,000 Cr.	
5	(g) Service cost	9,500 Dr.			9,500 Cr.	
6	(h) Interest cost	19,200 Dr.			19,200 Cr.	
7	(i) Actual/expected return	11,100 Cr.				11,100 Dr.
8	(j) Contribution		20,000 Cr.			20,000 Dr.
9	(k) Benefits paid				8,000 Dr.	8,000 Cr.
10	Expense entry, 2014	97,600 Dr.		97,600 Cr.		
11	Contribution entry, 2014		20,000 Cr.	20,000 Dr.		
12	Balance, Dec. 31, 2014			78,600 Cr.	212,700 Cr.	134,100 Dr.
13						

An entry is needed on December 31, 2014, to formally record the pension expense under IFRS and ASPE for the year.

Pension Expense	97,600
Net Defined Benefit Liability/Asset	97,600

$$A = L + SE$$
$$+97,600 \quad -97,600$$

Cash flows: No effect

When the company made its contributions to the pension fund during the year, the following entry was recorded:

Net Defined Benefit Liability/Asset	20,000
Cash	20,000

$$A = L + SE$$
$$-20,000 \quad -20,000$$

Cash flows: ↓ 20,000 outflow

Because the expense exceeds the funding, the Net Defined Benefit Liability/Asset account increases during the year by the $77,600 difference ($97,600 less $20,000). In 2014, for the same reasons as in 2013, the balance of the Accrued Benefit Liability/Asset account ($78,600) is equal to the funded status, the difference between the DBO of $212,700 and the plan assets of $134,100.

2015 Work Sheet and Entries with Actuarial Gains/Losses. Refer back to the pension plan activities for Zarle Corporation in Illustration 19-8 and review what happens during 2015. No additional plan amendments were made in this year; therefore, there are no past service costs to be recognized in 2015. However, there is an actuarial loss in 2015. The loss came about because the actuary updated the underlying actuarial assumptions used in calculating the DBO at December 31, 2015. The change in assumptions resulted in an increase in the balance of this obligation. If the obligation had been reduced, this would have been an actuarial gain. For 2015, assume that the contribution made by Zarle to the plan occurred on July 1, 2015, rather than at the end of the year.

Under the ASPE immediate recognition approach to pension accounting, the increase in the obligation caused by the actuarial loss is recognized as pension expense in the same accounting period. The immediate recognition in pension expense of both past service costs and actuarial gains and losses can cause significant variability in the pension expense recognized each year. However, both the funded status and statement of financial position pension account are reported at up-to-date funding-related values.

Actuarial gains and losses are discussed more fully in Appendix 19B.

Illustration 19-11

Pension Work Sheet under ASPE—2015

	A	B	C	D	F	G
			General Journal Entries		Memo Record	
2	Items	Annual Pension Expense	Cash	Accrued Benefit Liability/Asset	Accrued Benefit Obligation	Plan Assets
3	Balance, Dec. 31, 2014			78,600 Cr.	212,700 Cr.	134,100 Dr.
4	(l) Service cost	13,000 Dr.			13,000 Cr.	
5	(m) Interest cost	21,270 Dr.			21,270 Cr.	
6	(n) Actual return	12,000 Cr.				12,000 Dr.
7	(o) Contribution		24,000 Cr.			24,000 Dr.
8	(p) Benefits paid				10,500 Dr.	10,500 Cr.
9	(q) Actuarial loss	28,530 Dr.			28,530 Cr.	
10	Expense entry, 2015	50,800 Dr.		50,800 Cr.		
11	Contribution entry, 2015		24,000 Cr.	24,000 Dr.		
12	Balance, Dec. 31, 2015			105,400 Cr.	265,000 Cr.	159,600 Dr.
13						

The work sheet in Illustration 19-11 presents all the pension transactions and information used by Zarle Corporation in 2015 under ASPE (where ASPE uses the term "ABO" instead of "DBO"). The beginning balances for this year are identical to the 2014 ending balances from Illustration 19-10.

Entries (l), (m), (n), (o), and (p) are similar to the entries that were explained in 2013 and 2014. Entry (q) records the increase in the accrued benefit obligation that results from a change in actuarial assumptions. Using up-to-date actuarial assumptions at December 31, 2015, the actuary calculates the ending balance to be $265,000. Since the memo record balance at December 31 is $236,470 (equal to $212,700 + $13,000 + $21,270 − $10,500), there is a difference of $28,530 ($265,000 − $236,470). This $28,530 increase in the employer's obligation is the actuarial loss.

The journal entry on December 31, 2015, to formally record pension expense for the year under ASPE is as follows:

<table>
<tr><td>Pension Expense</td><td>50,800</td><td></td></tr>
<tr><td>Accrued Benefit Liability/Asset</td><td></td><td>50,800</td></tr>
</table>

A = L + SE
+50,800 −50,800

Cash flows: No effect

The company has already recorded the $24,000 contribution during the year as follows under both ASPE and IFRS:

<table>
<tr><td>Accrued Benefit Liability/Asset</td><td>24,000</td><td></td></tr>
<tr><td>Cash</td><td></td><td>24,000</td></tr>
</table>

A = L + SE
−24,000 −24,000

Cash flows: ↓ 24,000 outflow

As illustrated previously for the 2013 and 2014 work sheets, the $105,400 credit balance of the Accrued Benefit Liability/Asset account reported on the statement of financial position at December 31, 2015, is once again equal to the funded status of $265,000 − $159,600 = $105,400. Anyone reading Zarle Corporation's financial statements would expect to see a net liability of $105,400 on the company's statement of financial position if the pension fund was actually underfunded by $105,400. This is an advantage of the immediate recognition approach.

On the other hand, pension expense on the income statement is highly variable from year to year due to the immediate recognition of actuarial gains and losses and past service costs directly in expense. Management, however, generally thinks that immediate recognition of these costs gives a false picture of the company's risk. The fluctuations in pension expense are felt to be beyond management's control, and over the longer term many of the actuarial gains and losses are expected to reverse. As a result, historically there has been support for a deferral and amortization approach to accounting for defined benefit plans. More recently, IFRS makes use of other comprehensive income to minimize the impact of actuarial gains and losses on net income and earnings per share, as illustrated below:

	A	B	C	D	E	F	G
1		General Journal Entries				Memo Record	
2	Items	Remeasure-ment (Gain) Loss OCI	Annual Pension Expense	Cash	Net Defined Benefit Liability/ Asset	Defined Benefit Obligation	Plan Assets
3	Balance, Dec. 31, 2014				78,600 Cr.	212,700 Cr.	134,100 Dr.
4	(l) Service cost		13,000 Dr.			13,000 Cr.	
5	(m) Interest cost		21,270 Dr.			21,270 Cr.	
6	(n) Expected return		14,610 Cr.				14,610 Dr.
7	(o) Remeasurement loss on plan assets	2,610 Dr.					2,610 Cr.
8	(p) Contribution			24,000 Cr.	24,000 Cr.		24,000 Dr.
9	(q) Benefits paid					10,500 Dr.	10,500 Cr.
10	(r) Actuarial loss	28,530 Dr.				28,530 Cr.	
11	Expense entry, 2015	31,140 Dr.	19,660 Dr.		50,800 Cr.		
12	Contribution entry, 2015			24,000 Cr.	24,000 Dr.		
13	Balance, Dec. 31, 2015				105,400 Cr.	265,000 Cr.	159,600 Dr.
14							

Illustration 19-12

Pension Work Sheet under IFRS—2015

The work sheet in Illustration 19-12 presents all the pension transactions and information used by Zarle Corporation in 2015 under IFRS. The beginning balances for this year are identical to the 2014 ending balances from Illustration 19-10.

Entries (l), (m), (p), and (q) are similar to the entries that were explained for ASPE with Illustration 19-11. Entry (n) indicates the expected return on the plan assets based on the same discount rate that was used for the DBO. Recall that we are assuming that the 2015 contribution occurred on July 1, 2015; therefore, the funds were available to earn interest for half of the year.[22] The expected return on plan assets is therefore [$134,100 + (24,000 × $^6/_{12}$)] × 10% = $14,610]. Entry (o) represents the remeasurement loss on the plan assets that is calculated as the difference between the expected return and the actual return of $12,000. Entry (r) records the increase in the defined benefit obligation that results from a change in actuarial assumptions, calculated as explained above for ASPE. However, under IFRS, this actuarial loss is recorded as part of the remeasurement gain or loss that is reported in other comprehensive income on the statement of comprehensive income.

The journal entry on December 31, 2015, to formally record pension expense for the year under IFRS is as follows:

Pension Expense	19,660	
Remeasurement Loss (OCI)	31,140	
Net Defined Benefit Liability/Asset		50,800

A	=	L	+	SE
		+50,800		−50,800

Cash flows: No effect

Other Considerations

Limit on the Carrying Amount of a Net Defined Benefit Asset. Although the illustrations provided in this chapter result in net defined benefit liabilities being reported on the statement of financial position, net defined benefit assets are also found on corporate statements of financial position. The accounting standards provide for an **asset ceiling test** on the balance of any benefit asset reported on the statement of financial position.

Similar to most assets we have studied, there is a limit on the carrying amount of a net defined benefit asset resulting from a defined benefit plan. In general, if the fair value of the plan assets is greater than the future benefits the company is expected to receive from the assets, a valuation allowance is needed to reduce the asset's reported amount. Generally, the "asset ceiling" limit is determined the same way under IFRS as ASPE and considers benefits to the company in the form of refunds from the plan or reductions in future contributions to the plan. Calculations differ under the deferral and amortization approach of ASPE as companies would first need to take into account unamortized costs/losses in excess of unamortized gains.

Although the calculations required are not explained in this text, you should be aware that the change in the valuation allowance in the year is recognized as a component of the pension expense in income in the year. In addition, the net defined benefit asset is reported based on the asset ceiling on the statement of financial position.[23]

Underlying Concept

The measurement of an asset always takes into account the amount of the future benefits expected from the recognized item.

Other Benefits. This chapter presents the basics of accounting for employee future benefits. In addition to the valuation of the funded status asset, further complexities arise from obligation settlements, benefits provided through insurance contracts or other arrangements, plan curtailments, termination benefits, and multi-employer plans.

Other Defined Benefit Plans

Other Post-Employment and Long-Term Employee Benefit Plans with Benefits that Vest or Accumulate

Objective 8

Account for defined benefit plans with benefits that vest or accumulate other than pension plans.

In addition to pension plans, companies provide their employees with other post-employment benefits as part of their compensation package. These may include such benefits as health care, prescription drugs, life insurance, dental and eye care, legal and tax services, tuition assistance, or free or subsidized travel. In the past, most companies accounted for the cost of these employee future benefits as an expense in the period when the benefits were provided to the retirees, their spouses, dependants, and beneficiaries; that is, on a pay-as-you-go basis. In 2000, the Canadian standard changed to require companies to account for all defined benefit plans where the benefits vest or accumulate on the same basis as they account for defined benefit pension plans.

In 1990, the FASB issued *Statement No. 106, Employers' Accounting for Post-Retirement Benefits Other Than Pensions.* This standard required a change from the pay-as-you-go method of accounting for these benefits to an accrual basis, similar to pension accounting. When the standard was first applied, the effect on most U.S. companies was significant. For example, **General Motors** announced a U.S. $20.8-billion charge against its 1992 earnings as a result of adopting the new standard, and this was at a time when the company's net book value before the charge was approximately U.S. $28 billion! The impact of a subsequent change in Canada was not as significant as in the United States because of broader health-care coverage paid for by the government. A Financial Executives Institute Canada study estimated a total Canadian unreported liability of $52 billion, almost entirely unfunded. In both countries, the requirement to measure the outstanding obligation and related costs resulted in corporate management paying much closer attention to the benefit packages that are offered to employee groups, supporting the saying that "you only control what gets measured and reported."

What Do the Numbers Mean?

Sources: Doron P. Levin, "Company Reports: G.M. Lost $23.5 Billion Last Year," *The New York Times,* February 12, 1993; T. Ross Archibald and Darroch Robertson, "Survey of Pension Plans in Canada," Financial Executives Institute Canada, 1993; Paul Fronstein, "Retiree Health Benefits: Trends and Outlook," *Issue Brief,* Employee Benefit Research Institute, August 2001.

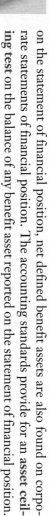

Unlike pension benefits, companies tend not to prefund (set aside assets in advance for) their other post-employment benefit plans. The major reason is that payments to prefund health-care costs, for example, are not tax-deductible, unlike contributions to a pension trust. Although these two types of retirement benefits appear similar, there are also some other significant differences, as indicated in Illustration 19-13.

Item	Pensions	Health-Care Benefits
Funding	Generally funded	Generally not funded
Benefit	Well-defined and level dollar amount	Generally uncapped and great variability
Beneficiary	Retiree (maybe some benefit to surviving spouse)	Retiree, spouse, and other dependants
Benefit payable	Monthly	As needed and used
Predictability	Variables are reasonably predictable	Utilization difficult to predict; level of cost varies geographically and fluctuates over time

Illustration 19-13

Differences between Pensions and Post-Retirement Health-Care Benefits

Measuring the net cost of the post-retirement benefits for the period is complex. Estimates of these costs may have a large margin of error. This is due to the uncertainties in forecasting health-care costs, rates of usage, changes in government health programs, and the differences in non-medical assumptions (such as the discount rate, employee turnover, rate of early retirement, and spouse-age difference). However, not recognizing an obligation and expense before paying the benefits is considered to not be a faithful representation of financial position and performance.

Under ASPE, the basic concepts, accounting terminology, recognition and measurement criteria, and measurement methods that apply to defined benefit pensions for the most part **also apply to the requirements for other benefits** that vest or accumulate based on the service provided by employees. Examples of such benefits are sabbaticals where unrestricted time off with pay is granted for services provided, service-related long-term disability benefits, or sick days not used that accumulate and are paid out on retirement.[24] Assume, for example, that an employee benefit plan provides a cash bonus of $500 per year of service when an employee retires or has his or her employment terminated for other reasons, on condition that the employee has worked there for at least 10 years. Because the right to the benefit is earned by providing service and the benefit increases with the length of service provided, the cost and related liability are accrued starting from the date of employment. The measurement of the obligation and expense takes into consideration the probabilities related to employee turnover. The fact that the benefits do not vest for 10 years does not eliminate the need to recognize the cost and liability over the first 10 years of employment.

Under IFRS, a distinction is made between post-employment plans such as pensions and post-employment health-care benefits, and short-term employee benefits such as paid annual leave (vacation pay), sick leave, and profit-sharing and bonus plans. The short-term employee benefits that accumulate are generally recognized (without discounting) at the amount expected to be paid in exchange for the services provided (IAS 19.11). Short-term benefits were covered in more detail in Chapter 13. Other long-term benefits include items such as paid absences for long service, unrestricted sabbaticals, and long-term benefits that depend on length of service. IFRS requires the same recognition and measurement for these long-term benefits as for post-employment benefits such as pension plans. However, remeasurements of the net defined benefit liability (asset) related to these benefits should be reflected in income (not OCI). For termination benefits, IFRS requires the cost of the benefits to be recognized at the earlier of when the company can no longer withdraw an offer of the benefits and when it recognizes the related restructuring costs.

Other Employee Benefit Plans with Benefits that Do Not Accumulate

Both ASPE and IFRS make no attempt to accrue the benefit costs and liabilities related to employee benefits that do not accumulate with additional service. In this case, there is no basis on which to assign the costs to periods other than the period when the benefits are taken. A good example is costs associated with parental leave or unused sick pay that do not change with an employee's length of service. Instead, both the total cost and liability are recognized when the event occurs that obligates the company to provide the benefits. This is referred to as an "event accrual" method of accounting for benefits and is explained in Chapter 13.

PRESENTATION, DISCLOSURE, AND ANALYSIS

Presentation

Objective 9

Identify the types of information required to be presented and disclosed for defined benefit plans, prepare basic schedules, and be able to read and understand such disclosures.

Statement of Financial Position Presentation of Defined Benefit Assets and Liabilities

Entities with two or more defined benefit plans are required to separately measure the benefit cost, defined benefit obligation, and plan assets for each funded benefit plan. If all the plans result in a net defined benefit liability on the balance sheet or all result in a net defined benefit asset, the plans can be reported together in the financial statements. However, because companies generally do not have the legal right, and do not intend to use the assets of one plan to pay for the benefits of other plans, a net defined benefit asset of one plan and a net defined benefit liability of another are required to be reported separately on the balance sheet or statement of financial position.

Neither IFRS nor ASPE provides any guidance on how to determine whether net defined benefit assets and liabilities for defined benefit plans are current or long-term, so companies revert to basic underlying principles to determine the classification. Most such assets and liabilities are found in the long-term classifications on both sides of the balance sheet.

Income Statement Presentation of Benefit Cost

IFRS and ASPE identify the components that make up the benefit costs for the period, and both indicate that a portion of these costs may be required to be treated as a product cost in inventory or capitalized in a property, plant, and equipment asset. However, neither IFRS nor ASPE dictates how the components of benefit costs are to be reported on the income statement. Companies therefore have the option of reporting current service cost, interest cost, and the expected return on plan assets as separate components, as part of similar expenses, or in total as a single benefit cost. Many companies report all the components together as a single benefit cost.

Disclosure

Disclosure Requirements

For a phenomenon as significant and specialized as pensions and other defined benefit plans, it is not surprising that there are extensive reporting and disclosure requirements. While ASPE requires only a limited set of basic information in addition to the accounting policy choices the entity has made, IAS 19 *Employee Benefits* requires a high level of accountability from companies for the effect of such plans on their current and future performance, financial position, and risk.

Under ASPE, separate disclosures are required for plans that provide pension benefits and other types of employee future benefits, and most of these are for defined benefit plans. This includes:

- a description of each type of plan and any major changes in the terms of the plan during the year;
- the effective date of the most recent actuarial valuation for funding purposes;
- the year-end funded status, including the fair value of the plan assets and accrued benefit obligation; and
- an explanation of any difference between the amount reported on the balance sheet and the plans' funded status.

It is expected that any additional information needed by users is available from the company.

The objective under IFRS is to provide disclosures for a broad range of users with no access to additional information. The information should describe:

- the characteristics of the defined benefit plans and risks associated with them;
- the amounts in the statements arising from the plans; and
- how the defined benefit plans help them assess the amounts, timing, and likelihood of the cash flows that are associated with future benefits (IFRS 19.135).

In addition to a description of each defined benefit plan or groupings of similar plans, and what accounting choices were made where choices are permitted, the following types of information are also required:

- **Reconciliations** of the opening to closing balances of the present value of the net defined benefit liability/asset, plan assets, and the DBO
- **Amounts included in periodic net income:** the amount included in expense, such as current service cost, interest expense, and return on plan assets, along with amounts recognized in OCI such as actuarial gains and losses from changes in assumptions
- **Sensitivity information for each significant actuarial assumptions,** including the impact on the DBO
- Many other disclosures, including details relating to classes of items making up the fair value of plan assets, asset-liability matching strategies, and funding arrangements that affect future contributions

Disclosure Illustration

Real World Emphasis

Companies organize their disclosures in a variety of acceptable ways. **Marks and Spencer Group plc,** with 731 stores in the UK and another 387 internationally, is a food and general merchandise (clothing and home) retailer. Its 2012 accounting policy note and specific consolidated statement of financial position note on pension provisions are set out in Illustration 19-14, providing a comprehensive example of disclosures required under IFRS.[25] As you can tell, the disclosures are extensive! The M&S financial statements for its year ended March 31, 2012, are reported in millions of pounds (£m).

It is particularly interesting to note the cumulative actuarial losses recognized in equity totalling £1,412.8 million at the end of fiscal 2012 as in part H of Note 11. The actuarial loss of £189.9 million in the year, reflects an actual positive adjustment on the plan assets of £581.0 million offset by a £770.9 million actuarial loss on liabilities, relating mostly to changes in actuarial assumptions. This charge bypasses the consolidated income statement and earnings per share, and is reflected entirely in other comprehensive income. Look through the other parts of this note and see if you can relate the information to what has been explained in the chapter.

Illustration 19-14

Illustrative Disclosure—Marks and Spencer Group plc, March 31, 2012

1) Accounting policies (selected excerpts)

Pensions

Funded pension plans are in place for the Group's UK employees and some employees overseas.

For defined benefit pension schemes, the difference between the fair value of the assets of the defined benefit obligation is recognised as an asset or liability in the statement of financial position. The defined benefit obligation is actuarially calculated using the projected unit credit method.

The service cost of providing retirement benefits to employees during the year, together with the cost of any benefits relating to past service, is charged to operating profit in the year.

A credit representing the expected return on the assets of the retirement benefit schemes during the year is included within finance income. This is based on the market value of the assets of the schemes at the start of the financial year.

A charge is also made within finance income representing the expected increase in the liabilities of the retirement benefit schemes during the year. This arises from the liabilities of the schemes being one year closer to payment.

Actuarial gains and losses are recognised immediately in the statement of comprehensive income.

Payments to defined contribution retirement benefit schemes are charged as an expense as they fall due.

Critical accounting estimates and judgements

D. Post-retirement benefits

The determination of the pension cost and defined benefit obligation of the Group's defined benefit pension schemes depends on the selection of certain assumptions which include the discount rate, inflation rate, salary growth, mortality and expected return on scheme assets. Differences arising from actual experiences or future changes in assumptions will be reflected in subsequent periods. See note 11 for further details of assumptions and note 12 for critical judgements associated with the Marks & Spencer UK Pension Scheme interest in the Marks and Spencer Scottish Limited Partnership.

Note 11 Retirement benefits (excerpts)

The Group provides pension arrangements for the benefit of its UK employees through the Marks & Spencer UK Pension Scheme. This has a defined benefit section, which was closed to new entrants with effect from 1 April 2002, and a defined contribution section which has been open to new members with effect from 1 April 2003.

The defined benefit section operates on a final salary basis and at the year end had some 14,000 active members (last year 15,000), 56,000 deferred members (last year 56,000) and 51,000 pensioners (last year 51,000). At the year end, the defined contribution section had some 9,000 active members (last year 9,000) and some 2,000 deferred members (last year 2,000).

The Group also operates a small defined benefit pension scheme in the Republic of Ireland. Retirement benefits also include a UK post-retirement healthcare scheme and unfunded retirement benefits.

Within the total Group retirement benefit cost of £32.1m (last year £22.4m excluding a one-off pension credit of £10.7m), £12.0m (last year £1.0m) relates to the UK defined benefit section, £15.9m (last year £14.3m) to the UK defined contribution section and £4.2m (last year £7.1m) to other retirement benefit schemes.

A. Pensions and other post-retirement liabilities

	2012 £m	2011 £m
Total market value of assets	6,186.4	5,398.1
Present value of scheme liabilities	(6,095.1)	(5,215.5)
Net funded pension plan asset	91.3	182.6
Unfunded retirement benefits	(0.8)	(0.9)
Post-retirement healthcare	(12.5)	(13.2)
Net retirement benefit asset	78.0	168.5
Analysed in the statement of financial position as:		
Retirement benefit asset	91.3	182.6
Retirement benefit deficit	(13.3)	(14.1)
	78.0	168.5

B. Financial assumptions

A full actuarial valuation of the UK Defined Benefit Pension Scheme was carried out at 31 March 2009 and showed a deficit of £1.3bn. A funding plan of £800m was agreed with the Trustees. The difference between the valuation and the funding plan is expected to be met by investment returns on the existing assets of the pension scheme. The financial assumptions for the UK scheme and the most recent actuarial valuations of the other post-retirement schemes have been updated by independent qualified actuaries to take account of the requirements of IAS 19 – 'Employee Benefits' in order to assess the liabilities of the schemes and are as follows:

(continued)

Illustration 19-14

Illustrative Disclosure—Marks and Spencer Group plc, March 31, 2012 (continued)

	2012 %	2011 %
Rate of increase in salaries	1.0	1.0
Rate of increase in pensions in payment for service	2.3-3.1	2.4-3.4
Discount rate	4.6	5.5
Inflation rate	3.1	3.4
Long-term healthcare cost increases	7.1	7.4

The inflation rate of 3.1% reflects the Retail Price Index (RPI) rate. In line with changes to legislation certain benefits have been calculated with reference to the Consumer Price Index (CPI) as the inflationary measure and in these instances a rate of 2.1% (last year 2.7%) has been used. Last year, the change from RPI to CPI for deferred revaluation was included in the results, resulting in a gain of approximately £170m, taken as an actuarial gain on the obligation.

The amount of the surplus varies if the main financial assumptions change, particularly the discount rate. If the discount rate increased/decreased by 0.1% the IAS 19 surplus would increase/decrease by c.£110m (last year £90m). If the inflation rate increased by 0.1%, the IAS 19 surplus would decrease by c.£75m and if the inflation rate decreased by 0.1%, the IAS 19 surplus would increase by c.£65m.

C. Demographic assumptions

Apart from cash commutation and post-retirement mortality, the demographic assumptions are in line with those adopted for the last formal actuarial valuation of the scheme performed as at 31 March 2009. The allowance for cash commutation reflects actual scheme experience. The post-retirement mortality assumptions are based on an analysis of the pensioner mortality trends under the scheme for the period to March 2009 updated to allow for anticipated longevity improvements over the subsequent years. The specific mortality rates used are based on the SAPS tables, adjusted to allow for the experience of scheme pensioners. The life expectancies underlying the valuation are as follows:

		2012 years	2011 years
Current pensioners (at age 65)	– males	22.1	22.0
	– females	23.4	23.4
Future pensioners (at age 65)	– males	23.2	23.2
	– females	24.3	24.3

An increase of one year in the life expectancies would decrease the IAS 19 surplus by c.£200m.

H. Cumulative actuarial gains and losses recognised in equity

	2012 £m	2011 £m
Loss at start of year	(1,222.9)	(1,508.9)
Net actuarial (losses)/gains recognised in the year	(189.9)	286.0
Loss at end of year	**(1,412.8)**	**(1,222.9)**

Analysis

With all the information that is reported in the notes to the financial statements, what should an analysis focus on? The most important elements are the major assumptions that underlie the calculations, the status of the plan, and the company's future cash requirements.

As was indicated earlier in the chapter, the defined benefit obligation and pension expense are based on several estimates that, if altered, can significantly change the amounts. Aside from actuarial assumptions relating to items such as turnover, mortality, and the rate of compensation and health-care increases, the choice of discount rate used to measure the DBO, the current service cost, and the interest cost are also key variables. A one-percentage-point difference in the discount rate could have a 10% or 20% effect on the discounted value. This rate is required to be disclosed so that readers can assess it for reasonableness and compare it with those used by other companies in the industry.

A company's actual cash flow related to pensions is often very different from the pension costs recognized on the income statement, and analysts often try to determine the company's future cash commitments. The disclosure requirements of the standards help somewhat in this regard. They require companies to report the cash impact of the plans in the current period and an estimate of the cash impact for the next fiscal year.

What Do the Numbers Mean?

The new IFRS accounting standards for post-retirement benefits effective January 1, 2013, require companies to record their previously unrecognized past service costs, actuarial gains and losses, and any transition costs in other comprehensive income and to recognize the plan's net benefit asset or liability on the statement of financial position. Previously, companies used the deferral and amortization approach under IFRS, and unamortized amounts were disclosed but not recognized in the accounts. As a result, the balance sheet benefit asset or liability would not portray the entity's real resource or obligation as measured by the funded status of its plan. Did the change make much difference to Canadian companies?

Canadian companies following pre-2011 Canadian standards applied the deferral and amortization approach as described in Appendix 19B of this chapter for private enterprises. In 2011, companies adopting IFRS could choose to recognize actuarial gains or losses in the period they occur (IAS 19.93), and could choose to recognize the actuarial gains or losses in OCI. Companies choosing to do so end up with a net defined benefit liability or asset on the balance sheet similar to the amount required under the new employee benefits requirements issued by the IASB in June 2011 (effective January 1, 2013).

For some companies, the adjustment to the new requirements was relatively minor. For others, it was very significant. The following table shows the net benefit asset or liability that was reported on a sample of Canadian companies' statements of financial position on December 31, 2011; the funded status of the benefit plans at the same year-end date; and the unrecognized, unamortized balances related to items such as the pension asset limits (for BCE Inc.) under IFRS. To put the numbers in perspective, the net benefit asset (A) or liability (L) for each company three years earlier (prior to adopting IFRS) is provided.

Company	Net Benefit Asset (A) or Liability (L) Reported on SFP	Funded Status of Plan at Date of the SFP	Unrecognized, Unamortized, Off-Balance Sheet Amounts in 2011	Net Benefit Asset (A) or Liability (L) Reported on SFP Prior to New Requirements
	$	$	$	$
Potash Corp. (Cdn. $ million)	162 (L)	164 (L)	2 (L)	Dec. 31, 2008 105(A)
Bombardier Inc. (U.S. $ million)	2,847 (L)	2,847 (L)	0 (L)	Jan. 31, 2009 271 (A)
BCE Inc. (Cdn. $ million)	1,257 (L)	1,088 (L)	169 (A)	Dec. 31, 2008 989 (A)
Telus Corporation (Cdn. $ million)	1,002 (L)	1,002 (L)	0 (L)	Dec. 31, 2008 1,232 (A)

The major accomplishment of changes to the accounting standards is to require recognition of the previously "unrecognized" amounts in the SFP liability account, instead of just in the notes. IFRS requires that the amounts brought on to the SFP be recognized in OCI. As you can tell from the numbers presented in the table, such a change to the standards had a significant effect on many Canadian public companies' debt to equity ratio and other provisions that underlie existing debt agreements. For example, all of the companies in the table had a net benefit asset on their financial statements prior to the change (see final column), but show a net benefit liability that closely reflects their funded status at the end of 2011 (see columns 2 and 3).

Hopefully, the effect on private company financial statements would not be as significant. Changing from the deferral and amortization approach to the immediate recognition approach approved by ASPE would have a similar effect on the benefit liability as the change noted above. The effect would be dampened, however, if the funded status under the immediate recognition approach is based on a measure of the ABO developed for funding rather than for accounting purposes.

Law

IFRS/ASPE COMPARISON

A Comparison of IFRS and ASPE

Objective 10

Identify differences between the IFRS and ASPE accounting for employee future benefits and what changes are expected in the near future.

Both ASPE and IFRS agree on the objective of accounting for the cost of employee future benefits: to recognize a liability and a cost in the reporting period in which an employee has provided the service that gives rise to the benefits. This is based on the fact that the obligation to provide benefits arises as the employees provide the service. Two different approaches are permitted under ASPE, and there are minor differences in how the immediate recognition approach is applied under ASPE and IFRS. These differences are highlighted in Illustration 19-15.

	Accounting Standards for Private Enterprises (ASPE)—*CICA Handbook*, Part II, Section 3461 (and proposed Section 3462)	IFRS—IAS 19 (effective Jan. 1, 2013)	References to Related Illustrations and Select Brief Exercises
Scope	The standard does not apply to benefits provided during an employee's active employment.	The standard is broader in scope, covering all employee benefits.	N/A
Recognition— defined contribution plans	The standard covers treatment of past service costs and the possibility of an interest cost element.	The standard does not make any reference to past service costs. Amounts are undiscounted as they are current in nature.	N/A
Recognition— defined benefit plans with benefits that vest or accumulate	Two approaches are permitted: an immediate recognition approach and a deferral and amortization approach. (The deferral and amortization approach would be eliminated under new Section 3462.)	Only one approach is permitted: an immediate recognition approach.	Illustration 19-12 (IFRS) and Illustration 19B-5 (ASPE–Deferral and Amortization)
	The immediate recognition model uses a funding valuation measure of the ABO and recognizes past service costs. (Under new Section 3462, valuation would be measured using either the funding valuation or a separate valuation for accounting purposes, and the term "ABO" would be replaced by "DBO.")	Under IFRS, there is no separate funding valuation measure permitted for financial accounting purposes.	N/A
	Under immediate recognition, actuarial gains and losses are recognized immediately in the benefit cost and accrued liability, along with current service cost, interest cost, and the actual return on plan assets.	The IAS 19 approach is similar, but remeasurement gains and losses including actuarial gains and losses are recognized in other comprehensive income.	Illustrations 19-11 and 19-12
	The same standards apply generally to all employee future benefit plans with benefits that vest or accumulate.	The same standards apply only to other long-term benefit plans.	N/A

(continued)

Illustration 19-15

IFRS and ASPE Comparison Chart

Illustration 19-15
IFRS and ASPE Comparison Chart (continued)

	Accounting Standards for Private Enterprises (ASPE)—*CICA Handbook*, Part II, Section 3461 (and proposed Section 3462)	IFRS—IAS 19 (effective Jan. 1, 2013)	References to Related Illustrations and Select Brief Exercises
Measurement —ABO/DBO and plan assets (*Note:* ASPE uses the term "ABO" and IFRS uses the term "DBO" to refer to the benefit obligation).	While the ABO and plan assets should be measured as at the date of the annual financial statements, a date up to three months earlier may be used as long as it is consistently used. This exception is not indicated when using the immediate recognition approach. (Under proposed Section 3462, the term "DBO" would be used and the DBO and plan assets would be measured as at the balance sheet date. However, measurement of the DBO could take place at an earlier date and then be updated to reflect the DBO at the balance sheet date.)	The plan assets and DBO are required to represent reporting date values.	N/A
—discount rate	Use of a current rate can be either the current yield on debt instruments (such as high-quality corporate bonds) or a current settlement rate.	Use of a current rate can only be the current yield on high-quality debt instruments such as high-quality corporate bonds.	N/A
	Under the deferral and amortization approach (ASPE), the expected return on plan assets could be different from the discount rate used for the ABO. (Under proposed Section 3462, deferral and amortization is not permitted, and the same discount rate is used for plan assets and the DBO.)	The same discount rate is used for plan assets and the DBO.	N/A
—past service costs	Past service costs are amortized over the period deemed to benefit from the plan initiation or amendment if the deferral and amortization approach is used. This is usually the expected period until the employees are eligible for the plan's full benefits, but may be shorter. Under the immediate recognition approach, past service costs are recognized immediately.	Past service costs are recognized immediately in net income.	Illustration 19-10 (IFRS) and Illustration 19B-6 (ASPE-Deferral and Amortization) BE19-2, BE19-9, BE19-11, BE19-12, and BE19-13
—actuarial gains and losses (deferral and amortization approach)	The minimum amount of actuarial gains and losses that are amortized to expense is dictated by the corridor approach. A larger amount can be recognized, even to the extent of immediate recognition. No amount is permitted to be recognized in OCI.	The deferral and amortization approach is not permitted under IFRS.	Illustrations 19B-1 and 19B-2 (ASPE-Deferral and Amortization) BE19-10 and BE19-14

(*continued*)

	Accounting Standards for Private Enterprises (ASPE)—CICA Handbook, Part II, Section 3462	IFRS—IAS 19 (effective Jan. 1, 2013)	References to Related Illustrations and Select Brief Exercises
—actuarial gains and losses (immediate recognition approach)	(Under proposed Section 3462, the deferral and amortization approach would not be permitted.) The entity recognizes the entire amount of actuarial gains and losses in net income.	The entity recognizes the amount of actuarial gains and losses in OCI instead of net income.	Illustrations 19-11 and 19-12
Disclosure	Only basic information is required to be disclosed.	Extensive disclosures are required, particularly for post-retirement pensions and health-related defined benefit plans.	Illustration 19-14

Illustration 19-15

IFRS and ASPE Comparison Chart (continued)

Looking Ahead

Updates to IAS 19, published in 2011, with an effective date of January 1, 2013, created additional differences between the ASPE requirements and those of IFRS. These are expected to be taken into account in the replacement of *CICA Handbook*, Part II, Section 3461 with Section 3462. (An Exposure Draft of Section 3462 was issued in January 2012, and the revised standard is expected to be issued in the second quarter of 2013, with a planned implementation date of January 1, 2014.)

SUMMARY OF LEARNING OBJECTIVES

1 **Understand the importance of pensions from a business perspective.**

A pension plan, together with post-retirement health care, is often part of an employee's overall compensation package. The size of these plans, in terms of both the number of employees and cost of benefits, has made their costs very large (on average) in relation to companies' financial position, results of operations, and cash flows. With the vast majority of defined benefit plans being underfunded, more and more companies are moving toward defined contribution plans.

2 **Identify and account for a defined contribution benefit plan.**

Defined contribution plans are plans that specify how contributions are determined rather than what benefits the individual will receive. They are accounted for similar to a cash basis.

3 **Identify and explain what a defined benefit plan is and the related accounting issues.**

Defined benefit plans specify the benefits that the employee is entitled to. Defined benefit plans whose benefits vest or accumulate typically provide for the benefits to be a function of the employee's years of service and, for pensions, compensation level. In general, the employer's obligation for such a plan and the associated cost is accrued as an expense as the employee provides the service. An actuary usually determines the required amounts.

4 **Explain what the employer's benefit obligation is, identify alternative measures for this obligation, and prepare a continuity schedule of transactions and events that change its balance.**

The employer's benefit obligation is the actuarial present value of the benefits that have been earned by employees for services they have provided up to the date of the statement of financial position. The vested benefit method, accumulated benefit method, and projected benefit method are three methods that could be used to measure companies' obligations. The third method is the one used to determine the defined benefit obligation, basing the calculation of the deferred compensation amount on both vested and non-vested service using future salaries. This last method is used under both IFRS and ASPE. The funding approach specified by legislation is the measurement of the obligation under ASPE's immediate recognition approach. The DBO is increased by current service cost, interest cost, plan amendments that usually increase employee entitlements for prior service, and by actuarial losses. It is reduced by payment of pension benefits and by actuarial gains.

5 Identify transactions and events that change benefit plan assets, and calculate the balance of the assets.

Plan assets are increased by company and employee contributions and the actual return that is earned on fund assets (including realized and unrealized gains and losses), and are reduced by pension benefits paid to retirees.

6 Explain what a benefit plan's funded status is, calculate it, and identify what transactions and events change its amount.

A plan's funded status is the difference between the defined benefit obligation and the plan assets at a point in time. It tells you the extent to which a company has a net obligation (underfunded) or a surplus (overfunded) relative to the benefits that are promised. All items that change the plan assets and DBO with the exception of the payments to retirees change the funded status.

7 Identify the components of pension expense, and account for a defined benefit pension plan under the immediate recognition approach.

Pension expense under the immediate recognition approach is a function of: (1) service cost, (2) interest on the liability, (3) actual return on plan assets, (4) past service costs, and (5) net actuarial gains or losses. Under ASPE, all are immediately included in current expense in their entirety. The pension obligation amount is determined under a funding basis measure. Under IFRS, pension costs relating to current service, past service, and net interest on the net defined benefit obligation are included in pension expense. Actuarial gains and losses, and any return on plan assets excluding amounts included in the net interest on the net defined benefit obligation (asset), are recognized in OCI.

8 Account for defined benefit plans with benefits that vest or accumulate other than pension plans.

Under ASPE, any non-pension defined benefit plans with benefits that vest or accumulate are accounted for in the same way as defined benefit pension plans. Under IFRS, short-term employee benefits are generally recognized (without discounting) at the amount expected to be paid in exchange for the services provided. Other long-term benefits include items such as short-term absences for long service, unrestricted sabbaticals, and long-term disability plans. IFRS requires the same recognition and measurement for these long-term benefits as for pension plans. Specifically, changes in the liabilities related to these benefits should be reflected in income. For termination benefits, IFRS requires the cost of the benefits to be recognized at the earlier of when the company can no longer withdraw an offer of employment and when it recognizes the related restructuring costs.

9 Identify the types of information required to be presented and disclosed for defined benefit plans, prepare basic schedules, and be able to read and understand such disclosures.

ASPE requires a description of the plans, major changes made in the plans, dates of the actuarial valuations, the fair value of the plan assets, the ABO, and the funded status and how this relates to the balance sheet account. IFRS requires substantial information, such as reconciliations of changes in the DBO and plan assets, details of amounts included in net income, underlying assumptions and sensitivity analysis, and other information related to help determine cash flows.

10 Identify differences between the IFRS and ASPE accounting for employee future benefits and what changes are expected in the near future.

IAS 19 is broader based and covers more employee benefits than does *CICA Handbook*, Part II, Section 3461. ASPE permits a choice of the immediate recognition approach or the deferral and amortization approach, whereas IFRS permits only the former approach, but with options within it. With recent changes to IAS 19, most companies are expected to recognize the net defined benefit liability (or asset) on the statement of financial position with items such as current service cost, past service cost and interest on the DBO and plan assets recognized in net income, and remeasurement changes and actuarial gains and losses reported in OCI. At the present time, ASPE still allows companies to use the deferral and amortization approach, although this option is expected to be eliminated eventually.

KEY TERMS

APPENDIX 19A

EXAMPLE OF A ONE-PERSON PLAN

Objective 11

Explain and apply basic calculations to determine current service cost, the defined benefit obligation, and past service cost for a one-person defined benefit pension plan.

The following simplified example is provided to help you better visualize and understand some of the new concepts introduced in this chapter. It uses an actuarial valuation done for accounting purposes.

Assume that Lee Sung, age 30, begins employment with HTSM Corp. on January 1, 2013, at a starting salary of $37,500. It is expected that Lee will work for HTSM Corp. for 35 years, retiring on December 31, 2047, when Lee is 65 years old. Taking into account estimated compensation increases of approximately 4% per year, Lee's salary at retirement is expected to be $150,000. Further assume that mortality tables indicate the life expectancy of someone age 65 in 2047 is 12 years.

The timeline in Illustration 19A-1 provides a snapshot of much of this information.

Illustration 19A-1

Timeline

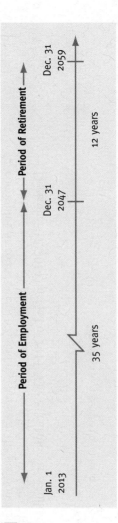

HTSM Corp. sponsors a defined benefit pension plan for its employees with the following **pension benefit formula**:

Annual pension benefit on retirement = 2% of salary at retirement for each year of service, or
= 2% final salary × years of service

In order to measure 2013 pension costs, dollars paid in the future must be discounted to their present values. A **discount rate of 6%** is assumed to be the current yield on high-quality debt instruments.

Current Service Cost

Year 2013

How much pension does Lee Sung earn for the one year of service in 2013? Applying the pension formula **using projected salaries:**

Annual pension benefit on retirement	= 2% × $150,000 × 1 year
	= $3,000 per year of retirement

That is, by virtue of working one year, Lee Sung has earned an entitlement to a pension of $3,000 per year for life.

To determine the company's cost (expense) in 2013 related to this benefit, HTSM discounts these future payments to their present value at December 31, 2013. This is a two-step process. **First**, the pension annuity of $3,000 per year for an estimated 12 years is discounted to its present value on December 31, 2047, the employee's retirement date. Because this is still 34 years in the future at December 31, 2013, the **second** step discounts the annuity's present value at the beginning of retirement to its present value at the end of 2013. The calculations are as follows:

PV of $3,000 annuity (n = 12, i = 6%) at Dec. 31, 2047	= $3,000 × 8.38384
	(Table A-4)
	= $25,151.52
PV of amount of $25,151.52 (n = 34, i = 6%) at Dec. 31, 2013	= $25,151.52 × 0.13791
	(Table A-2)
	= $3,469

Therefore, the current service cost to HTSM of the pension benefit earned by Lee Sung in 2013 is $3,469. This is a primary component of the period's pension expense.

Year 2014

The calculation of HTSM's current service cost for 2014 is identical to 2013, assuming a continuing discount rate of 6% and no change in the pension formula. The only difference is that the $3,000 of pension benefit earned by Lee Sung in 2014 is discounted back to December 31, 2014, instead of 2013. The calculation is as follows:

Annual pension benefit on retirement	= 2% × $150,000 × 1 year
	= $3,000 per year of retirement
PV of $3,000 annuity (n = 12, i = 6%) at Dec. 31, 2047	= $3,000 × 8.38384
	(Table A-4)
	= $25,151.52
PV of amount of $25,151.52 (n = 33, i = 6%) at Dec. 31, 2014	= $25,151.52 × 0.14619
	(Table A-2)
	= $3,677

Therefore, the current service cost to HTSM of the pension benefit earned by Lee Sung in 2014 is $3,677.

Defined Benefit Obligation (DBO)

At December 31, 2014

The defined benefit obligation calculation is similar to the current service cost calculation except that it represents the present value of the pension benefits that have **accumulated for employee services provided to date as determined under the pension benefit formula**. Because 2013 was the first year of employment, we assume that the DBO at December 31, 2013, is $3,469, the same as the current service cost. At December 31, 2014, the DBO is determined as follows:

Pension benefit earned to Dec. 31, 2014	= 2% × $150,000 × 2 years	
	= $6,000 per year of retirement	
PV of $6,000 annuity (*n* = 12, *i* = 6%) at Dec. 31, 2047	= $6,000 × 8.38384	
	(Table A-4)	
	= $50,303.04	
PV of amount of $50,303.04 (*n* = 33, *j* = 6%) at Dec. 31, 2014	= $50,303.04 × 0.14619	
	(Table A-2)	
	= $7,354	

The defined benefit obligation at the end of 2014 is $7,354. Further, we can reconcile the opening DBO at January 1, 2014, with the ending DBO at December 31, 2014:

DBO, January 1, 2014	$3,469
Add interest on the outstanding obligation: $3,469 × 6% × 1 year	208
Add 2014 current service cost	3,677
DBO, December 31, 2014	$7,354

At December 31, 2047

If Lee Sung works for the full 35 years, assuming no change in the $150,000 final salary estimate, pension benefit formula, discount rate, and life expectancy, the DBO on retirement is as follows:

Pension benefit earned to Dec. 31, 2047	= 2% × $150,000 × 35 years	
	= $105,000 per year of retirement	
PV of $105,000 annuity (*n* = 12, *i* = 6%) at Dec. 31, 2047	= $105,000 × 8.38384	
	(Table A-4)	
	= $880,303	

At December 31, 2047, HTSM has an obligation with a present value of $880,303. If the company had set aside assets (that is, funded the plan) each year in an amount equal to the current service cost and the funds had earned exactly 6%, the fund assets would have accumulated to $880,303 as well. The company needs to have this amount of cash in order to purchase an annuity that will pay Lee Sung an annual pension of $105,000 for life, which under actuarial calculations is estimated to be 12 years.

Past Service Cost

Now assume that Lee Sung had worked for HTSM's subsidiary company for six years prior to working for HTSM. Further assume that, on December 31, 2017, in determining Lee's pension benefits on retirement, HTSM agrees to give Lee credit for the years that he worked for the subsidiary company before 2013. What is the cost—the past service cost—of this to HTSM? We can determine this by calculating the company's DBO before and after the pension amendment:

	Before credit for prior service	After credit for prior service
Pension benefit earned to Dec. 31, 2017:	2% × $150,000 × 5 yrs = $3,000 × 5 = $15,000 per year	2% × $150,000 × 11 yrs = $3,000 × 11 = $33,000 per year
PV of pension earned to date at Dec. 31, 2047: (PV factor, annuity: $n = 12$, $i = 6$)	$15,000 × 8.38384 = $125,757.60	$33,000 × 8.38384 = $276,666.72
PV of pension earned to date at Dec. 31, 2017: (PV factor, amount: $n = 30$, $i = 6$)	$125,757.60 × 0.17411 = $21,896	$276,666.72 × 0.17411 = $48,170

DBO at Dec. 31, 2017, **after** prior service recognized	$48,170
DBO at Dec. 31, 2017, **before** prior service recognized	21,896
Past service cost incurred	$26,274

Giving credit for prior years of service is not the only event that creates a past service cost. Another common cause of past service cost is a change in the pension benefit formula. For example, if HTSM had agreed to change the formula to 2½% of final salary per year worked, this would have a significant effect on the DBO amount as soon as the formula was changed. A one-half-percentage-point increase on a base rate of 2% is a 25% increase!

11 Explain and apply basic calculations to determine current service cost, the defined benefit obligation, and past service cost for a one-person defined benefit pension plan.

The current service cost is a calculation of the present value of the benefits earned by employees that is attributable to the current period. The defined ben-

efit obligation is the present value of the accumulated benefits earned to a point in time, according to the pension formula and using projected salaries. Past service cost is the present value of the additional benefits granted to employees in the case of a plan amendment.

EXAMPLE OF THE DEFERRAL AND AMORTIZATION APPROACH

Objective 12

Identify the components of pension benefit cost, and account for a defined benefit pension plan when using the deferral and amortization approach under ASPE; determine the pension plan accounts reported in the financial statements and explain their relationship to the funded status of the plan.

The following example illustrates the **deferral and amortization approach**, which is an option for accounting for pensions under ASPE (and was allowed under IFRS until January 1, 2013). At the time this book went to press, the AcSB was considering eliminating the deferral and amortization approach under ASPE; however, it may be several years until it is completely phased out in Canada.

Deferral and Amortization Approach

One of the major differences between the accounting for defined benefit plans using the deferral and amortization approach and the immediate recognition approach is the valuation of the DBO or ABO that is used. (Under ASPE, the term "accrued benefit obligation" or ABO is used, so that is the term we use in this appendix.) Under the deferral and amortization approach, the actuarial valuation of the ABO is **not** the one developed for funding purposes, but rather it is one developed specifically for accounting purposes. The second difference relates to the treatment of the **past service costs** and **actuarial gains and losses**. The **deferral and amortization approach** provides opportunities to delay the recognition of both in relation to the benefit plan expense and the accrued benefit liability/asset on the statement of financial position. (Note that ASPE uses the term "accrued benefit liability" in relation to the deferral and amortization approach and that is what we use in this appendix.) We begin with a discussion of each of these two components before applying this approach to a specific company.

Past Service Costs

Underlying Concept

The matching concept is at the core of the deferral and amortization approach.

One question that standard setters have wrestled with is whether the past service costs or credits that are associated with the adoption or amendment of pension plans should be fully recognized in expense, and therefore net income, when the plan is initiated or amended. Those advocating the deferral and amortization approach to pension benefit accounting take the position that these costs should not be recognized immediately in expense. The rationale for deferral is that the employer would not provide credit for past years of service unless it is expected to receive benefits in the future; based on this reasoning, the past service costs should not be recognized immediately in expense.

In line with this position, the ASPE deferral and amortization standard specifies that the past service cost is deferred initially and recognized as an expense on a straight-line basis over the period in which the firm expects to realize the economic benefits from the change in plan. This is normally the expected period from the time of adoption or amendment until the employee is eligible for the plan's full benefits.[26] The period benefiting may actually be shorter than this, justifying a faster recognition of the past service costs. For example, consider a situation in which a company has a history of making plan amendments as a result of renegotiating a union agreement every three years. In this case, writing off the costs to expense on a straight-line basis over three years may be acceptable. If a plan amendment reduces the entity's ABO, the resulting past service **benefit** is amortized in the same way.

Under the deferral and amortization approach, notice that if only a portion of the past service cost is recognized in expense, that is all that is recognized in the statement of financial position liability (or asset) account as well. The remaining unamortized amounts remain off-balance sheet. Past service costs that have not yet been amortized to income are known as **unamortized past service costs** or **unrecognized past service costs**. We will come back to this feature when we work through an example later.

Actuarial Gains and Losses

Of great concern to companies that have pension plans are the uncontrollable and unexpected swings in pension expense that can be caused by (1) large and sudden changes in the market value of plan assets, and (2) changes in actuarial assumptions that affect the amount of the accrued benefit obligation. These two events are the sources of actuarial gains and losses. If these gains or losses are fully included in pension expense in the period in which they occur, substantial fluctuations in pension expense result. This was illustrated in the Zarle Corporation example in the chapter when the immediate recognition approach was used. Therefore, ASPE allow companies to reduce this volatility by choosing the deferral and amortization approach of accounting for defined benefit plans, and IFRS allows items such as this to be charged to OCI.

Asset Gains and Losses. The return on plan assets is a component of pension expense that normally reduces the expense amount. Because significant changes in the actual return from year to year could result in unacceptable fluctuations in the reported pension expense, the deferral and amortization approach uses a long-term **expected** rate of return instead of the **actual** rate of return. This is consistent with the actuary's use of a long-run average rate when developing a funding pattern for an employer to ensure that funds are set aside to pay expected benefits in the future.

To determine the expected return component of pension expense, the fair value of plan assets at the beginning of the year is adjusted for additional contributions and payments to retirees during the year and then the weighted average balance of the plan assets is multiplied by the expected long-term rate of return (the actuary's rate).

Liability Gains and Losses. Actuarial (experience) gains and losses on plan liabilities, on the other hand, arise from differences between the actuary's assumptions and actual experience, and from changes in the assumptions that are used by the actuary in calculating the ABO.

To illustrate, assume that the expected accrued benefit obligation of Zarle Corporation based on adding up the individual components is $212,700 at December 31, 2014. If the company's actuaries, using revised estimates at December 31, 2014, calculate an accrued benefit obligation of $213,500, then the company has suffered an actuarial loss of $800 ($213,500 − $212,700). If the actuary calculates a reduced obligation, the result is an actuarial gain. The ABO is adjusted to its most recent estimate and the difference is deferred with actuarial gains and losses (both asset and liability gains and losses) accumulated in prior years. The balance of the accumulated net actuarial gain or loss is reported off-balance sheet, in the notes to the financial statements.

Corridor Amortization for Net Actuarial Gains and Losses. Because actuarial gains and losses can and are expected to offset each other over time, the accumulated unrecognized or unamortized net actuarial gain or loss may not actually grow very large. In fact, this is the reason that is given for not including these gains and losses directly in pension expense each year. But it is possible that no offsetting will occur and that the balance of the accumulated net gain or loss will continue to grow. To limit its growth, the **corridor approach** is used to amortize the balance. The corridor approach amortizes the net accumulated gain or loss when its balance is considered too large. It is considered **too large** and must be amortized **only if it exceeds the arbitrarily selected criterion of 10% of the larger of the accrued benefit obligation and the fair value of the plan assets at the first of the year.**[27] That is, the corridor is a range. The accumulated

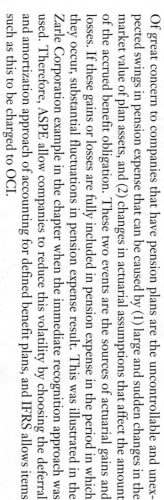

gains or losses only have to be amortized when the total accumulated amount falls outside that range.

Illustration 19B-1 presents assumed data on an ABO and plan assets over the six-year period from 2012 to 2017. We use these data to explain how the corridor approach works.

Illustration 19B-1

Calculation of the Corridor

	Beginning-of-the-Year Balances		
	Accrued Benefit Obligation	Fair Value of Plan Assets	Corridor[a] ± 10%
2012	**$1,000,000**	$ 900,000	$100,000
2013	**1,200,000**	1,100,000	120,000
2014	1,300,000	**1,700,000**	170,000
2015	1,500,000	**2,250,000**	225,000
2016	1,700,000	**1,750,000**	175,000
2017	**1,800,000**	1,700,000	180,000

[a] The corridor is 10% of the larger (in **boldface**) of the accrued benefit obligation and the fair plan asset value.

If the balance of the accumulated net gain or loss stays within the corridor limits for each year, no amortization is required—the balance is carried forward unchanged. This becomes easier to see when the data are shown in a graph as in Illustration 19B-2.

Illustration 19B-2

Graphic Illustration of the Corridor

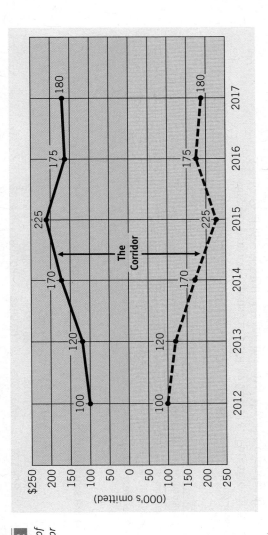

If the accumulated net gain or loss **at the start of the fiscal year** is more than the corridor limit, the **amount in excess of the limit** must be amortized. The minimum amortization is the accumulated net gain or loss in excess of the corridor amount divided by the **expected average remaining service life** of the employee group that is covered by the plan.[28] The expected average remaining service life of an employee group, known as **EARSL**, is the total number of years of future service that the group is expected to render divided by the number of employees in the group. Any systematic method of amortization may be used instead of the amount determined under this approach, as long as it results in faster recognition of actuarial gains and losses and is used consistently for both gains and losses. It can even be applied to amounts within the range established by the corridor.

Illustration of the Corridor Approach.   In applying the corridor approach, remember that **all calculations are based on beginning-of-the-period balances only.** That is, amortization of the excess is included as a component of pension expense only if the unamortized net gain or loss **at the beginning of the year** exceeds the **beginning-of-the-year corridor.** If there is no accumulated net gain or loss at the beginning of the period, there will be no actuarial gain or loss component of pension expense in the current period.

To illustrate the amortization procedure, assume that a company provides the following information:

	2013	2014	2015
Accrued benefit obligation, January 1	$2,100,000	$2,600,000	$2,900,000
Fair value of fund assets, January 1	2,600,000	2,800,000	2,700,000
Net actuarial loss (gain) in year	400,000	300,000	(170,000)
Corridor: 10% of greater of opening ABO and plan assets	260,000	280,000	290,000

Illustration 19B-3 shows how the amortization of the accumulated net loss is determined in each of the three years, assuming the employee group's average remaining service life is five and a half years and remains at that level throughout the three-year period.

Year	(a) Corridor for Year (see above)	(b) Unrecognized net loss (gain), first of year	(c) Excess loss (gain) to be amortized (b) − (a)	(d) Amortization of (c) over 5.5 years	(e) Actuarial loss (gain) in year (see above)	(f) Unrecognized net loss (gain), end of year (b) − (d) + (e)
2013	$260,000	—	—	—	$400,000	$400,000
2014	280,000	$400,000	$120,000	$21,818	300,000	678,182
2015	290,000	678,182	388,182	70,579	(170,000)	437,603

Notice that the unrecognized net actuarial gain or loss is a cumulative number:

	Opening balance of the accumulated net actuarial gain or loss
±	Asset and liability gains and losses in the current year
−	Current year's amortization and transfer to expense, if any
=	Ending balance of the accumulated net actuarial gain or loss

As Illustration 19B-3 shows, the $400,000 accumulated loss at the beginning of 2014 increases pension expense in 2014 by $21,818. This amount is small in comparison with the total loss of $400,000 and indicates that the corridor approach dampens the effects (reduces the volatility) of these gains and losses on pension expense and net income. The rationale for the corridor is that gains and losses result from refinements in estimates as well as real changes in economic value and that, over time, some of these gains and losses will cancel each other out. It therefore seems reasonable that gains and losses should not be recognized fully as a component of pension expense in the period in which they arise.

Note that the gains and losses go through three stages of smoothing. First, the asset gain or loss is smoothed by using the expected return. Then the accumulated net actuarial gain or loss at the beginning of the year is amortized to expense only if it is greater than the corridor. Finally, the excess is spread over the remaining service life of the current employees. Similar to past service costs that are not recognized immediately, any actuarial gains and losses that are deferred are also not captured in the statement of financial position benefit asset or liability account. The unamortized amounts, therefore, are off-balance sheet items.

Other Options within the Deferral and Amortization Approach. ASPE also allows a company to choose to recognize actuarial gains and losses in income in the same period in which they occur.

Illustration of the Deferral and Amortization Approach

We now walk through an example to illustrate the approach permitted as an option by ASPE. The transactions and events that affect the pension accounts of Trans Corp. over the three-year period 2013 to 2015 are listed in Illustration 19B-4.

Illustration 19B-4

Trans Corp. Pension Plan, 2013–2015

	2013	2014	2015
Fair value of plan assets, first of year	$150,000	$161,500	$195,500
Accrued benefit obligation (ABO) for accounting purposes, start of year	150,000	289,000	363,300
Current service cost for year	16,000	17,500	19,000
Interest or discount rate on the liability	9%	9%	9%
Cost of past service benefits granted, effective December 31, 2013	120,000	-0-	-0-
Amortization of past service cost	-0-	?	?
Expected earnings on plan assets for year	10%	10%	10%
Actual earnings on plan assets for year	10,000	16,000	28,000
Employer contributions for year (funding)	12,000	30,000	64,000
Benefits paid to retirees by trustee for year	10,500	12,000	15,500
Actuarial loss on liability due to change in actuarial assumptions	-0-	42,790	-0-
Amortization of accumulated actuarial gain/loss	-0-	?	?
Plan assets, end of year	161,500	195,500	272,000
Accrued benefit obligation (ABO), end of year	289,000	363,300	399,497
Funded status, end of year—over- or (under)-funded	(127,500)	(167,800)	(127,497)

2013 Work Sheet and Entries.

The work sheet in Illustration 19B-5 sets out the format and information that Trans Corp. needs for 2013.

Illustration 19B-5

Trans Corp. Work Sheet—2013

Items	General Journal Entries			Accrued Benefit Obligation	Memo Record		
	Annual Pension Expense	Cash	Accrued Benefit Liability/ Asset		Plan Assets	Unrecognized Past Service Cost	Unrecognized Actuarial Gain or Loss
Balance, Jan. 1, 2013			-0-	150,000 Cr.	150,000 Dr.	-0-	-0-
(a) Service cost	16,000 Dr.			16,000 Cr.			
(b) Interest cost	13,500 Dr.			13,500 Cr.			
(c) Expected return	15,000 Cr.				15,000 Dr.		
(d) Asset loss					5,000 Cr.		5,000 Dr.
(e) Past service cost				120,000 Cr.		120,000 Dr.	
(f) Amortization of past service cost	-0-					-0-	
(g) Contribution		12,000 Cr.			12,000 Dr.		
(h) Benefits paid				10,500 Dr.	10,500 Cr.		
(i) Amortization of actuarial gain/loss	-0-						-0-
Expense entry, 2013	14,500 Dr.		14,500 Cr.				
Contribution entry, 2013		12,000 Cr.	12,000 Dr.				
Balance, Dec. 31, 2013			2,500 Cr.	289,000 Cr.	161,500 Dr.	120,000 Dr.	5,000 Dr.

The beginning balances of the accrued benefit obligation and the pension plan assets are recorded on the work sheet's first line in the memo record. They are not recorded in the accounts and, therefore, are not reported as a liability and an asset on Trans Corp.'s statement of financial position. Although they are off-balance sheet, the January 1, 2013 funded status of $0 is the same as the balance of $0 in the Accrued Benefit Liability/Asset account on the statement of financial position on that date. This will happen only when there are no deferred balances relating to past service costs and actuarial gains or losses.

Let's walk through the events of 2013 and see how they are accounted for if Trans Corp. chooses a deferral and amortization accounting policy under ASPE.

Entries (a), the service cost, and (b), the interest cost, are both recognized directly in expense. Note that the interest is calculated on the weighted average balance of the ABO outstanding for the year. The increase is due to the granting of past service benefits was not effective until December 31. No part of it was outstanding during the year, and therefore it is not included in the interest component. Unless stated otherwise, we assume that the service cost, contributions into the fund, and benefits paid are all December 31 transactions.

Items (c) and (d) are related. Item (c), which represents the return on plan assets, is the **expected return**, used to smooth the amount of pension expense. The expected return is 10% of the weighted-average outstanding balance of fund assets for the year, in this case 10% of $150,000 or $15,000. This is higher than the actual return of $10,000. Entry (d) shows the resulting asset actuarial loss of $5,000 ($15,000 − $10,000), which, instead of being recognized in pension expense in 2013, is deferred as an unrecognized actuarial loss in the memo accounts.

The cost of the past service benefits granted effective December 31, 2013, is shown in (e). This is another component that is deferred to an off-balance sheet memo account and later amortized. Because the costs are effective only on the last day of the year, no amount is amortized into pension expense in 2013 in item (f).

The employer contributions and benefits paid by the fund in (g) and (h) are treated the same way as under the immediate recognition approach. They do not affect the expense. The last item (i) is the amortization of the net accumulated actuarial gain or loss in the year. Because the amortization is based on the opening balance of this amount, and the opening balance was $0, there is no amortization recognized in expense in 2013.

The expense is made up of five components: the current service cost, interest cost, expected return on assets, and two amortization amounts—for the past service costs and actuarial gains or losses. In this year, both amortization amounts were $0. The entry needed on December 31, 2013, to record the pension expense for the year is:

Pension Expense	14,500	
Accrued Benefit Liability/Asset		14,500

A = L + SE
  +14,500 −14,500
Cash flows: No effect

When the company made its contributions to the pension fund late in the year, the following entry was recorded:

Accrued Benefit Liability/Asset	12,000	
Cash		12,000

A = L + SE
−12,000 −12,000
Cash flows: ↓ 12,000 outflow

Because the expense exceeds the funding, the Accrued Pension Liability account increases during the year by the $2,500 difference ($14,500 less $12,000). At December 31, 2013, the balance of the Accrued Benefit Liability account ($2,500) is equal to the balance in the memo accounts. These now include the deferred and unamortized past service costs and actuarial losses:

	At Dec. 31, 2013
Accrued benefit obligation	$289,000 Cr.
Plan assets	161,500 Dr.
Funded status—net liability (underfunded)	127,500 Cr.
Unrecognized past service cost	120,000 Dr.
Unrecognized actuarial loss	5,000 Dr.
Accrued benefit liability on statement of financial position	$ 2,500 Cr.

2014 Work Sheet and Entries.

Continuing the Trans Corp. example set out in Illustration 19B-4 into 2014, we start by recording the opening balances at January 1, 2014, on the 2014 work sheet in Illustration 19B-6. Items (j) and (k) record the current service cost and interest as components of pension expense, and (o) and (p) have been explained previously. The interest cost is 9% of $289,000 or $26,010. The expected return (l) is 10% of $161,500 or $16,150. The actual return of $16,000 was $150 less than what was expected, resulting in an actuarial loss of $150 in (m) that is deferred.

The amortization of the past service costs deferred on December 31, 2013, requires an explanation. On that date, the plan amendment granted employees prior service benefits that had a present value of $120,000. Under the deferral and amortization approach, we need to determine how these costs will be amortized into expense. In this case, we assume the average remaining service life to full benefit eligibility of the employee group covered by the amendment is four years. The annual amortization amount is $120,000 ÷ 4 = $30,000, effective January 1, 2014. The amortization of these costs in (n) reduces the unamortized balance as they are recognized as part of pension expense in the income statement in each year from 2014 to 2017.

Entry (q) records the increase in the accrued benefit obligation that results from a change in actuarial assumptions. The actuary has calculated the ending balance of the ABO to be $363,300. Since the memo record balance at December 31 is $320,510 (equal to $289,000 + $17,500 + $26,010 − $12,000), there is a difference of $42,790 ($363,300 − $320,510). This $42,790 increase in the employer's obligation is an actuarial loss that is deferred by including it in the unrecognized actuarial gain/loss balance.

Illustration 19B-6

Trans Corp. Work Sheet—2014

	A	B	C	D		F	G	H	I
1		**General Journal Entries**				**Memo Record**			
2	Items	Annual Pension Expense	Cash	Accrued Benefit Liability/ Asset		Accrued Benefit Obligation	Plan Assets	Unrecognized Past Service Cost	Unrecognized Actuarial Gain or Loss
3	Balance, Jan. 1, 2014			2,500 Cr.		289,000 Cr.	161,500 Dr.	120,000 Dr.	5,000 Dr.
4	(j) Service cost	17,500 Dr.				17,500 Cr.			
5	(k) Interest cost	26,010 Dr.				26,010 Cr.			
6	(l) Expected return	16,150 Cr.					16,150 Dr.		
7	(m) Asset loss						150 Cr.		150 Dr.
8	(n) Amortization of past service cost	30,000 Dr.						30,000 Cr.	
9	(o) Contribution		30,000 Cr.				30,000 Dr.		
10	(p) Benefits paid					12,000 Dr.	12,000 Cr.		
11	(q) Actuarial loss (liability)					42,790 Cr.			42,790 Dr.
12	(r) Amortization of actuarial gain/loss	–0–							–0–
13	Expense entry, 2014	57,360 Dr.		57,360 Cr.					
14	Contribution entry, 2014		30,000 Cr.	30,000 Dr.					
15	Balance, Dec. 31, 2014			29,860 Cr.		363,300 Cr.	195,500 Dr.	90,000 Dr.	47,940 Dr.
16									

Is any amortization of the accumulated actuarial losses needed in 2014? Let's check:

Net accumulated actuarial loss at January 1, 2014		$ 5,000
Corridor: 10% of larger of ABO and fund assets		
at January 1, 2014 (10% × 289,000)		28,900
Excess of actuarial loss over corridor		$ 0

Assuming Trans Corp. follows a policy of recognizing the minimum amount required under the corridor approach, there is no amortization in 2014.

Again, the pension expense is made up of the same five items: service cost, interest cost, expected return, and any amortization of deferred past service costs and actuarial losses. The entry needed on December 31, 2014, to formally record the expense for the year is:

Pension Expense	57,360	
Accrued Benefit Liability/Asset		57,360

A = L + SE
+57,360 −57,360
Cash flows: No effect

The following entry was recorded in late December 2014:

Accrued Benefit Liability/Asset	30,000	
Cash		30,000

A = L + SE
−30,000 −30,000
Cash flows: ↓ 30,000 outflow

Because the expense exceeds the funding, the Accrued Pension Liability account increases during the year by the $27,360 difference ($57,360 less $30,000). In 2014, as in 2013, the balance of the Accrued Pension Liability account ($29,860) is equal to the balances in the memo accounts, as shown in the following reconciliation.

	At Dec. 31, 2014
Accrued benefit obligation	$363,300 Cr.
Plan assets	195,500 Dr.
Funded status—net liability (underfunded)	167,800 Cr.
Unrecognized past service cost	90,000 Dr.
Unrecognized actuarial loss	47,940 Dr.
Accrued pension liability on statement	137,940 Dr.
of financial position	$ 29,860 Cr.

2015 Work Sheet and Entries. We continue with the Trans Corp. data set out in Illustration 19B-4. The work sheet in Illustration 19B-7 presents the pension information that the company needs for 2015. The beginning balances recorded on the work sheet's first line are the ending balances from the 2014 pension work sheet in Illustration 19B-6.

Items	General Journal Entries			Memo Record			
	Annual Pension Expense	Cash	Accrued Benefit Liability/Asset	Accrued Benefit Obligation	Plan Assets	Unrecognized Past Service Cost	Unrecognized Actuarial Gain or Loss
3 Balance, Jan. 1, 2015			29,860 Cr.	363,300 Cr.	195,500 Dr.	90,000 Dr.	47,940 Dr.
4 (s) Service cost	19,000 Dr.			19,000 Cr.			
5 (t) Interest cost	32,697 Dr.			32,697 Cr.			
6 (u) Expected return	19,550 Cr.				19,550 Dr.		
7 (v) Asset gain					8,450 Dr.		8,450 Cr.
8 (w) Amortization of past service cost	30,000 Dr.					30,000 Cr.	
9 (x) Contribution		64,000 Cr.			64,000 Dr.		
10 (y) Benefits paid				15,500 Dr.	15,500 Cr.		
11 (z) Actuarial loss (liability)				–0–			–0–
12 (aa) Amortization of actuarial gain/loss	1,451 Dr.						1,451 Cr.
13 Expense entry, 2015	63,598 Dr.		63,598 Cr.				
14 Contribution entry, 2015		64,000 Cr.	64,000 Dr.				
15 Balance, Dec. 31, 2015			29,458 Cr.	399,497 Cr.	272,000 Dr.	60,000 Dr.	38,039 Dr.
16							

Illustration 19B-7

Trans Corp. Work Sheet—2015

Entries (s), (t), (w), (x), and (y) are similar to the entries that were explained in 2013 and 2014 for these components. Entries (u) and (v) are related to each other as explained earlier, but this time the company experienced an actuarial gain. The gain is deferred.

Trans Corp. checks to see whether any of the accumulated unrecognized actuarial loss should be amortized to expense in 2015 using the following analysis:

Accumulated actuarial losses at January 1, 2015	$47,940
Corridor: 10% of larger of DBO and fund assets	
at January 1, 2015 = 10% × 363,300	36,330
Excess of actuarial loss over corridor	$11,610

Now we see that the losses at the start of the year are high enough to be amortized. Assuming an expected average remaining service life of the affected employee group of eight years, the amortization amount in 2015 is $11,610 ÷ 8 = $1,451.

Note that the pension expense is made up of the same five items: service cost, interest cost, expected return, and any amortization of deferred past service costs and actuarial losses. The entry to record the expense for 2015 is:

Pension Expense	63,598	
Accrued Benefit Liability/Asset		63,598

A = L + SE
+63,598 −63,598

Cash flows: No effect

The company's contribution for the year was:

Accrued Benefit Liability/Asset	64,000	
Cash		64,000

A = L + SE
−64,000 −64,000

Cash flows: ↓ 64,000 outflow

The credit balance of the Accrued Pension Liability account reported on the statement of financial position at December 31, 2015, of $29,458 is equal to the net of the balances in the memo accounts at the same date.

	At Dec. 31, 2015
Accrued benefit obligation	$399,497 Cr.
Plan assets	272,000 Dr.
Funded status—net liability (underfunded)	127,497 Cr.
Unrecognized amounts:	
Past service cost	$60,000 Dr.
Net actuarial losses	38,039 Dr. 98,039 Dr.
Accrued benefit liability on statement of financial position	$ 29,458 Cr.

Comparison of Results: Deferral and Amortization versus Immediate Recognition

What is the result of applying the deferral and amortization approach rather than immediate recognition? You should notice two major differences in the reported results.

First, the expense reported over the three years is smoothed considerably under the deferral and amortization approach, making the net income reported less volatile than under the immediate recognition option. The second difference relates to how well the amount reported as the balance sheet liability or asset represents the funded status of the plan. As you saw earlier, the immediate recognition approach tracks the funded status directly, although under ASPE it incorporates an ABO measured for funding purposes rather than an ABO based on projected salaries. Under the deferral and amortization approach, the effects of many of the events that change the funded status are not recognized until future years. This is evident from the reconciliations of the funded status to the accrued benefit liability in the Trans Corp. example above.

12 Identify the components of pension benefit cost, and account for a defined benefit pension plan when using the deferral and amortization approach under ASPE; determine the pension plan accounts reported in the financial statements and explain their relationship to the funded status of the plan.

Pension cost under the deferral and amortization approach is a function of: (1) service cost, (2) interest on the liability, (3) expected return on plan assets, (4) past service costs, and (5) net actuarial gain or loss. Items (1) to (3) are included in current expense entirely, while items (4) and (5) are usually recognized through a process of amortization. The unamortized balances of items (4) and (5) are

reported in the notes to the financial statements. An accrued benefit liability or asset is reported in the balance sheet. Under the deferral and amortization approach, the balance is equal to the funded status adjusted for any unamortized past service costs and unamortized actuarial gains and losses. The pension expense is reported in the income statement.

Quiz

KEY TERMS

corridor approach, p. 1232

deferral and amortization approach, p. 1231

EARSL, p. 1233

expected average remaining service life, p. 1233

unamortized net actuarial gain or loss, p. 1232

unamortized past service costs, p. 1232

unrecognized net actuarial gain or loss, p. 1232

unrecognized past service costs, p. 1232

Brief Exercises

Note: All assignment material with an asterisk (*) relates to one of the appendices to the chapter. Unless otherwise indicated, assume that all current service costs, benefit payments, and company contributions are made at the end of the period.

(LO 1) **BE19-1** Murray Enterprises Inc. sponsors a defined benefit plan for its 500 employees. On December 31, 2014, the company's actuary provided the following information related to the plan: defined benefit obligation $7.5 million, and fair value of plan assets $6 million. Annual pension expense was $2 million in 2014. Murray Enterprises' statement of financial position as of December 31, 2014, shows total assets of $6 million and total liabilities of $6.5 million (which includes a net defined benefit liability of $1.5 million). There were no actuarial gains or losses or remeasurement gains or losses in 2014. Murray Enterprises follows IFRS. (a) Discuss the effect of the pension plan on Murray Enterprises' statement of financial position as of December 31, 2014. (b) Discuss some of the costs of the pension plan to Murray Enterprises' business.

(LO 2) **BE19-2** Ditek Corp. provides a defined contribution pension plan for its employees. The plan requires Ditek to contribute 3% of employees' gross pay to a fund trustee each year. Ditek's total payroll for 2014 was $2,732,864. At the start of 2014, Ditek revised the terms of the plan, which resulted in past service costs of $845,350. Ditek expects to realize the economic benefits from the plan change over five years, beginning in 2014. (a) Calculate Ditek's pension expense for 2014 assuming that the company follows IFRS. (b) Calculate Ditek's pension expense for 2014 assuming that the company follows ASPE and uses the deferral and amortization approach.

(LO 2, 3) **BE19-3** Tyshynski Corp. has recently decided to implement a pension plan for its employees; however, it is unsure if it would like to structure the pension as a defined contribution plan or a defined benefit plan. As requested by management, prepare a short memo outlining the nature of both plans, along with the accounting treatment of each plan.

(LO 4) **BE19-4** Cotter Corp. reports the following information (in hundreds of thousands of dollars) to you about its defined benefit pension plan for 2014:

Actual return on plan assets	11	Current service cost	21
Benefits paid to retirees	8	Interest cost	9
Contributions from employer	20	Opening balance, defined benefit obligation (DBO)	92
Cost of plan amendment in year	13	Opening balance, plan assets	100

Provide a continuity schedule for the DBO for the year. Cotter follows IFRS.

(LO 5) **BE19-5** For Castor Corporation, year-end plan assets were $1,750,000. At the beginning of the year, plan assets were $1,350,000. During the year, contributions to the pension fund were $170,000, while benefits paid were $140,000. Calculate Castor's actual return on plan assets.

(LO 5, 6) **BE19-6** Refer to the information for Cotter Corp. in BE19-4, and provide a continuity schedule for the plan assets for the year. Is the plan overfunded or underfunded?

(LO 6, 12) ***BE19-7** At December 31, 2013, Glover Corporation has the following balances:

Accrued benefit obligation	$3,400,000
Plan assets at fair value	2,420,000
Unrecognized past service cost	990,000

Determine the account and its balance that should be reported on Glover Corporation's December 31, 2013 balance sheet if it is using the deferral and amortization approach under ASPE.

(LO 6, 12) ***BE19-8** Borke Corporation follows ASPE and uses the deferral and amortization approach to account for its defined benefit pension plan. The following information is available for Borke Corporation for 2013:

Current service cost	$29,000
Interest on ABO	22,000
Expected return on plan assets	20,000
Amortization of unrecognized past service cost	15,200
Amortization of unrecognized net actuarial loss	500

Calculate Borke's 2013 pension expense.

(LO 7) **BE19-9** Jonquière Corporation uses the immediate recognition approach to account for its defined benefit pension plan. The following information (in hundreds of thousands of dollars) is available for 2014:

Actual return on plan assets	9
Expected return on plan assets	11
Contributions from employer	20
Benefits paid to retirees	10
Actuarial loss due to change in actuarial assumptions	15

At the end of the year, Jonquière revised the terms of its pension plan, which resulted in past service costs of $35. Assuming that Jonquière follows IFRS, determine the company's 2014 pension expense and the effect of the pension plan on the company's shareholders' equity.

(LO 7) **BE19-10** Duster Corporation is a private company and has a defined benefit pension plan that is accounted for under the immediate recognition approach. The following information is available for Duster Corporation for 2014:

Current service cost	19
Interest cost	11
Opening balance, DBO	100
Opening balance, plan assets	100

(LO 7) **BE19-11** At January 1, 2013, Uddin Corporation had plan assets of $250,000 and a defined benefit obligation of the same amount based on projected costs. During 2013, the current service cost was $27,500, the discount rate on the DBO/plan assets was 10%, actual return on plan assets was $30,000, contributions by Uddin were $20,000, benefits paid were $17,500, and the cost of past service benefits granted effective December 31, 2013, was $29,000. (a) Prepare a pension work sheet for Uddin Corporation for 2013 assuming that Uddin follows IFRS. (b) Prepare a pension work sheet for Uddin Corporation for 2013 assuming that Uddin follows ASPE and has elected to apply the deferral and amortization approach.

(LO 7) **BE19-12** Refer to BE19-11. Calculate the pension expense for Uddin Corporation for 2013, assuming that Uddin follows ASPE and has elected to apply the immediate recognition approach.

(LO 7, 12) ***BE19-13** On January 1, 2013, Tuesbury Corporation amended its defined benefit pension plan, resulting in $1,125,000 in past service costs. Tuesbury Corporation expects to receive economic benefits, through increased employee productivity and morale, over the next 15 years, at which point the employees will be eligible for their full pension benefits. Currently, all employees who are affected by the plan amendment are already vested. (a) Calculate the past service costs to be included in the pension expense for the December 31, 2013 fiscal year, assuming that Tuesbury follows IFRS. (b) Calculate the past service costs to be included in the pension expense for the December 31, 2013 fiscal year, assuming that Tuesbury follows ASPE and has elected to apply the deferral and amortization approach.

(LO 7, 12) ***BE19-14** Petey Ltd. has a policy of obtaining an actuarial pension valuation every three years. Based on the individual components of its annual pension expense, Petey Ltd.'s defined benefit obligation as at December 31, 2013, was $356,700. An actuarial valuation revealed that the defined benefit obligation is actually $388,000. The difference is mostly the result of revised estimates given the recent stock market troubles. (a) Discuss the options available under IFRS to account for the actuarial loss. (b) Discuss the options available under ASPE to account for the actuarial loss.

Assuming that Duster follows IFRS, determine the 2014 effect of the pension plan on pension expense and the company's shareholders' equity.

Opening balance, DBO	$210,000
Opening balance, plan assets	200,000
Service cost	58,000
Employer contributions paid throughout 2014	77,000
Interest or discount rate on the DBO/plan assets	10%
Actual return on plan assets	25,000
Actuarial loss due to change in actuarial assumptions	14,000

(LO 8) **BE19-15** Legacy Corporation has the following information available concerning its post-retirement benefit plan for 2014:

Current service cost	$80,000
Interest cost	65,500
Expected return on plan assets, using discount rate	48,000

Assuming Legacy follows IFRS, calculate Legacy's 2014 post-retirement expense that will be included in net income.

(LO 11, 12) ***BE19-16** Saver Corporation amended its defined benefit pension plan at the beginning of its 2013 fiscal year, resulting in past service costs of $775,000. The average period to full eligibility of the affected group is 17.5 years. Saver follows ASPE and uses the deferral and amortization approach to account for its defined benefit pension plan. Calculate the past service cost that will be included in the fiscal 2013 pension expense.

(LO 12) ***BE19-17** Hunt Corporation had an accrued benefit obligation of $3.1 million and plan assets of $3.3 million at January 1, 2013. Hunt's unrecognized net actuarial loss was $475,000 at that time. The average remaining service period of Hunt's employees is 7.5 years. Hunt follows ASPE and uses the deferral and amortization approach to account for its defined benefit pension plan. Calculate Hunt's minimum amortization of the unrecognized actuarial loss for 2013.

Exercises

(LO 2) **E19-1 (Defined Contribution Plan)** Jabara Limited provides a defined contribution pension plan for its employees. The plan requires the company to deduct 5% of each employee's gross pay for each payroll period as the employee contribution. The company then matches this amount by an equal contribution. Both amounts are remitted to the pension trustee within 10 days of the end of each month for the previous month's payrolls. At November 30, 2014, Jabara reported $26,300 of combined withheld and matched contributions owing to the trustee. During December, Jabara reported gross salaries and wages expense of $276,100.

Instructions

(a) Prepare the entry to record the December payment to the plan trustee.

(b) What amount of pension expense will the company report for December 2014?

(c) Determine the appropriate pension account and its balance to be reported on the December 31, 2014 statement of financial position.

(LO 2) **E19-2 (Defined Contribution Plan)** Ad Venture Ltd. provides a defined contribution pension plan for its employees. Currently, the company has 40 full-time and 55 part-time employees. The pension plan requires the company to make an annual contribution of $2,000 per full-time employee, and $1,000 per part-time employee, regardless of their annual salary. In addition, employees can match the employer's contribution in any given year.

At the beginning of the year, 10 full-time and 15 part-time employees elected to contribute to their pension plan by matching the company's contribution. An equal amount of funds was withheld from the employees' cheques in order to fund their pension contribution. Both the employees' and employer's contributions are sent to the plan trustee at year end.

Instructions

(a) What amount of pension expense will the company report?

(b) Prepare a summary journal entry to record Ad Venture Ltd.'s payment to the plan trustee.

(LO 4, 5, 7, 9) **E19-3 (Continuity Schedules and Calculation of Pension Expense; Immediate Recognition Approach)** Rebek Corporation provides the following information about its defined benefit pension plan for the year 2014:

Current service cost	$ 225,000
Contribution to the plan	262,500
Past service cost	25,000
Actual and expected return on plan assets	160,000

Benefits paid	100,000
Net defined benefit liability at Jan. 1, 2014	400,000
Plan assets at Jan. 1, 2014	1,600,000
Defined benefit obligation at Jan. 1, 2014	2,000,000
Interest or discount rate on the DBO/plan assets	10%

Rebek follows IRFS.

Instructions

(a) Prepare a continuity schedule for 2014 for the defined benefit obligation.

(b) Prepare a continuity schedule for 2014 for the plan assets.

(c) Calculate pension expense for the year 2014.

(d) Prepare all pension journal entries recorded by Rebek in 2014.

(e) What pension amount will appear on Rebek's statement of financial position at December 31, 2014?

(LO 4, E19-4 **(Preparation of Pension Work Sheet)** Refer to the information in E19-3.
5, 7

Instructions

(a) Prepare a pension work sheet: insert the January 1, 2014 balances and show the December 31, 2014 balances.

(b) Prepare all journal entries.

(LO 4, *E19-5 **(Immediate Recognition Approach; Deferral and Amortization Approach; Changes in Pension**
5, 12) Accounts)

Instructions

Complete the following tables by indicating whether the following events increase (I), decrease (D), or have no effect (NE) on the employer's defined benefit obligation, the pension plan assets, the pension plan's funded status, and the pension expense.

(a) Assume that the company uses the immediate recognition approach under IFRS:

	Defined Benefit Obligation	Pension Plan Assets	Funded Status	Pension Expense	Remeasurement Gain (Loss) OCI
Current service cost					
Actual return on plan assets					
Expected return on plan assets					
Past service costs on date of plan revision (inception)					
Actuarial gain/loss					
Employer contributions					
Benefits paid to retirees					
An increase in the average life expectancy of employees					

(b) Assume that the company uses the deferral and amortization approach under ASPE:

	Accrued Benefit Obligation	Pension Plan Assets	Funded Status	Pension Expense
Current service cost				
Actual return on plan assets				
Expected return on plan assets				
Past service costs on date of plan revision (inception)				
Amortization of past service costs				
Actuarial gain/loss				
Amortization of actuarial gain/loss				
Employer contributions				
Benefits paid to retirees				
An increase in the average life expectancy of employees				

(LO 5) E19-6 (Calculation of Actual Return) Queensland Importers provides the following pension plan information:

Fair value of pension plan assets, Jan. 1, 2014	$1,418,750
Fair value of pension plan assets, Dec. 31, 2014	1,596,875
Contributions to the plan in 2014	212,500
Benefits paid retirees in 2014	218,750

Instructions

Calculate the actual return on the plan assets for 2014.

(LO 5, *E19-7 (Calculation of Actual Return, Gains and Losses, Corridor Test, Past Service Cost, Pension Expense, 9, 12) and Reconciliation) Berstler Limited sponsors a defined benefit pension plan, which it accounts for using the deferral and amortization approach under ASPE. The corporation's actuary provides the following information about the plan:

	Jan. 1, 2013	Dec. 31, 2013
Vested benefit obligation	$1,200	$1,520
Accumulated and accrued benefit obligation, funding basis	1,520	2,184
Accrued benefit obligation, accounting basis	2,240	2,916
Plan assets (fair value)	1,360	2,096
Discount rate and expected rate of return	10%	10%
Net defined benefit liability/asset	0	?
Unrecognized past service cost	880	?
Service cost for the year 2013		320
Contributions (funding in 2013)		640
Benefits paid in 2013		160

The average remaining service life and period to full eligibility is 20 years.

Instructions

(a) Calculate the actual return on the plan assets in 2013.

(b) Calculate the amount of the unrecognized net actuarial gain or loss as of December 31, 2013 (assume the January 1, 2013 balance was zero).

(c) Calculate the amount of actuarial gain or loss amortization for 2013 using the corridor approach. How will 2014's expense be affected, if at all?

(d) Calculate the amount of past service cost amortization for 2013.

(e) Calculate the pension expense for 2013.

(f) Prepare a schedule reconciling the plan's funded status with the amount reported on the December 31, 2013 balance sheet.

(LO 5, *E19-8 (Preparation of Pension Work Sheet) Refer to the information in E19-7 about Berstler Limited's defined 9, 12) benefit pension plan.

Instructions

(a) Prepare a 2013 pension work sheet with supplementary schedules of calculations.

(b) Prepare the journal entries at December 31, 2013, to record pension expense and the funding contributions.

(c) Prepare a schedule reconciling the plan's funded status with the pension amounts reported on the balance sheet.

(LO 6, 7, *E19-9 (ABO and Fund Asset Continuity Schedules; Immediate Recognition Approach) The following 10, 12) defined benefit pension data of Datek Corp. apply to the year 2013:

Accrued benefit obligation, funding basis, 1/1/13 (before amendment)	$280,000
Plan assets, 1/1/13	273,100
Net defined benefit liability, 1/1/13	6,900
On January 1, 2013, Datek Corp., through plan amendment, grants prior service benefits having a present value of	50,000
Discount rate and expected rate of return	9%
Annual pension service cost	29,000
Contributions (funding)	27,500
Actual return on plan assets	26,140
Benefits paid to retirees	20,000

The company uses the immediate recognition approach under ASPE.

Instructions

(a) Prepare a continuity schedule for the ABO for 2013.

(b) Prepare a continuity schedule for the plan assets for 2013.

(c) Calculate pension expense for 2013 and prepare the entry to record the expense.

(d) Identify the plan's funded status as the asset or liability reported on the December 31, 2013 statement of financial position.

(e) Assume that Datek Corp. uses the deferral and amortization approach to account for its pension plan, and that the funding basis valuation and the accounting basis valuation for the ABO are the same at January 1, 2013. Calculate the pension expense for 2013 assuming that the prior service benefits will be amortized over five years.

(f) Reconcile the difference between the pension expense as calculated with the immediate recognition approach versus the deferral and amortization approach.

(g) From the perspective of a creditor, discuss the effect of using the immediate recognition approach versus the deferral and amortization approach to account for the company's pension plan.

**Digging
Deeper**

**(LO 6, 7,
10, 12)** ***E19-10 (Pension Expense, Journal Entries)** The following information is available for Huntley Corporation's pension plan for the year 2013:

Expected return on plan assets	$ 15,000
Actual return on plan assets	17,000
Benefits paid to retirees	40,000
Contributions (funding)	95,000
Discount rate and expected rate of return	10%
Defined benefit obligation, Jan. 1, 2013	500,000
Service cost	65,000

Instructions

(a) Calculate pension expense for the year 2013, and provide the entries to recognize the pension expense and funding for the year, assuming that Huntley follows IFRS and accounts for its pension under the immediate recognition approach. Assume that the DBO provided at January 1, 2013, for accounting and funding purposes is the same.

(b) Calculate pension expense for the year 2013, and provide the entries to recognize the pension expense and funding for the year, assuming that Huntley follows ASPE and accounts for its pension under the deferral and amortization approach.

**(LO 6, 7,
10, 12)** ***E19-11 (Pension Expense, Journal Entries)** The following information is available for Argust Corporation's pension plan for the 2013 fiscal year:

Accrued benefit obligation, 1/1/13, accounting basis	$315,000
Accrued benefit obligation, 1/1/13, funding basis	255,000
Fair value of plan assets, 1/1/13	297,000
Current service cost	63,000
Discount rate	10%
Expected return on plan assets	7%
Actual return on plan assets	8%
Contributions (funding)	79,200
Benefits paid to retirees	43,200

On January 1, 2013, Argust Corp. amended its pension plan, resulting in past service costs with a present value of $140,400. The amendment of the pension plan is expected to provide future benefits for five years. Argust follows ASPE.

Instructions

(a) Identify the plan's funded status and the asset or liability reported on the December 31, 2013 balance sheet assuming that Argust Corp. accounts for its pension using the deferral and amortization approach.

(b) Calculate pension expense for 2013 assuming that Argust Corp. accounts for its pension using the deferral and amortization approach.

(c) Identify the plan's funded status and the asset or liability reported on the December 31, 2013 balance sheet assuming that Argust Corp. accounts for its pension using the immediate recognition approach.

(d) Calculate pension expense for 2013, assuming that Argust Corp. accounts for its pension using the immediate recognition approach.

(LO 6, 9, 12) ***E19-12 (Pension Expense, Journal Entries, Disclosure)** Griseta Limited sponsors a defined benefit pension plan for its employees, which it accounts for using the deferral and amortization approach under ASPE. The following data relate to the operation of the plan for the year 2013:

1. The actuarial present value of future benefits earned by employees for services rendered in 2013 amounted to $56,000.

2. The company's funding policy requires a contribution to the pension trustee of $145,000 for 2013.

3. As of January 1, 2013, the company had an accrued benefit obligation of $1 million and an unrecognized past service cost of $400,000. The fair value of pension plan assets amounted to $600,000 at the beginning of the year. The actual and expected return on plan assets was $54,000. The discount rate was 9%.

4. Amortization of past service costs was $40,000 in 2013.

5. No benefits were paid in 2013.

Instructions

(a) Determine the pension expense that should be recognized by the company in 2013.

(b) Prepare the journal entries to record pension expense and the employer's payment to the pension trustee in 2013.

(c) Determine the plan's funded status and reconcile this to the Net Defined Benefit Liability/Asset account on the December 31, 2013 balance sheet.

(d) Assuming Griseta is not a public company and does not have broad public accountability, prepare the required disclosures for the 2013 financial statements.

(e) Calculate the January 1, 2013 balance in Net Defined Benefit Liability/Asset account.

(LO 7) **E19-13 (Pension Expense; Immediate Recognition Approach)** The following information is in regard to Saverio Corp.'s defined benefit pension plan, which is accounted for using the immediate recognition approach:

Defined benefit obligation, 1/1/14 (before amendment)	$176,000
Plan assets, 1/1/14	155,000
Discount rate and expected return on fund assets	10%
Annual pension service cost	13,000
Actual return on plan assets	5%

On January 1, 2014, the company amended its pension plan, which resulted in additional prior service benefits being granted to current employees. The present value of the prior service benefits is $34,000, and the employees are expected to provide future benefits over the next seven years as a result of the pension change. Saverio follows IFRS.

Instructions

Calculate the pension expense that will be reported in net income for 2014.

(LO 7, 8) **E19-14 (Post-retirement Benefit Expense, Funded Status, and Reconciliation)** Rosek Inc. provides the following information related to its post-retirement health care benefits for the year 2014:

Defined post-retirement benefit obligation at Jan. 1, 2014	$110,000
Plan assets, Jan. 1, 2014	42,000
Actual return on plan assets, 2014	3,000
Discount rate and expected return on fund assets	10%
Service cost, 2014	57,000
Plan funding during 2014	22,000
Payments from plan to retirees	6,000
Actuarial loss on defined post-retirement benefit obligation, 2014 (end of year)	31,000

Rosek Corp. follows IFRS.

Instructions

(a) Calculate the post-retirement benefit expense for 2014.

(b) Calculate the post-retirement benefit remeasurement gain or loss–OCI for 2014.

(c) Determine the December 31, 2014 balance of the plan assets, the defined post-retirement benefit obligation, and the funded status.

(d) Determine the balance of the net post-retirement benefit liability/asset account on the December 31, 2014 statement of financial position.

(e) Reconcile the funded status with the amount reported on the statement of financial position at December 31, 2014.

(LO 7, 10, 12) *E19-15 (Pension Expense) The following facts apply to the pension plan of Yorke Inc. for the year 2013:

Plan assets, Jan. 1, 2013	$490,000
Defined benefit obligation, funding basis, Jan. 1, 2013	389,000
Defined benefit obligation, accounting basis, Jan. 1, 2013	490,000
Interest rate and expected rate of return	8.5%
Annual pension service cost	40,000
Contributions (funding)	30,000
Actual return on plan assets	49,700
Benefits paid to retirees	33,400

Instructions

(a) Calculate pension expense for the year 2013, and provide the entries to recognize the pension expense and contributions for the year assuming that Yorke follows ASPE and uses the deferral and amortization approach.

(b) Discuss what adjustments would need to be made to your calculation and entries in part (a) if York follows IFRS and uses the immediate recognition approach instead. Provide calculations wherever possible.

(LO 7, 10, 12) *E19-16 (Actuarial Gains and Losses) The actuary for the pension plan of Brush Inc. calculated the following net actuarial gains and losses:

As of January 1	Incurred during the Year	Net Gain or Loss
		(Gain) or Loss
2013	2013	$ 480,000
2014	2014	300,000
2015	2015	(210,000)
2016	2016	(290,000)

Other information about the company's defined benefit obligation and plan assets is as follows:

As of January 1	Accrued Obligation	Benefit Plan Assets
2013	$4,000,000	$2,400,000
2014	4,520,000	2,200,000
2015	4,980,000	2,600,000
2016	4,250,000	3,040,000

Brush Inc. has a stable labour force of 400 employees who are expected to receive benefits under the plan. Their expected average remaining service life is 12 years in each of the next four years. The beginning balance of unrecognized net actuarial gain/loss is zero on January 1, 2013. The plan assets' market-related value and fair value are the same for the four-year period. Brush Inc. follows ASPE and accounts for its pension plan under the deferral and amortization approach.

Instructions

(a) Prepare a schedule that shows the minimum amount of amortization of the unrecognized net actuarial gain or loss for each of the years 2013, 2014, 2015, and 2016. (Round to the nearest dollar.)

(b) What options are available under IFRS to account for the actuarial gains or losses?

(c) What other options are available under the ASPE deferral and amortization approach to account for the actuarial gains or losses?

(LO 8) E19-17 (Post-Retirement Benefit Expense Calculation and Entries) Opsco Corp. provides the following information about its post-retirement health care benefit plan for the year 2013:

Current service cost	$ 202,500
Contribution to the plan	47,250
Actual return on plan assets	141,750
Benefits paid	90,000
Plan assets at Jan. 1, 2013	1,597,500
Defined post-retirement benefit obligation at Jan. 1, 2013	1,822,500
Discount rate and expected rate of return on plan assets	9%

Opsco follows IFRS.

Instructions

Calculate the post-retirement benefit expense for 2013, and prepare all required journal entries related to the post-retirement benefit plan that were made by Opsco in 2013.

(LO 8) **E19-18 (Post-Retirement Benefit Work Sheet)** Refer to the information in E19-17.

Instructions

(a) Complete a post-retirement work sheet for 2013.

(b) Prepare all required journal entries related to the plan made by Opsco in 2013.

(LO 8) **E19-19 (Post-Retirement Benefit Reconciliation Schedule)** The following is partial information related to Stanley Ltd.'s non-pension, post-retirement benefit plan at December 31, 2013:

Accrued post-retirement benefit obligation, accounting basis	$190,000
Accrued post-retirement benefit obligation, funding basis	155,000
Plan assets (at fair value)	130,000
Past service cost arising in current year	12,000

Amortization expense of $1,000 was incurred in the year related to the past service costs.

Instructions

*(a) Prepare a schedule reconciling the funded status with the asset/liability reported on the statement of financial position at December 31, 2013, assuming that Stanley Ltd. applies the deferral and amortization approach under ASPE.

(b) Prepare a schedule reconciling the funded status with the asset/liability reported on the statement of financial position at December 31, 2013, assuming that Stanley Ltd. applies the immediate recognition approach under IFRS.

(LO 9) *E19-20 (Pension Calculations and Disclosures)** Mila Enterprises Ltd. provides the following information about its defined benefit pension plan:

Balances or Values at December 31, 2013

Defined benefit obligation	$2,737,000
Vested benefit obligation	1,645,852
Fair value of plan assets	2,278,329
Other pension plan data:	
Current service cost for 2013	94,000
Actual return on plan assets in 2013	130,000
Expected return on plan assets in 2013 using discount rate	175,680
Interest on Jan. 1, 2013 defined benefit obligation	253,000
Funding of plan in 2013	92,329
Benefits paid	140,000

Instructions

*(a) Prepare the required disclosures for Mila's financial statements for the year ended December 31, 2013, assuming the company is not a public company, does not have broad public accountability, and has chosen the defer and amortize approach under ASPE.

(b) Prepare the required disclosures that would be required if Mila's common shares were traded on the Toronto Stock Exchange.

(c) Calculate the January 1, 2013 balances for the pension-related accounts if Mila follows IFRS.

Digging Deeper

(LO 10, 12) **E19-21 (Average Remaining Service Life and Amortization)** Toroton Ltd. has six employees participating in its defined benefit pension plan. The pension plan vests after six years of employment. The current years of service and expected years of future service for these employees at the beginning of 2013 are as follows:

On January 1, 2013, the company amended its pension plan, resulting in past service cost of $340,000, of which $200,000 is attributable to employees whose benefits have vested.

Employee	Current Years of Service	Expected Future Years of Service
Brandon	5	3
Chiara	4	5
Mikayla	5	6
Angela	6	5
Paolo	6	4
Erminia	7	7

Instructions

*(a) Calculate the amount of past service cost amortization for the years 2013 through 2018 assuming the company accounts for past service costs using the deferral and amortization approach under ASPE.

(b) Calculate the amount of past service cost amortization for the years 2013 through 2018 assuming the company accounts for past service costs using the immediate recognition approach under IFRS.

(LO 11) ***E19-22 (Calculation of Current Service Cost and ABO)** Josit Ltd. initiated a one-person pension plan in January 2009 that promises the employee a pension on retirement according to the following formula: pension benefit = 2.5% of final salary per year of service after the plan initiation. The employee began employment with Josit early in 2006 at age 33, and expects to retire at the end of 2032, the year in which he turns 60. His life expectancy at that time is 21 years.

Assume that this employee earned an annual salary of $40,000 when he joined Josit, that his salary was expected to increase at a rate of 4% per year, and that this remains a reasonable assumption to date. Josit considers a discount rate of 6% to be appropriate.

Instructions

(a) What is the employee's expected final salary?

(b) What amount of current service cost should Josit recognize in 2014 relative to this plan?

(c) What is the amount of the accrued benefit obligation at December 31, 2014?

(LO 12) ***E19-23 (Application of the Corridor Approach)** Bunker Corp. has the following beginning-of-year present values for its accrued benefit obligation, and fair values for its pension plan assets:

	Accrued Benefit Obligation	Plan Assets
2012	$3,500,000	$3,325,000
2013	4,200,000	4,375,000
2014	5,075,000	4,550,000
2015	6,300,000	5,250,000

The average remaining service life per employee in 2012 and 2013 is 10 years, and in 2014 and 2015 is 12 years. The net actuarial gain or loss that occurred during each year is as follows: 2012, $490,000 loss; 2013, $157,500 loss; 2014, $17,500 loss; and 2015, $43,740 gain. There was no opening balance in the accumulated net actuarial gain/loss account on January 1, 2012. Bunker applies the deferral and amortization approach under ASPE.

Instructions

Using the corridor approach, calculate the minimum amount of net actuarial gain or loss that should be amortized and charged to pension expense in each of the four years.

Problems

P19-1 RWL Limited provides a long-term disability program for its employees through an insurance company. For an annual premium of $18,000, the insurance company is responsible for providing salary continuation to disabled employees on a long-term basis after a three-month waiting period. During the waiting period, RWL continues to pay the employee at full salary. The employees contribute to the cost of this plan through regular payroll deductions that amount to $6,000 for the year. In late October 2014, Tony Hurst, a department manager earning $5,400 per month, was injured and was not expected to be able to return to work for at least one year.

Instructions

Prepare all entries made by RWL in 2014 in connection with the benefit plan, as well as any entries required in 2015.

*P19-2 Halifax University recently signed a contract with the bargaining unit that represents full-time professors. The contract agreement starts on April 1, 2012, the start of the university's fiscal year.

The following excerpt outlines the portion of the signed agreement that relates to sabbaticals: *"Professors may apply for a one-year sabbatical leave after seven continuous years of employment, and must outline how their sabbatical plans will benefit the university."*

After completing the required amount of time, any professor may apply for the leave. The contract notes particular types of activities that the sabbatical is intended to promote, including formal research, continued professional development, and independent study and research. Individual professors are left to make their own choices for whichever of these activities to pursue while on sabbatical leave. As part of their agreement, they must continue to work for Halifax University one year after their sabbatical, or reimburse the university for funds they receive while on leave. The agreement states that professors receive 80% of their salary while on sabbatical leave. Professors may delay, or be asked to delay, their application for sabbatical, in which case they will receive 85% of their salary while on leave.

The issue of sabbatical had long been a point of contention with faculty at Halifax University, which is an independent institution, and they fought vehemently for the right to this paid leave that had not previously been in their collective agreement. The university is phasing in the unfunded sabbatical plan gradually, which means that the first professors will be eligible to apply for their sabbatical in seven years.

The controller has put together the following numbers of professors in each salary group:

Professors with salaries averaging $60,000	55
Professors with salaries averaging $70,000	40
Professors with salaries averaging $100,000	10

The union agreement calls for a wage increase of 2% per year in each of the next seven years. This is consistent with past union agreements for this bargaining unit. Five of the professors with salaries averaging $100,000 are scheduled to retire in four years. Halifax University expects to keep a similar composition of salaried professors in the future. Assume a discount rate of 6%. Halifax University applies the deferral and amortization approach for employee future benefits under ASPE.

Instructions

(a) Prepare any entries that are required at the March 31, 2013 fiscal year end assuming sabbaticals will be granted only if the sabbatical activities proposed by the applicants are expected to benefit the university in some way.

(b) Prepare any entries that are required at the March 31, 2013 fiscal year end assuming sabbaticals will be granted automatically with no restrictions on the professors' activities during the year.

(c) Five employees are granted approval to take sabbatical in the first year that they are eligible under the assumption in (b). Prepare the entry that will be required when the professors are paid, assuming that an amount of $367,000 has correctly been accrued for these employees.

(d) The contract allows employees of the bargaining unit to take up to 10 days of paid sick leave per year. Explain the accounting implications under the following assumptions:

1. The sick leave is allowed to be carried over for up to a one-year period following year end.

2. Any unused sick time is not eligible to be carried over to the following fiscal period.

P19-3 Dayte Corporation reports the following January 1, 2014 balances for its defined benefit pension plan, which it accounts for using the immediate recognition approach under IFRS: plan assets, $460,000; defined benefit obligation, $460,000. Other data relating to three years of operation of the plan are as follows:

	2014	2015	2016
Annual service cost	$36,800	$ 43,700	$ 59,800
Discount rate and expected rate of return	10%	10%	10%
Actual return on plan assets	39,100	50,370	55,200
Funding of current service cost	36,800	43,700	59,800
Funding of past service cost	—	69,000	80,500
Benefits paid	32,200	37,720	48,300
Past service cost (plan amended, 1/1/15)		368,000	
Change in actuarial assumptions establishes a Dec. 31, 2016 defined benefit obligation of			1,196,000

Digging Deeper

Instructions

(a) Prepare and complete a pension worksheet for 2014.

(b) Prepare a continuity schedule of the projected benefit obligation over the three-year period.

(c) Prepare a continuity schedule of the plan assets over the three-year period.

(d) Determine the pension expense for each of 2014, 2015, and 2016.

(e) Prepare the journal entries to reflect the pension plan transactions and events for each year.

(f) Prepare a schedule reconciling the pension plan's funded status with the pension amounts reported on the statement of financial position over the three-year period.

*(g) Determine the pension expense for each of 2014, 2015, and 2016 assuming that the company elects to apply the immediate recognition approach under ASPE.

P19-4 The following information is available for Mitten Corporation's defined benefit pension plan:

	2013	2014	2015
Defined benefit obligation, opening balance, funded basis	$155,000	?	?
Defined benefit obligation, opening balance, accounting basis	175,000	?	?
Fair value of plan assets	165,000	?	?
Current service cost	35,000	47,250	52,500
Discount rate and expected rate of return	7%	7%	7%
Actual return on plan assets	8%	6%	7%
Contributions (funding)	44,000	44,000	44,000
Benefits paid to retirees	24,000	26,000	28,000

On January 1, 2013, Mitten Corp. amended its pension plan, resulting in past service costs with a present value of $78,000. The amendment of the pension plan is expected to provide future benefits for three years.

Instructions

*(a) Identify the pension plan's funded status and the liability or asset reported on the December 31, 2013, 2014, and 2015 statements of financial position assuming that Mitten Corp. accounts for its pension plan with the deferral and amortization approach under ASPE.

*(b) Calculate pension expense for 2013, 2014, and 2015 assuming that Mitten Corp. accounts for its pension plan with the deferral and amortization approach under ASPE.

(c) Identify the pension plan's funded status and the liability or asset reported on the December 31, 2013, 2014, and 2015 statements of financial position assuming that Mitten Corp. accounts for its pension plan with the immediate recognition approach under IFRS.

(d) Calculate pension expense and remeasurement (gain) loss–OCI for 2013, 2014, and 2015 assuming that Mitten Corp. accounts for its pension plan with the immediate recognition approach under IFRS.

(e) Which method results in a better measure of expense over the three-year period?

(f) Which method results in a better measure of the funded status on the statement of financial position?

P19-5 You are the controller of a newly established technology firm that is offering a new pension plan to its employees. The plan was established on January 1, 2013, with an initial contribution by the employer equal to the actuarial estimate of the past service costs for the existing group of employees. These employees are expected to continue to work for the firm for 20 years, on average, prior to retirement. This benefit vested in two employees immediately at a cost of $20,000. The remaining $55,000 was for employees with an average of five years remaining until the benefits are vested. The company expects to realize the economic benefits from the change in plan over the next four years. The company is considering going public in the next five years, and the president has asked you to keep her aware of the accounting changes in moving from ASPE to IFRS. She wants to be sure that the company always chooses the accounting policies that are closest to IFRS so that changes in the future when the company goes public will be minimized. In addition, she is interested in demonstrating a history of profits so that the company can be taken public successfully. The following information is available for you to work with.

	2013	2014	2015
Fair value of plan assets, beginning of year†	$75,000	?	?
DBO for funding purposes, beginning of year†	70,000	?	?
DBO for accounting purposes, beginning of year†	75,000	?	?
Current service cost for year	12,000	$13,000	$12,500
Interest on the liability	8%	8%	8%
Past service costs granted	75,000	-0-	-0-
Expected earnings on plan assets	8%	8%	8%

†After the initial contribution.

	2013	2014	2015
Actual earnings on plan assets	6,500	10,000	8,000
Employer contributions for the year	12,000	15,000	12,000
Benefits paid to retirees by trustee	–0–	4,000	5,000

Instructions

(a) Without using a pension work sheet, determine the funded status of the pension plan and the amount reported on the statement of financial position at each year end, the pension expense for each of the three years, and the remeasurement (gain) loss recorded in OCI for each of the three years, using the immediate recognition approach under IFRS.

*(b) Without using a pension work sheet, determine the funded status of the pension plan and the amount reported on the balance sheet at each year end, and the pension expense for each of the three years using the deferral and amortization approach under ASPE.

(c) Explain the differences between the two approaches and make a recommendation to your employer about which approach should be used.

*P19-6 Branfield Corporation sponsors a defined benefit pension plan for its 100 employees. On January 1, 2013, the company's actuary provided the following information:

Unrecognized past service cost	$ 390,000
Pension plan assets (fair value)	1,040,000
Accrued benefit obligation	1,430,000

The participating employees' expected average remaining service life (EARSL) and average remaining service period to full eligibility is 8.5 years. All employees are expected to receive benefits under the plan. On December 31, 2013, the actuary calculated that the present value of future benefits earned for employee services rendered in the current year amounted to $213,200 and the accrued benefit obligation was $1,825,200. The expected return on plan assets and the discount rate on the accrued benefit obligation were both 10%. The actual return on plan assets is $80,600. The company funded the current service cost as well as $106,600 of the past service costs in the current year. No benefits were paid during the year. The company accounts for its pension plan with the deferral and amortization approach under ASPE.

Instructions

Round all answers to the nearest dollar.

(a) Determine the pension expense that the company will recognize in 2013, identifying each component clearly. (Do not prepare a work sheet.)

(b) Calculate the amount of any 2013 increase/decrease in unrecognized actuarial gains or losses, and the amount to be amortized in 2013 and 2014 under the corridor approach.

(c) Prepare the journal entries to record pension expense and the company's funding of the pension plan in 2013.

(d) Prepare a schedule that reconciles the plan's funded status with the net defined benefit liability/asset reported on the December 31, 2013 balance sheet.

(e) Assume that the liability loss on the accrued benefit obligation arose because of the disposal of a segment of Branfield's business. How should this loss be reported on the company's 2013 financial statements?

*P19-7 Manon Corporation sponsors a defined benefit pension plan, which it accounts for with the deferral and amortization approach under ASPE. The following pension plan information is available for 2013 and 2014:

	2013	2014
Plan assets (fair value), Dec. 31	$380,000	$465,000
Accrued benefit obligation, Jan.1	600,000	700,000
Net defined benefit liability/(asset), Jan. 1	40,000	?
Unrecognized past service cost, Jan. 1	250,000	240,000
Unrecognized net actuarial loss, Jan. 1	50,000	?
Current service cost	60,000	90,000
Actual and expected return on plan assets	24,000	30,000
Amortization of past service cost	10,000	12,000
Funding of current service costs	60,000	90,000
Funding of past service costs	50,000	30,000
Interest/settlement rate	9%	9%

The pension fund paid out benefits in each year. While there was an unrecognized actuarial gain/loss at January 1, 2013, no additional actuarial gains or losses were incurred in the two-year period.

Instructions

(a) Calculate pension expense for 2013 and 2014.

(b) Prepare all journal entries to record the pension expense and the company's pension plan funding for both years.

(c) Assuming that Manon is not a public company and does not have broad public accountability, prepare the required notes to the financial statements at December 31, 2014.

(d) Prepare the complete pension work sheets for Manon for 2013 and 2014.

*P19-8   Bouter Corporation Limited (BCL) began operations in 1993 and in 2003 adopted a defined benefit pension plan for its employees. By January 1, 2013, the accrued benefit obligation was $510,000. The Net Defined Benefit Liability/Asset account on the December 31, 2012 statement of financial position was reported as a $190,000 liability balance.

On January 2, 2013, BCL agreed to a new union contract that granted retroactive benefits for services that employees had provided in years before the pension plan came into effect. The actuary informed BCL's chief accountant that, using its normal discount rate of 6%, benefits relating to these past services would cost the company $240,000. The expected average remaining service life of the group expected to receive benefits under this plan at this date was 21 years, the same as the group's period to full eligibility.

On January 1, 2013, the fair value of the pension plan assets was $320,000. The actuary estimates that these assets should earn a long-term rate of return of 7%, although, due to a downturn in the market, the actual return reported for the 2013 year was a loss of $9,500. The workforce is made up of a relatively young group of employees, so payments to those who had retired came to only $48,000 during the year, with these payments being made close to year end. The actuary also reported that the current service cost for BCL's employees for 2013 was $107,500. It is the company's policy, on advice from the actuary, to contribute amounts to the pension plan equal to each year's current service cost and the amount of any expense related to past service costs. This payment was made just before BCL's fiscal year end of December 31, 2013.

At the end of 2013, the actuary revised some key estimates, resulting in an actuarial loss of $15,500 related to the accrued obligation. Assume that the ABO amounts under the funding and accounting basis are the same.

Instructions

(a) Calculate the pension expense that should be reported for BCL's year ended December 31, 2013, under both the immediate recognition approach and the deferral and amortization approach under ASPE.

(b) Reconcile the difference in pension expense between the immediate recognition approach and the deferral and amortization approach under ASPE.

(c) Calculate the amount in the pension account to be reported on the December 31, 2013 statement of financial position under both the immediate recognition approach and the deferral and amortization approach under ASPE.

(d) How does the method of accounting for the pension plan (immediate recognition approach versus deferral and amortization approach under ASPE) impact cash flows in light of the company's policy regarding its contributions to the pension plan?

*P19-9   Dubel Toothpaste Corporation initiated a defined benefit pension plan for its 50 employees on January 1, 2013. The insurance company that administers the pension plan provides the following information for the years 2013, 2014, and 2015:

	For Year Ended December 31		
	2013	2014	2015
Plan assets (fair value)	$50,000	$ 85,000	$170,000
Accrued benefit obligation	63,900	?	?
Net actuarial (gain) loss re: ABO	8,900	(24,500)	84,500
Net actuarial (gain) loss re: fund assets	?	?	(18,200)
Employer's funding contribution (made at end of year)	50,000	60,000	95,000

There were no balances as of January 1, 2013, when the plan was initiated. The long-term expected return on plan assets was 8% throughout the three-year period. The settlement rate that was used to discount the company's pension obligation was 13% in 2013, 11% in 2014, and 8% in 2015. The service cost component of net periodic pension expense amounted to the following: 2013, $55,000; 2014, $85,000; and 2015, $119,000. The average remaining service life per employee is 10 years for all years involved. No benefits were paid in 2013, but $30,000 was paid in 2014, and $35,000 in 2015 (all benefits were paid at the end of the year). The company had elected to use the deferral and amortization approach under ASPE.

Instructions

Depending on what your instructor assigns, do either (a), (b), (c), (e), and (f); or (d), (e), and (f). (Round all answers to the nearest dollar.)

(a) Prepare a continuity schedule for the accrued benefit obligation over the three-year period.

(b) Prepare a continuity schedule for the plan assets over the three-year period.

(c) Calculate the amount of net periodic pension expense that the company will recognize in each of 2013, 2014, and 2015.

(d) Prepare and complete a pension work sheet for each of 2013, 2014, and 2015.

(e) Determine the funded status at December 31, 2015, and the balance of the Accrued Benefit Liability/Asset account that will be reported on the December 31, 2015 balance sheet. Fully explain why these amounts differ.

(f) Discuss what options are available under ASPE in regard to accounting for any actuarial gains or losses.

P19-10 Ekedahl Inc. has sponsored a non-contributory defined benefit pension plan for its employees since 1992. Prior to 2013, the funding of this plan exactly equalled cumulative net pension expense. Other relevant information about the pension plan on January 1, 2013, is as follows:

1. The defined benefit obligation amounted to $1,250,000 and the fair and market-related value of pension plan assets was $750,000.

2. On December 30, 2012, the pension plan was amended and resulted in past service cost of $500,000.

3. The company has 200 employees who are expected to receive benefits under the plan. The employees' expected period to full eligibility is 13 years with an EARSL of 16 years. Assume there is no change in the length of these periods between 2013 and 2015.

On December 31, 2013, the defined benefit obligation was $1,187,500. The fair value of the pension plan assets amounted to $975,000 at the end of the year. A 10% discount rate and an 8% expected asset return rate were used in the actuarial present value calculations in the pension plan. The present value of benefits attributed by the pension benefit formula to employee service in 2013 amounted to $50,000. The employer's contribution to the plan assets was $143,750 in 2013. No pension benefits were paid to retirees during this period.

Instructions

Round all answers to the nearest dollar.

(a) Calculate the amount of past service cost that will be included as a component of pension expense in 2013, 2014, and 2015 under:

  1. The immediate recognition approach under ASPE

  *2. The deferral and amortization approach under ASPE

  3. The immediate recognition approach under IFRS

*(b) Assuming that Ekedahl accounts for its pension plan with the deferral and amortization approach under ASPE, determine the amount of any actuarial gains or losses in 2013 and the amount to be amortized to expense in 2013 and 2014.

(c) Calculate pension expense for the year 2013 under:

  1. The immediate recognition approach under ASPE

  *2. The deferral and amortization approach under ASPE

  3. The immediate recognition approach under IFRS

*(d) Prepare a schedule reconciling the plan's funded status with the pension amounts reported on the December 31, 2013 balance sheet assuming that Ekedahl accounts for its pension plan with the deferral and amortization approach under ASPE.

(e) Assume that Ekedahl's pension plan is contributory rather than non-contributory. Would any part of your answers above change? What would be the impact on the company's financial statements of a contributory plan?

Digging Deeper

P19-11 You are the auditor of Beaton and Gunter Inc., the Canadian subsidiary of a multinational engineering company that offers a defined benefit pension plan to its eligible employees. Employees are permitted to join the plan after two years of employment, and benefits vest two years after joining the plan. You have received the following information from the fund trustee for the year ended December 31, 2014:

Discount rate		5%
Expected long-term rate of return on plan assets		6.5%
Rate of compensation increase		3.5%

Defined Benefit Obligation

Defined benefit obligation at Jan. 1, 2014	$11,375,000
Current service cost	425,000
Interest cost	568,750
Benefits paid	756,250
Actuarial loss for the period	631,250

Plan Assets

Fair value of plan assets at Jan. 1, 2014	9,062,500
Actual return on plan assets, net of expenses	1,125,000
Employer contributions	493,750
Employee contributions	81,250
Benefits paid	756,250

Other relevant information:

1. The net defined benefit liability on January 1, 2014, is $2,312,500.

2. Employee contributions to the plan are withheld as payroll deductions, and are remitted to the pension trustee along with the employer contributions.

3. The EARSL is 10 years.

Instructions

(a) Prepare a pension work sheet for the company.

(b) Prepare the employer's journal entries to reflect the accounting for the pension plan for the year ended December 31, 2014.

(c) Prepare a schedule reconciling the plan's funded status with the pension amounts reported on the December 31, 2014 statement of financial position.

(d) Assume that interest rates are falling. Explain what effect this is likely to have on the funded status of the plan.

*P19-12 Donnie Harpin was recently promoted to assistant controller of Glomski Corporation, having previously served the company as a staff accountant. Glomski is a medium-sized company that reports under ASPE.

One of Harpin's new responsibilities is to prepare the annual pension accrual. Judy Gralapp, the corporate controller, provided Harpin with last year's working papers and information from the actuary's annual report. The pension work sheet for the prior year is as follows:

	General Journal Entries			Memo Records		
	Pension Expense	Cash	Accrued Pension Asset/Liability	Accrued Benefit Obligation	Plan Assets	Unrecognized Past Service Cost
June 1, 2011[1]				$(20,000)	$20,000	
Service cost[1]	$1,800			(1,800)		
Interest[2]	1,200			(1,200)		
Actual return[3]	(1,600)				1,600	
Contribution[1]		$(1,000)			1,000	
Benefits paid[1]				900	(900)	
Past service cost[4]				(2,000)		$2,000
Journal entries			$(1,400)			
	$1,400	$(1,000)	$(400)			
May 31, 2012 balance				$(24,100)	$21,700	$2,000

[1] Per actuary's report.

[2] Beginning accrued benefit obligation discount rate of 6%.

[3] Expected return was $1,600 (beginning plan assets expected return of 8%).

[4] A plan amendment that granted employees retroactive benefits for work performed in earlier periods took effect on May 31, 2012. The amendment increased the May 31, 2012 accrued benefit obligation by $2,000. No amortization was recorded in the fiscal year ended May 31, 2012.

The actuary's report for the year ended May 31, 2013, indicated no actuarial gains or losses in the fiscal year ended May 31, 2013. Other pertinent information from the report is as follows:

Contribution	$425	Actual return on plan assets	$1,736
Current service cost	$3,000	Benefits paid	$500
Discount rate	6%	Average remaining service life	10 years
Expected return	8%		
Average period to full eligibility	8 years		

Instructions

(a) Prepare the pension work sheet for Glomski Corporation for the year ended May 31, 2013.

(a) Prepare the necessary journal entries to reflect the accounting for Glomski Corporation's pension plan for the year ended May 31, 2013.

P19-13 Hass Foods Inc. sponsors a post-retirement medical and dental benefit plan for its employees. The company adopted the provisions of IAS 19 beginning January 1, 2014. The following balances relate to this plan on January 1, 2014:

Plan assets	$ 2,780,000
Defined post-retirement benefit obligation	3,439,800
Past service costs	–0–

As a result of the plan's operation during 2014, the following additional data were provided by the actuary.

1. The service cost for 2014 was $273,000.

2. The discount rate was 9%.

3. Funding payments in 2014 were $234,000.

4. The actual return on plan assets was $58,500.

5. The benefits paid on behalf of retirees from the plan were $171,600.

6. The average remaining service life to full eligibility was 20 years.

Instructions

(a) Calculate the post-retirement benefit expense for 2014.

(b) Prepare a continuity schedule for the defined post-retirement benefit obligation and for the plan assets from the beginning of the year to the end of 2014.

(c) At December 31, 2014, prepare a schedule reconciling the plan's funded status with the post-retirement amount reported on the statement of financial position.

(d) Explain in what ways, if any, the accounting requirements for this plan are different from the requirements for a defined benefit pension plan.

*P19-14. Refer to the example of HTSM Corp. in Appendix 19A and assume it is now 2015, three years after the defined benefit pension plan was initiated. In December 2015, HTSM's actuary provided the company with an actuarial revaluation of the plan. The actuary's assumptions included the following changes:

Estimated final salary on retirement	$145,000
Current settlement/discount rate	7%

Instructions

(a) Calculate the defined benefit obligation (DBO) at December 31, 2015, and the amount of any actuarial gain or loss.

(b) Based on the revised assumptions at the end of the year, determine what percentage increase or decrease there would be in the DBO for:

1. A 1% increase in the discount rate

2. A 1% decrease in the discount rate

(c) Determine the effect of the actuarial revaluation on the pension plan's funded status at December 31, 2015, and on pension expense for 2015 and for 2016.

(d) Based on the revised assumptions, recalculate the past service cost that was incurred by the company in 2016.

Case

Refer to the Case Primer on the Student Website and in *WileyPLUS* to help you answer this case.

CA19-1 Delmar Manufacturing Inc. is a provincial manufacturer of electronics. It has been in operation for over 25 years under ownership of the same two private shareholders. It has always offered its employees a very generous defined benefit (DB) pension plan as part of the compensation package. Delmar has recently undergone expansion, and in the last quarter of this fiscal year opened a new manufacturing plant in another province. As a result it also created a new DB pension plan for the employees of the new plant. Some of the employees at the new plant are current employees who were already participating in the existing DB pension plan and others are new employees recently hired and will be new to Delmar's pension plan. Existing employees were transferred into the new plan before the end of the fiscal year.

A review of the pension transactions for 2013 revealed the following:

1. For 2013, the service cost for Delmar employees is projected by the actuary to be $236,000. The current service cost is credited at the end of each fiscal year. Nothing has been recorded in the financials to reflect this.

2. The actuary has reviewed the new plan and determined that the past service costs for existing employees is $96,000 (a cumulative total over the period of the last 20 years). Delmar has not yet reflected this in its current results and is unclear on how to accurately reflect this in its financial statements. Delmar employees would be eligible for full benefits after a two-year vesting period.

3. Delmar's current borrowing rate and settlement rate is 8%. Delmar's management has specifically eliminated the option of purchasing an insurance contract for the future settlement of its pension liability. The current interest rate on high-quality corporate bonds is 9% and the pension committee has identified an expected rate of return of 10% on the plan assets.

4. The plan paid only $34,000 in benefits to its retirees for 2013 and Delmar contributed $88,000 to the plan throughout the year.

5. Due to declining economic conditions, the actuary has revised its assumption for age of retirement and final salary. This has resulted in an actuarial loss of $55,000. Delmar must also account for an actuarial loss of $19,000 resulting from differences in past assumptions and actual costs (experience losses). This has not yet been accounted for in the statements.

6. The actual return on plan assets was $16,500, significantly lower than projected.

7. The defined benefit obligation as determined by the actuarial valuation for funding purposes is equal to the defined benefit obligation used for accounting purposes. The fair value of the plan assets was $980,000 at the end of 2012.

Excerpts from Delmar's financial statements are provided below, prepared under ASPE using the immediate recognition approach.

	2012	2013
Total current assets	$ 2,078,900	$ 2,044,900
Fixed assets, at net book value	11,700,900	14,010,200
Total current liabilities	822,400	773,000
Long-term debt	345,900	333,800
Net accrued benefit obligation	2,165,000	?
Operating profit	1,890,000	1,345,000
Other revenue and other expenses	58,000	777,000
Costs—Expansion (*manufacturing facility*)	390,000	482,000
Interest expense		
Net income	$ 937,300	$ 55,900

Instructions

Delmar Manufacturing Inc.'s management is reviewing its current pension accounting in preparation for an upcoming meeting with the board of directors and its pension committee. Complete the necessary calculations needed to record the ending net accrued benefit obligation or asset following ASPE and using the immediate recognition approach. Management does not plan to change this accounting policy. In addition, assume the role of a consultant and discuss the financial reporting issues, particularly the implications for the financial statements and the differences in reporting and presentation under IFRS and ASPE. Provide guidance on which method would be preferable for Delmar.

Integrated Case

IC19-1 Martel Industries Limited is in the mining business. The company has significant exploration activities in many countries and has started to explore and develop oil and gas properties in the last few years. The company's shares trade on the national stock exchange. Martel has several significant loans with the Mining Bank Limited (MBL), which monitors its debt to equity ratio.

One of the company's largest ever silver mines is starting to produce (Mine A). In the past year, a significant amount has been spent getting the property ready for production. The company has had to borrow additional funds from MBL this year in order to complete the mine and has installed a complex underground railway system (railway cars and tracks) to assist in bringing the ore to the surface for processing. Martel has asked its engineers and geologists to estimate the amount of silver that exists in this property. The engineers and geologists have come up with a fairly wide range, with the top end of the range being three times the lower end of the range. The lower end of the range relates to silver ore reserves that can be proven and the upper end represents possible/probable silver ore reserves. The life of the mine is expected to be approximately 10 years, after which the company will probably just abandon the mine. The life of the railway tracks is 50 years and the railway cars 20 years. The company may be able to salvage the tracks and cars at the end of the 10-year period but is not sure if it would actually do this (and sell or reuse them) since the salvage costs would likely be high. As the ore is mined, it is stored in large piles waiting to be processed into silver. At year end, in anticipation of significant sales in the new year, the ore piles are very large.

Another mining property (Mine B) is just in the evaluation and exploration stage. The funds being spent on this property are also pretty significant and financed by borrowings. Primarily, the expenditures consist of geophysical studies, exploratory drilling, and sampling. Although the preliminary work that is being done points to a significant geological find of gold, there is still a large amount of uncertainty as to whether sufficient gold ore actually exists of a commercial grade. Nonetheless, the company is continuing to develop this property. A large amount of time has been spent on this particular property by Martel's senior management since this property is in a politically unstable country (Country C). Martel had to negotiate for several months for the rights to bring an exploration team into the country to begin the work. In addition, Martel had to pay a one-time fee to the resource minister of the government of Country C for this right. All costs have been capitalized.

Mine C has been actively producing copper for two years. During the current year, the government announced that it would be imposing stricter regulations on mining companies, requiring that they restore the land to its original condition. Although in the past Martel has tried to minimize any negative impact on the environment (there are numerous environmental groups that monitor the company's policies), senior management has admitted in private discussions within the firm that they have not met the proposed new standard. The amount would be material. As a matter of fact, the company may decide to close Mine C and abandon it. Mine C is in a country where Martel would likely not do business in the future due to the high incidence of earthquakes.

The oil and gas segment of the business has several producing wells. Luckily, they have not had any "dry wells" (that is, all properties that they explored resulted in producing wells). The oil rigs require major maintenance every two years. The costs to do this maintenance are pretty significant but given the risks involved, it is well worth it. The company stores its gas in underground storage caves. Approximately 25% of this gas will never be sold since it is required to pressurize the cave. The rest of the gas is generally sold.

During the year, the company put in place a new long-term benefit plan for Martel employees. Under the funding arrangement for the plan, the company will contribute to the plan annually an amount that is based on net income.

Instructions

Adopt the role of the company controller and discuss the financial reporting issues. Use the case analysis format discussed in class.

Writing Assignments

WA19-1 Shikkiah Corp. (which is a private enterprise) tries to attract the most knowledgeable and creative employees it can find. To help accomplish this, the company offers a special group of technology employees the right to a fully paid sabbatical leave after every five years of continuous service. It is the company's objective that the employees will come back renewed and with fresh ideas, but there are no restrictions on what they do during the sabbatical year.

Shikkiah hired three employees in early 2014 who were entitled to this benefit. Each new hire agreed to a starting salary of $80,000 per year.

Instructions

(a) Explain generally how this employee benefit should be accounted for by Shikkiah Corp. under ASPE and IFRS.

(b) Assume that you are the assistant to the company controller. In response to the controller's request, list all the information you need in order to calculate the amounts and prepare the adjusting entry that is required at December 31, 2014, relative to this plan under ASPE and IFRS. Include a brief discussion of the key information that you would need to provide to the actuary.

(c) Assume that the employees' activities during the sixth (the sabbatical) year are specified by the company: the employees must work on research and promotion activities that will benefit the company. Would your answer to part (a) change? If yes, explain why and how it would be accounted for. If not, explain why not.

WA19-2 Many business organizations have been concerned with providing for employee retirement since the late 1800s. During recent decades, a marked increase in this concern has resulted in the establishment of private pension and other post-retirement benefit plans in most sizable companies.

The substantial growth of these plans, both in the numbers of employees that they cover and in the types and value of retirement benefits, has increased the significance of the cost of these benefit plans in relation to the financial position, results of operations, and cash flows of many companies. In working with the benefit plans, accountants encounter a variety of terms. Each benefit plan component must be dealt with appropriately if generally accepted accounting principles are to be reflected in the financial statements of entities that offer these plans.

Instructions

(a) How does a contributory plan differ from a non-contributory plan?

(b) Differentiate between accounting for the employer and accounting for the benefit plan.

(c) Explain the terms "funded" and "net defined benefit liability or asset" as they relate to the employer and the benefit plan itself.

(d) Distinguish between each of the following sets of terms as they relate to pension plans and their treatment under ASPE and IFRS:

1. Current service cost and past service cost

2. Remeasurement gain/loss and actuarial experience gain/loss

(e) Explain how the accounting for other post-retirement benefit plans with benefits that vest or accumulate differs from the accounting for defined benefit pension plans, if there is any difference.

WA19-3 At the time of writing this book, two approaches were available for private enterprises: the immediate recognition approach and the deferral and amortization approach.

Instructions

Describe the advantages and disadvantages of the immediate recognition approach and the deferral and amortization approach. Explain any differences in the impact on the earnings and statement of financial position.

WA19-4 Research what Canadian companies have been doing in recent years in response to rising post-employment health care costs and the risks that are associated with defined benefit pension plans. Write a short report on your findings.

Instructions

Describe the advantages and disadvantages of the immediate recognition approach and the deferral and amortization approach. Explain any differences in the impact on the earnings and statement of financial position.

WA19-5 A ceiling test is required for companies that have pension plan assets.

Instructions

Explain how the asset ceiling test would be applied and why is it necessary. (See IFRIC 14 for information.)

WA19-6

Instructions

Write a brief essay highlighting the differences between IFRS and ASPE noted in this chapter, discussing the conceptual justification for each.

RESEARCH AND FINANCIAL ANALYSIS

RA19-1 BCE Inc.

Real World Emphasis

Obtain the annual statements for BCE Inc. for the year ended December 31, 2011, from the company's website or SEDAR (www.sedar.com).

Instructions

Refer to Note 20 of the 2011 financial statements of BCE Inc. and answer the following questions.

(a) Determine what the funded status is of the defined benefit (DB) pension plans and what the dollar amount of the over- or underfunding is at December 31, 2011, and December 31, 2010. Has the status improved or deteriorated since the end of the preceding year? What is the major reason for the change in BCE's funded status? What is the status of the plans in the net deficit position and what is the status of the plans in a net surplus position at December 31, 2011?

(b) What is the amount of the employee benefit asset or obligation reported on BCE's December 31, 2011 consolidated statement of financial position? Provide a reconciliation to the funded status reported in part (a). Comment on this reconciliation.

(c) What was the expected return on the pension plan assets in 2011? What was the actual return on the plan assets for the year?

(d) What was the cost that the company reported for its defined benefit plans? Describe the main components of the cost reported under IFRS. Estimate the amount of expense that would have been reported under the ASPE immediate recognition approach for December 31, 2011. Comment on any differences.

(e) What types of post-retirement plans does the company have? What was the total cost reported for these plans in Note 20 of the financial statements?

(f) What is the total expense for the defined contribution (DC) plans during 2011? During 2010?

RA19-2 Canadian National Railway Company

Real World Emphasis

Below is an excerpt from the note disclosure (excerpts from Note 12) of the Canadian National Railway Company's December 31, 2011 annual report.

(v) Components of net periodic benefit cost (income)

In millions		Pensions	
Year ended December 31,	2011	2010	2009
Service cost	$124	$ 99	$ 83
Interest cost	788	837	885
Curtailment gain	—	—	—
Settlement loss	3	—	—
Expected return on plan assets	(1,005)	(1,009)	(1,007)
Amortization of prior service cost	2	3	5
Recognized net actuarial loss (gain)	8	3	5
Net periodic benefit cost (income)	$ (80)	$ (70)	$ (34)

In millions	Pensions	
	Year ended December 31,	
	2011	2010
Change in benefit obligation		
Projected benefit obligation at beginning of year	$14,895	$13,708
Amendments	27	5
Interest cost	788	837
Service cost	577	1,118
Actuarial loss (gain)	124	99
Curtailment gain	—	—
Plan participants' contributions	54	99
Foreign currency changes	5	(12)
Benefit payments, settlements, and transfers	(922)	(910)
Projected benefit obligation at end of year	$15,548	$14,895
Component representing future salary increases	(437)	(439)
Accumulated benefit obligation at end of year	$15,111	$14,456
Change in plan assets		
Fair value of plan assets at beginning of year	$15,092	$14,332
Employer contributions	458	411
Plan participants' contributions	54	50
Foreign currency changes	1	(8)
Actual return on plan assets	36	1,217
Benefit payments, settlements, and transfers	(922)	(910)
Fair value of plan assets at end of year	$14,719	$15,092
Funded status (Excess (deficiency) of fair value of plan assets overprojected benefit obligation at end of year)	$ (829)	$ 197

Measurement date for all plans is December 31.
The projected benefit obligation and fair value of plan assets for the CN Pension Plan at December 31, 2011 were $14,514 million and $13,992 million respectively ($13,941 million and $14,343 million, respectively, at December 31, 2010.

Instructions

Using the above disclosure notes, answer the following questions.

(a) Is the company's pension plan in a surplus or deficit status position at December 31, 2011? At December 31, 2010?

(b) What is the amount reported for the net periodic benefit cost for December 31, 2011, and December 31, 2010? What could cause this trend?

(c) What was the amount of cash flow used to fund the plan for 2011 and 2010? Why would there be differences in the annual funding amounts? How does this compare with the expense that is showing for the company for the related years?

(d) Discuss whether or not you believe that the pension expense is faithfully presented in the profit or loss statement for the years 2011 and 2010.

RA19-3 Research Topic

Real World Emphasis

RONA Inc., **Bank of Montreal**, and **Air Canada** are all Canadian companies with defined benefit plans. Visit www.sedar.com to access financial statements for the 2011 fiscal year ends for RONA and Air Canada and for the 2012 fiscal year end for the Bank of Montreal.

Instructions

Analyze the notes to the financial statements of each of the three companies, and provide answers to the following questions.

(a) For each company, identify the following three assumptions:

1. The discount rate

2. The rate of compensation increase that was used to measure the projected benefit obligation

3. The expected long-term rate of return on plan assets

(b) Comment on any significant differences in the assumptions that are used by each firm.

(c) Did any of the companies change their assumptions during the period covered by the notes? If yes, what was the effect on each of the following: the current year's accrued benefit obligation, the plan assets, and the pension expense? Explain.

(d) Identify the types of plans and the assumptions that underlie any future benefit plans other than pensions. Are these similar across the three companies? Comment on how any differences would affect an intercompany analysis.

(e) Are the pension plans and post-retirement plans in a deficit or surplus position? What are the amounts that have been reported on the statements of financial position?

RA19-4 Research Topic

Real World Emphasis

The AcSB is proposing changes in the accounting of defined pension plans under ASPE as outlined in the chapter material. Access the January 2012 Exposure Draft for Employee Future Benefits from the www.frascanada.ca website.

Instructions

Write a brief essay highlighting the proposed changes in accounting for employee future benefits under the January 2012 Exposure Draft, discussing the related conceptual justification for each key change.

ENDNOTES

1 Statistics Canada, "Employer Pension Plans (Trusteed Pension Funds), First Quarter 2012," *The Daily*, September 12, 2012, available at http://www.statcan.gc.ca/.

2 Louise Egan and Susan Taylor, "Feds Take Tough Stance on Pension Fund Relief," Reuters, Canoe.ca, August 3, 2012.

3 When it is used as a verb, **fund** means to pay to a funding agency (for example, to fund future pension benefits or to fund pension cost). Used as a noun or an adjective, "fund" refers to assets that have accumulated in the hands of a funding agency (trustee) for the purpose of meeting pension benefits when they become due.

4 Increasingly, companies have hybrid plans that have characteristics of both defined contribution and defined benefit plans. Under ASPE, a company with a plan that has features of both types of plan should account for each component separately according to its substance.

5 *CICA Handbook—Accounting*, Part II, Section 3461.010 and IAS 19.8.

6 The benefit or pension cost and the benefit or pension expense for a period are the same amount unless some portion of the cost is treated as a product cost and charged to inventory, or is capitalized as a component of property, plant, and equipment, for example. In this chapter, these terms are generally used interchangeably.

7 There has been much litigation over the ownership of pension fund surpluses. The courts have increasingly determined that pension fund surpluses, or a significant portion of them, should accrue to the benefit of the employee group. Provincial pension legislation dictates how pension surpluses must be handled.

8 The employee is not 100% secure, however. If the health of the company sponsor is uncertain, the company's ability to meet any outstanding pension funding requirements may also be uncertain. This was very evident in the economic downturn of 2007 to 2009.

9 The general public has little understanding of what an actuary does, as illustrated by the following excerpt from *The Wall Street Journal: "A polling organization once asked the general public what an actuary was and received among its more coherent responses the opinion that it was a place where you put dead actors."*

10 When the term "present value of benefits" is used throughout this chapter, it really means the **actuarial present value** of benefits. Actuarial present value is the amount payable adjusted to reflect the time value of money and the probability of payment (by means of decreases for events such as death, disability, withdrawals, or retirement) between the present date and the expected date of payment. For simplicity, we will use the term "present value" instead of "actuarial present value" in our discussion.

11 ASPE refers to this method as the **projected benefit method prorated on services** (3461.047).

12 The service cost for funding purposes is usually calculated on a different basis.

13 *CICA Handbook—Accounting*, Part II, Section 3461.102.

14 IAS 19 uses the term "net interest" on the net defined benefit liability, but notes that this "can be viewed as comprising interest income on plan assets, interest cost on the defined benefit obligation and interest on the effect of the asset ceiling" (IAS 19.124).

15 In general, the current service cost has to be funded annually. If a plan is in a surplus position (that is, fund assets are greater than the accrued obligation), the company may be able to take a contribution holiday; in other words, to temporarily not make any contributions. If there is a funding deficiency, the extent of the shortfall is determined by two different valuations: one based on a going concern assumption and one based on a termination assumption. These dictate the additional funding that is required, and the period over which any deficiency must be funded. With the economic downturn and low interest rates in the last decade, many companies had difficulty dealing with unanticipated funding demands as pension obligations increased in value. A DBO based on current salary levels is common in determining the minimum funding requirements.

16 Under ASPE, the expected return may be based, instead, on a market-related value of the assets. The **market-related value of plan assets** is a calculated value that recognizes changes in fair value in a systematic and rational way over no more than five years (*CICA Handbook—Accounting*, Part II, Section 3461.089 and .090). Different ways of calculating a market-related value may be used for different asset classes. For example, an employer might use fair value for bonds and a five-year moving average for equities, as long as the method of determining market-related value is applied consistently from year to year for each asset class.

17 Under the deferral and amortization approach of ASPE described in Appendix 19B, entities may use a date up to three months before the year end if the timing is consistent from year to year. However, under the immediate recognition approach, the measures must represent balance sheet date values.

[18] When **Air Canada** filed for protection under the Companies' Creditors Arrangement Act in 2003, a $1.5-billion unfunded pension liability was listed as one of the key factors behind the company's insolvency. How to deal with this underfunded plan and unbooked liability was central to Air Canada's restructuring negotiations. The company faced similar problems in 2009 with its $3.2-billion pension deficit. In this case, the federal government stepped in with a legislated solution to help extremely troubled companies restructure such problems. The company continued to face underfunded pension liability issues in 2011 and 2012.

[19] In our examples we show the interest earned on the net defined benefit liability/asset in two pieces: the interest cost on the DBO and the interest earned on the plan assets. This has the same effect as calculating one interest amount on the net defined benefit liability (asset).

[20] This pension entry work sheet is based on Paul B.W. Miller, "The New Pension Accounting (part 2)," *Journal of Accountancy*, February 1987, pp. 86–94. Copyright 1987. American Institute of Certified Public Accountants, Inc.

[21] There is an exception. As explained later in the chapter, the balance sheet account may have to be adjusted for any valuation allowance that arises from the limit on the carrying amount of an accrued benefit asset based on the asset ceiling test.

[22] There would be a similar impact if we assume that the 2015 contributions are made evenly over the year in 2015. On average, half of the contributions would have been available to earn interest during the year, increasing expected return accordingly.

[23] The expected future benefits generally represent those that the company can realize from a plan surplus through amounts it can withdraw from the plan or reductions it can make in its future contributions. Under IFRS, the change in the valuation allowance made as a result of actuarial gains and losses recognized in other comprehensive income would be adjusted to OCI rather than net income.

[24] Sabbaticals where the employee is expected to use the compensated absence to perform research or other activities to the benefit of the organization do not need to be accrued over the period when the sabbatical is earned. Other benefits provided to employees during active employment, such as sick leave that does not accumulate and bonuses, are not covered by Employee Future Benefits under ASPE (*CICA Handbook–Accounting*, Part II, Section 3461.006).

[25] The M&S notes are based on IAS 19 requirements before the update to IAS 19 that was effective starting in 2013.

[26] *CICA Handbook–Accounting*, Part II, Section 3461.093. Note that this accounting treatment is consistent with the upper limit of the attribution period (that is, the expected period to full eligibility) that is used for attributing current service cost to accounting periods.

[27] ASPE also allows the "market-related" value of plan assets instead of fair value.

[28] *CICA Handbook–Accounting*, Part II, Section 3461.101.

Lease Reporting: Change in Flight Path on the Horizon

Courtesy WestJet

WITH A FLEET of over 100 aircraft, 44 of which are leased, WestJet has significant lease obligations. Several considerations factor into the lease versus buy decision for the Calgary-based airline, including the capital cost of the aircraft, the residual value risk, and the availability of the aircraft. Upon expiration of the lease, WestJet can choose to return the aircraft to the lessor or enter into negotiations to extend the lease.

There are also differences in how WestJet accounts for its leased aircraft versus its owned aircraft. All of WestJet's current aircraft leases are considered operating leases because they do not meet the test for capital leases: the airline will not own the aircraft at the end of the lease's term; the leases range from 8 to 14 years, just a portion of the aircraft's economic lives; and the lease payments are only a portion of the aircraft's fair value. WestJet does not include the future operating lease payments on the statement of financial position, but instead includes them in the notes to the financial statements as a commitment. The aircraft rental expense—that is, the lease payment—is included in the statement of earnings.

This may change, however, if the IASB implements its proposal requiring all leases to be capitalized, which could come into effect under IFRS starting January 1, 2015. This will affect WestJet's reporting of its liabilities since, as of January 2013, it had approximately U.S. $750 million in lease commitments that were not included in liabilities. If leases are capitalized, they would be reported as assets, with a corresponding liability.

WestJet's Executive Vice-President, Finance, and Chief Financial Officer, Vito Culmone, welcomes the proposed IFRS change. "In reviewing and planning our capital structure and our future debt obligations, we essentially do not differentiate between owned and leased aircraft. To that end, capitalizing aircraft leases will also enhance comparability among airlines and hopefully make it easier for the reader of the financial statements."

Capitalizing leases likely won't have much long-term effect on WestJet's debt covenants, profit and loss, or employee bonus plans, says Mr. Culmone.

Nor did this potential accounting change affect the company's decision to buy rather than lease all of its 20 new Bombardier Q-400 aircraft, which it needed for its 2013 launch of the WestJet Encore regional service to smaller communities across the country, such as Nanaimo and Fort St. John, B.C. "The buy versus lease decision is driven by several factors, but the accounting treatment has no bearing on our decision," Mr. Culmone says.

Leases

LEARNING OBJECTIVES

After studying this chapter, you should be able to:

1. Understand the importance of leases from a business perspective.

2. Explain the conceptual nature, economic substance, and advantages of lease transactions.

3. Identify and apply the criteria that are used to determine the type of lease for accounting purposes for a lessee under the classification approach.

4. Calculate the lease payment that is required for a lessor to earn a specific return.

5. Account for a lessee's basic capital (finance) lease.

6. Determine the effect of, and account for, residual values and bargain purchase options in a lessee's capital (finance) lease.

7. Account for an operating lease by a lessee and compare the operating and capitalization methods of accounting for leases.

8. Determine the statement of financial position presentation of a capital (finance) lease and identify other disclosures required.

9. Identify and apply the criteria that are used to determine the type of lease for a lessor under the classification approach.

10. Account for and report basic financing and manufacturer/dealer or sales-type leases by a lessor.

11. Account for and report financing and manufacturer/dealer or sales-type leases with guaranteed residual values or a bargain purchase option by a lessor.

12. Account for and report an operating lease by a lessor.

13. Identify differences in accounting between ASPE and IFRS, and what changes are expected in the near future.

After studying Appendix 20A, you should be able to:

14. Describe and apply the lessee's accounting for sale-leaseback transactions.

15. Explain the classification and accounting treatment for leases that involve real estate.

After studying Appendix 20B, you should be able to:

16. Explain and apply the contract-based approach to a basic lease for a lessee and lessor.

PREVIEW OF CHAPTER 20

Leasing continues to grow in popularity as a form of asset-based financing.[1] Instead of borrowing money to buy an airplane, a computer, a nuclear core, or a satellite, a company leases the item. Railroads lease huge amounts of equipment, many hotel and motel chains lease their facilities, most retail chains lease their retail premises and warehouses, and, as indicated in the opening vignette, most airlines lease their airplanes! Small and medium-sized enterprises also use leases as an important form of debt financing.

Because of the significance and popularity of lease arrangements, consistent accounting and complete reporting of these transactions are crucial. In this chapter, we look at these important issues related to leasing.

The chapter is organized as follows:

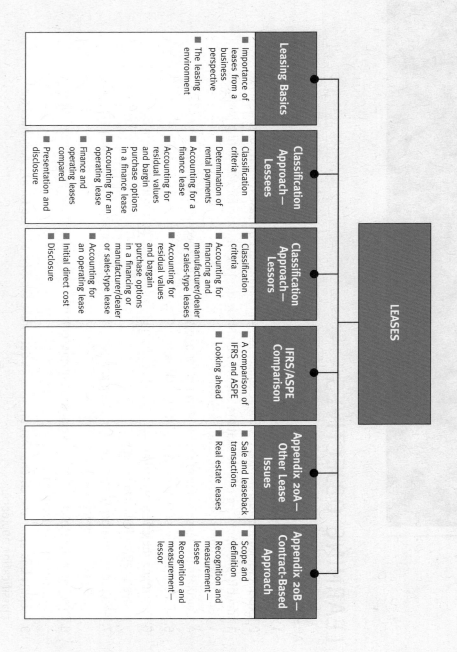

LEASES

Leasing Basics
- Importance of leases from a business perspective
- The leasing environment

Classification Approach— Lessees
- Classification criteria
- Determination of rental payments
- Accounting for a finance lease
- Accounting for residual values and bargain purchase options in a finance lease
- Accounting for an operating lease
- Finance and operating leases compared
- Presentation and disclosure

Classification Approach— Lessors
- Classification criteria
- Accounting for financing and manufacturer/dealer or sales-type leases
- Accounting for residual values and bargain purchase options in a financing or manufacturer/dealer or sales-type lease
- Accounting for an operating lease
- Initial direct cost
- Disclosure

IFRS/ASPE Comparison
- A comparison of IFRS and ASPE
- Looking ahead

Appendix 20A— Other Lease Issues
- Sale and leaseback transactions
- Real estate leases

Appendix 20B— Contract-Based Approach
- Scope and definition
- Recognition and measurement— lessee
- Recognition and measurement— lessor

LEASING BASICS

Importance of Leases from a Business Perspective

Objective 1

Understand the importance of leases from a business perspective.

Leasing is very attractive for many companies as a cost-effective way of financing property and equipment, especially for items whose technology becomes obsolete quite quickly. But the accounting for leases is very controversial. For many years standard setters have been concerned that financial statement preparers have avoided having to capitalize leases on their financial statements, by structuring leases in such a way that the lease liabilities remain "off–balance sheet." The substance of most lease arrangements is that companies are borrowing funds to acquire leased assets. However, the legal form of many leases allows companies to treat lease transactions simply as rent expense, with no separate recording of the related asset and liability.

The FASB and IASB are working to develop a new leasing standard. In a speech at the London School of Economics in November 2012, Hans Hoogervorst, Chairman of the IASB, noted that a significant source of off-balance sheet financing for companies is the leasing arrangements that they enter into. "For many companies, such as airlines and railway companies, the off–balance sheet financing numbers can be quite substantial," he said. "Companies tend to love off–balance sheet financing, as it masks the true extent of their leverage and many of those that make extensive use of leasing for this purpose are not happy" with the IASB-FASB project to get leases on the balance sheet, he said.

Hoogervoorst said there is a lack of transparency in leasing arrangements, so financial analysts have to "take an educated guess on what the real but hidden leverage of leasing is."[2] This leaves analysts and other financial statement users guessing, since management does not have to share the information needed to provide a proper estimate of the extent of leverage provided by lease financing.

The leasing industry predicts that the proposed new accounting rules would significantly hurt its business. Hoogervorst notes that a "recent report in the United States claimed that our joint efforts with the FASB to record leases on balance sheet[s] will lead to 190,000 jobs being lost in the US alone." He compares this with similar claims that were made when the IASB and the FASB required stock options to be expensed and pension liabilities to be put on the balance sheet.

We discuss the "players" involved in the leasing industry, and the changes being proposed by the IASB, further below. For now, it is important to note that accounting for leases is not just an accounting issue, but one of importance to financial institutions, leasing companies, and even the U.S. Congress (which was being heavily lobbied to keep leases off the balance sheets of corporations). It will be interesting to see if the FASB and the IASB succeed in their goal of improving the accounting for leases, like they did for pensions and stock options.

The Leasing Environment

Aristotle once said, "Wealth does not lie in ownership but in the use of things." Many Canadian companies have clearly come to agree with Aristotle as, rather than owning assets, they now are heavily involved in leasing them.

A **lease** is a contractual agreement between a **lessor** and a **lessee** that gives the lessee, for a specified period of time, the right to use specific property owned by the lessor in return for specified, and generally periodic, cash payments (rents). An essential element of the lease agreement is that the lessor transfers less than the total interest in the property. Because of the financial, operating, and risk advantages that the lease arrangement provides, many businesses and other types of organizations lease substantial amounts of property as an alternative to ownership. Any type of equipment or property can be leased, such as rail cars, helicopters, bulldozers, schools, golf club facilities, barges, medical scanners, computers, and so on. The largest class of leased equipment is information technology equipment. Next are assets in the transportation area, such as trucks, aircraft, and rail cars.

Ethics

Objective 2

Explain the conceptual nature, economic substance, and advantages of lease transactions.

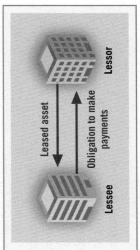

EXAMPLE

The lessee company gains the right to use the asset over the lease term in exchange for promising to make periodic rent or lease payments. The asset might be an automobile, a building, or any of a broad range of possible assets.

Law

Because a lease is a contract, the provisions that the lessor and lessee agree to can vary widely from lease to lease. Indeed, they are limited only by the ingenuity of the two parties to the contract and their advisors. The lease's duration—lease term—may be anything from a short period of time to the entire expected economic life of the asset. The **rental payments** may be the same amount from year to year, or they may increase or decrease; further, they may be predetermined or may vary with sales, the prime interest rate, the consumer price index, or some other factor. In most cases, the rent is set at an amount that enables the lessor to recover the asset's cost plus a fair return over the life of the lease.

The obligations for taxes, insurance, and maintenance (executory costs) may be the responsibility of either the lessor or the lessee, or they may be divided. In order to protect the lessor from default on the rents, the lease may include restrictions—comparable to those in bond indentures—that limit the lessee's activities in making dividend payments or incurring further debt. In addition, the lease contract may be non-cancellable or may grant the right to early termination on payment of a set scale of amounts plus a penalty. In case of default, the lessee may be liable for all future payments at once, and receive title to the property in exchange; or the lessor may have the right to sell the asset to a third party and collect from the lessee all or a portion of the difference between the sale price and the lessor's unrecovered cost.

When the lease term ends, several alternatives may be available to the lessee. These may range from simple termination to the right to renew or buy the asset at a nominal price.

Who Are the Players?

Who are the lessors referred to above? In Canada, lessors are usually one of three types of company:

1. Manufacturer finance companies
2. Independent finance companies
3. Traditional financial institutions

Manufacturer finance companies, or captive leasing companies as they are also called, are subsidiaries whose main business is to perform leasing operations for the parent company. **Honda Canada Finance Inc.** is an example of a captive leasing company. As soon as the parent company receives a possible order, its leasing subsidiary can quickly develop a lease-financing arrangement that facilitates the parent company's sale of its product.

An **independent finance company** acts as a financial intermediary by providing financing for transactions for manufacturers, vendors, or distributors. Your dentist, for example, when acquiring specialized equipment for his or her practice, may order the equipment through the manufacturer or distributor, who in turn may outsource the financing to a lessor such as an independent finance company.

Subsidiaries of domestic and foreign banks are examples of **traditional financial institutions** that provide leasing as another form of financing to their customers.

Advantages of Leasing

Although leasing does have disadvantages, the growth in its use suggests that it often has a genuine advantage over owning property. Some of the advantages are as follows.

100% Financing at Fixed Rates. Leases are often signed without requiring any money down from the lessee, helping to conserve scarce cash—an especially desirable feature for new and developing companies. In addition, lease payments often remain fixed (unchanging), which protects the lessee against inflation and increases in interest rates. The following comment about a conventional loan is typical: "Our local bank finally agreed to finance 80% of the purchase price but wouldn't go any higher, and they wanted a floating interest rate. We just couldn't afford the down payment and we needed to lock in a payment we knew we could live with."

Turning to the lessor's point of view, financial institutions and leasing companies find leasing profitable because it provides attractive interest margins.

Protection Against Obsolescence. Leasing equipment reduces the risk of obsolescence to the lessee, and in many cases passes the risk of residual value to the lessor. For example, a company that leases computers may have a lease agreement that permits it to turn in an old computer for a new model at any time, cancelling the old lease and writing a new one. The cost of the new lease is added to the balance due on the old lease, less the old computer's trade-in value. As one treasurer remarked, "Our instinct is to purchase." But when new computer innovations come along in a short time, "then leasing is just a heck of a lot more convenient than purchasing."

On the other hand, the lessor can benefit from the property reversion (that is, the return of the asset) at the end of the lease term. Residual values can produce very large profits. For example, **Citicorp** at one time assumed that the commercial aircraft it was leasing to the airline industry would have a residual value of 5% of their purchase price. As it turned out, however, the planes were worth 150% of their cost—a handsome price appreciation. Three years later these same planes slumped to 80% of their cost, but this was still a far greater residual value than the projected 5%.

Flexibility. Lease agreements may contain less restrictive provisions than other debt agreements. Innovative lessors can tailor a lease agreement to the lessee's specific needs. For instance, a ski lift operator using equipment for only six months of the year can arrange rental payments that fit well with the operation's revenue streams. In addition, because the lessor retains ownership and the leased property is the collateral, it is usually easier to arrange financing through a lease.

Less Costly Financing for Lessee, Tax Incentives for Lessor. Some companies find leasing cheaper than other forms of financing. For example, start-up companies in depressed industries or not-for-profit organizations may lease as a way of claiming tax benefits that might otherwise be lost. Investment tax credits and capital cost allowance deductions offer no benefit to companies that have little or no taxable income. Through leasing, these tax benefits are used by the leasing companies or financial institutions. They can then pass some of these tax benefits back to the asset's user through lower rental payments.

Off-Balance Sheet Financing. Certain leases do not add debt on a balance sheet or affect financial ratios, and may add to borrowing capacity.[3] **Off-balance sheet financing** has been critical to some companies. For example, airlines use lease arrangements extensively and this results in a great deal of off-balance sheet financing. Illustration 20-1 indicates that debt levels are understated by **WestJet Airlines Ltd.**, **Air Canada**, and **Canadian Pacific Railway Limited** (CP), a sample of Canadian companies in the transportation industry.

Underlying Concept

Some companies "double-dip" at the international level. The leasing rules of the lessor's and lessee's countries may differ, permitting both parties to own the asset. In such cases, both the lessor and lessee can receive the tax benefits related to amortization.

Illustration 20-1

Reported Debt and Unrecognized Operating Lease Obligations

	WestJet December 31, 2011 ($ thousands)	Air Canada December 31, 2011 ($ thousands)	CP December 31, 2011 ($ thousands)
Non-current liabilities, excluding deferred income taxes and deferred credits	$1,777,005	$10,486,000	$6,432,000
Shareholders' equity (deficit)	1,370,217	(4,085,000)	4,649,000
Unrecognized future minimum lease payments under existing operating leases (includes commitments for WestJet)	1,161,047	2,117,000	813,000

Conceptual Nature of a Lease

If an airline borrows $80 million on a 10-year note from the bank to purchase a Boeing 787 jet plane, it is clear that an asset and related liability should be reported on the company's balance sheet at that amount. If the airline purchases the 787 for $80 million directly from Boeing through an instalment purchase over 10 years, it is equally clear that an asset and related liability should be reported. (That is, the instalment purchase transaction should be "capitalized.") However, if the Boeing 787 is leased for 10 years through a non-cancellable lease transaction with payments of the same amount as the instalment purchase, there are differences of opinion about how this transaction should be reported. Three views on accounting for leases can be summarized as follows.

Do Not Capitalize Any Leased Assets—An Executory Contract Approach. Some argue that because the lessee does not own the property, it is not appropriate to capitalize the lease. Furthermore, a lease is an **executory contract** that requires continuing performance by both parties. Because other executory contracts (such as purchase commitments and employment contracts) are not currently capitalized, leases would not be capitalized either. The lessor would continue to recognize the leased item as an asset.

Capitalize Leases that Are Similar to Instalment Purchases—A Classification Approach. The **classification approach** says that transactions should be classified and accounted for according to their economic substance. Because instalment purchases are capitalized as property, plant, and equipment assets, leases that have similar characteristics to instalment purchases should be accounted for in the same way. In our earlier example, the airline is committed to the same payments over a 10-year period for either a lease or an instalment purchase; lessees simply make rental payments, whereas owners make mortgage payments. The financial statements should classify and report these transactions in the same way: recognizing the physical asset on the lessee's balance sheet where appropriate. Transactions not recognized as in-substance acquisitions of assets are classified as operating leases and accounted for differently;

Capitalize All Leases—A Contract-Based Approach. Under the contract-based approach, the leased asset that is acquired is not the physical property; rather, it is the **contractual right to use** the property that is conveyed under the lease agreement. The liability is the contractual obligation to make lease payments. Under this view, also called a property rights or **right-of-use approach**, it is justifiable to capitalize the fair value of the rights and obligations associated with a broad range of leases.[4] (The contract-based approach and right-of-use approach are explained in more detail in Appendix 20B.)

In short, the various viewpoints range from no capitalization to capitalization of all leases.

Current Standards

What do the current standards require? The standards in effect when this text went to print are consistent with the **classification approach** that capitalizes leases that are similar to an instalment purchase. These are classified as **capital** or **finance leases** and usually are recognized as items of property, plant, and equipment. The accounting treatment is based on the concept that **a lease that transfers substantially all of the benefits and risks of property ownership should be capitalized.**

By capitalizing the present value of the future rental payments, the **lessee** records an asset and a liability at an amount that is generally representative of the asset's fair value. The **lessor**, having transferred substantially all the benefits and risks of ownership, removes the asset from its statement of financial position (SFP), and replaces it with a receivable. The typical journal entries for the lessee and the lessor, assuming the leased equipment is capitalized, are shown at the top of Illustration 20-2. If the benefits and risks of ownership **are not transferred** from one party to the other, the lease is classified as an

operating lease. The accounting for an operating lease by the lessee and lessor is shown in the bottom of Illustration 20-2.

Illustration 20-2

Journal Entries for Finance and Operating Leases

	Lessee			Lessor		
Capital or Finance Lease	Equipment under Lease	xx		Lease Receivable	xx	
	Obligations under Lease		xx	Equipment		xx
	Depreciation Expense	x				
	Accumulated Depreciation —Leased Equipment		x			
	Obligations under Lease	x		Cash	x	
	Interest Expense	x		Interest Income		x
	Cash		x	Lease Receivable		x
Operating Lease	Rent Expense	x		Cash	x	
	Cash		x	Rent Revenue		x

When the asset is capitalized as an item of property, plant, and equipment, the lessee recognizes the depreciation. The lessor and lessee treat the lease rentals as the receipt and the payment of interest and principal. If the lease is not capitalized, no asset is recorded by the lessee and no asset is removed from the lessor's books. When a lease payment is made, the lessee records rent or lease expense and the lessor recognizes rental or lease income.

While the AcSB, FASB, and IASB standards were all consistent with the classification approach as this text went to print, these standards are expected to have a limited life going forward. Current thinking supports the **contract-based approach** and it is this concept that underlies the 2010 Exposure Draft issued by the IASB and FASB toward a new converged lease accounting standard.

The contract-based approach simply states that "lease contracts create assets and liabilities that should be recognized in the financial statements of lessees."[6] The most significant change that would result from the adoption of this approach would be the recognition on the statement of financial position of rights and obligations as assets and liabilities for what are now termed "operating" leases. These leases, as you can tell from Illustration 20-2, are now off-balance sheet items and are reported as an expense only as the lease payments are made. Under the contractual right-of-use approach, all leases covered by the expected standard are recognized as a type of intangible asset along with the contractual obligation (liability) to make lease payments in the future.

The next section of this chapter explains the basics of the classification approach that is currently in use. The basics of the contract-based approach in the 2010 Exposure Draft are set out in Appendix 20B and were expected to be updated as part of a new IFRS exposure draft in 2013.

CLASSIFICATION APPROACH— LESSEES

Classification Criteria

Objective 3

Identify and apply the criteria that are used to determine the type of lease for accounting purposes for a lessee under the classification approach.

Before discussing the accounting for the two classifications of leases required by current accounting standards, we begin by looking at how the classification decision is made by the lessee. From the lessee's standpoint, all leases are classified for accounting purposes as either operating leases or finance leases. As indicated previously, when the risks and benefits of ownership are transferred from the lessor to the lessee, the lease is accounted for as a capital lease (described as a finance lease under IFRS); otherwise, it is accounted for as an operating lease. The terms "capital lease" and "finance lease" are used interchangeably in this chapter. **What are the risks and benefits (or rewards) of ownership?** Benefits of ownership are the ability to use the asset to generate profits over its useful life, benefit from any

Underlying Concept

"According to the World Leasing Yearbook 2009, in 2007 the annual volume of leases amounted to U.S. $760 billion. However, the assets and liabilities arising from many of these contracts cannot be found" on entities' balance sheets.[5]

appreciation in the asset's value, and realize its residual value at the end of its economic life. The risks, on the other hand, are the exposure to uncertain returns, loss from use or idle capacity, and technological obsolescence.

Guidance is provided to help preparers determine the substance of the lease transaction under both ASPE and IAS 17 *Leases*, and the objective under both standards is the same. IAS 17 identifies numerous qualitative indicators to help identify whether a lease is a finance (capital) lease or not. Section 3065 of Part II of the *CICA Handbook*, on the other hand, provides fewer qualitative indicators, but includes a few quantitative indicators that end up being used extensively in making the classification decision. These quantitative factors are known as "bright lines" and they are key to those involved with the financial engineering of leases, done to obtain the accounting method preferred by the entity. The net effect is that entities applying IFRS make the classification decision based on principles, and those applying ASPE look to whether certain numerical thresholds have been met or missed.

IFRS Criteria

Under IFRS, any one or a combination of the following situations **normally indicates** that the risks and rewards of ownership are transferred to the lessee, and supports classification as a finance lease.

1. There is reasonable assurance that the lessee will obtain ownership of the leased property by the end of the lease term. If there is a bargain purchase option in the lease, it is assumed that the lessee will exercise it and obtain ownership of the asset. (Bargain purchase options will be discussed in the next section.)

2. The lease term is for the major part of the economic life of the asset, so that the lessee will receive substantially all of the economic benefits that are expected to be derived from using the leased property over its life.

3. The lease allows the lessor to recover substantially all of its investment in the leased property and to earn a return on the investment. Evidence of this is provided if the present value of the minimum lease payments is substantially all of the fair value of the leased asset.

4. The leased assets are so specialized that, without major modification, they are of use only to the lessee.

Other indicators that might suggest a transfer of the risks and benefits of ownership include situations where:

- the lessee absorbs the lessor's losses if the lessee cancels the lease,
- the lessee assumes the risk associated with the amount of the residual value of the asset at the end of the lease, or
- there is a bargain renewal option—when the lessee can renew the lease for an additional term at significantly less than the market rent.

The standard also states that these indicators are not always conclusive. The decision has to be made on the substance of each specific transaction. If the lessee determines that the risks and benefits of ownership have not been transferred to it, the lease is classified as an operating lease.

ASPE Criteria

ASPE assumes that the risks and benefits of ownership **are normally transferred to the lessee.** It requires that the lessee classify and account for the arrangement as a capital lease if **any one or more of** the following criteria is met:

1. There is reasonable assurance that the lessee will obtain ownership of the leased property, including through a bargain purchase option. This is identical to the first IFRS situation described above.

2. The lessee will benefit from most of the asset benefits due to the length of the lease term—identical to the second IFRS situation. **In addition, a numerical threshold is included:** this is usually assumed to occur if the lease term is 75% or more of the leased property's economic life.

3. The lessor recovers substantially all of its investment and earns a return on that investment as explained in the third IFRS criteria above. **In addition, a numerical threshold is included:** this is usually assumed if the present value of the minimum lease payments is equal to 90% or more of the fair value of the leased asset.

Under U.S. standards and ASPE, the numerical thresholds tend to be the key decision criteria, rather than using professional judgement as under IFRS.

IFRS and ASPE Requirements—A Closer Look

Aside from how the classification decision is made and the use of some different terminology, the remainder of lease accounting under both sets of standards is very similar.

Transfer of Ownership Test. The transfer of ownership criterion is not controversial and is easily applied in practice. The transfer may occur at the end of the lease term with no additional payment or through a bargain purchase option. A **bargain purchase option** is a provision that allows the lessee to purchase the leased asset for a price that is significantly lower than the asset's expected fair value when the lessee can exercise the option. At the beginning of the lease, the difference between the option price and the expected fair value in the future must be large enough to make it reasonably sure that the option will be exercised.

For example, assume that you were to lease a car for $599 per month for 40 months with an option to purchase it for $100 at the end of the 40-month period. If the car's estimated fair value is $3,000 at the end of the 40 months, the $100 option to purchase is clearly a bargain and, therefore, capitalization is required. It is assumed that an option that is a bargain will be acted on. In other situations, it may not be so clear whether the option price in the lease agreement is a bargain.

Economic Life Test. Under IFRS, the decision of whether the lease term is long enough to allow the lessee to derive the major part of the benefits offered by the asset requires judgement. Under ASPE, if the lease period is equal to or greater than 75% of the asset's economic life, it is assumed that most of the risks and rewards of ownership are going to accrue to the lessee.

The lease term is **generally considered the fixed, non-cancellable term of the lease.** However, this period can be extended if a bargain renewal option is provided in the lease agreement. A **bargain renewal option** is a provision that allows the lessee to renew the lease for a rental amount that is lower than the expected fair rental at the date when the option becomes exercisable. At the beginning of the lease, the difference between the renewal rental and the expected fair rental must be large enough to provide reasonable assurance that the option to renew will be exercised. With bargain renewal options, as with bargain purchase options, it is sometimes difficult to determine what a bargain is.

Estimating the economic life can also be a problem, especially if the leased item is a specialized asset or has been used for a long period of time. For example, determining the economic life of a nuclear core is extremely difficult because it is affected by much more than normal wear and tear.

Recovery of Investment by Lessor Test. The rationale for the recovery of investment by the lessor criterion is that if the present value of the payments is reasonably close to the asset's market price, the lessor is recovering its investment in the asset plus earning a return on the investment through the lease. The economic substance, therefore, is that the lessee is purchasing the asset. Applying this test requires an understanding of additional specific terms. For example, to calculate the present value of the minimum lease payments, three important factors are involved: (1) the minimum lease payments, (2) any executory costs, and (3) the discount rate.

Underlying Concept

In lease accounting, the importance of good definitions is clear. If the lease fits the definition of an asset in that it gives the lessee the economic benefits that flow from the possession or use of the leased property, then an asset should be recognized.

Finance

1. **Minimum Lease Payments:** Minimum lease payments from a lessee's perspective include the following:[7]

Minimum rental payments: The payments that the lessee is making or can be required to make to the lessor under the lease agreement, excluding contingent rent and executory costs (defined below).

Amounts guaranteed: Any amounts guaranteed by the lessee related to the residual value of the leased asset. The **residual value** is the asset's estimated fair value at the end of the lease term. The lessor often transfers the risk of loss in value to the lessee or to a third party by requiring a guarantee of the estimated residual value, either in whole or in part. The **guaranteed residual value** from the lessee's perspective is the maximum amount the lessor can require the lessee to pay at the end of the lease. The **unguaranteed residual value** is the portion of the residual value that is not guaranteed by the lessee or is guaranteed solely by a party that is related to the lessor. Often, no part of the residual is guaranteed.

Bargain purchase option: As explained above, this is an option that allows the lessee to acquire the leased asset at the end of the lease term for an amount considerably below the asset's value at that time. This may or may not be included in the lease conditions.

2. **Executory Costs:** Like most assets, leased property needs to be insured and maintained, and it may require the payment of property tax. These ownership-type expenses are called **executory costs.** If the lessor pays these costs, any portion of each lease payment that represents a recovery of executory costs from the lessee **is excluded** from the rental payments used in calculating the minimum lease payments. If the amount of the payment that represents executory costs cannot be determined from the lease contract, the lessee makes an estimate of the executory costs and excludes that amount. Many lease agreements, however, require the lessee to pay the executory costs directly. In these cases, the rental payments can be used without any adjustment in the minimum lease payments calculations.

3. **Discount Rate:** What discount rate should be used by the lessee in determining the present value of the minimum lease payments: the rate implicit in the lease, or the lessee's incremental borrowing rate? The **interest rate implicit in the lease** is the lessor's internal rate of return at the beginning of the lease that makes the present value of the minimum lease payments plus any unguaranteed residual values equal to the fair value of the leased asset.[8] The lessee's **incremental borrowing rate** is the interest rate that, at the beginning of the lease, the lessee would incur to borrow the funds needed to purchase the leased asset, assuming a similar term and using similar security for the borrowing.[9]

IFRS requires the interest rate implicit in the lease to be used whenever it is reasonably determinable; otherwise the incremental borrowing rate is used. ASPE specifies that the lower of the two rates is used.

There are two reasons for using these rates. First, the lessor's implicit rate is generally a more realistic rate to use in determining the amount, if any, to report as the asset and related liability for the lessee. Second, ASPE ensures that the lessee does not use an artificially high incremental borrowing rate **that would cause the present value of the minimum lease payments to be less than 90% of the property's fair value. This might make it possible to avoid capitalization of the asset and related liability!** Remember that the higher the discount rate that is used, the lower the discounted value. The lessee may argue that it cannot determine the implicit rate of the lessor and therefore the higher rate should be used. However, in many cases, the implicit rate that is used by the lessor is disclosed or can be estimated. Determining whether or not a reasonable estimate can be made requires judgement, particularly when using the incremental borrowing rate comes close to meeting the 90% test. **Because the leased property cannot be capitalized at more than its fair value,** the lessee is prevented from using an excessively low discount rate.

Specialized Nature of Leased Asset. When the leased assets are so specialized that they are useful only to the lessee except at great incremental cost, the substance of the transaction is one of financing the asset acquisition, with the risks and benefits associated with ownership of the asset transferred to the lessee.

Determination of Rental Payments

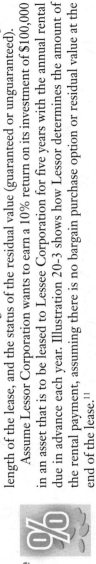

Objective 4

Calculate the lease payment that is required for a lessor to earn a specific return.

Finance

The lessor determines the rental amount to charge based on the rate of return—the implicit rate—that the lessor needs to receive in order to justify leasing the asset.[10] The key variables considered in deciding on the rate of return are the lessee's credit standing, the length of the lease, and the status of the residual value (guaranteed or unguaranteed).

Assume Lessor Corporation wants to earn a 10% return on its investment of $100,000 in an asset that is to be leased to Lessee Corporation for five years with the annual rental due in advance each year. Illustration 20-3 shows how Lessor determines the amount of the rental payment, assuming there is no bargain purchase option or residual value at the end of the lease.[11]

Illustration 20-3

Calculation of Lease Payments by Lessor

Investment to be recovered[a]	$100,000.00
Less: Present value of the amount to be recovered through a bargain purchase option or residual value at end of the lease term	–0–
Equals the present value of amount to be recovered through lease payments	$100,000.00
Five beginning-of-the-year lease payments to yield a 10% return: ($100,000 ÷ 4.16986[b])	$ 23,981.62

[a] If the lessor is not a manufacturer or dealer, then any initial direct costs of negotiating and arranging the lease are added to this amount.
[b] PV of an annuity due (Table A-5); $i = 10\%$, $n = 5$

If there is a bargain purchase option or a residual value, guaranteed or not, the lessor does not have to recover as much through the rental payments. In such cases, the present value of these other recoveries is deducted before determining the present value of the amount to be recovered through lease payments. This is illustrated later in the chapter in more detail.

What Do the Numbers Mean?

Lease this year's model for just $199 per month! Or 0% financing! Sometimes leasing just looks too good to be true...and sometimes it is. It pays to be familiar with what is involved in a typical leasing agreement such as you might encounter in a vehicle lease, and to do your homework before signing on the dotted line.

First, there is often an upfront payment required to cover freight costs and pre-delivery expenses, plus taxes on these. Add to this a requirement for an initial down payment plus the first month's rent in advance. Increasing this payment, of course, will lower your monthly rental. Do you have to pay a security deposit similar to one you would pay on an apartment you rent? Some leasing companies also charge an administration fee for acquiring the vehicle and processing the paperwork for you.

Check out all the conditions. How reasonable is the annual mileage allowance? How much do you have to pay per kilometre if you exceed the "free" amount? What happens at the end of the lease term? Do you have to ensure that the vehicle has a reasonable residual value at the end? What price will you have to pay to purchase the leased asset if that is an option?

Finally, what alternatives are there of acquiring the same asset? What are the cash flows associated with the financing of a direct purchase? Or borrowing the money elsewhere and paying cash for the car? The 0% financing might be at the expense of a sales price that is higher than you could otherwise negotiate. A $2,000 or more rebate today for a cash deal may make a difference to your decision. The bottom line: get familiar with the agreements, look at your options, evaluate the cash flows, and make your decision with full knowledge and understanding of what is involved.

We now turn to how **the lessee** accounts for agreements classified as capital or finance leases.

Accounting for a Finance Lease

Finance Lease Basics

Objective 5
Account for a lessee's basic capital (finance) lease.

Asset and Liability Recognition. In a capital or finance lease transaction, the lessee uses the lease **as a source of financing.** The lessor provides the leased asset to the lessee and finances the transaction by accepting installment payments. The lessee accounts for the transaction as if an asset is purchased and a long-term obligation is entered into. Over the life of the lease, the rental payments made by the lessee are a repayment of principal and interest on the outstanding balance.

The lessee recognizes the asset and liability at the lower of (1) **the present value of the minimum lease payments** as defined above and (2) the fair value of the leased asset at the lease's inception. The reason for this is that, like other assets, a leased asset cannot be recorded at more than its fair value.

Depreciable Amount, Period, and Method. Having capitalized the asset, its "cost" is allocated over its useful life.[12] You need to understand the terms of the lease and what is included in the capitalized value—the present value of the minimum lease payments—to determine the depreciable amount and its useful life.

For example, if it is a simple lease that transfers title to the asset at the end of the lease term for no additional payments, then the full capitalized value less any estimated residual value at the end of its useful life to the lessee is depreciated over the full useful life to the entity. If the lease contains a bargain purchase option, the assumption is that the lessee will acquire legal title to the asset and it will continue to use the asset. Once again, the entity allocates the full capitalized cost over the full useful life of the asset. It is a matter of thinking about it in terms of what physically happens to the asset.

Now consider a situation in which the lessee is obligated to make rental payments over the lease term and then return the asset to the lessor in whatever condition it is in at that time. All that is capitalized are the lease payments because this is all the lessee is responsible for. In this case, the full capitalized value is amortized over the time to the end of the lease. This changes if the lessee also takes on an obligation to guarantee the residual value of the asset at the end of the lease. Now the capitalized value includes the present value of the guaranteed residual. (You may want to review the definition of **minimum lease payments** to see that only the residual value guaranteed by the lessee is included!) Now, what will the entity depreciate? Because the leased asset (at the guaranteed residual value) is expected to be returned to the lessor, the lessee depreciates only the capitalized amount less the guaranteed residual amount over the period to the end of the lease.

Illustration 20-4 summarizes the depreciable amounts and depreciation period, and you are encouraged to understand the reason for each.

Illustration 20-4
Depreciable Amount and Period

	Included in Capitalized Asset Cost	Depreciable Amount	Depreciation Period
Asset reverts to lessor at end of lease term:			
– Lessee does not guarantee any residual value	Minimum rental payments	Full capitalized amount	Lease term

(continued)

Illustration 20-4

Depreciable Amount and Period (continued)

	Included in Capitalized Asset Cost	Depreciable Amount	Depreciation Period
– Lessee guarantees a residual value	Minimum rental payments plus residual value guarantee	Full capitalized amount minus undiscounted guaranteed residual value	Lease term
Lessee retains asset at end of lease term: – Title is transferred, no purchase option	Minimum rental payments	Full capitalized amount minus estimated residual value, if any, at end of useful life	Useful life of asset
– Title is transferred when bargain purchase option is exercised	Minimum rental payments plus bargain purchase option	Full capitalized amount minus estimated residual value, if any, at end of useful life	Useful life of asset

The lessee amortizes the leased asset by applying conventional depreciation methods that it uses for assets it owns.

Effective Interest Method. Over the term of the lease, the effective interest method is used to allocate each lease payment between principal and interest. In this way, the periodic interest expense is equal to a constant percentage of the obligation's outstanding balance. The discount rate used to determine how much of each payment represents interest is the same one the lessee used to calculate the present value of the minimum lease payments.

Finance Lease Method Illustration 1

We use the example of a lease agreement between Lessor Corporation and Lessee Corporation to illustrate the accounting for a finance lease. The contract calls for Lessor Corporation to lease equipment to Lessee Corporation beginning January 1, 2014. The lease agreement's provisions and other pertinent data are given in Illustration 20-5.

Illustration 20-5

Lease Agreement Terms and Conditions

1. The lease term is five years, the lease agreement is non-cancellable, and it requires equal rental payments of $25,981.62 at the beginning of each year (annuity due basis), beginning January 1, 2014. The lease contains no renewal options, and the equipment reverts to Lessor Corporation at the end of the lease.

2. The equipment has a fair value of $100,000 on January 1, 2014, an estimated economic life of five years, and no residual value. Lessee Corporation uses straight-line depreciation for similar equipment that it owns.

3. Lessee Corporation pays all executory costs directly to third parties except for maintenance fees of $2,000 per year, which are included in the annual payments to the lessor.

4. Lessee Corporation's incremental borrowing rate is 11% per year. Lessor Corporation set the annual rental to earn a rate of return on its investment of 10% per year; this fact is known to Lessee Corporation.

Finance

The lease meets the criteria for classification as a finance (capital) lease under both IFRS and ASPE for two reasons: (1) Lessor Corporation uses up all the benefits the leased asset has to offer over the five-year lease term (the 75% threshold under ASPE is therefore well met); and (2) the present value of the minimum lease payments is $100,000 (calculated below) and this is the same as the asset's fair value. It also exceeds the 90% of fair value threshold set out in ASPE. Only one of the capitalization criteria has to be met to justify classification as a capital or finance lease.

The **minimum lease payments** are $119,908.10 ($23,981.62 × 5), and the present value of the minimum lease payments is $100,000, as calculated in Illustration 20-6.[13] This is the amount that is capitalized as the leased asset and recognized as the lease obligation.

Illustration 20-6

Present Value of Minimum

PV of minimum
lease payments

= ($25,981.62 − $2,000) × present value of an annuity due of $1 for
5 periods at 10% (Table A-5)
= $23,981.62 × 4.16986
= $100,000

The lessor's implicit rate of interest rate of 10% is used in this case instead of the lessee's incremental borrowing rate of 11% either because (1) Lessee Corp. is a public company and this is the IFRS preferred rate, or (2) Lessee Corp. applies ASPE and this rate is lower than its incremental borrowing rate.[14]

The entry to record the lease on Lessee Corporation's books on January 1, 2014, is:

Equipment under Lease	100,000	
Obligations under Lease		100,000

The journal entry to record the first lease payment on January 1, 2014, is:

Maintenance and Repairs Expense (or Prepaid Expenses)	2,000.00	
Obligations under Lease	23,981.62	
Cash		25,981.62

Each lease payment of $25,981.62 consists of three elements: (1) a reduction in the principal of the lease obligation, (2) a financing cost (interest expense), and (3) executory costs (maintenance). The total financing cost of $19,908.10 over the lease's term is the difference between the present value of the minimum lease payments ($100,000) and the actual cash payments excluding the executory costs ($119,908.10). These amounts, along with the annual interest expense, are shown in the lease amortization schedule in Illustration 20-7.[15]

A = L + SE
+100,000 +100,000

Cash flows: No effect

A = L + SE
−25,981.62 −23,981.62 −2,000.00

Cash flows: ↓ 25,981.62 outflow

Illustration 20-7

Lease Amortization Schedule for Lessee—Annuity Due Basis

	A	B	C	D	E
1			**Lessee Corporation**		
			Lease Amortization Schedule		
			(Annuity due basis)		
2	Date	Annual Lease Payment	Interest (10%) on Unpaid Obligation	Reduction of Lease Obligation	Balance of Obligation
		(a)	(b)	(c)	(d)
3	1/1/14				$100,000.00
4	1/1/14	$ 23,981.62	$ −0−	$ 23,981.62	76,018.38
5	1/1/15	23,981.62	7,601.84	16,379.78	59,638.60
6	1/1/16	23,981.62	5,963.86	18,017.76	41,620.84
7	1/1/17	23,981.62	4,162.08	19,819.54	21,801.30
8	1/1/18	23,981.62	2,180.32*	21,801.30	−0−
9		$119,908.10	$19,908.10	$100,000.00	
10					

(a) Lease payment as required by lease, excluding executory costs.
(b) 10% of the preceding balance of (d) except for 1/1/14, since this is an annuity due, no time has elapsed at the date of the first payment and no interest has accrued.
(c) (a) minus (b).
(d) Preceding balance minus (c).
*Rounded by 19 cents.

Accrued interest is recorded at Lessee Corporation's fiscal year end, December 31, 2014, as follows:

Interest Expense	7,601.84	
Interest Payable		7,601.84

A	=	L	+	SE
		+7,601.84		−7,601.84

Cash flows: No effect

Using Lessee Corporation's normal depreciation policy, the following entry is made on December 31, 2014, to record the current year's depreciation of the leased equipment:

Depreciation Expense	20,000	
Accumulated Depreciation—Leased Equipment		20,000
($100,000 ÷ 5 years)		

A	=	L	+	SE
−20,000				−20,000

Cash flows: No effect

At December 31, 2014, the assets recorded under finance leases are identified separately on the lessee's SFP, or in a note cross-referenced to the SFP. Similarly, the related obligations are identified separately. The principal portion that is due within one year is classified with current liabilities and the remainder is reported with non-current liabilities. For example, the current portion of the December 31, 2014 total obligation of $76,018.38 **is the principal of the obligation that will be paid off within the next 12 months.** Therefore, the current portion is $16,379.78, as indicated on the amortization schedule. Illustration 20-8 shows the liability section of the December 31, 2014 SFP for the lease obligation and related accrued interest.

Current liabilities

Interest payable	$ 7,601.84
Obligations under lease, current portion	16,379.78

Non-current liabilities

Obligations under lease	$59,638.60

Illustration 20-8

Reporting Current and Non-Current Lease Liabilities

The journal entry to record the lease payment on January 1, 2015, is as follows:

Maintenance and Repairs Expense (or Prepaid Expenses)	2,000.00	
Interest Payable[a]	7,601.84	
Obligations under Lease	16,379.78	
Cash		25,981.62

[a] This entry assumes that the company does not prepare reversing entries. If reversing entries are used, Interest Expense is debited for this amount.

A	=	L	+	SE
−25,981.62		−23,981.62		−2,000.00

Cash flows: ↓ 25,981.62 outflow

Entries through to 2018 follow the same pattern as above. Other executory costs (insurance and maintenance) that are assumed by Lessee Corporation are recorded in the same way as the company records operating costs incurred on assets that it owns. **At the end of the lease,** the amount capitalized as leased equipment is fully depreciated and the lease obligation is fully discharged. If the equipment is not purchased, the lessee returns it to the lessor and removes the equipment and related accumulated depreciation accounts from the books. If instead the lessee purchases the equipment at the end of the lease for $5,000, and expects to use it for another two years, the following entry is made:

Equipment ($100,000 + $5,000)	105,000	
Accumulated Depreciation—Leased Equipment	100,000	
Equipment under Lease		100,000
Accumulated Depreciation—Equipment		100,000
Cash		5,000

Cash flows: ↓ 5,000 outflow

A	=	L	+	SE
0		0		0

Accounting for Residual Values and Bargain Purchase Options in a Finance Lease

Finance

Finance Lease Method Illustration 2

The Lessor/Lessee Corporation example above illustrates the lessee's accounting for a basic lease. Let's now see what the effects are of including residual value requirements in the lease agreement. If title does not pass to the lessee and there is no bargain purchase option, the lessee returns the asset to the lessor at the end of the lease. There is often a significant residual value at the end of the lease term, especially when the leased asset's economic life is longer than the lease.[16]

Guaranteed versus Unguaranteed. The residual value may be unguaranteed or guaranteed by the lessee. If the lessee agrees to pay for any loss in value below a stated amount at the end of the lease, the lessee agrees to pay for any loss in value below a stated amount at the end of the lease, the stated amount is the guaranteed residual value.

The guaranteed residual value is used in lease arrangements for good reason: it protects the lessor against any loss in estimated residual value, and so ensures that the lessor will get its desired rate of return on its investment. For **finance leases**, residual values guaranteed by the lessee affect the amounts that are recognized as the leased asset and lease obligation.

Effect on Lease Payments. A guaranteed residual value—by definition—is more likely to be realized than an unguaranteed residual value. As the risk of non-recovery is reduced, the lessor may reduce the required rate of return, and therefore the rental payments required.

Assume the same data as in the Lessee Corporation/Lessor Corporation example above in Illustration 20-5: Lessor wants to recover its net investment in the leased asset of $100,000 and earn a 10% return.[17] The asset reverts to Lessor at the end of the five-year lease term. Now assume that the asset is expected to have a residual value of $5,000 at the end of the lease. **Whether the residual value is guaranteed or not**, Lessor Corporation calculates the lease payments using the approach set out in Illustration 20-3. Illustration 20-9 shows the calculations when the residual value is included.

LESSOR'S CALCULATION OF LEASE PAYMENTS (10% ROI)
Guaranteed or Unguaranteed Residual Value

(Annuity due basis)

Investment in leased equipment to be recovered	$100,000.00
Less amount to be recovered through residual value, end of year 5:	
Present value of residual value ($5,000 × 0.62092, Table A-2)	3,104.60
Amount to be recovered by lessor through rental payments	$ 96,895.40
Five periodic lease payments ($96,895.40 ÷ 4.16986, Table A-5)	$ 23,237.09

Contrast this lease payment with the lease payment of $23,981.62 that was calculated in Illustration 20-3 when there was no residual value. The payments are lower because a portion of the lessor's net investment of $100,000 is recovered through the residual value.

The residual value amount is discounted in the calculation because it will not be received for five years.

Lessee Accounting with a Residual Value. If the residual value is guaranteed by the lessee, there are both economic and accounting consequences. The accounting difference is that the minimum lease payments that are capitalized as the leased asset are defined to **include the guaranteed** residual value. Unguaranteed residual values are excluded from "minimum lease payments." If the residual value is not guaranteed by the lessee, the lessee has no responsibility or obligation for the asset's condition at the end of the lease. The unguaranteed residual value, therefore, is not included in the calculation of the lease obligation either.

A guaranteed residual is similar to an additional lease payment that will be paid in property or cash, or both, at the end of the lease. Using the rental payments as calculated by the lessor in Illustration 20-9, the lessee's **minimum lease payments** are $121,185.45 ([$23,237.09 × 5] + $5,000). Illustration 20-10 shows the calculation of the present value of the minimum lease payments. This amount is capitalized as the leased asset and recognized as the lease liability.

Finance

LESSEE'S CAPITALIZED AMOUNT (10% RATE)
(Annuity due basis; guaranteed residual value)

Present value of five annual rental payments of $23,237.09, i = 10%: ($23,237.09 × 4.16986, Table A-5)	$ 96,895.40
Add: present value of guaranteed residual value of $5,000 due at end of five-year lease term: ($5,000 × 0.62092, Table A-2)	3,104.60
Lessee's capitalized amount	$100,000.00

A		B	C	D	E
	Lessee Corporation				
	Lease Amortization Schedule				
	(Annuity due basis, guaranteed residual value)				
			Interest (10%) on	Reduction of	
Date		Lease Payment	Unpaid Obligation	Lease Obligation	Lease Obligation
		(a)	(b)	(c)	(d)
1/1/14					$100,000.00
1/1/14		$ 23,237.09	$ -0-	$ 23,237.09	76,762.91
1/1/15		23,237.09	7,676.29	15,560.80	61,202.11
1/1/16		23,237.09	6,120.21	17,116.88	44,085.23
1/1/17		23,237.09	4,408.52	18,828.57	25,256.66
1/1/18		23,237.09	2,525.67	20,711.42	4,545.24
12/31/18		5,000.00*	454.76**	4,545.24	-0-
		$121,185.45	$21,185.45	$100,000.00	

(a) Annual lease payment as required by lease, excluding executory costs.
(b) Preceding balance of (d) × 10%, except 1/1/14.
(c) (a) minus (b).
(d) Preceding balance minus (c).
*Represents the guaranteed residual value.
**Rounded by 24 cents.

As Illustration 20-11 shows, Lessee Corporation's schedule of interest expense and amortization of the $100,000 lease obligation results in a $5,000 guaranteed residual value payment at the end of five years, on December 31, 2018.

The journal entries in the first column of Illustration 20-16 are based on a **guaranteed residual value**. The format of these entries is the same as illustrated earlier, but the amounts are different because of the capitalized residual value. As you might expect, the guaranteed residual value is subtracted from the cost of the leased asset in determining the depreciable amount. Assuming the straight-line method is used, the depreciation expense each year is $19,000 ([$100,000 − $5,000] ÷ 5). Note that the **undiscounted residual value is used** in this calculation, consistent with Chapter 11.

Illustration 20-12 shows how the leased asset and obligation are reported on the December 31, 2018 SFP, just before the lessee transfers the asset back to the lessor.

Illustration 20-12

Account Balances on Lessee's Books at End of Lease—Guaranteed Residual Value

Property, plant, and equipment		Current liabilities	
Equipment under lease	$100,000.00	Interest payable	$ 454.76
Less: Accumulated depreciation—leased equipment	95,000.00	Obligations under lease	4,545.24
	$ 5,000.00		$5,000.00

If the equipment's fair value is less than $5,000 at the end of the lease, Lessee Corporation records a loss. For example, assume that Lessee Corporation depreciated the leased asset down to its residual value of $5,000 but the asset's fair value at December 31, 2018, is only $3,000. In this case, Lessee Corporation records the following entry, assuming cash is paid to make up the residual value deficiency:

Loss on Lease	2,000.00	
Interest Payable	454.76	
Obligations under Lease	4,545.24	
Accumulated Depreciation—Leased Equipment	95,000.00	
Equipment under Lease		100,000.00
Cash		2,000.00

Finance

A = L + SE
−7,000 = −5,000 + −2,000

Cash flows: ↓ 2,000 outflow

If the fair value is more than $5,000, a gain may or may not be recognized. Gains on guaranteed residual values are shared between the lessor and lessee in whatever ratio the parties initially agreed to.

Lessee Accounting with an Unguaranteed Residual Value. From the lessee's viewpoint, an unguaranteed residual value has the same effect as no residual value on its calculation of the minimum lease payments, the leased asset, and lease obligation. Assume the same facts as those above except that the $5,000 residual value is **unguaranteed**. The annual lease payment is the same ($23,237.09) because, whether the residual is guaranteed or unguaranteed, Lessor Corporation's amount to be recovered through lease rentals is the same: $96,895.40. Lessee Corporation's minimum lease payments are $116,185.45 ($23,237.09 × 5). Illustration 20-13 calculates the capitalized amount for the lessee.

Illustration 20-13

Calculation of Lessee's Capitalized Amount—Unguaranteed Residual Value

LESSEE'S CAPITALIZED AMOUNT (10% RATE)		
(Annuity due basis, unguaranteed residual value)		
Present value of five annual rental payments of $23,237.09 i = 10%, $23,237.09 × 4.16986 (Table A-5)		$96,895.40
Unguaranteed residual value is not included in minimum lease payments		–0–
Lessee's capitalized amount		$96,895.40

With an unguaranteed residual, Lessee Corporation's amortization table for the $96,895.40 obligation is provided in Illustration 20-14.

	A	B	C	D	E
1			**Lessee Corporation** **Lease Amortization Schedule (10%)** **(Annuity due basis, unguaranteed residual value)**		
2	**Date**	**Lease Payment**	**Interest (10%) on Unpaid Obligation**	**Reduction of Lease Obligation**	**Lease Obligation**
3		(a)	(b)	(c)	(d)
4	1/1/14				$96,895.40
5	1/1/14	$ 23,237.09	$ –0–	$23,237.09	73,658.31
6	1/1/15	23,237.09	7,365.83	15,871.26	57,787.05
7	1/1/16	23,237.09	5,778.71	17,458.38	40,328.67
8	1/1/17	23,237.09	4,032.87	19,204.22	21,124.45
9	1/1/18	23,237.09	2,112.64*	21,124.45	–0–
10		$116,185.45	$19,290.05	$96,895.40	
12	(a) Annual lease payment as required by lease, excluding executory costs. (b) Preceding balance of (d) × 10%, except Jan. 1, 2014. (c) (a) minus (b). (d) Preceding balance minus (c). *Rounded by 19 cents.				

With no guarantee of the residual value, the journal entries needed to record the lease agreement and subsequent depreciation, interest, property tax, and payments are provided in the right-hand column of Illustration 20-16. The format of these entries is the same as illustrated earlier. Note that the leased asset is recorded at $96,895.40 and is depreciated over five years. Using straight-line depreciation, the depreciation expense each year is $19,379.08 ($96,895.40 ÷ 5). Illustration 20-15 shows how the asset and obligation are reported on the December 31, 2018 SFP, just before the lessee transfers the asset back to the lessor.

Property, plant, and equipment		**Current liabilities**	
Equipment under lease	$96,895	Obligations under lease	$–0–
Less: Accumulated depreciation —leased equipment	96,895		
	$ –0–		

Whether the asset's fair value at the end of the lease is $3,000 or $6,000, the only entry required is one to remove the asset and its accumulated depreciation from the books. There is no gain or loss to report.

Lessee Entries Involving Residual Values.

Lessee Corporation's entries for both a guaranteed and an unguaranteed residual value are shown side by side in Illustration 20-16.

Guaranteed Residual Value			**Unguaranteed Residual Value**		
Capitalization of Lease (January 1, 2014):					
Equipment under Lease	100,000.00		Equipment under Lease	96,895.40	
Obligations under Lease		100,000.00	Obligations under Lease		96,895.40
First Payment (January 1, 2014):					
Maintenance and Repairs Expense	2,000.00		Maintenance and Repairs Expense	2,000.00	
Obligations under Lease	23,237.09		Obligations under Lease	23,237.09	
Cash		25,237.09	Cash		25,237.09

(continued)

Guaranteed Residual Value			Unguaranteed Residual Value		

Adjusting Entry for Accrued Interest (December 31, 2014):

	Guaranteed Residual Value		Unguaranteed Residual Value	
Interest Expense	7,676.29		Interest Expense	7,365.83
Interest Payable		7,676.29	Interest Payable	7,365.83

Entry to Record Depreciation (December 31, 2014):

Depreciation Expense	19,000.00		Depreciation Expense	19,379.08
Accumulated Depreciation—			Accumulated Depreciation—	
Leased Equipment		19,000.00	Leased Equipment	19,379.08
([$100,000 − $5,000] ÷ 5 years)			($96,895.40 ÷ 5 years)	

Second Payment (January 1, 2015):

Maintenance and Repairs Expense	2,000.00		Maintenance and Repairs Expense	2,000.00
Obligations under Lease	15,560.80		Obligations under Lease	15,871.26
Interest Payable	7,676.29		Interest Payable	7,365.83
Cash		25,237.09	Cash	25,237.09

Illustration 20-16

Comparative Entries for Guaranteed and Unguaranteed Residual Values, Lessee Corporation *(continued)*

Lessee Accounting with a Bargain Purchase Option.

Based on the examples above, you may be able to deduce how the lessee would account for a lease when the terms include a bargain purchase option. The lessor gets a return on its investment in the leased asset from the option amount it will receive at the end of the lease (similar to the residual value calculations) and from the lease payments. Therefore the option amount is taken into consideration in determining the amount of the lease payments.

The lessee's accounting **assumes that the option will be exercised** and that the title to the leased property will be transferred to the lessee. Therefore, the bargain option price is included in the minimum lease payments and its present value is included as part of the leased asset and lease obligation.

There is **no difference** between the lessee's calculations and the amortization schedule for the lease obligation for a $5,000 **bargain purchase option** and those shown previously for the $5,000 **guaranteed residual value.** The only accounting difference is the calculation of the **annual depreciation of the asset.** In the case of a guaranteed residual value, the lessee depreciates the asset over the lease term because the asset will be returned to the lessor. In the case of a bargain purchase option, the lessee uses the asset's economic life and its estimated remaining value at the end of that time because it is assumed that the lessee will acquire title to the asset by exercising the option, and will then continue to use it.

Accounting for an Operating Lease

Objective 7

Account for an operating lease by a lessee and compare the operating and capitalization methods of accounting for leases.

In a lease agreement where the risks and benefits of ownership of the leased asset are not considered to be transferred to the lessee, a non-capitalization method is appropriate. Under this type of lease, **neither the leased asset nor the obligation to make lease payments is recognized in the accounts.** It is treated as an executory contract, and the lease payments are treated as rent expense.[18]

Refer back to the Lessor Corporation and Lessee Corporation example in Illustration 20-5 and assume now that the lease described there does not qualify as a finance or capital lease and, by default, is an operating lease. The charge to the income statement for rent expense each year is $25,981.62, the amount of the rental payment. The journal entry to record the payment each January 1 is as follows:

Prepaid Rent	25,981.62	
Cash		25,981.62

A	=	L	+	SE
0		0		0

Cash flows: ↓ 25,981.62 outflow

Assuming that adjusting entries are prepared only annually, the following entry is made at each December 31 fiscal year end:

Rent Expense	25,981.62	
Prepaid Rent		25,981.62

$$A = L + SE$$
$$-25,981.62 \quad -25,981.62$$

Cash flows: No effect

Both **ASPE** and **IFRS** agree that lease rentals are recognized on a straight-line basis over the term of the lease unless another systematic basis better represents the pattern of the benefits received. Complexities can arise, however, such as when lease inducements are offered. Assume that to motivate a lessee to sign a new five-year lease for office space at $3,000 each month, a lessor agrees to a three-month rent-free period at the beginning of the lease and a two-month rent-free period at the end. How much rent expense should be recognized in each accounting period?

The straight-line method is applied to the lease inducement example in the following way:

Lease term: 5 years × 12 months = 60 months
Total rent: 60 − 3 − 2 = 55 months × $3,000 = $165,000
Rent expense to be recognized each month: $165,000 ÷ 60 months = $2,750

That is, the total rent is recognized evenly over the lease term.

Finance and Operating Leases Compared

As indicated above, if the lease in Illustration 20-5 had been accounted for as an operating lease, the first-year charge to operations would have been $25,981.62, the amount of the rental payment. As a finance lease, however, the first-year charge is $29,601.84: straight-line depreciation of $20,000, interest expense of $7,601.84, and executory expenses of $2,000. Illustration 20-17 shows that, while the total charges to operations are the same over the lease term whether the lease is accounted for as a finance lease or as an operating lease, the charges are higher in the earlier years and lower in the later years under the finance lease treatment. The higher expense in the early years, along with the recognition of the lease obligation as a liability, are two reasons that lessees are reluctant to classify leases as finance leases. Lessees, especially when real estate leases are involved, claim that it is no more costly to operate the leased asset in the early years than in the later years; thus, they prefer an even charge like the operating method offers.

Illustration 20-17

Comparison of Charges to Operations—Finance versus Operating Leases

Lessee Corporation
Schedule of Charges to Operations
Finance Lease versus Operating Lease

	Finance Lease			Operating Lease		
Year	Depreciation	Executory Costs	Interest	Total Expense	Expense	Difference
2014	$ 20,000	$ 2,000	$ 7,601.84	$ 29,601.84	$ 25,981.62	$3,620.22
2015	20,000	2,000	5,963.86	27,963.86	25,981.62	1,982.24
2016	20,000	2,000	4,162.08	26,162.08	25,981.62	180.46
2017	20,000	2,000	2,180.32	24,180.32	25,981.62	(1,801.30)
2018	20,000	2,000	–0–	22,000.00	25,981.62	(3,981.62)
	$100,000	$10,000	$19,908.10	$129,908.10	$129,908.10	$ –0–

If an accelerated depreciation method is used, the difference between the amounts that are charged to operations under the two methods is even larger in the earlier and later years.

The most important and significant difference between the two approaches, however, is the effect on the statement of financial position. The finance lease approach initially reports an asset and related liability of $100,000 on the SFP, **whereas no such asset or liability is reported under the operating lease method.** Refer back to Illustration 20-1 to understand the significance of the amounts that are left off the statement of financial position for WestJet, Air Canada, and Canadian Pacific Railway. It is not surprising that the business community resists capitalizing leases, as the resulting **higher debt to equity ratio, reduced total asset turnover, and reduced rate of return on total assets** are seen as having a detrimental effect on the company.

And resist this they have! The intention of the Canadian standard was to have the accounting for leases based on whether or not the risks and benefits of ownership were transferred, similar to how the international standard works. However, because the standard specifies 75% of the asset's useful life and 90% of its fair value, management often interprets these numbers as "rates to beat." That is, leases are specifically engineered to ensure that ownership is not transferred and to have them come in just under the 75% and 90% hurdles so that the capitalization criteria are not met.

The experience with how this standard has been applied remains one of the key reasons why Canadian and international standard setters shy away from identifying specific numerical criteria in standards. They prefer to rely on principles-based, rather than rules-based, guidance.

Whether this resistance is reasonable is a matter of opinion. From a cash flow point of view—and excluding any cash flow effects that are associated with income tax differences—a company is in the same position whether the lease is accounted for as an operating or a finance lease. When arguing against capitalization, managers often state that capitalization can:

- more easily lead to violation of loan covenants;

- affect the amount of compensation that is received (for example, a stock compensation plan tied to earnings); and

- lower rates of return and increase debt to equity relationships, thus making the company less attractive to present and potential investors.[19]

Presentation and Disclosure

Current versus Non-Current Classification

The classification of the lessee's lease obligation was presented earlier for an **annuity due** situation. As indicated in Illustration 20-8, the lessee's current portion of the lease obligation is the reduction in its principal balance within 12 months from the date of the SFP **plus** interest accrued to the SFP date. Coincidentally, the total of these two amounts in the example is the same as the rental payment of $23,981.62 that will be made one day later on January 1 of the next year. In this example, the SFP date is December 31 and the due date of the lease payment is January 1, so the total of the principal reduction on January 1 and the interest accrued to December 31 is the same as the rental payment ($23,981.62). **This will happen only when the payment is due the day following the SFP date.** Understandably, this is not a common situation.

The following questions might now be asked. What happens if the lease payments fall as an **ordinary annuity** rather than an annuity due? What if the lease payment dates do not coincide with the company's fiscal year? To illustrate, assume that the lease in our original example from Illustration 20-5 was signed and effective on September 1, 2014, with the first lease payment to be made on September 1, 2015—an ordinary annuity situation. Assume also that we continue to use the other facts of the Lessee Corporation/Lessor Corporation example, excluding the executory costs. Because the rents are paid at the end of the lease periods instead of at the beginning, the five rents are set at $26,379.73 to earn the lessor an interest rate of 10%.[20] With both companies having December 31 year ends,

Illustration 20-18 provides the appropriate lease amortization schedule for this lease, based on the September 1 lease anniversary date each year.

Illustration 20-18

Lease Amortization Schedule—Ordinary Annuity Basis, Mid-Year Lease Date

	A	B	C	D	E
1			Lessee Corporation		
			Lease Amortization Schedule (10%) (Ordinary annuity basis)		
2	Date	Annual Lease Payment	Interest (10%)	Reduction of Principal	Balance of Lease Obligation
3	1/9/14				$100,000.00
4	1/9/15	$ 26,379.73	$10,000.00	$ 16,379.73	83,620.27
5	1/9/16	26,379.73	8,362.03	18,017.70	65,602.57
6	1/9/17	26,379.73	6,560.26	19,819.47	45,783.10
7	1/9/18	26,379.73	4,578.31	21,801.42	23,981.68
8	1/9/19	26,379.73	2,398.05*	23,981.68	–0–
9		$131,898.65	$31,898.65	$100,000.00	
11	*Rounded by 12 cents.				

At December 31, 2014, the lease obligation is still $100,000. How much should be reported in current liabilities on the December 31, 2014 SFP and how much in long-term liabilities? The answer here is the same as earlier: **the current portion is the principal that will be repaid within 12 months from the SFP date** (that is, $16,379.73). **In addition, any interest that has accrued up to the SFP date** (that is, 10% of $100,000 × 4/12 = $3,333) is reported in current liabilities. The long-term portion of the obligation is the principal that will **not** be repaid within 12 months from the SFP date, or $83,620.27. It helps if you can first correctly describe in words what makes up the current portion, then determine the numbers that correspond.

On December 31, 2015, the long-term portion of the lease is $65,602.57. The principal due within 12 months from December 31, 2015, or $18,017.70, is included as a current liability along with interest accrued to December 31, 2015, of $2,787 (10% of $83,620.27 × 4/12).

Disclosure

Capital/Finance Leases. Because a capital or finance lease recognizes the leased capital asset and a long-term liability, most of the required disclosures are identified in or are similar to those in the standards that cover property, plant, and equipment; intangible assets; impairment; financial instruments; and/or long-term liabilities. IFRS requires additional disclosures related to:

1. The net carrying amount of each class of leased asset

2. A reconciliation of the future minimum lease payments to their present value in total, and for the next year, years two to five, and beyond five years from the SFP date

3. The entity's material lease arrangements, especially concerning contingent rents, sublease payments, and restrictions imposed by lease agreements

Operating Leases. Both ASPE and IFRS require disclosure of the minimum lease payments for their operating leases extending into the future. Private enterprises report the total at the SFP date and those payable in each of the next five years. The IFRS requirement is similar, but extends the disclosures to include a description of significant lease arrangements and information about subleases and contingent rents.

Illustration of Lease Disclosures by a Lessee. The excerpts from the financial statements of Canadian Pacific Railway Limited for the year ended December 31, 2011, in

Real World Emphasis

Illustration 20-19

Illustration 20-19 show how this lessee company met the disclosure requirements for its leases under U.S. GAAP, similar to the ASPE requirements. The company reports in millions of Canadian dollars.

Capital Lease Disclosures by a Lease—Canadian Pacific Railway Limited

15 Properties

(in millions of Canadian dollars)	Average annual depreciation rate	2011			2010		
		Cost	Accumulated depreciation	Net book value	Cost Restated (note 2)	Accumulated depreciation	Net book value
Track and roadway	2.7%	$12,778	$3,552	$ 9,226	$11,980	$3,305	$ 8,675
Buildings	3.0%	453	225	198	440	266	174
Rolling stock	2.7%	3,390	1,362	2,028	3,245	1,319	1,926
Information systems(1)	9.5%	665	338	327	600	303	297
Other	4.8%	1,436	463	973	1,355	430	925
Total net properties		$18,722	$5,970	$12,752	$17,620	$5,623	$11,997

(2010 – $54 million; 2009 – $405 million).

(1) Net additions during 2011 were $91 million (2010 – $54 million; 2009 – $405 million).

CAPITAL LEASES INCLUDED IN PROPERTIES

(in millions of Canadian dollars)	2011			2010		
	Cost	Accumulated depreciation	Net book value	Cost	Accumulated depreciation	Net book value
Buildings	$ 1	$ —	$ 1	$ 1	$ —	$ 1
Rolling stock	515	165	350	517	152	365
Other	2	2	—	2	1	1
Total assets held under capital lease	$518	$167	$351	$520	$153	$367

During 2011, properties were acquired under the Company's capital program at an aggregate cost of $1,153 million (2010 – $743 million; 2009 – $703 million), none of which were acquired by means of capital leases (2010 – $1 million; 2009 – $1 million). Cash payments related to capital purchases were $1,104 million in 2011 (2010 – $726 million; 2009 – $703 million).

18 Long-term debt (excerpts)

(in millions of Canadian dollars)	Maturity	Currency in which payable	2011	2010
Obligations under capital leases (4.90% – 7.63%) (H)	2012-2026	US$	285	287
Obligations under capital leases (5.64% – 5.65%) (H)	Jan 2031	CDN$	3	3

Annual maturities and principal repayments requirements, excluding those pertaining to capital leases, for each of the five years following 2011 are (in millions): 2012 – $42; 2013 – $45; 2014 – $47; 2015 – $122; 2016 – $29.

H. At December 31, 2011, capital lease obligations included in long-term debt were as follows:

(in millions of Canadian dollars)

Minimum lease payments in:

Year	Capital leases
2012	$ 28
2013	29
2014	162
2015	14
2016	14
Thereafter	180
Total minimum lease payments	427
Less: Imputed interest	(139)
Present value of minimum lease payments	288
Less: Current portion	(8)
Long-term portion of capital lease obligations	$280

During the year the Company had no additions to property, plant and equipment under capital lease obligations (2010 – $1 million; 2009 – $1 million). The carrying value of the assets collateralizing the capital lease obligations was $351 million at December 31, 2011.

(continued)

29 Commitments and contingencies (excerpts)

Minimum payments under operating leases were estimated at $831 million in aggregate, with annual payments in each of the five years following 2011 of (in millions): 2012 – $145; 2013 – $131; 2014 – $96; 2015 – $83; 2016 – $65.

30 Guarantees (excerpts)

In the normal course of operating the railway, the Company enters into contractual arrangements that involve providing certain guarantees, which extend over the term of the contracts. These guarantees include, but are not limited to:

❑ residual value guarantees on operating lease commitments of $164 million at December 31, 2011

Illustration 20-19

Capital Lease Disclosures by a Lease—Canadian Pacific Railway Limited (continued)

Illustration 20-20

Lessee Disclosures under IFRS—WestJet Airlines Ltd. (in thousands)

Alternative Terminology

Although IFRS and ASPE use different terminology when discussing accounting for leases by lessors, the underlying journal entries and financial statement presentation are very similar.

Illustration 20-20 provides an additional example of disclosure related to lessees, this time under IFRS. The excerpts are taken from the December 31, 2011 financial statements of WestJet Airlines Ltd. WestJet has been part of the Canadian airline industry since 1996, and in 2011 flew over 16 million "guests" and had in excess of $3 billion in revenue. The company adopted IFRS in 2011 and reports in Canadian dollars.

1. Statement of significant accounting policies

(n) Leases

The determination of whether an arrangement is, or contains, a lease is made at the inception of the arrangement based on the substance of the arrangement and whether (i) fulfillment of the arrangement is dependent on the use of a specific asset and (ii) whether the arrangement conveys a right to use the asset.

Finance leases transfer substantially all the risks and rewards incidental to ownership. Finance leases are recognized as assets and liabilities on the consolidated statement of financial position at the fair value of the leased property or, if lower, the present value of the minimum lease payments, each determined at the inception of the lease. Any costs directly attributable to the finance lease are added to the cost of the leased asset. Minimum lease payments are apportioned between a finance charge, which produces a constant rate of interest on the outstanding liability, and a principal reduction of the lease liability. Depreciation of finance lease assets follows the same methods used for other similar owned assets over the term of the lease.

Operating leases do not result in the transfer of substantially all risks and rewards incidental to ownership. Non-contingent lease payments are recognized as an expense in the consolidated statement of earnings on a straight-line basis over the term of the lease.

11. Obligations under finance leases

The Corporation has entered into finance leases relating to a fuel storage facility and ground handling equipment. Future scheduled repayments of obligations under finance leases as at December 31, 2011 are as follows:

Within 1 year	245
1 – 3 years	490
3 – 5 years	490
Over 5 years	4,371
Total minimum lease payments	5,596
Less: Weighted average imputed interest at 5.28%	(2,347)
Net minimum lease payments	3,249
Less: Current portion of obligations under finance leases	(75)
Long term obligations under finance leases	3,174

18. Commitments (excerpts)

(b) Operating leases and commitments

The Corporation has entered into operating leases and commitments for aircraft, land, buildings, equipment, computer hardware, software licenses and satellite programming. As at December 31, 2011 the future payments in US dollars, where applicable, and Canadian dollar equivalents under operating leases and commitments are as follows:

(continued)

Illustration 20-20

Lessee Disclosures under IFRS—WestJet Airlines Ltd. (in thousands) (continued)

	USD	CAD
Within 1 year	191,462	219,271
1 – 3 years	371,634	400,588
3 – 5 years	262,846	279,747
Over 5 years	215,642	261,441
	1,041,584	1,161,047

As at December 31, 2011, the Corporation is committed to lease one additional 737-800 aircraft for a term of eight years in US dollars. This aircraft has been included in the above totals.

Objective 9

Identify and apply the criteria that are used to determine the type of lease for a lessor under the classification approach.

CLASSIFICATION APPROACH—LESSORS

Classification Criteria

Illustration 20-21

Classification of Leases from a Lessor's Perspective

From the **lessor's** standpoint, all leases are classified for accounting purposes as shown in Illustration 20-21:

Type	ASPE Terminology		IFRS Terminology
Operating	Operating lease		Operating lease
Sales-type	Sales-type lease or	=	Finance lease: Manufacturer or dealer lease or
Financing-type	Direct financing lease	=	Finance lease

The lessor considers the same factors as the lessee in determining whether the risks and benefits of ownership of the leased property are transferred. If they **are not transferred** to the lessee, the lessor accounts for the lease contract as an operating lease. If instead the risks and benefits of ownership **are transferred** to the lessee, the lessor accounts for the lease under ASPE terminology as either a sales-type or direct financing lease. Under IFRS, non-operating leases are called finance leases, mirroring the terminology used by the lessee. The substance of the types of non-operating leases is exactly the same under both—IFRS's manufacturer or dealer lease is equivalent to a sales-type lease, and a "finance lease" is equivalent to a direct-financing lease.

Under IFRS, the criteria to assess whether a lease is an operating lease or a finance lease are identical to the criteria used by the lessee, as explained earlier in this chapter. Under ASPE, the same criteria are also used, with the addition of two revenue recognition-based tests that must be passed:

1. Is the credit risk associated with the lease normal when compared with the risk of collection of similar receivables?

2. Can the amounts of any unreimbursable costs that are likely to be incurred by the lessor under the lease be reasonably estimated?

If collectibility of the amounts that are due under the contract is not reasonably assured or if the lessor still has to absorb an uncertain amount of additional costs associated with the agreement, then it is not appropriate to remove the leased asset from the lessor's books and recognize revenue. In short, if any one of the three ASPE criteria for classification as a capital lease is met and the answer to both of these additional two questions is also yes, then the arrangement is not an operating lease—it is either a sales-type or a direct financing lease.

How do you distinguish between a manufacturer/dealer or sales-type and a financing-type lease? This depends on the specific situation. Some manufacturers enter into lease agreements either directly or through a subsidiary captive leasing company as a way of facilitating the sale of their product. These transactions are usually manufacturer/dealer or sales-type lease arrangements. Other companies are in business to provide financing to the lessee for the acquisition of a variety of assets in order to generate financing income. They usually enter into direct financing, or finance leases.

The difference between these classifications **is the presence or absence of a manufacturer's or dealer's profit (or loss)**. A sales-type lease (a manufacturer or dealer lease) includes in the rental amount the recovery of a manufacturer's or dealer's profit as well as the asset's cost. The profit (or loss) to this lessor is the difference between the fair value of the leased property at the beginning of the lease, and the lessor's cost or carrying amount (book value). As indicated earlier, manufacturer/dealer or sales-type leases normally arise when manufacturers or dealers use leasing as a way of marketing their products.

Direct financing leases (or finance leases), on the other hand, generally result from arrangements with lessors that are engaged mostly in financing operations, such as lease-finance companies and a variety of financial intermediaries, such as banks or their finance subsidiaries. These lessors acquire the specific assets that lessees have asked them to acquire. Their business model is to earn interest income on the financing arrangement with the lessee.

All leases that are not financing or manufacturer/dealer or sales-type leases are classified and accounted for by the lessor as **operating leases**. Under ASPE, when both revenue recognition criteria are not met, it is possible that a lessor will classify a lease as an **operating** lease while the lessee will classify the same lease as a **capital** lease. When this happens, both the lessor and lessee carry the asset on their books and both depreciate the capitalized asset.

| Objective | 10 |

Account for and report basic financing and manufacturer/dealer or sales-type leases by a lessor.

Accounting for Financing and Manufacturer/ Dealer or Sales-Type Leases

For all leases that are not operating leases, the lessor recognizes the leased assets on the SFP as a receivable equal to its net investment in the lease. This applies under both sets of standards.

Accounting for a Financing-Type Lease

Direct or finance leases are, in substance, the financing of an asset by the lessor. The lessor removes the asset from its books and replaces it with a receivable. The accounts and information that are needed to record this type of lease are as follows.

LESSOR TERMINOLOGY

Term	Account	Explanation
Gross investment in lease	Lease Receivable	The undiscounted rental/lease payments (excluding executory costs) plus any guaranteed or unguaranteed residual value that accrues to the lessor at the end of the lease or any bargain purchase option.[a]
Unearned finance or interest income	Unearned Interest Income (contra account to Lease Receivable)	The difference between the undiscounted Lease Receivable and the fair value of the leased property.
Net investment in lease	Net of the two accounts above	The gross investment (the Lease Receivable account) less the Unearned Interest Income; i.e., the gross investment's present value.

[a] This is equal to the lessor's minimum lease payments, as defined, plus any unguaranteed residual value. To a lessor, the minimum lease payments are the same as the **minimum lease payments** as defined for the lessee plus any residual amounts guaranteed by parties unrelated to the lessee or lessor.

The net investment is the present value of the items that are included in the gross investment. The difference between these two accounts is the unearned interest. The unearned interest income is amortized and taken into income over the lease term by applying the effective interest method, using the interest rate implicit in the lease. This results in a constant rate of return being produced on the net investment in the lease.

Illustration of a Financing-Type Lease (Annuity Due).

The following lease example uses the same data as the Lessor Corporation/Lessee Corporation example in Illustration 20-5. The relevant information for Lessor Corporation from the illustration follows.

1. The lease has a **five-year term** that begins January 1, 2014, is non-cancellable, and requires equal **rental payments of $25,981.62** at the beginning of each year. Payments include **$2,000 of executory costs** (maintenance fee).

2. The equipment has a **cost and fair value of $100,000** to Lessor Corporation, an estimated **economic life of five years**, and **no residual value**. No initial direct costs are incurred in negotiating and closing the lease contract.

3. The lease contains no renewal options and the **equipment reverts to Lessor Corporation** at the end of the lease.

4. **Collectibility is reasonably assured** and **no additional costs** (with the exception of the maintenance fees being reimbursed by the lessee) are to be incurred by Lessor Corporation.

5. The interest rate implicit in the lease is 10%. Lessor Corporation set the annual lease payments to ensure a **10% return** on its investment, shown previously in Illustration 20-3.

The lease meets the criteria for classification as a financing-type lease as set out above. It is not a sales-type or manufacturer/dealer lease, because **there is no dealer profit** between the equipment's fair value and the lessor's cost.

Illustration 20-22 calculates the initial gross investment in the lease, which is the amount to be recognized in Lease Receivable.

Illustration 20-22

Calculation of Lease Receivable

Gross investment in the lease and lease receivable	= Total lease payments (excluding executory costs) plus residual value or bargain purchase option[21]
	= [($25,981.62 − $2,000) × 5] + $0
	= $119,908.10

The net investment in the lease is the present value of the gross investment, as determined in Illustration 20-23.

Illustration 20-23

Calculation of Net Investment in the Lease

Net investment in the lease	= Gross investment in the lease discounted at the rate implicit in the lease
	= $23,981.62 × 4.16986 (n = 5, i = 10) (Table A-5)
	+ $0 × 0.62092 (n = 5, i = 10) (Table A-2)
	= $100,000

The acquisition of the asset by the lessor, its transfer to the lessee, the resulting receivable, and the unearned interest income are recorded on January 1, 2014, as follows:

Equipment Acquired for Lessee	100,000	
Cash[22]		100,000

Illustration 20-22

A = L + SE
0   0   0

Cash flows: ↓ 100,000 outflow

A	=	L	+	SE
0		0		0

Cash flows: No effect

Lease Receivable	119,908.10	
Equipment Acquired for Lessee		100,000.00
Unearned Interest Income		19,908.10

The Unearned Interest Income account is classified on the SFP as a contra account to the receivable account. Although the lease receivable amount is **recorded** at the gross investment amount, it is generally **reported** on the SFP at the "net investment" amount and entitled "Net investment in finance leases."[23]

As a result of this entry, Lessor Corporation replaces its investment in the asset that it acquired for Lessee Corporation at a cost of $100,000, with a net lease receivable of $100,000. Similar to Lessee's treatment of interest, Lessor Corporation applies the effective interest method and recognizes interest income according to the unrecovered net investment balance, as shown in Illustration 20-24.

Illustration 20-24

Lease Amortization Schedule for Lessor—Annuity Due Basis

	A	B	C	D	E
1			**Lessor Corporation Lease Amortization Schedule (Annuity due basis)**		
2	**Date**	**Annual Lease Payment**	**Interest (10%) on Net Investment**	**Net Investment Recovery**	**Net Investment**
3		**(a)**	**(b)**	**(c)**	**(d)**
4	1/1/14				$100,000.00
5	1/1/14	$ 23,981.62	$ -0-	$ 23,981.62	76,018.38
6	1/1/15	23,981.62	7,601.84	16,379.78	59,638.60
7	1/1/16	23,981.62	5,963.86	18,017.76	41,620.84
8	1/1/17	23,981.62	4,162.08	19,819.54	21,801.30
9	1/1/18	23,981.62	2,180.32*	21,801.30	-0-
10		$119,908.10	$19,908.10	$100,000.00	

12 (a) Annual rental that provides a 10% return on net investment (exclusive of executory costs).
(b) 10% of the preceding balance of (d) except for 1/1/14.
(c) (a) minus (b).
(d) Preceding balance minus (c).
*Rounded by 19 cents.

On January 1, 2014, the entry to record the receipt of the first year's lease payment is as follows:

A	=	L	+	SE
+2,000				+2,000

Cash flows: ↑ 25,981.62 inflow

Cash	25,981.62	
Lease Receivable		23,981.62
Maintenance and Repairs Expense		2,000.00

On December 31, 2014, the interest income earned during the first year is recognized:

A	=	L	+	SE
+7,601.84				+7,601.84

Cash flows: No effect

Unearned Interest Income	7,601.84	
Interest Income		7,601.84

T accounts for the receivable and its unearned interest contra account, and the effect on the net investment after these entries are made and posted, are shown in Illustration 20-25.

Illustration 20-25

General Ledger Lease Asset Accounts

	Lease Receivable		Unearned Interest Income		Net Investment in Lease
Jan. 1/14	$119,908.10			$19,908.10	$100,000.00
Jan. 1/14		23,981.62			(23,981.62)
					76,018.38
Dec. 31/14				19,908.10	7,601.84
			7,601.84		83,620.22
	95,926.48		12,306.26		

At December 31, 2014, the net investment in finance leases is reported in Lessor Corporation's SFP among current and non-current assets, as appropriate. The principal portion that is due within 12 months is classified as a current asset and the remainder is reported with non-current assets.

The net investment at December 31, 2014, is $83,620.22, which is the balance at January 1, 2014, of $76,018.38 plus interest earned up to the SFP date of $7,601.84. The **current portion** is determined as follows:

Recovery of net investment within 12 months from Dec. 31, 2014	$16,379.78
Interest accrued to Dec. 31, 2014	7,601.84
Current portion of net investment	$23,981.62

The **long-term portion** is the $59,638.60 remainder. The lease amortization schedule in Illustration 20-24 indicates that this is the net investment that will still have to be recovered after 12 months from the date of the SFP.

Illustration 20-26 shows how the lease assets appear on the December 31, 2014 SFP.

Illustration 20-26

Statement of Financial Position Reporting by Lessor

Current assets	
Net investment in finance leases	$23,981.62
Non-current assets	
Net investment in finance leases	$59,638.60

The following entries record the receipt of the second year's lease payment and recognition of the interest earned in 2015:

Jan. 1, 2015	Cash	25,981.62
	Lease Receivable	23,981.62
	Maintenance and Repairs Expense	2,000.00

A = L + SE
+2,000 +2,000
Cash flows: ↑ 25,981.62 inflow

Dec. 31, 2015	Unearned Interest Income	5,963.86
	Interest Income	5,963.86

A = L + SE
+5,963.86 +5,963.86
Cash flows: No effect

Journal entries through to 2018 follow the same pattern except that no entry is recorded in 2018, the last year, for earned interest. Because the receivable is fully collected by January 1, 2018, there is no outstanding investment balance during 2018 for Lessor Corporation to earn interest on. When the lease expires, the gross receivable and the unearned interest have been fully written off. Note that Lessor Corporation records no depreciation. If the equipment is sold to Lessee Corporation for $5,000 when the lease expires, Lessor Corporation recognizes the disposition of the equipment as follows:

| Cash | 5,000 | |
| Gain on Sale of Equipment | | 5,000 |

| A | = | L | + | SE |
| +5,000 | | | | +5,000 |

Cash flows: ↑ 5,000 inflow

Accounting for a Manufacturer/Dealer or Sales-Type Lease

Accounting for a lease entered into by a manufacturer or dealer lessor is very similar to the accounting for a financing-type lease. The major difference is that the lessor in the manufacturer/dealer or sales-type lease has usually manufactured or acquired the leased asset in order to sell it and is looking, through the lease agreement, to make a profit on the "sale" of the asset as well as earn interest on the extended payment terms. The lessor expects to recover the asset's selling price through the lease payments. The cost or carrying amount on the lessor's books is usually less than the asset's fair value to the customer. The lessor, therefore, records a sale and the related cost of goods sold in addition to the entries made in the direct financing lease.

In addition to the gross investment in the lease, the net investment in the lease and the unearned interest income, the following information must be determined:

LESSOR TERMINOLOGY (continued)	
Term	Account	Explanation
Selling price of the asset	Sales	The present value of the Lease Receivable account reduced by the present value of any unguaranteed residual.[a]
Cost of the leased asset being sold	Cost of Goods Sold	The cost of the asset to the lessor, reduced by the present value of any unguaranteed residual.

[a] This is the present value of the minimum lease payments.

The same data from the earlier Lessor Corporation/Lessee Corporation example is used to illustrate the accounting for a manufacturer/dealer or sales-type lease. There is one exception: instead of the leased asset having a cost of $100,000 to Lessor Corporation, the assumption is that **Lessor Corporation manufactured the asset and that it is in Lessor's inventory at a cost of $85,000.** Lessor's regular selling price for this asset—its fair value—is $100,000, and Lessor wants to recover this amount through the lease payments.

The lessor's accounting entries to record the lease transactions are the same as the entries illustrated earlier for a financing-type lease, except for the entry at the lease's inception. **Sales and cost of goods sold are recorded in a manufacturer/dealer or sales-type lease.** The entries are as follows:

January 1, 2014

Lease Receivable ($23,981.62 × 5)	119,908.10	
Unearned Interest Income		19,908.10
Sales Revenue		100,000.00

| A | = | L | + | SE |
| +100,000 | | | | +100,000 |

Cash flows: No effect

| Cost of Goods Sold | 85,000.00 | |
| Inventory | | 85,000.00 |

| A | = | L | + | SE |
| −85,000 | | | | −85,000 |

Cash flows: No effect

	Cash	25,981.62	
	Lease Receivable		23,981.62
	Maintenance and Repairs Expense		2,000.00

Cash flows: ↑ 25,981.62 inflow

| A | = | L | + | SE |
| +2,000 | | +2,000 | | |

December 31, 2014

| | Unearned Interest Income | 7,601.84 | |
| | Interest Income | | 7,601.84 |

Cash flows: No effect

| A | = | L | + | SE |
| +7,601.84 | | | | +7,601.84 |

Compare the January 1, 2014 entries above with the entries for the financing-type lease. The manufacturer/dealer or sales-type lease recognizes that what is being recovered is the asset's selling price, so a sale is recorded. The cost of the inventory is transferred to cost of goods sold. With a manufacturer/dealer or sales-type lease, the lessor recognizes **a gross profit from the sale**, which is reported at the lease's inception, and also recognizes **interest** or **finance income** over the period of the lease until the receivable is no longer outstanding. A lessor with a financing-type lease reports **only finance income.**

Accounting for Residual Values and Bargain Purchase Options in a Financing or Manufacturer/Dealer or Sales-Type Lease

Objective 11

Account for and report financing and manufacturer/dealer or sales-type leases with guaranteed residual values or a bargain purchase option by a lessor.

Assume the same data as in the Lessee Corporation/Lessor Corporation example above and in Illustration 20-5: Lessor wants to recover its net investment in the leased asset of $100,000 and earn a 10% return.[24] The asset reverts to Lessor at the end of the five-year lease term. Now assume that the asset is expected to have a residual value of $5,000 at the end of the lease. **Whether the residual value is guaranteed or not**, Lessor Corporation calculates the lease payments using the same approach set out in Illustration 20-3. Illustration 20-9 shows the calculations when the residual value is included. As you can see from the Lessee Corporation/Lessor Corporation example, the lease payment was $23,237.09, both with the guarantee and without it.

Note that the accounting result is exactly **the same whether the situation involves a residual value or a bargain purchase option.** At the end of the lease term, the lessor either recovers an asset expected to have a value of $5,000, or the lessor expects to get a payment of $5,000 from the lessee for the residual value. In either case, the lessor expects to recover an additional $5,000 at the end of the lease term.

Financing-Type Lease

Illustration 20-27 provides the calculations that are the basis for the lessor's accounting for a financing-type lease, whether the residual value of $5,000 is guaranteed or unguaranteed or whether there is a $5,000 bargain purchase option. The example continues with the Lessee Corporation/Lessor Corporation data.

Illustration 20-27

Calculation of Financing-Type Lease Amounts by Lessor

Gross investment		
Net investment:		
PV of lease payments +	= ($23,237.09 × 5) + $5,000	= $121,185.45
PV of residual value	= $23,237.09 × 4.16986 (Table A-5) +	
	$5,000 × 0.62092 (Table A-2)	= 100,000.00
Unearned interest income		$ 21,185.45

Illustration 20-28 shows the lessor's amortization schedule, which is the same whether the residual value is guaranteed or unguaranteed.

Illustration **20-28**

Lease Amortization Schedule for Lessor—Residual Value or Bargain Purchase Option

	A	B	C	D	E
1			**Lessor Corporation** Lease Amortization Schedule (Annuity due basis, residual value or bargain purchase option)		
2	Date	Lease Payment Received (a)	Interest (10%) on Net Investment (b)	Net Investment Recovery (c)	Net Investment (d)
3					
4	1/1/14				$100,000.00
5	1/1/14	$ 23,237.09	$ –0–	$ 23,237.09	76,762.91
6	1/1/15	23,237.09	7,676.29	15,560.80	61,202.11
7	1/1/16	23,237.09	6,120.21	17,116.88	44,085.23
8	1/1/17	23,237.09	4,408.52	18,828.57	25,256.66
9	1/1/18	23,237.09	2,525.67	20,711.42	4,545.24
10	12/31/18	5,000.00*	454.76**	4,545.24	–0–
11		$121,185.45	$21,185.45	$100,000.00	
13	(a) Lease payment as required by lease, excluding executory costs. (b) Preceding balance of (d) × 10%, except January 1, 2014. (c) (a) minus (b). (d) Preceding balance minus (c). *Represents the residual value or bargain purchase option. **Rounded by 24 cents.				

Lessor Corporation's entries during the first year for this lease are shown in Illustration 20-29. Note the similarity between these entries and those of Lessee Corporation in Illustration 20-16.

Illustration **20-29**

Entries for Residual Value or Bargain Purchase Option, Lessor Corporation

Inception of Lease (January 1, 2014):

Lease Receivable	121,185.45	
Equipment Acquired for Lessee		100,000.00
Unearned Interest Income		21,185.45

First Payment Received (January 1, 2014):

Cash	25,237.09	
Lease Receivable		23,237.09
Maintenance and Repairs Expense		2,000.00

Adjusting Entry for Accrued Interest (December 31, 2014):

Unearned Interest Income	7,676.29	
Interest Income		7,676.29

Manufacturer/Dealer or Sales-Type Lease

The gross investment and the original amount of unearned interest income are the same for a manufacturer/dealer or sales-type lease and a financing-type lease, whether the residual value is guaranteed or whether there is a bargain purchase option of the same amount.

When recording **sales revenue** and **cost of goods sold**, however, there is a difference in accounting, **but only in the situation of an unguaranteed residual value.** A guaranteed residual value or bargain purchase option can be considered part of sales revenue because the lessor either knows or is fairly certain that the entire amount will be realized. There is less certainty, however, that any unguaranteed residual will be realized; therefore,

sales and cost of goods sold are only recognized for the portion of the asset that is sure to be realized. The gross profit amount reported on the asset's sale **is the same** whether the residual value is guaranteed or not, but the present value of any unguaranteed residual is not included in the calculation of **either the sales amount or the cost of goods sold.**

To illustrate a manufacturer/dealer or sales-type lease (a) with a guaranteed residual value or bargain purchase option and (b) without a guaranteed residual value, assume the same facts as in the preceding examples:

- the estimated residual value or option amount is $5,000 (the present value of which is $3,104.60);

- the annual lease payments are $23,237.09 (the present value of which is $96,895.40); and

- the leased equipment has an $85,000 cost to the manufacturer, Lessor Corporation.

In the case of residual values, assume that the leased asset's actual fair value at the end of the lease is $3,000.

Illustration 20-30 provides the calculations that are needed to account for this sales-type lease.

Illustration 20-30

Calculation of Lease Amounts by Lessor Corporation— Manufacturer/Dealer or Sales-Type Lease

	Manufacturer/Dealer or Sales-Type Lease	
	Guaranteed Residual Value or Bargain Purchase Option	Unguaranteed Residual Value
Gross investment	$121,185.45	$121,185.45
	([$23,237.09 × 5] + $5,000)	
Unearned interest income	$21,185.45	$21,185.45
	($121,185.45 − [$96,895.40 + $3,104.60])	
Sales	$100,000	$96,895.40
	($96,895.40 + $3,104.60)	
Cost of goods sold	$85,000	$81,895.40
		($85,000 − $3,104.60)
Gross profit	$15,000	$15,000
	($100,000 − $85,000)	($96,895.40 − $81,895.40)

The $15,000 gross profit that is recorded by Lessor Corporation at the point of sale is the same whether there is a $5,000 bargain purchase option or a residual value that is guaranteed or unguaranteed. However, the **sales revenue** and **cost of goods sold** amounts reported are **different.**

The 2014 and 2015 entries and the entry to record the asset's return at the end of the lease are provided in Illustration 20-31. The only differences are in the original entry that recognizes the lease and the final entry to record the asset's return to the lessor.

Illustration 20-31

Entries for Residual Values, Lessor Corporation— Manufacturer/Dealer or Sales-Type Lease

Guaranteed Residual Value/Bargain Purchase Option			Unguaranteed Residual Value		
To record lease at inception on January 1, 2014:					
Cost of Goods Sold	85,000.00		Cost of Goods Sold	81,895.40	
Lease Receivable	121,185.45		Lease Receivable	121,185.45	
Sales Revenue		100,000.00	Sales Revenue		96,895.40
Unearned Interest Income		21,185.45	Unearned Interest Income		21,185.45
Inventory		85,000.00	Inventory		85,000.00
To record receipt of the first lease payment on January 1, 2014:					
Cash	25,237.09		Cash	25,237.09	
Lease Receivable		23,237.09	Lease Receivable		23,237.09
Maintenance and Repairs Expense		2,000.00	Maintenance and Repairs Expense		2,000.00

(continued)

Guaranteed Residual Value/Bargain Purchase Option		Unguaranteed Residual Value	
To recognize interest income earned during the first year, December 31, 2014:			
Unearned Interest Income	7,676.29	Unearned Interest Income	7,676.29
Interest Income	7,676.29	Interest Income	7,676.29
(See lease amortization schedule, Illustration 20-28)			
To record receipt of the second lease payment on January 1, 2015:			
Cash	25,237.09	Cash	25,237.09
Lease Receivable	23,237.09	Lease Receivable	23,237.09
Maintenance and Repairs Expense	2,000.00	Maintenance and Repairs Expense	2,000.00
To recognize interest income earned during the second year, December 31, 2015:			
Unearned Interest Income	6,120.21	Unearned Interest Income	6,120.21
Interest Income	6,120.21	Interest Income	6,120.21
To record receipt of residual value at end of lease, December 31, 2018:			
Inventory	3,000	Inventory	3,000
Cash	2,000	Loss on Lease	2,000
Lease Receivable	5,000	Lease Receivable	5,000

Illustration 20-31

Entries for Residual Values, Lessor Corporation—Manufacturer/Dealer or Sales-Type Lease (continued)

A = L + SE
0   0   0

Cash flows: ↑ 5,000 inflow

If the situation included a $5,000 bargain purchase option that was exercised at the end of the lease, all the entries would be the same as those in the "Guaranteed Residual Value" column with one exception. The entry for the exercise of the option on December 31, 2018, is:

Cash	5,000	
Lease Receivable		5,000

The estimated unguaranteed residual value in all leases needs to be reviewed periodically by the lessor and the usual impairment standards apply to the lease-related accounts. If the estimate of the unguaranteed residual value declines, the accounting for the transaction must be revised using the changed estimate. The decline represents a reduction in the lessor's net investment and is recognized as a loss in the period when the residual estimate is reduced. Upward adjustments in estimated residual value are not recognized.

Accounting for an Operating Lease

Objective 12
Account for and report an operating lease by a lessor.

With an operating lease, the lessor records each rental receipt as rental income. The leased asset remains on the lessor's books and is depreciated in the normal manner, with the depreciation expense of the period matched against the rental income. An equal (straight-line) amount of rental income is recognized in each accounting period regardless of the lease provisions, unless another systematic and rational basis better represents the pattern in which the leased asset provides benefits. In addition to the depreciation charge, maintenance and other operating costs that are incurred during the period are also charged to expense.

To illustrate operating lease accounting, assume that the Lessor Corporation/Lessee Corporation lease agreement used throughout the chapter does not meet the capitalization criteria and is therefore classified as an operating lease. The entry to record the cash rental receipt, assuming the $2,000 is to cover the lessor's maintenance expense, is as follows:

Lessor Corporation records depreciation as follows, assuming the straight-line method, a cost basis of $100,000, and a five-year life with no residual value:

Depreciation Expense	20,000	
Accumulated Depreciation—Rental Equipment		20,000

A = L + SE
−20,000 = −20,000

Cash flows: No effect

If property taxes, insurance, maintenance, and other operating costs during the year are the lessor's obligation, they are recorded as expenses that are chargeable against the gross rental revenues reported.

Initial Direct Costs

Initial direct costs are generally defined as costs incurred by a lessor that are directly associated with negotiating and arranging a specific lease. Examples of such costs are commissions, legal fees, and costs of preparing and processing lease documents.

Because initial direct costs are treated somewhat differently between IFRS and ASPE in ways that do not result in material differences in the amount of income or assets reported, we do not provide details of the accounting for each classification of lease in this chapter. The important issue is that they are accounted for similar to other costs in that their effect is matched with the revenue of the accounting period benefiting from the lease.

In a **financing-type lease**, the initial direct costs are recognized in such a way that they are spread over the term of the lease. For a **manufacturer/dealer or sales-type lease**, the costs are recognized as an expense in the year they are incurred; that is, they are expensed in the same period that the gross profit on the sale is recognized. For **operating leases**, the lessor defers the initial direct costs and allocates them over the lease term in proportion to the amount of rental income that is recognized.

Disclosure

Financing and Manufacturer/Dealer or Sales-Type Leases

The ASPE requirements are limited to disclosure of the entity's net investment in direct financing and manufacturer/dealer or sales-type leases and the interest rate implicit in them, as well as the carrying amount of any impaired leases including the amount of the related impairment allowance.

The requirements of IAS 17 *Leases* are more extensive. Lessors must provide a reconciliation between the gross investment in the lease and the present value of the minimum lease payments, plus the amounts of both of these due within the next year, between years two and five, and beyond five years. Additional requirements include disclosing the amount of unearned finance income, unguaranteed residual values, contingent rental income in the year, the allowance for doubtful receivables, and general information about the lessor's leasing arrangements.

Operating Leases

Under ASPE, disclosures by the lessor are limited to the cost and related accumulated depreciation of property that is held for leasing purposes, along with the carrying amount of any impaired lease receivables and related allowance provided for impairment.

Cash 25,981.62
Rent Revenue 25,981.62

A = L + SE
+25,981.62 = +25,981.62

Cash flows: ↑ 25,981.62 inflow

The IFRS disclosures for operating leases are similar to those for finance leases. Lessors report the future minimum lease payments in total as well as the amounts due within one year, between years two and five, and beyond five years. The contingent rental income for the period and general information about the entity's leasing arrangements are also reported. For operating leases as well as for those that are not classified as operating in nature, additional requirements are imposed by other standards. These include the standards on property, plant, and equipment; financial instruments; investment property; and impairment, among others.

IFRS/ASPE Comparison

Objective 13
Identify differences in accounting between ASPE and IFRS, and what changes are expected in the near future.

A Comparison of IFRS and ASPE

Illustration 20-32 sets out material differences between existing IFRS and ASPE for lessees and lessors. In general, except for some terminology differences, the classification approach is applied in much the same way under both sets of standards after the initial classification of the lease has been made. Illustration 20-32 also sets out the major differences between this approach and the IFRS proposals that support a contract-based method, expanded upon in Appendix 20B.

Looking Ahead

As indicated at the beginning of this chapter, lease accounting is an area of accounting that is much abused through efforts by preparers to circumvent the provisions of the IFRS and ASPE standards. In practice, the accounting rules for capitalizing leases have been rendered partly ineffective by the strong motivation of lessees to resist capitalization. Leasing generally involves large dollar amounts that, if capitalized, materially increase reported liabilities and weaken debt to equity and other ratios. Lease capitalization is also resisted because charges to expense in the early years of the lease are higher when leases are capitalized than when they are treated as operating leases, often with no corresponding tax benefit.

As a consequence, much effort has been devoted, particularly in North America, to "beating" the profession's lease capitalization rules. To avoid asset capitalization, lease agreements are designed, written, and interpreted so that none of the three criteria is satisfied from the lessee's viewpoint. Under IFRS, similar leases are accounted for in different ways, and new positions being taken on asset and liability definition are driving standard setters to change the existing requirements.

The FASB and IASB have been working together to develop a new leasing standard with the aim of ending abuse. After receiving feedback on the August 2010 ED, the IASB and FASB tentatively decided in June 2012 on some modifications regarding its proposed lease standard. The major change is, in certain circumstances, allowing the straight-line approach (that is, a straight-line expense similar to what is done now for operating leases). For example, leases of property (land or a building—or part of a building—or both) would "be accounted for using the straight-line approach, unless the lease term is for the major part of the economic life of the underlying asset; or the present value of fixed lease payments accounts for substantially all of the fair value of the underlying asset." Also, leases of other assets would be accounted for using an approach similar to that proposed in the 2010 Leases ED, "unless the lease term is an insignificant portion of the economic life of the underlying asset; or the present value of the fixed lease payments is insignificant relative to the fair value of the underlying asset."[25] The proposals were being put in exposure draft form just as this text went to print. In Appendix 20B we take a closer look at what is being proposed.

The new standards will differ from the existing classification approach, as the highlights of the contract-based method summarized in the third column of Illustration 20-32 indicate. Contracts in which the substance of the lease is a purchase and sale would be accounted for as such, but most all other non-cancellable leases would be recognized on

Illustration 20-32 | IFRS and ASPE Comparison Chart

both the lessee's and lessor's statement of financial position as contract-based rights and obligations.

	Accounting Standards for Private Enterprises (ASPE)—CICA Handbook, Part II, Section 3065	IFRS—IAS 17	IASB Proposed Model— A Contract-Based Approach	References to related illustrations and select brief exercises
Scope and Definitions	Applies primarily to property, plant, and equipment assets.	Applies to a broader group of assets, including intangible assets.	Applies only to property, plant, and equipment assets.	N/A
Recognition – By lessee	Leases are either a capital or an operating lease to a lessee. Leases are either operating or a sales-type or direct financing lease to a lessor.	Leases are either a finance or an operating lease to a lessee. Leases are either an operating or a finance lease to a lessor.	No classification is needed, except that those leases that are an in-substance purchase and sale of the underlying asset do not qualify for treatment under the proposed standard.	N/A
	Leases where the risks and benefits of ownership are transferred to the lessee are capital leases to the lessee. The classification criteria include numerical thresholds that are often used.	Leases where the risks and benefits of ownership are transferred to the lessee are finance leases to the lessee. The degree to which the asset is specialized and of use only to the lessee without major expense to the lessor is an additional criterion considered, but no numerical thresholds are given for any criterion.	Lessee recognizes its contractual right to use the leased asset as an asset, and its obligation to make rental payments as a liability.	BE20-2 and BE20-23
– By lessor	ASPE does not recognize investment property outside the regular classification requirements.	A property interest under an operating lease may be recognized as an investment property and accounted for under the fair value model.	Under the performance obligation approach, the lessor recognizes the contract-based rental payments as a lease receivable and the obligation to provide the lessee with a right to use the asset as a liability. Revenue is recognized as a transfer from the liability as performance takes place.	Illustration 20-21
	Classification criteria include numerical thresholds; plus two revenue recognition criteria must be met to qualify as a sales-type or a direct financing lease rather than an operating lease.	A lessor considers the same criteria as the lessee to determine whether the lease is a finance lease or an operating lease. A finance lease could be one entered into by a manufacturer or dealer, or not. The result is similar to ASPE.		N/A
Measurement	For capital leases, the lessee uses the lower of the lessee's incremental borrowing rate and the rate implicit in the lease to determine the capitalized amount of the leased asset.	For finance leases, the lessee uses the interest rate implicit in the lease whenever it can be reasonably determined; otherwise the incremental borrowing rate is used.	Measurement by both lessee and lessor take into account probability-weighted expected outcomes of rental payments, residual values, and options; and a lease term equal to the longest possible term that is more likely than not to occur. Lessee and lessor measurements will differ on the expected payments/	BE20-3

(continued)

	Accounting Standards for Private Enterprises (ASPE)—CICA Handbook, Part II, Section 3065	IFRS—IAS 17	IASB Proposed Model—A Contract-Based Approach	References to related illustrations and select brief exercises
Disclosure – Lessee	Most capital lease disclosures are similar to the disclosures required for plant and equipment assets and long-term liabilities in general.	Most finance lease disclosures are similar to the disclosures covering the asset and liability in other IFRS. Additional disclosures are required about material lease arrangements including contingent rents, sublease payments, and lease-imposed restrictions for both operating and finance leases.	receipts, for example, where the lessor recognizes only the amounts that can be reliably measured. Lease rights are reported with property, plant, and equipment on the statement of financial position.	Illustrations 20-19 and 20-20
– Lessor	For operating leases, the lessor discloses only the cost and net carrying amount of assets held for leasing purposes and impairment information. There are minimum requirements related to the net investment in direct financing and sales-type leases, the interest rate implicit in the lease, and impairment information.	For operating leases, the lessor reports information about the future minimum lease payments due within one year, years two to five, and after five years, as well as about the entity's leasing arrangements in general. For finance leases, a reconciliation is required between gross investment and net investment; the amounts of both due within one year, years two to five, and after five years; and supplementary information about unguaranteed residual values, unearned finance income, contingent rentals, impairments, and general lease arrangement information.	The leased asset, lease receivable, and performance obligation are reported separately, but presented as one net asset or net obligation on the statement of financial position under the performance obligation approach.	N/A
Appendix 20A —Sale-leaseback transactions: – Recognition	The deferred gain on sale recognized by a lessee on a capital leaseback is amortized on the same basis as the depreciation of the leased asset. The gain on an operating leaseback is deferred and amortized unless the lease is for only a minor portion of the original asset.	The deferred gain on sale recognized by a lessee on a finance leaseback is recognized over the lease term. The gain on an operating leaseback is deferred and amortized only for that portion of the sales price that exceeds fair value of the asset sold. A loss is recognized immediately, unless subsequent rents are less than market rates. In this case, the loss is deferred and amortized.	The transaction is accounted for as a sale and leaseback only if the underlying asset has been "sold." Gains and losses are recognized if all assets are at fair value; otherwise, the asset, liabilities, gains, and losses are adjusted to reflect current market rental amounts.	BE20-18 N/A

(continued)

Illustration 20-32

IFRS and ASPE Comparison Chart (continued)

Accounting Standards for Private Enterprises (ASPE)—CICA Handbook, Part II, Section 3065	IFRS—IAS 17	IASB Proposed Model—A Contract-Based Approach	References to related illustrations and select brief exercises
When ownership of the leased asset is not expected to be transferred to the lessee by the end of the lease either directly or through a bargain purchase option and the fair value of the land is significant relative to the building, a lease involving both land and building is treated as two separate leases based on the relative fair value of each.	A bargain purchase option is not considered in determining whether title will be transferred by the end of the lease. Ordinarily, a lease of land and building are treated as two separate leases, with the lease payments separated based on the relative fair value of the leasehold interests, rather than the fair value of the leased property.		BE20-20 and BE20-21

Appendix 20A—Real estate leases:
– Recognition

SUMMARY OF LEARNING OBJECTIVES

1 Understand the importance of leases from a business perspective.

Leases represent a significant source of off-balance sheet financing for companies. One of the issues identified by the IASB in existing accounting standards is the lack of transparency in financial reporting of leases, leaving users like financial analysts having to guess the extent of debt and leverage of many companies.

2 Explain the conceptual nature, economic substance, and advantages of lease transactions.

A lease is a contract between two parties that gives the lessee the right to use property that is owned by the lessor. In situations where the lessee obtains the use of the majority of the economic benefits inherent in a leased asset, the transaction is similar in substance to acquiring an asset. Therefore, the lessee recognizes the asset and associated liability and the lessor transfers the asset under one of the approaches to lease accounting. The major advantages of leasing for the lessee relate to the cost and flexibility of the financing, and protection against obsolescence. For the lessor, the finance income is attractive.

3 Identify and apply the criteria that are used to determine the type of lease for accounting

purposes for a lessee under the classification approach.

A lease is classified as a capital or finance lease where the risks and benefits of owning the leased asset are transferred to the lessee, which is evidenced by one or more of the following: (1) the transfer of title, (2) the use of the majority of the asset services inherent in the leased asset, (3) the recovery by the lessor of substantially all of its investment in the leased asset plus a return on that investment, or (4) under IFRS, in some cases the degree of specialization of the specific asset. If none of these criteria is met, the lease is classified as an operating lease.

4 Calculate the lease payment that is required for a lessor to earn a specific return.

The lessor determines the investment that it wants to recover from a leased asset. If the lessor has acquired an asset for the purpose of leasing it, the lessor usually wants to recover the asset's cost. If the lessor participates in leases as a way of selling its product, it usually wants to recover the sales price. The lessor's investment in the cost or selling price can be recovered in part through a residual value if the asset will be returned to the lessor, or through a bargain purchase price that it expects the lessee to pay, if a bargain purchase is part of the lease agreement. In addition to these sources, the lessor recovers its investment through the lease payments. The periodic lease payment, therefore, is the annuity amount whose present value exactly equals the amount to be recovered through lease payments.

5 Account for a lessee's basic capital (finance) lease.

As a capital lease, called a finance lease under IFRS, the asset is capitalized on the lessee's SFP and a liability is recognized for the obligation owing to the lessor. The amount capitalized is the present value of the minimum lease payments (in effect the payments, excluding executory costs) that the lessee has agreed to take responsibility for. The asset is then depreciated in the same way as other capital assets owned by the lessee. Payments to the lessor are divided into an interest portion and a principal payment, using the effective interest method.

6 Determine the effect of, and account for, residual values and bargain purchase options in a lessee's capital (finance) lease.

When a lessee guarantees a residual value, it is obligated to return either the leased asset or cash, or a combination of both, in an amount that is equal to the guaranteed value. The lessee includes the guaranteed residual in the lease obligation and leased asset value. The asset is depreciated to this value by the end of the lease term. If the residual is unguaranteed, the lessee takes no responsibility for the residual and it is excluded from the lessee's calculations.

7 Account for an operating lease by a lessee and compare the operating and capitalization methods of accounting for leases.

A lessee recognizes the lease payments that are made as rent expense in the period that is covered by the lease, usually based on the proportion of time. Over the term of a lease, the total amount that is charged to expense is the same whether the lease has been treated as a capital/finance lease or as an operating lease. The difference relates to (1) the timing of recognition for the expense (more is charged in the early years for a finance lease), (2) the type of expense that is charged (depreciation and interest expense for a finance lease versus rent expense for an operating lease), and (3) the recognition of an asset and liability on the SFP for a finance lease versus non-recognition for an operating lease. Aside from any income tax differences, the cash flows for a lease are the same whether it is classified as an operating or finance lease.

8 Determine the statement of financial position presentation of a capital (finance) lease and identify other disclosures required.

The current portion of the obligation is the principal that will be repaid within 12 months from the SFP date. The current portion also includes the amount of interest that has accrued up to the SFP date. The long-term portion of the obligation or net investment is the principal balance that will not be paid within 12 months of the SFP date. Lessees disclose the same information as is required for capital assets and long-term debt in general. In addition, details are required of the future minimum lease payments for each of the next five years, and under IFRS, information about its leasing arrangements is required.

9 Identify and apply the criteria that are used to determine the type of lease for a lessor under the classification approach.

If a lease, in substance, transfers the risks and benefits of ownership of the leased asset to the lessee (decided in the same way as for the lessee) and revenue recognition criteria related to collectibility and ability to estimate any remaining unreimbursable costs are met, the lessor accounts for the lease as either a direct financing or a sales-type lease. Under IFRS, it is classified either as a financing, or a manufacturer or dealer lease. The existence of a manufacturer's or dealer's profit on the amount to be recovered from the lessee is the difference between a manufacturer/dealer or sales-type lease and a direct financing lease, as the objective is only to generate finance income in the latter. If any one of the capitalization or revenue recognition criteria is not met, the lessor accounts for the lease as an operating lease. While the revenue recognition criteria are not set out in IAS 17, they would be applied in general before any revenue is recognized by the lessor.

10 Account for and report basic financing and manufacturer/dealer or sales-type leases by a lessor.

In a finance lease, the lessor removes the cost of the leased asset from its books and replaces it with its net investment in the lease. This is made up of two accounts: (1) the gross investment or lease receivable, offset by (2) the portion of these amounts that represents unearned interest. The net investment represents the present value of the lease payments and the residual value or bargain purchase option amounts. As the lease payments are received, the receivable is reduced. As time passes, the unearned interest is taken into income based on the implicit rate of return that applies to the net investment. Under a manufacturer/dealer or sales-type lease, the accounting is similar except that the net investment represents the sale amount the lessor wants to recover. The lessor also transfers the inventory "sold" to cost of goods sold.

11 **Account for and report financing and manufacturer/dealer or sales-type leases with guaranteed residual values or a bargain purchase option by a lessor.**

For both types of lease, the net investment in the lease includes the estimated residual value whether it is guaranteed or not, or the bargain purchase option amount. Under a manufacturer/dealer or sales-type lease, both the sale and cost of goods sold amounts are reduced by any unguaranteed residual values.

12 **Account for and report an operating lease by a lessor.**

The lessor records the lease payments received from the lessee as rental income in the period covered by

the lease payment. Because the leased asset remains on the lessor's books, the lessor records depreciation expense. Separate disclosure is required of the cost and accumulated amortization of property held for leasing purposes, and the amount of rental income earned.

13 **Identify differences in accounting between ASPE and IFRS, and what changes are expected in the near future.**

Under the classification approach, ASPE is substantially the same as the IFRS requirements. Different terminology is used and the classification requirements that differentiate between a capital/finance lease and an operating lease under IFRS are based more on principles and judgement than ASPE. A new lease standard was expected to be issued by the IASB and FASB after a 2013 exposure draft, and it was expected to significantly change the approach to lease accounting. Under the revisions planned, a contract-based or right-of-use approach is used by both lessee and lessor.

APPENDIX 20A

OTHER LEASE ISSUES

Sale and Leaseback Transactions

Objective 14

Describe and apply the lessee's accounting for sale-leaseback transactions.

Sale-leaseback describes a transaction in which a property owner (the seller-lessee) sells a property to another party (the purchaser-lessor) and, at the same time, leases the same asset back from the new owner. The property generally continues to be used without any interruption. This type of transaction is fairly common.[26]

For example, a company buys land, constructs a building to its specifications, sells the property to an investor, and then immediately leases it back from the investor. From the seller's viewpoint, the advantage of a sale and leaseback usually has to do with financing. If an equipment purchase has already been financed, and rates have subsequently decreased, a sale-leaseback can allow the seller to refinance the purchase at lower rates. Alternatively, a sale-leaseback can also provide additional working capital when liquidity is tight.

To the extent that, after the sale, the seller-lessee continues to use the same asset it has sold, **the sale-leaseback is really a form of financing**, and therefore it is reasonable that no gain or loss is recognized on the transaction. In substance, the seller-lessee is simply borrowing funds. On the other hand, if the seller-lessee gives up the ownership risks and benefits associated with the asset, the transaction is clearly a sale, and gain or loss recognition is appropriate. Accounting standards indicate that the lease should be accounted for as a finance/capital or operating lease by the seller-lessee and as a finance-type or operating lease by the purchaser-lessor, as appropriate under the lease accounting standards.

When a seller-lessee leases back only a portion of the asset sold, such as one floor of a 10-floor building sold, or a lease term of two years when the remaining useful life is six years, then the transaction does not meet the definition of a sale-leaseback transaction. In such a case, the sale and the lease are accounted for as separate transactions based on the underlying substance of each.

Seller-Lessee Accounting

If the lease meets the criteria to be classified as a **capital or finance lease**, the seller-lessee accounts for the transaction as a sale, and the lease as a capital or finance lease. Any profit on the sale of the assets that are leased back **is deferred and amortized** over the lease term (under IFRS) or on the same basis as the depreciation of the leased assets (if ASPE). If the leased asset is land only, the amortization is on a straight-line basis over the lease term.

For example, if Lessee Inc. sells equipment having a book value of $580,000 and a fair value of $623,110 to Lessor Inc. for $623,110 and leases the equipment back for $50,000 a year for 20 years, the profit of $43,110 (that is, $623,110 − $580,000) is deferred and amortized over the 20-year period. The $43,110 is credited originally to a Deferred Profit on Sale-Leaseback account.

If none of the capital lease criteria is met, the seller-lessee accounts for the transaction as a sale, and the lease as an **operating lease**. Under IFRS, if the terms of the sale/operating lease transaction are clearly fair value amounts, the profit or loss on disposal is recognized in net income immediately. If the selling price is less than fair value, the same rule applies unless the future rentals are also below a market rent to compensate. If so, the loss is deferred and amortized over the period the asset is expected to be used. If the selling price is more than fair value, the amount above fair value is deferred and amortized over the same period.

Under ASPE, the profit or loss on sale of a property sold and leased back under an operating lease arrangement is deferred and amortized in proportion to the rental payments over the period of time that it is expected the lessee will use the assets.

The standards require, however, that when there is a legitimate loss on the sale of an asset—that is, when the asset's **fair value is less than its carrying amount**—the loss is recognized immediately. For example, if Lessee Inc. sells equipment that has a book value of $650,000 and a fair value of $600,000, the difference of $50,000 is charged directly to a loss account.

Purchaser-Lessor Accounting

Under a sale and leaseback transaction, the purchaser-lessor applies the regular lease standards. This type of transaction results in either an operating or direct-financing type lease on the part of the lessor.

Sale-Leaseback Illustration

To illustrate the accounting treatment for a sale-leaseback transaction, assume that on January 1, 2015, Lessee Inc. sells a used Boeing 767, having a cost of $85.5 million and a carrying amount on Lessee's books of $75.5 million, to Lessor Inc. for $80 million, and then immediately leases the aircraft back under the following conditions:

1. The term of the non-cancellable lease is 15 years, and the agreement requires equal annual rental payments of $10,487,443, beginning January 1, 2015.

2. The aircraft has a fair value of $80 million on January 1, 2015, and an estimated economic life of 15 years.

3. Lessee Inc. pays all executory costs.

4. Lessee Inc. depreciates similar aircraft that it owns on a straight-line basis over 15 years.

5. The annual payments assure the lessor a 12% return, which is the same as Lessee's incremental borrowing rate.

6. The present value of the minimum lease payments is $80 million, or $10,487,443 × 7.62817 (Table A-5: $i = 12, n = 15$).

This is a capital or finance lease to Lessee Inc. because the lease term covers the entire useful life of the asset and because the lessor recovers its investment in the aircraft and earns the required rate of return from the minimum lease payments. Assuming that the appropriate revenue recognition criteria are met, Lessor Inc. classifies this arrangement as a finance-type lease.

Illustration 20A-1 shows the journal entries related to this lease for both Lessee Inc. and Lessor Inc. for the first year.

<table>
<tr><td>Illustration 20A-1</td><td>Comparative Entries for Sale-Leaseback for Lessee and Lessor</td></tr>
</table>

Lessee Inc.			Lessor Inc.		
Sale of aircraft by Lessee Inc. to Lessor Inc., January 1, 2015, and leaseback transaction:					
Cash	80,000,000		Aircraft Acquired for Lessee	80,000,000	
Accumulated Depreciation	10,000,000		Cash		80,000,000
Aircraft		85,500,000			
Deferred Profit on					
Sale-Leaseback		4,500,000			
Aircraft under Lease	80,000,000		Lease Receivable	157,311,645[a]	
Obligations under Lease		80,000,000	Aircraft Acquired for Lessee		80,000,000
			Unearned Interest Income		77,311,645
			[a]($10,487,443 × 15 = $157,311,645)		
First lease payment, January 1, 2015:					
Obligations under Lease	10,487,443		Cash	10,487,443	
Cash		10,487,443	Lease Receivable		10,487,443
Executory costs incurred and paid by Lessee Inc. throughout 2015:					
Operating Expenses	xxx				
Cash or Accounts Payable		xxx			
Depreciation expense for 2015 on the aircraft, December 31, 2015:					
Depreciation Expense	5,333,333				
Accumulated Depreciation—					
Leased Aircraft		5,333,333			
($80,000,000 ÷ 15)				(No entry)	

(continued)

Lessee Inc.		Lessor Inc.	

Amortization of deferred profit on sale-leaseback by Lessee Inc.., December 31, 2015:

			(No entry)
Deferred Profit on			
Sale-Leaseback	300,000		
Depreciation Expense[b]		300,000	
($4,500,000 ÷ 15)			

[b]alternatively a gain account could be credited

Interest for 2015, December 31, 2015:

			Unearned Interest Income	8,341,507	
Interest Expense	8,341,507[c]		Interest Income		8,341,507[c]
Interest Payable		8,341,507[c]			

[c] Lease obligation or net investment in the lease of ($80,000,000 − $10,487,443) × 12% × 12/12

Illustration 20A-1

Comparative Entries for Sale-Leaseback for Lessee and Lessor (continued)

Looking ahead to expected changes in the lease accounting standards, it is likely that the standards on sale-leasebacks will also change. One area of controversy is the reporting of a deferred gain as a liability when there is no obligation to a creditor or other party. As recent standards support an asset-liability approach to income measurement, deferred charges and deferred credits that do not meet the definitions of assets and liabilities, respectively, are not likely to remain. Also, the international lease standard considers an issue that ASPE does not. IAS 17 *Leases* recognizes that if the leaseback is an operating lease, the sale has actually transferred the risks and benefits of ownership to the purchaser. The international standard therefore allows a gain to be recognized, but only if the transaction takes place at fair value.

Disclosure and Example

There are no specific disclosure requirements for a sale-leaseback transaction other than the ones that are required for financial reporting and leases in general. Illustration 20A-2 provides an example of how Netherlands-based **Koninklijke Ahold N.V.** reports its sale-leaseback transaction. Ahold is an international food retailing group of companies with supermarket operations in Europe and the United States.

Real World Emphasis

Illustration 20A-2

Example of Sale-Leaseback Disclosure—Koninklijke Ahold N.V.

3 Significant accounting policies —

Sale and leaseback

The gain or loss on sale and operating leaseback transactions is recognized in the income statement immediately if (i) Ahold does not maintain or maintains only minor continuing involvement in these properties, other than the required lease payments and (ii) these transactions occur at fair value. Any gain or loss on sale and finance leaseback transactions is deferred and amortized over the term of the lease. In classifying the leaseback in a sale and leaseback transaction, similar judgments have to be made as described under "Leases."

In some sale and leaseback arrangements, Ahold sells a property and only leases back a portion of that property. These properties generally involve shopping centers, which contain an Ahold store as well as other stores leased to third-party retailers. Ahold recognizes a sale and the resulting profit on the portion of the shopping center that is not leased back to the extent that (i) the property is sold for fair value and (ii) the risks and rewards of owning stores that are not leased back to Ahold have been fully transferred to the buyer. The leaseback of the Ahold store and any gain on the sale of the Ahold store is accounted for under the sale and leaseback criteria described above.

In some sale and leaseback arrangements, Ahold subleases the property to third parties (including franchisees) or maintains a form of continuing involvement in the property sold, such as earn-out provisions or obligations or options to repurchase the property. In such situations, the transaction generally does not qualify for sale and lease-back accounting, but rather is accounting for as a financing transaction (financing). The carrying amount of the asset remains on the balance sheet and the sale proceeds are recorded as a financing obligation. The financing obligation is amortized over the lease term, using either the effective interest rate or Ahold's cost of debt rate, whichever is higher. Once Ahold's continuing involvement ends, the sale is accounted for under the sale and leaseback criteria described above.

(continued)

Illustration 20A-2

Example of Sale-Leaseback
Disclosure—Koninklijke
Ahold N.V. (continued)

25 Other non-current liabilities

€ million	January 1, 2012	January 2, 2011
Step rent accruals	187	168
Deferred income	29	35
Other	14	14
Total other non-current liabilities	230	217

Step rent accruals relate to the equalization of rent payments from lease contracts with scheduled fixed rent increases throughout the life of the contract.

Deferred income predominantly represents the non-current portions of deferred gains on sale and leaseback transactions.

Objective 15

Explain the classification and accounting treatment for leases that involve real estate.

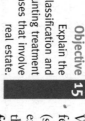

Real Estate Leases

When a capital or finance lease involves land, and ownership of the land will not be transferred to the lessee, capitalizing the land on the lessee's SFP would result in no expense (such as depreciation) being recognized for its use over the term of the lease. Then, at the end of the lease, a loss equal to the capitalized value of the land would be recognized when the land is transferred back to the lessor. This explains why **special guidance is needed for leases that involve land.**

Land

If land is the only leased asset, and title to the property is transferred to the lessee by the end of the lease, the **lessee** accounts for the arrangement as a capital or finance lease, and the **lessor** accounts for it either as a manufacturer/dealer or sales-type lease or as a direct financing lease, whichever is appropriate. If the title is not transferred, it is accounted for as an operating lease.

Land and Building

If land and a building are leased together, IFRS requires that each be considered separately when classifying the lease. The minimum lease payments are allocated on the basis of the relative fair values of the leasehold interest in each component.[27] If this can't be determined reliably, the entire lease is classified as a finance lease, unless it is clear that both are operating leases. If the portion determined to be for the land is immaterial, the whole arrangement may be accounted for as a single unit.

Under ASPE, the lessee can capitalize land separately from the building when title is expected to be transferred, either directly or through a bargain purchase option. The minimum lease payments in this case are allocated based on the relative fair values of the land and the building. If title is not expected to be transferred, the accounting depends on the fair value of the land relative to the building. If it is minor, the land and building are treated as a single unit when classifying the lease; if significant, the land and building are considered separately, with the land portion classified as an operating lease.

SUMMARY OF LEARNING OBJECTIVES FOR APPENDIX 20A

14 Describe and apply the lessee's accounting for sale-leaseback transactions.

A sale and leaseback is accounted for by the lessee as if the two transactions were related. In general, any gain or loss, with the exception of a real (economic) loss, is deferred by the lessee and recognized in income over the lease term. For an operating lease under ASPE, the seller-lessee takes the deferred gain or loss into income in proportion to the rental payments made. Under IFRS, if the transaction is done at fair value, the gain or loss may be taken to income immediately. For a finance lease, the deferred gain or loss is taken into income over the same period

and basis as the depreciation of the leased asset (ASPE) or over the term of the lease (IFRS).

15 Explain the classification and accounting treatment for leases that involve real estate.

Because the capitalization of land by the lessee in a capital or finance lease that does not transfer title results in an unwanted and unintended effect on the lessee's financial statements, the portion of such leases that relates to land is accounted for as an operating lease. If the relative value of the land is minor, however, the minimum lease payments are fully capitalized as building.

KEY TERM

sale-leaseback, p. 1308

APPENDIX 20B

CONTRACT-BASED APPROACH

Objective 16
Explain and apply the contract-based approach to a basic lease for a lessee and lessor.

The IASB and the FASB have been working since 2006 on a joint project to replace their accounting standards on leases. They released a discussion paper in 2009 that set out preliminary views on significant aspects of a new accounting model for lessee accounting and identified issues that need to be addressed for the lessor. This was followed by an August 2010 Exposure Draft. After studying the responses and further discussion, the IASB expected to issue a new Exposure Draft of a revised, and common, lease accounting standard in 2013.[28]

Significant Change

EXAMPLE

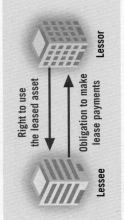

The lessor transfers the right to use the asset over the lease term to the lessee in exchange for the lessee's promise to make periodic rent or lease payments.

Right to use the leased asset

Lessor

Lessee

Obligation to make lease payments

Law

The accounting model proposed is a contract-based approach first introduced to you in Chapter 6 and then discussed again earlier in this chapter. In essence, the lessee recognizes a "right-of-use asset" representing its right to use the leased item over the lease term along with a liability that captures its obligation to make lease payments. While this looks similar to the capital/finance lease situation set out earlier in the chapter, it is a very different concept. Under the **classification approach,** the lessee recognizes a lease as the leased property itself when there is a transfer of the risks and benefits of ownership and when this is an in-substance instalment purchase of the asset. The **contract-based approach** sees the asset taken on by the lessee as the contractual right to use the asset, not the transfer of the asset itself. In addition, this approach is much broader, capturing most arrangements that are now considered operating leases. However, in June 2012, after receiving comments and feedback on the 2010 Exposure Draft (ED), the IASB indicated that it will allow some additional exceptions in its 2013 ED. These exceptions are discussed in the "Looking Ahead" section of this chapter.

Let's see what the basics of this new approach are.

Scope and Definition

A **lease** is defined in the joint FASB-IASB project as "a contract in which the right to use a specified asset is conveyed, for a period of time, in exchange for consideration."[29]

The intent of the 2010 ED was to set out the accounting treatment for non-cancellable lease contracts where the contractual **right to use** the asset is transferred from a lessor to a lessee. For this reason, contracts that actually transfer **control of the underlying asset** itself or almost all of the risks and benefits associated with ownership **are excluded from the new standard.** Such in-substance purchases by the lessee include:

- contracts in which the title to the property is transferred automatically at the end of the lease,

- those with a bargain purchase option that is reasonably certain to be exercised,

- those in which the contract is expected to cover almost all of the useful life of the asset, and

- contracts where the lessor's return is fixed.

These situations are excluded because they are in-substance acquisitions of the asset itself. In such cases, the accounting would be similar to present-day capital or finance leases.

Recognition and Measurement—Lessee

Initial Measurement

Under the contract-based approach, the assets and liabilities arise and are recognized at the start of the lease contract. At this point, the right-of-use asset and the liability to make lease payments are usually equal.

The Liability to Make Lease Payments. The liability recognized by the lessee is measured at the present value of the lease payments.[30] While this sounds straightforward at first, a number of decisions need to be made before the resulting amounts are determined and then discounted.

1. Do contingent rentals—additional rents that become payable based on the level of sales or other variable—have to be considered?

2. How are any guarantees of residual values at the end of the lease factored into the calculations?

3. Lease contracts often contain renewal or purchase options, sometimes at bargain prices and other times at market rates, or options to end the lease early. Are these considered?

4. What discount rate is used?

The new proposals take the position that the contractual obligation to pay rent **includes amounts payable under contingent rental arrangements** over the term of the lease and **amounts expected to be payable under residual value guarantees.** Therefore, such amounts are estimated in advance, are measured using probability-weighted expected values, and are included in the lease payments as part of the initial liability recognized. Note, however, that it is only the cash flows that are expected to be made in the future related to these items that are included, not the full amount of the residual value, for example, unless that is expected to be the amount of the deficiency. However, purchase options are not considered to be a lease payment and are not included.

An associated issue is one of determining the **term of the lease.** This decision, in turn, affects the number of periods over which the minimum and contingent rentals are payable, as well as the amount of any residual value deficiency or purchase option amount to be received. Taking all relevant factors into account, including the possibility of early termination and the renewal of the lease at market rates, an entity identifies the **probability of occurrence for each possible lease term,** and uses this in its calculations.

The third variable in measuring the lease payments is the discount rate itself. Here the standard setters propose the use of the lessee's incremental borrowing rate. However, if the rate implicit in the lease can be readily determined, this alternative rate can be used.

The Right-of-Use Asset. The asset recognized under the contract-based approach is measured initially at cost, based on the present value of the lease payments as described above for the lease obligation. Consistent with a cost model, any of the lessee's initial direct costs of negotiating and arranging the lease are also capitalized.

Measurement after Recognition

The Lease Liability. The lease obligation is accounted for at amortized cost using the effective interest method. As lease payments are made, the contractual obligation is reduced, with each payment separated into interest and principal reduction amounts. Interest is calculated using the original discount rate established when the obligation was first recognized, applied to the outstanding principal balance.

The estimates used to determine the lease term and contingent rental amounts are reassessed at every reporting date if new events or circumstances indicate that there might be a material change in the amount of the obligation. If there is, the liability is remeasured. Illustration 20B-1 sets out the August 2010 ED proposals for any resulting changes in the amount of the obligation.

Illustration 20B-1

Changes in Contractual Lease Obligation—Accounting Requirements

	Changes in Contractual Lease Obligation	Remeasurement of Contractual Lease Obligation
Cause	A change in the obligation from changes in amounts payable for contingent rentals, residual value guarantees, and term option penalties	A change in the obligation to pay rentals as a result of a probability reassessment of the lease term
Accounting	Change related to current or prior periods: – Recognize in net income Change relating to future periods: – Adjust the carrying amount of the right-of-use asset	All changes: – Adjust the carrying amount of the liability to make lease payments

The Right-of-Use Asset. Accounting for the right-of-use asset after initial recognition and measurement is consistent with its nature; it is similar to the accounting requirements for an intangible asset. Most will continue to be accounted for at amortized cost, taking into account any changes in amount resulting from remeasurements if it chooses to revalue that class of property, plant, and equipment in accordance with IAS 16.

The asset's cost should be amortized to expense on a systematic basis over the term of the lease (or the useful life if shorter) using a method that best represents the pattern of benefits received from the asset used. The proposals do specify, however, that "amortization" expense, not "rent" expense, is recognized on the income statement.

Also consistent with other standards, if the right-of-use assets are revalued, gains and losses on revaluation would be recognized in accordance with IAS 38 *Intangible Assets*. The right-of-use asset would also be considered for impairment under the requirements of IAS 36 *Impairment of Assets*.

Illustration of Contract-Based Lessee Accounting

We now walk through an example of how a lease is accounted for under the contract-based approach. Assume that EE Corporation, a lessee, enters into a non-cancellable lease contract with OR Limited, a lessor, on September 1, 2015. Assume that the signing and delivery of the lease happened on the same day. The terms and conditions of the lease are set out in Illustration 20B-2.

Illustration 20B-2

Terms, Conditions, and Other Information Related to the Lease Contract

Leased asset	Manufacturing equipment
Economic life of equipment	7 years
Lease term	September 1, 2015, to August 31, 2019
Lease payment per year, payable in advance	$5,000
Contingent rental payments	Not required
Renewal option	Renewable for additional 2 years at option of lessee at $4,500 per year
Expected value of asset (not guaranteed)	
– August 31, 2019	$6,000
– August 31, 2021	$1,000
Title to leased equipment	Retained by lessor
Rate implicit in the lease	9%
Lessee's incremental borrowing rate	9%
Fair value of leased asset, September 1, 2015	$24,000
Lessor's initial direct costs	$365
Lessee's expectations:	
– Most likely lease term (option will be taken to renew lease for additional 2 years)	Lease will expire on August 31, 2021; lease term is 6 years.
Lessor's expectations:	
– Most likely lease term	Lessee will renew the lease for 2 years on August 31, 2019; a 6-year lease term
– Probability-weighted expected value of residual at end of lease term	$1,000

Because EE Corporation now has the right to use the manufacturing equipment owned by OR Limited (an asset) and an obligation to make lease payments (a liability), the right-of-use asset and liability at acquisition are measured and recognized. The obligation is the minimum lease payments, including contingent rentals and possible payments under guarantees, all discounted using the lessee's incremental borrowing rate based on the probability of occurrence of each lease term. Illustration 20B-3 shows that the initial measure of the obligation and asset, assuming a probable lease term of 6 years, is $23,769.

Illustration 20B-3

Initial Measurement of Right-of-Use Asset and Obligations

Contractual Rights and Obligations under Lease, September 1, 2015		
Present value of amounts payable under the lease contract, i = 9:		
$5,000 annuity due × 3.53130 (n = 4) [Table A-5]	=	$17,656
$4,500 sum × 0.70843 ($n$ = 4) [Table A-2]	=	3,188
$4,500 sum × 0.64993 ($n$ = 5) [Table A-2]	=	2,925
		$23,769

The initial entries to recognize the contract and the first payment on September 1, 2015, are:

Right-of-Use Asset 23,769
Obligations under Lease 23,769

> A = L + SE
> +23,769 +23,769
> Cash flows: No effect

Obligations under Lease 5,000
Cash 5,000

> A = L + SE
> −5,000 −5,000
> Cash flows: ↓ 5,000 outflow

At December 31, 2015, EE Corporation's year end, the company recognizes the amortization of lease rights that have been used up and interest expense on the obligation since September 1, 2015:

Amortization Expense 1,320
Right-of-Use Asset[a] 1,320
($23,769 ÷ 6 years) × 4/12

[a]The August 2010 Leases ED made no reference to separate disclosures of accumulated amortization amounts, although it indicated that the asset was to be reported with property, plant, and equipment assets. Use of an accumulated amortization account would also be correct.

> A = L + SE
> −1,320 −1,320
> Cash flows: No effect

Interest Expense 563
Interest Payable 563
[($23,769 − $5,000) × .09 × 4/12)]

> A = L + SE
> +563 −563
> Cash flows: No effect

Recognition and Measurement—Lessor

The standard setters initially decided that the lessor should take either a performance obligation or a derecognition approach to accounting for the lease contract. The transaction is represented by the following illustration under the performance obligation approach. This approach would be used if the lessor retains significant risks and benefits with the leased asset.

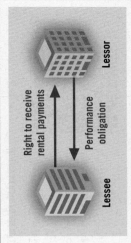

EXAMPLE

The contract gives the lessor an entitlement to receive rental payments from the lessee. In turn, the lessor is obligated to allow the lessee to use the leased item; having done that, the lessor satisfies the performance obligation and recognizes revenue.

Alternatively, if the lessor does not retain exposure to significant risks and benefits associated with the underlying asset, the lessor would apply the derecognition approach, which is discussed briefly later in this appendix. Similar to the lessee's accounting, the contractual rights and obligations are recognized at the date of inception of the lease.

Lease Assets

The lessor measures the lease receivable (that is, the right to receive lease payments) at the present value of the rental payments to be received, discounted at the interest rate the lessor is charging the lessee, increased by any initial direct costs incurred by the lessor. Although the lease term chosen by the lessor is also based on the probability of occurrence of each possible lease term, its expectations may differ from those of the lessee. The measurement of the expected value of contingent rents, expected residual values, or purchase options mirror those of the lessee, but here again, different amounts may result. Also note that amounts are recognized by the lessor only to the extent that they can be measured reliably.

After its initial recognition, the lease receivable is accounted for at amortized cost, using the effective interest method. Subsequent adjustments made to the receivable as a result of changes in either the expected values of the amounts to be received or the lease term are accounted for as set out in Illustration 20B-4. The leased asset itself remains in the accounts, depreciated over its useful life.

	Remeasurement of Contractual Lease Obligation	
Cause	A change in the receivable from changes in expected rent payments and residual value	A change in the receivable as a result of a reassessment of the lease term
Accounting	Treat as an adjustment to the original transaction price. For a change related to a satisfied performance obligation: – Recognize in net income For a change related to an unsatisfied performance obligation: – Adjust the carrying amount of the lease liability	All changes: – Adjust the carrying amount of the lease liability

Quiz

Illustration 20B-4

Changes in Lease Receivable—Accounting Requirements

The Lease Liability

Initially, the lessor's obligation to allow the lessee to use an asset it owns is measured at the present value of the lease payments that are also recognized in the lease receivable. After this, as the lessor meets the performance obligation, the lease liability is decreased and revenue is recognized in a systematic and rational manner based on the pattern of the asset's use by the lessee.

Under a performance obligation approach to lessor accounting, the leased asset itself remains on the lessor's SFP at the same time that the lessor recognizes the new Lease Receivable asset and the Lease Liability. All three accounts are reported separately on the SFP, but totalled to one net lease asset or net lease liability amount. Interest income, lease income, and depreciation expense are presented separately in the income statement.

Lessor Accounting—A Derecognition Approach

The **derecognition approach** removes the portion of the underlying leased asset that is given up in the lease agreement from the SFP and recognizes a lease receivable, representing the right to receive lease payments. Any remaining portion of the carrying value of the underlying asset that the lessor retains is classified as a "residual asset." The derecognition approach is explained further in the August 2010 ED.

SUMMARY OF LEARNING OBJECTIVE FOR APPENDIX 20B

16 Explain and apply the contract-based approach to a basic lease for a lessee and lessor.

The contract-based approach to lease accounting assumes that the asset transferred by the lease contract from the lessor to the lessee is the right to use the leased property. The lessee recognizes this right-of-use as an asset and recognizes the obliga-

tion to make rental payments as an obligation. The lessor recognizes the contractual right to receive lease payments as an asset—a receivable—and recognizes its performance obligation to permit the lessee to use the asset as a liability. As performance takes place, the lessor recognizes revenue.

KEY TERM

performance obligation, p. 1317

Brief Exercises

Note: All assignment material with an asterisk (*) relates to an appendix to the chapter.

(LO 3) **BE20-1** Piper Corporation recently signed a lease for equipment from Photon Inc. The lease term is five years and requires equal rental payments of $32,000 at the beginning of each year. The equipment has a fair value at the lease's inception of $140,000, an estimated useful life of eight years, and no residual value. Piper pays all executory costs directly to third parties. Photon set the annual rental to earn a rate of return of 8%, and this fact is known to Piper. The lease does not transfer title or contain a bargain purchase option. How should Piper classify this lease using ASPE?

(LO 3) **BE20-2** Blane Inc. entered into a five-year lease of equipment from Zdrinka Inc. At the lease's inception, it is estimated that the equipment has an economic life of eight years and fair value of $250,000. Present value of minimum lease payments amounts to $215,606.50. The lease does not transfer title or contain a bargain purchase option. (a) Assume that Blane follows IFRS. How should Blane classify this lease? (b) Assume that Blane follows ASPE. How should Blane classify this lease?

(LO 3) **BE20-3** Diamond Corporation entered into a finance or capital lease on January 1, 2014. The lease term is six years and requires annual rental payments of $30,000 at the beginning of each year. Diamond's incremental borrowing rate is 8% and the rate implicit in the lease is 9%. (a) Calculate the capitalized amount of the leased asset if Diamond follows IFRS. (b) Calculate the capitalized amount of the leased asset if Diamond follows ASPE.

(LO 5) **BE20-4** Lalonde Ltd., a public company following IFRS, recently signed a lease for equipment from Costner Ltd. The lease term is five years and requires equal rental payments of $25,173 at the beginning of each year. The equipment has a fair value at the lease's inception of $112,400, an estimated useful life of five years, and no residual value. Lalonde pays all executory costs directly to third parties. The appropriate interest rate is 6%. Prepare Lalonde's journal entries at the inception of the lease.

(LO 4) **BE20-5** Use the information for Lalonde and Costner from BE20-4. Explain, using numbers, how Costner determined the amount of the lease payment of $25,173.

(LO 5) **BE20-6** McCormick Corporation Ltd., a public company following IFRS, recorded a finance lease at $150,000 on May 1, 2014. The interest rate is 10%. McCormick Corporation made the first lease payment of $25,561 on May 1, 2014. The lease requires a total of eight annual payments. The equipment has a useful life of eight years with no residual value. Prepare McCormick Corporation's December 31, 2014 adjusting entries.

(LO 5) **BE20-7** Use the information for McCormick Corporation from BE20-6. Assume that at December 31, 2014, McCormick made an adjusting entry to accrue interest expense of $8,296 on the lease. Prepare McCormick's May 1, 2015 journal entry to record the second lease payment of $25,561. Assume that no reversing entries are made.

(LO 6) **BE20-8** Merrill Corporation, which uses ASPE, enters into a six-year lease of equipment on September 13, 2014, that requires six annual payments of $28,000 each, beginning September 13, 2014. In addition, Merrill guarantees the lessor a residual value of $17,000 at lease end. The equipment has a useful life of six years. Prepare Merrill's September 13, 2014 journal entries, assuming an interest rate of 9%.

(LO 6) BE20-9 Use the information for Merrill Corporation from BE20-8. Assume that a residual value of $17,000 is expected at the end of the lease, but that Merrill does not guarantee the residual value. Prepare Merrill's September 13, 2014 journal entries, assuming an interest rate of 9% and that Merrill also uses ASPE.

(LO 11) BE20-10 Use the information for Merrill Corporation from BE20-8. Assume that for Moxey Corporation, the lessor, collectibility is reasonably predictable, there are no important uncertainties concerning costs, and the equipment's carrying amount is $121,000. Prepare Moxey's September 13, 2014 journal entries.

(LO 7) BE20-11 Wing Corporation enters into a lease with Sharda Inc., a lessor, on August 15, 2014, that does not transfer ownership or contain a bargain purchase option. Both Wing and Sharda use IFRS. The lease covers three years of the equipment's eight-year useful life, and the present value of the minimum lease payments is less than 90% of the equipment's fair value. Prepare Wing's journal entry to record its August 15, 2014 annual lease payment of $31,500. Wing has a November 30 year end.

(LO 12) BE20-12 Use the information for Wing Corporation and Sharda Inc. from BE20-11. Assume that Sharda, the lessor, has a June 30 year end. Prepare Sharda's entry on August 15, 2014, and any adjusting entry needed on June 30, 2015.

(LO 9, 10) BE20-13 Lai Corporation, which uses ASPE, leased equipment that was carried at a cost of $175,000 to Swander Inc., the lessee. The term of the lease is five years, beginning January 1, 2014, with equal rental payments of $40,584 at the beginning of each year. Swander pays all executory costs directly to third parties. The equipment's fair value at the lease's inception is $175,000. The equipment has a useful life of six years with no residual value. The lease has an implicit interest rate of 8%, no bargain purchase option, and no transfer of title. Collectibility is reasonably assured, with no additional costs to be incurred by Lai. Prepare Lai Corporation's January 1, 2014 journal entries at the inception of the lease.

(LO 9, 10) BE20-14 Use the information for Lai Corporation from BE20-13. Assume that instead of costing Lai $175,000, the equipment was manufactured by Lai at a cost of $137,500 and the equipment's regular selling price is $175,000. Prepare Lai Corporation's January 1, 2014 journal entries at the inception of the lease and the entry at December 31, 2014, to record interest.

(LO 10) BE20-15 Use the information for Lai Corporation from BE20-13. Assume that the direct financing lease was recorded at a present value of $175,000. Prepare Lai's December 31, 2014 entry to record interest.

(LO 11) BE20-16 Regina Corporation, which uses ASPE, manufactures replicators. On May 29, 2014, it leased to Barnes Limited a replicator that cost $265,000 to manufacture and usually sells for $410,000. The lease agreement covers the replicator's five-year useful life and requires five equal annual rentals of $95,930 each, beginning May 29, 2014. The equipment reverts to Regina at the end of the lease, at which time it is expected that the replicator will have a residual value of $40,000, which has been guaranteed by Barnes, the lessee. An interest rate of 12% is implicit in the lease agreement. Collectibility of the rentals is reasonably assured, and there are no important uncertainties concerning costs. Prepare Regina's May 29, 2014 journal entries.

(LO 11) BE20-17 Use the information for Regina Corporation from BE20-16. Assume instead that the residual value is not guaranteed. Prepare Regina's May 29, 2014 journal entries.

(LO 14) *BE20-18 On January 1, 2014, Clark Inc. sold a piece of equipment to Daye Ltd. for $200,000, and immediately leased it back. At the time, the equipment was carried on Clark's books at a cost of $300,000, less accumulated depreciation of $120,000. The lease is a finance or capital lease to Clark, with a lease term of five years. The equipment under finance or capital lease will be depreciated in Clark's books over five years using double-declining balance depreciation. (a) Calculate the amortization of the deferred gain on sale to be recorded at the end of 2014, if Clark follows IFRS. (b) Calculate the amortization of the deferred gain on sale to be recorded at the end of 2014, if Clark follows ASPE.

(LO 14, 15) *BE20-19 On January 1, 2014, Ryan Animation Ltd., which uses IFRS, sold a truck to Letourneau Finance Corp. for $35,000 and immediately leased it back. The truck was carried on Ryan Animation's books at $53,000, net of $26,000 of accumulated depreciation. The term of the lease is five years, and title transfers to Ryan Animation at lease end. The lease requires five equal rental payments of $17,147, with each payment made at year end. The appropriate rate of interest is 10%, and the truck has a useful life of five years with no salvage value. Prepare Ryan Animation's 2014 journal entries.

(LO 15) *BE20-20 Lessee Corp. agreed to lease property from Lessor Corp. effective January 1, 2014, for an annual payment of $23,576.90, beginning January 1, 2014. The property is made up of land with a fair value of $100,000 and a two-storey office building with a fair value of $150,000 and a useful life of 20 years. The implicit interest rate is 8%, the lease term is 20 years, and title to the property is transferred to Lessee at the end of the lease term. Prepare the required entries made by Lessee Corp. on January 1, 2014, and at its year end of December 31, 2014. Both Lessee and Lessor use ASPE.

(LO 15) ***BE20-21** Use the information provided in BE20-20 about Lessee Corp. Assume that title to the property will not be transferred to Lessee by the end of the lease term and that there is also no bargain purchase option, but that the lease does meet other criteria to qualify as a capital lease. Prepare the required entries made by Lessee Corp. on January 1, 2014, and at its year end of December 31, 2014.

(LO 16) ***BE20-22** Langlois Services Inc. is using the contract-based approach to account for a lease of a truck. The lease includes a residual value guarantee at the end of the term of the lease of $16,000. Langlois estimates that the likelihood for the residual value of $16,000 has a 50% certainty. Langlois feels that there is a 30% chance that the residual value will be $12,000 and a 20% chance that it will be $10,000. Calculate the probability weighted value of the residual guarantee that needs to be included in the lease payments liability recorded by Langlois when the lease is signed.

(LO 16) ***BE20-23** On January 1, 2014, Quong Corporation (the lessee) entered into a four-year, non-cancellable equipment lease contract with Zareiga Inc. (the lessor). The present value of the minimum lease payments required was $116,025. Also at lease inception, it was estimated that the equipment's economic life was eight years, and that its fair value was $150,000. The lease does not transfer title or contain a bargain purchase option. (a) Assume that Quong follows ASPE. How should Quong classify this lease? (b) Assume that Quong follows IFRS and uses the classification approach to accounting for leases. How should Quong classify this lease? (c) Assume that Quong follows IFRS and uses the contract-based approach to accounting for leases. How should Quong account for this lease at lease inception?

Exercises

(LO 3, 5, 6) **E20-1 (Lessee Entries and Capital Lease with Unguaranteed Residual Value—Lease and Fiscal Year Differ)** On September 1, 2014, Wong Corporation, which uses ASPE, signed a five-year, non-cancellable lease for a piece of equipment. The terms of the lease called for Wong to make annual payments of $13,668 at the beginning of each lease year, starting September 1, 2014. The equipment has an estimated useful life of six years and a $9,000 unguaranteed residual value. The equipment reverts back to the lessor at the end of the lease term. Wong uses the straight-line method of depreciation for all of its plant assets, has a calendar year end, prepares adjusting journal entries at the end of the fiscal year, and does not use reversing entries. Wong's incremental borrowing rate is 10%, and the lessor's implicit rate is unknown.

Instructions

(a) Explain why this is a capital lease to Wong.

(b) Using time value of money tables, a financial calculator, or computer spreadsheet functions, calculate the present value of the minimum lease payments for the lessee.

(c) Prepare all necessary journal entries for Wong for this lease, including any year-end adjusting entries through September 1, 2015.

(d) Would this also be a capital lease if the lessee reported under IFRS?

Digging Deeper

(LO 7) **E20-2 (Lessee Entries, Operating Lease, Comparison)** Refer to the data and other information provided in E20-1. Assume that the machine has an estimated economic life of seven years and that its fair value on September 1, 2014, is $79,000.

Instructions

(a) Explain why this lease is now considered an operating lease.

(b) Prepare all necessary journal entries for Wong Corporation for this lease, including any year-end adjusting entries through December 31, 2015.

(c) Identify what accounts will appear on Wong's December 31, 2014 balance sheet and income statement relative to this lease.

(d) How would Wong's December 31, 2014 balance sheet and income statement differ from your answer to part (c) if the lease were a capital lease as described in E20-1?

(e) From the perspective of an investor, discuss the effect of accounting for this lease as an operating lease rather than as a capital lease.

Digging Deeper

(LO 3, 5, 6) **E20-3 (Lessee Calculations and Entries; Capital Lease with Guaranteed Residual Value)** New Bay Corporation leases an automobile with a fair value of $21,500 from Simon Motors, Inc. on the following lease terms:

1. It is a non-cancellable term of 55 months.

2. The rental is $425 per month at the end of each month (the present value at 1% per month is $17,910).

3. The estimated residual value after 55 months is $2,500 (the present value at 1% per month is $1,446). New Bay Corporation guarantees the residual value of $2,500.

4. The automobile's estimated economic life is 72 months.

5. New Bay Corporation's incremental borrowing rate is 12% a year (1% a month). Simon's implicit rate is unknown.

Instructions

(a) Assuming that New Bay Corporation reports under ASPE, explain why this is a capital lease.

(b) What is the present value of the minimum lease payments for New Bay?

(c) Record the lease on New Bay Corporation's books at the date of inception.

(d) Record the first month's depreciation on New Bay Corporation's books (assume the straight-line depreciation method).

(e) Record the first month's lease payment.

(f) Would this lease be considered a capital lease if the company reported under IFRS?

(LO 3, 5, 6, 8) **E20-4 (Lessee Entries; Finance Lease with Executory Costs and Unguaranteed Residual Value)** On January 1, 2014, Fine Corp., which uses IFRS, signs a 10-year, non-cancellable lease agreement to lease a specialty loom from Sheffield Corporation. The following information concerns the lease agreement.

1. The agreement requires equal rental payments of $73,580 beginning on January 1, 2014.

2. The loom's fair value on January 1, 2014, is $450,000.

3. The loom has an estimated economic life of 12 years, with an unguaranteed residual value of $12,000. Fine Corp. depreciates similar equipment using the straight-line method.

4. The lease is non-renewable. At the termination of the lease, the loom reverts to the lessor.

5. Fine's incremental borrowing rate is 12% per year. The lessor's implicit rate is not known by Fine Corp.

6. The yearly rental payment includes $2,470.29 of executory costs related to insurance on the loom.

Instructions

(a) Prepare an amortization schedule for the term of the lease to be used by Fine. Use a computer spreadsheet.

(b) Prepare the journal entries on Fine Corp.'s books to reflect the signing of the lease agreement and to record the payments and expenses related to this lease for the years 2014 and 2015 as well as any adjusting journal entries at its fiscal year ends of December 31, 2014, and 2015.

(c) Prepare Fine Corp.'s required note disclosure on the lease for the fiscal year ending December 31, 2015.

(LO 3, 5, 6) E20-5 (Lessee Entries; Finance Lease with Executory Costs and Unguaranteed Residual Value—Lease and Fiscal Years Differ)

Instructions

Refer to the data and other information provided in E20-4, but now assume that Fine's fiscal year end is May 31. Prepare the journal entries on Fine Corp.'s books to reflect the lease signing and to record payments and expenses related to this lease for the calendar years 2014 and 2015. Fine does not prepare reversing entries.

(LO 3, 5, 6, 11, 13) E20-6 (Type of Lease, Lessee Entries with Bargain Purchase Option) The following facts are for a non-cancellable lease agreement between Hebert Corporation and Russell Corporation, a lessee:

Inception date	July 1, 2014
Annual lease payment due at the beginning of each year, starting July 1, 2014	$20,066.26
Bargain purchase option price at end of lease term	$ 4,500.00
Lease term	5 years
Economic life of leased equipment	10 years
Lessor's cost	$60,000.00
Fair value of asset at July 1, 2014	$88,000.00
Lessor's implicit rate	9%
Lessee's incremental borrowing rate	9%

The collectibility of the lease payments is reasonably predictable, and there are no important uncertainties about costs that have not yet been incurred by the lessor. The lessee assumes responsibility for all executory costs. Both Russell and Hebert use ASPE.

Instructions

Answer the following, rounding all numbers to the nearest cent.

(a) Discuss the nature of this lease to Russell Corporation, the lessee.

(b) Discuss the nature of this lease to Hebert Corporation, the lessor.

(c) Prepare a lease amortization schedule for the lease obligation using a computer spreadsheet for Russell Corporation for the five-year lease term.

(d) Prepare the journal entries on the lessee's books to reflect the signing of the lease and to record the payments and expenses related to this lease for the years 2014 and 2015. Russell's annual accounting period ends on December 31, and Russell does not use reversing entries.

(e) Discuss the differences, if any, in the classification of the lease to Russell Corporation (the lessee) or to Hebert Corporation (the lessor) if both were using IFRS in their financial reporting.

(LO 6, 9, 10, 11) **E20-7 (Lessor Entries with Bargain Purchase Option)** A lease agreement between Hebert Corporation and Russell Corporation is described in E20-6.

Instructions

Provide the following for Hebert Corporation, the lessor, rounding all numbers to the nearest cent.

(a) Calculate the amount of gross investment at the inception of the lease.

(b) Calculate the amount of net investment at the inception of the lease.

(c) Prepare a lease amortization schedule using a computer spreadsheet for Hebert Corporation for the five-year lease term.

(d) Prepare the journal entries to reflect the signing of the lease and to record the receipts and income related to this lease for the years 2014, 2015, and 2016. The lessor's accounting period ends on December 31, and Hebert Corporation does not use reversing entries.

(LO 3, 5, 8) **E20-8 (Lessee Calculations and Entries; Capital Lease; Disclosure)** On December 31, 2014, Xu Ltd., which uses ASPE, entered into an eight-year lease agreement for a conveyor machine. Annual lease payments are $28,500 at the beginning of each lease year, which ends December 31, and Xu made the first payment on January 1, 2015. At the end of the lease, the machine will revert to the lessor. However, conveyor machines are only expected to last for eight years and have no residual value. At the time of the lease agreement, conveyor machines could be purchased for approximately $166,000 cash. Equivalent financing for the machine could have been obtained from Xu's bank at 10.5%. Xu's fiscal year coincides with the calendar year and Xu uses straight-line depreciation for its conveyor machines.

Instructions

(a) Calculate the present value of the minimum lease payments using a financial calculator or work sheet functions.

(b) Explain why this is a capital lease to Xu Ltd. Document your calculations in arriving at your explanation.

(c) Prepare an amortization schedule for the term of the lease to be used by Xu Ltd. Use a computer spreadsheet.

(d) Prepare the journal entries on Xu Ltd.'s books to reflect the signing of the lease agreement and to record the payments and expenses related to this lease for the years 2015 and 2016 as well as any adjusting journal entries at its fiscal year ends of December 31, 2015, and 2016.

(e) Prepare a partial comparative balance sheet at December 31, 2016, and 2015, for all of the accounts related to this lease for Xu Ltd. Be specific about the classifications that should be used.

(f) Provide Xu Ltd.'s required note disclosure concerning the lease for the fiscal year ending December 31, 2016.

(g) What is the significance of the difference between the amount of the present value of the minimum lease payments calculated in part (a) and the approximate selling price of the machine of $166,000?

Digging Deeper

(LO 3, 5, 8) **E20-9 (Amortization Schedule and Journal Entries for Lessee)** Oakridge Leasing Corporation, which uses ASPE, signs an agreement on January 1, 2014, to lease equipment to LeBlanc Limited. The following information relates to the agreement.

1. The term of the non-cancellable lease is five years, with no renewal option. The equipment has an estimated economic life of six years.

2. The asset's fair value at January 1, 2014, is $80,000.

3. The asset will revert to the lessor at the end of the lease term, at which time the asset is expected to have a residual value of $7,000, which is not guaranteed.

4. LeBlanc Limited assumes direct responsibility for all executory costs, which include the following annual amounts: $900 to Rocky Mountain Insurance Corporation for insurance and $1,600 to James County for property taxes.

5. The agreement requires equal annual rental payments of $18,142.95 to the lessor, beginning on January 1, 2014.

6. The lessee's incremental borrowing rate is 11%. The lessor's implicit rate is 10% and is known to the lessee.

7. LeBlanc Limited uses the straight-line depreciation method for all equipment.

8. LeBlanc uses reversing entries when appropriate.

Instructions

Answer the following, rounding all numbers to the nearest cent.

(a) Use a computer spreadsheet to prepare an amortization schedule for LeBlanc Limited for the lease term.

(b) Prepare all of LeBlanc's journal entries for 2014 and 2015 to record the lease agreement, the lease payments, and all expenses related to this lease. Assume that the lessee's annual accounting period ends on December 31.

(c) Provide the required note disclosure for LeBlanc Limited concerning the lease for the fiscal year ending December 31, 2015.

(d) Would this lease be considered a capital lease if the company reported under IFRS? Would the note disclosure required in (c) above need to be modified under IFRS?

(LO 3, 5, 9, 10, 13) **E20-10 (Lease Payment Calculation and Lessee-Lessor Entries—Capital/Manufacturer/Dealer or Sales-Type Lease)** On January 1, 2014, Lavery Corporation leased equipment to Flynn Corporation. Both Lavery and Flynn use ASPE and have calendar year ends. The following information pertains to this lease.

1. The term of the non-cancellable lease is six years, with no renewal option. The equipment reverts to the lessor at the termination of the lease, at which time it is expected to have a residual value (not guaranteed) of $6,000. Flynn Corporation depreciates all its equipment on a straight-line basis.

2. Equal rental payments are due on January 1 of each year, beginning in 2014.

3. The equipment's fair value on January 1, 2014, is $144,000 and its cost to Lavery is $111,000.

4. The equipment has an economic life of seven years.

5. Lavery set the annual rental to ensure a 9% rate of return. Flynn's incremental borrowing rate is 10% and the lessor's implicit rate is unknown to the lessee.

6. Collectibility of lease payments is reasonably predictable and there are no important uncertainties about any unreimbursable costs that have not yet been incurred by the lessor.

Instructions

(a) Explain clearly why this lease is a capital lease to Flynn and a manufacturer/dealer or sales-type lease to Lavery.

(b) Using time value of money tables, a financial calculator, or computer spreadsheet functions, calculate the amount of the annual rental payment.

(c) Prepare all necessary journal entries for Flynn for 2014.

(d) Prepare all necessary journal entries for Lavery for 2014.

(e) Discuss the differences, if any, in the classification of the lease to Lavery Corporation (the lessor) or to Flynn Corporation (the lessee) if both were using IFRS.

(LO 3, 5, 9, 13) **E20-11 (Type of Lease and Amortization Schedule)** Victoria Leasing Corporation, which uses ASPE, leases a new machine that has a cost and fair value of $95,000 to Black Corporation on a three-year, non-cancellable contract. Black Corporation agrees to assume all risks of normal ownership, including such costs as insurance, taxes, and maintenance. The machine has a three-year useful life and no residual value. The lease was signed on January 1, 2014, and Victoria Leasing Corporation expects to earn a 9% return on its investment. The annual rentals are payable on each December 31, beginning December 31, 2014. Black Corporation has an excellent credit rating and so Victoria Leasing is reasonably assured of the collections under the lease.

Instructions

(a) Discuss the nature of the lease arrangement and the accounting method that each party to the lease should apply.

(b) Provide a calculation proving the relationship between the annual lease payment and the present value of minimum lease payments.

(c) Use a computer spreadsheet to prepare an amortization schedule that would be suitable for both the lessor and the lessee and that covers all the years involved.

(d) Discuss the differences, if any, in the classification of the lease to Victoria Leasing Corporation (the lessor) or to Black Corporation (the lessee) if both were using IFRS in their financial reporting.

(LO 3, 7) E20-12 (Operating Lease versus Capital Lease) You are a senior auditor auditing the December 31, 2014 financial statements of Deng, Inc., a manufacturer of novelties and party favours and a user of ASPE. During your inspection of the company garage, you discovered that a 2013 Shirk automobile is parked in the company garage but is not listed in the equipment subsidiary ledger. You ask the plant manager about the vehicle, and she tells you that the company did not list the automobile because the company was only leasing it. The lease agreement was entered into on January 1, 2014, with Quick Deal New and Used Cars. You decide to review the lease agreement to ensure that the lease should be given operating lease treatment, and you discover the following lease terms.

1. It is a non-cancellable term of 50 months.
2. The rental is $220 per month at the end of each month. (The present value at 1% per month is $8,623.)
3. The estimated residual value after 50 months is $2,100. (The present value at 1% per month is $1,277.) Deng guarantees the residual value of $2,100.
4. The automobile's estimated economic life is 60 months.
5. Deng's incremental borrowing rate is 12% per year (1% per month).

Instructions

Write a memo to your supervisor, the audit partner in charge of this audit, to discuss the situation. Be sure to include the following:

(a) why you inspected the lease agreement,

(b) what you determined about the lease, and

(c) how you advised your client to account for this lease.

Explain every journal entry that you believe is necessary to record this lease properly on the client's books.

(LO 3, E20-13 (IFRS versus Contract-Based Lease and Journal Entries for Lessee) Cuomo Mining Corporation, a 7, 16) public company whose stock trades on the Toronto Stock Exchange, uses IFRS. The vice-president of finance has asked you, the assistant controller, to prepare a comparison of the company's current accounting of a lease with the contract-based approach, which is expected to be implemented in the near future. The lease you are going to use for this comparison was signed by Cuomo on April 1, 2014, with Bertrand Ltd. for a piece of excavation equipment. The following information relates to the agreement.

1. The term of the non-cancellable lease is three years, with a renewal option of one additional year at the annual rate of 125% of the initial payment. The equipment has an estimated economic life of 10 years.

2. The asset's fair value at April 1, 2014, is approximately $1 million.

3. The asset will revert to Bertrand at the end of the initial term of the lease, or at the end of the renewal period should Cuomo exercise that option. The excavation equipment is expected to have a fair value of $600,000 on March 31, 2016, and $500,000 on March 31, 2017, which is not guaranteed.

4. Cuomo assumes direct responsibility for all executory costs for excavation equipment.

5. The initial term of the lease agreement requires equal annual rental payments of $135,000 to Bertrand, beginning on April 1, 2014.

6. The lessee's incremental borrowing rate is 9%. Bertrand's implicit rate is 8% and is known to Cuomo.

7. Cuomo has a calendar year end.

You have established that it has always been Cuomo's intention to exercise the renewal period on account of the nature of the asset. Cuomo's operations manager says that there is a 70% chance that the renewal period will be exercised.

Instructions

Answer the following, rounding all numbers to the nearest dollar.

Part 1

Using the current accounting under IFRS:

(a) Determine the accounting treatment of the lease agreement and obligation to Cuomo. What were the conditions that would need to be in place for the lease to be classified as a finance lease?

(b) Record all transactions concerning the lease for Cuomo for the fiscal year 2014.

*Part 2

Using the proposed contract-based approach:

(c) Determine the amount of the liability for lease payments at the signing of the lease.

(d) Use a computer spreadsheet to prepare an amortization schedule for Cuomo for the lease term including the expected lease renewal.

(e) Prepare all of Cuomo's journal entries for fiscal years 2014 and 2015 to record the lease agreement and the lease payments.

Part 3

Prepare a table of Cuomo's statement of financial position disclosure of all of the amounts that would appear concerning the right and the liability at December 31, 2015. Follow with the statement of income disclosure for the fiscal year ending December 31, 2015. Be specific concerning classifications. Include a second column to show the amounts Cuomo reports for the same period following IFRS.

(LO 5, 9, 10) E20-14 (Calculation of Rental, Amortization Table, Journal Entries for Lessor—Lease and Fiscal Year Differ) Zoppas Leasing Corporation, which has a fiscal year end of October 31 and uses IFRS, signs an agreement on January 1, 2014, to lease equipment to Irvine Limited. The following information relates to the agreement.

1. The term of the non-cancellable lease is six years, with no renewal option. The equipment has an estimated economic life of eight years.

2. The asset's cost to Zoppas, the lessor, is $305,000. The asset's fair value at January 1, 2014, is $305,000.

3. The asset will revert to the lessor at the end of the lease term, at which time the asset is expected to have a residual value of $45,626, which is not guaranteed.

4. Irvine Limited, the lessee, assumes direct responsibility for all executory costs.

5. The agreement requires equal annual rental payments, beginning on January 1, 2014.

6. Collectibility of the lease payments is reasonably predictable. There are no important uncertainties about costs that have not yet been incurred by the lessor.

Instructions

Answer the following, rounding all numbers to the nearest dollar.

(a) Assuming that Zoppas Leasing desires a 10% rate of return on its investment, use time value of money tables, a financial calculator, or computer spreadsheet functions to calculate the amount of the annual rental payment that is required.

(b) Prepare an amortization schedule using a computer spreadsheet that would be suitable for the lessor for the lease term.

(c) Prepare all of the journal entries for the lessor for 2014 and 2015 to record the lease agreement, the receipt of lease payments, and the recognition of income. Assume that Zoppas prepares adjusting journal entries only at the end of the fiscal year.

(LO 5, 9, E20-15 (Lessor Entries, Determination of Type of Lease, Lease Payment Calculation, Spreadsheet 10, 11) Application, Financial Statement Amounts) Turpin Corp., which uses ASPE, leases a car to Jaimne DeLory on June 1, 2014. The term of the non-cancellable lease is 48 months. The following information is provided about the lease.

1. The lessee is given an option to purchase the automobile at the end of the lease term for $5,000.

2. The automobile's fair value on June 1, 2014, is $29,500. It is carried in Turpin's inventory at $21,200.

3. The car has an economic life of seven years, with a $1,000 residual value at the end of that time. The car's estimated fair value is $10,000 after four years, with a $1,000 residual value at the end of that time. The car's estimated fair value is $10,000 after four years, $7,000 after five years, and $2,500 after six years.

4. Turpin wants to earn a 12% rate of return (1% per month) on any financing transactions.

5. Jaimne DeLory represents a reasonable credit risk and no future costs are anticipated in relation to this lease.

6. The lease agreement calls for a $1,000 down payment on June 1, 2014, and 48 equal monthly payments on the first of each month, beginning June 1, 2014.

Instructions

(a) Determine the amount of the monthly lease payment using present value tables, a financial calculator, or computer spreadsheet functions. Round to the nearest cent.

(b) What type of lease is this to Turpin Corp.? Explain.

(c) Prepare a lease amortization schedule for the 48-month lease term using a computer spreadsheet.

(d) Prepare the entries that are required, if any, on December 31, 2014, Turpin's fiscal year end.

(e) How much income will Turpin report on its 2014 income statement relative to this lease?

(f) What is the net investment in the lease to be reported on the December 31, 2014 statement of financial position? How much is reported in current assets? In non-current assets?

(LO 5, 10, 11) E20-16 (Lessor Entries, Financing Lease with Option to Purchase, Lessee Capitalizable Amount) Castle Leasing Corporation, which uses IFRS, signs a lease agreement on January 1, 2014, to lease electronic equipment to Wai Corporation, which also uses IFRS. The term of the non-cancelable lease is two years and payments are required at the end of each year. The following information relates to this agreement.

1. Wai Corporation has the option to purchase the equipment for $13,000 upon the termination of the lease.

2. The equipment has a cost and fair value of $135,000 to Castle Leasing Corporation. The useful economic life is two years, with a residual value of $13,000.

3. Wai Corporation is required to pay $5,000 each year to the lessor for executory costs.

4. Castle Leasing Corporation wants to earn a return of 10% on its investment.

5. Collectibility of the payments is reasonably predictable, and there are no important uncertainties surrounding the costs that have not yet been incurred by the lessor.

Instructions

(a) Using time value of money tables, a financial calculator, or computer spreadsheet functions, calculate the lease payment that Castle Leasing would require from Wai Corporation.

(b) What classification will Wai Corporation give to the lease? What classification will be given to the lease by Castle Leasing Corporation?

(c) What classification would be adopted by Wai Corporation and Castle Leasing Corporation had they both been using ASPE?

(d) Prepare a lease amortization table for Castle Leasing for the term of the lease.

(e) Prepare the journal entries on Castle Leasing's books to reflect the payments received under the lease and to recognize income for the years 2014 and 2015.

(f) Assuming that Wai Corporation exercises its option to purchase the equipment on December 31, 2015, prepare the journal entry to reflect the sale on Castle Leasing's books.

(g) What amount would Wai Corporation capitalize and recognize as a liability on signing the lease? Explain.

(LO 5, 10, 11) E20-17 (Rental Amount Calculation, Lessor Entries, Disclosure—Financing Lease with Unguaranteed Residual Value) On January 1, 2014, Vick Leasing Inc., a lessor that uses IFRS, signed an agreement with Rock Corporation, a lessee, for the use of a compression system. The system cost $415,000 and was purchased from Manufacturing Solutions Ltd. specifically for Rock Corporation. Annual payments are made each January 1 by Rock. In addition to making the lease payment, Rock also reimburses Vick $4,000 each January 1 for a portion of the maintenance expenditures, which cost Vick Leasing a total of $6,000 per year. At the end of the five-year agreement, the compression equipment will revert to Vick and is expected to have a residual value of $25,000, which is not guaranteed. Collectibility of the rentals is reasonably predictable, and there are no important uncertainties surrounding the costs that have not yet been incurred by Vick Leasing Inc.

Instructions

(a) Assume that Vick Leasing Inc. has a required rate of return of 8%. Calculate the amount of the lease payments that would be needed to generate this return on the agreement if payments were made each:

1. January 1   2. December 31

(b) Use a computer spreadsheet to prepare an amortization table that shows how the lessor's net investment in the lease receivable will be reduced over the lease term if payments are made each:

1. January 1   2. December 31

(c) Assume that the payments are due each January 1. Prepare all journal entries and adjusting journal entries for 2014 and 2015 for the lessor, assuming that Vick has a calendar year end. Include the payment for the purchase of the equipment for leasing in your entries and the annual payment for maintenance.

(d) Provide the note disclosure concerning the lease that would be required for Vick Leasing Inc. at December 31, 2015. Assume that payments are due each January 1.

(LO 7, 8, 12) E20-18 (Accounting and Disclosure for an Operating Lease—Lessee and Lessor) On May 1, 2014, a machine was purchased for $1,750,000 by Pomeroy Corp. The machine is expected to have an eight-year life with no salvage value and is to be depreciated on a straight-line basis. The machine was leased to St. Isidor Inc. on May 1, 2014, at an annual rental of $480,000. Other relevant information is as follows.

1. The lease term is three years.

2. Pomeroy Corp. incurred maintenance and other executory costs of $61,000 for the fiscal year ending December 31, 2014, related to this lease.

3. The machine could have been sold by Pomeroy Corp. for $1,850,000 instead of leasing it.

4. St. Isidor is required to pay a rent security deposit of $65,000 and to prepay the last month's rent of $40,000 on signing the lease.

5. Both Pomeroy and St. Isidor use IFRS.

Instructions

(a) How much should Pomeroy Corp. report as income before income tax on this lease for 2014?

(b) What amount should St. Isidor Inc. report for rent expense for 2014 on this lease?

(c) What financial statement disclosures relative to this lease are required for each company's December 31, 2014 year end assuming ASPE had been used for each company?

(d) What additional disclosures, if any, apply if both companies use IFRS?

(LO 7, 12) E20-19 (Accounting for an Operating Lease—Lease and Fiscal Year Differ) On July 1, 2014, Morrison Corp. leased a building to Wisen Inc. Both companies use IFRS. The relevant information on the lease is as follows.

1. The lease arrangement is for 10 years.

2. The leased building cost $5.5 million and was purchased by Morrison for cash on July 1, 2014.

3. The building is depreciated on a straight-line basis. Its estimated economic life is 40 years.

4. Lease payments are $325,000 per year and are made at the end of the lease year, and so the first lease payment was made June 30, 2015.

5. Property tax expense of $57,000 and insurance expense of $11,000 on the building were incurred by Morrison for the 2014 fiscal year. Payment for these two items was made on July 1, 2014.

6. Both the lessor and the lessee have their fiscal years on a calendar-year basis.

Instructions

(a) Prepare the journal entries and any year-end adjusting journal entries made by Morrison Corp. in 2014.

(b) Prepare the journal entries and any year-end adjusting journal entries made by Wisen Inc. in 2014.

(c) If Morrison paid $30,000 to a real estate broker on July 1, 2014, as a fee for finding the lessee, how much should Morrison Corp. report as an expense for this fee item in 2014?

(d) Would any of the accounting treatment you have provided in parts (a) through (c) above change if Morrison had been using ASPE?

Digging Deeper

(LO 9, 10) E20-20 (Lessor Entries—Manufacturer/Dealer or Sale Type Lease) Pucci Corporation, a machinery dealer whose stock trades on the Toronto Stock Exchange, and so uses IFRS, leased a machine to Ernst Corporation on January 1, 2014. The lease is for a six-year period and requires equal annual payments of $24,736 at the beginning of each year. The first payment is received on January 1, 2014. Pucci had purchased the machine during 2013 for $99,000. Collectibility of lease payments is reasonably predictable, and no important uncertainties exist about costs that have not yet been incurred by Pucci. Pucci set the annual rental amount to ensure an 8% rate of return. The machine has an economic life of six years, with no residual value, and reverts to Pucci at the termination of the lease.

Instructions

(a) Using time value of money tables, a financial calculator, or computer spreadsheet functions, calculate the amount of each of the following:

1. Gross investment

2. Unearned interest income

3. Net investment in the lease

(b) Prepare all necessary journal entries for Pucci for 2014.

(LO 12) E20-21 (Operating Lease for Lessee and Lessor with Initial Costs) On February 20, 2014, Sigouin Inc. purchased a machine for $1.6 million for the purpose of leasing it. The machine is expected to have a 10-year life with no residual value, and will be depreciated on the straight-line basis. The machine was leased to Densmore Corporation on March 1, 2014, for a four-year period at a monthly rental of $26,500. There is no provision for the renewal of the lease or purchase of the machine by the lessee at the expiration of the lease term. Sigouin paid $36,000 to a third party for commissions associated with negotiating the lease in February 2014. Both Sigouin Inc. and Densmore Corporation use ASPE.

Instructions

(a) What expense should Densmore Corporation record based on the above facts for the year ended December 31, 2014? Show supporting calculations in good form.

(b) What income or loss before income tax should Sigouin record based on the above facts for the year ended December 31, 2014?

(c) Would your answer to parts (a) and (b) above be different if both companies used IFRS?

(AICPA adapted)

(LO 14) ***E20-22 (Sale-Leaseback—Lessee and Lessor Entries)** On January 1, 2014, Hein Corporation sells equipment to Liquidity Finance Corp. for $720,000 and immediately leases the equipment back. Both Hein and Liquidity use ASPE. Other relevant information is as follows.

1. The equipment's carrying value on Hein's books on January 1, 2014, is $640,000.

2. The term of the non-cancellable lease is 10 years. Title will transfer to Hein at the end of the lease.

3. The lease agreement requires equal rental payments of $117,176.68 at the end of each year.

4. The incremental borrowing rate of Hein Corporation is 12%. Hein is aware that Liquidity Finance Corp. set the annual rental to ensure a rate of return of 10%.

5. The equipment has a fair value of $720,000 on January 1, 2014, and an estimated economic life of 10 years, with no residual value.

6. Hein pays executory costs of $11,000 per year directly to appropriate third parties.

Instructions

(a) Prepare the journal entries for both the lessee and the lessor for 2014 to reflect the sale and leaseback agreement. No uncertainties exist and collectibility is reasonably certain.

(b) What is Hein's primary objective in entering a sale-leaseback arrangement with Liquidity Finance Corp.? Would you consider this transaction to be a red flag to creditors, demonstrating that Hein is in financial difficulty?

(LO 14) ***E20-23 (Lessee-Lessor, Sale-Leaseback)** Presented below are four independent situations. All the companies involved use ASPE.

1. On December 31, 2014, Zarle Inc. sold equipment to Orfanakos Corp. and immediately leased it back for 10 years. The equipment's selling price was $520,000, its carrying amount $400,000, and its estimated remaining economic life 12 years.

2. On December 31, 2014, Tessier Corp. sold a machine to Cross Ltd. and simultaneously leased it back for one year. The machine's selling price was $480,000, its carrying amount was $420,000, and it had an estimated remaining useful life of 14 years. The rental payments' present value for one year is $35,000.

3. On January 1, 2014, McKane Corp. sold an airplane with an estimated useful life of 10 years. At the same time, McKane leased back the plane for 10 years. The airplane's selling price was $500,000, the carrying amount $379,000, and the annual rental $73,975.22. McKane Corp. intends to depreciate the leased asset using the straight-line depreciation method.

4. On January 1, 2014, Barnes Corp. sold equipment with an estimated useful life of five years. At the same time, Barnes leased back the equipment for two years under a lease classified as an operating lease. The equipment's selling price (fair value) was $212,700, the carrying amount was $300,000, the monthly rental under the lease was $6,000, and the rental payments' present value was $115,753.

Instructions

(a) For situation 1: Determine the amount of unearned profit to be reported by Zarle Inc. from the equipment sale on December 31, 2014.

(b) For situation 2: At December 31, 2014, how much should Tessier report as unearned profit from the sale of the machine?

(c) For situation 3: Discuss how the gain on the sale should be reported by McKane at the end of 2014 in the financial statements.

Digging Deeper

(d) For situation 4: For the year ended December 31, 2014, identify the items that would be reported on Barness's income statement related to the sale-leaseback transaction.

(LO 14) *E20-24 (Land Lease, Lessee and Lessor) On September 15, 2014, Local Camping Products Limited, the lessee, entered into a 20-year lease with Sullivan Corp. to rent a parcel of land at a rate of $30,000 per year. Both Local and Sullivan use ASPE. The annual rental is due in advance each September 15, beginning in 2014. The land has a current fair value of $195,000. The land reverts to Sullivan at the end of the lease. Local Camping's incremental borrowing rate and Sullivan's implicit interest rate are both 8%.

Instructions

(a) Prepare Local Camping Products' required journal entries on September 15, 2014, and at December 31, 2014, its year end.

(b) Explain how and why these entries might differ if Local were leasing equipment instead of land.

(c) Prepare the entries required on Sullivan's books at September 15, 2014, and at December 31, 2014, its year end.

(LO 15) *E20-25 (Real Estate Lease) Rancour Ltd., which uses ASPE, recently expanded its operations into an adjoining municipality and, on March 30, 2014, signed a 15-year lease with its Municipal Industrial Commission (MIC). The property has a total fair value of $150,000 on March 30, 2014, with one third of the amount attributable to the land and two thirds to the building. The land is expected to double in value over the next 15 years, while the building will depreciate by 60%. The lease includes a purchase option at the end of the lease that allows Rancour to receive title to the property for a payment of $90,000.

Rancour is required to make rental payments of $10,000 annually, with the first payment due March 30, 2014. The MIC's implicit interest rate, known to all, is 7%. The building's economic life is estimated at 20 years, at which time it will have a small residual value of $10,000.

Instructions

(a) Prepare the entries required by Rancour on the signing of the lease and the payment of the first lease payment.

(b) Assuming that Rancour's year end is December 31, prepare the entries that are required on December 31, 2014; March 30, 2015; and December 31, 2015. Rancour does not use reversing entries.

Problems

P20-1 Interior Design Inc. (ID) is a privately owned business that produces interior decorating options for consumers. ID has chosen to follow ASPE. The software that it purchased 10 years ago to present clients with designs that are unique to their offices is no longer state-of-the-art, and ID is faced with making a decision on the replacement of its software. The company has two options:

1. Enter into a lease agreement with Precision Inc. whereby ID makes an upfront lease payment of $12,000 on January 1, 2015, and annual payments of $4,500 over the next five years on each December 31. At the end of the lease, ID has the option to buy the software for $5,000. The first annual lease payment is on December 31, 2015.

2. Enter into a lease agreement with Graphic Design Inc. on January 1, 2015, whereby ID makes five annual lease payments of $6,500, beginning on January 1, 2015. ID may purchase the software at the end of the lease period for $200. This is considered a bargain price compared with the offer of $5,000 in the proposal from Precision Inc.

Under both options, the software will require annual upgrades that are expected to cost $1,500 per year. These upgrade costs are in addition to the lease payments that are required under the two independent options. As this additional cost is the same under both options, ID has decided to ignore it in making its choice.

The Precision agreement requires a licensing fee of $1,000 to be renewed annually. If ID decides on the Precision option, the licensing fee will be included in the annual lease payment of $4,500. Both Precision Inc. and Graphic Design Inc. offer software programs of similar quality and ease in use, and both provide adequate support. The software under each offer is expected to be used for up to eight years, although this depends to some extent on technological advances in future years. Both offers are equivalent in terms of the product and service.

It is now early October 2014, and ID hopes to have the software in place by its fiscal year end of December 31, 2014. ID is currently working on preparing its third-quarter financial statements, which its bank is particularly interested in seeing in order to ensure that ID is respecting its debt to equity ratio covenant in its loan agreement with the bank. The interest rate on the bank loan, which is ID's only source of external financing, is 10% per year. ID would have preferred to be in a position where it could buy rather than lease the software, but the anticipated purchase price of $30,000 exceeds the limits that the bank set for ID's borrowing.

Instructions

(a) Discuss the nature of the lease arrangement under each of the two lease options offered to Interior Design and the corresponding accounting treatment that should be applied.

(b) Prepare all necessary journal entries and adjusting journal entries for Interior Design under the Precision Inc. option, from lease inception on January 1, 2015, through to December 31, 2015 excluding the $1,500 annual upgrade.

(c) Prepare an amortization schedule using a computer spreadsheet that would be suitable for the lease term in the Graphic Design Inc. option.

(d) Prepare all necessary journal entries and adjusting journal entries for Interior Design under Graphic Design's option, from lease inception on January 1, 2015, through to January 1, 2016 excluding the $1,500 annual upgrade.

(e) Summarize and contrast the effects on Interior Design's financial statements for the year ending December 31, 2015, using the entries prepared in parts (b) and (d) above. Include in your summary the total differential cash outflows that would be made by Interior Design during 2015 under each option.

(f) Discuss the qualitative considerations that should enter into Interior Design's decision on which lease to sign. Which lease do you think will most likely be chosen by Interior Design? Why?

(g) What are the long-term and short-term implications of the choice between these two options? How do these implications support the direction in which GAAP is headed in the future concerning the accounting for leases?

Digging Deeper

P20-2 You have just been hired as the new controller of SWT Services Inc., and on the top of the stack of papers on your new desk is a bundle of draft contracts with a note attached. The note says, "Please help me to understand which of these leases would be best for our situation." The note is signed by the president of SWT Services Inc. You have reviewed the proposed contracts and asked a few questions. In the process, you have become aware that the company is facing a large cutback in capital spending to deal with the effect of competition in the industry. A new customer service system that is heavily IT based is critical in meeting the challenge head on. In order to meet this commitment, you need to identify the lease that will have the lowest total cost in the coming year and overall. As well, you will need to address the cash demands of each choice. The leases are for telecommunications and computer equipment and software. The following information is available.

Lease One: The equipment and software has a fair value of $487,694 and an expected life of six years. The lease has a five-year term. Annual rent is paid each January 1, beginning in 2014, in the amount of $104,300. The implicit rate of the lease is not known by SWT. Insurance and operating costs of $23,500 are to be paid directly by SWT to the lessor in addition to the lease payments. At the end of the lease term, the equipment will revert to the lessor, who will be able to sell it for $85,000. If the lessor is unable to sell the equipment for this amount, SWT will be required to make up the difference. SWT will likely purchase the equipment for $85,000 if any payments are required under this clause of the lease.

Lease Two: The equipment and software have a fair value of $444,404 and an expected life of seven years. The lease has a five-year term beginning January 1, 2014, with a two-year renewal period. Annual lease payments are made beginning December 31, 2014, in the amount of $137,500. This lease has an implicit rate of 8%. Insurance and operating costs of $26,500 are included in the lease payment. At the end of the initial lease term, the equipment can be leased for another two years for $27,500 per year, including insurance and operating costs, and then at the end of that two-year period, the equipment will belong to SWT.

SWT uses ASPE and has a December year end. SWT's incremental borrowing rate is 10%.

Instructions

(a) Prepare a memo to the president explaining which lease will have the lowest cost in the initial year of the lease and overall cost for the full term of the lease, including any renewal period for Lease Two. Include in your analysis a comparison of the cash flow requirement under each option for the term of the lease including any renewal option.

(b) Which lease do you recommend the company sign, assuming both will meet the company's requirements and the equipment proposed in both leases is similar? Bring as many arguments to your recommendation as possible to allow the president to be fully advised of the factors leading to your recommendation.

P20-3 On January 1, 2014, Hunter Ltd. entered into an agreement to lease a truck from Situ Ltd. Both Hunter and Situ use IFRS. The details of the agreement are as follows:

Carrying value of truck for Situ Ltd.	$20,691
Fair value of truck	$20,691
Economic life of truck	5 years
Lease term	3 years
Rental payments (at beginning of each month)	$620
Executory costs included in rental payments each month for insurance	$20
Incremental borrowing rate for Hunter Ltd.	12%
Hunter Ltd. guarantees Situ Ltd. that at the end of the lease term Situ Ltd. will realize $3,500 from selling the truck	

Additional information:

1. There are no abnormal risks associated with the collection of lease payments from Hunter.

2. There are no additional unreimbursable costs to be incurred by Situ in connection with the leased truck.

3. At the end of the lease term, Situ sold the truck to a third party for $3,200, which was the truck's fair value at December 31, 2013. Hunter paid Situ the difference between the guaranteed residual value of $3,500 and the proceeds obtained on the resale.

4. Hunter knows the interest rate that is implicit in the lease.

5. Hunter knows the amount of executory costs included in the minimum lease payments.

6. Hunter uses straight-line depreciation for its trucks.

Instructions

(a) Discuss the nature of this lease for both Hunter Ltd. (the lessee) and Situ Ltd. (the lessor).

(b) Assume that the effective interest of 12% had not been provided in the data. Prove the effective interest rate of 12% using a financial calculator or computer spreadsheet function.

(c) Prepare a lease amortization schedule for the full term of the lease using a computer spreadsheet.

(d) Prepare the journal entries that Hunter would make on January 1, 2014, and 2015, and any year-end adjusting journal entries at December 31, 2014, related to the lease arrangement, assuming that Hunter does not use reversing entries.

(e) Identify all accounts that will be reported by Hunter Ltd. on its comparative statement of financial position at December 31, 2015, and 2014, and comparative income statement for the fiscal years ending December 31, 2015, and 2014. Include all the necessary note disclosures on the transactions related to this lease for Hunter and be specific about the classifications in each statement.

(f) Prepare the journal entry for Hunter's payment on December 31, 2016, to Situ to settle the guaranteed residual value deficiency. Assume that no accruals for interest have been recorded as yet during 2016, but that the 2016 depreciation expense for the truck has been recorded.

(g) Prepare Hunter's partial comparative statement of cash flows for the years ended December 31, 2015, and 2014, for all transactions related to the above information. Be specific about the classifications in the financial statement.

Digging Deeper

P20-4 Refer to the information in P20-3.

Instructions

(a) Prepare the journal entries that Situ would make on January 1, 2014, and the adjusting journal entries at December 31, 2014, to record the annual interest income from the lease arrangement, assuming that Situ has a December 31 fiscal year end.

(b) Identify all accounts that will be reported by Situ Ltd. on its comparative income statement for the fiscal years ending December 31, 2015, and 2014, and its comparative statement of financial position at December 31, 2015, and 2014. Be specific about the classifications in each statement.

(c) Prepare a partial comparative statement of cash flows for Situ for the years ended December 31, 2015, and 2014, for all transactions related to the information in P20-3. Be specific about the classifications in the financial statement.

Digging Deeper

P20-5 LePage Manufacturing Ltd. agrees to lease equipment to Labonté Corporation on July 15, 2014. Both LePage and Labonté use ASPE. The following information relates to the lease agreement.

1. The lease term is seven years, with no renewal option, and the equipment has an estimated economic life of nine years.

2. The equipment's cost is $420,000 and the asset's fair value on July 15, 2014, is $560,000.

3. At the end of the lease term, the asset reverts to LePage, the lessor. The asset is expected to have a residual value of $80,000 at this time, and this value is guaranteed by Labonté. Labonté depreciates all of its equipment on a straight-line basis.

4. The lease agreement requires equal annual rental payments, beginning on July 15, 2014.

5. LePage usually sells its equipment to customers who buy the product outright, but Labonté was unable to get acceptable financing for an outright purchase. LePage's credit investigation on Labonté revealed that the company's financial situation was deteriorating. Because Labonté had been a good customer many years ago, LePage agreed to enter into this lease agreement, but used a higher than usual 15% interest rate in setting the lease payments. Labonté is aware of this rate.

6. LePage is uncertain about what additional costs it might have to incur in connection with this lease during the lease term, although Labonté has agreed to pay all executory costs directly to third parties.

7. LePage incurred legal costs of $4,000 in early July 2014 in finalizing the lease agreement.

Instructions

(a) Discuss the nature of this lease for both the lessee and the lessor.

(b) Using time value of money tables, a financial calculator, or computer spreadsheet functions, calculate the amount of the annual rental payment that is required.

(c) Prepare the journal entries that Labonté would make in 2014 and 2015 related to the lease arrangement, assuming that the company has a December 31 fiscal year end and that it does not use reversing entries.

(d) From the information you have calculated and recorded, identify all balances related to this lease that would be reported on Labonté's December 31, 2014 balance sheet and income statement, and where each amount would be reported.

(e) Prepare the journal entries that Le Page would make in 2014 and 2015 related to the lease arrangement, assuming that the company has a December 31 fiscal year end and does not use reversing entries.

(f) From the information you have calculated and recorded, identify all balances related to this lease that would be reported on LePage's December 31, 2014 balance sheet and income statement, and where each amount would be reported.

(g) Comment briefly on the December 31, 2014 reported results in parts (d) and (f) above.

P20-6 Synergetics Inc. leased a new crane to Gumowski Construction under a six-year, non-cancellable contract starting February 1, 2014. The lease terms require payments of $21,500 each February 1, starting February 1, 2014. Synergetics will pay insurance, taxes, and maintenance charges on the crane, which has an estimated life of 12 years, a fair value of $160,000, and a cost to Synergetics of $160,000. The crane's estimated fair value is $50,000 at the end of the lease term. No bargain purchase or renewal options are included in the contract. Both Synergetics and Gumowski adjust and close books annually at December 31 and use IFRS. Collectibility of the lease payments is reasonably certain and there are no uncertainties about unreimbursable lessor costs. Gumowski's incremental borrowing rate is 8% and Synergetics' implicit interest rate of 7% is known to Gumowski.

Instructions

(a) Identify the type of lease that is involved and give reasons for your classification. Also discuss the accounting treatment that should be applied by both the lessee and the lessor.

(b) Would the classification of the lease have been different if Synergetics and Gumowski had been using ASPE?

(c) Prepare all the entries related to the lease contract and leased asset for the year 2014 for the lessee and lessor, assuming the following executory costs: insurance of $450 covering the period February 1, 2014, to January 31, 2015; taxes of $200 for the remainder of calendar year 2014; and a one-year maintenance contract beginning February 1, 2014, costing $1,200. Straight-line depreciation is used for similar leased assets. The crane is expected to have a residual value of $20,000 at the end of its useful life.

(d) Identify what will be presented on the statement of financial position and income statement, and in the related notes, of both the lessee and the lessor at December 31, 2014.

P20-7 Ramey Corporation is a diversified public company with nationwide interests in commercial real estate development, banking, copper mining, and metal fabrication. The company has offices and operating locations in major cities throughout Canada. With corporate headquarters located in a metropolitan area of a western province, company executives must travel extensively to stay connected with the various phases of operations. In order to make business travel more efficient to areas that are not adequately served by commercial airlines, corporate management is currently evaluating the feasibility of acquiring a business aircraft that can be used by Ramey executives. Proposals for either leasing or purchasing a suitable aircraft have been analyzed, and the leasing proposal was considered more desirable.

The proposed lease agreement involves a twin-engine turboprop Viking that has a fair value of $1 million. This plane would be leased for a period of 10 years, beginning January 15, 2014. The lease agreement is cancellable only upon accidental destruction of the plane. An annual lease payment of $139,150 is due on January 15 of each year, with the first payment to be made on January 15, 2014. Maintenance operations are strictly scheduled by the lessor, and

Ramey will pay for these services as they are performed. Estimated annual maintenance costs are $6,900. The lessor will pay all insurance premiums and local business taxes, which amount to a combined total of $4,000 annually and are included in the annual lease payment of $139,150. Upon expiration of the 10-year lease, Ramey can purchase the Viking for $44,440. The plane's estimated useful life is 15 years, and its value in the used plane market is estimated to be $100,000 after 10 years. The residual value probably will never be less than $75,000 if the engines are overhauled and maintained as prescribed by the manufacturer. If the purchase option is not exercised, possession of the plane will revert to the lessor; there is no provision for renewing the lease agreement beyond its termination on January 15, 2024.

Ramey can borrow $1 million under a 10-year term loan agreement at an annual interest rate of 12%. The lessor's implicit interest rate is not expressly stated in the lease agreement, but this rate appears to be approximately 8% based on 10 net rental payments of $135,150 per year and the initial fair value of $1 million for the plane. On January 15, 2014, the present value of all net rental payments and the purchase option of $44,440 is 872,571 using the 12% interest rate. The present value of all net rental payments and the $44,440 purchase option on January 15, 2014, is $1,000,000 using the 8% interest rate implicit in the lease agreement. The financial vice-president of Ramey Corporation has established that this lease agreement is a financing lease as defined by the IFRS standards followed by Ramey.

Instructions

(a) IFRS indicates that the crucial accounting issue is whether the risks and benefits of ownership are transferred from one party to the other, regardless of whether ownership is transferred. What is meant by "the risks and benefits of ownership," and what factors are general indicators of such a transfer?

(b) Have the risks and benefits of ownership been transferred in the lease described above? What evidence is there?

(c) What is the appropriate amount for Ramey Corporation to recognize for the leased aircraft on its statement of financial position after the lease is signed?

(d) Independent of your answer in part (c), assume that the annual lease payment is $141,780, that the appropriate capitalized amount for the leased aircraft is $1 million on January 14, 2014, and that the interest rate is 9%. How will the lease be reported on the December 31, 2014 statement of financial position and related income statement? (Ignore any income tax implications.)

P20-8 The following facts pertain to a non-cancellable lease agreement between Woodhouse Leasing Corporation and McKee Electronics Ltd., a lessee, for a computer system:

Inception date	October 1, 2014
Lease term	6 years
Economic life of leased equipment	6 years
Fair value of asset at October 1, 2014	$150,690
Residual value at end of lease term	–0–
Lessor's implicit rate	8.5%
Lessee's incremental borrowing rate	8.5%
Annual lease payment due at the beginning of each year, beginning October 1, 2014	$ 30,500

The collectibility of the lease payments is reasonably predictable, and there are no important uncertainties about costs that have not yet been incurred by the lessor. McKee Electronics Ltd., the lessee, assumes responsibility for all executory costs, which amount to $2,500 per year and are to be paid each October 1, beginning October 1, 2014. (This $2,500 is not included in the rental payment of $30,500.) The asset will revert to the lessor at the end of the lease term. The straight-line depreciation method is used for all equipment.

The following amortization schedule has been prepared correctly for use by both the lessor and the lessee in accounting for this lease using ASPE. The lease is accounted for properly as a capital lease by the lessee and as a direct financing lease by the lessor.

Date	Annual Lease Payment/ Receipt	Interest (8.5%) on Unpaid Obligation/ Net Investment	Reduction of Lease Obligation/ Net Investment	Balance of Lease Obligation/ Net Investment
10/01/14				$150,690
10/01/14	$ 30,500	–0–	$ 30,500	120,190
10/01/15	30,500	$10,216	20,284	99,906
10/01/16	30,500	8,492	22,008	77,898
10/01/17	30,500	6,621	23,879	54,019
10/01/18	30,500	4,592	25,908	28,111
10/01/19	30,500	2,389	28,111	–0–
	$183,000	$32,310	$150,690	

Instructions

Answer the following questions, rounding all numbers to the nearest dollar.

(a) Assuming that McKee Electronics' accounting period ends on September 30, answer the following questions with respect to this lease agreement.

1. What items and amounts will appear on the lessee's income statement for the year ending September 30, 2015?
2. What items and amounts will appear on the lessee's balance sheet at September 30, 2015?
3. What items and amounts will appear on the lessee's income statement for the year ending September 30, 2016?
4. What items and amounts will appear on the lessee's balance sheet at September 30, 2016?

(b) Assuming that McKee Electronics' accounting period ends on December 31, answer the same questions as in part (a) above for the years ending December 31, 2014, and 2015.

(c) Discuss the differences, if any, in the classification of the lease to McKee Electronics Ltd. if the company were using IFRS in its financial reporting.

P20-9 Assume the same information as in P20-8.

Instructions

Answer the following questions, rounding all numbers to the nearest dollar.

(a) Assuming that Woodhouse Leasing Corporation's accounting period ends on September 30, answer the following questions with respect to this lease agreement.

1. What items and amounts will appear on the lessor's income statement for the year ending September 30, 2015?
2. What items and amounts will appear on the lessor's balance sheet at September 30, 2015?
3. What items and amounts will appear on the lessor's income statement for the year ending September 30, 2016?
4. What items and amounts will appear on the lessor's balance sheet at September 30, 2016?

(b) Assuming that Woodhouse Leasing Corporation's accounting period ends on December 31, answer the same questions as in part (a) above for the years ending December 31, 2014, and 2015.

(c) Discuss the differences, if any, in the classification of the lease to Woodhouse Leasing Corporation if the company were using IFRS in its financial reporting.

P20-10 In 2011, Yin Trucking Corporation, which follows ASPE, negotiated and closed a long-term lease contract for newly constructed truck terminals and freight storage facilities. The buildings were erected to the company's specifications on land owned by the company. On January 1, 2012, Yin Trucking Corporation took possession of the leased properties. On January 1, 2012, and 2013, the company made cash payments of $1,048,000 that were recorded as rental expenses.

Although the useful life of each terminal is 40 years, the non-cancellable lease runs for 20 years from January 1, 2012, with a purchase option available upon expiration of the lease.

The 20-year lease is effective for the period January 1, 2012, through December 31, 2031. Advance rental payments of $900,000 are payable to the lessor on January 1 of each of the first 10 years of the lease term. Advance rental payments of $320,000 are due on January 1 for each of the last 10 years of the lease. The company has an option to purchase all of these leased facilities for $1 million on December 31, 2031, although their fair value at that time is estimated at $3 million. At the end of 40 years, the terminals and facilities will have no remaining value. Yin Trucking must also make annual payments to the lessor of $125,000 for property taxes and $23,000 for insurance. The lease was negotiated to assure the lessor a 6% rate of return.

Instructions

Answer the following questions, rounding all numbers to the nearest dollar.

(a) Using time value of money tables, a financial calculator, or computer spreadsheet functions, calculate for Yin Trucking Corporation the amount, if any, that should be capitalized on its January 1, 2012 balance sheet.

(b) Assuming a capital lease and a capitalized value of terminal facilities at January 1, 2012, of $8.7 million, prepare journal entries for Yin Trucking Corporation to record the following:

1. The cash payment to the lessor on January 1, 2014
2. Depreciation of the cost of the leased properties for 2014 using the straight-line method
3. The accrual of interest expense at December 31, 2014

(c) What amounts would appear on Yin's December 31, 2014 balance sheet for the leased asset and the related liabilities under the lease arrangement described in part (b)?

P20-11 Lee Industries and Lor Inc. enter into an agreement that requires Lor Inc. to build three diesel-electric engines to Lee's specifications. Both Lee and Lor follow ASPE. Upon completion of the engines, Lee has agreed to lease them for a period of 10 years and to assume all costs and risks of ownership. The lease is non-cancellable, becomes effective on January 1, 2014, and requires annual rental payments of $620,956 each January 1, starting January 1, 2014.

Lee's incremental borrowing rate is 10%, and the implicit interest rate used by Lor Inc. is 8% and is known to Lee. The total cost of building the three engines is $3.9 million. The engines' economic life is estimated to be 10 years, with residual value expected to be zero. Lee depreciates similar equipment on a straight-line basis. At the end of the lease, Lee assumes title to the engines. Collectibility of the lease payments is reasonably certain and there are no uncertainties about unreimbursable lessor costs.

Instructions

Answer the following questions, rounding all numbers to the nearest dollar.

(a) Discuss the nature of this lease transaction from the viewpoints of both the lessee (Lee Industries) and lessor (Lor Inc.).

(b) Prepare the journal entry or entries to record the transactions on January 1, 2014, on the books of Lee Industries.

(c) Prepare the journal entry or entries to record the transactions on January 1, 2014, on the books of Lor Inc.

(d) Prepare the journal entries for both the lessee and lessor to record interest expense (income) at December 31, 2014. (Prepare a lease amortization schedule for the lease obligation for two years using a computer spreadsheet.)

(e) Show the items and amounts that would be reported on the balance sheet (ignore the notes) at December 31, 2014, for both the lessee and the lessor.

(f) Identify how the lease transactions would be reported on each company's statement of cash flows in 2014.

(g) Provide the note disclosure concerning the lease that would be required for the lessee, Lee Industries, on its financial statements for the fiscal year ending December 31, 2014.

(h) Provide the note disclosure concerning the lease that would be required for the lessor, Lor Inc., on its financial statements for the fiscal year ending December 31, 2014.

P20-12 Dubois Steel Corporation, as lessee, signed a lease agreement for equipment for five years, beginning January 31, 2014. Annual rental payments of $41,000 are to be made at the beginning of each lease year (January 31). The taxes, insurance, and maintenance costs are the lessee's obligation. The interest rate used by the lessor in setting the payment schedule is 9%; Dubois' incremental borrowing rate is 10%. Dubois is unaware of the rate being used by the lessor. At the end of the lease, Dubois has the option to buy the equipment for $4,000, which is considerably below its estimated fair value at that time. The equipment has an estimated useful life of seven years with no residual value. Dubois uses straight-line depreciation on similar equipment that it owns, and follows IFRS.

Instructions

Answer the following questions, rounding all numbers to the nearest dollar.

(a) Prepare the journal entry or entries, with explanations, that should be recorded on January 31, 2014, by Dubois.

(b) Prepare any necessary adjusting journal entries at December 31, 2014, and the journal entry or entries, with explanations, that should be recorded on January 31, 2015, by Dubois. (Prepare the lease amortization schedule for the lease obligation using a computer spreadsheet for the minimum lease payments.) Dubois does not use reversing entries.

(c) Prepare any necessary adjusting journal entries at December 31, 2015, and the journal entry or entries, with explanations, that should be recorded on January 31, 2016, by Dubois.

(d) What amounts would appear on Dubois' December 31, 2015 statement of financial position relative to the lease arrangement?

(e) What amounts would appear on Dubois' statement of cash flows for 2014 relative to the lease arrangement? Where would the amounts be reported?

(f) Assume that the leased equipment had a fair value of $200,000 at the inception of the lease, and that no bargain purchase option is available at the end of the lease. Determine what amounts would appear on Dubois' December 31, 2015 statement of financial position and what amounts would appear on the 2015 statement of cash flows relative to the leasing arrangements.

P20-13 CHL Corporation manufactures specialty equipment with an estimated economic life of 12 years and leases it to Provincial Airlines Corp. for a period of 10 years. Both CHL and Provincial Airlines follow ASPE. The equipment's normal selling price is $210,482 and its unguaranteed residual value at the end of the lease term is estimated to be $15,000. Provincial Airlines will pay annual payments of $25,000 at the beginning of each year and all maintenance, insurance, and taxes. CHL incurred costs of $105,000 in manufacturing the equipment and $7,000 in negotiating and closing the lease. CHL has determined that the collectibility of the lease payments is reasonably predictable, that no additional costs will be incurred, and that the implicit interest rate is 8%.

Instructions

Answer the following questions, rounding all numbers to the nearest dollar.

(a) Discuss the nature of this lease in relation to the lessor and calculate the amount of each of the following items:

   1. Gross investment   **3.** Sale price

   2. Unearned interest income   **4.** Cost of goods sold

(b) Prepare a 10-year lease amortization schedule for the lease obligation using a computer spreadsheet.

(c) Prepare all of the lessor's journal entries for the first year of the lease, assuming the lessor's fiscal year end is five months into the lease. Reversing entries are not used.

(d) Determine the current and non-current portion of the net investment at the lessor's fiscal year end, which is five months into the lease.

(e) Assuming that the $15,000 residual value is guaranteed by the lessee, what changes are necessary to parts (a) to (d)?

(f) Assuming that, as an alternative, CHL would consider leasing the equipment for 12 years, if it could recover the normal selling price of $210,482. How much would CHL charge the lessee annually for a 12 year lease? Assume the residual value at the end of 12 years would be $0, and that lease payments would be due at the start of each year.

P20-14 Assume the same data as in P20-13 and that Provincial Airlines Corp. has an incremental borrowing rate of 8%.

Instructions

Answer the following questions, rounding all numbers to the nearest dollar.

(a) Discuss the nature of this lease in relation to the lessee.

(b) What classification will Provincial Airlines Corp. give to the lease?

(c) What difference, if any, would occur in the classification of the lease if Provincial were using IFRS?

(d) Using time value of money tables, a financial calculator, or computer spreadsheet functions, calculate the amount of the initial obligation under capital leases.

(e) Prepare a 10-year lease amortization schedule for the lease obligation using a computer spreadsheet.

(f) Prepare all of the lessee's journal entries for the first year, assuming that the lease year and Provincial Airlines' fiscal year are the same.

(g) Prepare the entries in part (f) again, assuming that the residual value of $15,000 was guaranteed by the lessee.

(h) Prepare the entries in part (f) again, assuming a residual value at the end of the lease term of $45,000 and a purchase option of $15,000.

P20-15 Jennings Inc., which uses IFRS, manufactures an X-ray machine with an estimated life of 12 years and leases it to SNC Medical Centre for a period of 10 years. The machine's normal selling price is $343,734, and the lessee guarantees a residual value at the end of the lease term of $15,000. The medical centre will pay rent of $50,000 at the beginning of each year and all maintenance, insurance, and taxes. Jennings incurred costs of $210,000 in manufacturing the machine and $14,000 in negotiating and closing the lease. Jennings has determined that the collectibility of the lease payments is reasonably predictable, that there will be no additional costs incurred, and that its implicit interest rate is 10%.

Instructions

Answer the following questions, rounding all numbers to the nearest dollar.

(a) Discuss the nature of this lease in relation to the lessor and calculate the amount of each of the following items:

   1. Gross investment   **3.** Unearned interest income

   2. Sale price   **4.** Cost of goods sold

(b) Prepare a 10-year lease amortization schedule for the lease obligation.

(c) Prepare all of the lessor's journal entries for the first year.

(d) Identify the amounts to be reported on Jennings's statement of financial position, income statement, and statement of cash flows one year after signing the lease, and prepare any required note disclosures.

(e) Assume that SNC Medical Centre's incremental borrowing rate is 12% and that the centre knows that 10% is the rate implicit in the lease. Determine the depreciation expense that SNC will recognize in the first full year that it leases the machine.

(f) Assuming instead that the residual value is not guaranteed, what changes, if any, are necessary in parts (a) to (d) for the lessor and in part (e) for the lessee?

(g) Discuss how Jennings would have determined the classification of the lease if the company were using ASPE for its financial reporting.

P20-16 Lanier Dairy Ltd. leases its milk cooling equipment from Green Finance Corporation. Both companies use IFRS. The lease has the following terms.

1. The lease is dated May 30, 2014, with a lease term of eight years. It is non-cancellable and requires equal rental payments of $30,000 due each May 30, beginning in 2014.

2. The equipment has a fair value and cost at the inception of the lease of $211,902, an estimated economic life of 10 years, and a residual value (which is guaranteed by Lanier Dairy) of $23,000.

3. The lease contains no renewal options and the equipment reverts to Green Finance Corporation on termination of the lease.

4. Lanier Dairy's incremental borrowing rate is 6% per year; the implicit rate is also 6%.

5. Lanier Dairy uses straight-line depreciation for similar equipment that it owns.

6. Collectibility of the payments is reasonably predictable, and there are no important uncertainties about costs that have not yet been incurred by the lessor.

Instructions

(a) Describe the nature of the lease and, in general, discuss how the lessee and lessor should account for the lease transaction.

(b) Prepare the journal entries for the lessee and lessor at May 30, 2014, and at December 31, 2014, which is the lessee's and lessor's year ends.

(c) Prepare the journal entries at May 30, 2015, for the lessee and lessor. Assume reversing entries are not used.

(d) What amount would have been capitalized by the lessee upon inception of the lease if:
1. The residual value of $23,000 had been guaranteed by a third party, not the lessee?
2. The residual value of $23,000 had not been guaranteed at all?

(e) On the lessor's books, what amount would be recorded as the net investment at the inception of the lease, assuming:
1. Green Finance had incurred $1,200 of direct costs in processing the lease?
2. The residual value of $23,000 had been guaranteed by a third party?
3. The residual value of $23,000 had not been guaranteed at all?

(f) Assume that the milk cooling equipment's useful life is 20 years. How large would the residual value have to be at the end of 8 years in order for the lessee to qualify for the operating method? Assume that the residual value would be guaranteed by a third party. (*Hint:* The lessee's annual payments will be appropriately reduced as the residual value increases.)

(g) Discuss how Jennings would have determined the classification of the lease if the company were using ASPE for its financial reporting.

P20-17 Fram Fibreglass Corp. (FFC) is a private New Brunswick company, using ASPE, that manufactures a variety of fibreglass products for the fishing and food services industry. With the traditional fishery in decline over the past few years, FFC found itself in a tight financial position in early 2014. Revenues had levelled off, inventories were over-stocked, and most operating costs were increasing each year.

The Royal Montreal Bank, which FFC has dealt with for 20 years, was getting anxious as FFC's loans and line of credit were at an all-time high, the most recent loan carrying an interest rate of 15%. In fact, the bank had just recently imposed stipulations on FFC that prevented the company from paying out any dividends or increasing its debt to equity ratio above current levels without the bank's prior approval.

The vice-president of finance, Joe Blowski, CMA, knew that with aggressive investment in new equipment, the company could go after new markets in the construction industry. He had investigated the cost of the necessary equipment and found that $50,000 of new capital investment would allow the company to get started. All it needed was the financing. Joe set up appointments with Kirk Cullen, the loans officer at the provincial Industrial Development Bank, and with Heidi Hazen, the manager of the local office of Municipal Finance Corp.

Kirk Cullen was very receptive to Joe's request. He indicated that the Industrial Development Bank would be interested in working with FFC, and could provide him with a lease on the equipment he identified. Heidi Hazen also welcomed the business, suggesting a lease arrangement between Municipal Finance Corp. and FFC as well. Two days later, Joe had proposals from both lenders on his desk.

You are an accounting major and co-op student placed with FFC for your final work term. On his way out of the office for a meeting, Joe provides you with the two proposals and asks, just before the elevator door closes, "Would you please review these and give me your analysis and recommendation on which proposal to accept, if either?" The details of the two proposals are as follows:

	Industrial Development Bank Proposal	Municipal Finance Corp. Proposal
Selling price of equipment	$50,000	$50,000
Lease term	April 23, 2014 to April 22, 2019	May 1, 2014 to April 30, 2019
Economic life of equipment	7 years	7 years
Residual value, end of lease term	$10,000	$10,000
Residual value guaranteed	no	by lessee
Annual rental payment	$12,000 in advance	$11,681 in advance
Executory costs	$1,020 per year included in rent	$300 per year in addition to rent
Interest rate implicit in lease	12%	unknown
Equipment returned at end of lease	yes	yes

Instructions

Prepare the required report for Joe.

P20-18 Mulholland Corp., a lessee, entered into a non-cancellable lease agreement with Galt Manufacturing Ltd., a lessor, to lease special purpose equipment for a period of seven years. Both Mulholland and Galt follow ASPE. The following information relates to the agreement:

Lease inception	May 2, 2014
Annual lease payment due at the beginning of each lease year	$?
Residual value of equipment at end of lease term, guaranteed by an independent third party	$100,000
Economic life of equipment	10 years
Usual selling price of equipment	$415,000
Manufacturing cost of equipment on lessor's books	$327,500
Lessor's implicit interest rate, known to lessee	12%
Lessee's incremental borrowing rate	12%
Executory costs per year to be paid by lessee, estimated	$ 14,500

The leased equipment reverts to Galt Manufacturing at the end of the lease, although Mulholland has an option to purchase it at its expected fair value at that time.

Instructions

(a) Using time value of money tables, a financial calculator, or computer spreadsheet functions, calculate the lease payment determined by the lessor to provide a 12% return.

(b) Prepare a lease amortization table for Galt Manufacturing, the lessor, covering the entire term of the lease.

(c) Assuming that Galt Manufacturing has a December 31 year end, and that reversing entries are not made, prepare all entries made by the company up to and including May 2, 2016.

(d) Identify the balances and classification of amounts that Galt Manufacturing will report on its December 31, 2014 balance sheet, and the amounts on its 2014 income statement and statement of cash flows related to this lease.

(e) Assuming that Mulholland has a December 31 year end, and that reversing entries are not made, prepare all entries made by the company up to and including May 2, 2016. Assume payments of executory costs of $14,000, $14,400, and $14,950 covering fiscal years 2014, 2015, and 2016, respectively.

(f) Identify the balances and classification of amounts that Mulholland will report on its December 31, 2014 balance sheet, and the amounts on its 2014 income statement and statement of cash flows related to this lease.

(g) On whose balance sheet should the equipment appear? On whose balance sheet does the equipment currently get reported?

*P20-19 Your employer, Wagner Inc., is a large Canadian public company that uses IFRS. You are working on a project to determine the effect of the proposed contract-based approach on the corporate accounting for leases. To get started on the project, you have collected the following information with respect to a lease for a fleet of trucks used by Wagner to transport completed products to warehouses across the country. The trucks have an economic life of eight years. The lease term is from July 1, 2014, to June 30, 2021, and the company intends to lease the equipment for this period of time, so the lease term is seven years. The lease payment per year is $545,000, payable in advance, with no other payments required, and no renewal option or bargain purchase option available. The expected value of the fleet of trucks at June 30, 2021, is $450,000; this value is guaranteed by Wagner. The leased trucks must be returned to the lessor at the end of the lease. Wagner's management is confident that with an aggressive maintenance program, Wagner has every reason to believe that the asset's residual value will be more than the guaranteed amount at the end of the lease term. Wagner's incremental borrowing rate is 8%, and the rate implicit in the lease is not known. At the time the lease was signed, the fair value of the leased trucks was $3,064,470.

Instructions

(a) Based on the original information:

1. Using time value of money tables, a financial calculator, or computer spreadsheet functions, determine the contractual obligations and rights under the lease at July 1, 2014.

2. Prepare an amortization schedule for the obligation over the term of the lease.

3. Prepare the journal entries and any year-end (December 31) adjusting journal entries made by Wagner Inc. in 2014 and up to and including July 1, 2015.

(b) Immediately after the July 1, 2015 lease payments, based on the feedback of the staff in operations, management reassesses its expectations for the guaranteed residual value. Management now estimates the fleet of trucks to have a value of $400,000 with a 60% probability and $300,000 with a 40% probability.

1. Calculate the probability-weighted expected value of the residual at the end of the lease term. Also calculate the present value at July 1, 2015, of any additional cash flows related to the residual value guarantee.

2. Prepare any necessary entry to implement the revision to the contractual lease rights and obligation at July 1, 2015.

3. Revise the amortization schedule effective January 1, 2015, for the lease, including any liability related to the residual value guarantee.

4. Prepare the year-end adjusting journal entries made by Wagner Inc. for fiscal year 2015.

P20-20 Sanderson Inc., a pharmaceutical distribution firm, is providing a BMW car for its chief executive officer as part of a remuneration package. Sanderson has a calendar year end, issues financial statements annually, and follows ASPE. You have been assigned the task of calculating and reporting the financial statement effect of several options Sanderson is considering in obtaining the vehicle for its CEO.

Option 1: Obtain financing from Western Bank to finance an outright purchase of the BMW from BMW Canada, which regularly sells and leases luxury vehicles.

Option 2: Sign a lease with BMW Canada and exercise the option to renew the lease at the end of the initial term.

Option 3: Sign a lease with BMW Canada and exercise the option to purchase at the end of the lease. The amount of the option price is financed with a bank loan.

For the purpose of your comparison, you can assume a January 1, 2014 purchase and you can also exclude all amounts for any provincial sales taxes, GST, and HST on all the proposed transactions. You can also assume that Sanderson uses the straight-line method of depreciating automobiles. Assume that for options 1 and 2, the BMW is sold on January 1, 2019, for $10,000.

Sanderson does not expect to incur any extra kilometre charges because it is likely that the BMW won't be driven that much by the CEO. However, there is a 10% chance that an extra 10,000 km will be driven and a 15% chance that an extra 20,000 km will be used.

Terms and values concerning the asset that are common to all options are the following:

	January 1, 2014
Date of purchase or signing of lease	January 1, 2014
Purchase price equal to fair value at January 1, 2014	$79,000
Cost to BMW Canada	$70,000
Physical life	8 years
Useful life to Sanderson	5 years
Residual value at January 1, 2019, equal to Sanderson	$10,000
Fair value at January 1, 2017	$39,500

Borrowing terms with Western Bank for purchase: Option 1

Loan amount	$79,000
Fixed bank rate for loan to purchase	7%
Term of loan to purchase	5 years
Repayment terms	Quarterly instalment note
First payment due	April 1, 2014

For Option 2:

Terms, conditions, and other information related to the initial lease with BMW Canada:

Lease term	36 months
First lease payment date	January 1, 2014
Monthly lease payment	$1,392.21
Maximum number of kilometres allowed under lease	72,000

Excess kilometre charge beyond 72,000 km	25 cents
Option to purchase price at end of lease	50% of original fair value
Date of payment for option to purchase	January 1, 2017
Maintenance and insurance	paid by Sanderson
Interest rate stated in lease—annual	6%
Sanderson's incremental borrowing rate	7%

Terms, conditions, and other information related to the renewal option for lease with BMW Canada:

Renewal lease term	24 months
Renewal option first lease payment date	January 1, 2017
Monthly lease payment	$1,371.00
Maximum number of kilometres allowed under renewal lease	48,000
Excess kilometre charge beyond 48,000 km	25 cents
Option to purchase at end of renewal option	none
Maintenance and insurance	paid by Sanderson
Renewal option	none
Interest rate stated in renewal lease	7%
Sanderson's incremental borrowing rate (projected)	8%

Borrowing terms with Western Bank to exercise option to purchase: Option 3

Loan amount	$39,500
Bank rate January 1, 2017	8%
Term of loan January 1, 2017	2 years
Repayment terms	Quarterly instalment note
First payment due	April 1, 2017

Instructions

(a) For Option 1:

1. Using a financial calculator or computer spreadsheet, calculate the quarterly blended payments that will be due to Western Bank on the instalment note.

2. Prepare an amortization schedule for the loan with Western Bank for the term of the lease.

3. Record all of the necessary transactions on January 1, 2014, the first loan payment, and for any adjusting journal entries at the end of the fiscal year 2014.

(b) For Option 2:

1. Using a financial calculator or computer spreadsheet, determine how BMW Canada arrived at the amounts of the monthly payment for the original lease and for the lease renewal option, allowing it to recover its investment.

2. Assume that the original lease is signed and Sanderson Inc. has no intention of exercising the lease renewal. Determine the classification of the three-year lease for Sanderson Inc.

3. Assume that Sanderson fully intends to exercise the renewal option offered by BMW Canada. Determine the classification of the lease for Sanderson Inc.

4. Prepare a lease amortization schedule for the term of the lease for Sanderson Inc.

5. Record all of the necessary transactions on January 1, 2014, for the first two lease payments and for any adjusting journal entries at the end of the fiscal year 2014 for Sanderson Inc.

(c) For Option 3:

1. Determine the classification of the lease for Sanderson Inc.

2. Record all of the necessary transactions concerning the lease on January 1, 2014, and for any adjusting journal entries at the end of the fiscal year ending December 31, 2014.

3. Using a financial calculator, or computer spreadsheet functions, calculate the quarterly blended payments that will be due to Western Bank on the instalment note used to finance the purchase.

4. Prepare an amortization schedule for the loan with Western Bank.

5. Record all of the necessary transactions concerning exercising the option to purchase on January 1, 2017, the signing of the instalment note payable to the bank, the first loan payment, and any adjusting journal entries at the end of the fiscal year ending December 31, 2017.

*(d) Use the contract-based approach in the proposed standards and assume the information in Option 2. Update, if necessary, and reproduce the amortization table needed under this approach for the first 13 payments of the lease. Prepare the journal entries on January 1 and February 1, 2014, and for any adjusting journal entries at the end of the fiscal year ending December 31, 2014.

(e) Assume that the amount paid by Sanderson on July 1, 2017, equals the amount calculated based on probability weighting for the excess charge for kilometres driven. How would you account for the penalty Sanderson expects to pay?

(f) Prepare a table of the financial statement results from the above three options and the contract-based approach of part (d). Your table should clearly show all of the classifications and amounts for the statement of financial position at December 31, 2014, and the income statement for the 2014 fiscal year.

(g) Calculate the amount of the expense for the BMW for the total five-year period based on each of the three assumptions, as well as under the contract-based approach assuming that Sanderson follows Option 2. Include any penalty payment for excess kilometres driven for Option 2.

(h) Based on the results obtained in part (g), provide Sanderson with additional considerations that should be taken into account before making a choice between the different options.

P20-21 Use the information for P20-20.

Instructions

Under Option 2:

(a) Assume that at the signing of the original lease, Sanderson Inc. has no intention of exercising the lease renewal. Determine the classification of the three-year lease for BMW Canada.

(b) Prepare the journal entry to show how BMW Canada records the collection of the first lease payment on January 1, 2014.

(c) Assume now that Sanderson Inc. signs the renewal option at the same time that it enters into the original lease agreement.

1. Prepare a lease amortization schedule including the renewal period for BMW Canada.

2. Determine the classification of the lease for BMW Canada.

3. Record all of the necessary transactions on January 1, 2014, for the first two lease payments collected and for any adjusting journal entries at the end of the fiscal year ending December 31, 2014, for BMW Canada.

*P20-22 The head office of North Central Ltd. has operated in the western provinces for almost 50 years. North Central uses IFRS. In 1998, new offices were constructed on the same site at a cost of $9.5 million. The new building was opened on January 4, 1999, and was expected to be used for 35 years, at which time it would have a value of approximately $2 million.

In 2014, as competitors began to consider merger strategies among themselves, North Central felt that the time was right to expand the number of its offices throughout the province. This plan required significant financing and, as a source of cash, North Central looked into selling the building that housed its head office. On June 29, 2014, Rural Life Insurance Company Ltd. purchased the building (but not the land) for $8 million and immediately entered into a 20-year lease with North Central to lease back the occupied space. The terms of the lease were as follows.

1. It is non-cancellable, with an option to purchase the building at the end of the lease for $1 million.

2. The annual rental is $838,380, payable on June 29 each year, beginning on June 29, 2014.

3. Rural Life expects to earn a return of 10% on its net investment in the lease, the same as North Central's incremental borrowing rate.

4. North Central is responsible for maintenance, insurance, and property taxes.

5. Estimates of useful life and residual value have not changed significantly since 1996.

Instructions

(a) Prepare all entries for North Central Ltd. from June 29, 2014, to December 31, 2015. North Central has a calendar year fiscal period.

(b) Assume instead that there was no option to purchase, that $8 million represents the building's fair value on June 29, 2014, and that the lease term was 12 years. Prepare all entries for North Central from June 29, 2014, to December 31, 2015.

(c) Besides the increase in cash that it needs from the sale of the building, what effect should North Central expect to see on the net assets appearing on its statement of financial position immediately after the sale and leaseback?

*P20-23 Zhou Ltd. is a private corporation, which uses ASPE, and whose operations rely considerably on a group of technology companies that experienced operating difficulties from 2011 to 2013. As a result, Zhou suffered temporary cash flow problems that required it to look for innovative means of financing. In 2014, Zhou's management therefore decided to enter into a sale and leaseback agreement with a major Canadian leasing company, Intranational Leasing.

Digging
Deeper

Immediately after its September 30, 2014 year end, Zhou sold one of its major manufacturing sites to Intranational Leasing for $1,750,000, and entered into a 15-year agreement to lease back the property for $175,000 per year. The lease payment is due October 1 of each year, beginning October 1, 2014.

Zhou's carrying amount of the property when sold was $250,000. The lease agreement gives Zhou the right to purchase the property at the end of the lease for its expected fair value at that time of $2.5 million. In 2014, the land is estimated to be worth 40% of the total property value, and the building, 60%. Zhou uses a 10% declining-balance method of amortizing its buildings, and has a 7% incremental borrowing rate.

Instructions

(a) Prepare all entries that are needed by Zhou to recognize the sale and leaseback transaction on October 1, 2014; any adjusting entries that are required on September 30, 2015; and the October 1, 2015 transaction. Reversing entries are not used.

(b) Prepare all necessary note disclosures and amounts that are to be reported on Zhou's September 30, 2015 balance sheet, income statement, and statement of cash flows for its year ended September 30, 2015.

(CICA adapted)

Cases

Refer to the Case Primer on the Student Website and in *WileyPLUS* to help you answer these cases.

CA20-1 Crown Inc. (CI) is a private company that manufactures a special type of cap that fits on a bottle. At present, it is the only manufacturer of this cap and therefore enjoys market security. The machinery that makes the cap has been in use for 20 years and is due for replacement. CI has the option of buying the machine or leasing it. Currently, CI is leaning toward leasing the machine since it is expensive to buy and funds would have to be borrowed from the bank. The company's debt to equity ratio is currently marginal, and if the funds were borrowed, the debt to equity ratio would surely worsen. CI's top management is anxious to maintain the ratio at its present level.

The dilemma for CI is that if it leases the machine, it may have to set up a long-term obligation under the lease and this would also affect the debt to equity ratio. Since this is clearly unacceptable, CI decided to see if the leasing company, Anchor Limited, could do anything to help with the situation. After much negotiation, the following terms were agreed upon and written into the lease agreement.

1. Anchor Limited would manufacture and lease to CI a unique machine for making caps.

2. The lease would be for a period of 12 years.

3. The lease payments of $150,000 would be paid at the end of each year.

4. CI would have the option to purchase the machine for $850,000 at the end of the lease term, which is equal to the expected fair market value at that time; otherwise, the machine would be returned to the lessor.

5. CI also has the option to lease the machine for another eight years at $150,000 per year.

6. The rate that is implicit in the lease is 9%.

The new machine is expected to last 20 years. Since it is a unique machine, Anchor Limited has no other use for it if CI does not either purchase it at the end of the lease or renew the lease. If CI had purchased the asset, it would have cost $1.9 million. Although it was purposefully omitted from the written lease agreement, there was an understanding that CI would either renew the lease or exercise the purchase option.

Instructions

Assume the role of CI's auditors and discuss the nature of the lease, noting how it should be accounted for. The company controller has confided in you that the machine will likely be purchased at the end of the lease. Assume that you are aware of top management's position on adding debt to the balance sheet. Management has also asked you to compare the accounting under ASPE and IFRS.

CA20-2 Kelly's Shoes Limited used to be a major store in Canada before it went bankrupt and was bought by Bears Shoes Limited. Many of the stores were anchor tenants in medium- to large-sized retail shopping malls. This space was primarily leased under non-cancellable real estate leases as disclosed in note 16 to the consolidated financial statements. Aggregate commitments under both capital and operating leases amounted to over $1.3 million.

As part of Kelly's restructuring and downsizing plans prior to its bankruptcy, the company announced at the beginning of the year that it planned to close down 31 of its 85 stores by June 30. Subsequently, it announced that it might keep certain stores open until February in the following year if the landlords were prepared to provide an appropriate level of financial support. Kelly's also announced that landlords who allowed the stores to close June 30 (the earlier date) would be given a bonus of three months of rent.

Writing Assignments

Ethics

WA20-1

Cuby Corporation entered into a lease agreement for 10 photocopy machines for its corporate headquarters. The lease agreement qualifies as an operating lease in all ways except that there is a bargain purchase option. After the five-year lease term, the corporation can purchase each copier for $1,000, when the anticipated market value of each machine will be $2,500.

Glenn Beckert, the ethical accountant and CFO, thinks the financial statements must recognize the lease agreement as a finance lease because of the bargain purchase clause. The controller, Tareek Koba, disagrees: "Although I don't know much about the copiers themselves, there is a way to avoid recording the lease liability." She argues that the corporation might claim that copier technology advances rapidly and that by the end of the lease term—five years in the future—the machines will most likely not be worth the $1,000 bargain price.

Instructions

Answer the following questions.

(a) Is there an ethical issue at stake? Explain.

(b) Should the controller's argument be accepted if she does not really know much about copier technology? Would your answer be different if the controller were knowledgeable about how quickly copier technology changes?

(c) What should Beckert do? Be sure to take into account the ethical repercussions of your recommendations.

(d) What would be the impact of these arguments on the company's statement of financial position under the contract-based approach for reporting leases? What impact would Koba's argument have in this case?

WA20-2

Sporon Corp. is a fast-growing Canadian private company in the manufacturing, distribution, and retail of specially designed yoga and leisure wear. Sporon has recently signed 10 new leases for new retail locations and is looking to sign about 30 more over the next year as the company expands its retail outlets. All of the leases also have a contingent rent that is based on a percentage of annual sales in each location over a certain amount. The threshold and the percentage vary between locations. The contingent rent is payable annually on the anniversary date of the lease. The company has currently assessed these to be operating, as they have no conditions that meet the capitalization criteria under ASPE. All of these payments on these leases are expensed as incurred.

The company has also moved into a new state-of-the-art manufacturing and office facility designed specifically for its needs, and signed a 20-year lease with PPS Pension Inc., the owner. As this building lease also does not meet any of the criteria for a capital lease under ASPE, Sporon accounts for this lease as an operating lease. As a result, it expenses both the monthly rental and the annual payment that it agreed on with PPS to cover property tax increases above the 2013 base property tax cost. The tax increase amount is determined by PPS and is payable by September 30 each year.

The small group of individuals who own the company are very interested in the company's annual financial statements as they expect, if all goes well, to take the company public by 2015. For this and other reasons, Sporon's chief financial officer, Louise Bren, has been debating whether or not to adopt IFRS or ASPE for the 2014 year end.

Louise has also been following the new changes that are being proposed by the IASB to adopt the contract-based approach.

Instructions

(a) Explain to Louise Bren to what extent, if any, adjustments will be needed to Sporon's financial statements for the leases described above, based on existing private enterprise and international accounting standards.

(b) Assume that the joint IASB-FASB study group supports the contract-based approach for leases. Prepare a short report for the CFO that explains the conceptual basis for this approach and that identifies how Sporon Corp.'s statement of financial position, statement of comprehensive income, and cash flow statement will likely differ under revised leasing standards based on this approach.

(c) Prepare a short, but informative, appendix to your report in part (b) that addresses how applying such a revised standard might affect a financial analyst's basic ratio analysis of Sporon Corp.'s profitability (profit margin, return on assets, return on equity); risk (debt to equity, times interest earned); and solvency (operating cash flows to total debt).

WA20-3

In May 2010, the IASB expressed an interest in using a hybrid of two models for lessor accounting. One model is the performance obligation model and one is called the derecognition model. Both of these models are

---

Instructions

Assume the role of Kelly's management and discuss the financial reporting issues that the company had to deal with before its bankruptcy. Discuss any differences between IFRS and ASPE.

discussed in the discussion paper entitled document "Preliminary Views: Leases, July 17, 2009". The discussion paper is available on the IASB website at www.ifrs.org.

Instructions

(a) Describe the "performance obligation approach" for lessor accounting with respect to its concept, impact on the statement of financial position, and impact on the statement of comprehensive income.

(b) Describe the "derecognition approach" for lessor accounting with respect to its concept, impact on the statement of financial position, and impact on the statement of comprehensive income.

(c) Using the information below, determine what the statement of financial position would look like at the inception of the lease under the two alternatives:

The Lessor has entered into a six-year lease for a piece of machinery. The Lessor carries the machinery on its books at $100,000. The present value of the lease payments to be received for the lease is determined to be $92,900. Show the assets and liabilities that would be shown on the statement of financial position under the two different alternatives.

WA20-4 On October 30, 2014, Truttman Corp. sold a five-year-old building with a carrying value of $10 million at its fair value of $13 million and leased it back. There was a gain on the sale. Truttman pays all insurance, maintenance, and taxes on the building. The lease provides for 20 equal annual payments, beginning October 30, 2014, with a present value equal to 85% of the building's fair value and sales price. The lease's term is equal to 73% of the building's useful life. There is no provision for Truttman to reacquire ownership of the building at the end of the lease term. Truttman has a December 31 year end.

Instructions

(a) Why would Truttman have entered into such an agreement?

(b) In reaching a decision on how to classify a lease, why is it important to compare the equipment's fair value with the present value of the lease payments, and its useful life with the lease term? What does this information tell you under ASPE and IFRS?

(c) Assuming that Truttman would classify this as an operating lease, determine how the initial sale and the sale-leaseback transaction would be reported under ASPE and IFRS for the 2014 year. What would be the implications if the selling price had been $14 million, $1 million greater than the fair value of the building?

(d) Assuming that Truttman would classify this as a finance lease, determine how the initial sale and the sale-leaseback transaction would be reported under ASPE and IFRS for the 2014 year.

WA20-5

Instructions

Write a brief essay highlighting the differences between IFRS and ASPE and the contract-based approach noted in this chapter, discussing the conceptual justification for each.

RESEARCH AND FINANCIAL ANALYSIS

RA20-1 Shoppers Drug Mart Corporation

Real World Emphasis

Refer to the 2011 year-end financial statements and accompanying notes of **Shoppers Drug Mart Corporation** at the end of this volume or on the company's website and then answer the following questions about the company.

Instructions

(a) Review the notes and determine how Shoppers Drug Mart accounts for its leasing transactions. Is Shoppers the lessor or lessee? What types of leases does it have?

(b) Identify all accounts on the consolidated statements of financial position and the consolidated income statement, along with their dollar amounts, that relate to any lease agreements that the company is a party to.

(c) Identify the line account(s) on the consolidated statements of cash flows where the cash lease payments are reported. Explain your answer.

(d) Calculate Shoppers' return on total assets and total debt to equity ratios for 2011.

(e) Assume the IASB develops a revised lease accounting standard using the contract-based approach. Would there be any impact to the financial statement of Shoppers Drug Mart? If so, what would the impact be?

Real World Emphasis

RA20-2 Canadian National Railway Company and Canadian Pacific Railway Limited

The accounting for operating leases is a controversial issue. Many observers argue that firms that use operating leases are using significantly more assets and are more highly leveraged than their financial statements indicate. As a result, analysts often use footnote disclosures to reconstruct and then capitalize operating lease obligations. One way to do so is to increase a firm's assets and liabilities by the present value of all its future minimum rental payments.

Instructions

Go to the SEDAR website (www.sedar.com) or the websites of the companies and access the financial statements of **Canadian National Railway Company** (CNR) and **Canadian Pacific Railway Limited** (CPR) for their years ended December 31, 2011. Refer to the financial statements and notes to the financial statements and answer the following questions.

(a) Identify all lease arrangements that are indicated in each company's financial statements and notes. For each lease arrangement, give the title and balances of the related lease accounts that are included in the financial statements.

(b) Have CNR and CPR provided all the lease disclosures as required by the accounting standards?

(c) What are the terms of these leases?

(d) What amount did each company report as its future minimum annual rental commitments under capital leases? Under operating leases? Are there significant differences between the two companies and the way they provide for their physical operating capacity, or are they basically similar?

(e) Calculate the debt to equity ratio for each company at December 31, 2011.

(f) Assuming that the contract-based approach is adopted by both companies, what would be the impact on the companies' debt-to-total assets ratios? Where necessary estimate the impact on the statement of financial position using 7% as the lessee's implied borrowing rate. What information is missing from the companies' notes to make a more accurate calculation of the impact of adopting the contract-based approach?

(g) Recalculate the ratios in part (e), incorporating the adjustments made in part (f) above. Comment on your results.

(h) What do you believe are the advantages of adopting the contract-based approach when trying to compare companies? Relate your discussion to your analysis above for CNR and CPR.

Real World Emphasis

RA20-3 Indigo Books & Music Inc.

Indigo Books & Music Inc., operating under Indigo, Chapters, Coles, The World's Biggest Bookstore, SmithBooks, The Book Company, and chapters.indigo.ca, has 245 stores across Canada. Through the SEDAR website (www.sedar.com) or the company's website, access the financial statements of Indigo Books & Music Inc. for its 52 weeks ending March 31, 2012. Refer to the financial statements and notes to the financial statements and answer the following questions.

Instructions

(a) Identify all lease arrangements that are indicated in the company's financial statements, including the notes. Indicate any balances related to these leases that are reported on the income statement and statement of financial position.

(b) Calculate the following ratios for Indigo based on the 2012 published financial statements:

1. Debt to equity ratio

2. Capital asset turnover ratio

3. Total asset turnover ratio

4. Return on investment (net income to total assets)

(c) Assume that the company adopts the contract-based approach as set out in the IASB's 2010 Exposure Draft. Assuming an interest rate of 6%, estimate the impact of the adoption on the 2012 statements of financial position. Also, estimate the impact on the 2012 income statement. List any assumptions that you have made. To help with the analysis, below is the information on operating lease payments that were committed to as of March 31, 2012 (excerpts from note 13).

The Company's contractual obligations due over the next five fiscal years and thereafter are summarized below:

(millions of dollars)	Operating leases	Capital leases	Total
2013	58.5	1.1	59.6
2014	46.4	0.7	47.1
2015	31.0	0.4	31.4
2016	22.0	—	22.0
2017	15.0	—	15.0
Thereafter	22.8	—	22.8
Total obligations	195.7	2.2	197.9

The Company entered into capital lease agreements for certain equipment. The obligations under these capital leases is \$2.2 million (2011 – \$3.3 million), of which \$1.1 million (2011 – \$1.3 million) is included in the current portion of long-term debt. The remainder of the capital lease obligations have been included in the non-current portion of long-term debt.

(d) Using your estimate of the amount to capitalize for Indigo, recalculate the debt-to-equity and total asset turnover ratios in part (b) above. Compare the recalculated ratios with the original results and comment on the differences.

RA20-4 Research an Automobile Lease

Instructions

Contact an automobile dealership and find out the full out-of-pocket cost of purchasing a specific model of car if you were to pay cash for it. Also find out the details of the costs that are associated with leasing the same model car. Answer the following questions.

(a) What terms and conditions are associated with the lease? In other words, specify the lease term, residual values and whether they are guaranteed by the lessee or not, the lessor's implicit interest rate, any purchase options, and so on.

(b) What cash flows are associated with the lease?

(c) Which do you think is the better deal (pay cash or lease)? Briefly explain.

ENDNOTES

1 Asset-based financing is the financing of equipment through a secured loan, conditional sales contract, or lease.

2 Hans Hoogervoorst, "Accounting Harmonisation and Global Economic Consequences," public lecture at the London School of Economics, November 6, 2012, available at www.ifrs.org/Alerts/Conference/Documents/HH-LSE-November-2012.pdf.

3 As shown in this chapter, some lease arrangements are not capitalized on the balance sheet. This keeps the liabilities section free from large commitments that, if recorded, would have a negative effect on the debt to equity ratio. The reluctance to record lease obligations as liabilities is one of the main reasons that some companies resist capitalized lease accounting.

4 The property rights approach was originally recommended in *Accounting Research Study No. 4* (New York: AICPA, 1964), pp. 10–11. In the 1990s, this view received additional support. See Warren McGregor, "Accounting for Leases: A New Approach," Special Report (Norwalk, Conn.: FASB, 1996).

5 IASB, Snapshot: *Leases—Preliminary Views* (of Discussion paper DP/2009/1), March 2009, page 2. Copyright © 2012 IFRS Foundation. All rights reserved. Reproduced by Wiley Canada with the permission of the IFRS Foundation ®. No permission granted to third parties to reproduce or distribute.

6 Ibid., page 4. Copyright © 2012 IFRS Foundation. All rights reserved. Reproduced by Wiley Canada with the permission of the IFRS Foundation ®. No permission granted to third parties to reproduce or distribute.

7 "Minimum lease payments" is defined differently for a lessor.

8 IAS 17.4 *Leases* requires the **interest rate implicit in the lease** to be the rate that equates the inflows with the fair value of the leased asset **plus any initial direct costs of the lessor**. If the lessor is a manufacturer or dealer, the initial direct costs are not included.

9 IAS 17.4 uses this as a secondary definition. It prefers the interest rate that the lessee would have to pay on a similar lease, if determinable.

10 In lease-versus-buy decisions and in determining the lessor's implicit rate, income tax effects must be factored in. A major variable is whether the Canada Revenue Agency requires the lease to be accounted for as a conditional sale; this is usually established based on whether the title is transferred by the end of the lease term or the lessee has a bargain purchase option. Tax shields that relate to the rental payment and capital cost allowance significantly affect the return and an investment's net present value.

11 Alternatively, use Excel or other spreadsheet program to calculate the required payments. With Excel, use the following series of keystrokes: FORMULAS/INSERTFUNCTION/PMT. Fill in the variables that you are prompted to enter.

12 An exception to measuring the leased asset at amortized cost is made when a lessee leases investment property under a finance lease. In such a case, the investment property may be accounted for at fair value under IAS 40 *Investment Property*.

13 Alternatively, using Excel or another spreadsheet program, enter the following series of key strokes: FORMULAS/INSERTFUNCTION/PV. Fill in the required variables that the program asks for. Note that the interest rate must be provided with the % sign or be in decimal form.

14 If Lessee Corporation had an incremental borrowing rate of 9% (lower than the 10% rate used by Lessor Corporation) or it did not know the rate used by Lessor, the present value calculation yields a capitalized amount of $101,675.35 ($23,981.62 × 4.23972). Because this amount exceeds the asset's fair value, Lessee Corporation capitalizes the $100,000 and uses 10% as its effective rate for amortization of the lease obligation.

15 This is a task well suited for Excel or other spreadsheet program. Set up the schedule headings, and use formulas to perform the calculations for you.

16 When the lease term and the economic life are not the same, the asset's residual value at the end of the lease and at the end of its useful life will differ. The residual value at the end of an asset's economic life is sometimes referred to as salvage value, and it is generally a small amount.

17 Technically, the rate of return that is demanded by the lessor would differ depending on whether the residual value was guaranteed or unguaranteed. To simplify the illustrations, we ignore this difference in this chapter.

18 Under IAS 40 *Investment Property*, a lessee is able to classify a property interest under an operating lease as an investment property. If this option is taken, the investment property must be accounted for under the fair value model. There is no corresponding private enterprise concept.

19 One study indicates that management's behaviour did change as a result of the profession's requirements to capitalize certain leases. Many companies restructured their leases to avoid capitalization; others increased their purchases of assets instead of leasing; and others, faced with capitalization, postponed their debt offerings or issued shares instead. It is interesting to note that the study found no significant effect on share or bond prices as a result of capitalization of leases. A. Rashad Abdel-khalik, "The Economic Effects on Lessees of *FASB Statement No. 13*, Accounting for Leases," Research Report (Stamford, Conn.: FASB, 1981).

20 The rent is now calculated as $100,000 \div 3.79079 = \$26,379.73$. The denominator is the factor for $n = 5$ and $i = 10$ for an ordinary annuity (Table A-4).

21 Under IFRS, a lessor who is not a manufacturer or dealer also includes any initial direct costs associated with negotiating and arranging the lease. In this example, these costs are $0.

22 The lessor usually finances the purchase of this asset over a term that generally coincides with the term of the lease. Because the lessor's cost of capital is lower than the rate that is implicit in the lease, the lessor earns a profit represented by the interest spread.

23 While lessees may record and report the lease obligation on a net basis, lessors tend to recognize the gross amount in receivables. Unlike the lessee, lessors may have hundreds or thousands of lease contracts to administer and the amounts to be collected are the gross receivables. Therefore, for administrative simplicity, the amounts that are received are a direct reduction of the receivable, and the interest is determined and adjusted for separately.

24 Technically, the rate of return that is demanded by the lessor would differ depending on whether the residual value was guaranteed or unguaranteed. To simplify the illustrations, we ignore this difference in the chapter.

25 See the IFRS website for details, www.ifrs.org/Current-Projects/IASB-Projects/Leases/Meeting-Summaries-and-Observer-Notes/Pages/IASBJune2012.aspx, accessed November 30, 2012.

26 *Financial Reporting in Canada—2008* (CICA, 2008) reports that out of 200 companies surveyed, 27 companies provided disclosure related to current or prior years' sale-leaseback transactions.

27 Allocating based on the value of leasehold interests is not the same thing as based on relative fair values of the underlying assets. Because the land will revert to the lessor and maintain its value, unlike the building, the rental payments charged for the land will not be based on recovering its full fair value.

28 The description of the proposed standards included in this text are based on the tentative decisions reached by the FASB and IASB that were reported in the February 19, 2010 and May 14, 2010 *Leases Project Update*, the latter accessed at www.fasb.org on May 19, 2010.

29 IASB *Exposure Draft*, *Leases* (Appendix A), August, 2010; accessed at www.ifrs.org on November 27, 2012.

30 The proposals allow an exemption for short-term leases. A short-term lease is an agreement with an expected total term of less than 12 months. From the lessee's point of view, the right-of-use asset and lease obligation are both reported gross; that is, on an undiscounted basis. The lessor also has an option to use this simplified accounting.

Standards Change Is Constant

THE 2011 MOVE from Canadian generally accepted accounting principles (GAAP) to International Financial Reporting Standards (IFRS) for publicly accountable companies was the biggest change that corporations and those affected by accounting standards had ever seen. But the standards will continue to evolve.

"What you'll find is a regime of constant change of standards," says Ron Salole, Vice-President, Standards at the Canadian Institute of Chartered Accountants, who is a non-voting member of the Canadian Accounting Standards Board (AcSB). "We have always introduced changes because businesses change, new types of transactions and new types of financial instruments are thought of, and there are no standards to deal with those types of issues, so we are constantly trying to bring in standards to reflect what is happening in the business world." As an example, more amended and new international standards came into effect on January 1, 2013, including revisions to IFRS 10 dealing with consolidated financial statements and IAS 19 regarding post-retirement benefits. Additional amended and new standards were expected to take effect on January 1, 2015, or 2016.

More changes to IFRS will also be likely once the International Accounting Standards Board implements its new conceptual framework, a project that had been dormant for some time and is expected to be revived. Existing IFRS will likely

have to be aligned with the new framework, Mr. Salole says.

Much further down the road, integrated reporting may be introduced, issuing more reader-friendly financial statements along with information on companies' environmental sustainability initiatives, human resources, and other things, he says.

For Canadian companies following Accounting Standards for Private Enterprises (ASPE), however, the rate of standards change will likely be slower than that for public companies using IFRS, Mr. Salole says. That's mainly because the AcSB wants to keep ASPE as straightforward as possible. Under the old Canadian GAAP, which applied to all sizes of enterprises, private companies, which tend to be smaller, felt that there was "standards overload."

The AcSB developed ASPE to reduce the accounting complexities for Canadian private enterprises, effectively cutting their disclosure requirements in half. With the old Canadian GAAP, "Whereas the larger companies and the public companies had the resources and the wherewithal to be able to handle some of those complexities, the smaller companies that had to apply the same standards just did not have the ability to be able to do it. They were totally fraught with frustration and difficulties," Mr. Salole says. The AcSB expects to implement changes to the ASPE standards no more than once every two years.

21 | Accounting Changes and Error Analysis

LEARNING OBJECTIVES

After studying this chapter, you should be able to:

1. Identify and differentiate among the types of accounting changes.

2. Identify and explain alternative methods of accounting for accounting changes.

3. Identify the accounting standards for each type of accounting change under ASPE and IFRS.

4. Apply the retrospective application method of accounting for a change in accounting policy and identify the disclosure requirements.

5. Apply retrospective restatement for the correction of an accounting error and identify the disclosure requirements.

6. Apply the prospective application method for an accounting change and identify the disclosure requirements for a change in an accounting estimate.

7. Identify economic motives for changing accounting methods and interpret financial statements where there have been retrospective changes to previously reported results.

8. Identify the differences between ASPE and IFRS related to accounting changes.

After studying Appendix 21A, you should be able to:

9. Correct the effects of errors and prepare restated financial statements.

PREVIEW OF CHAPTER 21

As our opening story indicates, 2011 was a huge year for change for many Canadian companies. When new standards are adopted and when accounting errors are uncovered and changes in accounting estimates are made, companies must follow specific accounting and reporting requirements. To ensure comparability, standard setters have standardized how accounting changes, error corrections, and related earnings per share information are accounted for and reported. In this chapter, we discuss these reporting standards, which help investors better understand a company's financial condition and performance. In the appendix, we look at how to analyze and correct the accounts when there have been numerous errors. The chapter is organized as follows:

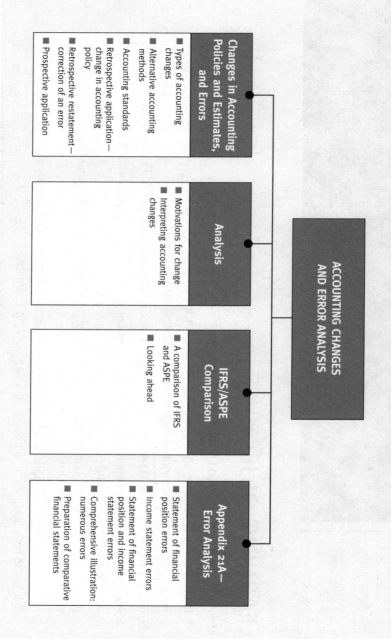

ACCOUNTING CHANGES AND ERROR ANALYSIS

Changes in Accounting Policies and Estimates, and Errors
- Types of accounting changes
- Alternative accounting methods
- Accounting standards
- Retrospective application—change in accounting policy
- Retrospective restatement—correction of an error
- Prospective application

Analysis
- Motivations for change
- Interpreting accounting changes

IFRS/ASPE Comparison
- A comparison of IFRS and ASPE
- Looking ahead

Appendix 21A—Error Analysis
- Statement of financial position errors
- Income statement errors
- Statement of financial position and income statement errors
- Comprehensive illustration: numerous errors
- Preparation of comparative financial statements

CHANGES IN ACCOUNTING POLICIES AND ESTIMATES, AND ERRORS

Financial press readers regularly see headlines about companies that report accounting changes and related events. Why do these accounting changes occur?

First, the accounting profession may mandate new accounting methods or standards. In addition to the major changes that Canadian companies underwent when they adopted either IFRS or ASPE in 2011, specific standards change from time to time. For example, revisions were made to the standards relating to post-employment benefits in 2011 (effective 2013), and the IASB issued a standard on fair value measurements in the same year (also effective 2013). Second, changing economic conditions may cause a company to revise its methods of accounting. Third, changes in technology and in operations may require a company to revise estimates of the service lives, depreciation pattern, or expected residual value of depreciable assets. Lastly, corrections are needed when accounting errors are discovered.

How should these changes be accounted for and disclosed so that the financial information's usefulness is maintained?

Before the existence of a standard for accounting changes, companies had considerable flexibility and were able to use alternative accounting treatments for what were basically equivalent situations. The overall objectives of accounting and disclosure standards for accounting changes, therefore, are to limit the types of changes permitted, standardize the reporting for each type of change, and ensure that readers of accounting reports have the necessary information to understand the effects of such changes on the financial statements.

Types of Accounting Changes

Objective 1

Identify and differentiate among the types of accounting changes.

ASPE and IFRS have established reporting frameworks that cover three types of accounting changes:

1. **A change in accounting policy.** Changes in the choice of "specific principles, bases, conventions, rules, and practices applied by an entity in preparing and presenting financial statements" are all changes in accounting policies.[1] The initial adoption of a new accounting standard and a change from a weighted average cost flow formula to one based on FIFO (as long as this results in reliable and more relevant information) are both examples of a change in policy.

2. **A change in accounting estimate.** A change in an accounting estimate is an adjustment to the carrying amount of an asset or a liability or the amount of an asset's periodic consumption, and results from either an assessment of the present status of or the expected future benefits and obligations associated with an asset or liability.[2] Examples include a change in the estimate of the service life of an asset that is subject to depreciation, and a change in the estimate of the net realizable value of accounts receivable.

3. **Correction of a prior period error.** Prior period errors are omissions from or mistakes in the financial statements of one or more prior periods that are caused by the misuse of, or failure to use, reliable information that existed when those financial statements were completed and could reasonably have been found and used in their preparation and presentation.[3] An example is the failure to recognize depreciation on a group of capital assets that were used in operations for a specific prior period.

Each of these classifications is discussed separately below.

Another major type of change occurs when the specific entities making up the reporting entity change due to a business combination or the disposal of a major part of a company's operations. These are not included in this chapter. Discontinued operations were explained in Chapter 4, and business combinations and other reporting entity changes are covered in most advanced accounting courses.

Changes in Accounting Policies

Choices of Accounting Policies. Before discussing what is involved in a change in accounting policy, it is a good idea to review the issues related to an entity making the **initial choice** of accounting policy based on GAAP.

ASPE describes what makes up GAAP and the GAAP hierarchy.[4] The **GAAP hierarchy** is the guidance to follow when there is no primary source of generally accepted accounting principles that covers a specific situation. ASPE identifies two levels of GAAP:

1. Primary sources of GAAP

2. Policies that are consistent with the primary sources of GAAP, and are developed by exercising professional judgement and applying concepts set out in Section 1000, Financial Statement Concepts

The first level, the **primary sources of GAAP**, lists these sources in order of authority, as follows:

(a) Sections 1400 to 3870, including Appendices; and

(b) Accounting Guidelines, including Appendices.

The second level—policies consistent with the primary sources, applying professional judgement, and the concepts in Section 1000—is used only when primary sources of GAAP do not deal with the specific issue. Section 1100 provides additional guidance on applying secondary sources and addresses the topic of consistency in accounting policies. It indicates that similar transactions, events, and circumstances are accounted for and presented in a consistent manner in an entity's financial statements.

IFRS requires a similar **hierarchy**. The **primary sources** to look to are the IFRS and guidance that is an integral part of the specific standard. When no such source exists, judgement is used to determine the accounting treatment. Judgement takes into account the definitions of elements, recognition criteria, and measurement concepts and the underlying qualities of financial statement information found in the Framework for the Preparation and Presentation of Financial Statements. It ensures that the method chosen results in consistency with the treatment that primary sources would require for similar situations.

Under both ASPE and IFRS, if GAAP specifically requires or permits categorization of items and different policies to be used, such as with depreciation methods, different methods may be used. Once an appropriate method is chosen from among those allowed, this method is then applied consistently to each category. Both sets of standards also identify other sources that could be considered and applied, such as the pronouncements of standard-setting bodies with similar conceptual frameworks, as long as the result is consistent with the hierarchy set out above.

GAAP Requirements for Changes in Accounting Policies.
Having been introduced to the original choice of policy, we can now ask what conditions must exist for an entity to be allowed to change its policy. Under IFRS, one of the following two situations is required for a change in an accounting policy to be acceptable:

1. the change is required by a primary source of GAAP, or

2. a voluntary change results in the financial statements presenting reliable and more relevant information about the effects of the transactions, events, or conditions on the entity's financial position, financial performance, or cash flows.[5]

ASPE permits a third type of accounting policy change to be made without having to meet the "reliable, but more relevant" test in the second situation above. It allows the following voluntary changes in policy to be made:

3. between or among alternative ASPE methods of accounting and reporting

(a) for investments in subsidiary companies, and in companies where the investor has significant influence or joint control;

(b) for expenditures during the development phase on internally generated intangible assets;

(c) for defined benefit plans;

(d) for accounting for income taxes; and

(e) for measuring the equity component of a financial instrument that has both a liability and equity component at zero.[6]

Specific transitional provisions that indicate how any changes are to be accounted for are often identified in new or revised standards. The second situation permitting a change in policy—a **voluntary change**—underscores one of the principles underlying both ASPE and IFRS: for a change in accounting policy to be acceptable, the new policy chosen must result in financial information that remains reliable and is more relevant than under the previous policy. The change would be unacceptable if it produces more reliable but less relevant information. The assumption, therefore, is also that the use of another method that remains reliable and is equally relevant would not meet the criterion for being an acceptable change. The onus is on management to explain why a different method is more relevant than the method that is currently being applied.

A change in the measurement basis of an asset or liability is typically a change in accounting policy. An IFRS example of an acceptable voluntary change might be the move from a cost basis to the fair value model for measuring investment property. Another possible example, this time related to ASPE, is the change made by a company that constructs its own long-lived assets if it moves from expensing all interest charges as they are incurred to capitalizing interest during construction. In both cases, management can likely explain in what way the resulting financial information has become more relevant and remains reliable.

But determining what is "more relevant" is not always obvious in financial reporting. How is relevance measured? One enterprise might argue that a change in accounting policy from FIFO to a weighted average cost formula better matches current costs and current revenues, providing more predictive, and therefore more relevant, information. Conversely, another enterprise might change from a weighted average cost formula to FIFO because it wants to report a more current and relevant ending inventory amount that also has better predictive value. The decision has to be made based on the situation in each specific case.

The requirement based on relevance and reliability links back to the two primary qualitative characteristics of accounting information that make it useful. The main purpose of the qualitative characteristics is their use as evaluative criteria in choosing among accounting alternatives. Any new or revised standard that is issued as a primary source of GAAP has been evaluated against these characteristics as part of its development.

The third situation allowed under ASPE as an acceptable change in accounting policy refers to standards where accounting policy choices have to be made. These changes are treated as voluntary changes, but they do not have to meet the "reliable and more relevant" hurdle required of other voluntary changes. Although not specifically stated in the actual standard, once that choice has been made, the same policy is followed consistently.

It is not always obvious whether an accounting change is, in fact, a change in accounting policy. It is clearly **not** a change in policy if either one of the following two situations is evident:

1. A different policy is applied to transactions, events, or conditions that are different in substance from those that previously occurred.

2. A different policy is applied to transactions, events, or conditions that either did not occur previously or that were immaterial.

Consider, for example, a company that begins to capitalize interest during the construction of its own long-lived assets. If the company was not involved in any self-construction activities previously, the new policy of capitalizing interest would not be considered a change in accounting policy. Another example is applying a new "defer and amortize" policy for development expenditures. If these costs were immaterial previously but are now significant, the change in materiality justifies the new policy. This is not a change in methods of accounting for similar events and circumstances. In each of these examples, the method that was used previously was appropriate for the circumstances that existed then; the new policy is appropriate for the changed circumstances.

What happens if the accounting policy that was previously followed was not acceptable, or if the policy was applied incorrectly? Rather than being a change in accounting policy, these changes to a generally accepted accounting method are considered corrections of an error. A switch from the cash basis of accounting to the accrual basis is considered an error correction. If a company incorrectly deducted residual values when calculating double-declining depreciation on tangible capital assets and later recalculates the depreciation without deducting the estimated residual value, the change is considered the correction of an error.

Underlying Concept

Relevance and reliability are used in accounting standards as criteria in the choice of accounting methods.

Finally, companies often change how they allocate or group items within categories on the financial statements. When an item is reclassified on the financial statements of the prior period(s) in order to make the statements comparable, this is considered a change in presentation only and not, in itself, a change in accounting policy. As with retrospective changes in accounting policy, IAS 1 *Presentation of Financial Statements* requires that an "extra" statement of financial position (SFP)—an opening SFP for the earliest comparative period presented—be provided in such a case.[7]

Changes in Accounting Estimates

In preparing financial statements, estimates of the effects of future conditions and events are often made. As future conditions and events and their effects cannot be known with certainty, estimation requires the use of judgement. The following are a few of the many examples of accounting items that require estimates:

1. Uncollectible receivables

2. Inventory obsolescence

3. Fair value of financial assets or financial liabilities

4. Useful lives of, the pattern of consumption of the future economic benefits that are embodied in, and the residual values of depreciable assets

5. Liabilities for warranty costs

The use of reasonable estimates is considered an essential part of the accounting process. And it is normal to expect that accounting estimates will change over time as new events occur, circumstances change, more experience is acquired, or additional information is obtained. By its very nature, a change in estimate does not relate to past periods. Instead, and as its definition reinforces, the change is brought about by assessing the present status and future expectations associated with specific assets and liabilities.

Sometimes it is difficult to differentiate between a change in an estimate and a change in an accounting policy. Assume, for example, that a company changes its method of depreciation for its property, plant, and equipment. At first glance, this appears to be a change in an accounting policy. Or does the new method result from a change in the estimate of the pattern in which the assets' benefits are used by the entity? Assume that a company changes from deferring and amortizing certain development costs to recording them as expenses as they are incurred because the future benefits associated with these costs have become doubtful. Is this a change in policy or a change in estimate?

The definition of a change in accounting estimate clearly includes both of these scenarios. Further, **in cases where it is unclear whether a change is one of policy or of estimate**, the change is treated as a change in estimate. A revision of an estimate, such as a prior year's tax assessment not caused by errors, is given change-in-estimate treatment. It is clearly not the same thing as a correction of an error, which is discussed next.

Correction of a Prior Period Error

No business, large or small, is immune from errors. The risk of material errors, however, may be reduced by installing good internal controls and applying sound accounting procedures. The accounting standards define prior period errors and make a distinction between errors and changes in accounting estimates. Estimates, by their nature, are approximations whose values change as circumstances and conditions change and more information becomes available. Errors, on the other hand, are omissions or mistakes, either intentional or through oversight, that are not discovered until after the financial statements for a period have been issued.

The following are examples of accounting errors. The analysis assumes that the financial statements are intended to be in accordance with GAAP (IFRS or ASPE) except for the error:

1. A change from an accounting policy that is not generally accepted to an accounting policy that is acceptable, or the inappropriate application of an acceptable accounting policy. The rationale adopted is that the prior periods were incorrectly presented. Example: a change from a FIFO cost formula to specific identification where the inventory items are not ordinarily interchangeable (for instance jewelry).

2. Arithmetic mistakes. Example: the incorrect totalling of the inventory count sheets in calculating total inventory cost.

3. Previous estimates were not prepared in good faith. Example: based on information that was available when an amortization rate was determined, an entity used a clearly unrealistic rate.

4. An omission due to an oversight. Example: the failure to accrue certain revenues at the end of the period.

5. A recognition error. Example: the recognition of a cost as an asset instead of as an expense.

6. A misappropriation of assets. Example: the correction of a previous year's financial statements because inventory theft was discovered.

A problem may arise in distinguishing between the correction of an accounting error and a change in estimate. What is the correct treatment of the settlement of litigation (not previously accrued) related to a reassessment of a prior year's income taxes? How do we determine whether the information was overlooked in earlier periods (an error) or whether it results from new information, more experience, or subsequent developments (a change in estimate)? This decision is important because, depending on the answer, a different accounting treatment is applied. The general rule is that when a careful estimate later proves to be incorrect, the change is considered a change in estimate. This is the case with most unaccrued tax litigation settlements. Only when the estimate was obviously calculated incorrectly because of lack of expertise or it was done in bad faith should the adjustment be considered an error correction. There is no clear separating line here. Good judgement must take all the circumstances into account.

Alternative Accounting Methods

Objective 2

Identify and explain alternative methods of accounting for accounting changes.

Three approaches have been suggested for reporting changes in the accounts:

1. **Retrospective:** Retrospective application (also known as **retroactive application**) requires applying a new accounting policy in the accounts as if the new method had always been used. The cumulative effect of the change on the financial statements at the beginning of the period is calculated and an adjustment is made to the financial statements. In addition, all prior years' financial statements that are affected are restated on a basis that is consistent with the newly adopted policy. Advocates of this position argue that only by restating prior periods can accounting changes lead to comparable information. If this approach is not used, the years before the change will be reported using one method and the current and following years will present financial statements on a different basis. Consistency is considered essential in providing meaningful earnings-trend data and other financial relationships that are necessary to evaluate a business.

2. **Current:** The cumulative effect of the change on the financial statements at the beginning of the period is calculated. This **"catch-up" adjustment** is then reported in the current year's income statement. Advocates of this position argue that restating financial statements for prior years' results in a loss of confidence by investors in financial reports. How will a present or prospective investor react when told that the earnings reported five years ago have changed? Restatement, if permitted, might also upset many contractual and other arrangements that were based on the old figures.

For example, profit-sharing arrangements based on the old policy might have to be recalculated and completely new distributions made. This might create numerous legal problems. Many practical difficulties also exist: the cost of restatement may be excessive, or restatement may be impossible based on the data available.

3. **Prospective** (in the future): With prospective application, previously reported results remain; no change is made. Opening balances are not adjusted, and no attempt is made to correct or change past periods. Instead, the new policy or estimate is applied to balances existing at the date of the change, with effects of the change reported in current and future periods. Supporters of this position argue that once management presents financial statements based on acceptable accounting principles, methods, and estimates, they are final; management cannot change prior periods by adopting new methods and calculations. According to this line of reasoning, a cumulative adjustment in the current year is not appropriate, because such an approach includes amounts that have little or no relationship to the current year's income or economic events.

Objective 3
Identify the accounting standards for each type of accounting change under ASPE and IFRS.

Accounting Standards

Illustration 21-1 identifies the accounting standards for each type of accounting change. These are more fully explained and illustrated below.

Illustration 21-1

Accounting Changes—GAAP Accounting Methods

Type of Accounting Change	Accounting Method Applied
Change in accounting policy—on adoption of a primary source of GAAP	Apply the method that is approved in the transitional provisions of the primary source. If there is none, use retrospective application to the extent that it is practicable. If retrospective application is impracticable, apply prospectively.
Change in accounting policy—voluntary	Use retrospective application to the extent practicable. If impracticable, apply prospectively.
Change in accounting estimate	Apply prospectively.
Correction of an error	Use retrospective restatement.

As indicated, **only two of the general approaches are permitted: retrospective and prospective treatment.** When new or revised primary sources of GAAP are adopted, recommendations are usually included that specify how an entity should handle the transition. The **transitional provisions** are sometimes complex. Those involving new disclosures (for example, Financial Instruments—Disclosures) tend to be applied prospectively. Those that require existing SFP items to be remeasured (for example, Employee Benefits) tend to require retrospective application by adjusting the opening asset and liability measurements and retained earnings and other equity balances. Some particularly major changes permit a choice of either prospective or retrospective application. The transitional provisions also set out specific disclosures that are required when the new or revised primary sources are adopted.

For all accounting changes, the requirements apply to each incident—it is not appropriate to net the effects of two or more changes when considering materiality. Let's turn now to how these methods are applied. Retrospective application and restatement are discussed first, followed by prospective application.

Retrospective Application—Change in Accounting Policy

Objective 4

Apply the retrospective application method of accounting for a change in accounting policy and identify the disclosure requirements.

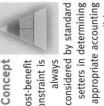

Underlying Concept

The cost-benefit constraint is always considered by standard setters in determining appropriate accounting policies.

When an entity voluntarily changes one of its accounting policies, retrospective application is considered the most informative method of accounting for these changes and reporting their effects on the financial statements. This method is often recommended in the specific transitional provisions of a new or revised primary source of GAAP as well.

The underlying principle of the retrospective application method is that all comparative periods are presented as if the new accounting policy had always been used. This outcome provides the best information to users who assess trends in financial information for prediction purposes. Specifically, retrospective application means that the opening balance of each affected component of equity is adjusted for the earliest prior period that is presented. In addition, all other affected comparative amounts that are disclosed for each prior period that is provided are presented as if the new accounting policy had always been in use.

Faced with having to retrospectively restate its financial statements of prior periods, an entity may find that data from specific prior periods may not be available, or may only be available at too high a cost. A limited version of retrospective application may need to be applied if it is impracticable to do the restatements; that is, if the entity cannot determine the effects on a specific prior period or the cumulative effect of the change in policy for all comparative prior periods after making all reasonable efforts to do so.

The accounting standards clearly explain what is meant by **impracticable**. It is considered impracticable to apply a change to a particular prior period if any of the following situations are true:

1. The effects of the retrospective application cannot be determined.

2. Assumptions are needed about what management's intents were in that prior period.

3. Significant estimates must be made that need to take into account circumstances that existed in that prior period, and it is no longer possible to do this.

Partial retrospective application is allowed only when one or more of these three limitations exist. If the cumulative effect cannot be determined even on the opening balances of the current period, then a change in accounting policy is accounted for prospectively.

Retrospective Application with Full Restatement of Comparative Information

Retrospective application with full restatement of all comparative information is applied as follows:

1. An accounting entry is made to recognize the effects of the new accounting policy that is being applied retrospectively, along with any related income tax effects.

2. Financial statement amounts for prior periods that are included for comparative purposes are restated to give effect to the new accounting policy. The entity adjusts the opening balance of the specific components of equity that are affected for the earliest prior period included in the report, along with other relevant accounts affected for each period.

3. Disclosures are made that enable users of the financial statements to understand the effects of any changes on the financial statements so that the statements remain comparable to those of other years and of other entities.

To illustrate full retrospective application, assume that Denson Ltd. follows ASPE and has expensed all interest costs incurred on self-constructed assets since beginning its major capital upgrading project in 2012. The company recognizes deferred/future taxes. In 2014, the company changes its accounting policy to one of capitalizing all avoidable interest costs related to the self-constructed assets. Management believes that this approach provides a more relevant measure of income earned as well as a better reflection of the asset's cost. Shareholders and financial analysts are better able to assess a period's operating performance and prospects for the future with information that is reported under this changed accounting policy. The company is subject to a 30% tax rate. Denson has also expensed interest for tax purposes and plans to continue using this method in the future. Illustration 21-2 provides the information for analysis.

Illustration 21-2

Data for Full Retrospective Application Example

Interest Expensed Policy
Reported in Prior Years

	2014	2013	2012
Income Statement			
Income before income tax	$ 190,000	$ 160,000	$ 400,000
Income tax—30%	57,000	48,000	120,000
Net income	$ 133,000	$ 112,000	$ 280,000
Statement of Retained Earnings			
Opening balance	$1,752,000	$1,640,000	$1,360,000
Net income	133,000	112,000	280,000
Closing balance	$1,885,000	$1,752,000	$1,640,000

Incomes if **Interest Capitalization Policy** Had Been Used

	2014	2013	2012
Income Statement			
Income before income tax	$ 200,000	$ 180,000	$ 600,000
Income tax—30%	60,000	54,000	180,000
Net income	$ 140,000	$ 126,000	$ 420,000

Differences in Income, Income Tax, and Net Income
Using Interest Capitalization Policy

	2014	2013	2012
Increase in income before tax	$ 10,000	$ 20,000	$ 200,000
Increase in income tax expense	3,000	6,000	60,000
Increase in net income	$ 7,000	$ 14,000	$ 140,000

Accounting Entry to Recognize the Change. The first step is to make the accounting entry to recognize this change in accounting policy. Because the 2014 accounts have not yet been closed, any adjustments that are needed to 2014's income are made to the income statement and balance sheet accounts themselves, while any changes to prior years are made through retained earnings.

The entry to record the change effective January 1, 2014, is:

Buildings	220,000	
Deferred Tax Liability		66,000
Retained Earnings		154,000

A	=	L	+	SE
+220,000	=	+66,000	+	+154,000

Cash flows: No effect

The Buildings account, net of its accumulated depreciation, is increased by $220,000. This represents the additional costs charged to the capital asset account for interest, less the related increase in the accumulated depreciation account from the increased depreciation expense since the assets were completed and used in operations ($200,000 + $20,000). The $220,000 adjustment brings these accounts to what the January 1, 2014 balances would have been if the revised policy had been in effect since the beginning of

Alternative Terminology

IFRS uses the terms current tax expense (income) and deferred tax expense (income), whereas ASPE suggests current income tax expense (benefit) and future income tax expense (benefit). We use the ASPE term "benefit" rather than "income" when describing tax-related income statement accounts, and we use the other terms interchangeably in this text.

construction. In reality, both the asset account and its contra account—the accumulated depreciation—are affected. The adjustment is shown as a net amount so you can focus on the other balance sheet effects.

The Deferred Tax Liability credit recognizes the tax effects of the taxable temporary difference; that is, the difference between the carrying amount and tax basis of the capital asset account. In future periods, because taxable income will be higher than accounting income as a result of this temporary difference at January 1, 2014, a deferred tax liability is recognized.[8] The adjustment to Retained Earnings is the accumulated after-tax effect of the new policy up to the beginning of the current year and represents all changes to prior years' incomes ($140,000 + $14,000 = $154,000). The entry corrects the accounts to January 1, 2014, and the revised policy is applied to the current year's operations.

The next step is to prepare the comparative financial statements by restating them as if the new policy had been in use from the beginning of 2012, the first year that Denson Ltd. incurred interest costs on self-constructed assets.

Financial Statement Presentation. Illustration 21-3 shows what the bottom portion of the income statement for Denson Ltd. looks like after giving effect to the retrospective change in accounting policy. It also presents the restated statements of retained earnings.[9]

Illustration 21-3

Comparative Income Statements and Statements of Retained Earnings

DENSON LTD.
Statement of Income
Year Ended December 31

	2014	2013 (restated)	2012 (restated)
Income before income tax	$ 200,000	$ 180,000	$ 600,000
Income tax—30%	60,000	54,000	180,000
Net income	$ 140,000	$ 126,000	$ 420,000

DENSON LTD.
Statement of Retained Earnings
Year Ended December 31

	2014 (restated)	2013 (restated)	2012 (restated)
Opening balance	$1,906,000	$1,780,000	$1,360,000
Net income	140,000	126,000	420,000
Closing balance	$2,046,000	$1,906,000	$1,780,000

The Buildings; Accumulated Depreciation; and Deferred Tax Liability accounts on the comparative balance sheet now appear as if the new accounting policy had always been used. This is the objective of retrospective application. However, it is important for the financial statement reader to be alerted to the fact that Denson did change a key policy in the year. The disclosure requirements are identified after our next illustration.

Retrospective Application with Partial Restatement of Comparative Information

Impracticability. As indicated earlier, retrospectively restating the financial statements of a prior year requires information that may, in many cases, be impracticable to obtain, even though the cumulative effect can be determined. For many reasons, however, it was not practicable for some companies to retroactively determine the effect of the new standard on specific prior years—a necessary condition for restatement. The standard's transitional provisions therefore permitted a partial retrospective application.

Thus, if the effect of a change in policy can be determined for some of the prior periods, the change in policy is applied retrospectively with restatement to the carrying

Underlying Concept

Applying full retrospective treatment and providing the related disclosures that are required is an attempt to restore the comparability of the income statements.

amounts of assets, liabilities, and affected components of equity at the beginning of the earliest period for which restatement is possible. This could even be the current year. An adjustment is made to the opening balances of the equity components for that earliest period, similar to the adjustments in the full restatement that was illustrated above.

While estimates can be used to allow some restatements to be made retrospectively, estimates should not be made for this purpose after the fact if it is impossible to objectively assess circumstances and conditions in prior years that need to be known in order to develop those estimates. It is not appropriate to apply hindsight in developing measurements that need to be used. Measurements must be based on conditions that existed and were known in the prior period.

If the entity cannot practicably determine the cumulative effect of the change even at the beginning of the current period, retrospective treatment cannot be applied. Instead, the entity applies the new accounting policy **prospectively** from the earliest date that is practicable. This situation may arise if the necessary data were not collected and cannot be recreated appropriately.

Example—Statement of Retained Earnings. In the Denson Ltd. example in Illustrations 21-2 and 21-3, the company was able to determine the effect of the change in accounting policy on each prior year affected. What would happen if the company had been using a policy of expensing interest on self-constructed assets for many years and management concluded that it was impracticable to determine the effects on specific years any further back than 2013? It knows what the effect is on the January 1, 2013 capital assets, deferred income tax liability, and retained earnings, but it does not know the income effects on specific years prior to that date. In this case, management is only able to determine the information provided in Illustration 21-4.

Illustration 21-4

Data for Partial Retrospective Application Example

	Interest Expensed Policy Reported in Prior Years			
Income Statement	2014	2013	2012	
Income before income tax	$ 190,000	$ 160,000	$ 400,000	
Income tax—30%	57,000	48,000	120,000	
Net income	$ 133,000	$ 112,000	$ 280,000	

	Incomes if **Interest Capitalization Policy** Had Been Used			
Statement of Retained Earnings	2014	2013	2012	
Opening balance	$1,752,000	$1,640,000	$1,360,000	
Net income	133,000	112,000	280,000	
Closing balance	$1,885,000	$1,752,000	$1,640,000	

	Differences in Income, Income Tax, and Net Income Using Interest Capitalization Policy			
Income Statement	2014	2013	2012	
Income before income tax	$ 200,000	$ 180,000	Unknown	
Income tax—30%	60,000	54,000		
Net income	$ 140,000	$ 126,000		

	2014	2013	2012	
Increase in income before tax	$ 10,000	$ 20,000	Unknown	
Increase in income tax expense	3,000	6,000		
Increase in net income	$ 7,000	$ 14,000		

When it is impracticable to determine the effects on a specific period that is presented for comparative purposes, the accounting standard indicates that the relevant assets and liabilities of the earliest prior period for which the effect is known should be adjusted, along with the opening balances of that period's equity accounts.

The journal entry to record the change in accounting policy is the same as the one that was made for the full restatement above:

Buildings	220,000	
Deferred Tax Liability		66,000
Retained Earnings		154,000

A	=	L	+	SE
+220,000		+66,000		+154,000

Cash flows: No effect

Illustration 21-5 shows how the comparative financial statements are presented when only partial retrospective restatement is possible.

Illustration 21-5

Partial Retrospective Application—Comparative Income Statements and Statements of Retained Earnings

DENSON LTD.
Statement of Income
Year Ended December 31

	2014	2013 (restated)	2012
Income before income tax	$ 200,000	$ 180,000	$ 400,000
Income tax—30%	60,000	54,000	120,000
Net income	$ 140,000	$ 126,000	$ 280,000

DENSON LTD.
Statement of Retained Earnings
Year Ended December 31

	2014 (restated)	2013 (restated)	2012
Opening balance, as previously reported		$1,640,000	
Change in capitalization of interest accounting policy		140,000	
Opening balance, as restated	$1,906,000	1,780,000	$1,360,000
Net income	140,000	126,000	280,000
Closing balance	$2,046,000	$1,906,000	$1,640,000

As the illustration shows, the 2012 financial statements are not restated. Instead, the effect of the policy change is carried back only to January 1, 2013, and the retained earnings amount at that date is adjusted for the cumulative effect of the change to that date. The new policy is applied in the 2013 and 2014 comparative income statements and balance sheets, and is supported by the required disclosures.

An expanded retained earnings statement is included in this presentation to show the type of adjustment that is needed to restate the beginning balance of retained earnings for the earliest prior period that is presented. In 2013, the beginning balance is adjusted for the excess of the "capitalization of interest" incomes over the "interest expensed" incomes prior to 2013 ($140,000). The restated balance is the amount that the opening balance would have been if the new policy had always been in effect. In 2014, the restated opening balance is what would have been in the accounts if the new policy had always been applied.

Partial Retrospective Application Example—Statement of Changes in Equity.
Let us assume now that Denson Ltd. prepares a statement of changes in equity rather than a statement of retained earnings. The same requirements apply, but the statement is formatted in a different way. We assume that Denson Ltd. has had share capital outstanding of $2 million since the beginning of its 2012 fiscal year, and the same change in interest capitalization

policy applies. Illustration 21-6 shows how the change would be presented in a comparative statement of changes in equity.

DENSON LTD.
Statement of Changes in Equity
Year Ended December 31, 2014

	Share Capital	Retained Earnings	Total
Balance, January 1, 2012	$2,000,000	$1,360,000	$3,360,000
Net income 2012		280,000	280,000
Balance December 31, 2012, as previously reported	$2,000,000	$1,640,000	$3,640,000
Cumulative effect of change in interest capitalization accounting policy		140,000	140,000
Balance January 1, 2013, as restated	$2,000,000	$1,780,000	$3,780,000
Net income 2013 (restated)		126,000	126,000
Balance December 31, 2013, as restated	$2,000,000	$1,906,000	$3,906,000
Net income 2014		140,000	140,000
Balance December 31, 2014	$2,000,000	$2,046,000	$4,046,000

This adjustment process might appear complicated at first. It may be helpful at this point for you to try to develop the revised income and retained earnings statements on your own assuming the interest capitalization policy had always been used. You should end up with the results in Illustrations 21-3, 21-5, and 21-6.

Is there any **effect on the statement of cash flows?** As you might expect, past cash flows for prior periods do not change just because we change an accounting policy in 2014. However, the category of cash flow will change in our example. Instead of all the interest paid being reported as an operating outflow, the restated financial statements report the capitalized interest as an investing outflow, thereby increasing the cash flow from operations above the amount previously reported. In other situations, the cash flow from operations does not change. Illustration 21-7 provides an example from **Canadian Pacific Railway Limited**. In that example, cash provided by operating activities and cash used in investing activities both decreased.

Continuing with our Denson Ltd. example, if the company had been unable to determine the effect on 2013's income, the adjustment would have been made instead to the opening balance of 2014's retained earnings. In the most limited circumstances, if it were not practicable to determine the cumulative effect even at the beginning of 2014, retrospective application is not possible and Denson would apply the new accounting policy on a prospective basis from the earliest possible date in the current year. The prospective method is explained later in the chapter where it is applied to changes in estimates.

Disclosures Required for a Change in Accounting Policy

Whether the change in accounting policy is due to an initial application of a primary source of GAAP or to a voluntary change, considerable information is required to be reported under both ASPE and IFRS. This helps readers understand why the change was made and what its effects are on previous and the current period financial statements. The information below is required to be disclosed in the period of the change, if practicable, regardless of whether the change was accounted for retrospectively or prospectively:

1. For an initial application of an IFRS or primary source, its title, the nature of the change and that it is made according to its transitional provisions, and what the provisions are

2. The nature of any voluntary change, and why the new policy provides reliable and more relevant information

3. The effects of the change, to the extent practicable, on each financial statement line item affected in the current period and on periods before those presented

4. Where full retrospective application is impracticable, additional information about why that is so, the periods affected, and how the change was handled

As indicated earlier in the chapter, under ASPE some voluntary accounting policy choice changes are exempt from having to provide "reliable and more relevant" information. Under IFRS, the information set out above is also required when a transitional provision or voluntary change might have an **effect on future periods**. Related to this disclosure is a requirement to report information about new standards that have been issued but are not yet effective and have not been applied. The entity discloses any reasonably reliable information that would be useful in assessing the effect of the new primary source on its financial statements when it will be first applied.

A limited amount of additional information is required to be disclosed under IFRS. This includes line-item adjustments for all prior periods presented and, for entities required to report earnings per share amounts, the adjustments needed to basic and fully diluted earnings per share (EPS) because of the accounting change. An opening balance sheet at the beginning of the earliest comparative period is also required.

Canadian Pacific Railway Limited (CPR) is a well-known Canadian transportation icon. Illustration 21-7 provides excerpts from CPR's financial statements for its year ended December 31, 2010, that indicate its disclosures related to a variety of accounting policy changes. These provide good examples of the retrospective application of voluntary changes in accounting policy as well as changes under the transitional requirements of primary sources of GAAP.

Real World Emphasis

Illustration 21-7

Example of Disclosure of Changes in Accounting Policy—Canadian Pacific Railway Limited

CANADIAN PACIFIC RAILWAY LIMITED
CONSOLIDATED STATEMENT OF CHANGES IN SHAREHOLDERS' EQUITY
December 31, 2010

(in millions of Canadian dollars)	Share capital	Additional paid-in capital	Accumulated other comprehensive loss	Retained earnings	Total shareholders' equity
Balance at December 31, 2007	$1,209.5	$47.6	$ (855.4)	$3,792.9	$4,194.6
Adjustment for change in accounting policy (Note 2)	—	—	2.0	(51.1)	(49.1)
Balance at December 31, 2007, as restated	1,209.5	47.6	(853.4)	3,741.8	4,145.5
Net income	—	—	—	627.8	627.8
Other comprehensive loss	—	—	(371.8)	—	(371.8)
Dividends declared	—	—	—	(152.2)	(152.2)
Stock compensation expense	—	7.7	—	—	7.7
Shares issued under stock option plans	32.8	(14.7)	—	—	18.1
Balance at December 31, 2008, as restated	1,242.3	40.6	(1,225.2)	4,217.4	4,275.1
Net income	—	—	—	550.0	550.0
Other comprehensive loss	—	—	(519.5)	—	(519.5)
Dividends declared	—	—	—	(166.5)	(166.5)
Shares issued (Note 25)	495.2	—	—	—	495.2
Stock compensation recovery	—	(1.8)	—	—	(1.8)
Shares issued under stock option plans	33.6	(8.0)	—	—	25.6
Balance at December 31, 2009, as restated	1,771.1	30.8	(1,744.7)	4,600.9	4,658.1
Net income	—	—	—	650.7	650.7
Other comprehensive loss	—	—	(341.1)	—	(341.1)
Dividends declared	—	—	—	(178.6)	(178.6)
Stock compensation expense	—	1.2	—	—	1.2
Shares issued under stock option plans	41.7	(7.3)	—	—	34.4
Balance at December 31, 2010	$1,812.8	$24.7	$(2,085.8)	$5,073.0	$4,824.7

See Notes to Consolidated Financial Statements.

(continued)

ACCOUNTING FOR TRANSFERS OF FINANCIAL ASSETS

The FASB has released additional guidance with respect to the accounting and disclosure of transfers of financial assets such as securitized accounts receivable. Although the Company currently does not have an accounts receivable securitization program, the guidance, which includes revisions to the derecognition criteria in a transfer and the treatment of qualifying special purpose entities, would be applicable to any future securitization. The new guidance is effective for the Company from January 1, 2010. The adoption of this guidance had no impact to the Company's financial statements.

FAIR VALUE MEASUREMENT AND DISCLOSURE

In January 2010, the FASB amended the disclosure requirements related to fair value measurements. The update provides for new disclosures regarding transfers in and out of Level 1 and Level 2 financial asset and liability categories and expanded disclosures in the Level 3 reconciliation (see Note 21 for a definition of Level 1, 2 and 3 financial asset and liability categories). The update also provides clarification that the level of disaggregation should be at the class level and that disclosures about inputs and valuation techniques are required for both recurring and nonrecurring fair value measurements that fall in either Level 2 or Level 3. New disclosures and clarifications of existing disclosures are effective for interim and annual reporting periods beginning after December 15, 2009, except for the expanded disclosures in the Level 3 reconciliation, which are effective for fiscal years beginning after December 15, 2010. The Company has adopted this guidance resulting in expanded note disclosure in Note 21.

RAIL GRINDING

During the second quarter of 2010, the Company changed its accounting policy for the treatment of rail grinding costs. In prior periods, CP had capitalized such costs and depreciated them over the expected economic life of the rail grinding. The Company concluded that, although the accounting treatment was within acceptable accounting standards, it is preferable to expense the costs as incurred, given the subjectivity in determining the expected economic life and the associated depreciation methodology. The accounting policy change has been accounted for on a retrospective basis. The effects of the adjustment to January 1, 2010 resulted in an adjustment to decrease net properties by $89.0 million, deferred income taxes by $26.3 million, and shareholders' equity by $62.7 million. As a result of the change the following increases (decreases) to financial statement line items occurred:

(in millions of Canadian dollars, except per share data)	For the year ended December 31		
	2010	2009	2008
Changes to Consolidated Statement of Income and Comprehensive Income (Loss)			
Depreciation and amortization	$ (15.7)	$ (14.0)	$ (8.9)
Compensation and benefits	2.3	2.8	2.7
Fuel	—	0.1	0.1
Materials	0.8	1.8	1.7
Purchased services and other	13.8	15.9	15.4
Total operating expenses	1.2	6.6	11.0
Income tax expense	(0.7)	(1.2)	(3.2)
Net income	$ (0.5)	$ (5.4)	$ (7.8)
Basic earnings per share	$ —	$ (0.03)	$ (0.05)
Diluted earnings per share	$ —	$ (0.03)	$ (0.05)
Other comprehensive income (loss)	0.9	2.4	(2.8)
Comprehensive income (loss)	$ 0.4	$ (3.0)	$ (10.6)
Changes to Consolidated Statement of Cash Flows			
Cash provided by operating activities (decrease)	$ (16.9)	$ (20.6)	$ (19.9)
Cash used in investing activities (decrease)	$ (16.9)	$ (20.6)	$ (19.9)

	As at December 31,		As at January 1, 2008
	2010	2009	2008
Changes to Consolidated Balance Sheet			
Net properties	$ (88.6)	$ (89.0)	$ (86.2)	$ (70.6)
Deferred income tax liability	(26.3)	(26.3)	(26.5)	(21.5)
Accumulated other comprehensive loss (income)	2.5	1.6	(0.8)	2.0
Retained earnings	(64.8)	(64.3)	(58.9)	(51.1)

Illustration 21-7

Example of Disclosure of Changes in Accounting Policy—Canadian Pacific Railway Limited (continued)

CPR decided to adopt U.S. GAAP for its financial reporting in 2011.[10] Therefore, it was not affected by the transition to IFRS.

You will learn in the discussion of accounting errors that is covered next that retrospective restatements to correct errors are handled in the same way as retrospective application of a change in accounting policy. The Canadian Pacific Railway Limited example can be reviewed for that type of change as well. In addition, notice that retained earnings is not the only equity account that may be subject to restatement.

Retrospective Restatement—Correction of an Error

Objective 5

Apply retrospective restatement for the correction of an accounting error and identify the disclosure requirements.

Although the general approach to accounting for an error correction is similar to accounting for a change in accounting policy, the accounting standards make a distinction between the two: prior financial statements with material errors were never prepared in accordance with GAAP, unlike those that used a different, but acceptable, accounting policy. The term **retrospective restatement** is used in the case of an error correction. The result is the correction of amounts that were reported in the financial statements of prior periods as if the error had never occurred. Specifically, retrospective restatement takes place in the first set of financial statements that is completed after the error's discovery by:

- restating the comparative amounts for the prior period(s) presented in which the error occurred or
- if the error took place before the earliest prior period provided, restating the opening amounts of assets, liabilities, and equity for the earliest period presented.

ASPE allows only full retrospective restatement. An accounting error, by its definition and nature, can be traced to a specific prior year; therefore, full retrospective changes to all prior years that are affected are required.

IFRS, on the other hand, accept that there may be situations where it may be impracticable to determine the accounting adjustment needed for a specific prior period or for the cumulative effect of an error. In such a case, partial retrospective restatement is allowed, similar to the requirements for an accounting policy change.

- If the effect on each prior period presented cannot be determined, the opening amounts of the SFP elements for the earliest period the effects can be determined are restated. This may be the current period.
- If the cumulative effect on prior periods cannot be determined from the earliest possible date practicable.

Retrospective Restatement—Affecting One Prior Period

As soon as they are discovered, errors are corrected retrospectively by proper entries in the accounts and are reflected in the financial statements. In the year in which the error is discovered, the correction is recorded as an adjustment to the beginning balance of retained earnings. If comparative statements are presented, the prior statements that are affected are restated to correct the error so that they appear as if the error had never occurred. The accounting and reporting is similar to the examples of retrospective application for a voluntary change in accounting policy.

To illustrate, assume that the bookkeeper for Selectric Corporation discovered in 2014 that in 2013 the accountant had failed to record in the accounts $20,000 of depreciation expense on a newly constructed building. The company follows ASPE and recognizes deferred taxes. Selectric's tax rate is 30%.

As a result of the $20,000 depreciation error in 2013, the following balances are incorrect:

Depreciation expense (2013) was understated by:	$20,000
Accumulated depreciation at December 31, 2013/January 1, 2014, was understated by:	20,000
Deferred tax expense (2013) was overstated by ($20,000 × 30%):	6,000
Net income (2013) was overstated by ($20,000 − $6,000):	14,000
Deferred tax liability at December 31, 2013/January 1, 2014, was overstated by $20,000 × 30%):	6,000

The entry needed in 2014 to correct the omission of $20,000 of depreciation in 2013, assuming the books for 2013 have been closed, is:

Retained Earnings	14,000	
Deferred Tax Liability	6,000	
Accumulated Depreciation—Buildings		20,000

$$A = L + SE$$
$$-20,000 \quad -6,000 \quad -14,000$$

Cash flows: No effect

The Retained Earnings account is adjusted because all 2013 income statement accounts were closed to retained earnings at the end of that year. The journal entry to record the error correction is the same whether single-period or comparative financial statements are prepared; however, presentation on the financial statements will differ. If single-period financial statements are presented, the error is reported as an adjustment to the opening balance of retained earnings of the period in which the error is discovered, as Illustration 21-8 shows.

Retained earnings, January 1, 2014		
As previously reported (assumed)		$350,000
Correction of an error (depreciation)	$(20,000)	
Less: Applicable income tax reduction	6,000	
		(14,000)
Restated balance of retained earnings, January 1, 2014		336,000
Add: Net income 2014 (assumed)		400,000
Retained earnings, December 31, 2014		$736,000

If comparative financial statements are prepared, adjustments are made to correct the amounts of all affected accounts in the statements of all periods that are reported. The data for each year that is presented are restated to the correct amounts. In addition, the opening balance of retained earnings for the earliest period being reported is adjusted for any cumulative change in amounts that relates to periods that are prior to the reported periods. In the case of Selectric Corporation, the error of omitting the depreciation of $20,000 in 2013, which was discovered in 2014, results in restating the 2013 financial statements when they are presented for comparison with those of 2014. Illustration 21-9 shows the changes that need to be made to the previously reported amounts on the comparative statements.

Comparative Balance Sheet (restated) December 31, 2013	
Accumulated depreciation, buildings	+$20,000
Deferred tax liability	− 6,000
Retained earnings	− 14,000

Comparative Income Statement (restated) Year ended December 31, 2013	
Depreciation expense	+$20,000
Deferred tax expense	− 6,000
Net income	− 14,000

Comparative Statement of Retained Earnings Year ended December 31, 2013 (restated)	
Opening balance, January 1	no change
Net income	−$14,000
Ending balance, December 31	−$14,000

Selectric's 2014 financial statements (presented in comparative form with those of 2013) are prepared as if the error had not occurred; the only exception to this is the restated opening balance of retained earnings at January 1, 2014. In addition, a note to the 2014 financial statements is required that provides all appropriate disclosures.

Retrospective Restatement—Affecting Multiple Prior Periods

Assume that when preparing the financial statements for the year ended December 31, 2014, the controller of Shilling Corp. discovered that a property purchased in mid-2011 for $200,000 had been charged entirely to the Land account in error. The $200,000 cost should have been allocated between Land ($50,000) and Building ($150,000). The building was expected to be used for 20 years and then sold for $70,000 (not including the land). The company follows ASPE and recognizes deferred/future taxes. Prior to discovery of this error, Shilling Corp.'s accounting records reported the information in Illustration 21-10.

Illustration **21-10**

Accounting Records before Restatement

	2014 (books not closed)	2013
Revenues	$402,000	$398,000
Expenses	329,000	320,000
Income before tax	73,000	78,000
Income tax expense (30%)	21,900	23,400
Net income	$ 51,100	$ 54,600
Retained earnings, January 1	$294,000	$242,000
Net income for year	51,100	54,600
Dividends declared	(2,100)	(2,600)
Retained earnings, December 31	$343,000	$294,000

Retrospective restatement is required, so the first step is to determine the effect of this error on all prior periods. Preparing an appropriate analysis provides backup for the required correcting entry and helps in the restatement of the financial statements. The specific analysis differs for each situation encountered. However, each analysis requires identifying two things: first, what is in the books and records now; and second, what would have been in the accounts if the error had not occurred. The correcting entry then adjusts what is there now to what should be there. Illustration 21-11 shows the analysis that underlies the correcting entry to Shilling's accounts. Assume that the tax records were not updated for the building acquisition and therefore no CCA was claimed on the building over the years. Go through each line, making sure that you understand the source of each number.

Illustration **21-11**

Analysis of Error on Shilling's Records

	2014	2013	2012	2011
Income statement effects:				
Correct amount of depreciation expense ($150,000 − $70,000) ÷ 20 = $4,000 per year	$ 4,000	$ 4,000	$ 4,000	$ 2,000
Correct amount of tax benefit related to depreciation = 30% of depreciation expense	1,200	1,200	1,200	600
Income was overstated each year by:	$ 2,800	$ 2,800	$ 2,800	$ 1,400
Balance sheet effects, end of each year:				
Land reported	$200,000	$200,000	$200,000	$200,000
Correct land balance	50,000	50,000	50,000	50,000
Building reported	–0–	–0–	–0–	–0–
Correct building balance	150,000	150,000	150,000	150,000
Accumulated depreciation reported	–0–	–0–	–0–	–0–
Correct accumulated depreciation	14,000	10,000	6,000	2,000
Deferred tax asset reported re: building	–0–	–0–	–0–	–0–
Correct deferred tax asset balance (= 30% of temporary difference at year end)[11]	4,200	3,000	1,800	600

The correcting entry needed at the 2014 year end when the error is discovered is taken directly from the analysis in Illustration 21-11.

Building (150,000 − 0)	150,000
Depreciation Expense (4,000 − 0)	4,000
Deferred Tax Asset (4,200 − 0)	4,200
Retained Earnings (Jan. 1, 2014. 2,800 + 2,800 + 1,400)	7,000
Land (200,000 − 50,000)	150,000
Accumulated Depreciation—Buildings (14,000 − 0)	14,000
Current Tax Benefit (1,200 − 0)	1,200

A = L + SE
−9,800   −9,800
Cash flows: No effect

Let's review this entry. The objective is to correct the accounts so the amounts in the records are the same as they would have been if there had been no error. The Building account would have had a $150,000 balance, but now stands at $0, so we need to debit $150,000 to Building. Depreciation expense should have been taken on the building in 2014 but was not, so the current year's expense needs to be recognized. With income statement items, because all accounts get closed out each year to Retained Earnings, the correction to depreciation expense for 2011 to 2013 must be to Retained Earnings. The depreciation expense for 2014 has not yet been closed out, so the adjustment is made directly to the expense. The same explanation applies to the adjustment to Current Tax Benefit. In 2014, the adjustment is made to the expense account but for 2011 to 2013, it is made to Retained Earnings. In effect, the $7,000 adjustment to decrease the January 1, 2014 Retained Earnings balance represents the 2011 to 2013 Depreciation Expense correction of $10,000, net of the related Current Tax Benefit correction for the same three-year period of $3,000.

Three other balance sheet accounts need correcting. The Land account, now at $200,000, must be reduced to $50,000. The Accumulated Depreciation now stands at $0 but should be $14,000. Lastly, the Deferred Tax Asset account related to the temporary deductible difference between the tax basis (UCC) of the building and its revised carrying amount is recognized.

Now that the records have been adjusted, the accounting error has to be reported on the comparative statements for 2013, assuming that only one year's comparative statements are provided. These financial statements are presented "as if the error had never occurred." If the error occurred before the earliest period that is presented, as in this situation, then the opening balances of the related assets, liabilities, and equity for the earliest prior period presented are restated. The required income statements and statements of retained earnings are presented in Illustration 21-12.

Illustration 21-12

Retrospective Restatement of Comparative Statements—Shilling Corp.

Income Statement

	2014	2013 (restated)
Revenues	$402,000	$398,000
Expenses	333,000[a]	324,000[b]
Income before tax	69,000	74,000
Income tax expense	20,700[c]	22,200[d]
Net income	$ 48,300	$ 51,800

Statement of Retained Earnings

	2014	2013 (restated)
Retained earnings, January 1, as previously reported	$329,000 + $4,000 [a]	$287,000
Cumulative effect of accounting error, net of tax benefit of $1,800		(4,200)
Retained earnings, January 1, as restated	$320,000 + $4,000 [b]	237,800
Net income	48,300	51,800
Less: Dividends declared	(2,100)	(2,600)
Retained earnings, December 31	$333,200	$287,000

[c] $21,900 − $1,200
[d] $23,400 − $1,200

The adjustments to the income statement are relatively straightforward as the expenses and income tax lines are simply changed to the corrected amounts. The earliest retained earnings balance that is reported now has to be restated to what it would have been if the error had never occurred.

For the 2013 statement of retained earnings, the previously reported opening retained earnings balance (that is, the 2012 ending balance) is adjusted for the effects on income (and therefore retained earnings) prior to January 1, 2013. The cumulative adjustment at this date is $4,200. This reflects the $6,000 of additional depreciation expense ($2,000 + $4,000) reduced by the $1,800 of related income tax benefit ($600 + $1,200) to January 1, 2013. If the error had not been made, the balance of retained earnings at January 1, 2013, would have been $237,800. The revised 2013 net income of $51,800 is added to this and the 2013 dividends are deducted in determining the corrected December 31, 2013 balance of retained earnings.

For 2014, the restated opening retained earnings for 2014 of $287,000 is the balance that would have been reported if the error had never occurred. The correct income for 2014 is added to this and the 2014 dividends are deducted to give the retained earnings at the end of 2014. It is not an accounting error in the current year.

The comparative balance sheet for 2013 is designated as "restated" and information is disclosed about the effect on each financial statement line item that has been affected. Under IFRS, an opening January 1, 2013 comparative SFP must also be presented with the correct amounts reported.

It may be useful to revisit the Canadian Pacific Railway Limited example in Illustration 21-7 to review how this company applied retrospective adjustments. Although the examples provided were not error corrections, the general approach is the same. Also notice that equity accounts other than retained earnings are changed using the same approach when changes affect them.

Disclosures Required for the Correction of an Accounting Error

The disclosures required when a company corrects an error in a prior period are few, but informative. The following are disclosed in the year of the correction, but are not necessary in subsequent periods:

1. The nature of the error

2. The amount of the correction made to each affected financial statement item for each prior period presented

3. The amount of the correction made at the beginning of the earliest prior period presented

IAS 8 *Accounting Policies, Changes in Accounting Estimates and Errors* requires two additional disclosures. Because IAS 8 recognizes that it may not be practicable to determine the correction's effect on each specific prior period, an entity is required to provide information about the circumstances leading to any impracticality and how such an error has been corrected. Also, the effect of the correction on both basic and fully diluted earnings per share is reported for each prior period presented. IAS 1 *Presentation of Financial Statements* also requires an opening SFP for the earliest comparative period presented.

Objective **6**

Apply the prospective application method for an accounting change and identify the disclosure requirements for a change in an accounting estimate.

Prospective Application

As explained above, the effects of changes in estimates are handled prospectively. That is, no changes are made to previously reported results—they are made forward from the time of the change in estimate. Changes in estimates are viewed as normal recurring corrections and adjustments—the natural result of the accounting process—and retrospective treatment is therefore not appropriate. Opening balances are not adjusted, and no attempt is made to "catch up" for prior periods. The financial statements of prior periods are not restated.

Instead, the effect of a change in estimate is accounted for by including it in net income or comprehensive income, as appropriate, in (1) the period of change if the change affects that period only, or (2) the period of change and future periods if the change affects both. If the estimate relates to the balance of an asset, liability, or equity item, the item's carrying amount is changed.

The circumstances related to a change in estimate are different from those related to a change in accounting policy. If changes in estimates were handled on a retroactive basis, continual adjustments of prior years' income would occur. It seems proper to accept the view that, because new conditions or circumstances exist, the revision fits the new situation and should be handled in the current and future periods only.

As indicated earlier in the chapter, **it is also appropriate to apply prospective treatment to a change in accounting policy** if it is impracticable to determine the effect of the change even as far back as the beginning of the current period. In such a situation, the new accounting policy is only applied to transactions and events that occur after the accounting policy is changed.

Illustration—Change in Estimate

To illustrate the accounting for a change in estimate, assume that Underwriter Labs Inc. purchased a building for $300,000 that was originally estimated to have a useful life of 15 years and no residual value. Depreciation of $20,000 per year has been recorded for five years on a straight-line basis. In 2014, the total useful life estimate is revised to 25 years. The accounts at the beginning of the sixth year are as follows:

Building	$300,000
Less accumulated depreciation at end of 2013: 5 × $20,000 =	100,000
Carrying amount of building, January 1, 2014	$200,000

Assuming no entry has yet been made in 2014, the entry to record depreciation for 2014 is:

Depreciation Expense	10,000	
Accumulated Depreciation—Buildings		10,000

The $10,000 depreciation charge is calculated in Illustration 21-13.

$$\text{Depreciation charge} = \frac{\text{Carrying amount of asset} - \text{Residual value}}{\text{Remaining service life}} = \frac{\$200,000 - \$0}{25 \text{ years} - 5 \text{ years}} = \$10,000$$

Illustration 21-13

Depreciation after Change in Estimate

A	=	L	+	SE
−10,000				−10,000

Cash flows: No effect

Prospective treatment applied to a change in accounting policy simply means that the new policy is applied to the current balance of the related asset, liability, and/or equity item after the date of change.

Disclosure Requirements for a Change in an Accounting Estimate

Disclosures for changes in estimates have the same objective as other types of changes: to provide information that is useful in assessing the effects of the change on the financial statements. In addition to reporting the nature and amount of any change in estimate that affects the current period, as required under ASPE, IFRS also requires reporting of the nature and amount of any change that is expected to affect future periods, unless it is impracticable to estimate its effect. If impracticable to estimate, this fact is disclosed.

Do companies have to disclose changes in accounting estimates made as part of normal operations, such as bad debt allowances or inventory obsolescence? Materiality plays an important role here, as it does with other accounting standards. Although the change may have little effect in the current year, the effect on future periods has to be considered.

Example of Disclosure of a Change in Estimate

Qantas Airways Limited, an international airline headquartered in Sydney, Australia, reports under international reporting standards. Illustration 21-14 captures Qantas's disclosure about a change in accounting estimate it reported in its financial statements for its year ended June 30, 2010, followed by disclosures from its financial statements for the year ended June 30, 2011.

Real World Emphasis

Illustration 21-14

Example of Disclosure of a Change in Accounting Estimate—Qantas Airways Limited

2010:

Change in accounting estimates – passenger aircraft residual value
Effective 1 January 2010, the estimated residual values of passenger aircraft were revised to between nil and 10 per cent of acquisition cost. The estimated residual values had been between nil and 20 per cent.

These changes resulted in an increase in depreciation expense of the Qantas Group for the period from 1 January 2010 to 30 June 2010 of $50 million. The annual impact of these changes will progressively decrease until the end of the estimated useful lives of the affected assets.

Change in accounting estimates – software
The Qantas Group revised the estimated useful lives of core system software from five to 10 years effective 1 January 2009. The net effect of the change in the current financial year was a decrease in amortisation expense of the Qantas Group by $26 million (2009: $17 million).

Change in accounting estimates – Qantas Frequent Flyer
Qantas Frequent Flyer changed the accounting estimates of the fair value of points and breakage expectation effective 1 January 2009. The launch of the Qantas Frequent Flyer enhanced program in July 2008 has improved the reliability of Management's estimate of the fair value of the award for which points are expected to be redeemed. The effect of this change is being applied prospectively from 1 January 2009 for new points issued. Unredeemed points as at 1 January 2009 remain deferred at the previous estimate and will be redeemed at this value until these points are extinguished.

If the accounting estimates had not been changed, the reported revenue of the Qantas Group would be lower by $153 million (2009: $164 million of which $84 million relates to a non-recurring benefit arising from the direct earn conversion implemented in 2009).

2011:

Change in accounting estimates – Passenger Aircraft Residual Value
From 1 January 2010 the estimated residual values of passenger aircraft were revised to between nil and 10 per cent of acquisition cost. The estimated residual values had been between nil and 20 per cent. These changes resulted in an increase in depreciation expense of $93 million (2010: $50 million) to the Qantas Group for the year ended 30 June 2011.

Change in Accounting Estimates – Major Cyclical Maintenance Costs for Operating Leased Aircraft
Historically the costs of major cyclical maintenance checks for operating leased aircraft were expensed as incurred, as the difference from capitalising and depreciating these amounts over the shorter of their useful life or the remaining lease term was immaterial.

During the year ended 30 June 2011 the difference between expensing the maintenance checks as incurred and capitalising/ depreciating became material due to the average age and resultant maintenance profile of the operating leased aircraft. Therefore, from 1 July 2010 the Qantas Group has capitalised and depreciated the costs of these checks over the shorter of their useful life or the remaining lease term. Maintenance checks covered by third party agreement where there is a transfer of risk and legal obligation continue to be expensed on the basis of hours flown. This aligns the maintenance accounting for operating leased aircraft with owned and finance leased aircraft.

This change resulted in $50 million of maintenance costs being capitalised in property, plant and equipment as at 30 June 2011 (net of depreciation). The effect of this change in the current year profit and loss was an increase in depreciation expense of $5 million and a decrease in aircraft operating variable expense of $55 million.

Summary of Accounting Changes

Developing recommendations for reporting accounting changes has helped resolve several significant and long-standing accounting problems. Yet, because of the diversity of situations and of characteristics of the items that are encountered in practice, applying professional judgement is still very important. The primary objective is to serve the user of the financial statements. Achieving this requires accuracy, full disclosure, and the avoidance of any misleading inferences.

The major accounting approaches that were presented in earlier discussions are summarized in Illustration 21-15.

Illustration 21-15

Accounting Approaches to Accounting Changes

Accounting Change	Accounting Method to Apply			
	Method Indicated in the Standard	Retrospective		Prospective
		Full Retrospective	Partial Retrospective	
CHANGE IN ACCOUNTING POLICY				
On adoption of, or change in, a primary source of GAAP— transitional provision included: IFRS and ASPE	✓			
On adoption of, or change in, a primary source of GAAP— no transitional provision or if it is a voluntary change: IFRS and ASPE		✓ if practicable	✓ if retrospective treatment is not practicable	✓ if retrospective treatment is not practicable
Change within the allowed accounting policy choices identified in *CICA Handbook*, Part II, Section 1506: ASPE only		✓ if practicable	✓ if retrospective treatment is not practicable	✓ if retrospective treatment is not practicable
CORRECTION OF AN ERROR IFRS only		✓ if practicable	✓ if full retrospective treatment is not practicable	✓ if full retrospective treatment is not practicable
ASPE only		✓ if practicable	✓ if full retrospective treatment is not practicable	✓ if full retrospective treatment is not practicable
CHANGE IN ACCOUNTING ESTIMATE IFRS and ASPE				✓

ANALYSIS

Motivations for Change

Understanding how an entity chooses its accounting methods and procedures is complex. The complexity is due to the fact that managers, and others, have an interest in how the financial statements make the company appear. Managers naturally want to show their financial performance in the best light. A favourable profit picture can influence investors, and a strong liquidity position can influence creditors. Too favourable a profit picture, however, can provide union negotiators with ammunition during bargaining talks. Also, if the federal government has established price controls, managers might believe that a trend of lower profits might persuade the regulatory authorities to grant their company a price increase. Hence, managers might have varying profit motives, depending on the economy and who they want to impress.

Objective 7

Identify economic motives for changing accounting methods and interpret financial statements where there have been retrospective changes to previously reported results.

Research has provided insights into why companies may prefer certain accounting methods.[12] Some of these reasons are as follows.

1. **Political costs:** As companies become larger and more politically visible, politicians and regulators devote more attention to them. The larger the firm, the more likely it is to become subject to legislation such as anti-competition regulations and the more likely it is to be required to pay higher taxes. Therefore, companies that are politically visible may try to report income numbers that are low in order to avoid the scrutiny of regulators. By reporting low income numbers, companies hope to reduce their exposure to being viewed as a monopoly power. This practice can have an effect on other concerned parties as well. For example, labour unions may be less eager to demand wage increases if reported income is low. Researchers have found that the larger a company is, the more likely it is to adopt approaches that decrease income when it selects its accounting methods.

2. **Capital structure:** Several studies have found that a company's capital structure can affect the selection of accounting methods. For example, a company with a high debt-to-equity ratio is more likely to be constrained by debt covenants. A company may be considered in default on its bonds if the debt-to-equity ratio is too high. As a result, this type of company is more likely to select accounting methods that will increase net income—such as capitalizing interest instead of expensing it, or using the full cost method instead of the successful efforts approach for exploration and development costs in the oil and gas industry.

3. **Bonus payments:** Studies have found that if compensation plans tie managers' bonus payments to income, management may select accounting methods that maximize bonus payments.

4. **Smooth earnings:** Substantial increases in earnings attract the attention of politicians, regulators, and competitors. In addition, large increases in income create problems for management because the same results are difficult to achieve in subsequent years. Compensation plans may adjust to these higher numbers as a baseline and make it difficult for management to achieve its profit goals and receive bonuses in the following years. On the other hand, decreases in earnings might signal that the company is in financial trouble. Furthermore, significant changes in income raise concerns on the part of shareholders, lenders, and other interested parties about the riskiness of the company. For all these reasons, companies have an incentive to "manage" or "smooth" their earnings. Management typically believes that steady growth of 10% each year is much better than 30% growth one year followed by a 10% decline the next. In other words, management usually prefers to report gradually increasing income and it sometimes changes accounting methods to ensure such a result.

Ethics

Management pays careful attention to the accounting it follows and often changes accounting methods, not for conceptual reasons, but rather for economic reasons. As indicated throughout this textbook, such arguments have come to be known as **economic consequences** arguments, since they focus on the supposed impact of accounting on the behaviour of investors, creditors, competitors, governments, and the managers of the reporting companies themselves, rather than address the conceptual justification for accounting standards.[13]

To counter these pressures, standard setters have declared, as part of their conceptual framework, that they will assess the merits of proposed standards from a position of **neutrality**. That is, the soundness of standards should not be evaluated on the grounds of their possible impact on behaviour. It is not the standard setter's place to choose standards according to the kinds of behaviour that they want to promote or discourage. At the same time, the reality is that accounting numbers influence behaviour. Nonetheless, the justification for accounting choices should be conceptual, and not viewed in terms of their economic impact.

Underlying Concept

Neutrality is an aspect of reliability and faithful representation.

Interpreting Accounting Changes

What effect do accounting changes have on financial statement analysis? Not surprisingly, they often make it difficult to develop meaningful trend data, which undermines one of the major reasons that accounting information has been found useful in the past.

The year 2011 was huge for companies in Canada, both public and private. Public companies had to switch to IFRS and private companies following GAAP had the choice to switch to IFRS or ASPE for years beginning on or after January 1, 2011. The switchover required a significant number of accounting changes. The AcSB and IASB drafted separate standards (Section 1500 and IFRS 1, respectively) that provided some guidance on the move to IFRS or ASPE.

In principle, the changes were to be made retrospectively but because of costs and practical considerations, both standard-setting bodies provided some relief by allowing exemptions from the retrospective requirement. For instance, for property, plant, and equipment, entities were allowed to use fair value as an estimate of cost as at the transition date. Both standards required significant disclosures, including three statements of financial positions (with one of these being an opening statement for the comparative year). Reconciliations between equity and income under pre-changeover GAAP to IFRS and/or ASPE were required in sufficient detail to allow users to fully understand the impact.

Companies produced their 2010 financial statements as usual under pre-changeover GAAP and then in 2011 had to produce the 2011 statements under IFRS or ASPE with restated 2010 comparatives. Illustration 21-16 contains some excerpts from the financial statements of **Air Canada** for the 2011 year.

Illustration 21-16

Excerpt from Air Canada Financial Statements— Transition to IFRS

CONSOLIDATED STATEMENT OF FINANCIAL POSITION

(Canadian dollars in millions)		December 31, 2011	December 31, 2010	January 1, 2010
ASSETS				
Current				
Cash and cash equivalents	Note 3P	$ 848	$ 1,090	$ 1,115
Short-term investments	Note 3Q	1,251	1,102	292
Total cash, cash equivalents and short-term investments		2,099	2,192	1,407
Restricted cash	Note 3R	76	80	78
Accounts receivable		712	641	701
Aircraft fuel inventory		92	67	63
Spare parts and supplies inventory		93	88	64
Prepaid expenses and other current assets	Note 3S	255	279	338
Total current assets		3,327	3,347	2,651
Property and equipment	Note 5	5,088	5,629	6,287
Intangible assets	Note 6	312	317	329
Goodwill	Note 7	311	311	311
Deposits and other assets	Note 8	595	549	547
Total assets		**$ 9,633**	**$ 10,153**	**$ 10,125**
LIABILITIES				
Current				
Accounts payable and accrued liabilities		$ 1,175	$ 1,182	$ 1,246
Advance ticket sales		1,554	1,375	1,288
Current portion of long-term debt and finance leases	Note 9	424	567	468
Total current liabilities		3,153	3,124	3,002

(continued)

Long-term debt and finance leases	Note 9	3,906	4,028	4,313
Pension and other benefit liabilities	Note 10	5,563	3,328	3,940
Maintenance provisions	Note 11	548	493	461
Other long-term liabilities	Note 12	469	468	429
Total liabilities		**$ 13,639**	**$ 11,441**	**$ 12,145**

EQUITY

Shareholders' equity

Share capital	Note 14	840	846	844
Contributed surplus		58	54	53
Deficit		(4,983)	(2,334)	(2,881)
Accumulated other comprehensive loss	Note 18	–	–	(184)
Total shareholders' equity		(4,085)	(1,434)	(2,168)
Non-controlling interests		79	146	148
Total equity		**(4,006)**	**(1,288)**	**(2,020)**
Total liabilities and equity		**$ 9,633**	**$ 10,153**	**$ 10,125**

2. BASIS OF PREPARATION AND ADOPTION OF IFRS

The Corporation prepares its financial statements in accordance with Canadian generally accepted accounting principles ("GAAP") as defined in the Handbook of the Canadian Institute of Chartered Accountants – Part 1 ("CICA Handbook"). In 2010, the CICA Handbook was revised to incorporate International Financial Reporting Standards ("IFRS") as issued by the International Accounting Standards Board, and to require publicly accountable enterprises to apply IFRS effective for years beginning on or after January 1, 2011. Accordingly, these are the Corporation's first annual consolidated financial statements prepared in accordance with IFRS. In these financial statements, the term "Canadian GAAP" refers to GAAP in Canada before the adoption of IFRS and the term "GAAP" refers to generally accepted accounting principles in Canada after the adoption of IFRS.

These financial statements have been prepared in accordance with GAAP. Subject to certain transition elections and exceptions disclosed in Note 25, the Corporation has consistently applied the accounting policies used in the preparation of its opening IFRS statement of financial position at January 1, 2010 throughout all periods presented, as if these policies had always been in effect. Note 25 discloses the impact of the transition to IFRS on the Corporation's reported statement of financial position, statement of operations and cash flows, including the nature and effects of significant changes in accounting policies from those used in the Corporation's consolidated financial statements for the year ended December 31, 2010 prepared under Canadian GAAP.

These financial statements were approved by the Board of Directors of the Corporation for issue on February 9, 2012.

Reconciliation of the Consolidated Statement of Operations as previously reported under Canadian GAAP to IFRS

(Canadian dollars in millions except per share figures)		Year ended December 31, 2010		
		Canadian GAAP(1)	Adjustment	IFRS
Operating revenues				
Passenger		$ 9,427	$	$ 9,427
Cargo		466		466
Other		893		893
Total revenues		10,786	–	10,786
Operating expenses				
Aircraft fuel		2,652		2,652
Wages, salaries and benefits	Note ii	1,885	28	1,913
Airport and navigation fees		961		961
Capacity purchase agreements		971		971
Depreciation, amortization and impairment	Note iii & v	679	122	801
Aircraft maintenance	Note iii & vi	682	(28)	654
Sales and distribution costs		581		581
Food, beverages and supplies		279		279

(continued)

Illustration 21-16

Excerpt from Air Canada Financial Statements– Transition to IFRS (continued)

Real World Emphasis

Communications and information technology	Note iv	195	195
Aircraft rent		346	353
Other 1,194 – 1,194		7	
Total operating expenses		10,425	10,554
Operating income before exceptional item		**361**	**232**
Provision adjustment for cargo investigations, net		46	46
Operating income		407	278
Non-operating income (expense)			
Foreign exchange gain	Note i, ii & vi	145	184
Interest income		19	19
Interest expense	Note i	(378)	(397)
Net financing expense relating to employee benefit liabilities	Note ii		39
Interest capitalized		1	(75)
Loss on assets	Note iii	(7)	1
Loss on financial instruments recorded at fair value		(3)	(1)
Other	Note vi	(20)	(11)
		(243)	(303)
Income (loss) before the following items		**164**	**(189)**
Non-controlling interest	Note i	(9)	9
Recovery of (provision for) income taxes			
Current		4	(25)
Deferred	Note v	(52)	49
		(48)	24
Net income (loss) for the year		$ 107	$ (24)

(1) Air Canada revised the presentation of certain operating expenses on the statement of operations for the year ended December 31, 2010 to conform to current year presentation. These revisions include a new expense line category within operating expenses referred to as Sales and distribution costs which includes sales commissions, credit card fees and other sales and distribution costs, including fees paid to global distribution system providers. The expense line category related to Capacity purchase agreements has been expanded to include fees paid under all capacity purchase arrangements, including those paid to Jazz and those paid to other carriers operating flights on behalf of Air Canada under commercial agreements.

Air Canada included additional details and disclosures as required under IFRS 1. Note 25 (the main financial statement note in the Air Canada statements that dealt with the change) is approximately 10 pages and therefore has not been replicated here. It is worthwhile to study some of these disclosures to see just how much the switch to IFRS affected the numbers. As can be seen above, net income for Air Canada went from $107 million to a loss of $24 million. The deficit went from $620 million to $2,334 million. Needless to say, a thorough understanding of the changes is necessary to interpret the impact on the various financial statement ratios.

Financial statement readers should look closely at all accounting changes and adjust any trend data appropriately. Although most adjustments result in no change in the company's cash position, some adjustments can end up converting previously reported operating cash flows to investment or financing flows. Most changes tend to shift earnings from one accounting period to another. The disclosures required by the accounting standards are the best source of input for the analysis.

Objective 8 IFRS/ASPE COMPARISON

Identify the differences between ASPE and IFRS related to accounting changes.

A Comparison of IFRS and ASPE

IFRS and ASPE standards covering how to choose accounting policies initially and how to account for changes in policy, corrections of errors, and changes in estimates are very similar. The significant differences between the two sets of GAAP are identified in Illustration 21-17.

Illustration 21-17

IFRS and ASPE Comparison Chart

	Accounting Standards for Private Enterprises (ASPE)—*CICA Handbook*, Part II, Sections 1100 and 1506	IFRS—IAS 1and 8	References to Related Illustrations and Select Brief Exercises
Accounting policies	Accounting policies applied are determined by applying the primary sources of GAAP—the principles and policies set out in Part II of the CICA Handbook, first in Sections 1400 to 3870, and then in the Accounting Guidelines. If not dealt with in a primary source or if additional guidance is needed, management uses policies consistent with the primary sources, and that are developed using professional judgement and the concepts in Section 1000.	Accounting policies applied are determined by applying the IFRS. If there is no specific IFRS that applies, management applies judgement in determining a policy that is relevant to the needs of users and is reliable. Judgement considers first the requirements of IFRS in similar situations, and then the definitions, recognition criteria, and elements in the Framework for the Preparation and Presentation of Financial Statements.	N/A
Changes in accounting policy	Other than a change in accounting policy that is required by a primary source of GAAP, an accounting policy can be changed under two circumstances: (1) when it results in reliable and more relevant information; and (2) when the choice is related to a change in GAAP methods within a number of specifically identified accounting standards.	Other than a change in accounting policy that is required by an IFRS, an accounting policy can be changed only under one circumstance: when it results in reliable and more relevant information.	N/A
Correction of an error	ASPE assumes that the correction can be made to each specific prior period. No allowance is made for impracticability.	IFRS permits other than full retrospective restatement in the situation that it is impracticable to determine the period-specific effects or cumulative effect of the error.	Illustration 21-15
Presentation and disclosure	There is no requirement for an additional balance sheet for retrospective treatment of an accounting policy or retrospective restatement, or reclassification of items in the financial statements.	When applying retrospective treatment for a change in accounting policy or restatement due to correction of an error, or when an entity reclassifies items in the financial statements, an opening SFP must be presented for the earliest comparative period reported.	Illustration 21-16
	There is no requirement to report on issued standards that are not yet effective.	Information about the effect of issued standards that are not yet effective is required to be disclosed.	

Looking Ahead

The accounting standards covering accounting changes as identified in this chapter have been updated relatively recently and no significant changes are expected to these standards—IFRS or ASPE—in the immediate future.

SUMMARY OF LEARNING OBJECTIVES

1 Identify and differentiate among the types of accounting changes.

There are three types of accounting changes. (1) Change in accounting policy: a change in the specific principles, bases, rules, or practices that an entity applies in the preparation of its financial statements. (2) Change in an accounting estimate: a change in the carrying amount of an asset or liability or the amount of an asset's periodic consumption from reassessing the current status of the asset or liability or the expected future benefits or obligations associated with it. (3) Correction of a prior period error: a change caused by an omission from or misstatement in prior years' financial statements from the misuse of or failure to use reliable information that existed at the time the statements were completed and that could have been used in their preparation and presentation.

2 Identify and explain alternative methods of accounting for accounting changes.

Accounting changes could be accounted for retrospectively, currently, or prospectively. The retrospective method requires restatement of prior periods as if the accounting change had been used from the beginning, or the error had never been made. The current method calculates a catch-up adjustment related to the effect on all prior years, and reports it in the current period. Prospective treatment requires making no adjustment for past effects, but instead, beginning to use the new method in the current and future periods.

3 Identify the accounting standards for each type of accounting change under ASPE and IFRS.

A change in accounting policy due to the initial application of a new primary source of GAAP is accounted for according to the transitional provisions of that standard. If none is provided, or if it is a voluntary change, retrospective application is used. A change in an accounting estimate is accounted for prospectively. Errors are corrected through full retrospective restatement.

4 Apply the retrospective application method of accounting for a change in accounting policy and identify the disclosure requirements.

Comparative periods are presented as if the new accounting policy had always been applied. The opening balance of each affected component of equity is adjusted for the earliest prior period presented, and all other affected comparative amounts for each prior period provided are restated. When the effects on particular prior periods are impracticable to determine, the cumulative effect of the change is shown as an adjustment to the beginning retained earnings of the earliest prior period possible. Required disclosures therefore include identifying the nature of the change, the effect on each financial statement item affected, the amounts relating to periods prior to those that are presented, and why full retrospective application was not applied, if applicable. If the change resulted from applying transitional provisions, information about the standards and the provisions is provided, including, if under IFRS, the effects on future periods. If it is a voluntary change, excluding specific ASPE accounting changes, the reasons why the new policy results in more relevant information are disclosed. Information about the future effect of changes in primary sources of GAAP that are issued but not yet effective is also required under IFRS.

5 Apply retrospective restatement for the correction of an accounting error and identify the disclosure requirements.

Comparative amounts for prior periods affected are restated, unless under IFRS it is not practicable to identify the effect on specific past periods. If the error is in a period before the earliest comparative statements included, the opening balances of the earliest comparative period are restated. An opening SFP is required under IFRS for the earliest comparative period presented as is information about the nature of any impracticality. The nature of the error and the amount of the adjustment to each comparative financial statement line item and to EPS are all required disclosures.

6 Apply the prospective application method for an accounting change and identify the disclosure requirements for a change in an accounting estimate.

Under prospective treatment, only the current and future fiscal periods are affected. There is no adjustment of current-year opening balances and no attempt is made to "catch up" for prior periods. The nature and amount of a change in an accounting estimate that affects the current period or, under IFRS, is expected to affect future periods, is required to be disclosed.

7 Identify economic motives for changing accounting methods and interpret financial statements where there have been retrospective changes to previously reported results.

Some of the aspects that affect decisions about the choice of accounting methods are (1) political costs,

(2) the capital structure, (3) bonus payments, and (4) the desire to smooth earnings. Financial statement users should analyze the information presented about accounting changes and adjust any trend information affected.

8 Identify the differences between ASPE and IFRS related to accounting changes.

The accounting standards under ASPE are very similar to those under IFRS. Minor differences exist, such as IAS 8's permitting partial retrospective treatment for the correction of an accounting error, ASPE allowing specific voluntary changes without justification on a "reliable and more relevant" basis, and IFRS requiring additional disclosures.

KEY TERMS

APPENDIX 21A

ERROR ANALYSIS

Objective 9
Correct the effects of errors and prepare restated financial statements.

In the past, it was unusual to see the correction of material errors in the financial statements of large corporations. Internal control procedures and the diligence of the accounting staff were normally sufficient to find and correct any major errors in the system before the statements were released. However, in the past decade, there were a number of well-publicized cases of major companies restating past results. For example, numerous companies in the United States and Canada, including Apple Inc., Pixar Inc., and Research In Motion, restated past financial statements for a number of years due to improper dating of stock option grants. Many top executives have signed settlements for large sums of money with their shareholders over these events. Smaller businesses may face different problems. These enterprises may not be able to afford an internal audit staff or be able to implement the necessary control procedures to ensure that accounting data are recorded accurately.

Restatements sometimes occur because of financial fraud. Financial frauds involve the intentional misstatement or omission of material information in the organization's financial reports. Common methods of financial fraud manipulation include recording fictitious revenues, concealing liabilities or expenses, and artificially inflating reported assets. Financial frauds made up only 8% of the frauds in a recent study on fraud but caused a median loss of $1 million—by far the most costly category of fraud. Presented below is a chart that compares loss amounts for 2012, 2010, and 2008 for financial statement fraud, corruption, and asset misappropriation.

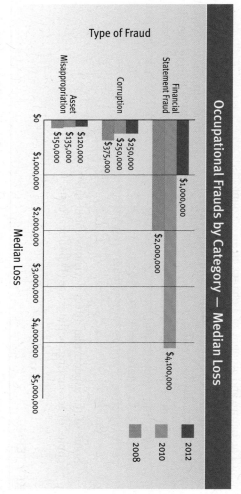

Occupational Frauds by Category — Median Loss

Type of Fraud (y-axis): Financial Statement Fraud, Corruption, Asset Misappropriation

Median Loss (x-axis): $0, $1,000,000, $2,000,000, $3,000,000, $4,000,000, $5,000,000

Legend: 2012, 2010, 2008

Values shown:
- Financial Statement Fraud: $1,000,000; $2,000,000; $4,100,000
- Corruption: $250,000; $250,000; $375,000
- Asset Misappropriation: $120,000; $135,000; $150,000

Companies must increase their efforts to protect their statements from the negative effects of fraud.

Source: Report to the Nations on Occupational Fraud and Abuse: 2012 Global Fraud Study, Association of Certified Fraud Examiners (2012), p. 11.

In practice, firms often do not correct errors that are discovered unless they have a significant effect on the financial statements. For example, the failure to record accrued wages of $5,000 when the total payroll for the year is $1,750,000 and net income is $940,000 is not considered significant, and no correction is made. Obviously, defining materiality is difficult, and experience and judgement are used to determine whether adjustment is necessary for a given error. All errors discussed in this section are assumed to be material and to require adjustment. For simplicity, we have chosen to ignore the tax effects initially so that you can focus instead on the direct effects of the errors themselves.

The accountant must answer three questions in error analysis:

1. What type of error is involved?

2. What entries are needed to correct the error?

3. How are financial statements to be restated once the error is discovered?

As indicated earlier, the standards usually require that errors be corrected retrospectively with restatement, meaning that the elements of the financial statements are adjusted as if the error had never occurred. Three types of errors can occur. Because each type has its own peculiarities, it is important to understand their differences.

Statement of Financial Position Errors

Statement of financial position errors affect only the presentation of an asset, liability, or shareholders' equity account. Examples are classifying a short-term receivable as part of the investment section, a note payable as an account payable, or plant assets as inventory. Reclassification of the item to its proper position is needed when the error is discovered. If comparative statements that include the error year are prepared, the SFP for the error year is restated.

Income Statement Errors

These errors affect only income statement accounts. Errors involve the improper classification of revenues or expenses, such as recording interest revenue as part of sales, purchases as bad debt expense, or amortization expense as interest expense. An income statement classification error has no effect on the SFP or on net income. If a reclassification error is discovered in the year the error is made, an entry is needed to correct it. If the error occurred in prior periods, no entry is needed at the date of discovery because the accounts for the year of the misclassification have all been closed to retained earnings and the current year is correctly stated. If comparative statements that include the error year are prepared, the income statement for the error year is restated.

Statement of Financial Position and Income Statement Errors

The third type of error involves both the statement of financial position and the income statement. For example, assume that accrued wages were overlooked by the accounting staff at the end of the accounting period. The error's effect is to understate expenses and liabilities, and overstate net income for that accounting period. This type of error affects both the SFP and the income statement and is either a counterbalancing or a non-counterbalancing error.

Counterbalancing errors are errors that will be offset or that will self-correct over two periods. In the previous illustration, the failure to record accrued wages is considered a counterbalancing error because, after a two-year period, the error will no longer be present. In other words, the failure to record accrued wages in year one means that (1) wages expense for the first period is understated, (2) net income for the first period is overstated, (3) accrued wages payable (a liability) at the end of the first period is understated, and (4) retained earnings at the end of the first period is overstated. In period two, wages expense is overstated and net income is understated, but both accrued wages payable (a liability) and retained earnings at the end of the second period **are now correct. For the two years combined, total wages expense and net income are correct,** as are the ending SFP amounts of wages payable and retained earnings. Most errors in accounting that affect both the SFP and income statement are counterbalancing errors.

Non-counterbalancing errors are errors that are not offset in the next accounting period. An example is the failure to capitalize equipment that has a useful life of five years. If we expense this asset immediately, expenses will be overstated in the first period but understated in the next four periods. At the end of the second period, the error's effect is not fully offset. Net income is only correct overall at the end of five years, because the asset will have been fully depreciated at this point, assuming it has no residual value. Thus, **non-counterbalancing errors are those that take longer than two periods to correct themselves.**

Only in rare instances does an error never reverse. This would occur, for example, if land were initially expensed. Because land is not subject to depreciation, the error is not offset until the land is sold.

Counterbalancing Errors

The usual types of counterbalancing errors are illustrated on the following pages. In studying these illustrations, several points should be remembered. **First**—and this is key—**the entries will differ depending on whether or not the books have been closed for the period in which the error is found.**

1. When the books have been closed:
   (a) If the error is already counterbalanced, no entry is necessary.
   (b) If the error is not yet counterbalanced, an entry is necessary to adjust the present balance of retained earnings and the other affected SFP account(s).

2. When the books have not been closed:

(a) If the error is already counterbalanced and the company is in the second year, an entry is necessary to correct the current period income statement account(s) and to adjust the beginning balance of retained earnings.

(b) If the error is not yet counterbalanced, an entry is necessary to adjust the beginning balance of retained earnings and correct the affected current period income statement account(s) and SFP account(s).

Second, if comparative statements are presented, it is necessary to restate the amounts for comparative purposes. **Restatement is necessary even if a correcting journal entry is not required.** To illustrate, assume that Sanford Cement Ltd. failed to accrue revenue in 2012 when it was earned, but recorded the revenue in 2013 when it was received. The error is discovered in 2015. No entry is necessary to correct this error, because the effects have been counterbalanced by the time the error is discovered in 2015. However, if comparative financial statements for 2012 through to 2015 are presented, the accounts and related amounts for the years 2012 and 2013 are restated for financial reporting purposes.

The following are examples of counterbalancing errors. Income tax effects have been ignored for now. Work with the entries until you understand each one. In addition, the 2014 comparative financial statements would need to be restated.

1. **Failure to record accrued wages:** On December 31, 2014, accrued wages of $1,500 were not recognized. The entry in 2015 to correct this error, assuming that the books have not been closed for 2015, is:

Retained Earnings	1,500	
Salaries and Wages Expense		1,500

The rationale for this entry is as follows: When the wages relating to 2014 were paid in 2015, an additional debit of $1,500 was made to 2015 Wages Expense, overstating this account by $1,500. Because 2014 wages were not recorded as Salaries and Wages Expense for 2014, net income for 2014 was overstated by $1,500. Because 2014 net income was overstated by $1,500, the 2015 opening Retained Earnings were also overstated by $1,500, because net income is closed to Retained Earnings.

If the books have been closed for 2015, no entry is made, because the error is counter-balanced.

2. **Failure to record prepaid expenses:** In January 2014, a two-year insurance policy costing $1,000 was purchased. Insurance Expense was debited, and Cash was credited. No adjusting entries were made at the end of 2014. The entry on December 31, 2015, to correct this error, assuming that the books have not been closed for 2015, is:

Insurance Expense	500	
Retained Earnings		500

Cash flows: No effect

A	=	L	+	SE		
0		0		0		

If the books are closed for 2015, no entry is made, because the error is counter-balanced.

3. **Understatement of unearned revenue:** On December 31, 2014, cash of $50,000 was received as a prepayment for renting office space for the following year. The entry that was made when the rent payment was received was a debit to Cash and a credit to Rent Revenue. No adjusting entry was made as at December 31, 2014. The entry on December 31, 2015, to correct this error, assuming that the books have not been closed for 2015, is:

Cash flows: No effect

A	=	L	+	SE		
0		0		0		

| Retained Earnings | 50,000 | |
| Rent Revenue | | 50,000 |

If the books are closed for 2015, no entry is made, because the error is counterbalanced.

4. **Overstatement of accrued revenue:** On December 31, 2014, interest income of $8,000 was accrued that applied to 2015. The entry made on December 31, 2014, was to debit Interest Receivable and credit Interest Income. The entry on December 31, 2015, to correct this error, assuming that the books have not been closed for 2015, is:

| Retained Earnings | 8,000 | |
| Interest Income | | 8,000 |

If the books have been closed for 2015, no entry is made, because the error is counterbalanced.

5. **Overstatement of purchases:** The accountant recorded a purchase of merchandise for $9,000 in 2014 that applied to 2015. The physical inventory for 2014 was correctly stated. The company uses the periodic inventory method. The entry on December 31, 2015, to correct this error, assuming that the books have not been closed, is:

| Purchases | 9,000 | |
| Retained Earnings | | 9,000 |

If the 2015 books were closed, no entry is made, because the error is counterbalanced.

6. **Understatement of ending inventory:** On December 31, 2014, the physical inventory count was understated by $25,000 because the inventory crew failed to count one section of a merchandise warehouse. The entry on December 31, 2015, to correct this error, assuming the 2015 books have not yet been closed and the ending inventory has not yet been adjusted to the inventory account, is:

| Inventory | 25,000 | |
| Retained Earnings | | 25,000 |

If the books are closed for 2015, no entry needs to be made, because the error has been counterbalanced.

7. **Overstatement of purchases and inventories:** Sometimes, both the physical inventory and the purchases are incorrectly stated. Assume that 2015 purchases of $9,000 were incorrectly recorded as 2014 purchases and that 2014 ending inventory was overstated by the same amount. The entry on December 31, 2015, to correct this error before the 2015 books are closed and the correct ending inventory is adjusted to the inventory account is:

| Purchases | 9,000 | |
| Inventory | | 9,000 |

The net income for 2014 is correct because the overstatement of purchases was offset by the overstatement of ending inventory in cost of goods sold. Similar to the other

A = L + SE
0   0   0

Cash flows: No effect

A = L + SE
0   0   0

Cash flows: No effect

A = L + SE
0   0   0

Cash flows: No effect

A   = L +   SE
+25,000   0   +25,000

Cash flows: No effect

A   = L +   SE
−9,000   0   −9,000

Cash flows: No effect

examples of counterbalancing errors, no entry is required if the 2015 books have already been closed. Regardless, the 2014 comparative statements need to be restated.

Non-Counterbalancing Errors

Because non-counterbalancing errors do not self-correct over a two-year period, the entries for them are more complex, and correcting entries are needed even if the books have been closed. The best approach is to identify what the relevant account balances are in the accounts, what they should be, and then bring them to the correct balances through correcting entries. Examples follow. Here, as well, the prior year's financial statements need to be restated.

1. **Failure to record depreciation:** Assume that a machine with an estimated five-year useful life was purchased on January 1, 2014, for $10,000. The accountant incorrectly expensed this machine in 2014 and the error was discovered in 2015. If we assume that the company uses straight-line depreciation on similar assets, the entry on December 31, 2015, to correct this error, given that the 2015 books are not yet closed, is:

Machinery	10,000	
Depreciation Expense	2,000	
Retained Earnings		8,000
Accumulated Depreciation—Machinery		4,000

Retained Earnings:

Expense reported in 2014	$10,000	
Correct depreciation for 2014 (20% × $10,000)	(2,000)	
Retained earnings understated as at Dec. 31, 2014, by	$ 8,000	

Accumulated Depreciation, Dec. 31, 2015:

Accumulated depreciation (20% × $10,000 × 2)	$ 4,000	

If the books have been closed for 2015, the entry is:

Machinery	10,000	
Retained Earnings		6,000
Accumulated Depreciation—Machinery		4,000

Retained Earnings:

Retained earnings understated as at Dec. 31, 2014, by	$ 8,000	
Correct depreciation for 2015 (20% × $10,000)	(2,000)	
Retained earnings understated as at Dec. 31, 2015, by	$ 6,000	

2. **Failure to adjust for bad debts:** Assume that a company has been using the direct writeoff method when the allowance method should have been applied. Thus, the following bad debt expense has been recognized as the debts have actually become uncollectible.

	2014	2015
From 2014 sales	$550	$690
From 2015 sales		700

The company estimates that an additional $1,400 will be written off in 2016, of which $300 applies to 2014 sales and $1,100 to 2015 sales.[14] The entry on December 31, 2015, to correct the accounts for bad debt expense, assuming that the books have not been closed for 2015, is:

A = L + SE
+6,000 +6,000

Cash flows: No effect

A = L + SE
+6,000 +6,000

Cash flows: No effect

Bad Debt Expense		410	
Retained Earnings		990	
Allowance for Doubtful Accounts			1,400

Allowance for doubtful accounts:
Additional $300 for 2014 sales and $1,100 for 2015 sales = $1,400.

Bad debt expense corrections needed:

	2014	2015
Accounts written off by year of sale ($550 + $690 = $1,240)	$1,240	$ 700
Additional bad debts anticipated (total of $1,400)	300	1,100
Correct amount of bad debt expense each year	1,540	1,800
Bad debt expense previously recorded	(550)	(1,390)
Bad debt expense adjustment needed	$ 990	$ 410

A = L + SE
−1,400 0 −1,400

Cash flows: No effect

If the books have been closed for 2015, the entry is:

| Retained Earnings | 1,400 | |
| Allowance for Doubtful Accounts | | 1,400 |

A = L + SE
−1,400 0 −1,400

Cash flows: No effect

Income Tax Effects

As mentioned earlier, the income tax effects are not reported with the above correcting entries in order to make it easier for you to focus on the effects of the errors themselves. Once you understand the correcting entries, it is easier to add the income tax effects, as we will do now.

If a correction **increases a previous year's income** (either by an increase in revenue or a decrease in expense), the income tax expense for that period will usually be increased: more income, more tax. If the correction **reduces a previous year's income** (either by a decrease in revenue or an increase in expense), the income tax expense for that period will usually be reduced: less income, less tax. The net correction to retained earnings, therefore, is made net of tax. Note that for counterbalancing errors, the income tax effects also offset each other over the two-year period, assuming tax rates have not changed.

Because the tax return for the previous period has already been filed, most adjustments of the previous year's income affects Income Tax Payable. The Deferred Tax Asset/Liability account is affected only when the treatment for income taxes in the previous year is a permitted tax treatment. Examples include the depreciation and bad debt non-counterbalancing error situations below. In both these cases, taxable income was correct as it was calculated in the prior year, but now the amount of the related temporary difference has changed.

Illustration 21A-1 identifies the **correcting entries** that are needed, including the tax effects for the counterbalancing and non-counterbalancing examples we just walked through. A 30% income tax rate is assumed for all years.

Illustration 21A-1
Correcting Entries with Income Tax Effects

Error	Not Closed		Closed
COUNTERBALANCING ERRORS			
1. Accrued Wages			
Retained Earnings	1050		−No Entry−
Income Tax Payable	450		
Salaries and Wages			
Expense		1,500	

(continued)

Correcting Entries with Income Tax Effects (continued)

Illustration 21A-1

Error		Not Closed	Closed
2. Prepaid expenses			
Insurance Expense		500	
Retained Earnings			350
Income Tax Payable			150
3. Unearned Revenue			
Retained Earnings		35,000	–No Entry–
Income Tax Payable		15,000	
Rent Revenue		50,000	
4. Accrued Revenue			
Retained Earnings		5,600	–No Entry–
Income Tax Payable		2,400	
Interest Income		8,000	
5. Overstatement of Purchases			
Purchases		9,000	–No Entry–
Retained Earnings		6,300	
Income Tax Payable		2,700	
6. Understatement of Ending Inventory			
Inventory		25,000	–No Entry–
Retained Earnings		17,500	
Income Tax Payable		7,500	
7. Overstatement of Purchases and Inventories			
Purchases		9,000	–No Entry–
Inventory		9,000	
NON-COUNTERBALANCING ERRORS			
1. Depreciation			
Machinery	10,000		Machinery 10,000
Depreciation Expense	2,000		
Accumulated Depreciation		4,000	Accumulated Depreciation 4,000
—Machinery			—Machinery
Retained Earnings		5,600	Retained Earnings 4,200
Deferred Tax Asset/Liability		2,400	Deferred Tax Asset/Liability 1,800
2. Bad Debts			
Bad Debt Expense		410	
Retained Earnings		693	Retained Earnings 980
Deferred Tax Asset/Liability		297	Deferred Tax Asset/Liability 420
Allowance for Doubtful			Allowance for Doubtful
Accounts		1,400	Accounts 1,400

Comprehensive Illustration: Numerous Errors

In some circumstances, a combination of errors occurs, and a work sheet is prepared to help with the analysis. To demonstrate the use of a work sheet, the following problem is presented for solution. The mechanics of how the work sheet is prepared should be clear from the format of the solution. The tax effects are omitted.

The income statements of Hudson Corporation for the three years ended December 31, 2013, 2014, and 2015, show the following net incomes:

2013	$17,400
2014	20,200
2015	11,300

An examination of the company's accounting records for these years reveals that several errors were made in arriving at the net incomes reported. The following errors were discovered:

1. Wages earned by workers but not paid at December 31 were consistently omitted from the records. The amounts omitted were:

December 31, 2013	$1,000
December 31, 2014	1,400
December 31, 2015	1,600

These amounts were recorded as expenses when they were paid; that is, in the year following the year when they were earned by the employees.

2. The merchandise inventory on December 31, 2013, was overstated by $1,900 as a result of errors made in the footings (totals) and extensions on the inventory sheets.

3. Insurance of $1,200 that is applicable to 2015 was expensed on December 31, 2014.

4. Interest receivable in the amount of $240 was not recorded on December 31, 2014.

5. On January 2, 2014, a piece of machinery costing $3,900 was sold for $1,800. At the date of sale, the equipment had accumulated depreciation of $2,400. The proceeds on the sale were credited to Gain on Sale of Machinery in 2014. In addition, depreciation was recorded for this equipment in both 2014 and 2015 at the rate of 10% of cost.

The **first** step in preparing the work sheet is to prepare a schedule showing the corrected net incomes for each of the years ended December 31, 2013, 2014, and 2015. Each correction of the amount that was originally reported is clearly labelled. The **next step** is to indicate the SFP accounts affected as at December 31, 2015, if any. The completed work sheet for Hudson Corporation is provided in Illustration 21A-2.

Illustration 21A-2

Work Sheet to Correct Income and SFP Errors

Hudson Corporation
Work Sheet to Correct Income and SFP Errors

	Work Sheet Analysis of Changes in Net Income				SFP Correction at December 31, 2015		
Year	2013	2014	2015	Totals	Debit	Credit	Account
Net income as reported	$17,400	$20,200	$11,300	$48,900			
Wages unpaid, 12/31/13	(1,000)	1,000		–0–			
Wages unpaid, 12/31/14		(1,400)	1,400	–0–			
Wages unpaid, 12/31/15			(1,600)	(1,600)		$1,600	Salaries and Wages Payable
Inventory overstatement, 12/31/13	(1,900)	1,900		–0–			
Unexpired insurance, 12/31/14		1,200	(1,200)	–0–			
Interest receivable, 12/31/14		240	(240)	–0–			
Correction for entry made on sale of equipment, 1/2/14[a]		(1,500)		(1,500)	$2,400		Accumulated Depreciation—Machinery
Overcharge of depreciation, 2014		390	390	390	390	3,900	Accumulated Depreciation—Machinery / Machinery / Accumulated Depreciation—Machinery

(continued)

Hudson Corporation
Work Sheet to Correct Income and SFP Errors

	A	B	C	D	E	F	G	H	I
14									
15		Work Sheet Analysis of Changes in Net Income					SFP Correction at December 31, 2015		
16	Year	2013	2014	2015	Totals		Debit	Credit	Account
17	Overcharge of depreciation, 2015			390	390		390		Accumulated Depreciation— Machinery
18	Corrected net income	$14,500	$22,030	$10,050	$46,580				
19	ªCalculations								

Calculations	
Cost	$ 3,900
Accumulated depreciation	2,400
Carrying amount	1,500
Proceeds from sale	1,800
Gain on sale	300
Income reported	1,800
Adjustment	$(1,500)

20	

Illustration 21A-2

Work Sheet to Correct Income and SFP Errors (continued)

Correcting entries **if the books have not been closed for 2015** are:

	Debit	Credit
Retained Earnings	1,400	
Salaries and Wages Expense		1,400

(To correct wages expense charged to 2015 that should have been charged to prior year)

	Debit	Credit
Salaries and Wages Expense	1,600	
Salaries and Wages Payable		1,600

(To record wages expense and accrual for wages at 2015 year end)

	Debit	Credit
Insurance Expense	1,200	
Retained Earnings		1,200

(To correct insurance expense charged to 2014 that should have been charged to 2015)

	Debit	Credit
Interest Income	240	
Retained Earnings		240

(To correct interest income recognized in 2015 that should have been reported in 2014)

	Debit	Credit
Retained Earnings	1,500	
Accumulated Depreciation—Machinery	2,400	
Machinery		3,900

(To record writeoff of machinery and correction of the gain reported in 2014)

Accumulated Depreciation—Machinery	780	
Depreciation Expense		390
Retained Earnings		390

(To correct charges made in error to depreciation expense in 2014 and 2015)

If the books have been closed for 2015, the correcting entries are:

| Retained Earnings | 1,600 | |
| Salaries and Wages Payable | | 1,600 |

(To correct the cumulative effect of accrued wages errors to December 31, 2015)

Retained Earnings	1,500	
Accumulated Depreciation—Machinery	2,400	
Machinery		3,900

(To record writeoff of machinery and correction of the gain reported in 2014)

| Accumulated Depreciation—Machinery | 780 | |
| Retained Earnings | | 780 |

(To correct charges made in error to depreciation expense in 2014 and 2015)

Preparation of Comparative Financial Statements

Up to now, our discussion of error analysis has been concerned with identifying the type of error involved and then accounting for its correction in the accounting records. Equally important is how the corrections are presented on comparative financial statements. In annual reports or other documents, five- or 10-year financial summaries are often provided. Illustration 21A-3, explained below, shows how a typical year's financial statements are restated, assuming that many different errors have been corrected. Dick & Wally's Outlet Ltd. is a small retail outlet in the town of Priestly Sound. Lacking expertise in accounting, its management does not keep adequate records. As a result, numerous errors occurred in recording accounting information:

1. The bookkeeper, by mistake, failed to record a cash receipt of $1,000 on the sale of merchandise in 2015.

2. Accrued wages at the end of 2014 were $2,500; at the end of 2015, $3,200. The company does not accrue wages; all wages are charged to Administrative Expense.

3. The 2015 beginning inventory was understated by $5,400 because goods in transit at the end of last year were not counted. The purchase entry was made early in 2015. The debit was charged to Retained Earnings in 2015.

4. No allowance had been set up for estimated uncollectible receivables. Dick and Wally decided to set up such an allowance for the estimated probable losses at December 31, 2015, for 2014 accounts of $700, and 2015 accounts of $1,500. They also decided to correct the charge against each year so that it shows the losses (actual and estimated) relating to that year's sales. Accounts have been written off to bad debt expense (selling expense) as follows:

	In 2014	In 2015
2014 accounts	$400	$2,000
2015 accounts		1,600

5. Unexpired insurance not recorded at the end of 2014 was $600, and at the end of 2015, $400. All insurance is charged to Administrative Expense. Unexpired insurance will be included in Prepaid Insurance on the SFP.

6. An account payable at the end of 2015 of $6,000 should have been a note payable.

7. During 2014, a truck that cost $10,000 and had a carrying amount of $4,000 was sold for $7,000. At the time of sale, Cash was debited and Gain was credited for $7,000.

8. As a result of transaction 7, the company overstated depreciation expense (an administrative expense) in 2014 by $800 and in 2015 by $1,200.

9. In a physical count, the company determined the 2015 ending inventory to be $40,000.

Illustration 21A-3 presents a work sheet that begins with the unadjusted trial balance of Dick & Wally's Outlet. The correcting entries and their effect on the financial statements can be determined by examining the work sheet. The numbers in parentheses show which transaction number the correction relates to.

Illustration 21A-3

Work Sheet to Adjust Financial Statements

Dick & Wally's Outlet

Work Sheet Analysis to Adjust Financial Statements for the Year 2015

	A	B	C	D	E	F	G	H	I	J	K	L
		Trial Balance Unadjusted		Adjustments				Income Statement Adjusted			SFP Adjusted	
1		Debit	Credit	Debit	Credit			Debit	Credit		Debit	Credit
2												
3												
4	Cash	3,100		(1) 1,000							4,100	
5	Accounts Receivable	17,600									17,600	
6	Notes Receivable	8,500									8,500	
7	Inventory, Jan. 1, 2015	34,000		(3) 5,400				39,400				
8	Property, Plant, and Equipment	112,000			(7) 10,000ᵃ						102,000	
9	Accumulated Depreciation—Trucks		83,500	(7) 6,000ᵃ (8) 2,000								75,500
10												
11	Investment in Associate	24,300									24,300	
12	Accounts Payable		14,500	(6) 6,000								8,500
13	Notes Payable		10,000		(6) 6,000							16,000
14	Common Shares		43,500									43,500
15	Retained Earnings		20,000	(4) 2,700ᵇ (7) 4,000ᵃ	(3) 5,400 (5) 600							
16				(2) 2,500	(8) 800							
17												
18	Sales Revenue		94,000		(1) 1,000				95,000			
19	Purchases	21,000						21,000				
20	Selling Expenses	22,000			(4) 500ᵇ			21,500				
21	Administrative Expenses	23,000		(2) 700 (5) 400	(5) 600 (8) 1,200			22,700				
22												
23	Totals	265,500	265,500								17,600	

(continued)

Dick & Wally's Outlet
Work Sheet Analysis to Adjust Financial Statements for the Year 2015

	Trial Balance Unadjusted		Adjustments		Income Statement Adjusted		SFP Adjusted	
	Debit	Credit	Debit	Credit	Debit	Credit	Debit	Credit
Salaries and Wages Payable				(2) 3,200				3,200
Allowance for Doubtful Accounts				(4) 2,200[b]				2,200
Prepaid Insurance			(5) 400				400	
Inventory, Dec. 31, 2015						(9) 40,000	(9) 40,000	
Net Income					30,400			30,400
Totals			31,300	31,300	135,000	135,000	196,900	196,900

[a] Machinery

Proceeds from sale	$ 7,000
Carrying amount of machinery	4,000
Gain on sale	3,000
Income credited	7,000
Retained earnings adjustment	$(4,000)

[b] Bad Debts

	For Sales in	
	2014	2015
Bad debts charged	$2,400	$1,600
Other bad debts anticipated	700	1,500
	3,100	3,100
Charges made in year	400	3,600
Bad debt adjustment	$2,700	$(500)

SUMMARY OF LEARNING OBJECTIVE FOR APPENDIX 21A

9 Correct the effects of errors and prepare restated financial statements.

Three types of errors can occur: (1) errors that affect only the SFP, (2) errors that affect only the income statement, and (3) errors that affect both the SFP and the income statement. This last type of error is classified either as (a) a counterbalancing error, where the effects are offset or corrected over two periods; or (b) a non-counterbalancing error, where the effects take longer than two periods to correct themselves.

KEY TERMS

counterbalancing errors, p. 1383   non-counterbalancing errors, p. 1383

Quiz

Brief Exercises

Note: In the end-of-chapter material that follows, the simplifying assumption is made that all companies use the term "deferred" (used by IFRS) rather than the term "future" (used by ASPE) for the income tax accounts related to temporary differences. It is also assumed that where warranties are used as an example of a temporary/timing difference, the company is following the expense warranty approach, and not accounting for the warranty as a separate performance obligation. All assignment material with an asterisk (*) relates to the appendix to the chapter.

(LO 1) BE21-1 Wensley Manufacturing Corp. is preparing its year-end financial statements and is considering the accounting for the following items:

1. The vice president of sales had indicated that one product line has lost its customer appeal and will be phased out over the next three years. Therefore, a decision has been made to lower the estimated lives on related production equipment from the remaining five years to three years.

2. The Hightone Building was converted from a sales office to offices for the Accounting Department at the beginning of this year. Therefore, the expense related to this building will now appear as an administrative expense rather than a selling expense on the current year's income statement.

3. Estimating the lives of new products in the Leisure Products Division has become very difficult because of the highly competitive conditions in this market. Therefore, the practice of deferring and amortizing preproduction costs has been abandoned in favour of expensing such costs as they are incurred.

Wensley follows IFRS. Explain whether each of the above items is a change in principle, a change in estimate, an error, or not any of these.

(LO 1) BE21-2 Palmer Corp. is evaluating the appropriate accounting for the following items under ASPE:

1. Management has decided to switch from the FIFO inventory cost formula to the weighted average cost inventory cost formula for all inventories.

2. When the year-end physical inventory adjustment was made for the current year, the controller discovered that the prior year's physical inventory sheets for an entire warehouse were mislaid and excluded from last year's count.

3. Palmer's Custom Division manufactures large-scale, custom-designed machinery on a contract basis. Management decided to switch from the completed-contract method to the percentage-of-completion method of accounting for long-term contracts because they are now able to estimate the progress toward completion (whereas they were not able to measure this before).

Explain whether each of the above items is a change in accounting principle, a change in estimate, or an error.

(LO 3, 5) BE21-3 At the beginning of 2014, Becky Corporation discovered that depreciation expense in the years prior to 2014 was incorrectly calculated and recorded. For the years prior to 2014, total depreciation expense of $117,000 was recorded, whereas correct total depreciation expense was $76,000. The tax rate is 30%. Becky follows ASPE and the deferred taxes method of accounting for income taxes. Prepare Becky's 2014 journal entry with respect to the depreciation expense that was recorded in the years prior to 2014.

(LO 4) BE21-4 Crosbie, Inc. changed from the weighted average cost formula to the FIFO cost formula in 2014. The increase in the prior year's income before tax as a result of this change is $435,000. The tax rate is 30%. Prepare Crosbie's 2014 journal entry to record the change in accounting policy, assuming that the company's financial statements are reliable and more relevant as a result of the change.

(LO 5) BE21-5 In 2014, Dody Corporation discovered that equipment purchased on January 1, 2012, for $75,000 was expensed in error at that time. The equipment should have been depreciated over five years, with no residual value. The tax rate is 32%. Prepare Dody's 2014 journal entry to correct the error and record 2014 depreciation.

(LO 5, 8, 9) *BE21-6 At January 1, 2014, Baker Corp. reported retained earnings of $2 million. In 2014, Baker discovered that 2013 depreciation expense was understated in error by $500,000. In 2014, net income was $900,000 and dividends declared were $250,000. The tax rate is 25%. Baker follows ASPE, and the deferred taxes method of accounting for income taxes. (a) Prepare a 2014 statement of retained earnings for Baker Corp. (b) Briefly explain how your answer would change if Baker were to follow IFRS.

(LO 6) BE21-7 Willow Corporation decided at the beginning of 2014 to change from the declining-balance method of depreciating its capital assets to the straight-line method because the straight-line method better represents the pattern of benefits provided by the capital assets. For years prior to 2014, total depreciation expense under the two methods was as follows: declining balance, $155,000; and straight-line, $60,000. The tax rate is 30%. Willow follows ASPE, and the taxes payable method of accounting for income taxes. Prepare Willow's 2014 journal entry, if any, to record the change in estimate.

(LO 6) **BE21-8** Corning Corporation purchased a computer system (accounted for as Office Equipment) for $60,000 on January 1, 2012. It was depreciated based on a seven-year life and an $18,000 residual value. On January 1, 2014, Corning revised these estimates to a total useful life of four years and a residual value of $10,000. Prepare Corning's entry to record 2014 depreciation expense. Assume that Corning follows IFRS and uses straight-line depreciation.

(LO 6) **BE21-9** Bailey Corp. changed depreciation methods in 2014 from straight-line to double-declining-balance because management gathered evidence that the assets were being used differently than previously thought. The assets involved were acquired early in 2011 for $185,000 and had an estimated useful life of eight years, with no residual value. The 2014 income using the double-declining-balance method was $490,000. Bailey had 10,000 common shares outstanding all year. What is the effect of the accounting change on the reported income and EPS for 2014? Bailey follows IFRS. Ignore income tax.

(LO 9) ***BE21-10** Indicate the effect—Understated (U), Overstated (O), or No Effect (NE)—that each of the following errors has on 2013 net income and 2014 net income:

	2013	2014
Wages payable were not recorded at Dec. 31, 2013.	___	___
Equipment purchased in 2012 was expensed.	___	___
Equipment purchased in 2013 was expensed.	___	___
Ending inventory at Dec. 31, 2013, was overstated.	___	___
Patent amortization was not recorded in 2014.	___	___

Exercises

(LO 1, 2, 3, 5) **E21-1** **(Long-Term Contracts)** In 2013, Sader Construction Company Ltd. applied the completed-contract method of accounting for long-term construction contracts. However in 2014, Sader discovered that the percentage-of-completion method should have been applied instead. For tax purposes, the company uses the completed-contract method and will continue this approach in the future. Sader follows ASPE, and will apply the percentage-of-completion method in 2014 and in the future. Sader applies the deferred taxes method of accounting for income taxes, and is subject to a tax rate of 30%. The appropriate information related to this change is as follows:

Pre-Tax Income Using:

	Percentage-of-Completion	Completed-Contract	Difference
2013	$820,000	$620,000	$200,000
2014	700,000	480,000	220,000

Instructions

(a) Calculate the net income to be reported in 2014.

(b) Provide the necessary entry(ies) in 2014 to adjust the accounting records with respect to the revenue recognition method applied in 2013.

(c) Assume that as at the end of 2014, just prior to recording the entry(ies) in part (b), Sader has a current ratio of 0.95. From the perspective of a creditor, discuss the effect of the entry(ies) in part (b) on Sader's current ratio.

Digging Deeper

(LO 1, 2, 3, 4, 5) **E21-2** **(Determine Type of Change and Method of Accounting; Prepare Journal Entries)** Bennett Corp., which began operations in January 2011, follows IFRS and is subject to a 30% income tax rate. In 2014, the following events took place:

1. The company switched from the zero-profit method to the percentage-of-completion method of accounting for its long-term construction projects. This change was a result of experience with the project and improved ability to estimate the costs to completion and therefore the percentage complete.

2. Due to a change in maintenance policy, the estimated useful life of Bennett's fleet of trucks was lengthened.

3. It was discovered that a machine with an original cost of $100,000, residual value of $10,000, and useful life of four years was expensed in error on January 23, 2013, when it was acquired. This situation was discovered after preparing the 2014 adjusting entries but prior to calculating income tax expense and closing the accounts. Bennett uses straight-line depreciation and takes a full year of depreciation in the year of acquisition. The asset's cost had been appropriately added to the CCA class in 2013 before the CCA was calculated and claimed.

4. As a result of an inventory study early in 2014 after the accounts for 2013 had been closed, management decided that the weighted average costing formula would provide a more relevant presentation in the financial statements than does FIFO costing. In making the change to weighted average cost, Bennett determined the following:

Date	Inventory—FIFO Cost	Inventory—Weighted Average Cost
Dec. 31, 2013	$ 90,000	$ 80,000
Dec. 31, 2012	130,000	100,000
Dec. 31, 2011	200,000	150,000

Instructions

(a) Analyze each of the four 2014 events described above. For each event, identify the type of accounting change that has occurred, and indicate whether it should be accounted for with full retrospective application, partial retrospective application, or prospectively.

(b) Prepare any necessary journal entries that would be recorded in 2014 to account for events 3 (ignore taxes) and 4.

(LO 1, 2, 3, 5, 6, 7) **E21-3   (Change in Estimate, Error Correction)** Field Corp.'s controller was preparing the year-end adjusting entries for the company's year ended December 31, 2014, when the V.P. Finance called him into her office.

"Jean-Pierre," she said, "I've been considering a couple of matters that may require different treatment this year. First, the patent we acquired in early January 2012 for $410,000 will now likely be used until the end of 2016 and then be sold for $110,000. We previously thought that we'd use it for 10 years in total and then be able to sell it for $50,000. We've been using straight-line amortization on the patent.

"Secondly, I just discovered that the property we bought midway through 2011 for $135,000 was charged entirely to the Land account instead of being allocated between Land ($33,750) and Building ($101,250). The building should be of use to us for a total of 20 years. At that point, it'll be sold and we should be able to realize at least $37,000 from the sale of the building.

"Please let me know how these changes should be accounted for and what effect they will have on the financial statements."

Instructions

Answer the following, ignoring tax considerations.

(a) Briefly identify the accounting treatment that should be applied to each accounting change that is required.

(b) Assuming that no amortization has been recorded as yet for the patent for 2014, prepare the December 31, 2014 entries that are necessary to make the accounting changes and to record patent amortization expense for 2014.

(c) Identify, and calculate where possible, the required disclosures for each change.

(d) Discuss the timing of applying the change in the patent's useful life and residual value. Since the determination of the change was done as part of the year-end process, should the change be applied to 2014 going forward, or to 2015 going forward? What are the implications of each approach?

(e) Could Field's controller consider the patent to be impaired instead of revising its useful life and residual value? What criteria should the controller look at to determine the appropriate treatment?

Digging Deeper

(LO 1, 2, 3, 8) **E21-4   (Accounting for Accounting Changes)** The following are various types of accounting changes:

___ **1.** Change in a plant asset's residual value

___ **2.** Change due to an overstatement of inventory

___ **3.** Change from sum-of-the-years'-digits to straight-line method of depreciation because of a change in the pattern of benefits received

___ **4.** Change in a primary source of GAAP

___ **5.** Decision by management to capitalize interest. The company is reporting a self-constructed asset for the first time.

___ **6.** Change in the rate used to calculate warranty costs

___ **7.** Change from an unacceptable accounting principle to an acceptable accounting principle

___ **8.** Change in a patent's amortization period

___ **9.** Change from the zero-profit method to the percentage-of-completion method on construction contracts. This change was a result of experience with the project and improved ability to estimate the costs to completion and therefore the percentage complete.

___ **10.** Recognition of additional income tax owing from three years ago as a result of improper calculations by the accountant, who was not familiar with income tax legislation and income tax returns

Instructions

(a) For each change or error, use the following code letters to indicate how it would be accounted for assuming the company follows IFRS:

Accounted for in the current year only (CY)
Accounted for prospectively (P)
Accounted for retrospectively (R)
None of the above, or unable to tell. Explain. (NA)

(b) Identify the type of change for each of the situations in items 1 to 10.

(c) Now assume that the company follows ASPE. Identify the situations in part (a) that would be accounted for differently under ASPE than IFRS.

(d) What are the conditions that must exist for an entity to be allowed to change an accounting policy?

Digging Deeper

(LO 2, 3, 5, 6, 9) ***E21-5** **(Change in Estimate and Error, Financial Statements)** The comparative statements for Hessey Inc. follow:

	2014	2013
Sales	$340,000	$270,000
Cost of sales	200,000	142,000
Gross profit	140,000	128,000
Expenses	88,000	50,000
Net income	$ 52,000	$ 78,000

	2014	2013
Retained earnings (Jan. 1)	$125,000	$ 72,000
Net income	52,000	78,000
Dividends	(30,000)	(25,000)
Retained earnings (Dec. 31)	$147,000	$125,000

The following additional information is provided:

1. In 2014, Hessey decided to change its depreciation method from sum-of-the-years'-digits to the straight-line method due to a change in pattern of usage. The assets were purchased at the beginning of 2013 for $90,000 with an estimated useful life of four years and no residual value. (The 2014 income statement contains depreciation expense of $27,000 on the assets purchased at the beginning of 2013.)

2. In 2014, the company discovered that the ending inventory for 2013 was overstated by $20,000; ending inventory for 2014 is correctly stated.

Hessey follows ASPE.

Instructions

(a) Prepare the revised statements of retained earnings for 2013 and 2014, assuming comparative statements (ignore income tax effects). Do not prepare notes to the financial statements.

(b) Identify other possible accounting treatments for the change in depreciation method under alternative circumstances.

(LO 4) **E21-6** **(Accounting Change—Inventory)** Linden Corporation started operations on January 1, 2009, and has used the FIFO cost formula since its inception. In 2015, it decides to switch to the weighted average cost formula. You are provided with the following information.

	Net Income		Retained Earnings (Ending Balance)
	Under FIFO	Under Weighted Average Cost	Under FIFO
2009	$100,000	$ 92,000	$100,000
2010	70,000	65,000	160,000
2011	90,000	85,000	235,000
2012	120,000	130,000	340,000
2013	300,000	293,000	590,000
2014	305,000	310,900	780,000

(LO 4) E21-7 (Accounting Change—Measurement Model for Investment Property) Golden Properties Corporation purchased a parcel of land in 2012 for $1 million with the intent to construct a building on the property in the near future. At the time of purchase, and in the subsequent financial statements for the years ended December 31, 2012, and 2013, Golden applied the cost model and measured and reported the land at its acquisition cost as allowed in IAS 16. Golden follows IFRS. Management decided in early 2014 that the land qualifies as an investment property under IAS 40 and that Golden is to apply the fair value model of accounting for investment properties effective immediately because the company believes that changing the measurement model will provide more relevant information. Independent appraisals indicate that the land's fair value at December 31, 2012, and 2013, was $980,000 and $1,050,000, respectively. Golden's reported retained earnings at December 31, 2012, and 2013, were $230,000 and $290,000, respectively.

Instructions

Answer the following, ignoring tax considerations.

(a) Prepare the original statements of financial position and income statements for the affected accounts.

(b) Prepare Golden's journal entry, if any, to record the change in accounting policy.

(c) Prepare the restated statements of financial position and income statements for the affected accounts.

(LO 4, 5) E21-8 (Various Changes in Policy—Inventory Methods) Yuan Instrument Corp., a small company that follows ASPE, began operations on January 1, 2011, and uses a periodic inventory system. The following net income amounts were calculated for Yuan under three different inventory cost formulas:

	FIFO	Weighted Average Cost	LIFO
2011	$26,000	$24,000	$20,000
2012	30,000	25,000	21,000
2013	28,000	27,000	24,000
2014	34,000	30,000	26,000

Instructions

Answer the following, ignoring tax considerations.

(a) Assume that in 2014, Yuan changed from the weighted average cost formula to the FIFO cost formula and it was agreed that the FIFO method provided more relevant financial statement information. Prepare the necessary journal entry for the change that took place during 2014, and provide all the information that is needed for reporting on a comparative basis.

(b) Assume that in 2014, Yuan, which had been using the LIFO method since incorporation in 2011, changed to the FIFO cost formula in order to comply with *CICA Handbook*, Part II, Section 3031, since LIFO is not a permitted inventory cost flow assumption under GAAP. The company applies the new policy retrospectively. Prepare the necessary journal entry for the change, and provide all the information that is needed for reporting on a comparative basis.

(LO 6) E21-9 (Change in Estimate—Depreciation) Oliver Inc. acquired the following assets in January 2011:

Equipment: estimated useful life, 5 years; residual value, $15,000		$465,000
Building: estimated useful life, 30 years; no residual value		$780,000

The equipment was depreciated using the double-declining-balance method for the first three years for financial reporting purposes. In 2014, the company decided to change the method of calculating depreciation to the straight-line method for the equipment because of a change in the pattern of benefits received, but no change was made in the estimated useful life or residual value. It was also decided to change the building's total estimated useful life from 30 years to 40 years, with no change in the estimated residual value. The building is depreciated on the straight-line method.

Instructions

(a) Prepare the journal entry to record depreciation expense for the equipment in 2014. (Ignore tax effects and round to the nearest dollar.)

(b) Prepare the journal entry to record the depreciation expense for the building in 2014. (Ignore tax effects and round to the nearest dollar.)

(LO 5) **E21-10** **(Error Correction Entries)** The first audit of the books of Gomez Limited was recently carried out for the year ended December 31, 2014. Gomez follows IFRS. In examining the books, the auditor found that certain items had been overlooked or might have been incorrectly handled in the past:

1. At the beginning of 2012, the company purchased a machine for $450,000 (residual value of $45,000) that had a useful life of six years. The bookkeeper used straight-line depreciation, but failed to deduct the residual value in calculating the depreciation base for the three years.

2. At the end of 2013, the company accrued sales salaries of $36,000 in excess of the correct amount.

3. A tax lawsuit that involved the year 2012 was settled late in 2014. It was determined that the company owed an additional $73,000 in tax related to 2012. The company did not record a liability in 2012 or 2013, because the possibility of losing was considered remote. The company charged the $73,000 to retained earnings in 2014 as a correction of a prior year's error.

4. Gomez purchased another company early in 2010 and recorded goodwill of $450,000. Gomez amortized $22,500 of goodwill in 2010, and $45,000 in each subsequent year.

5. In 2014, the company changed its basis of inventory costing from FIFO to weighted average cost. The change's cumulative effect was to decrease net income of prior years by $39,000. The company debited this cumulative effect to Retained Earnings. The weighted average cost formula was used in calculating income for 2014.

6. In 2014, the company wrote off $87,000 of inventory that it discovered, in 2014, had been stolen from one of its warehouses in 2013. This loss was charged to a loss account in 2014.

Instructions

(a) Prepare the journal entries in 2014 to correct the books where necessary, assuming that the 2014 books have not been closed. Assume that the change from FIFO to weighted average cost can be justified as resulting in more relevant financial information. Disregard the effects of corrections on income tax.

(b) Identify the type of change for each of the six items.

(c) Redo part (a) but include the effects of income tax, assuming the company has a tax rate of 25%.

(LO 5, 9) *E21-11** **(Error Analysis and Correcting Entry)** You have been engaged to review the financial statements of Lindsay Corporation. In the course of your examination of the work of the bookkeeper hired during the year that just ended, you noticed a number of irregularities for the past fiscal year:

1. Year-end wages payable of $4,100 were not recorded, because the bookkeeper thought that "they were immaterial."

2. Accrued vacation pay for the year of $29,400 was not recorded, because the bookkeeper "never heard that you had to do it."

3. Insurance that covers a 12-month period and was purchased on November 1 was charged to insurance expense in the amount of $2,760 "because the amount of the cheque is about the same every year."

4. Reported sales revenue for the year was $2,310,000 and included all sales taxes charged for the year. The sales tax rate is 5%. Because the sales tax is forwarded to the provincial ministry of revenue, the bookkeeper thought that "the sales tax is a selling expense" and therefore debited the Sales Tax Expense account. At the end of the fiscal year, the balance in the Sales Tax Expense account was $101,300.

Instructions

Prepare the necessary correcting entries, assuming that Lindsay Corporation uses a calendar-year basis and that the books for the fiscal year that just ended are not yet closed.

(LO 5, 9) *E21-12** **(Error Analysis and Correcting Entries)** A partial trial balance of Lindy Corporation at December 31, 2014, follows:

	Dr.	Cr.
Supplies	$ 4,100	
Salaries and wages payable		$ 3,900
Interest receivable	5,500	
Prepaid insurance	93,000	
Unearned rent revenue		–0–
Interest payable		15,000

Additional adjusting data:

1. A physical count of supplies on hand on December 31, 2014, totalled $2,100. Through an oversight, the Salaries and Wages Payable account was not changed during 2014. Accrued salaries and wages on December 31, 2014, amounted to $5,100.

2. The Interest Receivable account was also left unchanged during 2014. Accrued interest on investments amounted to $4,750 on December 31, 2014.

3. The unexpired portions of the insurance policies totalled $65,000 as at December 31, 2014.

4. A cheque for $44,000 was received on January 1, 2014, for the rent of a building for both 2014 and 2015. The entire amount was credited to rental income.

5. Depreciation for the year was recorded in error as $5,350 rather than the correct figure of $53,500.

6. A further review of prior years' depreciation calculations revealed that depreciation of $13,500 had not been recorded. It was decided that this oversight should be corrected by adjusting prior years' income.

Assume that Lindy applies IFRS.

Instructions

(a) Assuming that the books have not been closed, what adjusting entries are necessary at December 31, 2014? Ignore income tax considerations.

(b) Assuming that the books have been closed, what adjusting entries are necessary at December 31, 2014? Ignore income tax considerations.

(c) Discuss the nature of the adjustments that are needed and how the situations could have occurred. Are they all accounting errors, or are they part of the normal accounting cycle? (*Hint:* Revisit the topic of adjusting entries in Chapter 3.) How should management present the adjustments for these items on its financial statements and in the notes?

(LO 5, 6, 9) ***E21-13** **(Error and Change in Estimate—Depreciation)** Katherine Ltd. purchased a machine on January 1, 2011, for $1,350,000. At that time, it was estimated that the machine would have a 10-year life and no residual value. On December 31, 2014, the firm's accountant found that the entry for depreciation expense had been omitted in 2012. In addition, management informed the accountant that it planned to switch to double-declining-balance depreciation because of a change in the pattern of benefits received, starting with the year 2014. At present, the company uses the straight-line method for depreciating equipment.

Instructions

(a) Prepare the general journal entries, if any, the accountant should make at December 31, 2014. (Ignore tax effects.)

(b) Assume the same information as above, but factor in tax effects. The company has a 25% tax rate for 2011 to 2014.

(LO 5, 9) ***E21-14** **(Error Analysis)** Neilson Tool Corporation's December 31 year-end financial statements contained the following errors:

	December 31, 2013	December 31, 2014
Ending inventory	$9,600 overstated	$8,100 understated
Depreciation expense	$2,300 overstated	—

An insurance premium of $66,000 covering the years 2013, 2014, and 2015 was prepaid in 2013, with the entire amount charged to expense that year. In addition, on December 31, 2014, fully depreciated machinery was sold for $15,000 cash, but the entry was not recorded until 2015. There were no other errors during 2013 or 2014, and no corrections have been made for any of the errors. Neilson follows ASPE.

Instructions

Answer the following, ignoring income tax considerations.

(a) Calculate the total effect of the errors on 2014 net income.

(b) Calculate the total effect of the errors on the amount of Neilson's working capital at December 31, 2014.

Digging Deeper

(c) Calculate the total effect of the errors on the balance of Neilson's retained earnings at December 31, 2014.

(d) Assume that the company has retained earnings on January 1, 2013, and 2014, of $1,250,000 and $1,607,000, respectively; net income for 2013 and 2014 of $422,000 and $375,000, respectively; and cash dividends declared for 2013 and 2014 of $65,000 and $45,000, respectively, before adjustment for the above items. Prepare a revised statement of retained earnings for 2013 and 2014.

(e) Outline the accounting treatment required by ASPE in this situation and explain how these requirements help investors.

(Adapted from CGA-Canada Examination)

(LO 5, 9) ***E21-15 (Error Analysis)** The before-tax income for Marcel Corp. for 2013 was $101,000; for 2014, it was $77,400. However, the accountant noted that the following errors had been made:

1. Sales for 2013 included $38,200 that had been received in cash during 2013, but for which the related products were delivered in 2014. Title did not pass to the purchaser until 2014.

2. The inventory on December 31, 2013, was understated by $8,640. The December 31, 2014 ending inventory has not yet been adjusted to the Inventory account.

3. The bookkeeper, in recording interest expense for both 2013 and 2014 on bonds payable, made the following entry each year:

Interest Expense	15,000	
Cash		15,000

The bonds have a face value of $250,000 and pay a stated interest rate of 6%. They were issued at a discount of $15,000 on January 1, 2013, to yield an effective interest rate of 7%. (Use the effective interest method.)

4. Ordinary repairs to equipment had been charged in error to the Equipment account during 2013 and 2014. In total, repairs in the amount of $8,500 in 2013 and $9,400 in 2014 were charged in this way. The company applies a rate of 10% to the balance in the Equipment account at year end in determining its depreciation charges.

Assume that Marcel Corp. applies IFRS.

Instructions

(a) Prepare a schedule showing the calculation of corrected income before tax for 2013 and 2014.

(b) Prepare the journal entries that the company's accountant would prepare in 2014, assuming the errors are discovered while the 2014 books are still open. Ignore income tax.

Digging Deeper

(c) From the perspective of an investor, comment on the quality of Marcel Corp.'s earnings as reported in 2013 and 2014.

(LO 5, 9) ***E21-16 (Error Analysis)** When the records of Hilda Corporation were reviewed at the close of 2014, the following errors were discovered.

	2013			2014		
	Over-statement	Under-statement	No Effect	Over-statement	Under-statement	No Effect
1. Failure to record amortization of patent in 2014						
2. Failure to record the correct amount of ending 2013 inventory (the amount was understated because of a calculation error)						
3. Failure to record merchandise purchased in 2013 (it was also omitted from ending inventory in 2013 and remained unsold at the end of 2014)						
4. Failure to record accrued interest on notes payable in 2013 (the amount was recorded when paid in 2014)						
5. Failure to reflect supplies on statement of financial position at end of 2013						

(LO 6) **E21-17** **(Depreciation Changes)** On January 1, 2010, Zui Corporation purchased a building and equipment that had the following useful lives, residual values, and costs:

> Building: 40-year estimated useful life, $50,000 residual value, $1,200,000 cost
> Equipment: 12-year estimated useful life, $10,000 residual value, $130,000 cost

The building was depreciated under the double-declining-balance method through 2013. In 2014, the company decided to switch to the straight-line method of depreciation because of a change in the pattern of benefits received. In 2015, Zui decided to change the equipment's total useful life to nine years, with a residual value of $5,000 at the end of that time. The equipment is depreciated using the straight-line method.

Instructions

(a) Prepare the journal entry(ies) necessary to record the depreciation expense on the building in 2014. (Ignore tax effects.)

(b) Calculate the depreciation expense on the equipment for 2014. (Ignore tax effects.)

(LO 6) **E21-18** **(Change in Estimate—Depreciation)** Ingles Corp. changed from the straight-line method of depreciation on its plant assets acquired early in 2012 to the double-declining-balance method in 2014 because of a change in the pattern of benefits received (before finalizing its 2014 financial statements). The assets had an eight-year life and no expected residual value. Information related to both methods follows:

Year	Double-Declining-Balance Depreciation	Straight-Line Depreciation	Difference
2012	$250,000	$125,000	$125,000
2013	187,500	125,000	62,500
2014	140,625	125,000	15,625

Net income for 2013 was reported at $270,000; income for 2014 before depreciation and income tax is $300,000. Assume an income tax rate of 30%.

Instructions

The change from the straight-line method to the double-declining-balance method is considered a change in estimate.

(a) What net income is reported for 2014?

(b) What is the amount of the adjustment to opening retained earnings as at January 1, 2014?

(c) What is the amount of the adjustment to opening retained earnings as at January 1, 2013?

(d) Prepare the journal entry(ies), if any, to record the adjustment in the accounting records, assuming that the accounting records for 2014 are not yet closed.

(LO 7) **E21-19** **(Political Motivations for Policies)** Ever since the unethical actions of some employees of Enron Corp. first came to light, ethics in accounting has been in the news with increasing frequency. The unethical actions of the employees essentially involved their selection of certain accounting policies for the company.

In many instances, GAAP does allow firms some flexibility in their choice of legitimate accounting policies. This is true, for example, in choosing an inventory cost formula. However, the company's choice of policies may ultimately be influenced by several specific factors.

Instructions

State three of these factors and explain why each of them may influence an accounting policy choice.

(Adapted from CGA-Canada Examination)

Problems

P21-1 Beliveau Company, a small company following ASPE, is adjusting and correcting its books at the end of 2014. In reviewing its records, it compiles the following information.

1. Beliveau has failed to accrue sales commissions payable at the end of each of the last two years, as follows:

Dec. 31, 2013	$3,500
Dec. 31, 2014	$2,500

Instructions

For each item, indicate by a check mark in the appropriate column whether the error resulted in an overstatement or understatement, or had no effect on net income for the years 2013 and 2014.

2. In reviewing the December 31, 2014 inventory, Beliveau discovered errors in its inventory-taking procedures that have caused inventories for the last three years to be incorrect, as follows:

Dec. 31, 2012   Understated $16,000
Dec. 31, 2013   Understated $19,000
Dec. 31, 2014   Overstated $ 6,700

Beliveau has already made an entry that recognized the incorrect December 31, 2014 inventory amount.

3. In 2014, Beliveau changed the depreciation method on its office equipment from double-declining-balance to straight-line because of a change in the pattern of benefits received. The equipment had an original cost of $100,000 when purchased on January 1, 2012. It has a 10-year useful life and no residual value. Depreciation expense recorded prior to 2014 under the double-declining-balance method was $36,000. Beliveau has already recorded 2014 depreciation expense of $12,800 using the double-declining-balance method.

4. Before 2014, Beliveau accounted for its income from long-term construction contracts on the completed-contract basis because it was unable to reliably measure the degree of completion or the estimated costs to complete. Early in 2014, Beliveau changed to the percentage-of-completion basis for financial accounting purposes. The change was a result of experience with the project and improved ability to estimate the costs to completion and therefore the percentage complete. The completed-contract method will continue to be used for tax purposes. Income for 2014 has been recorded using the percentage-of-completion method. The following information is available:

Pre-Tax Income

	Percentage-of-Completion	Completed-Contract
Prior to 2014	$150,000	$105,000
2014	60,000	20,000

Instructions

Prepare the necessary journal entries at December 31, 2014, to record the above corrections and changes as appropriate. The books are still open for 2014. As Beliveau has not yet recorded its 2014 income tax expense and payable amounts, tax effects for the current year may be ignored. Beliveau's income tax rate is 25%. Assume that Beliveau applies the taxes payable method of accounting for income taxes.

P21-2 Leader Enterprises Ltd. follows IFRS and reported income before income tax of $176,000, $180,000, and $198,000 in each of the years 2012, 2013, and 2014, respectively. The following information is also available.

1. In 2014, Leader lost a court case in which it was the defendant. The case was a patent infringement suit, and Leader must now pay a competitor $25,000 to settle the suit. No previous entries had been recorded in the books relative to this case as Leader's management felt the company would win.

2. A review of the company's provision for uncollectible accounts during 2014 resulted in a determination that 1% of sales is the appropriate amount of bad debt expense to be charged to operations, rather than the 1.5% used for the preceding two years. Bad debt expense recognized in 2013 and 2012 was $25,000 and $17,500, respectively. The company would have recorded $22,500 of bad debt expense under the old rate for 2014. No entry has yet been made in 2014 for bad debt expense.

3. Leader acquired land on January 1, 2011, at a cost of $40,000. The land was charged to the equipment account in error and has been depreciated since then on the basis of a five-year life with no residual value.

4. During 2014, the company changed from the double-declining-balance method of depreciation for its building to the straight-line method because of a change in the pattern of benefits received. The building cost $1,280,000 to build in early 2012, and no residual value is expected after its 40-year life. Total depreciation under both methods for the past three years is as follows. Double-declining-balance depreciation has been used in 2014.

	Straight-Line	Double-Declining-Balance
2012	$32,000	$64,000
2013	32,000	60,800
2014	32,000	57,760

5. Late in 2014, Leader determined that a piece of specialized equipment purchased in January 2011 at a cost of $54,000 with an estimated life of five years and residual value of $4,000 is now expected to continue in use until the end of 2018 and have a residual value of $2,000 at that time. The company has been using straight-line depreciation for this equipment, and depreciation for 2014 has already been recognized based on the original estimates.

6. The company has determined that a $225,000 note payable that it issued in 2012 has been incorrectly classified on its statement of financial position. The note is payable in annual instalments of $25,000, but the full amount of the note has been shown as a long-term liability with no portion shown in current liabilities. Interest expense relating to the note has been properly recorded.

Instructions

(a) For each of the accounting changes, errors, or transactions, present the journal entry(ies) that Leader needs to make to correct or adjust the accounts, assuming the accounts for 2014 have not yet been closed. If no entry is required, write "none" and briefly explain why. Ignore income tax considerations.

(b) Prepare the entries required in (a) but where retrospective adjustments are made, adjust the entry to include taxes at 25%.

Digging
Deeper

(c) For each of the accounting changes, identify the type of change involved and whether retrospective or prospective treatment is required.

P21-3 As at December 31, 2014, Wilson Corporation is having its financial statements audited for the first time ever. The auditor has found the following items that might have an effect on previous years.

1. Wilson purchased equipment on January 2, 2011, for $130,000. At that time, the equipment had an estimated useful life of 10 years, with a $10,000 residual value. The equipment is depreciated on a straight-line basis. On January 2, 2014, as a result of additional information, the company determined that the equipment had a total useful life of seven years with a $6,000 residual value.

2. During 2014, Wilson changed from the double-declining-balance method for its building to the straight-line method because the company thinks the straight-line method now more closely follows the benefits received from using the assets. The current year depreciation was calculated using the new method following straight-line depreciation. In case the following information was needed, the auditor provided calculations that present depreciation on both bases. The building had originally cost $1.2 million when purchased at the beginning of 2012 and has a residual value of $120,000. It is depreciated over 20 years. The original estimates of useful life and residual value are still accurate.

	2014	2013	2012
Straight-line	$54,000	$ 54,000	$ 54,000
Double-declining-balance	97,200	108,000	120,000

3. Wilson purchased a machine on July 1, 2011, at a cost of $160,000. The machine has a residual value of $16,000 and a useful life of eight years. Wilson's bookkeeper recorded straight-line depreciation during each year but failed to consider the residual value.

4. Prior to 2014, development costs were expensed immediately because they were immaterial. Due to an increase in development phase projects, development costs have now become material and management has decided to capitalize and depreciate them over three years. The development costs meet all six specific conditions for capitalization of development phase costs. Amounts expensed in 2011, 2012, and 2013 were $300, $500, and $1,000, respectively. During 2014, $4,500 was spent and the amount was debited to Deferred Development Costs (an asset account).

Instructions
Do the following, ignoring income tax considerations.

(a) Prepare the necessary journal entries to record each of the changes or errors. The books for 2014 have not been closed. Ignore income taxes.

(b) Calculate the 2014 depreciation expense on the equipment.

(c) Calculate the comparative net incomes for 2013 and 2014, starting with income before the effects of any of the changes identified above. Income before depreciation expense was $600,000 in 2014 and $420,000 in 2013.

(d) From the perspective of an investor, comment on the quality of Wilson Corporation's earnings as reported in 2013 and 2014.

Digging
Deeper

P21-4 You are the auditor of Maglite Services Inc., a privately owned full-service cleaning company following ASPE that is undergoing its first audit for the period ending September 30, 2014. The bank has requested that Maglite have its statements audited this year to satisfy a condition of its debt covenant. It is currently October 1, 2014, and the company's books have been closed. As part of the audit, you have found the following situations:

1. Despite having high receivables, Maglite has no allowance for doubtful accounts, and cash collections have slowed dramatically. Unfortunately, Maglite is owed $5,000 by Brad's Fast Foods at the end of fiscal 2014. Brad's has received substantial media attention during the past year due to Department of Health investigations that ultimately resulted in the closure of the company's operations; the owner has apparently moved to the Bahamas. No

2. Maglite's only capital asset on its books is an advanced cleaning system that has a cost of $35,000 and a carrying amount of $20,825. Maglite has been depreciating this asset using the capital cost allowance used for tax purposes for the two years prior to its year ended September 30, 2014, at the rate of 30%. Useful life at the time of purchase was estimated to be 10 years. Maglite would like to change to a straight-line approach to provide more relevant information to its statement users. Management anticipates that the asset will continue to be of use for four years after the September 30, 2014 year end and will have no residual value. Since the company's accountant was uncertain about how to deal with the change in policy, depreciation expense has not been recorded for the fiscal year.

3. Maglite purchased a computer at the beginning of the fiscal year and immediately expensed its $3,000 cost. Upon questioning, one of the owners said he thought the computer would likely not need to be replaced for at least two more years.

4. You notice that there are no supplies on the statement of financial position. Company management explains that it expenses all supplies when purchased. The company had $1,500 of cleaning supplies on hand at the end of September 2014, which is about $500 higher than the balance that was on hand at the end of the previous year.

5. Maglite started this year to keep a small amount of excess cash in trading investments which are bought and sold on the local stock exchange. At the end of September 2014, the fair value of this portfolio was $15,000 and the carrying value of the investments was $12,000 (which represented the cost of the investments).

Instructions

(a) Assuming that the company's books are closed, prepare any journal entries that are required for each of the transactions. Ignore income tax considerations.

(b) For each of the items, discuss the type of change that is involved and how it is accounted for on the current and comparative financial statements.

(c) If Maglite elected to follow IFRS, discuss how this might change your answers to (a).

(d) Repeat part (a) assuming that the books are open.

P21-5 The founder, president, and major shareholder of Hawthorne Corp. recently sold his controlling interest in the company to a national distributor in the same line of business. The change in ownership was effective June 30, 2014, halfway through Hawthorne's current fiscal year.

During the due diligence process of acquiring the company and over the last six months of 2014, the new senior management team had a chance to review the company's accounting records and policies. Hawthorne follows ASPE. Although EPS are not part of ASPE, management calculates EPS for its own purposes and applies the IFRS guidelines. By the end of 2014, the following decisions had been made.

1. Hawthorne's policy of expensing all interest as incurred will be changed to correspond to the policy of the controlling shareholder whereby interest on self-constructed assets is capitalized. This policy will be applied retrospectively, and going forward it will simplify the consolidation process for the parent company. The major effect of this policy is to reduce interest expense in 2012 by $9,200 and to increase the cost of equipment by the same amount. The equipment was put into service early in 2013. Hawthorne uses straight-line depreciation for equipment and a five-year life. Because the interest has already been deducted for tax purposes, the change in policy results in a taxable temporary difference.

2. Deferred development costs of $12,000 remained in long-term assets at December 31, 2013. These were being written off on a straight-line basis with another three years remaining at that time. On reviewing the December 31, 2014 balances (after an additional year of depreciation), management decided that there were no further benefits to be received from these deferrals and there likely had not been any benefits for the past two years. The original costs were tax deductible when incurred.

3. A long-term contract with a preferred customer was completed in December 2014. When discussing payment with the customer, it came to light that a down payment of $30,000 made by the customer on the contract at the end of 2012 had been taken into revenue (and into taxable income) when received. The revenue should have been recognized in 2014 on completion of the contract.

Hawthorne's financial statements (summarized) were as follows at December 31, 2013 and 2014, before any corrections related to the information above. The December 31, 2014 statements are in draft form only and the 2014 accounts have not yet been closed.

---

adjustment has been made for this balance. Company management estimates that an allowance for doubtful accounts of $47,000 is required. During the 2014 fiscal year, the company wrote off $38,000 in receivables, and it estimates that its September 30, 2013 allowance for doubtful accounts should have been $30,000.

Statement of Financial Position
December 31

Assets	2014	2013	Liabilities and Equity	2014	2013
Current assets	$192,300	$168,400	Current liabilities	$117,000	$103,000
Long-term assets	322,000	311,000	Long-term liabilities	166,000	153,000
	$514,300	$479,400	Share capital (10,000 shares)	50,000	50,000
			Retained earnings	181,300	173,400
				$514,300	$479,400

Income Statement
Year Ended December 31

	2014	2013
Revenues	$475,000	$460,000
Expenses	378,000	376,000
Income tax (30% effective rate)	97,000	84,000
	29,100	25,200
Net income	$ 67,900	$ 58,800
Earnings per share	$ 6.79	$ 5.88
Dividends declared, per share	$ 6.00	$ 2.50

Instructions

(a) Prepare any December 31, 2014 journal entries that are necessary to put into effect the decisions made by senior management. Where retrospective adjustments are made, record the journal entry to include the effect of taxes.

(b) Prepare the comparative statement of financial position, income statement, and statement of retained earnings that will be issued to shareholders for the year ended December 31, 2014.

(c) Prepare the required note disclosures for the accounting changes.

(d) Assume now that Hawthorne follows IFRS instead of ASPE. Briefly comment on the changes, if any, to the accounting treatment for the three decisions in items 1 to 3 above.

P21-6 On December 31, 2014, before the books were closed, management and the accountant at Madrasa Inc. made the following determinations about three depreciable assets.

1. Depreciable asset A (building) was purchased on January 2, 2011. It originally cost $540,000 and the straight-line method was chosen for depreciation. The asset was originally expected to be useful for 10 years and have no residual value. In 2014, the decision was made to change the depreciation method from straight-line to double-declining balance due to a change in the pattern of benefits received. The estimates relating to useful life and residual value remained unchanged.

2. Depreciable asset B (machinery) was purchased on January 3, 2010. It originally cost $180,000 and the straight-line method was chosen for depreciation. The asset was expected to be useful for 15 years and have no residual value. In 2014, the decision was made to shorten this asset's total life to nine years and to estimate the residual value at $3,000.

3. Depreciable asset C (equipment) was purchased on January 5, 2010. The asset's original cost was $160,000 and this amount was entirely expensed in 2010 in error. This particular asset has a 10-year useful life and no residual value. The straight-line method is appropriate.

Additional information:

1. Income in 2014 before depreciation expense amounted to $400,000.

2. Depreciation expense on assets other than A, B, and C totalled $55,000 in 2014.

3. Income in 2013 was reported at $370,000.

4. In both 2013 and 2014, 100,000 common shares were outstanding. No dividends were declared in either year.

Madrasa follows IFRS.

Digging Deeper

Instructions

Answer the following questions, ignoring all income tax effects.

(a) Prepare any necessary entries in 2014. Ignore income taxes.

(b) Calculate the adjusted net income and earnings per share for 2013 and 2014.

(c) Prepare comparative retained earnings statements for Madrasa Inc. for 2013 and 2014. The company reported retained earnings of $200,000 at December 31, 2012.

(d) Prepare the required note disclosures for each of these changes.

(e) How would the changes to Madrasa's depreciable assets be reflected on the statement of cash flows?

P21-7 Sharma Corporation has decided that, in preparing its 2014 financial statements under IFRS, two changes should be made from the methods used in prior years:

1. Depreciation. Sharma has used the tax basis (CCA) method of calculating depreciation for financial reporting purposes. During 2014, management decided that the straight-line method should have been used to calculate depreciation for financial reporting purposes for the years prior to 2014 and going forward. The following schedule identifies the excess of depreciation based on CCA over depreciation based on straight-line, for the past years and for the current year:

	Excess of CCA-based Depreciation over Straight-Line Depreciation Calculated for Financial Statement Purposes
Prior to 2013	$1,365,000
2013	106,050
2014	103,950
	$1,575,000

Depreciation is charged to cost of sales and to selling, general, and administrative expenses on the basis of 75% and 25%, respectively.

2. Bad debt expense. In the past, Sharma recognized bad debt expense equal to 1.5% of net sales. After careful review, it has been decided that a rate of 1.75% is more appropriate for 2014. Bad debt expense is charged to selling, general, and administrative expenses. The following information is taken from preliminary financial statements, which were prepared before including the effects of the two changes.

SHARMA CORPORATION
Condensed Statement of Financial Position
December 31, 2014

Assets	2014	2013
Current assets	$28,340,000	$29,252,000
Plant assets, at cost	45,792,000	43,974,000
Less: Accumulated depreciation	23,761,000	22,946,000
Other long-term assets*	15,221,000	14,648,000
	$65,592,000	$64,928,000

Liabilities and Shareholders' Equity	2014	2013
Current liabilities	$21,124,000	$23,650,000
Long-term debt	15,154,000	14,097,000
Share capital	11,620,000	11,620,000
Retained earnings	17,694,000	15,561,000
	$65,592,000	$64,928,000

*Includes deferred tax asset of $225,000 (2014) and $234,000 (2013), with the latter amount being the result of deductible temporary differences that occurred before 2013.

SHARMA CORPORATION
Condensed Income Statement
Year Ended December 31, 2014

	2014	2013
Net sales	$80,520,000	$78,920,000
Cost of goods sold	54,847,000	53,074,000
	25,673,000	25,846,000
Selling, general, and administrative expenses	19,540,000	18,411,000
	6,133,000	7,435,000
Other expense, net	(1,198,000)	(1,079,000)
Income before income tax	4,935,000	6,356,000
Income tax	1,480,500	1,906,800
Net income	$ 3,454,500	$ 4,449,200

There have been no temporary differences between any book and tax items prior to the above changes except for those that involve the allowance for doubtful accounts. For tax purposes, bad debts are deductible only when they are written off. The tax rate is 30%.

Instructions

(a) For each of the items that follow, calculate the amounts that would appear on the comparative (2014 and 2013) financial statements of Sharma Corporation after adjustment for the two accounting changes. Show amounts for both 2014 and 2013, and prepare supporting schedules as necessary.

1. Accumulated depreciation
2. Deferred tax asset/liability
3. Selling, general, and administrative expenses
4. Current income tax expense
5. Deferred tax expense

(b) Prepare the comparative financial statements that will be issued to shareholders for Sharma's year ended December 31, 2014. Assume that no dividends were declared in 2013.

P21-8 Both the management of Kimmel Instrument Corporation, a small company that follows IFRS, and its independent auditors recently concluded that the company's results of operations will be reliable and more relevant in future years if Kimmel changes its method of costing inventory from FIFO to weighted average cost. The following data are a five-year income summary using FIFO and a schedule of what the inventories might have been if they had been stated using the weighted average cost method.

KIMMEL INSTRUMENT CORPORATION
Statement of Income and Retained Earnings for the Years Ended May 31

	2010	2011	2012	2013	2014
Sales—net	$13,964	$15,506	$16,673	$18,221	$18,898
Cost of goods sold					
Beginning inventory	1,000	1,100	1,000	1,115	1,237
Purchases	13,000	13,900	15,000	15,900	17,100
Ending inventory	(1,100)	(1,000)	(1,115)	(1,237)	(1,369)
Total	12,900	14,000	14,885	15,778	16,968
Gross profit	1,064	1,506	1,788	2,443	1,930
Administrative expenses	700	763	832	907	989
Income before taxes	364	743	956	1,536	941
Income taxes (30%)	109	223	287	461	282
Net income	255	520	669	1,075	659
Retained earnings—beginning	1,206	1,461	1,981	2,650	3,725
Retained earnings—ending	$ 1,461	$ 1,981	$ 2,650	$ 3,725	$ 4,384
Earnings per share	$ 2.55	$ 5.20	$ 6.69	$ 10.75	$ 6.59

KIMMEL INSTRUMENT CORPORATION
SCHEDULE OF INVENTORY BALANCES USING AVERAGE COST METHOD
Year Ended May 31

2009	2010	2011	2012	2013	2014
$950	$1,124	$1,091	$1,270	$1,480	$1,699

Instructions

(a) Prepare comparative statements for the five years that would be suitable for inclusion in the historical summary portion of Kimmel's annual report, assuming that Kimmel had changed its inventory costing method to weighted average cost in 2014. Indicate the effects on net income and earnings per share for the years involved. (All amounts except EPS are rounded up to the nearest dollar.)

(b) Prepare the statement of retained earnings for 2014, with comparative statements for 2013 and 2012 to be issued to shareholders, assuming retrospective treatment.

(c) Identify all statement of financial position accounts that require restatement on the comparative May 31, 2013 and 2012 statements of financial position issued to shareholders in 2014.

(d) Assume that the data for the years 2009 to 2013 were not available. Briefly explain how to account for this inability to apply full retrospective application under both ASPE and IFRS, and prepare the statement of retained earnings for 2014, with a comparative statement for 2013 to be issued to shareholders as an illustration to aid in the explanation.

P21-9   You have been assigned to examine the financial statements of Picard Corporation for the year ended December 31, 2014, as prepared following IFRS. Picard uses a periodic inventory system. You discover the following situations:

1. The physical inventory count on December 31, 2013, improperly excluded merchandise costing $26,000 that had been temporarily stored in a public warehouse.

2. The physical inventory count on December 31, 2014, improperly included merchandise with a cost of $15,400 that had been recorded as a sale on December 27, 2014, and was being held for the customer to pick up on January 4, 2015.

3. A collection of $6,700 on account from a customer received on December 31, 2014, was not recorded in 2014.

4. Depreciation of $4,600 for 2014 on delivery trucks was not recorded.

5. In 2014, the company received $3,700 on a sale of fully depreciated equipment that originally cost $25,000. The company credited the proceeds from the sale to the Equipment account.

6. During November 2014, a competitor company filed a patent infringement suit against Picard, claiming damages of $620,000. The company's legal counsel has indicated that an unfavourable verdict is probable and a reasonable estimate of the court's award to the competitor is $450,000. The company has not reflected or disclosed this situation in the financial statements.

7. A large piece of equipment was purchased on January 3, 2014, for $41,000 and was charged in error to Maintenance and Repairs Expense. The equipment is estimated to have a service life of eight years and no residual value. Picard normally uses the straight-line depreciation method for this type of equipment.

8. Picard has a portfolio of temporary investments reported as trading investments at fair value. No adjusting entry has been made yet in 2014. Information on carrying amounts and fair value is as follows:

	Carrying Amount	Fair Value
Dec. 31, 2013	$95,000	$95,000
Dec. 31, 2014	$94,000	$82,000

9. At December 31, 2014, an analysis of payroll information showed accrued salaries of $10,600. The Accrued Salaries Payable account had a balance of $16,000 at December 31, 2014, which was unchanged from its balance at December 31, 2013.

10. An $18,000 insurance premium paid on July 1, 2013, for a policy that expires on June 30, 2016, was charged to insurance expense.

11. A trademark was acquired at the beginning of 2013 for $36,000. Through an oversight, no amortization has been recorded since its acquisition. Picard expected the trademark to benefit the company for a total of approximately 12 years.

Instructions

Assume that the trial balance has been prepared, the ending inventory has not yet been recorded, and the books have not been closed for 2014. Assuming also that all amounts are material, prepare journal entries showing the adjustments that are required. Ignore income tax considerations.

P21-10 On May 5, 2015, you were hired by Gavin Inc., a closely held company that follows ASPE, as a staff member of its newly created internal auditing department. While reviewing the company's records for 2013 and 2014, you discover that no adjustments have yet been made for the items listed below.

1. Interest income of $18,800 was not accrued at the end of 2013. It was recorded when received in February 2014.

2. Equipment costing $18,000 was expensed when purchased on July 1, 2013. It is expected to have a four-year life with no residual value. The company typically uses straight-line depreciation for all fixed assets.

3. Research costs of $36,000 were incurred early in 2013. They were capitalized and were to be amortized over a three-year period. Amortization of $12,000 was recorded for 2013 and $12,000 for 2014. For tax purposes, the research costs were expensed as incurred.

4. On January 2, 2013, Gower leased a building for five years at a monthly rental of $9,000. On that date, the company paid the following amounts, which were expensed when paid for both financial reporting and tax purposes:

Security deposit	$35,000
First month's rent	9,000
Last month's rent	9,000
	$53,000

5. The company received $42,000 from a customer at the beginning of 2013 for services that it is to perform evenly over a three-year period beginning in 2013. None of the amount received was reported as unearned revenue at the end of 2013. The $42,000 was included in taxable income in 2013.

6. Merchandise inventory costing $16,800 was in the warehouse at December 31, 2013, but was incorrectly omitted from the physical count at that date. The company uses the periodic inventory method.

Gavin follows the taxes payable method of accounting for income taxes.

Instructions

Using the table that follows, enter the appropriate dollar amounts in the appropriate columns to indicate the effect of any errors on the net income figure reported on the income statement for the year ending December 31, 2013, and the retained earnings figure reported on the statement of financial position at December 31, 2014. Assume that all amounts are material and that an income tax rate of 25% is appropriate for all years. Assume also that each item is independent of the other items. It is not necessary to total the columns on the grid.

	Net Income for 2013		Retained Earnings at Dec. 31, 2014	
Item	Understated	Overstated	Understated	Overstated

P21-11 Kesterman Corporation is in the process of negotiating a loan for expansion purposes. Kesterman's books and records have never been audited and the bank has requested that an audit be performed and that IFRS be followed. Kesterman has prepared the following comparative financial statements for the years ended December 31, 2014 and 2013.

KESTERMAN CORPORATION
Statement of Financial Position
as at December 31, 2014 and 2013

	2014	2013
Assets		
Current assets		
Cash	$163,000	$ 82,000
Accounts receivable	392,000	296,000
Allowance for doubtful accounts	(37,000)	(18,000)
Fair value–net income investments	78,000	78,000
Inventory	207,000	202,000
Total current assets	803,000	640,000

Plant assets

Property, plant, and equipment	167,000	169,500
Accumulated depreciation	(121,600)	(106,400)
Plant assets (net)	45,400	63,100
Total assets	$848,400	$703,100

Liabilities and Shareholders' Equity

Liabilities

Accounts payable	$121,400	$196,100

Shareholders' equity

Common shares, no par value,
50,000 authorized, 20,000 issued and

outstanding	260,000	260,000
Retained earnings	467,000	247,000
Total shareholders' equity	727,000	507,000
Total liabilities and shareholders' equity	$848,400	$703,100

KESTERMAN CORPORATION
Statement of Income
for the Years Ended December 31, 2014 and 2013

	2014	2013
Sales	$1,000,000	$900,000
Cost of sales	430,000	395,000
Gross profit	570,000	505,000
Operating expenses	210,000	205,000
Administrative expenses	140,000	105,000
	350,000	310,000
Net income	$ 220,000	$195,000

During the audit, the following additional facts were determined:

1. An analysis of collections and losses on accounts receivable during the past two years indicates a drop in anticipated bad debt losses. After consulting with management, it was agreed that the loss experience rate on sales should be reduced from the recorded 2% to 1.5%, beginning with the year ended December 31, 2014.

2. An analysis of the fair value-net income investments revealed that the total fair value for these investments as at the end of each year was as follows:

Dec. 31, 2013	$78,000
Dec. 31, 2014	$65,000

3. Inventory at December 31, 2013, was overstated by $8,900 and inventory at December 31, 2014, was overstated by $13,600.

4. On January 2, 2013, equipment costing $30,000 (estimated useful life of 10 years and residual value of $5,000) was incorrectly charged to operating expenses. Kesterman records depreciation on the straight-line basis. In 2014, fully depreciated equipment (with no residual value) that originally cost $17,500 was sold as scrap for $2,800. Kesterman credited the $2,800 in proceeds to the equipment account.

5. An analysis of 2013 operating expenses revealed that Kesterman charged to expense a four-year insurance premium of $4,700 on January 15, 2013.

6. The analysis of operating expenses also revealed that operating expenses were incorrectly classified as part of administrative expenses in the amount of $15,000 in 2013 and $35,000 in 2014.

Instructions

(a) Prepare the journal entries to correct the books at December 31, 2014. The books for 2014 have not been closed. Ignore income tax.

(b) Beginning with reported net income, prepare a schedule showing the calculation of corrected net income for the years ended December 31, 2014 and 2013, assuming that any adjustments are to be reported on comparative statements for the two years. Ignore income tax. (Do not prepare financial statements.)

(c) Prepare a schedule showing the calculation of corrected retained earnings at January 1, 2014.

P21-12   Kitchener Corporation has followed IFRS and used the accrual basis of accounting for several years. A review of the records, however, indicates that some expenses and revenues have been handled on a cash basis because of errors made by an inexperienced bookkeeper. Income statements prepared by the bookkeeper reported $29,000 net income for 2013 and $37,000 net income for 2014. Further examination of the records reveals that the following items were handled improperly:

1. Rent of $1,300 was received from a tenant in December 2013, but the full amount was recorded as income at that time even though the rental related to 2014.

2. Wages payable on December 31 have been consistently omitted from the records of that date and have been entered instead as expenses when paid in the following year. The amounts of the accruals that were recorded in this way were as follows:

Dec. 31, 2012	$1,100	
Dec. 31, 2013	1,500	
Dec. 31, 2014	940	

3. Invoices for office supplies purchased have been charged to expense accounts when received. Inventories of supplies on hand at the end of each year have been ignored, and no entry has been made for them. The inventories were as follows:

Dec. 31, 2012	$1,300	
Dec. 31, 2013	740	
Dec. 31, 2014	1,420	

Instructions

(a) Prepare a schedule that shows the corrected net income for the years 2013 and 2014. All listed items should be labelled clearly. Ignore income tax considerations.

(b) Prepare the required journal entries to correct the 2014 net income. Assume that the books are open and ignore income tax considerations.

(c) Assume that Kitchener had unadjusted retained earnings of $95,000 at January 1, 2013, and of $124,000 at January 1, 2014. Prepare a schedule that shows the corrected opening retained earnings balances.

(d) Assume that Kitchener had total net sales revenue of $1.2 million and $1.1 million in 2013 and 2014, respectively. From the perspective of an investor, discuss the effects of the errors on Kitchener's profit margin in 2013 and 2014.

Digging Deeper

P21-13   You have been asked by a client to review the records of Inteq Corporation, a small manufacturer of precision tools and machines that follows ASPE. Your client is interested in buying the business, and arrangements were made for you to review the accounting records. Your examination reveals the following:

1. Inteq Corporation commenced business on April 1, 2011, and has been reporting on a fiscal year ending March 31. The company has never been audited, but the annual statements prepared by the bookkeeper reflect the following income before closing and before deducting income tax:

Year Ended March 31	Income Before Taxes
2012	$ 71,600
2013	111,400
2014	103,580

2. A relatively small number of machines have been shipped on consignment. These transactions have been recorded as ordinary sales and billed in this way, with the gross profit on each sale being recognized when the machine was shipped. On March 31 of each year, the amounts for machines billed and in the hands of consignees were as follows:

2012	$6,500
2013	none
2014	5,590

The sales price was determined by adding 30% to cost. Assume that the consigned machines are sold the following year.

3. On March 30, 2013, two machines were shipped to a customer on a C.O.D. basis. The sale was not entered until April 5, 2013, when $6,100 cash was received. The machines were not included in the inventory at March 31, 2013. (Title passed on March 30, 2013.)

4. All machines are sold subject to a five-year warranty. It is estimated that the expense ultimately to be incurred in connection with the warranty will amount to 0.5% of sales. The company has charged an expense account for actual warranty costs incurred. Sales per books and warranty costs were as follows:

Year Ended March 31	Sales	Actual Warranty Costs Incurred for Sales Made in			Total
		2012	2013	2014	
2012	$ 940,000	$760			$ 760
2013	1,010,000	360	$1,310		1,670
2014	1,795,000	320	1,620	$1,910	3,850

5. A review of the corporate minutes reveals that the manager is entitled to a bonus of 0.5% of the income before deducting income tax and the bonus. The bonuses have never been recorded or paid.

6. Bad debts have been recorded on a direct writeoff basis. Experience of similar enterprises indicates that losses will approximate 0.25% of sales. Bad debts written off and expensed were as follows:

	Bad Debts Incurred on Sales Made in			Total
	2012	2013	2014	
2012	$750			$ 750
2013	800	$ 520		1,320
2014	350	1,800	$1,700	3,850

7. The bank deducts 6% on all contracts that it finances. Of this amount, 0.5% is placed in a reserve to the credit of Inteq Corporation and is refunded to Inteq as financed contracts are paid in full. The reserve established by the bank has not been reflected in Inteq's books. On the books of the bank for each fiscal year, the excess of credits over debits (the net increase) to the reserve account for Inteq were as follows:

2012	$ 3,000
2013	3,900
2014	5,100
	$12,000

8. Commissions on sales have been entered when paid. Commissions payable on March 31 of each year were as follows:

2012	$1,400
2013	800
2014	1,120

Instructions

(a) Present a schedule showing the revised income before income tax for each of the years ended March 31, 2012, 2013, and 2014. Make calculations to the nearest dollar.

(b) Prepare the journal entry or entries that you would give the bookkeeper to correct the books. Assume that the books have not yet been closed for the fiscal year ended March 31, 2014. Disregard corrections of income tax.

(AICPA adapted)

P21-14 Bayberry Corporation performs year-end planning in November each year before its fiscal year ends in December. The preliminary estimated net income following IFRS is $4.2 million. The CFO, Rita Warren, meets with the company president, Jim Bayberry, to review the projected numbers.

The corporation has never used robotic equipment before, and Warren assumed an accelerated method because of the rapidly changing technology in robotic equipment. The company normally uses straight-line depreciation for production equipment. The investment securities held at year end were purchased during 2014, and are accounted for using the fair value through other comprehensive income (FV-OCI) model.

Bayberry explains to Warren that it is important for the corporation to show a $7-million income before tax because Bayberry receives a $1-million bonus if the income before tax and bonus reaches $7 million. He also cautions that the company does not want to pay more than $2.5 million in income tax to the government. Warren presents the following projected information.

Ethics

BAYBERRY CORPORATION
Projected Income Statement
Year Ended December 31, 2014
($000s)

Sales		$29,000
Cost of goods sold	$14,000	
Depreciation	2,600	
Operating expenses	6,400	23,000
Income before income tax		6,000
Provision for income tax		1,800
Net income		$ 4,200

SELECTED STATEMENT OF FINANCIAL POSITION INFORMATION
December 31, 2014
($000s)

Estimated cash balance	$ 5,000
Investment securities (FV-OCI) (at cost)	10,000

Security	Cost	Estimated Fair Value
A	$ 2,000	$ 2,200
B	4,000	3,900
C	3,000	3,000
D	1,000	1,800
Total	$10,000	$10,900

Other information ($000s) at December 31, 2014:

Equipment	$ 3,000
Accumulated depreciation (5 years, straight-line)	1,200
New robotic equipment (purchased 1/1/14)	5,000
Accumulated depreciation (5 years, double-declining-balance)	2,000

Instructions

(a) What can Warren do within IFRS to accommodate the president's wishes to achieve $7 million of income before tax and bonus? Present the revised income statement based on your decision.

(b) Are the actions ethical? Who are the stakeholders in this decision, and what effect does Bayberry's actions have on their interests?

(c) Are there any cash flow implications of the choices made to achieve the president's wishes?

(d) Assume instead that Bayberry Corporation follows ASPE instead of IFRS. Briefly comment on the changes, if any, to the accounting treatment of the items discussed above.

Digging Deeper

Case

Refer to the Case Primer on the Student Website and in *WileyPLUS* to help you answer this case.

Ethics

CA21-1 Andy Frain is an audit senior of a large public accounting firm who has just been assigned to the Usher Corporation's annual audit engagement. Usher is a public company and has been a client of Frain's firm for many years. Usher is a fast-growing business in the commercial construction industry. In reviewing the fixed asset ledger, Andy discovered a series of unusual accounting changes, in which the useful lives of assets, depreciated using the straight-line method, were substantially lowered near the mid-point of the original estimate. For example, the useful life of one dump truck was changed from 10 to 6 years during its fifth year of service. Upon further investigation, Andy was told by Sucharita Nasab, Usher's accounting manager, "I don't really see your problem. After all, it's perfectly legal to change an accounting estimate. Besides, our CEO likes to see big earnings!"

Instructions

Discuss the issues.

Integrated Cases

IC21-1 Temple Limited is in the real estate business. After several years of economic growth, most of the company's assets are now worth significantly more than the amount that is recognized on the financial statements. Wanting to capitalize on this positive trend, the company is ready to expand and is looking at developing a new property in the Bahamas that will cost $300 million. Currently, the company's debt to equity ratio is 5:1 and the company needs to raise funds for the expansion. Lendall Bank, the company's primary lender, understands that there is hidden value in the statement of financial position and is willing to finance the project.

Temple is now concerned about how the capital markets will react to this increase in debt. The company's shares list on the TSX and, therefore, IFRS is a constraint. Under IFRS, fair value accounting is permitted for real estate as an accounting policy choice.

Instructions

Adopt the role of Temple Limited's controller and write a memo to address the CEO's concerns.

IC21-2 Sunlight Equipment Manufacturers (SEM) makes barbecue equipment. The company has historically been very profitable; however, in the last year and a half, things have taken a turn for the worse due to higher consumer interest rates and a slowdown in the economy. On its 2014 draft year-end statements, the company is currently showing a break-even position before any final year-end adjustments. The company had fired its CEO, Sam Lazano, at the beginning of the year and a turnaround specialist was hired—Agneta Lundstrom. Agneta has a reputation of being able to come into companies that are suffering and make them profitable within two years. Agneta has agreed with SEM's board of directors that she will be paid a $1-million bonus if the company has a combined two-year profit of $5 million by the end of 2015.

Among other things, Agneta instituted a more aggressive sales policy for SEM's customers, who are mainly retailers, as well as a new remuneration policy for sales staff. Agneta attributed the company's poor performance to untrained sales staff whose remuneration and bonus scheme was not properly aligned to maximize sales. Under the new remuneration policy, sales staff is paid salary as well as a bonus, which is a percent of gross sales as at year end. The sales staff has responded well and sales have increased by 20%.

The new sales policy is as follows:

- Cash down payment of 20% with remaining payment for shipment once the barbecues are sold by the customer to a third party.

- If the customers double their normal order, no down payment is required.

- The barbecues may be stored on the premises of SEM. Many customers have taken the company up on this offer in order to double the size of their purchase.

- Any unsold barbecues are allowed to be returned after year end.

Under the new policy, sales have increased dramatically, with many customers taking advantage of the new terms. As at year end, legal title to all barbecues has passed to the customers. Only customers with excellent credit history have been allowed to purchase under the new policy. The company has accrued bonuses for almost all its sales staff.

The increased profits from these sales have been offset by the accrual of $500,000 of Agneta's bonus. She is very confident that she will be able to turn the company around and so has accrued part of her bonus. She has also decided to change several accounting policies, including the following:

- Depreciation on machinery switched to straight-line from double-declining-balance. Note that the equipment is about 2 years old with an estimated life of 10 years. Agneta felt that the double-declining-balance method was arbitrary and noted that several of their competitors used the straight-line method. Machinery is most useful when new since it requires less downtime for fixing.

Another problem that Agneta had identified was in inventory management. Agneta was convinced that inventory was being stolen and/or "lost" due to poor tracking. SEM had therefore hired a company, Software Limited, to install a new inventory tracking system during the year. Midway through the year, Software Limited had gone bankrupt and was not able to finish the installation. The installation was a customized job and as at year end, the system was not functioning yet. SEM has not been able to find a company to replace Software Limited. To date, $2 million has been spent on the new system. Agneta had capitalized the costs and noted she was confident that she would be able to find a company that could successfully complete the installation.

Instructions

Adopt the role of the company's auditors and discuss the financial reporting issues for the 2014 year end. The company is a private company but would like the statements to be prepared in accordance with IFRS.

Writing Assignments

WA21-1   It is December 2014 and Cranmore Inc. recently hired a new accountant, Jodie Larson. Although Cranmore is a private company, it follows IFRS. As part of her preparation of the 2014 financial statements for Cranmore Inc., Jodie has proposed the following accounting changes.

1. At December 31, 2013, Cranmore had a receivable of $250,000 from Michael Inc. on its statement of financial position that had been owed since mid-2012. In December 2014, Michael Inc. was declared bankrupt and no recovery is expected. Jodie proposes to write off the receivable in 2014 against retained earnings as a correction of a 2012 error.

2. Jodie proposes to change from double-declining-balance to straight-line depreciation for the company's manufacturing assets because of a change in the pattern in which the assets provide benefits to the company. If straight-line depreciation had been used for all prior periods, retained earnings would have been $380,800 higher at December 31, 2013. The change's effect just on 2014 income is a reduction of $48,800.

3. For equipment in the leasing division, Jodie proposes to adopt the sum-of-the-years'-digits depreciation method, which the company has never used before. Cranmore began operating its leasing division in 2014. If straight-line depreciation were used, 2014 income would be $110,000 higher.

4. Cranmore has decided to adopt the revaluation method for reporting and measuring its land, with this policy being effective from January 1, 2014. At December 31, 2013, the land's fair value was $900,000. The land's book value at December 31, 2013, was $750,000. (*Hint:* Refer to IAS 8 for the treatment of this specific change in policy.)

5. Cranmore has investments that are recorded at FV-OCI. At December 31, 2013, an error was made in the calculation of the fair values of these investments. The amount of the error was an overstatement of the fair value by $200,000.

Cranmore's income tax rate is 30%.

Instructions

(a) For each of the changes described above, identify whether the situation is a change in policy, a change in estimate, or the correction of an error. Justify your answer.

(b) For each of the changes described above, determine whether a restatement of January 1, 2014 retained earnings is required. What is the amount of the adjustment, if any? Prepare the required journal entries to record any adjustments.

(c) Prepare the statement of changes in equity. An excerpt from the statement of changes in equity for December 31, 2013, is provided below:

	Share Capital	Retained Earnings	AOCI Investments at FV through OCI	Total
Opening—January 1, 2013	$1,000,000	$2,500,000	$ 650,000	$4,150,000
Comprehensive income	–0–	910,000	475,000	1,385,000
Closing balance—December 31, 2013	$1,000,000	$3,410,000	$1,125,000	$5,535,000

The profit or loss is $1,350,000 and the other comprehensive income is $150,000 (relating to the change in value of the FV-OCI Investment during 2014) for the 2014 year. There were no shares issued or repurchased during the year. There are no other changes to the equity accounts for 2014.

(d) Identify what disclosures are required in the notes to the financial statements as a result of each of these changes.

WA21-2   Various types of accounting changes can affect the financial statements of a private business enterprise differently. Assume that each item on the following list would have a material effect on the financial statements of a private enterprise in the current year:

1. A change to the income taxes payable method from the tax liability method

2. A change in the estimated useful life of previously recorded capital assets where the straight-line depreciation method is used

3. A change from deferring and amortizing development costs to immediate recognition. The change to immediate recognition arises because the company does not have the resources to market the new product adequately.

4. A change from including the employer share of CPP and EI premiums as a separate payroll tax expense to including them with salaries and wages expense on the income statement

5. The correction of a mathematical error in inventory costing that was made in a prior period

6. A change from straight-line amortization to a double-declining method in recognition of the effect that technology has on the pattern of benefits received from the asset's use

7. A change from presenting unconsolidated statements (using the cost method for the subsidiaries) to presenting consolidated statements for the company and its two long-held subsidiaries

8. A change in the method of accounting for leases for tax purposes to conform with the financial accounting method; as a result, both future and current taxes payable changed substantially

9. A change from the periodic inventory method to the perpetual method with the introduction of scanning equipment and updated computer software

10. A change in an accounting method due to a change in a primary source of GAAP

Instructions

Identify the type of accounting change that is described in each item, and indicate whether the prior years' financial statements must be restated when they are presented in comparative form with the current year's statements. Also indicate if the company is required to justify the change.

WA21-3 Ali Reiners, a new controller of Luftsa Corp., is preparing the financial statements for the year ended December 31, 2014. Luftsa is a publicly traded entity and therefore follows IFRS. As a result of this review, Ali has found the following information.

1. Luftsa has been offering a loyalty rewards program to its customers for about five years. In the past, the company has not recorded any accrual related to the accumulated points as the amounts were not significant. However, with recent changes to the plan in 2014, the loyalty points are now accumulating much more rapidly and have become material. Ali has decided that effective January 1, 2014, the company will defer the revenue related to these points at the time of each sale, which will result in a liability.

2. In 2014, Luftsa decided to change its accounting policy for depreciating property, plant, and equipment to depreciate based on components and also to adopt the revaluation model. The company hired specialized appraisers at January 1, 2014, to determine the fair values, useful lives, and depreciable amounts for all of the components of the assets. In prior years, the company did not have sufficient documentation to be able to apply component accounting, and the appraisers were not able to determine this information.

3. One division of Luftsa Corp., Rosentiel Co., has consistently shown an increasing net income from period to period. On closer examination of its operating statement, Ali Reiners noted that inventory obsolescence charges are much lower than in other divisions. In discussing this with the division's controller, Ali learned that the controller knowingly makes low estimates related to the writeoff of inventory in order to manage his bottom line.

4. In 2014, the company purchased new machinery that is expected to increase production dramatically, particularly in the early years. The company has decided to depreciate this machinery on an accelerated basis, even though other machinery is depreciated on a straight-line basis.

5. All products sold by Luftsa are subject to a three-year warranty. It has been estimated that the expense ultimately to be incurred on these machines is 1% of sales. In 2014, because of a production breakthrough, it is now estimated that 0.5% of sales is sufficient. In 2012 and 2013, warranty expense was calculated as $64,000 and $70,000, respectively. The company now believes that warranty costs should be reduced by 50%.

6. In reviewing the capital asset ledger in another division, Usher Division, Ali found a series of unusual accounting changes in which the useful lives of assets were substantially reduced when halfway through the original life estimate. For example, the useful life of one truck was changed from 10 to 6 years during its fifth year of service. The divisional manager, who is compensated in large part by bonuses, indicated on investigation, "It's perfectly legal to change an accounting estimate. We always have better information after time has passed."

Instructions

Ali Reiners has come to you for advice about each of the situations. Prepare a memorandum to the controller, indicating the appropriate accounting treatment that should be given to each situation. For any situations where there might be ethical considerations, identify and assess the issues and suggest what should be done.

WA21-4 Rydell Manufacturing Ltd. is preparing its year-end financial statements. Rydell is a private enterprise. The controller, Theo Kimbria, is confronted with several decisions about statement presentation for the following items.

1. The company has decided to change its depreciation method for the machinery to units of production rather than the straight-line method. This is due to the way in which the machinery is now being used.

2. Trying to meet the criteria for capitalization of the development costs has become very difficult because of the highly competitive conditions in this market. Therefore, the practice of deferring and amortizing development costs has been abandoned in favour of expensing these costs as they are incurred.

Ethics

3. When the year-end physical inventory adjustment was made for the current year, the controller discovered that the prior year's physical inventory sheets for an entire section of warehouse had been mislaid and left out of last year's count.

4. The method of accounting that is used for financial reporting purposes for certain receivables has been approved for tax purposes during the current tax year by the Canada Revenue Agency. This change for tax purposes will cause both current taxes payable and future tax liabilities to change substantially.

5. Management has decided to switch from the FIFO inventory valuation method to the average cost inventory valuation method for all inventories.

Instructions

For each of the five changes that Rydell Manufacturing Ltd. made in the current year, advise Theo on whether the change is a change in accounting policy, a change in estimate, the correction of an error, or none of these. Explain if the accounting treatment would be different under ASPE or IFRS. Provide a short explanation for your choice. Determine if retrospective or prospective application would be required in each case and what information would be required in any note disclosure. If the information that is provided is insufficient for you to determine the nature of the change, identify what additional information you need and how this might affect your response.

(CMA adapted. Used with permission.)

WA21-5 ASPE does not permit the correction of an error to be accounted for using partial retrospective restatement or prospective restatement. However, IAS 8 does allow partial retrospective restatement or even prospective treatment for error corrections.

Instructions

(a) Write a short memorandum that is suitable for being presented to your class in support of the Canadian position for private enterprises.

(b) Write a short memorandum suitable for presentation to your class in support of the international position.

WA21-6 At a recent conference on financial accounting and reporting, three participants provided examples of similar accounting changes that they had encountered in the last few months. They all involved the current portion of long-term debt.

1. The first participant explained that it had just recently come to her attention that the current portion of long-term debt was incorrectly calculated in the last three years of her company's financial statements due to an error in an accounting software product.

2. The second participant explained that his company had just decided to change its definition of what is "current" to make it closer to the "operating cycle," which is approximately 18 months. The company had been using "12 months from the SFP date."

3. The third participant said that her company has decided to change from a "12 months from the SFP date" definition to one based on the company's operating cycle, which is now close to two years. She explained that the company's strategic plan over the last three years had moved the company into bidding on and winning significant longer-term contracts and that the average life of these contracts has now lengthened to about two years.

Instructions

As a panellist at this conference who is expected to respond to the participants, prepare a brief report on the advice you would give on how each situation should be handled under IFRS. Identify what steps each participant should take and what disclosures, if any, each would be required to report.

WA21-7

Instructions

Write a brief essay highlighting the differences between IFRS and accounting standards for private enterprises noted in this chapter, discussing the conceptual justification for each.

WA21-8

Instructions

Briefly discuss the motivation for adopting IFRS and discuss the merits of the changes. Include a discussion of changes to key ratios. Are these changes beneficial to the financial community?

RESEARCH AND FINANCIAL ANALYSIS

Real World Emphasis

RA21-1 Shoppers Drug Mart

Refer to the specimen financial statements at the end of the book, which show excerpts from the 2011 year-end financial statements and accompanying notes of **Shoppers Drug Mart**. The full financial statements are available on SEDAR. In the notes, the company refers to accounting standards that have been retrospectively applied, standards that have been prospectively applied, and standards that have been issued but are not yet effective.

Instructions

(a) Review Note 30 from the financial statements, and explain how the IFRS standards have been adopted and retrospectively applied. Indicate and explain the following:

1. On what date did the company adopt IFRS?

2. What were some of the elections to retrospective restatement that were applied?

3. What items required restatement and what was their impact (exclude tax impact) on the income statement for the year ended January 1, 2011, and the statement of financial position at January 3, 2010, and January 1, 2011? Consider putting the solution in table format.

(b) What disclosure did the company provide on standards that were issued, but were not effective?

RA21-2 Canadian Tire Corporation, Limited

Real World Emphasis

Access the annual report for Canadian Tire Corporation, Limited for the year ended December 31, 2011, from SEDAR (www.sedar.com).

Instructions

(a) Reviewing the consolidated statement of changes in shareholders' equity, discuss whether Canadian Tire reported any accounting changes in the years presented. Which accounts were impacted and by how much?

(b) Identify and explain each accounting change that the company implemented in 2011. How was each accounting change applied? If the change was due to an amendment of the standards, provide the details of the effective date of the changes. Classify each change as being one of the following:

1. A change in accounting policy mandated by a change in a primary source of GAAP

2. A voluntary change in accounting policy

3. A change in estimate

For each change reported above, explain whether the change was retrospectively or prospectively applied. What was the impact of each change on the financial statements of Canadian Tire in each year presented?

(c) The company also provides details for future accounting changes. Describe the note disclosure provided for these.

RA21-3 Research Case–Transitional Provisions

The IASB is working to update a major portion of the standards and has a put a project plan in place that outlines the timelines for these various updates. The following are examples of topics where new standards are proposed to be released (or already have been released): Consolidation (IAS 27), financial instruments (IFRS 9), joint arrangements (IAS 31), non-financial liabilities, and fair value measurements.

Instructions

Using the IASB website (www.ifrs.org), identify new standards that have been recently released. Review the transitional provisions, if any, for each of these standards identified. Write a report on the accounting requirements for each change in the year when it becomes effective. Discuss whether the requirements seem reasonable, and whether they are consistent from one standard to another.

RA21-4 Loblaw Companies Limited

Access the 2011 year-end financial statements and accompanying notes of **Loblaw Companies Limited** from SEDAR (www.sedar.com).

Instructions

Review the notes to the financial statements, in particular Note 31 detailing the transition to IFRS. Indicate and explain the following:

(a) On what date did the company adopt IFRS?

(b) Discuss some of the larger changes to total equity caused by the transition from pre-changeover GAAP to IFRS.

(c) What was the total impact from the transition on the total equity of the company? How would this change affect key financial ratios of the company? Recalculate these key ratios and discuss the potential impact.

ENDNOTES

1 *CICA Handbook–Accounting*, Part II, Section 1506.05 and IAS 8 *Accounting Policies, Changes in Accounting Estimates and Errors*, para. 5. Copyright © 2012 IFRS Foundation. All rights reserved. Reproduced by Wiley Canada with the permission of the IFRS Foundation ®. No permission granted to third parties to reproduce or distribute.

2 Ibid.

3 Ibid.

4 *CICA Handbook–Accounting*, Part II, Section 1100 *Financial Statement Concepts*

5 IAS 8.14. If an entity changes its accounting policy by following a source other than a primary source of GAAP, this is treated as a voluntary change in policy (IAS 8.21). Under both sets of GAAP, early adoption of a new accounting standard is not considered a voluntary change in policy.

6 *CICA Handbook–Accounting*, Part II, Section 1506.09.

7 IAS 1.10.

8 Think this through. The book value of the PP&E asset has just been increased, but no change has been made to the UCC. Future depreciation expense is based on the larger carrying amount, but this won't be permitted for tax purposes; the costs were actually deducted for tax purposes previously. Therefore, future taxable income will be higher than accounting income.

9 Although ASPE refers to the preparation of a statement of retained earnings, there is no requirement to prepare it in this form. Because changes in all shareholders' equity accounts are required to be reported, it is equally acceptable to prepare a statement of changes in equity. An example of this is shown in Illustration 21-6.

10 The Canadian Accounting Standards Board required Canadian publicly accountable enterprises to adopt IFRS on January 1, 2011, unless, as permitted by Canadian securities regulators, registrants adopted U.S. GAAP on or before that same date.

11 The correct deferred tax asset amount is 30% of the difference between the asset's tax basis and its carrying amount. Because no CCA has been claimed, the correct tax basis at December 31, 2014, is $150,000, its capital cost. The correct carrying amount at December 31, 2014, is $150,000 – $14,000 = $136,000. The temporary difference is $150,000 – $136,000 = $14,000 and the deferred tax asset is $14,000 × 30% = $4,200.

12 See Ross L. Watts and Jerold L. Zimmerman, "Positive Accounting Theory: A Ten-Year Perspective," *The Accounting Review* (January 1990) for an excellent review of research findings related to management incentives in selecting accounting methods.

13 Economic consequences arguments—and there are many of them—constitute manipulation through the use of lobbying and other forms of pressure brought on standard setters. We have seen examples of these arguments in the oil and gas industry about successful efforts versus full cost, in the technology area with the issue of mandatory expensing of research and most development costs, and with stock options and other issues.

14 Note that this example may be using hindsight in order to derive the amounts needing correction in each specific year, and therefore, the entity may contend that it is impracticable to retrospectively restate past amounts. Retrospective restatement does not endorse the use of hindsight, so the adjustment may actually need to be made on a partial retrospective basis or even only in the current year.

Tracing the Flow of Cash

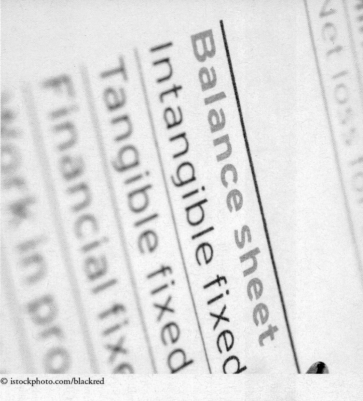

FINANCIAL STATEMENTS must be useful to users, but what exactly users want and need, and how best to achieve usefulness, is a source of debate. A good example is how to prepare the statement of cash flows.

IFRS and U.S. GAAP allow companies to prepare their statements using either one of two methods: the direct method or the indirect method. Both methods result in the same figure for net operating cash flows, but they arrive at that number in different ways. The direct method follows the trail of gross cash and cash equivalents coming in from customers, and payments going out to suppliers, employees, and others. The indirect method takes an indirect route to arrive at net cash flows, working backwards from accrual based net profit and making numerous adjustments to arrive at cash from operating activities.

Supporters of the direct method argue that it's more useful because it discloses actual sources and uses of cash, allows for more ratio analysis, and is more understandable to financial statement readers. Opponents of the direct method argue that it is costly and time-consuming to compile and reveals too much information to competitors.

Many financial statement users prefer the direct method. A 2009 survey of members of the CFA Institute, a global association of investment professionals, found that nearly two out of three respondents felt that information about operating cash flows presented using the direct method allowed them to better forecast future cash flows, assess a company's quality of earnings, and understand the relationship between a company's cash flows and its assets, liabilities, income, expenses, gains, and losses.

But most companies actually use the indirect method for their cash flow statements. A 1995 survey by the Canadian Institute of Chartered Accountants found that only 1 in 300 responding firms used the direct method. Companies do occasionally switch from one method to the other. For example, Toronto-based natural resources company Hawk Uranium Inc. (now called Noble Mineral Exploration Inc) changed from the indirect to the direct method during its 2008 fiscal year. In 2011, U.K.-based Camco International Ltd., a global developer of clean energy projects, switched from the direct to the indirect method. Neither company explained their rationale in their annual reports.

Companies may soon no longer have a choice, however. As part of their ongoing joint financial statement presentation project, the IASB and FASB were expected to propose that in future, companies must use the direct method to prepare their statement of cash flows.

Sources: "REG – Camco International – Final Results," Reuters, May 22, 2012; "CFA Institute Member Poll: Cash Flow Survey," Charlottesville, VA: CFA Institute, July 2009; Hawk Uranium Inc., 2008 Consolidated Financial Statements; Christine Yap, "International Harmonisation of Accounting Standards: The Case for a Mandatory Requirement for the Direct Method of Reporting Operating Cash Flows," *International Business & Economics Research Journal*, Vol. 3, No. 3 (2004), pp. 67–80.

22 | Statement of Cash Flows

LEARNING OBJECTIVES

After studying this chapter, you should be able to:

1. Understand the importance of cash flows from a business perspective.

2. Describe the purpose and uses of the statement of cash flows.

3. Define cash and cash equivalents.

4. Identify the major classifications of cash flows and explain the significance of each classification.

5. Prepare the operating activities section of a statement of cash flows using the direct versus the indirect method.

6. Prepare a statement of cash flows using the direct method.

7. Prepare a statement of cash flows using the indirect method.

8. Identify the financial presentation and disclosure requirements for the statement of cash flows.

9. Read and interpret a statement of cash flows.

10. Identify differences in ASPE and IFRS, and explain what changes are expected to standards for the statement of cash flows.

After studying Appendix 22A, you should be able to:

11. Use a work sheet to prepare a statement of cash flows.

PREVIEW OF CHAPTER 22

Examining a company's income statement may provide insights into its profitability, but it does not provide much information about its liquidity and financial flexibility. The purpose of this chapter is to highlight the requirements for the reporting of cash flow statements found in ASPE and in IFRS. We explain the main components of this statement and the type of information it provides, and demonstrate how to prepare, report on, and interpret such a statement. The chapter ends with a comparison of ASPE and IFRS standards for the statement of cash flows. The chapter is organized as follows:

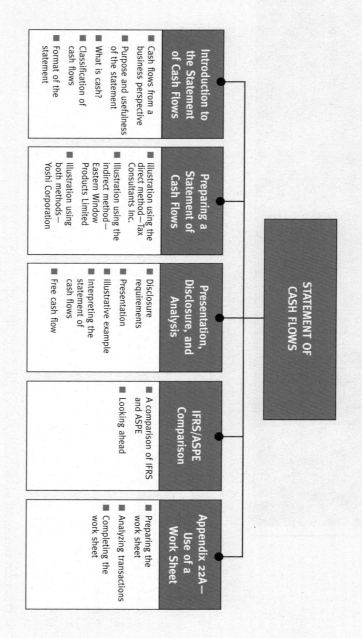

STATEMENT OF CASH FLOWS

Introduction to the Statement of Cash Flows
- Cash flows from a business perspective
- Purpose and usefulness of the statement
- What is cash?
- Classification of cash flows
- Format of the statement

Preparing a Statement of Cash Flows
- Illustration using the direct method—Tax Consultants Inc.
- Illustration using the indirect method— Eastern Window Products Limited
- Illustration using both methods— Yoshi Corporation

Presentation, Disclosure, and Analysis
- Disclosure requirements
- Presentation
- Illustrative example
- Interpreting the statement of cash flows
- Free cash flow

IFRS/ASPE Comparison
- A comparison of IFRS and ASPE
- Looking ahead

Appendix 22A— Use of a Work Sheet
- Preparing the work sheet
- Analyzing transactions
- Completing the work sheet

INTRODUCTION TO THE STATEMENT OF CASH FLOWS

Cash Flows from a Business Perspective

Cash Flows from a Business Perspective

Why do companies go bankrupt? One of the main causes is a lack of cash flow. In particular, one sign of a healthy company is positive cash flow from operations. Companies can use these funds to finance expansion, to issue dividends, or to ensure that they remain solvent during economic downturns. As one of Canada's largest banks has pointed out, cash flow is the lifeblood for businesses. "You may anticipate large profits tomorrow, but if you can't pay your bills today, you may not get a chance to realize those profits."[1]

Given the importance of cash flows for business, it is not surprising that the cash flow statement has grown in significance for companies and standard setters over the past 25 years. In addition, many consider the cash flow statement to be less susceptible to earnings management than the statement of comprehensive income, which has more subjective accruals for items such as bad debts expense, inventory obsolescence, and restructuring costs.

The statement of cash flows helps users answer many questions. For example, will the company be able to continue to pay dividends? How did it finance the acquisition of its new subsidiary? Will the company have sufficient cash to meet the debt that is maturing next year? How did cash increase when there was a net loss for the period? How were the proceeds of the bond issue used? How was the expansion in plant and equipment financed? Or, as the opening story discusses, how should cash flow from operations be provided to best assist financial statement users? These questions cannot be answered by reviewing the statement of financial position and statement of income or comprehensive income alone. A statement of cash flows is needed.

Purpose and Usefulness of the Statement

A key use of the statement of cash flows by investors and creditors is the assessment of companies' earnings quality. (For example, it allows an easy comparison of net profit and cash flow from operations.) It is also used to assess companies' ability to repay their debts as they come due and their ability to generate cash for long-run success. We focus on the uses of the statement below.

The primary purpose of the **statement of cash flows** is to provide information about an entity's cash receipts and cash payments during a period. A secondary objective is to provide information on a cash basis about its operating, investing, and financing activities. The statement of cash flows therefore reports cash receipts, cash payments, and the net change in cash resulting from an enterprise's operating, investing, and financing activities during a period. It does so in a format that reconciles the beginning and ending cash balances.

The information in a statement of cash flows enables investors, creditors, and others to assess the following:

1. **Liquidity and solvency of an entity—its capacity to generate cash and its needs for cash resources.** To assess an entity's ability to generate cash to pay maturing debt, to maintain and increase productive capacity, and to distribute a return to owners, it is important to determine both the timing and degree of certainty of expected cash inflows.

2. **Amounts, timing, and uncertainty of future cash flows.** Historical cash flows are often useful when predicting future cash flows. Readers can examine the relationships between items such as sales and net income and the cash flow from operating activities, or cash flow from operating activities and increases or decreases in cash. They can then make better predictions of the amounts, timing, and uncertainty of future cash flows than is possible using accrual-based data alone.

3. **Reasons for the difference between net income and cash flow from operating activities.** The net income number is important because it provides information on an enterprise's success or failure from one period to another. But some people are critical of accrual basis income because so many estimates are needed to calculate it. As a result, the number's reliability is often challenged. This usually does not occur with cash. Readers of the financial statements benefit from knowing the reasons for the difference between net income and cash flow from operating activities. It allows them to make their own assessment of the income number's reliability.

Because of the importance of this information, the statement of cash flows is required to be included in all ASPE and IFRS financial statements.

What Is Cash?

As part of a company's cash management system, short-term, near-cash investments are often held, instead of cash alone, because this allows the company to earn a return on cash balances that exceed its immediate needs. It is also common for an organization to have an agreement with a bank that allows its account to fluctuate between a positive balance and an overdraft. Because a company's cash activity and position are more appropriately described by including these other cash management activities, **cash flows** are defined in terms of inflows and outflows of cash and cash equivalents.

Cash is defined as cash on hand and demand deposits. **Cash equivalents** are short-term, highly liquid investments that are readily convertible to known amounts of cash and have an insignificant risk of change in value.[2] Cash equivalents are made up of **non-equity investments** that are acquired with short maturities—generally three months or less when they are acquired—and include such short-term investments as treasury bills, commercial paper, and money market funds that are acquired with cash in excess of current needs. IAS 7 *Statement of Cash Flows* does permit preferred shares acquired close to their maturity date to be included because they are cash equivalents in substance. In addition, **bank overdrafts** that are repayable on demand and fluctuate often between positive and negative balances are included in cash and cash equivalents under both sets of standards if they result from and are an integral part of an organization's cash management policies. Otherwise, amounts borrowed from a bank are generally considered financing activities.

Throughout this chapter, the use of the term "cash" should be interpreted generally to mean "cash and cash equivalents."

Classification of Cash Flows

The statement of cash flows (or cash flow statement as it is referred to under IFRS) classifies cash receipts and cash payments according to whether they result from an operating, investing, or financing activity. The transactions and other events that are characteristic of each kind of activity and the significance of each type of cash flow are as follows.

1. **Operating activities** are the enterprise's principal revenue-producing activities and other activities that are not investing or financing activities. Operating flows generally involve the cash effects of transactions that determine net income, such as collections from customers on the sale of goods and services, and payments to suppliers for goods and services acquired, to the Canada Revenue Agency for income taxes, and to employees for salaries and wages.

   The amount of cash that is provided by or used in operations is key information for financial statement users. Operating cash flows—derived mainly from receipts from customers—are needed to maintain the organization's systems: to meet payrolls, to pay suppliers, to cover rentals and insurance, and to pay taxes. In addition, surplus cash flows from operations are needed to repay loans, to take advantage of new investment opportunities, and to pay dividends without having to seek new external financing.

2. **Investing activities** involve the acquisition and disposal of long-term assets and other investments that are not included in cash equivalents or those acquired for trading purposes. Investing cash flows are a result of activities such as making and collecting loans and acquiring and disposing of investments and productive long-lived assets. They also include cash payments for and receipts from a variety of derivative products, unless such contracts are entered into for trading or financing purposes.

   The use of cash in investing activities tells the financial statement reader whether the entity is ploughing cash back into additional long-term assets that will generate profits and increase cash flows in the future, or whether the stock of long-term productive assets is being decreased by conversion into cash.

3. **Financing activities** result in changes in the size and composition of the enterprise's equity capital and borrowings. Financing cash flows result from activities that include obtaining cash from issuing debt and repaying amounts borrowed, and obtaining capital from owners and providing them with a return on, and a return of, their investment. Details of cash flows related to financing activities allow readers to assess the potential for future claims to the organization's cash and to identify major changes in the form of financing, especially between debt and equity.

Illustration 22-1 identifies an enterprise's typical cash receipts and payments and classifies them, according to ASPE, as to whether they result from operating, investing, or financing activities. Note the following.

1. The **operating** cash flows are related almost entirely to **working capital accounts** (that is, **current asset and current liability accounts**).

2. The **investing** cash flows generally involve **long-term asset items.**

3. The **financing** cash flows are derived mainly from changes in **long-term liability and equity accounts.** IFRS's requirements are similar, but not identical.

Illustration 22-1

Classification of Typical Cash Inflows and Outflows under ASPE

Types of Cash Flows	Relationship to the Balance Sheet
OPERATING	
Cash inflows	
From cash sales and collections from customers on account	
From returns on loans (interest) and equity securities (dividends)	Generally related to changes in non-cash current assets and current liabilities
From receipts for royalties, rents, and fees	
Cash outflows	
To suppliers on account	
To, and on behalf of, employees for services	
To governments for taxes	
To lenders for interest	
To others for expenses	
INVESTING	
Cash inflows	
From proceeds on the sale of property, plant, and equipment	
From proceeds on the sale of debt or equity securities of other entities	Generally related to changes in long-term assets
From the collection of principal on loans to other entities	
Cash outflows	
For purchases of property, plant, and equipment	
For purchases of debt or equity securities of other entities	
For loans to other entities	
FINANCING	
Cash inflows	
From proceeds on the issuance of equity securities	
From proceeds on the issuance of debt (bonds and notes)	Generally related to changes in long-term liabilities and equity
Cash outflows	
For payments of dividends to shareholders	
For redemptions of long-term debt or reacquisitions of share capital	
For reductions of capital lease obligations	

Some transactions that you might think are investing or financing activities may actually be operating cash flows. Under ASPE, for example, cash dividends and interest received and cash dividends and interest paid **that are included in determining net income** are classified as **operating** flows. Any dividends or interest paid **that are charged directly against retained earnings, however,** are reported as **financing** flows.[3]

Under IFRS, however, a choice is allowed. Interest paid and received and dividends received (excluding those received from an associate—a significant influence investment)[4] can be recognized as operating flows because they are included in determining net income. Alternatively, interest paid could be a financing outflow while interest and dividends received could be considered investment flows. A choice is also permitted for dividends paid: a financing flow as a return to equity holders, or an operating flow as a measure of the ability of operations to cover returns to shareholders. However management views these specific flows, once the choice is made, it is applied consistently from period to period. Illustration 22-2 summarizes these types of cash flows.

Illustration 22-2

Interest and Dividends: ASPE versus IFRS Classification

	Interest and Dividends Paid	Interest and Dividends Received
ASPE	Operating: if recognized in net income	Operating
	Financing: if charged to retained earnings	
	Choice: Operating or financing	
IFRS	Choice: Operating or financing	Choice: Operating or investing

Although they are reported on the income statement, some items are the result of an investing or financing activity. For example, the sale of property, plant, and equipment is an investing activity even though the cash proceeds received on the sale are reported in income. In this case, the cash proceeds received on the sale are properly classified as an investing cash inflow. The gain or loss, therefore, must be **excluded** in determining cash flows from operating activities. Similarly, cash paid to extinguish a debt is a financing activity, not an operating activity, and the gain or loss on repayment is excluded from operating cash flow. The cash paid to redeem the debt, not the amount of the gain or loss, is the actual cash flow and the repayment is clearly a financing activity.

Outflows to purchase investments and loans that are acquired specifically **for trading purposes**, and the proceeds on their sale, are treated the same as flows related to inventories acquired for resale; that is, as operating cash flows. If investments are acquired for other purposes, the cash flows are investing flows.

Income taxes present another complexity. While income tax expense can be identified with specific operating, investing, and financing transactions, the related cash payments for taxes usually cannot. For this reason, income tax payments are classified as operating cash flows unless they can be specifically identified with financing and investing activities.

How should **significant non-cash transactions** that affect an organization's assets and capital structure, such as those listed below, be handled?

1. The acquisition of assets by assuming directly related liabilities (including capital lease obligations) or by issuing equity securities

2. Exchanges of non-monetary assets

3. The conversion of debt or preferred shares to common shares

4. The issue of equity securities to retire debt

Because the statement of cash flows reports only the cash effect of activities, significant investing and financing transactions that do not affect cash are excluded from the statement. They are required to be disclosed elsewhere in the financial statements.[5]

Generally, companies move through several life-cycle stages of development, and each stage has implications for its cash flows. As the following graph shows, the pattern of cash flows from operating, financing, and investing activities varies depending on the stage of the cycle.

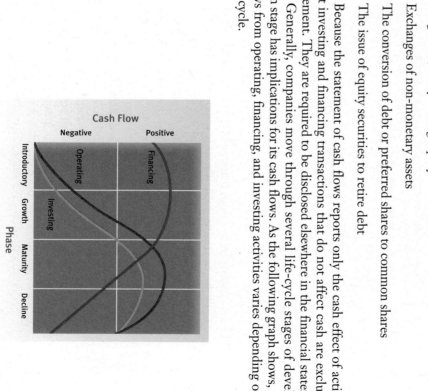

Cash Flow

In the introductory phase, the product is likely not generating much revenue, although significant cash is being spent to build up the company's inventories. Therefore, operating cash flow is negative. Because the company is making heavy investments to get a product off the ground, the cash flow associated with investing activities is also negative. Financing cash flows are positive as funds are raised to pay for the investments and cover the operating shortfall.

As the product moves to the growth and maturity phases, these relationships reverse. The product generates more cash from operations, which is used to cover investments that are needed to support the product, and less cash is needed from financing. So is a negative operating cash flow bad? Not always. It depends to a great extent on the product life cycle.

Source: Adapted from Paul D. Kimmel, Jerry J. Weygandt, and Donald E. Kieso, *Financial Accounting: Tools for Business Decision Making*, 5th ed. (New York: John Wiley & Sons, 2009), p. 606.

Format of the Statement

Formatting Basics

Objective 5
Prepare the operating activities section of a statement of cash flows using the direct versus the indirect method.

The three activities discussed in the preceding section guide the general format of the statement of cash flows. The operating activities section usually appears first, and is followed by the investing and financing activities sections. The individual inflows and outflows from investing and financing activities are reported separately; that is, they are reported gross, not netted against one another. Thus, a cash outflow from the purchase of property is reported separately from the cash inflow from the sale of property. Similarly, the cash inflow from issuing debt is reported separately from the cash outflow for the retirement of debt. If they are not reported separately, it is harder to see how extensive the enterprise's investing and financing activities are and therefore it is more difficult to assess future cash flows.[6]

Illustration 22-3 sets out a basic or "skeleton" format of a statement of cash flows. Note that the statement also provides a reconciliation between the beginning-of-the-period cash and the end-of-the-period cash reported in the comparative statement of financial position.

Illustration 22-3

Format of the Statement of Cash Flows—Indirect Method

COMPANY NAME
Statement of Cash Flows
Period Covered

Cash flows from operating activities			
Net income			XXX
Adjustments to reconcile net income to cash provided by (used in)			
operating activities: (List of individual items)		XX	
Net cash provided by (used in) operating activities			XX
			XXX
Cash flows from investing activities			
(List of individual inflows and outflows)		XX	
Net cash provided by (used in) investing activities			XXX
Cash flows from financing activities			
(List of individual inflows and outflows)		XX	
Net cash provided by (used in) financing activities			XXX
Net increase (decrease) in cash			XXX
Cash at beginning of period			XXX
Cash at end of period			XXX

Illustration 22-3 presents the net cash flow from operating activities indirectly by making the necessary adjustments to the net income reported on the income statement.

This is referred to as the **indirect method** (or reconciliation method). The cash flow from operating activities could be calculated directly by identifying the sources of the operating cash receipts and payments. This approach, shown in Illustration 22-4, is referred to as the **direct method**.

Cash flows from operating activities	
Cash receipts from customers	XX
Cash receipts from other revenue sources	XX
Cash payments to suppliers for goods and services	(XX)
Cash payments to and on behalf of employees	(XX)
Cash payments of income taxes	(XX)
Net cash provided by (used in) operating activities	**XXX**

Standard setters have wrestled with the issue of which method should be used. Both IFRS and ASPE encourage, but do not require, use of the direct method because it provides additional information.[7]

Direct versus Indirect Methods

In general, public companies tend to prefer the indirect method of calculating cash flows, although commercial lending officers and other investors tend to prefer the direct method because of the additional information that it provides.

Arguments in Favour of the Direct Method. The main advantage of the direct method is that it shows operating cash receipts and payments. That is, it is more consistent with the objective of a statement of cash flows—to provide information about the entity's cash receipts and cash payments—than the indirect method.

Supporters of the direct method argue that knowing the specific sources of operating cash receipts and the purposes of operating cash payments in past periods is useful in estimating future operating cash flows. Furthermore, information about the amounts of major classes of operating cash receipts and payments is more useful than information only about their arithmetic sum (the net cash flow from operating activities).

Many preparers of financial statements say that they do not currently collect information in a manner that allows them to determine amounts such as cash received from customers or cash paid to suppliers. But supporters of the direct method believe that the incremental cost of accumulating such operating cash receipts and payments data is not significant, especially with sophisticated database accounting systems underlying companies' financial reporting modules.[8]

Arguments in Favour of the Indirect Method. The main advantage of the indirect method is that it focuses on the differences between net income and cash flow from operating activities. That is, it provides a useful link between the statement of cash flows, the income statement, and the statement of financial position.

Preparers of financial statements argue that it is less costly to develop information that adjusts net income to net cash flow from operating activities. Supporters of the indirect method also state that the direct method, which effectively reports income statement information on a cash rather than an accrual basis, may suggest incorrectly that net cash flow from operating activities is as good as, or better than, net income as a measure of performance.

As the indirect method has been used almost exclusively in the past, both preparers and users are more familiar with it and this helps perpetuate its use. Each method provides useful information. The best solution may lie in mandating the direct method, which comes closer to meeting the statement's objectives, and requiring supplementary disclosure of a reconciliation of net income to cash flow from operations. The FASB and

IASB have done some work on a joint project dealing with financial statement presentation that includes significant changes to the statement of cash flows. An update on this project is provided in the Looking Ahead section at the end of this chapter.

PREPARING A STATEMENT OF CASH FLOWS

The statement of cash flows was previously called the statement of changes in financial position.[9] By analyzing the changes in all non-cash accounts on the statement of financial position from one period to the next, it is possible to identify and summarize the sources of all cash receipts and all cash disbursements. Illustration 22-5 explains why this is true.

$$A = L + SE$$
$$\Delta A = \Delta(L + SE)$$
$$\Delta A = \Delta L + \Delta SE$$
$$\Delta(Cash + non\text{-}cash\ A) = \Delta L + \Delta SE$$
$$\Delta Cash + \Delta non\text{-}cash\ A = \Delta L + \Delta SE$$
$$\Delta Cash = \Delta L + \Delta SE - \Delta non\text{-}cash\ A$$

Note: Δ is a symbol meaning "change in."

Unlike the other financial statements, which are prepared directly from the adjusted trial balance, the statement of cash flows is usually based on an analysis of the changes in the accounts on the statement of financial position over the accounting period. **Information to prepare this statement comes from the following three sources.**

1. **Comparative statement of financial positions** provide the amount of the changes in each asset, liability, and equity account from the period's beginning to end.

2. **The current income statement** provides details about the most significant changes in the statement of financial position retained earnings account and information about expenses that did not use cash and about revenues that did not generate cash.

3. **Selected transaction data** from the general ledger provide additional information needed to determine how cash was generated or used during the period.

Many small and medium-sized enterprises prepare the cash flow statement by manually accumulating these three sources of information, despite advances in technology. Alternatively, some companies have unique spreadsheet programs that generate the cash flow statement from a combination of their income statement data, changes in statement of financial position accounts, and other cash flow details provided as input. Larger organizations with sophisticated enterprise resource planning systems and databases can create template-based cash flow reports or generate server-based cash flow calculations in real time.

Whether you are preparing a cash flow statement manually, developing a spreadsheet template for use in its preparation, or interpreting a completed statement that has been presented to you, familiarity with the **manual steps** involved in the statement's preparation explained below will increase your understanding of this important financial statement.

Step 1: *Determine the change in cash.* This procedure is straightforward because the difference between the beginning and ending balances of cash and cash equivalents can easily be calculated by examining the comparative statement of financial positions. **Explaining this change is the objective of the analysis that follows.**

Step 2: *Record information from the income statement on the statement of cash flows.*[10] This is the starting point for calculating cash flows from operating activities. **Whenever**

subsequent analyses indicate that the actual operating cash flow and the amount reported on the income statement are different, the income statement number is adjusted.

Most adjustments fall into one of three categories:

Category 1. Amounts that are reported as revenues and expenses on the income statement and that are not the same as cash received from customers and cash paid to suppliers of goods and services. Companies receive cash from customers for revenue reported in a previous year, and do not receive cash for all the revenue reported as earned in the current period. Similarly, cash payments are made in the current period to suppliers for goods and services acquired, used, and recognized in a preceding period. In addition, not all amounts that are recognized as expense in the current year are paid for by year end. Most of the adjustments for these differences are related to receivables, payables, and other working capital accounts.

Category 2. Some expenses, such as depreciation and amortization, that represent costs that were incurred and paid for in a previous period. While there was a cash flow associated with the original acquisition of the asset (an investing flow), there is no cash flow associated with the amortization of these assets over the periods they are used.

Category 3. Amounts that are reported as gains or losses on the income statement but that are not usually the same as the cash amount from the transaction and, in many cases, the underlying activity is not an operating transaction. For example, gains and losses on the disposal of long-term assets and on the early retirement of long-term debt are reported on the income statement. Analyze the statement of financial position accounts one at a time until all the changes have been explained and the related cash flows identified. The cash flow amounts are the **proceeds on disposal** of the asset and the **payment to retire the debt, not the amount of the reported gain or loss.**

Step 3: Analyze the change in each statement of financial position account, identify all cash flows associated with changes in the account balance, and record the effect on the statement of cash flows. This analysis identifies all investing and financing cash flows, and all adjustments that are needed to convert income reported on the income statement to cash flow from operations. Analyze the statement of financial position accounts one at a time until all the changes have been explained and the related cash flows identified.

Step 4: Complete the statement of cash flows. Calculate subtotals for the operating, investing, and financing categories and ensure that the net change in cash you determined is equal to the actual change in cash for the period.[11]

We now work through these four steps to prepare the statements of cash flows for three different companies of increasing complexity.

Illustration Using the Direct Method—Tax Consultants Inc.

Our first example focuses on the direct method, because several simple examples using the indirect method were already included in Chapter 5. Tax Consultants Inc. began operations on January 1, 2013, when it issued 20,000 common shares for $20,000 cash. The company rented its office space and furniture and equipment, and performed tax consulting services throughout its first two years. The 2014 comparative statements of financial position and the income statement and additional information for 2014 are presented in Illustration 22-6.

COMPARATIVE STATEMENTS OF FINANCIAL POSITION

			Change
Assets	Dec. 31, 2014	Dec. 31, 2013	Increase/Decrease
Cash	$ 89,000	$40,000	(a) **$49,000 increase**
Accounts receivable	66,000	30,000	(b) **36,000 increase**
	$155,000	$70,000	
Liabilities and Shareholders' Equity			
Accounts payable	$ 35,000	$30,000	(c) **5,000 increase**
Common shares	80,000	20,000	(d) **60,000 increase**
Retained earnings	40,000	20,000	(e) **20,000 increase**
	$155,000	$70,000	

INCOME STATEMENT
For the Year Ended December 31, 2014

Revenues	$125,000
Operating expenses	85,000
Income before income taxes	40,000
Income tax expense	6,000
Net income	$ 34,000

Additional information:
An examination of selected data indicates that a dividend of $14,000 was declared during the year.

Step 1: ***Determine the change in cash.*** This first step is a straightforward calculation. Tax Consultants Inc. had $40,000 cash on hand at the beginning of 2014 and $89,000 on hand at the end of 2014; thus, the change in cash was an increase of $49,000.

Step 2: ***Record information from the income statement on the statement of cash flows.*** Most cash activity in any organization is related to operations, so the second step takes information from the operating statement (the income statement) and reports it on the statement of cash flows under the heading "Cash flows from operating activities." The specific information that is taken from the income statement and reported on the statement of cash flows in this step **depends on whether the indirect or the direct method is used.** Regardless of the method, this information will be converted from the accrual basis to the cash basis through adjustments in Step 3.

Under the direct method, skeleton headings similar to the ones in Illustration 22-4 are set up under "Cash flows from operating activities," as shown in Illustration 22-7. The number and descriptions of these headings vary from company to company. Amounts reported on the income statement are then transferred on a line-by-line basis to the heading that comes closest to representing the type of cash flow, until all components of net income have been transferred.

Illustration 22-7

Direct Method

DIRECT METHOD

	Income		Adjustments		Cash Flow
Cash flows from operating activities					
Cash received from customers	+125,000	=	XXX		XXX
Cash paid to suppliers	− 85,000	=	XX		XX
Income taxes paid	− 6,000	=	XX		XX
	+ **34,000**				XXX
Cash flows from investing activities					
Cash flows from financing activities					

The three headings in Illustration 22-7 are appropriate for Tax Consultants Inc. Because all income statement amounts are transferred to the Operating Activities section, the net amount transferred is equal to the amount of net income—the same as under the starting point of the indirect method.

In Step 3, adjustments are made to the appropriate line within the Operating Cash Flow section whenever the analysis indicates an operating cash flow that is not equal to the revenue or expense amount reported on the income statement. Revenues of $125,000 will be converted into the amount of cash received from customers; operating expenses of $85,000 will be adjusted to the amount of cash payments made to suppliers; and income tax expense of $6,000 will become income tax payments remitted to the government. Under this method, the specific revenue and expense lines are adjusted. Under the indirect method discussed in the second example below, it is only the bottom-line net income number that is adjusted, **but they are identical amounts.**

Step 3: Analyze the change in each statement of financial position account, identify all cash flows associated with changes in the account balance, and record the effect on the statement of cash flows. By analyzing the change in each account, transactions that involve cash can be identified and their effects can be recorded on the statement of cash flows.

Because the change in each account on the statement of financial position has to be explained, begin with the first non-cash asset and work down systematically through each asset, liability, and equity account. The results of Step 3 are provided in Illustration 22-8, where each item is referenced to the related calculation in Illustration 22-6.

CASH FLOWS FROM OPERATING ACTIVITIES

	Income	Adjustments	Cash Flow
Cash received from customers	+125,000	−36,000 (b)	+89,000
Cash paid to suppliers	− 85,000	+ 5,000 (c)	−80,000
Income taxes paid	− 6,000	− 6,000	− 6,000
	+ 34,000 (e)	**+ 3,000**	**+ 3,000**

CASH FLOWS FROM INVESTING ACTIVITIES

			−0−

CASH FLOWS FROM FINANCING ACTIVITIES

Proceeds from issue of common shares			+60,000 (d)
Dividends paid			−14,000 (e)
			+46,000

Increase in cash			+49,000 (a)

Note: items (a) to (e) refer to calculations from Illustration 22-6.

(a) **Change in Cash.** The cash balance increased by $49,000 during the year.

(b) **Accounts Receivable.** During the year, Tax Consultants' receivables increased by $36,000. Because this account increases by the amount of revenue that is recognized and decreases by cash received from customers, the cash received from customers must have been $36,000 less than the revenue reported on the 2014 income statement (item b). Therefore, an adjustment is needed in the Operating Activities section of the statement of cash flows. Using the direct method, the revenue line is reduced directly.

(c) **Accounts Payable.** Accounts Payable increases by purchases on account and decreases by payments on account. Tax Consultants' purchases must have been $5,000 higher than payments during 2014. A $5,000 adjustment is needed to convert the purchases included in net income to the amount paid to suppliers. Under the direct method, the $5,000 adjustment (item c) is made to the cash paid to suppliers line where the cost of the goods and services purchased was presented.

(d) **Common Shares.** The increase in this account resulted from the issue of shares that was recorded in this entry:

Cash		
Common Shares		60,000
	60,000	

The $60,000 inflow of cash (item d) is reported on the statement of cash flows as a financing inflow.

(e) **Retained Earnings.** In this account, the $20,000 increase (item e) is explained by net income and dividends paid. We already recognized the net income as the starting point in calculating cash flows from operations. The remaining change in the account is explained by the dividend-related entry:

Retained Earnings	14,000	
Cash		14,000

Assuming Tax Consultants Inc. reports under ASPE, the $14,000 dividend payment is reported as a financing outflow. The entire dividend must have been paid in cash because the company does not report a Dividends Payable account.

The changes in all statement of financial position accounts have been explained and their cash effects have been reported appropriately on the statement of cash flows. The statement can now be completed.

Step 4: Complete the statement of cash flows. Calculate subtotals for each of the operating, investing, and financing sections, and then the change in cash for the year. This should agree with the change identified in Step 1.

The completed statement illustrating the direct method is shown in Illustration 22-9.

Illustration 22-9

Completed Statement of Cash Flows—Tax Consultants Inc.

STATEMENT OF CASH FLOWS
Direct Method

Cash flows from operating activities		
Cash received from customers		$89,000
Less cash payments:		
To suppliers	$80,000	
For income taxes	6,000	86,000
		3,000
Cash flows from investing activities		–0–
Cash flows from financing activities		
Proceeds on issue of common shares		60,000
Payment of dividends		(14,000)
		46,000
Increase in cash during year		49,000
Opening cash balance		40,000
Cash, December 31, 2014		$89,000

The $49,000 cash increase (item a) came from a combination of net operating inflows of $3,000 and net financing inflows (primarily from the sale of common shares) of $46,000. Net cash provided by operating activities is the same whether the direct or indirect method is used. The $3,000 contribution to cash from operations is a result of cash collections from customers ($89,000) being only a little more than the operating cash outflows to suppliers ($80,000) and to the government for taxes ($6,000). The major source of cash flow for the company related to the issuance of common shares.

Illustration Using the Indirect Method—Eastern Window Products Limited

Objective 7

Prepare a statement of cash flows using the indirect method.

To illustrate the preparation of a more complex statement of cash flows, we use the operations of Eastern Window Products Limited (EWPL) for its 2014 year. EWPL has been operating for several years, and the company's comparative statements of financial position at December 31, 2014, and 2013, its statement of income and retained earnings for the year ended December 31, 2014, and other information are provided in Illustration 22-10.

For purposes of this example, EWPL could be reporting under either ASPE or IFRS. Assume, if a publicly accountable enterprise, that company management has chosen to present interest paid as an operating flow and dividends paid as a financing flow.

Illustration 22-10

Comparative Statements of Financial Position and Statement of Income and Retained Earnings—EWPL

STATEMENTS OF FINANCIAL POSITION – DECEMBER 31

	2014	2013	Change Increase/Decrease
	$	$	$
Cash	37,000	59,000	22,000 decrease
Accounts receivable	46,000	56,000	10,000 decrease
Inventory	82,000	73,000	9,000 increase
Prepaid expenses	6,000	7,500	1,500 decrease
Land	70,000	-0-	70,000 increase
Buildings	200,000	-0-	200,000 increase
Accumulated depreciation—buildings	(6,000)	-0-	6,000 increase
Equipment	68,000	63,000	5,000 increase
Accumulated depreciation—equipment	(19,000)	(10,000)	9,000 increase
	484,000	248,500	
Accounts payable	70,000	59,100	10,900 increase
Income taxes payable	4,000	1,000	3,000 increase
Salaries and wages payable	2,000	2,700	700 decrease
Mortgage payable	152,400	-0-	152,400 increase
Bonds payable	50,000	40,000	10,000 increase
Common shares	80,000	72,000	8,000 increase
Retained earnings	125,600	73,700	51,900 increase
	484,000	248,500	

STATEMENT OF INCOME AND RETAINED EARNINGS
Year Ended December 31, 2014

Sales revenue		$592,000
Less: Cost of goods sold		355,000
Gross profit		237,000
Salaries and wages expense	$55,000	
Interest expense	16,200	
Depreciation expense	15,000	
Other operating expenses	51,000	137,200
Income before income tax		99,800
Income tax expense		39,900
Net income		59,900
Retained earnings, January 1		73,700
Dividends declared		(8,000)
Retained earnings, December 31		$125,600

Additional information:

The company obtained a mortgage of $155,000 from a large Canadian bank to help finance the acquisition of the land and building during 2014.

Step 1: *Determine the change in cash.* Cash decreased by $22,000 during the year. There are no cash equivalents.

Step 2: *Record information from the income statement on the statement of cash flows.*
Under the **indirect method**, record the $59,900 net income in the Operating Activities section of the statement of cash flows.

Under the **direct method**, set up skeleton headings for the types of operating cash flows involved. Illustration 22-11 suggests that six headings are likely appropriate for EWPL, including an "Other expenses/losses" section that includes items such as depreciation expense that do not fall under the other headings. Because all income statement amounts are transferred to the Operating Activities section, the net amount transferred is the same as under the indirect method.

As you proceed through Step 3 using the direct method, the following will occur:

- Sales revenue of $592,000 will be converted into cash received from customers.

- Cost of goods sold of $355,000 and other operating expenses of $51,000 will be adjusted to an amount that represents cash payments to suppliers for goods and services acquired.

- Salaries and wages expense of $55,000 will become cash payments made to and on behalf of employees.

- Interest expense of $16,200 becomes interest payments made.

- Income tax expense of $39,900 becomes income tax payments remitted to the government.

As you review the adjustments being made for operating activities, note that the same adjustments are made under both the direct and indirect methods. However, under the indirect method we start with net income, while under the direct method we adjust each of the components of the statement of income individually. We review these adjustments in detail in Illustration 22-11.

Illustration **22-11**
Statement of Cash Flows
Working Paper—EWPL

CASH FLOWS FROM OPERATING ACTIVITIES
Indirect Method

Net income	+ 59,900
Adjustments: Decrease in accounts receivable	+ 10,000 (a)
Increase in inventory	− 9,000 (b)
Decrease in prepaid expenses	+ 1,500 (c)
Depreciation expense—building	+ 6,000 (e)
Depreciation expense—equipment	+ 9,000 (g)
Increase in accounts payable	+ 10,900 (h)
Increase in income taxes payable	+ 3,000 (i)
Decrease in wages payable	− 700 (j)
	+ 90,600

Direct Method

	Income	Adjustments	Cash Flow
Cash received from customers	+592,000	+ 10,000 (a)	+602,000
Cash paid to suppliers for goods and services	−355,000 −51,000	− 9,000 (b) + 1,500 (c) + 10,900 (h)	−402,600
Cash paid to employees	− 55,000	− 700 (j)	−55,700
Cash interest paid	− 16,200		−16,200
Income taxes paid	− 39,900	+ 3,000 (i)	−36,900
Other expenses/losses—depreciation	− 15,000	+ 6,000 (e) + 9,000 (g)	—
	+ 59,900		+ 90,600

(continued)

Illustration 22-11

Statement of Cash Flows
Working Paper—EWPL
(continued)

CASH FLOWS FROM INVESTING ACTIVITIES

Purchase of land and building	–270,000 (d)
Purchase of equipment	– 5,000 (f)
	–275,000

CASH FLOWS FROM FINANCING ACTIVITIES

Mortgage payable	+155,000 (d)
Repayment of mortgage payable	– 2,600 (d)
Bonds issued	+ 10,000 (l)
Shares issued	+ 8,000 (m)
Dividends paid	– 8,000 (n)
	+162,400

CHANGE IN CASH ‑ 22,000

Step 3: **Analyze the change in each statement of financial position account, identify any cash flows associated with a change in the account balance, and record the effect on the statement of cash flows.** The results of this step are provided in Illustration 22-11 above, where each item is referenced to the analysis that follows.

(a) **Accounts Receivable.** During the year, EWPL's receivables decreased by $10,000. Because Accounts Receivable is increased by revenue that is recognized and decreased by cash received from customers, the cash inflow from customers must have been $10,000 more than the revenue reported on the 2014 income statement. Under the indirect method, $10,000 is added to the net income number. Under the direct method, the revenue amount is increased directly.

(b) **Inventory.** Inventory increased by $9,000. Because Inventory is increased by the purchase of goods and is reduced by transferring costs to cost of goods sold, EWPL must have purchased $9,000 more inventory than it sold and, therefore, $9,000 more than the costs included in cost of goods sold on the income statement. The first part of this analysis (as summarized in the next paragraph) does not tell us how much cash was paid for the purchases; it only converts cost of goods sold to the cost of purchases in the year. The analysis of Accounts Payable (see item [h] below) converts the amount purchased to the cash payments to suppliers.

Cost of goods sold of $355,000 was deducted in calculating net income. Under the indirect method, net income must be further reduced by $9,000 to adjust for cash used to purchase goods that are still in inventory. Under the direct method, the $9,000 adjustment is made directly to the cost of goods sold line to adjust it to the cost of goods purchased.

(c) **Prepaid Expenses.** Prepaid Expenses decreased by $1,500. Because this account is increased by the acquisition of goods and services before they are used, and decreased by transferring the cost of the goods and services used up to expense—the same as for inventory—EWPL must have recognized $1,500 more expense than the amount purchased. The expenses reported on the income statement, therefore, have to be reduced by $1,500 to convert them to the cost of goods and services purchased. Under the indirect method, $1,500 is added back to the income reported. Under the direct method, the appropriate expense is reduced directly for the $1,500. When the Accounts Payable account is analyzed below, the purchases of prepaid expenses will be adjusted to cash paid to suppliers.

(d) **Land, Buildings.** The statements of financial position indicate an increase in Land of $70,000 and an increase in the Buildings account of $200,000, suggesting an investing cash outflow of $270,000. The investment in real property, however, is often financed by obtaining a mortgage payable from a bank or other third party that results in a lower direct cash outlay. A review of the records indicates that EWPL obtained a $155,000 mortgage in acquiring the land and building. Under ASPE and IFRS, this is treated like a cash inflow followed by a cash outflow of $155,000 (the $270,000 cost of the land and building being partly financed by the mortgage of $155,000).[12] It is often useful to consider the underlying journal entries:

Cash	155,000	
Mortgage Payable		155,000
Land	70,000	
Buildings	200,000	
Cash		270,000

This entry explains the change in the Land and the Buildings accounts on the statement of financial position. It also explains part of the change in the Mortgage Payable account (see item [k] below), and identifies the details of the net outflow of cash of $115,000. This land and building is reported as an **investing** cash flow on the statement, with the mortgage as a financing cash flow.

(e) **Accumulated Depreciation—Buildings.** The $6,000 increase in this account is due entirely to the recognition of depreciation expense for the year:

Depreciation Expense	6,000	
Accumulated Depreciation—Buildings		6,000

The entry records a non-cash event. Under the indirect method, $6,000 is added back to net income because depreciation expense did not use up any cash. Under the direct method, depreciation expense is adjusted directly. After adding back the $6,000 for depreciation expense here and the $9,000 from (g) below, depreciation expense is fully eliminated under the direct method.

(f) **Equipment.** EWPL purchased $5,000 of equipment during 2014. This resulted in an investing outflow of cash of $5,000.

(g) **Accumulated Depreciation—Equipment.** The $9,000 increase in this account is due to depreciation expense for the year. As explained in item (e), the operating activities section is adjusted for this non-cash expense.

(h) **Accounts Payable.** The Accounts Payable account is increased by the cost of purchases and decreased by payments on account. EWPL's cash payments to suppliers, therefore, must have been $10,900 less than the goods and services purchased during the year. In steps (b) and (c) above, cost of goods sold and other operating expenses were adjusted to convert them to the cost of goods and services purchased. A further adjustment of $10,900 is required to adjust the purchases to the amount of cash that was actually paid.

Under the indirect method, $10,900 is added back to net income to reflect the fact that the amounts deducted for purchases did not use an equivalent amount of cash. Under the direct method, the $10,900 adjustment reduces the cost of goods and other operating expenses purchased to the cash outflow for these purchases.

(i) **Income Taxes Payable.** This liability account is increased by the income tax expense reported and is decreased by payments to the government. Income tax expense, therefore, was $3,000 higher than the payments. Under the indirect method, the $3,000 difference is added back to net income. Under the direct method, a similar adjustment is made to the income tax expense line.

(j) **Wages Payable.** Similar to other current payables, this account is increased by amounts recognized as expense and decreased by payments; in this case, to employees.

Alternative Terminology

As discussed in Chapter 18, IFRS uses the terms current tax expense (income) and deferred tax expense (income), whereas ASPE recommends the use of the terms current income tax expense (benefit) and future income tax expense (benefit). We use the terms interchangeably. To simplify matters, in most of our examples in Chapter 22, we do not split the expense between current and deferred; instead we use the more general term income tax expense.

The $700 decrease indicates that cash outflows were $700 more than wages expense. Under the indirect method, an additional $700 is deducted from the reported income. Salaries and wages expense is adjusted under the direct method.[13]

(k) **Mortgage Payable.** The cash flow associated with part of the change in this account was identified above in item (d). If the account increased by $155,000 when the property was acquired, principal payments of $2,600 must have been made to reduce the balance to $152,400. The entry underlying this transaction is:

Mortgage Payable	2,600	
Cash		2,600

This is a financing outflow.

(l) **Bonds Payable.** The increase in this account is explained by the following entry:

Cash	10,000	
Bonds Payable		10,000

The $10,000 cash received from the bond issue is a financing cash inflow.

(m) **Common Shares.** The $8,000 increase in this account resulted from the issue of shares.

Cash	8,000	
Common Shares		8,000

The $8,000 cash received is a financing inflow.

(n) **Retained Earnings.** Net income accounts for $59,900 of the increase in retained earnings. We recognized this on the statement of cash flows already as the starting point in calculating cash flows from operations. The remainder of the change is explained by the entry for dividends:

Retained Earnings	8,000	
Cash		8,000

The payment of dividends that is charged to retained earnings is classified as a financing outflow. This treatment is required under ASPE, and permitted under IFRS—the alternative being to recognize it as an operating outflow under IFRS.

As the changes in all statement of financial position accounts have now been explained and all cash flows have been identified, the statement can be completed.

Step 4:   Complete the statement of cash flows. Subtotals are calculated for each section of the statement and the calculated change in cash is compared with the change identified in Step 1. Both indicate a $22,000 decrease in EWPL's cash balance during 2014.

A statement in good form is then prepared from the working paper developed in Illustration 22-11, using more appropriate descriptions and explanations. Illustration 22-12 shows what the final statement might look like if the indirect method is chosen. The additional disclosures that are provided are discussed in a later section of the chapter.

Illustration 22-12

EWPL Statement of Cash Flows, 2014—Indirect Method

EASTERN WINDOW PRODUCTS LIMITED
Statement of Cash Flows
Year Ended December 31, 2014

Cash provided by (used in) operations

Net income		$ 59,900
Add back non-cash expense—depreciation		15,000
Add (deduct) changes in non-cash working capital[a]		
– accounts receivable	$10,000	
– inventory	(9,000)	
– prepaid expenses	1,500	
– accounts payable	10,900	
– income taxes payable	3,000	
– wages payable	(700)	15,700
		90,600

Cash provided by (used in) investing activities

Purchase of property, plant, and equipment		(275,000)

Cash provided by (used in) financing activities

Issuance of mortgage payable	155,000	
Payment on mortgage payable	(2,600)	
Proceeds on issue of bonds	10,000	
Dividends paid	(8,000)	
Proceeds on issue of common shares	8,000	162,400
Decrease in cash		(22,000)
Cash balance, beginning of year		59,000
Cash balance, end of year		$ 37,000

Notes:
1. Cash consists of cash on hand and balances with banks.
2. Cash payments during the year for interest and income taxes were $16,200 and $36,900, respectively.

[a] Many companies provide only the subtotal on the statement of cash flows and report the details in a note to the financial statements.

Illustration 22-13 presents the Operating Activities section of the statement of cash flows if the direct method had been used. Of course, it results in the same total cash flow provided by operations as the indirect method (see Illustration 22-11).

Illustration 22-13

Operating Activities Section, Direct Method—EWPL

Cash provided by (used in) operations

Received from customers	$ 602,000
Payments to suppliers	(402,600)
Payments to and on behalf of employees	(55,700)
Interest payments	(16,200)
Income taxes paid	(36,900)
	$ 90,600

Illustration Using Both Methods—Yoshi Corporation

The next step is to see how the same principles are applied to more complex situations. Some of these complexities are illustrated through our next example of a **publicly accountable entity**, Yoshi Corporation, as we use the same approach as in the two previous examples. Although Yoshi Corporation applies IFRS, almost all of the situations are treated the same as if the company applied ASPE. If you prefer a more structured method of accumulating the information for the statement of cash flows than what is shown here, we recommend that you refer to the work sheet approach in Appendix 22A.

Illustrations 22-14, 22-15, 22-16, and 22-17 provide the comparative statements of financial position of Yoshi Corporation at December 31, 2014, and 2013; the statement of comprehensive income; the statement of changes in equity for the year ended December 31, 2014; and selected additional information.

Illustration 22-14

Comparative Statements of Financial Position—Yoshi Corporation

YOSHI CORPORATION
Comparative Statements of Financial Position
December 31, 2014, and 2013

	2014 $	2013 $	Change Increase/Decrease $
Assets			
Cash	5,000	32,000	27,000 decrease
Cash equivalents	14,000	4,000	10,000 increase
FV-NI investments	25,000	30,000	5,000 decrease
Accounts receivable	106,500	52,700	53,800 increase
Allowance for doubtful accounts	(2,500)	(1,700)	800 increase
Inventory	303,000	311,000	8,000 decrease
Prepaid expenses	16,500	17,000	500 decrease
Investment in Associate (Portel Corp.)	18,500	15,000	3,500 increase
FV-OCI investments (Hyco Ltd.)	17,500	13,000	4,500 increase
Land	190,000	30,000	160,000 increase
Deferred development costs	131,500	82,000	49,500 increase
Equipment	187,000	142,000	45,000 increase
Accumulated depreciation—equipment	(29,000)	(31,000)	2,000 decrease
Buildings	262,000	262,000	-0-
Accumulated depreciation—buildings	(74,100)	(71,000)	3,100 increase
Goodwill	7,600	10,000	2,400 decrease
Total assets	1,178,500	897,000	
Liabilities			
Accounts payable	130,000	131,000	1,000 decrease
Dividends payable, term preferred shares	2,000	-0-	2,000 increase
Accrued liabilities	43,000	39,000	4,000 increase
Income taxes payable	3,000	16,000	13,000 decrease
Bonds payable	97,800	97,500	300 increase
Term preferred shares	60,000	-0-	60,000 increase
Deferred tax liability	10,000	6,000	4,000 increase
Total liabilities	345,800	289,500	
Shareholders' Equity			
Common shares	225,400	88,000	137,400 increase
Retained earnings	602,800	518,500	84,300 increase
Accumulated other comprehensive income	4,500	1,000	3,500 increase
Total shareholders' equity	832,700	607,500	
Liabilities and shareholders' equity	1,178,500	897,000	

Illustration 22-15

Statement of Comprehensive Income—Yoshi Corporation

YOSHI CORPORATION
Statement of Comprehensive Income
Year Ended December 31, 2014

Net sales	$923,200
Investment income (Equity in earnings of Portel Corp.)	5,500
Investment income, FV-NI investments	1,300
Gain on sale of land	10,500
	940,500

(continued)

Illustration 22-15

Statement of Comprehensive Income—Yoshi Corporation (continued)

Expenses		
Cost of goods sold	$395,400	
Salaries and wages	200,000	
Selling and administrative	134,600	
Depreciation	14,600	
Interest and dividend expense	11,300	
Loss on impairment (goodwill)	2,400	
Other expenses and losses	12,000	770,300
Income before income tax		170,200
Income tax: Current	49,500	
Deferred	3,000	52,500
Net income		117,700
Other comprehensive income		
Unrealized gain (OCI) net of deferred tax of $1,000		3,500
Comprehensive income		$121,200

Illustration 22-16

Statement of Changes in Equity—Yoshi Corporation

YOSHI CORPORATION
Statement of Changes in Equity
Year Ended December 31, 2014

	Common Shares $	Retained Earnings $	AOCI $	Total $
Balance, January 1, 2014	88,000	518,500	1,000	607,500
2% stock dividend issued	15,000	(15,000)		-0-
Proceeds on sale of shares	144,000			144,000
Shares purchased and cancelled	(21,600)	(12,400)		(34,000)
Net income		117,700		117,700
Cash dividend declared		(6,000)		(6,000)
Unrealized gain, (OCI)			3,500	3,500
Balance, December 31, 2014	225,400	602,800	4,500	832,700

Illustration 22-17

Additional Information— Yoshi Corporation

YOSHI CORPORATION
Additional Information

1. Cash equivalents represent money-market instruments with original maturity dates of less than 90 days.

2. FV-NI investments in ABC Company at the beginning of the year were sold during the year for $32,300. Additional investments in XYZ Limited, also accounted for at FV-NI, were acquired at a cost of $26,000 and were still held at the end of the year.

3. During 2014, accounts receivable of $1,450 were written off.

4. Yoshi accounts for its 22% interest in Portel Corp. using the equity method. Portel Corp. paid a dividend in 2014 and Yoshi's share of Portel's net income was $5,500.

5. The investment in shares of Hyco Ltd. was purchased in July 2013 for $12,000 and classified for accounting purposes at FV-OCI.

6. During 2014, Yoshi incurred $200,000 of development costs that met the criteria for deferral as an intangible asset. During the year, $40,000 of this asset was amortized.

7. Land in the amount of $54,000 was purchased by issuing term preferred shares. The term preferred shares issued for land (and those issued for cash) are classified as financial liabilities.

8. An analysis of the equipment account and related accumulated depreciation indicates the following:

Equipment:

Balance, January 1, 2014	$142,000
Cost of equipment purchased	73,000
Cost of equipment sold (sold at a loss of $1,500)	(28,000)
Balance, December 31, 2014	$187,000

(continued)

Illustration 22-17

*Additional Information—
Yoshi Corporation (continued)*

Accumulated depreciation:

Balance, January 1, 2014	$ 31,000
Accumulated depreciation on equipment sold	(13,500)
Depreciation expense, 2014	11,500
Balance, December 31, 2014	$ 29,000

9. The bonds payable, issued in 2012, were issued at a discount and have a maturity value of $100,000.

10. Changes in other statement of financial position accounts resulted from usual transactions and events.

Step 1: **Determine the change in cash.** Yoshi's cash and cash equivalents include holdings of money-market instruments as well as cash balances, with a decrease in cash of $17,000 that needs to be explained. This is the difference between the opening cash and cash equivalents of $36,000 ($32,000 + $4,000) and the ending cash and cash equivalents of $19,000 ($5,000 + $14,000).

Step 2: **Record information from the income statement on the statement of cash flows.** Under the **indirect method**, the net income of $117,700 is inserted as the starting point, as shown in Illustration 22-18.

Illustration 22-18

*Statement of Cash Flows
Working Paper—Yoshi
Corporation*

CASH FLOWS FROM OPERATING ACTIVITIES
Indirect Method

	Adjustments	Cash Flow
Net income		+117,700
Adjustments: Decrease in FV-NI investments	+ 5,000 (a)	
Increase in accounts receivable, net of writeoffs	− 55,250 (b)	+ 55,250 (b)
Bad debt expense	+ 2,250 (c)	
Decrease in inventory	+ 8,000 (d)	
Decrease in prepaid expenses	+ 500 (e)	
Equity method investment income	− 2,000 (f)	
Dividend from equity method investment	+ 5,500 (f)	
Amortization of development costs	+ 40,000 (h)	
Gain on sale of land	− 10,500 (i)	
Loss on disposal of equipment	+ 1,500 (j)	
Depreciation expense—equipment	+ 11,500 (j)	
Depreciation expense—buildings	+ 3,100 (k)	
Impairment loss—goodwill	+ 2,400 (l)	
Decrease in accounts payable	− 1,000 (m)	
Increase in dividends payable on term preferred shares	+ 2,000 (n)	
Increase in accrued liabilities	+ 4,000 (o)	
Decrease in income taxes payable	− 13,000 (p)	
Amortization of bond discount	+ 300 (q)	
Increase in deferred tax liability (net income)	+ 3,000 (s)	
		+118,000

Direct Method

	Income	Adjustments	Cash Flow
Receipts from customers	+923,200	− 55,250 (b)	+867,950
Received from investment in Portel Corp.	+ 5,500	− 5,500 (f)	+ 2,000
		+ 2,000 (f)	
Received on FV-NI investment transactions	+ 1,300	+ 5,000 (a)	+ 6,300
Payments for goods and services	−395,400	+ 2,250 (c)	
	−134,600	+ 8,000 (d)	
	− 12,000	+ 500 (e)	
		+40,000 (h)	
		+ 1,500 (j)	
		+ 1,000 (m)	
		− 490,750	

Illustration 22-18

Statement of Cash Flows Working Paper—Yoshi Corporation (continued)

	Income	Adjustments	Cash Flow
Payments to employees	–200,000	+ 4,000 (o)	–196,000
Interest and dividend payments	– 11,300	+ 2,000 (n)	– 9,000
		+ 300 (q)	
Income taxes paid	– 52,500	– 13,000 (p)	– 62,500
		+ 3,000 (s)	
Other items:			
Depreciation expense	– 14,600	+ 11,500 (j)	—
		+ 3,100 (k)	—
Impairment loss	– 2,400	+ 2,400 (l)	—
Gain on sale of land	+ 10,500	– 10,500 (i)	—
	+ 117,700		+ 118,000
CASH FLOWS FROM INVESTING ACTIVITIES			
Development costs incurred			– 200,000 (h)
Proceeds on sale of land			+ 15,000 (i)
Purchase of equipment			– 73,000 (j)
Proceeds on sale of equipment			+ 13,000 (j)
			– 245,000
CASH FLOWS FROM FINANCING ACTIVITIES			
Proceeds on issue of term preferred shares			+ 6,000 (r)
Proceeds on issue of common shares			+ 144,000 (t)
Dividends paid on common shares			– 6,000 (u)
Payment to repurchase common shares			– 34,000 (t)
			+ 110,000
CHANGE IN CASH			– 17,000

Using the **direct method**, skeleton headings that cover each potential type of cash flow—from customer receipts to income taxes—are set up within the Operating Activities section of the statement of cash flows working paper, as shown in Illustration 22-18. The statement of comprehensive income provides clues about the types of operating cash flows and how they should be described. For example, the equity basis income from the investment in Portel Corp. is not a cash flow, but it will be replaced after adjustment with any dividends received from the investment.

Each amount that makes up the net income of $117,700 is transferred to the most appropriate skeleton heading on the working paper. Amounts reported as cost of goods sold, selling and administrative expense, and other expenses and losses form the base for what will eventually be "Cash paid to suppliers for goods and services." Income tax expense is included on the line that will be adjusted to "Income taxes paid." The unrealized gain on the FV-OCI investment and the tax on it are not included, but will be taken into account later.

Note that this illustration begins with **net income,** consistent with the international standard. Other companies, however, may decide to begin with comprehensive income, or even income before taxes. As long as the relationship of the beginning number to net income is obvious, the objective of the standard is met. If a number other than net income is used, the adjustments that follow will also be different, but the final statement will report the same total amounts and types of cash flows and change in cash balances as under the approach used here.

Step 3: *Analyze the change in each statement of financial position account, identify any cash flows associated with a change in the account balance, and record the effect on the statement of cash flows.* The analysis begins with the FV-NI investments that are held for trading purposes.

(a) **FV-NI Investments.** Based on information provided in Illustration 22-17, we can reproduce the entries made during the year to this account.

Cash	32,300	
FV-NI Investments		30,000
Investment Income or Loss		2,300
FV-NI Investments	26,000	
Cash		26,000
Investment Income or Loss	1,000	
FV-NI Investments		1,000

These entries tell us three things.

1. They explain the change in the FV-NI Investments account during the year.
2. They indicate what makes up the investment income on the FV-NI investments of $1,300 (the $2,300 realized gain on sale of shares of ABC Company and the unrealized loss on shares of XYZ Limited of $1,000).
3. They indicate that the cash effect of these transactions is +$32,300 − $26,000 = +$6,300.

The net cash flow is an **operating** flow because the FV-NI securities were acquired for trading purposes. We have already included an inflow of $1,300 in the operating section for investment income, so an adjustment is needed there for an additional $5,000 under the direct method.

Under the indirect method, $5,000 is added to the net income number to increase the cash inflow from the $1,300 already included as part of net income to the actual $6,300 net cash inflow that was generated. The $5,000 is split on the final statement of cash flows as $1,000 relating to the adding back of unrealized loss on FV-NI investments, and the other $4,000 as part of the decrease in FV-NI investments relating to non-cash working capital items.

(b) **Accounts Receivable.** Unlike the previous two company illustrations, Yoshi reports both the accounts receivable and its contra allowance account. The receivable control account is increased by sales on account and reduced by accounts written off and cash received on account. The 2014 receivable T account is shown below, with the sales amount taken from the income statement. The cash received on account, the only missing information, must have been $867,950. This was determined by solving for the one unknown credit entry: $52,700 + $923,200 − $1,450 − x = $106,500. The cash received, therefore, was $923,200 − $867,950 = $55,250 less than the revenue reported on the income statement.

Accounts Receivable			
Jan.1	52,700		
Sales on account	923,200	1,450	Accounts written off (given)
		?	Cash received on account
Dec. 31	106,500		
	106,500		

(c) **Allowance for Doubtful Accounts.** This account had an opening balance of $1,700, was increased by bad debt expense, was reduced by accounts written off, and ended the year at $2,500. With accounts written off of $1,450, bad debt expense must have been $2,250 ($1,700 + bad debt expense − $1,450 = $2,500; or prepare a T account to determine this). Because bad debt expense does not use cash, the net income number in the Operating Activities section must be adjusted.

Using the indirect method, $55,250 is deducted from the net income reported. Under the direct method, the revenue of $923,200 is adjusted directly by $55,250 to convert it to cash received from customers (see Illustration 22-18).

Under the indirect method, the $2,250 is added back to net income. Under the direct method, the $2,250 adjustment reduces the expense line that includes bad debt expense. In this example, it is assumed to be included in selling and administrative expenses.

The only time it is necessary to analyze the Accounts Receivable and the Allowance accounts separately is when using the direct method. This is because two adjustments are needed: one to adjust the revenue reported ($55,250) and the other to adjust the non-cash bad debt expense ($2,250). When using the indirect method, both adjustments correct the one net income number. The analysis is easier, therefore, if you focus on the change in the net accounts receivable and make one adjustment to the net income number.[14]

(d) **Inventory.** Because the Inventory account is increased by the cost of goods purchased and decreased by the transfer of costs to cost of goods sold, the $8,000 decrease in the Inventory account indicates that purchases were $8,000 less than transfers to cost of goods sold. Using the indirect method, $8,000 is added back to the net income number. The direct method adjusts cost of goods sold directly to convert it to the cost of goods purchased. The analysis of Accounts Payable in step (m) will convert the purchases to cash paid to suppliers.

(e) **Prepaid Expenses.** This account decreased by $500 because the costs that were charged to the income statement were $500 more than the costs of acquiring prepaid goods and services in the year. For reasons similar to the inventory analysis in step (d), $500 is either added back to net income under the indirect method, or used to adjust the expense line associated with the prepaid expense under the direct method. We assume that the prepaid expenses were charged to selling and administrative expenses when they were used. So, under the direct method, payments for goods and services are reduced by $500.

(f) **Investment in Associate (Portel Corp.).** The journal entries that explain the increase of $3,500 in this account are:

Investment in Associate	5,500	
Investment Income or Loss		5,500
(To record investment income of Portel Corp. using the equity method)		
Cash	2,000	
Investment in Associate		2,000
(To record the dividend received from Portel Corp.)		

The $5,500 investment income amount is reported on the income statement, and the dividend amount is derived from the change in the account balance. Cash did not change as a result of the investment income; therefore, an adjustment is needed to reduce the net income number. Under the indirect method, the $5,500 is deducted to offset the $5,500 reported. Under the direct method, the $5,500 adjustment is made to the specific revenue line. This adjustment eliminates the equity-method investment income reported.

The second entry indicates a dividend cash inflow of $2,000. In this case, an adjustment is needed to the net income reported in operating activities because it does not include the cash dividend. Unlike dividends received from other types of investments, those received from associates (significantly influenced investees) require an adjustment to be reported in operating flows. Using the indirect method, $2,000 is added to net income. Under the direct method, $2,000 is added to the same line as the $5,500 deduction above, as this completes the adjustment of the non-cash equity-basis investment income to cash received from the investment in Portel.

(g) **Investment in Shares of Hyco Ltd.** The entry that explains the change in this investment classified as an FV-OCI investment is:

FV-OCI Investments	4,500	
Unrealized Gain or Loss—OCI		4,500
(To adjust investment to fair value at year end.)		

The entry explains the change in the investment account and the source of $4,500 of the increase to other comprehensive income. No cash flow is involved and no income statement amount is affected. Therefore, no amounts are reported on the statement of cash flows and no adjustment is needed in the operating section (see also part(s) below).

If an FV-OCI investment had been acquired or sold in the year, there would be investing cash flows to capture on the statement. In the case of a disposal, any realized holding gain or loss transferred (recycled) from OCI to net income would need to be eliminated in the operating activities section.

(h) **Deferred Development Costs.** The two transactions that affected this intangible asset account in the current year are summarized in the following journal entries:

Deferred Development Costs	200,000	
Cash		200,000
(To record capitalized development costs.)		
Development Expenses	40,000	
Deferred Development Costs		40,000
(To record the amortization of deferred development costs.)		

The first entry indicates a cash outflow of $200,000. This is an investing outflow and is recognized in the statement's Investing Activities section.

The second entry did not affect cash. As explained earlier, it is important to be alert to non-cash amounts that are included in net income. This $40,000 expense did not use any cash; an adjustment to net income is therefore needed under the indirect method. Under the direct method, the adjustment is made to the specific expense: in this case, assumed to be selling and administrative expenses.

(i) **Land.** This account increased by $49,500. Because you know that land was purchased at a cost of $54,000 during the year, there must have been a disposal of land with a cost of $4,500. Knowing there was a gain on sale of land of $10,500, the entries that affect this account in 2014 must have been:

Land	54,000	
Term Preferred Shares		54,000
(To record purchase of land through issue of term preferred shares.)		
Cash	15,000	
Land		4,500
Gain on Disposal of Land		10,500
(To record disposal of land costing $4,500.)		

The first entry indicates that there were no cash flows associated with this transaction. Although this investment and financing transaction is not reported on the statement of cash flows, information about such non-cash transactions is a required disclosure elsewhere in the financial statements.

The second entry identifies a cash inflow of $15,000 on land disposal. This is an investing inflow because it affects the company's stock of non-current assets, so it is included on the statement of cash flows in the investing cash flow section.

The second transaction also results in a gain of $10,500 on the income statement. By starting with "net income" in the statement's Operating Cash Flow section in Step 2, the $10,500 gain is included in income as if the gain had generated $10,500 of operating cash flows. This is incorrect for two reasons. First, the cash inflow was $15,000, not $10,500. Second, the cash flow was an investing, not an operating, flow. An adjustment is needed, therefore, to deduct $10,500 from the income reported using the indirect method or from the gain on sale of land line if the direct method is used.

(j) **Equipment and Accumulated Depreciation—Equipment.** All the information that is needed to reproduce the entries made to these accounts in 2014 was provided in Illustrations 22-14, 22-15, and 22-17.

Equipment	73,000	
Cash		73,000
Cash	13,000	
Loss on Disposal of Equipment	1,500	
Accumulated Depreciation—Equipment	13,500	
Equipment		28,000
Depreciation Expense	11,500	
Accumulated Depreciation—Equipment		11,500

The first entry explains a cash outflow of $73,000 due to the purchase of equipment, which is an investing activity.

The second entry records the disposal of an asset that cost $28,000 and has accumulated depreciation of $13,500; that is, a carrying amount of $14,500. To be sold at a loss of $1,500, the proceeds on disposal must have been $13,000.

The analysis of this entry is similar to the land disposal in step (i).

1. The cash effect is an inflow of $13,000. This is an investing receipt.

2. The transaction results in a loss of $1,500 that is reported in 2014 income. Because the cash effect was not a $1,500 cash payment and because it was not an operating flow, an adjustment is needed in the Operating Cash Flow section. The $1,500 loss is added back to net income under the indirect method, or to the appropriate line (other expenses and losses) under the direct method.

The third entry reflects the annual depreciation expense. Depreciation does not use cash, so an adjustment is also needed to add this amount back to net income. Under the direct method, the depreciation line itself is corrected.

(k) **Buildings and Accumulated Depreciation—Buildings.** There was no change in the asset account during the year and, since there is no additional information, the increase in the accumulated depreciation account must have been due entirely to the depreciation recorded for the year. The $3,100 non-cash expense is an adjustment in the Operating Activities section, similar to depreciation on equipment discussed above.

(l) **Goodwill.** The $2,400 decrease in Goodwill is the result of the following entry:

Loss on Impairment (Goodwill)	2,400	
Goodwill		2,400

There was no effect on cash. Under the indirect method, $2,400 is added back to net income; under the direct method, the impairment loss line itself is offset.

(m) **Accounts Payable.** Because Accounts Payable is increased by purchases on account for operations and decreased by payments to suppliers, cash outflows to suppliers must have been $1,000 higher than purchases in 2014. Previous adjustments to the working paper in (d) and (e) converted expenses reported on the income statement to the cost of goods and services purchased. The analysis of accounts payable completes this by converting the purchases' amount to the cash paid for purchases. The indirect method deducts an additional $1,000 from the net income reported, while the direct method adjusts the expense line.

(n) **Dividends Payable on Term Preferred Shares.** The $2,000 increase indicates that dividends paid were $2,000 less than the dividends declared on these shares. Because the term preferred shares are liabilities in substance, the dividends on these shares are treated the same as interest on debt: they are deducted as dividend expense on the income statement. Under the indirect method, $2,000 is added back to net income because the cash outflow was less than the dividend expense reported. Under the direct method, the line item that includes the dividend expense is reduced. This assumes Yoshi reports interest paid as an operating outflow, and this treatment is required by ASPE and permitted under IFRS.

If Yoshi follows a policy of reporting interest paid (and dividends on in-substance financial liabilities) as financing outflows, as is permitted under IFRS, the amount recognized in net income and reported in operating flows on the working paper is eliminated and the correct cash outflow is reported in the financing activities section.

(o) **Accrued Liabilities.** This account is increased by expenses recognized and decreased by payments of the accrued amounts. During 2014, the payments must have been $4,000 less than the expenses reported: $4,000 is therefore added back to net income under the indirect method. Using the direct method, you must determine which expenses should be adjusted. If it was interest expense that was accrued and paid, the interest expense line is adjusted; if it was wages and salaries payable, the salaries and wages expense is adjusted. In Illustration 22-18, we assume the accruals relate to accrued payroll costs.

(p) **Income Taxes Payable.** This account is increased by tax expense and decreased by payments to the tax authorities. The $13,000 reduction indicates that the cash outflows were $13,000 more than the expense recognized. Net income is adjusted downward by $13,000 under the indirect method and the income tax line is adjusted under the direct method.

(q) **Bonds Payable.** In the absence of other information, we assume the change in the Bonds Payable account was increased through amortization of the discount.

Interest Expense	300	
Bonds Payable		300

The entry results in an expense with no corresponding use of cash. An adjustment of $300 is added back to net income under the indirect method, or to the interest expense line under the direct method.[15] The adjustment is identical if Yoshi accounts for the discount as a separate contra account.

(r) **Term Preferred Shares.** Term preferred shares of $60,000 were issued during the year, with $54,000 of this amount issued in exchange for land. This transaction was analyzed in (i) above. Without information to the contrary, we assume that the remaining issue of term preferred shares was for cash and recorded with this entry:

Cash	6,000	
Term Preferred Shares		6,000

This is reported as a financing inflow.

(s) **Deferred Tax Liability.** The increase in this account's credit balance was a result of the following two entries:

Deferred Tax Expense	3,000	
Deferred Tax Liability		3,000
Deferred Tax Expense—OCI	1,000	
Deferred Tax Liability		1,000

No part of the expense reported used cash. Therefore the $3,000 tax expense included in net income is added back under the indirect method and a similar adjustment is made to the income tax expense line under the direct method. The $1,000 amount reported in OCI did not use cash and it is not on the working paper; therefore, no adjustment needs to be made for it.

(t) **Common Shares.** The following entries summarize the changes to this account (see also the Statement of Changes in Equity):

Retained Earnings	15,000	
Common Shares		15,000
Cash	144,000	
Common Shares		144,000
Common Shares	21,600	
Retained Earnings	12,400	
Cash		34,000

The first entry records the stock dividend, which neither used nor provided cash. The issue of a stock dividend is not a financing and/or investing transaction, and therefore, is **not** required to be reported on the statement of cash flows. The second entry records a $144,000 inflow of cash as a result of issuing shares, so it is reported as a financing inflow on the working paper.

The third entry records the purchase and cancellation of shares in the year. Although IFRS does not provide specific guidance on the repurchase of a company's own shares, these entries are reasonable based on the information provided in Illustration 22-16. As the entry shows, the transaction used $34,000 cash. This financing flow is reported on the working paper.

(u) **Retained Earnings.** The statement of changes in equity also explains the $84,300 increase in this account. The $15,000 decrease due to the stock dividend was analyzed above as having no effect on cash flow. The cash flow associated with the $12,400 "loss" on the repurchase and cancellation of the common shares has already been dealt with in (t). The $117,700 increase due to net income and the cash flows associated with it have already been included in the Operating Activities section of the statement of cash flows. The $6,000 decrease due to dividends paid on the common shares could be either a financing or an operating outflow. This depends on the company's policy and how it has reported the dividend in the past. We assume it is a financing flow.

ASPE requires this dividend to be reported as a financing flow. Under IFRS, if the dividend on common shares is treated as an operating flow, the net income number (or the specific line item affected) is adjusted for the outflow.

The changes in all statement of financial position accounts have now been analyzed and those that affect cash have been recorded on the statement of cash flows working paper. **The following general statements summarize the approach to the analysis.**

1. For most current asset and current liability accounts, focus on the transactions that increase and decrease each account. Compare the effect on the income statement with the amount of the related cash flow, and then adjust the income number(s) in the Operating Activities section of the statement accordingly.

2. For non-current asset and non-current liability accounts in general, reconstruct summary journal entries that explain how and why each account changed. Then analyze each entry as follows:

(a) What is the cash flow? The cash effect is the amount of the debit or credit to cash (or cash equivalents) in the entry.

(b) Is the cash flow an investing or financing flow? If so, update the working paper.

(c) Identify all debits or credits to income statement accounts where the operating cash flow is not equal to the amount of revenue, gain, expense, or loss that is reported. Each of these requires an adjustment to the income number(s) that were originally reported in the Operating Activities section. Update the working paper.

While the transactions entered into by Yoshi Corporation represent a good cross-section of common business activities, they do not cover all possible situations. The general principles and approaches used in the above analyses, however, can be applied to most other transactions and events.

Step 4: Complete the statement of cash flows. Determine subtotals for each major classification of cash flow and ensure that the statement reconciles to the actual change in cash identified in Step 1.

The working paper prepared in Illustration 22-18 is presented with more appropriate descriptions and complete disclosure to comply with IFRS and to enable readers to better interpret the information. Illustration 22-19 presents a completed statement of cash flows for Yoshi Corporation, using the direct method to explain the operating flows.

Illustration 22-19
Statement of Cash Flows—
Yoshi Corporation
(Direct Method)

YOSHI CORPORATION
Statement of Cash Flows
Year Ended December 31, 2014

Cash provided by (used in) operations		
Received from customers		$ 867,950
Dividends received on significant influence investment		2,000
Net cash received on FV-NI investment transactions		6,300
Payments to suppliers		(490,750)
Payments to and on behalf of employees		(196,000)
Payments for interest, and dividends on term preferred shares		(9,000)
Income taxes paid		(62,500)
		118,000
Cash provided by (used in) investing activities		
Investment in development costs	$(200,000)	
Purchase of equipment	(73,000)	
Proceeds on sale of land	15,000	
Proceeds on sale of equipment	13,000	(245,000)
Cash provided by (used in) financing activities		
Proceeds on issue of common shares	144,000	
Proceeds on issue of term preferred shares	6,000	
Repurchase and cancellation of common shares	(34,000)	
Dividends paid on common shares	(6,000)	110,000
Decrease in cash and cash equivalents		(17,000)
Cash and cash equivalents, January 1		36,000
Cash and cash equivalents, December 31 (Note 1)		$ 19,000

Note 1. Cash and cash equivalents are defined as cash on deposit and money-market instruments with original maturity dates of 90 days or less.

Note 2. Term preferred shares valued at $54,000 were issued during the year as consideration for the purchase of land.

For those who prefer the indirect method of reporting operating cash flows, Illustration 22-20 indicates how the statement's Operating Activities section might look.

Illustration 22-20

Cash Provided by Operations—Yoshi Corporation (Indirect Method)

Cash provided by (used in) operations			
Net income			$117,700
Add back non-cash expenses:			
Depreciation expense	$ 14,600		
Unrealized loss on FV-NI investments	1,000		
Impairment loss—goodwill	2,400		
Amortization of discount on bond	300		
Amortization of development costs	40,000		
Deferred income taxes	3,000		61,300
Equity in income of Portel Corp. in excess of dividends received			(3,500)
Deduct non-operating gains and losses:			
Gain on sale of land	(10,500)		
Loss on disposal of equipment	1,500		(9,000)
Changes in non-cash working capital accounts (see Note A)			(48,500)
			$118,000

Note A—changes in non-cash working capital:		
FV-NI investments		$ 4,000
Accounts receivable, net		(53,000)
Inventory		8,000
Prepaid expenses		500
Accounts payable		(1,000)
Dividends payable, term preferred shares		2,000
Accrued liabilities		4,000
Income taxes payable		(13,000)
		($48,500)

How would this statement differ if ASPE had been followed instead of IFRS? Because we assumed that Yoshi follows the same reporting options for interest and dividends paid **permitted** under IFRS that are **required** under ASPE, the statements could be identical. The amount of cash generated or used by each type of activity and the change in cash are the same. Alternative presentations are permitted under IFRS, however, so the way the information is presented may differ. If the company had chosen different policies for reporting interest and dividends paid, the cash amounts in the operating and financing categories would change, but the net change in cash would not.

PRESENTATION, DISCLOSURE, AND ANALYSIS

Disclosure Requirements

Objective 8

Identify the financial presentation and disclosure requirements for the statement of cash flows.

The specific items that require disclosure are similar for IFRS and ASPE, with the latter requiring less disclosure. In addition to reporting cash flows according to operating, investing, and financing classifications, the standards call for disclosure of the items set out in Illustration 22-21.

Illustration 22-21

Disclosures Required for the Statement of Cash Flows

IFRS	ASPE
Separately disclose interest received and paid and dividends received and paid.	Separately present interest and dividends paid and charged to retained earnings as a financing activity; classify as operating if received/paid and including in determination of net income.
Separately disclose cash flows from taxes on income.	Not required.

(continued)

IFRS	ASPE
Disclose and provide relevant information about significant non-cash investing and financing transactions.	Same as IFRS requirement.
Report policy on what makes up cash and cash equivalents, and reconcile the change in amounts to the same amounts reported on the statement of financial position.	Same as IFRS requirement.
Report and explain amount of cash and cash equivalents that have restrictions on their use.	Disclosure of the amount of cash and cash equivalents that is restricted.

IFRS also identifies other information that may be helpful to users in assessing an entity's financial position and liquidity, and encourages the disclosure of this information along with a related commentary. Examples include:

- the amount of additional cash available under existing borrowing agreements;

- investing cash flows related to maintaining operating capacity and those for increasing operating capacity; and

- the operating, investing, and financing cash flows of each reportable segment.

Presentation

As indicated earlier in the chapter, entities can choose between the direct and indirect methods of presenting operating cash flows on the statement, although the direct method is preferred and encouraged by standard setters. Both ASPE and IFRS describe the indirect method as reconciling the net income (or, under IFRS, the profit and loss) to cash flow from operating activities. However, it is common in IFRS-prepared statements to see companies begin with **income before tax or income before interest and taxes.** The reason for this approach is that all other adjustments can be made and then the cash actually paid out for taxes and interest can be reported as separate figures. This allows entities to meet some of the disclosure requirements on the face of the statement.[16]

Illustration 22-22 provides an example of this presentation by **British Airways plc** in its financial statements for the year ended December 31, 2011 (reported in millions of pounds, £). Notice that the opening "operating profit" is actually before finance costs (interest) and income tax expense. The actual cash flows for these two costs are reported at the bottom of the operating activities section.

Cash flow statements

	Group	
£ million	12 mths. to 31 Dec. 2011	9 mths. to 31 Dec. 2010
Cash flow from operating activities		
Operating profit	518	342
Depreciation, amortisation and impairment	683	570
Operating cash flow before working capital changes	1,201	912
Movement in inventories, trade and other receivables	(460)	12
Movement in trade and other payables and provisions	404	(28)
Payments in respect of restructuring	(11)	(14)
Payments in settlement of competition investigation	(147)	—
Cash generated from operations	987	879
Interest paid	(147)	(87)
Taxation	(4)	—
Net cash generated from operating activities	836	792

Both sets of standards require, for the most part, the reporting of gross cash inflows and outflows from investing and financing activities rather than netted amounts. Other significant requirements relate to financial institutions, foreign currency cash flows, and business combinations and disposals. These are left to a course in advanced financial accounting.

Illustrative Example

Stantec Inc.'s consolidated statements of cash flow for its years ended December 31, 2011, and 2010, are provided in Illustration 22-23. Stantec, a Canadian-based company, provides professional engineering consulting services mostly for infrastructure and facilities projects in North America. Note that this company uses the direct method to present its operating cash flows, and its financial statements are presented in accordance with IFRS. Some of the required disclosures are presented on the face of the statement itself, although many companies provide them in notes to the financial statements. Although not required, Stantec also provides a reconciliation of its net income with the cash flows from operations in Note 33. This is shown in Illustration 22-23 as well. Take a minute to review the statement of cash flows for the differences in cash activity from one year to the next.

Real World Emphasis

Illustration 22-23

Statement of Cash Flows— Stantec Inc.

Consolidated Statements of Cash Flows

Years ended December 31 *(In thousands of Canadian dollars)*	Notes	2011 $	2010 $
CASH FLOWS FROM (USED IN) OPERATING ACTIVITIES			
Cash receipts from clients		1,611,974	1,499,392
Cash paid to suppliers		(496,270)	(508,637)
Cash paid to employees		(943,439)	(821,360)
Interest received		1,953	3,111
Interest paid		(16,604)	(16,775)
Finance costs paid		(2,546)	(1,773)
Income taxes paid		(50,282)	(51,548)
Income taxes recovered		9,800	9,522
Cash flows from operating activities	33	**114,586**	**111,932**
CASH FLOWS FROM (USED IN) INVESTING ACTIVITIES			
Business acquisitions, net of cash acquired	7	(76,434)	(106,393)
Dividends from equity investments		175	2,852
Increase in investments held for self-insured liabilities		(8,393)	(7,301)
Proceeds on disposition of investments and other assets		10,767	1,283
Purchase of intangible assets		(3,958)	(3,262)
Purchase of property and equipment		(21,832)	(25,725)
Proceeds on disposition of property and equipment		291	412
Proceeds on sale of equity investments	14	—	9,980
Cash flows used in investing activities		**(99,384)**	**(128,154)**
CASH FLOWS FROM (USED IN) FINANCING ACTIVITIES			
Repayment of bank debt		(229,449)	(140,002)
Proceeds from bank debt		80,736	216,948
Proceeds from senior secured notes		125,000	—
Transaction costs on senior secured notes		(1,115)	
Repayment of acquired bank indebtedness	7	(3,389)	(3,895)
Payment of finance lease obligations		(5,449)	(5,356)
Repurchase of shares for cancellation	25	(11,074)	(4,887)
Proceeds from issue of share capital		2,867	3,044
Cash flows (used in) from financing activities		**(41,873)**	**65,852**
Foreign exchange gain (loss) on cash held in foreign currency		51	(1,589)
Net (decrease) increase in cash and cash equivalents		**(26,620)**	**48,041**
Cash and cash equivalents, beginning of the year	8	62,731	14,690
Cash and cash equivalents, end of the year	8	**36,111**	**62,731**

(continued)

Illustration 22-23

Statement of Cash Flows—Stantec Inc. (continued)

33. Cash Flows From Operating Activities

Cash flows from (used in) operating activities determined by the indirect method are as follows:

(In thousands of Canadian dollars)

	For the year ended December 31	
	2011 $	2010 $
CASH FLOWS FROM (USED IN) OPERATING ACTIVITIES		
Net income for the year	12,662	94,741
Add (deduct) items not affecting cash:		
Depreciation of property and equipment	27,933	25,461
Impairment of goodwill	90,000	—
Amortization of intangible assets	18,395	17,289
Deferred income tax	4,281	(2,397)
Loss on dispositions of investments and property and equipment	1,298	586
Share-based compensation expense	5,575	2,822
Provision for self-insured liability and claims	11,463	10,962
Other non-cash items	(9,155)	(5,908)
Share of income from equity investments	(793)	(2,209)
Gain on sale of equity investments	—	(7,183)
	161,659	134,164
Trade and other receivables	11,917	11,647
Unbilled revenue	(26,685)	(1,250)
Prepaid expenses	(2,166)	4,055
Trade and other payables	(15,936)	(22,975)
Billings in excess of costs	(7,247)	(13,158)
Income taxes payable	(6,956)	(551)
	(47,073)	(22,232)
Cash flows from operating activities	114,586	111,932

Contrast the direct method in the operating activities section of Stantec's cash flow statements in Illustration 22-23 with the same section prepared under the indirect method. It is surprising that the cash flow from operations determined under two such different methods actually has the same meaning!

Interpreting the Statement of Cash Flows

Objective 9

Read and interpret a statement of cash flows.

Underlying Concept

Consolidated statements of cash flows may be of limited use to analysts evaluating multinational entities. With so much data brought together, users of the statements are not able to determine "where in the world" the funds are sourced and used.

As you can tell, companies have some flexibility in how information is reported in the statement of cash flows. The way in which the information is summarized and described can improve the information content and help users interpret and understand the significance of the cash flow data.

One way to approach an analysis of the statement is to begin by focusing on the three subtotals and determining what they tell you about which activities (operating, investing, and financing) generated cash for the company and which used cash. After this general assessment, delve deeper into the details within each section.

As an example, the statement of cash flows of Stantec Inc. in Illustration 22-23 indicates that, in 2011, excess operating cash flows of almost $114.6 million allowed the company to internally finance all of its investment activities of $99.4 million during the year. Due to healthy cash balances at the start of the year, Stantec also used almost $41.9 million to reduce its debt. The net result was a $26.6-million reduction in cash and cash equivalents over the year, with the ending balance considerably less than the opening amount.

The 2010 story was different. In 2010, Stantec's cash from operations was similar to 2011. The operating cash flows of almost $112 million, along with financing activities that generated another $65.9 million, was more than enough to cover the company's needs for investment capital of $128.2 million. This resulted in an increase in cash of about $48 million over the year. Each company and each statement of cash flows tells a different story, but the questions they answer remain the same: Where did the cash come from, and how was it used? Each story has to be read and interpreted in conjunction with the other financial statements and the MD&A.

Operating Activities

Whether a company uses the direct or indirect method, **the net operating cash flows tell you the same thing: the extent to which cash receipts from customers and other operating sources were able to cover cash payments to suppliers of goods and services and to employees, and for other operating expenditures.** This is how the approximately $115 million cash provided by operating activities at Stantec in 2011 and the $112 million in 2010 are interpreted.

Stantec has a growth strategy that it has identified as combining internal growth and acquisition of firms that will help move it toward becoming a top 10 global design firm. This means that it wants to generate cash from operations and use those flows to finance its business acquisitions. As a service provider, the company is not capital intensive; that is, it does not have large investments in property, plant, and equipment assets. The company, therefore, when compared with some large manufacturers, does not have a significant physical asset base to use as collateral for long-term borrowing. Instead, goodwill from its many acquisitions is the largest asset on its statement of financial position.

While the direct method provides more detail about the specific sources and uses of cash and is particularly useful in comparisons with previous years, the indirect method explains the relationship between the accrual-based net income and the cash from operations. Stantec's largest adjustment between these two numbers, as is the case with many companies, is typically the add-back of depreciation and amortization expense, and, in this company's case, impairment charges related to goodwill. This is the major reason why its operating cash flows are so much higher than the net income the company reports.

Deferred income tax and a variety of other expenses are adjusted because their cash effects are felt in different periods than their income statement effects. A positive adjustment in the current year often means that the related cash outflow will be felt in a subsequent year.[17]

An adjustment for the "changes in non-cash working capital balances" is found in the operating activities section of almost every statement of cash flows prepared under the indirect method and this can have a significant effect on the operating cash flow reported. The details, such as those provided in Note 33 in Illustration 22–23, should be reviewed. The change in these accounts reduced the operating cash flows otherwise generated, similar to the working capital changes in the preceding year. Although accounts receivable collections added to the cash flow, the paydown of trade and other payables and increases in unbilled revenue had the opposite effect.

These changes need to be analyzed carefully. For example, consider the case of **Aptalis Pharma Inc.**, which reported cash flow from operating activities of more than U.S. $63 million in 2010, substantially higher than the cash used in operating activities of U.S. $49 million the next year (the year ended September 30, 2011). However, U.S. $107.2 million of the cash flow from operations in 2010 came from a loss on disposal of a product line and a writedown of assets. A further U.S. $23.4 million was from higher than usual collections of accounts receivable (which help to offset a loss of U.S. $170.4 million). In this case, the operating cash flows in the period under review (2010) do not represent operating cash flows that are likely to be repeated in subsequent years. This was shown clearly in 2011, when cash flows from operations were U.S. $112.1 million lower than 2010.

Users of financial statements need to look beyond the amount of cash generated or used in operations, and analyze the reasons for the operating cash flows. The objective of the analysis is to assess whether the cash flow levels are sustainable and likely to be repeated in the future, or whether they are the result of payment deferrals and one-time events.

Investing Activities

Consistent with its strategic goals, Stantec reports significant cash outlays for business acquisitions in 2010 and 2011, explained in more detail in another note. Because investments in new business assets are the source of future operating cash flows, it is important to understand whether the new investment just maintains the existing capacity of a company, or whether the investment increases the potential for higher levels of operating cash flows in the future. For companies with substantial property, plant, and equipment, how do the new amounts invested compare with the stock of existing property, plant, and equipment, and with the depreciation charges for the year? Also, what types of assets have been purchased? Are they investments in new technologies and development expenditures? Or are existing assets being disposed of, reducing the potential for operating flows in the future?

Stantec appears to be investing in the future by making acquisitions as part of its growth strategy. These, in turn, are generating operating cash flows to allow for the internal financing of further acquisitions.

Financing Activities

The operating and investing flows tell just part of a company's cash story for the period. The financing activities section completes the picture. It clearly captures what changes took place to the firm's capital structure and whether the entity increased or reduced the claims of creditors to cash in the future.

In contrast to its 2010 financing activities, Stantec used much of the excess cash balances it had built up to repay a net amount of almost $149 million of its bank debt. This net reduction in debt was largely offset by proceeds from senior secured notes issued, and these two areas accounted for almost all of the cash used in financing activities.

As indicated above, the methods of financing are usually related to the types of assets acquired. For example, purchases of intangibles and development expenditures are often difficult to use as collateral and, therefore, they are generally financed internally from operating cash flows or externally through new equity.

Details of cash flows related to financing activities allow readers to assess the potential for future claims on the organization's cash and, as indicated above, to identify major shifts in the form of financing, especially between debt and equity. Will there be increased demand for future cash for interest claims and debt repayment? Companies in a growth stage may report significant amounts of cash generated from financing activities—financing that is needed to handle the significant investment activity. As growth levels off and operations begin to generate positive cash flows, financing flows tend to reverse as debt is repaid and, if appropriate, shares are redeemed. The required disclosure of long-term debt repayments over the next five years is an excellent source of information about upcoming demands on an organization's cash for financing purposes.

Due to recent concerns about a general decline in the quality of earnings, some investors have been focusing more on cash flow. Management has an incentive to make cash flow look good, because the capital markets pay a premium for companies that generate a lot of cash from operations rather than through borrowings. However, just as they can with earnings, companies have ways to pump up cash flow from operations.

One way that companies can boost their operating cash flow is by securitizing receivables. Chapter 7 discussed how companies can speed up cash collections by selling their receivables. For example, **Oxford Industries,** an apparel company, once reported a $74 million increase in cash flow from operations. This seemed impressive until you read the fine print, which indicated that a major portion of the increase was due to the sale of receivables. While it originally appeared that the company's core operations had improved, Oxford did little more than accelerate collection of its receivables. In fact, operating cash flow would have been negative without the securitization.

Operating cash flows can also be manipulated by having too liberal a policy of capitalizing expenditures as property, plant, and equipment instead of expensing them as incurred. Such a policy leads to these costs being treated as investment flows. They are not deducted in determining net income or cash from operations. Even when depreciated, the costs end up having no effect on operating cash flow. **WorldCom** was able to conceal almost U.S. $4 billion of decline in its operations this way; **Adelphia Communications** overstated its operating cash flow by U.S. $102 million this way; and closer to home, **Atlas Cold Storage** later reported a similar situation, although on a smaller scale.

The point is that operating cash flow, like earnings, can be of high or low quality. You should be careful when comparing companies' operating cash flows, even if they are in the same industry. Consider the different effect on operating cash flow of one company that rents its premises under operating leases with another that owns its property or has capital lease arrangements. Or compare one company that capitalizes interest and overhead as part of self-constructed assets with one that expenses these costs, or a company that capitalizes internal-use computer software with one that absorbs the costs as they are incurred. In all cases, one set of policies results in investing or financing outflows of cash, while the other set reports reduced operating cash flows. And, unlike revenue and expense accruals and deferrals that are reported on an income statement, where the effect reverses over time, the effects on the classifications in the statement of cash flows are permanent.

Sources: Gerald I. White, Ashwinpaul C. Sondhi, and Dov Fried, *The Analysis and Use of Financial Statements,* 3rd ed. (New York: John Wiley & Sons, Inc., 2003), p. 96; "Atlas Cold Storage Fires CFO, Suspends Q3 Distribution," CBCNews.ca, December 4, 2003; Deborah Solomon, "Adelphia Overstated Cash Flow, Revenue for the Past Two Years," *The Wall Street Journal,* June 11, 2002.

Free Cash Flow

Introduced in Chapter 5 and publicized by many companies in recent years, a non-GAAP performance measure used by many companies is **free cash flow** (FCF). As the name suggests, this is an indicator of financial flexibility that uses information provided on the statement of cash flows. Free cash flow is net operating cash flows reduced by the capital expenditures that are needed to sustain the current level of operations. The resulting cash flow is the discretionary cash that a company has available for increasing its capacity and acquiring new investments, paying dividends, retiring debt, repurchasing its shares, or simply adding to its liquidity.

The calculation of this measure varies by company as some entities deduct all capital expenditures because it is impossible to separate sustaining expenditures from the total. Others also deduct current dividends. FCF measures are more useful to investors if information is also provided about how they are calculated.

In general, companies with significant free cash flow have a strong degree of financial flexibility. They are able to take advantage of new opportunities or cope well during poor economic times without jeopardizing current operations.

IFRS/ASPE COMPARISON

A Comparison of IFRS and ASPE

Objective 10

Identify differences in ASPE and IFRS, and explain what changes are expected to standards for the statement of cash flows.

Because the most recent pre-2011 Canadian standard on the statement of cash flows was based on the international standard of the same name, ASPE and IAS 7 are very similar. Illustration 22-24 sets out the few areas where there are differences between them.

	Accounting Standards for Private Enterprises (ASPE)—*CICA Handbook*, Part II, Section 1540	IFRS—IAS 7	References to Related Illustrations and Select Brief Exercises
Definitions and Scope	Cash equivalents exclude all equity investments.	Preferred shares acquired close to their maturity date may be included in cash equivalents.	BE22-2
Presentation	Interest and dividends received are presented as operating cash flows. Interest and dividends paid are operating flows if recognized in net income. If charged directly to retained earnings, they are presented as financing cash flows.	Interest and dividends received may be classified and presented as either operating or investing cash flows. Interest and dividends paid are either operating or financing outflows.	Illustration 22-2, BE22-4
Disclosure	Interest and dividends paid and charged to retained earnings must be disclosed separately as a financing activity.	Separate disclosure is required for each of interest and dividends received and paid.	Illustration 22-21
	Income taxes paid **are encouraged (but not required)** to be disclosed.	Income taxes paid **are** required to be disclosed.	BE22-13
	The amount of cash and cash equivalents whose use is restricted is required to be disclosed.	Restrictions on the use of cash and cash equivalents and an explanation of the amount of cash and cash equivalents not available for use is required to be disclosed.	Illustration 22-21

Illustration 22-24

IFRS and ASPE Comparison

Looking Ahead

The most influential event on the horizon with the potential to affect the reporting of cash flows is Phase B of the joint FASB-IASB Financial Statement Presentation project.[18] From the IASB's perspective, Phase B is intended to replace existing IAS 1 *Presentation of Financial Statements* and IAS 7 *Statement of Cash Flows*. The IASB had planned an exposure draft in 2010 and a final standard expected in 2011, but then decided to do more outreach activities before finishing and publishing the exposure draft and final standard. The outreach activities focus on the perceived benefits and costs of the proposals and the effects on financial institutions. A reasonable period will be provided, however, before the new requirements must be applied.

As part of a 2012 Exposure Draft relating to its Annual Improvements Project, the IASB proposed an amendment to standards for statement of cash flow statements. The change would require capitalized borrowing costs relating to property, plant, and equipment; intangibles; and other long-term assets to be included as an investing activity. If approved, this change would start to be applied for annual periods beginning on or after January 1, 2014.

Chapter 4 in Volume 1 of this text introduced the major changes being considered for the reporting model by presenting the chart reproduced in Illustration 22-25, taken from an October 2008 presentation of the preliminary views document by the IASB.

Illustration 22-25

Financial Statement Presentation Proposals

Proposed format for the presentation of financial statements

Statement of financial position	Statement of comprehensive income	Statement of cash flows
Business	Business	Business
• Operating assets and liabilities	• Operating income and expenses	• Operating cash flows
• Investing assets and liabilities	• Investing income and expenses	• Investing cash flows

Statement of financial position	Statement of comprehensive income	Statement of cash flows
Financing • Financing assets • Financing liabilities	Financing • Financing asset income • Financing liability expenses	Financing • Financing asset cash flows • Financing liability cash flows
Income taxes	Income taxes on continuing operations (business and financing)	Income taxes
Discontinued operations	Discontinued operations net of tax	Discontinued operations
	Other comprehensive income, net of tax	
Equity		Equity

Illustration 22-25

Financial Statement Presentation Proposals (continued)

What would the statement of cash flows look like under these proposals? Illustration 22-26 sets out the proposed format from the 2008 Discussion Paper. As you can see, the cash flow information provided about business-related operating activities is expected to increase significantly.[19]

Illustration 22-26

Proposed Statement of Cash Flows Presentation

TOOLCO STATEMENT OF CASH FLOWS
(proposed format)

	For the year ended 31 December	
	2014	2013
BUSINESS		
Operating		
Cash received from wholesale customers	2,108,754	1,928,798
Cash received from retail customers	703,988	643,275
Total cash collected from customers	2,812,742	2,572,073
Cash paid for goods		
Materials purchases	(935,544)	(785,000)
Labour	(418,966)	(475,313)
Overhead—transport	(128,640)	(108,000)
Pension	(170,100)	(157,500)
Overhead—other	(32,160)	(27,000)
Total cash paid for goods	(1,685,409)	(1,552,813)
Cash paid for selling activities		
Advertising	(65,000)	(75,000)
Wages, salaries and benefits	(58,655)	(55,453)
Other	(13,500)	(12,500)
Total cash paid for selling activities	(137,155)	(142,953)
Cash paid for general and administrative activities		
Wages, salaries and benefits	(332,379)	(314,234)
Contributions to pension plan	(170,100)	(157,500)
Capital expenditures	(54,000)	(50,000)
Lease payments	(50,000)	—
Research and development	(8,478)	(7,850)
Settlement of share-based remuneration	(3,602)	(3,335)
Other	(12,960)	(12,000)
Total cash paid for general and administrative activities	(631,519)	(544,919)
Cash flow before other operating activities	358,657	331,388
Cash from other operating activities		
Disposal of property, plant and equipment	37,650	—
Investment in associate A	—	(120,000)
Sale of receivable	8,000	10,000
Settlement of cash flow hedge	3,402	3,150
Total cash received (paid) for other operating activities	49,052	(106,850)

(continued)

Illustration 22-26

Proposed Statement of Cash Flows Presentation
(continued)

	For the year ended 31 December	
	2014	2013
Net cash from operating activities	407,709	224,538
Investing		
Purchase of available-for-sale financial assets	—	(130,000)
Sale of available-for-sale financial assets	56,100	51,000
Dividends received	54,000	50,000
Net cash from investing activities	110,100	(29,000)
NET CASH FROM BUSINESS ACTIVITIES	517,809	195,538

Other items being considered include eliminating the term "cash equivalents" and treating them instead in the same way as other short-term investments, presenting bank overdrafts in the debt category of the financing section of the statement, and requiring the direct method for reporting operating cash flows. A reconciliation between operating income and operating cash flows and information about significant non-cash transactions may also be included as a supplement to the statement of cash flows.

SUMMARY OF LEARNING OBJECTIVES

1 Understand the importance of cash flows from a business perspective.

One sign of a healthy company is positive cash flow from operations. Companies can use these funds to finance expansion, to issue dividends, or to ensure that they remain solvent during economic downturns. Given the importance of cash flows for business, it is not surprising that the statement of cash flows has grown in importance for companies and standard setters over the past 25 years. Many also consider it to be less susceptible to earnings management than the statement of comprehensive income.

2 Describe the purpose and uses of the statement of cash flows.

The primary purpose of this statement is to provide information about an entity's cash receipts and cash payments during a period. A secondary objective is to report the entity's operating, investing, and financing activities during the period. The statement's objective is to provide information about historical changes in an enterprise's cash so that investors and creditors can assess the amount, timing, and degree of certainty associated with an entity's future cash flows, as well as the organization's needs for cash and how cash will be used.

3 Define cash and cash equivalents.

The definition of cash is related to an organization's cash management activities. Cash and cash equivalents include cash on hand, demand deposits, and short-term, highly liquid non-equity investments

that are convertible to known amounts of cash with insignificant risk of changes in value. These amounts are reduced by bank overdrafts that fluctuate from positive to negative balances and that are repayable on demand. IFRS allows preferred shares acquired within a short period of their maturity to be included as a cash equivalent.

4 Identify the major classifications of cash flows and explain the significance of each classification.

Cash flows are classified into those resulting from operating, investing, and financing activities. A company's ability to generate operating cash flows affects its capacity to pay dividends to shareholders, to take advantage of investment opportunities, to provide internal financing for growth, and to meet obligations when they fall due. The amount of cash spent on investing activities affects an organization's potential for future cash flows. Cash invested in increased levels of productive assets forms the basis for increased future operating cash inflows. Financing cash activities affect the firm's capital structure and, therefore, the requirements for future cash outflows.

5 Prepare the operating activities section of a statement of cash flows using the direct versus the indirect method.

The direct method presents operating cash flows in a manner similar to a condensed cash basis income statement. The accrual amounts are listed and adjusted whenever the cash received or paid out differs from the revenues, gains, expenses, and losses reported in net income, and for non-operating gains and losses.

6 Prepare a statement of cash flows using the direct method.

The direct method involves determining the change in cash and cash equivalents during the period, inserting line items from the income statement as the starting point within the statement's Operating Activities section, and analyzing the changes in all accounts on the statement of financial position to identify all transactions that have an impact on cash. Those with a cash impact are recorded on the statement of cash flows. To ensure that all cash flows have been identified, the results recorded on the statement are compared with the change in cash during the period. The statement is then prepared with required disclosures.

7 Prepare a statement of cash flows using the indirect method.

The steps using the indirect method are the same as in Objective 6 above, with one exception. Rather than starting with line items from the income statement in the Operating Activities section, the net income amount is the beginning point. All the same adjustments are then made to adjust net income to a cash basis, but the style and format of the Operating Activities sections differ.

8 Identify the financial presentation and disclosure requirements for the statement of cash flows.

Under IFRS, disclosure is required of cash flows associated with interest and dividends received and paid, the definition and components of cash and cash equivalents reconciled to the amounts reported on the statement of financial position, and the amount of and explanation for cash and cash equiva-

lents not available for use. All income tax cash flows are reported as operating flows unless they can be linked directly to investing or financing flows. Choices are available under IFRS for the reporting of interest and dividends received (operating or investing) and interest and dividends paid (operating or financing). Gross amounts should be reported except in specifically permitted circumstances, and non-cash investing and financing transactions are excluded from the statement of cash flows, but details about these are reported elsewhere on the financial statements. ASPE presentation requirements are very similar, but required disclosures are limited to interest and dividends paid and charged to retained earnings and the amount of any restricted cash. In addition, interest and dividends received are both operating flows, and interest and dividends paid are operating flows unless they were charged directly to retained earnings.

9 Read and interpret a statement of cash flows.

The first step in reading and interpreting a statement of cash flows is to look at the subtotals for the three classifications of activities and the overall change in cash. This provides a high-level summary of the period's cash flows. Next, analyze the items within each section for additional insights, keeping alert for accounting policies that affect the type of cash flow reported. Familiarity with the company's business and strategic direction is very useful in interpreting the statement.

10 Identify differences in ASPE and IFRS, and explain what changes are expected to standards for the statement of cash flows.

There are no significant differences between ASPE and IFRS related to the statement of cash flows except for the definition of cash equivalents and the presentation and disclosure requirements identified above.

KEY TERMS

cash, p. 1426
cash equivalents, p. 1426
cash flows, p. 1426
direct method, p. 1430

financing activities, p. 1426
free cash flow (FCF), p. 1459
indirect method, p. 1430
investing activities, p. 1426

operating activities, p. 1426
significant non-cash transactions, p. 1428
statement of cash flows, p. 1425

APPENDIX 22A

USE OF A WORK SHEET

When many adjustments are needed, or there are other complicating factors, a work sheet is often used to assemble and classify the data that will appear on the statement of cash flows. The work sheet (or spreadsheet when using computer software) is merely a device that aids in the preparation of the statement; using one is optional. The skeleton format of the work sheet for preparing the statement of cash flows using the indirect method is shown in Illustration 22A-1.

Illustration 22A-1

Format of Work Sheet for Preparing Statement of Cash Flows

	A	B	C		E	F
			Statement of Cash Flows for the Year Ended…			
1						
2	**Statement of Financial Position Accounts**	**End of Last Year Balances**	**Debits**		**Credits**	**End of Current Year Balances**
3	Debit balance					
4	accounts	XX	XX		XX	XX
5	Totals	XX	XX		XX	XX
6						
7	Credit balance					
8	accounts	XX	XX		XX	XX
9	Totals	XX	XX		XX	XX
10						
11	Cash Flows					
12	**Operating activities**					
13	Net income		XX			
14	Adjustments		XX		XX	
15	**Investing activities**					
16	Receipts (dr.) and					
17	payments (cr.)		XX		XX	
18	**Financing activities**					
19	Receipts (dr.) and					
20	payments (cr.)		XX		XX	
21	Totals		XX		XX	
22	Increase (cr.) or decrease (dr.) in cash		XX or		XX	
	Totals		XX		XX	

The following guidelines are important in using a work sheet.

1. In the Statement of Financial Position Accounts section, accounts with debit balances are listed separately from those with credit balances. This means, for example, that Accumulated Depreciation is listed under credit balances and not as a contra account under the debit balances. The beginning and ending balances of each account are entered. As the analysis proceeds, each line that relates to a statement of

financial position account should balance. That is, the beginning balance plus or minus the reconciling item(s) must equal the ending balance. When all statement of financial position accounts agree in this way, all changes in account balances have been identified and reconciled and the analysis is complete.

2. The bottom portion of the work sheet is an area to record the operating, investing, and financing cash flows. This section provides the detail for the change in the cash balance during the period—information that is used to prepare the formal statement of cash flows. Inflows of cash are entered as debits in the reconciling columns and outflows of cash are entered as credits in the reconciling columns. Thus, in this section, the sale of equipment for cash at book value is entered as a debit under inflows of cash from investing activities. Similarly, the purchase of land for cash is entered as a credit under outflows of cash for investing activities.

3. The reconciling items shown in the work sheet are not entered in any journal or posted to any account. They do not represent either adjustments or corrections of the statement of financial position accounts. They are only used to make it easier to prepare the statement of cash flows.

Preparing the Work Sheet

The preparation of a work sheet involves a series of steps.

Step 1: Enter the statement of financial position accounts and their beginning and ending balances in the appropriate Statement of Financial Position Accounts section.

Step 2: Enter the debits and credits from the summary entries that explain the changes in each statement of financial position account (other than cash). Identify all entries that affect cash, and enter these amounts in the reconciling columns at the bottom of the work sheet.

Step 3: After the analysis is complete and the changes in all statement of financial position accounts have been reconciled, enter the increase or decrease in cash on the statement of financial position cash line (or lines, if cash equivalents) and at the bottom of the work sheet. The totals of the reconciling columns should balance.

To illustrate the procedure for preparing the work sheet, we use the same comprehensive illustration for Yoshi Corporation, a publicly accountable enterprise reporting under IFRS that was used in the chapter. We will initially use the indirect method for calculating net cash provided by operating activities. An illustration of the direct method is also provided. The financial statements and other data related to Yoshi Corporation for its year ended December 31, 2014, are presented in Illustrations 22-14, 22-15, 22-16, and 22-17. Most of the analysis was discussed earlier in the chapter and additional explanations related to the work sheet are provided in the discussion here.

Analyzing Transactions

Before the analysis begins, Yoshi's statement of financial position accounts are transferred to the work sheet's opening and ending balance columns. The following discussion explains the individual adjustments that appear on the work sheet in Illustration 22A-2. The discussion assumes that you are familiar with the analysis of the Yoshi illustration earlier in the chapter.

Illustration 22A-2

Work Sheet for Preparation of Statement of Cash Flows— Yoshi Corporation

Yoshi Corporation
Work Sheet for Preparation of Statement of Cash Flows
Year Ended December 31, 2014

	Account	Balance 12/31/13	Reconciling Items—2014 Debits	Reconciling Items—2014 Credits	Balance 12/31/14
3	**Debits**				
4	Cash	32,000		(24) 27,000	5,000
5	Cash equivalents	4,000	(24) 10,000		14,000
6	FV-NI investments	30,000		(2) 5,000	25,000
7	Accounts receivable	52,700	(3) 55,250	(3) 1,450	106,500
8	Inventory	311,000		(4) 8,000	303,000
9	Prepaid expenses	17,000		(5) 500	16,500
10	Investment in Associate (Portel Corp.)	15,000	(6) 5,500	(6) 2,000	18,500
11	FV-OCI investments (Hyco Ltd.)	13,000	(7) 4,500		17,500
12	Deferred development costs	30,000	(8) 200,000	(8) 40,000	190,000
13	Land	82,000	(9) 54,000	(9) 4,500	131,500
14	Equipment	142,000	(10) 73,000	(10) 28,000	187,000
15	Buildings	262,000			262,000
16	Goodwill	10,000		(11) 2,400	7,600
17	**Total debits**	1,000,700			1,284,100
19	**Credits**				
20	Allowance for doubtful accounts	1,700	(3) 1,450	(12) 2,250	2,500
21	Accumulated Depreciation—Equipment	31,000	(10) 13,500	(13) 11,500	29,000
22	Accumulated Depreciation—Buildings	71,000		(14) 3,100	74,100
23	Accounts payable	131,000	(15) 1,000		130,000
24	Dividends payable, term preferred shares	—		(16) 2,000	2,000
25	Accrued liabilities	39,000		(17) 4,000	43,000
26	Income tax payable	16,000	(18) 13,000		3,000
27	Bonds payable	97,500		(19) 300	97,800
28	Term preferred shares	—		(20) 60,000	60,000
30	Deferred tax liability	6,000		(21) 4,000	10,000
32	Common shares	88,000		(22) 144,000	225,400
33	Retained earnings	518,500	(22) 12,400; (22) 15,000; (22) 6,000	(1) 117,700	602,800
37	Accumulated other comprehensive income	1,000	(21) 1,000	(7) 4,500	4,500
38	**Total credits**	1,000,700			1,284,100
40	**Cash Flows**				
41	**Operating activities:**				
42	Net income		(1) 117,700		
43	Decrease in FV-NI investments		(2) 5,000		
44	Increase in accounts receivable			(3) 55,250	
45	Decrease in inventory		(4) 8,000		
46	Decrease in prepaid expenses		(5) 500		
47	Investment Income or Loss from Portel Corp.			(6) 5,500	
48	Dividend from Portel Corp.		(6) 2,000		
49	Amortization, deferred development costs		(8) 40,000		

(continued)

50	Gain on sale of land		(9)	10,500
51	Loss on disposal of equipment	(10) 1,500		
52	Loss on impairment (goodwill)	(11) 2,400		
53	Bad debt expense	(12) 2,250		
54	Depreciation expense—equipment	(13) 11,500		
55	Depreciation expense—buildings	(14) 3,100		
56	Decrease in accounts payable		(15)	1,000
57	Dividend expense, term preferred shares	(16) 2,000		
58	Increase in accrued liabilities	(17) 4,000		
59	Decrease in income taxes payable		(18)	13,000
60	Amortization of bond discount	(19) 300		
61	Deferred tax liability	(21) 3,000		
62				
63	**Investing activities:**			
64	Development costs incurred		(8)	200,000
65	Proceeds on disposal of land	(9) 15,000		
66	Purchase of equipment		(10)	73,000
67	Proceeds on sale of equipment	(10) 13,000		
68				
69	**Financing activities:**			
70	Proceeds on issue of term preferred shares	(20) 6,000		
71	Proceeds on sale of common shares	(22) 144,000	(22)	34,000
72	Repurchase of common shares		(23)	6,000
73	Dividend on common shares			
74	Decrease in cash and cash equivalents	(24) 17,000		885,450
75		885,450		885,450
76				
77				

Illustration 22A-2

Work Sheet for Preparation of Statement of Cash Flows—Yoshi Corporation (continued)

1. **Net Income.** Because so much of the analysis requires adjustments to convert accrual basis income to the cash basis, the net income number is usually the first reconciling item put in the work sheet. The entry to reflect this and the statement of financial position account affected is:

Net Income	117,700	
Retained Earnings		117,700

The credit to Retained Earnings explains part of the change in that account. We know that net income did not generate $117,700 of cash, so this number is considered a temporary one that will be adjusted whenever the subsequent analysis identifies revenues and expenses whose cash impact is different from the revenue and expense amounts that are included in net income. It is a starting point only.

2. **FV-NI Investments.** Based on the activity and adjustments in this account during 2014, the entry to explain the net change in its balance is as follows:

Cash ($32,300 – $26,000)	6,300	
FV-NI Investments		5,000
Investment Income or Loss ($2,300 – $1,000)		1,300

Because the cash flows related to investments held for trading purposes are all operating cash flows, the Operating Activities section should report $6,300 of net cash inflows. However, all that is reported so far is the $1,300 of investment income. Therefore, an adjustment of $5,000 is needed to adjust the investment income number to the cash flows from these FV-NI investments. This explains the $5,000 decrease in this account's balance during the year.

3. **Accounts Receivable.** The following two entries summarize the net change in this account and identify the other accounts that are affected:

Accounts Receivable	55,250	
Revenue		55,250
Allowance for Doubtful Accounts	1,450	
Accounts Receivable		1,450

Accounts Receivable increased by $53,800 during the year after writing off accounts totalling $1,450. The increase due to reporting revenue in excess of cash receipts therefore must have been $55,250. This requires an adjustment to the net income reported in the work sheet's Operating Activities section. The other entry explains changes in two statement of financial position accounts with no cash impact. Enter these on the work sheet.

4. **Inventory.** The entry to explain the net change in the Inventory account is as follows:

Cost of Goods Sold	8,000	
Inventory		8,000

The credit to inventories explains the change in that account. The debit is an expense of $8,000 that was deducted in calculating net income, but which did not use cash. This requires a debit column adjustment to the net income in the Operating Activities section.[20]

5. **Prepaid Expenses.** Assuming the prepaid expenses were selling in nature, the following entry summarizes the change in this account:

Selling Expenses	500	
Prepaid Expenses		500

The credit entry explains the change in the Prepaid Expenses account. The debit represents a non-cash expense deducted on the income statement, requiring an adjustment to the net income reported in the Operating Activities section.

6. **Investment in Associate (Portel Corp.).** Entries explaining the change in this account are:

Investment in Associate	5,500	
Investment Income or Loss		5,500
Cash	2,000	
Investment in Associate		2,000

The first entry explains part of the change in the investment account and identifies a non-cash revenue included in net income. The entry to adjust net income for this is a $5,500 credit. The second entry credit explains the remainder of the change in the statement of financial position account. The debit portion of the entry represents an operating inflow of cash that has not been included in net income. The Operating Activities section is adjusted to reflect this $2,000 operating cash inflow.

7. **FV-OCI Investments.** A single entry explains the change in this investment accounted for at FV-OCI.

| FV-OCI Investments | 4,500 | |
| Unrealized Gain or Loss—OCI | | 4,500 |

The entry explains the change in two statement of financial position accounts. The $4,500 was not an income statement item and it is not a cash transaction.

8. **Deferred Development Costs.** The entries to summarize the changes in this account are as follows:

Deferred Development Costs	200,000	
Cash		200,000
Development Expenses	40,000	
Deferred Development Costs		40,000

The first entry identifies an outflow of cash related to the investment in this non-current asset—an investing flow. The second entry recognizes the amortization of these deferred costs—a non-cash expense—reported in net income. The adjustment adds back (debits) $40,000 to the net income number. Remember to enter the transactions that explain changes in the statement of financial position accounts as you proceed.

9. **Land.** The entries affecting the Land account are:

Land	54,000	
Term Preferred Shares		54,000
Cash	15,000	
Land		4,500
Gain on Disposal of Land		10,500

The first entry explains changes in both the Land and Term Preferred Shares accounts—a significant non-cash transaction. The second entry identifies a $15,000 investing inflow of cash, a reduction of $4,500 in the Land account, and the difference of $10,500 representing a gain reported in net income that does not correspond to the actual cash flow. Net income is adjusted.

10. **Equipment.** The entries that affect the Equipment account are as follows:

Equipment	73,000	
Cash		73,000
Cash	13,000	
Loss on Disposal of Equipment	1,500	
Accumulated Depreciation—Equipment	13,500	
Equipment		28,000

The first entry identifies a $73,000 investing outflow of cash. The second entry explains the remainder of the change in the asset account and part of the change in the Accumulated Depreciation account, and identifies a $13,000 investing inflow of cash and a $1,500 non-cash loss that is reported in net income and needs to be adjusted.

11. **Goodwill.** The decrease in Goodwill is an impairment loss, recreated with this entry:

| Loss on Impairment (Goodwill) | 2,400 | |
| Goodwill | | 2,400 |

The impairment loss is a non-cash charge to the income statement. It therefore requires an adjustment to the net income included in the Operating Activities section.

12. **Allowance for Doubtful Accounts.** Part of the change in this account was explained previously in item 3 above. The remaining entry to this account recognized bad debt expense:

Bad Debt Expense	2,250	
Allowance for Doubtful Accounts		2,250

This completes the explanation of changes to the allowance account. In addition, it identifies a non-cash expense of $2,250, which requires an adjustment to net income in the Operating Activities section.

13. **Accumulated Depreciation—Equipment.** One of the changes in the Accumulated Depreciation account was explained previously in item 10. The other entry affecting this account is:

Depreciation Expense	11,500	
Accumulated Depreciation—Equipment		11,500

The entry identifies an $11,500 non-cash expense requiring an adjustment to net income and the cash flows from operations.

14. **Accumulated Depreciation—Buildings.** With no change in the Buildings account during the year, the only entry needed to explain the change in the Accumulated Depreciation account is:

Depreciation Expense	3,100	
Accumulated Depreciation—Buildings		3,100

This $3,100 non-cash expense requires an adjustment to the net income number in the Operating Activities section.

15. **Accounts Payable.** The summary entry to explain the net change in this account is:

Accounts Payable	1,000	
Cash		1,000

The reduction in the payables balance resulted from paying out $1,000 more cash than was recorded in purchases. Cost of goods sold and other expenses have already been adjusted to represent the goods and services purchased, so a $1,000 credit adjustment is needed to convert the purchases to the amount paid; that is, to the operating cash outflow.

16. **Dividends Payable on Term Preferred Shares.** The summary entry explaining the net change in this account is as follows:

Dividend Expense (income statement expense)	2,000	
Dividends Payable (on term preferred shares)		2,000

The increase in the liability account results from recognizing more dividends as an expense (these shares are a financial liability in substance) than dividends paid in the year. Therefore, $2,000 is added back to net income to adjust the operating cash flows to equal cash dividends paid in 2014.

17. **Accrued Liabilities.** The $4,000 increase in this account was caused by recognizing $4,000 more expense than payments in the year. The entry is as follows:

Salaries and Wages Expense (assumed)	4,000	
Accrued Liabilities		4,000

To adjust, $4,000 is added back (debited) to the cash provided by net income as reported.

18. **Income Taxes Payable.** The decrease in this account occurred because Yoshi Corporation paid out more cash than the expense reported, reflected by this entry:

Income Tax Payable	13,000	
Cash		13,000

Because the expense reported has been deducted in determining the income number, an additional $13,000 outflow is deducted or credited on the work sheet.

19. **Bonds Payable.** The change in the Bonds Payable account is assumed to be explained by the following entry as a result of amortizing the bond discount netted with the liability:

Interest Expense	300	
Bonds Payable		300

That is, $300 of the interest expense did not require any cash, so an adjustment is needed to the net income in the operating activities section.

20. **Term Preferred Shares.** Of the increase, $54,000 has already been explained above. The remaining increase is assumed to have resulted from the following entry, a $6,000 financing inflow:

Cash	6,000	
Term Preferred Shares		6,000

21. **Deferred Tax Liability.** The increase in this account is due to the deferral of the tax liability to future periods, reflected in this entry:

Deferred Tax Expense	3,000	
Deferred Tax Liability		3,000
Deferred Tax Expense—OCI	1,000	
Deferred Tax Liability		1,000

The change in the statement of financial position account is explained, and the non-cash portion of income tax expense is adjusted by adding back $4,000 to net income.

22. **Common Shares.** The following entries explain the change in this account over the year:

Retained Earnings	15,000	
Common Shares		15,000
Cash	144,000	
Common Shares		144,000
Common Shares	21,600	
Retained Earnings	12,400	
Cash		34,000

The first entry records the stock dividend. As discussed earlier, this is a non-cash activity that, although explaining the change in two statement of financial position accounts, is not part of the statement of cash flows. The second entry records the inflow of cash for shares sold—a financing activity. The third entry records the repurchase and cancellation of the company's own shares.

23. **Retained Earnings.** Most of the changes in this account have already been dealt with above. One additional entry is needed to explain the remainder of the change:

Retained Earnings (dividends)	6,000	
Cash		6,000

This entry records a financing outflow of cash for dividends on common shares.

Completing the Work Sheet

All that remains to complete the statement of financial position portion of the work sheet is to credit the Cash account by $27,000 and debit the Cash Equivalents by $10,000, netting to a $17,000 credit or decrease in cash. The $17,000 debit to balance this work sheet entry is inserted at the bottom of the work sheet. The debit and credit columns of the reconciling items are then totalled and balanced.

If the direct method of determining cash flows from operating activities is preferred, one change is needed to the above procedures. Instead of debiting the net income of $117,700 and using this as the starting point to represent cash inflows from operations, the individual revenues, expenses, gains, and losses (netting to $117,700) are transferred to the Operating Activities section line by line. When income statement items differ from the actual cash generated or used, adjustments are made to the specific line items affected.

The analysis is simplified if items that will be reported together on the final statement are grouped together, and if all income tax amounts are grouped as well. This step and the adjustments that are needed in the Operating Activities section are shown in Illustration 22A-3. The adjustments in the Operating Activities section are exactly the same as the ones that were made using the indirect method, except that they are made to a specific line item instead of net income.

Illustration 22A-3

Operating Activities Work Sheet—Direct Method

DIRECT METHOD

		Debits (inflows)		Credits (outflows)
Cash Flows				
Operating activities:				
Receipts from customers	(1)	923,200	(3)	55,250
Received from investment in associate				
(Portel Corp.)	(1)	5,500	(6)	5,500
	(6)	2,000		
Received on FV-NI investment transactions	(1)	1,300		
	(2)	5,000		
Payments for goods and services	(4)	8,000	(1)	395,400
	(5)	500	(1)	134,600
	(8)	40,000	(1)	12,000
	(10)	1,500	(15)	1,000
	(12)	2,250		
Payments to employees	(17)	4,000	(1)	200,000
Interest and dividend payments	(19)	300	(1)	11,300
	(16)	2,000		
Loss on Impairment (goodwill)	(11)	2,400	(1)	2,400
Income taxes paid	(21)	3,000	(1)	52,500
			(18)	13,000
Depreciation expense	(13)	11,500	(1)	14,600
	(14)	3,100		
Cash received on sale of land	(1)	10,500	(9)	10,500

The bottom part of the work sheet in Illustration 22A-2 (and above) provides the necessary information to facilitate the preparation of the formal statement shown in Illustrations 22-19 (direct method) and 22-20 (indirect method).

SUMMARY OF LEARNING OBJECTIVE FOR APPENDIX 22A

11 Use a work sheet to prepare a statement of cash flows.

A work sheet can be used to organize the analysis and cash flow information needed to prepare a statement of cash flows. This method accounts for all changes in the balances of non-cash statement of financial position accounts from the period's beginning to the end, identifying all operating, investing, and financing cash flows in the process. The statement of cash flows is prepared from the cash flow information accumulated at the bottom of the work sheet.

Quiz

Brief Exercises

All assignment material with an asterisk (*) relates to the appendix to the chapter.

(LO 3) **BE22-1** Stamford Corporation, a private company, has reported increasing profit every year for the past five years. Stamford would like to expand operations by adding three new retail stores within the next three years, and is seeking a loan from its bank to help fund the expansion. In Stamford's most recent statement of financial position, the company reported a positive cash balance, and a current ratio of 2. Stamford's controller believes that a statement of cash flows "would not be useful to the bank manager in making their decision because Stamford has a solid financial position and has had increasing profit every year for the past five years." From the perspective of Stamford's bank manager, (a) discuss the importance of positive cash flows, and (b) discuss the purpose and usefulness of the statement of cash flows.

(LO 3) **BE22-2** As of December 31, 2014, Bajac Inc. has the following balances: Cash in bank, $108,000; Investment in preferred shares (retractable, purchased by Bajac within 90 days of maturity date), $120,000; Investment in common shares (to be sold within 30 days); and Cash (legally restricted for an upcoming long-term debt retirement), $245,000. Determine the December 31, 2014 cash and cash equivalents amount for the 2014 statement of cash flows under (a) IFRS and (b) ASPE.

(LO 3) **BE22-3** Mullins Corp. reported the following items on its June 30, 2014 trial balance and on its comparative trial balance one year earlier:

	June 30, 2014	June 30, 2013
Cash in bank	$12,100	$ 9,460
Petty cash	100	125
Investment in shares of GTT Ltd. (to be sold within 60 days)	6,500	–0–
Investment in Canada 60-day treasury bills	22,000	28,300
Accounts payable	66,300	69,225
Temporary bank overdraft, chequing account	13,800	1,000

Determine the June 30, 2014 cash and cash equivalents amount for the 2014 statement of cash flows, and calculate the change in cash and cash equivalents since June 30, 2013.

(LO 4) **BE22-4** Maddox Corporation had the following activities in 2014.

1. Sold land for $180,000.

2. Purchased investment in common shares for $15,000, for trading purposes.

3. Purchased inventory for $845,000.

4. Received $73,000 cash from bank borrowings.

5. Received interest for $11,000.

6. Purchased equipment for $495,000.

7. Issued common shares for $350,000.

8. Recorded an unrealized gain of $3,000 on investments accounted for using the fair value through net income (FV-NI) model.

9. Purchased investments in bonds, reported at amortized cost for $61,000.

10. Declared and paid a dividend of $18,000 (charged to retained earnings).

11. Investments in bonds reported at amortized cost, with a carrying amount of $410,000, were sold for $415,000.

12. Dividends were received for $4,000.

Calculate the amount that Maddox should report as net cash provided (used) by investing activities on its statement of cash flows under (a) IFRS and (b) ASPE. Under IFRS, Maddox would adopt the policy of classifying interest and dividends paid as financing activities, and interest and dividends received as investing activities.

(LO 4) **BE22-5** Tang Corporation, which follows ASPE, had the following activities in 2014.

1. Paid $870,000 of accounts payable.

2. Paid $12,000 of bank loan interest.

3. Issued common shares for $200,000.

4. Paid $170,000 in dividends (charged to retained earnings).

5. Collected $150,000 in notes receivable.

6. Issued $410,000 of bonds payable.

7. Paid $20,000 on bank loan principal.

8. Issued a stock dividend in the amount of $11,000.

9. Received $5,000 in interest from an investment in bonds.

10. Purchased at a cost of $47,000 the corporation's own shares.

Calculate the amount that Tang should report as net cash provided (used) by financing activities in its 2014 statement of cash flows.

(LO 4) BE22-6 Watson Corporation, which uses ASPE, is using the indirect method to prepare its 2014 statement of cash flows. A list of items that may affect the statement follows:

—— **(a)** Increase in accounts receivable

—— **(b)** Decrease in accounts receivable

—— **(c)** Issue of shares

—— **(d)** Depreciation expense

—— **(e)** Sale of land at carrying amount

—— **(f)** Sale of land at a gain

—— **(g)** Payment of dividends charged to retained earnings

—— **(h)** Purchase of land and building

—— **(i)** Purchase of long-term investment in bonds, reported at amortized cost

—— **(j)** Increase in accounts payable

—— **(k)** Decrease in accounts payable

—— **(l)** Loan from bank by signing note payable

—— **(m)** Purchase of equipment by issuing a note payable

—— **(n)** Increase in inventory

—— **(o)** Issue of bonds

—— **(p)** Retirement of bonds

—— **(q)** Sale of equipment at a loss

—— **(r)** Purchase of corporation's own shares

—— **(s)** Acquisition of equipment using a capital/finance lease

—— **(t)** Conversion of bonds into common shares

—— **(u)** Goodwill impairment loss

Match each code in the list that follows to the items above to show how each item will affect Watson's 2014 statement of cash flows. Unless stated otherwise, assume that the transaction was for cash.

Code Letter	Effect
A	Added to net income in the operating section
D	Deducted from net income in the operating section
R-I	Cash receipt in investing section
P-I	Cash payment in investing section
R-F	Cash receipt in financing section
P-F	Cash payment in financing section
N	Non-cash investing and/or financing activity disclosed in notes to the financial statement

(LO 4, 8) BE22-7 In 2014, Abbotsford Inc. issued 1,000 common shares for land worth $149,000.

(a) Prepare Abbotsford's journal entry to record the transaction.

(b) Indicate the effect that the transaction has on cash.

(c) Indicate how the transaction is reported on the statement of cash flows.

(LO 4, 8) BE22-8 Wong Textiles Ltd. entered into a capital lease obligation during 2014 to acquire a cutting machine. The amount recorded to the Equipment under Capital Leases account and the corresponding Obligations under Capital

(LO 5, 6) BE22-9 Azure Corporation had the following 2014 income statement data:

Leases account was $85,000 at the date of signing the lease. Wong paid the first annual lease payment of $2,330 at the date of signing, and by the end of 2014 had recorded depreciation of $1,100 for the machine. Using the direct format, provide the necessary disclosure for these transactions on the statement of cash flows.

Sales	$205,000
Cost of goods sold	120,000
Gross profit	85,000
Operating expenses (includes depreciation of $21,000)	50,000
Net income	$ 35,000

The following accounts increased during 2014 by the amounts shown: Accounts Receivable, $17,000; Inventory, $11,000; Accounts Payable, $13,000; Mortgage Payable, $40,000. Prepare the cash flows from operating activities section of Azure's 2014 statement of cash flows using the direct method.

(LO 5, 7) BE22-10 Using the information from BE22-9 for Azure Corporation, prepare the cash flows from operating activities section of Azure's 2014 statement of cash flows using the indirect method.

(LO 6) BE22-11 At January 1, 2014, Apex Inc. had accounts receivable of $72,000. At December 31, 2014, the accounts receivable balance was $59,000. Sales revenue for 2014 was $420,000. Sales returns and allowances for the year were $10,000. Purchase discounts were in the amount of $4,200 and sales discounts were $1,000. Calculate Apex's 2014 cash receipts from customers.

(LO 6) BE22-12 Ciao Corporation had January 1 and December 31 balances as follows:

	1/1/14	12/31/14
Inventory	$90,000	$113,000
Accounts payable	61,000	69,000

For 2014, the cost of goods sold was $550,000. Calculate Ciao's 2014 cash paid to suppliers of inventory.

(LO 6) BE22-13 Kamsky Inc., which follows ASPE, had the following balances and amounts appear on its comparative financial statements at year end:

	Dec. 31, 2014	Dec. 31, 2013
Income taxes payable	$1,200	$1,400
Future tax asset (current)	300	-0-
Future tax liability (non-current)	1,950	1,600
Income tax expense	2,500	2,100
Future tax benefit	(600)	(200)

(a) Calculate income taxes paid and discuss the related disclosure requirements under ASPE, if any. (b) If Kamsky followed IFRS instead of ASPE, would the disclosure requirements for income taxes paid be any different?

(LO 6, 7) BE22-14 Majestic Corporation had the following 2014 income statement data:

Revenues	$100,000
Expenses	60,000
	$ 40,000

In 2014, Majestic had the following activity in selected accounts:

	Accounts Receivable				Allowance for Doubtful Accounts	
1/1/14	20,000					1,200 1/1/14
Revenues	100,000	1,000	Writeoffs	Writeoffs	1,000	1,540 Bad debt expense
12/31/14	29,000	90,000	Collections			12/31/14
					1,740	

Prepare Majestic's cash flows from operating activities section of the statement of cash flows using (a) the direct method, and (b) the indirect method.

(LO 7) BE22-15 October Corporation reported net income of $46,000 in 2014. Depreciation expense was $17,000 and unrealized losses on FV-NI investments were $3,000. The following accounts changed as indicated in 2014:

Accounts Receivable	$11,000 increase
Investments in Bonds, at Amortized Cost	16,000 increase
Deferred Tax Assets	2,000 decrease
Inventory	7,400 increase
Notes Payable (non-trade)	15,000 decrease
Accounts Payable	9,300 increase

Calculate the net cash provided by operating activities.

(LO 7) **BE22-16** In 2014, Oswald Corporation reported a net loss of $56,000. Oswald's only net income adjustments were depreciation expense of $87,000 and an increase in accounts receivable of $8,100. Calculate Oswald's net cash provided (used) by operating activities.

(LO 11) *BE22-17** Indicate in general journal form how the following items would be entered in a work sheet to prepare the statement of cash flows.

(a) Net income is $207,000.

(b) Cash dividends declared (charged to retained earnings) and paid totalled $60,000.

(c) Equipment was purchased for $114,000.

(d) Equipment that originally cost $40,000 and had accumulated depreciation of $32,000 was sold for $13,000.

Exercises

(LO 2, 7, 9) **E22-1** (Preparation of Statement from Transactions, and Explanation of Changes in Cash Flow) Strong House Inc. had the following condensed statement of financial position at the end of operations for 2013:

STRONG HOUSE INC.
Statement of Financial Position
For the Year Ended December 31, 2013

Cash	$ 10,000	Current liabilities	$ 14,500
Current assets (non-cash)	34,000	Long-term notes payable	30,000
Investment in bonds, at amortized cost	40,000	Bonds payable	32,000
Plant assets	57,500	Share capital	80,000
Land	38,500	Retained earnings	23,500
	$180,000		$180,000

Strong House Inc. follows IFRS and chooses to classify dividends paid as financing activities and interest paid as operating activities on the statement of cash flows.

During 2014, the following occurred:

1. Strong House Inc. sold part of its investment portfolio in bonds for $15,500, resulting in a gain of $500.

2. Dividends totalling $19,000 were paid to shareholders.

3. A parcel of land was purchased for $5,500.

4. Common shares with a fair value of $20,000 were issued.

5. Bonds payable of $10,000 were retired at par.

6. Heavy equipment was purchased through the issuance of $32,000 of bonds.

7. Net income for 2014 was $42,000 after allowing for depreciation on Strong House's plant assets of $13,550. The amount of interest paid during 2014 was $4,150 and the amount of income taxes paid was $19,500.

8. Both current assets (other than cash) and current liabilities remained at the same amount.

Instructions

(a) Prepare a statement of cash flows for 2014 using the indirect method.

(b) Draft a one-page letter to Mr. Gerald Brauer, president of Strong House Inc., in which you briefly explain the changes within each major cash flow category. Refer to the statement of cash flows whenever necessary.

(c) Prepare a statement of financial position at December 31, 2014, for Strong House Inc.

(d) Comment briefly about why the statement of cash flows used to be called a statement of changes in financial position.

(LO 4) E22-2 (Classification of Transactions and Calculation of Cash Flows) The following are selected statement of financial position accounts of Strong Ltd. at December 31, 2013, and 2014, and the increases or decreases in each account from 2013 to 2014. Also presented is the selected income statement and other information for the year ended December 31, 2014.

Statement of Financial Position (selected accounts)

	2014	2013	Increase (Decrease)
Assets			
Accounts receivable	$ 84,000	$ 74,000	$10,000
FV-NI investments	41,000	49,000	(8,000)
Property, plant, and equipment	177,000	147,000	30,000
Accumulated depreciation	(78,000)	(67,000)	11,000
Liabilities and shareholders' equity			
Bonds payable	149,000	146,000	3,000
Dividends payable	8,000	5,000	3,000
Common shares	31,000	22,000	9,000
Retained earnings	104,000	91,000	13,000

Income Statement (selected information)
For the Year Ended December 31, 2014

Sales revenue	$295,000
Depreciation expense	33,000
Gain on sale of FV-NI investments	5,000
Unrealized loss on FV-NI investments	3,000
Gain on sale of equipment	14,500
Net income	31,000

Additional information:

1. During 2014, equipment costing $45,000 was sold for cash.

2. Accounts receivable relate to sale of inventory.

3. During 2014, $20,000 of bonds payable were issued in exchange for property, plant, and equipment. All bonds were issued at par.

4. During the year, trading investments accounted for at FV-NI were sold for $22,000. Additional investments were purchased.

Instructions

Determine the category (operating, investing, or financing) and the amount that should be reported in the statement of cash flows for the following items, assuming Strong Ltd. follows ASPE:

(a) Cash received from customers

(b) Payments for purchases of property, plant, and equipment

(c) Proceeds from the sale of equipment

(d) Cash dividends paid

(e) Redemption of bonds payable

(f) Proceeds from the sale of FV-NI investments

(g) Purchase of FV-NI investments

(LO 4, 5, E22-3 (Statement of Cash Flows—Direct and Indirect Methods) Angus Farms Ltd., which uses ASPE, had the
6, 7, 8) following transactions during the fiscal year ending December 31, 2014.

1. On May 1, a used tractor was sold at auction. The information concerning this transaction included:

Original cost of the tractor	$52,000
Carrying amount of tractor at date of sale	14,000
Cash proceeds obtained at sale	22,500

2. After the seeding season, on June 15, 2014, a plough with an original cost of $6,000 and a carrying amount of $500 was discarded.

3. On September 1, 2014, a new plough was purchased for $7,700.

4. On December 30, a section of land was sold to a neighbouring farm called Clear Pastures Ltd. The original cost of the land was $45,000. To finance the purchase, Clear Pastures gave Angus a three-year mortgage note in the amount of $75,000 that carries interest at 5%, with interest payable annually each December 30.

5. On December 31, 2014, depreciation was recorded on the farm equipment in the amount of $12,600.

Instructions

(a) Prepare the journal entries that recorded the transactions during the year.

(b) Prepare the sections of the statement of cash flows of Angus Farms Ltd. to report the transactions provided, using the indirect format.

(c) Prepare the sections of the statement of cash flows of Angus Farms Ltd. to report the transactions provided, using the direct format.

(d) What results do you notice when comparing the information arrived at in parts (b) and (c) above?

(LO 4, 6, 7, 8, 9) **E22-4   (Statement Presentation of Transactions—Investment Using Equity Method)** The following selected account balances were taken from the financial statements of Blumberg Inc. concerning its long-term investment in shares of Black Inc. over which it has had significant influence since 2011:

	Dec. 31, 2014	Dec. 31, 2013
Investment in Black Inc.	$494,600	$422,000
Investment income recorded for Black	13,200	11,800

At December 31, 2014, the following information is available:

1. Blumberg purchased additional common shares in Black Inc. on January 2, 2014, for $65,000. As a result of this purchase, Blumberg's ownership interest in Black increased to 40%.

2. Black reported income of $33,000 for the year ended December 31, 2014.

3. Black declared and paid total dividends of $14,000 on its common shares for the year ended December 31, 2014.

Instructions

(a) Prepare a reconciliation of the Investment in Black Inc. account from December 31, 2013, to December 31, 2014, assuming Blumberg Inc. uses the equity method for this investment.

(b) Prepare a table that contrasts the direct and indirect methods for presenting all transactions related to the Black Inc. investment on Blumberg's statement of cash flows based on the assumption that Black uses IFRS and adopts the policy of classifying dividends received as investing activities. Be specific about the classification in the statement for each item that is reported.

(c) Prepare a table that contrasts the direct and indirect methods for presenting all transactions related to the Black Inc. investment on Blumberg's statement of cash flows based on the assumption that Black uses ASPE and must therefore classify dividends received as operating cash flows.

(LO 4, 7) **E22-5   (Partial Statement of Cash Flows—Indirect Method)** The following accounts appear in the ledger of Tanaka Limited, which uses IFRS, and has adopted the policy of classifying dividends paid as operating activities:

Retained Earnings		Dr.	Cr.	Bal.
Jan. 1, 2014	Credit balance			$ 42,000
Aug. 15	Dividends (cash)	$15,000		27,000
Dec. 31	Net income for 2014		$40,000	67,000

Machinery		Dr.	Cr.	Bal.
Jan. 1, 2014	Debit balance			$140,000
Aug. 3	Purchase of machinery	$62,000		202,000
Sept. 10	Cost of machinery constructed	48,000		250,000
Nov. 15	Machinery sold		$56,000	194,000

Accumulated Depreciation—Machinery		Dr.	Cr.	Bal.
Jan. 1, 2014	Credit balance			$84,000
Nov. 15	Accumulated depreciation on machinery sold	25,200		58,800
Dec. 31	Depreciation for 2014		$16,800	75,600

(LO 4, 7) E22-6 (Analysis of Changes in Capital Asset Accounts and Related Cash Flows) MacAskill Mills Limited, which uses ASPE, engaged in the following transactions in 2014.

1. The Land account increased by $58,000 over the year: Land that originally cost $60,000 was exchanged along with a cash payment of $3,000 for another parcel of land valued at $91,000. Additional land was acquired later in the year in a cash purchase.

2. The Equipment account had a balance of $67,500 at the beginning of the year and $62,000 at the end. The related Accumulated Depreciation account decreased over the same period from a balance of $24,000 to $15,200. Fully depreciated equipment that cost $10,000 was sold during the year for $1,000. In addition, equipment that cost $3,000 and had a carrying amount of $700 was discarded, and new equipment was acquired and paid for.

3. A five-year capital lease for specialized equipment was entered into halfway through the year. Under the terms of the lease, the company agreed to make five annual payments (in advance) of $25,000, after which the equipment will revert to the lessor. The present value of these lease payments at the 10% rate that is implicit in the lease was $104,247. The first payment was made as agreed.

Instructions

For each listed item:

(a) Prepare the underlying journal entries that were made by MacAskill Mills during 2014 to record all information related to the changes in each capital asset account and associated accounts over the year.

(b) Identify the amount(s) of the cash flows that result from the transactions and events recorded, and determine the classification of each one.

(c) Prepare the corresponding amounts to those prepared in part (b) for the operating activities section of the statement of cash flows prepared using the indirect method.

(d) Comment on the results obtained in (b) and (c) above.

(LO 4, 8) E22-7 (Statement Presentation of Transactions—Indirect Method) Each of the following items must be considered in preparing a statement of cash flows (indirect method) for Bastille Inc., which uses ASPE, for the year ended December 31, 2014.

1. Plant assets that cost $40,000 six years before and were being depreciated on a straight-line basis over 10 years with no estimated residual value were sold for $5,300.

2. During the year, 10,000 common shares were issued for $41 cash per share.

3. Uncollectible accounts receivable in the amount of $27,000 were written off against the allowance for doubtful accounts.

4. The company sustained a net loss for the year of $10,000. Depreciation amounted to $22,000. A gain of $9,000 was reported on the sale of land for $39,000 cash.

5. A three-month Canadian treasury bill was purchased for $50,000 on November 13, 2014. The company uses a cash and cash-equivalent basis for its statement of cash flows.

6. Patent amortization for the year was $18,000.

7. The company exchanged common shares for a 40% interest in TransCo Corp. for $900,000.

8. The company accrued an unrealized loss on investments accounted for at FV-NI.

Instructions

Identify where each item is reported in the statement of cash flows, if at all.

(LO 4, 8) E22-8 (Statement Presentation of Transactions—Equity Accounts) The following selected account balances are taken from the financial statements of Mandrich Inc. at year end and prepared using IFRS:

	2014	2013
Preferred shares classified as equity		
Common shares: 9,000 shares in 2014, 10,000 shares in 2013	$145,000	$145,000
Contributed surplus—reacquisition of common shares	142,000	160,000
Cash dividends—preferred	3,500	-0-
Stock dividends—common	6,250	6,250
Retained earnings (balance after closing entries)	14,000	4,000
	300,000	240,000

Instructions

Show how the information posted in the accounts is reported on a statement of cash flows by preparing a partial statement of cash flows using the indirect method. The loss on sale of machinery (November 15) was $5,800.

At December 31, 2014, the following information is available:

1. Mandrich Inc. repurchased 2,000 common shares during 2014. The repurchased shares had a weighted average cost of $32,000.

2. During 2014, 1,000 common shares were issued as a stock dividend.

3. Mandrich Inc. chooses to classify dividends paid as financing activities.

Instructions

(a) Calculate net income for the fiscal year ending December 31, 2014.

(b) Provide the necessary disclosure for all of Mandrich Inc.'s transactions on the statement of cash flows. Also state the section of the statement of cash flows in which each item is reported. Where there are choices or options in the classification, provide details of the options available.

(c) Does Mandrich Inc. have other choices in classifying dividends paid on the statement of cash flows?

(LO 4, 8, 9) E22-9 (Partial Statement of Cash Flows—Operating and Finance Leases) Wagner Inc. is a large Canadian public company that uses IFRS. A lease for a fleet of trucks has been capitalized and the lease amortization schedule for the first three lease payments appears below. The trucks have an economic life of eight years. The lease term is from July 1, 2013, to June 30, 2020, and the trucks must be returned to the lessor at the end of this period.

WAGNER INC.
Lease Amortization Schedule

Date	Annual Lease Payments	Interest (8%) on Unpaid Obligation	Reduction of Lease Obligation	Balance of Lease Obligation
				$3,064,470
July 1, 2013	$545,000		$545,000	2,519,470
July 1, 2014	545,000	$201,558	343,442	2,176,028
July 1, 2015	545,000	174,082	370,918	1,805,110

Instructions

(a) Prepare the journal entries and any year-end (December 31) adjusting journal entries made by Wagner Inc. in 2013 and 2014.

(b) Prepare a partial comparative statement of cash flows for the 2013 and 2014 fiscal years along with any additional disclosure notes. Wagner Inc. has adopted the policy of classifying any interest paid as operating activities on the statement of cash flows.

(c) Repeat parts (a) and (b) assuming that the lease must be recorded as an operating lease.

(d) From the perspective of an external user, which statement of cash flows seems to present a more favourable picture of Wagner Inc.'s financial performance? Comment briefly.

Digging Deeper

(LO 4, 8, 10) E22-10 (Classification of Major Transactions and Events) Dunrobin Industries Ltd., which uses IFRS, had the following transactions during its most recent fiscal year.

1. Acquired raw materials inventory.

2. Declared a cash dividend on common shares.

3. Collected cash from tenants for rents.

4. Acquired a 4% interest in a supplier company's shares accounted as FV-NI. (Management's intention is not to trade the shares.)

5. Made the annual contribution to the employees' pension plan.

6. Leased new equipment under a finance lease.

7. Leased additional office space under an operating lease.

8. Paid the semi-annual interest on outstanding debentures and amortized the associated premium.

9. Paid the supplier for the acquisition in item 1 above.

10. Acquired land by issuing preferred shares.

11. Paid the car dealership for a new fleet of vehicles for the sales staff.

12. Collected a dividend on the investment made in item 4 above.

13. Sold the old fleet of sales vehicles at an amount in excess of their carrying amount.

14. Distributed additional shares following a declaration of a 5% stock dividend.

Dunrobin Industries Ltd. has adopted the policy of classifying dividends received as investing activities, dividends paid as operating activities, and interest paid as a financing activity on the cash flow statement.

Instructions

Identify each transaction listed above as

(a) an operating activity,

(b) an investing activity,

(c) a financing activity,

(d) a significant non-cash investing or financing activity, or

(e) none of these options.

Where there are choices or options in the classification, provide details of the options available.

(LO 4,   **E22-11   (Classification of Transactions)** Baird Corp. had the following activity in its most recent year of operations:
8, 10)

1. Purchase of equipment

2. Redemption of bonds

3. Conversion of bonds into common shares

4. Sale of building

5. Depreciation of equipment

6. Exchange of equipment for furniture of equal fair value

7. Issue of common shares

8. Amortization of intangible assets

9. Purchase of company's own shares

10. Issue of bonds for land

11. Impairment loss on goodwill

12. Unrealized holding loss on investment accounted at fair value with gains and losses in net income

13. Payment of dividends on common shares

14. Increase in interest receivable on notes receivable

15. Pension expense in excess of amount funded

16. Signing of a finance lease agreement for equipment

17. Payment of a monthly finance lease obligation

18. Purchase of a treasury bill as a cash equivalent

19. Payment on an operating lease agreement

20. Unrealized gain accrued on FV-NI equity security investments

21. Redemption of preferred shares classified as debt

22. Payments of principal on an operating line of credit

23. Payment of interest on an operating line of credit

24. Receipt of interest income on a note receivable

25. Receipt of dividends on an investment in common shares

26. Purchase of an investment in retractable preferred shares (that will mature within 90 days of purchase date)

Instructions

(a) Assume that Baird Corp. follows IFRS, and that the company has adopted the policy of classifying dividends received as operating activities, dividends paid as operating activities, interest received as investing activities, and interest paid as a financing activity on the cash flow statement. Using the indirect method, classify the items as one of the following:

1. an operating activity, added to net income;

2. an operating activity, deducted from net income;

3. an investing activity;

4. a financing activity;

5. a significant non-cash investing or financing activity; or

6. none of these options.

Where there are choices or options in the classification, provide details of the options available.

(b) Assume instead that Baird Corp. is a private company and has decided to apply ASPE. Identify which, if any, of your previous answers in part (a) would change under this assumption.

(LO 5, 6) E22-12 (Preparation of Operating Activities Section—Direct Method) Ellis Corp.'s income statement for the year ended December 31, 2014, had the following condensed information:

Sales revenue	$778,000
Operating expenses (excluding depreciation)	$499,000
Depreciation expense	66,000
Unrealized loss on FV-NI investments	4,000
Loss on sale of equipment	14,000
	583,000
Income before income tax	195,000
Income tax expense	58,000
Net income	$137,000

There were no purchases or sales of trading (FV-NI) investments during 2014.
Ellis's statement of financial position included the following comparative data at December 31:

	2014	2013
FV-NI investments	$22,000	$26,000
Accounts receivable	35,000	54,000
Accounts payable	44,000	31,000
Income tax payable	6,000	8,500

Instructions

(a) Prepare the operating activities section of the statement of cash flows using the direct method.

(b) Assume that Ellis Corp.'s current cash debt coverage ratio in 2013 was 2. Calculate the company's current cash debt coverage ratio in 2014, and discuss the results from the perspective of a creditor.

(LO 5, 6, 7) E22-13 (Cash Provided by Operating, Writeoff, and Recovery of Accounts Receivable) The following are the transactions from Izzy Inc. concerning the allowance for doubtful accounts.

1. Writeoff of accounts receivable $5,000

2. Recovery of accounts previously written off   3,500

3. Accrual for bad debt expense   4,400

Assume these are the only transactions for the year.

Instructions

(a) Record the above transactions.

(b) Prepare the reporting necessary on a partial statement of cash flows using

1. the direct method, and

2. the indirect method.

(LO 5, 6, 7) E22-14 (Statement of Cash Flows—Direct and Indirect Methods) Tuit Inc., a greeting card company that follows ASPE, had the following statements prepared as of December 31, 2014:

TUIT INC.
Comparative Statement of Financial Position
December 31

	2014	2013
Cash and cash equivalents	$ 53,625	$ 25,000
Accounts receivable	58,000	51,000
Inventory	40,000	60,000
Prepaid rent	5,000	4,000
Equipment	154,000	130,000
Accumulated depreciation—equipment	(35,000)	(25,000)
Goodwill	20,000	50,000
Total assets	$295,625	$295,000
Accounts payable	$ 46,000	$ 40,000
Income tax payable	4,000	6,000
Salaries and wages payable	8,000	4,000
Short-term loans payable	8,000	10,000
Long-term loans payable	60,000	69,000
Common shares	130,000	130,000
Retained earnings	39,625	36,000
Total liabilities and shareholders' equity	$295,625	$295,000

TUIT INC.
Income Statement
Year Ending December 31, 2014

Sales revenue		$338,150
Cost of goods sold		165,000
Gross margin		173,150
Operating expenses		120,000
Operating income		53,150
Interest expense	$11,400	
Impairment loss—goodwill	30,000	
Gain on sale of equipment	(2,000)	39,400
Income before tax		13,750
Income tax expense		4,125
Net income		$ 9,625

Additional information:

1. Dividends on common shares in the amount of $6,000 were declared and paid during 2014.

2. Depreciation expense is included in operating expenses, as are salaries and wages expense of $69,000.

3. Equipment with a cost of $20,000 that was 70% depreciated was sold during 2014.

Instructions

(a) Prepare a statement of cash flows using the direct method.

(b) Prepare a statement of cash flows using the indirect method.

(c) Does Tuit Inc. have any options on how to classify interest and dividends paid on the statement of cash flows?

(d) From the perspective of an investor who is interested in investing in mature, successful companies, comment on Tuit Inc.'s sources and uses of cash by analyzing the company's statement of cash flows.

Digging Deeper

(LO 5, 6, 7, 8, 9) E22-15 (Statement of Cash Flows—Direct and Indirect Methods) Guas Inc., a major retailer of bicycles and accessories, operates several stores and is a publicly traded company. The company is currently preparing its statement of cash flows. The comparative statement of financial position and income statement for Guas as of May 31, 2014, are as follows:

GUAS INC.
Statement of Financial Position
May 31, 2014, and May 31, 2013

	2014	2013
Current assets		
Cash	$ 33,250	$ 20,000
Accounts receivable	74,800	55,600
Inventory	188,700	199,000
Prepaid expenses	8,800	7,000
Total current assets	305,550	281,600
Plant assets	596,500	501,500
Less: Accumulated depreciation	148,000	122,000
Net plant assets	448,500	379,500
Total assets	$754,050	$661,100
Current liabilities		
Accounts payable	$123,000	$115,000
Salaries and wages payable	61,000	72,000
Interest payable	24,700	22,600
Total current liabilities	208,700	209,600
Long-term debt		
Bonds payable	75,000	100,000
Total liabilities	283,700	309,600
Shareholders' equity		
Common shares	335,750	280,000
Retained earnings	134,600	71,500
Total shareholders' equity	470,350	351,500
Total liabilities and shareholders' equity	$754,050	$661,100

GUAS INC.
Income Statement
For the Year Ended May 31, 2014

Sales	$1,345,800
Cost of goods sold	814,000
Gross margin	531,800
Expenses	
Salaries and wages expense	207,800
Interest expense	66,700
Other expenses	24,800
Depreciation expense	26,000
Total operating expenses	325,300
Operating income	206,500
Income tax expense	65,400
Net earnings	$ 141,100

The following is additional information about transactions during the year ended May 31, 2014, for Guas Inc., which follows IFRS.

1. Plant assets costing $95,000 were purchased by paying $44,000 in cash and issuing 5,000 common shares.

2. The "other expenses" relate to prepaid items.

3. In order to supplement its cash, Guas issued 4,000 additional common shares.

4. There were no penalties assessed for the retirement of bonds.

5. Cash dividends of $78,000 were declared and paid at the end of the fiscal year.

Instructions

(a) Compare and contrast the direct method and the indirect method for reporting cash flows from operating activities.

(b) Prepare a statement of cash flows for Guas Inc. for the year ended May 31, 2014, using the direct method. Support the statement with appropriate calculations, and provide all required disclosures.

(c) Using the indirect method, calculate only the net cash flow from operating activities for Guas Inc. for the year ended May 31, 2014.

(d) Does Guas Inc. have a choice in how it classifies dividends paid on the statement of cash flows?

(e) Assume that you are a shareholder of Guas Inc. What do you think of the dividend payout ratio that is highlighted in the statement of cash flows?

(LO 5, 6, **E22-16** **(Statement of Cash Flows—Direct and Indirect Methods)** Information from the statement of financial
7, 8, 10) position and statement of income are given below for North Road Inc., a company following ASPE, for the year ended
December 31.

Comparative Statement of Financial Position, at December 31

	2014	2013
Cash	$ 92,700	$ 47,250
Accounts receivable	90,800	37,000
Inventory	121,900	102,650
Investments in land	84,500	107,000
Property, plant, and equipment	290,000	205,000
Accumulated depreciation	–49,500	–40,000
	$630,400	$458,900
Accounts payable	$ 52,700	$ 48,280
Accrued liabilities	12,100	18,830
Notes payable	140,000	70,000
Common shares	250,000	200,000
Retained earnings	175,600	121,790
	$630,400	$458,900

Statement of Income, Year Ended December 31, 2014

Revenues		
Sales		$297,500
Gain on sale of equipment		8,750
		306,250
Expenses		
Cost of goods sold	$ 99,460	
Depreciation expense	58,700	
Operating expenses	14,670	
Income tax expense	39,000	
Interest expense	2,940	214,770
Net income		$ 91,480

Additional information:

1. Investments in land were sold at cost during 2014.
2. Equipment costing $56,000 was sold for $15,550, resulting in a gain.
3. Common shares were issued in exchange for some equipment during the year. No other shares were issued.
4. The remaining purchases of equipment were paid for in cash.

Instructions

(a) Prepare a statement of cash flows for the year ended December 31, 2014, using the indirect method.
(b) Prepare the operating activities section of the statement of cash flows using the direct method.
(c) Does North Road Inc. have a choice in how it classifies dividends paid on the statement of cash flows?

(LO 5, 6, 7, 9) **E22-17 (Statement of Cash Flows—Indirect and Direct Methods)** Condensed financial data of Tobita Limited, which follows ASPE, for 2014 and 2013 follow:

TOBITA LIMITED
Comparative Statement of Financial Position
December 31

	2014	2013
Cash	$1,935	$1,150
FV-NI investments	1,300	1,420
Accounts receivable	1,750	1,300
Inventory	1,600	1,900
Plant assets	1,900	1,700
Accumulated depreciation	(1,200)	(1,170)
	$7,285	$6,300
Accounts payable	$1,200	$ 900
Accrued liabilities	200	250
Bonds payable	1,400	1,550
Share capital	1,900	1,700
Retained earnings	2,585	1,900
	$7,285	$6,300

TOBITA LIMITED
Income Statement
Year Ended December 31, 2014

Sales		$6,900
Cost of goods sold		4,700
Gross margin		2,200
Administrative expenses		910
Income from operations		1,290
Other expenses and gains		
Interest expense	$(20)	
Gain on sale of investments (FV-NI)	80	60
Income before tax		1,350
Income tax expense		405
Net income		$ 945

Additional information: During the year, $70 of common shares were issued in exchange for plant assets. No plant assets were sold in 2014.

Instructions

(a) Prepare a statement of cash flows using the indirect method.

(b) Prepare a statement of cash flows using the direct method.

(c) Does Tobita Limited have any options on how to classify interest and dividends paid on the statement of cash flows?

(d) What would you consider to be an alarming trend that is revealed by the statements that you have prepared? Is it as easy to notice this trend using the direct method, as in part (b)?

(LO 5, 7) **E22-18 (Preparation of Operating Activities Section—Indirect Method)** Data for Ellis Corp. are presented in E22-12.

Instructions

Prepare the operating activities section of the statement of cash flows using the indirect method.

(LO 6) **E22-19 (Statement of Cash Flows—Direct Method)** Huang Corp. uses the direct method to prepare its statement of cash flows and follows IFRS. Huang's trial balances at December 31, 2014, and 2013, was as follows:

	Dec. 31, 2014	Dec. 31, 2013
Debits		
Cash	$ 55,000	$ 31,000
Accounts Receivable	33,000	30,000
Inventory	31,000	47,000
Property, Plant, and Equipment	95,000	90,000
Cost of Goods Sold	253,000	380,000
Selling Expenses	138,000	172,000
Administrative Expenses	140,000	151,300
Interest Expense	15,600	28,600
Income Tax Expense	20,200	56,200
	$780,800	$986,100
Credits		
Allowance for Doubtful Accounts	$ 1,300	$ 1,100
Accumulated Depreciation	26,500	25,000
Accounts Payable	25,000	15,500
Income Taxes Payable	21,000	29,100
Deferred Income Tax Liability	5,300	4,600
8% Callable Bonds Payable	46,000	45,500
Common Shares	53,600	22,000
Retained Earnings	44,700	64,600
Sales Revenue	557,400	778,700
	$780,800	$986,100

Additional information:

1. Huang purchased $5,000 of equipment during 2014.
2. Bad debt expense for 2014 was $5,000 and writeoffs of uncollectible accounts totalled $4,800.
3. Huang has adopted the policy of classifying the payments of interest as financing activities on the statement of cash flows.

Instructions

Determine what amounts Huang should report in its statement of cash flows for the year ended December 31, 2014, for the following:

(a) Cash collected from customers

(b) Cash paid to suppliers of goods and services (excluding interest and income taxes)

(c) Cash paid for interest

(d) Cash paid for income taxes

(LO 6, 7) E22-20 (Accounting Cycle, Financial Statements, Cash Account, and Statement of Cash Flows) The following are transactions of Albert Sing, an interior design consultant, for the month of September 2014.

Sept.	1	Albert Sing began business as an interior design consultant, investing $31,000 for 8,000 common shares of the company, A.S. Design Limited.
	2	Purchased furniture and display equipment from Green Jacket Co. for $17,280.
	4	Paid rent for office space for the next three months at $680 per month.
	7	Employed a part-time secretary, Michael Bradley, at $300 per week.
	8	Purchased office supplies on account from Mann Corp. for $1,142.
	9	Received cash of $1,690 from clients for services performed.
	10	Paid miscellaneous office expenses, $430.
	14	Invoiced clients for consulting services, $5,120.
	18	Paid Mann Corp. on account, $600.
	19	Paid a dividend of $1.00 per share on the 5,000 outstanding shares.
	20	Received $980 from clients on account.
	21	Paid Michael Bradley two weeks of salary, $600.
	28	Invoiced clients for consulting services, $2,110.
	29	Paid the September telephone bill of $135 and miscellaneous office expenses of $85.

At September 30, the following information is available.

1. The furniture and display equipment has a useful life of five years and an estimated residual value of $1,500. Straight-line depreciation is appropriate.

2. One week's salary is owing to Michael Bradley.

3. Office supplies of $825 remain on hand.

4. Two months of rent has been paid in advance.

5. The invoice for electricity for September of $195 has been received, but not paid.

Instructions

(a) Prepare journal entries to record the transaction entries for September. Set up a T account for the Cash account and post all cash transactions to the account. Determine the balance of cash at September 30, 2014.

(b) Prepare any required adjusting entries at September 30, 2014.

(c) Prepare an adjusted trial balance at September 30, 2014.

(d) Prepare a statement of financial position and income statement for the month ended September 30, 2014.

(e) Prepare a statement of cash flows for the month of September 2014. Use the indirect method for the cash flows from operating activities.

(f) Recast the cash flow from operating activities section using the direct method.

(g) Compare the statement of cash flows in parts (e) and (f) with the Cash account prepared in part (a) above.

(h) As a creditor, what might you consider to be alarming that is revealed by the statement of cash flows prepared using the indirect method as required in part (e) above? Is this trend as easy to notice when the statement is prepared using the direct method as required in part (f) above?

(LO 7) E22-21   (Conversion of Net Income to Operating Cash Flow—Indirect Method) Shen Limited reported net income of $32,000 for its latest year ended March 31, 2014.

Instructions

For each of the five different situations involving the statement of financial position accounts that follow, calculate the cash flow from operations:

	Accounts Receivable March 31		Inventory March 31		Accounts Payable March 31	
	2014	2013	2014	2013	2014	2013
(a)	$20,000	$21,500	$16,500	$17,900	$ 9,000	$ 9,300
(b)	$23,000	$20,000	$17,300	$20,500	$14,600	$10,200
(c)	$20,000	–0–	$12,000	–0–	$ 7,000	–0–
(d)	$19,500	$21,000	$19,500	$15,600	$10,200	$14,100
(e)	$21,500	$24,000	$12,900	$14,000	$13,300	$11,300

(LO 11) *E22-22   (Work Sheet Analysis of Selected Transactions) The following transactions took place during the year 2014 for Mia Inc.

1. Convertible bonds payable with a carrying amount of $300,000 along with conversion rights of $9,000 were exchanged for unissued common shares.

2. The net income for the year was $410,000.

3. Depreciation charged on the building was $90,000.

4. Recorded the investment income earned from investment in Transot Ltd. using the equity method. Transot earnings for the year were $123,000 and Mia Inc. owns 28% of the outstanding common shares.

5. Old office equipment was traded in on the purchase of new equipment, resulting in the following entry:

Equipment	50,000	
Accumulated Depreciation—Equipment	30,000	
Equipment		40,000
Cash		34,000
Gain on Disposal of Equipment*		6,000

*The gain on disposal of equipment was credited to current operations as ordinary income.

6. Dividends in the amount of $123,000 were declared. They are payable in January 2015.

Instructions

For each item, use journal entries to show the adjustments and reconciling items that would be made on Mia Inc.'s work sheet for a statement of cash flows.

(LO 11) *E22-23 (Work Sheet Preparation) The comparative statement of financial position for Cosky Corporation follows:

	Dec. 31, 2014	Dec. 31, 2013
Cash	$ 16,500	$ 21,000
FV-NI investments	25,000	19,000
Accounts receivable	43,000	45,000
Allowance for doubtful accounts	(1,800)	(2,000)
Prepaid expenses	4,200	2,500
Inventory	81,500	65,000
Land	50,000	50,000
Buildings	125,000	73,500
Accumulated depreciation—buildings	(30,000)	(23,000)
Equipment	53,000	46,000
Accumulated depreciation—equipment	(19,000)	(15,500)
Delivery equipment	39,000	39,000
Accumulated depreciation—delivery equipment	(22,000)	(20,500)
Patents	15,000	-0-
	$379,400	$300,000
Accounts payable	$ 26,000	$ 16,000
Short-term notes payable (trade)	4,000	6,000
Accrued liabilities	3,000	4,600
Mortgage payable	73,000	53,400
Bonds payable	50,000	62,500
Share capital	150,000	106,000
Retained earnings	73,400	51,500
	$379,400	$300,000

Additional information:

1. Dividends of $15,000 were declared and paid in 2014.

2. There were no unrealized gains or losses on the FV-NI investments.

Instructions

Based on the information, prepare a work sheet for a statement of cash flows. Make reasonable assumptions as appropriate.

Problems

P22-1 Jeopardy Inc.'s CFO has just left the office of the company president after a meeting about the draft statement of financial position at April 30, 2014, and income statement for the year ended. (Both are reproduced below.) "Our liquidity position looks healthy," the president had remarked. "Look at the current and acid test ratios, and the amount of working capital we have. And between the goodwill writeoff and depreciation, we have almost $23 million of non-cash expenses. I don't understand why you've been complaining about our cash situation."

The CFO turns the draft financial statements over to you, the newest member of the accounting staff, along with extracts from the notes to the financial statements.

JEOPARDY INC.
Consolidated Statement of Financial Position
April 30, 2014, and 2013
(in $000s)

	2014	2013
Assets		
Cash and 60-day treasury bills	$ 3,265	$ 3,739
Accounts receivable	23,744	18,399
Inventory	26,083	21,561

	2014	2013
Income tax receivable	145	-0-
Prepaid expenses	1,402	1,613
Investments (Note 1)	54,639	45,312
Property, plant, and equipment (Note 2)	5,960	6,962
Deferred tax asset	37,332	45,700
Intangible assets—franchises (Note 3)	4,875	2,245
Goodwill	4,391	1,911
	-0-	12,737
	$107,197	$114,867

Liabilities

Current	2014	2013
Bank overdraft (temporary)	$ 6,844	$ 6,280
Accounts payable and accrued (Note 4)	3,243	4,712
Current portion of long-term debt	1,800	1,200
	11,887	12,192
Long-term debt (Note 5)	14,900	14,500

Shareholders' Equity

	2014	2013
Share capital (Note 6)	79,257	62,965
Retained earnings	1,153	25,210
	80,410	88,175
	$107,197	$114,867

Consolidated Statement of Income and Retained Earnings
Year Ended April 30, 2014, and 2013
(in $000s)

	2014	2013
Revenue		
Sales revenue	$89,821	$68,820
Interest and other	1,310	446
	91,131	69,266
Expenses		
Operating*	76,766	62,455
General and administrative*	13,039	12,482
Depreciation and amortization	10,220	11,709
Loss on impairment (goodwill)	12,737	-0-
Interest	1,289	1,521
Loss on sale of capital assets	394	-0-
	114,445	88,167
Loss before equity loss and income tax	(23,314)	(18,901)
Investment Income or Loss (Note 1)	(2,518)	100
Loss before income tax	(25,832)	(18,801)
Income tax	2,775	5,161
Net loss	(23,057)	(13,640)
Retained earnings, beginning of year	25,210	38,850
	2,153	25,210
Stock dividend	(1,000)	-0-
Retained earnings, end of year	$ 1,153	$25,210

*The operating and general and administrative expenses for 2014 include salaries and wages of $46,624.

Draft Notes to the Financial Statements
For the Year Ended April 30, 2014

Note 1. Investments

The company's investments at April 30 are as follows (in $000s):

	2014	2013
Compuco Ltd. (fair value 2014, $4.3 million)		
Shares, opening balance at equity	$6,962	$5,862
Equity income (loss)	(2,518)	100
	4,444	5,962
Shares, ending balance at equity	1,516	1,000
Other investments, at amortized cost	$5,960	$6,962

Note 2. Property, Plant, and Equipment

Additions to property, plant, and equipment for the current year amounted to $2,290,000. Proceeds from the disposal of property, plant, and equipment amounted to $250,000.

Note 3. Intangible Assets—Franchises

Franchise fees are amortized over the term of 10 years using the straight-line method.

Note 4. Accounts Payable and Accrued Liabilities (in $000s)

	2014	2013
Accounts payable—suppliers	$3,102	$4,562
Salaries and wages payable	141	150
	$3,243	$4,712

Note 5. Long-Term Debt (in $000s)

	2014	2013
Debentures	$12,500	$12,500
Bank term loans, due April 30, 2015, principal repayable at $150,000 a month (2013, at $100,000 a month)	4,200	3,200
	16,700	15,700
Current maturities	(1,800)	(1,200)
	$14,900	$14,500

Debentures bear interest at 9% per annum and are due in 2016. Bank term loans bear interest at 8% and the bank advanced $2.2 million during the year.

Note 6. Share Capital

On September 14, 2013, Jeopardy Inc. issued 3.8 million shares with special warrants. Net proceeds from issuing 3.8 million shares amounted to $14,393,000. Net proceeds from issuing 3.8 million warrants amounted to $899,000. On April 30, 2014, a stock dividend of $1 million was issued.

Instructions

Based on the assumption that Jeopardy Inc. follows ASPE:

(a) Prepare a statement of cash flows for the year ended April 30, 2014, on a non-comparative basis from the information provided. The CFO wants to use the direct method to report the company's operating cash flows this year. Include all required disclosures.

(b) Prepare a reconciliation of the 2014 net loss to cash provided from (used in) operations. This reconciliation is to be included in a note to the financial statements.

(c) Write a memo to the president of Jeopardy Inc. that explains why the company is experiencing a cash crunch when its liquidity ratios look acceptable and it has significant non-cash expenses.

P22-2 The following is Mann Corp.'s comparative statement of financial position at December 31, 2014, and 2013, with a column showing the increase (decrease) from 2013 to 2014:

(CICA adapted)

MANN CORP.
Comparative Statement of Financial Position

	2014	2013	Increase (Decrease)
Cash	$ 28,300	$ 44,400	$ (16,100)
Accounts receivable	846,400	766,700	79,700
Inventory	717,600	675,000	42,600
Property, plant, and equipment	3,066,400	2,866,400	200,000
Accumulated depreciation	(1,165,000)	(1,010,000)	155,000
Investment in Bligh Corp., at equity	288,000	266,000	22,000
Loan receivable	251,500	-0-	251,500
Total assets	$4,033,200	$3,608,500	
Bank loan	$ 142,600	$ 72,900	69,700
Accounts payable	753,600	814,600	(61,000)
Income tax payable	37,000	46,000	(9,000)
Dividends payable	65,000	85,000	(20,000)
Obligations under lease	270,000	-0-	270,000
Share capital, common	900,000	900,000	-0-
Retained earnings	1,865,000	1,690,000	175,000
Total liabilities and shareholders' equity	$4,033,200	$3,608,500	

Additional information:

1. On December 31, 2013, Mann acquired 25% of Bligh Corp.'s common shares for $266,000. On that date, the carrying value of Bligh's assets and liabilities was $1,064,000, which approximated their fair values. Bligh reported income of $88,000 for the year ended December 31, 2014. No dividend was paid on Bligh's common shares during the year.

2. During 2014, Mann loaned $285,000 to TMC Corp., an unrelated company. TMC made the first semi-annual principal repayment of $33,500, plus interest at 10%, on December 31, 2014.

3. On January 2, 2014, Mann sold equipment costing $70,000, with a carrying amount of $44,000, for $42,000 cash.

4. On December 31, 2014, Mann entered into a finance lease for equipment. The present value of the annual lease payments is $270,000, which equals the equipment's fair value. Mann made the first rental payment of $47,000 when due on January 2, 2015.

5. Net earnings for 2014 were $240,000. The amount of income taxes paid was $151,000.

6. The amount of interest paid during the year was $14,900 and the amount of interest earned was $9,400. Mann has adopted the policy of classifying interest received and interest paid as operating cash flows.

7. Mann declared and paid cash dividends for 2014 and 2013 as follows:

	2014	2013
Declared	Dec. 15, 2014	Dec. 15, 2013
Paid	Feb. 28, 2015	Feb. 28, 2014
Amount	$65,000	$85,000

8. The bank loan listed in the comparative statement of financial position represents a line of credit used to finance operating cash demands of the business. The limit set on the operating line by the lender is $600,000. Although the operating line functions similar to a bank overdraft, at no time during 2014 did the operating line become reduced to nil.

Instructions

(a) Prepare a statement of cash flows for Mann Corp. for the year ended December 31, 2014, using the indirect method, including any necessary additional note disclosures. Mann applies IFRS.

(b) Prepare a reconciliation of the change in Property, Plant, and Equipment's carrying amount to the amounts appearing on the statement of cash flows and corresponding notes.

(c) Financial statement preparers often use reconciliations of changes in major categories of statement of financial position accounts to balance the statement of cash flows, as required in part (b) above. What additional insight does this reconciliation reveal to a reader of the statement that is not as evident from the statement of cash flows?

(d) What other choices did Mann Corp. have available for the classification of interest received and paid? Would your opinion of Mann's liquidity position and ability to generate cash change from these alternative classifications?

(e) Is Mann Corp. in financial difficulty from a poor liquidity position and extremely small cash reserves? Comment.

(AICPA adapted)

P22-3 Comparative statement of financial position accounts of Laflamme Inc., which follows ASPE, and its statement of income for the year ending December 31, 2014, follow:

	December 31		
	2014	2013	Change
Cash	$ 46,000	$ 56,000	$ (10,000)
Cash equivalents (Note 1)	36,000	45,000	(9,000)
Accounts receivable	348,000	271,000	77,000
Prepaid insurance	16,000	35,000	(19,000)
Inventory	398,000	350,000	48,000
Supplies	13,000	17,000	(4,000)
Long-term investment, at equity (Note 7)	418,000	400,000	18,000
Land (Note 6)	640,000	500,000	140,000
Buildings (Note 3)	1,310,000	1,280,000	30,000
Accumulated depreciation—buildings	(400,000)	(360,000)	(40,000)
Equipment (Note 4)	632,000	640,000	(8,000)
Accumulated depreciation—equipment	(160,000)	(135,000)	(25,000)
Patent	100,000	100,000	
Accumulated amortization	(40,000)	(35,000)	(5,000)
	$3,357,000	$3,164,000	$193,000
Bank overdrafts (temporary)	$ –0–	$ 93,000	$ (93,000)
Accounts payable	165,000	150,000	15,000
Income tax payable	26,000	35,000	(9,000)
Accrued liabilities	57,000	41,000	16,000
Dividends payable	20,000	50,000	(30,000)
Long-term notes payable	420,000	460,000	(40,000)
Bonds payable	999,000	995,000	4,000
Preferred shares	504,000	380,000	124,000
Common shares	746,000	666,000	80,000
Retained earnings	420,000	294,000	126,000
	$3,357,000	$3,164,000	$193,000

Income Statement

Revenues		
Sales revenue	$999,000	
Investment income	90,000	$1,089,000
Expenses and Losses		
Cost of goods sold	314,000	
Sales commission expense	108,000	
Operating expenses (Note 5)	166,000	
Salaries and wages expense	104,000	
Interest expense	95,000	
Loss on sale of equipment (Note 4)	11,000	
Income tax expense	96,000	894,000
Net Income		$ 195,000

The following is additional information about Laflamme's transactions during the year ended December 31, 2014.

1. The cash equivalents are typically term deposits that are very liquid and mature on average in 60 days. The bank overdrafts are temporary and reverse within a few days. Laflamme has opted to show these as cash and cash equivalents on its statement of cash flows.
2. A stock dividend on common shares for $18,000 was declared and distributed during the year.
3. There were no disposals of buildings during the year 2014.
4. Equipment with an original cost of $46,000 and carrying amount of $14,000 was sold at a loss during the year.
5. All depreciation and amortization expense is included in operating expenses.

6. During the year, Laflamme obtained land with a fair value of $100,000 in exchange for its preferred shares.

7. Investment income includes the equity earnings of $62,000 from a long-term investment accounted for using the equity method and from interest revenue on the short-term investments referred to in item 1 above.

Instructions

(a) Prepare the statement of cash flows for the year ended December 31, 2014, for Laflamme Inc. using the indirect method. Prepare any additional disclosure notes that are required, including a table that shows the details of the cash and cash equivalents accounts at the end of each period.

(b) Prepare the operating activities section of the statement using the direct format.

(c) Does Laflamme Inc. have any options available to it concerning the classification of interest and dividends paid or received?

(d) If Laflamme Inc. chose to not treat the cash equivalents and the temporary bank overdrafts as cash and cash equivalents, how would transactions related to these accounts be reported on the statement of cash flows?

P22-4 Comparative statement of financial position accounts of Jensen Limited, which follows IFRS, appear below:

JENSEN LIMITED
Statement of Financial Position Accounts
December 31, 2014, and 2013

Debit balances	2014	2013
Cash	$ 80,000	$ 51,000
FV-NI investments	59,000	80,000
Accounts receivable	138,500	119,000
Inventory	75,000	61,000
Deferred tax asset	6,500	11,000
Equipment	70,000	48,000
Buildings	145,000	145,000
Land	40,000	25,000
	$614,000	$540,000

Credit balances	2014	2013
Allowance for doubtful accounts	$ 10,000	$ 8,000
Accumulated depreciation—equipment	21,000	14,000
Accumulated depreciation—buildings	37,000	28,000
Accounts payable	72,500	60,000
Income tax payable	12,000	10,000
Long-term notes payable	62,000	70,000
Accrued pension liability	7,500	10,000
Common shares	300,000	250,000
Retained earnings	92,000	90,000
	$614,000	$540,000

Data from Jensen's 2014 income statement follow:

Sales		$960,000
Less: Cost of goods sold		600,000
Gross profit		360,000
Less: Operating expenses		
(includes depreciation and bad debt expense)		250,000
Income from operations		110,000
Other revenues and expenses		
Interest expense	$ (10,000)	
Gain on FV-NI investments	24,000	
Loss on sale of equipment	(3,000)	11,000
Income before tax		121,000
Income tax		45,000
Net income		$ 76,000

Additional information:

1. Equipment that cost $10,000 and was 40% depreciated was sold in 2014.

2. Cash dividends were declared and paid during the year.

3. Common shares were issued in exchange for land.

4. FV-NI investments that had cost $35,000 and had a fair value of $37,000 at December 31, 2013, were sold during the year for proceeds of $50,000. Additional purchases of FV-NI investments were made during 2014.

5. Cost of goods sold includes $115,000 of direct labour and benefits and $11,700 of pension costs. Operating expenses include $76,000 of salaries and wages and $8,000 of pension expense.

6. Jensen has adopted the policy of classifying interest paid as operating activities and dividends paid as financing activities on the statement of cash flows.

7. No accounts receivable were written off during the year.

Instructions

(a) Prepare a statement of cash flows using the indirect method, including all required disclosures.

(b) Prepare the "Cash provided by (or used in) operating activities" section under the direct method.

(c) Does Jensen Limited have any options available for the classification of interest and dividends paid or received?

(d) Comment on the company's cash activities during the year.

(e) Assume that you are a shareholder of Jensen Limited. What do you think of the dividend payout ratio that is highlighted in the statement of cash flows?

Digging Deeper

P22-5 Ashley Limited, which follows ASPE, had the following information available at the end of 2014:

ASHLEY LIMITED
Comparative Statement of Financial Position
December 31, 2014, and 2013

	2014	2013
Cash	$ 25,400	$ 16,950
Accounts receivable	17,500	30,000
FV-NI investments	20,000	35,000
Inventory	42,000	12,000
Prepaid rent	3,000	
Prepaid insurance	2,100	900
Office supplies	1,000	750
Land	125,000	175,000
Buildings	350,000	350,000
Accumulated depreciation—Buildings	(105,000)	(87,500)
Equipment	525,000	400,000
Accumulated depreciation—Equipment	(130,000)	(112,000)
Patents	90,000	90,000
Accumulated amortization—Patents	(45,000)	(40,000)
Total assets	$921,000	$871,100
Temporary bank overdraft	$ -0-	$ 12,000
Accounts payable	22,000	20,000
Income tax payable	5,000	4,000
Salaries and wages payable	5,000	3,000
Short-term notes payable (trade)	10,000	10,000
Long-term notes payable (non-trade)	60,000	70,000
Deferred tax liability	30,000	25,000
Bonds payable	375,000	375,000
Common shares	260,000	237,500
Retained earnings	154,000	114,600
Total liabilities and shareholders' equity	$921,000	$871,100

ASHLEY LIMITED
Income Statement
Year Ended December 31, 2014

Sales revenue		$1,160,000
Cost of goods sold		(748,000)
Gross margin		412,000
Operating expenses		
Selling expenses	$ 19,200	
Administrative expenses	124,700	
Salaries and wages expense	92,000	
Depreciation and amortization expense	40,500	
Total operating expenses		(276,400)
Income from operations		135,600
Other revenues/expenses		
Gain on sale of land	8,000	
Investment income (Note 1)	6,400	
Interest expense	(51,750)	(37,350)
Income before taxes		98,250
Income tax expense		(39,400)
Net income		$ 58,850

Note 1: Investment income for the trading investments (FV-NI) includes dividend income of $2,400 and a gain on sale of $4,000 from investments at FV-NI.

Instructions

(a) Prepare a statement of cash flows for Ashley Limited using the direct method, accompanied by all required disclosures and a schedule that reconciles net income to cash flow from operations.

(b) Does Ashley Limited have any options available for the classification of interest and dividends paid or received?

(c) Prepare a memo for top management that summarizes and comments on the cash activities of Ashley in 2014.

(d) Management wants to provide more captions (headings) in the section for cash flow from operating activities. Recommend one additional caption that would help achieve this goal.

P22-6 Gao Limited, a publicly traded company, uses IFRS and had the following events and transactions occur in its fiscal year ending October 31, 2014. Although no dates are given, the events described are in chronological order.

1. Gao Limited repurchased common shares on the open market to allow stock options to its key employees to be exercised without a dilution effect resulting to the remaining shareholders. The weighted average issue price of the outstanding shares on the date of reacquisition was $34.20, and 4,000 shares were repurchased at a price of $44.40. On the date of declaration, Gao had contributed surplus for preferred share repurchases of $84,600 and contributed surplus for common share repurchases of $22,700.

2. Common shares were issued in partial settlement of a purchase of land. Gao paid $33,000 and 5,000 common shares for the land. On the date of the transaction, the common shares were trading at $41.50.

3. Gao has 8,000 preferred shares outstanding. These shares are limited in number and are not traded on the public stock exchange. Gao declared a property dividend to be paid to the preferred shareholders. Shareholders will receive for each preferred share held one share of Trivex Corp. Gao holds 8,000 shares of Trivex (2% of the outstanding shares), and had purchased them in 2012 for $68,400 (or $8.55 per share). The shares were held as an investment since 2012 and accounted for using the fair value through other comprehensive income (FV-OCI) model with recycling (transference). At the beginning of the fiscal year, the accumulated other comprehensive income had a debit balance in the amount of $2,350 relating only to the Trivex shares. The fair value of Trivex shares was $7.80 per share on the date of declaration of the property dividend. On the date of the dividend distribution, the fair value of the Trivex shares was $7.95. Because there were no longer any investments accounted for at FV-OCI, the reclassification entry needed to be recorded, in accordance with Gao's practice.

4. Gao declared a 5% stock dividend to the common shareholders. There were 43,200 common shares outstanding on the date of declaration and the market price of the common shares on that date was $39.70. The stock dividend was later distributed.

5. A shareholder, in an effort to persuade Gao to expand into her city, donated to the company a plot of land with an appraised value of $42,000.

Digging Deeper

6. Gao sold by subscription to an investment institution 10,000 common shares for $38.50 per share. The terms require 10% of the balance to be paid in cash immediately. The remainder is expected to be paid in fiscal year 2015.

7. Gao has term preferred shares on its statement of financial position. These shares are classified as debt. Gao declared a cash dividend of $3,800 on these shares. The dividend will be paid in the first week of the fiscal year 2015.

Instructions

(a) Prepare the underlying journal entries that were made by Gao Limited during 2014 to record all information related to the changes in each equity account and associated accounts over the year.

(b) Prepare the captions that would appear on Gao's statement of cash flows for the year ended October 31, 2014, using the indirect format. Include all necessary additional disclosures required under IFRS.

(c) How would your answer to parts (a) and (b) above change if the investments in Trivex were accounted for using the fair value through net income model?

(d) How would your answer to parts (a) and (b) above change if Gao were using ASPE?

P22-7 Comparative statement of financial position accounts of Secada Inc., which follows IFRS, follow:

SECADA INC.
Comparative Statement of Financial Position Accounts
December 31, 2014, and 2013

	December 31	
	2014	2013
Debit accounts		
Cash	$ 37,000	$ 33,750
Accounts receivable	67,500	60,000
Merchandise inventory	30,000	24,000
Long-term investments (FV-NI)	23,250	40,500
Machinery	30,000	18,750
Buildings	67,500	56,250
Land	7,500	7,500
	$262,750	$240,750
Credit accounts		
Allowance for doubtful accounts	$ 2,250	$ 1,500
Accumulated depreciation—machinery	5,625	2,250
Accumulated depreciation—buildings	13,500	9,000
Accounts payable	30,000	24,750
Accrued payables	2,375	1,125
Income taxes payable	1,000	1,500
Long-term note payable—non-trade	26,000	31,000
Common shares	150,000	125,000
Retained earnings	32,000	44,625
	$262,750	$240,750

Additional information:

1. Cash dividends declared during the year were $25,375.

2. A 20% stock dividend was declared during the year and $25,000 of retained earnings was capitalized.

3. Investments at FV-NI that cost $20,000 and had a fair value at December 31, 2013, of $24,750 were sold during the year for $23,750.

4. Machinery that cost $3,750 and had $750 of depreciation accumulated was sold for $2,200.

Secada's 2014 statement of income is as follows:

Sales revenue	$640,000
Less cost of goods sold	380,000
Gross margin	260,000
Less: Operating expenses (includes $8,625 depreciation and $5,400 bad debts)	180,450
Income from operations	79,550

Unrealized loss on FV-NI investments	$ (1,000)	
Loss on sale of machinery	(800)	(1,800)
Income before tax		77,750
Income tax expense		40,000
Net income		$37,750

Instructions

(a) Calculate net cash flow from operating activities using the direct method.

(b) Prepare a statement of cash flows using the indirect method.

(c) Assume that your investment club is considering investing in Secada Inc. Write a memo to the other members of the club about the company's cash activities during 2014.

(d) Management wants to provide more captions (headings) in the section on cash flow from operating activities. Recommend one additional caption that would help achieve that goal.

P22-8 Neilson Corp. reported $145,000 of net income for 2014. In preparing the statement of cash flows, the accountant noted several items that might affect cash flows from operating activities.

1. During 2014, Neilson reported a sale of equipment for $7,000. The equipment had a carrying amount of $23,500.

2. During 2014, Neilson sold 100 Lontel Corporation common shares at $200 per share. The acquisition cost of these shares was $145 per share. This investment was shown on Neilson's December 31, 2013 statement of financial position as an investment at fair value with gains and losses in net income.

3. During 2014, Neilson corrected an error for ending inventory of December 31, 2013. The debit to opening retained earnings was $14,600.

4. During 2014, Neilson revised its estimate for bad debts. Before 2014, Neilson's bad debt expense was 1% of its net sales. In 2014, this percentage was increased to 2%. Net sales for 2014 were $500,000, and net accounts receivable decreased by $15,000 during 2014.

5. During 2014, Neilson issued 500 common shares for a patent. The shares' market value on the transaction date was $23 per share.

6. Depreciation expense for 2014 was $38,000.

7. Neilson Corp. holds 40% of Nirbana Corporation's common shares as a long-term investment and exercises significant influence. Nirbana reported $27,000 of net income for 2014.

8. Nirbana Corporation paid a total of $2,800 of cash dividends to all shareholders in 2014.

9. During 2014, Neilson declared a 10% stock dividend, distributing 1,000 common shares. The market price at the date of issuance was $20 per share.

10. Neilson Corp. paid $10,000 in dividends: $2,500 of this amount was paid on term preferred shares classified as a long-term liability.

Instructions

(a) Prepare a schedule that shows the net cash flow from operating activities using the indirect method. Assume that no items other than the ones listed affected the calculation of 2014 cash flow from operating activities. Also assume that Neilson Corp. follows ASPE.

(b) Assume now that Neilson Corp. follows IFRS. What possible amounts might be reported?

P22-9 MFI Holdings Inc. follows IFRS and applies the FV-OCI model without recycling. MFI's statement of financial position contained the following comparative data at December 31:

Statement of financial position accounts:

	2014	2013
FV-OCI investments	$24,000	$37,900
Accumulated other comprehensive income (loss)	400	(2,400)

Partial statement of income and comprehensive income, 2014:

Dividend revenue	$ 200
Loss on sale of FV-OCI investments	300
Net income	XXX
Other comprehensive income	
Unrealized gains-OCI	2,500
Comprehensive income	$ XXX

Digging Deeper

At December 31, 2014, the following information is available:

1. MFI Holdings had a single investment in shares at December 31, 2013. The investment cost $40,300 and was sold during 2014 for $40,000.

2. During 2014, dividends of $200 were received on shares classified as investments at fair value with gains and losses in OCI.

3. Another investment, with the same classification, was purchased at a cost of $23,600. The fair value of this new investment at December 31, 2014, was $24,000.

4. MFI Holdings classifies dividends received as operating cash flows.

Instructions

(a) Calculate and reconcile the transactions that were recorded to the accounts Fair Value through Other Comprehensive Income Investments and Accumulated Other Comprehensive Income.

(b) Using the direct and the indirect methods, prepare a table that contrasts the presentation of all transactions related to the above financial statements and related investment transactions on MFI's statement of cash flows. Be specific about the classification within the statement for each item that is reported.

(c) How would your answer to parts (a) and (b) above change if the investments were accounted for using the fair value through net income model?

(d) Why would MFI not use the fair value through other comprehensive income model?

P22-10   The following accounts appear in the ledger of Samson Inc. Samson's shares trade on the Toronto and New York Stock Exchanges and so the company uses IFRS. Samson made a special election to account for shares held in Anderson Corp. as FV-OCI and to reclassify out of OCI and into net income investment holding gains that are realized. It also chooses to classify dividends received as operating cash flows. Samson's investment in Anderson Corp. is not strategic and is classified as a long-term investment.

			Dr.	Cr.	Bal.
		Investment in Anderson Corp.			
Dec. 1, 2013		Purchase of 40,000 shares	$893,500		$893,500
Dec. 31, 2013		Fair value adjustment 40,000 shares		$10,100	883,400
Aug. 15, 2014		Fair value adjustment of 3,000 shares	4,350		887,750
Aug. 15, 2014		Sale of 3,000 shares		70,605	817,145
Nov. 3, 2014		Purchase of 2,000 shares	35,480		852,625
Dec. 31, 2014		Fair value adjustment 39,000 shares	19,620		872,245
		Accumulated Other Comprehensive Income	Dr.	Cr.	Bal.
Dec. 31, 2013		Closing entry		$10,100	$ 10,100
Dec. 31, 2014		Closing entry	$ 10,100	20,378	(10,278)
		Dividend Revenue	Dr.	Cr.	Bal.
June 30, 2014		Dividends from Anderson Corp.		$35,700	$(35,700)
		Gain on Sale of Investments	Dr.	Cr.	Bal.
Aug. 15, 2014		Reclassification adjustment—3,000 shares		$ 3,592	$ (3,592)
		Unrealized Gain or Loss-OCI	Dr.	Cr.	Bal.
Dec. 31, 2013		Fair value adjustment of 40,000 shares	$ 10,100		$ 10,100
Dec. 31, 2013		Closing entry		$10,100	-0-
Aug. 15, 2014		Fair value adjustment of 3,000 shares		4,350	(4,350)
Aug. 15, 2014		Reclassification adjustment—3,000 shares	3,592		(758)
Dec. 31, 2014		Fair value adjustment of 39,000 shares		19,620	(20,378)
Dec. 31, 2014		Closing entry	20,378		-0-

Instructions

(a) Prepare a partial comparative statement of financial position for Samson Inc. at the fiscal year end of December 31, 2014.

(b) Prepare an income statement, a statement of comprehensive income, and a statement of changes in accumulated other comprehensive income for the year ended December 31, 2014.

(c) Prepare the journal entries dated June 30, August 15, and November 3, 2014. Provide explanations to the entries.

(d) Using the direct and the indirect methods, prepare a table that contrasts the presentation of all transactions recorded in the ledger accounts provided on Samson's statement of cash flows. Be specific about the classification within the statement for each item that is reported. What other choices could Samson have used in the classification of cash flows?

(e) How would your answer to parts (b) and (d) above change if the investments were accounted for using the fair value through net income model?

(f) Why would Samson not use the fair value through other comprehensive income model?

P22-11 Davis Inc. is a privately held company that uses ASPE. Davis had the following information available at March 31, 2014:

DAVIS INC.
Income Statement
For the Year Ended March 31, 2014

Sales revenue		$450,000
Cost of goods sold		260,000
Gross profit		190,000
Operating expenses		
Salaries and wages expense	$64,500	
Depreciation expense	7,500	
Rent expense	18,000	
Administrative expenses	21,000	
Amortization of patents	1,500	112,500
Operating income		77,500
Other revenues and expenses		
Bond interest expense	(6,750)	
Unrealized gains on FV-NI investments	3,000	
Investment income	12,500	
Gain on retirement of bonds	16,600	25,350
		102,850
Income tax expense—current	19,900	
Income tax expense—future	10,300	30,200
Net income		$ 72,650

Davis Inc.'s partial list of comparative account balances as of March 31, 2014, and 2013, is as follows:

	March 31		
	2014	**2013**	**Change**
Cash	$ 5,200	$ 4,400	$ 800
Investment in 30-day treasury bills	20,000	6,200	13,800
Accounts receivable	46,400	43,600	2,800
Inventory	35,800	29,600	6,200
Prepaid expenses	2,650	2,800	(150)
FV-NI Investments	5,230	2,230	3,000
Prepaid rent—long-term	4,000	-0-	4,000
Accounts payable, trade	22,800	24,200	(1,400)
Salaries and wages payable	500	1,300	(800)
Income tax payable	13,000	29,500	(16,500)
Interest payable	3,000	1,500	1,500
Accrued pension liability	8,500	6,900	1,600
Deferred tax liability	12,900	2,600	10,300

Additional information:

1. Bond interest expense includes $750 of bond discount amortized.

2. The investment income represents Davis Inc.'s reported income in its 40%-owned, significantly influenced investment in Jessa Ltd. Davis received a $2,000 dividend from Jessa on February 15, 2014.

3. During the year, the company retired $500,000 of its outstanding bonds payable, paying out $16,600 less than the price at which the bonds were carried on the books.

4. In early January 2014, Davis renewed and signed a four-year operating lease, agreeing to pay $4,000 each month in rent. The lessor required the payment of the rent for the first and last months of the lease at that time.

5. The change in the FV-NI investment is from the change in the market value of the securities for the fiscal year 2014. There were no purchases or sales of these securities during the 2014 fiscal year.

Note: There is insufficient information to allow you to prepare a complete statement of cash flows.

Instructions

(a) What is the amount of Davis Inc.'s change in cash to be explained on the statement of cash flows for the year ended March 31, 2014?

(b) Prepare the "Cash provided by (used in) operations" section of the statement of cash flows, assuming that the indirect method is used and all necessary information has been provided.

(c) Identify the amounts that would be reported within this section if the direct method were used for the following items:

1. Cash paid to and on behalf of employees
2. Cash received from customers
3. Income taxes paid
4. Cash paid to suppliers for goods and services
5. Interest paid

(d) Calculate the sum of the cash flows in part (c). Should the sum of the cash flows in the direct format equal the amount arrived at in part (a) for "Cash provided by (used in) operations"? If not, why not? If it should, do the amounts equal each other? Why or why not?

P22-12 The unclassified statement of financial position accounts for Sorkin Corporation, which is a public company using IFRS, for the year ended December 31, 2013, and its statement of comprehensive income and statement of cash flows for the year ended December 31, 2014, are as follows:

SORKIN CORPORATION
Statement of Financial Position Accounts
December 31, 2013
($ in millions)

Cash	$ 21
Accounts receivable	194
Inventory	200
Prepaid expenses	12
Long-term investment in shares of Stoker Inc.	125
Land	150
Buildings and equipment	400
Accumulated depreciation	(120)
Patents	60
Accumulated amortization patent	(28)
Goodwill	60
Total assets	$1,074

Accounts payable	$ 65
Salaries and wages payable	11
Bond interest payable	4
Income tax payable	14
Deferred tax liability	8
Bonds payable	250
Common shares	495
Retained earnings	227
Total liabilities and shareholders' equity	$1,074

SORKIN CORPORATION
Statement of Income
Year Ended December 31, 2014
($ in millions)

Revenues:		
Sales revenue	$410	
Unrealized gain on investments (FV-NI)	5	
Investment income	11	$426
Expenses and losses:		
Cost of goods sold	158	
Administrative expenses	22	

Digging Deeper

Salaries and wages expense	65
Depreciation and amortization expense	21
Bond interest expense	28
Loss from damaged equipment	18
Loss on impairment of goodwill	20
	332
Income before income tax	94
Income tax	27
Net income	$ 67

SORKIN CORPORATION
Statement of Cash Flows (Indirect Method)
For the Year Ended December 31, 2014

Cash flows from operating activities		
Net earnings		$67
Add back (deduct) non-cash revenues and expenses:		
Investment income from equity investment in Stoker Inc.	(11)	
Dividends received from equity investment in Stoker Inc.	6	
Loss from damaged equipment	18	
Depreciation expense	19	
Unrealized gain on FV-NI investments	(5)	
Amortization of patent	2	
Amortization of bond discount	3	
Loss on impairment of goodwill	20	52
Add (deduct) changes in non-cash working capital:		
Decrease in accounts receivable	4	
Increase in inventories	(5)	
Decrease in prepaid expenses	2	
Decrease in accounts payable	(15)	
Decrease in salaries and wages payable	(5)	
Increase in deferred tax liability	3	
Increase in bond interest payable	4	
Decrease in income taxes payable	(2)	(14)
Net cash provided by operating activities		105
Cash flows from investing activities:		
Proceeds from disposal of damaged equipment	10	
Purchase of land (Note 1)	(23)	
Purchase of FV-NI investments	(25)	
Net cash used by investing activities		(38)
Cash flows from financing activities:		
Dividends paid	(7)	
Redemption of serial bonds	(60)	
Issuance of preferred shares	75	
Repurchase of common shares	(9)	
Net cash used by financing activities		(1)
Net increase in cash		66
Cash, January 1, 2014		21
Cash, December 31, 2014		$87

Note 1. Non-cash investing and financing activities

(a) During the year, land was acquired for $46 million in exchange for cash of $23 million and a $23-million, four-year, 15% note payable to the seller.

(b) Equipment was acquired through a finance lease that was capitalized initially at $82 million.

Additional information:

1. The investment income represents Sorkin's reported income in its 35%-owned, significantly influenced investment in Stoker Inc. Sorkin received a dividend from Stoker during the year.

2. Early in 2014, Sorkin purchased shares for $25 million as an investment at fair value with gains and losses in net income. There were no purchases or sales of these shares during 2014, nor were there any dividends received from this investment.

3. A machine that originally cost $70 million became unusable due to a flood. Most major components of the machine were unharmed and were sold together for $10 million. Sorkin had no insurance coverage for the loss because its insurance policy did not cover floods.

4. Reversing differences in the year between pre-tax accounting income and taxable income resulted in an increase in future taxable amounts, causing the deferred tax liability to increase by $3 million.

5. On December 30, 2014, land costing $46 million was acquired by paying $23 million cash and issuing a $23-million, four-year, 15% note payable to the seller.

6. Equipment was acquired through a 15-year financing lease. The present value of minimum lease payments was $82 million when signing the lease on December 31, 2014. Sorkin made the initial lease payment of $2 million on January 1, 2015.

7. Serial bonds with a face value of $60 million were retired at maturity on June 20, 2014. In order to finance this redemption and have additional cash available for operations, Sorkin issued preferred shares for $75 million cash.

8. In February, Sorkin issued a 4% stock dividend (4 million shares). The market price of the common shares was $7.50 per share at that time.

9. In April 2014, 1 million common shares were repurchased for $9 million. The weighted average original issue price of the repurchased shares was $12 million.

Instructions

(a) Prepare the unclassified statement of financial position accounts for Sorkin Corporation for the year ended December 31, 2014, as a check on the statement of cash flows. Add whichever accounts you consider necessary.

(b) Prepare the operating activities section of the statement of cash flows for Sorkin Corporation using the direct method.

(c) How would the statement of cash flows differ if the terms on the purchase of land had been essentially the same except that the financing for the note payable had been negotiated with a mortgage company instead of the seller of the land?

Digging Deeper

P22-13 Seneca Corporation, which uses IFRS, has contracted with you to prepare a statement of cash flows. The controller has provided the following information:

	December 31	
	2014	2013
Cash	$ 38,700	$13,000
Accounts receivable	11,600	9,750
Inventory	10,600	9,100
FV-NI Investments	-0-	2,500
Buildings	-0-	27,700
Equipment	40,500	18,500
Patent	14,000	14,000
	$115,400	$94,550
Allowance for doubtful accounts	$ 1,400	$ 1,500
Accumulated depreciation—equipment	2,000	3,300
Accumulated depreciation—buildings	-0-	5,700
Accumulated amortization—patent	9,000	7,750
Accounts payable	4,400	3,300
Dividends payable	-0-	6,000
Notes payable, short-term (non-trade)	3,400	4,000
Long-term notes payable	30,500	25,000
Share capital	43,000	33,000
Retained earnings	21,700	5,000
	$115,400	$94,550

Additional information related to 2014 is as follows:

1. Equipment that cost $10,500 and was 50% depreciated at the time of disposal was sold for $2,600.

2. Common shares were issued to pay $10,000 of the long-term note payable.

3. Cash dividends paid were $6,000. Seneca has adopted the policy of classifying dividends paid as operating activities.

4. On January 1, 2014, a flood destroyed the building. Insurance proceeds on the building were $23,000.

5. Investments in shares, reported at fair value with gains and losses in net income, were sold at $3,300 above their cost. The fair value of these investments at December 31, 2013, equalled their original cost.

6. Cash of $17,000 was paid to acquire equipment.

7. A long-term note for $15,500 was issued in exchange for equipment.

8. Interest of $2,200 and income tax of $5,600 were paid in cash. Seneca has adopted the policy of classifying interest paid as financing activities.

Instructions

(a) Use the indirect method to analyze the above information and prepare a statement of cash flows for Seneca.

(b) Prepare a reconciliation of the change in property, plant, and equipment's carrying amount to the amounts appearing on the statement of cash flows and corresponding notes.

(c) Financial statement preparers often use reconciliations of changes in major categories of statement of financial position accounts to balance the statement of cash flows, as required in part (b) above. What additional insight does this reconciliation reveal to a reader of the statement that is not as evident from the statement of cash flows?

(d) Prepare a short analysis of Seneca's cash flow activity for 2014. The analysis is to be given to the controller.

(e) What choices, if any, are available for classifications for interest and dividends paid or received by Seneca?

(f) What kind of company would you expect to be revealed by the operating, investing, and financing sections of Seneca's statement of cash flows: a company that is severely troubled financially or a recently formed company that is experiencing rapid growth?

(g) Compare Seneca's net cash flow provided by operating activities with profit. Comment on the relationship between these two amounts from the perspective of an investor.

Digging Deeper

Case

Refer to the Case Primer on the Student Website and in *WileyPLUS* to help you answer this case.

CA22-1 Papadopoulos Limited (PL) sells retail merchandise in Canada. The company was incorporated last year and is now in its second year of operations. PL is owned and operated by the Papadopoulos family, and Iris Papadopoulos, the company president, has decided to expand into the American marketplace. In order to do this, bank financing will be necessary.

The books have been kept by Iris's daughter Tonya, who is studying accounting in university. Financial statements had only been prepared for tax purposes in the past. For the year ended December 31, 2014, Tonya prepared the following statement showing cash inflows and cash outflows:

Sources of cash:	
From shareholder loan	$150,000
From sales of merchandise	350,000
From truck financing	50,000
From term deposit cashed in	100,000
From interest income	10,000
Total sources of cash	$660,000
Uses of cash:	
For fixed asset purchases	$100,000
For inventory purchases	250,000
Operating expenses, including depreciation of $70,000	160,000
For purchase of investment	55,000
For purchase of truck	50,000
For interest on debt	30,000
Total uses of cash	$645,000
Net increase in cash	$ 15,000

Tonya showed the statement to her mother, noting that the bank was sure to give them a loan, especially since they were profitable in their second year and since cash had increased over the year, which shows that it had been a good year. Iris was not convinced, however, and decided to have the statement looked at by a "real" accountant.

Instructions

Adopt the role of the accountant and redraft the statement, if necessary, in good form for the bank. Discuss the company's financial position. Consider ASPE to be a constraint.

Integrated Case

IC22-1　Earthcom Inc. is in the telecommunications industry. The company builds and maintains telecommunication lines that are buried in the ground. The company is a public company and has been having some bad luck. One of its main underground telecommunications lines was cut by accident and the company cannot determine the exact location of the problem. As a result, many of the company's lines have lost service. Because Earthcom did not have a backup plan, it is uncertain about how long it will take to restore service. The affected customers are not happy and are threatening to sue. In order to try to calm them down, Earthcom has managed to purchase some capacity from a competitor. Unfortunately, the cost of the service is much higher than the revenues from Earthcom's customers. Earthcom is also currently spending quite a bit on consulting fees (on lawyers and damage control consultants).

In addition, Earthcom is spending a significant amount of money trying to track down the problem with its line, and although it has had no luck so far, the company recently announced that it was confident that services would be restored imminently. As a result of the work being done, Earthcom feels that it will be in a better position to restore service if this ever happens again.

The company has been upgrading many of its very old telecommunications lines that were beginning to degrade due to age. It has capitalized these amounts and they are therefore showing up as investing activities on the cash flow statement. The company's auditors have questioned this as they feel that the amounts should be expensed.

As a result of all this, Earthcom's share price has plummeted, making its stock options worthless. Management has historically been remunerated solely based on these stock options, however. The company's CFO meanwhile has just announced that he is leaving and is demanding severance pay for what he is calling constructive dismissal. He feels that because the stock options are worthless, he is working for free—which he cannot afford to do—and that the company has effectively fired him.

Instructions

Adopt the role of the company controller and discuss the financial reporting issues.

Writing Assignments

WA22-1　HTM Limited is a young and growing producer of electronic measurement instruments and technical equipment. You have been retained by HTM to advise it in preparing a statement of cash flows using the indirect method. For the fiscal year ended October 31, 2014, you have obtained the following information about certain HTM events and transactions. The company reports under IFRS.

1. Earnings reported for the fiscal year were $800,000.

2. Depreciation expense of $315,000 was included in the earnings reported.

3. Uncollectible accounts receivable of $40,000 were written off against the allowance for doubtful accounts. Also, $51,000 of bad debt expense was included in determining income for the year and was added to the allowance for doubtful accounts.

4. A gain of $9,000 was realized on the sale of a machine; it originally cost $75,000, of which $30,000 was depreciated to the date of sale.

5. The company has investments that are recorded at FV through OCI. The increase in the value of these investments that was included in other comprehensive income for the year was $30,000.

6. The company has an investment property, which is measured at fair value. At October 31, 2014, it was determined that the fair value of the building had declined by $45,000 and the appropriate adjustment was made.

7. On July 3, 2014, equipment was purchased for $700,000; HTM gave in exchange a payment of $75,000 cash, previously unissued common shares with a $200,000 market value, and a $425,000 mortgage note payable for the remainder.

8. On August 3, 2014, $800,000 in face value of HTM's 10% convertible debentures were converted into common shares. The bonds were originally issued at face value.

9. Bonds payable with a par value of $100,000, on which there was an unamortized bond discount of $2,000, were redeemed at 99.5.

10. On September 21, 2014, a new issue of $500,000 par value, 8% convertible bonds was issued at 101. Without the conversion feature, the bonds would have been issued at 99.

11. HTM's employees accrue benefits related to the company's unfunded post-retirement medical plan each year. At October 31, 2014, HTM recognized $49,000 of accrued expense for the current year.

Instructions

(a) Explain whether each of the 11 numbered items is a source of cash, a use of cash, or neither.

(b) Explain how each item that is a source or use of cash should be reported in HTM's statement of cash flows for the fiscal year ended October 31, 2014, assuming HTM uses the indirect approach for the Operating Activities section. For items that are neither a source nor use of cash, explain why this is true, and indicate the reporting, if any, that should be made of the item in the company's statement of cash flows for the year ended October 31, 2014.

WA22-2 The past few years have seen numerous changes in Canadian accounting standards, such as for investments, asset retirement obligations, and stock options, particularly for companies that have changed to IFRS or ASPE from pre-changeover Canadian GAAP. For the following scenarios, assume that IFRS has been adopted.

Instructions

For each accounting situation listed below, identify any related cash flows, and explain how the statement of cash flows is affected for companies with this type of transaction.

(a) Investments of securities purchased for trading held by a company are classified as fair value through net income. The investments do not meet the definition of cash equivalents, but are used to earn a return on excess cash until the cash is needed for operations. Small amounts of gains and losses on disposal, interest and dividends received, and changes in their fair values are reported in income.

(b) A company holds equity investments that are classified as fair value through OCI (without recycling). One security was disposed of at a gain during the year and the others have fair values that are higher than they were at the previous year end. Dividends have been received and reported in income.

(c) An investment in another company's bonds is recorded at amortized cost. The investment was acquired at a premium because the bond pays a higher rate of interest than the market rate.

(d) A company began development activities for a new mine site. As a result, it incurred an obligation related to the mine's eventual retirement, reporting it as an asset retirement obligation and as a portion of the mine's cost on its statement of financial position. The following year, the obligation was increased due to expanded mine activity as well as the accretion of the amount that was recognized in the preceding year representing interest.

(e) Stock options with a two-year vesting period were issued to the top executive team at the beginning of the current fiscal period. The fair value of the stock options was determined using the Black-Scholes formula.

(f) Stock options that were granted three years ago were exercised in the current year when the fair value of the company's shares was at an all-time high. The option or strike price was approximately half of the market share price when the options were exercised.

WA22-3 Durocher Guitar Corp. is in the business of manufacturing top-quality, steel-string folk guitars. Durocher is a private enterprise and follows ASPE. In recent years, the company has experienced working capital problems resulting from investments in new factory equipment, the unanticipated buildup of receivables and inventories, and the payoff of a mortgage on one of its manufacturing plants. The founder and president of the company, Laraine Durocher, has tried to raise cash from various financial institutions, but she has been unsuccessful because of the company's poor performance recently. In particular, the company's lead bank, First Provincial, is especially concerned about Durocher's inability to maintain a positive cash position. The commercial loan officer from First Provincial told Laraine Durocher, "I can't even consider your request for capital financing unless I see that your company is able to generate positive cash flows from operations."

Thinking about the banker's comment, Laraine Durocher came up with what she believes is a good plan: with a more attractive statement of cash flows, the bank might be willing to provide long-term financing. To "window dress" cash flows, the company can sell its accounts receivables to factors, liquidate its raw material inventories, and arrange a sale and leaseback for major components of its equipment. These rather costly transactions would generate lots of cash. It is your job, as the company's ethical accountant, to advise Laraine Durocher on this plan.

Ethics

Instructions

(a) Explain how each of these "solutions" would affect Durocher Guitar Corp.'s statement of cash flows. Be specific.

(b) What are the ethical issues related to Laraine Durocher's idea?

(c) What would you advise Laraine Durocher to do?

WA22-4 The statement of cash flows is one of the four main statements required in the preparation of a company's financial statements.

Instructions

(a) Explain what the purpose is of the statement of cash flows, and identify at least three reasons users might find it helpful.

(b) What is the definition of cash? What can be included in cash equivalents? How are bank overdrafts treated? State any differences between IFRS and ASPE.

(c) Identify and describe the three categories of activities that must be reported in the statement of cash flows. What is the relationship between these activities and a company's statement of financial position?

(d) Identify two methods of reporting cash flows from operations. Are both permitted under GAAP? Explain. Which method do you prefer? Why?

(e) Provide two examples of a non-cash investing and financing transaction, and describe the financial reporting requirements for such transactions.

(f) Assume that you overhear the following comment by an investor in the stock market: "You can't always trust the net income number reported, because of all the estimates and judgement that go into its determination. That's why I only look at the cash flow from operations in analyzing a company." Comment.

WA22-5 In October 2008, the IASB published a Discussion Paper entitled "Preliminary Views on Financial Statement Presentation" (see www.ifrs.org). Since then, there have been various meetings to discuss the comments received and proposed changes. This discussion paper made various proposals about changes to the statement of cash flows.

Instructions

Locate and read the Discussion Paper entitled "Preliminary Views on Financial Statement Presentation" and any Financial Statement Presentation project summaries and updates on the IASB website that relate to the statement of cash flows. Write a short report that you can present to your class on the decisions that have been made to date on this project that will affect the statement of cash flows and why. Describe how the statement will be different from what is now reported and any reconciliations that are proposed.

WA22-6

Instructions

Write a brief essay highlighting the differences between IFRS and ASPE noted in this chapter, discussing the conceptual justification for each.

RESEARCH AND FINANCIAL ANALYSIS

Real World Emphasis

RA22-1 Shoppers Drug Mart Corporation

Shoppers Drug Mart Corporation's 2011 financial statements can be found at the end of this volume or on the company website. The company is the licensor of full-service retail drug stores that sell pharmacy, health, and beauty products.

Instructions

Review the financial statements and notes of Shoppers Drug Mart and answer the following questions.

(a) Prepare a summary analysis of Shoppers Drug Mart's sources and uses of cash at the level of operating, investing, and financing subtotals only, for 2011 and 2010. Based on this, comment on the similarities and differences in the company's needs for cash and how they were met over the past three years.

(b) What method of reporting operating cash flows does Shoppers use in the statement of cash flows? Do you think this approach provides useful information to a potential investor?

(c) Using the information provided in the statement of cash flows, determine the balances of the Trade Receivables, Inventories, and Accounts Payable and Accrued Liabilities that would have been reported on the December 31, 2011 statement of financial position. Compare this with the actual balance at December 31, 2011, provided in the notes and explain any differences.

(d) Explain why interest paid has been deducted and finance expenses have been added on the statement of cash flows. Companies have a choice in classifying interest and finance costs. What choice did Shoppers make with respect to this?

(e) Based only on the information in the Financing Activities section of the statement of cash flows, can you tell whether the debt to equity ratio increased or decreased during the years ended December 31, 2011, and 2010? Explain.

(f) Is Shoppers' operating capability expanding or contracting? What type of assets is the company investing in? What is the likely effect of these investments on Shoppers' future operating and financing cash flows?

(g) Comment briefly on the company's solvency and financial flexibility.

RA22-2 Bombardier Inc.

Real World Emphasis

Access the financial statements of Bombardier Inc. for the years ended December 31, 2012, and December 31, 2011, from the company's website or SEDAR (www.sedar.com).

Instructions

Changes in non-cash working capital items can have a significant impact on operating cash flows. Using the financial statements, answer the following questions.

(a) What does Bombardier do? When is revenue and related costs recognized? Comment on the timing of revenue and expenses, and cash receipts and payments related to operating activities.

(b) What were Bombardier's net earnings from 2011 to 2012? What were the operating cash flow amounts for the same periods? Calculate the difference between net income and operating cash flows for each year. In which years was the operating cash flow higher or lower than net earnings? Calculate the year over year percentage changes in net earnings. Calculate the year over year percentage changes in operating cash flows. Comment on these differences in dollar amounts and year over year percentage changes.

(c) What is causing these differences in net income and operating cash flows to occur? Highlight significant differences and explain why these arise.

(d) Comment on the ability to predict cash flows for this company. Which approach in preparing operating cash flows (direct or indirect) would be most useful to potential investors?

RA22-3 AltaGas Ltd.

Real World Emphasis

AltaGas Ltd. capitalizes on the supply and demand dynamic for natural gas and power by owning and operating assets in gas, power, and utilities in places that provide a strategic competitive advantage.

Instructions

Access the financial statements for AltaGas for the year ended December 31, 2012, from the company's website or from SEDAR (www.sedar.com) and answer the following questions.

(a) Review the statement of cash flows for the two years 2011 and 2012. What are the total cash flows from (or used by) operations, investing activities, and financing activities? What sources of cash are available to fund the dividends and capital investments? Do you think that the dividends are sustainable?

(b) Using the net book value of property, plant, and equipment (PPE) at December 31, 2011, as the opening balance and items from the statement of cash flows, statement of earnings, and related note disclosures, try to reconcile the opening and closing balance for PPE for 2011.

RA22-4 Allon Therapeutics Inc. and Oncothyreon Inc.– Comparative Analysis

Real World Emphasis

Allon Therapeutics Inc. and Oncothyreon Inc. are both involved in the discovery, research, and development of therapeutic products. Allon Therapeutics focuses mainly on discovering and developing first drugs that impact the progression of neurodegenerative diseases, while Oncothyreon researches and develops therapeutic products for the treatment of cancer.

Instructions

From the company websites, obtain the comparative financial statements of Allon for its year ended December 31, 2010, and of Oncothyreon for its year ended December 31, 2010. Review the financial statements and answer the following questions.

(a) Compare the companies' statements of operations and comment on their results over the past two fiscal periods. What is the major reason for the results that are reported?

(b) How would you expect companies in this industry and stage of development to be financed? Why? Is this consistent with what is reported on their statement of financial position? Comment.

(c) For the two most recent years reported by each company, write a brief explanation of their cash activities at the subtotal level of operating, investing, and financing flows. Note any similarities and differences.

(d) How do the investments that Allon and Oncothyreon make differ from the investments made by companies in other industries? Describe the difference in general, and then specifically explain how it affects each of the financial statements.

(e) Are the companies liquid? Explain. On what does the solvency and financial flexibility of companies in this industry depend?

Real World Emphasis

RA22-5 Nestlé Group

Nestlé Group is one of the world's largest food and beverage companies, selling 10,000 different products ranging from milk and dairy, to chocolate and pet food. Access a copy of the company's comparative financial statements for the year ended December 31, 2012, from the company's website (www.nestle.com).

Instructions

(a) Prepare a summary report of Nestlé's cash activities during its year ended December 31, 2012, and 2011, at the subtotal level of operating, investing, and financing activities, and a comparative report for the preceding fiscal year. Are there major differences at this level between the two periods? Explain. How is the company using any excess operating cash flows after investing activities?

(b) Identify what major differences there are between the company's accrual-based income and its cash flow from operating activities over the past two years.

(c) Prepare a short report summarizing Nestlé's investing cash transactions and its financing cash transactions for 2012.

(d) How has the company classified interest paid, interest received, income taxes paid, dividends received, and dividends paid? What were the amounts for these items during 2012?

ENDNOTES

[1] TD Canada Trust, https://webinar.tdcanadatrust.com/7-tips-to-improve-your-business-cash-flow/?referral=0018

[2] *CICA Handbook–Accounting*, Part II, Section 1540.06(a) and (b), and IAS 7.6. Copyright © 2012 IFRS Foundation. All rights reserved. Reproduced by Wiley Canada with the permission of the IFRS Foundation ®. No permission granted to third parties to reproduce or distribute.

[3] Dividend payments that are recognized in the income statement relate to equity securities that are determined to be liabilities in substance. Interest payments that are charged to retained earnings relate to debt securities that are judged to be equity instruments in substance. The statement of cash flows, therefore, treats returns to in-substance equity holders as financing outflows and to those designated as creditors as operating outflows.

[4] IAS 7 *Statement of Cash Flows*, para .20, indicates that the undistributed income of an associate is an adjustment in determining cash from operations under the indirect method.

5 Note that an asset that is acquired and financed through a third party when the lender pays the seller directly is considered a cash inflow (financing) followed by a cash outflow (investing). If an existing mortgage is assumed when an asset is acquired, however, this does not result in a cash flow.

6 Netting is permitted in limited and specific circumstances. See *CICA Handbook–Accounting*, Part II, Section 1540.25 –.26 and IAS 7.22 – .24.

7 Unfortunately, use of the direct method is the exception. Companies suggest that it is costly for them to generate the information required by the direct method. However, the unpopularity of the direct method may also be due in part to the fact that accounting instructors tend to focus on the indirect method because that is what is used, and the indirect method is used because that is what accountants have been taught!

8 *CICA Handbook–Accounting*, Part II, Section 1540 also provides and explains, in an appendix, a simplified work sheet approach for companies to use in developing the information needed to present operating cash flows under the direct method.

9 Prior to the current standard on cash flows, significant non-cash transactions **were included** in the statement because of their effect on the entity's asset and capital structure. This difference shows the change in focus from a statement of changes in financial position (old terminology) to a statement of cash flows (new terminology), where only cash effects are reported.

10 Income statement information is used rather than information from the statement of comprehensive income because other comprehensive income amounts are non-cash and non-operating in nature.

11 On occasion, even experienced accountants get to this step and find that the statement does not balance! Don't despair. Determine the amount of your error and review your analysis until you find it.

12 If the mortgage payable had been directly assumed from the vendor of the land and building, the mortgage would have been considered a non-cash transaction with the vendor. (See *CICA Handbook–Accounting*, Part II, Sections 1540.42 and IAS 7.44.) The purchase of land and building and mortgage payable on the statement of cash flows would both have been reduced by $155,000.

13 For all current asset and current liability account changes that adjust accrual basis net income to cash flows from operations, a simple check can be made. The adjustment for all increases in current asset accounts should have the same effect within the Operating Activities section of the statement of cash flows. (For example, an increase in inventory implies more cash "tied up" in inventory and a decrease in cash flow.) All decreases in current asset accounts should represent increases in cash flows from operations. (For example, a decrease in accounts receivable suggests more cash collected from customers or an increase in cash flow.) All increases and decreases in current liability accounts should have the opposite effect of changes in current asset accounts. This is a useful mechanical procedure to double-check your adjustments.

14 For Yoshi Corporation, net receivables increased $53,000, from $51,000 ($52,700 – $1,700) at the beginning of the year to $104,000 ($106,500 – $2,500) at year end. The increase means that $53,000 of income was recognized that did not result in a corresponding cash flow. On the statement of cash flows under the indirect method, one adjustment to reduce net income by $53,000 is all that is needed.

15 *CICA Handbook–Accounting*, Part II, Sections 1540.32 and .33 explain how the amortization of a financial asset or financial liability acquired or issued at a premium or discount is reflected on the statement of cash flows. In general, any discount amortization is not a cash flow, while the amount received or paid in the case of a premium is split between interest (an operating flow) and repayment of principal (an investing or financing flow, as appropriate). IAS 7 *Statement of Cash Flows* does not make specific reference to this matter.

16 Another presentation alternative identified in IAS 7.20, although not widely used, is a variation of the indirect method: revenues and expenses are presented along with the changes in inventories and operating receivables and payables in the period.

17 A good example of this type of adjustment that you should be aware of is the adjustment for unfunded pension and other post-employment benefits expense that many companies report. The current year adjustment has a positive effect—it increases operating cash flows above the net income reported as no cash was paid out. However, very large amounts of operating cash outflows will be required in the future when these claims are eventually paid.

18 Phase A dealt with the question of what makes up a complete set of financial statements and is now complete and embedded in IAS 1. Phase B looks at how information is presented on the face of the financial statements, and Phase C will cover interim financial reporting.

19 Illustration 22-26 is based on the IASB Discussion Paper, Preliminary Views on Financial Statement Presentation, October 2008, p. 110. Other comments related to tentative decisions to date are based on IASB *Updates* to May 3, 2012. Illustration 22-26 focuses on the Operating and Investing activities from the proposed statement of cash flows. The sample SCF in the discussion paper also illustrates the format of the financing activities, income taxes, discontinued operations and equity aspects of the proposed SCF.

20 This is consistent with the analysis earlier in the chapter. If $8,000 of cost of goods sold came from a reduction in inventory levels, purchases for the year must have been $8,000 less than cost of goods sold. Therefore both analyses equally well convert the cost of goods sold to the level of purchases in the year.

Communicating Business Information

© istockphoto.com/Francois Hogue

IF YOU WANTED TO invest in a television station, magazine, baseball team, sports stadium, and cell phone provider, you would only have to buy one share: in Rogers Communications Inc.

Toronto-based Rogers, which dates back to the founding of the city's CFRB radio station in 1927 by Edward S. Rogers Sr., had revenues of more than $12.4 billion in 2011. It operates in telecommunications and media, and owns 100% of the Toronto Blue Jays Baseball Club and the Rogers Centre sports and entertainment stadium in downtown Toronto. With so many diverse businesses, how can a reader of Rogers' financial statements—such as a potential investor or analyst—know how each one is doing?

That's where segmented reporting comes in. IFRS requires companies such as Rogers, which became public in 1979, to report results in their financial statements according to reportable segments. IFRS sets out several criteria that a business unit must meet to be considered a reportable segment, including any segment whose revenues account for 10% or more of the company's total revenues.

In the case of Rogers, it reports results for each of three operating segments: Wireless, Cable, and Media. Wireless is the company's voice and data wireless communications operations. Cable is its cable television, telephone, and Internet operations. Media includes more than a dozen conventional and specialty television channels, 55 radio stations, 54 magazine and trade publications, the Rogers Centre, and Digital Media, which provides digital advertising to websites.

Rogers provides further breakdowns of financial information for parts of its Cable operations, which has three more reportable segments: cable, Rogers business solutions, and video. For its operating segments, the company generally provides more details of revenues, but not costs. For example, it states in its 2011 annual report that the revenues from its Media operating segment were $1.6 billion, of which $164 million came from the Blue Jays. But it does not state how much it spent on employee salaries and benefits per segment, so readers don't know how much the Blue Jays players' salaries cost, as an example.

Rogers also has investments in other companies, including some involved in television production and broadcast sales, plus a 37.5% ownership in Maple Leaf Sports & Entertainment Ltd., which owns and operates the Toronto Maple Leafs NHL team, the Toronto Raptors NBA team, and Toronto's Air Canada Centre, among other things. But the financial information for those companies is not reported on Rogers' financial statements since they are investments, not operating segments. Those investments are part of the assets reported on Rogers' statement of financial position.

Sources: Rogers Communications Inc., 2011 annual report; "A History of Rogers," corporate website, ww.rogers.com; "Rogers Communications to Invest in Maple Leaf Sports and Entertainment," company news release, December 9, 2011.

23 | Other Measurement and Disclosure Issues

LEARNING OBJECTIVES

After studying this chapter, you should be able to:

1. Understand the importance of disclosure from a business perspective.

2. Review the full disclosure principle and describe problems of implementation.

3. Explain the use of accounting policy notes in financial statement preparation.

4. Describe the disclosure requirements for major segments of a business.

5. Describe the accounting problems associated with interim reporting.

6. Discuss the accounting issues for related-party transactions.

7. Identify the difference between the two types of subsequent events.

8. Identify the major disclosures found in the auditor's report.

9. Describe methods used for basic financial statement analysis and summarize the limitations of ratio analysis.

10. Identify the major differences in accounting between ASPE and IFRS, and what changes are expected in the near future.

It is very important to read not only a company's financial statements, but also related information such as the president's letter and the management discussion and analysis. These additional documents **are just two ways in which companies disclose information to the public and stakeholders and they help to provide context for the financial statements within the annual report.** In this chapter, we cover a variety of disclosures contained in the notes to the financial statements, and other disclosures such as those that accompany the financial statements in the annual report to ensure that the statements are not misleading.

The chapter is organized as follows:

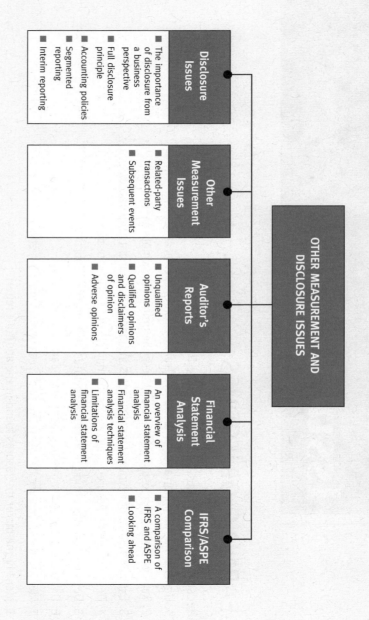

OTHER MEASUREMENT AND DISCLOSURE ISSUES

Disclosure Issues
- The importance of disclosure from a business perspective
- Full disclosure principle
- Accounting policies
- Segmented reporting
- Interim reporting

Other Measurement Issues
- Related-party transactions
- Subsequent events

Auditor's Reports
- Unqualified opinions
- Qualified opinions and disclaimers of opinion
- Adverse opinions

Financial Statement Analysis
- An overview of financial statement analysis
- Financial statement analysis techniques
- Limitations of financial statement analysis

IFRS/ASPE Comparison
- A comparison of IFRS and ASPE
- Looking ahead

DISCLOSURE ISSUES

The Importance of Disclosure from a Business Perspective

Objective 1

Understand the importance of disclosure from a business perspective.

Information disclosure is important to the proper functioning of capital markets and the allocation of capital. As we discussed in Chapter 1, the information provided in financial statements helps investors compare the performance of companies and assess the relative risks and returns of different investments. The full disclosure principle suggests that information relevant to decision-making should be included in the financial statements. But financial statements are not the only source of information for investors and creditors. For example, the Ontario Securities Commission (OSC) lists the following key disclosure documents for public companies on its website.[1]

- Annual information forms
- Financial statements
- Management information circulars
- Management's discussion and analysis (MD&A)
- Material change reports
- News releases relating to material changes and earnings releases
- Prospectuses

Finance

These disclosure documents can generally be found at www.sedar.com for Canadian public companies and investment funds.

The OSC notes that the "fact that documents are filed with the OSC does not make the company or fund immune from fraud or mean it is a 'good' investment. Investors still need to carefully choose their investments and who they deal with." However, an evaluation of the information provided freely by public (and some other) companies is a good starting point for investing decisions. You can begin by comparing the disclosures of the company you are interested in with disclosures made by other companies in that industry. By using publicly available information to assess the relative risks and rewards of the potential investments, and by being diligent in your assessment, you can assess the relative quality of companies you may be considering investing in (or working for).

Before we look at disclosure issues in more detail, a word of warning: not all disclosure is good disclosure. As we will see, too much disclosure can lead to information overload. Also, as the OSC notes in its "Guide for Investors: Researching Your Investments," companies and investors need to beware of the following:

- Misleading disclosure (inaccurate, incomplete, or unbalanced information)
- Selective disclosure (disclosing to a select group, rather than the general public)
- Untimely disclosure (being late with the disclosure of a material change in the business)

Law

- Insider trading (buying or selling a company's securities based on material information not disclosed to the public)

Investors should be wary of the extra risk involved in dealing with companies that have poor disclosure practices. Businesses should be aware that the four disclosure practices listed above often involve violations of securities law.

Full Disclosure Principle

Objective 2
Review the full disclosure principle and describe problems of implementation.

Some information is best provided in the financial statements and some is best provided by other means of financial reporting. For example, earnings and cash flows are readily available in financial statements, but investors might do better to look at comparisons with other companies in the same industry, which can be found in news articles or reports issued by analysts at brokerage firms.

Financial statements, notes to the financial statements, and supplementary information are all areas that are directly affected by GAAP. Other types of information that are found in the annual report, such as the management discussion and analysis, are not subject to GAAP. Illustration 23-1 shows the various types of financial information.

Illustration 23-1
Types of Financial Information

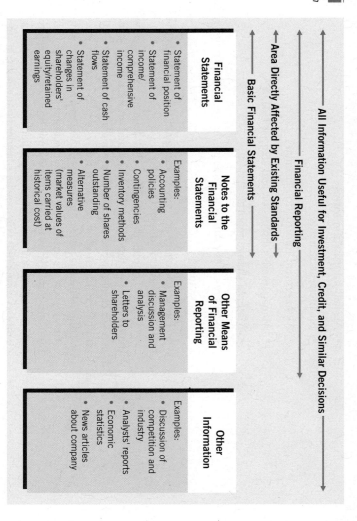

All Information Useful for Investment, Credit, and Similar Decisions

→ **Financial Reporting** →

Area Directly Affected by Existing Standards

Basic Financial Statements

Financial Statements	Notes to the Financial Statements	Other Means of Financial Reporting	Other Information
• Statement of financial position	Examples:	Examples:	Examples:
• Statement of income/comprehensive income	• Accounting policies	• Management discussion and analysis	• Discussion of competition and industry
• Statement of cash flows	• Contingencies	• Letters to shareholders	• Analysts' reports
• Statement of changes in shareholders' equity/retained earnings	• Inventory methods		• Economic statistics
	• Number of shares outstanding		• News articles about company
	• Alternative measures (market values of items carried at historical cost)		

Full Disclosure Principle Revisited

As indicated above and in Chapter 2, the accounting profession has adopted a **full disclosure principle** that calls for reporting of any financial facts that are significant enough to influence the judgement of an informed reader. In some situations, the benefits of disclosure may be apparent while the costs are uncertain. In other instances, the costs may be certain but the benefits of disclosure are less apparent. How much information is enough information? This is a difficult question to answer. While not enough information is clearly problematic, sometimes too much—often referred to as information overload—is equally problematic.

Different users want different information, and it becomes exceedingly difficult to develop disclosure policies that meet their varied objectives.

Underlying Concept

Deciding what information to provide, while taking into account different users' needs, is a good example of the trade-off between the cost-benefit constraint and the full disclosure principle.

Increase in Disclosure Requirements

Disclosure requirements for public companies have increased substantially over the past several decades.[2] As illustrated throughout this textbook, the accounting profession has issued many standards in the last two decades that have substantial disclosure provisions.

Accounting standards for private enterprises have fewer disclosure requirements than IFRS.[3] This is partly because many private enterprises have less complex business models and transactions. As well, many private companies are closely held, thus giving stakeholders greater access to information that may not be presented in the financial statements.

The reasons for the increase in disclosure requirements for public companies are varied. Some of them are as follows.

Complexity of the Business Environment. The increasing complexity of business operations in such areas as derivatives, leasing, business combinations, pensions, financing arrangements, and revenue recognition increases the difficulty of summarizing economic events. As a result, notes to the financial statements are used extensively to explain these transactions and their future effects.

Necessity for Timely Information. Today, more than ever before, users are demanding information that is current and predictive. As a result, more complete interim data are required.

Accounting as a Control and Monitoring Device. Governments have recently sought more information and public disclosure of such phenomena as management compensation, environmental pollution, related-party transactions, errors and irregularities, and illegal activities.

Accounting Policies

Objective 3
Explain the use of accounting policy notes in financial statement preparation.

As mentioned previously, notes are an integral part of a business enterprise's financial statements. However, they are frequently overlooked because they are highly technical and often appear in small print. Notes are the accountant's means of amplifying or explaining items that are presented in the main body of the statements. Information that is relevant to specific financial statement items can be explained in qualitative terms in notes, and additional quantitative data can be provided to expand the information in the financial statements. Notes can also be used to give information about restrictions that are imposed by financial arrangements or basic contractual agreements. Although notes may be technical and difficult to understand, they provide meaningful information for the financial statement user.

The **accounting policies** of any particular entity are the specific accounting principles and methods that are currently used and considered most appropriate to present fairly the enterprise's financial statements. Information about a reporting entity's accounting policies is essential for financial statement users in making economic decisions. The accounting policies disclosure should be given either as one of the first notes or in a separate Summary of Significant Accounting Policies section that immediately precedes the notes to the financial statements. The summary of significant accounting policies answers such questions as: What method of depreciation is used on plant assets? What valuation method is used on inventories? What amortization policy is followed in regard to intangible assets? How are marketing costs handled for financial reporting purposes?

Refer to the audited financial statements of **Shoppers Drug Mart** found at the end of this volume for an example of a note disclosure of accounting policies and other notes. Analysts carefully examine the summary of accounting policies section to determine whether the company is using conservative or aggressive accounting practices. For example, recognizing revenues prior to delivery of products might be considered an aggressive practice. On the other hand, using the successful efforts method for an oil and gas company would generally be viewed as a conservative practice.

As discussed in previous chapters, ASPE allows greater choice in accounting policies to allow for flexibility for private entities of differing sizes and complexity. In addition, ASPE allows entities to change accounting policies in certain instances without having to meet the criteria of providing reliable and more relevant information. For IFRS, the IASB has been attempting to reduce accounting policy choice to promote comparability. Changes in accounting policy under IFRS should be limited to new IFRS requirements or for a new policy that provides reliable and more relevant information.

Accounting Errors and Illegal Acts

Accounting errors are unintentional mistakes, whereas **irregularities** are intentional distortions of financial statements. As indicated in this textbook, when errors are discovered, the financial statements should be corrected. The same treatment should be given to irregularities. When an accountant or auditor discovers irregularities, however, a whole different set of suspicions, procedures, and responsibilities comes into play.

Illegal acts have been defined as "a violation of a domestic or foreign statutory law or government regulation attributable to the entity … or to management or employees acting on the entity's behalf."[4] The term "illegal act" is not meant to include personal misconduct by the entity's management or employees that may be unrelated to the enterprise's business activities. The accountant or auditor must evaluate the adequacy of disclosure in the financial statements and may have to assess whether the item should be recognized in the statement of financial position (SFP) or income statement. For example, if revenue is derived from an illegal act that is considered material in relation to the financial statements, this information should be disclosed. Furthermore, if the illegal act creates a liability to pay a fine, this must be reflected in the SFP and income statement.

Segmented Reporting

In the last several decades, business enterprises have at times diversified their operations by investing in various other businesses. As a result of such diversification efforts, investors and investment analysts have sought more information about the details behind conglomerate financial statements. Particularly, they want income statement, SFP, and cash flow information on the individual segments that together result in the total profit figure. Illustration 23-2 presents **segmented (disaggregated) financial information** for **British Airways plc.**

---

3 Segment information

a Business segments

The Group's network passenger and cargo operations are managed as a single business unit. The Leadership Team makes resource allocation decisions based on route profitability, which considers aircraft type and route economics, based primarily by reference to passenger economics with limited reference to cargo demand. The objective in making resource allocation decisions is to optimise consolidated financial results. While the operations of OpenSkies SASA (OpenSkies) and BA Cityflyer Limited (Cityflyer) are considered to be separate operating segments, their activities are considered to be sufficiently similar in nature to aggregate the two segments and report them together with the network passenger and cargo operations. Therefore, based on the way the Group treats the network passenger and cargo operations, and the manner in which resource allocation decisions are made, the Group has only one reportable operating segment for financial reporting purposes, reported as the 'airline business'.

Financial results from other operating segments are below the quantitative threshold for determining reportable operating segments and consist primarily of The Mileage Company Limited, British Airways Holidays Limited and Speedbird Insurance Company Limited.

For the year ended 31 December, 2011

£ million	Airline business	All other segments	Unallocated	Total
Revenue				
Sales to external customers	9,690	297		9,987
Inter-segment sales	106			106
Segment revenue	9,796	297		10,093
Segment result	488	30		518
Other non-operating expense	(32)			(32)
Profit before tax and finance costs	456	30		486
Net finance costs	192		(159)	33
Loss on sale of assets	(3)			(3)
Share of associates' profit	(6)			(6)
Revaluation of convertible bond derivative liability			169	169
Tax			(7)	(7)
Profit after tax	639	30	3	672
Assets and liabilities				
Segment assets	11,005	132		11,137
Investment in associates	232			232
Total assets	11,237	132		11,369
Segment liabilities		334		4,054
Unallocated liabilities*	3,720		4,533	4,533
Total liabilities	3,720	334	4,533	8,587
Other segment information				
Property, plant and equipment – additions (note 12d)	640	10		650

(continued)

Non-current assets held for sale – transfers in (note 14)	11		11
Intangible assets – additions (note 15c)	72		72
Depreciation, amortisation and impairment (note 4a)	681	2	683
Impairment of available-for-sale financial asset – including Flybe (note 9)	23		23
Exceptional items (note 4b):			
Restructuring	12		12
Net impairment reversal	8		8

*Unallocated liabilities primarily include current taxes of £12 million deferred taxes £778 million and borrowings of £3,743 million which are managed on a Group basis.

(The company also provides comparative information for the nine months ended December 31, 2010; in 2010 it changed its year end from March 31 to December 31.)

b Geographical segments – by area of original sale

	Group	
£ million	12 months to 31 December 2011	9 months to 31 December 2010
Europe:	**6,090**	**3,906**
UK	4,323	2,943
Continental Europe	1,767	963
The Americas	**2,163**	**1,493**
USA and Canada	1,921	1,334
The rest of the Americas	242	159
Africa, Middle East and Indian sub-continent	998	727
Far East and Australasia	736	557
Revenue	**9,987**	**6,683**

The total of non-current assets excluding available-for-sale financial assets, employee benefit assets, other non-current assets and derivative financial instruments located in the UK is £7,093 million (2010: £7,063 million) and the total of these non-current assets located in other countries is £326 million (2010: £364 million).

If the analyst has access to only the consolidated figures, information about the composition of these figures is hidden in aggregated totals. There is no way to tell from the consolidated data how much each product line contributes to the company's profitability, risk, and growth potential. For example, in the case of British Airways, the segmented data reveal that the airline business segment yields 94% of the operating profit while contributing 97% of the revenues, whereas all other segments generate 3% of revenues yet 6% of profits. How much the other segments contribute to revenues and profits would not be revealed otherwise.

Companies have always been somewhat hesitant to disclose segmented data for several reasons, including the following:

1. Without a thorough knowledge of the business and an understanding of such important factors as the competitive environment and capital investment requirements, the investor may find the segmented information meaningless or may even draw improper conclusions about the segments' reported earnings.

2. Additional disclosure may harm reporting firms because it may be helpful to competitors, labour unions, suppliers, and certain government regulatory agencies.

3. Additional disclosure may discourage management from taking intelligent business risks because segments that report losses or unsatisfactory earnings may cause shareholder dissatisfaction with management.

4. The wide variation among firms in the choice of segments, cost allocation, and other accounting problems limits the usefulness of segmented information.

5. The investor is investing in the company as a whole and not in the particular segments, and it should not matter how any single segment is performing if the overall performance is satisfactory.

6. Certain technical problems, such as classification of segments and allocation of segment revenues and costs (especially "common costs"), are challenging.

On the other hand, the advocates of segmented disclosures offer these reasons in support of the practice.

1. Segmented information is needed by the investor to make an intelligent investment decision regarding a diversified company.

   (a) Sales and earnings of individual segments are needed to forecast consolidated profits because of the differences among segments in growth rate, risk, and profitability.

   (b) Segmented reports disclose the nature of a company's businesses and the relative size of the components, which aids in evaluating the company's investment worth.

2. The absence of segmented reporting by a diversified company may put its unsegmented, single-product-line competitors at a competitive disadvantage because the conglomerate may obscure information that its competitors must disclose.

The development of accounting standards for segmented financial information has been a continuing process during the past quarter century. The basic reporting requirements are discussed next. Note that ASPE does not contain guidance for reporting segmented information.

The advocates of segmented disclosures appear to have a much stronger case. Many users indicate that segmented data are the most useful financial information provided, aside from the basic financial statements.

Objective of Reporting Segmented Information

The objective of reporting segmented financial data is to provide information about the different types of business activities in which an enterprise engages and the different economic environments in which it operates[5] so that users of financial statements can:

- better understand the enterprise's performance,

- better assess its prospects for future net cash flows, and

- make more informed judgements about the enterprise as a whole.

Basic Principles of Segmented Reporting

A company might meet the segmented reporting objective by providing complete sets of financial statements that are disaggregated in several ways: for example, by products or services, by geography, by legal entity, or by type of customer. However, it is not feasible to provide all that information in every set of financial statements. The IASB instead requires that financial statements include selected information about operating segments from the perspective of the **chief operating decision-maker**, who could, for example, be CEO or COO (chief operating officer). The chief operating decision-maker function refers to the executive, or group of executives or directors, that allocates resources and assesses the operating performance of the company's segments.[6] The method chosen is sometimes referred to as the **management approach**. The **management approach** is based on the way that management segments the company for making operating decisions, which is made evident by the company's organization structure. Because this approach focuses on information about the components of the business that management looks at in making its decisions about operating matters, the components are referred to as **operating segments**.

Identifying Operating Segments

An operating segment is a component of an enterprise that has all of the following characteristics:

1. It engages in business activities from which it earns revenues and incurs expenses.

2. Its operating results are regularly reviewed by the company's chief operating decision-maker to assess segment performance and allocate resources to the segment.

3. There is discrete financial information available on it.[7]

Information about two or more operating segments may be aggregated only if the segments have the same basic characteristics in all of the following areas:

1. The nature of the products and services provided

2. The nature of the production process

3. The type or class of customer

4. The methods of product or service distribution

5. If applicable, the nature of the regulatory environment

After the company decides on the segments for possible disclosure, a quantitative materiality test is made to determine whether the segment is significant enough to warrant actual disclosure. An operating segment is regarded as significant, and is therefore identified as a **reportable segment**, if it satisfies one or more of the following quantitative thresholds:[8]

1. Its reporting revenue (including both sales to external customers and intersegment sales or transfers) is 10% or more of the combined revenue of all the enterprise's operating segments.

2. The absolute amount of its reported profit or loss is 10% or more of the greater, in absolute amount, of:

   (a) the combined reported operating profit of all operating segments that did not incur a loss, and

   (b) the combined reported loss of all operating segments that reported a loss.

3. Its assets are 10% or more of the combined assets of all operating segments.

In applying these tests, three additional factors must be considered. First, segment data must explain a significant portion of the company's business. Specifically, the segmented results must equal or exceed 75% of the combined sales to unaffiliated customers for the entire enterprise. This test prevents a company from providing limited information on only a few segments and lumping all the rest into one category.[9]

Second, as the profession recognizes that reporting too many segments may overwhelm users with detailed information, it has therefore proposed 10 segments as a practical limit of the number of segments that a company should disclose.[10]

Third, if an operating segment does not meet any of the tests but management believes separate information would be useful to users, then the segment may be presented separately.

To illustrate these requirements, assume that a company has identified the six possible reporting segments shown in Illustration 23-3 (amounts in 000s).

Illustration 23-3

Data for Different Possible Reporting Segments

Segments	Total Revenue	Reported Profit (Loss)	Assets
A	$ 100	$10	$ 60
B	50	2	30
C	700	40	390
D	300	20	160
E	900	18	280
F	100	(5)	50
	$2,150	$85	$970

The respective tests may be applied as follows:

Revenue test: 10% × $2,150 = $215; C, D, and E meet this test.

Reported profit (loss) test:

10% × $90 = $9 (note that the $5 loss is excluded as it is a loss) A, C, D, and E meet this test.

Assets tests: 10% × $970 = $97; C, D, and E meet this test.

The reportable segments are therefore A, C, D, and E, assuming that these four segments have enough sales to meet the test of 75% of combined sales. The 75% test is calculated as follows:

75% of combined sales test: 75% × $2,150 = $1,612; the sales of A, C, D, and E total $2,000 ($100 + $700 + $300 + $900); therefore, the 75% test is met.

Measurement Principles

The accounting principles that an entity uses for segment disclosure do not need to be the same principles that are used to prepare the consolidated statements. This flexibility may at first appear inconsistent. But preparing segment information in accordance with generally accepted accounting principles would be difficult because some principles are not expected to apply at a segment level. Examples include accounting for the cost of company-wide employee benefit plans and accounting for income taxes in a company that files one overall tax return.

Allocations of joint, common, or company-wide costs solely for external reporting purposes are not required. **Common costs** are defined as any costs that are incurred for the benefit of more than one segment and whose interrelated nature prevents a completely objective division of the costs among the segments. For example, the company president's salary is difficult to allocate to various segments. Allocations of common costs are inherently arbitrary and may not be meaningful if they are not used for internal management purposes. There is a presumption instead that allocations to segments are either directly attributable to the segment or reasonably allocable to it. There should be disclosure of the choices that were made in measuring segmented information.

Segmented and Enterprise-Wide Disclosures

The IASB requires that an enterprise report the following:[11]

1. **General information** about its reportable segments. This includes factors that management considers most significant in determining the company's reportable segments, and the types of products and services from which each operating segment derives its revenues.

2. **Segment revenues, profit and loss, assets, liabilities, and related information.** This states total profit or loss and total assets and liabilities for each reportable segment. In addition, the following specific information about each reportable segment must be reported if the amounts are regularly reviewed by management:

   (a) Revenues from external customers (revenues from customers attributed to individual material foreign countries should be separately disclosed)

   (b) Revenues from transactions with other operating segments of the same enterprise

   (c) Interest revenue

   (d) Interest expense

   (e) Depreciation and amortization

   (f) Unusual items

   (g) Equity in the net income of investees and joint ventures that are accounted for using the equity method

   (h) Income tax expense or benefit

(i) Significant non-cash items other than depreciation and amortization expense

Note that the amount that is reported should be the amount reviewed by management (the chief operating decision-maker). Information about the basis of accounting and other details should be disclosed.

3. **Reconciliations.** An enterprise must provide a reconciliation of the following:

(a) The total of the segments' revenues to total revenues

(b) The total of the operating segments' profits or losses to its profits or losses before income taxes and discontinued operations

(c) The total of the operating segments' assets and liabilities to total assets and liabilities

Reconciliations for other significant items that are disclosed should also be presented and all reconciling items should be separately identified and described for all of the above.

4. **Products and services.** The amount of revenues from external customers.

5. **Geographic areas.** Revenues from external customers (Canada versus foreign) and capital assets and goodwill (Canada versus foreign) should be stated. Foreign information must be disclosed by country if the amounts are material.

6. **Major customers.** If 10% or more of the revenues are derived from a single customer, the enterprise must disclose the total amount of revenues from each of these customers by segment.

Interim Reporting

Objective 5
Describe the accounting problems associated with interim reporting.

One further source of information for the investor is interim reports. **Interim reports** cover periods of less than one year. While at one time annual reporting was considered sufficient in terms of providing timely information, demand quickly grew for quarterly information and now capital markets are moving rapidly to even more frequent disclosures. IFRS does not mandate which entities should provide interim information; however, it provides guidance (which entities are encouraged to follow) if the entity does provide the information. If the interim report is in compliance with IFRS, this should be disclosed. ASPE does not include standards for interim reporting.

Illustration 23-4 presents the disclosure of selected quarterly data for **Torstar Corporation**. The media company also disclosed consolidated statements of financial position, income, comprehensive income, changes in equity, and cash flows (along with related notes). The statements were accompanied by a management discussion of the operations, liquidity and capital resources, outlook, and risks and uncertainties. With such comprehensive coverage, the report gives a significant amount of information.

Illustration 23-4

Disclosure of Quarterly Consolidated Statement of Income—Torstar Corporation

TORSTAR CORPORATION
Consolidated Statement of Income
(Dollars in Thousands of Canadian Dollars except per share amounts)
(Unaudited)

	Three months ended March 31	
	2012	2011
Operating revenue	$ 350,755	$ 351,422
Salaries and benefits	(128,618)	(122,240)
Other operating costs	(181,905)	(187,503)
Amortization and depreciation	(9,253)	(7,780)
Restructuring and other charges (note 12)	(2,595)	(401)

(continued)

Illustration 23-4

*Disclosure of Quarterly
Consolidated Statement of
Income—Torstar Corporation
(continued)*

**Real World
Emphasis**

	Three months ended March 31	
	2012	2011
Operating profit		
Interest and financing costs (note 10(c))	28,384	33,498
Foreign exchange	(2,271)	(10,715)
Loss of associated businesses (note 7)	(6)	768
Other income (note 18)	(412)	(563)
Gain on sale of assets (note 18)	10,407	
	3,417	
Income and other taxes (note 5)	39,519	22,988
	(10,250)	(7,600)
Net income	$29,269	$15,388
Attributable to:		
Equity shareholders	$29,310	$15,472
Minority interests	($41)	($84)
Net income attributable to equity shareholders per Class A (voting) and Class B (non-voting) share (note 14(b)):		
Basic	$0.37	$0.20
Diluted	$0.37	$0.19

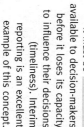

**Underlying
Concept**

For information
to be relevant,
it must be
available to decision-makers
before it loses its capacity
to influence their decisions
(timeliness). Interim
reporting is an excellent
example of this concept.

Because of the short-term nature of the information in these reports, however, there is considerable controversy about the general approach that should be taken. Supporters of the **discrete view** believe that each interim period should be treated as a separate accounting period. Deferrals and accruals would therefore follow the same principles that are used for annual reports. Accounting transactions should be reported as they occur, and expense recognition should not change with the period of time covered. Proponents of the **integral view**, on the other hand, believe that the interim report is an integral part of the annual report and that deferrals and accruals should take into consideration what will happen for the entire year. In this approach, estimated expenses are assigned to parts of a year based on the sales volume or some other activity base. IFRS generally favours the discrete view.

One notable exception to the discrete view is in calculating tax expense. Normally a company would prepare its tax return at year end and assess taxes payable and related tax balances. It is neither cost-effective nor feasible to do this for each interim period (since tax rates are often graduated and therefore increase with increasing taxable income), so annual estimates are made instead. Specifically, an estimate is made of interim taxable income and temporary differences and then the annual estimated tax rate is applied. **Another exception relates to the employer's portion of payroll taxes.** Although these taxes may be remitted by the employer early in the year (as required by law), they are assessed by the government on an annual basis. Therefore, for interim reporting periods, the total estimated annual amount is allocated to the interim periods, which means that the expense is recognized on an accrual basis as opposed to a cash basis.

Interim Reporting Requirements

As a general rule, the profession indicates that the same accounting principles that are used for annual reports should be used for interim reports. Revenues should be recognized in interim periods on the same basis as they are for annual periods. For example, if the percentage-of-completion method is used for recognizing revenue on an annual basis, then the same method should be applied to interim reports as well. Also, costs that are directly associated with revenues (product costs), such as materials, labour and related fringe benefits, and manufacturing overhead, should be treated in the same manner for interim reports as for annual reports.

Companies should also generally use the same inventory cost formulas (such as FIFO or weighted average) for interim reports that they use for annual reports. At a minimum, a condensed SFP, comprehensive income statement, statement of changes in equity, statement of cash flows, and selected notes are required.[12] Note that the standard requires companies to provide at least condensed statements but does not prevent companies from providing more detailed presentations. Condensed financial statements should include at least the same headings and subtotals as the most recent annual statements. The SFP should be presented as at the end of the current interim period with a comparative SFP as at the end of the immediately preceding fiscal year. The SFP should also be presented for the beginning of the earliest comparative period when an entity applies an accounting policy retrospectively or makes a retrospective restatement.

The income statement should be presented for the current interim period and interim year to date with comparatives. (Comparatives are comparable information for the previous period or year). For the statement of changes in equity, the information should be presented cumulatively for the current fiscal year to date with comparatives. Finally, for the cash flow statement, information should be presented cumulatively for the current fiscal year to date with comparatives.[13] Earnings per share (EPS) information is also required if an enterprise must present this information in its annual information.[14]

Regarding disclosure, the following interim data should be reported as a minimum:[15]

1. Whether the statements comply with IFRS

2. A statement that the company follows the same accounting policies and methods as the most recent annual financial statements including a description of new or changed policies

3. A description of any seasonality or cyclicality of interim period operations

4. The nature and amount of any unusual items

5. The nature and amount of changes in estimates

6. Issuances, repurchases, and repayments of debt and equity securities

7. Dividends paid

8. Information about reportable segments including revenues from external customers, intersegment revenues, segment profit or loss, total assets for which there is a material change, a description of differences from the last annual statements in the basis of segmentation, and reconciliation of segment profit or loss to the entity's total profit or loss before taxes and discontinued operations

9. Events subsequent to the interim period

10. Specific information about changes in the composition of the entity

11. Any other information that is required for fair presentation and/or is material to an understanding of the interim period

Unique Problems of Interim Reporting

Changes in Accounting. What happens if a company decides to change an accounting principle in the third quarter of a fiscal year? Should the adjustment for the cumulative effect of the change be charged or credited to that quarter? Presentation of a cumulative effect in the third quarter may be misleading because of the inherent subjectivity that is associated with the reported income of the first two quarters. In addition, a question arises as to whether such a change might not be used to manipulate a particular quarter's income. These changes should therefore be reflected by retroactive application to prior interim periods unless the data are not practicably available. The comparable interim periods of prior fiscal years should also be restated.[16]

Earnings per Share. Interim reporting of earnings per share numbers has all the problems that are involved in calculating and presenting annual earnings per share figures, and more. If shares are issued in the third period, EPS for the first two periods may not be indicative of year-end EPS. For purposes of calculating earnings per share and making the required disclosure determinations, each interim period should stand alone. That is, all applicable tests should be made for that single period.

Seasonality. Seasonality occurs when sales are compressed into one short period of the year while certain costs are fairly evenly spread throughout the year. For example, the natural gas industry has its heavy sales in the winter, while the beverage industry has its heavy sales in the summer.

In a seasonal business, wide fluctuations in profits occur because off-season sales do not absorb the company's fixed costs (for example, manufacturing, selling, and administrative costs that tend to remain fairly constant regardless of sales or production). Revenues and expenses should be recognized and accrued when they are earned or incurred according to IFRS. This is also true for interim periods. Thus, a company would only defer recognition of costs or revenues if it would be appropriate to do so at year end (in other words, the same tests are applied). As mentioned earlier in the text, deferral of costs is not appropriate unless the costs meet the definition of an asset.

Continuing Controversy. The profession has developed the stringent standards noted above for interim reporting and this has alleviated much of the controversy that existed regarding the discrete and integral perspectives.

There is still controversy, however, in regard to the independent auditor's involvement in interim reports. Many auditors are reluctant to express an opinion on interim financial information, arguing that the data are too tentative and subjective. Conversely, an increasing number of individuals are arguing for some type of examination of interim reports. A compromise may be a limited review of interim reports that provides some assurance that an examination has been conducted by an outside party and that the published information appears to be in accordance with generally accepted accounting principles.

Analysts want financial information as soon as possible, before it becomes old news. We may not be far from a system in which corporate financial records can be accessed at any time by computer. Investors might be able to access a company's financial records via computer whenever they wish and put the information in the format they need.[17] Thus, they could learn about sales slippage, cost increases, or earnings changes as they happen, rather than waiting until after the quarter has ended.

A steady stream of information from the company to the investor could be very positive because it might alleviate management's continual concern with short-run interim numbers. It would also alleviate many of the allocation problems that plague current GAAP.

Internet Financial Reporting and Continuous Disclosures

How can companies improve the usefulness of their financial reporting practices? Many companies are using the Internet's power and reach to provide more useful information to financial statement readers. Almost all large companies have websites, and a considerable proportion of these companies' websites contain links to their financial statements, annual reports, and other disclosures. The increased popularity of such reporting is not surprising, since the costs of printing and disseminating paper reports are reduced.

How does Internet financial reporting improve the overall usefulness of a company's financial reports? First, dissemination of reports via the Internet can allow firms to communicate with more users than is possible with traditional paper reports. In addition, Internet reporting allows users to take advantage of tools such as search engines and hyperlinks to quickly find information about the firm and, sometimes, to download the information for analysis, perhaps in computer spreadsheets. Finally, Internet reporting can help make financial reports more relevant by allowing companies to report expanded disaggregated data and more timely data than is possible through paper-based reporting. For example, some companies voluntarily report weekly sales data and segment operating data on their websites.

Given these benefits and ever-improving Internet tools, will it be long before electronic reporting entirely replaces paper-based financial disclosure? The main obstacles to achieving complete electronic reporting are **equality of access to electronic financial reporting and the reliability of the information that is distributed** via the Internet. Although companies may practise Internet financial reporting, they must still prepare traditional paper reports because some investors may not have Internet access. These investors would receive differential (less) information relative to wired investors if companies were to eliminate paper reports. In addition, at present, Internet financial reporting is a voluntary means of reporting. As a result, there are no standards for the completeness of reports on the Internet, nor is there a requirement that these reports be audited. One concern in this regard is that computer hackers could invade a company's website and corrupt the financial information that is there.

A great example of the use of technology and continuous reporting is the current practice of releasing quarterly results via the company website through video and live streaming. Investors and analysts can visit the company website and hear the earnings announcements first-hand.

While Internet financial reporting is gaining in popularity, until issues related to differential access to the Internet and the reliability of web-based information are addressed, we will also continue to see traditional paper-based reporting.

Other Measurement Issues

Related-Party Transactions

Objective 6

Discuss the accounting issues for related-party transactions.

Related-party transactions present especially sensitive and difficult problems. The accountant or auditor who has responsibility for reporting on these types of transactions has to be extremely careful to ensure that the rights of the reporting company and the needs of financial statement users are properly balanced.

IFRS deals only with disclosure requirements whereas ASPE requires that some related-party transactions be remeasured. **Related-party transactions** arise when a business engages in transactions in which one of the transacting parties has the ability to significantly influence the policies of the other, or in which a non-transacting party has the ability to influence the policies of the two transacting parties. Related parties include but are not limited to the following:

1. Companies or individuals who control, or are controlled by, or are under common control with the reporting enterprise

2. Investors and investees where there is significant influence or joint control

3. Company management

4. Members of immediate family of the above

5. The other party when a management contract exists[18]

Transactions between related parties cannot be presumed to be carried out at arm's length since there may not be the required conditions of competitive, free-market dealings. Transactions such as borrowing or lending money at abnormally low or high interest rates, real estate sales at amounts that differ significantly from appraised values, exchanges of nonmonetary assets, and transactions involving enterprises that have no economic substance ("shell corporations") suggest that related parties may be involved. **In each case, there is a measurement issue.** A basic assumption about financial information is that it is based on transactions that are between arm's-length parties. **Consequently, if this condition is not met, the transactions should at least be** disclosed as being between related parties. Furthermore, special measurement principles exist for related-party transactions and these may require a transaction to be remeasured under ASPE.

The accountant is expected to report the **economic substance rather than the legal form** of these transactions and to make adequate disclosures. The following disclosures are recommended:[19]

1. The nature of the relationship(s) involved

2. A description of the transactions

3. The recorded amounts of transactions

4. The measurement basis that was used

5. Amounts due from or to related parties and the related terms and conditions

6. Contractual obligations with related parties

7. Contingencies involving related parties

8. Under IFRS, management compensation and the name of the entity's parent company as well as its ultimate controlling entity or individual

Under ASPE, certain related-party transactions must be remeasured to the carrying amount of the underlying assets or services that were exchanged. **Carrying amount** is defined as the amount of the item transferred as recorded in the books of the transferor. **This is the case if the transaction is not in the normal course of business, there is no substantive change in ownership, and/or the exchange amount is not supported by independent evidence.** The argument to support remeasurement rests on the premise that, if the transaction is not an ordinary transaction for the enterprise, there might not be a reasonable measure of fair value. Furthermore, if there is no change in ownership, then no bargaining has taken place and, therefore, the price that is arrived at for the exchange may not represent a value that would have been arrived at had the transaction been at arm's length. **Transactions that are in the normal course of business that have no commercial substance must also be remeasured.** This argument rests on the premise that, if the transaction is not bona fide or authentic, there is no real exchange of risks and rewards of ownership and, therefore, no gain or loss should be recognized. **This is only an issue where the transaction is also a nonmonetary transaction.** A transaction has **commercial substance** when the entity's cash flows are expected to be significantly different after and as a result of the transaction. In making this determination, consider the risk, timing, and amount of cash flows. Finally, where products or properties are exchanged in the normal course of business to facilitate sales, the transaction is also recorded at carrying value.

Where transactions are remeasured to their carrying value, the difference between the carrying amounts of the items that have been exchanged is booked as a charge or credit to equity.[20] To illustrate, assume that Knudson Limited, a manufacturing company, sells land worth $20,000 to Bay Limited. The companies are related because the same shareholder has a 70% equity interest in each company (the rest of the shares are publicly traded). The land has a carrying value of $15,000 on Knudson's books. In exchange, Bay Limited, also a manufacturing company, transfers to Knudson a building that has a net book value of $12,000. This transaction is not in the **ordinary (normal) course of business** since both companies are manufacturers and would not normally be selling capital assets such as land and buildings. Based on this assessment, therefore, the transaction merits further analysis.

Illustration 23-5 is a decision tree[21] of the judgement that is necessary when determining how to treat related-party transactions.

Illustration 23-5

*Related-Party Transactions—
Decision Tree*

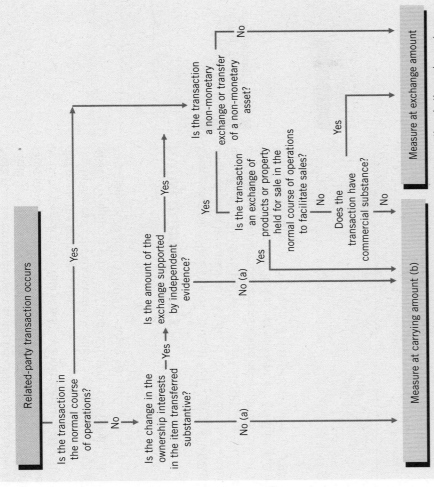

Related-party transaction occurs

Is the transaction in the normal course of operations? — Yes

No

Is the change in the ownership interests in the item transferred substantive? — Yes → Is the amount of the exchange supported by independent evidence? — Yes

No (a)

No (a)

Yes → Is the transaction an exchange of products or property held for sale in the normal course of operations to facilitate sales?

Yes → Is the transaction a non-monetary exchange or transfer of a non-monetary asset?

No

Does the transaction have commercial substance? — Yes

No

No

Measure at carrying amount (b)

Measure at exchange amount

(a) Carrying amount is used for both monetary and nonmonetary transactions in these circumstances.
(b) In rare circumstances, when the carrying amount of the item received is not available, a reasonable estimate of the carrying amount, based on the transferor's original cost, may be used to measure the exchange.

Looking at the decision tree, after deciding if the transaction is in the normal course of business, the next question is **whether there has been a substantive change in ownership.** Do different parties own the exchanged items after the transaction? Since the same controlling shareholder owns both assets before and after the transaction (even if indirectly through the companies), there is no substantive change in ownership.[22] The transaction would therefore be remeasured to carrying values with the following journal entry on the Knudson books:

Property, Plant, and Equipment	12,000	
Retained Earnings	3,000	
Land		15,000

A	=	L	+	SE
–3,000				–3,000

Cash flows: No effect

Bay would record the land at $15,000 and take the building off its books. The resulting credit would be booked to Contributed Surplus. Note that the difference between the carrying values is generally viewed as an equity contribution or distribution and is therefore booked through equity.

If, on the other hand, the transaction had been in the normal course of business and it had commercial substance, it would have been recorded at the exchange value. The exchange value is defined as the amount of consideration paid or received and agreed to by the related parties.[23] In this case, assume that the agreed-upon exchange value is $20,000.

Note that the exchange value is not necessarily equal to the fair value but it could be. It is whatever value the two parties agree on. ASPE notes that it is possible that the transaction value may approximate fair value but it is not necessary to establish what fair value would be if the transaction value is not an approximation. If cash were exchanged, this would determine the exchange value.

In this case, the transaction would be treated like a sale by both parties and Knudson would recognize a gain of \$5,000 (\$20,000 − \$15,000). Likewise, Bay would also recognize a gain of \$8,000 (\$20,000 − \$12,000).

Subsequent Events

Events that take place after the formal SFP date but before the financial statements are complete must be considered. Under IFRS, this date is the date that the statements are considered authorized for issue, whereas under ASPE, the date is a matter of judgement, taking into account management structure and procedures followed in completing the statements. These events are referred to as **subsequent events** since they occur subsequent to the SFP date. The subsequent events period is time-diagrammed in Illustration 23-6.

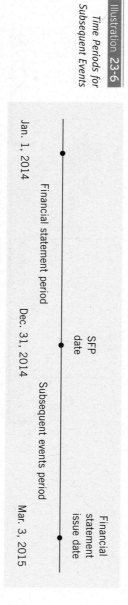

Illustration 23-6

Time Periods for Subsequent Events

Jan. 1, 2014	Dec. 31, 2014	Mar. 3, 2015
	SFP date	Financial statement issue date
Financial statement period	Subsequent events period	

A period of several weeks, and sometimes months, may lapse after the end of the year before the financial statement completion date. Taking, and pricing, the inventory, reconciling subsidiary ledgers with controlling accounts, preparing necessary adjusting entries, assuring that all transactions for the period have been entered, obtaining an audit of the financial statements by independent public accountants, and printing the annual report all take time. **During the period between the SFP date and after completion of the financial statements for distributions to shareholders and creditors, important transactions or other events may occur that materially affect the company's financial position or operating situation.**

Many readers of a recent SFP would believe that the balance sheet condition is constant and they therefore project it into the future. Readers therefore need to be made aware if the company has sold one of its plants, acquired a subsidiary, settled significant litigation, or experienced any other important event in the post-balance sheet period. Without an explanation in a note, the reader might be misled and draw inappropriate conclusions.

Two types of events or transactions that occur after the SFP date may have a material effect on the financial statements or may need to be considered to interpret these statements accurately:

1. **Events that provide additional evidence about conditions that existed at the SFP date, affect the estimates used in preparing financial statements, and, therefore, result in needed adjustments.** All information that is available prior to the issuance of the financial statements is used to evaluate previously made estimates. To ignore these subsequent events is to skip an opportunity to improve the financial statements' accuracy. This first type of event encompasses information that would have been recorded in the accounts if it had been known at the SFP date. For example, if a loss on an account receivable results from a customer's bankruptcy subsequent to the SFP date, the financial statements are adjusted before their issuance. The bankruptcy stems from the customer's poor financial health, which existed at the SFP date.

The same criterion applies to settlements of litigation. The financial statements must be adjusted if the events that gave rise to the litigation, such as personal injury or patent infringement, took place prior to the SFP date. If the event giving rise to the claim took place subsequent to the SFP date, no adjustment is necessary. Thus, a loss resulting from a customer's fire or flood after the SFP date is not indicative of conditions that existed at that date. Accordingly, adjustment of the financial statements is not appropriate.

2. **Events that provide evidence about conditions that did not exist at the SFP date but arise subsequent to that date and do not require adjustment of the financial statements.** Some of these events may have to be disclosed to keep the financial statements from being misleading. These disclosures take the form of notes, supplemental schedules, or even pro forma "as if" financial data prepared as if the event had occurred on the SFP date. The following are examples of such events that require disclosure if they are significant (but do not result in adjustment):

(a) A fire or flood that results in a loss

(b) A decline in the market value of investments

(c) A purchase of a business

(d) The start of legal action where the cause of action arose after the SFP date

(e) Changes in foreign currency rates

(f) An issuance of shares or debt

Illustration 23-7 presents an example of subsequent events disclosure from the February 2011 annual report of **Acasti Pharma Inc.**

Underlying Concept

The periodicity or time period assumption implies that an enterprise's economic activities can be divided into artificial time periods for purposes of analysis.

Real World Emphasis

Illustration 23-7

Subsequent Events Note Disclosure—Acasti Pharma Inc.

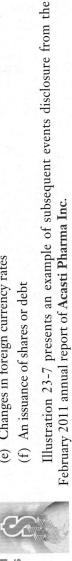

16. Subsequent events:

(a) On March 21, 2011, the outstanding Class B and Class C shares, 5,000,000 and 260,000, respectively, were converted into Class A shares by their holders on a 1:1 basis (the "Conversion"). Following the Conversion, the liability for convertible redeemable shares in the amount of $4,052,000 was extinguished, and the number of issued and outstanding Class A shares of the Company was 64,434,444. While the shares were redeemable on demand as of February 28, 2011, they have been classified as long-term liabilities at that date, as the conversion refinanced the obligation on a long-term basis.

(b) On March 21, 2011, the Company's Board of Directors amended the incentive stock option plan (the "Plan"). The amendments to the Plan are subject to the approval by the shareholders at their next annual meeting. The main modification to the Plan consists of an increase in the number of shares reserved for issuance of incentive stock options under the Plan to 6,443,444.

(c) On March 21, 2011, the Board of Directors approved the submission of a listing application to the TSX Venture Exchange, for the public listing of the Company's Class A shares. A copy of the Listing Application is available on SEDAR. The Company's shares began trading on March 31, 2011.

(d) On March 21, 2011, the Company entered into an agreement with Neptune in order to delay the due dates of the unpaid balance of the first minimum annual royalty payment, in the amount of $16,020, and of the second payment in the amount of $200,000, until August 7, 2012. Royalties accrued as of February 28, 2011 have therefore been classified as long-term liabilities in the balance sheet.

(e) Clinical research contract:

On March 24, 2011, the Company initiated a clinical research trial that is being conducted over a 24-month period at an estimated cost of $2,400,000.

(f) Rights offering:

On May 6, 2011, the Company's Board of Directors authorized, subject to regulatory approval, the issuance of rights to its shareholders to subscribe to additional Class A shares of the Company. The maximum number of shares to be issued following the rights offering will equal 15% of the Company's outstanding shares. If approved, the rights will be exercisable at a minimal price of $0.60 and not less than the discounted market price permitted by the TSX-Venture Exchange (the "Exchange"). The Company has received the Exchange's conditional approval, which is also subject to the Autorité des Marchés Financiers' (AMF) approval. The Company has also filed a request to obtain a prospectus exemption from the AMF. At May 17, 2011, approvals from the AMF for the rights offering and the exemption requested were pending.

Many subsequent events or developments are not likely to require either adjustment of the financial statements or disclosure. Typically, these are non-accounting events or conditions that management normally communicates by other means. These events include legislation, product changes, management changes, strikes, unionization, marketing agreements, and loss of important customers. What to include in the financial statements is a matter of professional judgement since all changes to the business will eventually affect performance one way or another.

Sometimes subsequent events are so pervasive—such as a rapid decline of the company's financial health—that they call into question the going concern assumption. Recall from earlier chapters that the going concern assumption presumes that an entity will continue to operate and will be able to realize its assets and discharge its liabilities in an orderly manner. This supports the use of the mixed fair value/historical cost measurement model. If the subsequent event calls the going concern assumption into question, the measurement model would perhaps change. The company would have to make a decision as to whether it should include additional note disclosures or whether the assets and liabilities should be remeasured to reflect net realizable values in a liquidation market.

Illustration 23-8 presents an excerpt from **Quintain Estates and Development plc's** annual report and accounts for the year ended March 31, 2012. Quintain lists on the London Stock Exchange. This note illustrates the concept of going concern. In this case, the value of the company's property has declined and, if it declines further, it could result in debt covenants being breached and loans being called. Note that the financial statements mention "gearing," which is a term commonly used in Britain to refer to financial leverage. Gearing, which is discussed in the note in relation to its debt covenants, is defined by the company in its annual report as "the ratio of net borrowings of the Company and its wholly owned subsidiaries to equity shareholders' funds adjusted for deferred tax and mark to market movements."

Illustration 23-8

Potential Going Concern Issues—Quintain Estate and Development plc

1.2 Going concern

The Group financial statements have been prepared on a going concern basis, which assumes that the Group will continue to meet its liabilities as they fall due. At 31 March 2012, the Group has prepared detailed cashflow forecasts which show that it has adequate committed undrawn facilities to finance its committed capital expenditure and other outflows, which will enable it to continue in operational existence for the foreseeable future. Further information regarding the Group's business activities, together with the factors likely to affect its future development, performance and position is set out in the Operational and Financial Review. In addition, notes 5.3 and 6.5 to these financial statements set out the Group's objectives, policies and processes for managing its capital, its financial risk management objectives, details of its financial instruments and hedging activities and its exposure to credit risk and liquidity risk.

The Group's key financial covenants are an interest cover covenant, which requires the Group's operating profit before net finance expenses plus realized profits on disposals over net finance expenses excluding mark to market movements on derivatives to be greater than 1.25x, and a gearing covenant, which requires the net borrowings of the Company and its wholly owned subsidiaries to be less than 110% of its equity, as defined in the banking covenants. The Group has a gearing ratio of 87% at 31 March 2012 and an interest cover ratio of 2.9x at 31 March 2012. The Group's forecasts show that the Group is expected to continue to meet both financial covenants for the foreseeable future.

Based on the above the directors believe it is appropriate to prepare the financial statements on a going concern basis.

Unincorporated Businesses

Throughout this text, the primary emphasis has been on incorporated businesses. Partnerships and sole proprietorships are another significant business form. These businesses are unincorporated and thus do not have share capital. This type of business has in the past decade become very popular as a tax shelter in the form of income trusts or investment trusts. Interestingly enough, while ownership of partnerships is generally private, ownership of income and investment trusts is often public. The partnership or trust units trade on various stock exchanges.

The accounting issues related to these types of entities are generally similar to those of incorporated companies, with a few exceptions.

1. It is critical to define the economic entity since unincorporated businesses are not separate legal entities. The financial statements should indicate clearly the name under

which the business is conducted and it should be clear that the business is unincorporated and that the statements do not include the assets and liabilities of the owners.

2. Salaries, interest, or similar items accruing to owners should be clearly indicated.

3. No provision for income taxes should be made. Since the businesses are not separate legal entities, the income is taxed in the hands of the unit holders.

Note that the owners' equity section would also include different terminology; for example, "capital" instead of common stock and "withdrawals" instead of dividends. ASPE provides guidance regarding unincorporated businesses in Section 1800 of Part II of the *CICA Handbook*, whereas there is no specific guidance under IFRS.

AUDITOR'S REPORTS

Objective 8

Identify the major disclosures found in the auditor's report.

Another important source of information that is often overlooked is the **auditor's report.** An auditor is an accounting professional who conducts an independent examination of the accounting data presented by a business enterprise. If the auditor is satisfied that the financial statements present the financial position, results of operations, and cash flows fairly in accordance with International Financial Reporting Standards, an unqualified opinion is expressed, as shown in Illustration 23-9.[24]

Illustration 23-9

Example of Auditors' Report under Canadian Auditing Standards

Real World Emphasis

INDEPENDENT AUDITOR'S REPORT

Report on the Financial Statements

[Appropriate Addressee]

We have audited the accompanying financial statements of ABC Company, which comprise the statement of financial position as at December 31, 20X1, and the statement of comprehensive income, statement of changes in equity and cash flow statement for the year then ended, and a summary of significant accounting policies and other explanatory information.

Management's Responsibility for the Financial Statements

Management is responsible for the preparation and fair presentation of these financial statements in accordance with International Financial Reporting Standards, and for such internal control as management determines is necessary to enable the preparation of financial statements that are free from material misstatement, whether due to fraud or error.

Auditor's Responsibility

Our responsibility is to express an opinion on these financial statements based on our audit. We conducted our audit in accordance with Canadian generally accepted auditing standards. Those standards require that we comply with ethical requirements and plan and perform the audit to obtain reasonable assurance about whether the financial statements are free from material misstatement.

An audit involves performing procedures to obtain audit evidence about the amounts and disclosures in the financial statements. The procedures selected depend on the auditor's judgment, including the assessment of the risks of material misstatement of the financial statements, whether due to fraud or error. In making those risk assessments, the auditor considers internal control relevant to the entity's preparation and fair presentation of the financial statements in order to design audit procedures that are appropriate in the circumstances, but not for the purpose of expressing an opinion on the effectiveness of the entity's internal control. An audit also includes evaluating the appropriateness of accounting policies used and the reasonableness of accounting estimates made by management, as well as evaluating the overall presentation of the financial statements.

We believe that the audit evidence we have obtained is sufficient and appropriate to provide a basis for our audit opinion.

Opinion

In our opinion, the financial statements present fairly, in all material respects, the financial position of ABC Company as at December 31, 20X1, and its financial performance and its cash flows for the year then ended in accordance with International Financial Reporting Standards.

[Auditor's signature]
[Date of the auditor's report]
[Auditor's address]

Source: ©2012. Reproduced from the *CICA Handbook–Assurance,* CAS 700, Illustration No. 1 with permission from the Canadian Institute of Chartered Accountants.

In preparing a report, an auditor follows procedures in accordance with the reporting standards articulated in the Canadian Auditing Standards.

Unqualified Opinions

In most cases, the auditor issues a standard **unqualified or clean opinion**. This means that the auditor expresses the opinion that the financial statements present fairly, in all material respects, the entity's financial position, results of operations, and cash flows in conformity with generally accepted accounting principles. Certain circumstances, although they do not affect the auditor's unqualified opinion, may require the auditor to add an explanatory paragraph to the audit report.

Qualified Opinions and Disclaimers of Opinion

In some situations, the auditor is required to express a qualified opinion. A **qualified opinion** contains an exception to the standard opinion. Ordinarily the exception is not significant enough to invalidate the statements as a whole; if it were, an adverse opinion would be given. Usually, the auditor may deviate from the standard unqualified short-form report on financial statements when something does not follow GAAP.

A qualified opinion states that, except for the effects of the matter related to the qualification, the financial statements present fairly, in all material respects, the financial position, results of operations, and cash flows in conformity with generally accepted accounting principles.

A qualified opinion might also be given where there is a scope limitation; that is, where the auditor has not been able to obtain sufficient and appropriate audit evidence. This might happen if there has been an accidental destruction by fire of company records, for instance. In this case, there would be a disclaimer that would note that the auditor is unable to give an opinion.

Adverse Opinions

An **adverse opinion** is required in any report in which the exceptions to fair presentation are so pervasive that in the independent auditor's judgement a qualified opinion is not justified. In such a case, the financial statements taken as a whole are not presented in accordance with GAAP. Adverse opinions are rare, because most enterprises change their accounting to conform to the auditor's desires.

FINANCIAL STATEMENT ANALYSIS

An Overview of Financial Statement Analysis

Objective 9
Describe methods used for basic financial statement analysis and summarize the limitations of ratio analysis.

In prior chapters, starting with Chapter 4, we discussed financial statement analysis and ratios as they applied to the specific topics from each chapter. In Chapter 5 (Appendix 5A) we also provided a summary of key ratios used in the text. In this section we provide a summary of the various aspects of financial statement analysis previously discussed, and provide an overview of some additional techniques of financial statement analysis.

An awareness of the particular accounting policies and methods used by a company to recognize items and measure amounts reported is important for interpreting and understanding the results of financial statement analysis. Examples of areas in which companies may choose different accounting policies include the capitalization or expensing of the interest related to financing asset construction (under ASPE), the method for amortizing long-lived assets, the valuation of inventory, and the method used to recognize revenue on long-term contracts. The particular choice can have a significant effect on whether items and amounts are reported, how they are measured, where they are reported, and trends over time for a given company. Also, if the financial statement analysis involves inter-company comparison, the use of different policies by the companies must be taken into consideration.

Within this general context, specific information from financial statements can be obtained by examining relationships between items on the statements and identifying trends in these relationships. Relationships are expressed numerically in ratios and percentages, and trends are identified through horizontal and trend analysis.

Several limitations must be considered when analyzing financial statements. For example, **financial statements report on the past.** As such, analysis of financial statement data is largely an examination of the past. Whenever such information is incorporated into a decision-making process, a critical assumption is that the past is a reasonable basis for predicting the future. This is usually a reasonable approach, but you should recognize this limitation.

Also, **while ratio and trend analyses will help identify strengths and weaknesses of a company, such analyses will not likely reveal why things are as they are.** Ratios and trends may serve as "red flags" to indicate problem areas. Finding answers about why usually requires an in-depth analysis and an awareness of many factors about a company that are not reported in the financial statements; for instance, the impact of inflation, actions of competitors, technological developments, or a strike at a major supplier's or buyer's business.

Another consideration is that a **single ratio, by itself, is not likely to be very useful.** For example, a current ratio of 2:1 (current assets are twice current liabilities) may be viewed as satisfactory. If, however, the industry average is 3:1, such a conclusion may be questioned. Even given this industry average, you may conclude that the particular company is doing well if the ratio last year was 1.5:1. Consequently, to derive meaning from ratios, some standard against which to compare them is needed. Such a standard may come from industry averages, past years' amounts, a particular competitor, or planned levels.

Finally, **awareness of the limitations of accounting numbers used in an analysis** is important. For example, the implications of different acceptable accounting policies on statements, ratios, and trends, particularly regarding comparability among companies and between a company and an industry average, must be recognized. More will be said about limitations and their consequences later in this chapter.

Financial Statement Analysis Techniques

Various techniques are used in the analysis of financial statement data.[25] These include **ratio analysis, percentage (common-size) analysis, and examination of related data** (that is, in notes and other sources). No one technique is more useful than another. Every situation faced by the analyst is different, and the answers needed are often obtained only on close examination of the interrelationships among all the data provided.

Ratio Analysis

Ratio analysis is a starting point in developing information desired by an analyst. A **ratio is** simply **an expression of the relationship between two numbers** drawn or derived from the financial statements. Ratios can be classified as shown in Illustration 23–10 (and as previously discussed in Appendix 5A).

Illustration 23-10

Major Types of Ratios

MAJOR TYPES OF RATIOS

Liquidity ratios. Measure the enterprise's short-term ability to pay its maturing obligations.

Activity ratios. Measure how effectively the enterprise is using its assets. Activity ratios also measure how liquid certain assets like inventory and receivables are; in other words, how fast the asset's value is realized by the company.

Profitability ratios. Measure financial performance and shareholder value creation for a specific time period.

Coverage or solvency ratios. Measure the degree of protection for long-term creditors and investors or a company's ability to meet its long-term obligations.

Generally, the liquidity ratios and coverage ratios reflect financial strength: the ability to satisfy the financial requirements of non-ownership interests in the business. Assessing management's performance is a prime reason for examining activity and profitability ratios. From such assessment, investors formulate opinions about returns from future ownership interest.

The calculation and use of individual ratios has been illustrated throughout each chapter in Volume 1 and Volume 2 of the textbook. This chapter does not repeat the details of how to use and interpret each ratio, so you may wish to refer back to the discussion of the individual ratios in prior chapters. The ratios are summarized in Illustration 23-11. The exercises and problems at the end of this chapter allow you to further consider the appropriate calculation and use of these ratios.

Illustration 23-11

A Summary of Financial Ratios

RATIO	FORMULA	WHAT IT MEASURES
I. Liquidity		
1. Current ratio	$\dfrac{\text{Current assets}}{\text{Current liabilities}}$	Short-term debt-paying ability
2. Quick or acid-test ratio	$\dfrac{\text{Cash, marketable securities, and receivables (net)}}{\text{Current liabilities}}$	Immediate short-term liquidity
3. Current cash debt coverage ratio	$\dfrac{\text{Net cash provided by operating activities}}{\text{Average current liabilities}}$	Company's ability to pay off its current liabilities in a specific year from its operations
II. Activity		
4. Receivables turnover	$\dfrac{\text{Net sales}}{\text{Average trade receivables (net)}}$	Liquidity of receivables
5. Inventory turnover	$\dfrac{\text{Cost of goods sold}}{\text{Average inventory}}$	Liquidity of inventory
6. Asset turnover	$\dfrac{\text{Net sales}}{\text{Average total assets}}$	How efficiently assets are used to generate sales
III. Profitability		
7. Profit margin on sales	$\dfrac{\text{Net income}}{\text{Net sales}}$	Net income generated by each dollar of sales
8. Rate of return on assets	$\dfrac{\text{Net income}}{\text{Average total assets}}$	Overall profitability of assets
9. Rate of return on common share equity	$\dfrac{\text{Net income minus preferred dividends}}{\text{Average common shareholders' equity}}$	Profitability of owners' investment

(continued)

RATIO	FORMULA	WHAT IT MEASURES
10. Earnings per share	$$\frac{\text{Net income minus preferred dividends}}{\text{Weighted average shares outstanding}}$$	Net income earned on each common share
11. Price earnings ratio	$$\frac{\text{Market price of shares}}{\text{Earnings per share}}$$	Ratio of the market price per share to earnings per share
12. Payout ratio	$$\frac{\text{Cash dividends}}{\text{Net income}}$$	Percentage of earnings distributed as cash dividends
IV. Coverage		
13. Debt to total assets	$$\frac{\text{Total debt}}{\text{Total assets}}$$	Percentage of total assets provided by creditors
14. Times interest earned	$$\frac{\text{Income before interest charges and taxes}}{\text{Interest charges}}$$	Ability to meet interest payments as they come due
15. Cash debt coverage ratio	$$\frac{\text{Net cash provided by operating activities}}{\text{Average total liabilities}}$$	Company's ability to repay its total liabilities in a specific year from its operations
16. Book value per share	$$\frac{\text{Common shareholders' equity}}{\text{Outstanding shares}}$$	Amount each share would receive if the company were liquidated at the amounts reported on the balance sheet

Illustration 23-11

A Summary of Financial Ratios (continued)

Percentage (Common-Size) Analysis

Analysts also use percentage analysis to help them evaluate an enterprise. **Percentage (common-size) analysis** consists of converting a series of related amounts to a series of percentages of a given base. All items in an income statement are frequently expressed as a percentage of net sales; a statement of financial position may be analyzed on the basis of total assets. This conversion is helpful in evaluating the relative size of items in a given year's financial statements and can ease comparison of amounts or changes in amounts over time. It is also very helpful for comparing companies of different size. To demonstrate, Illustration 23-12 provides a comparative percentage analysis of the change in expenses in MoreTek's income statement for the last two years. This approach, normally called **horizontal analysis**, indicates the proportionate change over a period of time. It is especially useful in evaluating a trend because absolute changes are often deceiving.

Illustration 23-12

Horizontal Analysis

	2014 (000s)	2013 (000s)	Difference	% Change
Cost of sales	$1,000	$850	$150	17.6
Depreciation and amortization	150	150	–0–	–0–
Selling and administrative expenses	225	150	75	50.0
Interest expense	50	25	25	100.0
Taxes	100	75	25	33.3

Another approach, called **vertical analysis**, is the proportional expression of each item on a financial statement in a given period to a base figure. For example, MoreTek's income statement using this approach with total revenue as the base figure appears in Illustration 23-13.

Illustration 23-13

Vertical Analysis

MORETEK CORPORATION
INCOME STATEMENT
(000,000 OMITTED)

	Amount	Percentage of Total Revenue
Net sales	$1,600.0	96
Other revenue	75.0	4
Total revenue	1,675.0	100
Less:		
Cost of sales	1,000.0	60
Depreciation and amortization	150.0	9
Selling and administrative expenses	225.0	13
Interest expense	50.0	3
Income taxes	100.0	6
Total expenses	1,525.0	91
Net income	$ 150.0	9

Reducing all the dollar amounts to a percentage of a base amount is frequently called common-size analysis because all of the statements and all of the years are reduced to a common size; that is, all of the elements within each statement are expressed in percentages of some common number.

For the statement of financial position, common-size analysis answers such questions as: What is the distribution of financing between current liabilities, long-term debt, and owners' equity? What is the mix of assets (percentage-wise) with which the enterprise has chosen to conduct its business? What percentage of current assets is in inventory, receivables, and so forth?

The income statement lends itself to an analysis because each item in it is related to a common amount, often net sales. It is informative to know what proportion of each sales dollar is absorbed by the various costs and expenses incurred by the enterprise.

Common-size analysis may be used for comparing one company's statements over different years to detect trends not evident from the comparison of absolute amounts. Also, common-size analysis eases inter-company comparisons regardless of their size because the financial statements are put into a comparable common-size format.

Limitations of Financial Statement Analysis

An underlying objective of decision-makers is to evaluate risk. Uncertainty is the major factor contributing to risk. Uncertainty is reduced and, therefore, awareness of risk is enhanced by decision-relevant information. We have argued that information in financial statements and ratio analysis based on this information can be decision-relevant and, consequently, useful in reducing uncertainty. Even so, a decision-maker should be aware that there are significant limitations regarding financial statement information and ratio analysis.

A CICA research study identified the following four sources of uncertainty as being important when considering the usefulness of financial statement information to a decision-maker.[26]

1. *Uncertainty about the nature and role of financial statements.* Misunderstanding the nature, purpose, terminology used, and method of preparation of financial statements can lead users to misinterpret and/or place inappropriate reliance on the information.

2. *Uncertainty about the nature of business operations portrayed in the financial statements.* The unpredictability of business activities due to factors such as economic environment, technology, and competitors' actions causes uncertainty. Knowledge of

the type of business activities carried out is important in determining the extent of the uncertainties that characterize these activities.

3. **Uncertainty due to limitations of financial statement measurements and disclosures.** The conceptual framework, *CICA Handbook* recommendations, and accounting practice dictate that various principles be followed and methods used. Uncertainty occurs when there is recognition that the resulting measurements and disclosures are not well understood or are thought to be incomplete or to lack relevance in a particular decision context.

4. **Uncertainty about management's motives and intentions.** Management is responsible for determining the accounting policies and methods used to prepare the financial statements. Choice of a policy or method should be based on reflecting underlying economic reality. This source of uncertainty suggests, however, that users may suspect that management's choices are more motivated by a need to "manage earnings" to maximize bonuses over time, or to avoid debt covenant violations.

There are other important limitations of ratio analysis. They include the following.

a. They are **based on historical cost**, which can lead to distortions in measuring performance.

b. **Estimated items** (such as depreciation, site restoration costs, and bad debts) **are significant**, and ratios based on significant estimates may be less credible

c. **Achieving comparability among companies in a given industry may be difficult.** For example, companies often apply different accounting policies that require that an analyst identify basic differences existing in their accounting and adjust the balances to achieve comparability.

This section has introduced you to the basic concepts and tools for financial statement analysis. Keep in mind that there are entire courses devoted to financial statement analysis, where additional tools are discussed and illustrated.

Objective 10

Identify the major differences in accounting between ASPE and IFRS, and what changes are expected in the near future.

IFRS/ASPE COMPARISON

A Comparison of IFRS and ASPE

Illustration 23-14

IFRS and ASPE Comparison Chart

Illustration 23-14 compares ASPE with the international standards regarding other measurement and disclosure issues.

	Accounting Standards for Private Enterprises (ASPE)—*CICA Handbook*, Part II, Sections 1100, 3820, and 3840	IFRS—IAS 8, 10, 24, and 34; IFRS 8	References to Related Illustrations and Select Brief Exercises
Disclosures	Generally less disclosure requirements due to the fact that many private entities have less complex business transactions and stakeholders have greater access to information about the entity.	Increased level of disclosures.	BE23-1
Accounting policies	Greater range of choice of policies to account for differing sizes and complexities of business entities. Entities need not meet the test of providing more relevant and reliable	The IASB is attempting to reduce choice in terms of accounting policies to promote comparability. Where there is an accounting change, the entity must prove that	N/A

(continued)

Illustration 23-14

IFRS and ASPE Comparison Chart (continued)

	Accounting Standards for Private Enterprises (ASPE)—CICA Handbook, Part II, Sections 1100, 3820, and 3840	IFRS—IAS 8, 10, 24, and 34; IFRS 8	References to Related Illustrations and Select Brief Exercises
	information in certain situations where accounting policies are changed.	the new policy provides reliable and more relevant information.	
Segmented reporting	No guidance provided.	Separate information should be presented for reportable segments including information about revenues, profits and loss, and assets and liabilities. These numbers must be reconciled to reported financial statements. In addition, information about the segment products and services as well as material customers and information by geographical areas should be disclosed.	BE23-6
Interim reporting	No guidance provided.	IFRS does not mandate which entities should provide interim information; however, it provides guidance (which entities are encouraged to follow) if the entity does provide the information. If the interim report is in compliance with IFRS, this should be disclosed. Basically, each interim period is considered a discrete period. The same accounting policies should be used as for the annual financial statements.	BE23-10
Related-party transactions	Related-party transactions are remeasured under certain situations (basically where the transaction has no economic substance or is not measurable).	IFRS only requires additional disclosures regarding related parties. It does not require remeasurement. In addition to the disclosure requirement under ASPE, management compensation, and the name of the entity's parent company as well as its ultimate controlling entity or individual, are required to be disclosed.	BE23-11 and BE23-12
Subsequent events	The subsequent event period ends when the statements are complete. The date is a matter of judgement, taking into account management structure and procedures followed in completing the statements.	The subsequent event period ends when the statements are authorized for issue.	BE23-16
Unincorporated business	Specific guidance includes requiring the statements to define the entity and disclose salaries and other items accruing to owners. No provision is made for income taxes.	IFRS does not provide guidance.	

Looking Ahead

Throughout this textbook, we have stressed the need to provide information that is useful to predict the amounts, timing, and uncertainty of future cash flows. To achieve this objective, judicious choices of alternative accounting concepts, methods, and means of disclosure must be made. You are probably surprised by the large number of choices among acceptable alternatives that accountants are required to make.

You should be aware, however, as Chapter 1 indicated, that accounting is greatly influenced by its environment. Because it does not exist in a vacuum, it seems unrealistic to assume that alternative presentations of certain transactions and events will be eliminated entirely. Nevertheless, we are hopeful that as the conceptual framework evolves the profession will be able to enhance its focus on the needs of financial statement users and eliminate diversity in presentation where appropriate. The profession must continue its efforts to develop a sound foundation upon which financial standards and practice can be built.

SUMMARY OF LEARNING OBJECTIVES

1 Understand the importance of disclosure from a business perspective.

Information disclosure is important to the proper functioning of capital markets and the allocation of capital. The information provided in financial statements helps investors compare the performance of companies and to assess the relative risks and returns of different investments. The full disclosure principle suggests that information relevant to decision-making should be included in the financial statements. But financial statements are just one of many sources of information for investors and creditors.

2 Review the full disclosure principle and describe problems of implementation.

The full disclosure principle calls for financial reporting of any financial facts that are significant enough to influence the judgement of an informed reader. Implementing the full disclosure principle is difficult because the cost of disclosure can be substantial and the benefits difficult to assess. Disclosure requirements for public entities have increased because of (1) the growing complexity of the business environment, (2) the necessity for timely information, and (3) the use of accounting as a control and monitoring device. For private entities, disclosure requirements have decreased due to the lesser complexity of many private entities and the fact that many stakeholders of private entities have greater access to information.

3 Explain the use of accounting policy notes in financial statement preparation.

Notes are the accountant's means of amplifying or explaining the items presented in the main body of the statements. Information that is pertinent to specific financial statement items can be explained in qualitative terms, and supplementary quantitative data can be provided to expand the information in the financial statements. Accounting policy notes explain the accounting methods and policies chosen by the company, thus allowing greater comparability between companies.

4 Describe the disclosure requirements for major segments of a business.

If only the consolidated figures are available to the analyst, much information regarding the composition of these figures is hidden in aggregated figures. There is no way to tell from the consolidated data how much each product line contributes to the company's profitability, risk, and growth potential. As a result, segment information is required by the profession for public entities.

5 Describe the accounting problems associated with interim reporting.

Interim reports cover periods of less than one year. There are two viewpoints regarding interim reports. The discrete view holds that each interim period should be treated as a separate accounting period. In contrast, the integral view holds that the interim report is an integral part of the annual report and that deferrals and accruals should take into consideration what will happen for the entire year. IFRS encourages the discrete view approach. The same accounting principles that are used for annual reports should generally be employed for interim reports; however, there are several unique reporting problems. Interim reporting is not mandated by accounting standard setters even for public entities.

6 Discuss the accounting issues for related-party transactions.

Related-party transactions pose special accounting issues. Since the transactions are not at arm's length, they may have to be remeasured under ASPE, as the exchange value is not necessarily representative of the market or fair value. In the absence of reliable information, the transaction may have to be remeasured to reflect historical values or costs. IFRS does not require remeasurement of related-party transactions whereas ASPE does.

7 Identify the difference between the two types of subsequent events.

The first type of events provides additional evidence about an event that existed at the SFP date. These events should be reflected in the SFP and income statement. The second type of event provides evidence about events or transactions that did not exist at the SFP date. These events should be disclosed in notes if they will have a material impact on the future of the company.

8 Identify the major disclosures found in the auditor's report.

If the auditor is satisfied that the financial statements present the financial position, results of operations, and cash flows fairly in accordance with generally accepted accounting principles, an unqualified opinion is expressed. A qualified opinion contains an exception to the standard opinion; ordinarily, the exception is not significant enough to invalidate the statements as a whole. An adverse opinion is required in any report in which the exceptions to fair presentation are so pervasive that a qualified opinion is not justified. A disclaimer of an opinion is appropriate when the auditor has gathered so little information on the financial statements that no opinion can be expressed.

9 Describe methods used for basic financial statement analysis and summarize the limitations of ratio analysis.

Various techniques are used in the analysis of financial statement data. These include ratio analysis, percentage (common-size) analysis, and examination of related data (in notes and other sources). No one technique is more useful than another. Every situation faced by the analyst is different, and the answers needed are often obtained only on close examination of the interrelationships among all the data provided. Ratio analysis is a starting point in developing information desired by an analyst. While the basic concepts and tools for analysis are provided, keep in mind that there are limitations inherent in individual financial statement analysis techniques. For more complex techniques, you should refer to textbooks and courses that focus entirely on financial statement analysis.

10 Identify the major differences in accounting between ASPE and IFRS, and what changes are expected in the near future.

Differences are noted in the chapter and the comparison chart.

KEY TERMS

Quiz

Brief Exercises

(LO 1) **BE23-1**   Discuss why full disclosure is essential to the proper functioning of capital markets, and why private companies following ASPE may be subject to fewer disclosure requirements.

(LO 2) **BE23-2**   What type of disclosure or accounting is necessary for each of the following items?

(a) Because of a general increase in the number of labour disputes and strikes, both within and outside the industry, there is more chance that a company will suffer a costly strike in the near future.

(b) A company reports a discontinued operation (net of tax) correctly on the income statement. No other mention is made of this item in the annual report.

(c) A company expects to recover a substantial amount in connection with a pending refund claim for a prior year's taxes. Although the claim is being contested, the company's lawyers have confirmed that they expect their client to recover the taxes.

(LO 2, 3) **BE23-3**   An annual report of Chignecto Industries states: "The company and its subsidiaries have long-term leases expiring on various dates after December 31, 2014. Amounts payable under such commitments, without reduction for related rental income, are expected to average approximately $5,711,000 annually for the next three years. Related rental income from certain subleases to others is estimated to average $3,094,000 annually for the next three years." What information is provided by this note?

(LO 2, 3) **BE23-4**   An annual report of **Ford Motor Company** states: "Net income a share is computed based upon the average number of shares of capital stock of all classes outstanding. Additional shares of common stock may be issued or delivered in the future on conversion of outstanding convertible debentures, exercise of outstanding employee stock options, and for payment of defined supplemental compensation. Had such additional shares been outstanding, net income a share would have been reduced by 10¢ in the current year and 3¢ in the previous year. ...As a result of capital stock transactions by the company during the current year (primarily the purchase of Class A Stock from Ford Foundation), net income a share was increased by 6¢." What information is provided by this note?

(LO 4) **BE23-5**   Bronwyn Mantini, a student of intermediate accounting, was heard to remark after a class discussion on segmented reporting: "All this is very confusing to me. First we are told that there is merit in presenting the consolidated results and now we are told that it is better to show segmented results. I wish they would make up their minds." Evaluate this comment.

(LO 4) **BE23-6**   Penner Corporation has seven industry segments with total revenues as follows:

	(thousands)			(thousands)
Gamma	$600		Suh	$225
Kennedy	650		Tsui	200
RGD	250		Nuhn	700
Red Moon	375			

Based only on the revenues test, which industry segments are reportable under ASPE?

(LO 4) **BE23-7**   Operating profits and losses for the seven industry segments of Penner Corporation are as follows:

	(thousands)			(thousands)
Gamma	$90		Suh	$ (20)
Kennedy	(40)		Tsui	34
RGD	25		Nuhn	100
Red Moon	50			

Based only on the operating profit (loss) test, which industry segments are reportable under IFRS?

(LO 4) **BE23-8**   Assets for the seven industry segments of Penner Corporation are as follows:

	(thousands)			(thousands)
Gamma	$500		Suh	$200
Kennedy	550		Tsui	150
RGD	400		Nuhn	475
Red Moon	400			

Based only on the assets test, which industry segments are reportable under IFRS?

(LO 5) BE23-9 What are the accounting problems related to the presentation of interim data?

(LO 5) BE23-10 How does seasonality affect interim reporting and how should companies overcome the seasonality problem? Is there more of an effect on interim reporting for companies following IFRS or ASPE?

(LO 6) BE23-11 Nguyen Limited purchases land from its president for $390,000 in cash, which is the appraised value of the land at the time of the purchase. The land was purchased by the president 15 years ago for $45,000. (a) Assume that Nguyen follows ASPE. Prepare the journal entry to record the purchase of the land. Use the decision tree in Illustration 23-5 to explain the basis for your answer. What information should be disclosed for this transaction? (b) How would your answer to part (a) change if Nguyen were to follow IFRS?

(LO 6) BE23-12 Textile manufacturer Fibreright Corp. exchanges computer software having a carrying amount of $11,000 with the real estate company Frederick Corp. The software that is received in exchange from Frederick Corp. has a carrying amount of $15,100, performs different functions, and has a fair value of $20,800. Both companies are 100% owned by the same individual and since they are closely held companies they both follow ASPE. Discuss how this transaction should be measured and prepare the journal entries for both companies to record the exchange. Use the decision tree in Illustration 23-5 to explain the reasoning for your answer.

(LO 6) BE23-13 How would the transaction in BE23-12 be recorded if it were arm's length?

(LO 6) BE23-14 How would the transaction in BE23-12 be recorded if the individual shareholder only owned 40% of the shares of each company? Assume that there is independent evidence to support the value of the computer software. Discuss and prepare journal entries. Use the decision tree in Illustration 23-5 to explain the reasoning for your answer.

(LO 6) BE23-15 The following information was described in a note of Cruton Packing Co., a public company that follows IFRS: "During August, Bigelow Products Corporation purchased 212,450 shares of the Company's common shares, which constitutes approximately 35% of the shares outstanding. Bigelow has since obtained representation on the Board of Directors. An affiliate of Bigelow Products Corporation acts as a food broker for Cruton Packing in the Toronto marketing area. The commissions for such services after August amounted to approximately $33,000." Why is this information disclosed?

(LO 7) BE23-16 Tonoma Corporation, a company that follows IFRS, is preparing its December 31, 2014 financial statements. The following two events occurred after December 31, 2014: (1) A flood loss of $80,000 occurred on March 1, 2015. (2) A liability, estimated at $140,000 at December 31, 2014, was settled on March 15, 2015, at $190,000. The statements were completed on March 10, 2015, and they were authorized for issue on March 17, 2015. (a) What effect do these subsequent events have on 2014 net income? (b) How would your answer to part (a) change if Tonoma were to follow ASPE?

(LO 7) BE23-17 What are the major types of subsequent events? Indicate how each of the following subsequent events would be reported:

(a) Collection of a note written off in a prior period

(b) Issuance of a large preferred share offering

(c) Acquisition of a company in a different industry

(d) Destruction of a major plant in a flood

(e) Death of the company's chief executive officer

(f) Additional wage costs associated with the settlement of a four-week strike

(g) Settlement of a federal income tax case at considerably more tax than was anticipated at year end

(h) Change in the product mix from consumer goods to industrial goods

(LO 8) BE23-18 What is the difference between an auditor's unqualified or "clean" opinion and a qualified opinion?

(LO 9) BE23-19 The income statements of Dwayne Corporation show the following amounts:

	2014	2013	2012
Net sales	$800	$780	$720
Cost of goods sold	560	546	468
Gross profit	240	234	252
Selling, general, and administrative expenses	200	156	115
Profit before tax	40	78	137

Using vertical (common-size) analysis, analyze Dwayne Corporation's declining profit before tax.

(LO 9) BE23-20 Referring to the CICA research study mentioned in this chapter, discuss some limitations of the financial statement analysis done in BE23-19.

Exercises

(LO 3) E23-1 (Illegal Acts) The detection and reporting of illegal acts by management or other employees is a difficult task. To fulfill their responsibilities, auditors must have a good knowledge of the client's business, including an understanding of the laws and regulations that govern the business and activities of their clients. In addition, accountants and auditors must be sensitive to factors in the company that may indicate an abnormally high risk of illegal acts by the company or its employees.

Instructions

(a) Identify some examples of illegal acts that may be committed by a company or its employees that, if violated, could reasonably be expected to result in a material misstatement in the financial statements.

(b) Explain how, if at all, an undetected illegal act by a client (for example, paying bribes to secure business, or violating pollution control laws and regulations) could affect the company's financial statements.

(c) Identify some factors that could indicate that the risk of violation of laws and regulations is greater than normal and that evaluation of note disclosure, or possibly recognition, of an illegal act may be required.

(LO 4) E23-2 (Segmented Reporting) LaGraca Inc. is involved in five separate industries. The following information is available for each of the five industries:

Operating Segment	Total Revenue	Operating Profit (Loss)	Assets
A	$140,000	$25,000	$240,000
B	40,000	8,000	11,000
C	26,000	–5,000	36,000
D	190,000	–2,000	49,000
E	2,000	500	15,000
	$398,000	$26,500	$351,000

Instructions

Determine which of the operating segments are reportable under IFRS based on each of the following:

(a) Revenue test

(b) Operating profit (loss) test

(c) Assets test

(LO 6) E23-3 (Related-Party Transaction) Maffin Corp. owns 75% of Grey Inc. Both companies are in the mining industry. During 2014, Maffin Corp. purchased a building from Grey Inc. for $1,000. The building's carrying amount in Grey Inc.'s financial statements is $700. Maffin's contributed surplus account contains a credit balance of $200 from previous related-party transactions. Grey's contributed surplus account is nil. There is no available independent evidence of the value of the building as it is a unique building in a remote part of the country. Maffin subsequently sold the building, during 2015, to an unrelated party for $1,100. Both Maffin and Grey follow ASPE.

Instructions

Using the related-party decision tree in Illustration 23-5, answer the following.

(a) How would both Maffin and Grey record the purchase and sale of the building during 2014?

(b) Record the subsequent sale of the building by Maffin during 2014.

(c) Assume that Maffin purchased the building from Grey for $500. How would your answer to part (a) change?

(d) Assume that the transaction is in the normal course of operations for both Maffin and Grey and that it has commercial substance. How would your answers to parts (a) and (b) change?

(e) Calculate the total impact on income of the purchase and sale of the building for 2014 and 2015 for the consolidated reporting unit of the two companies. What can you conclude from your calculation?

Digging Deeper

(LO 6) E23-4 (Related-Party Transaction) Verez Limited owns 90% of Consior Inc. During 2014, Verez acquired a machine from Consior in exchange for its own used machine. Both companies are in the consulting business. The agreed exchange amount is $1,000, although the transaction is nonmonetary. Consior Inc. carries its machine on its books at a carrying amount of $700, whereas Verez carries its machine on its books at a carrying amount of $900.

Neither company has a balance in the contributed surplus account relating to previous related-party transactions. Both Verez and Consior follow ASPE.

Instructions

Using the related-party decision tree in Illustration 23-5, prepare the journal entries to record the exchange for both Verez and Consior under the following assumptions.

(a) The transaction is not in the normal course of operations for either company, and the transaction has commercial substance.

(b) The transaction is not in the normal course of operations for either company, and the transaction does not have commercial substance.

(c) The transaction is in the normal course of operations for each company, and the transaction has commercial substance.

(d) The transaction is in the normal course of operations for each company, and the transaction does not have commercial substance.

(e) Briefly explain how your answers to parts (a) through (d) would change if both companies were to follow IFRS.

Digging
Deeper

(LO 7) **E23-5 (Subsequent Events)** Jason Corporation completed, authorized, and issued its financial statements following IFRS for the year ended December 31, 2014, on March 10, 2015. The following events took place in early 2015.

1. On January 10, 19,000 common shares were issued at $45 per share.

2. On March 1, Jason determined after negotiations with the Canada Revenue Agency that income tax payable for 2014 should be $1.2 million. At December 31, 2014, income tax payable was recorded at $1 million.

Instructions

(a) Discuss how these subsequent events should be reflected in the 2014 financial statements.

(b) The controller of Jason Corporation believes that the income tax payable as at December 31, 2014, should not be increased to $1.2 million, because the original estimate of $1 million was based on the information available at the time of accrual, and recorded in good faith. The controller feels that the revised estimate of $1.2 million should be treated prospectively as a change in estimate. Do you agree or disagree with the controller's proposed accounting treatment of the income tax payable as at December 31, 2014? Discuss your conclusion from the perspective of investors.

(LO 7) **E23-6 (Subsequent Events)** The following are subsequent (post-statement of financial position) events.

— **1.** Settlement of a federal tax case at a cost considerably higher than the amount expected at year end

— **2.** Introduction of a new product line

— **3.** Loss of an assembly plant due to fire

— **4.** Sale of a significant portion of the company's assets

— **5.** Retirement of the company president

— **6.** Prolonged employee strike

— **7.** Loss of a significant customer

— **8.** Issuance of a significant number of common shares

— **9.** Material loss on a year-end receivable because of a customer's bankruptcy

— **10.** Hiring of a new president

— **11.** Settlement of a prior year's litigation against the company

— **12.** Merger with another company of similar size

Instructions

For each of the above events, indicate whether the company should

(a) adjust the financial statements,

(b) disclose the event in notes to the financial statements, or

(c) neither adjust nor disclose.

(LO 9) E23-7 (Percentage Analysis) The financial statements of Mackay Corporation show the following information:

MACKAY CORPORATION
Statement of Financial Position
December 31, 2014

Assets	2014	2013
Cash	$ 285,000	$ 292,000
Accounts receivable	142,000	181,000
Investments—fair value through net income	133,000	132,000
Inventory	355,000	401,000
Plant assets (net)	442,000	465,000
Intangible assets	113,000	143,000
	$1,470,000	$1,614,000

Liabilities and Equity		
Accounts payable	$ 267,000	$ 337,000
Long-term debt	64,000	152,000
Share capital	326,000	326,000
Retained earnings	813,000	799,000
	$1,470,000	$1,614,000

MACKAY CORPORATION
Income Statement
Year Ended December 31, 2014

	2014	2013
Net sales	$ 805,000	$ 781,000
Cost of goods sold	527,000	530,000
Gross profit	278,000	251,000
Selling, general, and administrative expenses	140,000	111,000
Other expenses, net	118,000	110,000
Income before income tax	20,000	30,000
Income tax	6,000	9,000
Net income	$ 14,000	$ 21,000

Instructions

(a) Using horizontal analysis, analyze Mackay Corporation's change in liquidity, solvency, and profitability in 2014.

(b) Using vertical analysis, analyze Mackay Corporation's decline in net income in 2014.

(c) Referring to the CICA research study mentioned in this chapter, discuss some limitations of the financial statement analysis done in parts (a) and (b).

(LO 9) E23-8 (Analysis of Given Ratios) Robbins Company is a wholesale distributor of professional equipment and supplies. The company's sales have averaged about $900,000 annually for the 3-year period 2012–2014. The firm's total assets at the end of 2014 amounted to $850,000. The president of Robbins Company has asked the controller to prepare a report that summarizes the financial aspects of the company's operations for the past three years. This report will be presented to the board of directors at their next meeting. In addition to comparative financial statements, the controller has decided to present a number of relevant financial ratios which can assist in the identification and interpretation of trends. At the request of the controller, the accounting staff has calculated the following ratios for the 2012–2014:

	2012	2013	2014
Current ratio	1.80	1.89	1.96
Acid-test (quick) ratio	1.04	0.99	0.87
Accounts receivable turnover	8.75	7.71	6.42
Inventory turnover	4.91	4.32	3.72
Total debt to total assets	51.0%	46.0%	41.0%
Long-term debt to total assets	31.0%	27.0%	24.0%
Sales to fixed assets (fixed asset turnover)	1.58	1.69	1.79

	2012	2013	2014
Sales as a percent of 2012 sales	1.00	1.03	1.05
Gross margin percentage	36.0%	35.1%	34.6%
Net income to sales	6.9%	7.0%	7.2%
Return on total assets	7.7%	7.7%	7.8%
Return on equity	13.6%	13.1%	12.7%

In preparation of the report, the controller has decided first to examine the financial ratios independent of any other data to determine if the ratios themselves reveal any significant trends over the three-year period.

Instructions

(a) The current ratio is increasing while the acid-test (quick) ratio is decreasing. Using the ratios provided, identify and explain the contributing factor(s) for this apparently divergent trend.

(b) In terms of the ratios provided, what conclusion(s) can be drawn regarding the company's use of financial leverage during the 2012–2014 period?

(c) Using the ratios provided, what conclusion(s) can be drawn regarding the company's net investment in plant and equipment?

Problems

P23-1 Franklin Corporation is a diversified company that operates in five different industries: A, B, C, D, and E. The following information relating to each segment is available for 2014. Sales of segments B and C included intersegment sales of $20,000 and $100,000, respectively.

	A	B	C	D	E
Sales	$40,000	$ 80,000	$580,000	$ 35,000	$55,000
Cost of goods sold	19,000	50,000	270,000	19,000	30,000
Operating expenses	10,000	40,000	235,000	12,000	18,000
Total expenses	29,000	90,000	505,000	31,000	48,000
Operating profit (loss)	$11,000	$ (10,000)	$ 75,000	$ 4,000	$ 7,000
Assets	$35,000	$ 60,000	$500,000	$ 65,000	$50,000
Liabilities	$22,000	$ 31,000	$443,000	$ 12,000	$29,000

Instructions

(a) Determine which of the segments are reportable under IFRS based on each of the following:

1. Revenue test

2. Operating profit (loss) test

3. Assets test

(b) Prepare the necessary disclosures.

(c) The corporation's accountant recently commented, "If I have to disclose our segments individually, the only people who will gain are our competitors and the only people who will lose are our present shareholders." Evaluate this comment.

P23-2 In an examination of Daniel Corporation Ltd. as of December 31, 2014, you have learned that the following situations exist. No entries have been made in the accounting records for these items. Daniel follows IFRS.

1. The corporation erected its present factory building in 1999. Depreciation was calculated by the straight-line method, using an estimated life of 35 years. Early in 2014, the board of directors conducted a careful survey and estimated that the factory building had a remaining useful life of 25 years as of January 1, 2014.

2. An additional assessment of 2014 income tax was levied and paid in 2015.

3. When calculating the accrual for officers' salaries at December 31, 2014, it was discovered that the accrual for officers' salaries for December 31, 2013, had been overstated.

4. On December 15, 2014, Daniel Corporation Ltd. declared a stock dividend of 1,000 common shares per 100,000 of its common shares outstanding, distributable February 1, 2015, to the common shareholders of record on December 31, 2014.

5. Daniel Corporation Ltd., which is on a calendar-year basis, changed its inventory method as of January 1, 2014. The inventory for December 31, 2013, was costed by the average method, and the inventory for December 31,

Digging Deeper

2014, was costed by the FIFO method. Daniel is changing its inventory method because it would result in reliable and more relevant information.

6. Daniel has guaranteed the payment of interest on the 20-year first mortgage bonds of Bonbee Inc., an affiliate. Outstanding bonds of Bonbee Inc. amount to $150,000 with interest payable at 10% per annum, due June 1 and December 1 of each year. The bonds were issued by Bonbee Inc., on December 1, 2010, and the company has met all interest payments except for the payment due December 1, 2014. Daniel states that it will pay the defaulted interest to the bondholders on January 15, 2015.

7. During the year 2014, Daniel Corporation Ltd. was named as a defendant in a lawsuit for damages by Anand Shahid Corporation for breach of contract. The case was decided in favour of Anand Shahid Corporation, which was awarded $80,000 damages. At the time of the audit, the case was under appeal to a higher court.

Instructions

Describe fully how each of the items should be reported in the financial statements of Daniel Corporation Ltd. for the year 2014.

P23-3 Your firm has been engaged to examine the financial statements of Samson Corporation for the year 2014. The bookkeeper who maintains the financial records has prepared all the unaudited financial statements for the corporation since its organization on January 2, 2008. The client provides you with the information that follows:

SAMSON CORPORATION
Statement of Financial Position
As of December 31, 2014

Assets		Liabilities	
Current assets	$1,881,100	Current liabilities	$ 962,400
Other assets	5,121,900	Long-term liabilities	1,390,000
	$7,003,000	Capital	4,650,600
			$7,003,000

An analysis of current assets discloses the following:

Cash (restricted in the amount of $400,000 for plant expansion)	$ 571,000
Investments in land	185,000
Accounts receivable less allowance of $30,000	480,000
Inventories (FIFO flow assumption)	645,100
	$1,881,100

Other assets include:

Prepaid expenses	$ 47,400
Plant and equipment less accumulated depreciation of $1,430,000	4,130,000
Cash surrender value of life insurance policy	84,000
Notes receivable (short-term)	162,300
Goodwill	252,000
Land	446,200
	$5,121,900

Current liabilities include:

Accounts payable	$ 510,000
Notes payable (due 2016)	157,400
Estimated income taxes payable	145,000
Premium on common shares	150,000
	$ 962,400

Long-term liabilities include:

Unearned revenue	$ 489,500
Dividends payable (cash)	200,000
8% bonds payable (due May 1, 2019)	700,500
	$1,390,000

Capital includes:

Retained earnings	$2,810,600
Common shares; 200,000 authorized, 184,000 issued	1,840,000
	$4,650,600

The following supplementary information is also provided:

1. On May 1, 2014, the corporation issued at 93.4, $750,000 of bonds to finance plant expansion. The long-term bond agreement provided for the annual payment of interest every May 1. The existing plant was pledged as security for the loan. Use the effective interest method for discount amortization.

2. The bookkeeper made the following mistakes:

(a) In 2012, the ending inventory was overstated by $183,000. The ending inventories for 2013 and 2014 were correctly calculated.

(b) In 2014, accrued wages in the amount of $275,000 were omitted from the statement of financial position and these expenses were not charged on the income statement.

(c) In 2014, a gain of $175,000 (net of tax) on the sale of certain plant assets was credited directly to retained earnings.

3. A major competitor has introduced a line of products that will compete directly with Samson's primary line, which is now being produced in a specially designed new plant. Because of manufacturing innovations, the competitor's line will be of similar quality but priced 50% below Samson's line. The competitor announced its new line on January 14, 2015. Samson indicates that the company will meet the lower prices; the lower prices are still high enough to cover Samson's variable manufacturing and selling expenses, but will permit only partial recovery of fixed costs.

4. You learned on January 28, 2015, prior to completion of the audit, of heavy damage from a recent fire at one of Samson's two plants and that the loss will not be reimbursed by insurance. The newspapers described the event in detail.

Digging Deeper

Instructions

(a) Analyze the above information to prepare a corrected statement of financial position for Samson in accordance with IFRS. Prepare a description of any notes that might need to be prepared. The books are closed and adjustments to income are to be made through retained earnings.

(b) "The financial statements of a company are management's responsibility, not the accountant's." Discuss the implications of this statement.

P23-4 Radiohead Inc. produces electronic components for sale to manufacturers of radios, television sets, and digital sound systems. In connection with her examination of Radiohead's financial statements for the year ended December 31, 2014, Marg Zajic, CA, completed fieldwork two weeks ago. Ms. Zajic now is evaluating the significance of the following items prior to preparing her auditor's report. Except as noted, none of these items has been disclosed in the financial statements or notes.

Item 1

A 10-year loan agreement that the company entered into three years ago provides that, subsequent to the date of the agreement, dividend payments may not exceed net income earned after tax. The balance of retained earnings at the date of the loan agreement was $420,000. From that date through December 31, 2014, net income after tax has totalled $570,000 and cash dividends have totalled $520,000. Based on these data, the staff auditor who was assigned to this review concluded that there was no retained earnings restriction at December 31, 2014.

Item 2

Recently, Radiohead interrupted its policy of paying cash dividends quarterly to its shareholders. Dividends were paid regularly through 2013, discontinued for all of 2014 to finance the purchase of equipment for the company's new plant, and resumed in the first quarter of 2015. In the annual report, dividend policy is to be discussed in the president's letter to shareholders.

Item 3

A major electronics firm has introduced a line of products that will compete directly with Radiohead's primary line, which is now being produced in Radiohead's specially designed new plant. Because of manufacturing innovations, the competitor's line will be of similar quality but priced 50% below Radiohead's line. The competitor announced its new line during the week following the completion of Ms. Zajic's fieldwork. Ms. Zajic read the announcement in the newspaper and discussed the situation by telephone with Radiohead executives. Radiohead will meet the lower prices as they are still high enough to cover variable manufacturing and selling expenses, although they will permit only partial recovery of fixed costs.

Item 4

The company's new manufacturing plant, which cost $2.4 million and has an estimated life of 25 years, is leased from Armadillo National Bank at an annual rental of $600,000. The company is obligated to pay property tax, insurance, and maintenance. At the end of its 10-year non-cancellable lease, the company has the option of purchasing the property for $1. In Radiohead's income statement, the rental payment is reported on a separate line.

Instructions

For each of the items, discuss any additional disclosures in the financial statements and notes that the auditor should recommend to her client. The client follows IFRS. (Do not consider the cumulative effect of the four items.)

P23-5 You have completed your audit of Khim Inc. and its consolidated subsidiaries for the year ended December 31, 2014, and are satisfied with the results of your examination. You have examined the financial statements of Khim for the past three years. The corporation follows IFRS and is now preparing its annual report to shareholders. The report will include the consolidated financial statements of Khim and its subsidiaries, and your short-form auditor's report. During your audit, the following matters came to your attention.

1. A vice-president who is also a shareholder resigned on December 31, 2014, after an argument with the president. The vice-president is soliciting proxies from shareholders and expects to obtain enough proxies to gain control of the board of directors so that a new president will be appointed. The president plans to have a note prepared that would include information of the upcoming proxy fight, management's accomplishments over the years, and an appeal by management for the support of shareholders.

2. The corporation decides in 2014 to adopt the straight-line method of depreciation for plant equipment. The straight-line method will be used for new acquisitions and for previously acquired plant equipment that was being depreciated on an accelerated basis.

3. The Canada Revenue Agency is currently examining the corporation's 2012 federal income tax return. It is questioning the amount of a deduction claimed by the corporation's domestic subsidiary for a loss sustained in 2012. The examination is still in process, and any additional tax liability cannot be determined at this time. The corporation's tax lawyer believes that there will be no substantial additional tax liability.

Instructions

(a) Prepare the notes, if any, that you would suggest for each of the items.

(b) For each item that you decided did not require note disclosure, explain your reasons for not making the disclosure.

(AICPA adapted)

P23-6 The following excerpt is from the financial statements of **H. J. Heinz Company** and provides segmented geographic data:

The company is engaged principally in one line of business—processed food products—that represents more than 90% of consolidated sales. Information about the company business by geographic area is presented in the table below. There were no material amounts of sales or transfers between geographic areas or between affiliates, and no material amounts of United States export sales.

(in thousands of U.S. dollars)	Domestic	United Kingdom	Canada	Foreign Western Europe	Other	Total	Worldwide
Sales	$2,381,054	$547,527	$216,726	$383,784	$209,354	$1,357,391	$3,738,445
Operating income	246,780	61,282	34,146	29,146	25,111	149,685	396,465
Identifiable assets	1,362,152	265,218	112,620	294,732	143,971	816,541	2,178,693
Capital expenditures	72,712	12,262	13,790	8,253	4,368	38,673	111,385
Depreciation expense	42,279	8,364	3,592	6,355	3,606	21,917	64,196

Instructions

(a) Why does H. J. Heinz not prepare segment information on its products or services?

(b) Why are revenues by geographic area important to disclose?

P23-7 Three independent situations follow.

Situation 1

A company offers a one-year warranty for the product that it manufactures. A history of warranty claims has been compiled and the probable amount of claims on sales for any particular period can be determined.

Situation 2

Subsequent to the date of a set of financial statements, but before the date of authorization for issuing the financial statements, a company enters into a contract that will probably result in a significant loss to the company. The loss amount can be reasonably estimated.

Situation 3

A company has adopted a policy of recording self-insurance for any possible losses resulting from injury to others by the company's vehicles. The premium for an insurance policy for the same risk from an independent insurance company would have an annual cost of $4,000. During the period covered by the financial statements, there were no accidents involving the company's vehicles that resulted in injury to others.

Instructions

(a) Discuss the accrual or type of disclosure that is necessary under ASPE (if any) and the reason(s) why the disclosure is appropriate for each of the three independent situations.

(b) For situation 2, assume instead that the contract is a non-cancellable purchase contract that was entered into before the date of the financial statements. Discuss the accrual or type of disclosure that would be recorded under ASPE (if any). Provide support for the accrual or disclosure from the perspective of a user of the financial statements.

Digging Deeper

P23-8 Leopard Corporation is currently preparing its annual financial statements for the fiscal year ended April 30, 2014, following IFRS. The company manufactures plastic, glass, and paper containers for sale to food and drink manufacturers and distributors. Leopard maintains separate control accounts for its raw materials, work-in-process, and finished goods inventories for each of the three types of containers. The inventories are valued at the lower of cost and net realizable value.

The company's property, plant, and equipment are classified in the following major categories: land, office buildings, furniture and fixtures, manufacturing facilities, manufacturing equipment, and leasehold improvements. All fixed assets are carried at cost. The depreciation methods that are used depend on the type of asset (its classification) and when it was acquired.

Leopard plans to present the inventory and fixed asset amounts in its April 30, 2014 statement of financial position as follows:

Inventory	$4,814,200
Property, plant, and equipment (net of depreciation)	$6,310,000

Instructions

(a) What information regarding inventory and property, plant, and equipment must be disclosed by Leopard Corporation in the audited financial statements issued to shareholders, either in the body or the notes, for the 2013–14 fiscal year?

(b) Leopard Corporation's controller believes that to comply with the full disclosure principle, as much information as possible should be provided in the note disclosures, including, for example, the name of the supplier that each asset was purchased from and the current location of each asset. Comment on the usefulness of these additional disclosures from the perspective of a user of the financial statements.

(CMA adapted. Used with permission.)

Digging Deeper

P23-9 You are compiling the consolidated financial statements for Vu Corporation International (VCI), a public company. The corporation's accountant, Timothy Chow, has provided you with the following segment information.

Note 7: Major Segments of Business

VCI conducts funeral service and cemetery operations in Canada and the United States. Substantially all revenues of VCI's major segments of business are from unaffiliated customers. Segment information for fiscal 2014, 2013, and 2012, follows:

			(thousands)					
	Funeral	Floral	Cemetery	Corporate	Catering	Limousine	Consolidated	
Revenues:								
2014	$302,000	$10,000	$ 83,000	$ -0-	$7,000	$14,000	$416,000	
2013	245,000	6,000	61,000	-0-	4,000	8,000	324,000	
2012	208,000	3,000	42,000	-0-	1,000	6,000	260,000	
Operating Income:								
2014	$ 79,000	$ 1,500	$ 18,000	$(36,000)	$ 500	$14,000	$ 65,000	
2013	64,000	200	12,000	–28,000	200	8,000	48,800	
2012	54,000	150	6,000	–21,000	100	6,000	39,600	
Capital Expenditures:								
2014	$ 26,000	$ 1,000	$ 9,000	$ 400	$ 300	$ 1,000	$ 37,700	
2013	28,000	2,000	60,000	1,500	100	700	92,300	
2012	14,000	25	8,000	600	25	50	22,700	
Depreciation and								
Amortization:								
2014	$ 13,000	$ 100	$ 2,400	$ 1,400	$ 100	$ 200	$ 17,200	
2013	10,000	50	1,400	700	50	100	12,300	
2012	8,000	25	1,000	600	25	50	9,700	

(thousands)

	Funeral	Floral	Cemetery	Corporate	Catering	Limousine	Consolidated
Identifiable Assets:							
2014	$334,000	$1,500	$162,000	$114,000	$500	$8,000	$620,000
2013	322,000	1,000	144,000	52,000	1,000	6,000	526,000
2012	223,000	500	78,000	34,000	500	3,500	339,500
Liabilities:							
2014	$222,000	$1,230	$132,000	$99,000	$340	$6,000	$460,570
2013	209,000	900	119,000	74,000	750	4,100	407,750
2012	121,000	350	56,000	27,000	320	2,400	207,070

Instructions

Determine which of the segments must be reported separately and which can be combined under the category "Other." Then write a one-page memo to the company's accountant, Timothy Chow, that explains all of the following:

(a) Which segments must be reported separately and which ones can be combined

(b) Which criteria you used to determine the reportable segments

(c) What major items must be disclosed for each segment

P23-10 At December 31, 2014, Bouvier Corp. has assets of $10 million, liabilities of $6 million, common shares of $2 million (representing 2 million common shares of $1.00 par), and retained earnings of $2 million. Net sales for the year 2014 were $18 million, and net income was $800,000. As one of the auditors of this company, you are making a review of subsequent events on February 13, 2015, and you find the following.

1. On February 3, 2015, one of Bouvier's customers declared bankruptcy. At December 31, 2014, this company owed Bouvier $300,000, of which $40,000 was paid in January 2015.

2. On January 18, 2015, one of the client's three major plants burned.

3. On January 23, 2015, a strike was called at one of Bouvier's largest plants and it halted 30% of production. As of today (February 13), the strike has not been settled.

4. A major electronics enterprise has introduced a line of products that would compete directly with Bouvier's primary line, now being produced in a specially designed new plant. Because of manufacturing innovations, the competitor has been able to achieve quality similar to that of Bouvier's products, but at a price 30% lower. Bouvier officials say they will meet the lower prices, which are barely high enough to cover variable and fixed manufacturing and selling costs.

5. Merchandise traded in the open market is recorded in the company's records at $1.40 per unit on December 31, 2014. This price held for two weeks after the release of an official market report that predicted vastly excessive supplies; however, no purchases were made at $1.40. The price throughout the preceding year had been about $2.00, which was the level experienced over several years. On January 18, 2015, the price returned to $2.00 after public disclosure of an error in the official calculations of the prior December—the correction erased the expectations of excessive supplies. Inventory at December 31, 2014, was on a lower of cost or net realizable value basis.

6. On February 1, 2015, the board of directors adopted a resolution to accept the offer of an investment banker to guarantee the marketing of $1.2 million of preferred shares.

7. The company owns investments classified as trading securities accounted for using the fair value through net income model. The investments have been adjusted to fair value as of December 31, 2014. On January 21, 2015, the annual report of one of the investment companies has been issued for its year ended November 30, 2014. The investee company did not meet its earnings forecasts and the market price of the investment has dropped from $49 per share at December 31, 2014, to $27 per share on January 21, 2015.

Instructions

For each event, state how it will affect the 2014 financial statements, if at all. The company follows IFRS.

P23-11 (**Ratio Computations and Additional Analysis**) Bradburn Corporation was formed five years ago through an initial public offering (IPO) of common shares. Daniel Brown, who owns 15% of the common shares, was one of the organizers of Bradburn and is its current president. The company has been successful, but it is currently experiencing a shortage of funds. On June 10, 2014 Daniel Brown approached the Hibernia Bank, asking for a 24-month extension on two $35,000 notes, which are due on June 30, 2014, and September 30, 2014. Another note of $6,000 is due on March 31, 2015, but he expects no difficulty in paying this note on its due date. Brown explained that Bradburn's cash flow problems are due primarily to the company's desire to finance a $300,000 plant expansion over the next two fiscal years through internally generated funds. The commercial loan officer of Hibernia Bank requested financial reports for the last two fiscal years. These reports are reproduced below.

BRADBURN CORPORATION
Statement of Financial Position
March 31

Assets	2014	2013
Cash	$ 18,200	$ 12,500
Notes receivable	148,000	132,000
Accounts receivable (net)	131,800	125,500
Inventories (at cost)	105,000	50,000
Plant and equipment (net of depreciation)	1,449,000	1,420,500
Total assets	$1,852,000	$1,740,500

Equity and Liabilities		
Share capital—common (130,000 shares, $10 par)	$1,300,000	$1,300,000
Retained earnings[a]	388,000	282,000
Accrued liabilities	9,000	6,000
Notes payable	76,000	61,500
Accounts payable	79,000	91,000
Total equity and liabilities	$1,852,000	$1,740,500

[a]Cash dividends were paid at the rate of $1 per share in fiscal year 2013 and $2 per share in fiscal year 2014.

BRADBURN CORPORATION
Income Statement
For the Fiscal Years Ended March 31

	2014	2013
Sales	$3,000,000	$2,700,000
Cost of goods sold[a]	1,530,000	1,425,000
Gross margin	$1,470,000	$1,275,000
Operating expenses	860,000	780,000
Income before income tax	$ 610,000	$ 495,000
Income tax (30%)	183,000	148,500
Net income	$ 427,000	$ 346,500

[a]Depreciation charges on the plant and equipment of $100,000 and $102,500 for fiscal years ended March 31, 2013 and 2014, respectively, are included in cost of goods sold.

Instructions

(a) Compute the following items for Bradburn Corporation.

1. Current ratio for fiscal years 2013 and 2014.

2. Acid-test (quick) ratio for fiscal years 2013 and 2014.

3. Inventory turnover for fiscal year 2014.

4. Return on assets for fiscal years 2013 and 2014. (Assume total assets were $1,688,500 at 3/31/12.)

5. Percentage change in sales, cost of goods sold, gross margin, and net income after tax from fiscal year 2013 to 2014.

(b) Identify and explain what other financial reports and/or financial analyses might be helpful to the commercial loan officer of Hibernia Bank in evaluating Daniel Brown's request for a time extension on Bradburn's notes.

(c) Assume that the percentage changes experienced in fiscal year 2014 as compared with fiscal year 2013 for sales and cost of goods sold will be repeated in each of the next 2 years. Is Bradburn's desire to finance the plant expansion from internally generated funds realistic? Discuss.

(d) Should Hibernia Bank grant the extension on Bradburn's notes considering Daniel Brown's statement about financing the plant expansion through internally generated funds? Discuss.

Case

Refer to the Case Primer on the Student Website and in *WileyPLUS* to help you answer this case.

CA23-1 In June 2015, the board of directors for Holtzman Enterprises Inc. authorized the sale of $10 million of corporate bonds. Michelle Collins, treasurer for Holtzman Enterprises Inc., is concerned about the date when the bonds are issued. The company really needs the cash, but she is worried that if the bonds are issued before the company's year end (December 31, 2015), the additional liability will have an adverse effect on several important ratios. In July, she explains to company president Kenneth Holtzman that if they delay issuing the bonds until after December 31, the bonds will not affect the ratios until December 31, 2016. They will have to report the issuance as a subsequent event, which requires only footnote disclosure. Collins predicts that with expected improved financial performance in 2015, the ratios should be better.

Instructions

Adopt the role of Michelle Collins and discuss any issues. The company's shares trade on the local stock exchange.

Integrated Cases

IC23-1 Penron Limited is in the energy business of buying and selling gas and oil and related derivatives. It is a public company whose shares are widely held. It recently underwent a tremendous expansionary period over the past decade, and revenues quadrupled and continue to climb. Executives are remunerated using stock options, and the employee pension plan invests heavily in the company's stock. It is currently October 2014. The year end is December 31, 2014. Many of the benefit plans of the top executives vest at the end of the year. (That is, the executives will have legal entitlement to the benefits even if they leave the company.) As a matter of fact, there is a concern that several of these top executives will announce that they plan to leave the company right after the year-end financial statements are released.

Penron was seen as a "hot stock" by the marketplace. Numerous analysts followed the stock carefully and had been advising their clients to buy the stock as long as revenues and profits kept increasing. The third-quarter results had shown steadily increasing revenues and profits. The company had been signalling that this trend would continue through the fourth quarter.

During the fourth quarter, Penron sold some of its pipelines to LPL Corporation. The pipelines had not been in use for some time and were seen as non-essential assets. Over the past two years, Penron has steadily been divesting itself of non-essential assets. Penron had not written the pipelines down in the financial statements since they were able to sell them and recover twice their cost. This one deal was responsible for substantially all of the fourth-quarter profits. Under the terms of the deal, the pipelines were sold for $15 million cash.

LPL Corporation was owned by the president of Penron. The company had been established just before the pipeline deal was signed. Since LPL was a new company and otherwise had very few assets, it borrowed the money for the deal from the bank. The bank had requested that Penron guarantee the loan, which it did.

During the year, Penron issued Class A shares to certain executives of the company. The shares participate in the earnings of the entity much like the common shares of the company. (That is, dividends accrue to the shareholders out of the residual earnings after the preferred dividends have been paid.) They are mandatorily redeemable if a triggering event occurs, such as the resignation or termination of the shareholder. The shares are otherwise similar to common shares in that they have no preferential rights.

During the year, the company also began the planning stages for development of a new website that will allow customers to transact with the company. A significant amount of time was spent in this planning phase to determine the feasibility and desirability of this type of customer interface. Toward the end of the year, after lengthy discussion about whether or not to go down this path, the company began to acquire software and hardware to facilitate the new website. A large amount was spent on the site's graphic design and on its content.

Instructions

Assume the role of Penron's auditors and discuss the financial reporting issues for the year ended December 31, 2014.

IC23-2 Frangipani Ltd. (FL) is a new company that has just started up in January 2014. The company is the brainchild of Frank Frangi, who is working on developing a new process for a solar-powered car. To date, most of the year has been taken up with setting up the lab and working on the problem of how to power the vehicle using solar energy. The work has been financed equally by a government-sponsored bank loan and Frank's own personal capital, which he contributed to the company in return for 100% of the common shares upon incorporation. In addition, FL sold preferred shares to family members who are anxious to see how the project (and their investment) is progressing. Frank originally thought to take a salary from the company but has not yet done so this year due to the tight cash flow situation. FL has five scientists working for it. Instead of salary, the scientists have been awarded share appreciation rights that are settleable in cash or a variable number of shares at the option of the company.

Under the terms of the government-sponsored loan, FL agreed to do the following:

- Report to the government annually on its progress, including its ability to continue to operate.
- Maintain a debt to equity ratio of 1:1.
- The debt is forgivable if FL is successful in generating the new process within three years. The government will instead take back preferred shares.

The preferred shares have the following characteristics:

- Redeemable at the option of the company for common shares
- Redeemable at the option of the holder (in cash) if the company does not make a profit this year

During the year, FL has been selling advertising space on the company website. Frank is very interested in programming and has created a website that attracts a significant amount of traffic. The website includes several scientific and environmental blogs that many scientists and interested parties contribute to. As a matter of fact, many scientists help each other with practical and theoretical research questions. Since FL continually needs funds to further the work on the solar-powered vehicle, the advertising fees are paid upfront. FL has a clause in the advertising agreement that states the fees are non-refundable. In addition, the advertising fees are stipulated as being for one month's worth of advertising although it is commonly understood that FL displays the advertising for a year. At the end of November 2014, a significant amount of advertising dollars were received.

Frank and the scientists working on the car really feel that they have made significant breakthroughs this year and are close to reaching their goal and submitting the technology for patenting. On December 31, 2014, FL received a call from the company's patent lawyers stating that someone has already filed a patent for the technology that FL is developing. Frank was very angry to learn that it was one of the scientists who contributes to the FL blogs. Apparently someone had leaked critical information about the FL technology in an on-line discussion and the idea had been stolen. Frank has already contacted his friend who is a litigation lawyer and is confident he can prove the theft of the intellectual capital.

Instructions

Assume the role of the accountant for FL and discuss the financial reporting issues for the year ended December 31, 2014. The company follows ASPE.

Writing Assignments

WA23-1 International Financial Reporting Standards require that publicly traded companies provide segment information based on the management approach. An operating segment must engage in activities that generate revenue and incur expenses, and discrete information is available that is regularly reviewed by the chief operating decision maker. If an operating segment meets specific criteria, then it is reportable and disclosed in the notes to the financial statements.

Instructions

(a) What does financial reporting for segments of a business enterprise involve?

(b) What are the reasons for requiring financial data to be reported by segments?

(c) What are the possible disadvantages of requiring financial data to be reported by segments?

(d) What accounting difficulties are inherent in segment reporting?

WA23-2 J. J. Kersee Corporation is a publicly traded company and is currently preparing the interim financial data that it will issue to its shareholders and the securities commission at the end of the first quarter of its December 31, 2014 fiscal year. Kersee's financial accounting department has compiled the following summarized revenue and expense data for the first quarter of the year:

Sales	$60,000,000
Cost of goods sold	36,000,000
Variable selling expenses	2,000,000
Fixed selling expenses	1,500,000

In the first quarter, the company spent $2 million for television advertisements as a lump sum payment for the entire year. As the company believes that it will receive a benefit for the entire year for this expenditure, it has included only one quarter ($500,000) in the fixed selling expenses. Also, included in inventory is an unfavourable variance, due to prices, of $245,000 that has been deferred as Kersee anticipates that this will reverse before the third quarter is complete. J. J. Kersee Corporation must issue its quarterly financial statements in accordance with generally accepted accounting principles regarding interim financial reporting.

Instructions

(a) Explain whether Kersee should report its operating results for the quarter as if the quarter were an entirely separate reporting period or as if the quarter were an integral part of the annual reporting period.

(b) State how the sales, cost of goods sold, and fixed selling expenses would be reflected in Kersee Corporation's quarterly report prepared for the first quarter of the 2014 fiscal year. Briefly justify your presentation.

(c) What financial information, as a minimum, must Kersee Corporation disclose to its shareholders in its quarterly reports?

(CMA adapted. Used with permission.)

WA23-3 The following statement is an excerpt from a document on interim financial reporting:

Interim financial information is essential to provide investors and others with timely information about the progress of the enterprise. The usefulness of such information rests on the relationship that it has to the annual results of operations. Accordingly, the Board has concluded that each interim period should be viewed primarily as an integral part of an annual period.

In general, the results for each interim period should be based on the accounting principles and practices used by an enterprise in the preparation of its latest annual financial statements unless a change in an accounting practice or policy has been adopted in the current year. The Board has concluded, however, that certain accounting principles and practices followed for annual reporting purposes may require modification at interim reporting dates so that the reported results for the interim period may better relate to the results of operations for the annual period.

Instructions

Listed below are eight independent cases on how accounting facts might be reported on an individual company's interim financial reports. For each case, state whether the method that is proposed for interim reporting would be acceptable under IFRS for interim financial data. Support each answer with a brief explanation.

(a) King Limited takes a physical inventory at year end for annual financial statement purposes. Inventory and cost of sales reported in the interim quarterly statements are based on estimated gross profit rates because a physical inventory would require a stoppage of operations. The company does have reliable perpetual inventory records.

(b) Bounajm Limited is planning to report one fourth of its pension expense each quarter. In the current period, the company had a significant settlement and has also prorated this cost over the remaining months to the end of the fiscal year.

(c) Lopez Corp. wrote inventory down to reflect lower of cost or market in the first quarter. At year end, the market exceeds the original acquisition cost of this inventory. Consequently, management plans to write the inventory back up to its original cost as a year-end adjustment.

(d) Witt Corp. realized a large gain on the sale of investments at the beginning of the second quarter. The company wants to report one third of the gain in each of the remaining quarters.

(e) Marble Fixtures Limited has estimated its annual audit fee. It plans to prorate this expense equally over all four quarters.

(f) McNeil Inc. was reasonably certain that it would have an employee strike in the third quarter. As a result, it shipped heavily during the second quarter but plans to defer the recognition of the sales in excess of the normal sales volume. The deferred sales will be recognized as sales in the third quarter when the strike is in progress. McNeil management thinks that this better represents normal second- and third-quarter operations.

(g) At the end of the second quarter, Solace Inc. had reported an impairment loss on its goodwill related to the real estate division. At year end, this goodwill value has now increased to the amount it was prior to the writedown and the company plans to reverse this goodwill impairment loss since it is still all in the current year.

(h) Regent Corp. has a bonus plan whereby the employees will earn a bonus of 10% of the company's net income if the price of the company's share reaches a target price by the fiscal year end, which is December 31, 2014. It is now June 30, 2014, and the share price has been reached. Consequently, the company has accrued 10% of the reported net earnings for the interim period.

WA23-4

Instructions

Write a brief essay highlighting the differences between IFRS and ASPE noted in this chapter, discussing the conceptual justification for each.

WA23-5

Maude Limited's condensed financial statements provide the following information:

MAUDE LIMITED
Statement of Financial Position

	Dec. 31, 2014	Dec. 31, 2013
Cash	$ 60,000	$ 68,000
Accounts receivable (net)	198,000	80,000
Fair value-net income investments (short-term)	120,000	80,000
Inventory	520,000	640,000
Prepaid expenses	7,000	11,000
Total current assets	905,000	879,000
Property, plant, and equipment (net)	857,000	853,000
Total assets	$1,762,000	$1,732,000
Accounts payable	$ 420,000	$ 445,000
Other current liabilities	52,000	47,000
Bonds payable	600,000	600,000
Shareholders' equity	690,000	640,000
Total liabilities and shareholders' equity	$1,762,000	$1,732,000

INCOME STATEMENT
For the Year Ended December 31, 2014

Sales	$1,640,000
Cost of goods sold	(800,000)
Gross profit	840,000
Selling and administrative expense	(440,000)
Interest expense	(40,000)
Net income	$ 360,000

Instructions

(a) Determine the following:
1. Current ratio at December 31, 2014
2. Acid-test ratio at December 31, 2014
3. Accounts receivable turnover for 2014
4. Inventory turnover for 2014
5. Days payables outstanding for 2014
6. Rate of return on assets for 2014
7. Profit margin on sales

(b) Prepare a brief evaluation of the financial condition of Maude Limited and of the adequacy of its profits.

(c) In examining the other current liabilities on Maude Limited's statement of financial position, you notice that unearned revenues have declined in the current year compared with the previous year. Is this a positive indicator about the client's liquidity? Explain.

(d) Maude has a bonus plan for senior management based on a percentage of current year's profit. Management has approached you, the ethical accountant, as they would like to improve the company's profits for 2014. For example, they could discount the price of some of their goods to "move" profits from 2015 into 2014. Discuss how you would advise management in this situation.

Ethics

RESEARCH AND FINANCIAL ANALYSIS

RA23-1 Air Canada and British Airways plc

Access the annual report for Air Canada for the December 31, 2011 fiscal year end from the company's website (www.aircanada.com). Also, access the annual report for the year ended December 31, 2011, for **British Airways plc** from the company's parent website (www.iagshares.com).

Instructions

(a) What specific items do the airlines discuss in their accounting policies notes? (Prepare a list of the headings only.)

(b) Note the similarities and differences in regard to these notes. Comment on these and relate them to the nature of the two businesses.

(c) For what lines of business or segments do the companies present segmented information? What information is provided by segment? Which note disclosure is most useful and why?

(d) Note and comment on the similarities and differences between the auditors' reports submitted by the independent auditors.

RA23-2 Thomson Reuters Corporation

Access the financial statements for the year ended December 31, 2011, for **Thomson Reuters Corporation** from the company's website (www.thomsonreuters.com).

Instructions

(a) What were the related-party transactions that the company had during the year?

(b) Is the disclosure adequate or is there missing information? Is this information useful?

(c) What were the subsequent events that occurred for the company? What is the cut-off date that has been used (that is, the date of approval by the directors)?

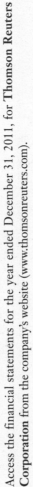

RA23-3 Nestlé Group

Access the interim financial report for the six-month period ended June 30, 2012, for the Nestlé Group from the company's website (www.nestle.com).

Instructions

(a) What are the period end dates that have been reported for the statement of comprehensive income, statement of financial position, statement of changes in equity, and statement of cash flows?

(b) On what basis have these interim statements been prepared? Summarize the type of information disclosed in note 1 for accounting policies.

(c) Describe the nature of information provided in the other notes.

(d) Is this information audited?

RA23-4 SEC Conversion to IFRS

In late 2008, the U.S. Securities Exchange Commission (SEC) published its roadmap to IFRS that would look at adopting IFRS in the United States.

Read the article entitled "IFRS: Dead in the USA?" by Lawrence Richter Quinn from *CA Magazine*, April 2010, which is available at www.camagazine.com.

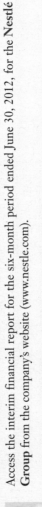

Instructions

(a) The article suggests that the SEC has been slow in providing guidance as to whether or not IFRS will be adopted in the United States. Outlined in the article are examples of how this indecision has cost companies. Explain how these costs might be incurred and the examples provided.

(b) What are the arguments for and against the SEC requiring companies to adopt IFRS?

(c) Research what recent announcements have been made by the SEC on this topic.

ENDNOTES

[1] See www.osc.gov.on.ca/en/Investors_disclosure-requirements_index.htm

[2] When European Union countries switched to IFRS from their national GAAP in 2005, it was felt that the required disclosures increased by 30%. (See Rafik Greiss and Simon Sharp, "IFRS Conversions: What CFOs Need to Know and Do," Toronto: CICA, 2008.)

[3] It is generally felt that disclosure requirements under ASPE should be approximately 40% to 50% less than under prior Canadian GAAP (see "Private Matters" by Jeff Buckstein, CA Magazine, May 2009).

[4] CICA Handbook–Assurance, Section 5136.03 and CAS 450.

[5] IFRS 8.1.

[6] IFRS 8.7.

[7] IFRS 8.5.

[8] IFRS 8.12 and .13. Copyright © 2012 IFRS Foundation. All rights reserved. Reproduced by Wiley Canada with the permission of the IFRS Foundation ®. No permission granted to third parties to reproduce or distribute.

[9] IFRS 8.13–.15.

[10] IFRS 8.19.

[11] IFRS 8.23, .27, .28 and .31–.34.

[12] IAS 34.8.

[13] IAS 34.20.

[14] IAS 34.11 and 11A.

[15] IAS 34.16A.

[16] IAS 34.43.

[17] A step in this direction is the OSC's mandate for companies to file their financial statements electronically through SEDAR (similar to the SEC requirement to use EDGAR in the United States). SEDAR provides interested parties with computer access to financial information such as annual reports, corporate prospectuses, and proxy materials.

[18] CICA Handbook–Accounting, Part II, Section 3840.04, and IAS 24.9.

[19] CICA Handbook–Accounting, Part II, Section 3840.51.

[20] CICA Handbook–Accounting, Part II, Section 3840.09.

[21] CICA Handbook–Accounting, Part II, Section 3840 DT.

[22] As a benchmark, a substantive change in ownership may be deemed to have occurred if an unrelated party has gained or given up at least 20% interest in the exchanged items (CICA Handbook–Accounting, Part II, Section 3840.35). In the example, if the controlling shareholder only owned, say, 70% of both companies and the shares were publicly traded, then one might argue that a substantive change in ownership may be evident—that is, the other 30% of the shareholders now own (indirectly, through their shareholdings) part of the asset where they did not before the transaction. This is not so clear-cut, however, since the majority shareholders still have a controlling interest, and no real bargaining would have happened between the noncontrolling interest shareholders and the majority shareholders. The resolution of this issue would be a matter of judgement.

[23] CICA Handbook–Accounting, Part II, Section 3840.03.

[24] See Canadian Auditing Standards for details (CAS 700 – Forming an Opinion and Reporting on Financial Statements).

[25] Using Ratios and Graphics in Financial Reporting, CICA Research Study (Toronto: CICA, 1993).

[26] J. E. Boritz, Approaches to Dealing with Risk and Uncertainty, pp. 44–45. CICA Research Report (Toronto: CICA, 1990).

Cumulative Coverage: Chapters 19 to 23

During 2014, you were hired as the chief financial officer for MC Travel Inc., a fairly young travel company that is growing quickly. A key accounting staff member has prepared the financial statements, but there are a couple of transactions that have not been recorded yet because she is waiting for your guidance regarding how these transactions should be recorded. In addition, the staff member is not confident in preparing cash flow statements, so you have been asked to prepare this statement for the 2014 year. MC Travel Inc. reports under ASPE.

The transactions that have not been recorded yet are as follows.

1. On January 1, 2012, the company purchased a small hotel property in Miami for $50 million, paying $10 million in cash and issuing a 5%, $40-million bond at par to cover the balance. The bond principal is payable on January 1, 2022. When you were hired and began to review the financial information from previous years, you quickly realized that the land portion of the total purchase price had been capitalized with the building, and depreciated. Depreciation has been incorrectly recorded on the building for 2012, 2013, and 2014, and the land is still included in the building account. The land portion of the purchase was appraised at $15 million in 2012, and the land is currently worth $17 million. The cost of the property is to be amortized over a 20-year period using the straight-line basis, and a residual value of $5 million. The company's tax rate is 30%.

2. During 2014, the president, who is also the principal shareholder in the business, transferred ownership of a vacant piece of land in the Caribbean to the company. A hotel will be constructed on this property beginning in 2015. The cost when the president purchased this property was $10 million, and the fair market value, based on a professional appraisal, at the time it was transferred to the company was $25 million. The president was issued 50,000 common shares in exchange for this land. This transaction has not yet been booked.

Additional information that you have gathered to assist in preparing the cash flow statement is as follows.

1. In 2014, equipment was purchased for $250,000. In addition, some equipment was disposed of during the year.

2. Investment income includes a dividend of $150,000 received on the temporary investment. Interest income of $106,000 was reinvested in fair value–net income investments.

Following are the financial statements for MC Travel Inc. for the 2014 and 2013 fiscal years.

MC TRAVEL INC.

Balance Sheet—December 31

	2014	2013
ASSETS—Current assets		
Cash	$ 7,600,000	$ 5,040,000
Fair value–net income investments	2,006,000	1,900,000
Accounts receivable	5,000,000	3,700,000
Allowance for doubtful accounts	–200,000	–100,500
Total current assets	14,406,000	10,539,500
Capital assets		
Land	250,000	250,000
Building and equipment	55,270,000	55,072,000
Accumulated depreciation	–7,425,000	–4,950,000
Total capital assets	48,095,000	50,372,000
Total assets	$62,501,000	$60,911,500
LIABILITIES AND SHAREHOLDERS' EQUITY—Current liabilities		
Accounts payable	$ 3,800,800	$ 4,100,750
Interest payable	30,000	15,000
Income taxes payable	350,000	250,000
Dividends payable	–0–	100,000
Total current liabilities	4,180,800	4,465,750

(continued)

Long-term liabilities	1,145,000	807,000
Long-term bank loan	40,000,000	40,000,000
5% bond payable—Miami property, due 2022	175,000	150,000
Future income tax liability	41,320,000	40,957,000
Total long-term liabilities	45,500,800	45,422,750
Total liabilities		
Shareholders' equity		
Common shares	1,000,000	1,000,000
Retained earnings	16,000,200	14,488,750
Total shareholders' equity	17,000,200	15,488,750
Total liabilities and shareholders' equity	$62,501,000	$60,911,500

MC TRAVEL INC.
Income Statement—Year Ended December 31, 2014

Sales Revenue		$37,500,000
Expenses: Salaries and wages	5,000,000	
Purchases from tour operators	22,500,000	
Depreciation expense	2,500,000	
Office, general, and selling expense	3,489,800	
Bad debt expense	150,000	
Interest on long-term debt	30,000	
Bond interest expense	2,000,000	
Total expenses		35,669,800
Income before other income and expenses		1,830,200
Investment income		256,000
Gain on sale of equipment		73,000
Income before income taxes		2,159,200
Income tax expense		647,750
Net income		$ 1,511,450

Instructions

From the information supplied, complete the necessary entries to record the two transactions that have not been recorded, and prepare a revised balance sheet and income statement for the year, keeping in mind that comparative figures will need to be restated. Once this is complete, prepare a statement of cash flows in good form using the direct method for the year ended December 31, 2014. Assume all transaction amounts have been reported in Canadian dollars.

Specimen Financial Statements

Shoppers Drug Mart

The following pages contain the financial statements, accompanying notes, and other information from the 2011 annual financial statements of Shoppers Drug Mart. Note 30 has been reproduced partially in the interest of brevity. The text of the full note and other financial information that is not reproduced here is available on WileyPLUS and the student website. The corporate profile below is taken from the company annual report.

Corporate profile

Shoppers Drug Mart Corporation is the licensor of full-service retail drug stores operating under the names Shoppers Drug Mart® and Pharmaprix®. Founded in 1962 by Toronto pharmacist Murray Koffler, the Company has grown to a network of more than 1,200 stores across Canada. These conveniently located stores are owned and operated by licensed Associate-owners, who have helped build a brand that is synonymous with exceptional service, value and trust. The Company also licenses or owns 58 medical clinic pharmacies operating under the names Shoppers Simply Pharmacy® and Pharmaprix Simplement Santé®, as well as eight luxury beauty destinations operating as Murale™.

With fiscal 2011 sales of approximately $10.5 billion, the Company is the leader in Canada's retail drug store marketplace and is the number one provider of pharmacy products and services. Shoppers Drug Mart has successfully leveraged its leadership position in pharmacy and its convenient store locations to capture a significant share of the market in front store merchandise, including over-the-counter medications, health and beauty aids, cosmetics and fragrances, seasonal products and everyday household essentials. The Company offers a broad range of high-quality private label products including Life Brand®, Quo®, Etival Laboratoire®, Baléa®, Everyday Market®, Simply Food®, Nativa® and Bio-Life®, among others, and value-added services such as the Healthwatch® program, which offers patient counselling and advice on medications, disease management and health and wellness, and the Shoppers Optimum® program, one of the largest retail loyalty card programs in Canada.

As well, the Company owns and operates 63 Shoppers Home Health Care® stores, which are engaged in the sale and service of assisted-living devices and equipment to institutional and retail customers. In addition to its retail network, the Company owns Shoppers Drug Mart Specialty Health Network Inc., a provider of specialty drug distribution, pharmacy and comprehensive patient support services, and Medi-System Technologies Inc., a provider of pharmaceutical products and services to long-term care facilities in Ontario and Alberta.

At this point, we recommend that you take 20 to 30 minutes to scan the statements and notes to familiarize yourself with the contents and accounting elements. Throughout the following chapters, when you are asked to refer to specific parts of Shoppers' financials, do so. Then, when you have completed reading this book, we challenge you to reread Shoppers' financials to see how much greater and more sophisticated your understanding of them has become.

Management's Report

Management's Responsibility for Financial Statements

Management is responsible for the preparation and presentation of the accompanying consolidated financial statements and all other information in the Annual Report. This responsibility includes the selection and consistent application of appropriate accounting principles and methods in addition to making the estimates, judgements and assumptions necessary to prepare the consolidated financial statements in accordance with Canadian generally accepted accounting principles, which complies with International Financial Reporting Standards. It also includes ensuring that the financial information presented elsewhere in the Annual Report is consistent with the consolidated financial statements.

In fulfilling its responsibilities, management has established and maintains systems of internal controls. Although no cost-effective system of internal controls will prevent or detect all errors and irregularities, these systems are designed to provide reasonable assurance regarding the reliability of the Company's financial reporting and preparation of the financial statements in accordance with Canadian generally accepted accounting principles. These systems include controls to provide reasonable assurance that resources are safeguarded from material loss or inappropriate use, that transactions are authorized, recorded and reported properly and that financial records are reliable for preparing the consolidated financial statements. Internal auditors, who are employees of the Company, review and evaluate internal controls on management's behalf. The consolidated financial statements have been audited by the independent auditors, Deloitte & Touche LLP, in accordance with generally accepted auditing standards. Their report follows.

The Board of Directors, acting through an Audit Committee which is comprised solely of directors who are not employees of the Company, is responsible for determining that management fulfils its responsibility for financial reporting and internal control. This responsibility is carried out through periodic meetings with senior officers, financial management, internal audit and the independent auditors to discuss audit activities, the adequacy of internal financial controls and financial reporting matters. The Audit Committee has reviewed these consolidated financial statements and the Management's Discussion and Analysis and has recommended their approval by the Board of Directors prior to their inclusion in this Annual Report.

Domenic Pilla
President and Chief Executive Officer

TORONTO, ONTARIO
FEBRUARY 9, 2012

Brad Lukow
Executive Vice-President and Chief Financial Officer

To the Shareholders of Shoppers Drug Mart Corporation

We have audited the accompanying consolidated financial statements of Shoppers Drug Mart Corporation, which comprise the consolidated balance sheets as at December 31, 2011, January 1, 2011, and January 3, 2010 and the consolidated statements of earnings, consolidated statements of comprehensive income, consolidated statements of changes in shareholders' equity and consolidated statements of cash flows for the 52 week periods ended December 31, 2011 and January 1, 2011, and a summary of significant accounting policies and other explanatory information.

Management's Responsibility for the Consolidated Financial Statements

Management is responsible for the preparation and fair presentation of these consolidated financial statements in accordance with International Financial Reporting Standards, and for such internal control as management determines is necessary to enable the preparation of consolidated financial statements that are free from material misstatement, whether due to fraud or error.

Auditor's Responsibility

Our responsibility is to express an opinion on these consolidated financial statements based on our audits. We conducted our audits in accordance with Canadian generally accepted auditing standards. Those standards require that we comply with ethical requirements and plan and perform the audit to obtain reasonable assurance about whether the consolidated financial statements are free from material misstatement.

An audit involves performing procedures to obtain audit evidence about the amounts and disclosures in the consolidated financial statements. The procedures selected depend on the auditor's judgment, including the assessment of the risks of material misstatement of the consolidated financial statements, whether due to fraud or error. In making those risk assessments, the auditor considers internal control relevant to the entity's preparation and fair presentation of the consolidated financial statements in order to design audit procedures that are appropriate in the circumstances, but not for the purpose of expressing an opinion on the effectiveness of the entity's internal control. An audit also includes evaluating the appropriateness of accounting policies used and the reasonableness of accounting estimates made by management, as well as evaluating the overall presentation of the consolidated financial statements.

We believe that the audit evidence we have obtained in our audits is sufficient and appropriate to provide a basis for our audit opinion.

Opinion

In our opinion, the consolidated financial statements present fairly, in all material respects, the financial position of Shoppers Drug Mart Corporation as at December 31, 2011, January 1, 2011 and January 3, 2010 and its financial performance and its cash flows for the 52 week periods ended December 31, 2011 and January 1, 2011 in accordance with International Financial Reporting Standards.

Deloitte & Touche LLP

Chartered Accountants,
Licensed Public Accountants

FEBRUARY 9, 2012
TORONTO, ONTARIO

Consolidated Statements of Earnings

For the 52 weeks ended December 31, 2011 and January 1, 2011
(in thousands of Canadian dollars, except per share amounts)

	Note	2011	2010[1]
Sales		$ 10,458,652	$ 10,192,714
Cost of goods sold	9	(6,416,208)	(6,283,634)
Gross profit		4,042,444	3,909,080
Operating and administrative expenses		(3,131,539)	(3,011,758)
Operating income	10, 11, 13	910,905	897,322
Finance expenses	12	(64,038)	(60,633)
Earnings before income taxes		846,867	836,689
Income taxes	14		
Current		(208,696)	(238,779)
Deferred		(24,237)	(6,059)
		(232,933)	(244,838)
Net earnings		$ 613,934	$ 591,851
Net earnings per common share			
Basic	25	$ 2.84	$ 2.72
Diluted	25	$ 2.84	2.72
Weighted average common shares outstanding (millions):			
Basic	25	216.4	217.4
Diluted	25	216.5	217.5
Actual common shares outstanding (millions)	24	212.5	217.5

[1] In preparing its 2010 comparative information, the Company has adjusted amounts reported previously in financial statements prepared in accordance with Canadian Generally Accepted Accounting Principles ("previous Canadian GAAP"). See Note 30 to these consolidated financial statements for an explanation of the transition to International Financial Reporting Standards ("IFRS").

The accompanying notes are an integral part of these consolidated financial statements.

Consolidated Statements of Comprehensive Income

For the 52 weeks ended December 31, 2011 and January 1, 2011
(in thousands of Canadian dollars)

	Note	2011	2010[1]
Net earnings		$ 613,934	$ 591,851
Other comprehensive income (loss), net of tax			
Effective portion of changes in fair value of hedges on interest rate derivatives (net of tax of $nil (2010: $525))	18	–	1,120
Effective portion of changes in fair value of hedges on equity forward derivatives (net of tax of $12 (2010: $205))	18	(39)	(521)
Net change in fair value of hedges on interest rate and equity forward derivatives transferred to earnings (net of tax of $163 (2010: $13))	18	411	33
Retirement benefit obligations actuarial losses (net of tax of $7,433 (2010: $2,905))	21	(21,943)	(8,150)
Other comprehensive loss, net of tax	7	(21,571)	(7,518)
Total comprehensive income		$ 592,363	$ 584,333

[1] In preparing its 2010 comparative information, the Company has adjusted amounts reported previously in financial statements prepared in accordance with previous Canadian GAAP. See Note 30 to these consolidated financial statements for an explanation of the transition to IFRS.

The accompanying notes are an integral part of these consolidated financial statements.

Consolidated Balance Sheets

As at December 31, 2011, January 1, 2011 and January 3, 2010
(in thousands of Canadian dollars)

	Note	December 31, 2011	January 1, 2011[1]	January 3, 2010[1]
Current assets				
Cash		$ 118,566	$ 64,354	$ 44,391
Accounts receivable		493,338	432,089	470,935
Inventory		2,042,302	1,957,525	1,852,441
Income taxes recoverable		—	20,384	—
Prepaid expenses and deposits		41,441	68,468	74,206
Total current assets		2,695,647	2,542,820	2,441,973
Non-current assets				
Property and equipment	15	1,767,543	1,677,340	1,541,841
Investment property	15	16,372	12,770	5,884
Goodwill	16	2,499,722	2,493,108	2,483,430
Intangible assets	17	281,737	272,217	258,766
Other assets		18,214	19,678	16,716
Deferred tax assets	14	21,075	26,264	28,456
Total non-current assets		4,604,663	4,501,377	4,335,093
Total assets		$ 7,300,310	$ 7,044,197	$ 6,777,066
Liabilities				
Bank indebtedness	19	$ 172,262	$ 209,013	$ 270,332
Commercial paper	19	—	127,828	260,386
Accounts payable and accrued liabilities	18	1,109,444	990,244	970,831
Income taxes payable		26,538	—	17,046
Dividends payable	24	53,119	48,927	46,748
Current portion of long-term debt	20	249,971	—	—
Provisions	22	12,024	12,562	11,009
Associate interest		152,880	138,993	130,189
Total current liabilities		1,776,238	1,527,567	1,706,541
Long-term debt	20	695,675	943,412	946,098
Other long-term liabilities	23	520,188	442,124	386,262
Provisions	22	1,701	1,852	1,062
Deferred tax liabilities	14	38,678	26,607	25,219
Total long-term liabilities		1,256,242	1,413,995	1,358,641
Total liabilities		3,032,480	2,941,562	3,065,182
Shareholders' equity				
Share capital	24	1,486,455	1,520,558	1,519,870
Treasury shares	24	(4,735)	—	—
Contributed surplus	26	10,246	11,702	10,274
Accumulated other comprehensive loss	7	(30,214)	(8,643)	(1,125)
Retained earnings		2,806,078	2,579,018	2,182,865
Total shareholders' equity		4,267,830	4,102,635	3,711,884
Total liabilities and shareholders' equity		$ 7,300,310	$ 7,044,197	$ 6,777,066

(1) In preparing its 2010 comparative information, the Company has adjusted amounts reported previously in financial statements prepared in accordance with previous Canadian GAAP. See Note 30 to these consolidated financial statements for an explanation of the transition to IFRS.

The accompanying notes are an integral part of these consolidated financial statements

On behalf of the Board of Directors:

Domenic Pilla
Director

Holger Kluge
Director

Consolidated Statements of Changes in Shareholders' Equity

For the 52 weeks ended December 31, 2011 and January 1, 2011
(in thousands of Canadian dollars)

	Note	Share Capital	Treasury Shares	Contributed Surplus	Accumulated Other Comprehensive Loss (Notes 18 and 21)	Retained Earnings	Total
Balance as at January 1, 2011 (1)		$ 1,520,558	$ —	$ 11,702	$ (8,643)	$ 2,579,018	$ 4,102,635
Total comprehensive income		—	—	—	(21,571)	613,934	592,363
Dividends	24	—	—	—	—	(215,671)	(215,671)
Share repurchases	24	(35,576)	(4,735)	—	—	(171,203)	(211,514)
Share-based payments	26	—	—	(1,210)	—	—	(1,210)
Share options exercised	26	1,466	—	(246)	—	—	1,220
Repayment of share-purchase loans	26	7	—	—	—	—	7
Balance as at December 31, 2011		**$ 1,486,455**	**$ (4,735)**	**$ 10,246**	**$ (30,214)**	**$ 2,806,078**	**$ 4,267,830**
Balance as at January 3, 2010 (1)		$ 1,519,870	$ —	$ 10,274	$ (1,125)	$ 2,182,865	$ 3,711,884
Total comprehensive income		—	—	—	(7,518)	591,851	584,333
Dividends	24	—	—	—	—	(195,698)	(195,698)
Share-based payments	26	—	—	1,592	—	—	1,592
Share options exercised	26	655	—	(164)	—	—	491
Repayment of share-purchase loans	26	33	—	—	—	—	33
Balance as at January 1, 2011 (1)		$ 1,520,558	$ —	$ 11,702	$ (8,643)	$ 2,579,018	$ 4,102,635

(1) In preparing its 2010 comparative information, the Company has adjusted amounts reported previously in financial statements prepared in accordance with previous Canadian GAAP. See Note 30 to these consolidated financial statements for an explanation of the transition to IFRS.

The accompanying notes are an integral part of these consolidated financial statements.

Consolidated Statements of Cash Flows

For the 52 weeks ended December 31, 2011 and January 1, 2011
(in thousands of Canadian dollars)

	Note	2011	2010[1]
Cash flows from operating activities			
Net earnings		$ 613,934	$ 591,851
Adjustments for:			
Depreciation and amortization	13, 15, 17	296,464	278,421
Finance expenses	12	64,038	60,633
Loss on sale or disposal of property and equipment, including impairments	15, 17	2,015	3,880
Share-based payment transactions	26	(1,210)	1,592
Recognition and reversal of provisions, net	22	9,218	12,160
Other long-term liabilities	23	296	18,491
Income tax expense	14	232,933	244,838
		1,217,688	1,211,866
Net change in non-cash working capital balances	27	32,166	(34,824)
Provisions used	22	(9,907)	(9,817)
Interest paid		(63,853)	(62,916)
Income taxes paid		(202,256)	(276,108)
Net cash from operating activities		**973,838**	**828,201**
Cash flows from investing activities			
Proceeds from disposition of property and equipment and investment property		55,459	60,538
Business acquisitions	8	(10,496)	(11,779)
Deposits		105	1,534
Acquisition or development of property and equipment	15	(341,868)	(415,094)
Acquisition or development of intangible assets	17	(53,836)	(56,625)
Other assets		1,464	(3,249)
Net cash used in investing activities		**(349,172)**	**(424,675)**
Cash flows from financing activities			
Repurchase of own shares	24	(206,779)	–
Proceeds from exercise of share options	26	1,220	491
Repayment of share-purchase loans	24	7	33
Repayment of bank indebtedness, net	19	(36,714)	(61,319)
Repayment of commercial paper, net	19	(128,000)	(133,000)
Revolving term debt, net	20	152	(1,298)
Payment of transaction costs for debt refinancing	20	(575)	(2,792)
Repayment of financing lease obligations	23	(2,173)	(1,436)
Associate interest		13,887	9,277
Dividends paid	24	(211,479)	(193,519)
Net cash used in financing activities		**(570,454)**	**(383,563)**
Net increase in cash		54,212	19,963
Cash, beginning of the year		64,354	44,391
Cash, end of the year		**$ 118,566**	**$ 64,354**

[1] In preparing its 2010 comparative information, the Company has adjusted amounts reported previously in financial statements prepared in accordance with previous Canadian GAAP. See Note 30 to these consolidated financial statements for an explanation of the transition to IFRS.

The accompanying notes are an integral part of these consolidated financial statements.

Notes to the Consolidated Financial Statements

December 31, 2011 and January 1, 2011 (in thousands of Canadian dollars, except per share data)

1. GENERAL INFORMATION

Shoppers Drug Mart Corporation (the "Company") is a public company incorporated and domiciled in Canada, whose shares are publicly traded on the Toronto Stock Exchange. The Company's registered address is 243 Consumers Road, Toronto, Ontario M2J 4W8, Canada.

The Company is a licensor of 1,199 Shoppers Drug Mart®/Pharmaprix® full-service retail drug stores across Canada. The Shoppers Drug Mart®/Pharmaprix® stores are licensed to corporations owned by pharmacists ("Associates"). The Company also licenses or owns 58 Shoppers Simply Pharmacy®/Pharmaprix Simplement Santé® medical clinic pharmacies and eight Murale™ beauty stores. In addition, the Company owns and operates 63 Shoppers Home Health Care® stores. In addition to its store network, the Company owns Shoppers Drug Mart Specialty Health Network Inc., a provider of specialty drug distribution, pharmacy and comprehensive patient support services, and MediSystem Technologies Inc., a provider of pharmaceutical products and services to long-term care facilities in Ontario and Alberta.

The majority of the Company's sales are generated from the Shoppers Drug Mart®/Pharmaprix® full-service retail drug stores and the majority of the Company's assets are used in the operations of these stores. As such, the Company presents one operating segment in its consolidated financial statement disclosures. The revenue generated by Shoppers Drug Mart®/Pharmaprix Simplement Santé®, MediSystem Technologies Inc. and Shoppers Drug Mart Specialty Health Network Inc. is included with prescription sales of the Company's retail drug stores. The revenue generated by Shoppers Home Health Care® and Murale™ is included with the front store sales of the Company's retail drug stores.

These consolidated financial statements of the Company as at and for the financial year ended December 31, 2011 include the accounts of Shoppers Drug Mart Corporation, its subsidiaries, and the Associate-owned stores that comprise the majority of the Company's store network. The financial year of the Company consists of a 52 or 53 week period ending on the Saturday closest to December 31. The current financial year is the 52 weeks ended December 31, 2011. The comparative financial year is the 52 weeks ended January 1, 2011. The Company has also presented the consolidated balance sheet as at January 3, 2010, the Company's date of transition to International Financial Reporting Standards ("IFRS").

2. BASIS OF PREPARATION

(a) Statement of Compliance

These consolidated financial statements have been prepared in accordance with Canadian Generally Accepted Accounting Principles ("Canadian GAAP"). These consolidated financial statements also comply with International Financial Reporting Standards ("IFRS") as issued by the International Accounting Standards Board ("IASB").

These are the Company's first consolidated financial statements prepared in accordance with IFRS. IFRS 1, "First-time Adoption of International Financial Reporting Standards", has been applied in the preparation of these financial statements. Consolidated financial statements of the Company had been prepared under previous Canadian GAAP, which differs in certain respects from IFRS. When preparing the Company's 2011 consolidated financial statements, management has amended certain accounting methods in order to comply with IFRS. The comparative consolidated financial statements reflect the adoption of IFRS.

An explanation of how the transition from previous Canadian GAAP to IFRS has affected the reported financial position, financial performance and cash flows of the Company is provided in Note 30 to these consolidated financial statements.

These consolidated financial statements were authorized for issuance by the Board of Directors of the Company on February 9, 2012.

(b) Use of Estimates and Judgements

The preparation of these consolidated financial statements in conformity with IFRS requires management to make certain judgements, estimates and assumptions that affect the application of accounting policies and the reported amounts of assets and liabilities and disclosure of contingent assets and liabilities at the date of these consolidated financial statements and the reported amounts of revenues and expenses during the reporting period.

Notes to the Consolidated Financial Statements (continued)
December 31, 2011 and January 1, 2011 (in thousands of Canadian dollars, except per share data)

2. BASIS OF PREPARATION (continued)

Judgement is commonly used in determining whether a balance or transaction should be recognized in the consolidated financial statements and estimates and assumptions are more commonly used in determining the measurement of recognized transactions and balances. However, judgement and estimates are often interrelated.

The Company has applied judgement in its assessment of the appropriateness of the consolidation of the Associate-owned stores, classification of items such as leases and financial instruments, the recognition of tax losses and provisions, determining the tax rates used for measuring deferred taxes, determining cash-generating units, identifying the indicators of impairment for property and equipment and intangible assets with finite useful lives, and the level of componentization of property and equipment.

Estimates are used when estimating the useful lives of property and equipment and intangible assets for the purpose of depreciation and amortization, when accounting for or measuring items such as inventory provisions, Shoppers Optimum® loyalty card program deferred revenue, assumptions underlying the actuarial determination of retirement benefit obligations, income and other taxes, provisions, certain fair value measures including those related to the valuation of business combinations, share-based payments and financial instruments and when measuring goodwill, indefinite useful life intangible assets and other assets for impairment. Actual results may differ from these estimates.

Estimates and underlying assumptions are reviewed on an ongoing basis. Revisions to accounting estimates are recognized in the period in which the estimates are revised and in any future periods affected.

3. SIGNIFICANT ACCOUNTING POLICIES

The accounting policies set out in these consolidated financial statements have been applied consistently to all periods presented in these consolidated financial statements.

(a) Basis of Consolidation

(i) Subsidiaries

Subsidiaries are entities controlled by the Company. Control exists where the Company has the power to govern the financial and operating policies of an entity so as to obtain benefits from its activities. All of the Company's subsidiaries are wholly-owned. The financial statements of subsidiaries are included in the Company's consolidated financial statements from the date that control commences until the date that control ceases.

(ii) Associate-owned Stores

Associate-owned stores comprise the majority of the Company's store network. The Company does not have any direct or indirect shareholdings in these Associates' corporations. The Associates' corporations remain separate legal entities. The Company consolidates the Associate-owned stores under IAS 27, "Consolidated and Separate Financial Statements" ("IAS 27"). The consolidation of the stores under IAS 27 was determined based on the concept of control under IAS 27 and determined primarily through the agreements with Associates ("Associate Agreements") that govern the relationship between the Company and the Associates.

(iii) Transactions Eliminated on Consolidation

Intra-company balances and transactions and any unrealized earnings and expenses arising from intra-company transactions, including those of the Associate-owned stores, are eliminated in preparing the consolidated financial statements.

(b) Basis of Measurement

These consolidated financial statements have been prepared on the historical cost basis except for certain financial instruments, deferred revenue related to the Shoppers Optimum® loyalty card program and the liabilities for the Company's long-term incentive plan and restricted share unit plan, which are measured at fair value (see Note 26 to these consolidated financial statements for further information on the long-term incentive plan and the restricted share unit plan). Any recognized impairment losses will also impact the historical cost of certain balances.

The methods used to measure fair values are discussed further in Note 4 to these consolidated financial statements.

(c) Revenue

(i) Sale of Goods and Services

Revenue is comprised primarily of retail sales, including prescription sales. Retail sales are recognized as revenue when the goods are sold to the customer. Revenue is net of returns and amounts deferred related to the issuance of points under the Shoppers Optimum® Loyalty Card Program (the "Program"). Where a sales transaction includes sales transaction points awarded under the Program, revenue allocated to the Program points is deferred based on the fair value of the awards and recognized as revenue when the Program points are redeemed and the Company fulfills its obligations to supply the awards.

Revenue is measured at the fair value of the consideration received or receivable from the customer for products sold or services supplied.

(ii) Shoppers Optimum® Loyalty Card Program

The Shoppers Optimum® Loyalty Card Program allows members to earn points on their purchases in Shoppers Drug Mart®, Pharmaprix®, Shoppers Simply Pharmacy®, Pharmaprix Simplement Santé®, Shoppers Home Health Care® and Murale™ stores at a rate of 10 points for each dollar spent on eligible products and services, plus any applicable bonus points. Members can then redeem points, in accordance with the Program rewards schedule or other offers, for qualifying merchandise at the time of a future purchase transaction.

When points are earned by Program members, the Company defers revenue equal to the fair value of the awards. The Program's deferred revenue is recognized within accounts payable and accrued liabilities in the Company's consolidated balance sheets. When awards are redeemed by Program members, the redemption value of the awards is charged against the deferred revenue balance and recognized as revenue.

The estimated fair value per point is determined based on the expected weighted average redemption levels for future redemptions based on the program reward schedule, including special redemption events. The trends in redemption rates (points redeemed as a percentage of points issued) are reviewed on an ongoing basis and the estimated fair value per point is adjusted based upon expected future activity.

(d) Vendor Rebates

The Company classifies rebates and other consideration received from vendors as a reduction to the cost of inventory. These amounts are recognized in cost of goods sold when the associated inventory is sold. Certain exceptions apply where the consideration received from the vendor is a reimbursement of a selling cost or a payment for services delivered to the vendor, in which case the consideration is reflected in cost of goods sold or operating and administrative expenses dependent on where the related expenses are recorded.

(e) Finance Expenses

Finance expenses are comprised of interest expense on borrowings and the amortization of transaction costs incurred in conjunction with debt transactions. All borrowing costs are recognized in earnings on an accrual basis using the effective interest method, net of amounts capitalized as part of the cost of qualifying property and equipment.

The Company's finance income is not significant.

(f) Borrowing Costs

Borrowing costs that are directly attributable to the acquisition, construction or development of a qualifying asset are recognized as part of the cost of that asset. Qualifying assets are those that require a substantial period of time to prepare for their intended use. All other borrowing costs are recognized as finance expenses in the period in which they are incurred.

The Company capitalizes borrowing costs at the weighted average interest rate on borrowings outstanding for the period. The Company commences capitalization of borrowing costs as part of the cost of a qualifying asset when activities are undertaken to prepare the asset for its intended use and when expenditures, including borrowing costs, are incurred for the asset. Capitalization of borrowing costs ceases when substantially all of the activities necessary to prepare the asset for its intended use are complete.

3. SIGNIFICANT ACCOUNTING POLICIES (continued)

(g) Income Taxes

Income tax expense is comprised of taxes currently payable on earnings and changes in deferred tax balances, excluding those changes related to business acquisitions. Income tax expense is recognized in net earnings except to the extent that it relates to items recognized either in other comprehensive income (loss) or directly in equity, in which case it is recognized in other comprehensive income (loss) or in equity respectively.

Current tax expense is comprised of the tax payable on the taxable income for the current financial year using tax rates enacted or substantively enacted at the reporting date, and any adjustment to income taxes payable in respect of previous years.

Deferred tax is recognized using the balance sheet method in respect of taxable temporary differences arising from differences between the carrying amount of assets and liabilities for tax purposes and their carrying amounts in the financial statements. Deferred tax is calculated at the tax rates that are expected to apply to temporary differences in the year they are expected to reverse and are based on the tax legislation that has been enacted or substantively enacted by the reporting date. Deferred tax is not recognized for the following temporary differences: the initial recognition of goodwill and the initial recognition of assets or liabilities in a transaction that is not a business acquisition and that affects neither accounting nor taxable earnings; and, differences relating to investments in subsidiaries to the extent that it is probable that they will not reverse in the foreseeable future. Deferred tax assets and liabilities are offset if there is a legally enforceable right to offset the recognized amounts and the Company intends to settle on a net basis or to realize the asset and settle the liability simultaneously.

A deferred tax asset is recognized to the extent that it is probable that future taxable earnings will be available against which the temporary difference can be utilized. Deferred tax assets are reviewed at each reporting date and are reduced to the extent that it is no longer probable that all or part of the related tax benefit will be realized.

(h) Earnings per Common Share

The Company presents basic and diluted earnings per share ("EPS") amounts for its common shares. Basic EPS is calculated by dividing the net earnings attributable to common shareholders of the Company by the weighted average number of common shares outstanding during the period. Diluted EPS is determined by dividing the net earnings attributable to common shareholders of the Company by the weighted average number of common shares outstanding after adjusting both amounts for the effects of all potential dilutive common shares, which are comprised of share options granted to employees. Anti-dilutive options are not included in the calculation of diluted EPS.

(i) Financial Instruments

(i) Classification of Financial Instruments

Financial instruments are recognized when the Company becomes a party to the contractual provisions of a financial instrument. Financial instruments are classified into one of the following categories: held for trading, held-to-maturity investments, loans and receivables, available-for-sale financial assets or financial liabilities. The classification determines the accounting treatment of the instrument. The classification is determined by the Company when the financial instrument is initially recorded, based on the underlying purpose of the instrument.

The Company's financial instruments are classified and measured as follows:

Financial Asset/Liability	Category	Measurement
Cash	Loans and receivables	Amortized cost
Accounts receivable	Loans and receivables	Amortized cost
Deposits[1]	Loans and receivables	Amortized cost
Long-term receivables[2]	Loans and receivables	Amortized cost
Bank indebtedness	Financial liabilities	Amortized cost
Commercial paper	Financial liabilities	Amortized cost
Accounts payable and accrued liabilities	Financial liabilities	Amortized cost
Dividends payable	Financial liabilities	Amortized cost
Long-term debt	Financial liabilities	Amortized cost
Other long-term liabilities	Financial liabilities	Amortized cost

Derivatives	Classification	Measurement
Interest rate derivatives[3]	Effective cash flow hedge	Fair value through other comprehensive income (loss)
Equity forward derivatives[3][4]	Derivative financial instrument	Fair value through earnings
Equity forward derivatives[3][4]	Effective cash flow hedge	Fair value through other comprehensive income (loss)

[1] The carrying value of deposits is recognized within prepaid expenses and deposits in the consolidated balance sheets.

[2] The carrying value of long-term receivables is recognized within other assets in the consolidated balance sheets.

[3] The carrying values of the Company's derivatives are recognized within other assets, accounts payable and accrued liabilities and other long-term liabilities in the consolidated balance sheets.

[4] The portion of the equity forward derivative agreements relating to the earned long-term incentive plan units and earned restricted share unit plan units is considered a derivative financial instrument. The portion of the equity forward derivative agreements relating to the unearned long-term incentive plan units and unearned restricted share unit plan units is considered an effective cash flow hedge. See Note 26 to these consolidated financial statements for further discussion of the long-term incentive plan and the restricted share unit plan.

Financial instruments measured at amortized cost are initially recognized at fair value and then subsequently at amortized cost using the effective interest method, less any impairment losses, with gains and losses recognized in earnings in the period in which the gain or loss occurs. Changes in the fair value of the Company's derivative instruments designated as effective cash flow hedges are recognized in other comprehensive income (loss) and changes in derivative instruments not designated as effective hedges are recognized within operating and administrative expenses in the Company's consolidated statements of earnings in the period of the change.

The Company categorizes its financial assets and financial liabilities that are recognized in the consolidated balance sheets at fair value using the fair value hierarchy. The fair value hierarchy has the following levels:

* Level 1 – quoted market prices in active markets for identical assets or liabilities;

* Level 2 – inputs other than quoted market prices included in Level 1 that are observable for the asset or liability, either directly (as prices) or indirectly (derived from prices); and

* Level 3 – unobservable inputs such as inputs for the asset or liability that are not based on observable market data.

The level in the fair value hierarchy within which the fair value measurement is categorized in its entirety is determined on the basis of the lowest level input that is significant to the fair value measurement in its entirety.

Notes to the Consolidated Financial Statements (continued)

December 31, 2011 and January 1, 2011 (in thousands of Canadian dollars, except per share data)

3. SIGNIFICANT ACCOUNTING POLICIES (continued)

(ii) Transaction Costs

Transaction costs are added to the initial fair value of financial assets and liabilities when those financial assets and liabilities are not measured at fair value subsequent to initial measurement. Transaction costs are amortized to net earnings, within finance expenses, using the effective interest method.

(iii) Derivative Financial Instruments and Hedge Accounting

The Company is exposed to fluctuations in interest rates by virtue of its borrowings under its bank credit facilities, commercial paper program and financing programs available to its Associates. Increases and decreases in interest rates will negatively or positively impact the financial performance of the Company. The Company may use, from time to time, interest rate derivatives to manage this exposure. The earnings or expense arising from the use of these instruments is recognized within finance expenses for the financial year.

The Company uses cash-settled equity forward agreements to limit its exposure to future price changes in the Company's share price for share unit awards under the Company's long-term incentive plan ("LTIP") and restricted share unit plan ("RSU Plan"). The earnings or expense arising from the use of these instruments is included in other comprehensive income (loss) and in operating and administrative expenses, based on the amounts considered to be a hedge or a derivative, respectively, for the financial year. See Note 26 to these consolidated financial statements for further discussion of the LTIP and RSU Plan.

The Company formally identifies, designates and documents all relationships between hedging instruments and hedged items, as well as its risk assessment objective and strategy for undertaking various hedge transactions. The Company assesses, both at the inception of the hedge and on an ongoing basis, including on re-designation, whether the derivatives that are used in hedging transactions are highly effective in offsetting changes in fair values or cash flows of hedged items. When such derivative instruments cease to exist or to be effective as hedges, or when designation of a hedging relationship is terminated, any associated deferred gains or losses are recognized in earnings in the same period as the corresponding gains or losses associated with the hedged item. When a hedged item ceases to exist, any associated deferred gains or losses are recognized in earnings in the period the hedged item ceases to exist.

(iv) Embedded Derivatives

Embedded derivatives (elements of contracts whose cash flows move independently from the host contract) are required to be separated and measured at their respective fair values unless certain criteria are met. The Company does not have any significant embedded features in contractual arrangements that require separate accounting or presentation from the related host contracts.

(v) Share Capital

Common Shares Common shares issued by the Company are recorded in the amount of the proceeds received, net of direct issue costs.

Repurchase of Share Capital The Company, from time to time, will repurchase its common shares under a Normal Course Issuer Bid. When common shares are repurchased, the amount of the consideration paid which includes directly attributable costs and is net of any tax effects, is recognized as a deduction from share capital. Any repurchased common shares are cancelled. The premium paid over the average book value of the common shares repurchased is charged to retained earnings. At the end of a reporting period, if there are shares that have not yet been cancelled, they are recognized as treasury shares at the purchase price of the transaction.

(f) Business Combinations

The Company applies the acquisition method in accounting for business combinations.

On acquisition, the assets, including intangible assets, and any liabilities assumed are measured at their fair value. Purchase price allocations may be preliminary when initially recognized and may change pending finalization of the valuation of the assets acquired. Purchase price allocations are finalized within one year of the acquisition and prior periods are restated to reflect any adjustments to the purchase price allocation made subsequent to the initial recognition.

The determination of fair values, particularly for intangible assets, is based on management's estimates and includes assumptions on the timing and amount of future cash flows. The Company recognizes as goodwill the excess of the purchase price of an acquired business over the fair value of the underlying net assets, including intangible assets, at the date of acquisition. Transaction costs are expensed as incurred. The date of acquisition is the date on which the Company obtains control over the acquired business.

(k) Inventory

Inventory is comprised of merchandise inventory, which includes prescription inventory, and is valued at the lower of cost and estimated net realizable value. Cost is determined on the first-in, first-out basis. Cost includes all direct expenditures and other appropriate costs incurred in bringing inventory to its present location and condition. The Company classifies rebates and other consideration received from a vendor as a reduction to the cost of inventory unless the rebate relates to the reimbursement of a selling cost or a payment for services.

Net realizable value is the estimated selling price in the ordinary course of business, less the estimated selling expenses.

(l) Property and Equipment and Investment Property

(i) Recognition and Measurement

Items of property and equipment are carried at cost less accumulated depreciation and any recognized impairment losses (see (p) impairment).

Cost includes expenditures that are directly attributable to the acquisition of the asset. The cost of self-constructed assets includes the cost of materials and direct labour, any other costs directly attributable to bringing the assets to a working condition for their intended use, and, where applicable, the costs of dismantling and removing the items and restoring the site on which they are located. Borrowing costs are recognized as part of the cost of an asset, where appropriate.

Purchased software that is integral to the functionality of the related equipment is capitalized as part of that equipment.

When components of property and equipment have different useful lives, they are accounted for as separate items of property and equipment.

Gains and losses on disposal of an item of property and equipment are determined by comparing the proceeds from disposal with the carrying amount of property and equipment net, and are recognized net, within operating and administrative expenses, in net earnings.

Fully-depreciated items of property and equipment that are still in use continue to be recognized in cost and accumulated depreciation.

(ii) Subsequent Costs

The cost of replacing part of an item of property and equipment is recognized in the carrying amount of the item if it is probable that the future economic benefits embodied within the part will flow to the Company and its cost can be measured reliably. The carrying amount of the replaced part is de-recognized. The costs of repairs and maintenance of property and equipment are recognized in earnings as incurred.

3. SIGNIFICANT ACCOUNTING POLICIES (continued)

(iii) Depreciation

Depreciation is recognized in earnings on a straight-line basis over the estimated useful lives of each component of an item of property and equipment. Land is not depreciated. The Company commences recognition of depreciation in earnings when the item of property and equipment is ready for its intended use.

The estimated useful lives for the current and comparative periods are as follows:

Buildings and their components	10 to 40 years
Equipment and fixtures	3 to 10 years
Computer equipment	2 to 10 years
Leasehold improvements	Lesser of term of the lease and useful life
Assets under financing leases	Lesser of term of the lease and useful life

Depreciation methods and useful lives are reviewed at each reporting date.

(iv) Investment Property

Investment property is carried at cost less accumulated depreciation and any recognized impairment losses.

(m) Goodwill

(i) Recognition and Measurement

The Company recognizes goodwill as the excess amount of the purchase price of an acquired business over the fair value of the underlying net assets, including intangible assets, at the date of acquisition. Goodwill is not amortized but is tested for impairment on an annual basis or more frequently if there are indicators that goodwill may be impaired (see (p) Impairment).

(ii) Acquisitions Prior to January 3, 2010

As described in Note 30 to these consolidated financial statements, as part of its transition to IFRS, the Company elected to apply IFRS 3, "Business Combinations" ("IFRS 3"), only to those business combinations that occurred on or after January 3, 2010. In respect of acquisitions prior to January 3, 2010, goodwill represents the amount recognized under previous Canadian GAAP.

(iii) Subsequent Measurement

Goodwill is measured at cost less any accumulated impairment losses.

(n) Intangible Assets

(i) Computer Software

The Company acquires computer software through purchases from vendors and internal development. Computer software that is an integral part of computer equipment is presented in property and equipment. All other computer software is treated as an intangible asset. The Company includes computer software under development in intangible assets. The assessment of whether computer software is an integral part of computer hardware is made when the software development project is complete and placed into use. Costs for internally developed computer software include directly attributable costs including direct labour and overheads associated with the software development project. Expenditures on research activities as part of internally developed computer software are recognized in earnings when incurred.

(ii) Other Intangible Assets

Other intangible assets that are acquired by the Company, other than as a result of a business acquisition, which have finite useful lives, are measured at cost less accumulated amortization and any accumulated impairment losses (see (p) Impairment). Other intangible assets that are acquired by the Company as a result of a business acquisition are measured at their fair values as at the date of acquisition.

(iii) Amortization

Amortization is recognized in earnings on a straight-line basis over the estimated useful lives of intangible assets from the date that they are available for their intended use. The estimated useful lives are as follows:

Prescription files	7 to 12 years
Customer relationships	5 to 25 years
Computer software	3 to 10 years
Other	Term of the lease or 3 years

Computer software under development is not amortized. Amortization methods and useful lives are reviewed at each reporting date.

(o) Leases

The Company leases most of its store locations and office space. Terms vary in length and typically permit renewal for additional periods. Leases for which substantially all the benefits and risks of ownership are transferred to the Company based on certain criteria are recorded as financing leases and classified as property and equipment, accounts payable and accrued liabilities and other long-term liabilities. All other leases are classified as operating leases under which minimum rent, including scheduled escalations, is expensed on a straight-line basis over the term of the lease, including any rent-free periods. Landlord inducements are deferred and amortized as reductions to rent expense on a straight-line basis over the same period.

In the normal course of business, the Company sells certain real estate properties and enters into leaseback arrangements for the area occupied by the Associate-owned stores. The leases are assessed as financing or operating in nature as applicable, and are accounted for accordingly. The gains realized on the disposal of the real estate properties related to sale-leaseback transactions, which are financing in nature, are deferred and amortized on a straight-line basis over the shorter of the lease term and the estimated useful life of the leased asset. The gains realized on the disposal of real estate properties related to sale-leaseback transactions, which are transacted at fair value and are operating in nature, are recognized within operating and administrative expenses in the consolidated statements of earnings. In the event the fair value of the asset at the time of the sale-leaseback transaction is less than its carrying value, the difference would be recognized within operating and administrative expenses in the consolidated statements of earnings.

Leases may include additional payments for real estate taxes, maintenance and insurance. These amounts are expensed in the period to which they relate.

(p) Impairment

(i) Financial Assets

A financial asset is assessed at each reporting date to determine whether there is any objective evidence that it is impaired. A financial asset is considered to be impaired if objective evidence indicates that one or more events, which have a negative effect on the estimated future cash flows of that asset, have occurred.

An impairment loss in respect of a financial asset measured at amortized cost is calculated as the difference between its carrying amount and the present value of the estimated future cash flows, discounted at the original effective interest rate.

Individually significant financial assets are tested for impairment on an individual basis. The remaining financial assets are assessed collectively in groups that share similar credit risk characteristics.

All impairment losses are recognized in the consolidated statements of earnings.

An impairment loss is reversed if the reversal can be objectively related to an event occurring after the impairment loss was recognized. For financial assets measured at amortized cost, the reversal is recognized in earnings.

Notes to the Consolidated Financial Statements

December 31, 2011 and January 1, 2011 (in thousands of Canadian dollars, except per share data)

3. SIGNIFICANT ACCOUNTING POLICIES (continued)

(ii) Property and Equipment and Intangible Assets with Finite Useful Lives

The carrying amount of property and equipment and intangible assets with finite useful lives is reviewed at each reporting date to determine whether there are any indicators of impairment. If any such indicators exist, then the recoverable amount of the asset is estimated as the higher of the fair value of the asset less costs to sell, or value-in-use. An impairment loss is recognized in net earnings for the amount by which the carrying amount of the asset exceeds its recoverable amount. For the purposes of assessing impairment, when an individual asset does not generate cash flows in and of itself, assets are then grouped and tested at the lowest level for which there are separately identifiable cash flows, called a cash-generating unit. The Company has determined that its cash generating units are primarily its retail stores.

(iii) Goodwill and Intangible Assets with Indefinite Useful Lives

For goodwill and intangible assets that have indefinite useful lives or that are not yet available for use, the carrying value is reviewed for impairment on an annual basis, or more frequently if there are indicators that impairment may exist.

Goodwill is allocated to cash-generating units expected to benefit from the synergies created from a business combination and to the lowest level at which management monitors goodwill. To review for impairment, the recoverable amount of each cash-generating unit to which goodwill is allocated is compared to its carrying value, including goodwill.

(iv) Recoverable Amount

The recoverable amount of an asset or cash-generating unit is the greater of its value-in-use and its fair value less costs to sell. In assessing value-in-use, the estimated future cash flows are discounted to their present value using a pre-tax discount rate that reflects current market assessments of the time value of money and the risks specific to the asset.

(v) Impairment Losses

An impairment loss is recognized if the carrying amount of an asset or its cash-generating unit exceeds its estimated recoverable amount. Impairment losses are recognized in operating and administrative expenses in the consolidated statements of earnings.

Impairment losses recognized in respect of cash-generating units are allocated first to reduce the carrying amount of any goodwill allocated to the cash-generating units and, then, to reduce the carrying amounts of the other assets in the cash-generating unit (group of units) on a pro rata basis.

An impairment loss in respect of goodwill is not reversed. In respect of other assets, impairment losses recognized in prior periods are assessed at each reporting date for any indicators that the loss has decreased or no longer exists. An impairment loss is reversed if there has been a change in the estimates used to determine the recoverable amount. An impairment loss is reversed only to the extent that the carrying amount of the asset does not exceed the carrying amount that would have been determined, net of depreciation or amortization, if no impairment loss had been recognized.

(q) Bank Indebtedness

Bank indebtedness is comprised of corporate bank overdraft balances, corporate and Associate-owned store bank lines of credit and outstanding cheques.

(r) Employee Benefits

(i) Defined Benefit Plans

The Company maintains registered defined benefit pension plans under which benefits are available to certain employee groups. The Company also makes supplementary retirement benefits available to certain employees under a non-registered defined benefit pension plan.

The Company accrues for its defined benefit plans under the following policies:

- The cost of pensions and other retirement benefits earned by employees is actuarially determined using the projected unit credit method (also known as the projected benefit method pro-rated on service) and management's best estimate of expected plan investment performance, salary escalation, retirement ages of employees and their expected future longevity.

- For the purposes of calculating the expected return on plan assets, those assets are valued at fair value.

- The Company recognizes actuarial gains and losses in other comprehensive income (loss) in the period in which those gains and losses occur.

The pension plans are funded through contributions based on actuarial cost methods as permitted by applicable pension regulatory bodies. Benefits under these plans are based on the employees' years of service and final average earnings.

(ii) Defined Contribution Plans

The Company maintains a defined contribution plan for a small number of employees. Required contributions are recognized as an expense when the employees have rendered service.

(iii) Other Long-term Employee Benefits

The Company maintains post-retirement benefit plans, other than pensions, covering benefits such as health and life insurance for certain retirees. The cost of these plans is charged to earnings as benefits are earned by employees on the basis of service rendered.

(s) Share-based Payment Transactions

The grant date fair value of stock options granted to employees is recognized as employee compensation expense, with a corresponding increase in equity, over the period that the employees become unconditionally entitled to the options. Fair value is measured using the Black-Scholes option-pricing model. If the Company can reasonably estimate forfeitures of vested options, the amount expensed is adjusted for estimated forfeitures. For amounts that have been recognized related to options not yet vested that are subsequently forfeited, the amounts recognized as expenses and equity are reversed.

The fair value of the amount payable to employees in respect of cash-settled share-based payments is recognized as an expense, with a corresponding increase in liabilities, over the period that the employees become unconditionally entitled to payment. The fair value of the liability is re-measured at each reporting date and at settlement date. Any changes in the fair value of the liability are recognized within operating and administrative expenses in the consolidated statements of earnings.

(t) Provisions

Provisions are recognized when there is a present legal or constructive obligation as a result of a past event, it is probable that an outflow of economic benefits will be required to settle the obligation and that obligation can be measured reliably. If the effect of the time value of money is material, provisions are discounted using a current pre-tax rate that reflects the risks specific to the liability. Provisions are reviewed on a regular basis and adjusted to reflect management's best current estimates. Due to the judgmental nature of these items, future settlements may differ from amounts recognized. Provisions are comprised of estimated insurance claims, litigation settlements and store closing costs.

(i) Insurance Claims

The insurance claim provision is management's best estimate of future payments for current insurance claims that are below the Company's deductible limits and is based on determinations made by an independent insurance adjuster. The timing of utilization of the provision will vary according to the individual claims.

(ii) Litigation Claims

A provision for legal claims is recognized when it is probable that a settlement will be made in respect of a claim.

(iii) Store Closing Costs

The Company records a provision for store closings when it vacates current leased-store locations and relocates.

3. SIGNIFICANT ACCOUNTING POLICIES (continued)

(u) Associate Interest

Associate interest reflects the investment the Associates have in the net assets of their businesses. Under the terms of the Company's agreements with Associates (the "Associate Agreements"), the Company agrees to purchase the assets that the Associates use in store operations, primarily at the carrying value to the Associate, when Associate Agreements are terminated by either party.

(v) New Standards and Interpretations Not Yet Adopted

A number of new standards, amendments to standards and interpretations have been issued but are not yet effective for the financial year ended December 31, 2011, and accordingly, have not been applied in preparing these consolidated financial statements:

(i) Financial Instruments – Disclosures

The IASB has issued an amendment to IFRS 7, "Financial Instruments: Disclosures" ("IFRS 7 amendment"), requiring incremental disclosures regarding transfers of financial assets. This amendment is effective for annual periods beginning on or after July 1, 2011. The Company will apply the amendment at the beginning of its 2012 financial year and does not expect the implementation to have a significant impact on the Company's disclosures.

(ii) Deferred Taxes – Recovery of Underlying Assets

The IASB has issued an amendment to IAS 12, "Income Taxes" ("IAS 12 amendment"), which introduces an exception to the general measurement requirements of IAS 12 in respect of investment properties measured at fair value. The IAS 12 amendment is effective for annual periods beginning on or after January 1, 2012. The Company will apply the amendment at the beginning of its 2012 financial year and does not expect the implementation to have a significant impact on its results of operations, financial position and disclosures.

(iii) Financial Instruments

The IASB has issued a new standard, IFRS 9, "Financial Instruments" ("IFRS 9"), which will ultimately replace IAS 39, "Financial Instruments: Recognition and Measurement" ("IAS 39"). The replacement of IAS 39 is a multi-phase project with the objective of improving and simplifying the reporting for financial instruments and the issuance of IFRS 9 is part of the first phase of this project. IFRS 9 uses a single approach to determine whether a financial asset or liability is measured at amortized cost or fair value, replacing the multiple rules in IAS 39. For financial assets, the approach in IFRS 9 is based on how an entity manages its financial instruments in the context of its business model and the contractual cash flow characteristics of the financial assets. IFRS 9 requires a single impairment method to be used, replacing multiple impairment methods in IAS 39. For financial liabilities measured at fair value, fair value changes due to changes in an entity's credit risk are presented in other comprehensive income. IFRS 9 is effective for annual periods beginning on or after January 1, 2015 and must be applied retrospectively. The Company is assessing the impact of the new standard on its results of operations, financial position and disclosures.

(iv) Fair Value Measurement

The IASB has issued a new standard, IFRS 13, "Fair Value Measurement" ("IFRS 13"), which provides a standard definition of fair value, sets out a framework for measuring fair value and provides for specific disclosures about fair value measurements. IFRS 13 applies to all International Financial Reporting Standards that require or permit fair value measurements or disclosures. IFRS 13 defines fair value as the price that would be received to sell an asset or paid to transfer a liability in an orderly transaction between market participants at the measurement date. IFRS 13 is effective for annual periods beginning on or after January 1, 2013 and must be applied retrospectively. The Company is assessing the impact of IFRS 13 on its results of operations, financial position and disclosures.

(v) Consolidated Financial Statements

The IASB has issued a new standard, IFRS 10, "Consolidated Financial Statements" ("IFRS 10"), which establishes the principles for the presentation and preparation of consolidated financial statements when an entity controls one or more other entities. IFRS 10 establishes control as the basis for consolidation and defines the principle of control. An investor controls an investee if the investor has power over the investee, exposure or rights to variable returns from its involvement with the investee and the ability to use its power over the investee to affect the amount of the investor's returns. IFRS 10 was issued as part of the IASB's broader project on interests in all types of entities. This project also resulted in the issuance of additional standards as described in (vi) to (ix) below. IFRS 10 is effective for annual periods beginning on or after January 1, 2013 and must be applied retrospectively. The Company is assessing the impact of IFRS 10 on its results of operations, financial position and disclosures.

(vi) Joint Arrangements

The IASB has issued a new standard, IFRS 11, "Joint Arrangements" ("IFRS 11"), which establishes the principles for financial reporting by parties to a joint arrangement. IFRS 11 supersedes IAS 31, "Interests in Joint Ventures" and SIC Interpretation 13, "Jointly Controlled Entities – Non-Monetary Contributions by Venturers". The standard defines a joint arrangement as an arrangement where two or more parties have joint control, with joint control being defined as the contractually agreed sharing of control where decisions about relevant activities require unanimous consent of the parties sharing control. The standard classifies joint arrangements as either joint operations or joint investments and the classification determines the accounting treatment. IFRS 11 is effective for annual periods beginning on or after January 1, 2013 and must be applied retrospectively. The Company is assessing the impact of IFRS 11 on its results of operations, financial position and disclosures.

(vii) Disclosure of Interests in Other Entities

The IASB has issued a new standard, IFRS 12, "Disclosure of Interests in Other Entities" ("IFRS 12"), which integrates and provides consistent disclosure requirements for all interests in other entities such as subsidiaries, joint arrangements, associates and unconsolidated structured entities. IFRS 12 is effective for annual periods beginning on or after January 1, 2013 and must be applied retrospectively. The Company is assessing the impact of IFRS 12 on its disclosures.

(viii) Separate Financial Statements

The IASB has issued a revised standard, IAS 27, "Separate Financial Statements" ("IAS 27"), which contains the accounting and disclosure requirements for investments in subsidiaries, joint ventures and associates when an entity prepares separate (non-consolidated) financial statements. IAS 27 is effective for annual periods beginning on or after January 1, 2013 and must be applied retrospectively. IAS 27 will not have an impact on the Company's consolidated results of operations, financial position and disclosures.

(ix) Investments in Associates and Joint Ventures

The IASB has issued a revised standard, IAS 28, "Investments in Associates and Joint Ventures" ("IAS 28"), which prescribes the accounting for investments in associates and sets out the requirements for the application of the equity method when accounting for investments in associates and joint ventures. IAS 28 is effective for annual periods beginning on or after January 1, 2013 and must be applied retrospectively. The Company is assessing the impact of IAS 28 on its results of operations, financial position and disclosures.

(x) Presentation of Financial Statements – Other Comprehensive Income

The IASB issued an amendment to IAS 1, "Presentation of Financial Statements" (the "IAS 1 amendment") to improve consistency and clarity of the presentation of items of other comprehensive income. A requirement has been added to present items in other comprehensive income grouped on the basis of whether they may be subsequently reclassified to earnings in order to more clearly show the effects the items of other comprehensive income may have on future earnings. The IAS 1 amendment is effective for annual periods beginning on or after July 1, 2012 and must be applied retrospectively. The Company is assessing the impact of the IAS 1 amendment on its presentation of other comprehensive income.

Notes to the Consolidated Financial Statements
December 31, 2011 and January 1, 2011 (in thousands of Canadian dollars, except per share data)

3. SIGNIFICANT ACCOUNTING POLICIES (continued)

(xi) Post-Employment Benefits

The IASB has issued amendments to IAS 19, "Employee Benefits" ("IAS 19"), which eliminates the option to defer the recognition of actuarial gains and losses through the "corridor" approach, revises the presentation of changes in assets and liabilities arising from defined benefit plans and enhances the disclosures for defined benefit plans. IAS 19 is effective for annual periods beginning on or after January 1, 2013 and must be applied retrospectively. The Company is assessing the impact of IAS 19 on its results of operations, financial position and disclosures.

4. DETERMINATION OF FAIR VALUES

A number of the Company's accounting policies and disclosures require the determination of fair value, for both financial and non-financial assets and liabilities. Fair values have been determined for measurement and/or disclosure purposes based on the following methods. When applicable, further information about the assumptions made in determining the fair values is disclosed in the notes specific to that asset or liability.

(a) Non-derivative Financial Assets

The fair values of cash, accounts receivable and deposits approximate their carrying values due to their short-term maturities.

The fair values of long-term receivables approximate their carrying values due to their current market rates. Long-term receivables are recognized within other assets in the consolidated balance sheets.

(b) Property and Equipment Acquired in a Business Combination

The fair values of property and equipment recognized as a result of a business combination are based on the amount for which an item of property and equipment could be exchanged on the date of valuation between knowledgeable, willing parties in an arm's length transaction.

(c) Investment Property

The fair value of investment property is determined by comparison to comparable properties or recent nearby sale transactions as well as a review of recent property tax assessments.

(d) Intangible Assets Acquired in a Business Combination

The fair values of prescription files and customer relationships acquired in a business combination are based on the discounted cash flows that the prescription files and customer relationships, respectively, are expected to generate using an estimated rate of return.

The fair values of other intangible assets acquired in a business combination are based on external valuations, discounted cash flows expected to be derived from the use and eventual sale of these assets, or other methods appropriate to the nature of the assets.

(e) Derivatives

The fair value of the interest rate derivative was valued using the one-month Reuters Canadian Dealer Offered Rate Index as the Company's interest rate derivative agreement had a reset term of one month. The primary valuation input for the determination of the equity forward derivatives is the Company's common share price.

(f) Non-derivative Financial Liabilities

The fair values of bank indebtedness, commercial paper, accounts payable and accrued liabilities and dividends payable approximate their carrying values due to their short-term maturities. The fair values of the revolving term facility and other long-term liabilities approximate their carrying values due to the current market rates associated with those instruments. The fair values of medium-term notes are determined by discounting the associated future cash flows using current market rates for items of similar risk.

(g) Share-based Payment Transactions

The grant-date fair values of employee stock options granted to employees are measured using the Black-Scholes option-pricing model (the "model"). Measurement inputs to the model include share price on measurement date, exercise price of the instruments, expected volatility, weighted average expected life of the instruments (based on historical experience and general option holder behaviour), expected dividends and the risk-free interest rate (based on government bonds). The fair value of the amount payable to employees in respect of cash-settled share-based payments is measured based on the Company's common share price.

5. FINANCIAL RISK MANAGEMENT OBJECTIVES AND POLICIES RELATED TO FINANCIAL INSTRUMENTS

Financial Risk Management Objectives and Policies

In the normal course of business, the Company is exposed to financial risks that have the potential to negatively impact its financial performance. The Company may use derivative financial instruments to manage certain of these risks. The Company does not use derivative financial instruments for trading or speculative purposes. These risks are discussed in more detail below.

Interest Rate Risk

Interest rate risk is the risk that fair value of future cash flows associated with the Company's financial assets or liabilities will fluctuate due to changes in market interest rates.

The Company, including its Associate-owned store network, is exposed to fluctuations in interest rates by virtue of its borrowings under its bank credit facilities, commercial paper program and financing programs available to its Associates. Increases or decreases in interest rates will positively or negatively impact the financial performance of the Company.

The Company monitors market conditions and the impact of interest rate fluctuations on its fixed and floating rate debt instruments on an ongoing basis and may use interest rate derivatives to manage this exposure. Until December 2010, the Company used interest rate derivatives to manage a portion of the interest rate risk on its commercial paper. The Company was party to an agreement converting an aggregate notional principal amount of $50,000 of floating rate commercial paper debt into fixed rate debt at a rate of 4.18%, which expired in December 2010. Throughout 2011, the Company no longer had interest rate derivative agreements to convert its floating rate debt into fixed rate debt. See Note 18 to these consolidated financial statements for further discussion of the derivative agreement.

As at December 31, 2011, the Company had $166,592 (2010: $304,410) of unhedged floating rate debt. During the current financial year, the Company's average outstanding unhedged floating rate debt was $386,193 (2010: $538,243). Had interest rates been higher or lower by 50 basis points during the current financial year, net earnings for the financial year would have decreased or increased, respectively, by approximately $1,396 (2010: $1,885) as a result of the Company's exposure to interest rate fluctuations on its unhedged floating rate debt.

Credit Risk

Credit risk is the risk that the Company's counterparties will fail to meet their financial obligations to the Company, causing a financial loss.

Accounts receivable arise primarily in respect of prescription sales billed to governments and third-party drug plans and, as a result, collection risk is low. There is no concentration of balances with debtors in the remaining accounts receivable. The Company does not consider its exposure to credit risk to be material.

Notes to the Consolidated Financial Statements (continued)
December 31, 2011 and January 1, 2011 (in thousands of Canadian dollars, except per share data)

5. FINANCIAL RISK MANAGEMENT OBJECTIVES AND POLICIES RELATED TO FINANCIAL INSTRUMENTS (continued)

Liquidity Risk

Liquidity risk is the risk that the Company will be unable to meet its obligations relating to its financial liabilities.

The Company prepares cash flow budgets and forecasts to ensure that it has sufficient funds through operations, access to bank facilities and access to debt and capital markets to meet its financial obligations, capital investment program requirements and fund new investment opportunities or other unanticipated requirements as they arise. The Company manages its liquidity risk as it relates to financial liabilities by monitoring its cash flow from operating activities to meet its short-term financial liability obligations and planning for the repayment of its long-term financial liability obligations through cash flow from operating activities and/or the issuance of new debt or equity.

The contractual maturities of the Company's financial liabilities in the consolidated balance sheet as at December 31, 2011 are as follows:

	Carrying Amount	Payments Due in the Next 90 Days	Payments Due Between 90 Days and Less Than a Year	Payments Due Between 1 Year and Less Than 2 Years	Payments Due After 2 Years	Total Contractual Cash Flows
Bank indebtedness	$ 172,262	$ 172,262	$ –	$ –	$ –	$ 172,262
Accounts payable and accrued liabilities	1,055,891	1,032,431	23,460	–	–	1,055,891
Derivatives	915	–	793	122	–	915
Dividends payable	53,119	53,119	–	–	–	53,119
Medium-term notes	945,494	262,488	28,943	474,202	256,487	1,022,120
Revolving-term debt	152	–	–	–	152	152
Other long-term liabilities	231,970	–	–	18,478	213,492	231,970
Total	**$ 2,459,803**	**$ 1,520,300**	**$ 53,196**	**$ 492,802**	**$ 470,131**	**$ 2,536,429**

The contractual maturities of the Company's financial liabilities in the consolidated balance sheet as at January 1, 2011, were as follows:

	Carrying Amount	Payments Due in the Next 90 Days	Payments Due Between 90 Days and Less Than a Year	Payments Due Between 1 Year and Less Than 2 Years	Payments Due After 2 Years	Total Contractual Cash Flows
Bank indebtedness	$ 209,013	$ 209,013	$ –	$ –	$ –	209,013
Commercial paper	127,828	128,000				128,000
Accounts payable and accrued liabilities	930,910	920,384	10,526	–	–	930,910
Derivatives	2,257	–	674	1,583	–	2,257
Dividends payable	48,927	48,927	–	–	–	48,927
Medium-term notes	946,641	12,488	34,943	291,430	730,690	1,069,551
Other long-term liabilities	167,709	–	–	19,207	148,502	167,709
Total	$ 2,433,285	$ 1,318,812	$ 46,143	$ 312,220	$ 879,192	$ 2,556,367

The accounts payable and accrued liabilities and other long-term liabilities amounts exclude certain liabilities that are not considered financial liabilities. The medium-term note amounts, which are recognized within long-term debt in the consolidated balance sheets, include principal and interest liabilities.

6. CAPITAL MANAGEMENT

The Company's primary objectives when managing capital are to profitably grow its business while maintaining adequate financing flexibility to fund attractive new investment opportunities and other unanticipated requirements or opportunities that may arise. Profitable growth is defined as earnings growth commensurate with the additional capital being invested in the business in order that the Company earns an attractive rate of return on that capital. The primary investments undertaken by the Company to drive profitable growth include additions to the selling square footage of its store network via the construction of new, relocated and expanded stores, including related leasehold improvements and fixtures and the purchase of sites as part of a land bank program, as well as the acquisition of independent drug stores or their prescription files. In addition, the Company makes capital investments in information technology and its distribution capabilities to support an expanding store network. The Company also provides working capital to its Associates via loans and/or loan guarantees. The Company largely relies on its cash flow from operations to fund its capital investment program and dividend distributions to its shareholders. This cash flow is supplemented, when necessary, through the borrowing of additional debt. No changes were made to these objectives during the financial years ended December 31, 2011 and January 1, 2011.

The Company considers its total capitalization to be bank indebtedness, commercial paper, long-term debt (including the current portion thereof), financing lease obligations and shareholders' equity, net of cash. The Company also gives consideration to its obligations under operating leases when assessing its total capitalization. The Company manages its capital structure with a view to maintaining investment grade credit ratings from two credit rating agencies. In order to maintain its desired capital structure, the Company may adjust the level of dividends paid to shareholders, issue additional equity, repurchase shares for cancellation or issue or repay indebtedness. The Company has certain debt covenants and was in compliance with those covenants as at December 31, 2011, January 1, 2011 and January 3, 2010.

The Company monitors its capital structure principally through measuring its net debt to shareholders' equity and net debt to total capitalization ratios, and ensures its ability to service its debt and meet other fixed obligations by tracking its financing and other fixed charges coverage ratios.

The following table provides a summary of certain information with respect to the Company's capital structure and financial position at the end of the periods indicated.

	December 31, 2011	January 1, 2011	January 3, 2010
Cash	$ (118,566)	$ (64,354)	$ (44,391)
Bank indebtedness	172,262	209,013	270,332
Commercial paper	–	127,828	260,386
Current portion of long-term debt	249,971	–	–
Long-term debt	695,675	943,412	946,098
Financing lease obligations	120,810	79,031	56,670
Net debt	1,120,152	1,294,930	1,489,095
Shareholders' equity	4,267,830	4,102,635	3,711,884
Total capitalization	$ 5,387,982	$ 5,397,565	$ 5,200,979
Net debt:Shareholders' equity	0.26:1	0.32:1	0.40:1
Net debt:Total capitalization	0.21:1	0.24:1	0.29:1
EBITDA:Cash interest expense[1],[2]	18.73:1	18.62:1	19.59:1

[1] For the purposes of calculating the ratios, earnings before interest, taxes, depreciation and amortization ("EBITDA") is comprised of EBITDA for the 52 week periods ended December 31, 2011 and January 1, 2011. The EBITDA for the 52 week period ended January 3, 2010 has not been adjusted for the impact of adopting IFRS. EBITDA is not addressed in IFRS. Such financial measures do not have standardized meanings prescribed by IFRS and therefore may not be comparable to similar measures presented by other reporting issuers.

[2] Cash interest expense is also not addressed in IFRS. Cash interest expense is comprised of finance expense for the 52 week periods ended December 31, 2011 and January 1, 2011. It excludes finance income, finance expenses associated with financing leases and the amortization of deferred financing costs and includes capitalized interest. The cash interest expense for the 52 week period ended January 3, 2010 has not been adjusted for the impact of adopting IFRS.

Notes to the Consolidated Financial Statements (continued)

December 31, 2011 and January 1, 2011 (in thousands of Canadian dollars, except per share data)

6. CAPITAL MANAGEMENT (continued)

As measured by the ratios set out above, the Company maintained its desired capital structure and financial position during the financial year.

The following table provides a summary of the Company's credit ratings at December 31, 2011:

	Standard & Poor's	DBRS Limited
Corporate credit rating	BBB+	—
Senior unsecured debt	BBB+	A (low)
Commercial paper	—	R-1 (low)

There were no changes to the Company's credit ratings during the financial years ended December 31, 2011 and January 1, 2011.

On April 8, 2010, DBRS Limited placed the short and long-term ratings of the Company under review with negative implications. The rating action was in response to the Ontario Ministry of Health and Long-Term Care's April 7, 2010 announcement with respect to further drug reform in the province. On July 30, 2010, DBRS Limited confirmed the short and long-term ratings of the Company and changed the ratings trend from under review with negative implications to stable.

7. ACCUMULATED OTHER COMPREHENSIVE LOSS

	December 31, 2011	January 1, 2011	January 3, 2010
Unrealized loss on the interest rate derivative (net of tax of $nil, $nil and $525, respectively)	$ —	$ —	(1,120)
Unrealized loss on equity forward derivatives (net of tax of $44, $195 and $2, respectively)	(121)	(493)	(5)
Actuarial losses on retirement benefit obligations (net of tax of $10,338, $2,905 and $nil, respectively)	(30,093)	(8,150)	—
Accumulated other comprehensive loss	$ (30,214)	$ (8,643)	(1,125)

During the current financial year, amounts previously recorded in accumulated other comprehensive loss related to the equity forward derivatives of $411 (2010: $33) were recognized in net earnings in the consolidated statements of earnings.

8. BUSINESS ACQUISITIONS

In the normal course of business, the Company acquires the assets or shares of pharmacies. The total cost of these acquisitions during the financial year ended December 31, 2011 of $10,496 (2010: $11,779) was allocated primarily to goodwill and other intangible assets based on their fair values. The goodwill acquired represents the benefits the Company expects to receive from the acquisitions. See Note 16 to these consolidated financial statements for further details on goodwill. The Company expects $814 (2010: $8,258) of acquired goodwill will be deductible for tax purposes.

The values of assets acquired and liabilities assumed have been valued at the acquisition date using fair values. See Note 4 to these consolidated financial statements for the methods used in determining fair values, except as shown below. The intangible assets acquired are composed of prescription files. In determining the fair value of prescription files acquired, the Company applied a pre-tax discount rate of 9 percent (2010: 8 percent) to the estimated expected future cash flows.

The Company did not incur any acquisition related costs for acquisitions during the financial year end December 31, 2011 (2010: $38 relating primarily to legal fees). Acquisition-related costs were recognized within operating and administrative expenses in the Company's consolidated statement of earnings for the financial year ended January 1, 2011.

The operations of the acquired pharmacies have been included in the Company's results of operations from the date of acquisition.

Funds Held in Escrow

As at January 1, 2011, the Company had amounts held in escrow of $105 with respect to a number of offers to acquire certain pharmacies. These amounts were recognized within the prepaid expenses and deposits balance in the consolidated balance sheets.

9. COST OF GOODS SOLD

During the current financial year, the Company recorded $39,943 (2010: $37,884) as an expense for the write-down of inventory as a result of net realizable value being lower than cost in cost of goods sold in the consolidated statements of earnings. During the financial years ended December 31, 2011 and January 1, 2011, the Company did not reverse any significant inventory write-downs recognized in previous years.

10. OPERATING AND ADMINISTRATIVE EXPENSES

During the financial year ended January 1, 2011, the Company recognized an expense of $10,282 in operating and administrative expenses related to the settlement of a long-standing legal dispute related to a commercial arrangement with one of the Company's ancillary businesses.

11. EMPLOYEE BENEFITS EXPENSE

Employee benefits expense, recognized within operating and administrative expenses, is as follows:

	Note	2011	2010
Wages and salaries		$ 1,391,430	$ 1,325,489
Statutory deductions		164,528	155,721
Expense related to pension and benefits	21	6,130	6,059
Share-based payment transactions	26	2,135	12,618
		$ 1,564,223	1,499,887

12. FINANCE EXPENSES

The components of the Company's finance expenses are as follows:

	2011	2010
Finance expense on bank indebtedness	$ 5,907	$ 5,642
Finance expense on commercial paper	1,702	4,269
Finance expense on long-term debt	52,626	50,961
Finance expense on financing leases	6,859	4,757
	67,094	65,629
Finance expense capitalized	(3,050)	(4,996)
	$ 64,038	$ 60,633

The amount of finance expense capitalized is based on the Company's weighted average cost of borrowing and is attributed to those items of property and equipment which meet the definition of a qualifying asset. A qualifying asset is defined as an asset that requires a substantial period of time to get ready for its intended use or sale.

Notes to the Consolidated Financial Statements (continued)
December 31, 2011 and January 1, 2011 (in thousands of Canadian dollars, except per share data)

13. DEPRECIATION AND AMORTIZATION EXPENSE

The components of the Company's depreciation and amortization expense, recognized within operating and administrative expenses, are as follows:

	Note	2011	2010
Property and equipment	15	$ 250,965	$ 238,008
Investment property	15	325	420
Intangible assets	17	46,392	43,077
		$ 297,682	$ 281,505

These amounts include net gains and losses on the disposition of property and equipment and intangible assets and any impairment losses recognized by the Company. During the financial year ended December 31, 2011, the Company recognized a net loss of $1,498 (2010: a net gain of $6,818) on the disposal of property and equipment and a net loss of $24 (2010: $9) on the disposition of intangible assets. During the financial year ended December 31, 2011, the Company did not recognize any impairment losses on property and equipment. During the financial year ended January 1, 2011, the Company recognized an impairment loss on store assets in property and equipment of $10,338. During the financial years ended December 31, 2011 and January 1, 2011, the Company did not recognize any impairment losses on intangible assets.

14. INCOME TAX EXPENSE AND DEFERRED TAX ASSETS AND LIABILITIES

	2011	2010
Current income tax expense		
Current period	$ 201,905	$ 239,379
Adjustment for prior periods	6,791	(600)
	208,696	238,779
Deferred income tax expense		
Origination and reversal of temporary differences	26,843	3,303
Reduction in tax rate	1,834	1,969
Adjustment for prior periods	(4,440)	787
	24,237	6,059
Total income tax expense	$ 232,933	$ 244,838

The effective income tax rate is comprised of the following:

	2011		2010	
Net earnings for the financial year	$ 613,934		$ 591,851	
Total income tax expense	232,933		244,838	
Earnings before income tax expense	$ 846,867		$ 836,689	
Income tax using the Combined Canadian federal and provincial statutory tax rate	$ 229,738	27.13%	$ 240,992	28.80%
Reduction in tax rate	1,834	0.22%	1,969	0.24%
Non-deductible expenses	(990)	(0.12%)	1,690	0.20%
Adjustments for prior periods	2,351	0.28%	187	0.02%
Effective income tax rate	$ 232,933	27.51%	$ 244,838	29.26%

The effective income tax rate for the financial year ended December 31, 2011 declined from the prior financial year due to reductions in statutory income tax rates.

Movement in Deferred Tax Assets (Liabilities) Related to Temporary Differences during the Financial Year

	Balance, January 1, 2011	Recognized in Earnings	Recognized in Equity	Acquired in Business Combinations (Note 8)	Balance, December 31, 2011
Deferred revenue	$ 6,746	$ (26,840)	$ –	$ –	$ (20,094)
Deferred rent obligations	33,585	1,489	–	–	35,074
Derivatives	195	–	(151)	–	44
Property and equipment and investment property	(59,710)	5,241	–	–	(54,469)
Goodwill and intangible assets	(19,968)	1,122	–	(305)	(19,151)
Retirement benefit obligations	3,876	(1,566)	7,433	–	9,743
Provisions	12,822	(572)	–	–	12,250
Non-capital loss carryforwards	17,645	(5,691)	–	–	11,954
Capital loss carryforwards	5,151	192	–	–	5,343
Other items	(685)	2,388	–	–	1,703
Deferred tax assets (liabilities)	$ (343)	$ (24,237)	$ 7,282	$ (305)	$ (17,603)

	Balance, January 3, 2010	Recognized in Earnings	Recognized in Equity	Acquired in Business Combinations (Note 8)	Balance, January 1, 2011
Deferred revenue	$ 5,346	$ 1,400	$ –	$ –	$ 6,746
Deferred rent obligations	30,859	2,726	–	–	33,585
Derivatives	527	–	(332)	–	195
Property and equipment and investment property	(50,450)	(9,260)	–	–	(59,710)
Goodwill and intangible assets	(21,562)	1,688	–	(94)	(19,968)
Retirement benefit obligations	3,070	(2,099)	2,905	–	3,876
Provisions	11,156	1,666	–	–	12,822
Non-capital loss carryforwards	19,784	(2,139)	–	–	17,645
Capital loss carryforwards	5,215	(64)	–	–	5,151
Other items	(708)	23	–	–	(685)
Deferred tax assets (liabilities)	$ 3,237	$ (6,059)	$ 2,573	$ (94)	$ (343)

Deferred tax assets are recognized for non-capital loss carryforwards to the extent that the realization of the related tax benefit through future profits is probable and for capital loss carryforwards to the extent that the Company can realize capital gains on the sale of assets.

December 31, 2011 and January 1, 2011 (in thousands of Canadian dollars, except per share data)

15. PROPERTY AND EQUIPMENT AND INVESTMENT PROPERTY

	Properties Under Development	Land	Buildings	Equipment, Fixtures and Computer Equipment	Leasehold Improvements	Assets Under Financing Leases (Note 23)	Total
Cost							
Balance at January 1, 2011	$ 72,035	$ 70,411	$ 206,472	$ 1,135,805	$ 1,179,795	$ 83,082	$ 2,747,600
Additions:							
– Asset acquisitions	9,979	–	–	–	–	43,952	53,931
– Development	9,990	3,688	25,738	168,204	131,667	–	339,287
Transfers	(20,662)	6,147	8,791	752	320	–	(4,652)
Computer software transfers from intangible assets	–	–	–	1,330	–	–	1,330
Disposals	–	(14,768)	(26,958)	(23,563)	(20,337)	–	(85,626)
Retirements	–	–	–	534	–	–	534
Balance at December 31, 2011	$ 71,342	$ 65,478	$ 214,043	$ 1,283,062	$ 1,291,445	$ 127,034	$ 3,052,404
Depreciation							
Balance at January 1, 2011	$ –	$ –	$ 16,102	$ 655,467	$ 355,523	$ 11,446	$ 1,038,538
Depreciation for the financial year	–	–	11,542	140,537	92,423	4,965	249,467
Transfers	–	–	(216)	375	(123)	–	36
Computer software transfers from intangible assets	–	–	–	(18)	–	–	(18)
Disposals	–	–	(3,103)	(19,792)	(11,807)	–	(34,702)
Retirements	–	–	–	(182)	–	–	(182)
Balance at December 31, 2011	$ –	$ –	$ 24,325	$ 776,387	$ 436,016	$ 16,411	$ 1,253,139
Impairment losses							
Balance at January 1, 2011	$ –	$ –	$ –	$ 16,257	$ 15,465	$ –	31,722
Impairment loss	–	–	–	–	–	–	–
Balance at December 31, 2011	$ –	$ –	$ –	$ 16,257	$ 15,465	$ –	31,722
Net book value							
At December 31, 2011	$ 71,342	$ 65,478	$ 189,718	$ 490,418	$ 839,964	$ 110,623	$ 1,767,543

	Properties Under Development	Land	Buildings	Equipment, Fixtures and Computer Equipment	Leasehold Improvements	Assets Under Financing Leases (Note 23)	Total
Cost							
Balance at January 3, 2010	$ 113,478	$ 57,683	$ 144,515	$ 1,048,056	$ 1,022,868	$ 59,382	$ 2,445,982
Additions:							
– Asset acquisitions	11,139	531	695	–	–	23,700	36,065
– Development	94,745	327	5,206	135,454	166,986	–	402,718
Transfers	(143,302)	27,880	97,365	(1,223)	11,943	–	(7,337)
Computer software transfers from intangible assets	–	–	–	1,395	–	–	1,395
Disposals	(4,025)	(16,010)	(41,309)	(45,515)	(22,002)	–	(128,861)
Retirements	–	–	–	(2,362)	–	–	(2,362)
Balance at January 1, 2011	$ 72,035	$ 70,411	$ 206,472	$ 1,135,805	$ 1,179,795	$ 83,082	$ 2,747,600
Depreciation							
Balance at January 3, 2010	$ –	$ –	$ 24,412	$ 561,691	$ 288,519	$ 8,135	$ 882,757
Depreciation for the financial year	–	–	8,759	136,933	85,487	3,311	234,490
Transfers	–	–	732	(439)	(293)	–	–
Disposals	–	–	(17,801)	(41,255)	(18,190)	–	(77,246)
Retirements	–	–	–	(1,463)	–	–	(1,463)
Balance at January 1, 2011	$ –	$ –	$ 16,102	$ 655,467	$ 355,523	$ 11,446	$ 1,038,538
Impairment losses							
Balance at January 3, 2010	$ –	$ –	$ –	$ 10,502	$ 10,882	$ –	21,384
Impairment loss	–	–	–	5,755	4,583	–	10,338
Balance at January 1, 2011	$ –	$ –	$ –	$ 16,257	$ 15,465	$ –	31,722
Net book value							
At January 1, 2011	$ 72,035	$ 70,411	$ 190,370	$ 464,081	$ 808,807	$ 71,636	$ 1,677,340
At January 3, 2010	$ 113,478	$ 57,683	$ 120,103	$ 475,863	$ 723,467	$ 51,247	$ 1,541,841

During the financial year ended December 31, 2011, the Company recognized depreciation expense of $249,467 (2010: $234,490), an impairment loss on store assets of $nil (2010: $10,338) and a loss on disposal of property and equipment of $1,498 (2010: a net gain of $6,818) within operating and administrative expenses in the consolidated statements of earnings.

Impairment Loss

During the financial year ended December 31, 2011, the Company reviewed its long-lived assets for indicators of impairment at the cash-generating unit level and determined that an impairment test was not necessary.

During the financial year ended January 1, 2011, the Company reviewed its long-lived assets for indicators of impairment at the cash-generating unit level and determined that a test for impairment was necessary on certain of its store assets. This resulted in the identification of an impairment charge of $7,554, which is net of taxes of $2,784. The impaired assets consist primarily of equipment, fixtures, computer equipment and leasehold improvements at certain of the Company's newer stores. The recoverable amount of the impaired assets was determined through a value-in-use methodology using a pre-tax discount rate of 8 percent.

During the financial years ended December 31, 2011 and January 1, 2011, the Company did not record any reversals of previously recorded impairment charges.

Property under Development

During the financial year ended December 31, 2011, the Company acquired properties with the intention of developing retail stores on the sites. The cost of acquisition was $9,979 (2010: $11,139).

Notes to the Consolidated Financial Statements (continued)
December 31, 2011 and January 1, 2011 (in thousands of Canadian dollars, except per share data)

15. PROPERTY AND EQUIPMENT AND INVESTMENT PROPERTY (continued)

Investment Property

	Land	Building	Total	Land	Building	Total
			2011			2010
Cost						
Balance, beginning of financial year	$ 8,084	$ 5,995	$ 14,079	$ 3,729	$ 3,044	$ 6,773
Transfers	4,325	327	4,652	4,386	2,951	7,337
Disposals	(723)	(2)	(725)	(31)	–	(31)
Balance, end of financial year	$ 11,686	$ 6,320	$ 18,006	8,084	$ 5,995	14,079
Amortization						
Balance, beginning of financial year	$ –	$ 1,309	$ 1,309	$ –	$ 889	889
Amortization for the financial year	–	325	325	–	420	420
Transfers	–	–	–	–	–	–
Balance, end of financial year	$ –	$ 1,634	$ 1,634	$ –	$ 1,309	1,309
Net book value			$ 16,372			$ 12,770
Net book value at January 3, 2010						$ 5,884

The fair value of investment property approximates its carrying value.

16. GOODWILL

	Note	2011	2010
Cost			
Balance, beginning of the financial year		$ 2,493,108	$ 2,483,430
Additions			
– business acquisitions	8	10,496	11,779
Transfers		(3,882)	(2,101)
Balance, end of the financial year		$ 2,499,722	$ 2,493,108

During the financial year ended December 31, 2011, the Company transferred $3,882 (2010: $2,101) from goodwill related to business acquisitions transacted during the financial year to prescription files, which are recognized within intangible assets, net of deferred taxes.

Impairment Testing of Goodwill

For the purpose of impairment testing, goodwill is allocated to the group of cash-generating units which represent the lowest level within the group at which the goodwill is monitored for internal management purposes.

The aggregate carrying amounts of goodwill allocated to each unit are as follows:

	December 31, 2011	January 1, 2011	January 3, 2010
Goodwill allocated to the store network	$ 2,474,540	$ 2,467,926	$ 2,458,248
Goodwill allocated to Shoppers Home Health Care®	25,182	25,182	25,182
	$ 2,499,722	$ 2,493,108	$ 2,483,430

During the financial years ended December 31, 2011 and January 1, 2011, the Company performed impairment testing of goodwill in accordance with the Company's accounting policy. No impairment was identified.

The Company uses the value-in-use method for determining the recoverable amount of the group of cash-generating units to which goodwill is allocated. The values assigned to the key assumptions represent management's assessment of future trends in the retail and drug industry and are based on both external sources and internal sources (historical data). Key assumptions include comparable store sales growth, gross margin rates, changes in employee wages and benefits, occupancy cost changes and other operating expense changes. The Company has projected cash flows based on the most recent three-year budgets and forecasts. For the purposes of the impairment test, the Company has adjusted budgets and forecasts to reflect a zero growth assumption at the time the test was performed. Years four and five of the projection continue to reflect a zero growth rate and terminal value growth of two percent after the fifth year is used for the present value calculation.

The Company has used a pre-tax discount rate of 9 percent (2010 – 8 percent), which is based on the Company's weighted average cost of capital with appropriate adjustments for the risks associated with the group of cash-generating units to which goodwill is allocated and market data from a comparable industry grouping. Cash flow projections are discounted over a five-year period.

The above estimates are particularly sensitive in the following areas:

- An increase in one percentage point in the discount rate used would have decreased the excess of fair value over the carrying value of goodwill by approximately $1,600 (2010: $1,300).

- A 10 percent decrease in future planned revenues would have decreased the excess of fair value over the carrying value of goodwill by approximately $1,200 (2010: $900).

17. INTANGIBLE ASSETS

	Note	Prescription Files	Customer Relationships	Computer Software	Computer Software Under Development	Other	Total
Cost							
Balance at January 1, 2011		$ 129,803	$ 43,600	$ 211,162	$ 52,412	8,824	$ 445,801
Additions							
– purchases		–	7,136	1,381	–	696	9,213
– development		–	–	–	44,624	–	44,624
– business acquisitions	8, 15	4,184	–	–	–	–	4,184
Transfers	16	–	–	74,260	(75,337)	(253)	(1,330)
Disposals		–	–	–	(24)	–	(24)
Balance at December 31, 2011		$ 133,987	$ 50,736	$ 286,803	$ 21,675	9,267	$ 502,468
Amortization							
Balance at January 1, 2011		$ 49,675	$ 9,959	$ 108,463	$ –	5,487	$ 173,584
Amortization for the financial year		14,697	3,732	27,932	–	804	47,165
Transfers		–	–	11	–	(29)	(18)
Balance at December 31, 2011		$ 64,372	$ 13,691	$ 136,406	$ –	6,262	$ 220,731
Net book value							
At December 31, 2011		$ 69,615	$ 37,045	$ 150,397	$ 21,675	3,005	$ 281,737

17. INTANGIBLE ASSETS (continued)

	Note	Prescription Files	Customer Relationships	Computer Software	Computer Software Under Development	Other	Total
Cost							
Balance at January 3, 2010		$ 127,701	$ 43,600	$ 170,285	$ 39,639	$ 7,274	$ 388,499
Additions							
– purchases		–	–	10,963	–	–	10,963
– development		–	–	–	44,112	1,550	45,662
– business acquisitions	8, 15	1,577	–	–	–	–	1,577
Transfers	15, 16	525	–	29,944	(31,339)	–	(870)
Disposals		–	–	(30)	–	–	(30)
Balance at January 1, 2011		$ 129,803	$ 43,600	$ 211,162	$ 52,412	$ 8,824	$ 445,801
Amortization							
Balance at January 3, 2010		$ 34,288	$ 6,448	$ 84,639	$ –	$ 4,358	$ 129,733
Amortization for the financial year		15,387	3,511	23,845	–	1,129	43,872
Disposals		–	–	(21)	–	–	(21)
Balance at January 1, 2011		$ 49,675	$ 9,959	$ 108,463	$ –	$ 5,487	$ 173,584
Net book value							
At January 1, 2011		$ 80,128	$ 33,641	$ 102,699	$ 52,412	$ 3,337	$ 272,217
At January 3, 2010		$ 93,413	$ 37,152	$ 85,646	$ 39,639	$ 2,916	$ 258,766

During the financial year ended December 31, 2011, the Company recognized amortization expense of $46,368 (2010: $43,068), operating expense of $797 (2010: $804) and a pre-tax loss on disposal of intangible assets of $24 (2010: $9) within operating and administrative expenses in the consolidated statements of earnings.

Impairment Loss

During the financial years ended December 31, 2011 and January 1, 2011, the Company reviewed its definite life intangible assets for indicators of impairment at the cash-generating unit level and determined that an impairment test was not necessary. An impairment loss and any subsequent reversals, if any, are recognized within operating and administrative expenses in the consolidated statements of earnings.

18. FINANCIAL INSTRUMENTS

See Note 5 to these consolidated financial statements for a discussion of the Company's exposure to risks from its use of financial instruments.

Interest Rate Derivatives

Until December 2010, the Company used interest rate derivatives to manage a portion of the interest rate risk on its commercial paper. The Company was party to an agreement converting an aggregate notional principal amount of $50,000 of floating rate commercial paper debt into fixed rate debt at a rate of 4.18%, which expired in December 2010. The Company recorded a net loss of $3,766 over the life of the agreement that expired in 2010 as finance expense on commercial paper. As at January 1, 2011, the Company no longer had any interest rate derivative agreements to convert its floating rate debt into fixed rate debt and the Company did not enter into any new interest rate derivative agreements during the financial year ended December 31, 2011.

Based on the market value of the interest rate derivative agreement at January 3, 2010, the Company recognized a liability of $1,645, all of which was presented in accounts payable and accrued liabilities. During the financial year ended January 1, 2011, the Company assessed that the interest rate derivative was an effective hedge for the floating interest rates on the associated commercial paper debt.

Equity Forward Derivatives

The Company uses cash-settled equity forward agreements to limit its exposure to future price changes in the Company's share price for share unit awards under the Company's LTIP and RSU Plan. The earnings or expense arising from the use of these instruments is recognized within operating and administrative expenses on the consolidated statements of earnings for the financial year.

Based on the market values of the equity forward agreements at December 31, 2011, the Company recognized a liability of $916 (2010: $2,257), of which $794 (2010: $674) is presented in accounts payable and accrued liabilities and $122 (2010: $1,583) is presented in other long-term liabilities. Based on the market values of the equity forward agreements at January 3, 2010, the Company recognized a net liability of $910, of which $286 was presented in other assets and $1,196 was presented in accounts payable and accrued liabilities. During the financial years ended December 31, 2011 and January 1, 2011, the Company assessed that the percentages of the equity forward derivatives in place related to unearned units under the LTIP and RSU Plan were effective hedges for its exposure to future changes in the market price of its common shares in respect of the unearned units.

Fair Value of Financial Instruments

The fair value of financial assets and financial liabilities measured at fair value in the consolidated balance sheet as at December 31, 2011 is as follows:

	Level 1	Level 2	Level 3	Total
Equity forward derivatives	$ –	$ (916)	$ –	$ (916)
Total	$ –	$ (916)	$ –	$ (916)

The fair value of financial assets and financial liabilities measured at fair value in the consolidated balance sheet as at January 1, 2011 is as follows:

	Level 1	Level 2	Level 3	Total
Equity forward derivatives	$ –	$ (2,257)	$ –	$ (2,257)
Total	$ –	$ (2,257)	$ –	$ (2,257)

The fair value of financial assets and financial liabilities measured at fair value in the consolidated balance sheet as at January 3, 2010 is as follows:

	Level 1	Level 2	Level 3	Total
Interest rate derivative	$ –	$ (1,645)	$ –	$ (1,645)
Equity forward derivatives	$ –	$ (910)	$ –	$ (910)
Total	$ –	$ (2,555)	$ –	$ (2,555)

The fair values of the interest rate derivative and equity forward derivatives are determined based on current market rates and on information received from the Company's counterparties to the agreements. The interest rate derivative was valued using the one-month Reuters Canadian Dealer Offered Rate Index. The primary valuation input for the equity forward derivatives is the Company's common share price.

For financial assets and liabilities that are valued at other than fair value on the consolidated balance sheets: cash, accounts receivable, deposits, bank indebtedness, commercial paper, accounts payable and accrued liabilities and dividends payable, fair values approximate their carrying values at December 31, 2011, January 1, 2011 and January 3, 2010 due to their short-term maturities. The fair values of long-term receivables, revolving term facility and other long-term liabilities approximate their carrying values at December 31, 2011, January 1, 2011, and January 3, 2010 due to the current market rates associated with these instruments. The fair value of the medium-term notes at December 31, 2011 was approximately $984,442 (2010: $997,345, 2009: $1,007,522) compared to a carrying value of $950,000 (2010 and 2009: $950,000) (excluding transaction costs) due to decreases in market interest rates for similar instruments.

Notes to the Consolidated Financial Statements (continued)
December 31, 2011 and January 1, 2011 (in thousands of Canadian dollars, except per share data)

19. BANK INDEBTEDNESS AND COMMERCIAL PAPER

Bank Indebtedness

The Associate-owned stores borrow under their bank line of credit agreements guaranteed by the Company. The Company has entered into agreements with banks to guarantee a total of $520,000 (2010 and 2009: $520,000) of lines of credit. At December 31, 2011, the Associate-owned stores utilized $166,592 (2010: $176,410, 2009: $254,332) of the available lines of credit.

Commercial Paper

Commercial paper is issued with maturities from overnight to 90 days at floating interest rates based on bankers' acceptance rates. Until December 2010, the Company used interest rate derivative agreements to manage a portion of the interest rate risk on its commercial paper. The Company was party to an agreement converting an aggregate notional principal amount of $50,000 of floating rate commercial paper debt into fixed rate debt at a rate of 4.18%, which expired in December 2010. The Company recorded a net loss of $3,766 over the life of the agreement that expired in 2010 as finance expense on commercial paper in the consolidated statement of earnings. As at January 1, 2011, the Company no longer had any interest rate derivative agreements to convert its floating rate debt into fixed rate debt. During the financial year ended December 31, 2011, the Company did not enter into any interest rate derivative agreements to convert its floating rate debt into fixed rate debt. See Notes 5 and 18 to these consolidated financial statements for further discussion of the derivative agreement.

20. LONG-TERM DEBT

	Face Value as at December 31, 2011	Maturity	December 31, 2011	January 1, 2011	January 3, 2010
Medium-term notes					
Series 2 Notes – 4.99%	$ 450,000	June 2013	$ 449,298	$ 448,704	$ 447,977
Series 3 Notes – 4.80%	250,000	January 2012	249,971	249,305	248,640
Series 4 Notes – 5.19%	250,000	January 2014	249,081	248,632	248,183
			948,350	946,641	944,800
Less: current portion of long-term debt			(249,971)	–	–
			698,379	946,641	944,800
Revolving term facility	$ 725,000	December 2015	152	–	1,298
Less: financing costs			(2,856)	(3,229)	–
			(2,704)	(3,229)	1,298
Total long-term debt			$ 695,675	$ 943,412	$ 946,098

As at December 31, 2011, $9,598 (2010: $137,053) of the $725,000 (2010: $750,000) revolving term facility was utilized as follows: drawings on the revolving term facility $152 (2010: $nil), $9,446 (2010: $9,053) relating to letters of credit and trade finance guarantees and $nil (2010: $128,000) relating to commercial paper issued by the Company. As at January 3, 2010, the revolving term facility was $800,000 and was utilized as follows: $8,322 related to letters of credit and trade finance guarantees and $261,000 relating to commercial paper issued by the Company.

2011 Debt Refinancing Transactions

On October 27, 2011, the Company amended its previously existing $750,000 revolving term credit facility that was to mature on December 10, 2014. The credit facility was amended to reduce the size of the credit facility to $725,000, to extend the maturity date by one year to December 10, 2015, reduce the applicable stamping fee on bankers' acceptance borrowings from 150 basis points per annum to 100 basis points per annum and reduce the applicable commitment fee rate on undrawn amounts to 20 basis points per annum from 37.5 basis points per annum. The consolidated net debt position of the Company remained substantially unchanged as a result of this refinancing. The new credit facility is available for general corporate purposes, including backstopping the Company's $500,000 commercial paper program. The Company recognized financing costs related to the credit facility of $575, the unamortized portion of which was netted against the long-term debt balance on the consolidated balance sheets.

2010 Debt Refinancing Transactions

On December 10, 2010, the Company entered into a $750,000 revolving term credit facility. This credit facility, which was to mature on December 10, 2014, replaced the Company's previously existing $800,000 revolving term credit facility that was to mature on June 6, 2011. The credit facility, as was the case with the credit facility it replaced, was available for general corporate purposes, including backstopping the Company's $500,000 commercial paper program. The Company recognized financing costs related to the credit facility of $3,281, the unamortized portion of which was netted against the long-term debt balance on the consolidated balance sheets.

Minimum Repayments

Future minimum required repayments of long-term debt are as follows:

Medium-term notes	
2012 – Series 3	$ 250,000
2013 – Series 2	450,000
2014 – Series 4	250,000
	$ 950,000

See Note 31 Subsequent Events for additional discussion of long-term debt transactions.

21. RETIREMENT BENEFIT OBLIGATIONS

	Note	December 31, 2011	January 1, 2011	January 3, 2010
Present value of defined benefit obligation for unfunded plans		$ (6,380)	$ (5,750)	$ (5,172)
Present value of defined benefit obligation for partially funded plans		(140,340)	(110,774)	(90,138)
Total present value of defined benefit obligations		(146,720)	(116,524)	(95,310)
Fair value of plan assets		108,616	106,040	85,199
Defined benefit liability included in other long-term liabilities	23	$ (38,104)	$ (10,484)	$ (10,111)

Information about the Company's pension and other post-retirement benefit plans is as follows:

	2011		2010	
	Pension Plans	Other Benefit Plans	Pension Plans	Other Benefit Plans
Fair value of plan assets				
Fair value of plan assets, beginning of the financial year	$ 106,040	$ –	$ 85,199	$ –
Expected return on plan assets	6,718	–	5,659	–
Actuarial gains/(losses)	(7,588)	–	2,161	–
Company contributions	7,262	625	16,230	510
Plan participants' contributions	1,292	–	1,237	–
Benefits paid	(5,108)	(625)	(4,446)	(510)
Fair value of plan assets, end of the financial year	$ 108,616	$ –	$ 106,040	$ –
Present value of the defined benefit obligation				
Defined benefit obligation, beginning of the financial year	$ 110,774	$ 5,750	$ 90,138	$ 5,172
Current service cost	6,200	306	5,936	287
Interest cost	6,044	298	5,200	295
Plan participants' contributions	1,292	–	1,237	–
Actuarial losses	21,138	651	12,709	506
Benefits paid	(5,108)	(625)	(4,446)	(510)
Present value of the defined benefit obligations, end of the financial year	$ 140,340	$ 6,380	$ 110,774	$ 5,750
Net defined benefit liability	$ 31,724	$ 6,380	$ 4,734	$ 5,750

21. RETIREMENT BENEFIT OBLIGATIONS (continued)

The significant actuarial assumptions adopted are as follows:

	2011			2010		
	Registered Pension Plans	Non-registered Pension Plans	Other Benefit Plans	Registered Pension Plans	Non-registered Pension Plans	Other Benefit Plans
Defined benefit obligations, end of the financial year						
Discount rate	4.25%	4.25%	4.25%	5.25%	5.00%	5.00%
Rate of compensation increase	4.00%	4.00%	4.00%	4.00%	4.00%	4.00%
Net benefit expense for the financial year						
Discount rate	5.25%	5.00%	5.00%	6.00%	5.75%	5.25%
Expected rate of return on plan assets	7.50%	3.75%	N/A	7.50%	3.75%	N/A
Rate of compensation increase	4.00%	4.00%	4.00%	4.00%	4.00%	4.00%

The discount rate is based on current market interest rates at the end of the Company's fiscal year, assuming a portfolio of corporate AA rated bonds with terms to maturity that, on average, match the terms of the accrued retirement benefit obligations. A 1.0% increase in the assumed discount rate would decrease the amount of the Company's accrued retirement benefit obligations and retirement benefit expense in respect of its registered and non-registered defined benefit plans by $23,049 and $1,843, respectively. Conversely, a 1.0% decrease in the assumed discount rate would increase the amount of the Company's accrued retirement benefit obligations and retirement benefit expense in respect of its registered and non-registered defined benefit plans by $27,318 and $1,933, respectively.

The expected long-term rate of return on plan assets is based on the asset mix of invested assets and historical returns. A 1.0% increase in the assumed long-term rate of return on plan assets would decrease the amount of the Company's retirement benefit expense in respect of its registered and non-registered defined benefit plans by $928. Conversely, a 1.0% decrease in the assumed long-term rate of return on plan assets would increase the amount of the Company's retirement benefit expense in respect of its registered and non-registered defined benefit plans by $928.

A 1.0% increase in the assumed rate of compensation increase would increase the amount of the Company's accrued retirement benefit obligations and retirement benefit expense in respect of its registered and non-registered defined benefit plans by $4,414 and $708, respectively. Conversely, a 1.0% decrease in the assumed rate of compensation increase would decrease the amount of the Company's accrued retirement benefit obligations and retirement benefit expense in respect of its registered and non-registered defined benefit plans by $4,214 and $732, respectively.

The expected health care cost trend rate is based on historical trends and external data. The health care cost trend rate used was 8.0% for 2011 (2010: 8.0%), with 8.0% being the trend rate for 2012. The trend rate is then reduced by 0.5% in each of the following years until reaching the ultimate trend rate of 5.0% for 2018 and later years. A 1.0% change in the assumed health care cost trend rate would result in an impact of $639 (2010: $570) on the retirement benefit obligation and a pre-tax impact of $38 (2010: $30) on the benefits expense recognized in earnings.

Assumptions regarding future mortality are based on published statistics and mortality tables. The current longevities underlying the values of the liabilities in the defined benefit plans as at December 31, 2011 and January 1, 2011 are as follows:

	Males	Females
Longevity at age 65 for current pensioners	19.7	22.1
Longevity at age 65 for current member aged 45	21.2	22.9

The calculation of the defined benefit obligation is sensitive to the mortality assumptions set out above. As the actuarial estimates of mortality continue to be refined, an increase of one year in the lives shown above is considered reasonably possible in the next financial year.

The experience adjustments are as follows:

	2011		2010	
	Pension Plans	Other Benefit Plans	Pension Plans	Other Benefit Plans
Asset experience adjustments				
Asset (gain)/loss during the financial year	$ 7,588	$ –	$ (2,161)	$ –
Liability experience adjustments				
Liability loss during the financial year	$ –	$ –	$ –	$ 506
Liability assumptions				
Liability loss during the financial year	$ 21,138	$ 651	$ 12,709	$ N/A

The components of the Company's pension and other post-retirement benefit plans expense are as follows:

	2011		2010	
	Pension Plans	Other Benefit Plans	Pension Plans	Other Benefit Plans
Current service costs	$ 6,200	$ 306	$ 5,936	$ 287
Interest on obligation	6,044	298	5,200	295
Expected return on plan assets	(6,718)	–	(5,659)	–
Expense recognized in operating and administrative expenses	$ 5,526	$ 604	$ 5,477	$ 582

The actual loss on plan assets for the financial year was $870 (2010: gain of $7,820).

The Company recognized the following actuarial losses for the financial year in other comprehensive income (loss):

	2011		2010	
	Pension Plans	Other Benefit Plans	Pension Plans	Other Benefit Plans
Cumulative amount, beginning of the financial year	$ (10,548)	$ (506)	$ –	$ –
Recognized during the financial year	(28,726)	(651)	(10,548)	(506)
Cumulative amount, end of the financial year	$ (39,274)	$ (1,157)	$ (10,548)	$ (506)

Cash payments for employee future benefits, which consist of the Company's contributions to the pension plans and cash payments made directly to beneficiaries of the other benefit plans, totalled $7,887 (2010: $16,740). The Company expects to make contributions to the pension plans and cash payments to beneficiaries of the other benefit plans of $6,302 in 2012.

The assets of the registered pension plans consist of cash, contributions receivable and investments held in a Master Trust for the benefit of the Company's pension plans. The assets held by the Master Trust are invested in a limited number of pooled funds, based on market values as at November 30, 2011, 2010 and 2009, respectively, as follows:

	December 31, 2011	January 1, 2011	January 3, 2010
Equity	57%	60%	61%
Fixed income	42%	39%	39%
Cash and cash equivalents	1%	1%	–
	100%	100%	100%

There were no significant changes in the assets held by the Master Trust between November 30, 2011 and December 31, 2011, between November 30, 2010 and January 1, 2011 and between November 30, 2009 and January 3, 2010.

Notes to the Consolidated Financial Statements (continued)
December 31, 2011 and January 1, 2011 (in thousands of Canadian dollars, except per share data)

21. RETIREMENT BENEFIT OBLIGATIONS (continued)

The assets of the non-registered plan consist of investments and refundable tax on account with Canada Revenue Agency. The investments are in pooled funds with an allocation of 59% equities, 40% bonds and 1% cash and cash equivalents based on market values as at November 30, 2011. The investments were in pooled funds with an allocation of 61% equities, 38% bonds and 1% cash and cash equivalents as at November 30, 2010 and 60% equities, 39% bonds and 1% cash and cash equivalents based on market values as at November 30, 2009. There were no significant changes in the allocation of investments between November 30, 2011 and December 31, 2011, between November 30, 2010 and January 1, 2011 and between November 30, 2009 and January 3, 2010.

22. PROVISIONS

	2011	2010
Balance, beginning of the financial year	$ 14,414	$ 12,071
Provisions made	8,980	12,341
Provisions used	(9,907)	(9,817)
Provisions reversed	(192)	(306)
Unwind of discount	430	125
Balance, end of the financial year	$ 13,725	$ 14,414
Balance, end of the financial year, presented as follows:		
Current liabilities	$ 12,024	$ 12,562
Long-term liabilities	1,701	1,852
	$ 13,725	$ 14,414

The Company has been served with a Statement of Claim in a proposed class proceeding that has been filed in the Ontario Superior Court of Justice by two of its licensed Associate-owners, claiming various declarations and damages of $1,000,000 on behalf of a proposed class comprised of all of its current and former licensed Associate-owners resident in Canada, other than in Québec. The claim alleges, among other things, that Shoppers Drug Mart and two of its affiliates breached contractual and other duties to its Associate-owners by collecting, receiving and/or retaining funds and/or benefits that are in excess of those permitted to be collected, received and/or retained by the applicable agreements. The Company believes that the claim is without merit and will vigorously defend the claim. However, there can be no assurance that the outcome of this claim will be favourable to the Company or that it will not have a material adverse impact on the Company's financial position. The amount payable, if any, is not reasonably determinable at this time.

In addition, the Company is involved in certain legal claims arising in the normal course of business. In the opinion of the Company's management, the eventual settlement of such claims will not have a significant effect on the Company's financial position or results of operations. Management has recorded a provision for these claims based on its best estimate of the final settlements.

23. OTHER LONG-TERM LIABILITIES

The components of the Company's other long-term liabilities are as follows:

	Note	December 31, 2011	January 1, 2011	January 3, 2010
Deferred rent obligations		$ 338,721	$ 330,295	$ 300,826
Retirement benefit obligations	21	38,104	10,484	10,111
Deferred gains on sale-leaseback transactions on financing leases		12,525	7,769	6,754
Financing lease obligations	15, 28	117,911	76,918	55,500
Long-term incentive plan and restricted share unit plan	26	8,134	11,900	4,531
Unrealized loss on derivatives	18	122	1,583	–
Other		4,671	3,175	8,540
		$ 520,188	$ 442,124	$ 386,262

Deferred Rent Obligations

The deferred rent obligations represent the difference between rent expense and cash rent payments and the deferral of landlord inducements.

Sale-leaseback Transactions

During the financial year ended December 31, 2011, the Company sold certain real estate properties for net proceeds of $54,210 (2010: $57,307) and entered into lease agreements for the area used by the Associate-owned stores. The leases have been accounted for as operating or financing leases as appropriate. During the financial year ended December 31, 2011, the Company recognized gains on disposal of $9,935 (2010: $14,182), of which $5,250 (2010: $1,597) were deferred under financing lease treatment. The deferred gains are presented in other long-term liabilities on the consolidated balance sheets and are being amortized over lease terms of 15–20 years.

24. SHARE CAPITAL

Share Capital and Contributed Surplus

Authorized

Unlimited number of common shares

Unlimited number of preferred shares, issuable in series without nominal or par value

Outstanding

	2011		2010	
	Number of Common Shares	Stated Value	Number of Common Shares	Stated Value
Beginning balance	217,452,068	$ 1,520,558	217,431,898	$ 1,519,870
Shares issued for cash	109,729	1,220	20,170	491
Shares repurchased in cash	(5,086,200)	(35,576)	–	–
Repayment of share purchase loans	–	7	–	33
Exercise of share options	–	246	–	164
Ending balance	212,475,597	$ 1,486,455	217,452,068	$ 1,520,558

The Company also has issued share options. See Note 26 to these consolidated financial statements for further details on the Company's issued share options.

Individual shareholder agreements address matters related to the transfer of certain shares issued to the Company's management and Associates, including shares issued under certain options granted to management. In particular, each provides, subject to certain exceptions, for a general prohibition on any transfer of a member of management's or Associate's shares for a period of five years from the date that the individual entered into the shareholder agreement.

The holders of common shares are entitled to receive dividends as declared from time to time and are entitled to one vote per share at meetings of the Company.

Normal Course Issuer Bid

On February 10, 2011, the Company implemented a normal course issuer bid to repurchase, for cancellation, up to 8,700,000 of its common shares, representing approximately 4.0% of the Company's then outstanding common shares. Repurchases will be effected through the facilities of the Toronto Stock Exchange (the "TSX") and may take place over a 12-month period ending no later than February 14, 2012. Repurchases will be made at market prices in accordance with the requirements of the TSX.

From February 10, 2011 to December 31, 2011, the Company purchased and cancelled 5,086,200 common shares under the normal course issuer bid at a cost of $206,779. The premium paid over the average book value of the common shares repurchased of $171,203 has been charged to retained earnings. The Company purchased an additional 115,900 shares at the end of the financial year at a cost of $4,735. These shares were cancelled subsequent to the end of the financial year. The cost of this latter purchase is recorded as treasury shares in Shareholders' Equity as at December 31, 2011.

24. SHARE CAPITAL (continued)

Dividends

The following table provides a summary of the dividends declared by the Company:

Declaration Date	Record Date	Payment Date		Dividend per Common Share
February 10, 2011	March 31, 2011	April 15, 2011	$	0.250
April 27, 2011	June 30, 2011	July 15, 2011	$	0.250
July 21, 2011	September 30, 2011	October 14, 2011	$	0.250
November 9, 2011	December 30, 2011	January 13, 2012	$	0.250
February 11, 2010	March 31, 2010	April 15, 2010	$	0.225
April 28, 2010	June 30, 2010	July 15, 2010	$	0.225
July 22, 2010	September 30, 2010	October 15, 2010	$	0.225
November 9, 2010	December 31, 2010	January 14, 2011	$	0.225

On February 9, 2012, the Board of Directors declared a dividend of 26.5 cents per common share payable April 13, 2012 to shareholders of record as of the close of business on March 30, 2012.

25. EARNINGS PER COMMON SHARE

Basic Net Earnings per Common Share

The calculation of basic net earnings per common share at December 31, 2011 was based on net earnings for the financial year of $613,934 (2010: $591,851) and a weighted average number of shares outstanding (basic) of 216,420,096 (2010: 217,435,868). The weighted average number of shares outstanding (basic) is calculated as follows:

Weighted Average Shares Outstanding (Basic)

	Note	2011	2010
Issued shares, beginning of the financial year	24	217,452,068	217,431,898
Effect of share options exercised		52,350	8,094
Effect of shares repurchased		(1,082,326)	–
Effect of share purchase loans		(1,996)	(4,124)
Weighted average number of shares outstanding (basic), end of the financial year		216,420,096	217,435,868

Diluted Net Earnings per Common Share

The calculation of diluted net earnings per common share at December 31, 2011 was based on net earnings for the financial year of $613,934 (2010: $591,851) and a weighted average number of shares outstanding, after adjustment for the effects of all potentially dilutive shares, of 216,504,784 (2010: 217,537,709). The weighted average number of shares outstanding (diluted) is calculated as follows:

Weighted Average Shares Outstanding (Diluted)

	2011	2010
Weighted average number of shares outstanding (basic), end of the financial year	216,420,096	217,435,868
Potentially dilutive share options	84,688	101,841
Weighted average number of shares outstanding (diluted), end of the financial year	216,504,784	217,537,709

The average market value of the Company's shares for purposes of calculating the effect of dilutive share options was based on quoted market prices for the period that the stock options were outstanding. Anti-dilutive stock options have been excluded.

26. SHARE-BASED PAYMENTS

The Company established stock option plans for certain employees and its Board of Directors, as described below, and has reserved 20,000,000 common shares for issuance under the plans. Effective February 2007, non-employee directors are no longer eligible to participate in the stock option plans. The Company established deferred share unit plans for its Chief Executive Officer and non-employee directors, which are described below. The Company uses the fair value method to account for stock options issued under employee and director stock option programs. The fair value of each option is established on the date of the grant using the Black-Scholes options-pricing model.

The Company recognized the following compensation expense or reversal of compensation expense associated with stock options issued under the employee plan ("share plan") and the director stock option plan in the financial years ended December 31, 2011 and January 1, 2011:

	Note	2011	2010
Options granted in 2006		$ (921) $	395
Options granted in 2010		(637)	1,197
Options granted in 2011		348	–
Total net (reversal of) expenses recognized in operating and administrative expenses	11	$ (1,210) $	1,592

During the financial year ended December 31, 2011, the Company recognized compensation expense of $505 (2010: $1,592) associated with the stock options outstanding and reversed compensation expense of $1,715 (2010: $nil), the latter as a result of the departure of certain management personnel.

Employee Stock Option Plan

Options issued to certain employees have an exercise price per share of no less than the fair market value on the date of the option grant. These options include awards for shares that vest based on the passage of time, performance criteria, or both.

The following is a summary of the status of the share plan and changes during the current and prior financial years:

	2011		2010	
	Options on Common Shares	Weighted Average Exercise Price Per Share	Options on Common Shares	Weighted Average Exercise Price Per Share
Outstanding, beginning of the financial year	803,492 $	39.53	541,542 $	36.59
Granted	253,186	41.80	282,120	44.09
Exercised	(109,729)	12.15	(20,170)	24.54
Forfeited/cancelled including repurchased	(566,072)	45.38	–	–
Outstanding, end of the financial year	380,877 $	40.23	803,492 $	39.53
Options exercisable, end of the financial year	88,917 $	33.47	451,372 $	35.62

	2011 Outstanding Options			2011 Exercisable Options	
Range of Exercise Price	Number of Options Outstanding	Weighted Average Contractual Life (Years)	Weighted Average Exercise Price Per Share	Number of Exercisable Options	Weighted Average Exercise Price Per Share
$23.48 – $26.57	32,390	0.61 $	23.68	32,388 $	23.68
$29.30 – $36.41	29,253	2.68	34.39	29,253	34.39
$40.81 – $44.09	319,234	6.29	42.43	27,276	44.09
	380,877	5.53 $	40.23	88,917 $	33.47

Notes to the Consolidated Financial Statements (continued)

December 31, 2011 and January 1, 2011 (in thousands of Canadian dollars, except per share data)

26. SHARE-BASED PAYMENTS (continued)

Options Granted Prior to the Company's 2010 Financial Year

Time-based options are exercisable 20% per year on the anniversary of the grant date in each of the five subsequent years. Performance-based options are exercisable 20% per year on the anniversary of the grant date in each of the five subsequent years, provided that the Company achieves specified earnings-based performance targets. As at December 31, 2011, all performance targets have been achieved.

Upon the termination of an option holder's employment, all unexercisable options expire immediately and exercisable options expire within 180 days of the date of termination. The share plan provides that the Company may pay, in cash, certain terminated option holders the appreciated value of the options to cancel exercisable options.

Subject to certain prior events of expiry, such as the termination of employment for cause, all exercisable options expire on the tenth anniversary of the date of grant.

Options Granted During the Company's 2010 and 2011 Financial Years

In February 2011 and 2010, the Company granted awards of time-based options under the share plan in respect of the Company's 2010 and 2009 financial years, respectively, to certain senior management, with one-third of such options vesting each year.

In November 2011, the Company granted an award of time-based options under the share plan to the Company's Chief Executive Officer, with one-fourth of such options vesting each year.

The following assumptions were used in the Black-Scholes option-pricing model to calculate the fair value for those options granted during the financial years ended December 31, 2011 and January 1, 2011:

	November 2011	February 2011	2010
Fair value per unit at grant date	$ 5.89	$ 6.32	$ 6.94
Share price	$ 42.28	$ 40.81	$ 44.09
Exercise price	$ 42.28	$ 40.81	$ 44.09
Valuation assumptions:			
Expected life	5 years	5 years	5 years
Expected dividends	2.37%	2.45%	2.10%
Expected volatility (based on historical share price volatility)	19.86%	19.32%	18.70%
Risk-free interest rate (based on government bonds)	1.39%	2.63%	2.54%

Upon the termination of an option holder's employment, all unexercisable options expire immediately and exercisable options expire within 180 days of the date of termination. The share plan provides that the Company may pay, in cash, certain terminated option holders the appreciated value of the options to cancel exercisable options.

Subject to certain prior events of expiry, such as termination of the employment for cause, all exercisable options expire on the seventh anniversary of the date of grant.

Director Stock Option Plan

Prior to February 2007, under the Company's director stock option plan, participating directors were issued time-based options to purchase 60,000 common shares. The options have an exercise price per share at fair market value on the date of the option grant, which is normally the date the option holder becomes a director. One-third of the options become exercisable in each of the following three years on the anniversary of the date of grant. Unexercisable options expire upon the option holder ceasing to be a director. Exercisable options expire on the earlier of (i) depending on the circumstances of the option holder ceasing to be a director and the determination of the Human Resources and Compensation Committee, 180 or 365 days of the option holder ceasing to be a director or (ii) the expiry date of the options, which is on the tenth anniversary of the date of grant.

A summary of the status of the director stock option plan and changes during the financial years ending December 31, 2011 and January 1, 2011 is presented below:

	2011		2010	
	Options on Common Shares	Weighted Average Exercise Price Per Share	Options on Common Shares	Weighted Average Exercise Price Per Share
Outstanding, beginning of the financial year	346,000 $	40.38	346,000 $	40.38
Exercised	–	–	–	–
Forfeited/cancelled including repurchased	–	–	–	–
Outstanding, end of the financial year	346,000 $	40.38	346,000 $	40.38
Options exercisable, end of the financial year	346,000 $	40.38	346,000 $	40.38

2011 Outstanding and Exercisable Options

Exercise Price	Number of Options Outstanding	Weighted Average Contractual Life (Years)	Weighted Average Exercise Price Per Share
$26.95	60,000	1.8 $	26.95
$41.80	106,000	3.6	41.80
$44.02	180,000	4.1	44.02
	346,000	3.5 $	40.38

Deferred Share Unit Plan for Non-employee Directors

The Company maintains a deferred share unit ("DSU") plan to provide non-employee directors with the option to elect to receive DSUs in lieu of cash payment for all or a portion of their director fees. When such an election is made, the Company credits to the account of each non-employee director a number of DSUs (each equivalent in value to a common share) equal to the amount of fees divided by the fair market value of the common shares. The directors' accounts are credited with dividend equivalents in the form of additional DSUs if and when the Company pays dividends on the common shares. Upon the director ceasing to be a member of the Board of Directors, the director shall receive a cash amount equal to the number of DSUs in his or her account multiplied by the fair market value of the common shares on the date the director ceases to be a member of the Board of Directors or on a later date selected by the director, which shall in any event be a date prior to the end of the following calendar year. During the current financial year, the Company recorded $1,487 (2010: $801) in director fee compensation, which is included in operating and administrative expenses in the consolidated statements of earnings.

Non-employee directors who are not holders of unvested stock options to purchase common shares of the Company are eligible to receive an annual award of DSUs in the amount of up to $60.

The non-executive Chair of the Board of Directors receives an annual fee of $120 in addition to the director fees and annual award of DSUs, one-half of which the Chair may elect, in whole or in part, to be received in DSUs and the other half of which is payable in DSUs.

During the current financial year, the Company issued an aggregate of 31,039 DSUs (2010: 30,569 DSUs) at a weighted average grant date fair value of $40.70 (2010: $41.34). During the financial year ended December 31, 2011, no director (2010: one director) ceased being a member of the Board of Directors and thus, the Company did not make any cash payments (2010: $147 cash payment which was the equivalent of 3,926 DSUs). As at December 31, 2011, there were 128,995 DSUs (2010: 97,956 DSUs) outstanding.

Notes to the Consolidated Financial Statements (continued)

December 31, 2011 and January 1, 2011 (in thousands of Canadian dollars, except per share data)

26. SHARE-BASED PAYMENTS (continued)

Chief Executive Officer Deferred Share Unit Plan

In November 2011, the Company established a deferred share unit plan for its Chief Executive Officer ("CEO DSU Plan") and granted time-based deferred share units ("DSUs") under the CEO DSU Plan, which vest 100% after three years. At the award date, the Company converted compensation awarded to the Chief Executive Officer into a number of DSUs based on the weighted average fair value at the award date. The Company records the compensation expense related to the granted DSUs evenly over the vesting period.

In addition, the Human Resource and Compensation Committee of the Board of Directors can mandate that all or a specified percentage of the Chief Executive Officer's short-term incentive compensation in respect of a calendar year be paid in the form of DSUs. Subject to any such determination, the Human Resource and Compensation Committee may permit the Chief Executive Officer to elect to receive an additional percentage of the Chief Executive Officer's short-term incentive compensation in respect of any calendar year in the form of DSUs. If such a mandate or election is made, the Company will credit to the account of the Chief Executive Officer a number of DSUs (each equivalent in value to a common share) equal to the amount of short-term incentive compensation divided by the fair value of the common shares. The date the short-term incentive compensation is payable is the award date of the DSUs, which will be fully vested at that time. The Chief Executive Officer's account is credited with dividend equivalents in the form of additional DSUs if and when the Company pays dividends on its common shares.

Upon the termination of employment, the Company will arrange to purchase shares, equal to the number of Chief Executive Officer DSUs on account of the Chief Executive Officer, on the secondary market. These shares will be held on behalf of the Chief Executive Officer for a one-year period.

Long-term Incentive Plan

Prior to 2010, the Company maintained a long-term incentive plan ("LTIP") pursuant to which certain employees were eligible to receive an award of share units equivalent in value to common shares of the Company ("share units"). Awards of share units under the LTIP were made in February of the financial year immediately following the financial year in respect of which the award was earned.

During the financial years ended December 31, 2011 and January 1, 2011, the Company did not award any share units under the Company's LTIP. During the financial years ended December 31, 2011 and January 1, 2011, the Company paid out the fully-vested awards granted in 2009 and 2008, respectively.

During the current financial year, the Company cancelled 18,289 share units (2010: nil) under the LTIP as a result of the departure of certain management personnel.

During the current financial year, the Company recognized compensation expense of $337 (2010: $2,221) associated with the LTIP share units outstanding and reversed compensation expense of $537 (2010: $nil), the latter as a result of the cancellation of previously granted share units under the LTIP.

As at December 31, 2011, there were no share units (2010: 148,086 share units) outstanding under the LTIP and the Company did not have any liability associated with the share units earned by the employees under the LTIP (2010: the liability associated with the share units earned by the employees under the LTIP was recognized within accounts payable and accrued liabilities in the consolidated balance sheet and was carried at the market value of the Company's shares at the end of the financial year).

In December 2011, the Company's cash-settled equity forward agreement, which related to the share units granted in 2009 under the LTIP, matured. Until December 2011, a percentage of the equity forward derivatives, which related to unearned share units under the LTIP, was designated as a hedge. As at December 31, 2011, the Company no longer has any cash-settled equity forward agreements related to the share units granted under the LTIP.

Restricted Share Unit Plan

In February 2011 and 2010, the Company made grants of restricted share units ("RSUs"), in respect of the 2010 and 2009 financial years under the Company's restricted share unit plan ("RSU Plan") and, for certain senior management, grants of RSUs, combined with grants of stock options under the Company's share plan.

During the current financial year, the Company awarded 193,474 RSUs (2010: 350,384 RSUs) at a grant-date fair value of $40.81 (2010: $44.09), which vest 100% after three years. Full vesting of RSUs will be phased in for employees who received an award under the Company's LTIP in respect of a financial year prior to the Company's 2009 financial year.

During the current financial year, the Company cancelled 80,537 RSUS (2010: nil) as a result of the departure of certain management personnel.

As at December 31, 2011, there were 381,380 RSUs (2010: 326,117 RSUs) outstanding.

During the financial year ended December 31, 2011, the Company recognized compensation expense of $4,973 (2010: $8,804) associated with the RSUs granted during the financial year and reversed compensation expense of $1,428 (2010: $nil), the latter as a result of the cancellation of previously granted RSUs.

As at December 31, 2011, the liability associated with the RSUs is recognized within accounts payable and accrued liabilities and other long-term liabilities in the Company's consolidated balance sheets and is carried at the market value of the Company's shares at the end of the respective financial year.

The Company entered into cash-settled equity forward agreements to limit its exposure to future price changes in the Company's share price for the Company's RSUs. These agreements mature in December 2012 and December 2013.

A percentage of the equity forward derivatives, related to unearned RSUs, has been designated as a hedge.

27. NET CHANGE IN NON-CASH WORKING CAPITAL BALANCES

	2011	2010
Accounts receivable	$ (36,242)	$ 38,846
Inventory	(84,242)	(103,749)
Prepaid expenses	32,759	4,218
Accounts payable and accrued liabilities	119,891	25,861
	$ 32,166	$ (34,824)

Notes to the Consolidated Financial Statements (continued)
December 31, 2011 and January 1, 2011 (in thousands of Canadian dollars, except per share data)

28. CONTINGENCIES, COMMITMENTS AND GUARANTEES

Obligations under Operating Leases

As at December 31, 2011, the minimum lease payments (exclusive of taxes, insurance and other occupancy charges) on a calendar year basis under long-term leases for store locations and office space are as follows:

	2012	2013	2014	2015	2016	Thereafter	Total
Minimum lease payments	$ 406,831 $	408,198 $	397,259 $	382,422 $	369,568	$ 2,335,088	$ 4,299,366
Less: sub-lease revenue	3,409	2,756	2,046	1,707	1,317	3,316	14,551
Total operating lease obligations	$ 403,422	$ 405,442 $	395,213 $	380,715 $	368,251	$ 2,331,772	$ 4,284,815

Obligations under Financing Leases

As at December 31, 2011, the minimum lease payments on a calendar year basis for the Company's assets under financing leases are as follows:

	2012	2013	2014	2015	2016	Thereafter	Total
Minimum lease payments	$ 11,583 $	11,634 $	11,811 $	11,943 $	12,268	$ 161,549 $	220,788
Less: financing expenses included in minimum lease payments	8,684	8,479	8,254	8,000	7,717	58,844	99,978
Total financing lease obligations	$ 2,899 $	3,155 $	3,557 $	3,943 $	4,551	$ 102,705 $	120,810

The Company has financing lease obligations for buildings. The leases have an average interest rate of 7% (2010: 8 percent) and an average remaining term of approximately 17 years (2010: 17 years).

Distribution Services

The Company has entered into an agreement with a third party to provide inventory distribution services to the Company's locations to December 31, 2012. Under the terms of this agreement, the third party will charge the Company specified costs incurred to provide the distribution services, plus an annual management fee.

Information Services

The Company has entered into agreements with several third parties to provide information services to the Company. These agreements have terms of 5 years. The Company has committed to annual payments over the next five years as follows:

Minimum commitment	
2012	$ 8,952
2013	7,050
2014	6,665
2015	4,066
2016	1,744
Total	$ 28,477

Litigation

See Note 22 to these consolidated financial statements for a discussion of the Company's exposure to litigation claims.

Other

In the normal course of business, the Company enters into significant commitments for the purchase of goods and services, such as the purchase of inventory or capital assets, most of which are short-term in nature and are settled under normal trade terms.

The Company is involved in and could potentially be subject to various claims by third parties arising out of its business including, but not limited to, contract, product liability, labour and employment, regulatory and environmental claims. In addition, the Company is subject to regular audits from federal and provincial tax authorities relating to income, capital and commodity taxes, and as a result of these audits, may receive reassessments. While income, capital and commodity tax filings are subject to audits and reassessments, management believes that adequate provisions have been made for all income and other tax obligations. However, changes in the interpretations or judgements may result in an increase or decrease in the Company's income, capital, or commodity tax provisions in the future. The amount of any such increase or decrease cannot be reasonably estimated.

29. RELATED PARTY TRANSACTIONS

Key Management Personnel Compensation

Key management personnel are those individuals having authority and responsibility for planning, directing and controlling the activities of the Company including the Company's Board of Directors. The Company considers key management to be the members of the Board of Directors and the Chief Executive Officer.

Key management personnel may also participate in the Company's stock-based compensation plans and the Company's LTIP and RSU Plan. See Note 26 to these consolidated financial statements for further details on the Company's share-based payment plans.

Key management personnel compensation is comprised of:

	2011	2010
Salaries and directors' fees	$ 5,134 $	1,638
Statutory deductions	104	105
Expense related to pension and benefits	293	1,745
Share-based payment transactions	(734)	5,120
	$ 4,797 $	8,608

Key management personnel may purchase goods for personal and family use from the Company on the same terms as those available to all other employees of the Company.

Principal Subsidiaries

All of the Company's subsidiaries are wholly-owned. Intra-company balances and transactions and any unrealized earnings and expenses arising from intra-company transactions are eliminated in preparing the consolidated financial statements. Principal subsidiary companies as at December 31, 2011 were as follows:

Shoppers Home Health Care (Canada) Inc.
Shoppers Drug Mart Specialty Health Network Inc.
MediSystem Technologies Inc.
Shoppers Drug Mart Inc.
Shoppers Drug Mart (London) Limited
Pharmaprix Inc.
911979 Alberta Ltd.
Shoppers Realty Inc.
Sanis Health Inc.

The list excludes non-trading companies that have no material effect on the accounts of the Company.

The Associate-owned stores are each operated through a corporation owned by the Associates. See Note 3(a)(ii) to these consolidated financial statements for a further discussion.

30. EXPLANATION OF TRANSITION TO IFRS

As stated in Note 2(a) to these consolidated financial statements, these are the Company's first consolidated financial statements prepared in accordance with IFRS. Prior to the adoption of IFRS, the Company prepared its financial statements in accordance with Canadian Generally Accepted Accounting Principles ("previous GAAP").

The accounting policies set out in Note 3 to these consolidated financial statements have been applied in preparing the financial statements for the financial year ended December 31, 2011, the comparative information presented in these financial statements for the financial year ended January 1, 2011 and in the preparation of an opening IFRS balance sheet at January 3, 2010 (the Company's date of transition).

In preparing its opening IFRS balance sheet, the Company has adjusted amounts reported previously in financial statements prepared in accordance with previous GAAP based on IFRS 1, "First-time Adoption of International Financial Reporting Standards" ("IFRS 1"), elections and exceptions and IFRS policy choices. An explanation of how the transition from previous GAAP to IFRS has affected the Company's financial performance, financial position and cash flows is set out in the following tables and the notes that accompany the tables.

31. SUBSEQUENT EVENTS

Subsequent to the end of the financial year, on January 6, 2012, the Company filed with the securities regulators in each of the provinces of Canada, a final short form base shelf prospectus (the "Prospectus") for the issuance of up to $1,000,000 of medium-term notes. Subject to the requirements of applicable law, medium-term notes can be issued under the Prospectus for up to 25 months from the date of the final receipt. No incremental debt was incurred by the Company as a result of this filing.

On January 20, 2012, $250,000 of three-year medium-term notes (the "Series 3 Notes"), were repaid in full, along with all accrued and unpaid interest owing on the final semi-annual interest payment. The repayment was financed through the combination of available cash and commercial paper issued under the Company's commercial paper program. The net debt position of the Company remained substantially unchanged as a result of these refinancing activities.

On February 9, 2012, the Board of Directors declared a dividend of 26.5 cents per common share payable April 13, 2012 to shareholders of record as of the close of business on March 30, 2012.

The consolidated financial statements were authorized for issue by the Board of Directors on February 9, 2012.

Table A-1
FUTURE VALUE OF 1
(FUTURE VALUE OF A SINGLE SUM)

$$FVF_{n,i} = (1+i)^n$$

(n) periods	2%	2½%	3%	4%	5%	6%	8%	9%	10%	11%	12%	15%
1	1.02000	1.02500	1.03000	1.04000	1.05000	1.06000	1.08000	1.09000	1.10000	1.11000	1.12000	1.15000
2	1.04040	1.05063	1.06090	1.08160	1.10250	1.12360	1.16640	1.18810	1.21000	1.23210	1.25440	1.32250
3	1.06121	1.07689	1.09273	1.12486	1.15763	1.19102	1.25971	1.29503	1.33100	1.36763	1.40493	1.52088
4	1.08243	1.10381	1.12551	1.16986	1.21551	1.26248	1.36049	1.41158	1.46410	1.51807	1.57352	1.74901
5	1.10408	1.13141	1.15927	1.21665	1.27628	1.33823	1.46933	1.53862	1.61051	1.68506	1.76234	2.01136
6	1.12616	1.15969	1.19405	1.26532	1.34010	1.41852	1.58687	1.67710	1.77156	1.87041	1.97382	2.31306
7	1.14869	1.18869	1.22987	1.31593	1.40710	1.50363	1.71382	1.82804	1.94872	2.07616	2.21068	2.66002
8	1.17166	1.21840	1.26677	1.36857	1.47746	1.59385	1.85093	1.99256	2.14359	2.30454	2.47596	3.05902
9	1.19509	1.24886	1.30477	1.42331	1.55133	1.68948	1.99900	2.17189	2.35795	2.55803	2.77308	3.51788
10	1.21899	1.28008	1.34392	1.48024	1.62889	1.79085	2.15892	2.36736	2.59374	2.83942	3.10585	4.04556
11	1.24337	1.31209	1.38423	1.53945	1.71034	1.89830	2.33164	2.58043	2.85312	3.15176	3.47855	4.65239
12	1.26824	1.34489	1.42576	1.60103	1.79586	2.01220	2.51817	2.81267	3.13843	3.49845	3.89598	5.35025
13	1.29361	1.37851	1.46853	1.66507	1.88565	2.13293	2.71962	3.06581	3.45227	3.88328	4.36349	6.15279
14	1.31948	1.41297	1.51259	1.73168	1.97993	2.26090	2.93719	3.34173	3.79750	4.31044	4.88711	7.07571
15	1.34587	1.44830	1.55797	1.80094	2.07893	2.39656	3.17217	3.64248	4.17725	4.78459	5.47357	8.13706
16	1.37279	1.48451	1.60471	1.87298	2.18287	2.54035	3.42594	3.97031	4.59497	5.31089	6.13039	9.35762
17	1.40024	1.52162	1.65285	1.94790	2.29202	2.69277	3.70002	4.32763	5.05447	5.89509	6.86604	10.76126
18	1.42825	1.55966	1.70243	2.02582	2.40662	2.85434	3.99602	4.71712	5.55992	6.54355	7.68997	12.37545
19	1.45681	1.59865	1.75351	2.10685	2.52695	3.02560	4.31570	5.14166	6.11591	7.26334	8.61276	14.23177
20	1.48595	1.63862	1.80611	2.19112	2.65330	3.20714	4.66096	5.60441	6.72750	8.06231	9.64629	16.36654
21	1.51567	1.67958	1.86029	2.27877	2.78596	3.39956	5.03383	6.10881	7.40025	8.94917	10.80385	18.82152
22	1.54598	1.72157	1.91610	2.36992	2.92526	3.60354	5.43654	6.65860	8.14028	9.93357	12.10031	21.64475
23	1.57690	1.76461	1.97359	2.46472	3.07152	3.81975	5.87146	7.25787	8.95430	11.02627	13.55235	24.89146
24	1.60844	1.80873	2.03279	2.56330	3.22510	4.04893	6.34118	7.91108	9.84973	12.23916	15.17863	28.62518
25	1.64061	1.85394	2.09378	2.66584	3.38635	4.29187	6.84847	8.62308	10.83471	13.58546	17.00000	32.91895
26	1.67342	1.90029	2.15659	2.77247	3.55567	4.54938	7.39635	9.39916	11.91818	15.07986	19.04007	37.85680
27	1.70689	1.94780	2.22129	2.88337	3.73346	4.82235	7.98806	10.24508	13.10999	16.73865	21.32488	43.53532
28	1.74102	1.99650	2.28793	2.99870	3.92013	5.11169	8.62711	11.16714	14.42099	18.57990	23.88387	50.06561
29	1.77584	2.04641	2.35657	3.11865	4.11614	5.41839	9.31727	12.17218	15.86309	20.62369	26.74993	57.57545
30	1.81136	2.09757	2.42726	3.24340	4.32194	5.74349	10.06266	13.26768	17.44940	22.89230	29.95992	66.21177
31	1.84759	2.15001	2.50008	3.37313	4.53804	6.08810	10.86767	14.46177	19.19434	25.41045	33.55511	76.14354
32	1.88454	2.20376	2.57508	3.50806	4.76494	6.45339	11.73708	15.76333	21.11378	28.20560	37.58173	87.56507
33	1.92223	2.25885	2.65234	3.64838	5.00319	6.84059	12.67605	17.18203	23.22515	31.30821	42.09153	100.69983
34	1.96068	2.31532	2.73191	3.79432	5.25335	7.25103	13.69013	18.72841	25.54767	34.75212	47.14252	115.80480
35	1.99989	2.37321	2.81386	3.94609	5.51602	7.68609	14.78534	20.41397	28.10244	38.57485	52.79962	133.17552
36	2.03989	2.43254	2.89828	4.10393	5.79182	8.14725	15.96817	22.25123	30.91268	42.81808	59.13557	153.15185
37	2.08069	2.49335	2.98523	4.26809	6.08141	8.63609	17.24563	24.25384	34.00395	47.52807	66.23184	176.12463
38	2.12230	2.55568	3.07478	4.43881	6.38548	9.15425	18.62528	26.43668	37.40434	52.75616	74.17966	202.54332
39	2.16474	2.61957	3.16703	4.61637	6.70475	9.70351	20.11530	28.81598	41.14479	58.55934	83.08122	232.92482
40	2.20804	2.68506	3.26204	4.80102	7.03999	10.28572	21.72452	31.40942	45.25926	65.00087	93.05097	267.86355

Table A-2

PRESENT VALUE OF 1

(PRESENT VALUE OF A SINGLE SUM)

$$PVF_{n,i} = \frac{1}{(1+i)^n} = (1+i)^{-n}$$

(n) periods	2%	2½%	3%	4%	5%	6%	8%	9%	10%	11%	12%	15%
1	.98039	.97561	.97087	.96156	.95238	.94340	.92593	.91743	.90909	.90090	.89286	.86957
2	.96117	.95181	.94260	.92456	.90703	.89000	.85734	.84168	.82645	.81162	.79719	.75614
3	.94232	.92860	.91514	.88900	.86384	.83962	.79383	.77218	.75132	.73119	.71178	.65752
4	.92385	.90595	.88849	.85480	.82270	.79209	.73503	.70843	.68301	.65873	.63552	.57175
5	.90583	.88385	.86261	.82193	.78353	.74726	.68058	.64993	.62092	.59345	.56743	.49718
6	.88797	.86230	.83748	.79031	.74622	.70496	.63017	.59627	.56447	.53464	.50663	.43233
7	.87056	.84127	.81309	.75992	.71068	.66506	.58349	.54703	.51316	.48166	.45235	.37594
8	.85349	.82075	.78941	.73069	.67684	.62741	.54027	.50187	.46651	.43393	.40388	.32690
9	.83676	.80073	.76642	.70259	.64461	.59190	.50025	.46043	.42410	.39092	.36061	.28426
10	.82035	.78120	.74409	.67556	.61391	.55839	.46319	.42241	.38554	.35218	.32197	.24719
11	.80426	.76214	.72242	.64958	.58468	.52679	.42888	.38753	.35049	.31728	.28748	.21494
12	.78849	.74356	.70138	.62460	.55684	.49697	.39711	.35554	.31863	.28584	.25668	.18691
13	.77303	.72542	.68095	.60057	.53032	.46884	.36770	.32618	.28966	.25751	.22917	.16253
14	.75788	.70773	.66112	.57748	.50507	.44230	.34046	.29925	.26333	.23199	.20462	.14133
15	.74301	.69047	.64186	.55526	.48102	.41727.	.31524	.27454	.23939	.20900	.18270	.12289
16	.72845	.67362	.62317	.53391	.45811	.39365	.29189	.25187	.21763	.18829	.16312	.10687
17	.71416	.65720	.60502	.51337	.43630	.37136	.27027	.23107	.19785	.16963	.14564	.09293
18	.70016	.64117	.58739	.49363	.41552	.35034	.25025	.21199	.17986	.15282	.13004	.08081
19	.68643	.62553	.57029	.47464	.39573	.33051	.23171	.19449	.16351	.13768	.11611	.07027
20	.67297	.61027	.55368	.45639	.37689	.31180	.21455	.17843	.14864	.12403	.10367	.06110
21	.65978	.59539	.53755	.43883	.35894	.29416	.19866	.16370	.13513	.11174	.09256	.05313
22	.64684	.58086	.52189	.42196	.34185	.27751	.18394	.15018	.12285	.10067	.08264	.04620
23	.63416	.56670	.50669	.40573	.32557	.26180	.17032	.13778	.11168	.09069	.07379	.04017
24	.62172	.55288	.49193	.39012	.31007	.24698	.15770	.12641	.10153	.08170	.06588	.03493
25	.60953	.53939	.47761	.37512	.29530	.23300	.14602	.11597	.09230	.07361	.05882	.03038
26	.59758	.52623	.46369	.36069	.28124	.21981	.13520	.10639	.08391	.06631	.05252	.02642
27	.58586	.51340	.45019	.34682	.26785	.20737	.12519	.09761	.07628	.05974	.04689	.02297
28	.57437	.50088	.43708	.33348	.25509	.19563	.11591	.08955	.06934	.05382	.04187	.01997
29	.56311	.48866	.42435	.32065	.24295	.18456	.10733	.08216	.06304	.04849	.03738	.01737
30	.55207	.47674	.41199	.30832	.23138	.17411	.09938	.07537	.05731	.04368	.03338	.01510
31	.54125	.46511	.39999	.29646	.22036	.16425	.09202	.06915	.05210	.03935	.02980	.01313
32	.53063	.45377	.38834	.28506	.20987	.15496	.08520	.06344	.04736	.03545	.02661	.01142
33	.52023	.44270	.37703	.27409	.19987	.14619	.07889	.05820	.04306	.03194	.02376	.00993
34	.51003	.43191	.36604	.26355	.19035	.13791	.07305	.05340	.03914	.02878	.02121	.00864
35	.50003	.42137	.35538	.25342	.18129	.13011	.06763	.04899	.03558	.02592	.01894	.00751
36	.49022	.41109	.34503	.24367	.17266	.12274	.06262	.04494	.03235	.02335	.01691	.00653
37	.48061	.40107	.33498	.23430	.16444	.11579	.05799	.04123	.02941	.02104	.01510	.00568
38	.47119	.39128	.32523	.22529	.15661	.10924	.05369	.03783	.02674	.01896	.01348	.00494
39	.46195	.38174	.31575	.21662	.14915	.10306	.04971	.03470	.02430	.01708	.01204	.00429
40	.45289	.37243	.30656	.20829	.14205	.09722	.04603	.03184	.02210	.01538	.01075	.00373

Table A-3

FUTURE VALUE OF AN ORDINARY ANNUITY OF 1

$$FVF\text{-}OA_{n,i} = \frac{(1+i)^n - 1}{i}$$

(n) periods	2%	2½%	3%	4%	5%	6%	8%	9%	10%	11%	12%	15%
1	1.00000	1.00000	1.00000	1.00000	1.00000	1.00000	1.00000	1.00000	1.00000	1.00000	1.00000	1.00000
2	2.02000	2.02500	2.03000	2.04000	2.05000	2.06000	2.08000	2.09000	2.10000	2.11000	2.12000	2.15000
3	3.06040	3.07563	3.09090	3.12160	3.15250	3.18360	3.24640	3.27810	3.31000	3.34210	3.37440	3.47250
4	4.12161	4.15252	4.18363	4.24646	4.31013	4.37462	4.50611	4.57313	4.64100	4.70973	4.77933	4.99338
5	5.20404	5.25633	5.30914	5.41632	5.52563	5.63709	5.86660	5.98471	6.10510	6.22780	6.35285	6.74238
6	6.30812	6.38774	6.46841	6.63298	6.80191	6.97532	7.33592	7.52334	7.71561	7.91286	8.11519	8.75374
7	7.43428	7.54743	7.66246	7.89829	8.14201	8.39384	8.92280	9.20044	9.48717	9.78327	10.08901	11.06680
8	8.58297	8.73612	8.89234	9.21423	9.54911	9.89747	10.63663	11.02847	11.43589	11.85943	12.29969	13.72682
9	9.75463	9.95452	10.15911	10.58280	11.02656	11.49132	12.48756	13.02104	13.57948	14.16397	14.77566	16.78584
10	10.94972	11.20338	11.46338	12.00611	12.57789	13.18079	14.48656	15.19293	15.93743	16.72201	17.54874	20.30372
11	12.16872	12.48347	12.80780	13.48635	14.20679	14.97164	16.64549	17.56029	18.53117	19.56143	20.65458	24.34928
12	13.41209	13.79555	14.19203	15.02581	15.91713	16.86994	18.97713	20.14072	21.38428	22.71319	24.13313	29.00167
13	14.68033	15.14044	15.61779	16.62684	17.71298	18.88214	21.49530	22.95339	24.52271	26.21164	28.02911	34.35192
14	15.97394	16.51895	17.08632	18.29191	19.59863	21.01507	24.21492	26.01919	27.97498	30.09492	32.39260	40.50471
15	17.29342	17.93193	18.59891	20.02359	21.57856	23.27597	27.15211	29.36092	31.77248	34.40536	37.27972	47.58041
16	18.63929	19.38022	20.15688	21.82453	23.65749	25.67253	30.32428	33.00340	35.94973	39.18995	42.75328	55.71747
17	20.01207	20.86473	21.76159	23.69751	25.84037	28.21288	33.75023	36.97371	40.54470	44.50084	48.88367	65.07509
18	21.41231	22.38635	23.41444	25.64541	28.13238	30.90565	37.45024	41.30134	45.59917	50.39593	55.74972	75.83636
19	22.84056	23.94601	25.11687	27.67123	30.53900	33.75999	41.44626	46.01846	51.15909	56.93949	63.43968	88.21181
20	24.29737	25.54466	26.87037	29.77808	33.06595	36.78559	45.76196	51.16012	57.27500	64.20283	72.05244	102.44358
21	25.78332	27.18327	28.67649	31.96920	35.71925	39.99273	50.42292	56.76453	64.00250	72.26514	81.69874	118.81012
22	27.29898	28.86286	30.53678	34.24797	38.50521	43.39229	55.45676	62.87334	71.40275	81.21431	92.50258	137.63164
23	28.84496	30.58443	32.45288	36.61789	41.43048	46.99583	60.89330	69.53194	79.54302	91.14788	104.60289	159.27638
24	30.42186	32.34904	34.42647	39.08260	44.50200	50.81558	66.76476	76.78981	88.49733	102.17415	118.15524	184.16784
25	32.03030	34.15776	36.45926	41.64591	47.72710	54.86451	73.10594	84.70090	98.34706	114.41331	133.33387	212.79302
26	33.67091	36.01171	38.55304	44.31174	51.11345	59.15638	79.95442	93.32398	109.18177	127.99877	150.33393	245.71197
27	35.34432	37.91200	40.70963	47.08421	54.66913	63.70577	87.35077	102.72314	121.09994	143.07864	169.37401	283.56877
28	37.05121	39.85990	42.93092	49.96758	58.40258	68.52811	95.33883	112.96822	134.20994	159.81729	190.69889	327.10408
29	38.79223	41.85630	45.21885	52.96629	62.32271	73.63980	103.96594	124.13536	148.63093	178.39719	214.58275	377.16969
30	40.56808	43.90270	47.57542	56.08494	66.43885	79.05819	113.28321	136.30754	164.49402	199.02088	241.33268	434.74515
31	42.37944	46.00027	50.00268	59.32834	70.76079	84.80168	123.34587	149.57522	181.94343	221.91317	271.29261	500.95692
32	44.22703	48.15028	52.50276	62.70147	75.29883	90.88978	134.21354	164.03699	201.13777	247.32362	304.84772	577.10046
33	46.11157	50.35403	55.07784	66.20953	80.06377	97.34316	145.95062	179.80032	222.25154	275.52922	342.42945	644.66553
34	48.03380	52.61289	57.73018	69.85791	85.06696	104.18376	158.62667	196.98234	245.47670	306.83744	384.52098	765.36535
35	49.99448	54.92821	60.46208	73.65222	90.32031	111.43478	172.31680	215.71076	271.02437	341.58955	431.66350	881.17016
36	51.99437	57.30141	63.27594	77.59831	95.83632	119.12087	187.10215	236.12472	299.12681	380.16441	484.46312	1014.34568
37	54.03425	59.73395	66.17422	81.70225	101.62814	127.26812	203.07032	258.37595	330.03969	422.98249	543.59869	1167.49753
38	56.11494	62.22730	69.15945	85.97034	107.70955	135.90421	220.31595	282.62978	364.04343	470.51056	609.83053	1343.62216
39	58.23724	64.78298	72.23423	90.40915	114.09502	145.05846	238.94122	309.06646	401.44778	523.26673	684.01020	1546.16549
40	60.40198	67.40255	75.40126	95.02552	120.79977	154.76197	259.05652	337.88245	442.59256	581.82607	767.09142	1779.09031

Table A-4

PRESENT VALUE OF AN ORDINARY ANNUITY OF 1

$$PVF\text{-}OA_{n,\,i} = \dfrac{1 - \dfrac{1}{(1+i)^n}}{i}$$

(n) periods	2%	2½%	3%	4%	5%	6%	8%	9%	10%	11%	12%	15%
1	.98039	.97561	.97087	.96154	.95238	.94340	.92593	.91743	.90909	.90090	.89286	.86957
2	1.94156	1.92742	1.91347	1.88609	1.85941	1.83339	1.78326	1.75911	1.73554	1.71252	1.69005	1.62571
3	2.88388	2.85602	2.82861	2.77509	2.72325	2.67301	2.57710	2.53130	2.48685	2.44371	2.40183	2.28323
4	3.80773	3.76197	3.71710	3.62990	3.54595	3.46511	3.31213	3.23972	3.16986	3.10245	3.03735	2.85498
5	4.71346	4.64583	4.57971	4.45182	4.32948	4.21236	3.99271	3.88965	3.79079	3.69590	3.60478	3.35216
6	5.60143	5.50813	5.41719	5.24214	5.07569	4.91732	4.62288	4.48592	4.35526	4.23054	4.11141	3.78448
7	6.47199	6.34939	6.23028	6.00205	5.78637	5.58238	5.20637	5.03295	4.86842	4.71220	4.56376	4.16042
8	7.32482	7.17014	7.01969	6.73274	6.46321	6.20979	5.74664	5.53482	5.33493	5.14612	4.96764	4.48732
9	8.16224	7.97087	7.78611	7.43533	7.10782	6.80169	6.24689	5.99525	5.75902	5.53705	5.32825	4.77158
10	8.98259	8.75206	8.53020	8.11090	7.72173	7.36009	6.71008	6.41766	6.14457	5.88923	5.65022	5.01877
11	9.78685	9.51421	9.25262	8.76048	8.30641	7.88687	7.13896	6.80519	6.49506	6.20652	5.93770	5.23371
12	10.57534	10.25776	9.95400	9.38507	8.86325	8.38384	7.53608	7.16073	6.81369	6.49236	6.19437	5.42062
13	11.34837	10.98319	10.63496	9.98565	9.39357	8.85268	7.90378	7.48690	7.10336	6.74987	6.42355	5.58315
14	12.10625	11.69091	11.29607	10.56312	9.89864	9.29498	8.24424	7.78615	7.36669	6.98187	6.62817	5.72448
15	12.84926	12.38138	11.93794	11.11839	10.37966	9.71225	8.55948	8.06069	7.60608	7.19087	6.81086	5.84737
16	13.57771	13.05500	12.56110	11.65230	10.83777	10.10590	8.85137	8.31256	7.82371	7.37916	6.97399	5.95424
17	14.29187	13.71220	13.16612	12.16567	11.27407	10.47726	9.12164	8.54363	8.02155	7.54879	7.11963	6.04716
18	14.99203	14.35336	13.75351	12.65930	11.68959	10.82760	9.37189	8.75563	8.20141	7.70162	7.24967	6.12797
19	15.67846	14.97889	14.32380	13.13394	12.08532	11.15812	9.60360	8.95012	8.36492	7.83929	7.36578	6.19823
20	16.35143	15.58916	14.87747	13.59033	12.46221	11.46992	9.81815	9.12855	8.51356	7.96333	7.46944	6.25933
21	17.01121	16.18455	15.41502	14.02916	12.82115	11.76408	10.01680	9.29224	8.64869	8.07507	7.56200	6.31246
22	17.65805	16.76541	15.93692	14.45112	13.16300	12.04158	10.20074	9.44243	8.77154	8.17574	7.64465	6.35866
23	18.29220	17.33211	16.44361	14.85684	13.48857	12.30338	10.37106	9.58021	8.88322	8.26643	7.71843	6.39884
24	18.91393	17.88499	16.93554	15.24696	13.79864	12.55036	10.52876	9.70661	8.98474	8.34814	7.78432	6.43377
25	19.52346	18.42438	17.41315	15.62208	14.09394	12.78336	10.67478	9.82258	9.07704	8.42174	7.84314	6.46415
26	20.12104	18.95061	17.87684	15.98277	14.37519	13.00317	10.80998	9.92897	9.16095	8.48806	7.89566	6.49056
27	20.70690	19.46401	18.32703	16.32959	14.64303	13.21053	10.93516	10.02658	9.23722	8.54780	7.94255	6.51353
28	21.28127	19.96489	18.76411	16.66306	14.89813	13.40616	11.05108	10.11613	9.30657	8.60162	7.98442	6.53351
29	21.84438	20.45355	19.18845	16.98371	15.14107	13.59072	11.15841	10.19828	9.36961	8.65011	8.02181	6.55088
30	22.39646	20.93029	19.60044	17.29203	15.37245	13.76483	11.25778	10.27365	9.42691	8.69379	8.05518	6.56598
31	22.93770	21.39541	20.00043	17.58849	15.59281	13.92909	11.34980	10.34280	9.47901	8.73315	8.08499	6.57911
32	23.46833	21.84918	20.38877	17.87355	15.80268	14.08404	11.43500	10.40624	9.52638	8.76860	8.11159	6.59053
33	23.98856	22.29188	20.76579	18.14765	16.00255	14.23023	11.51389	10.46444	9.56943	8.80054	8.13535	6.60046
34	24.49859	22.72379	21.13184	18.41120	16.19290	14.36814	11.58693	10.51784	9.60858	8.82932	8.15656	6.60910
35	24.99862	23.14516	21.48722	18.66461	16.37419	14.49825	11.65457	10.56682	9.64416	8.85524	8.17550	6.61661
36	25.48884	23.55625	21.83225	18.90828	16.54685	14.62099	11.71719	10.61176	9.67651	8.87859	8.19241	6.62314
37	25.96945	23.95732	22.16724	19.14258	16.71129	14.73678	11.77518	10.65299	9.70592	8.89963	8.20751	6.62882
38	26.44064	24.34860	22.49246	19.36786	16.86789	14.84602	11.82887	10.69082	9.73265	8.91859	8.22099	6.63375
39	26.90259	24.73034	22.80822	19.58448	17.01704	14.94907	11.87858	10.72552	9.75697	8.93567	8.23303	6.63805
40	27.35548	25.10278	23.11477	19.79277	17.15909	15.04630	11.92461	10.75736	9.77905	8.95105	8.24378	6.64178

Table A-5

PRESENT VALUE OF AN ANNUITY DUE OF 1

$$PVF\text{-}AD_{n,i} = 1 + \frac{1 - \frac{1}{(1+i)^{n-1}}}{i}$$

(n) periods	2%	2½%	3%	4%	5%	6%	8%	9%	10%	11%	12%	15%
1	1.00000	1.00000	1.00000	1.00000	1.00000	1.00000	1.00000	1.00000	1.00000	1.00000	1.00000	1.00000
2	1.98039	1.97561	1.97087	1.96154	1.95238	1.94340	1.92593	1.91743	1.90909	1.90090	1.89286	1.86957
3	2.94156	2.92742	2.91347	2.88609	2.85941	2.83339	2.78326	2.75911	2.73554	2.71252	2.69005	2.62571
4	3.88388	3.85602	3.82861	3.77509	3.72325	3.67301	3.57710	3.53130	3.48685	3.44371	3.40183	3.28323
5	4.80773	4.76197	4.71710	4.62990	4.54595	4.46511	4.31213	4.23972	4.16986	4.10245	4.03735	3.85498
6	5.71346	5.64583	5.57971	5.45182	5.32948	5.21236	4.99271	4.88965	4.79079	4.69590	4.60478	4.35216
7	6.60143	6.50813	6.41719	6.24214	6.07569	5.91732	5.62288	5.48592	5.35526	5.23054	5.11141	4.78448
8	7.47199	7.34939	7.23028	7.00205	6.78637	6.58238	6.20637	6.03295	5.86842	5.71220	5.56376	5.16042
9	8.32548	8.17014	8.01969	7.73274	7.46321	7.20979	6.74664	6.53482	6.33493	6.14612	5.96764	5.48732
10	9.16224	8.97087	8.78611	8.43533	8.10782	7.80169	7.24689	6.99525	6.75902	6.53705	6.32825	5.77158
11	9.98259	9.75206	9.53020	9.11090	8.72173	8.36009	7.71008	7.41766	7.14457	6.88923	6.65022	6.01877
12	10.78685	10.51421	10.25262	9.76048	9.30641	8.88687	8.13896	7.80519	7.49506	7.20652	6.93770	6.23371
13	11.57534	11.25776	10.95400	10.38507	9.86325	9.38384	8.53608	8.16073	7.81369	7.49236	7.19437	6.42062
14	12.34837	11.98319	11.63496	10.98565	10.39357	9.85268	8.90378	8.48690	8.10336	7.74987	7.42355	6.58315
15	13.10625	12.69091	12.29607	11.56312	10.89864	10.29498	9.24424	8.78615	8.36669	7.98187	7.62817	6.72448
16	13.84926	13.38138	12.93794	12.11839	11.37966	10.71225	9.55948	9.06069	8.60608	8.19087	7.81086	6.84737
17	14.57771	14.05500	13.56110	12.65230	11.83777	11.10590	9.85137	9.31256	8.82371	8.37916	7.97399	6.95424
18	15.29187	14.71220	14.16612	13.16567	12.27407	11.47726	10.12164	9.54363	9.02155	8.54879	8.11963	7.04716
19	15.99203	15.35336	14.75351	13.65930	12.68959	11.82760	10.37189	9.75563	9.20141	8.70162	8.24967	7.12797
20	16.67846	15.97889	15.32380	14.13394	13.08532	12.15812	10.60360	9.95012	9.36492	8.83929	8.36578	7.19823
21	17.35143	16.58916	15.87747	14.59033	13.46221	12.46992	10.81815	10.12855	9.51356	8.96333	8.46944	7.25933
22	18.01121	17.18455	16.41502	15.02916	13.82115	12.76408	11.01680	10.29224	9.64869	9.07507	8.56200	7.31246
23	18.65805	17.76541	16.93692	15.45112	14.16300	13.04158	11.20074	10.44243	9.77154	9.17574	8.64465	7.35866
24	19.29220	18.33211	17.44361	15.85684	14.48857	13.30338	11.37106	10.58021	9.88322	9.26643	8.71843	7.39884
25	19.91393	18.88499	17.93554	16.24696	14.79864	13.55036	11.52876	10.70661	9.98474	9.34814	8.78432	7.43377
26	20.52346	19.42438	18.41315	16.62208	15.09394	13.78336	11.67478	10.82258	10.07704	9.42174	8.84314	7.46415
27	21.12104	19.95061	18.87684	16.98277	15.37519	14.00317	11.80998	10.92897	10.16095	9.48806	8.89566	7.49056
28	21.70690	20.46401	19.32703	17.32959	15.64303	14.21053	11.93518	11.02658	10.23722	9.54780	8.94255	7.51353
29	22.28127	20.96489	19.76411	17.66306	15.89813	14.40616	12.05108	11.11613	10.30657	9.60162	8.98442	7.53351
30	22.84438	21.45355	20.18845	17.98371	16.14107	14.59072	12.15841	11.19828	10.36961	9.65011	9.02181	7.55088
31	23.39646	21.93029	20.60044	18.29203	16.37245	14.76483	12.25778	11.27365	10.42691	9.69379	9.05518	7.56598
32	23.93770	22.39541	21.00043	18.58849	16.59281	14.92909	12.34980	11.34280	10.47901	9.73315	9.08499	7.57911
33	24.46833	22.84918	21.38877	18.87355	16.80268	15.08404	12.43500	11.40624	10.52638	9.76860	9.11159	7.59053
34	24.98856	23.29188	21.76579	19.14765	17.00255	15.23023	12.51389	11.46444	10.56943	9.80054	9.13535	7.60046
35	25.49859	23.72379	22.13184	19.41120	17.19290	15.36814	12.58693	11.51784	10.60858	9.82932	9.15656	7.60910
36	25.99862	24.14516	22.48722	19.66461	17.37419	15.49825	12.65457	11.56682	10.64416	9.85524	9.17550	7.61661
37	26.48884	24.55625	22.83225	19.90828	17.54685	15.62099	12.71719	11.61176	10.67651	9.87859	9.19241	7.62314
38	26.96945	24.95732	23.16724	20.14258	17.71129	15.73678	12.77518	11.65299	10.70592	9.89963	9.20751	7.62882
39	27.44064	25.34860	23.49246	20.36786	17.86789	15.84602	12.82887	11.69082	10.73265	9.91859	9.22099	7.63375
40	27.90259	25.73034	23.80822	20.58448	18.01704	15.94907	12.87858	11.72552	10.75697	9.93567	9.23303	7.63805

Accounting errors Unintentional mistakes, not intentional distortions, in financial statements.

Accounting income Income before taxes. Also known as *Accounting profit*, "income for financial reporting purposes," or "income for book purposes."

Accounting policies The specific accounting principles and methods that are currently employed and considered most appropriate to present fairly a company's financial statements.

Accounting profit See *Accounting income.*

Accretion Under ASPE, the increase in the carrying amount of an asset retirement obligation due to passage of time.

Accrued benefit obligation (ABO) for accounting purposes ASPE terminology for the present value of vested and non-vested benefits earned to the balance sheet date, with the benefits measured using employees' future salary levels. Known as the defined benefit obligation for accounting purpose under IFRS.

Accrued benefit obligation (ABO) for funding purposes ASPE terminology for the present value of vested and non-vested benefits earned to the balance sheet date, with the benefits measured using employees' future salary levels and based on the most recent actuarial valuation report prepared for funding of the pension plan.

Accumulated benefit method A method used to measure the pension obligation. The calculation of the deferred compensation amount is based on all years of service performed by employees under the plan, vested and non-vested, using current salary levels.

Accumulated other comprehensive income The cumulative change in equity that is due to the revenues and expenses, and gains and losses, that stem from non-shareholder transactions that are excluded from the calculation of net income.

Accumulated rights Rights to benefits accumulated by employees that can be carried forward to future periods if not used in the period in which they were earned.

Acid-test ratio A liquidity ratio that relates total current liabilities to highly liquid assets such as cash, marketable securities, and receivables. Also known as *Quick ratio.*

Actual return The return on pension plan assets that takes into account actual changes in the market values of plan assets as well as the interest and dividends earned.

Actuarial assumptions Predictions made by actuaries regarding factors necessary to operate a pension plan, such as mortality rates, employee turnover, interest and earnings rates, early retirement frequency, and future salaries.

Actuarial gains and losses Gains and losses in a pension fund related to the defined benefit obligation (the liability) resulting from a change in actuarial assumptions or an experienced gain or loss.

Actuaries Individuals who are trained through a rigorous certification program to assign probabilities to future events and their financial effects.

Adverse opinion Audit opinion required when the exceptions to fair presentation are so material that in the independent auditor's judgement a qualified opinion is not justified.

Antidilutive securities Securities that upon conversion or exercise would increase earnings per share, or reduce the loss per share.

Asset ceiling test An analysis required of any end-of-period defined benefit asset to ensure that it is not reported at an amount in excess of the benefits that will be received from it in the future.

Asset retirement obligation (ARO) An existing legal obligation associated with the retirement of a tangible long-lived asset that results from its acquisition, construction, development, or normal operations, in the period it is incurred, provided a reasonable estimate can be made of its fair value. Also known as *Site restoration obligation.*

Asset-based financing The financing of equipment through a secured loan, conditional sales contract, or a lease.

Asset-linked debt See *Commodity-backed debt.*

Attribution period The accounting period beginning at the date of hire and ending when the employee obtains full eligibility for benefits.

Auditor's report The communication by the auditor as to his or her opinion regarding the fair presentation of an entity's financial statements.

Bargain purchase option A provision allowing the lessee to purchase the leased property for a price that is significantly lower than the property's expected fair value at the date the option becomes exercisable.

Bargain renewal option A provision allowing the lessee to renew the lease for a rental that is lower than the expected fair rental at the date the option becomes exercisable.

Basic EPS (earnings per share) Net income available to common shareholders divided by the number of outstanding common shares.

Basic or inherent rights Three rights inherent in shares where restrictive provisions are absent. These rights are to share proportionately in profits and losses, to share proportionately in management, and to share proportionately in corporate assets upon liquidation.

Bearer bond A bond that is not recorded in the owner's name and may be transferred simply from one owner to another. Also known as *Coupon bond.*

Benefit cost The annual amount that the company is obligated to contribute to a defined contribution (DC) plan.

Bifurcation The separation of proceeds into two or more amounts. For instance, it is used in accounting for bundled sales and convertible bonds (by the issuer).

Bond indenture A contract that is a promise to pay a sum of money at a designated maturity date, as well as periodic interest at a specified rate on the maturity amount (face value).

Bonus Amount paid by an employer to an employee in addition to regular salary or wage, often dependent on the company's yearly profit.

Book value method A method of accounting for the conversion of debt to equity whereby the equity is measured at the book value of the debt converted.

Book value per share Common shareholders' equity divided by the number of common shares outstanding.

Call option A derivative instrument where the option holder has the right, but not the obligation, to buy shares at a preset price.

Callable bonds and notes Bonds that give the issuer the right to call and retire the bonds prior to maturity.

Callable debt Debt that is due on demand (that is, callable) by the creditor.

Callable/redeemable (preferred) shares Shares that allow the issuing corporation to "call" or redeem at its option the outstanding preferred shares at specified future dates and at stipulated prices.

Capital leases Leases where the risks and rewards of ownership transfer from the lessor to the lessee. Evaluated based on stipulated criteria. Also known as *Finance leases*.

Carrying amount The amount at which the underlying assets or services that were exchanged are measured in certain related-party transactions. It is the amount of the item transferred as recorded in the books of the transferor.

Carrying value The value at which an item such as a bond is recorded on the balance sheet.

Cash flows The inflows and outflows of cash and cash equivalents.

Cash equivalents Short-term, highly liquid investments that are readily convertible to known amounts of cash and have an insignificant risk of change in value.

Cash flow hedge A hedge that deals with exposures to future variable cash flows, such as future interest payments on variable rate debt.

Change in accounting estimate An adjustment in the carrying amount of an asset or a liability or the amount of an asset's periodic consumption resulting either from an assessment of the present status of the asset or liability, or of the expected future benefits and obligations associated with the asset.

Change in accounting policy A change from one generally accepted accounting principle or the methods used in their application to another.

Chief operating decision-maker The person who has final say on operating matters and who regularly reviews operating segments.

Classification approach An approach where transactions should be classified and accounted for according to their economic substance.

Clean opinion The opinion expressed by the auditor that the financial statements present fairly, in all material respects, the entity's financial position, results of operations, and cash flows, in conformity with generally accepted accounting principles. Also known as *Unqualified opinion*.

Collateral trust bonds or notes Bonds or notes that are secured with assets (often shares and bonds of other corporations).

Combination plans Stock compensation plans that combine features from different types of compensation plans such as stock option plans and share appreciation rights plans. Also known as *Tandem plans*.

Commercial substance What a transaction has when the entity's cash flows are expected to be significantly different after, and as a result of, the transaction.

Commodity-backed debts Bonds that are redeemable in measures of a commodity, such as barrels of oil or tonnes of coal. Also known as *Asset-linked debt*.

Common costs Costs incurred for the benefit of more than one segment and whose interrelated nature prevents a completely objective division of costs among segments.

Common shares Shares that represent the residual ownership interest in the company, bear the ultimate risks of loss, and receive the benefits of success.

Compensated absences Absences from employment, e.g., vacation, illness, and holidays, for which employees will be paid.

Compensatory stock option plans (CSOPs) Stock options to remunerate parties including managers.

Complex capital structure What a corporation has when it has convertible securities, options, warrants, or other rights that upon conversion or exercise could dilute earnings per share.

Comprehensive revaluation The revaluation of a company's liabilities and assets following a financial reorganization in cases where the same party no longer controls the company.

Constructive obligation An obligation that arises from past or present company practice that signals that the entity acknowledges a potential economic burden.

Contingency An existing condition or situation involving uncertainty as to possible gain or loss and that will not be resolved until a future event or events occur or fail to occur.

Contingent liability An obligation incurred as a result of a loss contingency, dependent upon the occurrence or nonoccurrence of one or more future events to confirm either its existence or the amount payable.

Contingently issuable shares Additional shares a company promises to issue if a certain future event occurs.

Contract-based approach An approach where the leased asset that is acquired is not seen to be the physical property; rather, it is seen as the contractual right to use the property that is conveyed under the lease agreement.

Contractual commitments Agreements entered into by companies with customers, suppliers, employees, and other parties. They are not liabilities at balance sheet date, but commit the company and how its assets will be used into the future. Also known as *Contractual obligations*.

Contractual obligations See *Contractual commitments*.

Contributed (paid-in) capital The total amount provided by the shareholders to the corporation for use in the business.

Contributory plans A pension plan where the employees bear part of the stated benefits' cost or voluntarily make payments to increase their benefits.

Convertible bonds Bonds that can be converted into other securities of the corporation for a specified time after issuance. See *Convertible debt*.

Convertible debt Debt the holder can convert into other securities such as common shares. Certain bonds or other financial instruments give the issuer the option to repay or settle. Also known as *Contractual commitments*.

Convertible (preferred) shares Shares where the shareholders may at their option exchange preferred shares for common shares at a predetermined ratio.

Correction of a prior period error Correction of errors that occurred as a result of mathematical mistakes, mistakes in applying accounting principles, fraud, or oversight or misinterpretation of facts that existed at the time financial statements were prepared, e.g., the incorrect application of the retail inventory method for determining the final inventory value.

Corridor approach Under the ASPE deferral and amortization method, an approach to actuarial gains and losses that amortizes the net accumulated gain or loss when its balance is considered too large.

Counterbalancing errors Errors that reverse or correct themselves in subsequent periods.

Counterparty The other party to a contract.

Coupon bond A bond that is not recorded in the owner's name and may be transferred simply from one owner to another. Also known as *Bearer bond.*

Coupon rate The fixed rate of interest that is paid by the issuer of a bond annually or semi-annually during the life of the bond. Also known as *Nominal rate* or *Stated rate.*

Credit risk The risk that the other party to the contract will fail to fulfill its obligation under the contract and cause the company loss.

Cumulative (preferred) shares Preferred shares where dividends not paid in any year must be made up in a later year before any profits can be distributed to common shareholders.

Currency risk The risk that the fair value or future cash flows of a financial instrument will fluctuate because of changes in foreign exchange rates.

Current liability Amounts payable within one year from the date of the balance sheet or within the normal operating cycle where this is longer than a year.

Current maturities of long-term debt Bonds, mortgage notes, and other long-term indebtedness that mature within 12 months from the balance sheet date and are reported as current liabilities.

Current ratio The ratio of total current assets to total current liabilities.

Current service cost The cost of pension benefits that are to be provided in the future in exchange for the services that employees provide in the current period.

Customer advances Deposits received from customers that are returnable. Deposits may guarantee performance of a contract or service.

Days payables outstanding A ratio indicating how long it takes a company to pay its trade payables, thereby determining the average age of payables.

Debenture bond A bond that is unsecured.

Debt settlement The early repayment or refunding of debt (before maturity).

Debt to total assets ratio A ratio that measures the percentage of total assets provided by creditors by dividing total debt (both current and long-term liabilities) by total assets.

Deductible temporary difference A deductible amount that will decrease taxable income in future years.

Deep discount bonds or notes Bonds sold at a discount that provide the buyer's total interest payoff at maturity. Also known as *Zero-interest debentures, bonds, or notes.*

Defeasance The elimination of an obligation to a creditor. If a company wishes to extinguish or pay off debt prior to its due date, it must set aside sufficient money in a trust or other arrangement and allow the trust to repay the original debt (principal and interest) directly to the creditor as it becomes due according to the original agreement.

Deferral and amortization approach A method of accounting for defined benefit plans under ASPE that uses the accrued benefit obligation and provides opportunities to delay the recognition of both past service costs and actuarial gains and losses as part of the benefit plan expense and as part of the accrued benefit asset/liability on the balance sheet.

Deferred tax asset Under IFRS, an asset representing a reduction in taxes payable or the increase in taxes refundable in future years as a result of a deductible temporary difference that exists at the end of the current year. Also known (under ASPE) as *Future income tax asset.*

Deferred tax expense The change in the statement of financial position deferred income tax asset or liability account from the beginning to the end of the accounting period.

Deferred tax liability Under IFRS, a liability representing an increase in taxes payable or the decrease in taxes refundable in future years as a result of a taxable temporary difference at the end of the current year. Also known (under ASPE) as *Future income tax liability.*

Defined benefit (DB) plan A pension plan that defines the benefits that an employee will receive at retirement.

Defined benefit obligation IFRS terminology for the present value of vested and non-vested benefits earned to the date of the statement of financial position, with the benefits measured using employees' future salary levels. Also known as *Defined benefit obligation (DBO) for accounting purposes under IFRS,* and the *Accrued benefit obligation for accounting purposes under ASPE.*

Defined benefit obligation (DBO) for accounting purposes See *Defined benefit obligation* and *Accrued benefit obligation for accounting purposes.*

Defined contribution (DC) plan A pension plan that specifies how contributions are determined rather than the benefits that the individual is to receive or the method of determining those benefits.

Derivative instruments Financial instruments that transfer risks from one party to another with little or no upfront investment. Derivatives derive their value from changes in the value of things such as shares, interest rates, and exchange rates.

Diluted EPS (earnings per share) Earnings per share that includes the effect of all dilutive potential common shares outstanding during the period.

Direct financing leases Leases where no manufacturer's or dealer's profit is present, resulting from arrangements with lessors who are primarily engaged in financing operations, such as lease financing companies, banks, insurance companies, and pension trusts.

Direct method A method of preparing the cash flow statement where cash flow from operating activities is calculated directly by identifying the sources of the operating cash receipts and payments.

Discount The difference between the face value and the market price of a bond.

Discrete view The notion that each interim period should be treated as a separate accounting period.

Dividend payable An amount that a corporation owes to its shareholders because the board of directors has authorized a dividend payment.

Dividends Profit distribution to shareholders.

Dividends in kind Dividends payable in corporation assets other than cash. Also known as "property dividends."

Earned capital Capital that is created by the business operating profitably.

Economic consequences Arguments to change accounting methods based on economic reasons, rather than conceptual reasons, that focus on the supposed impact of accounting on the behaviour of investors, creditors, competitors, and governments.

Effective interest method Method of amortizing bond discounts/premiums and estimating the carrying value and amortized cost of a bond whereby the interest expense recognized is based on the effective interest rate/yield. The effective interest rate is the rate needed to discount the stated interest and principal payments such that the present value of the cash flows equals the current carrying value of the instrument.

Effective tax rate Total income tax expense divided by pre-tax income reported on the financial statements.

Effective yield The interest rate actually earned by the bondholders. See also Market rate.

Embedded derivatives A derivative such as a call or put option that is contained in (embedded in) a financial instrument such as a debenture.

Employee stock option or purchase plans (ESOPs) Stock options used to give employees an opportunity to own part of the company, issued to a wide group of people (such as all employees).

Equity instrument Any contract that evidences a residual interest in the assets of an entity after deducting all of its liabilities.

Event accrual method A method of accounting for non-accumulating compensated absences whereby a liability is not recorded until the obligating event occurs.

Executory contract A contract that is entered into where both parties agree to do something in the future. The contract is initially unexecuted until the goods in question or consideration is exchanged at that future point in time.

Executory costs Insurance, maintenance, and property tax expenses.

Exercise period The period (specified by the terms of a financial instrument) during which the holder or issuer of the instrument may exercise their rights. For instance, an option gives the holder the right to buy or sell shares at a predetermined price for a certain time period.

Exercise price The predetermined price (specified by the terms of a financial instrument) at which either the holder or the issuer of the instrument may exercise their rights. For instance, an option gives the holder the right to buy or sell shares at a predetermined price.

Expected return The return on pension plan assets based on the expected long-term rate of return on plan assets applied to the fair value (or the market-related value) of the plan assets.

Expected average remaining service life (EARSL) The total number of years of future service that an employee group is expected to render divided by the number of employees in the group.

Expense approach A method of accounting for the liability arising from product guarantees where the outstanding liability is measured at the cost of the economic resources needed to meet the obligation.

Experience gain or loss In relation to pension plans, the difference between what has occurred and the previous actuarial assumptions as to what was expected.

Extinguishment of debt The discharge, cancellation or expiry of debt.

Face value The value that the bond is worth at the date it is to be repaid. Also known as *Maturity value*, *Par value*, or *Principal amount*.

Fair value hedge A hedge that deals with exposures to changes in fair values of recognized assets or liabilities or unrecognized firm commitments.

Fair value option A financial reporting option that allows financial instruments to be recorded using fair value–net income.

Finance leases Leases where the risks and rewards of ownership transfer from the lessor to the lessee. Evaluated based on stipulated criteria. Also known as *Capital leases*.

Financial guarantees Legally binding undertakings to stand in the place of the party for whom the guarantee is given to discharge their obligation in the event of them failing to do so.

Financial instruments Contracts that create both a financial asset for one party and a financial liability or equity instrument for the other party.

Financial liabilities Contractual obligations to deliver cash or other financial assets to another party, or to exchange financial instruments with another party under conditions that are potentially unfavourable.

Financial reorganization A substantial realignment of an enterprise's equity and non-equity interests such that the holders of one or more of the significant classes of non-equity interests and the holders of all of the significant classes of equity interests give up some (or all) of their rights and claims on the enterprise.

Financing activities Activities that result in changes in the size and composition of a company's equity capital and borrowings.

Forward contract A contract in which the parties to the contract each commit upfront to buy or sell something in the future, including things such as foreign currency or commodities.

Free cash flow Net operating cash flows reduced by the capital expenditures that are needed to sustain the current level of operations.

Fresh start accounting The result of a financial reorganization, which allows a company in financial difficulty to continue with its plans without recovering from a deficit.

Full disclosure principle Financial reporting of financial facts that are significant enough to influence the judgement of an informed reader.

Full retrospective application The restatement of a company's financial reports for prior periods incorporating a recent change in accounting policy.

Funded In relation to pension plans, a term describing when the employer (company) sets funds aside for future pension benefits by making payments to a funding agency that is responsible for accumulating the pension plan assets and for making payments to the recipients as the benefits come due.

Funded status The difference between the defined benefit obligation and the pension assets' fair value at any point in time (overfunded/surplus or underfunded/deficit).

Future income tax asset Under ASPE, an asset representing a reduction in taxes payable or the increase in taxes refundable in future years as a result of a deductible temporary difference that exists at the end of the current year. Also known (under IFRS) as *Deferred tax asset*.

Future income tax expense The change in the future tax account balance from the beginning to the end of the accounting period.

Future income tax liability Under ASPE, a liability representing an increase in taxes payable or the decrease in taxes refundable in future years as a result of a taxable temporary difference at the end of the current year. Also known (under IFRS) as *Deferred tax liability*.

Future income taxes method A method for calculating income taxes that adjusts for the effects of any changes in future income tax assets and liabilities and recognizes these effects as future income tax expense. Also known as *Temporary difference approach*.

GAAP hierarchy The Generally Accepted Accounting Principles hierarchy that supports decisions about which principles and methods determine accepted accounting practice at a particular time.

Grant date The date that stock options are received.

Gross investment in lease The undiscounted rental/lease payments (excluding executory costs) plus any guaranteed or unguaranteed residual value that accrues to the lessor at the end of the lease or any bargain purchase option.

Guaranteed residual value The amount at which the lessor has the right to require the lessee to purchase the asset, or the amount the lessee or the third-party guarantor guarantees the lessor will realize.

Hedging A strategy whereby an entity enters into a contract with another party in order to reduce exposure to existing risks.

Horizontal analysis An approach to financial statement analysis that indicates the proportionate change over a period of time.

Hybrid/compound instruments Compound financial instruments that have both an equity component and a liability component.

If-converted method The method used to measure the dilutive effects of a potential conversion of convertible debt or preferred shares on earnings per share.

Illegal acts "A violation of a domestic or foreign statutory law or government regulation attributable to the entity," as defined by the *CICA Handbook*.

Immediate recognition approach An approach to accounting for defined benefit pension plans where the pension expense is made up of all items affecting the funded status during the period except the company contributions into the plan assets, including current service cost and interest cost, actual return on plan assets, past service cost, and actuarial gains and losses.

Impracticable Not practical due to lack of information or where costs exceed benefits.

Imputed interest rate The approximate or appropriate interest rate used to calculate the market value of a note where such value is not readily ascertainable.

In the money What happens to options if the holder of the options stands to benefit from exercising them.

In-substance common shares Shares with the same characteristics as common shares but that cannot be called common shares for legal purposes.

Income available to common shareholders Net income after deducting preferred share dividends.

Income bonds Bonds where no interest is paid unless the issuing company is profitable.

Income tax benefit An income tax related income statement account with a credit balance. Also known as *Tax income*.

Incremental borrowing rate The interest rate that, at the lease's inception, the lessee would have incurred to borrow, over a similar term and with similar security for the borrowing, the funds necessary to purchase the leased asset.

Incremental method See *Residual value method*.

Indirect method A method of preparing the cash flow statement where cash flow from operating activities is derived indirectly by making the necessary adjustments to net income reported on the income statement.

Induced conversion The conversion of securities whereby an issuer offers additional consideration (a sweetener), such as cash or common shares, to induce the conversion.

Initial direct costs "Those costs incurred by the lessor that are directly associated with negotiating and executing a specific leasing transaction," as defined by the *CICA Handbook*.

Input tax credit The GST or HST a company pays on goods and services it purchases from its suppliers.

Integral view The belief that the interim report is an integral part of the annual report and that deferrals and accruals should take into consideration what will happen for the entire year.

Interest rate implicit in the lease The discount rate that corresponds to the lessor's internal rate of return on a lease.

Interest rate risk The risk that the fair value or future cash flows of a financial instrument will fluctuate because of changes in market interest rates.

Interest rate swap A derivative contract under which the parties agree to exchange future payments that are based on the difference between a fixed interest rate and a variable interest rate.

Interim reports Reports covering periods of less than one year.

Interperiod tax allocation The recognition of deferred tax liabilities and assets for the future tax consequences of events that have already been recognized in the financial statements or tax returns.

Intraperiod tax allocation The approach to allocating taxes within the financial statements of the current period.

Intrinsic value When valuing a derivative, the difference between the fair value and the strike price of the underlying at any point in time.

Intrinsic value method A method to determine the value of an employee compensation plan where the cost of the plan is based on the share's fair value less the exercise price.

Investing activities Activities that involve the acquisition and disposal of long-term assets and other investments that are not included in operating activities.

Investment grade securities Securities that are high quality, not speculative.

Junk bonds Bonds that are unsecured and extremely risky.

Large stock dividend A stock dividend of more than 20% to 25% of the number of shares previously outstanding.

Lease A contractual agreement between a lessor and a lessee that gives the lessee the right to use specific property, owned by the lessor, for a specified time in return for stipulated, and generally periodic, cash payments (rents).

Lease term The fixed, non-cancellable term of the lease.

Legal capital The value at which a company's shares are recorded on its books.

Lessee The party that has the right to use specific property, owned by the lessor, for a specified time in return for stipulated, and generally periodic, cash payments (rents).

Lessor The party that owns the property and rents it out to the lessee.

Leverage The use of debt financing to maximize shareholder value. A company borrows funds and invests them at a higher rate of return such that the difference in rates accrues to the existing shareholders.

Leveraged buyout A buyout where management or another employee group purchases the company shares and finances the purchase, using the company's assets as collateral.

Liability Obligations of an entity arising from past transactions or events, the settlement of which may result in the transfer or use of assets, provision of services, or other yielding of economic benefits in the future.

Limited liability A feature of share ownership where shareholders are only liable on behalf of the corporation up to the amount of their original investment.

Line of credit An agreement a company enters into with its bank to make multiple borrowings up to a negotiated limit, instead of having to negotiate a new loan every time the company needs funds. Also known as *Revolving debt*.

Liquidating dividends Dividends that are a return of capital and not a return on capital or a share of earnings; they result in a decrease in the capital of the company.

Liquidity A company's ability to convert assets into cash to pay off its current liabilities in the course of business.

Liquidity risk The risk that an entity will have difficulty meeting obligations that are associated with financial liabilities.

Loan foreclosure What arises when a creditor takes the underlying security (the asset) in lieu of payment of the loan.

Long-term debt Probable future sacrifices of economic benefits arising from present obligations that are not payable within a year or the operating cycle of the business, whichever is longer.

Loss carryback What occurs when a corporation elects to carry a tax loss back against the taxable income of the immediately preceding three years.

Loss carryforward What occurs when a corporation chooses to carry a tax loss that it earned in tax years ending after 2005 forward to the 20 years that immediately follow the loss.

Loss for income tax purposes A loss resulting when tax-deductible expenses and losses exceed taxable revenues and gains. Also known as *Tax loss*.

Loyalty programs Promotions by a company promising future benefits to customers in exchange for specified purchases from the company.

Lump-sum sales Instances where two or more classes of shares are offered for sale at a single payment.

Management approach A method of reporting segmented information on general purpose financial statements whereby selected information on a single basis of segmentation is based on the way management reviews the company for making operating decisions.

Manufacturer's or dealer's profit The profit or loss to the lessor, which is the difference between the fair value of the leased property at the lease's inception and the lessor's cost or carrying amount (book value).

Manufacturer or dealer lease A lease whereby a manufacturer's or dealer's profit is incorporated. Also known as a sales-type lease.

Market rate The effective yield or actual return that bond investors earn.

Market risk The risk that the fair value or future cash flows of a financial instrument will fluctuate because of changes in market prices.

Market-related value of plan assets A calculated value that recognizes changes in a pension plan's fair value in a systematic and rational manner over no more than five years.

Maturity value The value that a bond is worth at the date it is to be repaid. Also known as *Face value, Par value, or Principal amount*.

Minimum lease payments Those payments that the lessee is obligated to make in connection with the leased property. They include the total of the minimum rental payments, the guaranteed residual value, the penalty for failure to renew or extend the lease, and the bargain purchase option.

More likely than not A probability of greater than 50%. Also known as *Probable*.

Mortgage bonds or notes Debt secured by real estate.

Net investment in lease The gross investment (the receivable) less the unearned finance or interest revenue included therein.

Neutrality A position of assessment whereby methods are evaluated for conceptual reasons, not economic reasons, and not on the grounds of their possible impact on behaviour.

Nominal rate The fixed rate of interest that is paid by the issuer of a bond annually or semi-annually during the life of the bond. Also known as *Coupon rate or Stated rate*.

Non-accumulating compensated absences Benefits that employees are entitled to by virtue of their employment and the occurrence of an obligating event. The rights to these benefits do not vest and are accounted for differently than those that accumulate with service.

Non-contributory plans Pension plans in which the employer bears the entire cost of the benefit plan.

Non-counterbalancing errors Errors that do not reverse or correct themselves in subsequent periods.

Nonmonetary reciprocal transaction A transaction in which stock may be awarded directly as compensation for services provided by an employee. The transaction is nonmonetary because it involves little or no cash and it is reciprocal because it is a two-way transaction.

Notes payable Written promises to pay a certain sum of money on a specified future date. They may arise from purchases, financing, or other transactions.

Off-balance sheet financing Financing obtained through non-traditional sources such that the related debt is not recognized on the statement of financial position (or balance sheet).

Operating activities A company's principal revenue-producing activities and other activities that are not investing or financing activities.

Operating cycle The period of time elapsing between the acquisition of goods and services involved in operations and the final cash realization resulting from sales and subsequent collections.

Operating lease A lease where the risks and benefits of ownership are not transferred from the lessor to the lessee (and none of the capitalization criteria are met).

Operating segments A component of an enterprise that engages in business activities from which it earns revenues and incurs expenses, whose operating results are reviewed by the company's *chief operating decision-maker* to assess segment performance and allocate resources to the segments, and for which discrete financial information is available.

Originating difference The cause of the initial difference between the carrying value and the tax base of an asset or liability, or of an increase in the temporary difference, regardless of whether the asset or liability's tax base exceeds or is exceeded by its carrying amount.

Other price risk The risk that the fair value or future cash flows will fluctuate because of change in market condition other than those related to interest rates or foreign currency exchange rates.

Overfunded A term describing a pension plan with accumulated assets that are greater than the related obligation.

Par value The value that a bond is worth at the date it is to be repaid. Also known as *Face value, Maturity value,* or *Principal amount.*

Par value shares Shares that have a fixed per-share amount for each share certificate.

Partial retrospective application A measure of change in accounting policy for previous periods excluding those where it is not practicable to retroactively determine the effect of the new standard.

Participating (preferred) shares Preferred shares where holders share proportionately with the common shareholders in any profit distributions beyond the prescribed rate.

Past service cost The amount of an employer's obligation to make contributions to a pension plan for employee services that were provided before the start of the plan (or an amendment to the plan).

Payout ratio A measure of profitability, which is the ratio of cash dividends to net income.

Payroll deductions Deductions made from employee payroll, including employee income taxes, Canada (Quebec) Pension Plan, employment insurance, and miscellaneous items such as other insurance premiums, employee savings, and union dues.

Pension cost Current service, past service, and net interest on the net defined benefit obligation that are included in pension expense. Under IFRS, costs related to actuarial gains and losses, and the return on plan assets excluding amounts included in the net interest on the net defined benefit obligation (asset), are recognized in other comprehensive income.

Pension expense Service cost (current and past service) and net interest (the net of interest on the defined benefit obligation and pension plan assets). Under ASPE's immediate recognition approach, it also includes actuarial gains and losses.

Pension plan An arrangement whereby an employer provides benefits (payments) to employees after they retire for services they provided while they were working.

Percentage (common-size) analysis An approach to financial statement analysis whereby a series of related amounts are converted to a series of percentages of a given base.

Performance obligation An obligation that arises when an entity promises to deliver something or provide a service in the future.

Permanent differences A difference between taxable and accounting income that will not reverse in future periods.

Perpetual bonds or notes Debt issues that have unusually long terms; that is, 100 years or more or never repayable.

Plan assets Pension assets that have been set aside in a trust or other legal entity that is separate from the employer company.

Potential common/ordinary share A security or other contract that upon conversion or exercise could dilute earnings per common share.

Preemptive right A right to share proportionately in any new issues of share of the same class.

Preferred dividends in arrears Accumulated but undeclared dividends on cumulative preferred shares.

Preferred shares A special class of shares that have certain preferential rights, such as a prior claim on earnings.

Premium The difference between the market price and the face value of a bond.

Premiums Offers, such as silverware, dishes, and small appliances, to customers on a limited or continuing basis for the return of items such as boxtops, certificates, coupons, labels, or wrappers.

Price earnings ratio An oft-quoted statistic used by analysts in discussing the investment possibility of an enterprise, calculated by dividing the share's market price by its earnings per share.

Primary financial instruments Instruments that include basic financial assets and liabilities, such as receivables and payables, as well as equity instruments such as shares.

Primary sources of GAAP The key financial reporting requirements as specified under IFRS and ASPE.

Principal amount The value that the bond is worth at the date it is to be repaid. Also known as *Face value, Maturity value,* or *Par value.*

Prior period errors Omissions from or misstatements in the financial statements of one or more prior periods that are caused by the misuse of, or failure to use, reliable information that existed when those financial statements were completed and could reasonably have been found and used in their preparation and presentation.

Probable See *More likely than not.*

Profit-sharing A type of plan where payments are made to employees in addition to the regular salary or wage. The payments may be a percentage of the employees' regular rates of pay, or they may depend on productivity increases or the amount of the company's annual profit.

Projected benefit method A measure of the pension obligation where the calculation of the deferred compensation amount is based on both vested and non-vested service using future salaries.

Proportional method A method of allocating a price to each unit of a transaction involving multiple units. It requires determining the fair value of each item and allocating the purchase price based on the relative fair values. Also known as *Relative fair value method.*

Prospective application The application of a new accounting policy whereby previously reported results remain and the new policy is adopted for the current and future periods only.

Provisions Liabilities of uncertain timing or amount.

Purchased options Call or put options purchased by a company, which has the right but not the obligation to exercise the option.

Put option A derivative where the option holder has the right but not the obligation to sell shares at a preset price.

Qualified opinion The opinion expressed by the auditor that contains an exception to the standard opinion.

Quick ratio A liquidity ratio that relates total current liabilities to highly liquid assets such as cash, marketable securities, and receivables. Also known as *Acid-test ratio*.

Rate of return on common shareholders' equity A ratio that measures profitability from the common shareholders' viewpoint. It shows how many dollars of net income were earned for each dollar invested by the owners.

Related-party transactions What arises when a business engages in transactions in which one of the transacting parties has the ability to significantly influence the policies of the other, or in which a non-transacting party has the ability to influence the policies of the two transacting parties.

Relative fair value method A method of allocating a price to each unit of a transaction involving multiple units. It requires determining the fair value of each item and allocating the purchase price based on the relative fair values. Also known as *Proportional method*.

Registered bonds Bonds issued in the owner's name that require surrender of the certificate and issuance of a new certificate to complete a sale.

Refunding The replacement of an existing debt with new debt.

Rental payments The payments that the lessee makes to the lessor in return for the right to use the lessor's property for a specified period of time.

Reportable segment A significant operating segment for which separate information is reported, if it satisfies one or more quantitative thresholds relating to revenues, profits, assets, or certain other factors.

Residual value An asset's estimated fair value at the end of the lease term.

Residual value method Method of allocating the value of a transaction whereby only one component is valued (the one that is easier to value, often the debt component). The other component is valued at whatever is left. Also known as *Incremental method*.

Restrictive covenants Contractual requirements that are meant to restrict activities and protect both lenders and borrowers.

Retained earnings An enterprise's earned capital.

Retractable (preferred) shares Shares where the holder can put or sell their shares to the company, normally after having given adequate notice, and the company must then pay the holders for the shares.

Retroactive application The application of a new accounting policy whereby its cumulative effect on the financial state-ments is calculated at the beginning of the period as if it had always been used. Also known as *Retrospective application*.

Retrospective application The application of a new accounting policy whereby its cumulative effect on the financial statements is calculated at the beginning of the period as if it had always been used. Also known as *Retroactive application*.

Retrospective restatement Accounting for an error correction where corrections are reported in the financial statements as though the error had never occurred.

Return on plan assets Actual changes in the market values of pension fund assets as well as the interest and dividends earned.

Returnable cash deposits Deposits received from customers that are returnable. Deposits may guarantee performance of a contract or service.

Revaluation adjustment The difference between the carrying values of a company's assets and liabilities before a financial reorganization and the new values after.

Revenue approach An approach to accounting for warranties whereby the proceeds received for any goods or services yet to be delivered or performed are unearned at the point of sale. Until the revenue is earned, the obligation is reported at its sales or fair value. The liability is then reduced as the revenue is earned.

Revenue bond Bonds where interest is paid from a specified revenue source.

Reverse treasury stock method Method of calculating diluted earnings per share for (written) put options and forward purchase contracts. It assumes that (1) the company will issue sufficient common shares at the beginning of the year in the marketplace (at the average market price) to generate sufficient funds to buy the shares under the option/forward, and (2) the proceeds from the above will be used to buy back the shares under the option/forward at the beginning of the year.

Reversible differences Situations where the accounting treatment and the tax treatment are the same, but the timing of when they are included in accounting income and when they are included in taxable income differs. Also known as *Timing differences*.

Revolving debt An agreement a company enters into with its bank to make multiple borrowings up to a negotiated limit, instead of having to negotiate a new loan every time the company needs funds. Also known as *Line of credit*.

Right-of-use approach A method of capitalizing leases whereby the asset that is acquired is not the physical property that is leased but is the right to use the property that is conveyed under the lease agreement.

Sale-leaseback A transaction in which a property owner (the seller-lessee) sells a property to another party (the purchaser-lessor) and, at the same time, leases the same asset back from the new owner.

Sales-type lease A lease whereby a manufacturer's or dealer's profit is incorporated. Also known as a manufacturer or dealer lease.

Secured debt Debt that is backed by a pledge of some form of collateral.

Securitization The selling of a pool of company assets such as accounts receivable to a limited/special purpose entity for cash. The limited/special purpose entity issues ownership interests (securities) to investors who then own part of the pool of assets.

Segmented (disaggregated) financial information Financial information that is presented in a note to the financial statements by operating segment.

Serial bonds or notes Bond issues that mature in instalments.

Service period The period in which an employee performs a service to the organization.

Settlement date The date at which parties to an interest rate swap contract exchange cash under the terms of the contract.

Settlement rate The rate implied in an insurance contract that could be purchased to effectively settle a pension obligation.

Share appreciation rights (SARs) Rights given to an executive or employee to receive compensation equal to the share appreciation, which is defined as the excess of the shares' market price at the date of exercise over a pre-established price. This share appreciation may be paid in cash, shares, or a combination of both.

Short-term obligations expected to be refinanced Those debts that are scheduled to mature within a year or operating cycle, where the company intends to refinance those debts.

Significant non-cash transactions Transactions not using cash that affect an organization's asset and capital structure, such as an acquisition of assets by assuming liabilities, exchanges of nonmonetary assets, and issuance of equity securities to retire debt.

Simple capital structure A corporation's capital structure consisting only of common shares or including no potential common shares.

Site restoration obligation An existing legal obligation associated with the retirement of a tangible long-lived asset that results from its acquisition, construction, development, or normal operations, in the period it is incurred, provided a reasonable estimate can be made of its fair value. Also known as *Asset retirement obligation*.

Special purpose entity An entity created by a company to perform a special project or function, such as accessing financing. Also known as *Variable interest entity*.

Speculating The process of taking on additional risk in the hope of making future gains.

Stand-ready obligation A type of liability that is unconditional whereby the obligor stands prepared to fulfill the terms of the contract when required, such as an insurance contract or warranty.

Stated rate The interest rate written in terms of the bond indenture. Also known as *Coupon rate* or *Nominal rate*.

Statement of cash flows A financial statement providing information about an entity's cash receipts and cash payments broken down into operating, investing, and financing cash flows.

Stock dividend Dividends that are issued to shareholders in stock and no assets are distributed. Each shareholder has exactly the same proportionate interest in the corporation and the same total book value after the stock dividend was issued as before it was declared.

Stock split A device whereby a company increases the number of shares outstanding. For instance in a 2-for-1 split, an existing share would be worth two shares after the split.

Straight-line method An amortization or depreciation method where a constant amount is depreciated each year.

Strike price The agreed upon price at which an option may be settled.

Subscribed shares Shares that are sold but their full price is not received immediately. Usually a partial payment is made and the share is not issued until the full subscription price is received.

Subsequent events Events that take place after the formal balance sheet date but before the financial statements are approved for release.

Substantively enacted rate A tax rate used for accounting purposes where there is persuasive evidence of the government's ability and commitment to implement it.

Swap contract A derivative contract under which two parties agree to exchange payment at future points in time (usually based on interest or foreign currency rates).

Tandem plans Stock compensation plans that combine features from different types of compensation plans such as stock option plans and share appreciation rights plans. Also known as *Combination plans*.

Tax base/basis The measurement under existing law applicable to a present asset, liability, or equity instrument recognized for tax purposes as a result of one or more past events.

Tax base of a liability A liability's carrying amount on the statement of financial position reduced by any amount that will be deductible for tax purposes in future periods.

Tax base of an asset The amount that can be deducted in determining taxable income when the carrying amount of that asset is recovered.

Tax income See *Income tax benefit*.

Tax loss A loss resulting when tax-deductible expenses and losses exceed taxable revenues and gains. Also known as *Loss for income tax purposes*.

Taxable income In tax accounting, the amount on which income tax payable is calculated. Also known as *Taxable profit*.

Taxable profit See *Taxable income*.

Taxable temporary difference A temporary difference that will result in taxable amounts in future years when the carrying amount of the asset is received or the liability is settled.

Taxes payable method A differential reporting method whereby total income tax expense (benefit) is equal to income taxes currently payable (receivable).

Temporary difference The difference between the tax base of an asset or liability and its reported (carrying or book) amount in the statement of financial position that will result in taxable amounts or deductible amounts in future years.

Temporary difference approach A method for calculating income taxes that adjusts for the effects of any changes in future income tax assets and liabilities and recognizes these effects as future income tax expense. Also known as *Future income taxes method*.

Term bonds or notes Bond issues that mature on a single date.

Time value A measurement that takes into account the fact that cash flows will occur over time and that future cash flows are worth less than current cash flows.

Times interest earned ratio A ratio that indicates the company's ability to meet interest payments as they come due. It is calculated by dividing income before interest expense and income taxes by interest expense.

Timing differences Situations where the accounting treatment and the tax treatment are the same, but the timing of when they are included in accounting income and when they are included in taxable income differs. Also known as *Reversible differences*.

Trade accounts payable Balances owed to others for goods, supplies, or services purchased on open account.

Trade notes payable Notes required as part of the sales/purchases transaction in lieu of the normal extension of open account credit.

Trade payables Amounts that the entity owes to suppliers for providing goods and services related to normal business operations.

Trading on equity The practice of using borrowed money at fixed interest rates or issuing preferred shares with constant dividend rates in hopes of obtaining a higher rate of return on the money used.

Transitional provisions The recommendations usually included when new or revised primary sources of GAAP are adopted that specify how an entity should handle the change to a new accounting method.

Treasury shares Shares that are reacquired by a corporation and held in the corporation for reissue.

Treasury stock method A method of calculating earnings per share where options, warrants, and their equivalents are included in the calculation.

Troubled debt restructuring When a creditor "for economic or legal reasons related to the debtor's financial difficulties grants a concession to the debtor that it would not otherwise consider." It usually involves either the settlement of the debt at less than its carrying amount or a continuation of the debt with a modification of terms.

Unamortized net actuarial gain or loss Under ASPE, the portion of the actuarial gains and losses that has been reflected in the accrued benefit obligation and/or pension plan assets, but that has not yet been included in the benefit expense and the accrued benefit asset/liability in the financial statements. Also known as *Unrecognized net actuarial gain or loss.*

Unamortized past service costs Under ASPE, the portion of the past service costs that has been reflected in the accrued benefit obligation, but that has not yet been included in the benefit expense and the accrued benefit asset/liability in the financial statements. Also known as *Unrecognized past service costs.*

Unconditional obligation An unconditional promise or other requirement to provide or forgo economic resources, such as the requirement to pay interest on borrowed money.

Underfunded A term describing a pension plan with more liabilities than assets.

Unearned revenue Revenue received by a company for goods or services that have not yet been provided by the company.

Unguaranteed residual value The portion of the residual value that is not guaranteed, or is guaranteed solely by a party related to the lessor.

Unqualified opinion The opinion expressed by the auditor that the financial statements present fairly, in all material respects, the entity's financial position, results of operations, and cash flows, in conformity with generally accepted accounting principles. Also known as *Clean opinion.*

Unrecognized net actuarial gain or loss Under ASPE, the portion of the actuarial gains and losses that has been reflected in the accrued benefit obligation and/or pension plan assets, but that has not yet been included in the benefit expense and the accrued benefit asset/liability in the financial statements. Also known as *Unamortized net actuarial gain or loss.*

Unrecognized past service costs Under ASPE, the portion of the past service costs that has been reflected in the accrued benefit obligation, but that has not yet been included in the benefit expense and the accrued benefit asset/liability in the financial statements. Also known as *Unamortized past service costs.*

Valuation allowance An impairment allowance for the portion of the asset deemed not more likely than not to be realized.

Variable interest entity An entity that a company creates so that it can perform a special function or project. Also known as *Special purpose entity.*

Vertical analysis An approach to financial statement analysis whereby each item on a financial statement in a given period is expressed proportionately to a base figure.

Vest To earn the rights to. An employee's award becomes vested at the date that the employee's right to receive or retain shares of stock or cash under the award is no longer contingent on remaining in the employer's service.

Vested benefit obligation A measure of a company's pension obligation including only vested benefits and calculated using current salary levels.

Vested benefits Benefits that an employee is entitled to receive even if he or she provides no additional services to the company.

Vested rights Rights that an employee has to some of the benefits that accumulate with service, even if his or her employment is terminated.

Vesting The principle that an employee keeps the rights to receive a benefit even if the employee no longer works for the entity.

Vesting period The period over which an employee becomes legally entitled to receive a benefit. It is normally the service period.

Voluntary change A change in accounting policy by a company that is not required by GAAP but is made to facilitate the provision of reliable and more relevant information to users of financial information.

Warranty A promise made by a seller to a buyer to make good on a product's deficiency of quantity, quality, or performance.

Weighted average number of shares The number of shares outstanding, weighted by the fraction of the period they are outstanding.

Written options Call or put options that are issued by a company. If exercised by the holder, the company is obligated to perform under the contract.

Zero-interest debentures, bonds, or notes Bonds sold at a discount that provide the buyer's total interest payoff at maturity. Also known as *Deep discount bonds or notes.*

Company Index

Subject Index